ERIC AMBLER

ERIC AMBLER

THE MASK OF DIMITRIOS

JOURNEY INTO FEAR

JUDGMENT ON DELTCHEV

THE SCHIRMER INHERITANCE

PASSAGE OF ARMS

THE LIGHT OF DAY

Heinemann/Octopus

The Mask of Dimitrios first published in Great Britain in 1939
by Hodder & Stoughton Ltd
Journey into Fear first published in Great Britain in 1940
by Hodder & Stoughton Ltd
Judgment on Deltchev first published in Great Britain in 1951
by Hodder & Stoughton Ltd
The Schirmer Inheritance first published in Great Britain in 1953
by William Heinemann Ltd
Passage of Arms first published in Great Britain in 1959
by William Heinemann Ltd
The Light of Day first published in Great Britain in 1962
by William Heinemann Ltd

This edition first published in 1978
jointly by

William Heinemann Limited
15–16 Queen Street
London W1

Secker & Warburg Limited
14 Carlisle Street
London W1

and
Octopus Books Limited
59 Grosvenor Street
London W1

ISBN 0 905712 25 0

Printed in Great Britain by
Jarrold and Sons Limited, Norwich

CONTENTS

ERIC
AMBLER

The Mask of Dimitrios

To Alan and Félice Harvey

'But the iniquity of oblivion blindely scattereth her poppy, and deals with the memory of men without distinction to merit of perpetuity . . . Without the favour of the everlasting register, the first man had been as unknown as the last, and Methuselah's long life had been his only Chronicle.'

SIR THOMAS BROWNE: *Hydriotaphia*

The characters in this book are entirely imaginary, and have no relation to any living person.

Chapter One

Origins of an Obsession

A Frenchman named Chamfort, who should have known better, once said that chance was a nickname for Providence.

It is one of those convenient, question-begging aphorisms coined to discredit the unpleasant truth that chance plays an important, if not predominant, part in human affairs. Yet it was not entirely inexcusable. Inevitably, chance does occasionally operate with a sort of fumbling coherence readily mistakable for the workings of a self-conscious Providence.

The story of Dimitrios Makropoulos is an example of this.

The fact that a man like Latimer should so much as learn of the existence of a man like Dimitrios is alone grotesque. That he should actually see the dead body of Dimitrios, that he should spend weeks that he could ill afford probing into the man's shadowy history, and that he should ultimately find himself in the position of owing his life to a criminal's odd taste in interior decoration are breath-taking in their absurdity.

Yet, when these facts are seen side by side with the other facts in the case, it is difficult not to become lost in superstitious awe. Their very absurdity seems to prohibit the use of the words 'chance' and 'coincidence'. For the sceptic there remains only one consolation: if there should be such a thing as a superhuman Law, it is administered with sub-human inefficiency. The choice of Latimer as its instrument could have been made only by an idiot.

During the first fifteen years of his adult life, Charles Latimer became a lecturer in political economy at a minor English university. By the time he was thirty-five he had, in addition, written three books. The first was a study of the influence of Proudhon on nineteenth century Italian political thought. The second was entitled: *The Gotha Programme of 1875*. The third was an assessment of the economic implications of Rosenberg's *Der Mythus des zwanzigsten Jahrhunderts*.

It was soon after he had finished correcting the bulky proofs of the last work, and in the hope of dispelling the black depression which was the aftermath of his temporary association with the philosophy of National Socialism and its prophet, Dr Rosenberg, that he wrote his first detective story.

A Bloody Shovel was an immediate success. It was followed by '*I*,' said the Fly and *Murder's Arms*. From the great army of university professors who write detective stories in their spare time, Latimer soon emerged as one of the shamefaced few who could make money at the sport. It was, perhaps, inevitable that, sooner or later, he would become a professional writer in name as well as in fact. Three things hastened the transition. The first was a disagreement with the university authorities over what he held to be a matter of principle. The second was an illness. The third was the fact that he happened to be unmarried. Not long after the publication of *No Doornail This* and following the illness, which had made inroads on his constitutional reserves, he wrote, with only mild reluctance, a letter of resignation and went abroad to complete his fifth detective story in the sun.

It was the week after he had finished that book's successor that he went to Turkey. He had spent a year in and near Athens and was longing for a change of scene. His health was much improved but the prospect of an English autumn was uninviting. At the suggestion of a Greek friend he took the steamer from the Piraeus to Istanbul.

It was in Istanbul and from Colonel Haki that he first heard of Dimitrios.

A letter of introduction is an uneasy document. More often than not, the bearer of it is only casually acquainted with the giver who, in turn, may know the person to whom it is addressed even less well. The chances of its presentation having a satisfactory outcome for all three are slender.

Among the letters of introduction which Latimer carried with him to Istanbul was one to a Madame Chávez, who lived, he had been told, in a villa on the Bosphorus. Three days after he arrived, he wrote to her and received in reply an invitation to join a four day party at the villa. A trifle apprehensively, he accepted.

For Madame Chávez, the road from Buenos Ayres had been as liberally paved with gold as the road to it. A very handsome Turkish woman, she had successfully married and divorced a wealthy Argentine meat broker and, with a fraction of her gains from these transactions, had purchased a small palace which had once housed a minor Turkish royalty. It stood, remote and inconvenient of access, overlooking a bay of fantastic beauty and, apart from the fact that the supplies of fresh water were insufficient to serve even one of its nine bathrooms, was exquisitely appointed. But for the other guests and his hostess's Turkish habit of striking her servants violently in the face when they displeased her (which was often), Latimer, for whom such grandiose discomfort was a novelty, would have enjoyed himself.

The other guests were a very noisy pair of Marseillais, three Italians, two young Turkish naval officers and their 'fiancées' of the moment and an assortment of Istanbul business men with their wives. The greater part of the time they spent in drinking Madame Chávez's seemingly inexhaustible supplies of Dutch gin and dancing to a gramophone attended by a servant who went on steadily playing records whether the guests happened to be dancing at the moment or not. On the pretext of ill-health, Latimer excused himself from much of the drinking and most of the dancing. He was generally ignored.

It was in the late afternoon of his last day there and he was sitting at the end of the vine-covered terrace out of earshot of the gramophone, when he saw a large chauffeur-driven touring car lurching up the long, dusty road to the villa. As it roared into the courtyard below, the occupant of the rear seat flung the door open and vaulted out before the car came to a standstill.

He was a tall man with lean, muscular cheeks whose pale tan contrasted well with a head of grey hair cropped Prussian fashion. A narrow frontal bone, a long beak of a nose and thin lips gave him a somewhat predatory air. He could not be less than fifty, Latimer thought, and studied the waist below the beautifully cut officer's uniform in the hope of detecting the corsets.

He watched the tall officer whip a silk handkerchief from his sleeve, flick some invisible dust from his immaculate patent-leather riding boots, tilt his cap raffishly and stride out of sight. Somewhere in the villa, a bell pealed.

Colonel Haki, for this was the officer's name, was an immediate success with the party. A quarter of an hour after his arrival, Madame Chávez, with an air of shy confusion clearly intended to inform her guests that she regarded herself as hopelessly compromised by the Colonel's unexpected appearance, led him on to the terrace and introduced him. All smiles and gallantry, he clicked heels, kissed hands, bowed, acknowledged the salutes of the naval officers and ogled the businessmen's wives. The performance so fascinated Latimer that, when his turn came to be introduced, the sound of his own name made him jump. The Colonel pump-handled his arm warmly.

'Damned pleased indeed to meet you, old boy,' he said.

'*Monsieur le Colonel parle bien anglais*,' explained Madame Chávez.

'*Quelques mots*,' said Colonel Haki.

Latimer looked amiably into a pair of pale grey eyes. 'How do you do?'

'Cheerio–all–the–best,' replied the Colonel with grave courtesy, and passed on to kiss the hand of, and to run an appraising eye over, a stout girl in a bathing costume.

It was not until late in the evening that Latimer spoke to the Colonel again. The Colonel had injected a good deal of boisterous vitality into the party; cracking jokes, laughing loudly, making humorously brazen advances to the wives and rather more surreptitious ones to the unmarried women. From time to time his eye caught Latimer's and he grinned deprecatingly. 'I've got to play the fool like this–it's expected of me,' said the grin; 'but don't think I like it.' Then, long after dinner, when the guests had begun to take less interest in the dancing and more in the progress of a game of mixed strip poker, the Colonel took him by the arm and walked him on to the terrace.

'You must excuse me, Mr Latimer,' he said in French, 'but I should very much like to talk with you. Those women–phew!' He slid a cigarette case under Latimer's nose. 'A cigarette?'

'Thank you.'

Colonel Haki glanced over his shoulder. 'The other end of the terrace is more secluded,' he said; and then, as they began to walk: 'you know, I came up here to-day specially to see you. Madame told me you were here and really I could not resist the temptation of talking with the writer whose works I so much admire.'

Latimer murmured a non-committal appreciation of the compliment. He was in a difficulty, for he had no means of knowing whether the Colonel was thinking in terms of political economy or detection. He had once startled and irritated a kindly old don who had professed interest in his 'last book', by asking the old man whether he preferred his corpses shot or bludgeoned. It sounded affected to ask which set of books was under discussion.

Colonel Haki, however, did not wait to be questioned. 'I get all the latest *romans policiers* sent to me from Paris,' he went on. 'I read nothing but *romans policiers*. I would like you to see my collection. Especially I like the English and American ones. All the best of them are translated into French. French writers themselves, I do not find sympathetic. French culture is not such as can produce a *roman policier* of the first order. I have just added your *Une Pelle Ensanglantée* to my library. Formidable! But I cannot quite understand the significance of the title.'

Latimer spent some time trying to explain in French the meaning of 'to call a spade a bloody shovel' and to translate the play on words which had given (to those readers with suitable minds) the essential clue to the murderer's identity in the very title.

Colonel Haki listened intently, nodding his head and saying, 'Yes, I see, I see it clearly now,' before Latimer had reached the point of the explanation.

'Monsieur,' he said when Latimer had given up in despair, 'I wonder whether you would do me the honour of lunching with me one day this week. I think,' he added mysteriously, 'that I may be able to help you.'

Latimer did not see in what way he could be helped by Colonel Haki but said that he would be glad to lunch with him. They arranged to meet at the Pera Palace Hotel three days later.

It was not until the evening before it that Latimer thought very much more about the luncheon appointment. He was sitting in the lounge of his hotel with the manager of his bankers' Istanbul branch.

Collinson, he thought, was a pleasant fellow but a monotonous companion. His conversation consisted almost entirely of gossip about the doings of the English and American colonies in Istanbul. 'Do you know the Fitzwilliams,' he would say. 'No? A pity, you'd like them. Well, the other day . . .' As a source of information about Kemal Ataturk's economic reforms he had proved a failure.

'By the way,' said Latimer after listening to an account of the goings-on of the Turkish-born wife of an American car salesman, 'do you know of a man named Colonel Haki?'

'Haki? What made you think of him?'

'I'm lunching with him to-morrow.'

Collinson's eyebrows went up. '*Are* you, by Jove!' He scratched his chin. 'Well I know *of* him.' He hesitated. 'Haki's one of those people you hear a lot about in this place but never seem to get a line on. One of the people behind the scenes, if you get me. He's got more influence than a good many of the men who are supposed to be at the top at Ankara. He was one of the Gazi's own particular men in Anatolia in 1919, a deputy in the Provisional Government. I've heard stories about him then. Bloodthirsty devil by all accounts. There was something about torturing prisoners. But then both sides did that and I dare say it was the Sultan's boys that started it. I heard, too, that he can drink a couple of bottles of Scotch at a sitting and stay stone cold sober. Don't believe that though. How did you get on to him?'

Latimer explained. 'What does he do for a living?' he added. 'I don't understand these uniforms.'

Collinson shrugged. 'Well, I've *heard* on good authority that he's the head of the secret police, but that's probably just another story. That's the worst of this place. Can't believe a word they say in the Club. Why, only the other day . . .'

It was with rather more enthusiasm than before that Latimer went to his luncheon appointment the following day. He had judged Colonel Haki to be something of a ruffian and Collinson's vague information had tended to confirm that view.

The Colonel arrived, bursting with apologies, twenty minutes late, and hurried his guest straight into the restaurant. 'We must have a whisky-soda immediately,' he said and called loudly for a bottle of 'Johnnie'.

During most of the meal he talked about the detective stories he had read, his reactions to them, his opinions of the characters and his preference for murderers who shot their victims. At last, with an almost empty bottle of whisky at his elbow and a strawberry ice in front of him, he leaned forward across the table.

'I think, Mr Latimer,' he said again, 'that I can help you.'

For one wild moment Latimer wondered if he were going to be offered a job in the Turkish secret service; but he said: 'That's very kind of you.'

'It was my ambition,' continued Colonel Haki, 'to write a good *roman policier* of my own. I have often thought that I could do so if I had the time. That is the trouble—the time. I have found that out. But . . .' He paused impressively.

Latimer waited. He was always meeting people who felt that they could write detective stories if they had the time.

'But,' repeated the Colonel, 'I have the plot prepared. I would like to make you a present of it.'

Latimer said that it was very good indeed of him.

The Colonel waved away his thanks. 'Your books have given me so much pleasure, Mr Latimer. I am glad to make you a present of an idea for a new one. I have not the time to use it myself, and in any case,' he added magnanimously, 'you would make better use of it than I should.'

Latimer mumbled incoherently.

'The scene of the story,' pursued his host, his grey eyes fixed on Latimer's, 'is an English country house belonging to the rich Lord Robinson. There is a party for the English week-end. In the middle of the party, Lord Robinson is discovered in the library sitting at his desk—shot through the temple. The wound is singed. A pool of blood has formed on the desk and it has soaked into a paper. The paper is a new Will which the Lord was about to sign. The old Will divided his money equally between six persons, his relations, who are at the party. The new Will, which he has been prevented from signing by the murderer's bullet, leaves all to one of those relations. Therefore'—he pointed his ice cream spoon accusingly—'one of the five other relations is the guilty one. That is logical, is it not?'

Latimer opened his mouth, then shut it again and nodded.

Colonel Haki grinned triumphantly. 'That is the trick.'

'The trick?'

'The Lord was murdered by none of the suspects, but by the butler, whose wife had been seduced by this Lord! What do you think of that, eh?'

'Very ingenious.'

His host leaned back contentedly and smoothed out his tunic. 'It is only a trick, but I am glad you like it. Of course, I have the whole plot worked out in detail. The *flic* is a High Commissioner of Scotland Yard. He seduces one of the suspects, a very pretty woman, and it is for her sake that he solves the mystery. It is quite artistic. But, as I say, I have the whole thing written out.'

'I should be very interested,' said Latimer with sincerity, 'to read your notes.'

'That is what I hoped you would say. Are you pressed for time?'

'Not a bit.'

'Then let us go back to my office and I will show you what I have done. It is written in French.'

Latimer hesitated only momentarily. He had nothing better to do, and it might be interesting to see Colonel Haki's office.

'I should like to go back with you,' he said.

The Colonel's office was situated at the top of what might once have been a cheap hotel, but which, from the inside, was unmistakably a government building, in Galata. It was a large room at the end of a corridor. When they went in a uniformed clerk was bending over the desk. He straightened his back, clicked his heels and said something in Turkish. The Colonel answered him and nodded a dismissal. Latimer looked round him. Besides the desk there were several small chairs and an American ice-water maker. The walls were bare and the floor was covered with coconut matting. Long green sun lattices hanging outside the windows kept out most of the light. It was very cool after the heat of the car which had brought them.

The Colonel waved him to a chair, gave him a cigarette and began rummaging in a drawer. At last he drew out a sheet or two of typewritten paper and held it out.

'There you are, Mr Latimer. *The Clue of the Bloodstained Will*, I have called it, but I am not convinced that that is the best title. All the best titles have been used, I find. But I will think of some alternatives. Read it, and do not be afraid to say frankly what you think of it. If there are any details which you think should be altered, I will alter them.'

Latimer took the sheets and read while the Colonel sat on the corner of his desk and swung a long, gleaming leg.

Latimer read through the sheets twice and then put them down. He was feeling ashamed of himself because he had wanted several times to laugh. He should not have come. Now that he *had* come, the best thing he could do was to leave as quickly as possible.

'I cannot suggest any improvements at the moment,' he said slowly; 'of course, it all wants thinking over; it is so easy to make mistakes with problems of this sort. There is so much to be thought of. Questions of British legal procedure, for instance . . .'

'Yes, yes, of course.' Colonel Haki slid off the desk and sat down in his chair. 'But you think you can use it, eh?'

'I am very grateful indeed for your generosity,' said Latimer evasively.

'It is nothing. You shall send me a free copy of the book when it appears.' He swung round in his chair and picked up the telephone. 'I will have a copy made for you to take away.'

Latimer sat back. Well, that was that! It could not take long to make a copy. He listened to the Colonel talking to someone over the telephone and saw him frown. The Colonel put the telephone down and turned to him.

'You will excuse me if I deal with a small matter?'

'Of course.'

The Colonel drew a bulky manila file towards him and began to go through the papers inside it. Then he selected one and glanced down it. As he did so the uniformed clerk rapped on the door and marched in with a thin yellow folder under his arm. The Colonel took the folder and put it on the desk in front of him; then, with a word of instruction, he handed over *The Clue of the Bloodstained Will* to the clerk who clicked his heels and went out. There was silence in the room.

Latimer, affecting preoccupation with his cigarette, glanced across the desk. Colonel Haki was slowly turning the pages inside the folder, and on his face was a look that Latimer had not seen there before. It was the look of the expert attending to the business he understood perfectly. There was a sort of watchful repose in his face that reminded Latimer of a very old and experienced cat contemplating a very young and inexperienced mouse. In that moment he revised his ideas about Colonel Haki. He had been feeling a little sorry for him as one feels sorry for anyone who has unconsciously made a fool of himself. He saw now that the Colonel stood in need of no such consideration. As his long, yellowish fingers turned the pages of the folder, Latimer remembered a sentence of Collinson's: 'There was something about torturing prisoners.' He knew suddenly that he was seeing the real Colonel Haki for the first time. Then the Colonel looked up and his pale eyes rested thoughtfully on Latimer's tie.

For a moment Latimer had an uncomfortable suspicion that although the man across the desk appeared to be looking at his tie, he was actually looking into his mind. Then the Colonel's eyes moved upwards and he grinned slightly in a way that made Latimer feel as if he had been caught stealing something.

He said: 'I wonder if you are interested in *real* murderers, Mr Latimer.'

Chapter Two

The Dossier of Dimitrios

Latimer felt himself redden. From the condescending professional he had been changed suddenly into the ridiculous amateur. It was a little disconcerting.

'Well, yes,' he said slowly. 'I suppose I am.'

Colonel Haki pursed his lips. 'You know, Mr Latimer,' he said, 'I find the murderer in a *roman policier* much more sympathetic than a real murderer. In a *roman policier* there is a corpse, a number of suspects, a detective and a gallows. That is artistic. The real murderer is not artistic. I, who am a sort of policeman, tell you that squarely.' He tapped the folder on his desk. 'Here is a real murderer. We have known of his existence for nearly twenty years. This is his dossier. We know of one murder he may have committed. There are doubtless others of which we, at any rate, know nothing. This man is typical. A dirty type, common, cowardly, scum. Murder, espionage, drugs–that is the history. There were also two affairs of assassination.'

'Assassination! that argues a certain courage, surely?'

The Colonel laughed unpleasantly. 'My dear friend, Dimitrios would have nothing to do with the actual shooting. No! His kind never risk their skins like that. They stay on the fringe of the plot. They are the professionals, the *entrepreneurs*, the links between the businessmen, the politicians who desire the end but are afraid of the means, and the fanatics, the idealists who are prepared to die for their convictions. The important thing to know about an assassination or an attempted assassination is not who fired the shot, but who paid for the bullet. It is the rats like Dimitrios who can best tell you that. They are always ready to talk to save themselves the inconvenience of a prison cell. Dimitrios would have been the same as any other. Courage!' He laughed again. 'Dimitrios was a little cleverer than some of them. I'll grant you that. As far as I know, no government has ever caught him and there is no photograph in his dossier. But we knew him all right, and so did Sofia and Belgrade and Paris and Athens. He was a great traveller, was Dimitrios.'

'That sounds as though he's dead.'

'Yes, he is dead.' Colonel Haki turned the corners of his thin mouth down contemptuously. 'A fisherman pulled his body out of the Bosphorus last night. It is believed that he had been knifed and thrown overboard from a ship. Like the scum he was, he was floating.'

'At least,' said Latimer, 'he died by violence. That is something very like justice.'

'Ah!' The Colonel leaned forward. 'There is the writer speaking. Everything must be tidy, artistic, like a *roman policier*. Very well!' He pulled the dossier towards him and opened it. 'Just listen, Mr Latimer, to this. Then you shall tell me if it is artistic.'

He began to read.

'Dimitrios Makropoulos.' He stopped and looked up. 'We have never been able to find out whether that was the surname of the family that adopted him or an alias. He was known usually as Dimitrios.' He turned to the dossier again. 'Dimitrios Makropoulos. Born 1889 in Larissa, Greece. Found abandoned. Parents unknown. Mother believed Romanian. Registered as Greek subject and adopted by Greek family. Criminal record with Greek authorities. Details unobtainable.' He looked up at Latimer. 'That was before he came to our notice. We first heard of him at Izmir[1] in 1922, a few days after our troops occupied the town. A *deunme*[2] named

[1] Smyrna.
[2] Jew turned Moslem.

Sholem was found in his room with his throat cut: He was a moneylender and kept his money under the floorboards. These were ripped up and the money had been taken. There was much violence in Izmir at that time and little notice would have been taken by the military authorities. The thing might have been done by one of our soldiers. Then, another Jew, a relation of Sholem's, drew the attention of the military to a Negro named Dhris Mohammed, who had been spending money in the cafés and boasting that a Jew had lent him the money without interest. Inquiries were made and Dhris was arrested. His replies to the court martial were unsatisfactory and he was condemned to death. Then he made a confession. He was a fig-packer, and he said that one of his fellow workmen, whom he called Dimitrios, had told him of Sholem's wealth hidden under the floorboards of his room. They had planned the robbery together and had entered Sholem's room by night. It had been Dimitrios, he said, who had killed the Jew. He thought that Dimitrios, being registered as a Greek, had escaped and bought a passage on one of the refugee ships that waited at secret places along the coast.'

He shrugged. 'The authorities did not believe his story. We were at war with Greece, and it was the sort of story a guilty man might invent to save his neck. They found that there had been a fig-packer named Dimitrios, that his fellow workmen had disliked him and that he had disappeared.' He grinned. 'Quite a lot of Greeks named Dimitrios disappeared at that time. You could see their bodies in the streets and floating in the harbour. This Negro's story was unprovable. He was hanged.'

He paused. During this recital he had not once referred to the dossier.

'You have a very good memory for facts,' commented Latimer.

The Colonel grinned again. 'I was the president of the court martial. It was through that that I was able to mark down Dimitrios later on. I was transferred a year later to the secret police. In 1924 a plot to assassinate the Gazi was discovered. It was the year he abolished the Caliphate and the plot was outwardly the work of a group of religious fanatics. Actually the men behind it were agents of some people in the good graces of a neighbouring friendly government. They had good reasons for wishing the Gazi out of the way. The plot was discovered. The details are unimportant. But one of the agents who escaped was a man known as Dimitrios.' He pushed the cigarettes towards Latimer. 'Please smoke.'

Latimer shook his head. 'Was it the same Dimitrios?'

'It was. Now, tell me frankly, Mr Latimer. Do you find anything artistic there? Could you make a good *roman policier* out of that? Is there anything there that could be of the slightest interest to a writer?'

'Police work interests me a great deal–naturally. But what happened to Dimitrios? How did the story end?'

Colonel Haki snapped his fingers. 'Ah! I was waiting for you to ask that. I knew you would ask it. And my answer is this: it *didn't* end!'

'Then what happened?'

'I will tell you. The first problem was to identify Dimitrios of Izmir with Dimitrios of Edirné. [1] Accordingly we revived the affair of Sholem, issued a

---

[1] Adrianople.

warrant for the arrest of a Greek fig-packer named Dimitrios on a charge of murder and, with that excuse, asked foreign police authorities for assistance. We did not learn much, but what we did learn was sufficient. Dimitrios had been concerned with the attempted assassination of Stambulisky in Bulgaria which had preceded the Macedonian officers' *putsch* in 1923. The Sofia police know very little but that he was known there to be a Greek from Izmir. A woman with whom he had associated in Sofia was questioned. She stated that she had had a letter from him a short time before. He had given no address, but as she had had very urgent reasons for wishing to get in touch with him she had looked at the postmark. It was from Edirné. The Sofia police obtained a rough description of him that agreed with that given by the Negro in Izmir. The Greek police stated that he had had a criminal record prior to 1922 and gave those particulars of his origin. The warrant is probably still in existence; but we did not find Dimitrios with it.

'It was not until two years later that we heard of him again. We received an inquiry from the Yugoslav Government concerning a Turkish subject named Dimitrios Talat. He was wanted, they said, for robbery; but an agent of ours in Belgrade reported that the robbery was the theft of some secret naval documents and that the charge the Yugoslavs hoped to bring against him was one of espionage on behalf of France. By the first name and the description issued by the Belgrade police we guessed that Talat was probably Dimitrios of Izmir. About the same time our Consul in Switzerland renewed the passport, issued apparently at Ankara, of a man named Talat. It is a common Turkish name; but when it came to entering the record of the renewal it was found from the number that no such passport had been issued. The passport had been forged.' He spread out his hands. 'You see, Mr Latimer? There is your story. Incomplete. Inartistic. No detection, no suspects, no hidden motives, merely sordid.'

'But interesting, nevertheless,' objected Latimer. 'What happened over the Talat business?'

'Still looking for the end of your story, Mr Latimer? All right, then. Nothing happened about Talat. It is just a name. We never heard it again. If he used the passport we don't know. It does not matter. We have Dimitrios. A corpse, it is true, but we have him. We shall probably never know who killed him. The ordinary police will doubtless make their inquiries and report to us that they have no hope of discovering the murderer. This dossier will go into the archives. It is just one of many similar cases.'

'You said something about drugs.'

Colonel Haki began to look bored. 'Oh, yes. Dimitrios made a lot of money once I should think. Another unfinished story. About three years after the Belgrade affair we heard of him again. Nothing to do with us but the available information was added to the dossier as a routine matter.' He referred to the dossier. 'In 1929, the League of Nations Advisory Committee on the illicit drug traffic received a report from the French government concerning the seizure of a large quantity of heroin at the Swiss frontier. It was concealed in a mattress in a sleeping car coming from Sofia. One of the car attendants was found to be responsible for the smuggling but all he could or would tell the police was that the drug was to have been collected in Paris by a man who worked at the rail terminus. He did not know the man's name and had never spoken to him; but he described him. The man in question was later arrested. Questioned, he admitted the charge but claimed that he knew nothing of the destination of the drug. He received one consignment a month which was collected by a third man. The police set a trap for this third man and caught him only to find there was a fourth intermediary. They arrested six men in all in connection with that affair and only obtained one real clue. It was that the man at the head of this peddling organization was a man known as Dimitrios. Through the medium of the Committee, the Bulgarian government then revealed that they had found a clandestine heroin laboratory at Radomir and had seized two hundred and thirty kilos of heroin ready for delivery. The consignee's name was Dimitrios. During the next year the French succeeded in discovering one or two other large heroin consignments bound for Dimitrios. But they did not get very much nearer to Dimitrios himself. There were difficulties. The stuff never seemed to come in the same way twice and by the end of the year, 1930, all they had to show in the way of arrests were a number of smugglers and some insignificant pedlars. Judging by the amounts of heroin they did find, Dimitrios must have been making huge sums for himself. Then, quite suddenly, about a year after that, Dimitrios went out of the drug business. The first news the police had of this was an anonymous letter which gave the names of all the principal members of the gang, their life histories and details of how evidence against every one of them might be obtained. The French police had a theory at the time. They said that Dimitrios himself had become a heroin addict. Whether that is true or not, the fact is that by December, the gang was rounded up. One of them, a woman, was already wanted for fraud. Some of them threatened to kill Dimitrios when they were released from prison but the most any of them could tell the police about him was that his surname was Makropoulos and that he had a flat in the seventeenth *arrondissement*. They never found the flat and they never found Dimitrios.'

The clerk had come in and was standing by the desk.

'Ah,' said the Colonel, 'here is your copy.'

Latimer took it and thanked him rather absently.

'And that was the last you heard of Dimitrios?' he added.

'Oh, no. The last we heard of him was about a year later. A Croat attempted to assassinate a Yugoslav politician in Zagreb. In the confession he made to the police, he said that friends had obtained the pistol he used from a man named Dimitrios in Rome. If it was Dimitrios of Izmir he must have returned to his old profession. A dirty type. There are a few more like him who should float in the Bosphorus.'

'You say you never had a photograph of him. How did you identify him?'

'There was a French *carte d'identité* sewn inside the lining of his coat. It was issued about a year ago at Lyons to Dimitrios Makropoulos. It is a visitor's *carte* and he is described as being without occupation. That might mean anything. There was, of course, a photograph in it. We've turned it over to the French. They say that it is quite genuine.' He pushed the dossier aside and stood up. 'There's an inquest to-morrow. I have to go and have a look at the body in the police mortuary. That is a thing you do not have to contend with in books, Mr Latimer—a list of regulations. A man is found floating in the Bosphorus. A police matter, clearly. But because this man happens to be on my files, my organization has to deal with it also. I have my car waiting. Can I take you anywhere?'

'If my hotel isn't too much out of your way, I should like to be taken there.'

'Of course. You have the plot of your new book safely? Good. Then we are ready.'

In the car, the Colonel elaborated on the virtues of *The Clue of the Bloodstained Will.* Latimer promised to keep in touch with him and let him know how the book progressed. The car pulled up outside his hotel. They had exchanged farewells and Latimer was about to get out when he hesitated and then dropped back into his seat.

'Look here, Colonel,' he said, 'I want to make what will seem to you a rather strange request.'

The Colonel gestured expansively. 'Anything.'

'I have a fancy to see the body of this man Dimitrios. I wonder if it would be possible for you to take me with you.'

The Colonel frowned and then shrugged. 'If you wish to come, by all means do so. But I do not see . . .'

'I have never,' lied Latimer quickly, 'seen either a dead man or a mortuary. I think that every detective story writer should see those things.'

The Colonel's face cleared. 'My dear fellow, of course he should. One cannot write about that which one has never seen.' He signalled the chauffeur on. 'Perhaps,' he added as they drove off again, 'we can incorporate a scene in a mortuary in your new book. I will think about it.'

The mortuary was a small corrugated iron building in the precincts of a police station near the mosque of Nouri Osmanieh. A police official, collected *en route* by the Colonel, led them across the yard which separated it from the main building. The afternoon heat had set the air above the concrete quivering and Latimer began to wish that he had not come. It was not the weather for visiting corrugated iron mortuaries.

The official unlocked the door and opened it. A blast of hot, carbolic-laden air came out, as from an oven, to meet them. Latimer took off his hat and followed the Colonel in.

There were no windows and light was supplied by a single high-powered electric lamp in an enamel reflector. On each side of a gangway which ran down the centre, there were four high, wooden trestle tables. All but three were bare. The three were draped with stiff, heavy tarpaulins which bulged slightly above the lever of the other trestles. The heat was overpowering and Latimer felt the sweat begin to soak into his shirt and trickle down his legs.

'It's very hot,' he said.

The Colonel shrugged and nodded towards the trestles. 'They don't complain.'

The official went to the nearest of the three trestles, leaned over it and dragged the tarpaulin back. The Colonel walked over and looked down. Latimer forced himself to follow.

The body lying on the trestle was that of a short, broad-shouldered man of about fifty. From where he stood near the foot of the table, Latimer could see very little of the face, only a section of putty-coloured flesh and a fringe of tousled grey hair. The body was wrapped in a mackintosh sheet. By the feet was a neat pile of crumpled clothing: some underwear, a shirt, socks, a flowered tie and a blue serge suit stained nearly grey by sea water. Beside this pile was a pair of narrow, pointed shoes, the soles of which had warped as they had dried.

Latimer took a step nearer so that he could see the face.

No one had troubled to close the eyes and the whites of them stared upwards at the light. The lower jaw had dropped slightly. It was not quite the face that Latimer had pictured; rather rounder and with thick lips instead of thin, a face that would work and quiver under the stress of emotion. The cheeks were loose and deeply lined. But it was too late now to form any judgment of the mind that had once been behind the face. The mind had gone.

The official had been speaking to the Colonel. Now he stopped.

'Killed by a knife wound in the stomach, according to the doctor,' translated the Colonel. 'Already dead when he got into the water.'

'Where did the clothes come from?'

'Lyons, all except the suit and shoes which are Greek. Poor stuff.'

He renewed his conversation with the official.

Latimer stared at the corpse. So this was Dimitrios. This was the man who had, perhaps, slit the throat of Sholem, the Jew turned Moslem. This was the man who had connived at assassinations, who had spied for France. This was the man who had trafficked in drugs, who had given a gun to a Croat terrorist and who, in the end, had himself died by violence. This putty-coloured bulk was the end of an Odyssey. Dimitrios had returned at last to the country whence he had set out so many years before.

So many years. Europe in labour had through its pain seen for an instant a new glory, and then had collapsed to welter again in the agonies of war and fear. Governments had risen and fallen; men and women had worked, had starved, had made speeches, had fought, had been tortured, had died. Hope had come and gone, a fugitive in the scented bosom of illusion. Men had learned to sniff the heady dreamstuff of the soul and wait impassively while the lathes turned the guns for their destruction. And through those years, Dimitrios had lived and breathed and come to terms with his strange gods. He had been a dangerous man. Now, in the loneliness of death, beside the squalid pile of clothes that was his estate, he was pitiable.

Latimer watched the two men as they discussed the filling-in of a printed form the official had produced. They turned to the clothes and began making an inventory of them.

Yet at some time Dimitrios had made money, much money. What had happened to it? Had he spent it or lost it? 'Easy come, easy go,' they said. But had Dimitrios been the sort of man to let money go easily, howsoever he had acquired it? They knew so little about him! A few odd facts about a few odd incidents in his life, that was all the dossier amounted to. No more. It told you something. It told you that he had been unscrupulous, ruthless and treacherous. It told you that his way of life had been consistently criminal. But it did not tell you anything that enabled you to see the living man who had slit Sholem's throat, who had lived in a flat in Paris 17. And for every one of the crimes recorded in the dossier there must have been others, perhaps even more serious. What had happened in those two- and three-year intervals which the dossier bridged so casually? And what had happened since he had been in Lyons a year ago? By what route had he travelled to keep his appointment with Nemesis?

They were not questions that Colonel Haki would bother even to ask, much less to answer. He was the professional, concerned only with the unfanciful business of disposing of a decomposing body. But there must be people who knew and knew of Dimitrios, his friends (if he had had any), and his enemies, people in Smyrna, people in Sofia, people in Belgrade, in Adrianople, in Paris, in Lyons, people all over Europe, who *could* answer them. If you could find those people and get the answers you would have the material for what would surely be the strangest of biographies.

Latimer's heart missed a beat. It would be an absurd thing to attempt, of course. Unthinkably foolish. If one did it one would begin with, say, Smyrna and try to follow one's man step by step from there, using the dossier as a rough guide. It would be an experiment in detection really. One would, no doubt, fail to discover anything new; but there would be valuable data to be gained even from failure. All the routine inquiries over which one skated so easily in one's novels one would have to make oneself. Not that any man in his senses would dream of going on such a wild goose chase–heavens no! But it was amusing to play with the idea and if one were a little tired of Istanbul . . .

He looked up and caught the Colonel's eye.

The Colonel grimaced a reference to the heat of the place. He had finished his business with the official. 'Have you seen all you wanted to see?'

Latimer nodded.

Colonel Haki turned and looked at the body as if it were a piece of his own handiwork of which he was taking leave. For a moment or two he remained motionless. Then his right arm went out, and, grasping the dead man's hair, he lifted the head so that the sightless eyes stared into his.

'Ugly devil, isn't he,' he said. 'Life is very strange. I've known about him for nearly twenty years and this is the first time I've met him face to face. Those eyes have seen some things I should like to see. It is a pity that the mouth can never speak about them.'

He let the head go and it dropped back with a thud on to the table. Then, he drew out his silk handkerchief and wiped his fingers carefully. 'The sooner he's in a coffin the better,' he added as they walked away.

Chapter Three

Nineteen Twenty-two

In the early hours of an August morning in 1922, the Turkish Nationalist Army under the command of Mustafa Kemal Pasha attacked the centre of the Greek army at Dumlu Punar on the plateau two hundred miles west of

Smyrna. By the following morning, the Greek army had broken and was in headlong retreat towards Smyrna and the sea. In the days that followed, the retreat became a rout. Unable to destroy the Turkish army, the Greeks turned with frantic savagery to the business of destroying the Turkish population in the path of their flight. From Alashehr to Smyrna they burnt and slaughtered. Not a village was left standing. Amid the smouldering ruins the pursuing Turks found the bodies of the villagers. Assisted by the few half-crazed Anatolian peasants who had survived, they took their revenge on the Greeks they were able to overtake. To the bodies of the Turkish women and children were added the mutilated carcases of Greek stragglers. But the main Greek army had escaped by sea. Their lust for infidel blood still unsatisfied, the Turks swept on. On the ninth of September, they occupied Smyrna.

For a fortnight, refugees from the oncoming Turks had been pouring into the city to swell the already large Greek and Armenian populations. They had thought that the Greek army would turn and defend Smyrna. But the Greek army had fled. Now they were caught in a trap. The holocaust began.

The register of the Armenian Asia Minor Defence League had been seized by the occupying troops, and, on the night of the tenth, a party of regulars entered the Armenian quarters to find and kill those whose names appeared on the register. The Armenians resisted and the Turks ran amok. The massacre that followed acted like a signal. Encouraged by their officers, the Turkish troops descended next day upon the non-Turkish quarters of the city and began systematically to kill. Dragged from their houses and hiding places, men, women and children were butchered in the streets which soon became littered with mutilated bodies. The wooden walls of the churches, packed with refugees, were drenched with benzine and fired. The occupants who were not burnt alive were bayoneted as they tried to escape. In many parts looted houses had also been set on fire and now the flames began to spread.

At first, attempts were made to isolate the blaze. Then, the wind changed, blowing the fire away from the Turkish quarter, and further outbreaks were started by the troops. Soon, the whole city, with the exception of the Turkish quarter and a few houses near the Kassamba railway station, was burning fiercely. The massacre continued with unabated ferocity. A cordon of troops was drawn round the city to keep the refugees within the burning area. The streams of panic-stricken fugitives were shot down pitilessly or driven back into the inferno. The narrow, gutted streets became so choked with corpses that, even had the would-be rescue parties been able to endure the sickening stench that arose, they could not have passed along them. Smyrna was changed from a city into a charnel-house. Many refugees had tried to reach ships in the inner harbour. Shot, drowned, mangled by propellers, their bodies floated hideously in the blood-tinged water. But the quayside was still crowded with those trying frantically to escape from the blazing waterfront buildings toppling above them a few yards behind. It was said that the screams of these people were heard a mile out at sea. *Giaur Izmir*—infidel Smyrna—had atoned for its sins.

By the time that dawn broke on the fifteenth of September, over one hundred and twenty thousand persons had perished; but somewhere amidst that horror had been Dimitrios, alive.

As, sixteen years later, his train drew into Smyrna, Latimer came to the conclusion that he was being a fool. It was not a conclusion that he had reached hastily or without weighing carefully all the available evidence. It was a conclusion that he disliked exceedingly. Yet there were two hard facts that were inescapable. In the first place, he might have asked Colonel Haki for assistance in gaining access to the records of the court martial and confession of Dhris Mohammed and had not been able to think of a reasonable excuse for doing so. In the second place, he knew so little Turkish that, even assuming that he could gain access to the records without Colonel Haki's help, he would be unable to read them. To have set out at all on this fantastic and slightly undignified wild goose chase was bad enough. To have set out without, so to speak, a gun and ammunition with which to make the killing was crass idiocy. Had he not been installed within an hour of his arrival in an excellent hotel, had his room not possessed a very comfortable bed and a view across the gulf to the sun-drenched, khaki hills that lay beyond it, and, above all, had he not been offered a dry Martini by the French proprietor who greeted him, he would have abandoned his experiment in detection and returned forthwith to Istanbul. As it was . . . Dimitrios or no Dimitrios, he might as well see something of Smyrna now that he was in the place. He partly unpacked his suit-cases.

It has been said that Latimer possessed a tenacious mind. Perhaps it would have been more accurate to say that he did not possess the sort of mental air-lock system which enables its fortunate owner to dispose of problems merely by forgetting them. Latimer might banish the problem from his mind but it would soon return to nibble furtively at his consciousness. He would have an uneasy feeling that he had mislaid something without being quite sure what that something was. His thoughts would wander from the business in hand. He would find himself staring blankly into space until, suddenly, there was the problem, back again. Useless to reason that, as he himself had created it, he should, therefore, be able to destroy it. Useless to argue that it was futile and that the solution of it did not matter anyway. It had to be tackled. On his second morning in Smyrna, he shrugged his shoulders irritably, went to the proprietor of his hotel and asked to be put in touch with a good interpreter.

Fedor Muishkin was a self-important little Russian of about sixty with a thick, pendulous underlip which flapped and quivered as he talked. He had an office on the waterfront and earned his living by translating business documents and interpreting for the masters and pursers of foreign cargo vessels using the port. He had been a Menshevik and had fled from Odessa in 1919; but although, as the hotel proprietor pointed out sardonically, he now declared himself in sympathy with the Soviets, he had preferred not to return to Russia. A humbug, mind you, but at the same time a good interpreter. If you wanted an interpreter, Muishkin was the man.

Muishkin himself also said that he was the man. He had a high-pitched, husky voice and scratched himself a great deal. His English was accurate but larded with slang phrases that never seemed quite to fit their contexts. He said: 'If there is anything I can do for you just give me the wire. I'm dirt cheap.'

'I want,' Latimer explained, 'to trace the record of a Greek who left here in September, 1922.'

The other's eyebrows went up. 'Nineteen twenty-two, eh? A Greek who left here?' He chuckled breathlessly. 'A good many of them left here then.' He spat on one forefinger and drew it across his throat. 'Like that! It was damnawful the way those Turks treated those Greeks. Bloody!'

'This man got away on a refugee ship. His name was Dimitrios. He was believed to have conspired with a Negro named Dhris Mohammed to murder a moneylender named Sholem. The Negro was tried by a military court and hanged. Dimitrios got away. I want to inspect, if I can, the records of the evidence taken at the trial, the confession of the Negro and the inquiries concerning Dimitrios.'

Muishkin stared. 'Dimitrios?'

'Yes.'

'Nineteen twenty-two?'

'Yes.' Latimer's heart thumped. 'Why? Did you happen to know him?'

The Russian appeared to be about to say something and then to change his mind. He shook his head. 'No. I was thinking that it was a very common name. Have you permission to examine the police archives?'

'No. I was hoping that you might be able to advise me as to the best way of getting permission. I realise, of course, that your business is only concerned with making translations, but if you could help me in this matter I should be very grateful.'

Muishkin pinched his lower lip thoughtfully. 'Perhaps if you were to approach the British Vice-Consul and request him to secure permission . . .?' He broke off. 'But excuse me,' he said; 'why do you want these records? I ask, not because I cannot mind my own damn business, but that question may be asked by the police. Now,' he went on slowly, 'if it were a *legal* matter and quite above board and Bristol fashion. I have a friend with influence who might arrange the matter quite cheap.'

Latimer felt himself redden. 'As it happens,' he said as casually as he could, 'it *is* a legal matter. I could, of course, go to the Consul, but if you care to arrange this business for me then I shall be saved the trouble.'

'A pleasure. I shall speak to my friend to-day. The police, you understand, are damnawful and if I go to them myself it will cost plenty. I like to protect my clients.'

'That's very good of you.'

'Don't mention it.' A faraway look came into his eyes. 'I like you British, you know. You understand how to do business. You do not haggle like those damn Greeks. When a man says cash with order you pay cash with order. A deposit? O.K. The British play fair. There is a mutual confidence between all parties. A chap can do his best work under such circumstances. He feels . . .'

'How much?' interrupted Latimer.

'Five hundred piastres?' He said it hesitantly. His eyes were mournful. Here was an artist who had no confidence in himself, a child in business matters, happy only in his work.

Latimer thought for a moment. Five hundred piastres was less than a pound. Cheap enough. Then he detected a gleam in the mournful eyes.

'Two hundred and fifty,' he said firmly.

Muishkin threw up his hands in despair. He had to live. There was his friend, too. He had great influence.

Soon after, having paid over one hundred and fifty piastres on account of a finally agreed price of three hundred (including fifty piastres for the influential friend), Latimer left. It was understood that he would call in the following day to learn the result of the negotiations with the friend. He walked back along the quayside not unpleased with his morning's work. He would have preferred, it was true, to have examined the records himself and to have seen the translation done. He would have felt more like an investigator and less like an inquisitive tourist; but there it was. There was always the chance, of course, that Muishkin might have in mind the pocketing of an easy one hundred and fifty piastres; but somehow he did not think so. He was susceptible to impressions and the Russian had impressed him as being fundamentally, if not superficially, honest. And there could be no question of his being deceived by manufactured documents. Colonel Haki had told him enough about the Dhris Mohammed court martial to enable him to detect that sort of fraud. The only thing that could go wrong was that the friend would prove unworthy of his fifty piastres.

Muishkin's office was locked when he called the next day and although he waited for an hour on the filthy wooden landing outside it, the interpreter did not appear. A second call, later in the day, was equally abortive. He shrugged. It hardly seemed worth any man's while to embezzle five shillings worth of Turkish piastres. But he began to lose a little of his confidence.

It was restored by a note that awaited him at the hotel on his return. A page of wild handwriting explained that the writer had been called away from his office to interpret in a dispute between a Romanian second-mate and the dock police over the death by crowbar of a Greek stevedore, that he could pull out his own finger-nails one by one for causing Mister Latimer inconvenience, that his friend had arranged everything and that he would deliver the translation himself the following evening.

He arrived, sweating profusely, very shortly before the time of the evening meal, and Latimer was drinking an aperitif. Muishkin came towards him waving his arms and rolling his eyes despairingly and, throwing himself into an armchair, emitted a loud gasp of exhaustion.

'What a day! Such heat!' he said.

'Have you got the translation?'

Muishkin nodded wearily, his eyes closed. With what seemed a painful effort he put his hand in his inside pocket and drew out a bundle of papers secured by a wire clip. He thrust them into Latimer's hands–the dying courier delivering his last dispatch.

'Will you have a drink?' said Latimer.

The Russian's eyes flickered open and he looked round like a man regaining consciousness. He said: 'If you like. I will have an absinthe, please. *Avec de la glace.*'

The waiter took the order and Latimer sat back to inspect his purchase.

The translation was handwritten and covered twelve large sheets of paper. Latimer glanced through the first two or three pages. There was no doubt that it was all genuine. He began to read it carefully.

NATIONAL GOVERNMENT OF TURKEY
TRIBUNAL OF INDEPENDENCE

*By order of the officer commanding the garrison of Izmir, acting under the
Decree Law promulgated at Ankara on the eighteenth day of the sixth
month of nineteen twenty-two in the new calendar.*

*Summary of evidence taken before the Deputy President of the Tribunal,
Major-of-Brigade Zia Haki, on the sixth day of the tenth month of
nineteen twenty-two in the new calendar.*

The Jew, Zakari, complains that the murder of his cousin, Sholem,
was the work of Dhris Mohammed, a Negro fig-packer of Buja.

Last week, a patrol belonging to the sixtieth regiment discovered the
body of Sholem, a Duenme moneylender, in his room in an unnamed
street near the Old Mosque. His throat had been cut. Although this
man was neither the son of True Believers nor of good reputation, our
vigilant police instituted inquiries and discovered that his money had
been taken.

Several days later, the complainant, Zakari, informed the Commandant of Police that he had been in a café and seen the man Dhris
showing handfuls of Greek money. He knew Dhris for a poor man and
was surprised. Later, when Dhris had become drunk, he heard him
boast that the Jew Sholem had lent him money without interest. At that
time he knew nothing of the death of Sholem but when his relations told
him of it he remembered what he had seen and heard.

Evidence was heard from Abdul Hakk, the owner of the Bar Cristal,
who said that Dhris had shown this Greek money, a matter of several
hundreds of drachmas, and had boasted that he had had it from the Jew
Sholem without interest. He had thought this strange for Sholem was a
hard man.

A dock-worker named Ismail also deposed that he had heard this
from the prisoner.

Asked to explain how he came into possession of the money, the
murderer first denied that he had had the money or that he had ever
seen Sholem and said that as a True Believer, he was hated by the Jew
Zakari. He said that Abdul Hakk and Ismail had also lied.

Questioned sternly by the Deputy-President of the Tribunal, he then
admitted that he had had the money and that it had been given to him
by Sholem for a service he had done. But he could not explain what this
service had been and his manner became strange and agitated. He
denied killing Sholem and in a blasphemous way called upon the True
God to witness his innocence.

The Deputy-President then ordered that the prisoner be hanged, the
other members of the Tribunal agreeing that this was right and just.

Latimer had come to the end of a page. He looked at Muishkin. The
Russian had swallowed the absinthe and was examining the glass. He caught
Latimer's eye. 'Absinthe,' he said, 'is very good indeed. So cooling.'

'Will you have another?'

'If you like.' He smiled and indicated the papers in Latimer's hand. 'That's all right, eh?'

'Oh yes, it looks all right. But they are a little vague about their dates, aren't they? There is no doctor's report either, and no attempt to fix the time of the murder. As for the evidence, it seems fantastically feeble to me. Nothing was proved.'

Muishkin looked surprised. 'But why bother to prove? This Negro was obviously guilty. Best to hang him.'

'I see. Well, if you don't mind, I'll go on glancing through it.'

Muishkin shrugged, stretched himself luxuriously and signalled to the waiter. Latimer turned a page and went on reading.

STATEMENT MADE BY THE MURDERER, DHRIS MOHAMMED, IN THE
PRESENCE OF THE GUARD-COMMANDANT OF THE BARRACKS IN IZMIR
AND OTHER TRUE WITNESSES

It is said in the book that he shall not prosper who makes lies and I say these things in order to prove my innocence and to save myself from the gallows. I have lied but now I will tell the truth. I am a True Believer. There is no god but God.

I did not kill Sholem. I tell you I did not kill him. Why should I lie now? Yes, I will explain. It was not I but Dimitrios who killed Sholem.

I will tell you about Dimitrios and you will believe me. Dimitrios is a Greek. To Greeks he is a Greek but to True Believers he says that he is also a Believer and that it is only with the authorities that he is a Greek because of some paper signed by his foster-parents.

Dimitrios worked with others of us in the packing sheds and he was hated by many for his violence and for his bitter tongue. But I am a man who loves other men as brothers and I would speak with Dimitrios sometimes as he worked and tell him of the religion of God. And he would listen.

Then, when the Greeks were fleeing before the victorious army of the True God, Dimitrios came to my house and asked me to hide him from the terror of the Greeks. He said that he was a True Believer. So I hid him. Then, our Glorious army came to our aid. But Dimitrios did not go because he was, by reason of this paper signed by his foster-parents a Greek and in fear of his life. So he stayed in my house and when he went out dressed like a Turk. Then, one day, he said certain things to me. There was a Jew, Sholem, he said, who had much money, Greek pieces and some gold, hidden below the floor of his room. It was the time, he said, to take our revenge upon those who had insulted the True God and His Prophet. It was wrong, he said, that a pig of a Jew should have the money rightfully belonging to True Believers. He proposed that we should go secretly to Sholem, bind him and take his money.

At first I was afraid, but he put heart into me, reminding me of the book which says that whosoever fights for the religion of God, whether he be slain or victorious, will surely find a great reward. This is now my reward: to be hanged like a dog.

Yes, I will go on. That night after the curfew we went to the place where Sholem lived and crept up the stairs to his room. The door was bolted. Then Dimitrios knocked and called out that it was a patrol to search the house and Sholem opened the door. He had been in bed and he was grumbling at being woken from his sleep. When he saw us he called upon God and tried to close the door. But Dimitrios seized him and held him while I went in as we had arranged and searched for the loose board which concealed the money. Dimitrios dragged the old man across the bed and kept him down with his knee.

I soon found the loose board and turned round full of joy to tell Dimitrios. He had his back turned towards me and was pressing down on Sholem with the blanket to stifle his cries. He said that he himself would bind Sholem with rope which we had brought. I saw him now draw out his knife. I thought that he was meaning to cut the rope for some purpose and I said nothing. Then, before I could speak, he drove the knife into the old Jew's neck and pulled it across his throat.

I saw the blood bubble and spurt out as if from a fountain and Sholem rolled over. Dimitrios stood away and watched him for a moment then he looked at me. I asked him what he had done and he answered that it was necessary to kill Sholem for fear that he should point us out to the police. Sholem was still moving on the bed and the blood was still bubbling, but Dimitrios said that he was certainly dead. After that, we took the money.

Then, Dimitrios said that it was better that we should not go together but that each should take his share and go separately. That was agreed. I was afraid then, for Dimitrios had a knife and I had none and I thought he meant to kill me. I wondered why he had told me of the money. He had said that he needed a companion to search for the money while he held Sholem. But I could see that he had meant from the first to kill Sholem. Why then had he brought me? He could have found the money for himself after he had killed the Jew. But we divided the money equally and he smiled and did not try to kill me. We left the place separately. He had told me the day before that there were Greek ships lying off the coast near Smyrna and that he had overheard a man saying that the captains of these ships were taking refugees who could pay. I think that he escaped on one of those ships.

I see now that I was a fool of fools and that he was right to smile at me. He knew that when my purse becomes full my head becomes empty. He knew, God's curses fall upon him, that when I sin by becoming drunk I cannot stop my tongue from wagging. I did not kill Sholem. It was Dimitrios the Greek who killed him. Dimitrios . . . (*here followed a stream of obscenities*). There is no doubt in what I say. As God is God and as Muhammad is His Prophet, I swear that I have said the truth. For the love of God, have mercy.

A note was appended to this, saying that the confession had been signed with a thumb print and witnessed. The record went on:

The murderer was asked for a description of this Dimitrios and said: 'He has the look of a Greek but I do not think he is one because he hates his own countrymen. He is shorter than I am and his hair is long and straight. His face is very still and he speaks very little. His eyes are brown and tired-looking. Many men are afraid of him but I do not understand this as he is not strong and I could break him with my two hands.'

N.B. The height of this man is 185 centimetres.

Inquiries have been made concerning the man Dimitrios at the packing sheds. He is known and disliked. Nothing has been heard of him for several weeks and he is presumed to have died in the fire. This seems likely.

The murderer was executed on the ninth day of the tenth month of nineteen twenty-two in the new calendàr.

Latimer returned to the confession and examined it thoughtfully. It rang true; there was no doubt about that. There was a circumstantial feeling about it. The Negro, Dhris, had obviously been a very stupid man. Could he have invented those details about the scene in Sholem's room? A guilty man inventing a tale would surely have embroidered it differently. And there was his fear that Dimitrios might have been going to kill him. If he himself had been responsible for the killing he would not have thought of that. Colonel Haki had said that it was the sort of story that a man might invent to save his neck. Fear did stimulate even the most sluggish imaginations; but did it stimulate them in quite that sort of way? The authorities obviously had not cared very much whether the story was or was not true. Their inquiries had been pitiably half-hearted; yet even so they had tended to confirm the Negro's story. Dimitrios had been presumed to have died in the fire. There was no evidence offered to support the presumption. It had, no doubt, been easier to hang Dhris Mohammed than to conduct, amidst all the terrible confusion of those October days, a search for a hypothetical Greek named Dimitrios. Dimitrios had, of course, counted on that fact. But for the accident of the Colonel's transfer to the secret police, he would never have been connected with the affair.

Latimer had once seen a zoophysicist friend of his build up the complete skeleton of a prehistoric animal from a fragment of fossilized bone. It had taken the zoophysicist nearly two years and Latimer, the economist, had marvelled at the man's inexhaustible enthusiasm for the task. Now, for the first time, he understood that enthusiasm. He had unearthed a single twisted fragment of the mind of Dimitrios and now he wanted to complete the structure. The fragment was small enough but it was substantial. The wretched Dhris had never had a chance. Dimitrios had used the Negro's dull wits, had played upon his religious fanaticism, his simplicity, his cupidity with a skill that was terrifying. 'We divided the money equally and he smiled and did not try to kill me.' Dimitrios had smiled. And the Negro had been too preoccupied with his fear of the man whom he could have broken with his two hands to wonder about that smile until it was too late. The brown, tired-looking eyes had watched Dhris Mohammed and understood him perfectly.

Latimer folded up the papers, put them in his pocket and turned to Muishkin.

'One hundred and fifty piastres, I owe you.'

'Right,' said Muishkin into his glass. He had ordered and was now finishing his third absinthe. He set down his glass and took the money from Latimer. 'I like you,' he said seriously; 'you have no *snobisme*. Now you will have a drink with me, eh?'

Latimer glanced at his watch. It was getting late and he had had nothing to eat. 'I'd be glad to,' he answered; 'but why not have some dinner with me first?'

'Good!' Muishkin clambered laboriously to his feet. 'Good,' he repeated and Latimer saw that his eyes were unnaturally bright.

At the Russian's suggestion they went out to a restaurant, a place of subdued lights and red plush and gilt and stained mirrors, where French food was served. It was crowded and the atmosphere was thick with cigarette smoke. They sat down in upholstered chairs which exuded wafts of stale scent.

'*Ton*,' said Muishkin looking round. He seized the menu and after some deliberation chose the most expensive dish on it. With their food they drank a syrupy, resinous Smyrna wine. Muishkin began to talk about his life. Odessa, 1918. Stambul, 1919. Smyrna, 1921. Bolsheviks. Wrangel's army. Kiev. A woman they called The Butcher. They used the abattoir as a prison because the prison had become an abattoir. Terrible, damnawful atrocities. Allied army of occupation. The English sporting. American relief. Bed bugs. Typhus. Vickers guns. The Greeks–God, those Greeks! Fortunes waiting to be picked up. Kemalists. His voice droned on while outside, through the cigarette smoke, beyond the red plush and the gilt and the white table-cloths, the amethyst twilight had deepened into night.

Another bottle of syrupy wine arrived. Latimer began to feel sleepy.

'And after so much madness, where are we now?' demanded Muishkin. His English had been steadily deteriorating. Now, his lower lip wet and quivering with emotion, he fixed Latimer with the unwavering stare of the drunk about to become philosophical. 'Where now?' he repeated and thumped the table.

'In Smyrna,' said Latimer and realized suddenly that he had drunk too much of the wine.

Muishkin shook his head irritably. 'We grade rapidly to damnawful hell,' he declared. 'Are you a Marxist?'

'No.'

Muishkin leaned forward confidentially. 'Neither me.' He plucked at Latimer's sleeve. His lip trembled violently. 'I'm a swindler.'

'Are you?'

'Yes.' Tears began to form in his eyes. 'I damn well swindled you.'

'Did you?'

'Yes.' He fumbled in his pocket. 'You are no snob. You must take back fifty piastres.'

'What for?'

'Take them back.' The tears began to course down his cheeks and mingle with the sweat collecting on the point of his chin. 'I swindled you, Mister. There was no damn friend to pay, no permission, nothing.'

'Do you mean that you made up those records yourself?'

Muishkin sat up sharply. '*Je ne suis pas un faussaire*,' he asserted. He wagged a finger in Latimer's face. 'This type came to me three months ago. By paying large bribes–' the finger stabbed emphatically '–large bribes, he had obtained the permissions to examine the archives for the dossier on the murder of Sholem. The dossier was in the old Arabic script and he brought photographs of the pages to me to translate. He took the photographs back, but I kept the translation on file You see? I swindled you. You paid fifty piastres too much. Faugh!' He snapped his fingers. 'I could have swindled five hundred piastres, and you would have paid. I am too soft.'

'What did he want with this information?'

Muishkin looked sulky. 'I can mind my own damn nose in the business.'

'What did he look like?'

'He looked like a Frenchman.'

'What sort of a Frenchman?'

But Muishkin's head had sagged forward on to his chest and he did not answer. Then, after a moment or two, he raised his head and stared blankly at Latimer. His face was livid and Latimer guessed that he would very shortly be sick. His lips moved.

'*Je ne suis pas un faussaire*,' he muttered; 'three hundred piastres, dirt cheap!' He stood up suddenly, murmured, '*Excusez-moi*,' and walked rapidly in the direction of the toilet.

Latimer waited for a time then paid the bill and went to investigate. There was another entrance to the toilet and Muishkin had gone. Latimer walked back to his hotel.

From the balcony outside the window of his room, he could see over the bay to the hills beyond. A moon had risen and its reflection gleamed through the tangle of crane jibs along the quay where the steamers berthed. The searchlights of a Turkish cruiser anchored in the roadstead outside the inner port swung round like long white fingers, brushed the summits of the hills and were extinguished. Out in the harbour and on the slopes above the town pinpoints of light twinkled. A slight warm breeze off the sea had begun to stir the leaves of a rubber tree in the garden below him. In another room of the hotel a woman laughed. Somewhere in the distance a gramophone was playing a tango. The turntable was revolving too quickly and the sound was shrill and congested.

Latimer lit a final cigarette and wondered for the hundredth time what the man who looked like a Frenchman had wanted with the dossier of the Sholem murder. At last he pitched his cigarette away and shrugged. One thing was certain: he could not possibly have been interested in Dimitrios.

Chapter Four

Mr Peters

Two days later, Latimer left Smyrna. He did not see Muishkin again.

The situation in which a person, imagining fondly that he is in charge of his own destiny, is, in fact, the sport of circumstances beyond his control, is always fascinating. It is the essential element in most good theatre from the *Œdipus* of Sophocles to *East Lynne*. When, however, that person is oneself and one is examining the situation in retrospect, the fascination becomes a trifle morbid. Thus, when Latimer used afterwards to look back upon those two days in Smyrna, it was not so much his ignorance of the part he was playing but the bliss which accompanied the ignorance that so appalled him. He had gone into the business believing his eyes to be wide open, whereas, actually, they had been tightly shut. That, no doubt, could not have been helped. The galling part was that he had failed for so long to perceive the fact. Of course, he did himself less than justice; but his self-esteem had been punctured; he had been transferred without his knowledge from the role of sophisticated, impersonal weigher of facts to that of active participator in a melodrama.

Of the imminence of that humiliation, however, he had no inkling when, on the morning after his dinner with Muishkin, he sat down with a pencil and a notebook to arrange the material for his experiment in detection.

Some time early in October 1922, Dimitrios had left Smyrna. He had had money and had probably purchased a passage on a Greek steamer. The next time Colonel Haki had heard of him he had been in Adrianople two years later. In that interim, however, the Bulgarian police had had trouble with him in Sofia in connection with the attempted assassination of Stambulisky. Latimer was a little hazy as to the precise date of that attempt but he began to jot down a rough chronological table.

TIME	PLACE	REMARKS	SOURCE OF INFORMATION
1922 (October) . . .	Smyrna	Sholem	Police Archives
1923 (early part) . .	Sofia	Stambulisky	Colonel Haki
1924	Adrianople	Kemal attempt	Colonel Haki
1926	Belgrade	Espionage for France	Colonel Haki
1926	Switzerland	Talat passport	Colonel Haki
1929–31 (?)	Paris	Drugs	Colonel Haki
1932	Zagreb	Croat assassin	Colonel Haki
1937	Lyons	*Carte d'identité*	Colonel Haki
1938	Istanbul	Murdered	Colonel Haki

The immediate problem, then, was quite clearcut. In the six months following the murder of Sholem, Dimitrios had escaped from Smyrna, made his way to Sofia and become involved in a plot to assassinate the Bulgarian Prime Minister. Latimer found it a trifle difficult to form any estimate of the time required to become involved in a plot to kill a Prime Minister; but it was fairly certain that Dimitrios must have arrived in Sofia soon after his departure from Smyrna. If he had indeed escaped by Greek steamer he must have gone first to the Piraeus and Athens. From Athens he could have reached Sofia overland, via Salonika, or by sea, via the Dardanelles and the Golden Horn to Bourgaz or Varna, Bulgaria's Black Sea Port. Istanbul at that time was in Allied hands. He would have had nothing to fear from the Allies. The question was: what had induced him to go to Sofia?

However, the logical course now was to go to Athens and tackle the job of picking up the trail there. It would not be easy. Even if attempts had been made to record the presence of every refugee among the tens of thousands who had arrived, it was more than probable that what records still existed, if any, were incomplete. There was no point, however, in anticipating failure. He had several valuable friends in Athens and if there was a record in existence it was fairly certain that he would be able to get access to it. He shut up his notebook.

When the weekly boat to the Piraeus left Smyrna the following day, Latimer was among the passengers.

During the months following the Turkish occupation of Smyrna, more than eight hundred thousand Greeks returned to their country. They came, boatload after boatload of them, packed on the decks and in the holds. Many of them were naked and starving. Some still carried in their arms the dead children they had had no time to bury. With them came the diseases of typhus, typhoid and smallpox.

War-weary and ruined, gripped by a food shortage and starved of medical supplies, their motherland received them. In the hastily improvised refugee camps they died like flies. Outside Athens, on the Piraeus, in Salonika, masses of humanity lay rotting in the cold of a Greek winter. Then, the Fourth Assembly of the League of Nations, in session in Geneva, voted one hundred thousand gold francs to the Nansen relief organization for immediate use in Greece. The work of salvage began. Huge refugee settlements were organized. Food was brought and clothing and medical supplies. The epidemics were stopped. The survivors began to sort themselves into new communities. For the first time in history, large scale disaster had been halted by goodwill and reason. It seemed as if the human animal were at last discovering a conscience, as if it were at last becoming aware of its humanity.

All this and more, Latimer heard from a friend, one Siantos, in Athens. When, however, he came to the point of his inquiries, Siantos pursed his lips.

'A complete register of those who arrived from Smyrna? That is a tall order. If you had seen them come . . . So many and in such a state . . .' And then followed the inevitable question. 'Why are you interested?'

It had occurred to Latimer that this question was going to crop up again and again. He had accordingly prepared his explanation. To have told the truth, to have explained that he was trying, for purely academic reasons, to trace the history of a dead criminal named Dimitrios would have been a long and uneasy business. He was, in any case, not anxious to have a second opinion on his prospects of success. His own was depressing enough. What had seemed a fascinating idea in a Turkish mortuary might well, in the bright, warm light of a Greek autumn, appear merely absurd. Much simpler to avoid the issue altogether.

He answered: 'It is in connection with a new book I am writing. A matter of detail that must be checked. I want to see if it is possible to trace an individual refugee after so long.'

Siantos said that he understood and Latimer grinned ashamedly to himself. The fact that one was a writer could be relied upon to explain away the most curious extravagances.

He had gone to Siantos because he knew that the man had a Government post of some importance in Athens; but now his first disappointment was in store for him. A week went by and, at the end of it, Siantos was able to tell him only that a register was in existence, that it was in the custody of the municipal authorities and that it was not open to inspection by unauthorized persons. Permission would have to be obtained. It took another week, a week of waiting, of sitting in *kafenios*, of being introduced to thirsty men with connections in the municipal offices. At last, however, the permission was forthcoming and the following day Latimer presented himself at the bureau in which the records were housed.

The inquiry office was a bare tiled room with a counter at one end. Behind the counter sat the official in charge. He shrugged over the information Latimer had to give him. A fig-packer named Dimitrios? October 1922? It was impossible. The register had been compiled alphabetically by surname.

Latimer's heart sank. All his trouble, then, was to go for nothing. He had thanked the man and was turning away when he had an idea. There was just a remote chance . . .

He turned back to the official. 'The surname,' he said, 'may have been Makropoulos.'

He was dimly aware, as he said it, that behind him a man had entered the inquiry office through the door leading to the street. The sun was streaming obliquely into the room and for an instant a long, distorted shadow twisted across the tiles as the new-comer passed the window.

'Dimitrios Makropoulos?' repeated the official. 'That is better. If there was a person of that name on the register we will find him. It is a question of patience and organization. Please come this way.'

He raised the flap of the counter for Latimer to go through. As he did so he glanced over Latimer's shoulder.

'Gone!' he exclaimed. 'I have no assistance in my work of organization here. The whole burden falls upon my shoulders. Yet people have no patience. I am engaged for a moment. They cannot wait.' He shrugged. 'That is their affair. I do my duty. If you will follow me, please.'

Latimer followed him down a flight of stone stairs into an extensive basement occupied by row upon row of steel cabinets.

'Organization,' commented the official; 'that is the secret of modern statecraft. Organization will make a greater Greece. A new empire. But patience is necessary.' He led the way to a series of small cabinets in one corner of the basement, pulled open one of the drawers and began with his finger-nail to flick over a series of cards. At last he stopped at a card and examined it carefully before closing the drawer. 'Makropoulos. If there is a record of this man we shall find it in drawer number sixteen. That is organization.'

In drawer number sixteen, however, they drew a blank. The official threw up his hands in despair and searched again without success. Then inspiration came to Latimer.

'Try under the name of Talat,' he said desperately.

'But that is a Turkish name.'

'I know. But try it.'

The official shrugged. There was another reference to the main index. 'Drawer twenty-seven,' announced the official a little impatiently; 'are you sure that this man came to Athens? Many went to Salonika. Why not this fig-packer?'

This was precisely the question that Latimer had been asking himself. He said nothing and watched the official's finger-nail flicking over another series of cards. Suddenly it stopped.

'Have you found it?' said Latimer quickly.

The official pulled out a card. 'Here is one,' he said. 'The man was a fig-packer, but the name is Dimitrios Tala*dis*.'

'Let me see.' Latimer took the card. Dimitrios Taladis! There it was in black and white. He had found out something that Colonel Haki did not know. Dimitrios had used the name Talat before 1926. There could be no doubt that it *was* Dimitrios. He had merely tacked a Greek suffix on to the name. He stared at the card. And there were here some other things that Colonal Haki did not know.

He looked up at the beaming official. 'May I copy this?'

'Of course. Patience and organization, you see. My organization is for use. But I must not let the record out of my sight. That is the regulation.'

Under the now somewhat mystified eyes of the apostle of organization and patience Latimer began to copy the wording on the card into his note-book, translating it as he did so into English. He wrote:

NUMBER T.53462

NATIONAL RELIEF ORGANIZATION

Refugee Section: ATHINAI

Sex: Male. *Name:* Dimitrios Taladis. *Born:* Salonika, 1889. *Occupation:* Fig-packer. *Parents:* believed dead. *Identity Papers or Passport:* Identity card lost. Said to have been issued at Smyrna. *Nationality:* Greek. *Arrived:* October 1st, 1922. *Coming from:* Smyrna. *On examination:* Able-bodied. No disease. Without money. Assigned to camp at Tabouria. Temporary identity paper issued. *Note:* Left Tabouria on own initiative, November 29th, 1922: Warrant for arrest on charge of robbery and attempted murder, issued in Athinai, November 30th, 1922. Believed to have escaped by sea.

Yes, that was Dimitrios all right. The date of his birth agreed with that supplied by the Greek police (and based on information gained prior to 1922) to Colonel Haki. The place of birth, however, was different.

According to the Turkish dossier it had been Larissa. Why had Dimitrios bothered to change it? If he were giving a false name, he must have seen that the chances of its falsity being discovered by reference to the registration records were as great for Salonika as for Larissa.

Salonika 1889! Why Salonika? Then Latimer remembered. Of course! It was quite simple. In 1889 Salonika had been in Turkish territory, a part of the Ottoman Empire. The registration records of that period would, in all probability, not be available to the Greek authorities. Dimitrios had certainly been no fool. But why had he picked the name Taladis? Why had he not chosen a typical Greek name? The Turkish 'Talat' must have had some special association for him. As for his identity card issued in Smyrna, that would naturally be 'lost' since, presumably, it had been issued to him in the name of Makropoulos by which he was already known to the Greek police.

The date of his arrival fitted in with the vague allusions to time made in the court martial. Unlike the majority of his fellow refugees, he had been able-bodied and free from disease when he had arrived. Naturally. Thanks to Sholem's Greek money, he had been able to buy a passage to the Piraeus and travel in comparative comfort instead of being loaded on to a refugee ship with thousands of others. Dimitrios had known how to look after himself. The fig-packer had packed enough figs. Dimitrios the Man had been emerging from his chrysalis. No doubt he had had a substantial amount of Sholem's money left when he had arrived. Yet to the relief authorities he had been 'without money'. That had been sensible of him. He might otherwise have been forced to buy food and clothing for stupid fools who had failed to provide, as he had provided, for the future. His expenses had been heavy enough as it was; so heavy that another Sholem had been needed. No doubt he had regretted Dhris Mohammed's half share.

'Believed to have escaped by sea.' With the proceeds of the second robbery added to the balance from the first, he had no doubt been able to pay for his passage to Bourgaz. It would obviously have been too risky for him to have gone overland. He had only temporary identity papers and might have been stopped at the frontier, whereas in Bourgaz, the same papers issued by an international relief commission with considerable prestige would have enabled him to get through.

The official's much-advertised patience was showing signs of wearing thin. Latimer handed over the card, expressed his thanks in a suitable manner and returned thoughtfully to his hotel.

He was feeling pleased with himself. He had discovered some new information about Dimitrios and he had discovered it through his own efforts. It had been, it was true, an obvious piece of routine inquiry; but, in the best Scotland Yard tradition, it had called for patience and persistence. Besides, if he had not thought of trying the Talat name . . . He wished that he could have sent a report of his investigations to Colonel Haki, but that was out of the question. The Colonel would probably fail to understand the spirit in which the experiment in detection was being conducted. In any case, Dimitrios himself would by this time be mouldering below ground, his dossier sealed and forgotten in the archives of the Turkish secret police. The main thing now was to tackle the Sofia affair.

He tried to remember what he knew about postwar Bulgarian politics and speedily came to the conclusion that it was very little. In 1923 Stambulisky had, he knew, been head of a government of liberal tendencies; but of just how liberal those tendencies had been he had no idea. There had been an attempted assassination and later a military *coup d'état* carried out at the instigation, if not under the leadership of I.M.R.O., the International Macedonian Revolutionary Organization. Stambulisky had fled from Sofia, tried to organize a counter-revolution and been killed. That was the gist of the affair, he thought. But of the rights and wrongs of it (if any such distinction were possible), of the nature of the political forces involved, he was quite ignorant. That state of affairs would have to be remedied; and the place in which to remedy it would be Sofia.

That evening he asked Siantos to dinner. Latimer knew him for a vain, generous soul who liked discussing his friends' problems and was flattered when, by making judicious use of his official position, he could help them. After giving thanks for the assistance in the matter of the municipal register, Latimer broached the subject of Sofia.

'I am going to trespass on your kindness still further, my dear Siantos.'

'So much the better.'

'Do you know anyone in Sofia? I want a letter of introduction to an intelligent newspaper man there who could give me some inside information about Bulgarian politics in the 'twenties.'

Siantos smoothed his gleaming white hair and grinned admiringly. 'You writers have bizarre tastes. Something might be done. Do you want a Greek or a Bulgar?'

'Greek for preference. I don't speak Bulgarian.'

Siantos was thoughtful for a moment. 'There is a man in Sofia named Marukakis,' he said at last. 'He is the Sofia correspondent of a French news agency. I do not know him myself, but I might be able to get a letter to him from a friend of mine.' They were sitting in a restaurant, and now Siantos glanced round furtively and lowered his voice. 'There is only one trouble about him from your point of view. I happen to know that he has . . .' The voice sunk still lower in tone. Latimer was prepared for nothing less horrible than leprosy. '. . . Communist tendencies,' concluded Siantos in a whisper.

Latimer raised his eyebrows. 'I don't regard that as a drawback. All the Communists I have ever met have been highly intelligent.'

Siantos looked shocked. 'How can that be? It is dangerous to say such things, my friend. Marxist thought is forbidden in Greece.'

'When can I have that letter?'

Siantos sighed. 'Bizarre!' he remarked. 'I will get it for you to-morrow. You writers . . . !'

Within a week the letter of introduction had been obtained, and Latimer, having secured Greek exit and Bulgarian entry visas, boarded a night train for Sofia.

The train was not crowded and he had hoped to have a sleeping car compartment to himself; but five minutes before the train was due to start, luggage was carried in and deposited above the empty berth. The owner of the luggage followed very soon after it.

'I must apologize for intruding on your privacy,' he said to Latimer in English.

He was a fat, unhealthy-looking man of about fifty-five. He had turned to tip the porter before he spoke, and the first thing about him that impressed Latimer was that the seat of his trousers sagged absurdly, making his walk reminiscent of that of the hind legs of an elephant. Then Latimer saw his face and forgot about the trousers. There was the sort of sallow shape-lessness about it that derives from simultaneous over-eating and under-sleeping. From above two heavy satchels of flesh peered a pair of pale-blue, bloodshot eyes that seemed to be permanently weeping. The nose was rubbery and indeterminate. It was the mouth that gave the face expression. The lips were pallid and undefined, seeming thicker than they really were. Pressed together over unnaturally white and regular false teeth, they were set permanently in a saccharine smile. In conjunction with the weeping eyes above it, it created an impression of sweet patience in adversity, quite startling in its intensity. Here, it said, was a man who had suffered, who had been buffeted by fiendishly vindictive Fates as no other man had been buffeted, yet who had retained his humble faith in the essential goodness of Man: here, it said, was a martyr who smiled through the flames—smiled yet who could not but weep for the misery of others as he did so. He reminded Latimer of a high church priest he had known in England who had been unfrocked for embezzling the altar fund.

'The berth was unoccupied,' Latimer pointed out; 'there is no question of your intruding.' He noted with an inward sigh that the man breathed very heavily and noisily through congested nostrils. He would probably snore.

The new-comer sat down on his berth and shook his head slowly. 'How good of you to put it that way! How little kindliness there is in the world these days! How little thought for others!' The bloodshot eyes met Latimer's. 'May I ask how far you are going?'

'Sofia.'

'Sofia. So? A beautiful city, beautiful. I am continuing to Bucaresti. I do hope that we shall have a pleasant journey together.'

Latimer said that he hoped so too. The fat man's English was very accurate, but he spoke it with an atrocious accent which Latimer could not place. It was thick and slightly guttural, as though he were speaking with his mouth full of cake. Occasionally, too, the accurate English would give out in the middle of a difficult sentence, which would be completed in very fluent French or German. Latimer gained the impression that the man had learned his English from books.

The fat man turned and began to unpack a small attaché case containing a pair of woollen pyjamas, some bed socks and a dog-eared paper-backed book. Latimer managed to see the title of the book. It was called *Pearls of Everyday Wisdom* and was in French. The fat man arranged these things carefully on the shelf and then produced a packet of thin Greek cheroots.

'Will you allow me to smoke, please?' he said, extending the packet.

'Please do. But I won't smoke just now myself, thank you.'

The train had begun to gather speed and the attendant came in to make up their beds. When he had gone, Latimer partially undressed and laid down on his bed.

The fat man picked up the book and then put it down again.

'You know,' he said, 'the moment the attendant told me that there was an Englishman on the train, I knew that I should have a pleasant journey.' The smile came into play, sweet and compassionate, a spiritual pat on the head.

'It's very good of you to say so.'

'Oh, no, that is how I feel.' His eyes bleared as smoke irritated them. He dabbed at them with one of the bed socks. 'It is so silly of me to smoke,' he went on ruefully. 'My eyes are a little weak. The Great One in His wisdom has seen fit to give me weak eyes. No doubt He had a purpose. Perhaps it was that I might more keenly appreciate the beauties of His work—Mother Nature in all her exquisite raiment, the trees, the flowers, the clouds, the sky, the snow-capped hills, the wonderful views, the sunset in all its golden magnificence.'

'You ought to wear glasses.'

The fat man shook his head. 'If I needed glasses,' he said solemnly, 'the Great One would guide me to seek them.' He leaned forward earnestly. 'Do you not feel, my friend, that somewhere, above us, about us, within us, there is a Power, a Destiny, that directs us to do the things we do?'

'That's a large question.'

'But only because we are not simple enough, not humble enough, to understand. A man does not need a great education to be a philosopher. Let him only be simple and humble.' He looked at Latimer simply and humbly. 'Live and let live—that is the secret of happiness. Leave the Great One to answer the questions beyond our poor understanding. One cannot fight against one's Destiny. If the Great One wills that we shall do unpleasant things, depend upon it that He has a purpose even though that purpose is not always clear to us. If it is the Great One's will that some should become rich while others should remain poor, then we must accept His will.' He belched slightly and glanced up at the suit-cases above Latimer's head. The smile became tenderly whimsical. 'I often think,' he said, 'that there is much food for thought in a train. Don't you? A piece of luggage, for instance. How like a human being! On its journey through Life it will collect many brightly coloured labels. But the labels are only the outward appearances, the face that it puts upon the world. It is what is *inside* that is important. And so often—' he shook his head despondently '—so very often, the suit-case is empty of the Beautiful Things. Don't you agree with me?'

This was nauseating. Latimer emitted a non-committal grunt. 'You speak very good English,' he added.

'English is the most beautiful language, I think. Shakespeare, H. G. Wells—you have some great English writers. But I cannot yet express all my ideas in English. I am, as you will have noticed, more at ease with French.'

'But your own language . . . ?'

The fat man spread out large, soft hands on one of which twinkled a rather grubby diamond ring. 'I am a citizen of the world,' he said. 'To me, all countries, all languages are beautiful. If only men could live as brothers, without hatred, seeing only the beautiful things. But no! There are always Communists etcetera. It is, no doubt, the Great One's will.'

Latimer said, 'I think I'll go to sleep now.'

'Sleep!' apostrophized his companion raptly; 'the great mercy vouchsafed to us poor humans. My name,' he added inconsequentially, 'is Mister Peters.'

'It has been very pleasant to have met you, Mr Peters,' returned Latimer firmly. 'We get into Sofia so early that I shan't trouble to undress.'

He switched off the main light in the compartment leaving only the dark blue emergency light glowing and the small reading lights over the berths. Then he stripped a blanket off his bed and wrapped it round him.

Mr Peters had watched these preparations in wistful silence. Now, he began to undress, balancing himself dexterously against the lurching of the train as he put on his pyjamas. At last he clambered into his bed and lay still for a moment, the breath whistling through his nostrils. Then he turned over on his side, groped for his book and began to read. Latimer switched off his own reading lamp. A few moments later he was asleep.

The train reached the frontier in the early hours of the morning and he was awakened by the attendant for his papers. Mr Peters was still reading. His papers had already been examined by the Greek and Bulgarian officials in the corridor outside and Latimer did not have an opportunity of ascertaining the nationality of the citizen of the world. A Bulgarian customs official put his head in the compartment, frowned at their suit-cases and then withdrew. Soon the train moved on over the frontier. Dozing fitfully, Latimer saw the thin strip of sky between the blinds turn blue-black and then grey. The train was due in Sofia at seven. When, at last, he rose to dress and collect his belongings, he saw that Mr Peters had switched off his reading lamp and had his eyes closed. As the train began to rattle over the network of points outside Sofia, he gently slid the compartment door open.

Mr Peters stirred and opened his eyes.

'I'm sorry,' said Latimer, 'I tried not to waken you.'

In the semi-darkness of the compartment, the fat man's smile looked like a clown's grimace. 'Please don't trouble yourself about me,' he said. 'I was not asleep. I meant to tell you that the best hotel for you to stay at would be the Slavianska Besseda.'

'That's very kind of you; but I wired a reservation from Athens to the Grand Palace. It was recommended to me. Do you know it?'

'Yes. I think it is quite good.' The train began to slow down. 'Good-bye, Mr Latimer.'

'Good-bye.'

In his eagerness to get to a bath and some breakfast it did not occur to Latimer to wonder how Mr Peters had discovered his name.

Chapter Five

Nineteen Twenty-three

Latimer had thought carefully about the problem which awaited him in Sofia.

In Smyrna and Athens it had been simply a matter of gaining access to written records. Any competent private inquiry agents could have found out as much. Now, however, things were different. Dimitrios had, to be sure, a police record in Sofia; but, according to Colonel Haki, the Bulgarian police had known little about him. That they had, indeed, thought him of little importance was shown by the fact that it was not until they had received the Colonel's inquiry that they had troubled to get a description of him from the woman with whom he was known to have associated. Obviously it was what the police had *not* got in their records, rather than what they had got, which would be interesting. As the Colonel had pointed out, the important thing to know about an assassination was not who had fired the shot but who had paid for the bullet. What information the ordinary police had would no doubt be helpful; but their business would have been with shot-firing rather than bullet-buying. The first thing he had to find out was who had or might have stood to gain by the death of Stambulisky. Until he had that basic information it was idle to speculate as to the part Dimitrios had played. That the information, even if he did obtain it, might turn out to be quite useless as a basis for anything but a Communist pamphlet, was a contingency that he was not for the moment prepared to consider. He was beginning to like his experiment and was unwilling to abandon it easily. If it were to die, he would see that it died hard.

On the afternoon of his arrival he sought out Marukakis at the office of the French news agency and presented his letter of introduction.

The Greek was a dark, lean man of middle age with intelligent, rather bulbous eyes and a way of bringing his lips together at the end of a sentence as though amazed at his own lack of discretion. He greeted Latimer with the watchful courtesy of a negotiator in an armed truce. He spoke in French.

'What information is it that you need, monsieur?'

'As much as you can give me about the Stambulisky affair of 1923.'

Marukakis raised his eyebrows. 'So long ago? I shall have to refresh my memory. No, it is no trouble, I will gladly help you. Give me an hour.'

'If you could have dinner with me at my hotel this evening, I should be delighted.'

'Where are you staying?'

'The Grand Palace.'

'We can get a better dinner than that at a fraction of the cost. If you like, I will call for you at eight o'clock and take you to the place. Agreed?'

'Certainly.'

'Good. At eight o'clock then. *Au 'voir.*'

He arrived punctually at eight o'clock and led the way in silence across the Boulevard Maria-Louise and up the Rue Alabinska to a small side-street. Half way along it there was a grocer's shop. Marukakis stopped. He looked suddenly self-conscious. 'It does not look very much,' he said doubtfully; 'but the food is sometimes very good. Would you rather go to a better place?'

'Oh no, I'll leave it to you.'

Marukakis looked relieved. 'I thought that I had better ask you,' he said and pushed open the door of the shop.

By some extraordinary means five tables had been arranged inside. Two of the tables were occupied by a group of men and women noisily eating soup. They sat down at a third. A moustachioed man in shirt sleeves and a green baize apron lounged over and addressed them in Bulgarian.

'I think you had better order,' said Latimer.

Marukakis said something to the waiter who twirled his moustache and lounged away shouting at a dark opening in the wall that looked like the entrance to the cellar. A voice could be heard faintly acknowledging the order. The man returned with a bottle and three glasses.

'I have ordered vodka,' said Marukakis. 'I hope you like it.'

'Very much.'

'Good.'

The waiter filled the three glasses, took one for himself, nodded to Latimer and, throwing back his head, poured the vodka down his throat. Then he walked away.

'*A votre santé,*' said Marukakis politely. 'Now,' he went on as they set their glasses down, 'that we have drunk together and that we are comrades, I will make a bargain with you. I will give you the information and then you shall tell me why you want it. Does that go?'

'It goes.'

'Very well then.'

Soup was put before them. It was thick and highly spiced and mixed with sour cream. As they ate it Marukakis began to talk.

In a dying civilization, political prestige is the reward not of the shrewdest diagnostician but of the man with the best bedside manner. It is the decoration conferred on mediocrity by ignorance. Yet there remains one sort of political prestige that may still be worn with a certain pathetic dignity; it is that given to the liberal-minded leader of a party of conflicting doctrinaire extremists. His dignity is that of all doomed men: for, whether the two extremes proceed to mutual destruction or whether one of them prevails, doomed he is, either to suffer the hatred of the people or to die a martyr.

Thus it was with Monsieur Stambulisky, leader of the Bulgarian Peasant Agrarian Party, Prime Minister and Minister for Foreign Affairs. The Agrarian Party, faced by organized reaction, was immobilized, rendered powerless by its own internal conflicts. It died without firing a shot in its own defence.

The end began soon after Stambulisky returned to Sofia early in January 1923, from the Lausanne Conference.

On January the twenty-third, the Yugoslav (then Serbian) Government lodged an official protest in Sofia against a series of armed raids carried out by Bulgarian *comitadji* over the Yugoslav frontier. A few days later, on February the fifth, during a performance celebrating the foundation of the National Theatre in Sofia at which the King and Princesses were present, a bomb was thrown into the box in which sat several government ministers. The bomb exploded. Several persons were injured.

Both the authors and objects of these outrages were readily apparent.

From the start, Stambulisky's policy towards the Yugoslav Government had been one of appeasement and conciliation. Relations between the two countries had been improving rapidly. But an objection to this improvement came from the Macedonian Autonomists, represented by the notorious Macedonian Revolutionary Committee, which operated both in Yugoslavia and in Bulgaria. Fearing that friendly relations between the two countries might lead to joint action against them, the Macedonians set to work systematically to poison those relations and to destroy their enemy Stambulisky. The attacks of the *comitadji* and the theatre incident inaugurated a period of organized terrorism.

On March the eighth, Stambulisky played his trump card by announcing that the Narodno Sobranie would be dissolved on the thirteenth and that new elections would be held in April.

This was disaster for the reactionary parties. Bulgaria was prospering under the Agrarian Government. The peasants were solidly behind Stambulisky. An election would have established him even more securely. The funds of the Macedonian Revolutionary Committee increased suddenly.

Almost immediately an attempt was made to assassinate Stambulisky and his Minister of Railways, Atanassoff, at Haskovo on the Thracian frontier. It was frustrated only at the last moment. Several police officials responsible for suppressing the activities of the *comitadji*, including the Prefect of Petrich, were threatened with death. In the face of these menaces, the elections were postponed.

Then, on June the fourth, the Sofia police discovered a plot to assassinate not only Stambulisky but also Muravieff, the War Minister, and Stoyanoff, the Minister of the Interior. A young army officer, believed to have been given the job of killing Stoyanoff, was shot dead by the police in a gun fight. Other young officers, also under the orders of the terrorist Committee, were known to have arrived in Sofia, and a search for them was made. The police were beginning to lose control of the situation.

Now was the time for the Agrarian Party to have acted, to have armed their peasant supporters. But they did not do so. Instead, they played politics among themselves. For them, the enemy was the Macedonian Revolutionary Committee, a terrorist gang, a small organization quite incapable of ousting a government entrenched behind hundreds of thousands of peasant votes. They failed to perceive that the activities of the Committee had been merely the smoke-screen behind which the reactionary parties had been steadily making their preparations for an offensive. They very soon paid for this lack of perception.

At midnight on June the eighth all was calm. By four o'clock on the morning of the ninth, all the members of the Stambulisky Government, with the exception of Stambulisky himself, were in prison and martial law had been declared. The leaders of this *coup d'état* were the reactionaries Zankoff and Rouseff, neither of whom had ever been connected with the Macedonian Committee.

Too late, Stambulisky tried to rally his peasants to their own defence. Several weeks later he was surrounded with a few followers in a country house some hundreds of miles from Sofia and captured. Shortly afterwards and in circumstances which are still obscure, he was shot.

It was in this way that, as Marukakis talked, Latimer sorted out the facts in his own mind. The Greek was a fast talker but liable, if he saw the chance, to turn from fact to revolutionary theory. Latimer was drinking his third glass of tea when the recital ended.

For a moment or two he was silent. At last he said: 'Do you know who put up the money for the Committee?'

Marukakis grinned. 'Rumours began to circulate some time after. There were many explanations offered; but, in my opinion, the most reasonable and, incidentally, the only one I was able to find any evidence for, was that the money had been advanced by the bank which held the Committee's funds. It is called the Eurasian Credit Trust.'

'You mean that this bank advanced the money on behalf of a third party?'

'No, I don't. The bank advanced the money on its own behalf. I happened to find out that it had been badly caught owing to the rise in the value of the *Lev* under the Stambulisky administration. In the early part of 1923, before the trouble started in earnest, the *Lev* doubled its value in two months. It was about eight hundred to the pound sterling and it rose to about four hundred. I could look up the actual figures if you are interested. Anyone who had been selling the *Lev* for delivery in three months or more, counting on a fall, would face huge losses. The Eurasian Credit Trust was not, nor is for that matter, the sort of bank to accept a loss like that.'

'What sort of a bank is it?'

'It is registered in Monaco which means not only that it pays no taxes in the countries in which it operates but also that its balance sheet is not published and that it is impossible to find out anything about it. There are lots more like that in Europe. Its head office is in Paris but it operates in the Balkans. Amongst other things it finances the clandestine manufacture of heroin in Bulgaria for illicit export.'

'Do you think that it financed the Zankoff *coup d'état*?'

'Possibly. At any rate it financed the conditions that made the *coup d'état* possible. It was an open secret that the attempt on Stambulisky and Atanassoff at Haskovo was the work of foreign gunmen imported and paid by someone specially for the purpose. A lot of people said, too, that although there was a lot of talking and threatening the trouble would have died down if it had not been for foreign *agents provocateurs*.'

This was better than Latimer had hoped.

'Is there any way in which I can get details of the Haskovo affair?'

Marukakis shrugged. 'It is over fifteen years old. The police might tell you something but I doubt it. If I knew what you wanted to know . . .'

Latimer made up his mind. 'Very well, I said I would tell you why I wanted this information and I will.' He went on hurriedly. 'When I was in Stambul some weeks ago I had lunch with a man who happened to be the chief of the Turkish Secret Police. He was interested in detective stories and wanted me to use a plot he had thought of. We were discussing the respective merits of real and fictional murderers when, to illustrate his point, he read me the dossier of a man named Dimitrios Makropoulos or Dimitrios Talat. The man had been a scoundrel and a cut-throat of the worst sort. He had murdered a man in Smyrna and arranged to have another man hanged for it. He had been involved in three attempted assassinations including that of Stambulisky. He had been a French spy and he had organized a gang of drug pedlars in Paris. The day before I heard of him he had been found floating dead in the Bosphorus. He had been knifed in the stomach. For some reason or other I was curious to see him and persuaded this man to take me with him to the mortuary. Dimitrios was there on a table with his clothes piled up beside him.

'It may have been that I had had a good lunch and was feeling stupid but I suddenly had a curious desire to know more about Dimitrios. As you know, I write detective stories. I told myself that if, for once, I tried doing some detecting myself instead of merely writing about other people doing it, I might get some interesting results. My idea was to try to fill in some of the gaps in the dossier. But that was only an excuse. I did not care to admit to myself then that my interest was nothing to do with detection. It is difficult to explain but I see now that my curiosity about Dimitrios was that of the biographer rather than of the detective. There was an emotional element in it, too. I wanted to explain Dimitrios, to account for him, to understand his mind. Merely to label him with disapproval was not enough. I saw him not as a corpse in a mortuary but as a man, not as an isolate, a phenomenon, but as a unit in a disintegrating social system.'

He paused. 'Well, there you are, Marukakis! That is why I am in Sofia, why I am wasting your time with questions about things that happened fifteen years ago. I am gathering material for a biography that will never be written, when I ought to be producing a detective story. It sounds unlikely enough to me. To you it must sound fantastic. But it is my explanation.'

He sat back feeling very foolish. It would have been better to have told a carefully thought out lie.

Marukakis had been staring at his tea. Now he looked up.

'What is your own private explanation of your interest in this Dimitrios?'

'I've just told you.'

'No. I think not. You deceive yourself. You hope *au fond* that by rationalizing Dimitrios, by explaining him, you will also explain that disintegrating social system you spoke about.'

'That is very ingenious; but, if you will forgive my saying so, a little over-simplified. I don't think that I can accept it.'

Marukakis shrugged. 'It is my opinion.'

'It is very good of you to believe me.'

'Why should I not believe you? It is too absurd for disbelief. What do you know of Dimitrios in Bulgaria?'

'Very little. He was, I am told, an intermediary in an attempt to assassinate Stambulisky. That is to say there is no evidence to show that he was going to do any shooting himself. He left Athens, wanted by the police for robbery and attempted murder, towards the end of November 1922. I found that out myself. I also believe that he came to Bulgaria by sea. He was known to the Sofia police. I know that because in 1924 the Turkish secret police made inquiries about him in connection with another matter. The police here questioned a woman with whom he was known to have associated.'

'If she were still here and alive it would be interesting to talk to her.'

'It would. I've traced Dimitrios in Smyrna and in Athens where he called himself Taladis, but so far I have not talked to anyone who ever saw him alive. Unfortunately, I do not even know the woman's name.'

'The police records would contain it. If you like I will make inquiries.'

'I cannot ask you to take the trouble. If I like to waste my time reading police records there is nothing to prevent my doing so, but there is no reason why I should waste your time too.'

'There is plenty to prevent your wasting your time reading police records. In the first place, you cannot read Bulgarian and in the second place, the police would make difficulties. I am, God help me, an accredited journalist working for a French news agency. I have certain privileges. Besides—' he grinned—'absurd as it is, your detecting intrigues me. The baroque in human affairs is always interesting don't you think?' He looked round. The restaurant had emptied. The waiter was sitting asleep with his feet on one of the tables. Marukakis sighed. 'We shall have to wake the poor devil to pay him.'

On his third day in Sofia, Latimer received a letter from Marukakis.

> My dear Mr Latimer, *(he wrote in French)*
> Here, as I promised, is a précis of all the information about Dimitrios Makropoulos which I have been able to obtain from the police. It is not, as you will see, complete. That is interesting, don't you think! Whether the woman can be found or not, I cannot say until I have made friends with a few more policemen. Perhaps we could meet to-morrow.
> Assuring you of my most distinguished sentiments.
> N. Marukakis.

Attached to this letter was the précis:

POLICE ARCHIVES, SOFIA 1922–4

Dimitrios Makropoulos. *Citizenship:* Greek. *Place of birth:* Salonika. *Date:* 1889. *Trade:* Described as fig-packer. *Entry:* Varna, December 22nd, 1922, off Italian steamer *Isola Bella*. *Passport or Identity Card:* Relief Commission Identity Card No. T53462.

At police inspection of papers in Café Spetzi, rue Perotska. Sofia, June 6th 1923, was in company of woman named Irana Preveza, Greek-born Bulgar. D.M. known associate of foreign criminals. Proscribed for deportation, June 7th 1923. Released at request and on assurances of A. Vazoff, June 7th 1923.

In September 1924 request received from Turkish Government for information relating to a fig-packer named 'Dimitrios' wanted on a charge of murder. Above information supplied a month later. Irana Preveza when questioned reported receiving letter from Makropoulos at Adrianople. She gave following description:

Height: 182 centimetres. *Eyes:* brown. *Complexion:* dark, clean-shaven. *Hair:* dark and straight. *Distinguishing marks:* none.

At the foot of this *précis*, Marukakis had added a handwritten note.

N.B. This is an ordinary police dossier only. Reference is made to a second dossier on the secret file but it is forbidden to inspect this.

Latimer sighed. The second dossier contained no doubt, the details of the part played by Dimitrios in the events of 1923. The Bulgarian authorities had evidently known more about Dimitrios than they had been prepared to confide to the Turkish police. To know that the information was in existence, yet to be unable to get at it was really most irritating.

However, there was much food for thought in what information was available. The most obvious tit-bit was that on board the Italian steamer *Isola Bella* in December 1922, between the Piraeus and Varna in the Black Sea, the Relief Commission Identity Card number T.53462 had suffered an alteration. 'Dimitrios Taladis' had become 'Dimitrios Makropoulos'. Either Dimitrios had discovered a talent for forgery or he had met and employed someone with such a talent.

Irana Preveza! A real clue that and one that would have to be followed up very carefully. If she were still alive there must surely be some way of finding her. For the moment, however, that task would have to be left to Marukakis. Incidentally, the fact that she was of Greek extraction was suggestive, Dimitrios would probably not have spoken Bulgarian.

'Known associate of foreign criminals,' was distinctly vague. What sort of criminals? Of what foreign nationality? And to what extent had he associated with them? And why had attempts been made to deport him just two days before the Zankoff *coup d'état*? Had Dimitrios been one of the suspected assassins for whom the Sofia police had been searching during that critical week? Colonel Haki had pooh-poohed the idea of his being an assassin at all. 'His kind never risk their skins like that.' But Colonel Haki had not known everything about Dimitrios. And who on earth was the obliging A. Vazoff who had so promptly and effectively intervened on behalf of Dimitrios? The answers to those questions were, no doubt, in that secret second dossier. Most irritating!

As for the description, it might, like most other tabulated descriptions, have fitted tens of thousands of men. With most persons, recognition, even of an intimate, was based on the perception of vague, half-observed quantities which together formed a caricature significant more in its relation to the observer than to the observed. A short man, conscious of his lack of height, would describe a man of medium height as tall. For the ordinary business of hating and loving and getting from the cradle to the deathbed with the least possible discomfort, such caricatures were, no doubt, satisfactory. But he, Latimer, needed more. He needed a portrait of Dimitrios, a portrait by an artist, an arrangement of accented lines infused by some alchemy with the spirit of the sitter. And if that were not available he must make his own portrait of Dimitrios from what crude daubs he could find in police dossiers, superimposing them on one another in the hope that two dimensions might eventually become three.

He had sent a note to Marukakis, and on the following morning received a telephone call from him. They arranged to meet again for dinner that evening.

'Have you got any further with the police?'

'Yes. I will tell you everything when we meet this evening. Good-bye.'

By the time the evening came, Latimer was feeling very much as he had once used to feel while waiting for examination results: a little excited, a little apprehensive and very much irritated at the decorous delay in publishing information which had been in existence for several days. He smiled rather sourly at Marukakis.

'It is really very good of you to take so much trouble.'

Marukakis flourished a hand. 'Nonsense, my dear friend. I told you I was interested. Shall we go to the grocer's shop again? We can talk there quietly.'

From then until the end of the meal he talked incessantly about the position of the Scandinavian countries in the event of a major European War. Latimer began to feel as baleful as one of his murderers.

'And now,' said the Greek at last, 'as to this question of your Dimitrios, we are going on a little trip to-night.'

'What do you mean?'

'I said that I would make friends with some policeman and I have done so. As a result I have found out where Irana Preveza is now. It was not very difficult. She turns out to be very well known—to the police.'

Latimer felt his heart begin to beat a little faster. 'Where is she?' he demanded.

'About five minutes' walk away from here. She is the proprietress of a *Nachtlokal* called *La Vierge St Marie*.'

'*Nachtlokal?*'

He grinned. 'Well, you could call it a night club.'

'I see.'

'She has not always had her own place. For many years she worked either on her own or for other houses. But she grew too old. She had money saved, and so she started her own place. About fifty years of age, but looks younger. The police have quite an affection for her. She does not get up until ten in the evening, so we must wait a little before we try our luck at talking to her. Did you read her description of Dimitrios? No distinguishing marks! That made me laugh.'

'Did it occur to you to wonder how she knew that his height was exactly one hundred and eighty-two centimetres?'

Marukakis frowned. 'Why should it?'

'Very few people know even their own heights exactly.'

'What is your idea?'

'I think that that description came from the second dossier you mentioned, and not from the woman.'

'And so?'

'Just a moment. Do you know who A. Vazoff is?'

'I meant to tell you. I asked the same question. He was a lawyer.'

'Was?'

'He died three years ago. He left much money. It was claimed by a nephew living in Bucaresti. He had no relations living here.' Marukakis paused and then added innocently: 'He used to be on the board of directors of the Eurasian Credit Trust.'

'Vazoff!'

The Greek chuckled. 'I was keeping that as a little surprise for you later, but you may have it now. I found out from the files. Eurasian Credit Trust was not registered in Monaco until 1926. The list of directors prior to that date is still in existence and open to inspection if you know where to find it.'

'But,' spluttered Latimer, 'this is most important. Don't you see what . . .'

Marukakis interrupted him by calling for the bill. Then he glanced as Latimer slyly. 'You know,' he said, 'you English are sublime. You are the only nation in the world that believes that it has a monopoly of ordinary common sense.'

Chapter Six

Carte Postale

La Vierge St Marie was situated, with somewhat dingy logic, in a street of houses behind the church of Sveta Nedelja. The street was narrow, sloping and poorly lit. At first it seemed unnaturally silent. But behind the silence there were whispers of music and laughter—whispers that would start out suddenly as a door opened and then be smothered as it closed again. Two men came out of a doorway ahead of them, lit cigarettes and walked quickly away. The footsteps of another pedestrian approached and then stopped as their owner went into one of the houses.

'Not many people about now,' commented Marukakis; 'too early.'

Most of the doors were panelled with translucent glass and had dim lights showing through them. On some of the panels the number of the house was painted; painted rather more elaborately than was necessary for ordinary purposes. Other doors bore names. There was Wonderbar, O.K., Jymmies Bar, Stambul. Torquemada, Vitocha, Le Viol de Lucrece and, higher up the hill, La Vierge St Marie.

For a moment they stood outside it. The door looked less shabby than some of the others. Latimer felt to see if his wallet was safe in his pocket as Marukakis pushed open the door and led the way in. Somewhere in the place an accordion band was playing a paso-doble. They were in a narrow passage between walls coated unevenly with red distemper. The floor was carpeted. Facing them at the end of the passage was a small vestiaire. When they had entered, it had been empty except for a few hats and coats; but now a pallid man in a white jacket took his place behind the counter, and smiled a welcome. He said: '*Bonsoir, messieurs*,' took their hats and coats and indicated with a flourish a staircase leading down to the right in the direction of the music. It was labelled: BAR-DANCING CABARET.

They found themselves in a low-ceilinged room about thirty feet square. At regular intervals round the pale blue walls were placed oval mirrors supported by *papier-mâché* cherubims. The spaces between the mirrors were decorated haphazard with highly stylized pictures, painted on the walls, of monocled men with straw-coloured hair and nude torsoes, and women in riding clothes. In one corner of the room was a minute bar; in the opposite corner the platform on which sat the band—four listless Negroes in white 'Argentine' blouses. Near them was a blue plush curtained doorway. The rest of the wall space was taken up by small cubicles which rose to the shoulder height of those sitting at the tables set inside them. A few more tables encroached on the dance-floor in the centre.

When they came in there were about a dozen persons seated in the cubicles. The band was still playing and two girls who looked as though they might presently form part of the cabaret were dancing solemnly together.

'Too early,' repeated Marukakis; 'but it will be gayer soon.'

A waiter swept them to one of the cubicles and hurried away, to reappear a moment or two later with a bottle of local champagne.

'Have you got plenty of money with you?' murmured Marukakis; 'we shall have to pay at least two hundred leva for this poison.'

Latimer nodded. Two hundred leva was about ten shillings.

The band stopped. The two girls finished their dance, and one of them caught Latimer's eye. They walked over to the cubicle and stood smiling down. Marukakis said something. Still smiling, the two shrugged their shoulders and went away. Marukakis looked doubtfully at Latimer.

'I said that we had business to discuss, but that we would entertain them later. Of course, if you don't want to be bothered with them . . .'

'I don't,' said Latimer and then shuddered as he drank some of the champagne.

Marukakis sighed. 'It seems a pity. We shall have to pay for the wine. Someone may as well drink it.'

'Where is La Preveza?'

'She will be down at any moment now, I should think. Of course,' he added thoughtfully, 'we could go up to her.' He raised his eyes significantly towards the ceiling. 'It is really quite refined, this place. Everything seems to be most discreet.'

'If she will be down here soon there seems to be no point in our going up.' He felt an austere prig and wished that the wine had been drinkable.

'Just so,' said Marukakis gloomily.

But an hour and a half passed by before the proprietress of *La Vierge St Marie* put in an appearance. During that time things certainly did become gayer. More people arrived, mostly men, although among them were one or two peculiar-looking women. An obvious pimp, who looked very sober, brought in a couple of Germans who looked very drunk and might have been commercial travellers on the spree. A pair of rather sinister young men sat down and ordered Vichy water. There was a certain amount of coming and going through the plush-curtained door. The cubicles were all occupied and extra tables were set up on the dance-floor which soon became a congested mass of swaying sweating couples. Presently, however, the floor was cleared and a number of the girls who had disappeared some minutes before to replace their clothes with a bunch or two of artificial primroses and a great deal of sun-tan powder, did a short dance. They were followed by a youth dressed as a woman who sang songs in German; then they reappeared without their primroses to do another dance. This concluded the cabaret and the audience swarmed back on the dance-floor. The atmosphere thickened, became hotter and hotter.

Through smarting eyes Latimer was idly watching one of the sinister young men offering the other a pinch of what might have been snuff, but which was not, and wondering whether he should make another attempt to slake his thirst with the wine, when suddenly Marukakis touched his arm.

'That will be her,' he said.

Latimer looked across the room. For a moment a couple on the extreme corner of the dance-floor obstructed the view; then the couple moved an inch or two, and he saw her standing motionless by the curtained door by which she had entered.

She possessed that odd blousy quality that is independent of good clothes and well-dressed hair and skilful maquillage. Her figure was full but good and she held herself well; her dress was probably expensive, her thick, dark hair looked as though it had spent the past two hours in the hands of a hairdresser. Yet she remained, unmistakably and irrevocably, a slattern. There was something temporary, an air of suspended animation, about her. It seemed as if at any moment the hair should begin to straggle, the dress slip down negligently over one soft, creamy shoulder, the hand with the diamond cluster ring which now hung loosely at her side reach up to pluck at pink silk shoulder straps and pat abstractedly at the hair. You saw it in her dark eyes. The mouth was firm and good-humoured in the loose, raddled flesh about it; but the eyes were humid with sleep and the carelessness of sleep. They made you think of things you had forgotten, of clumsy gilt hotel chairs strewn with discarded clothes and of grey dawn light slanting through closed shutters, of attar of roses and of the musty smell of heavy curtains on brass rings, of the sound of the warm, slow breathing of a sleeper against the ticking of a clock in the darkness. Yet now the eyes were open and watchful, moving about while the mouth smiled a greeting here and there. Latimer watched her turn suddenly and go towards the bar.

Marukakis beckoned to the waiter and said something to him. The man hesitated and then nodded. Latimer saw him weave his way towards where Madame Preveza was talking to a fat man with his arm round one of the cabaret girls. The waiter whispered something. Madame Preveza stopped talking and looked at him. He pointed towards Latimer and Marukakis, and for a moment her eyes rested dispassionately on them. Then she turned away, said a word to the waiter and resumed her conversation.

'She'll come in a minute,' said Marukakis.

Soon she left the fat man and went on making her tour of the room, nodding, smiling indulgently. At last she reached their table. Involuntarily, Latimer got to his feet. The eyes studied his face.

'You wished to speak with me, messieurs?' Her voice was husky, a little harsh, and she spoke in strongly accented French.

'We should be honoured if you would sit at our table for a moment,' said Marukakis.

'Of course.' She sat down beside him. Immediately the waiter came up. She waved him away and looked at Latimer. 'I have not seen you before, monsieur. Your friend I have seen, but not in my place.' She looked sideways at Marukakis. 'Are you going to write about me in the Paris newspapers, monsieur? If so, you must see the rest of my entertainment—you and your friend.'

Marukakis smiled. 'No, madame. We are trespassing on your hospitality to ask for some information.'

'Information?' A blank look had come into the dark eyes. 'I know nothing of any interest to anybody.'

'Your discretion is famous, madame. This, however, concerns a man, now dead and buried, whom you knew over fifteen years ago.'

She laughed shortly and Latimer saw that her teeth were bad. She laughed again, uproariously, so that her body shook. It was an ugly sound that tore away her slumberous dignity, leaving her old. She coughed a little as the laughter died away. 'You pay the most delicate compliments, monsieur,' she gasped. 'Fifteen years! You expect me to remember a man that long? Holy Mother of Christ, I think you shall buy me a drink after all.'

Latimer beckoned to the waiter. 'What will you drink, madame?'

'Champagne. Not this filth. The waiter will know. Fifteen years!' She was still amused.

'We hardly dared to hope that you would remember,' said Marukakis a trifle coldly. 'But if a name means anything to you, it was Dimitrios—Dimitrios Makropoulos.'

She had been lighting a cigarette. Now she stopped still with the burning match in her fingers. Her eyes were on the end of the cigarette. For several seconds the only movement that Latimer saw in her face was the corners of her mouth turning slowly downward. It seemed to him that the noise about them had receded suddenly, that there was cotton wool in his ears. Then she slowly turned the match between her fingers and dropped it on to the plate in front of her. The eyes did not move. Then, very softly, she said: 'I don't like you here. Get out—both of you!'

'But . . .'

'Get out!' Still she did not raise her voice or move her head.

Marukakis looked across at Latimer, shrugged and stood up. Latimer followed suit. She glared up at them sullenly. 'Sit down,' she snapped; 'do you think I want a scene here?'

They sat down. 'If you will explain, madame,' said Marukakis acidly, 'how we can get out without standing up we should be grateful.'

The fingers of her right hand moved quickly and grasped the stem of a glass. For a moment Latimer thought that she was going to break it in the Greek's face. Then her fingers relaxed and she said something in Greek too rapid for Latimer to understand.

Marukakis shook his head. 'No, he is nothing to do with the police,' Latimer heard him reply. 'He is a writer of books and he seeks information.'

'Why?'

'He is curious. He saw the dead body of Dimitrios Makropoulos in Stambul a month or two ago, and he is curious about him.'

She turned to Latimer and gripped his sleeve urgently. 'He is dead? You are sure he is dead? You actually saw his body?'

He nodded. Her manner made him feel oddly like the doctor who descends the stairs to announce that all is over. 'He had been stabbed and thrown into the sea,' he added and cursed himself for putting it so clumsily. In her eyes was an emotion he could not quite identify. Perhaps, in her way, she had loved him. A slice of life! Tears should follow.

But there were no tears. She said.

'Had he any money on him?'

Slowly, uncomprehendingly, Latimer shook his head.

'*Merde!*' she said viciously; 'the son of a camel owed me a thousand French francs. Now I shall never see it back. *Salop!* Get out, both of you, before I have you thrown out!'

It was nearly half-past three before Latimer and Marukakis left *La Vierge St Marie.*

The preceding two hours they had spent in Madame Preveza's private office, a be-flowered room filled with furniture: a walnut grand piano draped in a white silk shawl with a fringe and pen-painted birds in the corners of it, small tables loaded with bric-à-brac, many chairs, a browning palm tree in a bamboo stand, a chaise-longue and a large roll-top desk in Spanish oak. They had reached it, under her guidance, via the curtained door, a flight of stairs and a dimly lit corridor with numbered doors on either side of it and a smell that reminded Latimer of an expensive nursing home during visiting hours.

The invitation had been the very last thing that he had expected. It had come close on the heels of her final exhortation to them to get out. She had become plaintive, apologized. A thousand francs was a thousand francs. Now she would never see it. Her eyes had filled with tears. To Latimer she had seemed fantastic. The money had been owing since 1923. She could not seriously have expected its return after fifteen years. Perhaps somewhere in her mind she had kept intact the romantic illusion that one day Dimitrios would walk in and scatter thousand franc notes like leaves about her. The fairy tale gesture! Latimer's news had shattered that illusion and when her first anger had gone she had felt herself in need of sympathy. Forgotten had been their request for information about Dimitrios. The bearers of the bad news must know how bad their news had been. She had been saying farewell to a legend. An audience had been necessary, an audience who would understand what a foolish, generous woman she was. Their drinks she had said, rubbing salt in the wound, were on the house.

They had seated themselves side by side on the chaise-longue while she had rummaged in the roll-top desk. From one of the innumerable pigeon-holes she had produced a small dog-eared notebook. The pages of it had rustled through her fingers. Then:

'February fifteenth, 1923,' she had said suddenly. The notebook had shut with a snap and her eyes had moved upwards calling upon Heaven to testify to the accuracy of the date. 'That was when the money became due to me. A thousand francs and he promised faithfully that he would pay me. It was due to me and he had received it. Sooner than make a big scene—for I detest big scenes—I said that he could borrow it. And he said that he would repay me, that in a matter of weeks he would be getting plenty of money. And he *did* get the money, but he did not pay me my thousand francs. After all I had done for him too!

'I picked that man up out of the gutter, messieurs. That was in December. Dear Christ, it was cold. In the eastern provinces people were dying quicker than you could have machine-gunned them—and I have seen people machine-gunned. At that time I had no place like this, you understand. Of course, I was a girl then. Often I used to be asked to pose for photographs. There was one that was my favourite. I had on just a simple drape of white chiffon, caught in at the waist with a girdle, and a crown of small white flowers. In my right hand which rested—so—upon a pretty, white column, I held a single red rose. It was used for postcards, *pour les amoureux*, and the photographer coloured the rose and printed a very pretty poem at the bottom of the card.' The dark, moist lids had dropped over her eyes and she had recited softly:

> '*Je veux que mon coeur vous serve d'oreiller,*
> '*Et à votre bonheur je saurai veiller.*

'Very pretty, don't you think?' The ghost of a smile had tightened her lips. 'I burnt all my photographs several years ago. Sometimes I am sorry for that but I think that I was right. It is not good to be reminded always of the past. That is why, messieurs, I was angry to-night when you spoke of Dimitrios; for he is of the past. One must think of the present and of the future.

'But Dimitrios was not a man who one forgets easily. I have known many men but I have been afraid of only two men in my life. One of them was the man I married and the other was Dimitrios. One deceives oneself you know. One thinks that one wants to be understood when one wants only to be half-understood. If a person really understands you, you fear him. My husband understood me because he loved me and I feared him because of that. But when he grew tired of loving me I could laugh at him and no longer fear him. Dimitrios was different. Dimitrios understood me better than I understood myself; but he did not love me. I do not think he could love anyone. I thought that one day I should be able to laugh at him too, but that day never came. You could not laugh at Dimitrios. I found that out. When he had gone I hated him and told myself that it was because of the thousand francs he owed to me. I wrote it down in my book as proof. But I was lying to myself. He owed me more than a thousand francs. He had always cheated me over the money. It was because I feared him and could not understand him as he understood me that I hated him.

'I was living in a hotel then. A filthy place, full of scum. The *patron* was a dirty bully, but friendly with the police; and while one paid for one's room one was safe, even if one's papers were not in order.

'One afternoon I was resting when I heard the *patron* shouting at someone in the next room. The walls were thin and I could hear everything. At first I paid no attention, for he was always shouting at someone, but after a while I began to listen because they were speaking in Greek and I understand Greek. The *patron* was threatening to call in the police if the room were not paid for. I could not hear what was said in reply for the other man spoke softly; but at last the *patron* went out and there was quiet. I was half-asleep when suddenly I heard the handle of my door being tried. The door was bolted. I watched the handle turn slowly as it was released again. Then there was a knock.

'I asked who was there but there was no answer. I thought that perhaps it was one of my friends and that he had not heard me so I went to the door and unbolted it. Outside was Dimitrios.

'He asked in Greek if he could come in. I asked him what he wanted and he said that he wanted to talk to me. I asked him how he knew that I spoke Greek but he did not answer. I knew now that he must be the man in the next room. I had passed him once or twice on the stairs and he had always seemed very polite and nervous as he stood aside for me. But now he was not nervous. I said that I was resting and that he could come to see me later if he wished. But he smiled and pushed the door open and came in and leaned against the wall.

'I told him to get out, that I would call the *patron;* but he only smiled and stayed where he was. He asked me then whether I had heard what the *patron* had said and I replied that I had not heard. I had a pistol in the drawer of my table and I went to it; but he seemed to guess what I was thinking for he moved across the room as if by accident and leaned against the table as if he owned the place. Then he asked me to lend him some money.

'I was never a fool. I had a thousand leva pinned high up in the curtain but only a few coins in my bag. I said that I had no money. He seemed not to take any notice of that and began to tell me that he had not eaten anything since the day before, that he had no money and that he felt ill. But all the time he talked his eyes were moving, looking at the things in the room. I can see him now. His face was smooth and oval and pale and he had very brown, anxious eyes that made you think of a doctor's eyes when he is doing something to you that hurts. He frightened me. I told him again that I had no money but that I had some bread if he wanted it. He said: 'Give me the bread.'

'I got the bread from the drawer and gave it to him. He ate it slowly, still leaning against the table. When he had finished he asked for a cigarette. I gave him one. Then he said that I needed a protector. I knew then what he was after. I said that I could manage my own affairs. He said that I was a fool and he could prove it. If I would do as he said he would get five thousand leva that day and give me half of it. I asked what he wanted me to do. He told me to write a note that he would dictate. It was addressed to a man whose name I had never heard and simply asked for five thousand leva. I thought he must be mad and to get rid of him I wrote the note and signed it 'Irana'. He said that he would meet me at a café that evening.

'I did not trouble to keep the appointment. The next morning he came again to my room. This time I would not let him in. He was very angry and said he had two thousand five hundred leva for me. Of course, I did not believe him but he pushed a thousand leva note under the door and said that I should have the rest when I let him in. So I let him in. He gave me immediately another fifteen hundred leva. I asked him where he had got it and he said that he had delivered the note himself to the man who had given him the money immediately.

'I have always been discreet. I am not interested in the real names of my friends. Dimitrios had followed one of them to his home had found out his real name and that he was an important man, and then, with my note in his hand, had threatened to tell his wife and daughters of our friendship unless he paid.

'I was very angry. I said that for the sake of two thousand five hundred leva I had lost one of my good friends. Dimitrios said that he could get me richer friends. He said, too, that he had given the money to me to show that he was serious and that he could have written the note himself and gone to my friend without telling me.

'I saw that this was true. I saw also that he might go to other friends unless I agreed with him. So Dimitrios became my protector and he *did* bring me richer friends. And he bought himself very smart clothes and sometimes went to the best cafés.

'But soon, someone I knew told me that he had become involved in politics and that he often went to certain cafés that the police watched. I told him that he was a fool, but he took no notice. He said that soon he would make a lot of money. And then he became suddenly angry and said that he would not stay behind for anyone, that he was tired of being poor. When I reminded him that it was because of me that he was not starving he turned upon me.

'"You!" he said; "do you think that you make money for me? There are thousands like you. I chose you because although you look soft and sentimental you are cunning and can keep your head. When I came in that day, I guessed that you had money hidden in the curtain because your sort always has money in the curtain. It is an old trick. But it was at your bag that you kept looking so anxiously. I knew then that you were sensible. But you have no imagination. You do not understand money. You can buy anything you fancy and in restaurants they look up to you. It is only those without imagination who stay poor. When you are rich people do not mind what you do. You have the power and that is what is important to a man!" And he went on to tell me about rich men he had seen in Smyrna, men who owned ships and grew figs and had great houses on the hills outside the town.

'Then, for a single moment, because when men become sentimental and tell me their dreams I despise them, I forgot my fear of Dimitrios. Sitting there in his smart clothes with his eyes on mine he appeared to me absurd. I laughed.

'He was always pale but now all the blood left his face and suddenly I was terrified. I thought he meant to kill me. He had a glass in his hand. Slowly he raised it then smashed it on the edge of the table. Then he got up and with the broken half in his hand came towards me. I screamed. He stopped and dropped the glass on the floor. It was stupid, he said, to be angry with me. But I knew why he had stopped. He had remembered that I would be useless to him with my face cut about.

'After that I did not see him much. Often he left Sofia for several days at a time. He did not tell me where he went and I did not ask. But I knew that he had made important friends, for, once, when the police were making difficulties about his papers, he laughed and told me not to worry about the police. They would not dare to touch him, he said.

'But one morning he came to me in great agitation. He looked as if he had been travelling all night and had not shaved for several days. I had never seen him so nervous. He took me by the wrists and said that if anyone asked me I must say that he had been with me for the last three days. I had not seen him for over a week but I had to agree and he went to sleep in my room.

'Nobody asked me about him; but later that day I read in the newspaper that an attempt had been made on Stambulisky at Haskovo and I guessed where Dimitrios had been. I was frightened. An old friend of mine, whom I had known before Dimitrios, wanted to give me an apartment of my own. When Dimitrios had had his sleep and gone, I went to my friend and said that I would take this apartment.

'I was afraid when I had done it, but that night I met Dimitrios and told him. I had expected him to be angry but he was quite calm and said that it would be best for me. Yet I could not tell what he was thinking because he always looked the same, like a doctor when he is doing something to you that hurts. I took courage and reminded him that we had some business to settle. He agreed and said that he would meet me three days later to give me all the money that was due to me.'

She had paused then and looked from Latimer to Marukakis with a faint, taut smile on her lips. There had been something defensive in the smile. She had shrugged her shoulders slightly.

'You think it curious that I should trust Dimitrios. You think that I was a fool. But because Dimitrios frightened me, I would trust him. To distrust him was to remind myself of the fear. All men can be dangerous, as tame animals in a circus can be dangerous when they remember too much. But Dimitrios was different. He had the appearance of being tame; but when you looked into his eyes you saw that he had none of the feelings that make ordinary men soft, that he was always dangerous. I trusted him because there was nothing else for me to do. But I also hated him.

'Three days later I waited for him in the café and he did not come. Several weeks after that I saw him and he said that he had been away but that if I would meet him on the following day, he would pay me the money he owed. The meeting place was a café in the Rue Perotska, a low place that I did not like.

'This time he came as he had promised. He said that he was in difficulties about money, that he had a great sum coming to him and that he would pay me within a few weeks.

'I wondered why he had kept the appointment merely to tell me that; but later I understood why. He had come to ask me a favour. He had to have certain letters received by someone he could trust. They were not his letters but those of a friend of his, a Turk named Talat. If this friend could give the address of my apartment, Dimitrios himself would collect the letters when he paid me my money.

'I agreed. I could do nothing else. It meant that if Dimitrios had to collect these letters from me he would have to pay me the money. But I knew in my heart and he knew too that he could have collected the letters and not paid me a sou and I could have done nothing.

'We were sitting there drinking coffee—for Dimitrios was very mean in cafés—when the police came in to inspect papers. It was quite usual at that time, but it was not good to be found in that café because of its reputation. Dimitrios had his papers in order but because he was a foreigner they took his name and mine because I was with him. When they had gone he was very angry; but I think he was angry not because of their taking his name but because they had taken my name as being with him. He was much put out and told me not to trouble about the letters as he would arrange for them with someone else. We left the café and that was the last time I saw him.'

She had had a Mandarine-Curaçao in front of her and now she had drunk it down thirstily. Latimer had cleared his throat.

'And the last you heard of him?'

Suspicion had flickered for an instant in her eyes. Latimer had said: 'Dimitrios is dead, madame. Fifteen years have gone by. Times have changed in Sofia.'

Her queer, taut smile had hovered on her lips.

'"Dimitrios is dead, madame." That sounds very curious to me. It is difficult to think of Dimitrios as dead. How did he look?'

'His hair was grey. He was wearing clothes bought in Greece and in France. Poor stuff.' Unconsciously he had echoed Colonel Haki's phrase.

'Then he did not become rich?'

'He did once become rich, in Paris, but he lost his money.'

She had laughed. 'That must have hurt him.' And then suspicion again: 'You know a lot about Dimitrios, monsieur. If he is dead . . . I don't understand.'

'My friend is a writer,' Marukakis had put in; 'he is naturally interested in human nature.'

'What do you write?'

'Detective stories.'

She had shrugged. 'You do not need to know human nature for that. It is for love stories and romances that one must know human nature. *Romans policiers* are ugly. *Folle Farine* I think is a lovely story. Do you like it?'

'Very much.'

'I have read it seventeen times. It is the best of Ouida's books and I have read them all. One day I shall write my memoirs. I have seen a lot of human nature you know.' The smile had become a trifle arch and she had sighed and fingered a diamond brooch.

'But you wish to know more of Dimitrios. Very well. I heard of Dimitrios again a year later. One day I received a letter from him, from Adrianople. He gave a Poste Restante address. The letter asked me if I had received any letters for this Talat. If I had I was to write saying so but to keep the letters. He said that I was to tell nobody that I had heard from him. He promised again to pay me the money he owed me. I had no letters addressed to Talat and wrote to tell him so. I also said that I needed the money because, now that he had gone away, I had lost all my friends. That was a lie but I thought that by flattering him I would perhaps get the money. I should have known

Dimitrios better. He did not even reply.

'A few weeks after that a man came to see me. A type of *fonctionnaire* he was, very severe and businesslike. His clothes looked expensive. He said that the police would probably be coming to question me about Dimitrios.

'I was frightened at that but he said that I had nothing to fear. Only I must be careful what I said to them. He told me what to say: how I must describe Dimitrios so that the police would be satisfied. I showed him the letter from Adrianople and it seemed to amuse him. He said that I could tell the police about the letter coming from Adrianople but that I must say nothing about this name Talat. He said that the letter was a dangerous thing to keep and burnt it. That made me angry but he gave me a thousand leva note and asked me if I liked Dimitrios, if I was a friend. I said that I hated him. Then he said that friendship was a great thing and that he would give me five thousand leva to say what he had told me to the police.'

She had shrugged. 'That is being serious, messieurs. Five thousand leva! When the police came I said what this man had asked me to say and the following day an envelope with five thousand leva in it arrived by post. There was nothing else in the envelope, no letter. That was all right. But listen! About two years later I saw this man in the street. I went up to him; but the *salop* pretended that he had not seen me before and called the police to me. Friendship is a great thing.'

She had picked up the book and put it back in its pigeon-hole.

'If you will excuse me, messieurs, it is time I returned to my guests. I think I have talked too much. You see, I know nothing about Dimitrios that is of any interest.'

'We have been most interested, madame.'

She had smiled. 'If you are not in a hurry, messieurs, I can show you more interesting things than Dimitrios. I have two most amusing girls who . . .'

'We are a little pressed for time, madame. Another night we should be delighted. Perhaps you would allow us to pay for your drinks.'

She had smiled. 'As you wish, but it has been most agreeable talking to you. No, no, please! I have a superstition about money being shown in my own private room. Please arrange it with the waiter at your table. You will excuse me if I don't come down with you? I have a little business to attend to. *Au 'voir, monsieur. Au 'voir, monsieur. A bientôt.*'

The dark, humid eyes had rested on them affectionately. Latimer had found himself feeling absurdly distressed at the leave-taking.

It had been a *gérant* who had responded to their request for a bill. He had had a brisk, cheerful manner.

'Eleven hundred leva, messieurs.'

'What!'

'The price you arranged with madame.'

'You know,' Marukakis remarked as they waited for their change, 'I think one does wrong to disapprove altogether of Dimitrios. He had his points.'

'Dimitrios was employed by Vazoff acting on behalf of the Eurasian Credit Trust to do work in connection with getting rid of Stambulisky. It would be interesting to know how they recruited him, but that is a thing we shall never know. However, they must have found him satisfactory because they employed him to do similar work in Adrianople. He probably used the name Talat there.'

'The Turkish police did not know that. They heard of him simply as "Dimitrios"', put in Latimer. 'What I cannot understand is why Vazoff—it obviously was Vazoff who visited La Preveza in 1924—allowed her to tell the police that she had had that letter from Adrianople.'

'For only one reason, surely. Because Dimitrios was no longer in Adrianople.' Marukakis stifled a yawn. 'It's been a curious evening.'

They were standing outside Latimer's hotel. The night air was cold. 'I think I'll go in now,' he said.

'You'll be leaving Sofia?'

'For Belgrade. Yes.'

'Then you are still interested in Dimitrios?'

'Oh, yes.' Latimer hesitated. 'I can't tell you how grateful I am to you for your help. It has been a miserable waste of time for you.'

Marukakis laughed and then grinned apologetically. He said: 'I was laughing at myself for envying you your Dimitrios. If you find out any more about him in Belgrade I should like you to write to me. Would you do that?'

'Of course.'

But Latimer was not to reach Belgrade.

He thanked Marukakis again and they shook hands; then he went into the hotel. His room was on the second floor. Key in hand, he climbed the stairs. Along the heavily carpeted corridors his footsteps made no sound. He put the key in the lock, turned it and opened the door.

He had been expecting darkness and the lights in the room were switched on. That startled him a little. The thought flashed through his mind that perhaps he had mistaken the room; but an instant later he saw something which disposed of that notion. That something was chaos.

Strewn about the floor in utter confusion were the contents of his suit-cases. Draped carelessly over a chair were the bedclothes. On the mattress, stripped of their bindings, were the few English books he had brought with him from Athens. The room looked as if a cageful of chimpanzees had been turned loose in it.

Dazed, Latimer took two steps forward into the room. Then a slight sound to the right of him made him turn his head. The next moment his heart jolted sickeningly.

The door leading to the bathroom was open. Standing just inside it, a disembowelled tube of toothpaste in one hand, a massive pistol held loosely in the other and on his lips a sweet, sad smile, was Mr Peters.

Chapter Seven

Half a Million Francs

Mr Peters took a firmer grasp of his pistol.

'Would you be so good,' he said gently, 'as to shut the door behind you? I think that if you stretched out your right arm you could do it without moving your feet.' The pistol was now levelled in an unmistakable fashion.

Latimer obeyed. Now, at last, he felt very frightened indeed. He was afraid that he was going to be hurt; he could already feel the doctor probing for the bullet. He was afraid that Mr Peters was not used to the pistol, that he might fire accidentally. He was afraid of moving his hand too quickly lest the sudden movement should be misinterpreted. The door closed. He began to shake from head to foot and could not decide whether it was anger, fear or shock that made him do so. Suddenly he made up his mind to say something.

'What the hell does this mean?' he demanded harshly and then swore. It was not what he had intended to say and he was a man who very rarely swore. He was sure now that it was anger that was making him tremble. He glowered into Mr Peters' wet eyes.

The fat man lowered his pistol and sat down on the edge of the mattress.

'This is most awkward,' he said unhappily. 'I did not expect you back so soon. Your *maison close* must have proved disappointing. The inevitable Armenian girls, of course. Appealing enough for a while and then merely dull. I often think that perhaps this great world of ours would be a better, finer place if . . .' He broke off. 'But we can talk about that another time.' Carefully he put the remains of the toothpaste tube on the bedside table. 'I had hoped to get things tidied a little before I left,' he added.

Latimer decided to play for time. 'Including the books, Mr Peters?'

'Ah, yes, the books!' He shook his head despondently. 'An act of vandalism. A book is a lovely thing, a garden stocked with beautiful flowers, a magic carpet on which to fly away to unknown climes. I am sorry. But it was necessary.'

'What was necessary? What are you talking about?'

Mr Peters smiled a sad, long-suffering smile. 'A little frankness, Mr Latimer, *please*. There could be only one reason why your room should be searched and you know it as well as I do. I can see your difficulty, of course. You are wondering exactly where I stand. If it is any consolation to you, however, I may say that my difficulty is in wondering exactly where *you* stand.'

This was fantastic. In his exasperation, Latimer forgot his fears. He took a deep breath.

'Now look here, Mr Peters, or whatever your name is, I am very tired and

I want to go to bed. If I remember correctly, I travelled with you in a train from Athens several days ago. You were, I believe, going to Bucharest. I, on the other hand, got off here in Sofia. I have been out with a friend. I return to my hotel to find my room in a disgusting mess, my books destroyed, and you flourishing a pistol in my face. I conclude that you are either a sneak thief or a drunk. But for your pistol, of which I am, I confess, afraid, I should already have rung for assistance. But it seems to me on reflection that thieves do not ordinarily meet their victims in first class sleeping cars, nor do they tear books to pieces. Again, you do not appear to be drunk. I begin, naturally, to wonder if, after all, you may not be mad. If you are, of course, I can do nothing but humour you and hope for the best. But if you are comparatively sane I must ask you once more for an explanation. I repeat, Mr Peters—what the hell does this mean?'

Mr Peters' tear-filled eyes were half-closed. 'Perfect,' he said raptly; 'perfect! No, no, Mr Latimer, keep away from the bell push, please. That is better. You know, for a moment I was almost convinced of your sincerity. Almost. But, of course, not quite. It really is not kind of you to try to deceive me. Not kind, not considerate and such a waste of time.'

Latimer took a step forward. 'Now listen to me . . .'

The pistol jerked upwards. The smile left Mr Peters' mouth and his flaccid lips parted slightly. He looked adenoidal and very dangerous. Latimer stepped back quickly. The smile slowly returned.

'Come now, Mr Latimer. A little frankness, please. I have the best of intentions towards you. I did not seek this interview. But since you have returned so unexpectedly, since I could no longer meet you on a basis of, may I say, disinterested friendship, let us be frank with one another.' He leaned forward a little. 'Why are you so interested in Dimitrios?'

'Dimitrios!'

'Yes, dear Mr Latimer, Dimitrios. You have come from the Levant. Dimitrios came from there. In Athens you were very energetically seeking his record in the relief commission archives. Here in Sofia you have employed an agent to trace his police record. Why? Wait before you answer. I have no animosity towards you. I bear you no ill-will. Let that be clear. But, as it happens, I, too, am interested in Dimitrios and because of that I am interested in you. Now, Mr Latimer, tell me frankly where you stand. What—forgive the expression, please—is your game?'

Latimer was silent for a moment. He was trying to think quickly and not succeeding. He was confused. He had come to regard Dimitrios as his own property, a problem as academic as that of the authorship of an anonymous sixteenth century lyric. And now, here was the odious Mr Peters, with his shabby god and his smiles and his pistol, claiming acquaintance with the problem as though he, Latimer, were the interloper. There was, of course, no reason why he should be surprised. Dimitrios must have been known to many persons. Yet he had felt instinctively that they must all have died with Dimitrios. Absurd, no doubt, but . . .

'Well, Mr Latimer.' The fat man's smile had lost none of its sweetness, but there was an edge to his husky voice that made Latimer think of a small boy pulling the legs off flies.

'I think,' he said slowly, 'that if I am going to answer questions, I ought to be allowed to ask some. In other words, Mr Peters, if you will tell me what *your* game is, I will tell you about mine. I have nothing at all to hide, but I have a curiosity to satisfy. And it really is no good your weighing your pistol so ominously. It is no longer an argument. It is of a large calibre and probably makes a considerable amount of noise when fired. Besides, you would gain nothing by shooting me. While I thought that you might fire it to protect yourself from arrest, it no doubt had its uses. Now, you might just as well put it away in your pocket.'

Mr Peters smiled on steadily. 'Very neatly and charmingly put, Mr Latimer. All the same, I think I shall keep my pistol for the moment.'

'As you please. Do you mind telling me what you hoped to find here–in the bindings of my books or in the tube of toothpaste?'

'I was looking for an answer to my question, Mr Latimer. But all I found was this.' He held up a sheet of paper. It was the chronological table which Latimer had jotted down in Smyrna. As far as he remembered, he had left it folded in a book he had been reading. 'You see, Mr Latimer, I felt that if you hid papers between the leaves of books, you might also hide more in-teresting papers in the bindings.'

'It wasn't intended to be hidden.'

But Mr Peters took no notice. He held up the paper delicately between a finger and thumb–a schoolmaster about to consider a schoolboy essay. He shook his head.

'And is this all you know about Dimitrios, Mr Latimer?'

'No.'

'Ah!' He gazed pathetically at Latimer's tie. 'Now who, I wonder, is this Colonel Haki, who seems so well informed and so indiscreet? The name is Turkish. And poor Dimitrios was taken from us at Istanbul, was he not? And you have come from Istanbul, haven't you?'

Involuntarily, Latimer nodded and then could have kicked himself, for Mr Peters' smile broadened.

'Thank you, Mr Latimer. I can see that you are prepared to be helpful. Now let us see. You were in Istanbul, and so was Dimitrios, and so was Colonel Haki. There was a note here about a passport in the name of Talat. Another Turkish name. And there is Adrianople and the phrase "Kemal attempt". "Attempt"–ah, yes! Now, I wonder if you translated that word literally from the French "*attentat*". You won't tell me? Well, well. I think that perhaps we may take that for granted. You know it almost looks as if you have been reading a Turkish police dossier. Now, doesn't it, eh?'

Latimer had begun to feel rather foolish. He said: 'I don't think you're going to get very far that way. You're forgetting that for every question you ask you're going to have to answer one. For example, I should very much like to know whether you ever actually met Dimitrios?'

Mr Peters contemplated him for a moment without speaking. Then: 'I don't think that you are very sure of yourself, Mr Latimer,' he said slowly. 'I have an idea that I could tell you much more than you could tell me.' He dropped the pistol into his overcoat pocket and got to his feet. 'I think I must be going,' he added.

This was not at all what Latimer expected or wanted, but he said 'Good night' calmly enough.

The fat man walked towards the door. But there he stopped. 'Istanbul,' Latimer heard him murmur thoughtfully. 'Istanbul. Smyrna 1922, Athens the same year, Sofia 1923. Adrianople—no, because he comes from Turkey.' He turned round quickly. 'Now, I wonder . . .' He paused, and then seemed to make up his mind. 'I wonder if it would be very stupid of me to imagine that you might be thinking of going to Belgrade in the near future. Would it, Mr Latimer?'

Latimer was taken by surprise, and, even as he began to say very decidedly that it would be more than stupid of Mr Peters to imagine any such thing, he knew by the other's triumphant smile that his surprise had been detected and interpreted.

'You will like Belgrade,' Mr Peters continued happily; 'such a beautiful city. The views from the Terazija and the Kalemegdan! Magnificent!'

Latimer pulled the bedclothes off the chair and sat down facing him.

'Mr Peters,' he said, 'in Smyrna I had occasion to examine certain fifteen-year-old police records. I afterwards found out that those same records had been examined three months previously by someone else. I wonder if you would like to tell me if that someone else was you.'

But the fat man's watery eyes were staring into vacancy. A slight frown gathered on his forehead. He said, as though he were listening to Latimer's voice for mistakes in intonation: 'Would you mind repeating that question?'

Latimer repeated the question.

There was another pause. Then Mr Peters shook his head decidely. 'No, Mr Latimer, it was not I.'

'But you were yourself making inquiries about Dimitrios in Athens, weren't you, Mr Peters? You were the person who came into the bureau while I was asking about Dimitrios, weren't you? You made a rather hurried exit, I seem to remember. Unfortunately I did not see it, but the official there commented on it. And it was design, not accident, that brought you to Sofia on the train by which I was travelling, wasn't it? You also took care to find out from me—very neatly, I admit—at which hotel I was staying, before I got off the train. That's right, isn't it?'

Mr Peters was smiling sunnily again. He nodded. 'Yes, Mr Latimer, all quite right. I know everything that you have done since you left the record bureau in Athens. I have already told you that I am interested in anyone who is interested in Dimitrios. Of course, you found out all about this man who had been before you in Smyrna?'

The last sentence was put in a little too casually. Latimer said: 'No, Mr Peters, I did not.'

'But surely you were interested?'

'Not very.'

The fat man sighed. 'I do not think that you are being frank with me. How much better if . . .'

'Listen!' Latimer interrupted rudely. 'I'm going to be frank. You are doing your level best to pump me. I'm not going to be pumped. Let that be clear. I made you an offer. You answer my questions and I'll answer yours. The only questions you've answered so far have been questions to which I had already guessed the answers. I still want to know why you are interested in this dead man Dimitrios. You said that you could tell me more than I could tell you. That may be so. But *I* have an idea, Mr Peters, that it is more important for you to have my answers than it is for me to have your answers. Breaking into hotel rooms and making this sort of mess isn't the sort of thing any man does in a spirit of idle inquiry. To be honest, I cannot for the life of me conceive of any reason for your interest in Dimitrios. It did occur to me that perhaps Dimitrios had kept some of that money he earned in Paris. . . . You know about that, I expect?' And in response to a faint nod from Mr Peters: 'Yes, I thought you might. But, as I say, it did occur to me that Dimitrios might have hidden his treasure and that you were interested in finding out where. Unfortunately my own information disposes of that possibility. His belongings were on the mortuary table beside him, and there wasn't a penny piece there. Just a bundle of cheap clothes. And as for . . .'

But Mr Peters had stepped forward and was staring down at him with a peculiar expression on his face. Latimer allowed the sentence he had begun to trail off lamely into silence. 'What is the matter?' he added.

'Did I understand you to say,' said the fat man slowly, 'that you actually saw the body of Dimitrios in the mortuary?'

'Yes; what of it? Have I carelessly let slip another useful piece of information?'

But Mr Peters did not answer. He had produced one of his thin cheroots and was lighting it carefully. Suddenly he blew out a jet of smoke and started to waddle slowly up and down the room, his eyes screwed up as if he were in great pain. He began to talk.

'Mr Latimer, we must reach an understanding. We must stop this quarrelling.' He halted in his tracks and looked down at Latimer again. 'It is absolutely essential, Mr Latimer,' he said, 'that I know what you are after. No, no, please! Don't interrupt me. I admit that I probably need your answers more than you need mine. But I cannot give you mine at present. Yes, yes, I heard what you said. But I am talking seriously. Listen, please.

'You are interested in the history of Dimitrios. You are thinking of going to Belgrade to find out more about him. You cannot deny that. Now, both of us know that Dimitrios was in Belgrade in 1926. Also, I can tell you that he was never there after 1926. Why are you interested? You will not tell me. Very well. I will tell you something more. If you go to Belgrade you will not discover a single trace of Dimitrios. Furthermore, you may find yourself in trouble with the authorities if you pursue the matter. There is only one man who could and would, under certain circumstances, tell you what you want to know. He is a Pole, and he lives near Geneva.

'Now then! I will give you his name and I will give you a letter to him. I will do that for you. But first I must know why you want this information. I thought at first that you might perhaps be connected with the Turkish police—there are so many Englishmen in the Near Eastern police depart-ments these days—but that possibility I no longer consider. Your passport describes you as a writer, but that is a very elastic term. Who are you, Mr Latimer, and what is your game?'

He paused expectantly. Latimer stared back at him with what he hoped was an inscrutable expression. Mr Peters, unabashed, went on:

'Naturally, when I ask what your game is, I use the phrase in a specific sense. Your game is, of course, to get money. But that is not the answer I need. Are you a rich man, Mr Latimer? No? Then what I have to say may be simplified. I am proposing an alliance, Mr Latimer, a pooling of resources. I am aware of certain facts which I cannot tell you about at the moment. You, on the other hand, possess an important piece of information. You may not know that it is important, but nevertheless it *is*. Now, my facts alone are not worth a great deal. Your piece of information is quite valueless without my facts. The two together, however, are worth at the very least'–he stroked his chin–'at the very least five thousand English pounds, a million French francs.' He smiled triumphantly. 'What do you say to that?'

'You will forgive me,' replied Latimer coldly, 'if I say that I cannot understand what you're talking about, won't you? Not that it makes any difference whether you do or don't. I am *tired*, Mr Peters, *very* tired. I want badly to go to bed.' He got to his feet and, pulling the bedclothes on to the bed, began to remake it. 'There is, I suppose, no reason why you should not know why I am interested in Dimitrios,' he went on as he dragged a sheet into position. 'The reason is certainly nothing to do with money. I write detective stories for a living. In Stambul I heard from a Colonel Haki, who is something to do with the police there, about a criminal named Dimitrios, who had been found dead in the Bosphorus. Partly for amusement–the sort of amusement that one derives from cross-word puzzles–partly from a desire to try my hand at practical detection, I set out to trace the man's history. That is all. I don't expect you to understand it. You are probably wondering at the moment why I couldn't think of a more convincing story. I am sorry. If you don't like the truth, you can lump it.'

Mr Peters had listened in silence. Now he waddled to the window, pitched out his cheroot and faced Latimer across the bed.

'Detective stories! Now, that is most interesting to me, Mr Latimer. I am so fond of them. I wonder if you would tell me the names of some of your books.'

Latimer gave him several titles.

'And your publisher?'

'English, American, French, Swedish, Norwegian, Dutch or Hungarian?'

'Hungarian, please.'

Latimer told him.

Mr Peters nodded slowly. 'A good firm, I believe.' He seemed to reach a decision. 'Have you a pen and paper, Mr Latimer?'

Latimer nodded wearily towards the writing-table. The other went to it and sat down. As he finished making the bed and began to collect his belongings from the floor, Latimer heard the hotel pen scratching over a piece of the hotel paper. Mr Peters was keeping his word.

At last he finished and the chair creaked as he got up. Latimer, who was replacing some shoe trees, straightened his back. Mr Peters had recovered his smile. Goodwill oozed from him like sweat.

'Here, Mr Latimer,' he announced, 'are three pieces of paper. On the first one is written the name of the man of whom I spoke to you. His name is Grodek–Wladyslaw Grodek. He lives just outside Geneva. The second is a letter to him. If you present that letter he will know that you are a friend of mine and that he can be frank with you. He is retired now, so I think I may safely tell you that he was at one time the most successful professional agent in Europe. More secret naval and military information has passed through his hands than through those of any other one man. It was always accurate, what is more. He dealt with quite a number of governments. His headquarters were in Brussels. To an author I should think he would be very interesting. You will like him, I think. He is a great lover of animals. A beautiful character *au fond*. Incidentally, it was he who employed Dimitrios in 1926.'

'I see. Thank you very much. What about the third piece of paper?'

Mr Peters hesitated. His smile became a little smug. 'I think you said that you were not rich.'

'No, I am not rich.'

'Half a million francs, two thousand five hundred English pounds, would be useful to you?'

'Undoubtedly.'

'Well, then, Mr Latimer, when you have tired of Geneva I want you to—how do you say?—to kill two birds with one stone.' He pulled Latimer's chronological table from his pocket. 'On this list of yours you have other dates besides 1926 still to be accounted for if you are to know what there is to know about Dimitrios. The place to account for them is Paris. That is the first thing. The second is that, if you will come to Paris, if you will put yourself in touch with me there, if you will consider, then, the pooling of resources, the alliance that I have already proposed to you, I can definitely guarantee that in a very few days you will have at least two thousand five hundred English pounds to pay into your account—half a million French francs!'

'I do wish,' retorted Latimer irritably, 'that you would be a little more explicit. Half a million francs for doing what? Who is going to pay this money? You are far too mysterious, Mr Peters—far too mysterious to be true.'

Mr Peters' smile tightened. Here was a Christian, reviled but unembittered, waiting steadfastly for the lions to be admitted into the arena.

'Mr Latimer,' he said gently, 'I know that you do not trust me. That is the reason why I have given you Grodek's address and that letter to him. I want to give you concrete evidence of my goodwill towards you, to prove that my word is to be trusted. And I want to show that I trust you, that I believe what you have told me. At the moment I cannot say more. But if you will believe in and trust me, if you will come to Paris, then here, on this piece of paper, is an address. When you arrive send a *pneumatique* to me. Do not call, for it is the address of a friend. If you will simply send a *pneumatique* giving me your address, I will be able to explain everything. It is perfectly simple.'

It was time, Latimer decided, to get rid of Mr Peters.

'Well,' he said, 'this is all very confusing. You seem to me to have jumped to a lot of conclusions. I had not definitely arranged to go to Belgrade. It is not certain that I shall have time to go to Geneva. As for going on to Paris, that is a thing which I could not possibly consider at the moment. I have a great deal of work to do, of course, and . . .'

Mr Peters buttoned up his overcoat. 'Of course.' And then, with a curious urgency in his tone: 'But if you *should* find time to come to Paris, do please send me that *pneumatique*. I have put you to so much trouble, I should like to make restitution in a practical way. Half a million francs is worth considering, eh? And I would guarantee it. But we must trust one another. That is most important.' He shook his head despondently. 'One goes through life like a flower with its face turned to the sun, ever seeking, ever hoping, wanting to trust others, but afraid to do so. How much better if we trusted one another, if we saw only the good things, the finer things in our fellow creatures! How much better if we were *frank* and *open*, if we went on our ways without the cloak of hypocrisy and lies that we wear now! It only causes trouble, and trouble is bad for business. Besides, life is so short. We are here on this globe for a short time only before the Great One recalls us.' He heaved a very noisy sigh. 'But you are a writer, Mr Latimer, and sensitive to these things. You could express them so much better than I could.' He held out his hand. 'Good night, Mr Latimer. I won't say "good-bye."'

Latimer took the hand. It was dry and very soft.

'Good night.'

At the door he half turned. 'Half a million francs, Mr Latimer, will buy a lot of good things. I do hope that we shall meet in Paris. Good night.'

'I hope so, too. Good night.'

The door closed and Mr Peters was gone; but to Latimer's overwrought imagination it seemed as if his smile, like the Cheshire cat's, remained behind him, floating in the air. He leaned against the door and surveyed for an instant the upturned suit-cases. Outside it was beginning to get light. He looked at his watch. Five o'clock. The business of clearing up the room could wait. He undressed and got into bed.

Chapter Eight

Grodek

It was eleven o'clock when Latimer, having been awake for about a quarter of an hour, finally opened his eyes. There, on the bedside table, were Mr Peters' three pieces of paper. They were an unpleasant reminder that he had some thinking to do and some decisions to make. But for their presence and the fact that in the morning light his room looked like a rag-picker's workshop, he might have dismissed his recollections of the visitation as being no more than part of the bad dreams which had troubled his sleep. He would have liked so to dismiss them. But Mr Peters, with his mystery, his absurd references to half millions of francs, his threats and his hintings, was not so easily disposed of. He . . .

Latimer sat up in bed and reached for the three pieces of paper.

The first, as Peters had said, contained the Geneva address:

Wladyslaw Grodek,
Villa Acacias,
Chambésy.
(At 7 km. from Geneva.)

The writing was scratchy, florid and difficult to read. The figure seven was made with a stroke across the middle in the French way.

He turned hopefully to the letter. It consisted of only six lines and was written in a language and with an alphabet which he did not recognize, but which he concluded was probably Polish. It began, as far as he could see, without any preliminary 'Dear Godek', and ended with an indecipherable initial. In the middle of the second line he made out his own name spelt with what looked like a 'Y' instead of an 'I'. He sighed. He could, of course, take the thing to a bureau and have it translated, but Mr Peters would no doubt have thought of that, and it was unlikely that the result would supply any sort of answer to the questions that he, Latimer, badly wanted answered: the questions of who and what was Mr Peters.

He turned to the second address:

Mr Peters,
aux soins de Caillé,
3, Impasse des Huit Anges,
Paris 7.

And that brought his thoughts back to their starting point. Why, in the name of all that was reasonable, should Mr Peters want him to go to Paris? What was this information that was worth so much money? Who was going to pay for it?

He tried to remember at exactly what point in their encounter Mr Peters had changed his tactics so abruptly. He had an idea that it had been when he had said something about having seen Dimitrios in the mortuary. But there could surely be nothing in that. Could it have been his reference to the 'treasure' of Dimitrios that had . . .

He snapped his fingers. Of course! What a fool not to think of it before! He had been ignoring an important fact. Dimitrios had not died a natural death. *Dimitrios had been murdered.*

Colonel Haki's doubts of the possibility of tracing the murderer and his own preoccupation with the past had caused him to lose sight of the fact or, at any rate, to see in it no more than a logical ending to an ugly story. He had failed to take into account the two consequent facts; that the murderer was still at large (and probably alive) and that there must have been a motive for the murder.

A murderer and a motive. The motive would be monetary gain. What money? Naturally, the money that had been made out of the drug-peddling business in Paris, the money that had so unaccountably disappeared. Mr Peters' references to half millions of francs did not seem quite as fantastic when you looked at the problem from that point of view. As for the murderer—why not Peters? It was not difficult to see him in the part. What was it he had said in the train? 'If the Great One wills that we shall do unpleasant things, depend upon it that He has a purpose even though that purpose is not always clear to us.' It was tantamount to a licence to murder. How odd if it had been his apology for the murder of Dimitrios! You could see his soft lips moving over the words as he pulled the trigger.

But at that Latimer frowned. No trigger had been pulled. Dimitrios had been stabbed. He began to reconstruct the picture in his mind, to see Peters stabbing someone. Yet the picture seemed wrong. It was difficult to see Peters wielding a stabbing knife. The difficulty made him begin to think again. There really was no reason at all even to suspect Peters of the murder. And even if there had been a reason, the fact of Peters' murdering Dimitrios for his money still did not explain the connection (if a connection existed) between that money and the half million francs (if they existed). And, anyway, what was this mysterious piece of information he was supposed to possess? It was all very like being faced by an algebraic problem containing many unknown quantities and having only one biquadratic equation with which to solve it. If he *were* to solve it . . .

Now why should Peters be so anxious for him to go to Paris? Surely it would have been just as simple to have pooled their resources (whatever that might mean) in Sofia. Confound Mr Peters! Latimer got out of bed and turned on his bath. Sitting in the hot, slightly rusty water he reduced his predicament to its essentials.

He had a choice of two courses of action.

He could go back to Athens, work on his new book and put Dimitrios and Marukakis and Mr Peters and this Grodek out of his mind. Or, he could go to Geneva, see Grodek (if there were such a person) and postpone making any decision about Mr Peters' proposals.

The first course was obviously the sensible one. After all, the justification of his researches into the past life of Dimitrios had been that he was making an impersonal experiment in detection. The experiment must not be allowed to become an obsession. He had found out some interesting things about the man. Honour should be satisfied. And it was high time he got on with the book. He had his living to earn and no amount of information about Dimitrios and Mr Peters or anyone else would compensate for a lean bank balance six months hence. As for the half million francs, that could not be taken seriously. Yes, he would return to Athens at once.

He got out of the bath and began to dry himself.

On the other hand there was the matter of Mr Peters to be cleared up. He could not reasonably be expected to leave these things as they were and hurry off to write a detective story. It was too much to ask of any man. Besides, here was *real* murder: not neat, tidy book-murder with corpse and clues and suspects and hangman, but murder over which a chief of police shrugged his shoulders, wiped his hands and consigned the stinking victim to a coffin. Yes, that was it. It was real. Dimitrios was or had been real. Here were no strutting paper figures, but tangible evocative men and women, as real as Proudhon, Montesquieu and Rosa Luxemburg.

Aloud Latimer murmured: 'Comfortable, very comfortable! You want to go to Geneva. You don't want to work. You're feeling lazy and your curiosity has been aroused. In any case, the detective story-writer has no business with reality except in so far as it concerns the technicalities of such things as ballistics, medicine, the laws of evidence and police procedure. Let that be quite clear. Now then! no more of this nonsense.'

He shaved, dressed, collected his belongings, packed and went downstairs to inquire about the trains to Athens. The reception clerk brought him a time-table and found the Athens page.

Latimer stared at it in silence for a moment. Then:

'Supposing,' he said slowly, 'that I wanted to go to Geneva from here.'

On his second evening in Geneva, Latimer received a letter bearing the Chambésy postmark. It was from Wladyslaw Grodek and was in answer to a letter Latimer had sent enclosing Mr Peters' note.

Herr Grodek wrote briefly and in French:

> Villa Acacias,
> Chambésy.
> Friday.
>
> My dear Mr Latimer,
> I should be pleased if you could come to the Villa Acacias for luncheon to-morrow. Unless I hear that you cannot come, my chauffeur will call at your hotel at eleven-thirty.
> Please accept the expression of my most distinguished sentiments.
> Grodek.

The chauffeur arrived punctually, saluted, ushered Latimer ceremoniously into a huge chocolate-coloured *coupé de ville*, and drove off through the rain as if he were escaping from the scene of a crime.

Idly, Latimer surveyed the interior of the car. Everything about it from the inlaid wood panelling and ivory fittings to the too-comfortable upholstery suggested money, a great deal of money. Money, he reflected, that, if Peters were to be believed, had been made out of espionage. Unreasonably he found it odd that there should be no evidence in the car of the sinister origin of its purchase price. He wondered what Herr Grodek would look like. He might possibly have a pointed white beard. Peters had said that he was a Polish national, a great lover of animals and a beautiful character *au fond*. Did that mean that superficially he was an ugly character? As for his alleged love of animals, that meant nothing. Great animal lovers were sometimes pathetic in their hatred of humanity. Would a professional spy, uninspired by any patriotic motives, hate the world he worked in? A stupid question.

For a time they travelled along the road which ran by the northerly shore of the lake; but at Pregny they turned to the left and began to climb a long hill. About a kilometre farther on, the car swung off into a narrow lane through a pine forest. They stopped before a pair of iron gates which the chauffeur got out to open. Then they drove on up a steep drive with a right-angle turn in the middle to stop at last before a large, ugly *chalet*.

The chauffeur opened the door and he got out and walked towards the door of the house. As he did so it was opened by a stout, cheerful-looking woman who looked as though she might be the housekeeper. He went in.

He found himself in a small lobby no more than six feet wide. On one wall was a row of clothes pegs draped carelessly with hats and coats, a woman's

and a man's, a climbing rope and an odd ski-stick. Against the opposite wall
were stacked three pairs of well-greased skis.

The housekeeper took his coat and hat and he walked through the lobby
into a large room.

It was built rather like an inn with stairs leading to a gallery which ran
along two sides of the room, and a vast cowled fireplace. A wood fire roared
in the grate and the pinewood floor was covered with thick rugs. It was very
warm and clean.

With a smiling assurance that Herr Grodek would be down immediately,
the housekeeper withdrew. There were arm chairs in front of the fire and
Latimer walked towards them. As he did so there was a quick rustle and a
Siamese cat leaped on to the back of the nearest chair and stared at him with
hostile blue eyes. It was joined by another. Latimer moved towards them
and they drew back arching their backs. Giving them a wide berth, Latimer
made his way to the fire. The cats watched him narrowly. The logs shifted
restlessly in the grate. There was a moment's silence; then Herr Grodek
came down the stairs.

The first thing that drew Latimer's attention to the fact was that the cats
lifted their heads suddenly, stared over his shoulder and then jumped
lightly to the floor. He looked round. The man had reached the foot of the
stairs. Now he turned and walked towards Latimer with his hand
outstretched and words of apology on his lips.

He was a tall, broad-shouldered man of about sixty with thinning grey
hair still tinged with the original straw colour which had matched the fair,
clean-shaven cheeks and blue-grey eyes. His face was pear-shaped, tapering
from a broad forehead, past a small tight mouth to a chin which receded
almost into the neck. You might have put him down as an Englishman or a
Dane of more than average intelligence; a retired consulting engineer,
perhaps. In his slippers and his thick baggy tweeds and with his vigorous,
decisive movements he looked like a man enjoying the well-earned fruits of
a blameless and worthy career.

He said: 'Excuse me, please, monsieur. I did not hear the car arrive.'

His French, though curiously accented, was very ready, and Latimer
found the fact incongruous. The small mouth would have been more at
home with English.

'It is very kind of you to receive me so hospitably, Monsieur Grodek. I
don't know what Peters said in his letter, because . . .'

'Because,' interrupted the tall man heartily, 'you very wisely have never
troubled to learn Polish. I can sympathize with you. It is a horrible tongue.
You have introduced yourself to Anton and Simone here.' He indicated the
cats. 'I am convinced that they resent the fact that I do not speak Siamese.
Do you like cats? Anton and Simone have critical intelligence, I am sure of
it. They are not like ordinary cats, are you, *mes enfants?*' He seized one of
them and held it up for Latimer's inspection. '*Ah, Simone cherie, comme tu es
mignonne! Comme tu es bête!*' He released it so that it stood on the palms of
his hands. '*Allez vite! Va promener avec ton vrai amant, ton cher Anton!*'
The cat jumped to the floor and stalked indignantly away. Grodek dusted
his hands lightly together. 'Beautiful, aren't they! And so human. They
become ill-tempered when the weather is bad. I wish so much that we could

have had a fine day for your visit, monsieur. When the sun is shining the view from here is very pretty.'

Latimer said that he had guessed from what he had seen that it would be. He was puzzled. Both his host and his reception were totally unlike those he had expected. Grodek might look like a retired consulting engineer, but he had a quality which seemed to render the simile absurd. It was a quality that derived somehow from the contrast between his appearance and his quick, neat gestures, the urgency of his small lips. You could picture him without effort in the role of lover; which was a thing, Latimer reflected, that you could say of few men of sixty and few of under sixty. He wondered about the woman whose belongings he had seen in the entrance lobby. He added lamely: 'It must be agreeable here in the summer.'

Grodek nodded. He had opened a cupboard by the fireplace. 'Agreeable enough. What will you drink? English whisky?'

'Thank you.'

'Good. I, too, prefer it as an aperitif.'

He began to splash whisky into two tumblers. 'In the summer I work outside. That is very good for me but not good for my work, I think. Do you find that you can work out of doors?'

'No, I don't. The flies. . . .'

'Exactly! the flies. I am writing a book, you know.'

'Indeed. Your memoirs?'

Grodek looked up from the bottle of soda water he was opening and Latimer saw a glint of amusement in his eyes as he shook his head. 'No, monsieur. A life of St Francis. I confidently expect to be dead before it is finished.'

'It must be a very exhaustive study.'

'Oh yes.' He handed Latimer a drink. 'You see, the advantage of St Francis from my point of view is that he has been written about so extensively that I need not go to original sources for my material. There is no serious research for me to do. The work therefore serves its purpose in permitting me to live here in almost absolute idleness with an easy conscience.' He raised his glass. '*A votre santé.*'

'*A la vôtre.*' Latimer was beginning to wonder if his host were, after all, no more than an affected ass. He drank a little of his whisky. 'I wonder,' he said, 'if Peters mentioned the purpose of my visit to you in the letter I brought with me from Sofia.'

'No, he did not. But I received a letter from him yesterday which did mention it.' He was putting down his glass and he gave Latimer a sidelong look as he added: 'It interested me very much.' And then: 'Have you known Peters long?'

There was an unmistakable hesitation at the name. Latimer guessed that the other's lips had been framing a word of a different shape.

'I have met him once or twice. Once in a train, once in my hotel. And you, monsieur? You must know him very well.'

Grodek raised his eyebrows. 'And what makes you so sure of that?'

Latimer smiled easily because he felt uneasy. He had, he felt, committed some sort of indiscretion. 'If he had not known you very well he would surely not have given me an introduction to you or asked you to give me information of so confidential a character.' He felt pleased with that speech.

Grodek regarded him thoughtfully and Latimer found himself wondering how on earth he could have been as foolish as to liken the man to a retired consulting engineer. For no reason that he could fathom, he wished suddenly that he had Mr Peters' pistol in his hand. It was not that there was anything menacing in the other's attitude. It was just that . . .

'Monsieur,' said Herr Grodek; 'I wonder what your attitude would be if I were to ask an impertinent question; if I were, for instance, to ask you to tell me seriously if a literary interest in human frailty were your only reason for approaching me.'

Latimer felt himself redden. 'I can assure you . . .' he began.

'I am quite certain that you can,' Grodek interrupted smoothly. 'But–forgive me–what are your assurances worth?'

'I can only give you my word, monsieur, to treat any information you may give me as confidential,' retorted Latimer stiffly.

The other sighed. 'I don't think I have made myself quite clear,' he said carefully. 'The information itself is nothing. What happened in Belgrade in 1926 is of little importance now. It is my own position of which I am thinking. To be frank, our friend Peters has been a little indiscreet in sending you to me. He admits it but craves my indulgence and asks me as a favour–he recalls that I am under a slight obligation to him–to give you the information you need about Dimitrios Talat. He explains that you are a writer and that your interest is merely that of a writer. Very well! There is one thing, however, which I find inexplicable.' He paused, picked up his glass and drained it. 'As a student of human behaviour, monsieur,' he went on, 'you must have noticed that most persons have behind their actions one stimulus which tends to dominate all others. With some of us it is vanity, with others the gratification of the senses, with still others the desire for money, and so on. Er–Peters happens to be one of those with the money stimulus very highly developed. Without being unkind to him, I think I may tell you that he has the miser's love of money for its own sake. Do not misunderstand me, please. I do not say that he will act only under the money stimulus. What I mean is that I cannot from my knowledge of Peters imagine him going to the trouble of sending you here to me and writing to me in the way he has written, in the interests of the English detective story. You see my point? I am a little suspicious. I still have enemies in this world. Supposing, therefore, that you will tell me just what your relations with our friend Peters are. Would you like to do that?'

'I should be delighted to do so. Unfortunately I can't. And for a simple reason. I don't know what those relations are myself.'

Grodek's eyes hardened. 'I was not joking.'

'Nor was I. I have been investigating the history of this man Dimitrios. While doing so I have met Peters. For some reason that I do not know of, he, too, is interested in Dimitrios. He overheard me making inquiries in the relief commission archives in Athens. He then followed me to Sofia and approached me there–behind a pistol. I may add–for an explanation of my interest in this man, who, by the way, was murdered before I ever heard of him. He followed this up with an offer. He said that if I would meet him in Paris and collaborate with him in some scheme he had in mind we should each profit to the tune of half a million francs. He said that I possessed a piece of information which, though valueless by itself, would, when used in conjunction with information in his possession, be of great value. I did not believe him and refused to have anything to do with his scheme. Accordingly, as an inducement to me and as evidence of his goodwill, he gave me the note to you. I had told him, you see, that my interest was that of a writer and admitted that I was about to go to Belgrade to collect more information there if I could. He told me that you were the only person who could supply it.'

Grodek's eyebrows went up. 'I don't want to seem too inquisitive, but I should like to know how you knew that Dimitrios Talat was in Belgrade in 1926.'

'I was told by a Turkish official with whom I became friendly in Istanbul. He described the man's history to me; his history, that is, as far as it was known in Istanbul.'

'I see. And what, may I ask, is this so valuable piece of information in your possession?'

'I don't know.'

Grodek frowned. 'Come now, monsieur. You ask for my confidences. The least you can do is to give me yours.'

'I am telling you the truth. I don't know. I talked fairly freely to Peters. Then, at one point in the conversation, he became excited.'

'At what point?'

'I was explaining, I think, how I knew that Dimitrios had no money when he died. It was after that he started talking about this million francs.'

'And how *did* you know?'

'Because when I saw the body everything taken from it was on the mortuary table. Everything, that is, except his *carte d'identité* which had been removed from the lining of his coat and forwarded to the French authorities. There was no money. Not a penny.'

For several seconds Grodek stared at him. Then he walked over to the cupboard where the drinks were kept. 'Another drink?'

He poured the drinks out in silence, handed Latimer his and raised his glass solemnly. 'A toast, monsieur. To the English detective story!'

Amused, Latimer raised his glass to his lips. His host had done the same. Suddenly, however, he choked and, dragging a handkerchief from his pocket, set his glass down again. To his surprise, Latimer saw that the man was laughing.

'Forgive me,' he gasped; 'a thought crossed my mind that made me laugh. It was'—he hesitated a fraction of a second—'it was the thought of our friend Peters confronting you with a pistol. He is quite terrified of firearms.'

'He seemed to keep his fears to himself quite successfully.' Latimer spoke a trifle irritably. He had a suspicion that there was another joke somewhere, the point of which he had missed.

'A clever man, Peters.' Grodek chuckled and patted Latimer on the shoulder. He seemed suddenly in excellent spirits. 'My dear chap, please don't say that I have offended you. Look, we will have luncheon now. I hope you will like it. Are you hungry? Greta is really a splendid cook and there is nothing Swiss about my wines. Afterwards, I will tell you about Dimitrios and the trouble he caused me, and Belgrade and 1926. Does that please you?'

'It's very good of you to put yourself out like this.'

He thought that Grodek was about to laugh again, but the Pole seemed to change his mind. He became instead very solemn. 'It is a pleasure, monsieur. Peters is a very good friend of mine. Besides, I like you personally, and we have so few visitors here.' He hesitated. 'May I be permitted as a friend to give you a word of advice?'

'Please do.'

'Then, if I were in your place, I should be inclined to take our friend Peters at his word and go to Paris.'

Latimer was perplexed. 'I don't know . . .' he began slowly.

But the housekeeper, Greta, had come into the room.

'Luncheon!' exclaimed Grodek with satisfaction.

Later, when he had an opportunity of asking Grodek to explain his 'word of advice', Latimer forgot to do so. By that time he had other things to think about.

Chapter Nine

Belgrade, 1926

Men have learned to distrust their imaginations. It is therefore, strange to them when they chance to discover that a world conceived in the imagination, outside experience, does exist in fact. The afternoon which Latimer spent at the Villa Acacias, listening to Wladyslaw Grodek, he recalls as, in that sense, one of the strangest of his life. In a letter (written in French) to the Greek, Marukakis, which he began that evening, while the whole thing was still fresh in his mind, and finished on the following day, the Sunday, he placed it on record.

Geneva.
Saturday.

My dear Marukakis,

I remember that I promised to write to you to let you know if I discovered anything more about Dimitrios. I wonder if you will be as surprised as I am that I have actually done so. Discovered something, I mean; for I intended to write to you in any case to thank you again for the help you gave me in Sofia.

When I left you there, I was bound, you may remember, for Belgrade. Why, then, am I writing from Geneva?

I was afraid that you would ask that question.

My dear fellow, I wish that I knew the answer. I know part of it. The man, the professional spy, who employed Dimitrios in Belgrade in

1926, lives just outside Geneva. I saw him to-day and talked with him about Dimitrios. I can even explain how I got into touch with him. I was introduced. But just why I was introduced and just what the man who introduced us hopes to get out of it I cannot imagine. I shall, I hope, discover those things eventually. Meanwhile, let me say that if you find this mystery irritating, I find it no less so. Let me tell you about Dimitrios.

Did you ever believe in the existence of the 'master' spy? Until to-day I most certainly did not. Now I do. The reason for this is that I have spent the greater part of to-day talking to one. I cannot tell you his name, so I shall call him, in the best spy-story tradition, 'G'.

G. was a 'master' spy (he has retired now) in the same sense that the printer my publisher uses is a 'master' printer. He was an employer of spy labour. His work was mainly (though not entirely) administrative in character.

Now I know that a lot of nonsense is talked and written about spies and espionage, but let me try to put the question to you as G. put it to me.

He began by quoting Napoleon as saying that in war the basic element of all successful strategy was surprise.

G. is, I should say, a confirmed Napoleon-quoter. No doubt Napoleon did say that or something like it. I am quite sure he wasn't the first military leader to do so. Alexander, Caesar, Genghis Khan and Frederick of Prussia all had the same idea. In 1918 Foch thought of it, too. But to return to G.

G. says that 'the experiences of the 1914–18 conflict' showed that in a future war (that sounds so beautifully distant, doesn't it?) the mobility and striking power of modern armies and navies and the existence of air forces would render the element of surprise more important than ever; so important, in fact, that it was possible that the people who got in with a surprise attack first might win the war. It was more than ever necessary to guard against surprise, to guard against it, moreover, *before* the war had started.

Now, there are roughly twenty-seven independent states in Europe. Each has an army and an air force and most have some sort of navy as well. For its own security, each of those armies, air forces and navies must know what each corresponding force in each of the other twenty-six countries is doing—what its strength is, what its efficiency is, what secret preparations it is making. That means spies—armies of them.

In 1926 G. was employed by Italy; and in the spring of that year he set up house in Belgrade.

Relations between Yugoslavia and Italy were strained at the time. The Italian seizure of Fiume was still as fresh in Yugoslav minds as the bombardment of Corfu; there were rumours, too (not unfounded as it was learned later in the year) that Mussolini contemplated occupying Albania.

Italy, on her side, was suspicious of Yugoslavia. Fiume was held under Yugoslav guns. A Yugoslav Albania alongside the Straits of Otranto was an unthinkable propositon. An independent Albania was tolerable only as long as it was under a predominantly Italian influence. It might be desirable to make certain of things. But the Yugoslavs might put up a fight. Reports from Italian agents in Belgrade indicated that in the event of war Yugoslavia intended to protect her seaboard by bottling herself up in the Adriatic with minefields laid just north of the Straits of Otranto.

I don't know much about these things, but apparently one does not have to lay a couple of hundred miles' worth of mines to make a two-hundred-miles wide corridor of sea impassable. One just lays one or two small fields without letting one's enemy know just where. It is necessary, then, for them to find out the positions of those minefields.

That, then, was G.'s job in Belgrade. Italian agents found out about the minefields. G., the expert spy, was commissioned to do the real work of discovering where they were to be laid, without—a most important point this—without letting the Yugoslavs find out that he had done so. If they did find out, of course, they would promptly change the positions.

In that last part of his task G. failed. The reason for his failure was Dimitrios.

It has always seemed to me that a spy's job must be an extraordinarily difficult one. What I mean is this. If I were sent to Belgrade by the British Government with orders to get hold of the details of a secret mine-laying project for the Straits of Otranto, I should not even know where to start. Supposing I knew, as G. knew, that the details were recorded by means of markings on a navigational chart of the Straits. Very well. How many copies of the chart are kept? I would not know. Where are they kept? I would not know. I might reasonably suppose that at least one copy would be kept somewhere in the Ministry of Marine; but the Ministry of Marine is a large place. Moreover, the chart will almost certainly be under lock and key. And even if, as seems unlikely, I were able to find in which room it is kept and how to get to it, how should I set about obtaining a copy of it without letting the Yugoslavs know that I had done so?'

When I tell you that within a month of his arrival in Belgrade, G. had not only found out where a copy of the chart was kept, but had also made up his mind how he was going to copy that copy *without the Yugoslavs knowing*, you will see that he is entitled to describe himself as competent.

How did he do it? What ingenious manoeuvre, what subtle trick made it possible? I shall try to break the news gently.

Posing as a German, the representative of an optical instrument-maker in Dresden, he struck up an acquaintance with a clerk in the Submarine Defence Department (which dealt with submarine nets, booms, mine-laying and mine-sweeping) of the Ministry of Marine!

Pitiful, wasn't it! The amazing thing is that he himself regards it as a very astute move. His sense of humour is quite paralysed. When I asked him if he ever read spy stories, he said that he did not, as they always seemed to him very naïve. But there is worse to come.

He struck up this acquaintance by going to the Ministry and asking the door-keeper to direct him to the Department of Supply, a perfectly normal request for an outsider to make. Having got past the door-keeper, he stopped someone in a corridor, said that he had been directed to the Submarine Defence Department and had got lost and asked to be re-directed. Having got to the S.D. Department, he marched in and asked if it was the Department of Supply. They said that it was not, and out he went. He was in there not more than a minute, but in that time he had cast a quick eye over the personnel of the department, or, at all events, those of them he could see. He marked down three. That evening he waited outside the Ministry until the first of them came out. This man he followed home. Having found out his name and as much as he could about him, he repeated the process on succeeding evenings with the other two. Then he made his choice. It fell on a man named Bulić.

Now, G.'s initial tactics may have lacked subtlety; but there was considerable subtlety in the way he developed them. He himself is quite oblivious of any distinction here. He is not the first successful man to misunderstand the reasons for his own success.

G.'s first piece of subtlety lay in his choice of Bulić as a tool.

Bulić was a disagreeable, conceited man of between forty and fifty, older than most of his fellow clerks and disliked by them. His wife was ten years younger than he, dissatisfied and pretty. He suffered from catarrh. He was in the habit of going to a café for a drink when he left the Ministry for the day, and it was in this café that G. made his acquaintance by the simple process of asking him for a match, offering him a cigar and, finally, buying him a drink.

You may imagine that a clerk in a government department dealing with highly confidential matters would naturally tend to be suspicious of café acquaintances who tried to pump him about his work. G. was ready to deal with those suspicions long before they entered Bulić's head.

The acquaintance ripened. G. would be in the café every evening when Bulić entered. They would carry on a desultory conversation. G., as a stranger to Belgrade, would ask Bulić's advice about this and that. He would pay for Bulić's drinks. He let Bulić condescend to him. Sometimes they would play a game of chess. Bulić would win. At other times they would play four-pack *bezique* with other frequenters of the café. Then, one evening, G. told Bulić a story.

He had been told by a mutual acquaintance, he said, that he, Bulić, held an important post in the Ministry of Marine.

For Bulić the 'mutual acquaintance' could have been one of several men with whom they played cards and exchanged opinions and who were vaguely aware that he worked in the Ministry. He frowned and opened his mouth. He was probably about to enter a mock-modest qualification of the adjective 'important', but G. swept on. As chief salesman for a highly respectable firm of optical instrument-makers, he was deputed to obtain an order due to be placed by the Ministry of Marine for binoculars. He had submitted his quotation and had hopes of securing the order but, as Bulić would know, there was nothing like a friend at court in these affairs. If, therefore, the good and influential Bulić would bring pressure to bear to see that the Dresden company secured the order, Bulić would be in pocket to the tune of twenty thousand dinar.

Consider that proposition from Bulić's point of view. Here was he, an insignificant clerk, being flattered by the representative of a great German company and promised twenty thousand dinar, as much as he ordinarily earned in six months, for doing precisely nothing. If the quotation were already submitted, there was nothing to be done there. It would stand its chance with the other quotations. If the Dresden company secured the order he would be twenty thousand dinar in pocket without having compromised himself in any way. If they lost it *he* would lose nothing except the respect of this stupid and misinformed German.

G. admits that Bulić did make a half-hearted effort to be honest. He mumbled something about his not being sure that his influence could help. This, G. chose to treat as an attempt to increase the bribe. Bulić protested that no such thought had been in his mind. He was lost. Within five minutes he had agreed.

In the days that followed, Bulić and G. became close friends. G. ran no risk. Bulić could not know that no quotation had been submitted by the Dresden company as all quotations received by the Department of Supply were confidential until the order was placed. If he were inquisitive enough to make inquiries, he would find, as G. had found by previous reference to the *Official Gazette,* that quotations for binoculars had actually been asked for by the Department of Supply.

G. now got to work.

Bulić, remember, had to play the part assigned to him by G., the part of influential official. G., furthermore, began to make himself very amiable by entertaining Bulić and the pretty but stupid Madame Bulić at expensive restaurants and night clubs. The pair responded like thirsty plants to rain. Could Bulić be cautious when, having had the best part of a bottle of sweet champagne, he found himself involved in an argument about Italy's overwhelming naval strength and her threat to Yugoslavia's seaboard? It was unlikely. He was a little drunk. His wife was present. For the first time in his dreary life, his judgment was being treated with the deference due to it. Besides, he had his part to play. It would not do to seem to be ignorant of what was going on behind the scenes. He began to brag. He himself had seen the very plans that in operation would immobilize Italy's fleet in the Adriatic. Naturally, he had to be discreet, but . . .

By the end of that evening G. knew that Bulić had access to a copy of the chart. He had also made up his mind that Bulić was going to get that copy for him.

He made his plans carefully. Then he looked round for a suitable man to carry them out. He needed a go-between. He found Dimitrios.

Just how G. came to hear of Dimitrios is not clear. I fancy that he was anxious not to compromise any of his old associates. One can conceive that his reticence might be understandable. Anyway, Dimitrios was recommended to him. I asked in what business the recommender was engaged. I hoped, I admit to be able to find some link with the Eurasian Credit Trust episode. But G. became vague. It was so very long ago. But he remembered the verbal testimonial which accompanied the recommendation.

Dimitrios Talat was a Greek-speaking Turk with an 'effective' passport and a reputation for being 'useful' and at the same time discreet. He was also said to have had experience in 'financial work of a confidential nature'.

If one did not happen to know just what he was useful for and the nature of the financial work he had done, one might have supposed that the man under discussion was some sort of accountant. But there is, it seems, a jargon in these affairs. G. understood it and decided that Dimitrios was the man for the job in hand. He wrote to Dimitrios–he gave me the address as though it were a sort of American Express poste restante–care of the Eurasion Credit Trust in Bucharest!

Dimitrios arrived in Belgrade five days later and presented himself at G.'s house just off the Knez Miletina.

G. remembers the occasion very well. Dimitrios, he says, was a man of medium height who might have been almost any age between thirty-five and fifty–he was actually thirty-seven. He was smartly dressed and . . . But I had better quote G.'s own words:

'He was chic in an expensive way, and his hair was becoming grey at the sides of his head. He had a sleek, satisfied, confident air and something about the eyes that I recognized immediately. The man was a pimp. I can always recognize it. Do not ask me how. I have a woman's instinct for these things.'

So there you have it. Dimitrios had prospered. Had there been any more Madame Preveza's? We shall never know. At all events, G. detected the pimp in Dimitrios and was not displeased. A pimp, he reasoned, could be relied upon not to fool about with women to the detriment of the business in hand. Also Dimitrios was of pleasing address. I think that I had better quote G. again:

'He could wear his clothes gracefully. Also he looked intelligent. I was pleased by this because I did not care to employ riff-raff from the gutters. Sometimes it was necessary but I never liked it. They did not always understand my curious temperament.'

G., you see, was fussy.

Dimitrios had not wasted his time. He could now speak both German and French with reasonable accuracy. He said:

'I came as soon as I received your letter. I was busy in Bucharest but I was glad to get your letter as I had heard of you.'

G. explained carefully and with circumspection (it did not do to give too much away to a prospective employee) what he wanted done. Dimitrios listened unemotionally. When G. had finished, he asked how much he was to be paid.

'Thirty thousand dinar,' said G.

'Fifty thousand,' said Dimitrios, 'and I would prefer to have it in Swiss francs.'

They compromised on forty thousand to be paid in Swiss francs. Dimitrios smiled and shrugged his agreement.

It was the man's eyes when he smiled, says G., that first made him distrust his new employee.

I found that odd. Could it be that there was honour among scoundrels, that G., being the man he was and knowing (up to a point) the sort of man Dimitrios was, would yet need a smile to awaken distrust? Incredible. But there was no doubt that he remembered those eyes very vividly. Preveza remembered them, too, didn't she? 'Brown, anxious eyes that made you think of a doctor's eyes when he is doing something to you that hurts.' That was it, wasn't it? My theory is that it was not until Dimitrios smiled that G. realized the quality of the man whose services he had bought. 'He had the appearance of being tame; but when you looked into his eyes you saw that he had none of the feelings that make ordinary men soft, that he was always dangerous.' Preveza again. Did G. sense the same thing? He may not have explained it to himself in that way—he is not the sort of man to set much store by feelings—but I think he may have wondered if he had made a mistake in employing Dimitrios. Their two minds were not so very dissimilar and that sort of wolf prefers to hunt alone. At all events, G. decided to keep a wary eye on Dimitrios.

Meanwhile, Bulić was finding life more pleasant than it had ever been before. He was being entertained at rich places. His wife, warmed by unfamiliar luxury, no longer looked at him with contempt and distaste in her eyes. With the money they saved on the meals provided by the stupid German she could drink her favourite cognac; and when she drank she became friendly and agreeable. In a week's time, moreover, he might become the possessor of twenty thousand dinar. There was a chance. He felt very well, he said one night, and added that cheap food was bad for his catarrh. That was the nearest he came to forgetting to play his part.

The order for the binoculars was given to a Czech firm. The *Official Gazette*, in which the fact was announced, was published at noon. At one minute past noon, G. had a copy and was on his way to an engraver on whose bench lay a half-finished copper die. By six o'clock he was waiting opposite the entrance to the Ministry. Soon after six, Bulić appeared. He had seen the *Official Gazette*. A copy was under his arm. His dejection was visible from where G. stood. G. began to follow him.

Ordinarily, Bulić would have crossed the road before many minutes had passed, to get to his café. To-night he hesitated and then walked straight on. He was not anxious to meet the man from Dresden.

G. turned down a side street and hailed a taxi. Within two minutes his taxi had made a detour and was approaching Bulić. Suddenly, he signalled to the driver to stop, bounded out on to the pavement and embraced Bulić delightedly. Before the bewildered clerk could protest, he was bundled into the taxi and G. was pouring congratulations and thanks into his ear and pressing a cheque for twenty thousand dinar into his hand.

'But I thought you'd lost the order,' mumbles Bulić at last.

G. laughs as if at a huge joke. 'Lost it!' And then he 'understands'.
'Of course! I forgot to tell you. The quotation was submitted through a
Czech subsidiary of ours. Look, does this explain it?' He thrusts one of
the newly printed cards into Bulić's hand. 'I don't use this card often.
Most people know that these Czechs are owned by our company in
Dresden.' He brushes the matter aside. 'But we must have a drink
immediately. Driver!'

That night they celebrated. His first bewilderment over, Bulić took
full advantage of the situation. He became drunk. He began to brag of
the potency of his influence in the Ministry until even G., who had
every reason for satisfaction, was hard put to it to remain civil.

But towards the end of the evening, he drew Bulić aside. Estimates,
he said, had been invited for rangefinders. Could he, Bulić assist? Of
course he could. And now Bulić became cunning. Now that the value of
his co-operation had been established, he had a right to expect
something on account.

G. had not anticipated this, but, secretly amused, he agreed at once.
Bulić received another cheque; this time it was for ten thousand dinar.
The understanding was that he should be paid a further ten thousand
when the order was placed with G.'s 'employers'.

Bulić was now wealthier than ever before. He had thirty thousand
dinar. Two evenings later, in the supper room of a fashionable hotel, G.
introduced him to a Freiherr von Kiessling. The Freiherr von
Kiessling's other name was, needless to say, Dimitrios.

'You would have thought,' says G., 'that he had been living in such
places all his life. For all I know, he may have been doing so. His
manner was perfect. When I introduced Bulić as an important official in
the Ministry of Marine, he condescended magnificently. With Madame
Bulić he was superb. He might have been greeting a princess. But I saw
the way his fingers moved across the palm of her hand as he bent to kiss
the back of it.'

Dimitrios had displayed himself in the supper room before G. had
affected to claim acquaintance with him in order to give G. time to
prepare the ground. The 'Freiherr', G. told the Bulićs after he had
drawn their attention to Dimitrios, was a very important man.
Something of a mystery, perhaps; but a very important factor in
international big business. He was enormously rich and was believed to
control as many as twenty-seven companies. He might be a useful man
to know.

The Bulićs were enchanted to be presented to him. When the
'Freiherr' agreed to drink a glass of champagne at their table, they felt
themselves honoured indeed. In their halting German they strove to
make themselves agreeable. This, Bulić must have felt, was what he had
been waiting for all his life: at last he was in touch with the people who
counted, the real people, the people who made men and broke them, the
people who might make him. Perhaps he saw himself a director of one
of the 'Freiherr's' companies, with a fine house and others dependent
on him, loyal servants who would respect him as a man as well as a
master. When, the next morning, he went to his stool in the Ministry,

there must have been joy in his heart, joy made all the sweeter by the faint misgivings, the slight prickings of conscience which could so easily be stilled. After all, G. had had his money's worth. He, Bulić, had nothing to lose. Besides, you never knew what might come of it all. Men had taken stranger paths to fortune.

The 'Freiherr' had been good enough to say that he would have supper with Herr G. and his two charming friends two evenings later.

I questioned G. about this. Would it not have been better to have struck while the iron was hot. Two days gave the Bulićs time to think. 'Precisely,' was G.'s reply; 'time to think of the good things to come, to prepare themselves for the feast, to dream.' He became preternaturally solemn at the thought and then, grinning, suddenly quoted Goethe at me. *Ach! warum, ihr Götter, ist unendlich, alles, alles, endlich unser Glück nur?* G., you see, lays claim to a sense of humour.

That supper was the critical moment for him. Dimitrios got to work on madame. It was such a pleasure to meet such pleasant people as madame–and of course, her husband. She–and her husband, naturally–must certainly come and stay with him in Bavaria next month. He preferred it to his Paris house and Cannes was sometimes chilly in the spring. Madame would enjoy Bavaria; and so, no doubt, would her husband. That was, if he could tear himself away from the Ministry.

Crude, simple stuff, no doubt; but the Bulićs were crude, simple people. Madame lapped it up with her sweet champagne while Bulić became sulky. Then the great moment arrived.

The flower girl stopped by the table with her tray of orchids. Dimitrios turned round and, selecting the largest and most expensive bloom, handed it with a little flourish to Madame Bulić with a request that she accept it as a token of his esteem. Madame would accept it. Dimitrios drew out his wallet to pay. The next moment a thick wad of thousand dinar notes fell from his breast pocket on to the table.

With a word of apology Dimitrios put the money back in his pocket. G., taking his cue, remarked that it was rather a lot of money to carry in one's pocket and asked if the 'Freiherr' always carried as much. No, he did not. He had won the money at Alessandro's earlier in the evening and had forgotten to leave it upstairs in his room. Did madame know Alessandro's? She did not. Both the Bulićs were silent as the 'Freiherr' talked on: they had never seen so much money before. In the 'Freiherr's' opinion Alessandro's was the most reliable gambling place in Belgrade. It was your own luck not the croupier's skill that mattered at Alessandro's. Personally he was having a run of luck that evening–this with velvety eyes on madame–and had won a little more than usual. He hesitated at that point. And then: 'As you have never been in the place, I should be delighted if you would accompany me as my guests later.'

Of course, they went; and, of course, they were expected and preparations had been made. Dimitrios had arranged everything. No roulette–it is difficult to cheat a man at roulette–but there was *trente et quarante*. The minimum stake was two hundred and fifty dinar.

They had drinks and watched the play for a time. Then G. decided that he would play a little. They watched him win twice. Then the 'Freiherr' asked madame if she would like to play. She looked at her husband. He said, apologetically, that he had very little money with him. But Dimitrios was ready for that. No trouble at all, Herr Bulić! He personally was well known to Alessandro. Any friend of his could be accommodated. If he should happen to lose a few dinar, Alessandro would take a cheque or a note.

The farce went on. Alessandro was summoned and introduced. The situation was explained to him. He raised protesting hands. Any friend of the 'Freiherr' need not even ask such a thing. Besides, he had not yet played. Time to talk of such things if he had a little bad luck.

G. thinks that if Dimitrios had allowed the two to talk to one another for even a moment, they would not have played. Two hundred and fifty dinar was the minimum stake, and not even the possession of thirty thousand could overcome their consciousness of the value in terms of food and rent of two hundred and fifty. But Dimitrios did not give them a chance to exchange misgivings. Instead, as they were waiting at the table behind G.'s chair, he murmured to Bulić that if he, Bulić, had time, he, the 'Freiherr', would like to talk business with him over luncheon one day that week.

It was beautifully timed. It could, I feel, have meant only one thing to Bulić: 'My dear Bulić, there really is no need for you to concern yourself over a paltry few hundred dinar. I am interested in you, and that means that your fortune is made. Please do not disappoint me by showing yourself less important than you seem now.'

Madame Bulić began to play.

Her first two hundred and fifty she lost on *couleur*. The second won on *inverse*. Then, Dimitrios, advising greater caution, suggested that she play *à cheval*. There was a *refait* and then a second *refait*. Ultimately she lost again.

At the end of an hour the five thousand dinar's worth of chips she had been given had gone. Dimitrios, sympathizing with her for her 'bad luck', pushed across some five hundred dinar chips from a pile in front of him and begged that she would play with them 'for luck'.

The tortured Bulić may have had the idea that these were a gift, for he made only the faintest sound of protest. That they had not been a gift he was presently to discover. Madame Bulić, thoroughly miserable now and becoming a little untidy, played on. She won a little; she lost more. At half-past two Bulić signed a promissory note to Alessandro for twelve thousand dinar. G. bought them a drink.

It is easy to picture the scene between the Bulićs when at last they were alone—the recriminations, the tears, the interminable arguments—only too easy. Yet, bad as things were, the gloom was not unrelieved; for Bulić was to lunch the following day with the 'Freiherr'. And they were to talk business.

They did talk business. Dimitrios had been told to be encouraging. No doubt he was. Hints of big deals afoot, of opportunities for making fabulous sums for those who were in the know, talk of castles in Bavaria—it would all be there. Bulić had only to listen and let his heart beat faster. What did twelve thousand dinar matter? You had to think in millions.

All the same, it was Dimitrios who raised the subject of his guest's debt to Alessandro. He supposed that Bulić would be going along that very night to settle it. He personally would be playing again. One could not, after all, win so much without giving Alessandro a chance to lose some more. Supposing that they went along together—just the two of them. Women were bad gamblers.

When they met that night Bulić had nearly thirty-five thousand dinar in his pocket. He must have added his savings to G.'s thirty thousand. When Dimitrios reported to G.—in the early hours of the following morning—he said that Bulić had, in spite of Alessandro's protests, insisted on redeeming his promissory note before he started to play. 'I pay my debts,' he told Dimitrios proudly. The balance of the money he spent, with a flourish, on five hundred dinar chips. To-night he was going to make a killing. He refused a drink. He meant to keep a cool head.

G. grinned at this and perhaps he was wise to do so. Pity is sometimes too uncomfortable; and I do find Bulić pitiable. You may say that he was a weak fool. So he was. But Providence is never quite as calculating as were G. and Dimitrios. It may bludgeon away at a man, but it never feels between his ribs with a knife. Bulić had no chance. They understood him and used their understanding with skill. With the cards as neatly stacked against me as they were against him, I should perhaps be no less weak, no less foolish. It is a comfort to believe that the occasion is unlikely to arise.

Inevitably he lost. He began to play with just over forty chips. It took him two hours of winning and losing to get rid of them. Then, quite calmly, he took another twenty on credit. He said that his luck must change. The poor wretch did not even suspect that he was being cheated. Why should be suspect? The 'Freiherr' was losing even more than he was. He doubled his stakes and survived for forty minutes. He borrowed again and lost again. He had lost thirty-eight thousand dinar more than he had in the world when, white and sweating, he decided to stop.

After that it was plain sailing for Dimitrios. The following night Bulić returned. They let him win thirty thousand back. The third night he lost another fourteen thousand. On the fourth night, when he was about twenty-five thousand in debt, Alessandro asked for his money. Bulić promised to redeem his notes within a week. The first person to whom he went for help was G.

G. was sympathetic. Twenty-five thousand was a lot of money, wasn't it? Of course, any money he used in connection with orders received was his employers', and he was not empowered to do what he liked with it. But he himself could spare two hundred and fifty for a few days if it were any help. He would have liked to do more, but . . . Bulić took the two hundred and fifty.

With it G. gave him a word of advice. The 'Freiherr' was the man to get him out of his difficulty. He never lent money—with him it was a question of principle, he believed—but he had a reputation for helping his friends by putting them in the way of earning quite substantial sums. Why not have a talk with him?

The 'talk' between Bulić and Dimitrios took place after a dinner in the 'Freiherr's' hotel sitting-room. G. was out of sight in the adjoining bedroom.

When Bulić at last got to the point, he asked about Alessandro. Would he insist on his money? What would happen if he were not paid?

Dimitrios affected surprise. There was no question, he hoped, of Alessandro's not being paid. After all, it was on his personal recommendation that Alessandro had given credit in the first place. He would not like there to be any unpleasantness. What sort of unpleasantness? Well, Alessandro held the promissory notes and could take the matter to the police. He hoped sincerely that that would not happen.

Bulić was hoping so, too. Now, he had everything to lose, including his post at the Ministry. It might even come out that he had taken money from G. That might even mean prison. Would they believe that he had done nothing in return for those thirty thousand dinar? It was madness to expect them to do so. His only chance was to get the money from the 'Freiherr'—somehow.

To his pleas for a loan Dimitrios shook his head. No. That would simply make matters worse, for then he would owe the money to a friend instead of to an enemy; besides, it was a matter of principle with him. At the same time, he wanted to help. There was just one way; but would Herr Bulić feel disposed to take it? That was the question. He scarcely liked to mention the matter; but, since Herr Bulić pressed him, he knew of certain persons who were interested in obtaining some information from the Ministry of Marine that could not be obtained through the usual channels. They could probably be persuaded to pay as much as fifty thousand dinar for this information if they could rely upon its being accurate.

G. said that he attributed quite a lot of the success of his plan (he deems it successful in the same way that a surgeon deems an operation successful when the patient leaves the operating theatre alive) to his careful use of figures. Every sum from the original twenty thousand dinar to the amounts of the successive debts to Alessandro (who was an Italian agent) and the final amount offered by Dimitrios was carefully calculated with an eye to its psychological value. That final fifty thousand, for example. Its appeal to Bulić was two-fold. It would pay off his debt and still leave him with nearly as much as he had had before he met the 'Freiherr'. To the incentive of fear they added that of greed.

But Bulić did not give in immediately. When he heard exactly what the information was, he became frightened and angry. The anger was dealt with very efficiently by Dimitrios. If Bulić had begun to entertain doubts about the *bona fides* of the 'Freiherr' those doubts were now made certainties; for when he shouted 'dirty spy', the 'Freiherr's' easy charm deserted him. Bulić was kicked in the stomach and then, as he bent forward retching, in the face. Gasping for breath and with pain and bleeding from the mouth, he was flung into a chair while Dimitrios explained coldly that the only risk he ran was in not doing as he was told.

His instructions were simple. Bulić was to get a copy of the chart and bring it to the hotel when he left the Ministry the following evening. An hour later the chart would be returned to him to replace in the morning. That was all. He would be paid when he brought the chart. He was warned of the consequences to himself if he should decide to go to the authorities with his story, reminded of the fifty thousand that awaited him and dismissed.

He duly returned the following night with the chart folded in four under his coat. Dimitrios took the chart into G. and returned to keep watch on Bulić while it was photographed and the negative developed. Apparently Bulić had nothing to say. When G. had finished he took the money and the chart from Dimitrios and went without a word.

G. says that in the bedroom at that moment, when he heard the door close behind Bulić and as he held the negative up to the light, he was feeling very pleased with himself. Expenses had been low; there had been no wasted effort; there had been no tiresome delays; everybody, even Bulić, had done well out of the business. It only remained to hope that Bulić would return the chart safely. There was really no reason why he should not do so. A very satisfactory affair from every point of view.

And then Dimitrios came into the room.

It was at that moment that G. realized that he had made one mistake.

'My wages,' said Dimitrios, and held out his hand.

G. met his employee's eyes and nodded. He needed a gun and he had not got one. 'We'll go to my house now,' he said and started towards the door.

Dimitrios shook his head deliberately. 'My wages are in your pocket.'

'Not your wages. Only mine.'

Dimitrios produced a revolver. A smile played about his lips. 'What I want is in your pocket, *mein Herr*. Put your hands behind your head.'

G. obeyed. Dimitrios walked towards him. G., looking steadily into those brown anxious eyes, saw that he was in danger. Two feet in front of him Dimitrios stopped. 'Please be careful, *mein Herr*.'

The smile disappeared. Dimitrios stepped forward suddenly and, jamming his revolver into G.'s stomach, snatched the negative from G.'s pocket with his free hand. Then, as suddenly, he stood back. 'You may go,' he said.

G. went. Dimitrios, in turn, had made *his* mistake.

All that night men, hastily recruited from the criminal cafés, scoured Belgrade for Dimitrios. But Dimitrios had disappeared. G. never saw him again.

What happened to the negative? Let me give you G.'s own words:

'When the morning came and my men had failed to find him, I knew what I must do. I felt very bitter. After all my careful work it was most disappointing. But there was nothing else for it. I had known for a week that Dimitrios had been in touch with a French agent. The negative would be in that agent's hands by now. I really had no choice. A friend of mine in the German Embassy was able to oblige me. The Germans were anxious to please Belgrade at the time. What more natural than that they should pass on an item of information interesting to the Yugoslav government?'

'Do you mean,' I said, 'that you deliberately arranged for the Yugoslav authorities to be informed of the removal of the chart and of the fact that it had been photographed?'

'Unfortunately, it was the only thing I could do. You see, I had to render the chart worthless. It was really very foolish of Dimitrios to let me go; but he was inexperienced. He probably thought that I should blackmail Bulić into bringing the chart out again. But I realized that I should not be paid much for bringing in information already in the possession of the French. Besides, my reputation would have suffered. I was very bitter about the whole affair. The only amusing aspect of it was that the French had paid over to Dimitrios half the agreed price for the chart before they discovered that the information on it had been rendered obsolete by my little *démarche*.'

'What about Bulić?'

G. pulled a face. 'Yes, I was sorry about that. I always have felt a certain responsibility towards those who work for me. He was arrested almost at once. There was no doubt as to which of the Ministry copies had been used. They were kept rolled in metal cylinders. Bulić had folded this one to bring it out of the Ministry. It was the only one with creases in it. His finger-prints did the rest. Very wisely he told the authorities all he knew about Dimitrios. As a result they sent him to prison for life instead of shooting him. I quite expected him to implicate me, but he didn't. I was a little surprised. After all it was I who introduced him to Dimitrios. I wondered at the time whether it was because he was unwilling to face an additional charge of accepting bribes or because he felt grateful to me for lending him that two hundred and fifty dinar. Probably he did not connect me with the business of the chart at all. In any case, I was pleased. I still had work to do in Belgrade, and being wanted by the police, even under another name, might have complicated my life. I have never been able to bring myself to wear disguises.'

I asked him one more question. Here is his answer:

'Oh, yes, I obtained the new charts as soon as they had been made. In quite a different way, of course. With so much of my money invested in the enterprise I could not return empty handed. It is always the same: for one reason or another there are always these delays, these wastages of effort and money. You may say that I was careless in my handling of Dimitrios. That would be unjust. It was a small error of judgment on my part, that is all. I counted on his being like all the other fools in the world, on his being too greedy; I thought he would wait until he had from me the forty thousand dinar due to him before he tried to take the photograph as well. He took me by surprise. That error of judgment cost me a lot of money.'

'It cost Bulić his liberty.' I am afraid I said it a trifle grimly, for he frowned.

'My dear Monsieur Latimer,' he retorted stiffly, 'Bulić was a traitor and he was rewarded according to his deserts. One cannot sentimentalize over him. In war there are always casualties. Bulić was very lucky. I should certainly have used him again, and he might ultimately have been shot. As it was, he went to prison. For all I know he is still in prison. I do not wish to seem callous, but I must say that he is better off there. His liberty? Rubbish! He had none to lose. As for his wife, I have no doubt that she has done better for herself. She always gave me the impression of wanting to do so. I do not blame her. He was an objectionable man. I seem to remember that he tended to dribble as he ate. What is more, he was a nuisance. You would have thought, would you not, that on leaving Dimitrios that evening he would have gone there and then to Alessandro to pay his debt? He did not do so. When he was arrested late the following day he still had the fifty thousand dinar in his pocket. More waste. It is at times like those, my friend, that one needs one's sense of humour.'

Well, my dear Marukakis, that is all. It is, I think, more than enough. For me, wandering among the ghosts of old lies, there is comfort in the thought that you might write to me and tell me that all this was worth finding out. You might. For myself, I begin to wonder. It is such a poor story, isn't it? There is no hero, no heroine; there are only knaves and fools. Or do I mean only fools?

But it really is too early in the afternoon to pose such questions. Besides, I have packing to do. In a few days I shall send you a post card with my name and new address on it in the hope that you will have time to write. In any case, we shall, I hope, meet again very soon. *Croyez en mes meilleurs souvenirs.*

Charles Latimer.

Chapter Ten

The Eight Angels

It was on a slate-grey November day that Latimer arrived in Paris.

As his taxi crossed the bridge to the Ile de la Cité, he saw for a moment a panorama of low, black clouds moving quickly in the chill, dusty wind. The long façade of the houses on the Quai de Corse were still and secretive. It was as if each window concealed a watcher. There seemed to be few people about. Paris, in that late autumn afternoon, had the macabre formality of a steel engraving.

It depressed him, and as he climbed the stairs of his hotel on the Quai Voltaire he wished fervently that he had gone back to Athens.

His room was cold. It was too early for an aperitif. He had been able to eat enough of his meal on the train to render an early dinner unnecessary. He decided to inspect the outside of number three, Impasse des Huit Anges. With some difficulty he found the Impasse tucked away in a side street off the Rue de Rennes.

It was a wide, cobbled passage shaped like an L and flanked at the entrance by a pair of tall iron gates. They were fastened back, against the walls that supported them, with heavy staples, and had evidently not been shut for years. A row of spiked railings separated one side of the Impasse from the blank side-wall of the adjoining block of houses. Another blank cement wall, unguarded by railings but protected by the words 'DEFENSE D'AFFICHER, LOI DU 10 AVRIL 1929' in weatherbeaten black paint, faced it.

There were only three houses in the Impasse. They were grouped out of sight of the road, in the foot of the L, and looked out through the narrow gap between the building on which bill-posting was forbidden and the back of a hotel over which drainpipes writhed like snakes, on to yet another sightless expanse of cement. Life in the Impasse des Huit Anges would, Latimer thought, be rather like a rehearsal for Eternity. That others before him had found it so was suggested by the fact that, of the three houses, two were shuttered and obviously quite empty, while the third, number three, was occupied on the fourth and top floors only.

Feeling as if he were trespassing, Latimer walked slowly across the irregular cobbles to the entrance of number three.

The door was open and he could see along a tiled corridor to a small, dank yard at the back. The concierge's room, to the right of the door, was empty and showed no signs of having been used recently. Beside it, on the wall, was nailed a dusty board with four brass name slots screwed to it. Three of the slots were empty. In the fourth was a grimy piece of paper with the name 'CAILLE' clumsily printed on it in violet ink.

There was nothing to be learned from this but the fact, which Latimer had not doubted, that Mr Peters' accommodation address existed. He turned and walked back to the street. In the Rue de Rennes he found a post office where he bought a *pneumatique* letter-card, wrote in it his name and that of his hotel, addressed it to Mr Peters and dropped it down the chute. He also sent a postcard to Marukakis. What happened now depended to a great extent on Mr Peters. But there was something he could and should do: that was to find out what, if anything, the Paris newspapers had had to say about the breaking up in December 1931 of a drug-peddling gang.

At nine o'clock the following morning, being without word from Peters, he decided to spend the morning with newspaper files.

The paper he finally selected for detailed reading had made a number of references to the case. The first was dated November 29, 1931. It was headed: 'DRUG TRAFFICKERS ARRESTED,' and went on:

'A man and a woman engaged in the distribution of drugs to addicts were arrested yesterday in the Alésia quarter. They are said to be members of a notorious foreign gang. The police expect to make further arrests within a few days.'

That was all. It read curiously, Latimer thought. Those three bald sentences looked as if they had been lifted out of a longer report. The absence of names, too, was odd. Police censorship, perhaps.

The next reference appeared on December the fourth under the heading:

'DRUG GANG, THREE MORE ARRESTS.'

'Three members of a criminal drug distributing organization were arrested late last night in a café near the Porte d'Orleans. Police entering the café to make the arrests were compelled to fire on one of the men who was armed and who made a desperate attempt to escape. He was slightly wounded. The other two, one of whom was a foreigner, did not resist.

'This brings the number of drug gang arrests to five, for it is believed that the three men arrested last night belonged to the same gang as the man and woman arrested a week ago in the Alésia quarter.

'The police state that still more arrests are likely to be made, as the Bureau Général des Stupéfiants has in its possession evidence implicating the actual organizers of the gang.

'Monsieur Auguste Lafon, director of the Bureau, said: "We have known of this gang for some time and have conducted painstaking investigations into their activities. We could have made arrests but we held our hands. It was the leaders, the big criminals whom we wanted. Without leaders, with their sources of supply cut off, the army of drug pedlars that infests Paris will be powerless to carry on their nefarious trade. We intend to smash this gang and others like it."'

Then, on December the eleventh, the newspapers reported: 'DRUG GANG SMASHED, NEW ARRESTS.'

'Now we have them all,' says Lafon. 'THE COUNCIL OF SEVEN.'

'Six men and one woman are now under arrest as a result of the attack launched by Monsieur Lafon, director of the Bureau Général des Stupéfiants, on a notorious gang of foreign drug traffickers operating in Paris and Marseilles.

'The attack began with the arrest two weeks ago of a woman and her male accomplice in the Alésia quarter. It reached its climax yesterday with the arrest in Marseilles of two men believed to be the remaining members of the gang's "Council of Seven", which was responsible for the organization of this criminal enterprise.

'At the request of the police we have hitherto remained silent as to the names of those arrested as it was desired not to put the others on their guard. Now that restriction has been lifted.

'The woman, Lydia Prokofievna, is a Russian who is believed to have come to France from Turkey with a Nansen passport in 1924. She is known in criminal circles as "The Grand Duchess". The man arrested with her was a Dutchman named Manus Visser who, through his association with Prokofievna, was sometimes referred to as "Monsieur le Duc".

'The names of the other five under arrest are; Luis Galindo, a naturalized Frenchman of Mexican origin, who now lies in hospital with a bullet wound in the thigh, Jean-Baptiste Lenôtre, a Frenchman from Bordeaux, and Jacob Werner, a Belgian, who were arrested with Galindo, Pierre Lamare or "Jo-jo", a Niçois, and Frederik Petersen, a Dane, who were arrested in Marseilles.

'In a statement to the press last night, Monsieur Lafon said: "Now we have them all. The gang is smashed. We have cut off the head and with it the brains. The body will now die a speedy death. It is finished."

'Lamare and Petersen are to be questioned by the examining magistrate to-day. It is expected that there will be a mass-trial of the prisoners.

'*See the special article, SECRETS OF THE DRUG GANGS, on page 3.*'

In England, Latimer reflected, Monsieur Lafon would have found himself in serious trouble. It hardly seemed worthwhile trying the accused after he and the press between them had already pronounced the verdict. But then, the accused was always guilty in a French trial. To give him a trial at all was, practically speaking, merely to ask him whether he had anything to say before he was sentenced.

He turned to the special article on page three.

The author, who called himself '*Veilleur*', revealed that the stuff known as morphine was an opium derivative with the formula $C_{17}H_{19}O_3N$ and that its usual medical form was morphine hydrochloride, that heroin (diacetyl-morphine), another opium derived alkaloid, was preferred to morphine by addicts because it acted more speedily and powerfully and was easier to take, that cocaine was made from the leaves of the coco bush and served up in the form of cocaine hydrochloride (formula $C_{17}H_{21}O_4N$, HCl) and that the effects of all three drugs were approximately the same, namely: that they were aphrodisiac, that they produced states of mental and physical exhilaration in the early stages and that eventually the addict suffered physical and moral degeneration and mental tortures of the most appalling kind. The traffic in these drugs, declared '*Veilleur*', was carried on on a gigantic scale and it was possible for anyone to obtain them in Paris and Marseilles. There were illicit factories in every country in Europe. World production of these drugs exceeded legitimate medical consumption many times over. There were millions of addicts in Western Europe. Drug smuggling was a vast well-organized business. There followed a list of recent seizures of illicit drugs: sixteen kilos of heroin found in each of six cases of machinery consigned from Amsterdam to Paris, twenty-five kilos of cocaine found between the false sides of a drum of oil consigned from New York to Cherbourg, ten kilos of morphine found in the false bottom of a cabin trunk landed at Marseilles, two hundred kilos of heroin found in an illicit factory in a garage near Lyons. The gangs that peddled these drugs were controlled by rich and outwardly respectable men. The police were bribed by these vermin. There were bars and dancings in Paris where the drugs were distributed under the very eyes of the police who were laughed at by the pedlars. '*Veilleur*' choked with indignation. Had he been writing three years later he would certainly have implicated Stavisky and half the Chamber of Deputies. But for once, he went on, the police had taken action. It was to be hoped that they would do so again. Meanwhile, however, there were thousands of Frenchmen—yes, *and* Frenchwomen!—suffering the tortures of the damned through this diabolical traffic which was sapping the virility of the nation. All of which suggested that, although '*Veilleur's*' heart was in the right place, he knew none of the secrets of the drug gangs.

With the arrest of the 'Council of Seven', interest in the case seemed to wane. The fact that 'The Grand Duchess' had been transferred to Nice to stand trial there for a fraud committed three years previously may have been responsible for this. The trial of the men was dealt with briefly. All were sentenced: Galindo, Lenôtre and Werner to fines of five thousand francs and three months' imprisonment, Lamare, Petersen and Visser to fines of two thousand francs and one month's imprisonment.

Latimer was amazed by the lightness of the sentences. '*Veilleur*', who bobbed up again to comment on the affair, was outraged but not amazed. But for the existence of a set of obsolete and wholly ridiculous laws, he thundered, the whole six would have been imprisoned for life. And which of them was the leader of the gang? Ah! Did the police suppose that these alley rats had financed an organization which, on the evidence given in court, had in one month taken delivery of and distributed heroin and morphine to the value of two and a half million francs? It was absurd. The police . . .

It was the nearest the newspaper got to the fact that the police had failed to find Dimitrios. That was not surprising. The police were not going to tell the press that the arrests were made possible only by a dossier obligingly supplied by some anonymous well-wisher whom they suspected of being the leader of the gang. All the same, it was irritating to find that he knew more than the newspaper he had relied upon to clarify the affair for him.

He was about to shut the file in disgust when his attention was caught by an illustration. It was a smudgy reproduction of a photograph of three of the prisoners being led from the court by detectives to whom they were handcuffed. All three had turned their faces away from the camera but the fact of their being handcuffed had prevented them from concealing themselves effectively.

Latimer left the newspaper office in better spirits than those in which he had entered it.

At his hotel a message awaited him. Unless he sent a *pneumatique* making other arrangements, Mr Peters would call upon him at six o'clock that evening.

Mr Peters arrived soon after half-past five. He greeted Latimer effusively.

'My *dear* Mr Latimer! I cannot tell you how pleased I am to see you. Our last meeting took place under such inauspicious circumstances that I hardly dared hope. . . . But let us talk of pleasanter things. Welcome to Paris! Have you had a good journey? You are looking well. Tell me, what did you think of Grodek? He wrote telling me how charming and sympathetic you were. A good fellow, isn't he? Those cats of his! He worships them.'

'He was very helpful. Do, please, sit down.'

'I knew he would be.'

For Latimer, Mr Peters' sweet smile was like the greeting of an old and detested acquaintance. 'He was also mysterious. He urged me to come to Paris to see you.'

'Did he?' Mr Peters did not seem pleased. His smile faded a little. 'And what else did he say, Mr Latimer?'

'He said that you were a clever man. He seemed to find something I said about you amusing.'

Mr Peters sat down carefully on the bed. His smile had quite gone. 'And what was it you said?'

'He insisted upon knowing what business I had with you. I told him all I could. As I knew nothing,' went on Latimer spitefully, 'I felt that I could safely confide in him. If you do not like that, I am sorry. You must remember that I am still in complete ignorance concerning this precious scheme of yours.'

'Grodek did not tell you?'

'No. Could he have done so?'

The smile once more tightened his soft lips. It was as if some obscene plant had turned its face to the sun. 'Yes, Mr Latimer, he could have done so. What you have told me explains the flippant tone of his letter to me. I am glad you satisfied his curiosity. The rich are so often covetous of others' goods in this world of ours. Grodek is a dear friend of mine but it is just as well that he knows that we stand in no need of assistance. He might otherwise be tempted by the prospect of gain.'

Latimer regarded him thoughtfully for a moment. Then: 'Have you got your pistol with you, Mr Peters?'

The fat man looked horrified. 'Dear me no, Mr Latimer. Why should I bring such a thing on a friendly visit to you?'

'Good,' said Latimer curtly. He backed towards the door and turned the key in the lock. The key he put in his pocket. 'Now then,' he went on grimly, 'I don't want to seem a bad host but there are limits to my patience. I have come a long way to see you and I still don't know why. I want to know why.'

'And so you shall.'

'I've heard that before,' answered Latimer rudely. 'Now before you start beating about the bush again there are one or two things *you* should know. I am not a violent man, Mr Peters. To be honest with you, I dread violence. But there are times when the most peace-loving among us must use it. This may be one of them. I am younger than you and, I should say, in better condition. If you persist in being mysterious I shall attack you. That is the first thing.

'The second is that I know who you are. Your name is not Peters but Petersen, Frederik Petersen. You were a member of the drug-peddling gang organized by Dimitrios and you were arrested in December 1931, fined two thousand francs and sentenced to one month's imprisonment.'

Mr Peters' smile was tortured. 'Did Grodek tell you this?' He asked the question gently and sorrowfully. The word 'Grodek' might have been another way of saying 'Judas'.

'No. I saw a picture of you this morning in a newspaper file.'

'A newspaper. Ah, yes! I could not believe that my friend Grodek . . .'

'You don't deny it?'

'Oh, no. It is the truth.'

'Well then, Mr Petersen . . .'

'Peters, Mr Latimer. I decided to change the name.'

'All right then—Peters. We come to my third point. When I was in Istanbul I heard some interesting things about the end of that gang. It was said that Dimitrios betrayed the lot of you by sending to the police, anonymously, a dossier convicting the seven of you. Is that true?'

'Dimitrios behaved very badly to us all,' said Mr Peters huskily.

'It was also said that Dimitrios had become an addict himself. Is that true?'

'Unhappily, it is. Otherwise I do not think he would have betrayed us. We were making so much money for him.'

'I was also told there was talk of vengeance, that you all threatened to kill Dimitrios as soon as you were free.'

'*I* did not threaten,' Mr Peters corrected him. 'Some of the others did so. Galindo, for example, was always a hot-head.'

'I see. You did not threaten; you preferred to act.'

'I don't understand you, Mr Latimer.' And he looked as if he really did not understand.

'No? Let me put it to you this way. Dimitrios was murdered near Istanbul roughly two months ago. Very shortly after the time when the murder could have taken place, you were in Athens. That is not very far from Istanbul, is it? Dimitrios, it is said, died a poor man. Now, is that likely? As you have just pointed out, his gang made a lot of money for him in 1931. From what I have heard of him, he was not the man to lose money he had made. Do you know what is in my mind, Mr Peters? I am wondering whether it would not be reasonable to suppose that you killed Dimitrios for his money. What have you to say to that?'

Mr Peters did not answer for a moment but contemplated Latimer unhappily in the manner of a good shepherd about to admonish an erring lamb.

Then he said: 'Mr Latimer, I think that you are very indiscreet.'

'Do you?'

'And also very fortunate. Just suppose that I had, as you suggest, killed Dimitrios. Think what I should be forced to do. I should be forced to kill you also, now shouldn't I?' He put his hand in his breast pocket. It emerged holding the pistol. 'You see, I lied to you just now. I admit it. I was so curious to know what you were going to do if you thought I was unarmed. Besides, it seemed so impolite to come here carrying a pistol. So I lied. Do you understand my feelings a little? I am so anxious to have your confidence.'

'All of which is as skilful a reply to an accusation of murder as one could wish for.'

Mr Peters put away his pistol wearily. 'Mr Latimer, this is not a detective story. There is no *need* to be so stupid. Even if you cannot be discreet, at least use your imagination. Is it likely that Dimitrios would make a Will in my favour? No. Then how do you suppose that I could kill him for his money? People in these days do not keep their wealth in treasure chests. Come now, Mr Latimer, let us please be sensible. Let us eat dinner together and then talk business. I suggest that after dinner we drink coffee in my apartment—it is a little more comfortable than this room—though if you would prefer to go to a café I shall understand. You probably disapprove of me. I really cannot blame you. But at least let us cultivate the illusion of friendship.'

For a moment Latimer felt himself warming to Mr Peters. True, the last part of his appeal had been accompanied by an almost visible accretion of self-pity; but he had not smiled. Besides, the man had already made him feel a fool: it would be too much if he made him feel a pompous ass as well. At the same time . . .

'I am as hungry as you,' he said; 'and I can see no reason why I should prefer a café to your apartment. At the same time, Mr Peters, anxious though I am to be friendly, I feel that I should warn you now that unless I have, this evening, a satisfactory explanation of your asking me to meet you here in Paris, I shall–half a million francs or no half a million francs–leave by the first available train. Is that clear?'

Mr Peters' smile returned. 'It could not be clearer, Mr Latimer. And may I say how much I appreciate your frankness?' The smile became rancid. 'How much better if we could always be so frank, if we could always open our hearts to our fellow men without fear, fear of being misunderstood, misinterpreted! How much easier this life of ours would be! But we are so blind, so very blind. If the Great One chooses that we should do things of which the world may disapprove, let us not be ashamed of those things. For we are, after all, merely doing his Will and how can we understand His purposes? How?'

'I don't know.'

'Ah! none of us knows, Mr Latimer. None of us knows–until he reaches The Other Side.'

'Quite so. Where shall we dine? There is a Danish place near here, isn't there?'

Mr Peters struggled into his overcoat. 'No, Mr Latimer, as you are doubtless well aware, there is not.' He sighed unhappily. 'It is unkind of you to make fun of me. And in any case I prefer French cooking.'

At his suggestion and expense they ate in a cheap restaurant in the Rue Jacob. Afterwards they went to the Impasse des Huit Anges.

'What about Caillé?' said Latimer as they climbed the dusty stairs.

'He is away. At the moment I am in sole possession.'

'I see.'

Mr Peters, who was breathing heavily by the time they had reached the second landing, paused for a moment. 'You have concluded, I suppose, that I am Caillé.'

'Yes.'

Mr Peters began to climb again. The stairs creaked under his weight. Latimer, following two or three stairs behind, was reminded of a circus elephant picking its way unwillingly up a pyramid of coloured blocks to perform a balancing trick. They reached the fourth floor. Mr Peters stopped and, standing panting before a battered door, hauled out a bunch of keys. A moment later he pushed open the door, pressed a switch and waved Latimer in.

The room ran from front to back of the house and was divided into two by a curtain to the left of the door. The half beyond the curtain was of a different shape from that which contained the door as it included the space between the end of the landing, the rear wall and the next house. The space formed an alcove. At each end of the room was a tall French window.

But if it was, architecturally speaking, the sort of room that one would expect to find in a French house of that type and age, it was in every other respect fantastic.

The first thing that Latimer saw was the dividing curtain. It was of imitation cloth of gold. The walls and ceiling were distempered an angry blue and bespattered with gold five-pointed stars. Scattered all over the floor, so that not a square inch of it showed, were cheap Moroccan rugs. They overlapped a good deal so that in places there were humps of three and even four thicknesses of rug. There were three huge divans piled high with cushions, some tooled leather ottoman seats and a Moroccan table with a brass tray upon it. In one corner stood an enormous brass gong. The light came from fretted oak lanterns. In the centre of it all stood a small chromium-plated electric radiator. There was a choking smell of upholstery dust.

'Home!' said Mr Peters. 'Take your things off, Mr Latimer; would you like to see the rest of the place?'

'Very much.'

'Outwardly, just another uncomfortable French house,' commented Mr Peters as he toiled up the stairs again; 'actually an oasis in a desert of discomfort. This is my bedroom.'

Latimer had another glimpse of French Morocco. This time it was adorned by a pair of crumpled flannel pyjamas.

'And the toilet.'

Latimer looked at the toilet and learned that his host had a spare set of false teeth.

'Now,' said Mr Peters, 'I will show you something curious.'

He led the way out on to the landing. Facing them was a large clothes cupboard. He opened the door and struck a match. Along the back of the cupboard was a row of metal clothes pegs. Grasping the centre one, he turned it like a latch and pulled. The back of the cupboard swung towards them and Latimer felt the night air on his face and heard the noises of the city.

'There is a narrow iron platform running along the outside wall to the next house,' explained Mr Peters. 'There is another cupboard there like this one. You can see nothing because there are only blank walls facing us. Equally, no one could see us should we choose to leave that way. It was Dimitrios who had this done.'

'Dimitrios!'

'Dimitrios owned all three of these houses. They were kept empty for reasons of privacy. Sometimes, they were used as stores. These two floors were used for meetings. Morally, no doubt, the houses still belong to Dimitrios. Fortunately for me, he took the precaution of buying them in my name. I also conducted the negotiations. The police never found out about them. I was able, therefore, to move in when I came out of prison. In case Dimitrios should ever wonder what had happened to his property, *I* took the precaution of buying them from myself in the name of Caille. Do you like Algerian coffee?'

'Yes.'

'It takes a little longer to prepare than French but I prefer it. Shall we go downstairs again?'

They went downstairs. Having seen Latimer uncomfortably ensconced amid a sea of cushions, Mr Peters disappeared into the alcove.

Latimer got rid of some of the cushions and looked about him. It was odd to feel that the house had once belonged to Dimitrios. Yet the evidence around him of the tenancy of the preposterous Mr Peters was a good deal odder. There was a small (fretted) shelf above his head. On it were paper-bound books. There was *Pearls of Everyday Wisdom*. That was the one he had been reading in the train from Athens. There was, besides, Plato's

Symposium, in French and uncut, an anthology called *Poèmes Erotiques*, which had no author's name on it and *had* been cut, Æsop's *Fables* in English, Mrs Humphry Ward's *Robert Elsmere* in French, a German gazetteer, and several books by Dr Frank Crane in a language which Latimer took to be Danish.

Mr Peters came back carrying a Moroccan tray on which were a curious looking coffee percolator, a spirit lamp, two cups and a Moroccan cigarette box. The spirit lamp he lighted and put under the percolator. The cigarettes he placed beside Latimer on the divan. Then he reached up above Latimer's head, brought down one of the Danish books and flicked over one or two of the pages. A small photograph fluttered to the floor. He picked it up and handed it to Latimer.

'Do you recognize him, Mr Latimer?'

It was a faded head and shoulders photograph of a middle aged man with . . .

Latimer looked up. 'It's Dimitrios!' he exclaimed. 'Where did you get it?'

Mr Peters took the photograph from Latimer's fingers. 'You recognize it? Good.' He sat down on one of the ottoman seats and adjusted the spirit lamp. Then he looked up. If it had been possible for Mr Peters' wet, lustreless eyes to gleam, Latimer would have said that they were gleaming with pleasure.

'Help yourself to cigarettes, Mr Latimer,' he said. 'I am going to tell you a story.'

Chapter Eleven

Paris, 1928–1931

'Often, when the day's work is done,' said Mr Peters reminiscently, 'I sit by the fire, like this, and wonder if my life has been as successful as it might have been. True, I have made money—a little property, some *rentes*, a few shares here and there—but it is not of money that I think. Money is not everything. What have I done with my life in this world of ours? I think sometimes that it would have been better if I had married and brought up a family; but I have always been too restless, too interested in this world of ours as a whole. Perhaps it is that I have never known what I have wanted of life. So many of us poor human creatures are like that. We go on year after year, ever seeking, ever hoping—for what? We do not know. Money? Only when we have little. I sometimes think that he who has only a crust is happier than many millionaires. For the man with a crust knows what he wants—two crusts. His life is not complicated by possessions. I only know that there *is* something that I want above all else. Yet, how shall I know what it is? I have'—he waved a hand towards the bookshelf—'sought consolation in philosophy and the arts. Plato, H.G.Wells; yes, I have read widely. These things comfort, yet they do not satisfy.' He smiled bravely, the victim of an almost unbearable *Weltschmerz*. 'We must all just wait until the Great One summons us.'

Waiting for him to go on, Latimer thought how difficult it was to dislike a man when he was making coffee for you. The stubby fingers gave the percolator lid a gentle, congratulatory pat. Mr Peters straightened his back and emitted a sigh of satisfaction.

'Yes, Mr Latimer, most of us go through life without knowing what we want of it. But Dimitrios, you know, was not like that. Dimitrios knew exactly what he wanted. He wanted money and he wanted power. Just those two things; as much of them as he could get. The curious thing is that I helped him to get them.

'It was in 1928 that I first set eyes on Dimitrios. It was here in Paris. I was, at the time, the part-owner, with a man named Giraud, of a *boîte* in the Rue Blanche. We called it *Le Kasbah Parisien* and it was a very gay and cosy place with divans and amber lights and rugs. I had met Giraud in Marrakesh and we decided that everything should be just like a place we knew there. Everything was Moroccan; everything, that is, except the band for dancing which was South American.

'We opened it in 1926 which was a good year in Paris. The Americans and English, but especially the Americans, had money to spend on champagne and the French used to come, too. Most Frenchmen are sentimental about Morocco unless they have done their military service there. And the *Kasbah was* Morocco. We had Arab and Senegalese waiters and the champagne actually came from Meknes. It was a little sweet for the Americans but very nice all the same and quite cheap.

'For two years we made money and then, as is the way with such places, the clientèle began to change in character. We had more French and fewer Americans, more *maquereaux* and fewer gentlemen, more *poules* and fewer *chic* ladies. We still made a profit but it was not as great and we had to do more for it. I began to think that it was time to move on.

'It was Giraud who brought Dimitrios to *Le Kasbah*.

'I had met Giraud when I was in Marrakesh. He was a half-caste, his mother being an Arab and his father a French soldier. He was born in Algiers and had a French passport.

'Mostly you would not have known that he had Arab blood. It was only when you saw him with Arabs that you knew. He never really liked Arabs. I never really liked him. It was not that he did not trust me–that was no more than hurtful to me–but that I could not trust him. If I had had enough money to open *Le Kasbah* by myself I would not have taken him as a partner. He would try to trick me over the accounts and though he never succeeded I did not like it. I cannot stand dishonesty. By the spring of 1928 I was very weary of Giraud.

'I do not know exactly how he met Dimitrios. I think that it was at some *boîte* higher up the Rue Blanche; for we did not open until eleven o'clock and Giraud liked to dance at other places beforehand. But, one evening, he brought Dimitrios into *Le Kasbah* and then took me aside. He remarked that profits had been getting smaller and said that we could make some money for ourselves if we did business with this friend of his, Dimitrios Makropoulos.

'The first time I saw Dimitrios I was not impressed by him. He was, I thought, just such a type of *maquereau* as I had seen before. His clothes fitted tightly and he had greying hair and polished finger-nails and he looked at women in a way that those who came to *Le Kasbah* would not like. But I went over to his table with Giraud and we shook hands. Then he pointed to the chair beside him and told me to sit down. One would have thought that I was a waiter instead of the *patron*.'

He turned his watery eyes to Latimer. 'You may think, Mr Latimer, that, for one who was not impressed, I remember the occasion very clearly. That is true. I do remember it clearly. You understand, I did not then know Dimitrios as I came to know him later. He made his impression without seeming to do so. At the time he irritated me. Without sitting down, I asked him what he wanted.

'For a moment he looked at me. He had very soft, brown eyes, you know. Then he said: "I want champagne, my friend. Have you any objection? I can pay for it, you know. Are you going to be polite to me or shall I take my business proposals to more intelligent people?"

'I am an even-tempered man. I do not like trouble. I often think how much pleasanter a place this world of ours would be if people were polite and softly spoken with one another. But there are times when it is difficult. I told Dimitrios that nothing would induce me to be polite to him and that he could go when he pleased.

'But for Giraud he would have gone and I should not be sitting here talking to you. Giraud sat down at the table with him, apologizing for me. Dimitrios was watching me while Giraud was speaking, and I could see that he was wondering about me.

'I was now quite sure that I did not want to do business of any kind with this Dimitrios; but because of Giraud I agreed to listen, and we sat down together while Dimitrios told us what his proposal was. He talked very convincingly, and at last I agreed to do what he wanted. We had been in association with Dimitrios for several months, when one day . . .'

'Just a moment,' interrupted Latimer; 'what was this association? Was this the beginning of the drug peddling?'

Mr Peters hesitated and frowned. 'No, Mr Latimer, it was not.' He hesitated again and then broke suddenly into French. 'I will tell you what our business together was if you insist; but it is so difficult to explain these things to a person who does not understand the *milieu*, who is not sympathetic. It involves matters so much outside your experience.'

Latimer's 'Indeed?' was a trifle acid.

'You see, Mr Latimer, I have read one of your books. It terrified me. There was about it an atmosphere of intolerance, of prejudice, of ferocious moral rectitude that I found quite unnerving. Please do not misunderstand me, Mr Latimer. I do not fear your moral censure, but I resent, quite definitely, your being shocked.'

'As you have not yet told me what I am expected to be shocked at,' Latimer pointed out irritably, 'it is a little difficult for me to answer you.'

'Yes, yes, of course. But, forgive me, does not your interest in Dimitrios arise largely from the fact that you are shocked by him?'

Latimer thought for a moment. 'I think that that may be true. But it is just because I am shocked by him that I am trying to understand, to explain him. I do not believe in the inhuman, professional devil that one reads about in crime stories; and yet everything that I have heard about Dimitrios suggests that he consistently acted with quite revolting inhumanity–not just once or twice, but consistently.'

'Are the desires for money and power inhuman? With money and power a vain man can do so much to give himself pleasure. His vanity was one of the first things that I noticed about Dimitrios. It was that quiet, profound vanity that makes the man who has it so much more dangerous than ordinary people with their peacock antics. Come now, Mr Latimer, be reasonable! The difference between Dimitrios and the more respectable type of successful business man is only a difference of method–legal method or illegal method. Both are in their respective ways equally ruthless.'

'Rubbish!'

'No doubt. It is interesting, though, is it not, to note that I am now attempting to defend Dimitrios against attack from the forces of moral rectitude. He would not, I feel sure, be at all grateful to me for doing so. Dimitrios was, for all his apparent *savoir faire*, hopelessly uneducated. The words "moral rectitude" would mean nothing to him. Ah! the coffee is ready.'

He poured it out in silence, raised his own cup to his nose and sampled the aroma. Then he put the cup down.

'Dimitrios,' he said, 'was connected at the time with what I believe you call the white slave traffic. It is such an interesting phrase to me. "Traffic"–a word full of horrible significance. "White slave"–consider the implications of the adjective. Does anyone talk nowadays about the *coloured* slave traffic? I think not. Yet the majority of the women involved are coloured. I fail to see why the consequences of the traffic should be any more disagreeable to a white girl from a Bucharest slum than to a negro girl from Dakar or a Chinese girl from Harbin. The League of Nations Committee is unprejudiced enough to appreciate that aspect of the question. They are intelligent enough, too, to mistrust the word "slave". They refer to the "traffic in women".

'I have never liked the business. It is impossible to treat human beings as one would treat ordinary inanimate merchandise. There is always trouble. Besides, the overhead expenses of a trafficker in what is considered a fair way of business are enormous. There are always false birth, marriage and death certificates to be obtained and travelling expenses and bribes to pay quite apart from the cost of maintaining several identities. You have no idea of the cost of forged documents, Mr Latimer. There used to be three recognized sources of supply: one in Zürich, one in Amsterdam and one in Brussels. All neutrals! Odd, isn't it? You used to be able to get a false-real Danish passport–that is, a real Danish passport treated chemically to remove the original entries and photograph and then filled in with new ones–for, let me see, about two thousand francs at the present rate of exchange. A real-false–manufactured from start to finish by the agent–would have cost you a little less, say fifteen hundred. Nowadays you would have to pay twice as much. Most of the business is done here in Paris now. It is the refugees, of course. The point is that a trafficker needs plenty of capital. If he is known, there are always plenty of people willing to provide it, but they expect fantastic dividends. It is better to have one's own capital.

'Dimitrios had his own capital; but he also had access to capital which was not his own. He represented certain very rich men. He was never at a loss for money. When he came to Giraud and me he was in a different sort of difficulty. Owing to League of Nations activities, the laws in quite a number of countries had been altered and tightened up in such a way that it was sometimes very difficult indeed to get women from one place to another. All very praiseworthy, but a great nuisance to men like Dimitrios. It was not that it made it impossible for them to do their business. It didn't. But it made things more complicated and expensive for them.

'Before Dimitrios came to us he had had a very simple technique. He knew people in Alexandria who would advise him about their requirements. Then he would go to, say, Poland, recruit the women, take them to France on their own passports and then ship them from Marseilles. That was all. It was enough to say that the girls were going to fulfil a theatrical engagement. When the regulations were tightened up, however, it was no longer as simple. The night he came to *Le Kasbah* he told us that he had just encountered his first trouble. He had recruited twelve women from a *Madame* in Vilna, but the Poles would not let him bring them out without guarantees as to their destination and the respectability of their future employment. Respectability! But that was the law.

'Naturally, Dimitrios had told the Polish authorities that he would provide the guarantees. It would have been fatal for him not to have done so, for then he would have been suspect. Somehow he had to obtain the guarantees. That was where Giraud and I came in. We were to say that we were employing the girls as cabaret dancers and deal with any inquiries that might be made by the Polish Consular authorities. As long as they stayed in Paris for a week or so, we were perfectly safe. If inquiries were made after that we knew nothing. They had completed their engagement and gone. Where they had gone to was no business of ours.

'That was the way Dimitrios put it to us. He said that for our part of the affair he would pay us five thousand francs. It was money easily earned, but I was doubtful; and it was Giraud who finally persuaded me to agree. But I told Dimitrios that my agreement only applied to this particular case and that I could not consider myself committed to helping him again. Giraud grumbled, but agreed to accept the condition.

'A month later Dimitrios came to see us again, paid us the balance of the five thousand francs and said that he had another job for us. I objected; but, as Giraud immediately pointed out, we had had no trouble on the first occasion and my objection was not very firm. The money was useful. It paid the South Americans for a week.

'I believe now that Dimitrios lied to us about that first five thousand francs. I do not think that we earned it. I think he gave it to us simply to gain our confidence. It was like him to do a thing like that. Another man might try to trick you into serving his ends; but Dimitrios bought you. Yet he bought you cheaply. He set one's common sense fighting against one's instinctive suspicions of him.

'I have said that we earned that first five thousand francs without trouble. The second caused us a lot of trouble. The Polish authorities made some *chi-chi* and we had the police visiting us and asking questions. Worse, we had to have these women in *Le Kasbah* to prove that we were employing them. They could not dance a step and were a great inconvenience to us, as we had to be amiable to them in case one should go to the police and tell the truth. They drank champagne all the time, and if Dimitrios had not agreed to pay for it we should have lost money.

'He was, of course, very apologetic and said that there had been a mistake. He paid us ten thousand francs for our trouble and promised that if we would continue to help him there would be no more Polish girls and no more *chi-chi*. After some argument we agreed, and for several months we were paid our ten thousand francs. We had during that time only occasional visits from the police, and there was no unpleasantness. But at last we had trouble again. This time it was because of the Italian authorities. Both Giraud and I were questioned by the examining magistrate for the district and kept for a day at the Commissariat. The day after that I quarrelled with Giraud.

'I say that I quarrelled. It would be more correct to say that our quarrel became open. I have told you that I did not like Giraud. He was crude and stupid and, as I have said, he sometimes tried to cheat me. He was suspicious, too; suspicious in a loud, stupid way like an animal; and he encouraged the wrong sort of clientèle. His friends were detestable: *maquereaux*, all of them. He used to call people *"mon gar"*. He would have been better as the *patron* of a *bistro*. For all I know he may be one now; but I think it more likely that he is in a prison. He often became violent when he was angry and sometimes injured people badly.

'That day after our unpleasantness with the police I said that we should have no more to do with this business of the women. That made him angry. He said that we should be fools to give up ten thousand francs a month because of a few police and that I was too nervous for his taste. I understood his point of view. He had had much to do with the police both in Marrakesh and Algiers, and he had a contempt for them. As long as he could keep out of prison and make money he was satisfied. I have never thought that way. I do not like the police to be interested in me, even though they cannot arrest me. Giraud was right. I was nervous. But although I understood his point of view I could not agree with it, and I said so. I also said that, if he wished, he could buy my share in *Le Kasbah Parisien* for the amount of money I had originally invested.

'It was a sacrifice on my part, you know, but I was tired of Giraud and wanted to be rid of him. I did get rid of him. He agreed immediately. That night we saw Dimitrios and explained the situation to him. Giraud was delighted with his bargain and enjoyed himself very much cracking clumsy jokes at my expense. Dimitrios smiled at these jokes; but when Giraud left us alone for a moment, he asked me to leave soon after he did and meet him at a café as he had something to say to me.

'I very nearly did not go. On the whole, I think that it was as well that I did go. I profited by my association with Dimitrios. There are, I think, very few associates of Dimitrios who could say as much; but I was lucky. Besides, I think that he had a respect for my intelligence. Generally he could bluff me, but not always.

'He was waiting in the café for me, and I sat down beside him and asked him what he wanted. I was never polite to him.

'He said: "I think you are wise to leave Giraud. The business with the women has become too dangerous. It was always difficult. Now I have finished with it."

'I asked him if he proposed to tell Giraud that and he smiled.

'"Not yet," he said; "not until you have your money from him."

'I said suspiciously that he was very kind, but he shook his head impatiently. "Giraud is a fool," he said. "If you had not been there with him, I should have made other arrangements about the women. Now, I am offering you a chance to work with me. I should be a fool if I made you angry with me to begin with by costing you your investment in *Le Kasbah*."

'Then he asked me if I knew anything about the heroin business. I did know a little about it. He then told me that he had sufficient capital to buy twenty kilogrammes a month and finance its distribution in Paris and asked me if I were interested in working for him.

'Now, twenty kilogrammes of heroin is a serious thing, Mr Latimer. It is worth a lot of money. I asked him how he proposed to distribute so much. He said that, for the moment, that would be his affair. What he wanted me to do was to negotiate the purchases abroad and find ways of bringing it into the country. If I agreed to his proposal I was to begin by going to Bulgaria as his representative, dealing with suppliers there of whom he already knew and arranging for the transport of the stuff to Paris. He offered me ten percent of the value of every kilo I supplied him with.

'I said that I would think it over, but my mind was already made up. With the price of heroin as it was then, I knew that I would make nearly twenty thousand francs a month. I also knew that he was going to make a great deal more than that for himself. Even if, with my commission and expenses, he had to pay in effect fifteen thousand francs a kilo for the stuff, it would be good business for him. Selling heroin by the gramme in Paris, one can get nearly one hundred thousand francs a kilo for it. With the commissions to the actual pedlars and others, he would make not less than thirty thousand francs on each kilo. That meant over half a million francs a month for him. Capital is a wonderful thing if one knows just what to do with it and does not mind a little risk.

'In the September of 1928 I went to Bulgaria for Dimitrios with instructions from him to get the first twenty kilos to him by November. He had already begun to make arrangements with agents and pedlars. The sooner I could get the stuff the better.

'Dimitrios had given me the name of a man in Sofia who would put me in touch with the suppliers. This man did so. He also arranged for the credits with which I was to make the purchases. He . . .'

Latimer had an idea. He said suddenly: 'What was this man's name?'

Mr Peters frowned at the interruption. 'I do not think that you ought to ask me that, Mr Latimer.'

'Was it Vazoff?'

Mr Peters' eyes watered at him. 'Yes, it was.'

'And were the credits arranged through the Eurasian Credit Trust?'

'You evidently know a great deal more than I had thought.' Mr Peters was obviously not pleased by the fact. 'May I ask . . . ?'

'I was guessing. But you need not have worried about compromising Vazoff. He died three years ago.'

'I am aware of it. Did you guess that Vazoff was dead? And how much more guessing have you done, Mr Latimer?'

'That is all. Please continue.'

'Frankness . . .' began Mr Peters and then stopped and drank his coffee. 'We will return to the subject,' he said at last. 'Yes, Mr Latimer, I admit that you are right. Through Vazoff, I purchased the supplies Dimitrios needed and paid for them with drafts on Eurasian Credit Trust of Sofia. There was no difficulty about that. My real task was to transport the stuff to France. I decided to send it by rail to Salonika and ship it from there to Marseilles.'

'As heroin?'

'Obviously not. But I must confess it was difficult to know how to disguise it. The only goods which come into France from Bulgaria regularly, and which would not, therefore, be subject to special examination by the French Customs, were things like grain and tobacco and attar of roses. Dimitrios was pressing for delivery and I was at my wits' end.' He paused dramatically.

'Well, how *did* you smuggle it?'

'In a coffin, Mr Latimer. The French, I reflected, are a race with a great respect for the solemnity of death. Have you ever attended a French funeral? *Pompe funèbre*, you know. It is most impressive. No Customs official, I felt certain, would care to play the ghoul. I purchased the coffin in Sofia. It was a beautiful thing with very fine carving on it. I also purchased a suit of mourning clothes and accompanied the coffin myself. I am a man who responds very readily to emotion and really I was most moved by the marks of simple respect for my grief shown by the stevedores who handled the coffin at the dock. Not even my own personal luggage was examined at the Customs.

'I had warned Dimitrios and a hearse was waiting for me and the coffin. I was pleased by my success, but Dimitrios, when I saw him, shrugged. I could not, he said very reasonably, arrive in France with a coffin every month. I think he thought the whole affair a little unbusinesslike. He was right, of course. He had, however, a suggestion. There was an Italian shipping line which ran one cargo steamer a month from Varna to Genoa. The stuff could be shipped to Genoa in small cases and manifested as special tobacco consigned to France. That would prevent the Italian Customs examining it. There was a man in Nice who could arrange for the transport of the stuff from Genoa by bribing the warehouse people to release it from bond and then smuggling it through by road. I wished to know how that would affect my financial interest in the supplies. He said that I should lose nothing as there was other work for me to do.

'It was curious how we all accepted his leadership almost without question. Yes, he had the money; but there was more than that to it. He dominated us because he knew precisely what he wanted and precisely how to get it with the least possible trouble and at the lowest possible cost. He knew how to find the people to work for him, too; and, when he had found them, he knew how to handle them.

'There were seven of us who took our instructions directly from Dimitrios and not one was the sort of person to take instructions easily. For instance, Visser, the Dutchman, had sold German machine guns to the Chinese, spied for the Japanese and served a term of imprisonment for killing a coolie in Batavia. He was not an easy man to handle. It was he who made the arrangements with the clubs and bars through which we reached the addicts.

'You see, the system of distribution was very carefully organized. Both Lenôtre and Galindo had for several years been peddling drugs which they bought from a man in the employ of a big French wholesale drug manufacturer. That sort of thing used to be quite easy before the 1931 regulations. Both those men knew well those who needed the stuff and where to find them. Before Dimitrios came on the scene they had been dealing mostly in morphine and cocaine and always they had been handicapped by limited supplies. When Dimitrios offered them unlimited supplies of heroin they were quite ready to abandon the wholesale chemist and sell their clients heroin.

'But that was only one part of the business. Drug addicts, you know, are always very eager to get other people to take drugs too. Consequently, your circle of consumers is ever widening. It is most important, as you may imagine, to see that when you are approached by new customers they are not representatives of the *Brigade des Stupéfiants* or similar undesirables. That was where Visser's work came in. The would-be buyer would come to, say, Lenôtre in the first place on the recommendation of a regular customer known to Lenôtre. But, on being asked for drugs, Lenôtre would pretend to be astonished. Drugs? He knew nothing of such things. Personally, he never used them. But, if one did use them, he had heard that the place to go to was the So-and-So Bar. At the So-and-So Bar which would be on Visser's list, the prospective customer would receive much the same sort of answer. Drugs? No. Nothing of that kind at the So-and-So Bar but if it should be possible to call in again the following night, there might possibly be someone who could help. The following night, the Grand Duchess would be there.

'She was a curious woman. She had been brought into the business by Visser and was, I think, the only one of us Dimitrios had not found for himself. She was very clever. Her capacity for weighing up complete strangers was extraordinary. She could, I think, tell the most convincingly disguised detective just by looking at him across a room. It was her business to examine the person who wanted to buy and decide whether he or she should be supplied or not and how much was to be charged. She was very valuable to us.

'The other man was the Belgian, Werner. It was he who dealt with the small pedlars. He had been a chemist at one time and he used to dilute the heroin. Dimitrios never mentioned that part of the business.

'Some dilution very soon became necessary. Within six months of our beginning, I had had to increase the monthly heroin supply to fifty kilos. And I had other work to do. Lenôtre and Galindo had reported in the early stages that, if they were to get all the business they knew of, they would have to have morphine and cocaine to sell as well as heroin. Morphine addicts did not always like heroin and cocaine addicts would sometimes refuse it if they could get cocaine elsewhere. I had then to arrange for supplies of morphine and cocaine. The morphine problem was a simple one as it could be supplied at the same time and by the same people as the heroin; but the cocaine was a different matter. For that, it waš necessary to go to Germany. I had plenty to do.

'We had our troubles, of course. They usually came to my part of the business. By the time we had been operating for a year, I had made several alternative arrangements for bringing in our supplies. In addition to the Genoa route for heroin and morphine which Lamare handled, I had come to terms with a sleeping car attendant on the Orient Express. He used to take the stuff aboard at Sofia and deliver it when the train was shunted into the siding in Paris. It was not a very safe route and I had to take elaborate precautions to protect myself in case of trouble, but it was rapid. Cocaine used to come in in cases of machinery from Germany. We had also begun to receive consignments of heroin from an Istanbul factory. These were brought by a cargo boat which left them floating outside the port of Marseilles in anchored containers for Lamare to collect at night.

'There was one week of disaster. In the last week of the June of 1929, fifteen kilos of heroin were seized on the Orient Express and the police arrested six of my men including the sleeping car attendant. That would have been bad enough; but during the same week Lamare had to abandon a consignment of forty kilos of heroin and morphine near Sospel. He himself escaped but we were in a serious difficulty, for the loss of those fifty-five kilos meant that we were left with only eight kilos to meet commitments for over fifty. None was due on the Istanbul boat for several days. We were in despair. Lenôtre and Galindo and Werner had a terrible time. Two of Galindo's clientèle committed suicide and in one of the bars there was a *fracas* in which Werner had his head cut.

'I did the best I could. I went to Sofia myself and brought back ten kilos in a trunk; but that was not enough. Dimitrios did not, I must say, blame me. It would have been unfair to have done so. But he was angry. He decided that, in future, reserve stocks must be held. It was soon after that week that he bought these houses. Until then we had always met him in a room over a café near the Porte d'Orléans. Now he said that these houses should be our headquarters. We never knew where he lived and could never get in touch with him until he chose to telephone one or other of us. We were to discover later that this ignorance of his address put us at a disastrous disadvantage. But other things happened before we made that discovery.

'The task of creating stocks was left to me. It was by no means easy. If we were both to create stocks and to maintain existing supplies we had to increase the size of the consignments. That meant that there was a greater risk of seizure. It also meant that we had to find more new methods of bringing the stuff in. Things were complicated, too, by the Bulgarian

Government's closing down the factory at Radomir from which we drew the bulk of our supplies. It soon opened again in a different part of the country; but inevitably there were delays. We were forced to rely more and more upon Istanbul.

'It was a trying time. In two months we lost by seizure no less than ninety kilos of heroin, twenty of morphine and five of cocaine. But, in spite of ups and downs, the stock increased steadily. By the end of 1930, we had, beneath the floorboards of those houses next door, two hundred and fifty kilos of heroin, two hundred odd kilos of morphine, ninety kilos of cocaine and a small quantity of prepared Turkish opium.'

Mr Peters poured out the remainder of the coffee and extinguished the spirit lamp. Then he took a cigarette, wetted the end of it with his tongue and lit it.

'Have you ever known a drug addict, Mr Latimer?' he asked suddenly.

'I don't think so.'

'Ah, you don't *think* so. You do not know for certain. Yes, it is possible for a drug-taker to conceal his little weakness for quite a time. But he–especially *she*–cannot conceal it indefinitely, you know. The process is always roughly the same. It begins as an experiment. It may make you feel sick the first time; but you will try again and the next time it will be as it should be. A delicious sensation, warm, brilliant. Time stands still; but the mind moves at a tremendous pace and, it seems to you, with incredible efficiency. You were stupid; you become highly intelligent. You were unhappy; you become carefree. What you do not like you forget; and what you do like you experience with an intensity of pleasure undreamed of. Three hours of Paradise. And afterwards it is not too bad; not nearly as bad as it was when you had too much champagne. You want to be quiet; you feel a little ill at ease; that is all. Soon you are yourself again. Nothing has happened to you except that you have enjoyed yourself amazingly. If you do not wish to take the drug again, you tell yourself you need not do so. As an intelligent person you are superior to the stuff. Then, therefore, there is no logical reason why you should not enjoy yourself again, is there? Of course there isn't! And so you do. But this time it is a little disappointing. Your half a gramme was not quite enough. Disappointment must be dealt with. You must wander in Paradise just once more before you decide not to take the stuff again. A trifle more; nearly a gramme perhaps. Paradise again and still you don't feel any the worse for it. And since you don't feel any the worse for it, why not continue? Everybody knows that the stuff does ultimately have a bad effect on you; but the moment you detect any bad effects *you* will stop. Only fools become addicts. One and a half grammes. It really is something to look forward to in life. Only three months ago everything was so dreary; but now . . . Two grammes. Naturally, as you are taking a little more it is only reasonable to expect to feel a little ill and depressed afterwards. It's four months now. You must stop soon. Two and a half grammes. Your nose and throat get so dry these days. Other people seem to get on your nerves, too. Perhaps it is because you are sleeping so badly. They make too much noise. They talk so loudly. And what are they saying? Yes, *what*? Things about *you*, vicious lies. You can see it in their faces. Three grammes. And there are other things to be considered; other dangers. You have to be careful. Food tastes horrible. You cannot remember things that you have to do; important things. Even if you should happen to remember them, there are so many other things to worry you apart from this beastliness of having to live. For instance, your nose keeps running: that is, it is not really running but you think it must be, so you have to keep touching it to make sure. Another thing: there is always a fly annoying you. This terrible fly *will* never leave you alone and in peace. It is on your face, on your hand, on your neck. You must pull yourself together. Three and a half grammes. You see the idea, Mr Latimer?'

'You don't seem to approve of drug-taking.'

'Approve!' Mr Peters stared, aghast. 'It is terrible, *terrible!* Lives are ruined. They lose the power to work yet they must find money to pay for their special stuff. Under such circumstances people become desperate and may even do something criminal to get it. I see what is in your mind, Mr Latimer. You feel that it is strange that I should have been connected with, that I should have made money out of, a thing of which I disapprove so sternly. But consider. If *I* had not made the money, someone else would have done so. Not one of those unfortunate creatures would have been any better off and I should have lost money.'

'What about this ever-increasing clientèle of yours? You cannot pretend that all of those your organization supplied were habitual drug-takers before you went to work.'

'Of course they were not. But that side of the business was nothing to do with *me*. That was Lenôtre and Galindo. And I may tell you that Lenôtre and Galindo and Werner, too, were themselves addicts. They used cocaine. It is harder on the constitution but, whereas one can become a dangerous heroin addict in a few months, one can spend several years killing oneself with cocaine.'

'What did Dimitrios take?'

'Heroin. It was a great surprise to us the first time we noticed it. We would meet him in this room as a rule at about six o'clock in the evening. It was on one of those evenings in the spring of 1931 when we had our surprise.'

'Dimitrios arrived late. That in itself was unusual; but we took little notice of it. As a rule, at these meetings, he would sit very quietly with his eyes half-closed, looking a little troubled as though he had a headache, so that even when one became used to him one constantly wished to ask if all was well with him. Watching him sometimes I used to be amazed at myself for allowing myself to be led by him. Then I would see his face change as he turned to meet some objection from Visser—it was always Visser who objected—and I would understand. Visser was a violent man and quick and cunning as well; but he seemed a child beside Dimitrios. Once when Dimitrios had been making a fool of him, Visser pulled out a pistol. He was white with rage. I could see his finger squeezing the trigger. If I had been Dimitrios, I should have prayed. But Dimitrios only smiled in the insolent way he had and, turning his back on Visser, began to talk to me about some business matter. Dimitrios was always quiet like that, even when he was angry.

'That was why we were so surprised that evening. He came in late and he stood inside the door looking at us for nearly a minute. Then he walked over to his place and sat down. Visser had been saying something about the *patron* of a café who had been making trouble and now he went on. There was nothing remarkable about what he was saying. I think he was telling Galindo that he must stop using the café as it was unsafe.

'Suddenly, Dimitrios leaned across the table, shouted "*Imbecile!*" and spat in Visser's face.

'Visser was as surprised as the rest of us. He opened his mouth to speak but Dimitrios did not give him time to say anything. Before we could grasp what was happening, he was accusing Visser of the most fantastic things. The words poured out and he spat again like a guttersnipe.

'Visser went white and got to his feet with his hand in the pocket where he kept his pistol; but Lenôtre, who was beside him, got up, too, and whispered something to him which made Visser take his hand from his pocket. Lenôtre was used to people who had been taking drugs and he and Galindo and Werner had recognized the signs as soon as Dimitrios had entered the room. But Dimitrios had seen Lenôtre whisper and turned to him. From Lenôtre he came to the rest of us. We were fools, he told us, if we thought that he did not know that we were plotting against him. He called us a lot of very unpleasant names in French and Greek. Then he began to boast that he was cleverer than the rest of us together, that but for him we should be starving, that he alone was responsible for our success (which was true although we did not like to be told it) and that he could do with us as he wished. He went on for half an hour, abusing us and boasting alternately. None of us said a word. Then, as suddenly as he had started, he stopped, stood up and walked out of the room.

'I suppose that we should have been prepared for treachery after that. Heroin addicts have a reputation for it. Yet we were not prepared. I think it may have been that we were so conscious of the amount of money he was making. I only know that, when he had gone, Lenôtre and Galindo laughed and asked Werner if the boss were paying for the stuff he used. Even Visser grinned. A joke was made of it, you see.

'Next time we saw Dimitrios he was quite normal and no reference was made to his outburst. But as the months went by, although we had no more outbursts, he became bad-tempered and little difficulties would make him angry. His appearance was changing, too. He looked thin and ill and his eyes were dull. He did not always come to the meetings.

'Then, we had our second warning.

'Early in September, he announced suddenly that he proposed to reduce the consignments for the next three months and use our stock. This startled us and there were many objections. I was one of the objectors. I had had a great deal of trouble building up the stock and did not want to see it distributed without reason. The others reminded him of the trouble they had had when supplies ran out before. But Dimitrios would not listen. He had been warned, he said, that there was to be a new drive by the police. Not only, he said, would so large a stock compromise us seriously if it were discovered; but its seizure would be a serious financial loss. He, too, was sorry to see it go but it was best to play for safety.

'I do not think that the notion that he might be liquidating his assets before he got out occurred to any of us; and you may say that for people of experience we were very trusting. You would be right to say that. With the exception of Visser we seemed always to be on the defensive in our dealings with Dimitrios. Even Lydia, who understood so much about people, was defeated by him. As for Visser, he was too paralysed by his own conceit to believe that anyone, even a drug addict, could betray him. Besides, why should we suspect him? We were making money, but he was making more, much more. What logical reason was there for suspecting him? Who could possibly have foreseen that he would become so unstable and behave like a madman?'

He shrugged. 'You know the rest. He turned informer. We were all arrested. I was in Marseilles with Lamare when we were caught. The police were quite clever. They watched us for a week before they took us. They hoped, I think, to catch us with some of the stuff. Luckily, we noticed them the day before we were due to take delivery of a big consignment from Istanbul. Lenôtre and Galindo and Werner were not so lucky. They had some of the stuff in their pockets. The police tried of course, to make me tell them about Dimitrios and showed me the dossier he had sent them. They might as well have asked me for the moon. Visser, I found out later, knew more than the rest of us but he did not tell the police what it was. He had other ideas. He told the police that Dimitrios had had an apartment in the seventeenth arrondissement. That was a lie. Visser wanted to get a lighter sentence than the rest of us. He did not. He died not long ago, poor fellow.' Mr Peters heaved a sigh and produced one of his cheroots.

Latimer touched his second cup of coffee. It was quite cold. He took a cigarette and accepted a light from his host's match.

'Well?' he said when he saw that the cheroot was alight. 'What then? I am still waiting to hear how I am to earn a half a million francs.'

Mr Peters smiled as if he were presiding at a Sunday School treat and Latimer had asked for a second currant bun. 'That, Mr Latimer, is part of another story.'

'What story?'

'The story of what happened to Dimitrios after he disappeared from view.'

'Well, what *did* happen to him?' Latimer demanded testily.

Without replying, Mr Peters picked up the photograph that lay on the table and handed it to him again.

Latimer looked at it and frowned. 'Yes, I've seen this. It's Dimitrios all right. What about it?'

Mr Peters smiled very sweetly and gently. 'That, Mr Latimer, is a photograph of Manus Visser.'

'What on earth do you mean?'

'I told you that Visser had other ideas about using the knowledge he had been clever enough to acquire about Dimitrios. What you saw on the mortuary table in Istanbul, Mr Latimer, was Visser after he had tried to put those ideas into practice.'

'But it was Dimitrios. I saw . . .'

'You saw the body of Visser, Mr Latimer, after Dimitrios had killed him. Dimitrios himself, I am glad to say, is alive and in good health.'

Chapter Twelve

Monsieur C.K.

Latimer stared. His jaw had dropped and he knew that he looked ridiculous and that there was nothing to be done about the fact. Dimitrios was alive. It did not even occur to him to question the statement seriously. He knew instinctively that it was true. It was as if a doctor had warned him that he was suffering from a dangerous disease of the symptoms of which he had been only vaguely aware. He was surprised beyond words, resentful, curious and a little frightened; while his mind began to work feverishly to meet and deal with a new and strange set of conditions. He shut his mouth, then opened it again to say, feebly: 'I can't believe it.'

Mr Peters was clearly gratified by the effect of his announcement.

'I scarcely hoped,' he said, 'that you would have had no suspicions of the truth. Grodek, of course, understood. He had been puzzled by certain questions I asked him some time ago. When you came he was even more curious. That was why he wanted to know so much. But as soon as you told him that you had seen the body in Istanbul, he understood. He saw at once that the one thing that rendered you unique from my point of view was the fact of your having seen the face of the man buried as Dimitrios. It was obvious. Not to you, perhaps. I suppose that when one sees a perfect stranger on a mortuary slab and a policeman tells one that his name is Dimitrios Makropoulos, one assumes, if one has your respect for the police, that one has the truth of the matter. I *knew* that it was not Dimitrios you saw. But–I could not prove it. You, on the other hand, can. *You* can identify Manus Visser.' He paused significantly and then, as Latimer made no comment, added: 'How did they identify him as Dimitrios?'

'There was a French *carte d'identité*, issued in Lyons a year ago to Dimitrios Makropoulos, sewn inside the lining of his coat.' Latimer spoke mechanically. He was thinking of Grodek's toast to the English detective story and of Grodek's inability to stop himself laughing at his own joke. Heavens! what a fool the man must have thought him!

'A French *carte d'identité*!' echoed Mr Peters. 'That I find amusing. Very amusing.'

'It had been pronounced genuine by the French authorities and it had a photograph in it.'

Mr Peters smiled tolerantly. 'I could get you a dozen genuine French *cartes d'identité*, Mr Latimer, each in the name of Dimitrios Makropoulos and each with a different photograph. Look!' He drew a green *permis de séjour* from his pocket, opened it and, with his fingers over the space taken up by the identifying particulars, displayed the photograph in it. 'Does that look very much like me, Mr Latimer?'

Latimer shook his head.

'And yet,' declared Mr Peters, 'it *is* a genuine photograph of me taken three years ago. I made no effort to deceive. It is simply that I am not *photogénique*, that is all. Very few men are. The camera is a consistent liar. Dimitrios could have used photographs of anyone with the same type of face as Visser. That photograph I showed you a few moments ago is of someone like Visser.'

'If Dimitrios is still alive, where is he?'

'Here in Paris.' Mr Peters leaned forward and patted Latimer's knee. 'You have been very reasonable, Mr Latimer,' he said kindly. 'I shall tell you everything.'

'It's very good of you,' said Latimer bitterly.

'No! no! You have a *right* to know,' said Mr Peters. He pursed his lips with the air of one who knows justice when he sees it. 'I shall tell you everything,' he said again and relit his cheroot.

'As you may imagine,' he went on, 'we were all very angry with Dimitrios. Some of us threatened revenge. But, Mr Latimer, I have never been one to beat my head against a wall. Dimitrios had disappeared and there was no way of finding him. The indignities of prison life a memory, I purged my heart of malice and went abroad to regain my sense of proportion. I became a wanderer, Mr Latimer. A little business here, a little business there, travel and meditation–that was my life. I could afford to sit, when I wished, in a café and see this world of ours go by and try to understand my fellow men. How little true understanding there is! As I go through this life of ours, Mr Latimer, I sometimes wonder if perhaps it is not all a dream and if one day we shall not wake up to find that we have only been asleep like children in a cradle rocked by the Great One. That will be a great day. I have, I know, done things of which I have been ashamed; but the Great One will understand. That is how I think of the Great One: as someone who understands that it is sometimes necessary, for business reasons, to do unpleasant things; someone who understands not as a judge in a courtroom,' he added a trifle vindictively, 'but as a *friend*.'

He wiped the corners of his mouth. 'You will think, Mr Latimer, that I am something of a mystic. Perhaps I am. I do not believe in coincidence. If the Great One wills that one shall meet a person, then one meets him. There is nothing strange about it. That was why, when I met Visser, I was not surprised. It was a little under two years ago that I met him, and in Rome.

'I had not, of course, seen him for five years. Poor fellow! he had had a bad time. A few months after his release from prison he was pressed for money and forged a cheque. They sent him back to prison for three years and then, when he came out, deported him. He was almost penniless and he could not work in France where he knew useful people. I could not blame him for feeling bitter.

'He asked me to lend him money. We had met in a café and he told me that he had to go to Zürich to buy a new passport but that he had no money. His Dutch passport was useless because it was in his real name. I would have liked to have helped him; for, although I had never liked him very much, I felt sorry for him. But I hesitated. So often one's generous instincts run away with one. I should have been wiser to have said at once that I had no money to lend; but as I hesitated he knew that I had money. It was a foolish mistake on my part I thought at the time. It is only since that I have learned that my generous instinct was working for my own good.

'He became very pressing and swore that he would pay me back. This life of ours is so difficult sometimes, is it not? A person swears that he will repay money and you know that he is sincere. Yet you know also that he may to-morrow tell himself with equal sincerity that your money is his by right of need, that you can afford to lose so insignificant a sum and that you must in any case pay for your magnanimity. And then he grows to dislike you and you have lost a friend as well as your money. I decided to refuse Visser.

'At my refusal he became angry and accused me of not trusting him to pay a debt of honour, which was a foolish way for him to talk. Then he pleaded with me. He could prove, he said, that he would be able to repay the money and began to tell me some interesting things.

'I have said that Visser had known a little more about Dimitrios than the rest of us. That was true. He had taken a lot of trouble finding it out. It was just after that evening when he had pulled out a pistol to threaten Dimitrios and Dimitrios had turned his back upon him. Nobody had treated him like that before and he wished to know more about the man who had humiliated him: that, at least, is what I believe. He himself said that he had suspected that Dimitrios would betray us; but that, I knew, was nonsense. Whatever his reason, however, he decided to follow Dimitrios when he left the Impasse.

'The first night that he tried he was unsuccessful. There was a large closed car waiting at the entrance to the Impasse and Dimitrios was driven off in it before Visser could find a taxi in which to follow. The second night he had a hired car ready. He did not come to the meeting but waited for Dimitrios in the Rue de Rennes. When the closed car appeared, Visser drove off after it. Dimitrios stopped outside a big apartment house in the Avenue de Wagram and went inside while the big car drove away. Visser noted the address and about a week later, at a time when he knew that Dimitrios would be here in this room, he called at the apartment house and asked for Monsieur Makropoulos. Naturally, the concièrge knew of no one of that name but Visser gave him money and described Dimitrios and found that he had an apartment there in the name of Rougemont.

'Now Visser, for all his conceit, was no fool. He knew that Dimitrios would have foreseen that he might be followed and guessed that the Rougemont apartment was not his only place. Accordingly he set himself to watch Monsieur Rougemont's comings and goings. It was not long before he discovered that there was another way out of the apartment house at the rear and that Dimitrios used to leave that way.

'One night when Dimitrios left by the back entrance Visser followed him. He did not have far to go. He found that Dimitrios lived in a big house just off the Avenue Hoche. It belonged, he found, to a titled and very *chic* woman. I shall call her Madame la Comtesse. Later Visser saw Dimitrios leave with her for the opera. Dimitrios was *en grande tenue* and they had a large Hispano to take them there.

'At that point Visser lost interest. He knew where Dimitrios lived. No doubt he felt that he had in some way obtained his revenge by discovering that much. He must, too, have been tired of waiting about in the streets. His curiosity was satisfied. What he had discovered was, after all, very much what he might have expected to discover. Dimitrios was a man with a large income. He was spending it in the same way as other men with large incomes.

'They told me that, when Visser was arrested in Paris, he said very little about Dimitrios. Yet he must have had ugly thoughts, for he was by nature a violent man and very conceited. It would have been useless, in any case, for him to have tried to have Dimitrios arrested, for he could only have sent them to the apartment in the Avenue de Wagram and the house of Madame la Comtesse off the Avenue Hoche, and he knew that Dimitrios would have gone away. He had, as I said, other ideas about his knowledge.

'I think that, to begin with, he had intended to kill Dimitrios when he found him; but as he began to get short of money his hatred of Dimitrios became more reasonable. He probably remembered the Hispano and the luxury of the house of Madame la Comtesse. She would perhaps be worried to hear that her friend made his money by selling heroin and Dimitrios might be ready to pay good money to save her that worry. But it was easier to think about Dimitrios and his money than it was to find them. For several months after he was released from prison early in 1932, Visser looked for Dimitrios. The apartment in the Avenue de Wagram was no longer occupied. The house of Madame la Comtesse was shut up and the concièrge said that she was in Biarritz. Visser went to Biarritz and found that she was staying with friends. Dimitrios was not with her. Visser returned to Paris. Then he had what I think was quite a good idea. He himself was pleased with it. Unfortunately for him, it came a little too late. He remembered one day that Dimitrios had been a drug addict, and it occurred to him that Dimitrios might have done what many other wealthy addicts do when their addiction reaches an advanced stage. He might have entered a clinic to be cured.

'There are five private clinics near Paris which specialize in such cures. On the pretext of making inquiries as to terms on behalf of an imaginary brother, Visser went to each one in turn, saying that he had been recommended by friends of Monsieur Rougemont. At the fourth his idea was proved to be good. The doctor in charge asked after the health of Monsieur Rougemont.

'I think that Visser derived a certain vulgar satisfaction from the thought of Dimitrios being cured of a heroin addiction. The cure is terrible, you know. The doctors go on giving the patient drugs, but gradually reduce the quantity. For him the torture is almost unbearable. He yawns and sweats and shivers for days, but he does not sleep and he cannot eat. He longs for death and babbles of suicide; but he has not the strength left to commit it. He begs for his drug and it is withheld. He . . . But I must not bore you with horrors, Mr Latimer. The cure lasts three months and costs five thousand francs a week. When it is over the patient may forget the torture and start taking drugs again. Or he may be wiser and forget Paradise. Dimitrios, it seems, was wise.

'He had left the clinic four months before Visser visited it; and so Visser had to think of another good idea. He *did* think of it, but it involved going to

Biarritz again and he had no money. He forged a cheque, cashed it and set off again. He reasoned that as Dimitrios and Madame la Comtesse had been friends, she would probably know his present whereabouts. But he could not simply go to her and ask for his address. Even if he could have invented a pretext for doing so, he did not know under what name Dimitrios was known to her. There were difficulties, you see. But he found a way to overcome them. For several days he watched the villa where she was staying. Then, when he had found out enough about it, he broke into her room one afternoon, when the house was empty except for two drowsy servants, and looked through her baggage. He was looking for letters.

'Dimitrios had never liked written records in our business, and he never corresponded with any of us. But Visser had remembered that on one occasion Dimitrios had scribbled an address for Werner on a piece of paper. I remembered the occasion myself. The writing had been curious: quite uneducated, with clumsy, badly formed letters and many flourishes. It was this writing that Visser was looking for. He found it. There were nine letters in the writing. All were from an expensive hotel in Rome. I beg your pardon, Mr Latimer. You said something?'

'I can tell you what he was doing in Rome. He was organizing the assassination of a Yugoslav politician.'

Mr Peters did not seem impressed. 'Very likely,' he said indifferently; 'he would not be where he is to-day without that special organizing ability of his. Where was I? Ah, yes! the letters.

'All were from Rome and all were signed with initials which I shall tell you were "C.K." The letters themselves were not what Visser had expected. They were very formal and stilted and brief. Most of them said no more than that the writer was in good health, that business was interesting and that he hoped to see his dear friend soon. No *tu-toi*, you know. But in one he said that he had met a relation by marriage of the Italian Royal family and in another that he had been presented to a Romanian diplomat with a title. He was very pleased with these encounters, it seems. It was all very *snob*, and Visser felt that Dimitrios would certainly wish to buy his friendship. He noted the name of the hotel and, leaving everything as he found it, went back to Paris *en route* for Rome. He arrived in Paris the following morning. The police were waiting for him. He was not, I should think, a very clever forger.

'But you may imagine the poor fellow's feelings. During the three interminable years that followed he thought of nothing but Dimitrios; of how near he had been to him and how far he was now. He seemed, for some strange reason, to regard Dimitrios as the one responsible for his being in prison again. The idea served to feed his hatred of him and strengthen his resolve to make him pay. He was, I think, a little mad. As soon as he was free he picked up a little money in Holland and went to Rome. He was over three years behind Dimitrios, but he was determined to catch up with him. He went to the hotel and, posing as a Dutch private detective, asked to be permitted to see the records of those who had stayed there three years before. The *affiches* had, of course, gone to the police, but they had the bills for the period in question and he had the initials. He was able to discover the name which Dimitrios had used. Dimitrios had also left a forwarding address. It was a Poste Restante in Paris.

'Visser was now in a new difficulty. He knew the name; but that was useless unless he could get into France to trace the owner of it. It was no use his writing his demands for money. Dimitrios would not go on calling for letters for three years. And yet he could not enter France without being stopped at the frontier or risking another term of imprisonment. He had somehow to get a new name and a new passport, and he had no money with which to do so.

'I lent him three thousand francs; and I will confess to you, Mr Latimer, that I felt myself to be truly stupid. Yet I was sorry for him. He was not the Visser I had known in Paris. Prison had broken him. Once his passions had been in his eyes, but now they were in his mouth and cheeks. One felt he was getting old. I gave him the money out of pity and to get rid of him. I did not believe his story. I never expected to hear from him again. You may, therefore, imagine my astonishment when, a year ago, I received here a letter from him enclosing a *mandat* for the three thousand francs.

'The letter was very short. It said: "I have found him as I said I would. Here, with my profound thanks, is the money you lent me. It is worth three thousand francs to surprise you." That was all. He did not sign it. He gave no address. The *mandat* had been bought in Nice and posted there.

'That letter made me think, Mr Latimer. Visser had recovered his conceit. He could afford to indulge it to the extent of three thousand francs. That meant that he had a great deal more money. Conceited persons dream of such gestures, but they very rarely make them. Dimitrios must have paid; and since he was not a fool he must have had a very good reason for paying.

'I was idle at the time, Mr Latimer; idle and a little restless. I had my books, it is true; but one wearies of books, the ideas, the affectations of other men. It might be interesting, I thought, to find Dimitrios for myself and share in Visser's good fortune. It was not greed that prompted me; I should not like you to think that. I was *interested*. Besides, I felt that Dimitrios owed me something for the discomforts and indignities I had experienced because of him. For two days I played with the idea. Then, on the third day I made up my mind. I set out for Rome.

'As you may imagine, Mr Latimer, I had a difficult time and many disappointments. I had the initials which Visser, in his eagerness to convince me, had revealed, but the only thing I knew about the hotel was that it was expensive. There are, unfortunately, a great many expensive hotels in Rome. I began to investigate them one after the other; but when, at the fifth hotel, they refused, for some reason, to let me see the bills for 1932, I abandoned the attempt. Instead, I went to an Italian friend of mine in one of the Ministries. He was able to use his influence on my behalf and, after a lot of *chi-chi* and expense, I was permitted to inspect the Ministry of Interior archives for 1932. I found out the name Dimitrios was using, and I also found out what Visser had not found out—that Dimitrios had taken the course, which I myself took in 1932, of purchasing the citizenship of a certain South American republic which is sympathetic in such matters if one's pocket-book is fat enough. Dimitrios and I had become fellow citizens.

'I must confess, Mr Latimer, that I went back to Paris with hope in my heart. I was to be bitterly disappointed. Our consul was not helpful. He said that he had never heard of Señor C.K. and that even if I were Señor C.K.'s dearest and oldest friend he could not tell me where he was. He was offensive, which was unpleasant; but also I could tell that he was lying when he said that he had no knowledge of Dimitrios. That was tantalizing. And yet another disappointment awaited me. The house of Madame la Comtesse off the Avenue Hoche had been empty for two years.

'You would think, would you not, that it would be easy to find out where a *chic* and wealthy woman was? It was most difficult. The *Bottin* gave nothing. Apparently she had no house in Paris. I was, I will confess, about to abandon the search when I found a way out of my difficulty. I reflected that a fashionable woman like Madame la Comtesse would be certain to have gone somewhere for the winter sports season that was just over. Accordingly, I commissioned Hachettes to purchase for me a copy of every French, Swiss, German and Italian winter sports and social magazine which had been published during the previous three months.

'It was a desperate idea, but it yielded results. You have no idea how many such magazines there are, Mr Latimer. It took me a little over a week to go through them all carefully, and I can assure you that by the middle of that week I was very nearly a social-democrat. By the end of it, however, I had recovered my sense of humour. If repetition makes nonsense of words it makes even more fantastic nonsense of smiling faces, even if their owners are rich. Besides, I had found what I wanted. In one of the German magazines for February there was a small paragraph which said that Madame la Comtesse was at St Anton for the winter sports. In a French magazine there was a *couturier's* picture of her in skating clothes. I went to St Anton. There are not many hotels there, and I soon found that Monsieur C.K. had been in St Anton at the same time. He had given an address in Cannes.

'At Cannes I found that Monsieur C.K. had a villa on the Estoril, but that he himself was abroad on business at the moment. I was not discontented. Dimitrios would return to his villa sooner or later. Meanwhile I set myself to discover something about Monsieur C.K.

'I have always said, Mr Latimer, that the art of being successful in this life of ours is the art of knowing the people who will be useful to one. I have in my time met and done business with many important people–people, you know, who are informed of what goes on and why–and I have always taken care to be helpful to them. It has paid me.

'So, where Visser might have had to prowl about in the darkness in search of his information, I was able to get mine from a friend. It proved easier than I had expected to do so, for I found that, in certain circles, Dimitrios, with the name of Monsieur C.K., had become quite important. In fact, when I learned just how important he had become, I was pleasantly surprised. I began to realize that Visser must be living on the money he got from Dimitrios. Yet what did Visser know? Only that Dimitrios had dealt illegally in drugs; a fact that it would be difficult for him to prove. He knew nothing about the dealings in women. I did. There must, I reasoned, be other things, too, which Dimitrios would prefer not to be generally known. If, before I approached Dimitrios, I could find out some of those things, my financial position would be very strong indeed. I decided to see some more of my friends.

'Two of them were able to help me. Grodek was one. A Romanian friend of mine was another. You know of Grodek's acquaintance with Dimitrios when he called himself Talat. The Romanian friend told me that in 1925 Dimitrios had had questionable financial dealings with Codreanu, the lamented leader of the Romanian Iron Guard, and that he was known to, but not wanted by, the Bulgarian police.

'Now there was nothing criminal about any of those affairs. Indeed, Grodek's information depressed me somewhat. It was unlikely that the Yugoslav Government would apply for extradition after so many years; while, as for the French, they might hold that, as Dimitrios had rendered some sort of service to the Republic in 1926, he was entitled to a little tolerance in the matter of dealings in drugs and women. I decided to see what I could find out in Greece. A week after I arrived in Athens and while I was still trying unsuccessfully to trace in the official records a reference to my particular Dimitrios, I read in an Athens' paper of the discovery, by the Istanbul police, of the body of a Greek from Smyrna with the name of Dimitrios Makropoulos.'

He raised his eyes to Latimer's. 'Do you begin to see, Mr Latimer, why I found your interest in Dimitrios a little difficult to explain?' And then, as Latimer nodded: 'I, too, of course, inspected the Relief Commission dossier; but I followed you to Sofia instead of going to Smyrna. I wonder if you would care to tell me now what you found out from the police records there?'

'Dimitrios was suspected of murdering a money-lender named Sholem in Smyrna in 1922. He escaped to Greece. Two years later, he was involved in an attempt to assassinate Kemal. He escaped again, but the Turks used the murder as a pretext for issuing a warrant for his arrest.'

'A murder in Smyrna! That makes it even clearer.' Mr Peters smiled. 'A wonderful man, Dimitrios, don't you think? So economical.'

'What do you mean?'

'Let me finish my story and you will see. As soon as I read that newspaper paragraph, I sent a telegram to a friend in Paris asking him to let me know the whereabouts of Monsieur C.K. He replied two days later, saying that Monsieur C.K. had just returned to Cannes after an Aegean cruise with a party of friends in a Greek yacht which he had chartered two months previously.

'Do you see now what had happened Mr Latimer? You tell me that the *carte d'identité* was a year old when they found it on the body. That means that it was obtained a few weeks before Visser sent me that three thousand francs. You see, from the moment Visser found Dimitrios, he was doomed. Dimitrios must have made up his mind at once to kill him. You can see why. Visser was dangerous. He was such a conceited fellow. He might have blurted out indiscretions at any time when he had been drinking and wanted to boast. He would have to be killed.

'Yet, see how clever Dimitrios was! He could have killed Visser at once, no doubt. But he did not do so. His economical mind had evolved a better plan. If it were necessary to kill Visser, could he not dispose of the body in

some advantageous way? Why not use it to safeguard himself against the
consequences of that old indiscretion in Smyrna? It was unlikely that there
would be consequences, but here was his chance to make certain of the fact.
The body of the villain, Dimitrios Makropoulos, would be delivered to the
Turkish police. Dimitrios, the murderer, would be dead and Monsieur
C.K. would be left alive to cultivate his garden. But he would require a
certain amount of co-operation from Visser himself. The man would have
to be lulled into feeling secure. So, Dimitrios smiled and paid up and set
about getting the identity card which was to go with Visser's dead body.
Nine months later, in June, he invited his good friend Visser to join him on a
yachting trip.'

'Yes, but how could he have committed the murder on the yachting trip?
What about the crew? What about the other passengers?'

Mr Peters looked knowing. 'Let me tell you, Mr Latimer, what I would
have done if I had been Dimitrios. I would have begun by chartering a
Greek yacht. There would be a reason for its being a Greek yacht: its home
port would be the Piraeus.

'I would have arranged for my friends, including Visser, to join the yacht
at Naples. Then I would have taken them on their cruise and returned a
month later to Naples, where I would have announced that the cruise would
end. They would disembark; but I should stay on board saying that I was
returning with the yacht to the Piraeus. Then I would take Visser aside
privately and tell him that I had some very secret business to transact in
Istanbul, that I proposed to go there on the yacht and that I should be glad
of his company. I would ask him not to tell the disembarking passengers
who might be angry because I had not asked them all and to return to the
yacht when they had gone. To poor, conceited Visser, the invitation would
be irresistible.

'To the captain I would say that Visser and I would leave the yacht at
Istanbul and return overland, after we had transacted our business, to Paris.
He would sail the yacht back to the Piraeus. At Istanbul Visser and I would
go ashore together. I should have left word with the crew that we would
send for our baggage when we had decided where we should be staying for
the night. Then, I would have taken him to a *boîte* I know of in a street off
the Grande Rue de Pera; and later that night I would find myself poorer by
ten thousand French francs, while Visser would be at the bottom of the
Bosphorus at a place where the current would carry him, when he was
rotten enough to float, out to Seraglio Point. Then I would take a room in a
hotel in the name and with the passport of Visser, and send a porter to the
yacht with a note authorizing him to collect both Visser's luggage and mine.
As Visser, I would leave the hotel in the morning for the station. His
baggage, which I should have searched overnight to see that there was
nothing in it to identify it as Visser's, I would deposit in the *consigne*. Then I
would take the train to Paris. If inquiries about Visser are ever made in
Istanbul, he left by train for Paris. But who is going to inquire? My friends
believe he left the yacht at Naples. The captain and crew of the yacht are not
interested. Visser has a false passport, he is a criminal: such a type has an
obvious reason for disappearing of his own free will. Finish!'

Mr Peters spread out his hands. 'That is how it would occur to me to deal with such a situation. Perhaps Dimitrios managed it a little differently; but that is what might well have happened. There is one thing, however, that I am quite sure he did. You remember telling me that some months before you arrived in Smyrna, someone examined the same police records that you examined there? That must have been Dimitrios. He was always very cautious. No doubt he was anxious to find out how much they knew about his appearance, before he left Visser for them to find.'

'But that man I told you about looked like a Frenchman.'

Mr Peters smiled reproachfully. 'Then you were *not* quite frank with me in Sofia, Mr Latimer. You *did* inquire about this mysterious man.' He shrugged. 'Dimitrios does look like a Frenchman now. His clothes are French.'

'You've seen him recently?'

'Yesterday. Though he did not see me.'

'You know exactly where he is in Paris, then?'

'Exactly. As soon as I discovered his new business I knew where to find him here.'

'And, now that you have found him, what next?'

Mr Peters frowned. 'Come now, Mr Latimer. I am sure that you are not quite as obtuse as all that. You know and can prove that the man buried in Istanbul is not Dimitrios. If necessary you could identify Visser's photographs on the police files. I, on the other hand, know what Dimitrios is calling himself now and where to find him. Our joint silence would be worth a lot of money to Dimitrios. With Visser's fate in mind, we shall know, too, how to deal with the matter. We shall demand a million francs. Dimitrios will pay us, believing that we shall come back for more. We shall not be as foolish as to endanger our lives in that way. We shall rest content with half a million each—nearly three thousand pounds sterling, Mr Latimer—and quietly disappear.'

'I see. Blackmail on a cash basis. No credit. But why bring me into the business? The Turkish police could identify Visser without my help.'

'How? They identified him as Dimitrios and buried him. They have seen perhaps a dozen or more dead bodies since then. Weeks have gone by. Are they going to remember Visser's face well enough to justify their beginning expensive extradition proceedings against a rich foreigner because of their fourteen-year-old suspicions about a sixteen-year-old murder? My dear Latimer! Dimitrios would laugh at me. He would do with me as he did with Visser: give me a few thousand francs here and there to keep me from making myself a nuisance with the French police and to keep me quiet until, for safety's sake, I could be killed. But you have seen Visser's body and identified it. You have seen the police records in Smyrna. He knows nothing about you. He will have to pay or run an unknown risk. He is too cautious for that. Listen. In the first place, it is essential that Dimitrios does not discover our identities. He will know me, of course, but he will not know my present name. In your case, we shall invent a name. Mr Smith, perhaps, as you are English. I shall approach Dimitrios in the name of Petersen and we shall arrange to meet him outside Paris at a place of our own choosing to receive our million francs. That is the last that he will see of either of us.'

Latimer laughed but not very heartily. 'And do you really suppose that I shall agree to this plan of yours?'

'If, Mr Latimer, your trained mind can evolve a more ingenious plan, I shall be only too happy to . . .'

'My trained mind, Mr Peters, is concerned with wondering how best to convey this information which you have given me to the police.'

Mr Peters' smile became thin. 'The police? What information, Mr Latimer?' he inquired softly.

'Why, the information that . . .' Latimer began impatiently and then stopped, frowning.

'Quite so,' nodded Mr Peters approvingly. 'You have no real information to convey. If you go to the Turkish police they will no doubt send to the French police for Visser's photographs and record your identification. What then? Dimitrios will be found to be alive. That is all. I have not, you may remember, told you the name that Dimitrios uses now or even his initials. It would be impossible for you to trace him from Rome as Visser and I traced him. Nor do you know the name of Madame la Comtesse. As for the French police, I do not think that they would be interested either in the fate of a deported Dutch criminal or excited by the knowledge that somewhere in France there is a Greek using a false name who killed a man in Smyrna in 1922. You see, Mr Latimer, you cannot act without me. If, of course, Dimitrios should prove difficult, then it might be desirable to take the police into our confidence. But I do not think that Dimitrios will be difficult. He is very intelligent. In any case, Mr Latimer, why throw away three thousand pounds?'

Latimer considered him for a moment. Then he said: 'Has it occurred to you that I might not want that particular three thousand pounds? I think, my friend, that prolonged association with criminals has made it difficult for you to follow some trains of thought.'

'This moral rectitude . . .' began Mr Peters wearily. Then he seemed to change his mind. He cleared his throat. 'If you wished,' he said with the calculated *bonhommie* of one who reasons with a drunken friend, 'we could inform the police *after* we had secured the money. Even if Dimitrios were able to prove that he had paid money to us, he could not, however unpleasant he wished to be, tell the police our names or how to find us. In fact, I think that that would be a very wise move on our part, Mr Latimer. We should then be quite sure that Dimitrios was no longer dangerous. We could supply the police anonymously with a dossier as Dimitrios did in 1931. The retribution would be just.' Then his face fell. 'Ah, no. It is impossible. I am afraid that the suspicions of your Turkish friends might fall upon you, Mr Latimer. We could not risk that, could we!'

But Latimer was scarcely listening. He knew that what he had made up his mind to say was foolish and he was trying to justify its folly. Peters was right. There was nothing he could do to bring Dimitrios to justice. He was left with a choice. Either he could go back to Athens and leave Peters to make the best deal he could with Dimitrios or he could stay in Paris to see the last act of the grotesque comedy in which he now found himself playing a part. The first alternative being unthinkable, he was committed to the second. He really had no choice. To gain time he had taken and lighted a cigarette. Now he looked up from it.

'All right,' he said slowly; 'I'll do what you want. But there are conditions.'

'Conditions?' Mr Peters' lips tightened. 'I think that a half share is more than generous, Mr Latimer. Why my trouble and expenses alone . . . !'

'Just a moment. I was saying, Mr Peters, that there are conditions. The first should be very easy for you to fulfil. It is simply that you yourself retain all the money that you are able to squeeze from Dimitrios. The second . . .' he went on and then paused. He had the momentary pleasure of seeing Mr Peters disconcerted. Then, he saw the watery eyes narrow quite appreciably. Mr Peters' words as they issued from his mouth were charged with suspicion.

'I don't think I quite understand, Mr Latimer. If this is a clumsy trick. . . .'

'Oh no. There is no trick, clumsy or otherwise, Mr Peters. "Moral rectitude" was your phrase, wasn't it? It will do. I am prepared, you see, to assist in blackmailing a person when that person is Dimitrios; but I am not prepared to share in the profits. So much the better for you, of course.'

Mr Peters nodded thoughtfully. 'Yes, I see that you might think like that. So much the better for me, as you say. But what is the other condition?'

'Equally inoffensive. You have referred mysteriously to Dimitrios's having become a person of importance. I make my helping you get your million francs conditional on your telling me exactly *what* he has become.'

Mr Peters thought for a moment, then shrugged. 'Very well. I see no reason why I should not tell you. It so happens that the knowledge cannot possibly be of any help to you in discovering his present identity. The Eurasian Credit Trust is registered in Monaco and the details of its registration are not therefore open to inspection. Dimitrios is a member of the Board of Directors.'

Chapter Thirteen

Rendezvous

It was two o'clock in the morning when Latimer left the Impasse des Huits Anges and began to walk slowly in the direction of the Quai Voltaire.

At the corner of the Boulevard St Germain there was a café open. He went inside and was served with a glass of beer by the bored mute behind the zinc. He drank some of his beer and gazed vacantly about him like a person who has strayed into a museum for shelter from the rain. He wished that he had gone straight to bed after all. He paid for the beer and took a taxi back to his hotel. He was tired, of course; that was the trouble.

In his room, Latimer sat down by the window and gazed out across the black river to the lights which it reflected and the faint glow in the sky beyond the Louvre. His mind was haunted by the past, by the confession of Dhris, the Negro, and by the memories of Irana Preveza, by the tragedy of Bulić and by a tale of white crystals travelling west to Paris, bringing money to the fig-packer of Izmir. Three human beings had died horribly and countless others had lived horribly that Dimitrios might take his ease. If there *were* such a thing as Evil, then this man. . . .

But it was useless to try to explain him in terms of Good and Evil. They were no more than baroque abstractions. Good Business and Bad Business were the elements of the new theology. Dimitrios was not evil. He was logical and consistent; as logical and consistent in the European jungle as the poison gas called Lewisite and the shattered bodies of children killed in the bombardment of an open town. The logic of Michelangelo's *David*, Beethoven's quartets and Einstein's physics had been replaced by that of the *Stock Exchange Year Book* and Hitler's *Mein Kampf*.

Yet, Latimer reflected, although you could not stop people buying and selling Lewisite, although you could do no more than 'deplore' a number of slaughtered children, there were in existence means of preventing one particular aspect of the principle of expediency from doing too much damage. Most international criminals were beyond the reach of man-made laws; but Dimitrios happened to be within reach of one law. He had committed at least two murders and had therefore broken the law as surely as if he had been starving and had stolen a loaf of bread.

It was easy enough, however, to say that he was within reach of the Law: it was not as easy to see how the Law was to be informed of the fact. As Mr Peters had so carefully pointed out, he, Latimer, had no information to give the police. But was that an altogether true picture of the situation? He *had* some information. He knew that Dimitrios was alive and that he was a director of the Eurasian Credit Trust, that he knew a French Countess who had had a house off the Avenue Hoche and that he or she had had an Hispano Suiza car, that both of them had been in St Anton that year for the winter sports and that he had chartered a Greek yacht in June, that he had a villa on the Estoril and that he was now the citizen of a South American republic. Surely, then, it must be possible to find the person with those particular attributes. Even if the names of the directors of the Eurasian Credit Trust were unobtainable, it ought to be possible to get the names of the men who had chartered Greek yachts in June, of the wealthy South Americans with villas on the Estoril and of the South American visitors to St Anton in February. If you could get those lists, all you would have to do would be to see which names (if there should be more than one) were common to the three.

But how did you get the lists? Besides, even if you could persuade the Turkish police to exhume Visser and then apply officially for all that information, what sort of proof would you have that the man you had concluded to be Dimitrios, was in fact, Dimitrios? And supposing that you could convince Colonel Haki of the truth, would he have enough evidence to justify the French extraditing a director of the powerful Eurasian Credit Trust? If it had taken twelve years to secure the acquittal of Dreyfus, it could take at least as many years to secure the conviction of Dimitrios.

He undressed wearily and got into bed.

It looked as if he were committed to Mr Peters' blackmailing scheme. Lying in a comfortable bed with his eyes closed, he found the fact that in a few days time he would be, technically speaking, one of the worst sorts of criminals no more than odd. Yet, at the back of his mind there was a certain discomfort. When the reason for it dawned on him, he was mildly shocked. The simple truth was that he was feeling afraid of Dimitrios. Dimitrios was a dangerous man; more dangerous by far than he had been in Smyrna and Athens and Sofia, because he now had more to lose. Visser had blackmailed him and died. Now, he, Latimer, was going to blackmail him. Dimitrios had never hesitated to kill a man if he had deemed it necessary to do so; and, if he had deemed it necessary in the case of a man who threatened to expose him as a drug pedlar, would he hesitate in the case of two men who threatened to expose him as a murderer?

It was most important to see that, hesitation or no hesitation, he was not given the opportunity. Mr Peters had proposed the taking of elaborate precautions.

The first contact with Dimitrios was to be established by letter. Latimer had seen a draft of the letter and had found it gratifyingly similar in tone to a letter he himself had written for a blackmailer in one of his books. It began, with sinister cordiality, by trusting that, after all these years, Monsieur C. K. had not forgotten the writer and the pleasant and profitable times they had spent together, went on to say how pleasing it was to hear that he was so successful and hoped sincerely that he would be able to meet the writer who would be at the So-and-So Hotel at nine o'clock on the Thursday evening of that week. The writer concluded with an expression of his *'plus sincere amitié'* and a significant little postscript to the effect that he had chanced to meet someone who had known their mutual friend Visser quite well, that this person was most anxious to meet Monsieur K. and that it would be so unfortunate if Monsieur K. could not arrange to keep the appointment on Thursday evening.

Dimitrios would receive that letter on the Thursday morning. At half-past eight on the Thursday evening, 'Mr Petersen' and 'Mr Smith' would arrive at the hotel chosen for the interview and 'Mr Petersen' would take a room. There they would await the arrival of Dimitrios. When the situation had been explained, Dimitrios would be informed that he would receive instructions as to the payment of the million francs on the following morning and told to go. 'Mr Petersen' and 'Mr Smith' would then leave.

Precautions would now have to be taken to see that they were not followed and identified. Mr Peters had not specified what sort of precautions but had given assurances that there would be no difficulties.

That same evening, a second letter would be posted to Dimitrios telling him to send a messenger with the million francs, in *mille* notes to a specified point on the road outside the cemetery of Neuilly at eleven o'clock on the Friday night. There would be a hired car waiting for him there with two men in it. The two men would have been recruited for the purpose by Mr Peters. Their business would be to pick up the messenger and drive along the Quai National in the direction of Suresnes until they were quite sure that they were not being followed and then to make for a point on the Avenue de la Reine near the Porte de St Cloud where 'Mr Petersen' and

'Mr Smith' would be waiting to receive the money. The two men would then drive the messenger back to Neuilly. The letter would specify that the messenger must be a woman.

Latimer had been puzzled by this last provision. Mr Peters had justified it by pointing out that if Dimitrios came himself there was just a chance that he might prove too clever for the men in the car and that 'Mr Petersen' and 'Mr Smith' would end up lying in the Avenue de la Reine with bullets in their backs. Descriptions were unreliable and the two men would have no certain means of knowing in the dark if a man presenting himself as the messenger were Dimitrios or not. They could make no such mistake about a woman.

Yes, Latimer reflected, it was absurd to imagine that there could be any danger from Dimitrios. The only thing he had to look forward to was the meeting with this curious man whose path he had stumbled across. It would be strange, after he had heard so much about him, to meet him face to face; strange to see the hand which had packed figs and driven the knife into Sholem's throat, the eyes which Irana Preveza and Wladyslaw Grodek and Mr Peters had remembered so well. It would be as if a waxwork in a chamber of horrors had come to life.

For a time he stared at the narrow gap between the curtains. It was getting light. Very soon he fell asleep.

He was disturbed towards eleven by a telephone call from Mr Peters, who said that the letter to Dimitrios had been posted and asked if they could have dinner together 'to discuss our plans for to-morrow'. Latimer was under the impression that their plans had already been discussed, but he agreed. The afternoon he spent alone at the Vincennes Zoo. The subsequent dinner was tedious. Little was said about their plans, and Latimer concluded that the invitation had been another of Mr Peters' precautions. He was making sure that his collaborator, who now had no financial interest in the business, had not changed his mind about collaborating. Latimer spent two hours listening to an account of Mr Peters' discovery of the works of Dr Frank Crane and a defence of his contention that *Lame and Lovely* and *Just Human* were the most important contributions to literature since *Robert Elsmere*.

On the pretext of having a headache, Latimer escaped soon after ten o'clock and went to bed. When he awoke the following morning he actually had a headache and concluded that the carafe burgundy which his host had recommended so warmly at dinner had been even cheaper than it had tasted. As his mind crept slowly back to consciousness he had, too, a feeling that something unpleasant had happened. Then he remembered. Of course! Dimitrios had by now received the first letter.

He sat up in bed to think about it and, after a moment or two, came to the profound conclusion that if it were easy enough to hate and despise blackmailing when one wrote and read about it, the act of blackmailing itself called for rather more moral hardihood, more firmness of purpose, than he, at any rate, possessed. It made no difference to remind oneself that Dimitrios was a criminal. Blackmail was blackmail, just as murder was murder. Macbeth would probably have hesitated at the last minute to kill a criminal Duncan just as much as he hesitated to kill the Duncan whose virtues pleaded like angels. Fortunately, or unfortunately, he, Latimer, had a Lady Macbeth in the person of Mr Peters. He decided to go out to breakfast.

The day seemed interminable. Mr Peters had said that he had arrangements to make in connection with the car and the men to drive in it, and that he would meet Latimer at a quarter to eight, after dinner. Latimer spent the morning walking aimlessly in the Bois and, in the afternoon, went to a cinema.

It was towards six o'clock and after he had left the cinema that he began to notice a slight breathless feeling in the region of the solar plexus. It was as if someone had dealt him a light blow there. He concluded that it was Mr Peters' corrosive burgundy fighting a rearguard action and stopped in one of the cafés on the Champs Elysées for an *infusion*. But the feeling persisted, and he found himself becoming more and more conscious of it. Then, as his gaze rested for a moment on a party of four men and women talking excitedly and laughing over some joke, he realized what was the matter with him. He did not want to meet Mr Peters. He did not want to go on this blackmailing expedition. He did not want to face a man in whose mind the uppermost thought would be to kill him as quickly and quietly as possible. The trouble was not in his stomach. He had cold feet.

The realization annoyed him. Why should he be afraid? There was nothing to be afraid of. This man Dimitrios was a clever and dangerous criminal, but he was far from being superhuman. If a man like Peters could . . . but then Peters was used to this sort of thing. He, Latimer, was not. He ought to have gone to the police as soon as he had discovered that Dimitrios was alive and risked being thought a troublesome crank. He should have realized before that, with Mr Peters' revelations, the whole affair had taken on a completely different complexion, that it was no longer one in which an amateur criminologist (and a fiction writer at that) should meddle. You could not deal with real murderers in this irresponsible fashion. His bargain with Mr Peters, for example: what would an English judge say to that? He could almost hear the words:

'As for the actions of this man Latimer, he has given an explanation of them which you may find difficult to believe. He is, we have been told, an intelligent man, a scholar who has held responsible posts in universities in this country and written works of scholarship. He is, moreover, a successful author of a type of fiction which, even if it is properly regarded by the average man as no more than the pabulum of adolescent minds, has, at least, the virtue of accepting the proposition that it is the business of right-thinking men and women to assist the police, should the opportunity present itself, in preventing crime and in capturing criminals. If you accept Latimer's explanation, you must conclude that he deliberately conspired with Peters to defeat the ends of justice and to act as an accessory before the fact of the crime of blackmail for the sole purpose of pursuing researches which he states had no other object than the satisfaction of his curiosity. You may ask yourselves if that would not have been the conduct of a mentally unbalanced child rather than that of an intelligent man. You must also weigh carefully the suggestion of the prosecution that Latimer did in fact share in the proceeds of this blackmailing scheme and that his explanation is no more than an effort to minimize his part in the affair.'

No doubt a French judge could make it sound even worse.

It was still too early for dinner. He left the café and walked in the direction of the Opéra. In any case, he reflected, it was too late now to do anything. He was committed to helping Mr Peters. But was it too late? If he went to the police now, this minute, something could surely be done.

He stopped. This minute! There had been an *agent* sauntering along the street through which he had just come. He retraced his steps. Yes, there was the man, leaning against the wall, swinging his baton and talking to someone inside a doorway. Latimer hesitated again, then crossed the road and asked to be directed to the police *Poste*. It was three streets away, he was told. He set off again.

The entrance to the *Poste* was narrow and almost entirely concealed by a group of three *agents* deep in a conversation which they did not interrupt as they made way for him. Inside was an enamelled plate indicating that inquiries should be made on the first floor and pointing to a flight of stairs with a thin iron banister rail on one side and a wall with a long, greasy stain on it on the other. The place smelt strongly of camphor and faintly of excrement. From a room adjacent to the entrance hall came a murmur of voices and the clacking of a typewriter.

His resolution ebbing with every step, he went up the stairs to a room divided into two by a high wooden counter, the outer edges of which had been worn smooth and shiny by the palms of innumerable hands. Behind the counter a man in uniform was peering with the aid of a hand-mirror into the inside of his mouth.

Latimer paused. He had yet to make up his mind how he was going to begin. If he said: 'I was going to blackmail a murderer to-night, but I have decided to hand him over to you instead,' there was more than a chance that they would think him mad or drunk. In spite of the urgent need for immediate action, he would have to make some show of beginning at the beginning. 'I was in Istanbul some weeks ago and was told of a murder committed there in 1922. Quite by chance, I have found that the man who did it is here in Paris and is being blackmailed.' Something like that. The uniformed man caught a glimpse of him in the mirror and turned sharply round.

'What do you want?'

'I should like to see Monsieur le Commissaire.'

'What for?'

'I have some information to give him.'

The man frowned impatiently. 'What information? Please be precise.'

'It concerns a case of blackmail.'

'You are being blackmailed?'

'No. Someone else is. It is a very complicated and serious affair.'

'Your *carte d'identité*, please.'

'I have no *carte d'identité*. I am a temporary visitor. I entered France four days ago.'

'Your passport, then.'

'It is at my hotel.'

The man stiffened. The frown of irritation left his face. Here was something that he understood and with which his long experience had enabled him to deal. He spoke with easy assurance.

'That is very serious, monsieur. You realize that? Are you English?'

'Yes.'

He drew a deep breath. 'You must understand, monsieur, that your papers must always be in your pocket. It is the law. If you saw a street accident and were required as a witness, the *agent* would ask to see your papers before you were permitted to leave the scene of the accident. If you had not got them, he could, if he wished, arrest you. If you were in a *boîte de nuit* and the police entered to inspect papers, you would certainly be arrested if you carried none. It is the law, you understand? I shall have to take the necessary particulars. Give me your name and that of your hotel, please.'

Latimer did so. The man noted them down, picked up a telephone and asked for '*Septième*'. There was a pause, then he read out Latimer's name and address and asked for confirmation that they were genuine. There was another pause, of a minute or two this time, before he began to nod his head and say: '*Bien, bien.*' Then he listened for a moment, said: '*Oui, c'est ca,*' and put the telephone back on its hook. He returned to Latimer.

'It is in order,' he said; 'but you must present yourself with your passport at the Commissariat of the Seventh Arrondissement within twenty-four hours. As for this complaint of yours, you can make that at the same time. Please remember,' he went on tapping his pencil on the counter for emphasis, 'that your passport must always be carried. It is obligatory to do so. You are English, and so nothing more need be made of the affair; but you must report to the Commissariat in your arrondissement, and in future always remember to carry your passport. Good day, sir.' He nodded benevolently with an air of knowing his duty to be well done.

Latimer went out in a very bad temper, Officious ass! But the man was right, of course. It had been absurd of him to go into the place without his passport. Complaint, indeed! In a sense he had had a narrow escape. He might have had to tell his story to the man. He might well have been under arrest by now. As it was, he had not told his story and was still a potential blackmailer.

Yet the visit to the police *Poste* had eased his conscience considerably. He did not feel quite as irresponsible as he had felt before. He had made an effort to bring the police into the affair. It had been an abortive effort; but short of collecting his passport from the other side of Paris and starting all over again (and that, he decided comfortably, was out of the question) there was nothing more he could do. He was due to meet Mr Peters at a quarter to eight in a café on the Boulevard Hausmann. But by the time he had finished a very light dinner the curious feeling had returned again to his solar plexus and the two brandies which he had with his coffee were intended to do more than pass the time. It was a pity, he reflected as he went on to keep his appointment, that he could not accept even a small share of the million francs. The cost of satisfying his curiosity was proving, in terms of frayed nerves and an uneasy conscience, practically prohibitive.

Mr Peters arrived ten minutes late with a large, cheap-looking suit-case and the too matter-of-fact air of a surgeon about to perform a difficult operation. He said, 'Ah, Mr Latimer!' and sitting down at the table, ordered a raspberry liqueur.

'Is everything all right?' Latimer felt that the question was a little theatrical, but he really wanted to know the answer to it.

'So far, yes. Naturally, I have had no word from him because I gave no address. We shall see.'

'What have you got in the suit-case?'

'Old newspapers. It is better to arrive at a hotel with a suit-case. I do not wish to have to fill up an *affiche* unless I am compelled to do so. I decided finally upon a hotel near to the Ledru-Rollin Metro. Very convenient.'

'Why can't we go by taxi?'

'We shall go by taxi. But,' added Mr Peters significantly, 'we shall return by the Metro. You will see.' His liqueur arrived. He poured it down his throat, shuddered, licked his lips and said that it was time to go.

The hotel chosen by Mr Peters for the meeting with Dimitrios was in a street just off the Avenue Ledru. It was small and dirty. A man in his shirt-sleeves came out of a room marked 'Bureau', chewing a mouthful of food.

'I telephoned for a room,' said Mr Peters.

'Monsieur Petersen?'

'Yes.'

The man looked them both up and down. 'It is a large room. Fifteen francs for one. Twenty francs for two. Service, twelve and a half percent.'

'This gentleman is not staying with me.'

The man took a key from a rack just inside the Bureau and, taking Mr Peters' suit-case, led the way upstairs to a room on the second floor. Mr Peters looked inside it and nodded.

'Yes, this will do. A friend of mine will call for me here soon. Ask him to come up, please.'

The man withdrew. Mr Peters sat on the bed and looked round approvingly. 'Quite nice,' he said, 'and very cheap.'

'Yes, it is.'

It was a long, narrow room with an old hair carpet, an iron bedstead, a wardrobe, two bentwood chairs, a small table, a screen and an enamelled iron *bidet*. The carpet was red; but by the washbasin was a threadbare patch, black and shiny with use. The wall-paper depicted a trellis supporting a creeping plant, a number of purple discs and some shapeless pink objects of a vaguely clinical character. The curtains were thick and blue and hung on brass rings.

Mr Peters looked at his watch. 'Twenty-five minutes before he is due. We had better make ourselves comfortable. Would you like the bed?'

'No, thank you. I suppose you will do the talking.'

'I think it will be best.' Mr Peters drew his pistol from his breast pocket, examined it to see that it was loaded and then dropped it into the right-hand pocket of his overcoat.

Latimer watched these preparations in silence. He was now feeling quite sick. He said suddenly: 'I don't like this.'

'Nor do I,' said Mr Peters soothingly; 'but we must take precautions. It is unlikely, I think, that they will be needed. You need have no fears.'

Latimer remembered an American gangster picture that he had once seen.

'What is to prevent him from walking in here and shooting us both?'

Mr Peters smiled tolerantly. 'Now, now! You must not let your imagination run away with you, Mr Latimer. Dimitrios would not do that. It would be too noisy and dangerous for him. Remember, the man downstairs will have seen him. Besides, that would not be his way.'

'What is his way?'

'Dimitrios is a very cautious man. He thinks very carefully before he acts.'

'He has had all day to think carefully.'

'Yes, but he does not yet know how much we know, and if anyone else knows what we know. He would have to discover those things. Leave everything to me, Mr Latimer. I understand Dimitrios.'

Latimer was about to point out that Visser had probably had the same idea, and then decided not to do so. He had another, more personal misgiving to air.

'You said that when Dimitrios paid us the million francs that would be the last he heard of us. Has it occurred to you that he may not be content to let things rest in that way? When he finds that we don't come back for more money he may decide to come after us.'

'After Mr Smith and Mr Petersen? We should be difficult to find under those names, my dear Mr Latimer.'

'But he knows your face already. He will see mine. He could recognize our faces, whatever we chose to call ourselves.'

'But first he would have to find out where we were.'

'My photograph has appeared once or twice in newspapers. It may do so again. Or supposing my publisher decided to spread my photograph over the jacket of a book. Dimitrios might easily happen to see it. There have been stranger coincidences.'

Mr Peters pursed his lips. 'I think you exaggerate, but'–he shrugged–'since you feel nervous perhaps you had better keep your face hidden. Do you wear spectacles?'

'For reading.'

'Then put them on. Wear your hat, too, and turn up the collar of your coat. You might sit in the corner of the room where it is not so light. In front of the screen. It will blur the outlines of your face. There.'

Latimer obeyed. When he was in position, with his collar buttoned across his chin and his hat tilted forward over his eyes, Mr Peters surveyed him from the door and nodded.

'It will do. I still think it unnecessary; but it will do. After making all these preparations we shall feel very foolish if he does not come.'

Latimer, who was feeling very foolish anyway, grunted. 'Is there any likelihood of his not coming?'

'Who knows?' Mr Peters sat on the bed again. 'A dozen things might happen to prevent him. He might not, for some reason, have received my letter. He may have left Paris yesterday. But, if he has received the letter, I think that he will come.' He looked at his watch again. 'Eight forty-five. If he *is* coming, he will soon be here.'

They fell silent. Mr Peters began to trim his nails with a pair of pocket scissors.

Except for the clicking of the scissors and the sound of Mr Peters' heavy breathing, the silence in the room was complete. To Latimer it seemed almost tangible; a dark grey fluid that oozed from the corners of the room. He began to hear the watch ticking on his wrist. He waited for what seemed an eternity before looking at it. When he did look it was ten minutes to nine. Another eternity. He tried to think of something to say to Mr Peters to pass the time. He tried counting the complete parallelograms in the pattern of the wall-paper between the wardrobe and the window. Now he thought he could hear Mr Peters' watch ticking. The muffled sound of someone moving a chair and walking about in the room overhead seemed to intensify the silence. Four minutes to nine.

Then, so suddenly that the sound seemed as loud as a pistol shot, one of the stairs outside the door creaked.

Mr Peters stopped trimming his nails, and, dropping the scissors on the bed, put his right hand in his overcoat pocket.

There was a pause. His heart beating painfully, Latimer gazed rigidly at the door. There was a soft knock.

Mr Peters stood up and, with his hand still in his pocket, went to the door and opened it.

Latimer saw him stare for a moment into the semi-darkness of the landing and then stand back.

Dimitrios walked into the room.

Chapter Fourteen

The Mask of Dimitrios

A man's features, the bone structure and the tissue which covers it, are the product of a biological process; but his face he creates for himself. It is a statement of his habitual emotional attitude; the attitude which his desires need for their fulfilment and which his fears demand for their protection from prying eyes. He wears it like a devil mask; a device to evoke in others the emotions complementary to his own. If he is afraid, then he must be feared; if he desires, then he must be desired. It is a screen to hide his mind's nakedness. Only a few men, painters, have been able to see the mind through the face. Other men in their judgments reach out for the evidence of word and deed that will explain the mask before their eyes. Yet, though they understand instinctively that the mask cannot be the man behind it, they are generally shocked by a demonstration of the fact. The duplicity of others must always be shocking when one is unconscious of one's own.

So, when at last Latimer saw Dimitrios and tried to read in the face of the man staring across the room at him the evil which he felt should be there, it was of that sense of shock which he was conscious. Hat in hand, in his dark, neat French clothes, with his slim, erect figure and sleek grey hair,

Dimitrios was a picture of distinguished respectability.

His distinction was that of a relatively unimportant guest at a large diplomatic reception. He gave the impression of being slightly taller than the one hundred and eighty-two centimetres with which the Bulgarian police had credited him. His skin had the creamy pallor which succeeds in middle age a youthful sallowness. With his high cheekbones, thin nose and beak-like upper lip he might well have been the member of an Eastern European delegation. It was only the expression of his eyes that fitted in with any of Latimer's preconceived ideas about his appearance.

They were very brown and seemed at first to be a little screwed up, as if he were short-sighted or worried. But there was no corresponding frown or contraction of the eyebrows; and Latimer saw that the expression of anxiety or short-sightedness was an optical illusion due to the height of the cheekbones and the way the eyes were set in the head. Actually, the face was utterly expressionless, as impassive as that of a lizard.

For a moment the brown eyes rested on Latimer; then, as Mr Peters closed the door behind him, Dimitrios turned his head and said in strongly accented French: 'Present me to your friend. I do not think that I have seen him before.'

Latimer very nearly jumped. The face of Dimitrios might not be revealing, but the voice certainly was. It was very coarse and sharp, with an acrid quality that made nonsense of any grace implicit in the words it produced. He spoke very softly, and it occurred to Latimer that the man was aware of the ugliness of his voice and tried to conceal it. He failed. Its promise was as deadly as the rattle of a rattlesnake.

'This is Monsieur Smith,' said Mr Peters. 'There is a chair behind you. You may sit down.'

Dimitrios ignored the suggestion. 'Monsieur Smith! An Englishman. It appears that you knew Monsieur Visser.'

'I have *seen* Visser.'

'That is what we wanted to talk to you about, Dimitrios,' said Mr Peters.

'Yes?' Dimitrios now sat down on the spare chair. 'Then talk and be quick. I have an appointment to keep. I cannot waste time in this way.'

Mr Peters shook his head sorrowfully. 'You have not changed at all, Dimitrios. Always impetuous, always a little unkind. After all these years no word of greeting, no word of regret for all the unhappiness you caused me. You know, it was most unkind of you to hand us all over to the police like that. We were your friends. Why did you do it?'

'You still talk too much,' said Dimitrios. 'What is it you want?'

Mr Peters sat down carefully on the edge of the bed. 'Since you insist on making this a purely business meeting—we want money.'

The brown eyes flickered towards him. 'Naturally. What do you want to give me for it?'

'Our silence, Dimitrios. It is very valuable.'

'Indeed? How valuable?'

'It is worth at the very least a million francs.'

Dimitrios sat back in the chair and crossed his legs. 'And who is going to pay you that for it?'

'You are, Dimitrios. And you are going to be glad to get it so cheaply.'

Then Dimitrios smiled.

It was a slow tightening of the small, thin lips; nothing more. Yet there was something inexpressibly savage about it; something that made Latimer feel glad that it was Mr Peters who had to face it. At that moment, he felt, Dimitrios was far more appropriate to a gathering of man-eating tigers than to a diplomatic reception, however large. The smile faded. 'I think,' he said, 'that you shall tell me now precisely what you mean.'

To Latimer, who would, he knew, have responded promptly to the menace in the man's voice, Mr Peters' bland hesitation was maddeningly reckless. He appeared to be enjoying himself.

'It is so difficult to know where to begin.'

There was no reply. Mr Peters waited for a moment and then shrugged. 'There are,' he went on, 'so many things that the police would be glad to know. For instance, I might tell them who it was who sent them that dossier in 1931. And it would be such a surprise for them to know that a respectable director of the Eurasian Credit Trust was really the Dimitrios Makropoulos who used to send women to Alexandria.'

Latimer thought that he saw Dimitrios relax a little in his chair. 'And you expect me to pay you a million francs for that? My good Petersen, you are childish.'

Mr Peters smiled. 'Very likely, Dimitrios. You were always inclined to despise my simple approach to the problems of this life of ours. But our silence on those matters would be worth a great deal to you, would it not?'

Dimitrios considered him for a moment. Then: 'Why don't you come to the point, Petersen? Or perhaps you are only preparing the way for your Englishman.' He turned his head. 'What have you to say, Monsieur Smith? Or is neither of you very sure of himself?'

'Petersen is speaking for me,' mumbled Latimer. He wished fervently that Mr Peters would get the business over.

'May I continue?' inquired Mr Peters.

'Go on.'

'The Yugoslav police, too, might be interested in you. If we were to tell them where Monsieur Talat . . .'

'*Par example!*' Dimitrios laughed malignantly. 'So Grodek has been talking. Not a sou for that, my friend. Is there any more?'

'Athens, 1922. Does that mean anything to you, Dimitrios? The name was Taladis, if you remember. The charge was robbery and attempted murder. Is that so amusing?'

Into Mr Peters' face had come the look of unsmiling, adenoidal viciousness that Latimer had seen for a moment or two in Sofia. Dimitrios stared at him unblinkingly. In an instant the atmosphere had become deadly with a naked hatred that to Latimer was quite horrible. He felt as he had once felt when, as a child, he had seen a street fight between two middle-aged men. He saw Mr Peters draw the pistol from his pocket and weigh it in his hands.

'You have nothing to say to that, Dimitrios? Then I shall go on. A little earlier that year you murdered a man in Smyrna, a moneylender. What was his name, Monsieur Smith?'

'Sholem.'

'Sholem, of course. Monsieur Smith was clever enough to discover that, Dimitrios. A good piece of work, don't you think? Monsieur Smith, you know, is very friendly with the Turkish police; almost, one might say, in their confidence. Do you still think that a million francs is a lot to pay, Dimitrios?'

Dimitrios did not look at either of them. 'The murderer of Sholem was hanged,' he said slowly.

Mr Peters raised his eyebrows. 'Can that be true, Monsieur Smith?'

'A Negro named Dhris Mohammed was hanged for the murder, but he made a confession implicating Monsieur Makropoulos. An order was issued for his arrest in 1924. The charge was murder; but the Turkish police were anxious to catch him for another reason. He had been concerned in an attempt to assassinate Kemal in Adrianople.'

'You see, Dimitrios, we are very well informed. Shall we continue?' He paused. Dimitrios still stared straight in front of him. Not a muscle of his face moved. Mr Peters looked across at Latimer. 'Dimitrios is impressed, I think. I feel sure he would like us to continue.'

When Latimer thinks of Dimitrios now it is that scene which he remembers: the squalid room with its nightmare wall-paper, Mr Peters sitting on the edge of the bed, his wet eyes half closed and the pistol in his hands, talking, and the man sitting between them, staring straight in front of him, his white face as still as that of a waxwork and as lifeless. The droning of Mr Peters' voice was punctuated by silences. To Latimer's overwrought nerves those silences were piercing in their intensity. But they were short, and after each one Mr Peters would drone on again: a torturer mumbling the repetition of his questions after each turn of the screw.

'Monsieur Smith has told you that he saw Visser. It was in a mortuary in Istanbul that he saw him. As I told you, he is very friendly with the Turkish police, and they showed him the body. They told him that it was the body of a criminal named Dimitrios Makropoulos. It was foolish of them to be so easily deceived, was it not? But even Monsieur Smith was deceived for a while. Fortunately I was able to tell him that Dimitrios was still alive.' He paused. 'You do not wish to comment? Very well. Perhaps you would like to hear how I discovered where you were and who you were.' Another silence. 'No? Perhaps you would like to know how I knew that you were in Istanbul at the time poor, silly Visser was killed; or how easily Monsieur Smith was able to identify a photograph of Visser with the dead man he saw in the mortuary.' Another silence. 'No? Perhaps you would like to be told how easy it would be for us to arouse the interest of the Turkish police in the curious case of a dead murderer who is alive, or of the Greek police in the case of the refugee from Smyrna who left Tabouria so suddenly. I wonder if you are thinking that it would be difficult for us to prove that you *are* Dimitrios Makropoulos, or Taladis, or Talat, or Rougemont, after such a long time has elapsed. Are you thinking that, Dimitrios? You do not wish to answer? Then let me tell you that it would be quite easy for us to prove. I could identify you as Makropoulos, and so could Werner or Lenôtre or Galindo or the Grand Duchess. One of them is sure to be alive and within reach of the police. Any of them would be glad to help to hang you.

Monsieur Smith can swear that the man buried in Istanbul is Visser. Then there is the crew of the yacht you chartered in June. They knew that Visser went with you to Istanbul. There is the concièrge in the Avenue de Wagram. He knew you as Rougemont. Your present passport would not be a very good protection to a man with so many false names, would it? And even if you submitted to a little *chantage* from the French and Greek police, Monsieur Smith's Turkish friends would not be so accommodating. Do you think that a million francs is too much to pay for saving you from the hangman, Dimitrios?'

He stopped. For several long seconds Dimitrios continued to stare at the wall. Then at last he stirred and looked at his small gloved hands. His words, when they came, were like stones dropped one by one into a stagnant pool. 'I am wondering,' he said, 'why you ask so little. Is this million all that you are asking?'

Mr Peters sniggered. 'You mean, are we going to the police when we have the million? Oh, no, Dimitrios. We shall be fair with you. This million is only a preliminary gesture of good will. There will be other opportunities for you. But you will not find us greedy.'

'I am sure of that. You would not want me to become desperate, I think. Are you the only ones who have this curious delusion that I killed Visser?'

'There is no one else. I shall want the million in *mille* notes to-morrow.'

'So soon?'

'You will receive instructions as to how you are to give them to us in the morning. If the instructions are not followed exactly you will not be given a second chance. The police will be approached immediately. Do you understand?'

'Perfectly.'

The words were spoken levelly enough. To a casual observer they might have been concluding an ordinary business deal. But neither of their voices was quite steady. To Latimer it seemed as if it were only the pistol that prevented Dimitrios from attacking and killing Mr Peters and only the thought of a million francs that prevented Mr Peters from shooting Dimitrios. Two lives hung by the thin steel threads of self-preservation and greed.

As Dimitrios stood up an idea seemed to occur to him. He turned to Latimer. 'You have been very silent, monsieur. I wonder if you have been understanding that your life is in your friend Petersen's hands. If, for example, he decided to tell me your real name and where you might be found, I should very likely have you killed.'

Mr Peters showed his white false teeth. 'Why should I deprive myself of Monsieur Smith's help? Monsieur Smith is invaluable. He can prove that Visser is dead. Without him you could breathe again.'

Dimitrios took no notice of the interruption. 'Well, Monsieur Smith?'

Latimer looked up into the brown anxious-seeming eyes and thought of Madame Preveza's phrase. They were certainly the eyes of a man ready to do something that hurt, but they could have belonged to no doctor. There was murder in them.

'I can assure you', he said, 'that Petersen has no inducement to kill me. You see . . .'

'You see,' put in Mr Peters quickly, 'we are not fools, Dimitrios. You can go now.'

'Of course.' Dimitrios went towards the door, but at the threshold he paused.

'What is it?' said Mr Peters.

'I should like to ask Monsieur Smith two questions.'

'Well?'

'How was this man whom you took to be Visser dressed when he was found?'

'In a cheap blue serge suit. A French *carte d'identité*, issued at Lyons a year previously, was sewn into the lining. The suit was of Greek manufacture, but the shirt and underwear were French.'

'And how was he killed?'

'He had been stabbed in the side and then thrown into the water.'

Mr Peters smiled. 'Are you satisfied, Dimitrios?'

Dimitrios stared at him. 'Visser,' he said slowly, 'was too greedy. You will not be too greedy, will you, Petersen?'

Mr Peters gave him stare for stare. 'I shall be very careful,' he said. 'You have no more questions to ask? Good. You will receive your instructions in the morning.'

Dimitrios went without another word. Mr Peters shut the door, waited a moment or two, then, very gently opened it again. Motioning to Latimer to remain where he was, he disappeared on to the landing. Latimer heard the stairs creak. A minute later he returned.

'He has gone,' he announced. 'In a few minutes we, too, shall go.' He sat down again on the bed, lit one of his cheroots and blew the smoke out as luxuriously as if he had just been released from bondage. His sweet smile came out again like a rose after a storm. 'Well,' he said, 'that was Dimitrios about whom you have heard such a great deal. What did you think of him?'

'I didn't know what to think. Perhaps, if I had not known so much about him, I should have disliked him less. I don't know. It is difficult to be reasonable about a man who is obviously wondering how quickly he can murder you.' He hesitated. 'I did not realize that you hated him so much.'

Mr Peters did not smile. 'I assure you, Mr Latimer, that it was a surprise to me to realize it. I did not like him. I did not trust him. After the way he betrayed us all, that was understandable. It was not until I saw him in this room just now that I realized that I hated him enough to kill him. If I were a superstitious man, I should wonder if perhaps the spirit of poor Visser had entered into me.' He stopped, then added '*Salop!*' under his breath. He was silent for a moment. Then he looked up. 'Mr Latimer, I must make an admission. I must tell you that even if you had agreed to the offer I made you, you would not have received your half million. I should not have paid you.' He shut his mouth tightly as if he were prepared to receive a blow.

'So I imagine,' said Latimer dryly. 'I very nearly accepted the offer just to see how you would cheat me. I take it that you would have made the real time for delivery of the money an hour or so earlier than you would have told me, and that, by the time I arrived on the scene, you and the money would have gone. Was that it?'

Mr Peters winced. 'It was very wise of you not to trust me, but very unkind. But I suppose that I cannot blame you.' He rubbed salt in the wound. 'The Great One has seen fit to make me what is known as a criminal, and I must tread the path to my Destiny with patient resignation. But it was not to abase myself that I admitted to having tried to deceive you. It was to defend myself. I would like to ask you a question.'

'Well?'

'Was it—forgive me—was it the thought that I might betray you to Dimitrios that made you refuse my offer to share the money with you?'

'It never occurred to me.'

'I am glad,' said Mr Peters solemnly. 'I should not like you to think that of me. You may dislike me, but I should not care to be thought cold-blooded. I may tell you that the thought did not occur to me either. There you see Dimitrios! We have discussed this matter, you and I. We have mistrusted one another and looked for betrayal. Yet it is Dimitrios who puts this thought in our heads. I have met many wicked and violent men, Mr Latimer, but I tell you that Dimitrios is unique. Why do you think he suggested to you that I might betray you?'

'I imagine that he was acting on the principle that the best way to fight two allies is to get them to fight each other.'

Mr Peters smiled. 'No, Mr Latimer. That would have been too obvious a trick for Dimitrios. He was suggesting to you in a very delicate way that *I* was the unnecessary partner and that you could remove me very easily by telling him where I could be found.'

'Do you mean that he was offering to kill you for me?'

'Exactly. He would have only you to deal with then. He does not know, of course,' added Mr Peters thoughtfully, 'that you do not know his present name.' He stood up and put on his hat. 'No, Mr Latimer, I do not like Dimitrios. Do not misunderstand me, please. I have no moral rectitude. But Dimitrios is a savage beast. Even now, though I know that I have taken every precaution, I am afraid. I shall take his million and go. If I could allow you to hand him over to the police when I have done with him, I would do so. He would not hesitate if the situation were reversed. But it is impossible.'

'Why?'

Mr Peters looked at him curiously. 'Dimitrios seems to have had a strange effect on you. No, to tell the police afterwards would be too dangerous. If we were asked to explain the million francs—and we could not expect Dimitrios to remain silent about them—we should be embarrassed. A pity. Shall we go now? I shall leave the money for the room on the table. They can take the suit-case for a *pourboire*.'

They went downstairs in silence. As they deposited the key, the man in his shirt-sleeves appeared with an *affiche* for Mr Peters to complete. Mr Peters waved him away. He would, he said, fill it in when he returned.

In the street he halted and faced Latimer.

'Have you ever been followed?'

'Not to my knowledge.'

'Then you will be followed now. I do not suppose that Dimitrios had any real hope of our leading him to our homes, but he was always thorough. He glanced over Latimer's shoulder. 'Ah, yes. He was there when we arrived. Do not look round, Mr Latimer. A man wearing a grey mackintosh and a dark soft hat. You will see him in a minute.'

The hollow feeling which had disappeared with the departure of Dimitrios jolted back into its position in Latimer's stomach. 'What are we to do?'

'Return by Metro, as I said before.'

'What good will that do?'

'You will see in a minute.'

The Ledru-Rollin Metro station was about a hundred yards away. As they walked towards it the muscles in Latimer's calves tightened and he had a ridiculous desire to run. He felt himself walking stiffly and self-consciously.

'Do not look round,' said Mr Peters again.

They walked down the steps to the Metro. 'Keep close to me now,' said Mr Peters.

He bought two second-class tickets and they walked on down the tunnel in the direction of the trains.

It was a long tunnel. As they pushed their way through the spring barriers, Latimer felt that he could reasonably glance behind him. He did so, and caught a glimpse of a shabby young man in a grey raincoat about thirty feet behind them. Now the tunnel split into two. One way was labelled: '*Direction* Pte de Charenton,' the other: '*Direction* Balard.' Mr Peters stopped.

'It would be wise now,' he said, 'if we appeared to be about to take leave of one another.' He glanced out of the corners of his eyes. 'Yes, he has stopped. He is wondering what is going to happen. Talk, please, Mr Latimer, but not too loudly. I want to listen.'

'Listen to what?'

'The trains. I spent half an hour here listening to them this morning.'

'What on earth for? I don't see . . .'

Mr Peters gripped his arm and he stopped. In the distance he could hear the rumble of an approaching train.

'*Direction* Balard,' muttered Mr Peters suddenly. 'Come along. Keep close to me and do not walk too quickly.'

They went on down the right-hand tunnel. The rumble of the train grew louder. They rounded a bend in the tunnel. Ahead was the green automatic gate.

'*Vite!*' cried Mr Peters.

The train was by now almost in the station. The automatic door began to swing slowly across the entrance to the platform. As Latimer reached it and passed through with about three inches to spare, he heard, above the hiss and screech of pneumatic brakes, the sound of running feet. He looked round. Although Mr Peters' stomach had suffered some compression, he had squeezed himself through on to the platform. But the man in the grey raincoat had, in spite of his last-minute sprint, left it too late. He now stood, red in the face with anger, shaking his fists at them from the other side of the automatic gate.

They got into the train a trifle breathlessly.

'Excellent!' puffed Mr Peters happily. 'Now do you see what I meant, Mr Latimer?'

'Very ingenious.'

The noise of the train made further conversation impossible. Latimer stared vacantly at a Celtique advertisement. So that was that. Colonel Haki had been right after all. The story of Dimitrios had no proper ending. Dimitrios would buy off Mr Peters and the story would merely stop. Somewhere, at some future time, Dimitrios might happen to find Mr Peters and then Mr Peters would die as Visser had died. Somewhere, at some time, Dimitrios himself would die: probably of old age. But he, Latimer, would not know about those things. He would be writing a detective story with a beginning, a middle and an end; a corpse, a piece of detection and a scaffold. He would be demonstrating that murder would out, that justice triumphed in the end and that the green bay tree flourished alone. Dimitrios and the Eurasian Credit Trust would be forgotten. It had all been a great waste of time.

Mr Peters touched his arm. They were at Chatelet. They got out and took the Porte d'Orléans *correspondance* to St Placide. As they walked down the Rue de Rennes, Mr Peters hummed softly. They passed a café.

Mr Peters stopped humming. 'Would you like some coffee, Mr Latimer?'

'No, thanks. What about your letter to Dimitrios?'

Mr Peters tapped his pocket. 'It is already written. Eleven o'clock is the time. The junction of the Avenue de la Reine and the Boulevard Jean Jaurés is the place. Would you like to be there, or are you leaving Paris to-morrow?' And then, without giving Latimer a chance to reply: 'I shall be sorry to say good-bye to you, Mr Latimer. I find you so sympathetic. Our association has, on the whole, been most agreeable. It has also been profitable to me.' He sighed. 'I feel a little guilty, Mr Latimer. You have been so patient and helpful and yet you go unrewarded. You would not,' he inquired a trifle anxiously, 'accept a thousand francs of the money? It would help to pay your expenses.'

'No, thank you.'

'No, of course not. Then, at least, Mr Latimer, let me give you a glass of wine. That it is! A celebration! Come, Mr Latimer. There is no taste in nothing. Let us collect the money together to-morrow night. You will have the satisfaction of seeing a little blood squeezed from this swine Dimitrios. Then we will celebrate with a glass of wine. What do you say to that?'

They had stopped at the corner of the street which contained the Impasse. Latimer looked into Mr Peters' watery eyes. 'I should say,' he said deliberately, 'that you are wondering if there is a chance that Dimitrios might decide to call your bluff and thinking that it might be a good idea to have me in Paris until you have the money actually in your pocket.'

Mr Peters' eyes slowly closed. 'Mr Latimer,' he said bitterly, 'I did not think . . . I would not have thought that you could have put such a construction on . . .'

'All right, I'll stay.' Irritably, Latimer interrupted him. He had wasted so many days: another one would make no difference. 'I'll come with you to-morrow, but only on these conditions. The wine must be champagne; it must come from France, not Meknes, and it must be a vintage *cuvée* of either 1919, 1920 or 1921. A bottle,' he added vindictively, 'will cost you at least one hundred francs.'

Mr Peters opened his eyes. He smiled bravely. 'You shall have it, Mr Latimer,' he said.

Chapter Fifteen

The Strange Town

Mr Peters and Latimer took up their positions at the corner of the Avenue de la Reine and the Boulevard Jean Jaurès at half-past ten, the hour at which the hired car was due to pick up the messenger from Dimitrios opposite the Neuilly cemetery.

It was a cold night, and as it began to rain soon after they arrived, they stood for shelter just inside the *porte cochère* of a building a few yards along the avenue in the direction of the Pont St Cloud.

'How long will they be getting here?' Latimer asked.

'I said that I would expect them by eleven. That gives them half an hour to drive from Neuilly. They could do it in less, but I told them to make quite certain that they were not followed. If they are in doubt they will return to Neuilly. They will take no chances. The car is a Renault *coupé-de-ville*. We must have patience.'

They waited in silence. Now and again Mr Peters would stir as a car that might have been the hired Renault approached from the direction of the river. The rain trickling down the slope formed by the subsidence of the cobbles formed puddles about their feet. Latimer thought of his warm bed and wondered if he would catch a cold. He had booked a seat in the Athens slip-coach of the Orient Express due to leave the following morning. A train would not be the best place to spend three days nursing a cold. He remembered that he had a small bottle of cinnamon extract somewhere in his luggage and resolved to take a dose before he went to bed.

His mind was occupied with this domestic matter when suddenly Mr Peters grunted: '*Attention!*'

'Are they coming?'

'Yes.'

Latimer looked over Mr Peters' shoulder. A large Renault was approaching from the left. As he looked it began to slow down as if the driver were uncertain of the way. It passed them, the rain glistening in the beams of the headlights, and stopped a few yards farther on. The outline of the driver's head and shoulders were just visible in the darkness, but blinds were pulled down over the rear windows. Mr Peters put his hand in his overcoat pocket.

'Wait here, please,' he said to Latimer, and walked towards the car.

'*Ca va?*' Latimer heard him say to the driver. There was an answering '*Oui*'. Mr Peters opened the rear door and leaned forward.

Almost immediately he withdrew a pace and closed the door. In his left hand was a package. '*Attendez*,' he said, and walked back to where Latimer was standing.

'All right?' said Latimer.

'I think so. Will you strike a match, please?'

Latimer did so. The package was the size of a large book, about two inches thick and was wrapped in blue paper and tied with string. Mr Peters tore away the paper at one of the corners and exposed a solid wad of *mille* notes. He sighed. 'Beautiful!'

'Aren't you going to count them?'

'That pleasure,' said Mr Peters seriously, 'I shall reserve for the comfort of my home.' He crammed the package into his overcoat pocket, stepped on to the pavement and raised his hand. The Renault started with a jerk, swung round in a wide circle and splashed away on its return journey. Mr Peters watched it go with a smile.

'A very pretty woman,' he said. 'I wonder who she can be. But I prefer the million francs. Now, Mr Latimer, a taxi and then your favourite champagne. We have earned it, I think.'

They found a taxi near the Porte de St Cloud. Mr Peters enlarged on his success.

'With a type like Dimitrios it is necessary only to be firm and circumspect. We put the matter to him squarely; we let him see that he has no choice but to agree to our demands, and it is done. A million francs. Very nice! One almost wishes that one had demanded two million. But it would have been unwise to be too greedy. As it is, he believes that we shall make fresh demands and that he has time to deal with us as he dealt with Visser. He will find that he has deceived himself. That is very satisfactory to me, Mr Latimer: as satisfying to my pride as it is to my pocket. I feel, too, that I have, in some measure, avenged poor Visser's death. It is at moments like these, Mr Latimer, that one realizes that if it sometimes appears as if the Great One has forgotten His children, it is only that we have forgotten Him. I have suffered. Now I have my reward.' He patted his pocket. 'It would be amusing to see Dimitrios when at last he realizes how he has been tricked. A pity that we shall not be there.'

'Shall you leave Paris immediately?'

'I think so. I have a fancy to see something of South America. Not my own adopted fatherland, of course. It is one of the terms of my citizenship that I never enter the country. A hard condition, for I would like for sentimental reasons to see the country of my adoption. But it cannot be altered. I am a citizen of the world and must remain so. Perhaps I shall buy an estate somewhere, a place where I shall be able to pass my days in peace when I am old. You are a young man, Mr Latimer. When one is my age, the years seem shorter and one feels that one is soon to reach a destination. It is as if one were approaching a strange town late at night when one is sorry to be leaving the warm train for an unknown hotel and wishing that the journey would never end.'

He glanced out of the window. 'We are nearly home. I have your champagne. It was, as you warned me, very expensive. But I have no objections to a little luxury. It is sometimes agreeable and, even when it is disagreeable, it serves to make us appreciate simplicity. Ah!' The taxi had stopped at the end of the Impasse. 'I have no change, Mr Latimer. That seems odd with a million francs in one's pocket, does it not? Will you pay, please?'

They walked down the Impasse.

'I think,' said Mr Peters, 'that I shall sell these houses before I go to South America. One does not want property on one's hands that is not yielding a profit.'

'Won't they be rather difficult to sell? The view from the windows is a little depressing, isn't it?'

'It is not necessary to be always looking out of the windows. They could be made into very nice houses.'

They began the long climb up the stairs. On the second landing Mr Peters paused for breath, took off his overcoat and got out his keys. They continued to climb to his door.

He opened it, switched on the light, and then, going straight to the largest divan, took the package from his overcoat pocket and undid the string. With loving care he extracted the notes from the wrappings and held them up. For once his smile was real.

'There, Mr Latimer! A million francs! Have you ever seen so much money at once before? Nearly six thousand English pounds!' He stood up. 'But we must have our little celebration. Take off your coat and I will get the champagne. I hope that you will like it. I have no ice, but I put it in a bowl of water. It will be quite cool.'

He walked towards the curtained-off part of the room.

Latimer had turned away to take off his coat. Suddenly he became aware that Mr Peters was still on the same side of the curtain and that he was standing motionless. He glanced round.

For a moment he thought that he was going to faint. The blood seemed to drain away suddenly from his head, leaving it hollow and light. A steel band seemed to tighten round his chest. He felt that he wanted to cry out, but all he could do was to stare.

Mr Peters was standing with his back to him, and his hands were raised above his head. Facing him in the gap between the gold curtains was Dimitrios, with a revolver in his hand.

Dimitrios stepped forward and sideways so that Latimer was no longer partly covered by Mr Peters. Latimer dropped his coat and put up his hands. Dimitrios raised his eyebrows.

'It is not flattering,' he said, 'for you to look so surprised to see me, Petersen. Or should I call you Caillé?'

Mr Peters said nothing. Latimer could not see his face, but he saw his throat move as if he were swallowing.

The brown eyes flickered to Latimer. 'I am glad that the Englishman is here, too, Petersen. I am saved the trouble of persuading you to give me his name and address. Monsieur Smith, who knows so many things and who was so anxious to keep his face hidden, is now shown to be as easy to deal with as you are, Petersen. You were always too ingenious, Petersen. I told you so once before. It was on the occasion when you brought a coffin from Salonika. You remember? Ingenuity is never a substitute for intelligence, you know. Did you really think that I should not see through you?' His lips twisted. 'Poor Dimitrios! He is very simple. He will think that I, clever Petersen, will come back for more, like any other blackmailer. He will not guess that I may be bluffing him. But, just to make sure that he does not guess, I will do what no other blackmailer ever did. I will tell him that I *shall* come back for more. Poor Dimitrios is such a fool that he will believe me. Poor Dimitrios has no intelligence. Even if he finds out from the records that, within a month of my coming out of prison, I had succeeded in selling three unsaleable houses to someone named Caillé, he will not dream of suspecting that I, clever Petersen, am also Caillé. Did you not know, Petersen, that before I bought these houses in your name they had been empty for ten years? You are such a fool.'

He paused. The anxious brown eyes narrowed. The mouth tightened. Latimer knew that Dimitrios was going to kill Mr Peters and that there was nothing that he could do about it. The wild beating of his heart seemed to be suffocating him.

'Drop the money, Petersen.'

The wad of notes hit the carpet and spread out like a fan.

Dimitrios raised the revolver.

Suddenly, Mr Peters seemed to realize what was about to happen. He cried out: 'No! You must . . .'

Then Dimitrios fired. He fired twice and with the ear-splitting noise of the explosions Latimer heard one of the bullets thud into Mr Peters' body.

Mr Peters emitted a long-drawn-out retching sound and sank forward on to his hands and knees with blood pouring from his neck.

Dimitrios stared at Latimer. 'Now you,' he said.

At that moment Latimer jumped.

Why he chose that particular moment to jump he never knew. He never even knew what prompted him to jump at all. He supposed that it was an instinctive attempt to save himself. Why, however, his instinct for self-preservation should have led him to jump in the direction of the revolver which Dimitrios was about to fire is inexplicable. But he did jump, and the jump did save his life; for, as his right foot left the floor, a fraction of a second before Dimitrios pressed the trigger, he stumbled over one of Mr Peters' thick tufts of rug and the shot went over his head into the wall.

Half dazed and with his forehead scorched by the blast from the muzzle of the revolver, he hurled himself at Dimitrios. They went down together with their hands at each other's throats, but immediately Dimitrios brought his knee up into Latimer's stomach and rolled clear of him.

He had dropped his revolver, and now he went to pick it up. Gasping for breath, Latimer scrambled towards the nearest movable object, which happened to be the heavy brass tray on top of one of the Moroccan tables, and flung it at Dimitrios. The edge of it hit the side of his head as he was reaching for the revolver and he reeled; but the blow stopped him for barely a second. Latimer threw the wooden part of the table at him and dashed forward. Dimitrios staggered back as the table caught his shoulder. The next moment Latimer had the revolver and was standing back, still trying to get his breath, but with his finger on the trigger.

His face sheet-white, Dimitrios came towards him. Latimer raised the revolver.

'If you move again, I shall fire.'

Dimitrios stood still. His brown eyes stared into Latimer's. His grey hair was tousled; his scarf had come out of his coat; he looked dangerous. Latimer was beginning to recover his breath, but his knees felt horribly weak, his ears were singing and the air he breathed reeked sickeningly of cordite fumes. It was for him to make the next move, and he felt frightened and helpless.

'If you move,' he repeated, 'I shall fire.'

He saw the brown eyes flicker towards the notes on the floor and then back to him. 'What are you going to do?' asked Dimitrios suddenly. 'If the police come we shall both have something to explain. If you shoot me you will get only that million. If you will release me I will give you another million as well. That would be good for you.'

Latimer took no notice. He edged sideways towards the wall, until he could glance quickly at Mr Peters.

Mr Peters had crawled towards the divan on which his overcoat lay, and was now leaning against it with his eyes half closed. He was breathing stertorously through the mouth. One bullet had torn a great gaping wound in the side of his neck from which the blood was welling. The second had hit him full in the chest and scorched the clothing. The wound was a round purple mess about two inches in diameter. It was bleeding very little. Mr Peters' lips moved.

Keeping his eyes fixed on Dimitrios, Latimer moved round until he was alongside Mr Peters.

'How do you feel?' he said.

It was a stupid question, and he knew it the moment the words had left his mouth. He tried desperately to collect his wits. A man had been shot and he had the man who shot him. He . . .

'My pistol,' muttered Mr Peters; 'get my pistol. Overcoat.' He said something else that was inaudible.

Cautiously, Latimer worked his way round to the overcoat and fumbled for the pistol. Dimitrios watched with a thin ghastly smile on his lips. Latimer found the pistol and handed it to Mr Peters. He grasped it with both hands and snicked back the safety catch.

'Now,' he muttered, 'go and get police.'

'Someone will have heard the shots,' said Latimer soothingly. 'The police will be here soon.'

'Won't find us,' whispered Mr Peters. 'Get police.'

Latimer hesitated. What Mr Peters said was true. The Impasse was hemmed in by blank walls. The shots might have been heard, but unless someone had happened to be passing the entrance to the Impasse during the few seconds in which they were fired, nobody would know where the sounds had come from.

'All right,' he said. 'Where is the telephone?'

'No telephone.'

'But . . .' He hesitated again. It might take ten minutes to find a policeman. Could he leave a badly wounded Mr Peters to watch a man like

Dimitrios? But there was nothing else for it. Mr Peters needed a doctor. The sooner Dimitrios was under lock and key the better. He knew that Dimitrios understood his predicament and the knowledge did not please him. He glanced at Mr Peters. He had the pistol resting on one knee and pointed at Dimitrios. The blood was still pouring from his neck. If a doctor did not attend to him soon he would bleed to death.

'All right,' he said. 'I'll be as quick as I can.'

He went towards the door.

'One moment, monsieur.' There was an urgency in the harsh voice that made Latimer pause.

'Well?'

'If you go he will shoot me. Don't you see that? Why not accept my offer?'

Latimer opened the door. 'If you try any tricks you will certainly be shot.' He looked again at the wounded man, huddled over the pistol. 'I shall be back with the police. Don't shoot unless you have to.'

Then, as he made to go, Dimitrios laughed. Involuntarily, Latimer turned. 'I should save that laugh for the executioner,' he snapped. 'You will need it.'

'I was thinking,' said Dimitrios, 'that in the end one is always defeated by stupidity. If it is not one's own it is the stupidity of others.' His face changed. 'Five million, monsieur,' he shouted angrily. 'Is it not enough or do you want this carrion to kill me?'

Latimer stared at him for a moment. The man was almost convincing. Then he remembered that others had been convinced by Dimitrios. He waited no longer. He heard Dimitrios shout something after him as he shut the door.

He was half way down the stairs when he heard the shots. There were four of them. Three cracked out in quick succession. Then, there was a pause before the last one. His heart in his mouth, he turned and ran back up to the room. It was only later that he found anything curious in the fact that, as he raced up the stairs, the fear uppermost in his mind was for Mr Peters.

Dimitrios was not a pleasant sight. Only one of the bullets from Mr Peters' heavy pistol had missed. Two had lodged in the body. The fourth, evidently fired at him after he had fallen to the floor, had hit him between the eyes and almost blown the top of his head off. His body was still twitching.

The pistol had slipped from Mr Peters' fingers and he was leaning, with his head on the edge of the divan, opening and shutting his mouth like a stranded fish. As Latimer stood there he choked suddenly and blood trickled from his mouth.

Scarcely knowing what he was doing, Latimer blundered through the curtain. Dimitrios was dead; Mr Peters was dying; and all he, Latimer, could think about was the effort required not to faint or vomit. He strove to pull himself together. He must do something. Mr Peters must have water. Wounded men always need water. There was a washbasin and beside it were some glasses. He filled one and carried it back into the room.

Mr Peters had not moved. His mouth and eyes were open. Latimer knelt down beside him and poured a little water into the mouth. It ran out again. He put down the glass and felt for the pulse. There was none.

Latimer got quicky to his feet and looked at his hands. There was blood on them. He went back to the washbasin, rinsed them and dried them on a small, dirty towel which hung from a hook.

He should, he knew, call the police immediately. Two men had killed each other. That was a matter for the police. Yet . . . what was he going to say to them? How was he going to explain his own presence there in that shambles? Could he say that he had been passing the end of the Impasse and had heard the shots? But someone might have noticed him with Mr Peters. There was the taxi-driver who had brought them. And when they found that Dimitrios had that day obtained a million francs from his bank . . . there would be endless questionings. Supposing they suspected him.

His brain seemed to clear suddenly. He must get out at once and he must leave no traces of his presence there. He thought quickly. The revolver in his pocket belonged to Dimitrios. It had his finger-prints on it. He took it out of his pocket, put on his gloves and wiped it all over carefully with his handkerchief. Then, setting his teeth, he went back into the room, knelt down beside Dimitrios and, taking his right hand, pressed the fingers round the butt and trigger. Removing the fingers and holding the revolver by the barrel, he then put it near the body on the floor.

He considered the *mille* notes strewn over the rug like so much waste-paper. To whom did they belong–Dimitrios or Mr Peters? There was Sholem's money there and the money stolen in Athens in 1922. There was the fee for helping to assassinate Stambulisky and the money of which Madame Preveza had been cheated. There was the price of the charts Bulić had stolen and part of the profits from the white slave and drug traffics. To whom did it belong? Well, the police would decide. Best to leave it as it was. It would give them something to think about.

There was, however, the glass of water. It must be emptied, dried and replaced with the other glasses. He looked round. Was there anything else? No. Nothing at all? Yes, one thing. His finger-prints were on the tray and the table. He wiped them. Nothing more? Yes. Finger-prints on the door-knobs. He wiped them. Anything else? No. He carried the glass to the wash-basin. The glass dried and replaced, he turned to go. It was then that he noticed the champagne which Mr Peters had bought for their celebration standing in a bowl of water. It was a Verzy 1921–half a bottle.

No one saw him leave the Impasse. He went to a café in the Rue de Rennes and ordered a cognac.

Now he began to tremble from head to foot. He had been a fool. He ought to have gone to the police. It was still not too late to go to them. Supposing the bodies remained undiscovered. They might lie there for weeks in that ghastly room with the blue walls and gold stars and rugs, while the blood congealed and hardened and collected dust and the flesh began to rot. It was horrible to think of. If only there were some way of telling the police. An anonymous letter would be too dangerous. The police would know immediately that a third person had been concerned in the affair and would not be satisfied with the simple explanation that the two men had killed each other. Then he had an idea. The main thing was to get the police to the house. Why they went was unimportant.

There was an evening paper in the rack. He took it to his table and read it through feverishly. There were two news items in it which suited his purpose. One was a report of the theft of some valuable furs from a warehouse in the Avenue de la Republique; the other was an account of the smashing of the shop window of a jeweller in the Avenue de Clichy and the escape of two men with a tray of rings.

He decided that the first would suit his purpose best, and, summoning the waiter, ordered another cognac together with writing materials. He drank the brandy at a gulp and put his gloves on. Then, taking a sheet of the letter paper, he examined it carefully. It was ordinary, cheap café notepaper. Having satisfied himself that there was no distinguishing mark of any kind on it, he wrote across the middle of it in capital letters: '*FAITES DES ENQUETES SUR CAILLÉ-3, IMPASSE DES HUITS ANGES.*' Then he tore the report of the fur robbery out of the paper, folded it inside the note and put the two in an envelope, which he addressed to the Commissaire of Police of the Seventh Arrondissement. Leaving the café, he bought a stamp at a tobacco kiosk and posted the letter.

It was not until four o'clock that morning, when he had lain awake in bed for two hours, that the nerves of his stomach succumbed at last to the strain which had been put upon them and he was sick.

Two days later a paragraph appeared in three of the Paris morning papers saying that the body of a South American named Frederik Peters, together with that of a man, at present unidentified, but believed to be a South American also, had been found in an apartment off the Rue de Rennes. Both men, the paragraph continued, had been shot and it was thought that they had killed one another in a revolver fight following a quarrel over money, a considerable sum of which was found in the apartment. It was the only reference to the affair, the attention of the public being divided at the time between a new international crisis and a hatchet murder in the suburbs.

Latimer did not see the paragraph until several days later.

Soon after nine o'clock on the morning of the day on which the police received his note, he left his hotel for the Gare de l'Est and the Orient Express. A letter had arrived for him by the first post. It had a Bulgarian stamp and a Sofia postmark and was obviously from Marukakis. He put it in his pocket unread. It was not until later in the day, when the express was racing through the hills west of Belfort, that he remembered it. He opened it and began to read:

My dear Friend,

Your letter delighted me. I was so pleased to get it. I was also a little surprised, for—forgive me, please—I did not seriously expect you to succeed in the difficult task which you had set yourself. The years bury so much of our wisdom that they are bound to bury most of our folly with it. Some time I hope to hear from you how a filly buried in Belgrade comes to be unearthed in Geneva.

I was interested in the reference to the Eurasian Credit Trust. Here is something that will interest you.

There has been recently, as you may know, a great deal of tension between this country and Yugoslavia. The Serbs, you know, have reason to feel tense. If Germany and vassal Hungary attacked her from the north, Italy attacked her through Albania from the south and by sea from the west, and Bulgaria attacked her from the east, she would be quickly finished. Her only chance would lie in the Russians outflanking the Germans and Hungarians with an attack launched through Romania along the Bukovina railway. But has Bulgaria anything to fear from Yugoslavia? Is she a danger to Bulgaria? The idea is absurd. Yet, for the past three months or four, there has been here a stream of propaganda to the effect that Yugoslavia is planning to attack Bulgaria. 'The menace across the frontier' is a typical phrase.

If such things were not so dangerous one would laugh. But one recognizes the technique. Such propaganda always begins with words but soon it proceeds to deeds. When there are no facts to support lies, facts must be made.

Two weeks ago there took place the inevitable frontier incident. Some Bulgarian peasants were fired upon by Yugoslavs (alleged to be soldiers), and one of the peasants was killed. There is much popular indignation, an outcry against the devilish Serbs. The newspaper offices are very busy. A week later the Government announces fresh purchases of anti-aircraft guns to strengthen the defences of the western Provinces. The purchases are made from a Belgian firm with the help of a loan negotiated by the Eurasian Credit Trust.

Yesterday a curious news item comes into this office.

As a result of careful investigations by the Yugoslav Government, it is shown that the four men who fired on the peasants were not Yugoslav soldiers, nor even Yugoslav subjects. They were of various nationalities and two had previously been imprisoned in Poland for terrorist activities. They had been paid to create the incident by a man about whom none of them knows anything more than that he came from Paris.

But there is more. Within an hour of that news item reaching Paris, I had instructions from the head office there to suppress the item and send out a *démenti* to all subscribers taking our French news. That is amusing, is it not? One would not have thought that such a rich organization as the Eurasian Credit Trust would be so sensitive.

As for your Dimitrios: what can one say?

A writer of plays once said that there are some situations that one cannot use on the stage; situations in which the audience can feel neither approval nor disapproval, sympathy nor antipathy; situations out of which there is no possible way that is not humiliating or distressing and from which there is no truth, however bitter, to be extracted. He was, you may say, one of those unhappy men who are confounded by the difference between the stupid vulgarities of real life and the ideal existence of the imagination. That may be. Yet, I have been wondering if, for once, I do not find myself in sympathy with him. Can one explain Dimitrios or must one turn away disgusted and defeated? I am tempted to find reason and justice in the fact that he died as violently and indecently as he lived. But that is too ingenuous a way out. It does not explain Dimitrios; it only apologizes for him. Special sorts of conditions must exist for the creation of the special sort of criminal that he typified. I have tried to define those conditions—but unsuccessfully. All I do know is that while might is right, while chaos and anarchy masquerade as order and enlightenment, those conditions will obtain.

What is the remedy? But I can see you yawning and remember that if I bore you you will not write to me again to tell me whether you are enjoying your stay in Paris, whether you have found any more Bulićs or Prevezas and whether we shall see you soon in Sofia. My latest information is that war will not break out until the spring; so there will be time for some ski-ing. Late January is quite good here. The roads are terrible, but the runs, when one gets to them, are quite good. I shall look forward eagerly to learning from you when you will come.

With my most sincere regards

N. Marukakis.

Latimer folded the letter and put it in his pocket. A good fellow,

Marukakis! He must write to him when he had the time. But just at the moment there were more important matters to be considered.

He needed, and badly, a motive, a neat method of committing a murder and an entertaining crew of suspects. Yes, the suspects must certainly be entertaining. His last book had been a trifle heavy. He must inject a little more humour into this one. As for the motive, money was always, of course, the soundest basis. A pity that Wills and life insurance were so outmoded. Supposing a man murdered an old lady so that his wife could have a private income. It might be worth thinking about. The scene? Well, there was always plenty of fun to be got out of an English country village, wasn't there? The time? Summer; with cricket matches on the village green, garden parties at the vicarage, the clink of tea-cups and the sweet smell of grass on a July evening. That was the sort of thing people liked to hear about. It was the sort of thing that he himself would like to hear about.

He looked out of the window. The sun had gone and the hills were receding slowly into the night sky. They would be slowing down for Belfort soon. Two more days to go! He ought to get some sort of a plot worked out in that time.

The train ran into a tunnel.

ERIC
AMBLER

Journey into Fear

The characters in this book are entirely imaginary, and
have no relation to any living person.

Chapter One

The steamer, *Sestri Levante*, stood high above the dock side, and the watery sleet, carried on the wind blustering down from the Black Sea, had drenched even the small shelter deck. In the after well the Turkish stevedores, with sacking tied round their shoulders, were still loading cargo.

Graham saw the steward carry his suitcase through a door marked PASSEGGIERI, and turned aside to see if the two men who had shaken hands with him at the foot of the gangway were still there. They had not come aboard lest the uniform of one of them should draw attention to him. Now they were walking away across the crane lines towards the warehouses and the dock gates beyond. As they reached the shelter of the first shed they looked back. He raised his left arm and saw an answering wave. They walked on out of sight.

For a moment he stood there shivering and staring out at the mist that shrouded the domes and spires of Istanbul. Behind the rumble and clatter of the winches, the Turkish foreman was shouting plaintively in bad Italian to one of the ship's officers. Graham remembered that he had been told to go to his cabin and stay there until the ship sailed. He followed the steward through the door.

The man was waiting for him at the head of a short flight of stairs. There was no sign of any of the nine other passengers.

'*Cinque, signore?*'

'Yes.'

'*Da queste parte.*'

Graham followed him below.

Number five was a small cabin with a single bunk, a combined wardrobe and washing cabinet, and only just enough floor space left over to take him and his suit-case. The port-hole fittings were caked with verdigris, and there was a strong smell of paint. The steward man-handled the suit-case under the bunk, and squeezed out into the alley-way.

'*Favorisca di darmi il suo biglietto ed il suo passaporto, signore. Li portero al Commissario.*'

Graham gave him the ticket and passport, and, pointing to the port-hole, made the motions of unscrewing and opening it.

The steward said, '*Subito, signore,*' and went away.

Graham sat down wearily on the bunk. It was the first time for nearly twenty-four hours that he had been left alone to think. He took his right hand carefully out of his overcoat pocket, and looked at the bandages swathed round it. It throbbed and ached abominably. If that was what a bullet graze felt like, he thanked his stars that the bullet had not really hit him.

He looked round the cabin, accepting his presence in it as he had accepted so many other absurdities since he had returned to his hotel in Pera the night before. The acceptance was unquestioning. He felt only as if he had lost something valuable. In fact, he had lost nothing of any value but a sliver of skin and cartilage from the back of his right hand. All that had happened to him was that he had discovered the fear of death.

By the husbands of his wife's friends, Graham was considered lucky. He had a highly paid job with a big armaments manufacturing concern, a pleasant house in the country an hour's drive from his office, and a wife whom everyone liked. Not that he didn't deserve it all. He was, though you would never think it to look at him, a brilliant engineer; quite an important one if some of the things you heard were true; something to do with guns. He went abroad a good deal on business. He was a quiet, likeable sort of chap, and generous with his whisky. You couldn't, of course, imagine yourself getting to know him very well (it was hard to say which was worse—his golf or his bridge), but he was always friendly. Nothing effusive; just friendly; a bit like an expensive dentist trying to take your mind off things. He looked rather like an expensive dentist, too, when you came to think of it: thin and slightly stooping, with well-cut clothes, a good smile, and hair going a bit grey. But if it was difficult to imagine a woman like Stephanie marrying him for anything except his salary, you had to admit that they got on extraordinarily well together. It only went to show . . .

Graham himself also thought that he was lucky. From his father, a diabetic schoolmaster, he had inherited, at the age of seventeen, an easy-going disposition, five hundred pounds in cash from a life insurance policy and a good mathematical brain. The first legacy had enabled him to endure without resentment the ministrations of a reluctant and cantankerous guardian; the second had made it possible for him to use the scholarship he had won to a university; the third resulted in his securing in his middle twenties a science doctorate. The subject of his thesis had been a problem in ballistics, and an abridged version of it had appeared in a technical journal. By the time he was thirty he was in charge of one of his employers' experimental departments, and a little surprised that he should be paid so much money for doing something he liked doing. That same year he had married Stephanie.

It never occurred to him to doubt that his attitude towards his wife was that of any other man towards a wife to whom he has been married for ten years. He had married her because he had been tired of living in furnished rooms, and had assumed (correctly) that she had married him to get away from her father—a disagreeable and impecunious doctor. He was pleased by her good looks, her good humour, and her capacity for keeping servants and making friends; and if he sometimes found the friends tiresome, was inclined to blame himself rather than them. She, on her part, accepted the fact that he was more interested in his work than in anyone or anything else as a matter of course and without resentment. She liked her life exactly as it was. They lived in an atmosphere of good-natured affection and mutual tolerance, and thought their marriage as successful as one could reasonably expect a marriage to be.

The outbreak of war in September 1939 had little effect on the Graham household. Having spent the previous two years with the certain knowledge that such an outbreak was as inevitable as the going down of the sun, Graham was neither astonished nor dismayed when it occurred. He had calculated to a nicety its probable effects on his private life, and by October he was able to conclude that his calculations had been correct. For him, the war meant more work; but that was all. It touched neither his economic nor his personal security. He could not, under any circumstances, become liable for combatant military service. The chances of a German bomber unloading its cargo anywhere near either his house or his office were remote enough to be disregarded. When he learned, just three weeks after the signing of the Anglo-Turkish treaty of alliance, that he was to go to Turkey on company business, he was troubled only by the dismal prospect of spending Christmas away from home.

He had been thirty-two when he had made his first business trip abroad. It had been a success. His employers had discovered that, in addition to his scientific ability, he had the faculty, unusual in a man with his particular qualifications, of making himself amiable to—and liked by—foreign government officials. In the years that followed, occasional trips abroad had become part of his working life. He enjoyed them. He liked the actual business of getting to a strange city almost as much as he liked discovering its strangeness. He liked meeting men of other nationalities, learning smatterings of their languages, and being appalled at his lack of understanding of both. He had acquired a wholesome dislike of the word 'typical.'

Towards the middle of November, he reached Istanbul, by train from Paris, and left it almost immediately for Izmir and, later, Gallipoli. By the end of December he had finished his work in those two places, and on the first of January took a train back to Istanbul, the starting point of his journey home.

He had had a trying six weeks. His job had been a difficult one made more difficult by his having to discuss highly technical subjects through interpreters. The horror of the Anatolian earthquake disaster had upset him nearly as much as it had upset his hosts. Finally, the train service from Gallipoli to Istanbul had been disorganized by floods. By the time he arrived back in Istanbul he was feeling tired and depressed.

He was met at the station by Kopeikin, the company's representative in Turkey.

Kopeikin had arrived in Istanbul with sixty-five thousand other Russian refugees in nineteen twenty-four, and had been, by turns, card-sharper, part owner of a brothel, and army clothing contractor before he had secured—the Managing Director alone knew how—the lucrative agency he now held. Graham liked him. He was a plump, exuberant man with large projecting ears, irrepressible high spirits, and a vast fund of low cunning.

He wrung Graham's hand enthusiastically. 'Have you had a bad trip? I am so sorry. It is good to see you back again. How did you get on with Fethi?'

'Very well, I think. I imagined something much worse from your description of him.'

'My dear fellow, you underrate your charm of manner. He is known to be difficult. But he is important. Now everything will go smoothly. But we will talk business over a drink. I have engaged a room for you–a room with a bath, at the Adler Palace, as before. For to-night I have arranged a farewell dinner. The expense is mine.'

'It's very good of you.'

'A great pleasure, my dear fellow. Afterwards we will amuse ourselves a little. There is a box that is very popular at the moment–Le Jockey Cabaret. You will like it, I think. It is very nicely arranged, and the people who go there are quite nice. No riff-raff. Is this your luggage?'

Graham's heart sank. He had expected to have dinner with Kopeikin, but he had been promising himself that about ten o'clock he would have a hot bath and go to bed with a Tauchnitz detective story. The last thing he wanted to do was to 'amuse' himself at Le Jockey Cabaret, or any other night place. He said, as they followed the porter out to Kopeikin's car: 'I think that perhaps I ought to get to bed early to-night, Kopeikin. I've got four nights in a train in front of me.'

'My dear fellow, it will do you good to be late. Besides, your train does not go until eleven to-morrow morning, and I have reserved a sleeper for you. You can sleep all the way to Paris if you feel tired.'

Over dinner at the Pera Palace Hotel, Kopeikin gave war news. For him, the Soviets were still 'the July assassins' of Nicholas the Second, and Graham heard much of Finnish victories and Russian defeats. The Germans had sunk more British ships and lost more submarines. The Dutch, the Danes, the Swedes and the Norwegians were looking to their defences. The world awaited a bloody spring. They went on to talk about the earthquake. It was half-past ten when Kopeikin announced that it was time for them to leave for Le Jockey Cabaret.

It was in the Beyoglu quarter; just off the Grande Rue de Pera, and in a street of buildings obviously designed by a French architect of the middle nineteen twenties. Kopeikin took his arm affectionately as they went in.

'It is a very nice place, this,' he said. 'Serge, the proprietor, is a friend of mine, so they will not cheat us. I will introduce you to him.'

For the man he was, Graham's knowledge of the night life of cities was surprisingly extensive. For some reason, the nature of which he could never discover, his foreign hosts always seemed to consider that the only form of entertainment acceptable to an English engineer was that to be found in the rather less reputable *Nachtlokalen*. He had been in such places in Buenos Ayres and in Madrid, in Valparaiso and in Bucharest, in Rome and in Mexico; and he could not remember one that was very much different from any of the others. He could remember the business acquaintances with whom he had sat far into the early morning hours drinking outrageously expensive drinks; but the places themselves had merged in his mind's eye into one prototypical picture of a smoke-filled basement room with a platform for the band at one end, a small space for dancing surrounded by tables, and a bar with stools, where the drinks were alleged to be cheaper, to one side.

He did not expect Le Jockey Cabaret to be any different. It was not.

The mural decorations seemed to have caught the spirit of the street outside. They consisted of a series of immense vorticisms involving sky-scrapers, coloured saxophone players, green all-seeing eyes, telephones, Easter Island masks, and ash-blond hermaphrodites with long cigarette holders. The place was crowded and very noisy. Serge was a sharp-featured Russian with bristly grey hair and the air of one whose feelings were constantly on the point of getting the better of his judgment. To Graham, looking at his eyes, it seemed unlikely that they ever did: but he greeted them graciously enough, and showed them to a table beside the dance floor. Kopeikin ordered a bottle of brandy.

The band brought an American dance tune, which they had been playing with painful zeal, to an abrupt end and began, with more success, to play a rumba.

'It is very gay here,' said Kopeikin. 'Would you like to dance? There are plenty of girls. Say which you fancy and I will speak to Serge.'

'Oh, don't bother. I really don't think I ought to stay long.'

'You must stop thinking about your journey. Drink some more brandy and you will feel better.' He got to his feet. 'I shall dance now and find a nice girl for you.'

Graham felt guilty. He should, he knew, be displaying more enthusiasm. Kopeikin was, after all, being extraordinarily kind. It could be no pleasure for him to try to entertain a train-weary Englishman who would have preferred to be in bed. He drank some more brandy determinedly. More people were arriving. He saw Serge greet them warmly and then, when their backs were turned, issue a furtive instruction to the waiter who was to serve them: a drab little reminder that Le Jockey Cabaret was in business neither for his own pleasure nor for theirs. He turned his head to watch Kopeikin dancing.

The girl was thin and dark and had very big teeth. Her red satin evening dress drooped on her as if it had been made for a bigger woman. She smiled a great deal. Kopeikin held her slightly away from him and talked all the time they were dancing. To Graham, he seemed, despite the grossness of his body, to be the only man on the floor who was completely self-possessed. He was the ex-brothel-proprietor dealing with something he understood perfectly. When the music stopped he brought the girl over to their table.

'This is Maria,' he said. 'She is an Arab. You would not think it to look at her, would you?'

'No, you wouldn't.'

'She speaks a little French.'

'*Enchanté, Mademoiselle.*'

'*Monsieur.*' Her voice was unexpectedly harsh, but her smile was pleasant. She was obviously good natured.

'Poor child!' Kopeikin's tone was that of a governess who hoped that her charge would not disgrace her before visitors. 'She has only just recovered from a sore throat. But she is a very nice girl and has good manners. *Assieds-toi*, Maria.'

She sat down beside Graham. '*Je prends du champagne*,' she said.

'*Oui, oui, mon enfant. Plus tard*,' said Kopeikin vaguely. 'She gets extra commission if we order champagne,' he remarked to Graham, and poured out some brandy for her.

She took it without comment, raised it to her lips, and said, '*Skal!*'

'She thinks you are a Swede,' said Kopeikin.

'Why?'

'She likes Swedes, so I said you were a Swede.' He chuckled. 'You cannot say that the Turkish agent does nothing for the company.'

She had been listening to them with an uncomprehending smile. Now, the music began again and, turning to Graham, she asked him if he would like to dance.

She danced well; well enough for him to feel that he, too, was dancing well. He felt less depressed and asked her to dance again. The second time she pressed her thin body hard against him. He saw a grubby shoulder strap begin to work its way out from under the red satin and smelt the heat of her body behind the scent she used. He found that he was getting tired of her.

She began to talk. Did he know Istanbul well? Had he been there before? Did he know Paris? And London? He was lucky. She had never been to those places. She hoped to go to them. And to Stockholm, too. Had he many friends in Istanbul? She asked because there was a gentleman who had come in just after him and his friend who seemed to know him. This gentleman kept looking at him.

Graham had been wondering how soon he could get away. He realized suddenly that she was waiting for him to say something. His mind had caught her last remark.

'Who keeps looking at me?'

'We cannot see him now. The gentleman is sitting at the bar.'

'No doubt he's looking at you.' There seemed nothing else to say.

But she was evidently serious. 'It is in you that he is interested, Monsieur. It is the one with the handkerchief in his hand.'

They had reached a point on the floor from which he could see the bar. The man was sitting on a stool with a glass of vermouth in front of him.

He was a short, thin man with a stupid face: very bony with large nostrils, prominent cheekbones, and full lips pressed together as if he had sore gums or were trying to keep his temper. He was intensely pale and his small, deep-set eyes and thinning, curly hair seemed in consequence darker than they were. The hair was plastered in streaks across his skull. He wore a crumpled brown suit with lumpy padded shoulders, a soft shirt with an almost invisible collar, and a new grey tie. As Graham watched him he wiped his upper lip with the handkerchief as if the heat of the place were making him sweat.

'He doesn't seem to be looking at me now,' Graham said. 'Anyway, I don't know him, I'm afraid.'

'I did not think so, Monsieur.' She pressed his arm to her side with her elbow. 'But I wished to be sure. I do not know him either, but I know the type. You are a stranger here, Monsieur, and you perhaps have money in your pocket. Istanbul is not like Stockholm. When such types look at you more than once, it is advisable to be careful. You are strong, but a knife in the back is the same for a strong man as for a small one.'

Her solemnity was ludicrous. He laughed; but he looked again at the man by the bar. He was sipping at his vermouth; an inoffensive creature. The girl was probably trying, rather clumsily, to demonstrate that her own intentions were good.

He said: 'I don't think that I need worry.'

She relaxed the pressure on his arm. 'Perhaps not, Monsieur.' She seemed suddenly to lose interest in the subject. The band stopped and they returned to the table.

'She dances very nicely, doesn't she?' said Kopeikin.

'Very.'

She smiled at them, sat down and finished her drink as if she were thirsty. Then she sat back. 'We are three,' she said and counted round with one finger to make sure they understood; 'would you like me to bring a friend of mine to have a drink with us? She is very sympathetic. She is my greatest friend.'

'Later, perhaps,' said Kopeikin. He poured her out another drink.

At that moment the band played a resounding 'chord-on' and most of the lights went out. A spotlight quivered on the floor in front of the platform.

'The *attractions*,' said Maria. 'It is very good.'

Serge stepped into the spotlight and pattered off a long announcement in Turkish which ended in a flourish of the hand towards a door beside the platform. Two dark young men in pale blue dinner jackets promptly dashed out on to the floor and proceeded to do an energetic tap dance. They were soon breathless and their hair became dishevelled, but the applause, when they had finished, was lukewarm. Then they put on false beards and, pretending to be old men, did some tumbling. The audience was only slightly more enthusiastic. They retired, rather angrily Graham thought, dripping with perspiration. They were followed by a handsome coloured woman with long thin legs who proved to be a contortionist. Her contortions were ingeniously obscene and evoked gusts of laughter. In response to shouts, she followed her contortions with a snake dance. This was not so successful, as the snake, produced from a gilt wicker crate as cautiously as if it had been a fully grown cobra, proved to be a small and rather senile python with a tendency to fall asleep in its mistress's hands. It was finally bundled back into its crate while she did some more contortions. When she had gone, the proprietor stepped once more into the spotlight and made an announcement that was greeted with clapping.

The girl put her lips to Graham's ear. 'It is Josette and her partner, José. They are dancers from Paris. This is their last night here. They have had a great success.'

The spotlight became pink and swept to the entrance door. There was a roll of drums. Then, as the band struck up the Blue Danube waltz, the dancers glided on to the floor.

For the weary Graham, their dance was as much a part of the cellar convention as the bar and the platform for the band: it was something to justify the prices of the drinks: a demonstration of the fact that, by applying the laws of classical mechanics, one small, unhealthy looking man with a broad sash round his waist could handle an eight stone woman as if she were a child. Josette and her partner were remarkable only in that, although they carried out the standard 'speciality' routine rather less efficiently than usual they managed to do so with considerably more effect.

She was a slim woman with beautiful arms and shoulders and a mass of gleaming fair hair. Her heavily lidded eyes, almost closed as she danced, and the rather full lips, fixed in a theatrical half-smile, contradicted in a curious way the swift neatness of her movements. Graham saw that she was not a dancer but a woman who had been trained to dance and who did so with a sort of indolent sensuality, conscious of her young-looking body, her long legs, and the muscles below the smooth surfaces of her thighs and stomach. If her performance did not succeed as a dancer, as an *attraction* at Le Jockey Cabaret it succeeded perfectly and in spite of her partner.

He was a dark, preoccupied man with tight, disagreeable lips, a smooth sallow face, and an irritating way of sticking his tongue hard in his cheek as he prepared to exert himself. He moved badly and was clumsy, his fingers shifting uncertainly as he grasped her for the lifts as if he were uncertain of the point of balance. He was constantly steadying himself.

But the audience was not looking at him, and when they had finished called loudly for an encore. It was given. The band played another 'chord-on.' Mademoiselle Josette took a bow and was presented with a bouquet of flowers by Serge. She returned several times and bowed and kissed her hand.

'She is quite charming, isn't she?' Kopeikin said in English as the lights went up. 'I promised you that this place was amusing.'

'She's quite good. But it's a pity about the moth-eaten Valentino.'

'José? He does very well for himself. Would you like to have her to the table for a drink?'

'Very much. But won't it be rather expensive?'

'Gracious no! She does not get commission.'

'Will she come?'

'Of course. The *patron* introduced me. I know her well. You might take to her, I think. This Arab is a little stupid. No doubt Josette is stupid, too, but she is very attractive in her way. If I had not learned too much when I was too young, I should like her myself.'

Maria stared after him as he went across the floor, and remained silent for a moment. Then she said: 'He is very good, that friend of yours.'

Graham was not quite sure whether it was a statement, a question, or a feeble attempt to make conversation. He nodded. 'Very good.'

She smiled. 'He knows the proprietor well. If you desire it, he will ask Serge to let me go when you wish instead of when the place closes.'

He smiled as regretfully as he could. 'I'm afraid, Maria, that I have to pack my luggage and catch a train in the morning.'

She smiled again. 'It does not matter. But I specially like the Swedes. May I have some more brandy, Monsieur?'

'Of course.' He refilled her glass.

She drank half of it. 'Do you like Mademoiselle Josette?'

'She dances very well.'

'She is very sympathetic. That is because she has a success. When people have a success they are sympathetic. José, nobody likes. He is a Spaniard from Morocco, and very jealous. They are all the same. I do not know how she stands him.'

'I thought you said they were Parisians.'

'They have danced in Paris. She is from Hungary. She speaks languages–German, Spanish, English–but not Swedish, I think. She has had many rich lovers.' She paused. 'Are you a business man, Monsieur?'

'No, an engineer.' He realised, with some amusement, that Maria was less stupid than she seemed, and that she knew exactly why Kopeikin had left them. He was being warned, indirectly but unmistakably, that Mademoiselle Josette was very expensive, that communication with her would be difficult, and that he would have a jealous Spaniard to deal with.

She drained her glass again, and stared vaguely in the direction of the bar. 'My friend is looking very lonely,' she said. She turned her head and looked directly at him. 'Will you give me a hundred piastres, Monsieur?'

'What for?'

'A tip, Monsieur.' She smiled, but in not quite so friendly a fashion as before.

He gave her a hundred piastre note. She folded it up, put it in her bag, and stood up. 'Will you excuse me, please. I wish to speak to my friend. I will come back if you wish.' She smiled.

He saw her red satin dress disappear in the crowd gathered round the bar. Kopeikin returned almost immediately.

'Where is the Arab?'

'She's gone to speak to her best friend. I gave her a hundred piastres.'

'A hundred! Fifty would have been plenty. But perhaps it is as well. Josette asks us to have a drink with her in her dressing-room. She is leaving Istanbul to-morrow, and does not wish to come out here. She will have to speak to so many people, and she has packing to do.'

'Won't we be rather a nuisance?'

'My dear fellow, she is anxious to meet you. She saw you while she was dancing.

'When I told her that you were an Englishman, she was delighted. We can leave these drinks here.'

Mademoiselle Josette's dressing-room was a space about eight feet square, partitioned off from the other half of what appeared to be the proprietor's office by a brown curtain. The three solid walls were covered with faded pink wall-paper with stripes of blue; and there were greasy patches here and there where people had leaned against them. The room contained two bent-wood chairs and two rickety dressing-tables littered with cream jars and dirty make-up towels. There was a mixed smell of stale cigarette smoke, face powder, and damp upholstery.

As they went in in response to a grunt of '*Entrez*' from the partner, José, he got up from his dressing-table. Still wiping the grease paint from his face, he walked out without a glance at them. For some reason, Kopeikin winked at Graham. Josette was leaning forward in her chair dabbing intently at one of her eyebrows with a swab of damp cotton-wool. She had discarded her costume, and put on a rose velvet house-coat. Her hair hung down loosely about her head as if she had shaken it out and brushed it. It was really, Graham thought, very beautiful hair. She began to speak in slow, careful English, punctuating the words with dabs.

'Please excuse me. It is this filthy paint. It . . . *Merde!*'

She threw the swab down impatiently, stood up suddenly, and turned to face them.

In the hard light of the unshaded bulb above her head she looked smaller than she had looked on the dance floor; and a trifle haggard. Graham, thinking of his Stephanie's rather buxom good looks, reflected that the woman before him would probably be quite plain in ten years' time. He was in the habit of comparing other women with his wife. As a method of disguising from himself the fact that other women still interested him, it was usually effective. But Josette was unusual. What she might look like in ten years' time was altogether beside the point. At that moment she was a very attractive, self-possessed woman with a soft, smiling mouth, slightly protuberant blue eyes, and a sleepy vitality that seemed to fill the room.

'This, my dear Josette,' said Kopeikin, 'is Mr Graham.'

'I enjoyed your dancing very much, Mademoiselle,' he said.

'So Kopeikin told me.' She shrugged. 'It could be better, I think, but it is very good of you to say that you like it. It is nonsense to say that Englishmen are not polite.' She flourished her hand round the room. 'I do not like to ask you to sit down in this filth, but please try to make yourself comfortable. There is José's chair for Kopeikin, and if you could push José's things away, the corner of his table will be for you. It is too bad that we cannot sit together in comfort outside, but there are so many of these men who make some *chi-chi* if one does not stop and drink some of their champagne. The champagne here is filthy. I do not wish to leave Istanbul with a headache. How long do you stay here, Mr Graham?'

'I, too, leave to-morrow.' She amused him. Her posturing was absurd. Within the space of a minute she had been a great actress receiving wealthy suitors, a friendly woman of the world, and a disillusioned genius of the dance. Every movement, every piece of affectation was calculated: it was as if she were still dancing.

Now she became a serious student of affairs. 'It is terrible, this travelling. And you go back to your war. I am sorry. These filthy Nazis. It is such a pity that there must be wars. And if it is not wars, it is earthquakes. Always death. It is so bad for business. I am not interested in death. Kopeikin is, I think. Perhaps it is because he is a Russian.'

'I think nothing of death,' said Kopeikin. 'I am concerned only that the waiter shall bring the drinks I ordered. Will you have a cigarette?'

'Please, yes. The waiters here are filthy. There must be much better places than this in London, Mr Graham.'

'The waiters there are very bad, too. Waiters are, I think, mostly very bad. But I should have thought you had been to London. Your English . . .'

Her smile tolerated his indiscretion, the depths of which he could not know. As well to have asked the Pompadour who had paid her bills. 'I learned it from an American and in Italy. I have a great sympathy for Americans. They are so clever in business, and yet so generous and sincere. I think it is most important to be sincere. Was it amusing dancing with that little Maria, Mr Graham?'

'She dances very well. She seems to admire you very much. She says that you have a great success. You do, of course.'

'A great success! Here?' The disillusioned genius raised her eyebrows. 'I hope you gave her a good tip, Mr Graham.'

'He gave her twice as much as was necessary,' said Kopeikin. 'Ah, here are the drinks!'

They talked for a time about people whom Graham did not know, and about the war. He saw that behind her posturing she was quick and shrewd, and wondered if the American in Italy had ever regretted his 'sincerity.' After a while Kopeikin raised his glass.

'I drink,' he said pompously, 'to your two journeys.' He lowered his glass suddenly without drinking. 'No, it is absurd,' he said, irritable. 'My heart is not in the toast. I cannot help thinking that it is a pity that there should be two journeys. You are both going to Paris. You are both friends of mine, and so you have'–he patted his stomach–'much in common.'

Graham smiled, trying not to look startled. She was certainly very attractive, and it was pleasant to sit facing her as he was; but the idea that the acquaintance might be extended had simply not occurred to him. He was confused by it. He saw that she was watching him with amusement in her eyes, and had an uncomfortable feeling that she knew exactly what was passing through his mind.

He put the best face on the situation that he could. 'I was hoping to suggest the same thing. I think you should have left me to suggest it, Kopeikin. Mademoiselle will wonder if I am as sincere as an American.' He smiled at her. 'I am leaving by the eleven o'clock train.'

'And in the first class, Mr Graham?'

'Yes.'

She put out her cigarette. 'Then there are two obvious reasons why we cannot travel together. I am not leaving by that train and, in any case, I travel in the second class. It is perhaps just as well. José would wish to play cards with you all the way, and you would lose your money.'

There was no doubt that she expected them to finish their drinks and go. Graham felt oddly disappointed. He would have liked to stay. He knew, besides, that he had behaved awkwardly.

'Perhaps,' he said, 'we could meet in Paris.'

'Perhaps.' She stood up and smiled kindly at him. 'I shall stay at the Hotel des Belges near Trinité, if it is still open. I shall hope to meet you again. Kopeikin tells me that as an engineer you are very well known.'

'Kopeikin exaggerates–just as he exaggerated when he said that we should not hinder you and your partner in your packing. I hope you have a pleasant journey.'

'It has been so good to meet you. It was so kind of you, Kopeikin, to bring Mr Graham to see me.'

'It was his idea,' said Kopeikin. 'Goodbye, my dear Josette, and *bon voyage*. We should like to stay, but it is late, and I insist on Mr Graham getting some sleep. He would stay talking until he missed the train if I permitted it.'

She laughed. 'You are very nice, Kopeikin. When I come next to Istanbul, I shall tell you first. *Au 'voir*, Mr Graham, and *bon voyage*.' She held out her hand.

'The Hotel des Belges near Trinité,' he said. 'I shall remember.' He spoke very little less than the truth. During the ten minutes that his taxi would take to get from the Gare de l'Est to the Gare St Lazare, he probably would remember.

She pressed his fingers gently. 'I'm sure you will,' she said. '*Au 'voir*, Kopeikin. You know the way?'

'I think,' said Kopeikin, as they waited for their bill, 'I think that I am a little disappointed in you, my dear fellow. You made an excellent impression. She was yours for the asking. You had only to ask her the time of her train.'

'I am quite sure that I made no impression at all. Frankly, she embarrassed me. I don't understand women of that sort.'

'That sort of woman, as you put it, likes a man who is embarrassed by her. Your diffidence was charming.'

'Heavens! Anyway, I said that I would see her in Paris.'

'My dear fellow, she knows perfectly well that you have not the smallest intention of seeing her in Paris. It is a pity. She is, I know, quite particular. You were lucky, and you chose to ignore the fact.'

'Good gracious, man, you seem to forget that I'm a married man!'

Kopeikin threw up his hands. 'The English point of view! One cannot reason; one can only stand amazed.' He sighed profoundly. 'Here comes the bill.'

On their way out they passed Maria sitting at the bar with her best friend, a mournful-looking Turkish girl. They received a smile. Graham noticed that the man in the crumpled brown suit had gone.

It was cold in the street. A wind was beginning to moan through the telephone wires bracketed on the wall. At three o'clock in the morning the city of Sulyman the Magnificent was like a railway station after the last train had gone.

'We shall be having snow,' said Kopeikin. 'Your hotel is quite near. We will walk if you like. It is to be hoped,' he went on as they began to walk, 'that you will miss the snow on your journey. Last year there was a Simplon Orient express delayed for three days near Salonika.'

'I shall take a bottle of brandy with me.'

'Kopeikin grunted. 'Still, I do not envy you the journey. I think perhaps I am getting old. Besides, travelling at this time . . .'

'Oh, I'm a good traveller. I don't get bored easily.'

'I was not thinking of boredom. So many unpleasant things can happen in war time.'

'I suppose so.'

Kopeikin buttoned up his overcoat collar. 'To give you only one example . . .

'During the last war an Austrian friend of mine was returning to Berlin from Zürich, where he had been doing some business. He sat in the train with a man who said that he was a Swiss from Lugano. They talked a lot on the journey. This Swiss told my friend about his wife and his children, his business, and his home. He seemed a very nice man. But soon after they had crossed the frontier, the train stopped at a small station and soldiers came on with police. They arrested the Swiss. My friend had also to leave the train as he was with the Swiss. He was not alarmed. His papers were in order. He was a good Austrian. But the man from Lugano was terrified. He turned very pale and cried like a child. They told my friend afterwards that the man was not a Swiss but an Italian spy and that he would be shot. My friend was upset. You see, one can always tell when a man is speaking about something he loves, and there was no doubt that all that this man had said about his wife and children was true: all except one thing—they were in Italy instead of Switzerland. War,' he added solemnly, 'is unpleasant.'

'Quite so.' They had stopped outside the Adler Palace Hotel. 'Will you come in for a drink?'

Kopeikin shook his head. 'It is kind of you to suggest it, but you must get some sleep. I feel guilty now at having kept you out so late, but I have enjoyed our evening together.'

'So have I. I'm very grateful to you.'

'A great pleasure. No farewells now. I shall take you to the station in the morning. Can you be ready by ten?'

'Easily.'

'Then good night, my dear fellow.'

'Good night, Kopeikin.'

Graham went inside, stopped at the hall porter's desk for his key and to tell the night porter to call him at eight. Then, as the power for the lift was switched off at night, he climbed wearily up the stairs to his room on the second floor.

It was at the end of the corridor. He put the key in the lock, turned it, pushed the door open and, with his right hand, felt along the wall for the light switch.

The next moment there was a splinter of flame in the darkness and an ear-splitting detonation. A piece of plaster from the wall beside him stung his cheek. Before he could move or even think, the flame and the noise came again and it seemed as if a bar of hot-white metal had been suddenly pressed against the back of his hand. He cried out with pain and stumbled forward out of the light from the corridor into the darkness of his room. Another shot scattered plaster behind him.

There was silence. He was half leaning, half crouching against the wall by the bed, his ears singing from the din of the explosions. He was dimly aware that the window was open and that someone was moving by it. His hand seemed to be numb, but he could feel blood beginning to trickle between his fingers.

He remained motionless, his heart hammering at his head. The air reeked of cordite. Then, as his eyes became used to the darkness, he saw that whoever had been at the window had left by it.

There would, he knew, be another light switch beside the bed. With his left hand he fumbled along the wall towards it. Then his hand touched the telephone. Hardly knowing what he was doing, he picked it up.

He heard a click as the night porter plugged in at the switchboard.

'Room thirty-six,' he said and was surprised to find that he was shouting. 'Something has happened. I need help.'

He put the telephone down, blundered towards the bathroom and switched on the light there. The blood was pouring from a great gash across the back of his hand. Through the waves of nausea flowing from his stomach to his head, he could hear doors being flung open and excited voices in the corridor. Someone started hammering at the door.

Chapter Two

The stevedores had finished loading and were battening down. One winch was still working but it was hoisting the steel bearers into place. The bulkhead against which Graham was leaning vibrated as they thudded into their sockets. Another passenger had come aboard and the steward had shown him to a cabin farther along the alleyway. The newcomer had a low, grumbling voice and had addressed the steward in hesitant Italian.

Graham stood up and with his unbandaged hand fumbled in his pocket for a cigarette. He was beginning to find the cabin oppressive. He looked at his watch. The ship would not be sailing for another hour. He wished he had asked Kopeikin to come aboard with him. He tried to think of his wife in England, to picture her sitting with her friends having tea; but it was as if someone behind him were holding a stereoscope to his mind's eyes; someone who was steadily sliding picture after picture between him and the rest of his life to cut him off from it; pictures of Kopeikin and Le Jockey Cabaret, of Maria and the man in the crumpled suit, of Josette and her partner, of stabbing flames in a sea of darkness and of pale, frightened faces in the hotel corridor. He had not known then what he knew now, what he learnt in the cold, beastly dawn that had followed. The whole thing had seemed different then: unpleasant, decidedly unpleasant, but reasonable, accountable. Now he felt as if a doctor had told him that he was suffering from some horrible and deadly disease; as if he had become part of a different world, a world of which he knew nothing but that it was detestable.

The hand holding the match to his cigarette was trembling. 'What I need,' he thought, 'is sleep.'

As the waves of nausea subsided and he stood there in the bathroom, shivering, sounds began once more to penetrate the blanket of cotton wool that seemed to have enveloped his brain. There was a sort of irregular thudding coming from a long distance. He realised that someone was still knocking at the bedroom door.

He wrapped a face towel round his hand, went back into the bedroom and switched on the light. As he did so, the knocking ceased and there was a clinking of metal. Someone had got a pass key. The door burst open.

It was the night porter who came in first, blinking round uncertainly. Behind him in the corridor were the people from the neighbouring rooms, drawing back now for fear of seeing what they hoped to see. A small, dark man in a red dressing-gown over blue striped pyjamas pushed past the night porter. Graham recognized the man who had shown him to his room.

'There were shots,' he began in French. Then he saw Graham's hand and went white. 'I . . . You are wounded. You are . . .'

Graham sat down on the bed. 'Not seriously. If you will send for a doctor to bandage my hand properly, I will tell you what has happened. But first: the man who fired the shots left through the window. You might try and catch him. What is below the window?'

'But . . .' began the man shrilly. He stopped, visibly pulling himself together. Then he turned to the night porter and said something in Turkish. The porter went out, shutting the door behind him. There was a burst of excited chatter from outside.

'The next thing,' said Graham, 'is to send for the manager.'

'Pardon, Monsieur, he has been sent for. I am the Assistant Manager.' He wrung his hands. 'What has happened? Your hand, Monsieur. . . . But the doctor will be here immediately.'

'Good. You'd better know what happened. I have been out this evening with a friend. I returned a few minutes ago. As I opened the door here, someone standing there just inside the window fired three shots at me. The second one hit my hand. The other two hit the wall. I heard him moving but I did not see his face. I imagine that he was a thief and that my unexpected return disturbed him.'

'It is an outrage!' said the Assistant Manager hotly. His face changed. 'A thief! Has anything been stolen, Monsieur?'

'I haven't looked. My suitcase is over there. It was locked.'

The Assistant Manager hurried across the room and went down on his knees beside the suitcase. 'It is still locked,' he reported with a sigh of relief.

Graham fumbled in his pocket. 'Here are the keys. You'd better open it.'

The man obeyed. Graham glanced at the contents of the case. 'It has not been touched.'

'A blessing!' He hesitated. He was obviously thinking fast. 'You say that your hand is not seriously hurt, Monsieur?'

'I don't think it is.'

'It is a great relief. When the shots were heard, Monsieur, we feared an unbelievable horror. You may imagine. . . . But this is bad enough.' He went to the window and looked out. 'The pig! He must have escaped through the gardens immediately. Useless to search for him.' He shrugged despairingly. 'He is gone now, and there is nothing to be done. I need not tell you, Monsieur, how profoundly we regret that this thing should happen to you in the Adler Palace. Never before has such a thing happened here.' He hesitated again and then went on quickly: 'Naturally, Monsieur, we shall do everything in our power to alleviate the distress which has been caused to you. I have told the porter to bring some whisky for you when he has telephoned for the doctor. English whisky! We have a special supply. Happily, nothing has been stolen. We could not, of course, have forseen that an accident of such a kind should happen; but we shall ourselves see that the best medical attention is given. And there will, of course, be no question of any charge for your stay here. But . . .'

'But you don't want to call in the police and involve the hotel. Is that it?'

The Assistant Manager smiled nervously. 'No good can be done, Monsieur. The police would merely ask questions and make inconveniences for all.' Inspiration came to him. 'For *all*, Monsieur,' he repeated emphatically. 'You are a business man. You wish to leave Istanbul this morning. But if the police are brought in, it might be difficult. There would be, inevitably, delays. And for what purpose?'

'They might catch the man who shot me.'

'But how, Monsieur? You did not see his face. You cannot identify him. There is nothing stolen by which he could be traced.'

Graham hesitated. 'But what about this doctor you are getting? Supposing he reports to the police the fact that there is someone here with a bullet wound.'

'The doctor's services, Monsieur, will be paid for liberally by the management.'

There was a knock at the door and the porter came in with whisky, soda-water, and glasses which he set down on the table. He said something to the Assistant Manager who nodded and then motioned him out.

'The doctor is on his way, Monsieur.'

'Very well. No, I don't want any whisky. But drink some yourself. You look as though you need it. I should like to make a telephone call. Will you tell the porter to telephone the Crystal Apartments in the rue d'Italie? The number is forty-four, nine hundred and seven, I think. I want to speak to Monsieur Kopeikin.'

'Certainly, Monsieur. Anything you wish.' He went to the door and called after the porter. There was another incomprehensible exchange. The Assistant Manager came back and helped himself generously to the whisky.

'I think,' he said, returning to the charge, 'that you are wise not to invoke the police, Monsieur. Nothing has been stolen. Your injury is not serious. There will be no trouble. It is thus and thus with the police here, you understand.'

'I haven't yet decided what to do,' snapped Graham. His head was aching violently and his hand was beginning to throb. He was getting tired of the Assistant Manager.

The telephone bell rang. He moved along the bed and picked up the telephone.

'Is that you, Kopeikin?'

He heard a mystified grunt. 'Graham? What is it? I have only just this moment come in. Where are you?'

'Sitting on my bed. Listen! Something stupid has happened. There was a burglar in my room when I got up here. He took pot shots at me with a gun before escaping via the window. One of them hit me in the hand.'

'Merciful God! Are you badly hurt?'

'No. It just took a slice off the back of my right hand. I don't feel too good, though. It gave me a nasty shock.'

'My dear fellow! Please tell me exactly what has happened.'

Graham told him. 'My suit-case was locked,' he went on, 'and nothing is missing. I must have got back just a minute or so too soon. But there are complications. The noise seems to have roused half the hotel, including the

Assistant Manager who is now standing about drinking whisky. They've sent for a doctor to bandage me up, but that's all. They made no attempt to get out after the man. Not, I suppose, that it would have done any good if they had, but at least they might have seen him. I didn't. They say he must have got away by the gardens. The point is that they won't call in the police unless I turn nasty and insist. Naturally, they don't want police tramping about the place, giving the hotel a bad name. They put it to me that the police would prevent my travelling on the eleven o'clock train if I lodged a complaint. I expect they would. But I don't know the laws of this place; and I don't want to put myself in a false position by failing to lodge a complaint. They propose, I gather, to square the doctor. But that's their look-out. What do *I* do?'

There was a short silence. Then: 'I think,' said Kopeikin, slowly, 'that you should do nothing at the moment. Leave the matter to me. I will speak to a friend of mine about it. He is connected with the police, and has great influence. As soon as I have spoken to him, I will come to your hotel.'

'But there's no need for you to do that, Kopeikin. I . . .'

'Excuse me, my dear fellow, there is every need. Let the doctor attend to your wound and then stay in your room until I arrive.'

'I wasn't going out,' said Graham, acidly; but Kopeikin had rung off.

As he hung up the telephone, the doctor arrived. He was thin and quiet, with a sallow face, and wore an overcoat with a black lamb's wool collar over his pyjamas. Behind him came the Manager, a heavy, disagreeable-looking man who obviously suspected that the whole thing was a hoax concocted expressly to annoy him.

He gave Graham a hostile stare, but before he could open his mouth his assistant was pouring out an account of what had occurred. There was a lot of gesturing and rolling of eyes. The Manager exclaimed as he listened, and looked at Graham with less hostility and more apprehension. At last the assistant paused, and then broke meaningly into French.

'Monsieur leaves Istanbul by the eleven o'clock train, and so does not wish to have the trouble and inconvenience of taking this matter to the police. I think you will agree, Monsieur le Directeur, that his attitude is wise.'

'Very wise,' agreed the Manager pontifically, 'and most discreet.' He squared his shoulders. 'Monsieur, we infinitely regret that you should have been put to such pain, discomfort and indignity. But not even the most luxurious hotel can fortify itself against thieves who climb through the windows. Nevertheless,' he went on, 'the Hotel Adler Palace recognizes its responsibilities towards its guests. We shall do everything humanly possible to arrange the affair.'

'If it would be humanly possible to instruct the doctor then to attend to my hand, I should be grateful.'

'Ah yes. The doctor. A thousand pardons.'

The doctor, who had been standing gloomily in the background, now came forward and began snapping out instructions in Turkish. The windows were promptly shut, the heating turned up, and the Assistant Manager dispatched on an errand. He returned, almost immediately, with an enamel bowl which was then filled with hot water from the bathroom.

The doctor removed the towel from Graham's hand, sponged the blood away and inspected the wound. Then he looked up and said something to the Manager.

'He says, Monsieur,' reported the Manager, complacently, 'that it is not serious—no more than a little scratch.'

'I already knew that. If you wish to go back to bed, please do so. But I should like some hot coffee. I am cold.'

'Immediately, Monsieur.' He snapped his fingers to the Assistant Manager, who scuttled out. 'And if there is anything else, Monsieur?'

'No, thank you. Nothing. Good night.'

'At your service, Monsieur. It is all most regrettable. Good night.'

He went. The doctor cleaned the wound carefully, and began to dress it. Graham wished that he had not telephoned Kopeikin. The fuss was over. It was now nearly four o'clock. But for the fact that Kopeikin had promised to call in to see him, he might have had a few hours' sleep. He was yawning repeatedly. The doctor finished the dressing, patted it reassuringly, and looked up. His lips worked.

'*Maintenant,*' he said laboriously, '*il faut dormir.*'

Graham nodded. The doctor got to his feet and repacked his bag with the air of a man who has done everything possible for a difficult patient. Then he looked at his watch and sighed. '*Trés tard,*' he said. '*Giteceğ-im. Adiyo, efendi.*'

Graham mustered his Turkish. '*Adiyo, hekim efendi. Cok teşekkür ederim.*'

'*Birşey değil. Adiyo.*' He bowed and went.

A moment later, the Assistant Manager bustled in with the coffee, set it down with a businesslike flourish clearly intended to indicate that he, too, was about to return to his bed, and collected the bottle of whisky.

'You may leave that,' said Graham; 'a friend is on his way to see me. You might tell the porter . . .'

But as he spoke, the telephone rang, and the night porter announced that Kopeikin had arrived. The Assistant Manager retired.

Kopeikin came into the room looking preternaturally grave.

'My dear fellow!' was his greeting. He looked round. 'Where is the doctor?'

'He's just left. Just a graze. Nothing serious. I feel a bit jumpy but, apart from that, I'm all right. It's really very good of you to turn out like this. The grateful management have presented me with a bottle of whisky. Sit down and help yourself. I'm having coffee.'

Kopeikin sank into the arm-chair. 'Tell me exactly how it happened.'

Graham told him. Kopeikin heaved himself out of the arm-chair and walked over to the window. Suddenly he stooped and picked something up. He held it up: a small brass cartridge case.

'A nine millimetre calibre self-loading pistol,' he remarked. 'An unpleasant thing!' He dropped it on the floor again, opened the window and looked out.

Graham sighed. 'I really don't think it's any good playing detectives, Kopeikin. The man was in the room: I disturbed him, and he shot at me. Come in, shut that window, and drink some whisky.'

'Gladly, my dear fellow, gladly. You must excuse my curiosity.'

Graham realized that he was being a little ungracious. 'It's extremely kind of you, Kopeikin, to take so much trouble. I seem to have made a lot of fuss about nothing.'

'It is good that you have.' He frowned. 'Unfortunately a lot more fuss must be made.'

'You think we ought to call in the police? I don't see that it can do any good. Besides, my train goes at eleven. I don't want to miss it.'

Kopeikin drank some whisky and put his glass down with a bang. 'I'm afraid, my dear fellow, that you cannot under any circumstances leave on the eleven o'clock train.'

'What on earth do you mean? Of course I can. I'm perfectly all right.'

Kopeikin looked at him curiously. 'Fortunately you are. But that does not alter facts.'

'Facts?'

'Did you notice that both your windows and the shutters outside have been forced open?'

'I didn't. I didn't look. But what of it?'

'If you will look out of the window you will see that there is a terrace below which gives on the garden. Above the terrace there is a steel framework which reaches almost to the second floor balconies. In the summer it is covered with straw matting so that people can eat and drink on the terrace, out of the sun. This man obviously climbed up by the framework. It would be easy. I could almost do it myself. He could reach the balconies of all the rooms on this floor of the hotel that way. But can you tell me why he chooses to break into one of the few rooms with both shutters and windows locked?'

'Of course I can't. I've always heard that criminals were fools.'

'You say nothing was stolen. Your suit-case was not even opened. A coincidence that you should return just in time to prevent him.'

'A lucky coincidence. For goodness' sake, Kopeikin, let's talk about something else. The man's escaped. That's the end of it.'

Kopeikin shook his head. 'I'm afraid not, my dear fellow. Does he not seem to you to have been a very curious thief? He behaves like no other hotel thief ever behaved. He breaks in, and through a locked window as well. If you had been in bed, he would certainly have awakened you. He must, therefore, have known beforehand that you were not there. He must also have discovered your room number. Have you anything so obviously valuable that a thief finds it worth his while to make such preparations? No. A curious thief! He carries, too, a pistol weighing at least a kilogramme with which he fires three shots at you.'

'Well?'

Kopeikin bounced angrily out of his chair. 'My dear fellow, does it not occur to you that this man was shooting to kill you, and that he came here for no other purpose?'

Graham laughed. 'Then all I can say is that he was a pretty bad shot. Now you listen to me carefully, Kopeikin. Have you ever heard the legend about Americans and Englishmen? It persists in every country in the world where English isn't spoken. The story is that all Americans and Englishmen are

millionaires, and that they always leave vast amounts of loose cash about the
place. And now, if you don't mind, I'm going to try to snatch a few hours'
sleep. It was very good of you to come round, Kopeikin, and I'm very
grateful, but now . . .'

'Have you ever,' demanded Kopeikin, 'tried firing a heavy pistol in a dark
room at a man who's just come through the door? There's no direct light
from the corridor outside. Merely a glow of light. Have you ever tried? No.
You might be able to see the man, but it's quite another thing to hit him.
Under these circumstances even a good shot might miss first time as this
man missed. That miss would unnerve him. He does not perhaps know that
Englishmen do not usually carry firearms. You may fire back. He fires again
quickly, and clips your hand. You probably cry out with pain. He probably
thinks that he has wounded you seriously. He fires another shot for luck,
and goes.'

'Nonsense, Kopeikin! You must be out of your senses. What conceivable
reason could anyone have for wanting to kill me? I'm the most harmless man
alive.'

Kopeikin glared at him stonily. 'Are you?'

'Now what does *that* mean?'

But Kopeikin ignored the question. He finished his whisky. 'I told you
that I was going to telephone a friend of mine. I did so.' He buttoned up his
coat deliberately. 'I am sorry to tell you, my dear fellow, that you must come
with me to see him immediately. I have been trying to break the news to you
gently, but now I must be frank. A man tried to murder you to-night.
Something must be done about it at once.'

Graham got to his feet. 'Are you mad?'

'No, my dear fellow, I am not. You ask me why anyone should want to
murder you. There is an excellent reason. Unfortunately, I cannot be more
explicit. I have my official instructions.'

Graham sat down. 'Kopeikin, *I* shall go crazy in a minute. Will you
kindly tell me what you are babbling about? Friend? Murder? Official
instructions? What is all this nonsense?'

Kopeikin was looking acutely embarrassed. 'I am sorry, my dear fellow. I
can understand your feelings. Let me tell you this much. This friend of
mine is not, strictly speaking, a friend at all. In fact, I dislike him. But his
name is Colonel Haki, and he is the head of the Turkish secret police. His
office is in Galata, and he is expecting us to meet him there now to discuss
this affair. I may also tell you that I anticipated that you might not wish to
go, and told him so. He said, forgive me, that if you did not go you would be
fetched. My dear fellow, it is no use your being angry. The circumstances
are exceptional. If I had not known that it was necessary both in your
interests and in mine to telephone him, I would not have done so. Now
then, my dear fellow, I have a taxi outside. We ought to be going.'

Graham got slowly to his feet again. 'Very well. I must say, Kopeikin,
that you have surprised me. Friendly concern, I could understand and
appreciate. But this . . . this hysteria is the last thing I should have expected
from you. To get the head of the secret police out of bed at this hour seems
to me a fantastic thing to do. I can only hope that he doesn't object to being
made a fool of.'

Kopeikin flushed. 'I am neither hysterical nor fantastic, my friend. I have something unpleasant to do, and I am doing it. If you will forgive my saying so, I think . . .'

'I can forgive almost anything except stupidity,' snapped Graham. 'However, this is your affair. Do you mind helping me on with my overcoat?'

They drove to Galata in grim silence. Kopeikin was sulking. Graham sat hunched up in his corner staring out miserably at the cold, dark streets, and wishing that he had not telephoned Kopeikin. It was, he kept telling himself, absurd enough to be shot at by a hotel sneak thief: to be bundled out in the early hours of the morning to tell the head of the secret police about it was worse than absurd; it was ludicrous. He felt, too, concerned on Kopeikin's account. The man might be behaving like an idiot; but it was not very pleasant to think of him making an ass of himself before a man who might well be able to do him harm in his business. Besides, he, Graham, had been rude.

He turned his head. 'What's this Colonel Haki like?'

Kopeikin grunted. 'Very *chic* and polished–a ladies' man. There is also a legend that he can drink two bottles of whisky without getting drunk. It may be true. He was one of Ataturk's men, a deputy in the provisional government of 1919. There is also another legend–that he killed prisoners by tying them together in pairs and throwing them into the river to save both food and ammunition. I do not believe everything I hear, nor am I a sentimentalist, but, as I told you, I do not like him. He is, however, very clever. But you will be able to judge for yourself. You can speak French to him.'

'I still don't see . . .'

'You will.'

They pulled up soon afterwards behind a big American car which almost blocked the narrow street into which they had turned. They got out. Graham found himself standing in front of a pair of double doors which might have been the entrance to a cheap hotel. Kopeikin pressed a bell push.

One of the doors was opened almost immediately by a sleepy-looking caretaker who had obviously only just been roused from his bed.

'*Haki efendi evde midir,*' said Kopeikin.

'*Efendi var-dir. Yokari.*' The man pointed to the stairs.

They went up.

Colonel Haki's office was a large room at the end of a corridor on the top floor of the building. The Colonel himself walked down the corridor to meet them.

He was a tall man with lean, muscular cheeks, a small mouth and grey hair cropped Prussian fashion. A narrow frontal bone, a long beak of a nose and a slight stoop gave him a somewhat vultural air. He wore a very well-cut officer's tunic with full riding breeches and very tight, shiny cavalry boots; he walked with the slight swagger of a man who is used to riding. But for the intense pallor of his face and the fact that it was unshaven, there was nothing about him to show that he had recently been asleep. His eyes were grey and very wide-awake. They surveyed Graham with interest.

'Ah! *Nasil-siniz. Fransizca konuşaiblir misin.* Yes? Delighted, Mr Graham. Your wound, of course.' Graham found his unbandaged hand being gripped with considerable force by long rubbery fingers. 'I hope that it is not too painful. Something must be done about this rascal who tried to kill you.'

'I'm afraid,' said Graham, 'that we have disturbed your rest unnecessarily Colonel. The man stole nothing.'

Colonel Haki looked quickly at Kopeikin.

'I have told him nothing,' said Kopeikin placidly. 'At your suggestion, Colonel, you may remember. I regret to say that he thinks I am either mad or hysterical.'

Colonel Haki chuckled. 'It is the lot of you Russians to be misunderstood. Let us go into my office where we can talk.'

They followed him: Graham with the growing conviction that he was involved in a nightmare and that he would presently wake up to find himself at his dentist's. The corridor was, indeed, as bare and featureless as the corridors of a dream. It smelt strongly, however, of stale cigarette smoke.

The Colonel's office was large and chilly. They sat down facing him across his desk. He pushed a box of cigarettes towards them, lounged back in his chair and crossed his legs.

'You must realize, Mr Graham,' he said suddenly, 'that an attempt was made to kill you to-night.'

'Why?' demanded Graham irritably. 'I'm sorry, but I don't see it. I returned to my room to find that a man had got in through the window. Obviously he was some sort of thief. I disturbed him. He fired at me and then escaped. That is all.'

'You have not, I understand, reported the matter to the police.'

'I did not consider that reporting it could do any good. I did not see the man's face. Besides, I am leaving for England this morning on the eleven o'clock train. I did not wish to delay myself. If I have broken the law in any way I am sorry.'

'*Zarar yok!* It does not matter.' The Colonel lit a cigarette and blew smoke at the ceiling. 'I have a duty to do, Mr Graham,' he said. 'That duty is to protect you. I am afraid that you cannot leave on the eleven o'clock train.'

'But protect me from *what?*'

'I will ask you questions, Mr Graham. It will be simpler. You are in the employ of Messrs Cator and Bliss, Ltd., the English armament manufacturers?'

'Yes. Kopeikin here is the company's Turkish agent.'

'Quite so. You are, I believe, Mr Graham, a naval ordnance expert.'

Graham hesitated. He had the engineer's dislike of the word 'expert.' His Managing Director sometimes applied it to him when writing to foreign naval authorities; but he could, on those occasions, console himself with the reflection that his managing director would describe him as a full-blooded Zulu to impress a customer. At other times he found the word unreasonably irritating.

'Well, Mr Graham?'

'I'm an engineer. Naval ordnance happens to be my subject.'

'As you please. The point is that Messrs Cator and Bliss, Ltd., have contracted to do some work for my Government. Good. Now, Mr Graham, I do not know exactly what that work is'–he waved his cigarette airily–'that is the affair of the Ministry of Marine. But I have been told some things. I know that certain of our naval vessels are to be rearmed with new guns and torpedo tubes and that you were sent to discuss the matter with our dockyard experts. I also know that our authorities stipulated that the new equipment should be delivered by the spring. Your company agreed to that stipulation. Are you aware of it?'

'I have been aware of nothing else for the past two months.'

'*Iyi dir!* Now I may tell you, Mr Graham, that the reason for that stipulation as to time was not mere caprice on the part of our Ministry of Marine. The international situation demands that we have that new equipment in our dockyards by the time in question.'

'I know that, too.'

'Excellent. Then you will understand what I am about to say. The naval authorities of Germany and Italy and Russia are perfectly well aware of the fact that these vessels are being rearmed and I have no doubt that the moment the work is done, or even before, their agents will discover the details known at the moment only to a few men, yourself among them. That is unimportant. No navy can keep that sort of secret: no navy expects to do so. We might even consider it advisable, for various reasons, to publish the details ourselves. But'–he raised a long, well-manicured finger–'at the moment you are in a curious position, Mr Graham.'

'That, at least, I can believe.'

The Colonel's small grey eyes rested on him coldly. 'I am not here to make jokes, Mr Graham.'

'I beg your pardon.'

'Not at all. Please take another cigarette. I was saying that at the moment your position is curious. Tell me! Have you ever regarded yourself as indispensable in your business, Mr Graham?'

Graham laughed. 'Certainly not. I could tell you the names of dozens of other men with my particular qualifications.'

'Then,' said Colonel Haki, 'allow me to inform you, Mr Graham, that for once in your life you *are* indispensable. Let us suppose for the moment that your thief's shooting had been a little more accurate and that at this moment you were, instead of sitting talking with me, lying in hospital on an operating table with a bullet in your lungs. What would be the effect on this business you are engaged in now?'

'Naturally, the company would send another man out immediately.'

Colonel Haki affected a look of theatrical astonishment. 'So? That would be splendid. So typically British! Sporting! One man falls–immediately another, undaunted, takes his place. But wait!' The Colonel held up a forbidding arm. 'Is it necessary? Surely, Mr Kopeikin here could arrange to have your papers taken to England. No doubt your colleagues there could find out from your notes, your sketches, your drawings, exactly what they wanted to know even though your company did not build the ships in question, eh?'

Graham flushed. 'I gather from your tone that you know perfectly well that the matter could not be dealt with so simply. I was forbidden, in any case, to put certain things on paper.'

Colonel Haki tilted his chair. 'Yes, Mr Graham,'–he smiled cheerfully–'I do know that. Another expert would have to be sent out to do some of your work over again.' His chair came forward with a crash. 'And meanwhile,' he said through his teeth, 'the spring would be here and those ships would still be lying in the dockyards of Izmir and Gallipoli, waiting for their new guns and torpedo tubes. Listen to me, Mr Graham! Turkey and Great Britain are allies. It is in the interests of your country's enemies that, when the snow melts and the rain ceases, Turkish naval strength should be exactly what it is now. *Exactly what it is now!* They will do anything to see that it is so. *Anything*, Mr Graham! Do you understand?'

Graham felt something tightening in his chest. He had to force himself to smile. 'A little melodramatic, aren't you? We have no proof that what you say is true. And, after all, this is real life, not . . .' He hesitated.

'Not what, Mr Graham?' The Colonel was watching him like a cat about to streak after a mouse.

' . . . the cinema, I was going to say, only it sounded a little impolite.'

Colonel Haki stood up quickly. 'Melodrama! Proof! Real life! The cinema! Impolite!' His lips curled round the words as if they were obscene. 'Do you think I care what you say, Mr Graham? It's your carcass I am interested in. Alive, it's worth something to the Turkish Republic. I'm going to see that it stays alive as long as I've any control over it. There is a war on in Europe. Do you understand *that*?'

Graham said nothing.

The Colonel stared at him for a moment and then went on quietly. 'A little more than a week ago, while you were still in Gallipoli, we discovered–that is, my agents discovered–a plot to murder you there. The whole thing was very clumsy and amateurish. You were to be kidnapped and knifed. Fortunately, we are not fools. *We* do not dismiss as melodramatic anything that does not please us. We were able to persuade the arrested men to tell us that they had been paid by a German agent in Sofia–a man called Moeller about whom we have known for some time. He used to call himself an American until the American Legation objected. His name was Fielding then. I imagine that he claims any name and nationality that happens to suit him. However, I called Mr Kopeikin in to see me and told him about it but suggested that nothing should be said about it to you. The less these things are talked about the better and, besides, there was nothing to be gained by upsetting you while you were so hard at work. I think I made a mistake. I had reason to believe that this Moeller's further efforts would be directed elsewhere. When Mr Kopeikin, very wisely, telephoned me immediately he knew of this fresh attempt, I realized that I had underestimated the determination of this gentleman in Sofia. He tried again. I have no doubt that he will try a third time if we give him a chance.' He leaned back in his chair. 'Do you understand now, Mr Graham? Has your excellent brain grasped what I have been trying to say? It is perfectly simple! Someone is trying to kill you.'

Chapter Three

On the rare occasions—when matters concerned with insurance policies had been under consideration—on which Graham had thought about his own death, it had been to reaffirm the conviction that he would die of natural causes and in bed. Accidents did happen, of course; but he was a careful driver, an imaginative pedestrian and a strong swimmer; he neither rode horses nor climbed mountains; he was not subject to attacks of dizziness; he did not hunt big game and he had never had even the smallest desire to jump in front of an approaching train. He had felt, on the whole, that the conviction was not unreasonable. The idea that anyone else in the world might so much as hope for his death had never occurred to him. If it had done so he would probably have hastened to consult a nerve specialist. Confronted by the proposition that someone was, in fact, not merely hoping for his death but deliberately trying to murder him, he was as profoundly shocked as if he had been presented with incontrovertible proofs that a^2 no longer equalled $b^2 + c^2$ or that his wife had a lover.

He was a man who had always been inclined to think well of his fellow creatures; and the first involuntary thought that came into his head was that he must have done something particularly reprehensible for anyone to want to murder him. The mere fact that he was doing his job could not be sufficient reason. He was not dangerous. Besides, he had a wife dependent on him. It was impossible that anyone should wish to kill him. There must be some horrible mistake.

He heard himself saying: 'Yes. I understand.'

He didn't understand, of course. It was absurd. He saw Colonel Haki looking at him with a frosty little smile on his small mouth.

'A shock, Mr Graham? You do not like it, eh? It is not pleasant. War is war. But it is one thing to be a soldier in the trenches; the enemy is not trying to kill you in particular because you are Mr Graham; the man next to you will do as well; it is all impersonal. When you are a marked man it is not so easy to keep your courage. I understand, believe me. But you have advantages over the soldier. You have only to defend yourself. You do not have to go into the open and attack. And you have no trench or fort to hold. You may run away without being a coward. You must reach London safely. But it is a long way from Istanbul to London. You must, like the soldier, take precautions against surprise. You must know your enemy. You follow me?'

'Yes, I follow you.'

His brain was icily calm now, but it seemed to have lost control of his body. He knew that he must try to look as if he were taking it all very philosophically, but his mouth kept filling with saliva, so that he was swallowing repeatedly, and his hands and legs were trembling. He told himself that he was behaving like a schoolboy. A man had fired three shots at him. What difference did it make whether the man had been a thief or an intending murderer? He had fired three shots, and that was that. But all the same, it did somehow make a difference . . .

'Then,' Colonel Haki was saying, 'let us begin with what has just happened.' He was obviously enjoying himself. 'According to Mr Kopeikin, you did not see the man who shot at you.'

'No, I didn't. The room was in darkness.'

Kopeikin chipped in. 'He left cartridge cases behind him. Nine millimetre calibre ejected from a self-loading pistol.'

'That does not help a great deal. You noticed nothing about him, Mr Graham?'

'Nothing, I'm afraid. It was all over so quickly. He had gone before I realised it.'

'But he had probably been in the room for some time waiting for you. You didn't notice any perfume in the room?'

'All I could smell was cordite.'

'What time did you arrive in Istanbul?'

'At about six p.m.'

'And you did not return to your hotel until three o'clock this morning. Please tell me where you were during that time.'

'Certainly. I spent the time with Kopeikin. He met me at the station, and we drove in a taxi to the Adler Palace where I left my suit-case and had a wash. We then had some drinks and dined. Where did we have the drinks, Kopeikin?'

'At the Rumca Bar.'

'Yes, that was it. We went on to the Pera Palace to dine. Just before eleven we left there, and went on to Le Jockey Cabaret.'

'Le Jockey Cabaret! You surprise me! What did you do there?'

'We danced with an Arab girl named Maria, and saw the cabaret.'

'We? Was there, then, only one girl between you?'

'I was rather tired, and did not want to dance much. Later we had a drink with one of the cabaret dancers, Josette, in her dressing-room.' To Graham it all sounded rather like the evidence of detectives in a divorce case.

'A nice girl, this Josette?'

'Very attractive.'

The Colonel laughed; the doctor keeping the patient's spirits up. 'Blonde or brunette?'

'Blonde.'

'Ah! I must visit Le Jockey. I have missed something. And what happened then?'

'Kopeikin and I left the place. We walked back to the Adler Palace together where Kopeikin left me to go on to his apartment.'

The Colonel looked humorously astonished. 'You left this dancing blonde?'—he snapped his fingers—'just like that? There were no—little games?'

'No. No little games.'

'Ah, but you have told me that you were tired.' He swung round suddenly in his chair to face Kopeikin. 'These women–this Arab and this Josette–what do you know of them?'

Kopeikin stroked his chin. 'I know Serge, the proprietor of Le Jockey Cabaret. He introduced me to Josette some time ago. She is a Hungarian, I believe. I know nothing against her. The Arab girl is from a house in Alexandria.'

'Very well. We will see about them later.' He turned again to Graham. 'Now, Mr Graham, we shall see what we can find out from you about the enemy. You were tired, you say?'

'Yes.'

'But you kept your eyes open, eh?'

'I suppose so.'

'Let us hope so. You realize that you must have been followed from the moment you left Gallipoli?'

'I hadn't realized that.'

'It must be so. They knew your hotel and your room in it. They were waiting for you to return. They must have known of every movement you made since you arrived.'

He got up suddenly and, going to a filing cabinet in the corner, extracted from it a yellow manilla folder. He brought it back and dropped it on the desk in front of Graham. 'Inside that folder, Mr Graham, you will find photographs of fifteen men. Some of the photographs are clear; most are very blurred and indistinct. You will have to do the best you can. I want you to cast your mind back to the time you boarded the train at Gallipoli yesterday, and remember every face you saw, even casually, between that time and three o'clock this morning. Then I want you to look at those photographs and see if you recognize any of the faces there. Afterwards Mr Kopeikin can look at them, but I wish you to see them first.'

Graham opened the folder. There was a series of thin white cards in it. Each was about the size of the folder, and had a photograph gummed to the top half of it. The prints were all the same size, but they had obviously been copied from original photographs of varying sizes. One was an enlargement of part of a photograph of a group of men standing in front of some trees. Underneath each print was a paragraph or two of typewritten matter in Turkish, presumably the description of the man in question.

Most of the photographs were, as the Colonel had said, blurred. One or two of the faces were, indeed, no more than blobs of grey with dark patches marking the eyes and mouths. Those that were clear looked like prison photographs. The men in them stared sullenly at their tormentors. There was one of a Negro wearing a tarboosh with his mouth wide open as if he were shouting at someone to the right of the camera. Graham turned the cards over, slowly and hopelessly. If he had ever seen any of these men in his life, he could not recognize them now.

The next moment his heart jolted violently. He was looking at a photograph taken in very strong sunshine of a man in a hard straw hat standing in front of what might have been a shop, and looking over his shoulder at the camera. His right arm and his body below the waist were out of the picture, and what was in was rather out of focus; in addition the photograph looked as if it had been taken at least ten years previously; but there was no mistaking the doughy, characterless features, the long-suffering mouth, the small deep-set eyes. It was the man in the crumpled suit.

'Well, Mr Graham?'

'This man. He was at Le Jockey Cabaret. It was the Arab girl who drew my attention to him while we were dancing. She said that he came in just after Kopeikin and me, and that he kept looking at me. She warned me against him. She seemed to think that he might stick a knife in my back and take my wallet.'

'Did she know him?'

'No. She said that she recognized the type.'

Colonel Haki took the card and leaned back. 'That was very intelligent of her. Did you see this man, Mr Kopeikin?'

Kopeikin looked, and then shook his head.

'Very well.' Colonel Haki dropped the card on the desk in front of him. 'You need not trouble to look at any more of the photographs, gentlemen. I know now what I wanted to know. This is the only one of the fifteen that interests us. The rest I put with it merely to make sure that you identified this one of your own accord.'

'Who is he?'

'He is a Romanian by birth. His name is supposed to be Petre Banat; but as Banat is the name of a Romanian province, I think it very probable that he never had a family name. We know, indeed, very little about him. But what we do know is enough. He is a professional gunman. Ten years ago he was convicted, in Jasi, of helping to kick a man to death, and was sent to prison for two years. Soon after he came out of prison he joined Codreanu's Iron Guard. In 1933 he was charged with the assassination of a police official at Bucova. It appears that he walked into the official's house one Sunday afternoon, shot the man dead, wounded his wife, and then calmly walked out again. He is a careful man, but he knew that he was safe. The trial was a farce. The court-room was filled with Iron Guards with pistols, who threatened to shoot the judge and everyone connected with the trial if Banat were convicted. He was acquitted. There were many such trials in Romania at that time. Banat was afterwards responsible for at least four other murders in Romania. When the Iron Guard was proscribed, however, he escaped from the country, and has not returned there. He spent some time in France until the French police deported him. Then he went to Belgrade. But he got into trouble there, too, and has since moved about Eastern Europe.

'There are men who are natural killers. Banat is one of them. He is very fond of gambling, and is always short of money. At one time it was said that his price for killing a man was as little as five thousand French francs and expenses.

'But all that is of no interest to you, Mr Graham. The point is that Banat is here in Istanbul. I may tell you that we receive regular reports on the activities of this man Moeller in Sofia. About a week ago it was reported that he had been in touch with Banat, and that Banat had afterwards left Sofia. I will admit to you, Mr Graham, that I did not attach any importance to the fact. To be frank, it was another aspect of this agent's activities which were interesting me at the time. It was not until Mr Kopeikin telephoned me that I remembered Banat and wondered if, by any chance, he had come to Istanbul. We know now that he is here. We know also that Moeller saw him just after those other arrangements for killing you had been upset. There can be no doubt, I think, that it was Banat who was waiting for you in your room at the Adler Palace.'

Graham strove to seem unimpressed. 'He looked harmless enough.'

'That,' said Colonel Haki, sagely, 'is because you are not experienced, Mr Graham. The real killer is not a mere brute. He may be quite sensitive. Have you studied abnormal psychology?'

'I'm afraid not.'

'It is very interesting. Apart from detective stories, Kraft-Ebbing and Steikel are my favourite reading. I have my own theory about men such as Banat. I believe that they are perverts with an *idée fixe* about the father whom they identify not with a virile god,–he held up a cautionary finger–'but with their own impotence. When they kill, they are thus killing their own weakness. There is no doubt of it, I think.'

'Very interesting, I feel sure. But can't you arrest this man?'

Colonel Haki cocked one gleaming boot over the arm of his chair, and pursed his lips. 'That raises an awkward problem, Mr Graham. In the first place, we have to find him. He will certainly be travelling with a false passport and under a false name. I can and, of course, will circulate his description to the frontier posts so that we shall know if he leaves the country by a normal route, but as for arresting him . . . You see, Mr Graham, the so-called democratic forms of government have serious drawbacks for a man in my position. It is impossible to arrest and detain people without absurd legal formalities.' He threw up his hands–a patriot bemoaning his country's decadence. 'On what charge can we arrest him, even if we catch him? We have no evidence against him. We could, no doubt, invent a charge and then apologize, but what good will it do? No! I regret it, but we can do nothing about Banat. I do not think it matters a great deal. They could always get someone else for the job. What we must think of now is the future. We must consider how to get you home safely.'

'I have, as I have already told you, a sleeping berth on the eleven o'clock train. I fail to see why I shouldn't use it. It seems to me that the sooner I leave here the better.'

Colonel Haki frowned. 'Let me tell you, Mr Graham, that if you were to take that or any other train, you would be dead before you reached Belgrade. Don't imagine for one moment that the presence of other travellers would deter them. You must not underrate the enemy, Mr Graham. It is a fatal mistake. In a train you would be caught like a rat in a trap. Picture it for yourself! There are innumerable stops between the Turkish and French frontiers. Your assassin might get on the train at any of them. Imagine yourself sitting there for hour after hour after hour trying to stay awake lest you should be knifed while you slept; not daring to leave the compartment for fear of being shot down in the corridor; living in terror of everyone–from the man sitting opposite to you in the restaurant car to the Customs officials. Picture it, Mr Graham, and then reflect that a trans-continental train is the safest place in the world in which to kill a man.

Consider the position! These people do not wish you to reach England. So they decide, very wisely and logically, to kill you. They have tried twice and failed. They will wait now to see what you will do. They will not try again in this country. They will know that you will now be too well protected. They will wait until you come out in the open. No! I am afraid that you cannot travel by train.'

'Then I don't see . . .'

'If,' continued the Colonel, 'the air line services had not been suspended we could send you by aeroplane to Brindisi. But they *are* suspended—the earthquake, you understand. Everything is disorganized. The planes are being used for relief work. But we can do without them. It will be best if you go by sea.'

'But surely . . .'

'There is an Italian shipping line which runs a weekly service of small cargo boats between here and Genoa. Sometimes, when there is a cargo, they go up as far as Constanza, but usually they run only as far as here, calling at the Piraeus on the way. They carry a few passengers, fifteen at the most, and we can make sure that every one of them is harmless before the boat is given its clearance papers. When you get to Genoa, you will have only the short train journey between Genoa and the French frontier to put you out of reach of German agents.'

'But as you yourself pointed out, time is an important factor. To-day is the second. I am due back on the eighth. If I have to wait for boats I shall be days late. Besides, the journey itself will take at least a week.'

'There will be no delay, Mr Graham,' sighed the Colonel. 'I am not stupid. I telephoned the port police before you arrived. There is a boat leaving in two days' time for Marseilles. It would have been better if you could have travelled on that even though it does not ordinarily take passengers. But the Italian boat leaves to-day at four-thirty in the afternoon. You will be able to stretch your legs in Athens to-morrow afternoon. You will dock in Genoa early Saturday morning. You can, if you wish and if your visas are in order, be in London by Monday morning. As I have told you, a marked man has advantages over his enemies. He can run away—disappear. In the middle of the Mediterranean, you will be as safe as you are in this office.'

Graham hesitated. He glanced at Kopeikin; but the Russian was staring at his finger nails.

'Well, I don't know, Colonel. This is all very good of you, but I can't help thinking that, in view of the circumstances which you have explained to me, I ought to get in touch with the British Consul here, or with the British Embassy, before deciding anything.'

Colonel Haki lit a cigarette. 'And what do you expect the Consul or the Ambassador to do? Send you home in a cruiser?' He laughed unpleasantly. 'My dear Mr Graham, I am not asking you to decide anything. I am telling you what you must do. You are, I must again remind you, of great value to my country in your present state of health. You must allow me to protect my country's interests in my own way. I think that you are probably tired now and a little upset. I do not wish to harass you, but I must explain that, if you do not agree to follow my instructions, I shall have no alternative but to arrest you, have an order issued for your deportation and put on board the *Sestri Levante* under guard. I hope that I make myself clear.'

Graham felt himself reddening. 'Quite clear. Would you like to handcuff me now? It will save a lot of trouble. You need . . .'

'I think,' put in Kopeikin hastily,'that I should do as the Colonel suggests, my dear fellow. It is the best thing.'

'I prefer to be my own judge of that, Kopeikin.' He looked from one to the other of them angrily. He felt confused and wretched. Things had been moving too quickly for him. Colonel Haki he disliked intensely. Kopeikin seemed to be no longer capable of thinking 'for himself. He felt that they were making decisions with the glib irresponsibility of schoolboys planning a game of Red Indians. And yet the devil of it was that those conclusions were inescapably logical. His life was threatened. All they were asking him to do was to go home by another and safer route. It was a reasonable request but . . . Then he shrugged his shoulders. 'All right. I seem to have no choice.'

'Exactly, Mr Graham.' The Colonel smoothed out his tunic with the air of one who has reasoned wisely with a child. 'Now we can make our arrangements. As soon as the shipping company's offices are open Mr Kopeikin can arrange for your passage and obtain a refund for your railway ticket. I will see that the names and particulars of the other passengers are submitted to me for approval before the ship sails. You need have no fears, Mr Graham, of your fellow travellers. But I am afraid that you will not find them very *chic* or the boat very comfortable. This line is actually the cheapest route to and from Istanbul if you live in the west. But you will not, I am sure, mind a little discomfort if you have peace of mind to compensate for it.'

'As long as I get back to England by the eighth, I don't care how I travel.'

'That is the right spirit. And now I suggest that you remain in this building until it is time for you to leave. We will make you as comfortable as possible. Mr Kopeikin can collect your suitcase from the hotel. I will see that a doctor looks at your hand later on to see that it is still all right.' He looked at his watch. 'The concierge can make us some coffee now. Later, he can get some food for you from the restaurant round the corner.' He stood up.'I will go and see about it now. We cannot save you from bullets to let you die of starvation, eh?'

'It's very kind of you,' said Graham; and then, as the Colonel disappeared down the corridor: 'I owe you an apology, Kopeikin. I behaved badly.'

Kopeikin looked distressed.'My dear fellow! You cannot be blamed. I am glad everything has been settled so quickly.'

'Quickly, yes.' He hesitated. 'Is this man Haki to be trusted?'

'You do not like him either, eh?' Kopeikin chuckled. 'I would not trust him with a woman; but with you—yes.'

'You approve of my going on this boat?'

'I do. By the way, my dear fellow,' he went on mildly; 'have you a gun in your luggage?'

'Good heavens, no!'

'Then you had better take this.' He pulled a small revolver out of his

overcoat pocket. 'I put it in my pocket when I came out after you telephoned. It is an old model with a safety catch, but reliable and fully loaded.'

'I don't think I'll need it.'

'No, but it will make you feel better to have it.'

'I doubt that. Still. . . .' He took the revolver and stared at it distastefully.
'I've never fired one of these things, you know.'

'It is easy. You release the safety catch, point it, pull the trigger and hope
for the best.'

'All the same . . .'

'Put it in your pocket. You can give it to the French Customs officials at
Modano.'

Colonel Haki returned. 'The coffee is being prepared. Now, Mr Graham,
we will decide how you are to amuse yourself until it is time for you to go.'
He caught sight of the revolver in Graham's hand. 'Ah-ha! You are arming
yourself!' He grinned. 'A little melodrama is sometimes unavoidable, eh, Mr
Graham?'

The decks were silent now and Graham could hear the sounds within the
ship: people talking, doors slamming, quick businesslike footsteps in the
alleyways. There was not long to wait now. Outside it was getting dark. He
looked back upon a day which had seemed interminable, surprised that he
could remember so little of it.

Most of it he had spent in Colonel Haki's office, his brain hovering
uncertainly on the brink of sleep. He had smoked innumerable cigarettes
and read some fortnight old French newspapers. There had been an article
in one of them, he remembered, about the French mandate in the
Cameroons. A doctor had been, reported favourably on the state of his
wound, dressed it and gone. Kopeikin had brought him his suitcase and he
had made a bungled attempt to shave with his left hand. In the absence of
Colonel Haki they had shared a cool and soggy meal from the restaurant.
The Colonel had returned at two to inform him that there were nine other
passengers travelling on the boat, four of them women, that none of them
had booked for the journey less than three days previously, and that they
were all harmless.

The gangway was down now and the last of the nine, a couple who
sounded middle-aged and spoke French, had come aboard and were in the
cabin next to his. Their voices penetrated the thin wooden bulkhead with
dismaying ease. He could hear almost every sound they made. They had
argued incessantly, in whispers at first as if they had been in church; but the
novelty of their surroundings soon wore off and they spoke in ordinary
tones.

'The sheets are damp.'

'No, it is simply that they are cold. In any case it does not matter.'

'You think not? You think not?' She made a noise in her throat. 'You may
sleep as you wish, but do not complain to me about your kidneys.'

'Cold sheets do not harm the kidneys, *chérie*.'

'We have paid for our tickets. We are entitled to comfort.'

'If you never sleep in a worse place you will be lucky. This is not the
Normandie.'

'That is evident.' The washing cabinet clicked open. 'Ah! Look at this. Look! Do you expect me to wash in it?'

'It is only necessary to run the water. A little dust.'

'Dust! It is *dirty*. Filthy! It is for the steward to clean it. I will not touch it. Go and fetch him while I unpack the luggage. My dresses will be crushed. Where is the W.C.?'

'At the end of the corridor.'

'Then find the steward. There is no room for two while I unpack. We should have gone by train.'

'Naturally. But it is I who must pay. It is I who must give the steward a tip.'

'It is you who make too much noise. Quickly. Do you want to disturb everyone?'

The man went out and the woman sighed loudly. Graham wondered whether they would talk all night. And one or both of them might snore. He would have to cough loudly once or twice so that they would realize how thin the partition was. But it was strangely comforting to hear people talking about damp sheets and dirty wash basins and W.C.'s as if–the phrase was in his mind before he realized it–as if they were matters of life and death.

Life and death! He got to his feet and found himself staring at the framed instructions for lifeboat drill.

'CINTURE DI SALVATAGGIO, CEINTURES DE SAUVETAGE, RETTUNGSGÜRTEL, LIFEBELTS. . . . *In case of danger, the signal will be given by six short blasts on the whistle followed by one long blast and the ringing of alarm bells. Passengers should then put on their lifebelts and assemble at boat station number 4.*'

He had seen the same sort of thing dozens of times before but now he read it carefully. The paper it was printed on was yellow with age. The lifebelt on top of the washing cabinet looked as if it had not been moved for years. It was all ludicrously reassuring. '*In case of danger. . . .*' In case! But you couldn't get away from danger! It was all about you, all the time. You could live in ignorance of it for years; you might go to the end of your days believing that some things couldn't possibly happen to *you*, that death could only come to you with the sweet reason of disease or an 'act of God'; but it was there just the same, waiting to make nonsense of all your comfortable ideas about your relations with time and chance, ready to remind you–in case you had forgotten–that civilization was a word and that you still lived in the jungle.

The ship swayed gently. There was a faint clanging from the engine room telegraph. The floor began to vibrate. Through the smeared glass of the porthole he saw a light begin to move. The vibration ceased for a moment or two; then the engines went astern and the water glass rattled in its bracket on the wall. Another pause and then the engines went ahead again, slowly and steadily. They were free of the land. With a sigh of relief he opened the cabin door and went up on deck.

It was cold but the ship had turned and was taking the wind on her port side. She seemed stationary on the oily water of the harbour but the dock lights were sliding past them and receding. He drew the cold air into his lungs. It was good to be out of the cabin. His thoughts no longer seemed to worry him. Istanbul, Le Jockey Cabaret, the man in the crumpled suit, the Adler Palace and its manager, Colonel Haki—they were all behind him. He could forget about them.

He began to pace slowly along the deck. He would, he told himself, be able to laugh at the whole business soon. It was already half-forgotten; there was already an air of the fantastic about it. He might almost have dreamed it. He was back in the ordinary world. He was on his way home.

He passed one of his fellow passengers, the first he had seen, an elderly man leaning on the rail staring at the lights of Istanbul coming into view as they cleared the mole. Now, as he reached the end of the deck and turned about, he saw that a woman in a fur coat had just come out of the saloon door and was walking towards him.

The light on the deck was dim and she was within a few yards of him before he recognized her.

It was Josette.

Chapter Four

For a moment they stared blankly at one another. Then she laughed. 'Merciful God! It is the Englishman. Excuse me, but this is extraordinary.'

'Yes, isn't it.'

'And what happened to your first-class compartment on the Orient Express?'

He smiled. 'Kopeikin thought that a little sea air would do me good.'

'And you needed doing good?' The straw-coloured hair was covered with a woollen scarf tied under the chin, but she held her head back to look at him as if she were wearing a hat that shaded her eyes.

'Evidently.' On the whole, he decided, she looked a good deal less attractive than she had looked in her dressing-room. The fur coat was shapeless, and the scarf did not suit her. 'Since we are talking about trains,' he added, 'what happened to your second-class compartment?'

She frowned with a smile at the corners of her mouth. 'This way is so much less expensive. Did I say that I was travelling by train?'

Graham flushed. 'No, of course not. In any case, I am delighted to see you again so soon. I have been wondering what I should do if I found that the Hotel des Belges was closed.'

She looked at him archly. 'Ah! You were really going to telephone me, then?'

'Of course. It was understood, wasn't it?'

She discarded the arch look and replaced it with a pout. 'I do not think that you are sincere after all. Tell me truthfully why you are on this boat.'

She began to walk along the deck. He could do nothing but fall in step beside her.

'You don't believe me?'

She lifted her shoulders elaborately. 'You need not tell me if you do not wish to. I am not inquisitive.'

He thought he saw her difficulty. From her point of view there could be only two explanations of his presence on the boat: either his claim to be travelling first class on the Orient Express had been a pretentious lie intended to impress her–in which case he would have very little money–or he had somehow discovered that she was travelling on the boat, and had abandoned the luxury of the Orient Express in order to pursue her–in which case he would probably have plenty of money. He had a sudden absurd desire to startle her with the truth.

'Very well,' he said. 'I am travelling this way to avoid someone who is trying to shoot me.'

She stopped dead. 'I think it is too cold out here,' she said calmly. 'I shall go in.'

He was so surprised that he laughed.

She turned on him quickly. 'You should not make such stupid jokes.'

There was no doubt about it; she was genuinely angry. He held up his bandaged hand. 'A bullet grazed it.'

She frowned. 'You are very bad. If you have hurt your hand I am sorry, but you should not make jokes about it. It is very dangerous.'

'Dangerous!'

'You will have bad luck, and so shall I. It is very bad luck to joke in that way.'

'Oh, I see.' He grinned. 'I'm not superstitious.'

'That is because you do not know. I would sooner see a raven flying than joke about killing. If you wish me to like you, you must not say such things.'

'I apologize,' said Graham, mildly. 'Actually I cut my hand with a razor.'

'Ah, they are dangerous things! In Algiers José saw a man with his throat cut from ear to ear with a razor.'

'Suicide?'

'No, no! It was his *petite amie* who did it. There was a lot of blood. José will tell you about it if you ask him. It was very sad.'

'Yes, I can imagine. José is travelling with you, then?'

'Naturally.' And then, with a sidelong look: 'He is my husband.'

Her husband! That explained why she 'put up with' José. It also explained why Colonel Haki had omitted to tell him that the 'dancing blonde' was travelling on the boat. Graham remembered the promptitude with which José had retired from the dressing-room. That, no doubt, had been a matter of business. *Attractions* at a place like Le Jockey Cabaret were not quite so attractive if they were known to have husbands in the vicinity. He said: 'Kopeikin didn't tell me that you were married.'

'Kopeikin is very nice, but he does not know everything. But I will tell you confidentially that with José and me it is an arrangement. We are partners, nothing more. He is jealous about me only when I neglect business for pleasure.'

She said it indifferently, as if she were discussing a clause in her contract.

'Are you going to dance in Paris now?'

'I do not know. I hope so; but so much is closed on account of the war.'

'What will you do if you can't get an engagement?'

'What do you think? I shall starve. I have done it before.' She smiled bravely. 'It is good for the figure.' She pressed her hands on her hips and looked at him, inviting his considered opinion. 'Do you not think it would be good for my figure to starve a little? One grows fat in Istanbul.' She posed. 'You see?'

Graham nearly laughed. The picture being presented for his approval had all the simple allure of a full-page drawing in *La Vie Parisienne*. Here was the 'business man's' dream come true: the beautiful blonde dancer, married but unloved, in need of protection: something expensive going cheap.

'A dancer's must be a very hard life,' he said dryly.

'Ah, yes! Many people think that it is so gay. If they knew!'

'Yes, of course. It is getting a little cold, isn't it? Shall we go inside and have a drink?'

'That would be nice.' She added with a tremendous air of candour: 'I am so glad we are travelling together. I was afraid that I was going to be bored. Now, I shall enjoy myself.'

He felt that his answering smile was probably rather sickly. He was beginning to have an uncomfortable suspicion that he was making a fool of himself. 'We go this way, I think,' he said.

The *salone* was a narrow room about thirty feet long, with entrances from the shelter deck and from the landing at the head of the stairs to the cabins. They were grey upholstered *banquettes* round the walls and, at one end, three round dining tables bolted down. Evidently there was no separate dining-room. Some chairs, a card table, a shaky writing desk, a radio, a piano and a threadbare carpet completed the furnishings. Opening off the room at the far end was a cubby hole with half doors. The lower door had a strip of wood screwed to the top of it to make a counter. This was the bar. Inside it, the steward was opening cartons of cigarettes. Except for him, the place was deserted. They sat down.

'What would you like to drink, Mrs . . .' began Graham tentatively.

She laughed. 'José's name is Gallindo, but I detest it. You must call me Josette. I would like some English whisky and a cigarette, please.'

'Two whiskies,' said Graham.

The steward put his head out and frowned at them. 'Viski? *E molto caro*,' he said warningly; '*très cher. Cinque lire.* Five lire each. Vair dear.'

'Yes, it is, but we will have them just the same.'

The steward retired into the bar, and made a lot of noise with the bottles.

'He is very angry,' said Josette. 'He is not used to people who order whisky.' She had obviously derived a good deal of satisfaction from the ordering of the whisky, and the discomfiture of the steward. In the light of the saloon her fur coat looked cheap and old; but she had unbuttoned it and arranged it round her shoulders as if it had been mink. He began, against his better judgment, to feel sorry for her.

'How long have you been dancing?'

'Since I was ten. That is twenty years ago. You see,' she remarked complacently, 'I do not lie to you about my age. I was born in Serbia, but I say that I am Hungarian because it sounds better. My mother and father were very poor.'

'But honest, no doubt.'

She looked faintly puzzled. 'Oh no, my father was not at all honest. He was a dancer, and he stole some money from someone in the troupe. They put him in prison. Then the war came, and my mother took me to Paris. A very rich man took care of us for a time, and we had a very nice apartment.' She gave a nostalgic sigh: an impoverished *grande dame* lamenting past glories. 'But he lost his money, and so my mother had to dance again. My mother died when we were in Madrid, and I was sent back to Paris, to a convent. It was terrible there. I do not know what happened to my father. I think perhaps he was killed in the war.'

'And what about José?'

'I met him in Berlin when I was dancing there. He did not like his partner. She was,' she added simply, 'a terrible bitch.'

'Was this long ago?'

'Oh, yes. Three years. We have been to a great many places.' She examined him with affectionate concern. 'But you are tired. You look tired. You have cut your face, too.'

'I tried to shave with one hand.'

'Have you got a very nice house in England?'

'My wife likes it.'

'*Oh lá-lá!* And do you like your wife?'

'Very much.'

'I do not think,' she said reflectively, 'that I would like to go to England. So much rain and fog. I like Paris. There is nothing better to live in than an apartment in Paris. It is not expensive.'

'No?'

'For twelve hundred francs a month one can have a very nice apartment. In Rome it is not so cheap. I had an apartment in Rome that was very nice, but it cost fifteen hundred lire. My fiancé was very rich. He sold automobiles.'

'That was before you married José?'

'Of course. We were going to be married but there was some trouble about his divorce from his wife in America. He always said that he would fix it, but in the end it was impossible. I was very sorry. I had that apartment for a year.'

'And that was how you learned English?'

'Yes, but I had learned a little in that terrible convent.' She frowned. 'But I tell you everything about myself. About you I know nothing except that you have a nice house and a wife, and that you are an engineer. You ask questions, but you tell me nothing. I still do not know why you are here. It is very bad of you.'

But he did not have to reply to this. Another passenger had entered the saloon, and was advancing towards them, clearly with the intention of making their acquaintance.

He was short, broad-shouldered and unkempt, with a heavy jowl and a fringe of scurfy grey hair round a bald pate. He had a smile, fixed like that of a ventriloquist's doll: a standing apology for the iniquity of his existence.

The boat had begun to roll slightly; but from the way he clutched for support at the backs of chairs as he crossed the room, it might have been riding out a full gale.

'There is lot of movement, eh?' he said in English, and subsided into a chair. 'Ah! That is better, eh?' He looked at Josette with obvious interest, but turned to Graham before he spoke again. 'I hear English spoken so I am interested at once,' he said. 'You are English, sir?'

'Yes. And you?'

'Turkish. I also go to London. Trade is very good. I go to sell tobacco. My name is Mr Kuvetli, sir.'

'My name is Graham. This is Señora Gallindo.'

'So good,' said Mr Kuvetli. Without getting up from his chair, he bowed from the waist. 'I don't speak English very well,' he added, unnecessarily.

'It is a very difficult language,' said Josette coldly. She was obviously displeased by the intrusion.

'My wife,' continued Mr Kuvetli, 'does not speak English any. So I do not bring her with me. She has not been to England.'

'But you have?'

'Yes, sir. Three times, and to sell tobacco. I do not sell much before, but now I sell lot. It is war. United States ships do not come to England any more. English ships bring guns and aeroplanes from U.S. and have no room for tobacco, so England now buys lot of tobacco from Turkey. It is good business for my boss. Firm of Pazar and Co.'

'It must be.'

'He would come to England himself, but cannot speak English any. Or he cannot write. He is very ignorant. I reply to all favours from England and elsewhere abroad. But he knows lot about tobacco. We produce best.' He plunged his hand into his pocket and produced a leather cigarette case. 'Please try cigarette made from tobacco by Pazar and Co.' He extended the case to Josette.

She shook her head. '*Teşekkür ederim.*'

The Turkish phrase irritated Graham. It seemed to belittle the man's polite efforts to speak a language to him.

'Ah!' said Mr Kuvetli, 'you speak my language. That is very good. You have been long in Turkey?'

'*Dört ay.*' She turned to Graham. 'I would like one of *your* cigarettes, please.'

It was a deliberate insult but Mr Kuvetli only smiled a little more. Graham took one of the cigarettes.

'Thank you very much. It's very good of you. Will you have a drink, Mr Kuvetli?'

'Ah, no thank you. I must go to arrange my cabin before it is dinner.'

'Then later, perhaps.'

'Yes, please.' With a broadened smile and a bow to each of them he got to his feet and made his way to the door.

Graham lit her cigarette. 'Was it absolutely necessary to be so rude to the poor man?'

She frowned. 'Turks! I do not like them. They are'—she ransacked the automobile salesman's vocabulary for an epithet–'they are goddammed dagoes. See how thick his skin is! He does not get angry. He only smiles.'

'Yes, he behaved very well.'

'I do not understand it,' she burst out angrily. 'In the last war you fought with France against the Turks. In the convent they told me much about it. They are heathen animals, these Turks. There were the Armenian atrocities and the Syrian atrocities and the Smyrna atrocities. Turks killed babies with their bayonets. But now it is all different. You like the Turks. They are your allies and you buy tobacco from them. It is the English hypocrisy. I am a Serb. I have a longer memory.'

'Does your memory go back to nineteen twelve? I was thinking of the Serbian atrocities in Turkish villages. Most armies commit what are called atrocities at some time or other. They usually call them reprisals.'

'Including the British army, perhaps?'

'You would have to ask an Indian or an Afrikaner about that. But every country has its madmen. Some countries have more than others. And when you give such men a licence to kill they are not always particular about the way they kill. But I'm afraid that the rest of their fellow countrymen remain human beings. Personally, I like the Turks.'

She was clearly angry with him. He suspected that her rudeness to Mr Kuvetli had been calculated to earn his approval and that she was annoyed because he had not responded in the way she had expected. 'It is stuffy in here,' she said, 'and there is a smell of cooking. I should like to walk outside again. You may come with me if you wish.'

Graham seized the opportunity. He said, as they walked towards the door: 'I think that I should unpack my suitcase. I shall hope to see you at dinner.'

Her expression changed quickly. She became an international beauty humouring with a tolerant smile the extravagances of a love-sick boy. 'As you wish. José will be with me later. I shall introduce you to him. He will want to play cards.'

'Yes, I remember you told me that he would. I shall have to try to remember a game that I can play well.'

She shrugged. 'He will win in any case. But I have warned you.'

'I shall remember that when I lose.'

He returned to his cabin and stayed there until the steward came round beating a gong to announce dinner. When he went upstairs he was feeling better. He had changed his clothes. He had managed to complete the shave which he had begun in the morning. He had an appetite. He was prepared to take an interest in his fellow passengers.

Most of them were already in their places when he entered the saloon.

The ship's officers evidently ate in their own quarters. Only two of the dining tables were laid. At one of them sat Mr Kuvetli, a man and woman who looked as if they might be the French couple from the cabin next to his, Josette, and with her a very sleek José. Graham smiled courteously at the assembly and received in return a loud 'good evening' from Mr Kuvetli, a lift of the eyebrows from Josette, a cool nod from José, and a blank stare from the French couple. There was about them an air of tension which seemed to him to be more than the ordinary restraint of passengers on a boat sitting down together for the first time. The steward showed him to the other table.

One of the places was already filled by the elderly man whom he had passed on his walk round the deck. He was a thick, round-shouldered man with a pale heavy face, white hair and a long upper lip. As Graham sat down next to him he looked up. Graham met a pair of prominent pale blue eyes.

'Mr Graham?'

'Yes. Good evening.'

'My name is Haller. Doctor Fritz Haller. I should explain that I am a German, a good German, and that I am on my way back to my country.' He spoke very good, deliberate English in a deep voice.

Graham realized that the occupants of the other table were staring at them in breathless silence. He understood now the air of tension.

He said calmly: 'I am an Englishman. But I gather you knew that.'

'Yes, I knew it.' Haller turned to the food in front of him. 'The Allies seem to be here in force and unhappily the steward is an imbecile. The two French people at the next table were placed here. They objected to eating with the enemy, insulted me and moved. If you wish to do the same I suggest that you do so now. Everyone is expecting the scene.'

'So I see.'

'On the other hand,' Haller continued, breaking his bread, 'you may find the situation humorous. I do myself. Perhaps I am not as patriotic as I should be. No doubt I should insult you before you insult me; but, quite apart from the unfair differences in our ages, I can think of no effective way of insulting you. One must understand a person thoroughly before one can insult him effectively. The French lady, for example, called me a filthy Bosche. I am unmoved. I bathed this morning and I have no unpleasant habits.'

'I see your point. But . . .'

'But there is a matter of etiquette involved. Quite so. Fortunately, I must leave that to you. Move or not, as you choose. Your presence here would not embarrass me. If it were understood that we were to exclude international politics from our conversation we might even pass the next half-hour in a civilized manner. However, as the newcomer on the scene, it is for you to decide.'

Graham picked up the menu. 'I believe it is the custom for belligerents on neutral ground to ignore each other if possible and in any case to avoid embarrassing the neutrals in question. Thanks to the steward, we cannot ignore each other. There seems to be no reason why we should make a difficult situation unpleasant. No doubt we can rearrange the seating before the next meal.'

Haller nodded approval. 'Very sensible. I must admit that I am glad of your company to-night. My wife suffers from the sea and will stay in her cabin this evening. I think that Italian cooking is very monotonous without conversation.'

'I am inclined to agree with you.' Graham smiled intentionally and heard a rustle from the next table. He also heard an exclamation of disgust from the French-woman. He was annoyed to find that the sound made him feel guilty.

'You seem,' said Haller, 'to have earned some disapproval. It is partly my fault. I am sorry. Perhaps it is that I am old, but I find it extremely difficult to identify men with their ideas. I can dislike, even hate an idea, but the man who has it seems to be still a man.'

'Have you been long in Turkey?'

'A few weeks. I came there from Persia.'

'Oil?'

'No, Mr Graham, archaeology. I was investigating the early pre-Islamic cultures. The little I have been able to discover seems to suggest that some of the tribes who moved westward to the plains of Iran about four thousand years ago assimilated the Sumerian culture and preserved it almost intact until long after the fall of Babylon. The form of perpetuation of the Adonis myth alone was instructive. The weeping for Tammuz was always a focal point of the pre-historic religions—the cult of the dying and risen god. Tammuz, Osiris and Adonis are the same Sumerian deity personified by three different races. But the Sumerians called this god Dumuzida. So did some of the pre-Islamic tribes of Iran! And they had a most interesting variation of the Sumerian epic of Gilgamish and Enkidu which I had not heard about before. But forgive me, I am boring you already.'

'Not at all,' said Graham politely. 'Were you in Persia for long?'

'Two years only. I would have stayed another year but for the war.'

'Did it make so much difference?'

Haller pursed his lips. 'There was a financial question. But even without that I think that I might not have stayed. We can learn only in the expectation of life. Europe is too preoccupied with its destruction to concern itself with such things. A condemned man is interested only in himself, the passage of hours and such intimations of immortality as he can conjure from the recesses of his mind.'

'I should have thought that a preoccupation with the past. . . .'

'Ah yes, I know. The scholar in his study can ignore the noise in the market place. Perhaps—if he is a theologian or a biologist or an antiquarian. I am none of those things. I helped in the search for a logic of history. We should have made of the past a mirror with which to see round the corner that separates us from the future. Unfortunately, it no longer matters what we could have seen. We are returning the way we came. Human understanding is re-entering the monastery.'

'Forgive me but I thought you said that you were a *good* German.'

He chuckled. 'I am old. I can afford the luxury of despair.'

'Still, in your place, I think that I should have stayed in Persia and luxuriated at a distance.'

'The climate, unfortunately, is not suitable for any sort of luxuriating. It is either very hot or very cold. My wife found it particularly trying. Are you a soldier, Mr Graham?'

'No an engineer.'

'That is much the same thing. I have a son in the army. He has always been a soldier. I have never understood why he should be my son. As a lad of fourteen he disapproved of me because I had no duelling scars. He disapproved of the English, too, I am afraid. We lived for some time in Oxford while I was doing some work there. A beautiful city! Do you live in London?'

'No in the North'

'I have visited Manchester and Leeds. I preferred Oxford. I live in Berlin myself. I don't think it is any uglier than London.' He glanced at Graham's hand. 'You seem to have had an accident.'

'Yes. Fortunately it's just as easy to eat ravioli with the left hand.'

'There is that to be said for it, I suppose. Will you have some of this wine?'

'I don't think so, thank you.'

'Yes, you're wise. The best Italian wines never leave Italy.' He dropped his voice. 'Ah! Here are the other two passengers.'

They looked like mother and son. The woman was about fifty and unmistakably Italian. Her face was very hollow and pale and she carried herself as if she had been seriously ill. Her son, a handsome lad of eighteen or so, was very attentive to her and glared defensively at Graham, who had risen to draw back her chair for her. They both wore black.

Haller greeted them in Italian to which the boy replied briefly. The woman inclined her head to them but did not speak. It was obvious that they wished to be left to themselves. They conferred in whispers over the menu. Graham could hear José talking at the next table.

'War!' he was saying in thick, glutinous French; 'it makes it very difficult for all to earn money. Let Germany have all the territory she desires. Let her choke herself with territory. Then let us go to Berlin and enjoy ourselves. It is ridiculous to fight. It is not businesslike.'

'Ha!' said the Frenchman. 'You, a Spaniard, say that! Ha! That is very good. Magnificent!'

'In the civil war,' said José, 'I took no sides. I had my work to do, my living to earn. It was madness. I did not go to Spain.'

'War is terrible,' said Mr Kuvetli.

'But if the Reds had won . . .' began the Frenchman.

'Ah yes!' exclaimed his wife. 'If the Reds had won. . . . They were anti-Christ. They burnt churches and broke sacred images and relics. They violated nuns and murdered priests.'

'It was all very bad for business,' repeated José obstinately. 'I know a man in Bilbao who had a big business. It was all finished by the war. War is very stupid.'

'The voice of the fool,' murmured Haller, 'with the tongue of the wise. I think that I will go and see how my wife is. Will you excuse me, please?'

Graham finished his meal virtually alone. Haller did not return. The mother and son opposite to him ate with their heads bent over their plates. They seemed to be in communion over some private sorrow. He felt as if he were intruding. As soon as he had finished he left the saloon, put on his overcoat and went out on deck to get some air before going to bed.

The lights on the land were distant now, and the ship was rustling through the sea before the wind. He found the companion way up to the boat deck and stood for a time in the lee of a ventilator idly watching a man with a lamp on the well deck below tapping the wedges which secured the hatch tarpaulins. Soon the man finished his task, and Graham was left to wonder how he was going to pass the time on the boat. He made up his mind to get some books in Athens the following day. According to Kopeikin, they would dock at the Piraeus at about two o'clock in the afternoon, and sail again at five. He would have plenty of time to take the tram into Athens, buy some English cigarettes and books, send a telegram to Stephanie and get back to the dock.

He lit a cigarette, telling himself that he would smoke it and then go to bed; but, even as he threw the match away, he saw that Josette and José had come on to the deck, and that the girl had seen him. It was too late to retreat. They were coming over to him.

'So you are here,' she said accusingly. 'This is José.'

José, who was wearing a very tight black overcoat and a grey soft hat with a curly brim, nodded reluctantly, and said '*Enchanté, Monsieur,*' with the air of a busy man whose time is being wasted.

'José does not speak English,' she explained.

'There is no reason why he should. It is a pleasure to meet you, Señor Gallindo,' he went on in Spanish. 'I very much enjoyed the dancing of you and your wife.'

José laughed harshly. 'It is nothing. The place was impossible.'

'José was angry all the time because Coco—the negress with the snake, you remember?—had more money from Serge than we did, although we were the principal attraction.'

José said something obscene in Spanish.

'She was,' said Josette, 'Serge's lover. You smile, but it is true. Is it not true, José?'

José made a loud noise with his lips.

'José is very vulgar,' commented Josette. 'But it is true about Serge and Coco. It is a very *drôle* story. There was a great joke about Fifi, the snake. Coco was very fond of Fifi, and always used to take it to bed with her. But Serge did not know that until he became her lover. Coco says that when he found Fifi in the bed, he fainted. She made him increase her wages to double before she would consent to Fifi's sleeping alone in its basket. Serge is no fool; even José says that Serge is no fool; but Coco treats him like dirt. It is because she has a very great temper that she is able to do it.'

'He needs to hit her with his fist,' said José.

'Ah! *Salaud!*' She turned to Graham. 'And you! Do you agree with José?'

'I have no experience of snake dancers.'

'Ah! You do not answer. You are brutes, you men!'

She was obviously amusing herself at his expense. He began to feel rather foolish. He said to José: 'Have you made this trip before?'

José stared suspiciously. 'No. Why? Have you?'

'Oh no.'

José lit a cigarette. 'I am already very tired of this ship,' he announced. 'It is dull and dirty, and it vibrates excessively. Also the cabins are too near the lavabos. Do you play poker?'

'I *have* played. But I don't play very well.'

'I told you!' cried Josette.

'She thinks,' said José sourly, 'that because I win I cheat. I do not care a damn what she thinks. People are not compelled by law to play cards with me. Why should they squeal like stuck pigs when they lose?'

'It is,' Graham agreed, 'illogical.'

'We will play now if you like,' said José as if someone had accused him of refusing a challenge.

'If you don't mind, I'd sooner leave it until to-morrow. I'm rather tired to-night. In fact, I think that if you will excuse me I shall get to bed now.'

'So soon!' Josette pouted, and broke into English. 'There is only one interesting person on the boat and he goes to bed. It is too bad. Ah yes, you are being very bad. Why did you sit next to that German at dinner?'

'He did not object to my sitting beside him. Why should *I* object? He is a very pleasant and intelligent old fellow.'

'He is a German. For you no German should be pleasant or intelligent. It is as the French people were saying. The English are not serious about these things.'

José turned suddenly on his heel. 'It is very boring to listen to English,' he said, 'and I am cold. I shall go and drink some brandy.'

Graham was beginning to apologize when the girl cut him short. 'He is very unpleasant to-day. It is because he is disappointed. He thought there were going to be some pretty little girls for him to roll his eyes at. He always has a great success with pretty little girls—and old women.'

She had spoken loudly, and in French. José, who had reached the top of the companion way, turned and belched deliberately before ascending.

'He is gone,' said Josette. 'I am glad. He has very bad manners.' She drew in her breath, and looked up at the clouds. 'It is a lovely night. I do not see why you wish to go to bed. It is early.'

'I'm very tired.'

'You cannot be too tired to walk across the deck with me.'

'Of course not.'

There was a corner of the deck below the bridge where it was very dark. She stopped there, turned abruptly and leaned with her back to the rail so that he was facing her.

'I think you are angry with me?'

'Good gracious, no! Why should I be?'

'Because I was rude to your little Turk.'

'He's not *my* little Turk.'

'But you are angry?'

'Of course not.'

She sighed. 'You are very mysterious. You have still not told me why you are travelling on this boat. I am very interested to know. It cannot be because it is cheap. Your clothes are expensive!'

He could not see her face, only a vague outline of her; but he could smell the scent she was using, and the mustiness of the fur coat. He said: 'I can't think why you should be interested.'

'But you know perfectly well that I am.'

She had come an inch or two nearer to him. He knew that, if he wanted to do so, he could kiss her and that she would return the kiss. He knew also that it would be no idle peck, but a declaration that their relationship was to be the subject of discussion. He was surprised to find that he did not reject the idea instantaneously, that the immediate prospect of feeling her full smooth lips against his was more than attractive. He was cold and tired; she was near, and he could sense the warmth of her body. It could do no one any harm if . . .

He said: 'Are you travelling to Paris via Modane?'

'Yes. But why ask? It is the way to Paris.'

'When we get to Modane I will tell you exactly why I travelled this way, if you are still interested.'

She turned and they walked on. 'Perhaps it is not so important,' she said. 'You must not think I am inquisitive.' They reached the companion way. Her attitude towards him had changed perceptibly. She looked at him with friendly concern. 'Yes, my dear sir, you are tired. I should not have asked you to stay up here. I shall finish my walk alone. Good night.'

'Good night, Señora.'

She smiled. 'Señora! You must not be so unkind. Good night.'

He went below amused and irritated by his thoughts. Outside the door of the saloon he came face to face with Mr Kuvetli.

Mr Kuvetli broadened his smile. 'First officer says we shall have good weather, sir.'

'Splendid.' He remembered with a sinking heart that he had invited the man to have a drink. 'Will you join me in a drink?'

'Oh no, thank you. Not now.' Mr Kuvetli placed one hand on his chest. 'Matter of fact, I have pain because of wine at table. Very strong acid stuff!'

'So I should imagine. Until to-morrow, then.'

'Yes, Mr Graham. You will be glad to arrive back at your home, eh?' He seemed to want to talk.

'Oh yes, very glad.'

'You go to Athens when we stop to-morrow?'

'I was thinking of doing so.'

'Do you know Athens well, I suppose?'

'I've been there before.'

Mr Kuvetli hesitated. His smile became oily. 'You are in a position to do me service, Mr Graham.'

'Oh yes?'

'I do not know Athens. I have never been. Would you allow me to go with you?'

'Yes, of course. I should be glad of company. But I was only going to buy some English books and cigarettes.'

'I am most grateful.'

'Not at all. We get in just after lunch, don't we?'

'Yes, yes. That is quite right. But I will find out exact time. You leave that to me.'

'Then that's settled. I think I shall go to bed now. Good night, Mr Kuvetli.'

'Good night, sir. And I thank you for your favour.'

'Not at all. Good night.'

He went to his cabin, rang for the steward and said that he wanted his breakfast coffee in his cabin at nine-thirty. Then he undressed and got into his bunk.

For a few minutes he lay on his back enjoying the gradual relaxing of his muscles. Now, at last, he could forget Haki, Kopeikin, Banat, and the rest of it. He was back in his own life, and could sleep. The phrase 'asleep almost as soon as his head touched the pillow' passed through his mind. That was how it would be with him. God knew he was tired enough. He turned on his side. But sleep did not come so easily. His brain would not stop working. It was as if the needle were trapped in one groove on the record. He'd made a fool of himself with that wretched woman Josette. He'd made a fool . . . He jerked his thoughts forward. Ah yes! He was committed to three unalloyed hours of Mr Kuvetli's company. But that was to-morrow. And now, sleep. But his hand was throbbing again, and there seemed to be a lot of noise going on. That boor José was right. The vibration *was* excessive. The cabins *were* too near the lavatories. There were footsteps overhead, too, people walking round the shelter deck. Round and round. Why, for Heaven's sake, must people always be walking?

He had been lying awake for half an hour when the French couple entered their cabin.

They were quiet for a minute or two, and he could only hear the sounds they made as they moved about the cabin, and an occasional grunted comment. Then the woman began.

'Well, that is the first evening over! Three more! It is too much to think of.'

'It will pass.' A yawn. 'What is the matter with the Italian woman and her son?'

'You did not hear? Her husband was killed in the earthquake at Erzurum. The first officer told me. He is very nice, but I had hoped that there would be at least one French person to talk to.'

'There are people who speak French. The little Turk speaks it very well. And there are others.'

'They are not French. That girl and that man—the Spaniard. They say that they are dancers, but I ask you.'

'She is pretty.'

'Certainly. I do not dispute it. But you need not think little thoughts. She is interested in the Englishman. I do not like him. He does not look like an Englishman.'

'You think the English are all *milords* with sporting clothes and monocles. Ha! I saw the Tommies in 1915. They are all small and ugly with very loud voices. They talk very quickly. This type is more like the officers who are thin and slow, and look as if things do not smell very nice.'

'This type is not an English officer. He likes the Germans.'

'You exaggerate. An old man like that! I would have sat with him myself.'

'Ah! So you say. I will not believe it.'

'No? When you are a soldier you do not call the Bosche "the filthy Bosche." That is for the women, the civilians.'

'You are mad. They are filthy. They are beasts like those in Spain who violated nuns and murdered priests.'

'But, my little one, you forget that there were many of Hitler's Bosches who fought *against* the Reds in Spain. You forget. You are not logical.'

'They are not the same as those who attack France. They were Catholic Germans.'

'You are ridiculous! Was I not hit in the guts by a bullet fired by a Bavarian Catholic in 'seventeen? You make me tired. You are ridiculous. Be silent.'

'No, it is you who . . .'

They went on. Graham heard little more. Before he could make up his mind to cough loudly, he was asleep.

He awoke only once in the night. The vibration had ceased. He looked at his watch, saw that the time was half-past two, and guessed that they had stopped at Chanaq to drop the pilot. A few minutes later, as the engines started again, he went to sleep again.

It was not until the steward brought his coffee seven hours later that he learned that the pilot cutter from Chanaq had brought a telegram for him.

It was addressed: 'GRAHAM, VAPUR SESTRI LEVANTE, CANAKKALE.' He read:

H. REQUESTS ME INFORM YOU B. LEFT FOR SOFIA HOUR AGO. ALL WELL. BEST WISHES. KOPEIKIN.

It had been handed in at Beyoglu at seven o'clock the previous evening.

Chapter Five

It was an Aegean day: intensely coloured in the sun and with small pink clouds drifting in a bleached indigo sky. A stiff breeze was blowing and the amethyst of the sea was broken with white. The *Sestri Levante* was burying her stem in it and lifting clouds of spray which the breeze whipped across the well-deck like hail. The steward had told him that they were within sight of the island of Makronisi and as he went out on deck he saw it: a thin golden line shimmering in the sun and stretched out ahead of them like a sand bar at the entrance to a lagoon.

There were two other persons on that side of the deck. There was Haller and with him, on his arm, a small desiccated woman with thin grey hair, who was evidently his wife. They were steadying themselves at the rail and he was holding his head up to the wind as if to draw strength from it. He had his hat off and the white hair quivered with the air streaming through it.

Evidently they had not seen him. He made his way up to the boat deck. The breeze there was stronger. Mr Kuvetli and the French couple stood by the rail clutching at their hats and watching the gulls following the ship. Mr Kuvetli saw him immediately and waved. He went over to them.

'Good morning. *Madame. Monsieur.*'

They greeted him guardedly but Mr Kuvetli was enthusiastic.

'It *is* good morning, eh? You sleep well? I look forward to our excursion this afternoon. Permit me to present Monsieur and Madame Mathis. Monsieur Graham.'

There was handshaking. Mathis was a sharp-featured man of fifty or so with lean jaws and a permanent frown. But his smile, when it came, was good and his eyes were alive. The frown was the badge of his ascendancy over his wife. She had bony hips and wore an expression which said that she was determined to keep her temper however sorely it were tried. She was like her voice.

'Monsieur Mathis,' said Mr Kuvetli, whose French was a good deal more certain than his English, 'is from Eskeshehir, where he has been working with the French railway company.'

'It is a bad climate for the lungs,' said Mathis. 'Do you know Eskeshehir, Monsieur Graham?'

'I was there for a few minutes only.'

'That would have been quite enough for me,' said Madame Mathis. 'We have been there three years. It was never any better than the day we arrived.

'The Turks are a great people,' said her husband. 'They are hard and they endure. But we shall be glad to return to France. Do you come from London, Monsieur?'

'No, the North of England. I have been in Turkey for a few weeks on business.'

'To us, war will be strange after so many years. They say that the towns in France are darker than the last time.'

'The towns are damnably dark both in France and in England. If you do not have to go out at night it is better to stay in.'

'It is war,' said Mathis sententiously.

'It is the filthy Bosche,' said his wife.

'War,' put in Mr Kuvetli, stroking an unshaven chin, 'is a terrible thing. There is no doubt of it. But the Allies must win.'

'The Bosche is strong,' said Mathis. 'It is easy to say that the Allies must win, but they yet have the fighting to do. And do we yet know whom we are going to fight or where? There is a front in the East as well as in the West. We do not yet know the truth. When that is known the war will be over.'

'It is not for us to ask questions,' said his wife.

His lips twisted and in his brown eyes was the bitterness of years. 'You are right. It is not for us to ask questions. And why? Because the only people who can give us the answers are the bankers and the politicians at the top, the boys with the shares in the big factories which make war materials. They will not give us answers. Why? Because they know that if the soldiers of France and England knew those answers they would not fight.'

His wife reddened. 'You are mad! Naturally the men of France would fight to defend us from the filthy Bosche.' She glanced at Graham. 'It is bad to say that France would not fight. We are not cowards.'

'No, but neither are we fools.' He turned quickly to Graham. 'Have you heard of Briey, Monsieur? From the mines of the Briey district comes ninety per cent. of France's iron ore. In 1914 those mines were captured by the Germans, who worked them for the iron they needed. They worked them hard. They have admitted since that without the iron they mined at Briey they would have been finished in 1917. Yes, they worked Briey hard. I, who was at Verdun, can tell you that. Night after night we watched the glare in the sky from the blast furnaces of Briey a few kilometres away; the blast furnaces that were feeding the German guns. Our artillery and our bombing aeroplanes could have blown those furnaces to pieces in a week. But our artillery remained silent; an airman who dropped one bomb on the Briey area was courtmartialled. Why?' His voice rose. 'I will tell you why,

Monsieur. Because there were orders that Briey was not to be touched. Whose orders? Nobody knew. The orders came from someone at the top. The Ministry of War said that it was the generals. The generals said that it was the Ministry of War. We did not find out the facts until after the war. The orders had been issued by Monsieur de Wendel of the Comité des Forges who owned the Briey mines and blast furnaces. We were fighting for our lives, but our lives were less important than that the property of Monsieur de Wendel should be preserved to make fat profits. No, it is not good for those who fight to know too much. Speeches, yes! The truth, no!'

His wife sniggered. 'It is always the same. Let someone mention the war and he begins to talk about Briey—something that happened twenty-four years ago.'

'And why not?' he demanded. 'Things have not changed so much. Because we do not know about such things until after they have happened it does not mean that things like it are not happening now. When I think of war I think also of Briey and the glare of the blast furnaces in the sky to remind myself that I am an ordinary man who must not believe all that he is told. I see the newspapers from France with the blanks in them to show where the censor has been at work. They tell me certain things, these newspapers. France, they say, is fighting with England against Hitler and the Nazis for democracy and liberty.'

'And you don't believe that?' Graham asked.

'I believe that *the peoples* of France and England are so fighting, but is that the same thing? I think of Briey and wonder. Those same newspapers once told me that the Germans were not taking ore from the Briey mines and that all was well. I am an invalid of the last war. I do not have to fight in this one. But I can think.'

He wife laughed again. 'Ha! It will be different when he gets to France again. He talks like a fool but you should take no notice, Messieurs. He is a good Frenchman. He won the Croix de Guerre.'

He winked. 'A little piece of silver outside the chest to serenade the little piece of steel inside, eh? It is the women, I think, who should fight these wars. They are more ferocious as patriots than the men.'

'And what do you think, Mr Kuvetli?' said Graham.

'Me? Ah, please!' Mr Kuvetli looked apologetic. 'I am neutral, you understand. I know nothing. I have no opinion.' He spread out his hands. 'I sell tobacco. Export business. That is enough.'

The Frenchman's eyebrows went up. 'Tobacco? So? I arranged a great deal of transport for the tobacco companies. What company is that?'

'Pazar of Istanbul.'

'Pazar?' Mathis looked slightly puzzled. 'I don't think . . .'

But Mr Kuvetli interrupted him. 'Ah! See! There is Greece!'

They looked. There, sure enough, was Greece. It looked like a low bank of cloud on the horizon beyond the end of the golden line of Makronisi, a line that was contracting slowly as the ship ploughed on its way through the Zea channel.

'Beautiful day!' enthused Mr Kuvetli. 'Magnificent!' He drew a deep breath and exhaled loudly. 'I anticipate very much to see Athens. We get to Piraeus at two o'clock.'

'Are you and Madame going ashore?' said Graham to Mathis.

'No, I think not. It is too short a time.' He turned his coat collar up and shivered. 'I agree that it is a beautiful day, but it is cold.'

'If you did not stand talking so much,' said his wife, 'you would keep warm. And you have no scarf.'

'Very well, very well!' he said irritably. 'We will go below. Excuse us, please.'

'I think that I, too, will go,' said Mr Kuvetli. 'Are you coming down, Mr Graham?'

'I'll stay a little.' He would have enough of Mr Kuvetli later.

'Then at two o'clock.'

'Yes.'

When they had gone he looked at his watch, saw that it was eleven-thirty, and made up his mind to walk round the boat deck ten times before he went down for a drink. He was, he decided as he began to walk, a good deal better for his night's rest. For one thing, his hand had ceased throbbing and he could bend the fingers a little, without pain. More important, however, was the fact that the feeling of moving in a nightmare which he had had the previous day had now gone. He felt whole again and cheerful. Yesterday was years away. There was, of course, his bandaged hand to remind him of it but the wound no longer seemed significant. Yesterday it had been a part of something horrible. To-day it was a cut on the back of his hand, a cut which would take a few days to heal. Meanwhile he was on his way home, back to his work. As for Mademoiselle Josette, he had had, fortunately, enough sense left not to behave really stupidly. That he should actually have wanted, even momentarily, to kiss her was fantastic enough. However, there were extenuating circumstances. He had been tired and confused; and, while she was a woman whose needs and methods of fulfilling them were only too apparent, she was undeniably attractive in a blowsy way.

He had completed his fourth circuit when the subject of these reflections appeared on the deck. She had on a camel hair coat instead of the fur, a green cotton scarf round her head in place of the woollen one, and wore sports shoes with cork 'platform' soles. She waited for him to come over to her.

He smiled and nodded. 'Good morning.'

She raised her eyebrows. 'Good morning! Is that all you have to say?'

He was startled. 'What should I say?'

'You have disappointed me. I thought that all Englishmen got out of bed early to eat a great English breakfast. I get out of bed at ten but you are nowhere to be found. The steward says that you are still in your cabin.'

'Unfortunately they don't serve English breakfasts on this boat. I made do with coffee and drank it in bed.'

She frowned. 'Now, you do not ask why I wished to see you. Is it so natural that I should wish to see you as soon as I left my bed?'

The mock severity was appalling. Graham said: 'I'm afraid I didn't take you seriously. Why *should* you want to find me ?'

'Ah, that is better. It is not good but it is better. Are you going into Athens this afternoon?'

'Yes.'

'I wished to ask you if you would let me come with you.'

'I see. I should be . . . '

'But now it is too late.'

'I'm so sorry,' said Graham happily. 'I should have been delighted to take you.'

She shrugged. 'It is too late. Mr Kuvetli, the little Turk has asked me and, *faute de mieux*, I accepted. I do not like him but he knows Athens very well. It will be interesting.'

'Yes, I should think it would be.'

'He is a very interesting man.'

'Evidently.'

'Of course, I might be able to persuade him . . .'

'Unfortunately, there is a difficulty. Last night Mr Kuvetli asked me if I minded his going with me as he had never been in Athens before.'

It gave him a great deal of pleasure to say it; but she was disconcerted only momentarily. She burst out laughing.

'You are not at all polite. Not at all. You let me say what you know to be untrue. You do not stop me. You are unkind.' She laughed again. 'But it is a good joke.'

'I'm really very sorry.'

'You are too kind. I wished only to be friendly to you. I do not care whether I go to Athens or not.'

'I'm sure Mr Kuvetli would be delighted if you came with us. So should I, of course. You probably know a great deal more about Athens than I do.'

Her eyes narrowed suddenly. 'What, please, do you mean by that?'

He had not meant anything at all beyond the plain statement. He said, with a smile that he intended to be reassuring: 'I mean that you have probably danced there.'

She stared at him sullenly for a moment. He felt the smile, still clinging fatuously to his lips, fading. She said slowly: 'I do not think I like you as much as I thought. I do not think that you understand me at all.'

'It's possible. I've known you for such a short time.'

'Because a woman is an artiste,' she said angrily, 'you think that she must be of the *milieu*.'

'Not at all. The idea hadn't occurred to me. Would you like to walk round the deck?'

She did not move. 'I am beginning to think that I do not like you at all.'

'I'm sorry. I was looking forward to your company on the journey.'

'But you have Mr Kuvetli,' she said viciously.

'Yes, that's true. Unfortunately, he's not as attractive as you are.'

She laughed sarcastically. 'Oh, you have seen that I am attractive? That is very good. I am so pleased. I am honoured.'

'I seem to have offended you,' he said. 'I apologize.'

She waved one hand airily. 'Do not trouble. I think that it is perhaps because you are stupid. You wish to walk. Very well, we will walk.'

'Splendid.'

They had taken three steps when she stopped again and faced him. 'Why do you have to take this little Turk to Athens?' she demanded. 'Tell him that you cannot go. If you were polite you would do that.'

'And take you? Is that the idea?'

'If you asked me, I would go with you. I am bored with this ship and I like to speak English.'

'I'm afraid that Mr Kuvetli might not think it so polite.'

'If you liked me it would not matter to you about Mr Kuvetli.' She shrugged. 'But I understand. It does not matter. I think that you are very unkind, but it does not matter. I am bored.'

'I'm sorry.'

'Yes, you are sorry. That is all right. But I am still bored. Let us walk.' And then, as they began to walk: 'José thinks that you are indiscreet.'

'Does he? Why?'

'That old German you talked to. How do you know that he is not a spy?'

He laughed outright. 'A spy! What an extraordinary idea!'

She glanced at him coldly. 'And why is it extraordinary?'

'If you had talked to him you would know quite well that he couldn't possibly be anything of the sort.'

'Perhaps not. José is always very suspicious of people. He always believes that they are lying about themselves.'

'Frankly, I should be inclined to accept José's disapproval of a person as a recommendation.'

'Oh, he does not disapprove. He is just interested. He likes to find things out about people. He thinks that we are all animals. He is never shocked by anything people do.'

'He sounds very stupid.'

'You do not understand José. He does not think of good things and evil things as they do in the convent, but only of things. He says that a thing that is good for one person may be evil for another, so that it is stupid to talk of good and evil.'

'But people sometimes do good things simply because those things *are* good.'

'Only because they feel nice when they do them—that is what José says.'

'What about the people who stop themselves from doing evil because it *is* evil?'

'José says that if a person *really* needs to do something he will not trouble about what others may think of him. If he is really hungry, he will steal. If he is in real danger, he will kill. If he is really afraid, he will be cruel. He says that it was people who were safe and well fed who invented good and evil so that they would not have to worry about the people who were hungry and unsafe. What a man does depends on what he needs. It is simple. You are not a murderer. You say that murder is evil. José would say that you are as much a murderer as Landru or Weidmann and that it is just that fortune has not made it necessary for you to murder anyone. Someone once told him that there was a German proverb which said that a man is an ape in velvet. He always likes to repeat it.'

'And do you agree with José? I don't mean about my being a potential murderer. I mean about why people are what they are.'

'I do not agree or disagree. I do not care. For me, some people are nice, some people are sometimes nice and others are not at all nice.' She looked at him out of the corners of her eyes. 'You are sometimes nice.'

'What do you think about yourself?'

She smiled. 'Me? Oh, I am sometimes nice, too. When people are nice to me, I am a little angel.' She added: 'José thinks that he is as clever as God.'

'Yes, I can see that he would.'

'You do not like him. I am not surprised. It is only the old women who like José.'

'Do *you* like him?'

'He is my partner. With us it is business.'

'Yes, you told me that before. But do you *like* him?'

'He makes me laugh sometimes. He says amusing things about people. You remember Serge? José said that Serge would steal straw from his mother's kennel. It made me laugh very much.'

'It must have done. Would you like a drink now?'

She looked at a small silver watch on her wrist and said that she would.

They went down. One of the ship's officers was leaning by the bar with a beer in his hand, talking to the steward. As Graham ordered the drinks, the officer turned his attention to Josette. He obviously counted on being successful with women; his dark eyes did not leave hers while he was talking to her. Graham, listening to the Italian with bored incomprehension, was ignored. He was content to be ignored. He got on with his drink. It was not until the gong sounded for lunch and Haller came in that he remembered that he had done nothing about changing his place at table.

The German nodded in a friendly way as Graham sat down beside him. 'I did not expect to have your company to-day.'

'I completely forgot to speak to the steward. If you . . .'

'No, please. I take it as a compliment.'

'How is your wife?'

'Better, though she is not yet prepared to face a meal. But she took a walk this morning. I showed her the sea. This is the way Xerxes' great ships sailed to their defeat at Salamis. For those Persians that grey mass on the horizon was the country of Themistocles and the Attic Greeks of Marathon. You will think that it is my German sentimentality but I must say that the fact that for me that grey mass is the country of Venizelos and Metaxas is as regrettable as it could be. I was at the German Institute in Athens for several years when I was young.'

'Shall you go ashore this afternoon?'

'I do not think so. Athens can only remind me of what I know already–that I am old. Do you know the city?'

'A little. I know Salamis better.'

'That is now their big naval base, isn't it?'

Graham said yes rather too carelessly. Haller glanced sideways and smiled slightly. 'I beg your pardon. I see that I am on the point of being indiscreet.'

'I shall go ashore to get some books and cigarettes. Can I get anything for you?'

'It is very kind of you, but there is nothing. Are you going alone?'

'Mr Kuvetli, the Turkish gentleman at the next table has asked me to show him round. He has never been to Athens.'

Haller raised his eyebrows. 'Kuvetli? So that is his name. I talked with him this morning. He speaks German quite well and knows Berlin a little.'

'He speaks English too, and very good French. He seems to have travelled a lot.'

Haller grunted. 'I should have thought that a Turk who had travelled a lot would have been to Athens.'

'He sells tobacco. Greece grows its own tobacco.'

'Yes, of course. I had not thought of that. I am apt to forget that most people who travel do so not to see but to sell. I talked with him for twenty minutes. He has a way of talking without saying anything. His conversation consists of agreements or indisputable statements.'

'I suppose it's something to do with his being a salesman. "The world is my customer and the customer is always right."'

'He interests me. In my opinion he is too simple to be true. The smile is a little too stupid, the conversation a little too evasive. He tells you some things about himself within the first minutes of your meeting him and then tells you no more. That is curious. A man who begins by telling you about himself usually goes on doing so. Besides, who ever heard of a simple Turkish business man? No, he makes me think of a man who has set out to create a definite impression of himself in people's minds. He is a man who wishes to be underrated.'

'But why? He's not selling us tobacco.'

'Perhaps, as you suggest, he regards the world as his customer. But you will have an opportunity of probing a little this afternoon.' He smiled. 'You see, I assume, quite unwarrantably, that you are interested. I must ask your pardon. I am a bad traveller who has had to do a great deal of travelling. To pass the time I have learned to play a game. I compare my own first impressions of my fellow travellers with what I can find out about them.'

'If you are right you score a point? If you are wrong you lose one?'

'Precisely. Actually I enjoy losing more than winning. It is an old man's game, you see.'

'And what is your impression of Señor Gallindo?'

Haller frowned. 'I am afraid that I am only too right about that gentleman. He is not really very interesting.'

'He has a theory that all men are potential murderers and is fond of quoting a German proverb to the effect that a man is an ape in velvet.'

'It does not surprise me,' was the acid reply. 'Every man must justify himself somehow.'

'Aren't you a little severe?'

'Perhaps. I regret to say that I find Señor Gallindo a very ill-mannered person.'

Graham's reply was interrupted by the entrance of the man himself, looking as if he had just got out of bed. He was followed by the Italian mother and son. The conversation became desultory and over-polite.

The *Sestri Levante* was tied up alongside the new wharf on the north side of the harbour of the Piraeus soon after two o'clock. As, with Mr Kuvetli, Graham stood on the deck waiting for the passenger gangway to be hoisted into position, he saw that Josette and José had left the saloon and were standing behind him. José nodded to them suspiciously as if he were afraid that they were thinking of borrowing money from him. The girl smiled. It was the tolerant smile that sees a friend disregarding good advice.

Mr Kuvetli spoke up eagerly. 'Are you going ashore, Monsieur-dame?'

'Why should we?' demanded José. 'It is a waste of time to go.'

But Mr Kuvetli was not sensitive. 'Ah! Then you know Athens, you and your wife?'

'Too well. It is a dirty town.'

'I have not seen it. I was thinking that if you and Madame were going, we might all go together.' He beamed round expectantly.

José set his teeth and rolled his eyes as if he were being tortured. 'I have already said that we are *not* going.'

'But it is very kind of you to suggest it,' Josette put in graciously.

The Mathis came out of the saloon. 'Ah!' he greeted them. 'The adventurers! Do not forget that we leave at five. We shall not wait for you.'

The gangway thudded into position and Mr Kuvetli clambered down it nervously. Graham followed. He was beginning to wish that he had decided to stay on board. At the foot of the gangway he turned and looked up–the inevitable movement of a passenger leaving a ship. Mathis waved his hand.

'He is very amiable, Monsieur Mathis,' said Mr Kuvetli.

'Very.'

Beyond the Customs shed there was a flyblown old Fiat landaulet with a notice on it in French, Italian, English and Greek, saying that an hour's tour of the sights and antiquities of Athens for four persons cost five hundred drachmas.

Graham stopped. He thought of the electric trains and trams he would have to clamber on to, of the hill up to the Acropolis, of the walking he would have to do, of the exhausting boredom of sightseeing on foot. Any way of avoiding the worst of it was, he decided, worth twenty shillingsworth of drachmas.

'I think,' he said, 'that we will take this car.'

Mr Kuvetli looked worried. 'There is no other way? It is very expensive.'

'That's all right. I'll pay.'

'But it is you who do favour to me. I must pay.'

'Oh, I should have taken a car in any case. Five hundred drachmas is not really expensive.'

Mr Kuvetli's eyes opened very wide. 'Five hundred? But that is for four persons. We are two.'

Graham laughed. 'I doubt if the driver will look at it that way. I don't suppose it costs him any less to take two instead of four.'

Mr Kuvetli looked apologetic. 'I have little Greek. You will permit me to ask him?'

'Of course. Go ahead.'

The driver, a predatory looking man wearing a suit several sizes too small for him and highly polished tan shoes without socks, had leapt out at their approach and was holding the door open. Now he began to shout. '*Allez! Allez! Allez!*' he exhorted them; '*très bon marché. Cinque-cento, solamente.*'

Mr Kuvetli strode forward, a stout, grubby little Daniel going out to do battle with a lean Goliath in stained blue serge. He began to speak.

He spoke Greek fluently; there was no doubt of it. Graham saw the surprised look on the driver's face replaced by one of fury as a torrent of words poured from Mr Kuvetli's lips. He was disparaging the car. He began to point. He pointed to every defect in the thing from a patch of rust on the luggage grid to a small tear in the upholstery, from a crack in the wind shield to a worn patch on the running board. He paused for breath and the angry driver seized the opportunity of replying. He shouted and thumped the door panels with his fist to emphasise his remarks and made long streamlining gestures. Mr Kuvetli smiled sceptically and returned to the attack. The driver spat on the ground and counter-attacked. Mr Kuvetli replied with a short, sharp burst of fire. The driver flung up his hands, disgusted but defeated.

Mr Kuvetli turned to Graham. 'Price,' he reported simply, 'is now three hundred drachmas. It is too much, I think, but it will take time to reduce more. But if you think . . .'

'It seems a very fair price,' said Graham hurriedly.

Mr Kuvetli shrugged. 'Perhaps. It could be reduced more, but . . .' He turned and nodded to the driver, who suddenly grinned broadly. They got into the cab.

'Did you say,' said Graham, as they drove off, 'that you had never been in Greece before?'

Mr Kuvetli's smile was bland. 'I know little Greek,' he said. 'I was born in Izmir.'

The tour began. The Greek drove fast and with dash, twitching the wheel playfully in the direction of slow moving pedestrians, so that they had to run for their lives, and flinging a running commentary over his right shoulder as he went. They stopped for a moment on the road by the Theseion and again on the Acropolis where they got out and walked round. Here, Mr Kuvetli's curiosity seemed inexhaustible. He insisted on a century by century history of the Parthenon and prowled round the museum as if he would have liked to spend the rest of the day there; but at last they got back into the car and were whisked round to the theatre of Dionysos, the arch of Hadrian, the Olympieion, and the Royal Palace. It was, by now, four o'clock and Mr Kuvetli had been asking questions and saying 'very nice' and '*formidable*' for well over the allotted hour. At Graham's suggestion they stopped in the Syntagma, changed some money and paid off the driver, adding that if he liked to wait in the square he could earn another fifty drachmas by driving them back to the wharf later. The driver agreed. Graham bought his cigarettes and books and sent his telegram. There was a band playing on the terrace of one of the cafés when they got back to the square and at Mr Kuvetli's suggestion they sat down at a table to drink coffee before returning to the port.

Mr Kuvetli surveyed the square regretfully. 'It is very nice,' he said with a sigh. 'One would like to stay longer. So many magnificent ruins we have seen!'

Graham remembered what Haller had said at lunch about Mr Kuvetli's evasions. 'Which is your favourite city, Mr Kuvetli?'

'Ah, that is difficult to say. All cities have their magnificences. I like all cities.' He breathed the air. 'It is most kind of you to bring me here to-day, Mr Graham.'

Graham stuck to the point. 'A great pleasure. But surely you have some preference.'

Mr Kuvetli looked anxious. 'It is so difficult. I like London very much.'

'Personally I like Paris better.'

'Ah, yes. Paris is also magnificent.'

Feeling rather baffled, Graham sipped his coffee. Then he had another idea. 'What do you think of Señor Gallindo, Mr Kuvetli?'

'Señor Gallindo? It is so difficult. I do not know him. His manner is strange.'

'His manner,' said Graham, 'is damnably offensive. Don't you agree?'

'I do not like Señor Gallindo very much,' conceded Mr Kuvetli. 'But he is Spanish.'

'What can that have to do with it? The Spanish are an exceedingly polite race.'

'Ah, I have not been to Spain.' He looked at his watch. 'It is quarter-past four now. Perhaps we should go, eh? It has been very nice this afternoon.'

Graham nodded wearily. If Haller wanted Mr Kuvetli 'probed' he could do the probing himself. His, Graham's, personal opinion was that Mr Kuvetli was an ordinary bore whose conversation, such as it was, sounded a little unreal because he used languages with which he was unfamiliar.

Mr Kuvetli insisted on paying for the coffee; Mr Kuvetli insisted on paying the fare back to the wharf. By a quarter to five they were on board again. An hour later Graham stood on deck watching the pilot's boat chugging back towards the greying land. The Frenchman, Mathis, who was leaning on the rail a few feet away, turned his head.

'Well, that's *that!* Two more days and we shall be in Genoa. Did you enjoy your excursion ashore this afternoon, Monsieur?'

'Oh, yes, thank you. It was . . .'

But he never finished telling Monsieur Mathis what it was. A man had come out of the saloon door some yards away and was standing blinking at the setting sun which streamed across the sea towards them.

'Ah, yes,' said Mathis. 'We have acquired another passenger. He arrived while you were ashore this afternoon. I expect that he is a Greek.'

Graham did not, could not, answer. He knew that the man standing there with the golden light of the sun on his face was not a Greek. He knew, too, that beneath the dark grey raincoat the man wore there was a crumpled brown suit with lumpy padded shoulders; that below the high-crowned soft hat and above the pale, doughy features with the self-conscious mouth was thinning curly hair. He knew that this man's name was Banat.

Chapter Six

Graham stood there motionless. His body was tingling as if some violent mechanical shock had been transmitted to it through his heels. He heard Mathis' voice a long way away, asking him what the matter was.

He said: 'I don't feel well. Will you excuse me, please?'

He saw apprehension flicker over the Frenchman's face and thought: 'He thinks I'm going to be sick.' But he did not wait for Mathis to say anything. He turned and, without looking again at the man by the saloon door, walked to the door at the other end of the deck and went below to his cabin.

He locked the door when he got inside. He was shaking from head to foot. He sat down on the bunk and tried to pull himself together. He told himself: 'There's no need to get worried. There's a way out of this. You've got to think.'

Somehow Banat had discovered that he was on the *Sestri Levante*. It could not have been very difficult. An inquiry made at the Wagon-Lit and shipping company offices would have been enough. The man had then taken a ticket for Sofia, left the train when it crossed the Greek frontier, and taken another train via Salonika to Athens.

He pulled Kopeikin's telegram out of his pocket and stared at it. 'All well!' The fools! The bloody fools! He'd distrusted this ship business from the start. He ought to have relied on his instinct and insisted on seeing the British Consul. If it had not been for that conceited imbecile Haki . . . But now he was caught like a rat in a trap. Banat wouldn't miss twice. My God, no! The man was a professional murderer. He would have his reputation to consider–to say nothing of his fee.

A curious but vaguely familiar feeling began to steal over him: a feeling that was dimly associated with the smell of antiseptics and the singing of a kettle. With a sudden rush of horror, he remembered. It had happened years ago. They had been trying out an experimental fourteen-inch gun on the proving ground. The second time they fired it, it had burst. There had been something wrong with the breech mechanism. It had killed two men outright and badly injured a third. This third man had looked like a great clot of blood lying there on the concrete. But the clot of blood had screamed: screamed steadily until the ambulance had come and a doctor had used a hypodermic. It had been a thin, high, inhuman sound; just like the singing of a kettle. The doctor had said that the man was unconscious even though he was screaming. Before they had examined the remains of the gun, the concrete had been swabbed down with a solution of lysol. He hadn't eaten any lunch. In the afternoon it had begun to rain. He . . .

He realised suddenly that he was swearing. The words were dropping from his lips in a steady stream, a meaningless succession of obscenities. He stood up quickly. He was losing his head. Something had got to be done; and done quickly. If he could get off the ship . . .

He wrenched the cabin door open and went out into the alleyway. The Purser was the man to see first. The Purser's office was on the same deck. He went straight to it.

The door of the office was ajar and the Purser, a tall, middle-aged Italian with the stump of a cigar in his mouth, was sitting in his shirt-sleeves before a typewriter and a stack of copies of Bills of Lading. He was copying details of the Bills on to the ruled sheet in the typewriter. He looked up with a frown as Graham knocked. He was busy.

'*Signore?*'

'Do you speak English?'

'No, *Signore.*'

'French?'

'Yes. What is it you wish?'

'I want to see the Captain at once.'

'For what reason, Monsieur?'

'It is absolutely necessary that I am put ashore immediately.'

The Purser put his cigar down and turned in his swivel chair.

'My French is not very good,' he said calmly. 'Do you mind repeating . . .?'

'I want to be put ashore.'

'Monsieur Graham, is it?'

'Yes.'

'I regret, Monsieur Graham. It is too late. The pilot boat has gone. You should have . . .'

'I know. But it is absolutely necessary that I go ashore now. No, I am not mad. I realize that under ordinary circumstances it would be out of the question. But the circumstances are exceptional. I am ready to pay for the loss of time and the inconvenience caused.'

The Purser looked bewildered. 'But why? Are you ill?'

'No, I . . .' He stopped and could have bitten his tongue off. There was no doctor aboard and the threat of some infectious disease might have been sufficient. But it was too late now. 'If you will arrange for me to see the Captain at once, I will explain why. I can assure you that my reasons are good ones.'

'I am afraid,' said the Purser stiffly, 'that it is out of the question. You do not understand . . .'

'All I am asking,' interrupted Graham desperately, 'is that you put back a short way and ask for a pilot boat. I am willing and able to pay.'

The Purser smiled in an exasperated way. 'This is a ship, Monsieur, not a taxi. We carry cargo and run to a schedule. You are not ill and . . .'

'I have already said that my reasons are excellent. If you will allow me to see the Captain . . .'

'It is quite useless to argue, Monsieur. I do not doubt your willingness or ability to pay the cost of a boat from the harbour. Unfortunately that is not the important thing. You say that you are not ill but that you have reasons. As you can only have thought of those reasons within the last ten minutes, you must not be angry if I say that they cannot be of very grave importance. Let me assure you, Monsieur, that nothing but proved and evident reasons of life and death will suffice to stop any ship for the convenience of one passenger. Naturally, if you can give me any such reasons I will place them before the Captain immediately. If not, then I am afraid your reasons must wait until we get to Genoa.'

'I assure you . . .'

The Purser smiled sorrowfully. 'I do not question the good faith of your assurances, Monsieur, but I regret to say that we need more than assurances.'

'Very well,' snapped Graham, 'since you insist on details I will tell you. I have just found that there is a man on this ship who is here for the express purpose of murdering me.'

The Purser's face went blank. 'Indeed, Monsieur?'

'Yes, I . . .' Something in the man's eyes stopped him. 'I suppose you've decided that I'm either mad or drunk,' he concluded.

'Not at all, Monsieur.' But what he was thinking was as plain as a pikestaff. He was thinking that Graham was just another of the poor lunatics with whom his work sometimes brought him in contact. They were a nuisance, because they wasted time. But he was tolerant. It was useless to be angry with a lunatic. Besides, dealing with them always seemed to emphasize his own sanity and intelligence: the sanity and intelligence which, had the owners been less short sighted, would long ago have taken him to a seat on the board of directors. And they made good stories to tell his friends when he got home. 'Imagine, Beppo! There was this Englishman, looking sane but really mad. He thought that someone was trying to murder him! Imagine! It is the whisky, you know. I said to him . . .' But meanwhile he would have to be humoured, to be dealt with tactfully. 'Not at all, Monsieur,' he repeated.

Graham began to lose control of his temper. 'You asked me for my reasons. I am giving them to you.'

'And I am listening carefully, Monsieur.'

'There is someone on this ship who is here to murder me.'

'And his name, Monsieur?'

'Banat. B-A-N-A-T. He is a Romanian. He . . .'

'One moment, Monsieur.' The Purser got a sheet of paper out of a drawer and ran a pencil down the names on it with ostentatious care. Then he looked up. 'There is no one of that name or nationality on the ship, Monsieur.'

'I was about to tell you, when you interrupted me, that the man is travelling on a false passport.'

'Then, please . . .?'

'He is the passenger who came aboard this afternoon.'

The Purser looked at the paper again. 'Cabin number nine. That is Monsieur Mavrodopoulos. He is a Greek business man.'

'That may be what his passport says. His real name is Banat and he is a Romanian.'

The Purser remained polite with obvious difficulty. 'Have you any proof of that, Monsieur?'

'If you radio Colonel Haki of the Turkish police at Istanbul, he will confirm what I say.'

'This is an Italian ship, Monsieur. We are not in Turkish territorial waters. We can refer such a matter only to the Italian police. In any case, we carry wireless only for navigational purposes. This is not the *Rex* or the *Conte di Savoia*, you understand. This matter must be left until we reach Genoa. The police there will deal with your accusation concerning the passport.'

'I don't care a damn about his passport,' said Graham violently. 'I'm telling you that the man intends to kill me.'

'And why?'

'Because he has been paid to do so; that is why. Now do you understand?'

The Purser got to his feet. He had been tolerant. Now the time had come to be firm. 'No, Monsieur, I do *not* understand.'

'Then if you cannot understand, let me speak to the Captain.'

'That will not be necessary, Monsieur. I understand enough.' He looked Graham in the eyes. 'In my opinion there are two *charitable* explanations of this matter. Either you have mistaken this Monsieur Mavrodopoulos for someone else, or you have had a bad dream. If it is the former, I advise you not to repeat your mistake to anyone else. I am discreet, but if Monsieur Mavrodopoulos should hear of it he might regard it as a reflection upon his honour. If it is the second, I suggest that you lie down in your cabin for a while. And remember that nobody is going to murder you on this ship. There are too many people about.'

'But don't you see . . .?' shouted Graham.

'I see,' said the Purser grimly, 'that there is another less charitable explanation of this matter. You may have invented this story simply because for some private reason you wish to be put ashore. If that is true, I am sorry. It is a ridiculous story. In any case, the ship stops at Genoa and not before. And now, if you will excuse me, I have work to do.'

'I demand to see the Captain.'

'If you will close the door as you leave,' said the Purser happily.

Almost sick with anger and fear, Graham went back to his cabin.

He lit a cigarette and tried to think reasonably. He should have gone straight to the Captain. He could still go straight to the Captain. For a moment he considered doing so. If he . . . But it would be useless and unnecessarily humiliating. The Captain, even if he could get to him and make him understand, would probably receive his story with even less sympathy. And he would still have no proof that what he said was true. Even if he could persuade the Captain that there was some truth in what he was saying, that he was not, in fact, suffering from some form of delusional insanity, the answer would be the same: 'Nobody is going to murder you on this ship. There are too many people about.'

Too many people about! They did not know Banat. The man who had walked into a police official's house in broad daylight, shot the official and his wife and then calmly walked out again, was not going to be unnerved so easily. Passengers had disappeared from ships in mid-ocean before. Sometimes their bodies had been washed ashore, and sometimes they hadn't. Sometimes the disappearances had been explained, and sometimes they hadn't. What would there be to connect this disappearance of an English engineer (who had behaved very queerly) from a ship at sea with Mr Mavrodopoulos, a Greek business man? Nothing. And even if the body of the English engineer were washed ashore before the fish had rendered it unidentifiable and it were found that he had been killed before he had entered the water, who was going to prove that Mr Mavrodopoulos–if by that time there were anything left of Mr Mavrodopoulos but the ashes of his passport–had been responsible for the killing? Nobody.

He thought of the telegram he had sent in Athens that afternoon. 'Home Monday,' he had said. Home Monday! He looked at his unbandaged hand and moved the fingers of it. By Monday they could be dead and beginning to decompose with the rest of the entity which called itself Graham. Stephanie would be upset, but she'd get over it quickly. She was resilient and sensible.

But there wouldn't be much money for her. She'd have to sell the house. He ought to have taken out more insurance. If only he'd known. But of course it was just because you *didn't* know that there were such things as insurance companies. Still, he could do nothing now but hope that it would be over quickly, that it wouldn't be painful.

He shivered and began to swear again. Then he pulled himself up sharply. He'd *got* to think of some way out. And not only for his own sake and Stephanie's. There was the job he had to do. 'It is in the interests of your country's enemies that when the snow melts and the rain ceases, Turkish naval strength shall be exactly what it is now. They will do anything to see that it is so.' Anything! Behind Banat was the German agent in Sofia and behind him was Germany and the Nazis. Yes, he'd *got* to think of some way out. If other Englishmen could die for their country, surely he could manage to stay alive for it. Then another of Colonel Haki's statements came back to him. 'You have advantages over the soldier. You have only to defend yourself. You do not have to go into the open. You may run away without being a coward.'

Well he couldn't run away now; but the rest of it was true enough. He didn't have to go out into the open. He could stay here in the cabin; have his meals here; keep the door locked. He could defend himself, too, if need be. Yes, by God! He had Kopeikin's revolver.

He had put it among the clothes in his suit-case. Now, thanking his stars that he had not refused to take it, he got it out and weighed it in his hand.

For Graham a gun was a series of mathematical expressions resolved in such a way as to enable one man, by touching a button, to project an armour-piercing shell so that it hit a target several miles away plumb in the middle. It was a piece of machinery no more and no less significant than a vacuum cleaner or a bacon slicer. It had no nationality and no loyalties. It was neither awe-inspiring nor symbolic of anything except the owner's ability to pay for it. His interest in the men who had to fire the products of his skill as in the men who had to suffer their fire (and, thanks to his employers' tireless internationalism, the same sets of men often had to do both) had always been detached. To him who knew what even one four-inch shell could accomplish in the way of destruction, it seemed that they should be—could only be—nerveless cyphers. That they were not was an evergreen source of astonishment to him. His attitude towards them was uncomprehending as that of the stoker of a crematorium towards the solemnity of the grave.

But this revolver was different. It wasn't impersonal. There was a relationship between it and the human body. It had, perhaps, an effective range of twenty-five yards or less. That meant that you could see the face of the man at whom you fired it both before and after you fired it. You could see and hear his agony. You couldn't think of honour and glory with a revolver in your hand, but only of killing and being killed. There was no machine to serve. Life and death were there in your hand in the shape of an elementary arrangement of springs and levers and a few grammes of lead and cordite.

He had never handled a revolver in his life before. He examined it carefully. Stamped above the trigger guard was 'Made in U.S.A.' and the name of an American typewriter manufacturer. There were two small sliding bosses on the other side. One was the safety catch. The other, when moved, released the breech which dropped sideways and showed that there were cartridges in all six chambers. It was beautifully made. He took the cartridges out and pulled the trigger once or twice experimentally. It was not easy with his bandaged hand, but it could be done. He put the cartridges back.

He felt better now. Banat might be a professional killer, but he was as susceptible to bullets as any other man. And *he* had to make the first move. One had to look at things from his point of view. He'd failed in Istanbul and he'd had to catch up with the victim again. He'd managed to get aboard the boat on which the victim was travelling. But did that really help him very much? What he had done in Romania as a member of the Iron Guard was beside the point now. A man could afford to be bold when he was protected by an army of thugs and an intimidated judge. It was true that passengers were sometimes lost off ships at sea; but those ships were big liners, not two thousand ton cargo boats. It really would be very difficult to kill a man on a boat of that size without anyone discovering that you had done so. You might be able to do it; that is if you could get your victim alone on deck at night. You could knife him and push him over the side. But you would have to get him there first, and there was more than a chance that you would be seen from the bridge. Or heard: a knifed man might make a lot of noise before he reached the water. And if you cut his throat there would be a lot of blood left behind to be accounted for. Besides, that was always assuming that you could use a knife so skilfully. Banat was a gunman, not a cut-throat. That confounded Purser was right. There were too many people about for anyone to murder him on the ship. As long as he was careful he would be all right. The real danger would begin when he got off the ship at Genoa.

Obviously, the thing for him to do there would be to go straight to the British Consul, explain all the circumstances, and secure police protection as far as the frontier. Yes, that was it. He had one priceless advantage over the enemy. *Banat did not know that he was identified.* He would be assuming that the victim was unsuspecting, that he could bide his time, that he could do his work between Genoa and the French frontier. By the time he discovered his mistake it would be too late for him to do anything about rectifying it. The only thing now was to see that he did not discover the mistake too soon.

Supposing, for instance, that Banat had noticed his hasty retreat from the deck. His blood ran cold at the idea. But no, the man had not been looking. The supposition showed, though, how careful he had to be. It was out of the question for him to skulk in his cabin for the rest of the trip. That would arouse immediate suspicion. He would have to look as unsuspecting as he could and yet take care not to expose himself to any sort of attack. He must make sure that if he were not in his cabin with the door locked, he was with or near one of the other passengers. He must even be amiable to 'Monsieur Mavrodopoulos.'

He unbuttoned his jacket and put the revolver in his hip pocket. It bulged absurdly and uncomfortably. He took the wallet out of his breast pocket and put the revolver there. That was uncomfortable, too, and the shape of it could be seen from the outside. Banat must not see that he was armed. The revolver could stay in the cabin.

He put it back in his suit-case and stood up, bracing himself. He'd go straight up to the saloon and have a drink now. If Banat were there, so much the better. A drink would help to ease the strain of the first encounter. He knew that it would be a strain. He had to face a man who had tried once to kill him and who was going to try again, and behave as if he had never seen or heard of him before. His stomach was already responding to the prospect. But he had to keep calm. His life, he told himself, might depend on his behaving normally. And the longer he hung about thinking it over, the less normal he would be. Better get it over with now.

He lit a cigarette, opened the cabin door and went straight upstairs to the saloon.

Banat was not there. He could have laughed aloud with relief. Josette and José were there with drinks in front of them, listening to Mathis.

'And so,' he was saying vehemently, 'it goes on. The big newspapers of the Right are owned by those whose interest it is to see that France spends her wealth on arms and that the ordinary people do not understand too much of what goes on behind the scenes. I am glad to be going back to France because it is my country. But do not ask me to love those who have my country in the palms of their hands. Ah, no!'

His wife was listening with tight-lipped disapproval. José was openly yawning. Josette was nodding sympathetically but her face lit up with relief when she saw Graham. 'And where has our Englishman been?' she said immediately. 'Mr Kuvetli has told everyone what a magnificent time you both had.'

'I've been in my cabin recovering from the afternoon's excitements.'

Mathis did not look very pleased at the interruption but said agreeably enough: 'I was afraid that you were ill, Monsieur. Are you better now?'

'Oh yes, thanks.'

'You have been ill?' demanded Josette.

'I felt tired.'

'It is the ventilation,' said Madame Mathis promptly. 'I myself have felt a nausea and a headache since I got on the ship. We should complain. But'–she made a derogatory gesture in the direction of her husband–'as long as he is comfortable all is well.'

Mathis grinned. 'Bah! It is seasickness.'

'You are ridiculous. If I am sick it is of you.'

José made a loud plopping noise with his tongue and leaned back in his chair, his closed eyes and tightened lips calling upon Heaven to deliver him from domesticity.

Graham ordered a whisky.

'Whisky?' José sat up whistling astonishment. 'The Englishman drinks whisky!' he announced and then, pursing his lips and screwing up his face to express congenital aristocratic idiocy, added: 'Some viskee, pliz, ol' bhoy!' He looked round, grinning, for applause.

'That is his idea of an Englishman,' Josette explained. 'He is very stupid.'

'Oh I don't think so,' said Graham; 'he has never been to England. A great many English people who have never been to Spain are under the impression that all Spaniards smell of garlic.'

Mathis giggled.

José half rose in his chair. 'Do you intend to be insulting?' he demanded.

'Not at all. I was merely pointing out that these misconceptions exist. You, for instance, do not smell of garlic at all.'

José subsided into his chair again. 'I am glad to hear you say so,' he said ominously. 'If I thought . . .'

'Ah! Be silent!' Josette broke in. 'You make yourself look a fool.'

To Graham's relief the subject was disposed of by the entrance of Mr Kuvetli. He was beaming happily.

'I come,' he said to Graham, 'to ask you to have a drink with me.'

'That's very good of you but I've just ordered a drink. Supposing you have one with me.'

'Most kind. I will take vermouth, please.' He sat down. 'You have seen we have new passenger?'

'Yes, Monsieur Mathis pointed him out to me.' He turned to the steward bringing him his whisky and ordered Mr Kuvetli's vermouth.

'He is Greek gentleman. Name of Mavrodopoulos. He is business man.'

'What business is he in?' Graham found, to his relief, that he could talk of Monsieur Mavrodopoulos quite calmly.

'That I do not know.'

'That I do not care,' said Josette. 'I have just seen him. Ugh!'

'What's the matter with him?'

'She likes only men who look clean and simple,' said José vindictively. 'This Greek looks dirty. He would probably smell dirty too, but he uses a cheap perfume.' He kissed his fingers to the air. '*Nuit de Petits Gars! Numero Soixante-neuf! Cinq francs la bouteille.*'

Madame Mathis' face froze.

'You are disgusting, José,' said Josette. 'Besides, your own perfume cost only fifty francs a bottle. It is filthy. And you must not say such things. You will offend Madame here who is not used to your jokes.'

But Madame Mathis had already taken offence. 'It is disgraceful,' she said angrily, 'that such things should be said when there are women present. With men alone it would not be polite.'

'Ah yes!' said Mathis. 'My wife and I are not hypocrites but there are some things that should not be said.' He looked as if he were pleased to be able, for once, to side with his wife. Her surprise was almost pathetic. They proceeded to make the most of the occasion.

She said: 'Monsieur Gallindo should apologize.'

'I must insist,' said Mathis, 'that you apologize to my wife.'

José stared at them in angry astonishment. 'Apologize? What for?'

'He will apologize,' said Josette. She turned to him and broke into Spanish. 'Apologize, you dirty fool. Do you want trouble? Don't you see he's showing off to the woman? He would break you in pieces.'

José shrugged. 'Very well.' He looked insolently at the Mathis. 'I apologize. What for, I do not know, but I apologize.'

'My wife accepts the apology,' said Mathis stiffly. 'It is not gracious but it is accepted.'

'An officer says,' remarked Mr Kuvetli tactfully, 'that we shall not be able to see Messina because it will be dark.'

But this elephantine change of subject was unnecessary for at that moment Banat came through the door from the promenade deck.

He stood there for an instant looking at them, his raincoat hanging open, his hat in his hand, like a man who has strayed into a picture gallery out of the rain. His white face was drawn from lack of sleep, there were circles under the small deep-set eyes, the full lips were twisted slightly as if he had a headache.

Graham's heart drummed sickeningly at the base of his skull. This was the executioner. The hand with the hat in it was the hand which had fired the shots which had grazed his own hand, now outstretched to pick up a glass of whisky. This was the man who had killed men for as little as five thousand francs and his expenses.

He felt the blood leaving his face. He had only glanced quickly at the man but the whole picture of him was in his mind; the whole picture from the dusty tan shoes to the new tie with the filthy soft collar and the tired, frowsty, stupid face. He drank some of his whisky and saw that Mr Kuvetli was bestowing his smile on the newcomer. The others were staring blankly.

Banat walked slowly over to the bar.

'*Bon soir, Monsieur,*' said Mr Kuvetli.

'*Bon soir.*' It was grunted almost inaudibly as if he were anxious not to commit himself to accepting something he did not want. He reached the bar and murmured something to the steward.

He had passed close to Madame Mathis and Graham saw her frown. Then he himself caught the smell of scent. It was attar of roses and very strong. He remembered Colonel Haki's question as to whether he had noticed any perfume in his room at the Adler Palace after the attacks. Here was the explanation. The man reeked of scent. The smell of it would stay with the things he touched.

'Are you going far, Monsieur?' said Mr Kuvetli.

The man eyed him. 'No. Genoa.'

'It is a beautiful city.'

Banat turned without answering to the drink the steward had poured out for him. He had not once looked at Graham.

'You are not looking well,' said Josette severely. 'I do not think you are sincere when you say that you are only tired.'

'You are tired?' said Mr Kuvetli in French. 'Ah, it is my fault. Always with ancient monuments it is necessary to walk.' He seemed to have given Banat up as a bad job.

'Oh, I enjoyed the walk.'

'It is the ventilation,' Madame Mathis repeated stubbornly.

'There *is*,' conceded her husband, 'a certain stuffiness.' He addressed himself very pointedly to exclude José from his audience. 'But what can one expect for so little money?'

'So little!' exclaimed José. 'That is very good. It is quite expensive enough for me. I am not a millionaire.'

Mathis flushed angrily. 'There are more expensive ways of travelling from Istanbul to Genoa.'

'There is always a more expensive way of doing anything,' retorted José.

Josette said quickly: 'My husband always exaggerates.'

'Travelling is very expensive to-day,' pronounced Mr Kuvetli.

'But . . .'

The argument rambled on, pointless and stupid; a mask for the antagonism between José and the Mathis. Graham listened with half his mind. He knew that sooner or later Banat must look at him and he wanted to see that look. Not that it would tell him anything that he did not already know, but he wanted to see it just the same. He could look at Mathis and yet see Banat out of the corner of his eye. Banat raised the glass of brandy to his lips and drank some of it; then, as he put the glass down, he looked directly at Graham.

Graham leaned back in his chair.

'. . . but,' Mathis was saying, 'compare the service one receives. On the train there is a *couchette* in a compartment with others. One sleeps—perhaps. There is waiting at Belgrade for the coaches from Bucharest and at Trieste for the coaches from Budapest. There are passport examinations in the middle of the night and terrible food in the day. There is the noise and there is the dust and soot. I cannot conceive . . .'

Graham drained his glass. Banat was inspecting him: secretly, as the hangman inspects the man whom he is to execute the following morning; mentally weighing him, looking at his neck, calculating the drop.

'Travelling is very expensive to-day,' said Mr Kuvetli again.

At that moment the dinner gong sounded. Banat put his glass down and went out of the room. The Mathis followed. Graham saw that Josette was looking at him curiously. He got to his feet. There was a smell of food coming from the kitchen. The Italian woman and her son came in and sat down at the table. The thought of food made him feel ill.

'You are sure you feel well?' said Josette as they went to the dinner tables. 'You do not look it.'

'Quite sure.' He cast about desperately for something else to say and uttered the first words that came into his head: 'Madame Mathis is right. The ventilation is not good. Perhaps we could walk on deck after dinner is over.'

She raised her eyebrows. 'Ah, now I know that you cannot be well! You are polite. But very well, I will go with you.'

He smiled fatuously, went on to his table, and exchanged reserved greetings with the two Italians. It was not until he sat down that he noticed that an extra place had been laid beside them.

His first impulse was to get up and walk out. The fact that Banat was on the ship was bad enough: to have to eat at the same table would be intolerable. But everything depended upon his behaving normally. He would *have* to stay. He must try and think of Banat as Monsieur Mavrodopoulos, a Greek business man, whom he had never seen or heard of before. He must . . .

Haller came in and sat down beside him. 'Good evening, Mr Graham. And did you enjoy Athens this afternoon?'

'Yes, thanks. Mr Kuvetli was suitably impressed.'

'Ah, yes, of course. You were doing duty as a guide. You must be feeling tired.'

'To tell you the truth, my courage failed me. I hired a car. The chauffeur

did the guiding. As Mr Kuvetli speaks fluent Greek, the whole thing went
off quite satisfactorily.'

'He speaks Greek and yet he has never been to Athens?'

'It appears that he was born in Smyrna. Apart from that, I regret to say, I
discovered nothing. My own private opinion is that he is a bore.'

'That is disappointing. I had hopes . . . However, it cannot be helped. To
tell you the truth, I wished afterwards that I had come with you. You went
up to the Parthenon, of course.'

'Yes.'

Haller smiled apologetically. 'When you reach my age you sometimes
think of the approach of death. I thought this afternoon how much I would
have liked to have seen the Parthenon just once more. I doubt if I shall have
another opportunity of doing so. I used to spend hours standing in the
shade by the Propylaea looking at it and trying to understand the men who
built it. I was young then and did not know how difficult it is for Western
man to understand the dream-heavy classical soul. They are so far apart.
The god of superlative shape has been replaced by the god of superlative
force and between the two conceptions there is all space. The destiny idea
symbolized by the Doric columns is incomprehensible to the children of
Faust. For us . . .' He broke off. 'Excuse me. I see that we have another
passenger. I suppose that he is to sit here.'

Graham forced himself to look up.

Banat had come in and was standing looking at the tables. The steward,
carrying plates of soup, appeared behind him and motioned him towards
the place next to the Italian woman. Banat approached, looked round the
table, and sat down. He nodded to them, smiling slightly.

'Mavrodopoulos,' he said. '*Je parle français un petit peu.*'

His voice was toneless and husky and he spoke with a slight lisp. The
smell of attar of roses came across the table.

Graham nodded distantly. Now that the moment had come he felt quite
calm.

Haller's look of strangled disgust was almost funny. He said pompously:
'Haller. Beside you are Signora and Signor Beronelli. This is Monsieur
Graham.'

Banat nodded to them again and said: 'I have travelled a long way to-day.
From Salonika.'

Graham made an effort. 'I should have thought,' he said, 'that it would
have been easier to go to Genoa by train from Salonika.' He felt oddly
breathless as he said it and his voice sounded strange in his own ears.

There was a bowl of raisins in the centre of the table and Banat put some
in his mouth before replying. 'I don't like trains,' he said shortly. He looked
at Haller. 'You are a German, Monsieur?'

Haller frowned. 'I am.'

'It is a good country, Germany.' He turned his attention to Signora
Beronelli. 'Italy is good, too.' He took some more raisins.

The woman smiled and inclined her head. The boy looked angry.

'And what,' said Graham, 'do you think about England?'

The small tired eyes stared into his coldly. 'I have never seen England.'
The eyes wandered away round the table. 'When I was last in Rome,' he

said, 'I saw a magnificent parade of the Italian army with guns and armoured cars and aeroplanes.' He swallowed his raisins. 'The aeroplanes were a great sight and made one think of God.'

'And why should they do that, Monsieur?' demanded Haller. Evidently he did not like Monsieur Mavrodopoulos.

'They made one think of God. That is all I know. You feel it in the stomach. A thunderstorm makes one think of God, too. But these aeroplanes were better than a storm. They shook the air like paper.'

Watching the full self-conscious lips enunciating these absurdities, Graham wondered if an English jury, trying the man for murder, would find him insane. Probably not, he killed for money, and the Law did not think that a man who killed for money was insane. And yet he *was* insane. His was the insanity of the sub-conscious mind running naked, of the 'throw back,' of the mind which could discover the majesty of God in thunder and lightning, the roar of bombing planes, or the firing of a five hundred pound shell; the awe-inspired insanity of the primaeval swamp. Killing, for this man, *could* be a business. Once, no doubt, he had been surprised that people should be prepared to pay so handsomely for the doing of something they could do so easily for themselves. But, of course, he would have ended by concluding, with other successful business men, that he was cleverer than his fellows. His mental approach to the business of killing would be that of the lavatory attendant to the business of attending to his lavatories or of the stockbroker towards the business of taking his commission: purely practical.

'Are you going to Rome now?' said Haller politely. It was the heavy politeness of an old man with a young fool.

'I go to Genoa,' said Banat.

'I understand,' said Graham, 'that the thing to see at Genoa is the cemetery.'

Banat spat out a raisin seed. 'That is so? Why?' Obviously, that sort of remark was not going to disconcert him.

'It is supposed to be very large, very well arranged, and planted with very fine cypresses.'

'Perhaps I shall go.'

The waiter brought soup. Haller turned rather ostentatiously to Graham and began once more to talk about the Parthenon. It seemed that he liked arranging his thoughts aloud. The resultant monologue demanded practically nothing of the listener but an occasional nod. From the Parthenon he wandered to pre-Hellenic remains, the Aryan hero tales, and the Vedic religion. Graham ate mechanically, listened, and watched Banat. The man put his food in his mouth as if he enjoyed it. Then, as he chewed, he would look round the room like a dog over a plate of scraps. There was something pathetic about him. He was—Graham realised it with a shock—pathetic in the way that a monkey, in its likeness to man, could be pathetic. He was not insane. He was an animal and dangerous.

The meal came to an end. Haller, as usual, went to his wife. Thankful for the opportunity, Graham left at the same time, got his overcoat, and went out on deck.

The wind had dropped and the roll of the ship was long and slow. She was making good speed and the water sliding along her plates was hissing and bubbling as if they were red hot. It was a cold, clear night.

The smell of attar of roses was at the back of his throat and in his nostrils. He drew the fresh unscented air into his lungs with conscious pleasure. He was, he told himself, over the first hurdle. He had sat face to face with Banat and talked to him without giving himself away. The man could not possibly suspect that he was known and understood. The rest of it would be easy. He had only to keep his head.

There was a step behind him and he swung round quickly, his nerves jumping.

It was Josette. She came towards him smiling. 'Ah! So this is your politeness. You ask me to walk with you, but you do not wait for me. I have to find you. You are very bad.'

'I'm sorry. It was so stuffy in the saloon that . . .'

'It is not at all stuffy in the saloon, as you know perfectly well.' She linked her arm in his. 'Now we will walk and you shall tell me what is *really* the matter.'

He looked at her quickly. 'What is *really* the matter! What do you mean?'

She became the *grande dame*. 'So you are not going to tell me. You will not tell me how you came to be on this ship. You will not tell me what has happened to-day to make you so nervous.'

'Nervous! But . . .'

'Yes, Monsieur Graham, nervous!' She abandoned the *grande dame* with a shrug. 'I am sorry but I have seen people who are afraid before. They do not look at all like people who are tired or people who feel faint in a stuffy room. They have a special look about them. Their faces look very small and grey round the mouth and they cannot keep their hands still.' They had reached the stairs to the boat deck. She turned and looked at him. 'Shall we go up?'

He nodded. He would have nodded if she had suggested that they jump overboard. He could think of only one thing. If *she* knew a frightened man when she saw one, then so did Banat. And if Banat had noticed. . . . But he couldn't have noticed. He couldn't. He . . .

They were on the boat deck now and she took his arm again.

'It is a very nice night,' she said. 'I am glad that we can walk like this. I was afraid this morning that I had annoyed you. I did not really wish to go to Athens. That officer who thinks he is so nice asked me to go with him but I did not. But I would have gone if you had asked me. I do not say that to flatter you. I tell you the truth.'

'It's very kind of you,' he muttered.

She mimicked him. '"It's very kind of you." Ah, you are so solemn. It is as if you did not like me.'

He managed to smile. 'Oh, I like you, all right.'

'But you do not trust me? I understand. You see me dancing in Le Jockey Cabaret and you say, because you are so experienced: "Ah! I must be careful of this lady." Eh? But I am a friend. You are so silly.'

'Yes, I am silly.'

'But you *do* like me?'

'Yes, I like you.' A stupid fantastic suggestion was taking root in his mind. He would tell her about Banat.

'Then you must trust me, also.'

'Yes, I must.' It was absurd, of course. He couldn't trust her. Her motives were as transparent as the day. He couldn't trust anybody. He was alone. If he had someone to talk to about it, though, it wouldn't be so bad. Now supposing Banat had seen that he was nervous and concluded that he was on his guard. Had he or hadn't he seen? She could tell him that.

'What are you thinking about?'

'To-morrow.' If anything happened to him there would be nobody to accuse Banat. He would go scot free to collect his wages. She was right. It was stupid to distrust her simply because she danced in night places. After all, Kopeikin had liked her and he was no fool about women.

They had reached the corner below the bridge structure. She stopped as he had known she would.

'If we stay here,' she said, 'I shall get cold. It will be better if we go on walking round and round and round the deck.'

'I thought you wanted to ask me questions.'

'I have told you I am not inquisitive.'

'So you did. Do you remember that yesterday evening I told you that I came on this ship to avoid someone who was trying to shoot me and that this'–he held up his right hand–'was a bullet wound?'

'Yes. I remember. It was a bad joke.'

'A very bad joke. Unfortunately, it happened to be true.'

It was out now. He could not see her face but he heard her draw in her breath sharply and felt her fingers dig into his arm.

'You are lying to me.'

'I'm afraid not.'

'But you are an engineer,' she said accusingly. 'You said so. What have you done that someone should wish to kill you?'

'I have done nothing.' He hesitated. 'I just happen to be on important business. Some business competitors don't want me to return to England.'

'Now you are lying.'

'Yes, I am lying, but not very much. I *am* on important business and there *are* some people who do not want me to get back to England. They employed men to kill me while I was in Gallipoli but the Turkish police arrested these men before they could try. Then they employed a professional killer to do the job. When I got back to my hotel after I left Le Jockey Cabaret the other night, he was waiting for me. He shot at me and missed everything except my hand.'

She was breathing quickly. 'It is atrocious! A bestiality! Does Kopeikin know of it?'

'Yes. It was partly his idea that I should travel on this boat.'

'But who are these people?'

'I only know one. His name is Moeller and he lives in Sofia. The Turkish police told me that he is a German agent.'

'The *salaud*! But he cannot touch you now.'

'Unfortunately he can. While I was ashore with Kuvetli this afternoon, another passenger came aboard.'

'The little man who smells? Mavrodopoulos? But. . . .'

'His real name is Banat and he is the professional killer who shot at me in Istanbul.'

'But how do you know?' she demanded breathlessly.

'He was at Le Jockey Cabaret watching me. He had followed me there to see that I was out of the way before he broke into my room at the hotel. It was dark in the room when he shot at me, but the police showed me his photograph later and I identified him.'

She was silent for a moment. Then she said slowly: 'It is not very nice. That little man is a dirty type.'

'No, it is not very nice.'

'You must go to the Captain.'

'Thanks. I've tried to see the Captain once. I got as far as the Purser. He thinks I'm either crazy, drunk, or lying.'

'What are you going to do?'

'Nothing for the moment. He doesn't know that I know who he is. I think that he will wait until we get to Genoa before he tries again. When we get there I shall go to the British Consul and ask him to advise the police.'

'But I think he *does* know that you suspect him. When we were in the *salone* before dinner and the Frenchman was talking about trains, this man was watching you. Mr Kuvetli was watching you also. You looked so curious, you see.'

His stomach turned over. 'You mean, I suppose, that I looked frightened to death. I was frightened. I admit it. Why shouldn't I? I am not used to people trying to kill me.' His voice had risen. He felt himself shaking with a sort of hysterical anger.

She gripped his arm again. 'Ssh! You must not speak so loudly.' And then: 'Does it matter so much that he knows?'

'If he knows, it means that he will have to act before we get to Genoa.'

'On this little ship? He would not dare.' She paused. 'José has a revolver in his box. I will try to get it for you.'

'I've got a revolver.'

'Where?'

'It's in my suitcase. It shows in my pocket. I did not want him to see that I knew I was in danger.'

'If you carry the revolver you will be in no danger. Let him see it. If a dog sees that you are nervous, he will bite you. With types like that you must show that you are dangerous and then they are afraid.' She took his other arm. 'Ah, you do not need to worry. You will get to Genoa and you will go to the British Consul. You can ignore this dirty beast with the perfume. By the time you get to Paris you will have forgotten him.'

'If I get to Paris.'

'You are impossible. Why should you not get to Paris?'

'You think I'm a fool.'

'I think perhaps you are tired. Your wound . . .'

'It was only a graze.'

'Ah, but it is not the size of the wound. It is the shock.'

He wanted suddenly to laugh. It was true what she was saying. He hadn't really got over that hellish night with Kopeikin and Haki. His nerves were on edge. He was worrying unnecessarily. He said: 'When we get to Paris,

Josette, I shall give you the best dinner it is possible to buy.'

She came close to him. 'I don't want you to give me anything, *chéri*. I want you to like me. You *do* like me?'

'Of course I like you. I told you so.'

'Yes, you told me so.'

His left hand touched the belt on her coat. Her body moved suddenly pressing against his. The next moment his arms were round her and he was kissing her.

When his arms grew tired, she leaned back, half against him, half against the rail.

'Do you feel better, *chéri*?'

'Yes, I feel better.'

'Then I will have a cigarette.'

He gave her the cigarette and she looked at him across the light of the match. 'Are you thinking of this lady in England who is your wife?'

'No.'

'But you *will* think of her?'

'If you keep talking about her I shall have to think about her.'

'I see. For you I am part of the journey from Istanbul to London. Like Mr Kuvetli.'

'Not quite like Mr Kuvetli. I shan't kiss Mr Kuvetli if I can help it.'

'What do you think about me?'

'I think that you're very attractive. I like your hair and your eyes and the scent you use.'

'That is very nice. Shall I tell you something, *chéri*?'

'What?'

She began to speak very softly. 'This boat is very small; the cabins are very small; the walls are very thin; and there are people everywhere.'

'Yes?'

'Paris is very large and there are nice hotels there with big rooms and thick walls. One need not see anyone one does not wish to see. And do you know, *chéri*, that if one is making a journey from Istanbul to London and one arrives in Paris, it is sometimes necessary to wait a week before continuing the journey?'

'That's a long time.'

'It is because of the war, you see. There are always difficulties. People have to wait days and days for permission to leave France. There is a special stamp that must be put in your passport, and they will not let you on the train to England until you have that stamp. You have to go to the Préfecture for it and there is a great deal of *chi-chi*. You have to stay in Paris until the old women in the Préfecture can find time to deal with your application.'

'Very annoying.'

She sighed. 'We could pass that week or ten days very nicely. I do not mean at the Hotel des Belges. That is a dirty place. But there is the Ritz Hotel and the Lancaster Hotel and the Georges Cinq. . . .' She paused and he knew that he was expected to say something.

He said it. 'And the Crillon and the Meurice.'

She squeezed his arm. 'You are very nice. But you understand me? An apartment is cheaper, but for so little time that is impossible. One cannot enjoy oneself in a cheap hotel. All the same I do not like extravagance. There are nice hotels for less than it costs at the Ritz or the Georges Cinq and one has more money to spend on eating and dancing at nice places. Even in war time there are nice places.' The burning end of her cigarette made and impatient gesture. 'But I must not talk about money. You will make the old women at the Préfecture give you your permit too soon and then I shall be disappointed.'

He said: 'You know, Josette, I shall begin in a minute to think that you are really serious.'

'And you think that I am not?' She was indignant.

'I'm quite sure of it.'

She burst out laughing. 'You can be rude very politely. I shall tell José that. It will amuse him.'

'I don't think I want to amuse José. Shall we go down?'

'Ah, you are angry! You think that I have been making a fool of you.'

'Not a bit.'

'Then kiss me.'

Some moments later she said softly: 'I like you very much. I would not mind very much a room for fifty francs a day. But the Hotel des Belges is terrible. I do not want to go back there. You are not angry with me?'

'No, I am not angry with you.' Her body was soft and warm and infinitely yielding. She had made him feel as if Banat and the rest of the journey really did not matter. He felt both grateful to and sorry for her. He made up his mind that, when he got to Paris, he would buy her a handbag and slip a thousand franc note in it before he gave it to her. He said: 'It's all right. You needn't go back to the Hotel des Belges.'

When at last they went down to the saloon it was after ten. José and Mr Kuvetli were there playing cards.

José was playing with thin-lipped concentration and took no notice of them; but Mr Kuvetli looked up. His smile was sickly.

'Madame,' he said ruefully, 'your husband plays cards very well.'

'He has had a lot of practice.'

'Ah, yes, I am sure.' He played a card. José slapped another one on top of it triumphantly. Mr Kuvetli's face fell.

'It is my game,' said José and gathered up some money from the table. 'You have lost eighty-four lire. If we had been playing for lire instead of centesimi I should have won eight thousand four hundred lire. That would be interesting. Shall we play another game?'

'I think that I will go to bed now,' said Mr Kuvetli hurriedly. 'Good night, Messieurs-dame.' He went.

José sucked his teeth as if the game had left an unpleasant taste in his mouth. 'Everyone goes to bed early on this filthy boat,' he said. 'It is very boring.' He looked up at Graham. 'Do you want to play?'

'I'm sorry to say that I must go to bed, too.'

José shrugged. 'Very well. Good-bye.' He glanced at Josette and began to deal two hands. 'I will play a game with you.'

She looked at Graham and smiled hopelessly. 'If I do not he will be disagreeable. Good night, Monsieur.'

Graham smiled and said good night. He was not unrelieved.

He got to his cabin feeling a good deal more cheerful than he had felt when he had left it earlier in the evening.

How sensible she was! And how stupid he'd been. With men like Banat it was dangerous to be subtle. If a dog saw that you were nervous, he bit you. From now on he would carry the revolver. What was more, he would use it if Banat tried any funny business. You had to meet force with force.

He bent down to pull his suitcase from under the bunk. He was going to get the revolver out then and there.

Suddenly he stopped. For an instant his nostrils had caught the sweet cloying smell of attar of roses.

The smell had been faint, almost imperceptible, and he could not detect it again. For a moment he remained motionless, telling himself that he must have imagined it. Then panic seized him.

With shaking fingers he tore at the latches on the suitcase and flung back the lid.

The revolver was gone.

Chapter Seven

He undressed slowly, got into his bunk and lay there staring at the cracks in the asbestos round a steam pipe which crossed the ceiling. He could taste Josette's lipstick in his mouth. The taste was all that was left to remind him of the self-assurance with which he had returned to the cabin; the self-assurance which had been swept away by fear welling up into his mind like blood from a severed artery; fear that paralyzed thought. Only his senses seemed alive.

On the other side of the partition, Mathis finished brushing his teeth and there was a lot of grunting and creaking as he clambered into the upper berth. At last he lay back with a sigh. •

'Another day!'

'So much the better. Is the porthole open?'

'Unmistakably. There is a very disagreeable current of air on my back.'

'We do not want to be ill like the Englishman.'

'That was nothing to do with the air. It was seasickness. He would not admit it because it would not be correct for an Englishman to be seasick. The English like to think that they are all great sailors. He is *drôle* but I like him.'

'That is because he listens to your nonsense. He is polite—too polite. He and that German greet each other now as if they were friends. *That* is not correct. If this Gallindo . . .'

'Oh, we have talked enough about him.'

'Signora Beronelli said that he knocked against her on the stairs and went on without apologizing.'

'He is a filthy type.'

There was a silence. Then:

'Robert!'

'I am nearly asleep.'

'You remember that I said that the husband of Signora Beronelli was killed in the earthquake?'

'What about it?'

'I talked to her this evening. It is a terrible story. It was not the earthquake that killed him. He was shot.'

'Why?'

'She does not wish everyone to know. You must say nothing of it.'

'Well?'

'It was during the first earthquake. After the great shocks were over they went back to their house from the fields in which they had taken refuge. The house was in ruins. There was part of one wall standing and he made a shelter against it with some boards. They found some food that had been in the house but the tanks had been broken and there was no water. He left her with the boy, their son, and went to look for water. Some friends who had a house near theirs were away in Istanbul. That house, too, had fallen, but he went among the ruins to find the water tanks. He found them and one of them had not been broken. He had nothing to take the water back in so he searched for a jug or a tin. He found a jug. It was of silver and had been partly crushed by the falling stones. After the earthquake, soldiers had been sent to patrol the streets to prevent looting, of which there was a great deal because valuable things were lying everywhere in the ruins. As he was standing there trying to straighten the jug, a soldier arrested him. Signora Beronelli knew nothing of this and when he did not come back she and her son went to look for him. But there was such chaos that she could do nothing. The next day she heard that he had been shot. Is that not a terrible tragedy?'

'Yes, it is a tragedy. Such things happen.'

'If the good God had killed him in the earthquake she could bear it more easily. But for him to be shot . . . ! She is very brave. She does not blame the soldiers. With so much chaos they cannot be blamed. It was the Will of the good God.'

'He is a comedian. I have noticed it before.'

'Do not blaspheme.'

'It is *you* who blaspheme. You talk of the good God as if He were a waiter with a fly swatter. He hits at the flies and kills some. But one escapes. Ah, *le salaud!* The waiter hits again and the fly is paste with the others. The good God is not like that. He does not make earthquakes and tragedies. He is of the mind.'

'You are insupportable. Have you no pity for the poor woman?'

'Yes, I pity her. But will it help her if we hold another burial service? Will it help her if I stay awake arguing instead of going to sleep as I wish? She told you this because she likes to talk of it. Poor soul! It eases her mind to become the heroine of a tragedy. The fact becomes less real. But if there is no audience, there is no tragedy. If she tells me, I, too, will be a good audience. Tears will come into my eyes. But you are not the heroine. Go to sleep.'

'You are a beast without imagination.'

'Beasts must sleep. Good night, *chéri!*'

'Camel!'

There was no answer. After a moment or two he sighed heavily and turned over in his bunk. Soon he began gently to snore.

For a time Graham lay awake listening to the rush of the sea outside and the steady throb of the engines. A waiter with a fly-swatter! In Berlin there was a man whom he had never seen and whose name he did not know, who had condemned him to death; in Sofia there was a man named Moeller who had been instructed to carry out the sentence; and here, a few yards away in cabin number nine, was the executioner with a nine-millimetre calibre self-loading pistol, ready, now that he had disarmed the condemned man, to do his work and collect his money. The whole thing was as impersonal, as dispassionate, as justice itself. To attempt to defeat it seemed as futile as to argue with the hangman on the scaffold.

He tried to think of Stephanie and found that he could not. The things of which she was a part, his house, his friends, had ceased to exist. He was a man alone, transported into a strange land with death for its frontiers: alone but for the one person to whom he could speak of its terrors. She was sanity. She was reality. He needed her. Stephanie he did not need. She was a face and a voice dimly remembered with the other faces and voices of a world he had once known.

His mind wandered away into an uneasy doze. Then he dreamed that he was falling down a precipice and awoke with a start. He switched on the light and picked up one of the books he had bought that afternoon. It was a detective story. He read a few pages and then put it down. He was not going to be able to read himself to sleep with news of 'neat, slightly bleeding' holes in the right temples of corpses lying 'grotesquely twisted in the final agony of death.'

He got out of his bunk, wrapped himself in a blanket, and sat down to smoke a cigarette. He would, he decided, spend the rest of the night like that: sitting and smoking cigarettes. Lying prone increased his sense of helplessness. If only he had a revolver.

It seemed to him as he sat there that the having or not having of a revolver was really as important to a man as the having or not having of sight. That he should have survived for so many years without one could only be due to chance. Without a revolver a man was as defenceless as a tethered goat in a jungle. What an incredible fool he had been to leave the thing in his suitcase! If only . . .

And then he remembered something Josette had said:

'José has a revolver in his box. I will try to get it for you.'

He drew a deep breath. He was saved. José had a revolver. Josette would get it for him. All would be well. She would probably be on deck by ten. He would wait until he was sure of finding her there, tell her what had happened, and ask her to get the revolver there and then. With luck he would have it in his pocket within half an hour or so of his leaving his cabin. He would be able to sit down to luncheon with the thing bulging in his pocket. Banat would get a surprise. Thank goodness for José's suspicious nature!

He yawned and put out his cigarette. It would be stupid to sit there all night: stupid, uncomfortable, and dull. He felt sleepy, too. He put the blanket back on the bunk and lay down once more. Within five minutes he was asleep.

When he again awoke, a crescent of sunlight slanting through the porthole was rising and falling on the white paint of the bulkhead. He lay there watching it until he had to get up to unlock the door for the steward bringing his coffee. It was nine o'clock. He drank the coffee slowly, smoked a cigarette, and had a hot sea-water bath. By the time he was dressed it was close on ten o'clock. He put on his coat and left the cabin.

The alleyway on to which the cabins opened was only just wide enough for two persons to pass. It formed three sides of a square, the fourth side of which was taken up by the stairs to the saloon and shelter deck and two small spaces in which stood a pair of dusty palms in earthenware tubs. He was within a yard or two of the end of the alleyway when he came face to face with Banat.

The man had turned into the alleyway from the space at the foot of the stairs, and by taking a pace backwards he could have given Graham room to pass; but he made no attempt to do so. When he saw Graham, he stopped. Then, very slowly, he put his hands in his pockets and leaned against the steel bulkhead. Graham could either turn round and go back the way he had come or stay where he was. His heart pounding at his ribs, he stayed where he was.

Banat nodded. 'Good morning, Monsieur. It is very fine weather to-day, eh?'

'Very fine.'

'For you, an Englishman, it must be very agreeable to see the sun.' He had shaved and his pasty jowl gleamed with unrinsed soap. The smell of attar of roses came from him in waves.

'Most agreeable. Excuse me.' He went to push by to the stairs.

Banat moved, as if by accident, blocking the way. 'It is so narrow! One person must give way to the other, eh?'

'Just so. Do you want to go by?'

Banat shook his head. 'No. There is no hurry. I was so anxious to ask you, Monsieur, about your hand. I noticed it last night. What is the matter with it?'

Graham met the small, dangerous eyes staring insolently into his. Banat knew that he was unarmed and was trying to unnerve him as well. And he was succeeding. Graham had a sudden desire to smash his knuckles into the pale, stupid face. He controlled himself with an effort.

'It is a small wound,' he said calmly. And then his pent up feelings got the better of him. 'A bullet wound, to be exact,' he added. 'Some dirty little thief took a shot at me in Istanbul. He was either a bad shot or frightened. He missed.'

The small eyes did not flicker but an ugly little smile twisted the mouth. Banat said slowly: 'A dirty little thief, eh? You must look after yourself carefully. You must be ready to shoot back next time.'

'I shall shoot back. There is not the slightest doubt of that.'

The smile widened. 'You carry a pistol, then?'

'Naturally. And now, if you will excuse me . . .' He walked forward intending to shoulder the other man out of the way if he did not move. But Banat moved. He was grinning now. 'Be very careful, Monsieur,' he said, and laughed.

Graham had reached the foot of the stairs. He paused and looked back. 'I don't think it will be necessary,' he said deliberately. 'These scum don't risk their skins with an armed man.' He used the word *excrément*.

The grin faded from Banat's face. Without replying he turned and went on to his cabin.

By the time Graham reached the deck, reaction had set in. His legs seemed to have gone to jelly and he was sweating. The unexpectedness of the encounter had helped and, all things considered, he had not come out of it too badly. He'd put up a bluff. Banat might conceivably be wondering if, after all, he had a second revolver. But bluff wasn't going to go very far now. The gloves were off. His bluff might be called. Now, whatever happened, he *must* get José's revolver.

He walked quickly round the shelter deck. Haller was there with his wife on his arm, walking slowly. He said good morning; but Graham did not want to talk to anyone but the girl. She was not on the shelter deck. He went on up to the boat deck.

She was there, but talking to the young officer. The Mathis and Mr Kuvetli were a few yards away. Out of the corner of his eye he saw them look at him expectantly but he pretended not to have seen them and walked over to Josette.

She greeted him with a smile and a meaning look intended to convey that she was bored with her companion. The young Italian scowled a good morning and made to take up the conversation where Graham had interrupted it.

But Graham was in no mood for courtesies. 'You must excuse me, Monsieur,' he said in French; 'I have a message for Madame from her husband.'

The officer nodded and stood aside politely.

Graham raised his eyebrows. 'It is a *private* message, Monsieur.'

The officer flushed angrily and looked at Josette. She nodded to him in a kindly way and said something to him in Italian. He flashed his teeth at her, scowled once more at Graham and stalked on.

She giggled. 'You were really very unkind to that poor boy. He was getting on so nicely. Could you think of nothing better than a message from José?'

'I said the first thing that came into my head. I had to speak to you.'

She nodded approvingly. 'That is very nice.' She looked at him slyly. 'I was afraid that you would spend the night being angry with yourself because of last night. But you must not look so solemn. Madame Mathis is very interested in us.'

'I'm feeling solemn. Something has happened.'

The smile faded from her lips. 'Something serious?'

'Something serious. I . . .'

She glanced over his shoulder. 'It will be better if we walk up and down and look as if we are talking about the sea and the sun. Otherwise they will be gossiping. I do not care what people say, you understand. But it would be embarrassing.'

'Very well.' And then, as they began to walk: 'When I got back to my cabin last night I found that my revolver had been stolen from my suitcase.'

She stopped. 'This is true?'

'Quite true.'

She began to walk again. 'It may have been the steward.'

'No. Banat had been in my cabin. I could smell that scent of his.'

She was silent for a moment. Then: 'Have you told anyone?'

'It's no use my making a complaint. The revolver will be at the bottom of the sea by now. I have no proof that Banat took it. Besides, they wouldn't listen to me after the scene I made with the Purser yesterday.'

'What are you going to do?'

'Ask you to do something for me.'

She looked at him quickly. 'What?'

'You said last night that José had a revolver and that you might be able to get it for me.'

'You are serious?'

'Never more so in all my life.'

She bit her lip. 'But what am I to say to José if he finds that it is gone?'

'Will he find out?'

'He may do.'

He began to get angry. 'It was, I think, your idea that you should get it for me.'

'It is so necessary that you should have a revolver? There is nothing that he can do.'

'It was also your idea that I should carry a revolver.'

She looked sullen. 'I was frightened by what you said about this man. But that was because it was dark. Now that it is daytime it is different.' She smiled suddenly. 'Ah, my friend, do not be so serious. Think of the nice time we will have in Paris together. This man is not going to make any trouble.'

'I'm afraid he is.' He told her about his encounter by the stairs, and added: 'Besides, why did he steal my revolver if he doesn't intend to make trouble?'

She hesitated. Then she said slowly: 'Very well, I will try.'

'Now?'

'Yes, if you wish. It is in his box in the cabin. He is in the *salone* reading. Do you want to wait here for me?'

'No, I'll wait on the deck below. I don't want to have to talk to these people here just now.'

They went down and stood for a moment by the rail at the foot of the companion way.

'I'll stay here.' He pressed her hand. 'My dear Josette, I can't tell you how grateful I am to you for this.'

She smiled as if at a small boy to whom she had promised sweets. 'You shall tell me that in Paris.'

He watched her go and then turned to lean against the rail. She could not be more than five minutes. He stared for a time at the long, curling bow wave streaming out and away to meet the transverse wave from the stern and be broken by it into froth. He looked at his watch. Three minutes. Someone clattered down the companion way.

'Good morning, Mr Graham. You feel all right to-day, eh?' It was Mr Kuvetli.

Graham turned his head. 'Yes, thanks.'

'Monsieur and Madame Mathis are hopeful to play some bridge this afternoon. Do you play?'

'Yes, I play.' He was not, he knew, being very gracious but he was terrified lest Mr Kuvetli should attach himself to him.

'Then perhaps we make party of four, eh?'

'By all means.'

'I do not play well. Is very difficult game.'

'Yes.' Out of the corner of his eye he saw Josette step through the door from the landing on to the deck.

Mr Kuvetli's eyes flickered in her direction. He leered. 'This afternoon then, Mr Graham.'

'I shall look forward to it.'

Mr Kuvetli went. Josette came up to him.

'What was he saying?'

'He was asking me to play bridge.' Something in her face set his heart going like a trip hammer. 'You've got it?' he said quickly.

She shook her head. 'The box was locked. He has the keys.'

He felt the sweat prickling out all over his body. He stared at her trying to think of something to say.

'Why do you look at me like that?' she exclaimed angrily. 'I cannot help it if he keeps the box locked.'

'No, you can't help it.' He knew now that she had not intended to get the revolver. She couldn't be blamed. He couldn't expect her to steal for him. He had asked too much of her. But he had been banking on that revolver of José's. Now, in God's name, what was he going to do?

She rested her hand on his arm. 'You are angry with me?'

He shook his head. 'Why should I be angry? I should have had the sense to keep my own revolver in my pocket. It's just that I was relying on your getting it. It's my own fault. But, as I told you, I'm not used to this sort of thing.'

She laughed. 'Ah, you need not worry; I can tell you something. This man does not carry a gun.'

'What! How do you know?'

'He was going up the stairs in front of me when I came back just now. His clothes are tight and creased. If he carried a revolver I would have seen the shape of it in his pocket.'

'You are sure of this?'

'Of course. I would not tell you if . . .'

'But a *small* gun . . .' He stopped. A nine millimetre self-loading pistol would *not* be a small gun. It would weigh about two pounds and would be correspondingly bulky. It would not be the sort of thing a man would carry about in his pocket if he could leave it in a cabin. If . . .

She was watching his face. 'What is it?'

'He'll have left his gun in his cabin,' he said slowly.

She looked him in the eyes. 'I could see that he does not go to his cabin for a long time.'

'How?'

'José will do it.'

'José?'

'Be calm. I will not have to tell José anything about you. José will play cards with him this evening.'

'Banat would play cards. He is a gambler. But will José ask him?'

'I shall tell José that I saw this man open a wallet with a lot of money in it. José will see that he plays cards. You do not know José.'

'You're sure you can do it?'

She squeezed his arm. 'Of course. I do not like you to be worried. If you take his gun then you will have nothing at all to fear, eh?'

'No, I shall have nothing at all to fear.' He said it almost wonderingly. It seemed so simple. Why hadn't he thought of it before? Ah, but he had not known before that the man did not carry his gun. Take the man's gun away from him and he couldn't shoot. That was logical. And if he couldn't shoot there was nothing to fear. That was logical too. *The essence of all good strategy is simplicity.*

He turned to her. 'When can you do this?'

'This evening would be best. José does not like so much to play cards in the afternoon.'

'How soon this evening?'

'You must not be impatient. It will be some time after the meal.' She hesitated. 'It will be better if we are not seen together this afternoon. You do not want him to suspect that we are friends.'

'I can play bridge with Kuvetli and the Mathis this afternoon. But how shall I know if it is all right?'

'I will find a way to let you know.' She leaned against him. 'You are sure that you are not angry with me about José's revolver?'

'Of course I'm not.'

'There is no one looking. Kiss me.'

'Banking!' Mathis was saying. 'What is it but usury? Bankers are money lenders, usurers. But because they lend other people's money or money that does not exist, they have a pretty name. They are still usurers. Once, usury was a mortal sin and an abomination, and to be a usurer was to be a criminal for whom there was a prison cell. To-day the usurers are the gods of the earth and the only mortal sin is to be poor.'

'There are so many poor people,' said Mr Kuvetli profoundly. 'It is terrible!'

Mathis shrugged impatiently. 'There will be more before this war is finished. You may depend upon it. It will be a good thing to be a soldier. Soldiers, at least, will be given food.'

'Always,' said Madame Mathis, 'he talks nonsense. Always, always. But when we get back to France it will be different. His friends will not listen so politely. Banking! What does he know about banking?'

'Ha! That is what the banker likes. Banking is a mystery! It is too difficult for ordinary men to understand.' He laughed derisively. 'If you make two and two equal five you *must* have a lot of mystery.' He turned aggressively to Graham. 'The international bankers are the real war criminals. Others do the killing but they sit, calm and collected, in their offices and make money.'

'I'm afraid,' said Graham, feeling that he ought to say something, 'that the only international banker I know is a very harassed man with a duodenal ulcer. He is far from calm. On the contrary, he complains bitterly.'

'Precisely,' said Mathis triumphantly. 'It is the System! I can tell you . . .'

He went on to tell them. Graham picked up his fourth whisky and soda. He had been playing bridge with the Mathis and Mr Kuvetli for most of the afternoon and he was tired of them. He had seen Josette only once during that time. She had paused by the card table and nodded to him. He had taken the nod to mean that José had risen to the news that Banat had money in his pocket and that sometime that evening it would be safe to go to Banat's cabin.

The prospect cheered and terrified him alternately. At one moment the plan seemed foolproof. He would go into the cabin, take the gun, return to his own cabin, drop the gun out of the porthole and return to the saloon with a tremendous weight lifted from his shoulders. The next moment, however, doubts would begin to creep in. It was *too* simple. Banat might be insane but he was no fool. A man who earned his living in the way Banat earned his and who yet managed to stay alive and free was not going to be taken in so easily. Supposing he should guess what his victim had in mind, leave José in the middle of the game, and go to his cabin! Supposing he had bribed the steward to keep an eye on his cabin on the grounds that it contained valuables! Supposing . . . ! But what was the alternative? Was he to wait passively while Banat chose the moment to kill him? It was all very well for Haki to talk about a marked man having only to defend himself; but what had he to defend himself with? When the enemy was as close as Banat was, the best defence was attack. Yes, that was it! Anything was better than just waiting. And the plan might well succeed. It was the simple plans of attack that *did* succeed. It would never occur to a man of Banat's conceit to suspect that two could play at the game of stealing guns, that the helpless rabbit might bite back. He'd soon find out his mistake.

Josette and José came in with Banat. José appeared to be making himself amiable.

'. . . it is only necessary,' Mathis was concluding, 'to say one word – Briey! when you have said that you have said all.'

Graham drained his glass. 'Quite so. Will you all have another drink?'

The Mathis, looking startled, declined sharply; but Mr Kuvetli nodded happily.

'Thank you, Mr Graham. I will.'

Mathis stood up, frowning. 'It is time that we got ready for dinner. Please excuse us.'

They went. Mr Kuvetli moved his chair over.

'That was very sudden,' said Graham. 'What's the matter with them?'

'I think,' said Mr Kuvetli carefully, 'that they thought you are making joke of them.'

'Why on earth should they think that?'

Mr Kuvetli looked sideways. 'You ask them to have to drink three times in five minutes. You ask them once. They say no. You ask them again. They say no again. You ask again. They do not understand English hospitality.'

'I see. I'm afraid that I was thinking of something else. I must apologize.'

'Please!' Mr Kuvetli was overcome. 'It is not necessary to apologize for hospitality. But'–he glanced hesitantly at the clock–'it is now nearly time for dinner. You allow me later to have this drink you so kindly offer?'

'Yes, of course.'

'And you will excuse me please, now?'

'By all means.'

When Mr Kuvetli had gone, Graham stood up. Yes, he'd had just one drink too many on an empty stomach. He went out on deck.

The starlit sky was hung with small smoky clouds. In the distance were the lights of the Italian coast. He stood there for a moment letting the icy wind sting his face. In a minute or two the gong would sound for dinner. He dreaded the approaching meal as a sick man dreads the approach of the surgeon with a probe. He would sit, as he had sat at luncheon, listening to Haller's monologues and to the Beronellis whispering behind their misery, forcing food down his throat to his unwilling stomach, conscious all the time of the man opposite to him–of why he was there and of what he stood for.

He turned round and leaned against a stanchion. With his back to the deck he found himself constantly looking over his shoulder to make sure that he was alone. He felt more at ease with no deck space behind him.

Through one of the saloon portholes he could see Banat with Josette and José. They sat like details in a Hogarth group; José tight-lipped and intent, Josette smiling, Banat saying something that brought his lips forward. The air in there was grey with tobacco smoke and the hard light from the unshaded lamps flattened their features. There was about them all the squalor of a flashlight photograph taken in a bar.

Someone turned the corner at the end of the deck and came towards him. The figure reached the light and he saw that it was Haller. The old man stopped.

'Good evening, Mr Graham. You look as if you are really enjoying the air. I, as you see, need a scarf and a coat before I can face it.'

'It's stuffy inside.'

'Yes. I saw you this afternoon very gallantly playing bridge.'

'You don't like bridge?'

'One's tastes change.' He stared out at the lights. 'To see the land from a ship or to see a ship from the land. I used to like both. Now I dislike both. When a man reaches my age he grows, I think, to resent subconsciously the movement of everything except the respiratory muscles which keep him alive. Movement is change and for an old man change means death.'

'And the immortal soul?'

Haller sniffed. 'Even that which we commonly regard as immortal dies sooner or later. One day the last Titian and the last Beethoven quartet will cease to exist. The canvas and the printed notes may remain if they are carefully preserved but the works themselves will have died with the last eye and ear accessible to their messages. As for the immortal soul, that is an eternal truth and the eternal truths die with the men to whom they were necessary. The eternal truths of the Ptolemaic system were as necessary to the mediaeval theologians as were the eternal truths of Kepler to the theologians of the Reformation and the eternal truths of Darwin to the nineteenth century materialists. The statement of an eternal truth is a prayer to lay a ghost—the ghost of primitive man defending himself against what Spengler calls the "dark almightiness".' He turned his head suddenly as the door of the saloon opened.

It was Josette standing there looking uncertainly from one to the other of them. At that moment the gong began to sound for dinner.

'Excuse me,' said Haller; 'I must see my wife before dinner. She is still unwell.'

'Of course,' said Graham hurriedly.

Josette came over to him as Haller went.

'What did he want, that old man?' she whispered.

'He was talking about life and death.'

'Ugh! I do not like him. He makes me shudder. But I must not stay. I came only to tell you that it is all right.'

'When are they going to play?'

'After dinner.' She squeezed his arm. 'He is horrible, this man Banat. I would not do this for anyone except you, *chéri*.'

'You know I am grateful, Josette. I shall make it up to you.'

'Ah, stupid!' She smiled at him fondly. 'You must not be so serious.'

He hesitated. 'Are you sure that you can keep him there?'

'You need not worry. I will keep him. But come back to the *salone* when you have been to the cabin so that I shall know that you have finished. It is understood, *chéri?*'

'Yes, it is understood.'

It was after nine o'clock and, for the past half hour, Graham had been sitting near the door of the saloon pretending to read a book.

For the hundredth time his eyes wandered to the opposite corner of the room where Banat was talking to Josette and José. His heart began suddenly to beat faster. José had a pack of cards in his hand. He was grinning at something Banat had said. Then they sat down at the card-table. Josette looked across the room.

Graham waited a moment. Then, when he saw them cutting for the deal, he got slowly to his feet and walked out.

He stood on the landing for a moment, bracing himself for what he had to do. Now that the moment had come he felt better. Two minutes—three at the most—and it would be over. He would have the gun and he would be safe. He had only to keep his head.

He went down the stairs. Cabin number nine was beyond his and in the middle section of the alleyway. There was no one about when he reached the palms. He walked on.

He had decided that any sort of stealth was out of the question. He must walk straight to the cabin, open the door and go in without hesitation. If the worst came to the worst and he was seen as he went in by the steward or anyone else, he could protest that he had thought that number nine was an empty cabin and that he was merely satisfying a curiosity to see what the other cabins were like.

But nobody appeared. He reached the door of number nine, paused for barely a second and then, opening the door softly, went in. A moment later he had shut the door behind him and put up the catch. If, for any reason, the steward should try to get in, he would assume that Banat was there when he found the door fastened.

He looked round. The porthole was closed and the air reeked of attar of roses. It was a two-berth cabin and looked strangely bare. Apart from the scent, there were only two indications that the cabin was occupied; the grey raincoat hanging with the soft hat behind the door and a battered composition suit-case under the lower berth.

He ran his hands over the raincoat. There was nothing in the pockets and he turned his attention to the suit-case.

It was unlocked. He pulled it out and threw back the lid.

The thing was crammed with filthy shirts and underwear. There were, besides, some brightly-coloured silk handkerchiefs, a pair of black shoes without laces, a scent spray and a small jar of ointment. The gun was not there.

He shut the case, pushed it back and opened the washing cabinet-cum-wardrobe. The wardrobe part contained nothing but a pair of dirty socks. On the shelf by the tooth-glass was a grey washcloth, a safety razor, a cake of soap and a bottle of scent with a ground glass stopper.

He was getting worried. He had been so sure that the gun would be there. If what Josette had said were true it *must* be there somewhere.

He looked round for other hiding places. There were the mattresses. He ran his hands along the springs beneath them. Nothing. There was the waste compartment below the washing cabinet. Again nothing. He glanced at his watch. He had been there four minutes. He looked round again desperately. It *must* be in there. But he had looked everywhere. He returned feverishly to the suit-case.

Two minutes later he slowly straightened his back. He knew now that the gun was not in the cabin, that the simple plan had been too simple, that nothing was changed. For a second or two he stood there helplessly, putting off the moment when he must finally admit his failure by leaving the cabin. Then the sound of footsteps in the alleyway nearby jarred him into activity.

The footsteps paused. There was the clank of a bucket being put down. Then the footsteps receded. He eased back the door catch and opened the door. The alleyway was empty. A second later he was walking back the way he had come.

He had reached the foot of the stairs before he allowed himself to think. Then he hesitated. He had told Josette that he would go back to the saloon. But that meant seeing Banat. He must have time to steady his nerves. He turned and walked back to his cabin.

He opened the door, took one step forward, and then stopped dead.

Sitting on the bunk with his legs crossed and a book resting on his knee was Haller.

He was wearing a pair of horn-rimmed reading glasses. He removed them very deliberately and looked up. 'I've been waiting for you, Mr Graham,' he said cheerfully.

Graham found his tongue. 'I don't . . .' he began.

Haller's other hand came from under the book. In it was a large self-loading pistol.

He held it up. 'I think,' he said, 'that this is what you have been looking for, isn't it?'

Chapter Eight

Graham looked from the gun to the face of the man who was holding it: the long upper lip, the pale blue eyes, the loose yellowish skin.

'I don't understand,' he said, and put out his hand to receive the gun. 'How . . .?' he began and then stopped abruptly. The gun was pointing at him and Haller's forefinger was on the trigger.

Haller shook his head. 'No, Mr Graham. I think I shall keep it. I came for a little talk with you. Supposing you sit down here on the bed and turn sideways so that we can face one another.'

Graham strove to conceal the deadly sickness that was stealing over him. He felt that he must be going mad. Amid the flood of questions pouring through his mind there was only one small patch of dry land: Colonel Haki had examined the credentials of all the passengers who had embarked at Istanbul and reported that none of them had booked for the journey less than three days prior to the sailing and that they were all harmless. He clung to it desperately.

'I don't understand,' he repeated.

'Of course you don't. If you will sit down I will explain.'

'I'll stand.'

'Ah, yes. I see. Moral support derived from physical discomfort. Remain standing by all means if it pleases you to do so.' He spoke with crisp condescension. This was a new Haller, a slightly younger man. He examined the pistol as if he were seeing it for the first time. 'You know, Mr Graham,' he went on thoughtfully, 'poor Mavrodopoulos was really upset by his failure in Istanbul. He is not, as you have probably gathered, very intelligent and, like all stupid people, he blames others for his own mistakes. He complains that you moved.' He shrugged tolerantly. 'Naturally you moved. He could hardly expect you to stand still while he corrected his aim. I told him so. But he was still angry with you, so when he came aboard I insisted on taking care of his pistol for him. He is young, and these Romanians are so hot-headed. I did not want anything premature to happen.'

'I wonder,' said Graham, 'if your name happens to be Moeller.'

'Dear me!' He raised his eyebrows. 'I had no idea that you were so well informed. Colonel Haki must have been in a very talkative mood. Did he know that I was in Istanbul?'

Graham reddened. 'I don't think so.'

Moeller chuckled. 'I thought not. Haki is a clever man. I have a great respect for him. But he is human and, therefore, fallible. Yes, after that fiasco in Gallipoli I thought it advisable to attend to things myself. And then, when everything had been arranged, you were inconsiderate enough to move and spoil Banat's shooting. But I bear you no ill will, Mr Graham. I was irritated at the time, of course. Mavrodopoulos . . .'

'Banat is easier to say.'

'Thank you. As I was saying, Banat's failure made more work for me. But now my irritation has passed. Indeed, I am quite enjoying the trip. I like myself as an archaeologist. I was a little nervous at first, but as soon as I saw that I had succeeded in boring you I knew that all was well.' He held up the book he had been reading. 'If you would like a record of my little speeches I can recommend this. It is entitled "The Sumerian Pantheon" and is by Fritz Haller. His qualifications are given on the title page: ten years with the German Institute in Athens, the period at Oxford, the degrees: it is all here. He seems to be an ardent disciple of Spengler. He quotes the Master a great deal. There is a nostalgic little preface which was most helpful and you will find the piece about eternal truths on page three hundred and forty-one. Naturally I paraphrased a little here and there to suit my own mood. And I drew freely on some of the longer footnotes. You see, the effect I wanted to create was that of an erudite but lovable old bore. I think you will agree that I did well.'

'So there *is* a Haller?'

Moeller pursed his lips. 'Ah, yes. I was sorry to inconvenience him and his wife, but there was no other way. When I found that you were to leave on this boat I decided that it would be helpful if I travelled with you. Obviously I could not have booked a passage at the last moment without attracting Colonel Haki's attention; I therefore took over Haller's tickets and passport. He and his wife were not pleased. But they are good Germans, and when it was made plain to them that their country's interests must come before their own convenience, they gave no more trouble. In a few days their passport will be returned to them with their own photographs restored to it. My only embarrassment has been the Armenian lady who is doing duty for Frau Professor Haller. She speaks very little German and is virtually a half-wit. I have been forced to keep her out of the way. I had no time to make better arrangements, you see. As it was, the man who found her for me had quite a lot of trouble convincing her that she wasn't being carried off to an Italian *bordello*. Female vanity is sometimes extraordinary.' He produced a cigarette case. 'I hope you don't mind my telling you all these little things, Mr Graham. It's just that I want to be frank with you. I think that an atmosphere of frankness is essential to any business discussion.'

'Business?'

'Just so. Now do please sit down and smoke. It will do you good.' He held out the cigarette case. 'Your nerves have been a little jumpy to-day, haven't they?'

'Say what you want to say and get out!'

Moeller chuckled. 'Yes, certainly a little jumpy!' He looked suddenly solemn. 'It is my fault, I'm afraid. You see, Mr Graham, I could have had this little talk with you before, but I wanted to make sure that you would be in a receptive frame of mind.'

Graham leaned against the door. 'I think that the best way I can describe my state of mind at the moment is to tell you that I have been seriously considering kicking you in the teeth. I could have done so from here before you could have used your gun.'

Moeller raised his eyebrows. 'And yet you didn't do it? Was it the thought of my white hairs that stopped you, or was it your fear of the consequences?' He paused. 'No answer? You won't mind if I draw my own conclusions, will you?' He settled himself a little more comfortably. 'The instinct for self-preservation is a wonderful thing. It is so easy for people to be heroic about laying down their lives for the sake of principles when they do not expect to be called upon to do so. When, however, the smell of danger is in their nostrils they are more practical. They see alternatives not in terms of honour or dishonour, but in terms of greater or lesser evils. I wonder if I could persuade you to see my point of view.'

Graham was silent. He was trying to fight down the panic which had seized him. He knew that if he opened his mouth he would shout abuse until his throat ached.

Moeller was fitting a cigarette into a short amber holder as if he had time to waste. Obviously he had not expected any answer to his question. He had the self-contained air of a man who is early for an important appointment. When he finished with the cigarette-holder he looked up. 'I like you, Mr Graham,' he said. 'I was, I have admitted, irritated when Banat made such a fool of himself in Istanbul. But now that I know you I am glad that he did so. You behaved gracefully over that awkwardness at the dinner-table the night we sailed. You listened politely to my carefully memorized rec-itations. You are a clever engineer, and yet you are not aggressive. I should not like to think of your being killed–murdered–by any employee of mine.' He lit his cigarette. 'And yet, the demands made upon us by our life's needs are so uncompromising. I am compelled to be offensive. I must tell you that, as things stand at present, you will be dead within a few minutes of your landing at Genoa on Saturday morning.'

Graham had himself in hand now. He said: 'I'm sorry to hear that.'

Moeller nodded approval. 'I am glad to see you take it so calmly. If I were in your place I should be very frightened. But then, of course'–the pale blue eyes narrowed suddenly–'*I* should know that there was no possible chance of my escaping. Banat, in spite of his lapse in Istanbul, is a formidable young man. And when I considered the fact that ready waiting for me in Genoa there would be reinforcements consisting of several other men quite as experienced as Banat, I should realise that there was not the remotest chance of my being able to reach any sort of sanctuary before the end came. I should be left with only one hope–that they did their work so efficiently that I should know very little about it.'

'What do you mean by "as things stand at present"?'

Moeller smiled triumphantly. 'Ah! I am so glad. You have gone straight to the heart of the matter. I mean, Mr Graham, that you need not necessarily die. There is an alternative.'

'I see. A lesser evil.' But his heart leaped in spite of himself.

'Scarcely an evil,' Moeller objected. 'An alternative and by no means an unpleasant one.' He settled himself more comfortably. 'I have already said that I liked you, Mr Graham. Let me add that I dislike the prospect of violence quite as whole-heartedly as you do. I am lily-livered. I admit it freely. I will go out of my way to avoid seeing the results of an automobile accident. So, you see, if there is any way of settling this matter without bloodshed I should be prejudiced in favour of it. And if you are still uncertain of my personal goodwill towards you, let me put the question in another and harder light. The killing would have to be hurried, would consequently subject the killers to additional risks and would, therefore, be expensive. Don't misunderstand me, please. I shall spare no expense if it is necessary. But, naturally enough, I hope it won't be necessary. I can assure you that no one, with the possible exception of yourself, will be more delighted than I am if we can dispose of this whole thing in a friendly way as between business men. I hope you will at least believe that I am sincere in that.'

Graham began to get angry. 'I don't care a damn whether you're sincere or not.'

Moeller looked crestfallen. 'No, I suppose you don't. I was forgetting that you have been under some nervous strain. You are naturally interested only in getting home safely to England. That may be possible. It just depends on how calmly and logically you can approach the situation. It is necessary, as you must have gathered, that the completion of the work you are doing should be delayed. Now, if you die before you get back to England, somebody else will be sent to Turkey to do your work over again. I understand that the work as a whole would thus be delayed for six weeks. I also understand that that delay would be sufficient for the purposes of those interested. You might, might you not, conclude from that that the simplest way of dealing with the matter would be to kidnap you in Genoa and keep you under lock and key for the requisite six weeks and then release you, eh?'

'You might.'

Moeller shook his head. 'But you would be wrong. You would disappear. Your employers and, no doubt, the Turkish Government would make inquiries about you. The Italian police would be informed. The British Foreign Office would address bombastic demands for information to the Italian Government. The Italian Government, conscious that its neutrality was being compromised, would bestir itself. I might find myself in serious difficulties, especially when you were released and could tell your story. It would be most inconvenient for me to be wanted by the Italian police. You see what I mean?'

'Yes, I see.'

'The straightforward course is to kill you. There is, however, a third possibility.' He paused and then said: 'You are a very fortunate man, Mr Graham.'

'What does *that* mean?'

'In times of peace only the fanatical nationalist demands that a man should surrender himself body and soul to the government of the country in which he was born. Yet, in war time, when men are being killed and there is emotion in the air, even an intelligent man may be so far carried away as to talk of his "duty to his country." You are fortunate because you happen to be in a business which sees these heroics for what they are: the emotional excesses of the stupid and brutish. "Love of country!" There's a curious phrase. Love of a particular patch of earth? Scarcely. Put a German down in a field in Northern France, tell him that it is Hanover, and he cannot contradict you. Love of fellow-countrymen? Surely not. A man will like some of them and dislike others. Love of the country's culture? The men who know most of their countries' cultures are usually the most intelligent and the least patriotic. Love of the country's government? But governments are usually disliked by the people they govern. Love of country, we see, is merely a sloppy mysticism based on ignorance and fear. It has its uses, of course. When a ruling class wishes a people to do something which that people does not want to do, it appeals to patriotism. And, of course, one of the things that people most dislike is allowing themselves to be killed. But forgive me. These are old arguments and I am sure you are familiar with them.'

'Yes, I'm familiar with them.'

'I am so relieved. I should not like to think that I had been wrong in judging you to be a man of intelligence. And it makes what I have to say so much easier.'

'Well, what *have* you got to say?'

Moeller stubbed his cigarette out. 'The third possibility, Mr Graham, is that you might be induced to retire from business for six weeks of your own free will—that you should take a holiday.'

'Are you mad?'

Moeller smiled. 'I see your difficulty, believe me. If you simply go into hiding for six weeks, it may be rather awkward to explain matters when you return home. I understand. Hysterical fools might say that in choosing to remain alive instead of choosing to be killed by our friend Banat you did something shameful. The facts that the work would have been delayed in any case and that you were of more use to your country and its allies alive than dead would be ignored. Patriots, in common with other mystics, dislike logical argument. It would be necessary to practise a small deception. Let me tell you how it could be arranged.'

'You're wasting your time.'

Moeller took no notice. 'There are some things, Mr Graham, which not even patriots can control. One of those things is illness. You have come from Turkey where, thanks to earthquakes and floods, there have been several outbreaks of typhus. What could be more likely than that the moment you get ashore at Genoa a mild attack of typhus should develop? And what then? Well, of course, you will be taken immediately to a private clinic and the doctor there will, at your request, write to your wife and employers in England. Of course, there will be the inevitable delays of war. By the time anyone can get to see you, the crisis will have passed and you will be convalescent: convalescent but much too weak to work or travel. But in six weeks' time you will have recovered sufficiently to do both. All will be well again. How does that appeal to you, Mr Graham? To me it seems the only solution satisfactory to both of us.'

'I see. You don't have the bother of shooting me. I'm out of the way for the requisite six weeks and can't tell tales afterwards without showing myself up. Is that it?'

'That's a very crude way of putting it; but you are quite right. That *is* it. How do you like the idea? Personally I should find the prospect of six weeks' absolute peace and quiet in the place I have in mind very attractive. It is quite near Santa Margherita, overlooking the sea and surrounded by pines. But then, I am old. You might fret.'

He hesitated. 'Of course,' he went on slowly, 'if you liked the idea, it might be possible to arrange for Señora Gallindo to share your six weeks' holiday.'

'What on earth do you mean?'

Moeller shrugged. 'Come now, Mr Graham! I am not short-sighted. If the suggestion really offends you, I apologize humbly. If not . . . I need hardly say that you would be the only patients there. The medical staff, which would consist of myself, Banat, and another man, apart from the servants, would be unobtrusive unless you were receiving visitors from England. However, that could be discussed later. Now what do you think?'

Graham steeled himself to make an effort. He said with deliberate ease: 'I think you're bluffing. Hasn't it occurred to you that I may not be such a fool as you think? I shall, of course, repeat this conversation to the Captain. There will be police inquiries when we reach Genoa. My papers are perfectly genuine. Yours are not. Nor are Banat's. I have nothing to hide. You have plenty to hide. So has Banat. You're relying on my fear of being killed forcing me to agree to this scheme of yours. It won't. It won't keep my mouth shut either. I admit that I have been badly scared. I have had a very unpleasant twenty-four hours. I suppose that's your way of inducing a receptive frame of mind. Well, it doesn't work with me. I'm worried all right; I should be a fool if I weren't; but I'm not worried out of my senses. You're bluffing, Moeller. That's what I think. Now you can get out.'

Moeller did not move. He said, as if he were a surgeon musing over some not entirely unforeseen complication: 'Yes, I was afraid you might misunderstand me. A pity.' He looked up. 'And to whom are you going to take your story in the first place, Mr Graham? The Purser? The third officer was telling me about your curious behaviour over poor Monsieur Mavrodopoulos. Apparently you have been making wild allegations to the effect that he is a criminal named Banat who wants to kill you. The ship's officers, including the Captain, seem to have enjoyed the joke very much. But even the best of jokes becomes tiresome if it is told too often. There would be a certain unreality about the story that I, too, was a criminal who wanted to kill you. Isn't there a medical name for that sort of delusion? Come now, Mr Graham! You tell me that you are not a fool. Please do not behave like one. Do you think that I should have approached you in this way if I had thought that you might be able to embarrass me in the way you suggest? I hope not. You are no less foolish when you interpret my reluctance to have you killed as weakness. You may prefer lying dead in a gutter with a bullet in your back to spending six weeks in a villa on the Ligurian Riviera; that is your affair. But please do not deceive yourself; those *are* the inevitable alternatives.'

Graham smiled grimly. 'And the little homily on patriotism is to still any qualms I might have about accepting the inevitable. I see. Well, I'm sorry, but it doesn't work. I still think you're bluffing. You've bluffed very well. I admit that. You had me worried. I really thought for a moment that I had to choose between possible death and sinking my pride–just like the hero in a melodrama. My real choice was, of course, between using my common sense and letting my stomach do my thinking for me. Well, Mr Moeller, if that's all you have to say . . .'

Moeller got slowly to his feet. 'Yes, Mr Graham,' he said calmly, 'that is all I have to say.' He seemed to hesitate. Then, very deliberately, he sat down again. 'No, Mr Graham, I have changed my mind. There *is* something else that I should say. It is just possible that on thinking this thing over calmly you may decide that you have been silly and that I may not be as clumsy as you now seem to think. Frankly, I don't expect you to do so. You are pathetically sure of yourself. But in case your stomach should after all take control, I think I should issue a warning.'

'Against what?'

Moeller smiled. 'One of the many things you don't seem to know is that Colonel Haki considered it advisable to install one of his agents on board to watch over you. I tried hard to interest you in him yesterday, but was unsuccessful. Ihsan Kuvetli is unprepossessing, I agree; but he has the reputation of being a clever little man. If he had not been a patriot, he would have been rich.'

'Are you trying to tell me that Kuvetli is a Turkish agent?'

'I am indeed, Mr Graham!' The pale blue eyes narrowed. 'The reason why I approached you this evening instead of to-morrow evening is because I wanted to see you before he made himself known to you. He did not, I think, find out who I was until to-day. He searched my cabin this evening. I think that he must have heard me talking to Banat; the partitions between the cabins are absurdly thin. In any case, I thought it likely that, realizing the danger you were in, he would decide that the time had come to approach you. You see, Mr Graham, with his experience, he is not likely to make the mistake that you are making. However, he has his duty to do and I have no doubt that he will have evolved some laborious plan for getting you to France in safety. What I want to warn you against is telling him of this suggestion I have made to you. You see, if you should after all come round to my way of thinking, it would be embarrassing for both of us if an agent of the Turkish Government knew of our little deception. We could scarcely expect him to keep silent. You see what I mean, Mr Graham? If you let Kuvetli into the secret you will destroy the only chance of returning to England alive that remains to you.' He smiled faintly. 'It's a solemn thought, isn't it?' He got up again and went to the door. 'That was all I wanted to say. Good night, Mr Graham.'

Graham watched the door close and then sat down on the bunk. The blood was beating through his head as if he had been running. The time for bluffing was over. He should be deciding what he was going to do. He had to think calmly and clearly.

But he could not think calmly and clearly. He was confused. He became conscious of the vibration and movement of the ship and wondered if he had imagined what had just happened. But there was the depression in the bunk where Moeller had been sitting and the cabin was filled with the smoke from his cigarette. It was Haller who was the creature of imagination.

He was conscious now more of humiliation than of fear. He had become almost used to the tight sensation in his chest, the quick hammering of his heart, the dragging at his stomach, the crawling of his spine which were his body's responses to his predicament. In a queer, horrible way it had been stimulating. He had felt that he was pitting his wits against those of an enemy—a dangerous enemy but an intellectual inferior—with a chance of winning. Now he knew that he had been doing nothing of the kind. The enemy had been laughing up their sleeves at him. It had never even occurred to him to suspect 'Haller.' He had just sat there politely listening to extracts from a book. Heavens, what a fool the man must think him! He and Banat between them had seen through him as if he were made of glass. Not even his wretched little passages with Josette had escaped their notice. Probably they had seen him kissing her. And as a final measure of their contempt for him, it had been Moeller who had informed him that Mr Kuvetli was a Turkish agent charged with his protection. Kuvetli! It was funny. Josette would be amused.

He remembered suddenly that he had promised to return to the saloon. She would be getting anxious. And the cabin was stifling. He could think better if he had some air. He got up and put on his overcoat.

José and Banat were still playing cards; José with a peculiar intentness as if he suspected Banat of cheating; Banat coolly and deliberately. Josette was leaning back in her chair smoking. Graham realised with a shock that he had left the room less than half an hour previously. It was amazing what could happen to your mind in so short a time; how the whole atmosphere of a place could change. He found himself noticing things about the saloon which he had not noticed before: a brass plate with the name of the builders of the ship engraved on it, a stain on the carpet, some old magazines stacked in a corner.

He stood there for a moment staring at the brass plate. The Mathis and the Italians were sitting there reading and did not look up. He looked past them and saw Josette turning her head back to watch the game. She had seen him. He went across to the farther door and out on to the shelter deck.

She would follow him soon to find out if he had been successful. He walked slowly along the deck wondering what he would say to her, whether or not to tell her about Moeller and his 'alternative'. Yes, he would tell her. She would tell him that he was all right, that Moeller was bluffing. But supposing Moeller *weren't* bluffing! 'They will do anything to see that it is so. *Anything*, Mr Graham! Do you understand?' Haki had not talked about bluffing. The wound under the grimy bandage on his hand did not feel like bluffing. And if Moeller wasn't bluffing, what was he, Graham, going to do?

He stopped and stared out at the lights on the coast. They were nearer now; near enough for him to see the movement of the boat in relation to them. It was incredible that this should be happening to him. Impossible! Perhaps, after all, he had been badly wounded in Istanbul and it was all a fantasy born of anaesthesia. Perhaps he would become conscious again soon to find himself in a hospital bed. But the teak rail, wet with dew, on which his hand rested was real enough. He gripped it in sudden anger at his own stupidity. He should be thinking, cudgelling his brains, making plans, deciding; doing something instead of standing there mooning. Moeller had left him over five minutes ago and here he was still trying to escape from his senses into a fairyland of hospitals and anaesthetics. What was he going to do about Kuvetli? Should he approach him or wait to be approached? What . . . ?

There were quick footsteps on the deck behind him. It was Josette, her fur coat thrown over her shoulders, her face pale and anxious in the dingy glare of the deck light. She seized his arm. 'What has happened? Why were you so long?'

'There was no gun there.'

'But there must be. Something has happened. When you walked into the *salone* just now you looked as if you had seen a ghost or were going to be sick. What is it, *chéri?*'

'There was no gun there,' he repeated. 'I searched carefully.'

'You were not seen?'

'No, I wasn't seen.'

She sighed with relief. 'I was afraid when I saw your face . . .' She broke off. 'But don't you see? It is all right. He does not carry a gun. There is no gun in his cabin. He has not got a gun.' She laughed. 'Perhaps he has pawned it. Ah, do not look so serious, *chéri*. He may get a gun in Genoa, but then it will be too late. Nothing can happen to you. You will be all right.' She put on a woebegone expression. 'I am the one who is in trouble now.'

'You?'

'Your smelly little friend plays cards very well. He is winning money from José. José does not like that. He will have to cheat and cheating puts him in a bad temper. He says that it is bad for his nerves. Really it is that he likes to win because he is a better player.' She paused and added suddenly: 'Please wait!'

They had reached the end of the deck. She stopped and faced him. 'What is the matter, *chéri?* You are not listening to what I am saying. You are thinking of something else.' She pouted. 'Ah, I know. It is your wife. Now that there is no danger you think of her again.'

'No.'

'You are sure?'

'Yes, I am sure.' He knew now that he did not want to tell her about Moeller. He wanted her to talk to him believing that there was no longer any danger, that nothing could happen to him, that he could walk down the gangway at Genoa without fear. Afraid to create his own illusion, he could live in one of her making. He managed to smile. 'You mustn't take any notice of me, Josette. I'm tired. You know, it's a very tiring business searching other people's cabins.'

Immediately she was all sympathy. '*Mon pauvre chéri*. It is my fault, not yours. I forget how unpleasant things have been for you. Would you like us to go back to the *salone* and have a little drink?'

He would have done almost anything for a drink but go back to the saloon where he could see Banat. 'No. Tell me what we shall do first when we arrive in Paris.'

She looked at him quickly, smiling. 'If we do not walk we shall get cold.'
She wriggled into her coat and linked her arm in his. 'So we are going to
Paris together?'

'Of course! I thought it was all arranged.'

'Oh yes, but'–she pressed his arm against her side–'I did not think that
you were serious. You see,' she went on carefully, 'so many men like to talk
about what will happen, but they do not always like to remember what they
have said. It is not that they do not mean what they say but that they do not
always feel the same. You understand me, *chéri*?'

'Yes, I understand.'

'I want you to understand,' she went on, 'because it is very important to
me. I am a dancer and must think of my career also.' She turned to him
impulsively. 'But you will think that I am selfish and I would not like you to
think that. It is just that I like you very much and do not wish you to do
anything simply because you have made a promise. As long as you
understand that, it is all right. We will not talk about it.' She snapped her
fingers. 'Look! When we get to Paris we will go straight to a hotel which I
know of near the St Philippe du Roule Metro. It is very modern and
respectable and if you wish we can have a bathroom. It is not expensive.
Then we will have champagne cocktails at the Ritz bar. They are only nine
francs. While we have those drinks we can decide where to eat. I am very
tired of Turkish foods and the sight of raviolo makes me ill. We must have
good French food.' She paused and added hesitantly, 'I have never been to
the Tour d'Argent.'

'You shall.'

'You mean it? I shall eat until I am as fat as a pig. After that we will begin.'

'Begin?'

'There are some little places that are still open late in spite of the police. I
will introduce you to a great friend of mine. She was the *sous-maquecée* of the
Moulin Galant when Le Boulanger had it and before the gangsters came.
You understand *sous-maquecée*?'

She laughed. 'It is very bad of me. I will explain to you another time. But
you will like Suzie. She saved a lot of money and now she is very
respectable. She had a place in the rue de Liège which was better than Le
Jockey Cabaret in Istanbul. She had to close it when the war came but she
has opened another place in an impasse of the rue Pigalle and those who are
her friends can go there. She has a great many friends and so she is making
money again. She is quite old and the police do not trouble her. She shrugs
her shoulders at them. Just because there is this filthy war there is no reason
why we should all be miserable. I have other friends in Paris, too. You will
like them when I introduce you. When they know that you are my friend
they will be polite. They are very polite and nice when you are introduced
by someone who is known in the quarter.'

She went on talking about them. Most of them were women (Lucette,
Dolly, Sonia, Claudette, Berthe) but there were one or two men (Jojo,
Ventura) who were foreigners and had not been mobilized. She spoke of
them vaguely but with an enthusiasm half defensive, half real. They might
not be rich as Americans understood being rich, but they were people of the
world. Each was remarkable in some particular. One was 'very intelligent,'

another had a friend in the Ministry of the Interior, another was going to buy a villa at Saint Tropez and invite all his friends there for the summer. All were 'amusing' and very useful if one wanted 'anything special.' She did not say what she meant by 'anything special' and Graham did not ask her. He did not object to the picture she was painting. The prospect of sitting in the Café Graf buying drinks for *bizness* men and women from the places up the hill seemed to him at that moment infinitely attractive. He would be safe and free; himself again; able to think his own thoughts, to smile without stretching his nerves to breaking point when he did so. It must happen. It was absurd that he should be killed. Moeller was right about one thing at least. He would be more use to his country alive than dead.

Considerably more! Even if the Turkish contract were delayed for six weeks it would still have to be fulfilled. If he were alive at the end of the six weeks he would be able to go on with it; perhaps he might even make up for some of the lost time. He was, after all, the company's chief designer and it would be difficult to replace him in war time. He had been truthful enough when he had told Haki that there were dozens of other men with his qualifications; but he had not thought it necessary to bolster Haki's argument by explaining that those dozens were made up of Americans, Frenchmen, Germans, Japanese and Czechs as well as Englishmen. Surely the sensible course would be the safe one. He was an engineer, not a professional secret agent. Presumably, a secret agent would have been equal to dealing with men like Moeller and Banat. He, Graham, was not. It was not for him to decide whether or not Moeller was bluffing. His business was to stay alive. Six weeks on the Ligurian Riviera could not do him any harm. It meant lying, of course: lying to Stephanie and to their friends, to his managing director and to the representatives of the Turkish Government. He couldn't tell them the truth. They would think that he ought to have risked his life. It was the sort of thing people did think when they were safe and snug in their arm-chairs. But if he lied, would they believe him? The people at home would; but what about Haki? Haki would smell a rat and ask questions. And Kuvetli? Moeller would have to do something about putting him off. It would be a tricky business; but Moeller would arrange things. Moeller was used to that sort of thing. Moeller. . . .

He stopped with a jerk. For God's sake, what was he thinking? He must be out of his senses! Moeller was an enemy agent. What he, Graham, had been turning over in his mind was nothing less than treason. And yet. . . . And yet what? He knew suddenly that something had snapped in his mind. The idea of doing a deal with an enemy agent was no longer unthinkable. He could consider Moeller's suggestion on its merits, coolly and calmly. He was becoming demoralized. He could no longer trust himself.

Josette was shaking his arm. 'What is it, *chéri*? What is the matter?'

'I've just remembered something,' he muttered.

'Ah!' she said angrily, 'that is not at all polite. I ask you if you wish to go on walking. You take no notice. I ask you again and you stop as if you were ill. You have not been listening to what I was saying.'

He pulled himself together. 'Oh yes, I've been listening, but something you said reminded me that if I am to stop in Paris I shall have to write several important business letters so that I can post them immediately I get there.' He added with a fair assumption of jauntiness: 'I don't want to work while I am in Paris.'

'If it is not these *salauds* who tried to kill you, it is business,' she grumbled. But she was apparently mollified.

'I'm sorry, Josette. It won't happen again. Are you sure you are warm? You wouldn't like a drink?' He wanted to get away now. He knew what he must do and was impatient to do it before he could begin to think.

But she took his arm again. 'No, it is all right. I am not angry and I am not cold. If we go up on the top deck you can kiss me to show that we are friends again. Soon I must go back to José. I said that I would only be a few minutes.'

Half an hour later he went down to his cabin, took off his coat and went to look for the steward. He found him busy with a mop and bucket in the lavatories.

'Signore?'

'I promised to lend Signor Kuvetli a book. What is the number of his cabin?'

'Three, signore.'

Graham walked back to cabin number three and stood for a moment hesitating. Perhaps he should think again before he did anything decisive, anything for which he might be sorry later. Perhaps it would be better if he left it until the morning. Perhaps . . .

He set his teeth, raised his hand and knocked on the door.

Chapter Nine

Mr Kuvetli was wearing an old red wool dressing-gown over a flannel night-shirt and his fringe of grey hair stood out from the sides of his head in ringlets. He had a book in his hand and looked as if he had been lying in his bunk reading. He stared at Graham blankly for a moment, then his smile returned.

'Mr Graham! Is very good to see you. What can I do, please?'

At the sight of him, Graham's heart sank. It was to this grubby little man with a stupid smile that he was proposing to commit his safety. But it was too late to turn back now. He said: 'I wonder if I could have a talk with you, Mr Kuvetli.'

Mr Kuvetli blinked a little shiftily. 'Talk? Oh, yes. Come in, please.'

Graham stepped into the cabin. It was as small as his own and very stuffy.

Mr Kuvetli smoothed out the blankets on his bunk. 'Please take seat.'

Graham sat down and opened his mouth to speak, but Mr Kuvetli forestalled him.

'Cigarette, please, Mr Graham?'

'Thank you.' He took a cigarette. 'I had a visit from Herr Professor Haller earlier this evening,' he added; and then, remembering that the bulkheads were thin, glanced at them.

Mr Kuvetli struck a match and held it out. 'Herr Professor Haller is very interesting man, eh?' He lit Graham's cigarette and his own and blew the match out. 'Cabins on both sides empty,' he remarked.

'Then . . .'

'Please,' interrupted Mr Kuvetli, 'will you allow me to speak French? My English is not very good, eh? Your French is very good. We understand better each.'

'By all means.'

'Now, then, we can talk easily.' Mr Kuvetli sat down beside him on the bunk. 'Monsieur Graham, I was going to introduce myself to you to-morrow. Now, Monsieur Moeller has saved me the trouble I think. You know that I am not a tobacco merchant, eh?'

'According to Moeller you are a Turkish agent acting under Colonel Haki's order. Is that so?'

'Yes, that is so. I will be truthful. I am surprised that you have not discovered me before this. When the Frenchman asked me what firm I belonged to I had to say Pazar and Co., because I had given that name to you. Unfortunately, the firm of Pazar and Co. does not exist. Naturally he was puzzled. I was able to prevent him from asking more questions then, but I expected him to discuss it with you later.' The smile had gone and with it the bright-eyed stupidity which, for Graham, had been the tobacco merchant. In its place was a firm determined mouth, and a pair of steady brown eyes which surveyed him with something very like good-humoured contempt.

'He did not discuss it.'

'And you did not suspect that I was avoiding his questions?' He shrugged. 'One always takes unnecessary precautions. People are so much more trusting than one suppose.'

'Why should I suspect?' Graham demanded irritably. 'What I cannot understand is why you did not approach me as soon as you knew that Banat was on the ship. I suppose,' he added spitefully, 'that you *do* know that Banat is on the ship?'

'Yes, I know,' said Mr Kuvetli airily. 'I did not approach you for three reasons.' He held up podgy fingers. 'Colonel Haki instructed me in the first place that your attitude to his efforts to protect you were unsympathetic and that unless it became necessary I would do better to remain unknown to you. Secondly, Colonel Haki has a low opinion of your ability to conceal your feelings and considered that if I wished to keep my true identity secret I had better not tell you of it.'

Graham was scarlet. 'And what about the third reason?'

'Thirdly,' continued Mr Kuvetli serenely, 'I wished to see what Banat and Moeller would do. You tell me that Moeller had talked to you. Excellent. I would like to hear what he had to say.'

Graham was angry now. 'Before I waste my time doing that,' he said coldly, 'supposing you show me your credentials. So far I have only Moeller's word and your own that you *are* a Turkish agent. I've already made some silly mistakes on this trip. I don't intend to make any more.'

To his surprise, Mr Kuvetli grinned. 'I am pleased to see that you are in such excellent spirits, Monsieur Graham. I was getting a little worried about you this evening. In this sort of situation, whisky does more harm to the nerves than good. Excuse me, please.' He turned to his jacket hanging on the hook behind the door and produced from the pocket of it a letter which he handed to Graham. 'That was given to me by Colonel Haki to give to you. I think you will find it satisfactory.'

Graham looked at it. It was an ordinary letter of introduction written in French on notepaper embossed with the title and address of the Turkish Ministry of the Interior. It was addressed to him personally and signed 'Zia Haki.' He put it in his pocket.

'Yes, Monsieur Kuvetli, it is quite satisfactory. I must apologize for doubting your word.'

'It was correct of you to do so,' said Mr Kuvetli primly. 'And now, Monsieur, tell me about Moeller. I am afraid Banat's appearance on the ship must have been a shock to you. I felt guilty about keeping you ashore in Athens. But it was for the best. As to Moeller . . .'

Graham looked at him quickly. 'Wait a minute! Do you mean to say that you knew Banat was coming aboard? Do you mean that you hung about in Athens asking all those fool questions solely in order to prevent my finding out before we sailed that Banat was on board?'

Mr Kuvetli looked sheepish. 'It was necessary. You must see . . .'

'Of all the damned . . .!' began Graham violently.

'One moment, please,' said Mr Kuvetli sharply. 'I have said that it was necessary. At Canakkale I received a telegram from Colonel Haki saying that Banat had left Turkey, that it was possible that he might try to join the ship at the Piraeus and . . .'

'You knew that! And yet . . .'

'Please, Monsieur! I will continue. Colonel Haki added that I was to keep you here on the ship. That was intelligent. On the ship nothing could happen to you. Banat might have been going to the Piraeus for the purpose of frightening you on to the land, where very unpleasant things could happen to you. Wait, please! I went to Athens with you partly to see that you were not attacked while you were ashore and partly so that if Banat did join the ship, you would not see him until we had sailed.'

'But why, in the name of goodness, didn't Colonel Haki arrest Banat or at least delay him until it was too late for him to reach the ship?'

'Because Banat would certainly have been replaced. We know all about Banat. A strange Monsieur Mavrodopoulos would have been a new problem.'

'But you say that Banat's, or, rather, Moeller's idea might have been to scare me off the boat. Banat could not know that I knew him?'

'You told Colonel Haki that Banat was pointed out to you in Le Jockey Cabaret. Banat was watching you then. He would probably know that you had noticed him. He is not an amateur. You see Colonel Haki's point of view? If they were hoping to drive you on to the land and kill you there, it would be better for them to attempt to do so and fail than for the attempt to be frustrated in time for them to make other arrangements. As it happens, however,' he went on cheerfully, 'their intention was not to drive you on to the land and my precautions were wasted. Banat did join the ship, but he stayed in his cabin until the pilot had been taken off.'

'Precisely!' snarled Graham. 'I could have gone ashore, taken a train and been safe in Paris by now.'

Mr Kuvetli considered the criticism for a moment and then slowly shook his head. 'I do not think so. You have forgotten Monsieur Moeller. I do not think that he and Banat would have stayed on the boat very long if you had not returned by sailing time.'

Graham laughed shortly. 'Did you know that then?'

Mr Kuvetli contemplated dirty fingernails. 'I will be very honest, Monsieur Graham. I did not know it. I knew *of* Monsieur Moeller, of course. I was, through an intermediary, once offered a large sum of money to work for him. I had seen a photograph of him. But photographs are mostly useless. I did not recognize him. The fact that he came aboard at Istanbul prevented my suspecting him. Banat's behaviour made me think that I had overlooked something, and when I saw him talking to the Herr Professor I made some inquiries.'

'He says that you searched his cabin.'

'I did. I found letters addressed to him in Sofia.'

'There has,' said Graham bitterly, 'been quite a lot of cabin searching. Last night Banat stole my revolver from my suit-case. This evening I went to his cabin and tried to find his gun, the gun he used on me in Istanbul. It was not there. When I returned to my cabin, Moeller was there with Banat's gun.'

Mr Kuvetli had been listening gloomily. 'If,' he said now, 'you will please tell me what Moeller had to say we shall both get to sleep much sooner.'

Graham smiled. 'You know, Kuvetli, I have had several surprises on this ship. You are the first pleasant one.' And then the smile faded. 'Moeller came to tell me that unless I agree to delay my return to England for six weeks I shall be murdered within five minutes of my landing in Genoa. He says that apart from Banat, he has other men waiting in Genoa to do the killing.'

Mr Kuvetli did not seem surprised. 'And where does he suggest that you should spend the six weeks?'

'In a villa near Santa Margherita. The idea is that I should be certified by a doctor as suffering from typhus and that I should stay in this villa as if it were a clinic. Moeller and Banat would be the medical staff if anyone should come out from England to see me. He proposes, you see, to involve me in the deception so that I cannot tell tales afterwards.'

Mr Kuvetli raised his eyebrows. 'And how was I concerned?'

Graham told him.

'And, believing Monsieur Moeller, you decided to ignore his advice and tell me about his suggestion?' Mr Kuvetli beamed approvingly. 'That was very courageous of you, Monsieur.'

Graham did not beam back. 'Do you think that I might have agreed?'

Mr Kuvetli's eyes widened. 'I think nothing,' he said hastily. 'But'–he hesitated–'when a person's life is in danger he is not always quite normal. He may do things which he would not do in the ordinary way. He cannot be blamed.'

Graham smiled. 'I will be frank with you. I came to you now instead of in the morning so that there could be no chance of my thinking things over and deciding to take his advice after all.'

'What is important,' said Mr Kuvetli cosily, 'is that you *have* in fact come to me. Did you tell him that you were going to do so?'

'No. I told him that I thought he was bluffing.'

'And *do* you think that he was?'

'I don't know.'

Mr Kuvetli scratched his armpits thoughtfully. 'There are so many things to be considered. And it depends on what you mean by saying that he is bluffing. If you mean that he could not or would not kill you, I think you are wrong. He could and would.'

'But how? I have a Consul. What is to prevent my getting into a taxi at the dock and going straight to the Consulate? I could arrange for some sort of protection there.'

Mr Kuvetli lit another cigarette. 'Do you know where the British Consulate-General in Genoa is?'

'The taxi-driver would know.'

'I can tell you myself. It is at the corner of the Via Ippolito d'Aste. This ship docks at the Ponte San Giorgio in the Vittorio Emanuele basin, several kilometres away from your Consulate. I have travelled this way before and so I know what I am saying. Genoa is a great port. I doubt, Monsieur Graham, whether you would complete one of those kilometres. They will be waiting for you with a car. When you took the taxi they would follow you as far as the Via Francia, then force the taxi on to the pavement and shoot you as you sit there.'

'I could telephone to the Consul from the dock.'

'Certainly you could. But you would have to go through the Customs shed first. You would then have to wait for the Consul to arrive. *Wait*, Monsieur! Do you understand what that means? Let us suppose that you were to reach the Consul by telephone immediately and convince him that your case was urgent. You would still have to wait at least half an hour for him. Let me tell you that your chances of surviving that half-hour would not be lessened if you spent it drinking prussic acid. To kill an unarmed, unguarded man is never difficult. Among the sheds on the quay it would be simplicity itself. No, I do not think Moeller is bluffing when he says that he can kill you.'

'But what about this proposal? He seemed very eager to persuade me to agree.'

Mr Kuvetli fingered the back of his head. 'There could be several explanations of that. For instance, it is possible that his intention is to kill you in any case and that he wishes to do so with as little trouble as possible. One cannot deny that it would be easier to kill you on the road to Santa Margherita than on the waterfront at Genoa.'

'That's a pleasing idea.'

'I am inclined to think that it is the correct one.' Mr Kuvetli frowned. 'You see, this proposal of his looks very simple—you are taken ill, there is a forged medical certificate, you get better, you go home. *Voila!* It is done. But think now of the actuality. You are an Englishman in a hurry to get to England. You land in Genoa. What would you do normally? Take the train for Paris, without a doubt. But what is it necessary to do now? You must, for some mysterious reason, remain in Genoa long enough to discover that you have typhus. Also you must not do what anyone else would do in those circumstances—you must not go to a hospital. You must instead go to a private clinic near Santa Margherita. Is it possible that it would not be thought in England that your behaviour was curious? I think not. Furthermore, typhus is a disease which must be notified to the authorities. That could not be done in this case because there would be no typhus and the medical authorities would soon discover the fact. And supposing your friends discover that your case has not been notified. They might. You are of some importance. The British Consul might be asked to investigate. And then what? No, I cannot see Monsieur Moeller taking such absurd risks. Why should he? It would be easier to kill you.'

'He says that he does not like having people killed if he can help it.'

Mr Kuvetli giggled. 'He must think you very stupid indeed. Did he tell you what he would do about my presence here?'

'No.'

'I am not surprised. For that plan to succeed as he explained it to you, there would be only one thing he could do—kill me. And even when he had killed me I would still embarrass him. Colonel Haki would see to that. I am afraid that Monsieur's proposal is not very honest.'

'It sounded convincing. I may say that he was prepared to allow Señora Gallindo to make up the party if I liked to take her along.'

Mr Kuvetli leered: a scurfy faun in a flannel night-shirt. 'And did you tell Señora Gallindo that?'

Graham flushed. 'She knows nothing of Moeller. I told her about Banat. I'm afraid I gave myself away last night when Banat came into the saloon. She asked me what was wrong and I told her. Anyway,' he added defensively but none too truthfully, 'I needed her help. It was she who arranged to keep Banat occupied while I searched his cabin.'

'By arranging for the good José to play cards with him? Quite so. As to the suggestion that she should accompany you, I think that, if you had accepted it, it would have been withdrawn. It would, no doubt, be explained that difficulties had arisen. Does José know of this business?'

'No. I don't think that she would tell him. She's trustworthy, I think,' he added with as much nonchalance as he could muster.

'No woman is trustworthy,' gloated Mr Kuvetli. 'But I do not begrudge you your amusements, Monsieur Graham.' He moistened his upper lip with the tip of his tongue and grinned. 'Señora Gallindo is very attractive.'

Graham checked the retort that rose to his lips. 'Very,' he said tersely. 'Meanwhile we have reached the conclusion that I shall be killed if I accept Moeller's proposal and killed if I don't.' And then he lost control of himself. 'For God's sake, Kuvetli,' he burst out in English, 'do you think it's pleasant for me to sit here listening to you telling me how easy it would be for these lice to kill me! What am I going to *do*?'

Mr Kuvetli patted his knee consolingly. 'My dear friend, I understand perfectly. I was merely showing you that it would be impossible for you to land in the ordinary way.'

'But what other way *can* I land? I'm not invisible.'

'I will tell you,' said Mr Kuvetli complacently. 'It is very simple. You see, although this ship does not actually reach the quayside for the landing of passengers until nine o'clock on Saturday morning, she arrives off Genoa in the early hours, at about four o'clock. Night pilotage is expensive. Accordingly, although she takes on a pilot as soon as it begins to get light, she does not move in until sunrise. The pilot boat . . .'

'If you're suggesting that I leave by the pilot boat, it's impossible.'

'For you, yes. For me, no. I am privileged. I have a diplomatic *laisser passer*.' He patted his jacket pocket. 'By eight o'clock I can be at the Turkish Consulate. Arrangements can be made for getting you away safely and taking you to the airport. The international train service is not as good as it used to be, and the Paris train does not leave until two o'clock in the afternoon. It is better that you do not remain so long in Genoa. We will charter a plane to take you to Paris immediately.'

Graham's heart began to beat faster. An extraordinary feeling of lightness and ease came over him. He wanted to laugh. He said stolidly: 'It sounds all right.'

'It will be all right, but precautions must be taken to see that it is so. If Monsieur Moeller suspects that there is a chance of your escaping, something unpleasant will happen. Listen carefully, please.' He scratched his chest and then held up a forefinger. 'First; you must go to Monsieur Moeller to-morrow and tell him that you agree to his suggestion that you should stay in Santa Margherita.'

'What!'

'It is the best way to keep him quiet. I leave you to choose your own opportunity. But I will suggest the following: it is possible that he will approach you again, and so perhaps it will be best if you give him time to do so. Wait until late in the evening. If he has not approached you by then, go to him. Do not appear to be too ingenuous, but agree to do what he wants. When you have done that, go to your cabin, lock the door, and remain there. Do not leave your cabin under any circumstances until eight o'clock the following morning. It might be dangerous.

'Now comes the important part of your instructions. At eight o'clock in the morning you must be ready with your baggage. Call the steward, tip him, and tell him to put your baggage in the Customs shed. There must be no mistake at this point. What you have to do is to remain on the ship until I come to tell you that the preparations have been made and that it is safe for you to land. There are difficulties. If you remain in your cabin the steward will make you go ashore with the rest, including Monsieur Moeller and Banat. If you go on deck, the same thing will happen. You must see that you are not forced to go ashore before it is safe for you to do so.'

'But how?'

'I am explaining that. What you must do is to leave your cabin and then, taking care that nobody sees you, to go into the nearest unoccupied cabin. You have cabin number five. Go into cabin number four. That is the next cabin to this. Wait there. You will be quite safe. You will have tipped the steward. If he thinks of you again at all it will be to assume that you have gone ashore. If he is asked about you he will certainly not look in unoccupied cabins. Monsieur Moeller and Banat will naturally be looking for you. You will have agreed to go with them. But they will have to go ashore to wait. By that time we shall be there and able to act.'

'Act?'

Mr Kuvetli smiled grimly. 'We shall have two men for every one of theirs. I do not think that they will try to stop us. Are you quite clear about what you have to do?'

'Quite clear.'

'There is a small matter. Monsieur Moeller will ask you if I have made myself known to you. You will, of course, say yes. He will ask you what I said. You will tell him that I offered to escort you to Paris myself and that when you insisted on going to the British Consul, I threatened you.'

'Threatened me!'

'Yes.' Mr Kuvetli was still smiling, but his eyes had narrowed a little. 'If your attitude towards me had been different it might have been necessary for me to threaten you.'

'What with?' Graham demanded spitefully. 'Death? That would have been absurd, wouldn't it?'

Mr Kuvetli smiled steadily. 'No, Monsieur Graham, not death but with the accusation that you had accepted bribes from an enemy agent to sabotage Turkish naval preparations. You see, Monsieur Graham, it is just as important for me that you return to England without delay as it is for Monsieur Moeller that you should not return.'

Graham stared at him. 'I see. And this is a gentle reminder that the threat still stands if I should allow myself to be persuaded that Moeller's proposal is, after all, acceptable. Is that it?'

Mr Kuvetli drew himself up. 'I am a Turk, Monsieur Graham,' he said with dignity, 'and I love my country. I fought with the Gazi for Turkey's freedom. Can you imagine that I would let one man endanger the great work we have done? I am ready to give my life for Turkey. Is it strange that I should not hesitate to do less unpleasant things?'

He had struck an attitude. He was ridiculous and yet, for the very reason that his words were at so odd a variance with his appearance, impressive. Graham was disarmed. He grinned. 'Not at all strange. You need have no fears. I shall do exactly what you have told me to do. But supposing he wants to know when our meeting took place?'

'You will tell the truth. It is just possible that you were seen to come to my cabin. You can say that I asked you to do so, that I left a note in your cabin. Remember, too, that we must not be seen in private conversation after this. It will be better if we do not have any sort of conversation. In any case there is nothing more to be said. Everything is arranged. There is only one other matter to be considered – Señora Gallindo.'

'What about her?'

'She has part of your confidence. What is her attitude?'

'She thinks that everything is all right now.' He paused. 'I said that I would travel with her to Paris.'

'And after?'

'She believes that I shall spend some time with her there.'

'You did not, of course, intend to do so.' He had the air of a schoolmaster dealing with a difficult pupil.

Graham hesitated. 'No, I suppose I didn't,' he said slowly. 'To tell you the truth, it has been pleasant to talk of going to Paris. When you're expecting to be killed . . .'

'But now that you are not expecting to be killed it is different, eh?'

'Yes, it's different.' Yet was it so different? He was not quite sure.

Mr Kuvetli stroked his chin. 'On the other hand it would be dangerous to tell her that you have changed your mind,' he reflected. 'She might be indiscreet–or angry, perhaps. Say nothing to her. If she discusses Paris, everything is as it was before. You can explain that you have business to do in Genoa after the ship docks and say that you will meet her on the train. That will prevent her looking for you before she goes ashore. It is understood?'

'Yes. It is understood.'

'She is pretty,' Mr Kuvetli went on thoughtfully. 'It is a pity that your business is so urgent. However, perhaps you could return to Paris when you have finished your work.' He smiled: the schoolmaster promising a sweet for good behaviour.

'I suppose I could. Is there anything else?'

Mr Kuvetli looked up at him slyly. 'No. That is all. Except that I must ask you to continue to look as *distrait* as you have been looking since we left the Piraeus. It would be a pity if Monsieur Moeller should suspect anything from your manner.'

'My manner? Oh, yes, I see.' He stood up and was surprised to find that his knees felt quite weak. He said: 'I've often wondered what a condemned man feels like when they tell him that he has been reprieved. Now I know.'

Mr Kuvetli smiled patronizingly. 'You feel very well, eh?'

Graham shook his head. 'No, Mr Kuvetli, I don't feel very well. I feel very sick and very tired and I can't stop thinking that there must be a mistake.'

'A mistake! There is no mistake. You need not worry. All will be well. Go to bed now, my friend, and in the morning you will feel better. A mistake!'

Mr Kuvetli laughed.

Chapter Ten

As Mr Kuvetli had prophesied, Graham did feel better in the morning. Sitting up in his bunk drinking his coffee, he felt curiously free and competent. The disease from which he had been suffering was cured. He was himself again, well and normal. He had been a fool to worry at all. He ought to have known that everything would be all right. War or no war, men like him weren't shot in the street. That sort of thing just didn't happen. Only the adolescent minds of the Moellers and the Banats could entertain such possibilities. He had no misgivings. Even his hand was better. In the night the bandage had slipped, taking with it the bloody dressing which had been sticking to the wound. He was able to replace it with a piece of lint and two strips of adhesive plaster. The change, he felt, was symbolic. Not even the knowledge that in the day before him he had some highly disagreeable things to do, could depress him.

The first thing he had to consider was, of course, his attitude towards Moeller. As Mr Kuvetli had pointed out, it was possible that the man would wait until the evening before making any attempt to find out if the line he had put out the previous evening had caught the fish. That meant that he, Graham, would have to sit through two meals with Moeller and Banat without giving himself away. That, certainly, would not be pleasant. He wondered whether it might not be safer to approach Moeller at once. It would, after all, be far more convincing if the victim made the first move. Or would it be less convincing? Should the fish still be struggling on the hook when the line was reeled in? Evidently Mr Kuvetli thought that it should. Very well. Mr Kuvetli's instructions should be followed exactly. The questions of how he was going to behave at lunch and dinner could be left to settle themselves when those times came. As for the actual interview with Moeller, he had ideas about making that convincing. Moeller should not have things all his own way. Rather to his surprise, he found that it was the thought of what he had to do about Josette which worried him most.

He was, he told himself, treating her shabbily. She had been kind to him in her way. Indeed, she could not have been kinder. It was no excuse to say that she had behaved badly over that business of José's revolver. It had been unfair of him to ask her to steal for him. José was, after all, her partner. It would not even be possible now for him to give her that handbag with a thousand-franc note in it, unless he left it for her on his way through Paris, and it was always possible that she would not go to the Hotel des Belges. It was no good protesting that she was out for what she could get. She had made no secret of the fact and he had tacitly accepted it. He was treating her shabbily, he told himself again. It was an attempt to rationalize his feelings about her and it was strangely unsuccessful. He was perplexed.

He did not see her until just before lunch, and then she was with José.

It was a wretched day. The sky was overcast and there was an icy northeast wind with a hint of snow in it. He had spent most of the morning in a corner of the saloon reading some old copies of *L'Illustration* he found there. Mr Kuvetli had seen and looked through him. He had spoken to no one except the Beronellis, who had given him a defensive '*buon giorno,*' and the Mathis, who had returned his greeting with a frigid bow. He had thought it necessary to explain to the Mathis that his rudeness of the previous evening had been unintentional and due to his feeling ill at the time. The explanation had been accepted by them with some embarrassment and it had occurred to him that they might have preferred a silent feud to an apology. The man had been particularly confused as if he were finding himself in some way ridiculous. They had soon decided that they must go for a walk on deck. Through the porthole Graham had seen them a few minutes later walking with Mr Kuvetli. The only other person on deck that morning had been Moeller's Armenian demonstrating pathetically, for there was a heavy swell, that her dislike of the sea was no mere figment of her 'husband's' imagination. Soon after twelve Graham had collected his hat and coat from his cabin and gone out for the stroll which he had decided should precede the drinking of a large whisky and soda.

He was on his way back to the saloon when he encountered Josette and José.

José stopped with an oath and clutched at his curly soft hat which the wind was trying to snatch from his head.

Josette met Graham's eyes and smiled significantly. 'José is angry again. Last night he played cards and lost. It was the little Greek, Mavrodopoulos. The attar of roses was too strong for the California Poppy.'

'He is no Greek,' said José sourly. 'He has the accent of a goat as well as the smell. If he is a Greek I will . . .' He said what he would do.

'But he can play cards, *mon cher caïd.*'

'He stopped playing too soon,' said José. 'You need not worry. I have not finished with him.'

'Perhaps he has finished with you.'

'He must be a very good player,' Graham put in tactfully.

José eyed him distastefully. 'And what do you know about it?'

'Nothing,' retorted Graham coldly. 'For all I know it may be simply that you are a very bad player.'

'You would like to play perhaps?'

'I don't think so. Cards bore me.'

José sneered. 'Ah, yes! There are better things to do, eh?' He sucked his teeth loudly.

'When he is bad-tempered,' Josette explained, 'he cannot be polite. There is nothing to be done with him. He does not care what people think.'

José pursed up his mouth into an expression of saccharine sweetness. '"He does not care what people think,"' he repeated in a high, derisive falsetto. Then his face relaxed. 'What do I care what they think?' he demanded.

'You are ridiculous,' said Josette.

'If they do not like it they can stay in the lavabos,' José declared aggressively.

'It would be a small price to pay,' murmured Graham.

Josette giggled. José scowled. 'I do not understand.'

Graham did not see that there was anything to be gained by explaining. He ignored José and said in English: 'I was just going to have a drink. Will you come?'

She looked doubtful. 'Do you wish to buy José a drink also?'

'Must I?'

'I cannot get rid of him.'

José was glowering at them suspiciously. 'It is not wise to insult me,' he said.

'No one is insulting you, imbecile. Monsieur here asks us to have drinks. Do you want a drink?'

He belched. 'I do not care who I drink with if we can get off this filthy deck.'

'He is so polite,' said Josette.

They had finished their drinks when the gong sounded. Graham soon found that he had been wise to leave the question of his attitude towards Moeller to answer itself. It was 'Haller' who appeared in answer to the gong;

a Haller who greeted Graham as if nothing had happened and who embarked almost immediately on a long account of the manifestations of An, the Sumerian sky god. Only once did he show himself to be aware of any change in his relationship with Graham. Soon after he began talking, Banat entered and sat down. Moeller paused and glanced across the table at him. Banat stared back sullenly. Moeller turned deliberately to Graham.

'Monsieur Mavrodopoulos,' he remarked, 'looks as if he has been frustrated in some way, as if he has been told that he may not be able to do something that he wishes to do very badly. Don't you think so, Mr Graham? I wonder if he is going to be disappointed.'

Graham looked up from his plate to meet a level stare. There was no mistaking the question in the pale blue eyes. He knew that Banat, too, was watching him. He said slowly: 'It would be a pleasure to disappoint Monsieur Mavrodopoulos.'

Moeller smiled and the smile reached his eyes. 'So it would. Now let me see. What was I saying? Ah, yes . . .'

That was all; but Graham went on with his meal, knowing that one at least of the day's problems was solved. He would not have to approach Moeller: Moeller would approach him.

But Moeller was evidently in no hurry to do so. The afternoon dragged intolerably. Mr Kuvetli had said that they were not to have any sort of conversation and Graham deemed it advisable to plead a headache when Mathis suggested a rubber of bridge. His refusal affected the Frenchman peculiarly. There was a troubled reluctance about his acceptance of it, and he looked as if he had been about to say something important and then thought better of it. There was in his eyes the same look of unhappy confusion that Graham had seen in the morning. But Graham wondered about it only for a few seconds. He was not greatly interested in the Mathis.

Moeller, Banat, Josette and José had gone to their cabins immediately after lunch. Signora Beronelli had been induced to make the fourth with the Mathis and Mr Kuvetli and appeared to be enjoying herself. Her son sat by her watching her jealously. Graham returned in desperation to the magazines. Towards five o'clock, however, the bridge four showed signs of disintegrating and, to avoid being drawn into a conversation with Mr Kuvetli, Graham went out on deck.

The sun, obscured since the day before, was pouring a red glow through a thinning of the clouds just above the horizon. To the east the long, low strip of coast which had been visible earlier was already enveloped in a slate grey dusk and the lights of a town had begun to twinkle. The clouds were moving quickly as for the gathering of a storm and heavy drops of rain began to slant in on to the deck. He moved backwards out of the rain and found Mathis at his elbow. The Frenchman nodded.

'Was it a good game?' Graham asked.

'Quite good. Madame Beronelli and I lost. She is enthusiastic, but inefficient.'

'Then, except for the enthusiasm, my absence made no difference.'

Mathis smiled a little nervously. 'I hope that your headache is better.'

'Much better, thank you.'

It had begun to rain in earnest now. Mathis stared out gloomily into the gathering darkness. 'Filthy!' he commented.

'Yes.'

There was a pause. Then:

'I was afraid,' said Mathis suddenly, 'that you did not wish to play with us. I could not blame you if such were the case. This morning you were good enough to make an apology. The true apology was due from me to you.'

He was not looking at Graham. 'I am quite sure . . .' Graham began to mumble, but Mathis went on as if he were addressing the seagulls following the ship. 'I do not always remember,' he said bitterly, 'that what to some people is good or bad is to others simply boring. My wife has led me to put too much faith in the power of words.'

'I'm afraid I don't understand.'

Mathis turned his head and smiled wryly. 'Do you know the word *encotillonné*?'

'No.'

'A man who is governed by his wife is *encotillonné*.'

'In English we say "hen-pecked." '

'Ah, yes?' Obviously he did not care what was said in English. 'I must tell you a joke about it. Once I was *encotillonné*. Oh, but very badly! Does that surprise you?'

'It does.' Graham saw that the man was dramatizing himself, and was curious.

'My wife used to have a very great temper. She still has it, I think, but now I do not see it. But for the first ten years of our marriage it was terrible. I had a small business. Trade was very bad and I became bankrupt. It was not my fault, but she always pretended that it was. Has your wife a bad temper, Monsieur?'

'No. Very good.'

'You are lucky. For years I lived in misery. And then one day I made a great discovery. There was a socialist meeting in our town and I went to it. I was, you must understand, a Royalist. My family had no money, but they had a little which they would have liked to use without their neighbours sniggering. I was of my family. I went to this meeting because I was curious. The speaker was good, and he spoke about Briey. That interested me because I had been at Verdun. A week later we were with some friends in the café and I repeated what I had heard. My wife laughed in a curious way. Then when I got home I made my great discovery. I found that my wife was a snob and more stupid than I had dreamed. She said that I had humiliated her by saying such things as if I believed them. All her friends were respectable people. I must not speak as if I were a workman. She cried. I knew then that I was free. I had a weapon that I could use against her. I used it. If she displeased me I became a socialist. To the smug little tradesmen whose wives were her friends I would preach the abolition of profit and the family. I bought books and pamphlets to make my arguments more damaging. My wife became very docile. She would cook things that I liked so that I would not disgrace her.' He paused.

'You mean that you don't believe all these things you say about Briey and banking and capitalism?' demanded Graham.

Mathis smiled faintly. 'That is the joke about which I told you. For a time I was free. I could command my wife and I became more fond of her. I was a manager in a big factory. And then a terrible thing happened. I found that I had begun to believe these things I said. The books I read showed me that I had found a truth. I, a Royalist by instinct, became a socialist by conviction. Worse, I became a socialist martyr. There was a strike in the factory and I, a manager, supported the strikers. I did not belong to a union. Naturally! And so I was dismissed. It was ridiculous.' He shrugged. 'So here I am! I have become a man in my home at the price of becoming a bore outside it. It is funny, is it not?'

Graham smiled. He had decided that he liked Monsieur Mathis. He said: 'It would be funny if it were wholly true. But I can assure you that it was not because I was bored that I did not listen to you last night.'

'You are very polite,' began Mathis dubiously; 'but . . .'

'Oh, there is no question of politeness. You see, I work for an armaments manufacturer, and so I have been more than interested in what you have had to say. On some points I find myself in agreement with you.'

A change came over the Frenchman's face. He flushed slightly; a small delighted smile hovered round his lips; for the first time Graham saw the tense frown relax. 'On which points do you *not* agree?' he demanded eagerly.

At that moment Graham realized that, whatever else had happened to him on the *Sestri Levante*, he had made at least one friend.

They were still arguing when Josette came out on deck. Unwillingly, Mathis interrupted what he was saying to acknowledge her presence.

'*Madame.*'

She wrinkled her nose at them. 'What are you discussing? It must be very important that you have to stand in the rain to talk about it.'

'We were talking politics.'

'No, no!' said Mathis quickly. 'Not politics, economics! Politics are the effect. We were talking about causes. But you are right. This rain is filthy. If you will excuse me, please, I will see what has happened to my wife.' He winked at Graham. 'If she suspects that I am making propaganda she will not be able to sleep to-night.'

With a smile and a nod he went. Josette looked after him. 'He is nice, that man. Why does he marry such a woman?'

'He is very fond of her.'

'In the way that you are fond of me?'

'Perhaps not. Would you rather we went in?'

'No. I came out for some air. It will not be so wet round on the other side of the deck.'

They began to walk round to the other side. It was dark now and the deck lights had been put on.

She took his arm. 'Do you realize that to-day we have not really seen each other until now? No! Of course you do not realise it! You have been amusing yourself with politics. It does not matter that I am worried.'

'Worried? What about?'

'This man who wants to kill you, imbecile! You do not tell me what you are going to do at Genoa.'

He shrugged. 'I've taken your advice. I'm not troubling about him.'

'But you will go to the British Consul?'

'Yes.' The moment had come when he must do some really steady lying. 'I shall go straight there. Afterwards I shall have to see one or two people on business. The train does not leave until two o'clock in the afternoon, so I think that I shall have time. We can meet on the train.'

She sighed. 'So much business! But I shall see you for lunch, eh?'

'I'm afraid it's unlikely. If we did arrange to meet I might not be able to keep the appointment. It'll be best if we meet on the train.'

She turned her head a little sharply. 'You are telling me the truth? You are not saying this because you have changed your mind?'

'My dear Josette!' He had opened his mouth to explain again that he had business to attend to, but had stopped himself in time. He must not protest too much.

She pressed his arm. 'I did not mean to be disagreeable, *chéri*. It is only that I wish to be sure. We will meet at the train if you wish it. We can have a drink together at Torino. We reach there at four and stop for half an hour. It is because of the coaches from Milano. There are some nice places to drink in Torino. After the ship here it will be wonderful.'

'It'll be splendid. What about José?'

'Ah, it does not matter about him. Let him drink by himself. After the way he was rude to you this morning, I do not care what José does. Tell me about the letters you are writing. Are they all finished?'

'I shall finish them this evening.'

'And after that, no more work?'

'After that, no more work.' He felt that he could not stand much more of this. He said: 'You'll get cold if we stay out here much longer. Shall we go inside?'

She stopped and withdrew her arm from his so that he could kiss her. Her back was taut as she strained her body against his. Seconds later she drew away from him, laughing. 'I must remember,' she said, 'not to say "whisky-soda," but "whisky and soda" now. That is very important, eh?'

'Very important.'

She squeezed his arm. 'You are nice. I like you very much, *chéri*.'

They began to walk back towards the saloon. He was grateful for the dimness of the lights.

He did not have long to wait for Moeller. The German agent had been in the habit of leaving the table and going to his cabin as soon as a meal was finished. To-night, however, Banat was the first to go, evidently by arrangement; and the monologue continued until the Beronellis had followed him. It was an account of comparisons made between the Sumero-Babylonian liturgies and the ritual forms of certain Mesopotamian fertility cults and it was with unmistakable triumph that he at last brought it to an end. 'You must admit, Mr Graham,' he added, lowering his voice, 'that I have done extremely well to remember so much. Naturally, I made a few mistakes, and a good deal was lost, I have no doubt, in my translation. The author would probably fail to recognize it. But to the uninitiated I should say it would be most convincing.'

'I have been wondering why you have taken so much trouble. You might have been talking Chinese for all the Beronellis knew or cared.'

Moeller looked pained. 'I was not talking for the Beronellis, but for my own private satisfaction. How stupid it is to say that the memory fails with the approach of old age. Would you think that I am sixty-six?'

'I'm not interested in your age.'

'No, of course not. Perhaps we could have a private talk. I suggest that we take a walk together on deck. It is raining, but a little rain will not hurt us.'

'My coat is on the chair over there.'

'Then I will meet you on the top deck in a few minutes' time.'

Graham was waiting at the head of the companionway when Moeller came up. They moved into the lee of one of the lifeboats.

Moeller came straight to the point.

'I gather that you have seen Kuvetli.'

'I have,' said Graham grimly.

'Well?'

'I have decided to take your advice.'

'At Kuvetli's suggestion?'

This, Graham reflected, was not going to be as easy as he had thought. He answered: 'At my own. I was not impressed by him. Frankly, I was amazed. That the Turkish Government should have put such a fool of a man on the job seems to me incredible.'

'What makes you think he is a fool?'

'He seems to think that you are making some attempt to bribe me and that I am inclined to accept the money. He threatened to expose me to the British Government. When I suggested that I might be in some personal danger he seemed to think that I was trying to trick him in some stupid way. If that's your idea of a clever man, I'm sorry for you.'

'Perhaps he is not used to dealing with the English brand of self-esteem,' Moeller retorted acidly. 'When did this meeting take place?'

'Last night, soon after I saw you.'

'And did he mention me by name?'

'Yes. He warned me against you.'

'And how did you treat the warning?'

'I said that I would report his behaviour to Colonel Haki. He did not, I must say, seem to care. But if I had any idea of securing his protection, I gave it up. I don't trust him. Besides, I don't see why I should risk my life for people who treat me as if I were some sort of criminal.'

He paused. He could not see Moeller's face in the darkness but he felt that the man was satisfied.

'And so you've decided to accept my suggestion?'

'Yes, I have. But,' Graham went on, 'before we go any farther, there are one or two things I want to get clear.'

'Well?'

'In the first place, there is this man Kuvetli. He's a fool, as I've said, but he'll have to be put off the scent somehow.'

'You need have no fears.' Graham thought he detected a note of contempt in the smooth heavy voice. 'Kuvetli will cause no trouble. It will be easy to give him the slip in Genoa. The next thing he will hear of you is that you are suffering from typhus. He will be unable to prove anything to the contrary.'

Graham was relieved. Obviously, Moeller thought him a fool. He said doubtfully: 'Yes, I see. That's all right, but what about this typhus? If I'm going to be taken ill I've got to be taken ill properly. If I were really taken ill I should probably be on the train when it happened.'

Moeller sighed. 'I see that you've been thinking very seriously, Mr Graham. Let me explain. If you were really infected with typhus you would already be feeling unwell. There is an incubation period of a week or ten days. You would not, of course, know what was the matter with you. By to-morrow you would be feeling worse. It would be logical for you to shrink from spending the night in a train. You would probably go to an hotel for the night. Then, in the morning, when your temperature began to rise and the characteristics of the disease became apparent, you would be removed to a clinic.'

'Then we shall go to an hotel to-morrow?'

'Exactly. There will be a car waiting for us. But I advise you to leave the arrangements to me, Mr Graham. Remember, I am just as interested as you are in seeing that nobody's suspicions are aroused.'

Graham affected to ponder this. 'All right then,' he said at last. 'I'll leave it to you. I don't want to be fussy, but you can understand that I don't want to have any trouble when I get home.'

There was a silence and for a moment he thought that he had overacted. Then Moeller said slowly: 'You have no reason to worry. We shall be waiting for you outside the Customs shed. As long as you do not attempt to do anything foolish—you might, for example, decide to change your mind about your holiday—everything will go smoothly. I can assure you that you will have no trouble when you get home.'

'As long as that's understood.'

'Is there anything else you want to say?'

'No. Good night.'

'Good night, Mr Graham. Until to-morrow.'

Graham waited until Moeller had reached the deck below. Then he drew a deep breath. It was over. He was safe. All he had to do now was to go to his cabin, get a good night's sleep and wait for Mr Kuvetli in cabin number four. He felt suddenly very tired. His body was aching as if he had been working too hard. He made his way down to his cabin. It was as he passed the landing door of the saloon that he saw Josette.

She was sitting on one of the *banquettes* watching José and Banat playing cards. Her hands were on the edge of the seat and she was leaning forward, her lips parted slightly, her hair falling across her cheeks. There was something about the pose that reminded him of the moment, years ago it seemed, when he had followed Kopeikin into her dressing-room at Le Jockey Cabaret. He half expected her to raise her head and turn towards him, smiling.

He realized suddenly that he was seeing her for the last time, that before another day had passed he would be for her merely a disagreeable memory, someone who had treated her badly. The realization was sharp and strangely painful. He told himself that he was being absurd, that it had always been impossible for him to stay with her in Paris and that he had known it all along. Why should the leave-taking trouble him now? And yet it did trouble him. A phrase came into his head: 'to part is to die a little.' He knew suddenly that it was not Josette of whom he was taking his leave, but of something of himself. In the back streets of his mind a door was slowly closing for the last time. She had complained that for him she was just a part of the journey from Istanbul to London. There was more to it than that. She was part of the world beyond the door, the world into which he had stepped when Banat had fired those three shots at him in the Adler Palace; the world in which you recognized the ape beneath the velvet. Now he was on his way back to his own world; to his house and his car and the friendly, agreeable woman he called his wife. It would be exactly the same as when he had left it. Nothing would be changed in that world; nothing, except himself.

He went on down to his cabin.

He slept fitfully. Once he awoke with a start, believing that someone was opening the door of his cabin. Then he remembered that the door was bolted and concluded that he had been dreaming. When next he awoke, the engines had stopped and the ship was no longer rolling. He switched on the light and saw that the time was a quarter past four. They had arrived at the entrance to Genoa harbour. After a while he heard the chugging of a small boat and a fainter clatter from the deck above. There were voices too. He tried to distinguish Mr Kuvetli's among them, but they were too muffled. He dozed.

He had told the steward to bring coffee at seven. Towards six, however, he decided that it was useless to try to sleep any more. He was already dressed when the steward arrived.

He drank his coffee, put the remainder of his things in his case and sat down to wait. Mr Kuvetli had told him to go into the empty cabin at eight o'clock. He had promised himself that he would obey Mr Kuvetli's instructions to the letter. He listened to the Mathis arguing over their packing.

At about a quarter to eight the ship began to move in. Another five minutes and he rang for the steward. By five to eight the steward had been, received with barely concealed surprise fifty lire, and gone, taking the suitcase with him. Graham waited another minute and then opened the door.

The alleyway was empty. He walked along slowly to number four, stopped as if he had forgotten something, and half turned. The coast was still clear. He opened the door, stepped quickly into the cabin, shut the door, and turned round.

The next moment he almost fainted.

Lying across the floor with his legs under the lower berth and his head covered with blood, was Mr Kuvetli.

Chapter Eleven

Most of the bleeding seemed to have been caused by a scalp wound on the back of the head; but there was another wound, which had bled comparatively little and which looked as if it had been made with a knife, low on the left side of the neck. The movements of the ship had sent the slowly congealing blood trickling to and from in a madman's scrawl across the linoleum. The face was the colour of dirty clay. Mr Kuvetli was clearly dead.

Graham clenched his teeth to prevent himself retching and held on to the washing cabinet for support. His first thought was that he must not be sick, that he must pull himself together before he called for help. He did not realize immediately the implications of what had happened. So that he should not look down again he had kept his eyes fixed on the porthole and it was the sight of the funnel of a ship lying beyond a long concrete jetty that reminded him that they were going into harbour. In less than an hour the gangways would be down. And Mr Kuvetli had not reached the Turkish Consulate.

The shock of the realization brought him to his senses. He looked down.

It was Banat's work without a doubt. The little Turk had probably been stunned in his own cabin or in the alleyway outside it, dragged out of sight into this, the nearest empty cabin, and butchered while he was still insensible. Moeller had decided to dispose of a possible threat to the smooth working of his arrangements for dealing with the principal victim. Graham remembered the noise which had awakened him in the night. It might have come from the next cabin. 'Do not leave your cabin under any circumstances until eight o'clock the following morning. It might be dangerous.' Mr Kuvetli had failed to take his own advice and it *had* been dangerous. He had declared himself ready to die for his country and he had so died. There he was, his chubby fists clenched pitifully, his fringe of grey hair matted with his blood and the mouth which had smiled so much half open and inanimate.

Someone walked along the alleyway outside and Graham jerked his head up. The sound and the movement seemed to clear his brain. He began to think quickly and coolly.

The way the blood had congealed showed that Mr Kuvetli must have been killed before the ship had stopped. Long before! Before he had made his request for permission to leave by the pilot boat. If he had made the request, a thorough search for him would have been made when the boat came alongside and he would have been found. He had not yet been found. He was not travelling with an ordinary passport but with a diplomatic *laisser passer* and so had not had to surrender his papers to the Purser. That meant that unless the Purser checked off the passenger list with the passport control officer at Genoa–and Graham knew from past experience that they did not always bother to do that at Italian ports–the fact that Mr Kuvetli did not land would not be noticed. Moeller and Banat had probably counted on the fact. And if the dead man's baggage had been packed, the steward would put it in the Customs shed with the rest and assume that its owner was lying low to avoid having to give a tip. It might be hours, days even, before the body were discovered if he, Graham, did not call anyone.

His lips tightened. He became conscious of a slow cold rage mounting in his brain, stifling his sense of self-preservation. If he did call someone he could accuse Moeller and Banat; but would he be able to bring the crime home to them? His accusation by itself would carry no weight. It might well be suggested that the accusation was a ruse to conceal his own guilt. The Purser, for one, would be glad to support that theory. The fact that the two accused were travelling with false passports could, no doubt, be proved, but that alone would take time. In any case, the Italian police would be amply justified in refusing him permission to leave for England. Mr Kuvetli had died in trying to make it possible for him to reach England safely and in time to fulfil a contract. That Mr Kuvetli's dead body should become the very means of preventing the fulfilment of that contract was stupid and grotesque; but if he, Graham, wanted to be sure of saving his own skin, that was what must happen. It was strangely unthinkable. For him, standing there above the dead body of the man whom Moeller had described as a patriot, there seemed to be only one thing of importance in the world–that Mr Kuvetli's death should be neither stupid nor grotesque, that it should be useless only to the men who had murdered him.

But if he were not going to raise the alarm and wait for the police, what was he going to do?

Supposing Moeller had planned this. Supposing he or Banat had overheard Mr Kuvetli's instructions to him and, believing that he was sufficiently intimidated to do anything to save himself, had thought of this way of delaying his return. Or they might be preparing to 'discover' him with the body and so incriminate him. But no: both those suppositions were absurd. If they had known of Mr Kuvetli's plan they would have let the Turk go ashore by the pilot boat. It would have been his, Graham's, body that would have been found and the finder would have been Mr Kuvetli. Obviously, then, Moeller could neither know of the plan nor suspect that the murder would be discovered. An hour from now he would be standing with Banat and the gunmen who were to meet him, waiting for the victim to walk unsuspectingly . . .

But the victim would not be unsuspecting. There was a very slender chance . . .

He turned and, grasping the handle of the door, began to turn it gently. He knew that if he thought twice about what he had decided to do he would change his mind. He must commit himself before he had time to think.

He opened the door a fraction of an inch. There was no one in the alleyway. A moment later, he was out of the cabin and the door of it was shut behind him. He hesitated barely a second. He knew that he must keep moving. Five steps brought him to cabin number three. He went in.

Mr Kuvetli's luggage consisted of one old-fashioned valise. It was standing strapped up in the middle of the floor, and perched on one of the straps was a twenty lire piece. Graham picked up the coin and held it to his nose. The smell of attar of roses was quite distinct. He looked in the wardrobe and behind the door for Mr Kuvetli's overcoat and hat, failed to find them, and concluded that they had been disposed of through the porthole. Banat had thought of everything.

He put the valise up on the berth and opened it. Most of the things on top had obviously been stuffed in anyhow by Banat, but lower down the packing had been done very neatly. The only thing of any interest to Graham, however, was a box of pistol ammunition. Of the pistol which fired them there was no sign.

Graham put the ammunition in his pocket and shut the valise again. He was undecided as to what he should do with it. Banat had obviously counted on its being taken to the Customs shed by the steward, who would pocket the twenty lire and forget about Mr Kuvetli. That would be all right from Banat's point of view. By the time the people in the Customs shed started asking questions about an unclaimed valise, Monsieur Mavrodopoulos would be non-existent. Graham, however, had every intention of remaining in existence if he could possibly do so. Moreover, he intended–with the same proviso–to use his passport to cross the Italian frontier into France. The moment Mr Kuvetli's body was found the rest of the passengers would be sought for questioning by the police. There was only one thing for it: Mr Kuvetli's valise would have to be hidden.

He opened the washing cabinet, put the twenty lire piece on the corner by the bowl, and went to the door. The coast was still clear. He opened the door, picked up the valise, and lugged it along the alleyway to cabin number four. Another second or two and he was inside with the door shut again.

He was sweating now. He wiped his hands and forehead on his handkerchief and then remembered that his fingerprints would be on the hard leather handle of the valise as well as on the door handle and washing cabinet. He went over these objects with his handkerchief and then turned his attention to the body.

Obviously the gun was not in the hip pocket. He went down on one knee beside the body. He felt himself beginning to retch again and took a deep breath. Then he leaned across, gripped the right shoulder with one hand and the right side of the trousers with the other and pulled. The body rolled on to its side. One foot slid over the other and kicked the floor. Graham stood up quickly. In a moment or two, however, he had himself in hand sufficiently to bend down and pull the jacket open. There was a leather holster under the left arm but the gun was not in it.

He was not unduly disappointed. The possession of the gun would have made him feel better but he had not been counting on finding it. A gun was valuable. Banat would naturally take it. Graham felt in the jacket pocket. It was empty. Banat had evidently taken Mr Kuvetli's money and *laisser passer* as well.

He got up. There was nothing more to be done there. He put on a glove, cautiously let himself out and walked along to cabin number six. He knocked. There was a quick movement from within and Madame Mathis opened the door.

The frown with which she had prepared to meet the steward faded when she saw Graham. She gave him a startled 'good morning.'

'Good morning, Madame. May I speak to your husband for a moment?' Mathis poked his head over her shoulder. 'Hullo! Good morning! Are you ready so soon?'

'Can I speak to you for a moment?'

'Of course!' He came out in his shirt sleeves and grinning cheerfully. 'I am important only to myself. I am easy to approach.'

'Would you mind coming into my cabin for a moment?'

Mathis glanced at him curiously. 'You look very serious, my friend. Yes, of course I will come.' He turned to his wife. 'I will be back in a minute, *chérie.*'

Inside the cabin, Graham shut the door, bolted it and turned to meet Mathis' puzzled frown.

'I need your help,' he said in a low voice. 'No, I don't want to borrow money. I want you to take a message for me.'

'If it is possible, of course.'

'It will be necessary to talk very quietly,' Graham went on. 'I do not want to alarm your wife unnecessarily and the partitions are very thin.'

Fortunately, Mathis missed the full implications of this statement. He nodded. 'I am listening.'

'I told you that I was employed by an armaments manufacturer. It is true. But in a sense I am also, at the moment, in the joint services of the British and Turkish Governments. When I get off this ship this morning, an attempt is going to be made by German agents to kill me.'

'This is true?' He was incredulous and suspicious.

'I am afraid it is. It would not amuse me to invent it.'

'Excuse me, I . . .'

'That's all right. What I want you to do is to go to the Turkish Consulate in Genoa, ask for the Consul and give him a message from me. Will you do that?'

Mathis stared hard at him for a moment. Then he nodded. 'Very well. I will do it. What is the message?'

'I should like to impress upon you first that this is a highly confidential message. Is that understood?'

'I can keep my mouth shut when I choose.'

'I know I can rely on you. Will you write the message down? Here is a pencil and some paper. You would not be able to read my writing. Are you ready?'

'Yes.'

'This is it: "Inform Colonel Haki, Istanbul, that agent I.K. is dead, but do not inform the police. I am forced to accompany German agents, Moeller and Banat, travelling with passports of Fritz Haller and Mavrodopoulos. I . . ."'

Mathis jaw dropped and he let out an exclamation. 'Is it possible!'

'Unfortunately, it is.'

'Then it was not seasickness that you had!'

'No. Shall I go on with the message?'

Mathis swallowed. 'Yes. Yes. I did not realize. . . . Please.'

'"I shall attempt to escape and reach you, but in the event of my death please inform British Consul that these men are responsible."' It was, he felt, melodramatic; but it was no more than he wished to say. He felt sorry for Mathis.

The Frenchman was staring at him with horror in his eyes. 'It is not possible,' he whispered. 'Why. . .?'

'I should like to explain but I am afraid that I can't. The point is, will you deliver the message for me?'

'Of course. But is there nothing else that I can do? These German agents—why can you not have them arrested?'

'For various reasons. The best way you can help me is to take this message for me.'

The Frenchman stuck out his jaw aggressively. 'It is ridiculous!' he burst out and then lowered his voice to a fierce whisper. 'Discretion is necessary. I understand that. You are of the British secret service. One does not confide these things but I am not a fool. Very well! Why do we not together shoot down these filthy Bosches and escape? I have my revolver and together. . . .'

Graham jumped. 'Did you say that you had a revolver—here?'

Mathis looked defiant. 'Certainly I have a revolver. Why not. In Turkey . . .'

Graham seized his arm. 'Then you can do something more to help me.'

Mathis scowled impatiently. 'What is that?'

'Let me buy your revolver from you.'

'You mean you are unarmed?'

'My own revolver was stolen. How much will you take for yours?'

'But. . . .'

'It will be more use to me than to you.'

Mathis drew himself up. 'I will not sell it to you.'

'But. . . .'

'I will give it to you. Here. . . .' He pulled a small Beretta automatic out of his hip pocket and thrust it in Graham's hand. 'No, please. It is nothing. I would like to do more.'

Graham thanked his stars for the impulse which had led him to apologize to the Mathis' the previous day. 'You have done more than enough.'

'Nothing! It is loaded, see? Here is the safety catch. There is a light pull on the trigger. You do not have to be a Hercules. Keep your arm straight when you fire . . . but I do not have to tell you.'

'I am grateful, Mathis. And you will go to the Turkish Consul as soon as you land.'

'It is understood.' He held out his hand. 'I wish you luck, my friend,' he said with emotion. 'If you are sure that there is nothing else that I can do. . . .'

'I am sure.'

A moment later Mathis had gone. Graham waited. He heard the Frenchman go into the next cabin and Madame Mathis' sharp voice.

'Well?'

'So you cannot mind your own business, eh? He is broke and I have lent him two hundred francs.'

'Imbecile! You will not touch it again.'

'You think not? Let me tell you he had given me a cheque.'

'I detest cheques.'

'I am not drunk. It is on an Istanbul bank. As soon as we arrive I shall go to the Turkish Consulate and see that the cheque is a good one.'

'A lot they will know—or care!'

'Enough! I know what I am doing. Are you ready? No! Then . . .'

Graham breathed a sigh of relief and examined the automatic. It was smaller than Kopeikin's revolver and much flatter. He worked the safety catch and fingered the trigger. It was a handy little weapon and looked as if it had been carefully used. He looked about him for a place to put it. It must not be visible from the outside yet he must be able to get at it quickly. He decided eventually on his top left hand waistcoat pocket. The barrel, slide and most of the trigger guard just fitted in. When he buttoned his jacket the butt was hidden while the lapels set in a way that concealed the bulge. What was more, he could, by touching his tie, bring his fingers within two inches of the butt. He was ready.

He dropped Mr Kuvetli's box of ammunition through the porthole and went up on deck.

They were in the harbour now and moving across to the west side. Towards the sea the sky was clear but a mist hung over the heights above the town, obscuring the sun and making the white amphitheatrical mass of buildings seem cold and desolate.

The only other person on deck was Banat. He was standing gazing out at the shipping with the absorbed interest of a small boy. It was difficult to realise that, at some moment in the last ten hours, this pale creature had come out of cabin number four with a knife which he had just driven into Mr Kuvetli's neck; that in his pocket at that moment were Mr Kuvetli's papers, Mr Kuvetli's money and Mr Kuvetli's pistol; that he intended to commit within the next few hours yet another murder. His very insignificance was horrible. It lent a false air of normality to the situation. Had Graham not been so acutely alive to the danger he was in, he would have been tempted to believe that the memory of what he had seen in cabin number four was the memory not of a real experience, but of something conceived in a dream.

He was no longer conscious of any fear. His body was tingling in a curious way; he was short of breath, and every now and again a wave of nausea would rise up from the pit of his stomach; but his brain seemed to have lost touch with his body. His thoughts arranged themselves with a quick efficiency that surprised him. He knew that short of abandoning all hope of reaching England in time to fulfil the Turkish contract by the specified date, his only chance of getting out of Italy alive lay in his beating Moeller at Moeller's own game. Mr Kuvetli had made it clear that Moeller's 'alternative' was a trick devised with the sole object of transferring the scene of the killing to a less public place than a main street of Genoa. In other words, he was to be 'taken for a ride.' In a very short time now, Moeller, Banat and some others would be waiting with a car outside the Customs shed ready, if necessary, to shoot him down there and then. If, however, he were considerate enough to step into the car they would take him away to some quiet place on the Santa Margherita road and shoot him there. There was just one weak spot in their plan. They thought that if he were to get into the car he would do so believing that he was to be driven to a hotel in order to make an elaborate show of falling ill. They were mistaken; and in their being mistaken they presented him with the beginnings of a way out. If he acted quickly and boldly he might be able to get through.

They would not, he reasoned, be likely to tell him as soon as he got in the car what they were going to do. The fiction about the hotel and the clinic near Santa Margherita would be maintained until the last moment. From their point of view, it would be much easier to drive through the narrow streets of Genoa with a man who thought he was going to have six weeks' holiday than with a man who had to be forcibly prevented from attracting the attention of passers-by. They would be inclined to humour him. They might even let him register at a hotel. In any case, it was unlikely that the car would go right through the city without being held up once by the traffic. His chances of escape lay in his being able to taken them by surprise. Let him once get free in a crowded street, and they would have great difficulty in catching him. His objective, then, would be the Turkish Consulate. He had chosen the Turkish Consulate rather than his own, for the simple reason that with the Turks he would have to do less explaining. A reference to Colonel Haki would simplify matters considerably.

The ship was approaching the berth now, and men were standing on the quay ready to catch the lines. Banat had not seen him, but now Josette and José came out on deck. He moved quickly round to the other side. Josette was the last person he wanted to talk to at that moment. She might suggest that they share a taxi to the centre of the city. He would have to explain why he was leaving the quay in a private car with Moeller and Banat. There might be all sorts of other difficulties. At that moment he came face to face with Moeller.

The old man nodded affably. 'Good morning, Mr Graham. I was hoping to see you. It will be pleasant to get ashore again, won't it?'

'I hope so.'

Moeller's expression changed slightly. 'Are you ready?'

'Quite.' He looked concerned. 'I haven't seen Kuvetli this morning. I hope everything is going to be all right.'

Moeller's eyes did not flicker. 'You need not worry, Mr Graham.' Then he smiled tolerantly. 'As I told you last night, you can safely leave everything to me. Kuvetli will not worry us. If necessary,' he went on blandly, 'I shall use force.'

'I hope that won't be necessary.'

'And so do I, Mr Graham! So do I!' He lowered his voice confidentially. 'But while we are on the subject of the use of force, may I suggest that you are not in too much of a hurry to land? You see, should you happen to land before Banat and myself have time to explain the new situation to those who are waiting, an accident might happen. You are so obviously an Englishman. They would have no difficulty in identifying you.'

'I had already thought of that.'

'Splendid! I am so glad that you are entering into the spirit of the arrangements.' He turned his head. 'Ah, we are alongside. I shall see you again in a few minutes, then.' His eyes narrowed. 'You won't make me feel that my confidence has been misplaced, will you, Mr Graham.'

'I shall be there.'

'I am sure that I can count on you.'

Graham went into the deserted saloon. Through one of the port-holes he could see that a section of the deck had been roped off. The Mathis and the Beronellis had already joined Josette, José and Banat and, as he watched, Moeller came up with his 'wife.' Josette was looking round as if she were expecting someone, and Graham guessed that his absence was puzzling her. It was going to be difficult to avoid an encounter with her. She might even wait for him in the Customs shed. He would have to forestall that.

He waited until the gangway had been hoisted into position and the passengers, headed by the Mathis, were beginning to troop down it, then went out and brought up the rear of the procession immediately behind Josette. She half turned her head and saw him.

'Ah! I have been wondering where you were. What have you been doing?'

'Packing.'

'So long! But you are here now. I thought that perhaps we could drive together and leave our luggage in the *consigne* at the station. It will save a taxi.'

'I'm afraid I shall keep you waiting. I have some things to declare. Besides, I must go to the Consulate first. I think that we had better keep to our arrangement to meet at the train.'

She sighed. 'You are so difficult. Very well, we will meet at the train. But do not be late.'

'I won't.'

'And be careful of the little *salaud* with the perfume.'

'The police will take care of him.'

They had reached the passport control at the entrance to the Customs shed and José, who had walked on ahead, was waiting as if the seconds were costing him money. She pressed Graham's hand hurriedly. '*Alors, chéri! A tout à l'heure.*'

Graham got his passport and slowly followed them through to the Customs shed. There was only one Customs officer. As Graham approached he disposed of Josette and José, and turned to the Beronelli's mountainous bundles. To his relief, Graham had to wait. While he was waiting he opened his case and transferred some papers that he needed to his pocket; but several more minutes passed before he was able to show his transit *visa*, have his suit-case chalked and give it to a porter. By the time he had made his way through the group of mourning relatives which had surrounded the Beronellis, Josette and José had gone.

Then he saw Moeller and Banat.

They were standing beside a big American saloon drawn up beyond the taxis. There were two other men on the far side of the car: one was tall and thin and wore a mackintosh and a workman's cap, the other was a very dark heavy-jowled man with a grey belted ulster and a soft hat which he wore without a dent in it. A fifth and younger man sat at the wheel of the car.

His heart thumping, Graham beckoned to the porter, who was making for the taxis, and walked towards them.

Moeller nodded as he came up. 'Good! Your luggage? Ah, yes.' He nodded to the tall man, who came round, took the case from the porter, and put it in the boot.

Graham tipped the porter and got in the car. Moeller followed him and sat beside him. The tall man got in beside the driver. Banat and the man in the ulster sat on the pull-down seats facing Graham and Moeller. Banat's face was expressionless. The man in the ulster avoided Graham's eyes and looked out of the window.

The car started. Almost immediately, Banat took out his pistol and snapped the safety catch.

Graham turned to Moeller. 'Is that necessary?' he demanded. 'I'm not going to escape.'

Moeller shrugged. 'As you please.' He said something to Banat who grinned, snapped the safety catch again and put the gun back in his pocket.

The car swung into the cobbled road leading to the dock gates.

'Which hotel are we going to?' Graham inquired.

Moeller turned his head slightly. 'I have not yet made up my mind. We can leave that question until later. We shall drive out to Santa Margherita first.'

'But . . .'

'There are no "buts." I am making the arrangements.' He did not bother to turn his head this time.

'What about Kuvetli?'

'He left by the pilot boat early this morning.'

'Then what's happened to him?'

'He is probably writing a report to Colonel Haki. I advise you to forget about him.'

Graham was silent. He had asked about Mr Kuvetli with the sole object of concealing the fact that he was badly frightened. He had been in the car less than two minutes, and already the odds against him had lengthened considerably.

The car bumped over the cobbles to the dock gates, and Graham braced himself for the sharp right turn that would take them towards the town and the Santa Margherita road. The next moment he lurched sideways in his seat as the car swerved to the left. Banat whipped out his gun.

Graham slowly regained his position. 'I'm sorry,' he said. 'I thought we turned right for Santa Margherita.'

There was no reply. He sat back in his corner trying to keep his face expressionless. He had assumed quite unwarrantably that it would be through Genoa itself, and on to the Santa Margherita road that he would be taken for his 'ride.' All his hopes had been based on the assumption. He had taken too much for granted.

He glanced at Moeller. The German agent was sitting back with his eyes closed: an old man whose work for the day was done. The rest of the day was Banat's. Graham knew that the small deep-set eyes were feeling for his, and that the long-suffering mouth was grinning. Banat was going to enjoy his work. The other man was still looking out of the window. He had not uttered a sound.

They reached a fork and turned to the right along a secondary road with a direction sign for Novi-Torino. They were going north. The road was straight and lined with dusty plane trees. Beyond the trees there were rows of grim-looking houses and a factory or two. Soon, however, the road began to rise and twist, and the houses and factories were left behind. They were getting into the country.

Graham knew that unless some wholly unexpected way of escape presented itself, his chances of surviving the next hour were now practically non-existent. Presently the car would stop. Then he would be taken out and shot as methodically and efficiently as if he had been condemned by a court martial. The blood was thundering in his head, and his breathing was quick and shallow. He tried to breathe slowly and deeply, but the muscles in his chest seemed incapable of making the effort. He went on trying. He knew that if he surrendered himself to fear now, if he let himself go, he would be lost, whatever happened. He must not be frightened. Death, he told himself, would not be so bad. A moment of astonishment, and it would be over. He had to die sooner or later, and a bullet through the base of the skull now would be better than months of illness when he was old. Forty years was not a bad lifetime to have lived. There were many young men in Europe at that moment who would regard the attainment of such an age as an enviable achievement. To suppose that the lopping off of thirty years or so from a normal span of life was a disaster was to pretend to an importance that no man possessed. Living wasn't even so very pleasant. Mostly it was a matter of getting from the cradle to the grave with the least possible discomfort; of satisfying the body's needs, and of slowing down the process of its decay. Why make such a fuss about abandoning so dreary a business? Why, indeed! And yet you did make a fuss . . .

He became conscious of the pistol pressing against his chest. Supposing they decided to search him! But no, they wouldn't do that. They'd taken one gun from him, and another from Mr Kuvetli. They would scarcely suspect that there was a third. There were five other men in the car, and four of them at least were armed. He had seven rounds in the pistol. He might be able to fire two of them before he himself were hit. If he waited until Banat's attention had wandered he might get off three or even four of them. If he were going to be killed, he'd see that the killing was as expensive as possible. He got a cigarette out of his pocket and then, putting his hand inside his jacket as if he were looking for a match, snicked off the safety catch. For a moment he considered drawing the Beretta there and then, and trusting to luck and the driver's swerving to survive Banat's first shot; but the gun in Banat's hand was steady. Besides, there was always a chance that something unexpected might happen to create a better opportunity. For instance, the driver might take a corner too fast and wreck the car.

But the car purred steadily on. The windows were tightly shut, and Banat's attar of roses began to scent the air inside. The man in the ulster was becoming drowsy. Once or twice he yawned. Then, obviously to give himself something to do, he brought out a heavy German pistol and examined the magazine. As he replaced it, his dull pouched eyes rested for a moment on Graham. He looked away again indifferently, like a passenger in a train with the stranger opposite to him.

They had been driving for about twenty-five minutes. They passed through a small straggling village with a single fly-blown-looking café with a petrol pump outside it and two or three shops, and began to climb. Graham was vaguely aware that the fields and farmlands which had flanked the road till then were giving way to clumps of trees and uncultivateable slopes, and guessed that they were getting into the hills to the north of Genoa and west of the railway pass above Pontedecimo. Suddenly the car swung left down a small side road between trees, and began to crawl in low gear up a long twisting hill cut in the side of a wooded slope.

There was a movement by his side. He turned quickly, the blood rushing up into his head, and met Moeller's eyes.

Moeller nodded. 'Yes, Mr Graham, this is just about as far as you are going.'

'But the hotel . . .?' Graham began to stammer.

The pale eyes did not flicker. 'I am afraid, Mr Graham, that you must be very simple. Or can it be that you think that I am simple?' He shrugged. 'No doubt it is unimportant. But I have a request to make. As you have already caused me so much trouble, discomfort and expense, would it be asking too much of you to suggest that you do not cause me any more? When we stop and you are asked to get out, please do so without argument or physical protest. If you cannot consider your own dignity at such a time, please think of the cushions of the car.'

He turned abruptly and nodded to the man in the ulster who tapped on the window behind him. The car jerked to a standstill, and the man in the ulster half rose and put his hand down on the latch which opened the door beside him. At the same moment Moeller said something to Banat. Banat grinned.

In that second Graham acted. His last wretched little bluff had been called. They were going to kill him, and did not care whether he knew it or not. They were anxious only that his blood should not soil the cushions he was sitting on. A sudden blind fury seized him. His self-control, racked out until every nerve in his body was quivering, suddenly went. Before he knew what he was doing, he had pulled out Mathis' pistol and fired it full in Banat's face.

Even as the din of the shot thudded through his head, he saw something horrible happen to the face. Then he flung himself forward.

The man in the ulster had the door open about an inch when Graham's weight hit him. He lost his balance, and hurtled backwards through the door. A fraction of a second later he hit the road with Graham on top of him.

Half stunned by the impact, Graham rolled clear and scrambled for cover behind the car. It could, he knew, last only a second or two now. The man in the ulster was knocked out; but the other two, shouting at the tops of their voices, had their doors open, and Moeller would not be long in picking up Banat's gun. He might be able to get in one more shot. Moeller, perhaps . . .

At that moment chance took a hand. Graham realised that he was crouching only a foot or so away from the car's tank, and with some wild notion of hindering the pursuit should he succeed in getting clear, he raised the revolver and fired again.

The muzzle of the revolver had been practically touching the tank when he pulled the trigger, and the sheet of flame which roared up sent him staggering back out of cover. Shots crashed out, and a bullet whipped by his head. Panic seized him. He turned and dashed for the trees, and the slope shelving from the edge of the road. He heard two more shots, then something struck him violently in the back, and a sheet of light flashed between his eyes and his brain.

He could not have been unconscious for more than a minute. When he came too he was lying face downwards on the surface of dead pine needles on the slope below the level of the road.

Dagger-like pains were shooting through his head. For a moment or two he did not try to move. Then he opened his eyes again and his gaze, wandering inch by inch away from him, encountered Mathis' pistol. Instinctively he stretched out his hand to take it. His body throbbed agonizingly, but his fingers gripped the pistol. He waited for a second or two. Then, very slowly, he drew his knees up under him, raised himself on his hands and began to crawl back to the road.

The blast of the exploding tank had scattered fragments of ripped panelling and smouldering leather all over the road. Lying on his side amid this wreckage was the man in the workman's cap. The mackintosh down his left side hung in charred shreds. What was left of the car itself was a mass of shimmering incandescence, and the steel skeleton buckling like paper in the terrific heat was only just visible. Farther up the road the driver was standing with his hands to his face, swaying as if he were drunk. The sickening stench of burning flesh hung in the air. There was no sign of Moeller.

Graham crawled back down the slope for a few yards, got painfully to his feet and stumbled away, down through the trees towards the lower road.

Chapter Twelve

It was after midday before he reached the café in the village and a telephone. By the time a car from the Turkish Consulate arrived, he had had a wash and fortified himself with brandy.

The Consul was a lean, business-like man, who spoke English as if he had been to England. He listened intently to what Graham had to say before he said much himself. When Graham had finished, however, the Consul squirted some more soda water into his vermouth, leaned back in his chair and whistled through his teeth.

'Is that all?' he inquired.

'Isn't it enough?'

'More than enough.' The Consul grinned apologetically. 'I will tell you, Mr Graham, that when I received your message this morning, I telegraphed immediately to Colonel Haki, reporting that you were very likely dead.

Allow me to congratulate you.'

'Thank you. I was lucky.' He spoke automatically. There seemed to be something strangely fatuous about congratulations on being alive. He said: 'Kuvetli told me the other night that he had fought for the Gazi and that he was ready to give his life for Turkey. You don't, somehow, expect people who say that sort of thing to be taken up on it so quickly.'

'That is true. It is very sad,' said the Consul. He was obviously itching to get to business. 'Meanwhile,' he continued adroitly, 'we must see that no time is lost. Every minute increases the danger of his body being found before you are out of the country. The authorities are not very well disposed towards us at the moment, and if he were found before you had left, I doubt if we could prevent your being detained for at least some days.

'What about the car?'

'We can leave the driver to explain that. If, as you say, your suit-case was destroyed in the fire, there is nothing to connect you with the accident. Are you feeling well enough to travel?'

'Yes. I'm bruised a bit and I still feel shaky, but I'll get over that.'

'Good. Then, all things considered, it will be as well if you travel immediately.'

'Kuvetli said something about a 'plane.'

'A 'plane? Ah! May I see your passport, please?'

Graham handed it over. The Consul flicked over the pages, shut the passport with a snap and returned it. 'Your transit visa,' he said, 'specifies that you are entering Italy at Genoa and leaving it at Bardonecchia. If you are particularly anxious to go by air we can get the visa amended, but that will take an hour or so. Also you will have to return to Genoa. Also, in case Kuvetli is found within the next few hours, it is better not to bring yourself to the notice of the police with a change of arrangements.' He glanced at his watch. 'There is a train to Paris which leaves Genoa at two o'clock. It stops at Asti soon after three. I recommend that you get on it there. I can drive you to Asti in my car.'

'I think some food would do me good.'

'My dear Mr Graham! How stupid of me! Some food. Of course! We can stop at Novi. You will be my guest. And if there is any whisky to be had we shall have it. There is nothing like whisky when one is depressed.'

Graham felt suddenly a little light-headed. He laughed.

The Consul raised his eyebrows.

'I'm sorry,' Graham said. 'You must excuse me. You see, it is rather funny. I had an appointment to meet someone on the two o'clock train. She'll be surprised to see me.'

He became conscious of someone shaking his arm and opened his eyes.

'Bardonecchia, *signore*. Your passport, please.'

He looked up at the wagon-lit attendant bending over him and realized that he had been asleep since the train had left Asti. In the doorway, partly silhouetted against the gathering darkness outside, were two men in the uniform of the Italian railway police.

He sat up with a jerk, fumbling in his pocket. 'My passport? Yes, of course.'

One of the men looked at the passport, nodded and dabbed at it with a rubber stamp.

'*Grazie, signore.* Have you any Italian bank-notes?'

'No.'

Graham put his passport back in his pocket, the attendant switched the light off again, and the door closed. That was that.

He yawned miserably. He was stiff and and shivering. He stood up to put his overcoat on and saw that the station was deep in snow. He had been a fool to go to sleep like that. It would be unpleasant to arrive home with pneumonia. But he was past the Italian passport control. He turned the heating on and sat down to smoke a cigarette. It must have been that heavy lunch and the wine. It . . . And then he remembered suddenly that he had done nothing about Josette. Mathis would be on the train, too.

The train started with a jerk and began to rumble on towards Modane.

He rang the bell and the attendant came.

'Signore?'

'Is there going to be a restaurant car when we get over the frontier?'

'No, signore.' He shrugged. 'The war.'

Graham gave him some French money. 'I want a bottle of beer and some sandwiches. Can you get them at Modane?'

The attendant looked at the money. 'Easily, signore.'

'Where are the second-class coaches?'

'In the front of the train, signore.'

The attendant went. Graham smoked his cigarette and decided to wait until the train had left Modane before he went in search of Josette.

The stop at Modane seemed interminable. At last, however, the French passport officials finished their work and the train began to move again.

Graham went out into the corridor.

Except for the dim blue safety lights, the train was in darkness now. He made his way slowly towards the second-class coaches. He had no difficulty in finding Josette and José. They were in a compartment by themselves.

She turned her head as he slid the door open and peered at him uncertainly. Then, as he moved forward into the blue glow from the ceiling of the compartment, she started up with a cry.

'But what has happened?' she demanded. 'Where have you been? We waited, José and I, until the last moment, but you did not come as you had promised. We waited. José will tell you how we waited. Tell me what happened.'

'I missed the train at Genoa. I had a long drive to catch it up.'

'You drove to Bardonecchia! It is not possible!'

'No. To Asti.'

There was a silence. They had been speaking in French. Now José gave a short laugh and, sitting back in his corner, began to pick his teeth with his thumbnail.

Josette dropped the cigarette she had been smoking on to the floor and trod on it. 'You got on the train at Asti,' she remarked lightly, 'and you wait until now before you come to see me? It is very polite.' She paused and then added slowly: 'But you will not keep me waiting like that in Paris, will you, *chéri?*'

He hesitated.

'Will you, *chéri*?' There was an edge to her voice now.

He said: 'I'd like to talk to you alone, Josette.'

She stared at him. Her face in that dim, ghastly light was expressionless. Then she moved towards the door. 'I think,' she said, 'that it will be better if you have a little talk with José.'

'José? What's José got to do with it? You're the person I want to talk to.'

'No, *chéri*. You have a little talk with José. I am not very good at business. I do not like it. You understand?'

'Not in the least.' He was speaking the truth.

'No? José will explain. I will come back in a minute. You talk to José now, *chéri*.'

'But . . .'

She stepped into the corridor and slid the door to behind her. He went to open it again.

'She will come back,' said José; 'why don't you sit down and wait?'

Graham sat down slowly. He was puzzled. Still picking his teeth, José glanced across the compartment. 'You don't understand, eh?'

'I don't even know what I'm supposed to understand.'

José peered at his thumbnail, licked it, and went to work again on an eye tooth. 'You like Josette, eh?'

'Of course. But . . .'

'She is very pretty, but she has no sense. She is a woman. She does not understand business. That is why I, her husband, always look after the business. We are partners. Do you understand that?'

'It's simple enough. What about it?'

'I have an interest in Josette. That is all.'

Graham considered him for a moment. He was beginning to understand only too well. He said: 'Say exactly what you mean, will you?'

With the air of making a decision, José abandoned his teeth and twisted on his seat so that he was facing Graham. 'You are a business man, eh?' he said briskly. 'You do not expect something for nothing. Very well. I am her manager and I do not give anything for nothing. You want to amuse yourself in Paris, eh? Josette is a very nice girl and very amusing for a gentleman. She is a nice dancer, too. Together we earn at least two thousand francs a week in a nice place. Two thousand francs a week. That is something, eh?'

Memories were flooding into Graham's mind: of the Arab girl, Maria, saying, 'She has many lovers'; of Kopeikin saying, 'José? He does well for himself'; of Josette herself saying of José that he was jealous of her only when she neglected business for pleasure; of innumerable little phrases and attitudes. 'Well?' he said coldly.

José shrugged. 'If you are amusing yourself, we cannot earn our two thousand francs a week by dancing. So, you see, we must get it from somewhere else.' In the semi-darkness, Graham could see a small smile twist the black line of José's mouth. 'Two thousand francs a week. It is reasonable, eh?'

It was the voice of the philosopher of the apes in velvet. '*Mon cher caïd*' was justifying his existence. Graham nodded. 'Quite reasonable.'

'Then we can settle it now, eh?' José went on briskly. 'You are experienced, eh? You know that it is the custom.' He grinned and then quoted: '"*Chéri, avant que je t'aime t'oublieras pas mon petit cadeau.*"'

'I see. And who do I pay? You or Josette?'

'You pay it to Josette if you like, but that would not be very *chic* eh? I will see you once a week.' He leaned forward and patted Graham's knee. 'It is serious, eh? You will be a good boy? If you were, for example, to begin now. . . .'

Graham stood up. He was surprised at his own calmness. 'I think,' he said, 'that I should like to give the money to Josette herself.'

'You don't trust me, eh?'

'Of course I trust you. Will you find Josette?'

José hesitated, then, with a shrug, got up and went out into the corridor. A moment later he returned with Josette. She was smiling a little nervously.

'You have finished talking to José, *chéri?*'

Graham nodded pleasantly. 'Yes. But, as I told you, it was you I really wanted to talk to. I wanted to explain that I shall have to go straight back to England after all.'

She stared at him blankly for a moment; then he saw her lips drawing in viciously over her teeth. She turned suddenly on José.

'You dirty Spanish fool!' She almost spat the words at him. 'What do you think I keep you for? Your dancing?'

José's eyes glittered dangerously. He slid the door to behind him. 'Now,' he said, 'we will see. You shall not speak to me so or I shall break your teeth.'

'*Salaud!* I shall speak to you as I like.' She was standing quite still, but her right hand moved an inch or two. Something glittered faintly. She had slipped the diamanté bracelet she was wearing over her knuckles.

Graham had seen enough violence for one day. He said quickly: 'Just a moment. José is not to blame. He explained matters very tactfully and politely. I came, as I said, to tell you that I have to go straight back to England. I was also going to ask you to accept a small present. It was this.' He drew out his wallet, produced a ten-pound note, and held it near the light.

She glanced at the note and then stared at him sullenly. 'Well?'

'José made it clear that two thousand francs was the amount I owed. This note is only worth just over seventeen hundred and fifty. So, I am adding another two hundred and fifty francs.' He took the French notes out of his wallet, folded them up in the larger note and held them out.

She snatched them from him. 'And what do you expect to get for this?' she demanded spitefully.

'Nothing. It's been pleasant being able to talk to you.' He slid the door open. 'Good-bye, Josette.'

She shrugged her shoulders, stuffed the money into the pocket of her fur coat and sat down again in her corner. 'Good-bye. It is not my fault if you are stupid.'

José laughed. 'If you should think of changing your mind, Monsieur,' he began mincingly, 'we . . .'

Graham shut the door and walked away along the corridor. His one desire was to get back to his own compartment. He did not notice Mathis until he had almost bumped into him.

The Frenchman drew back to let him pass. Then, with a gasp, he leaned forward.

'Monsieur Graham! Is it possible?'

'I was looking for you,' said Graham.

'My dear friend. I am so glad. I was wondering. . . . I was afraid. . . .'

'I caught the train at Asti.' He pulled the Beretta from his pocket. 'I want to return this to you with my thanks. I'm afraid that I haven't had time to clean it. It has been fired twice.'

'Twice!' Mathis' eyes widened. 'You killed them both?'

'One of them. The other died in a road accident.'

'A road accident!' Mathis chuckled. 'That is a new way to kill them!' He looked at the pistol affectionately. 'Perhaps I will not clean it. Perhaps I will keep it as it is as a souvenir.' He glanced up. 'It was all right, that message I delivered?'

'Quite all right, and thank you again.' He hesitated. 'There's no restaurant car on the train. I have some sandwiches in my compartment. If you and your wife would care to join me. . . .'

'You are kind, but no thank you. We get off at Aix. It will not be long now. My family lives there. It will be strange to see them after so long. They . . .'

The door of the compartment behind him opened and Madame Mathis peered into the corridor. 'Ah, there you are!' She recognized Graham and nodded disapprovingly.

'What is it, *chérie*?'

'The window. You open it, and go out to smoke. I am left to freeze.'

'Then you may shut it, *chérie*.'

'Imbecile! It is too stiff.'

Mathis sighed wearily and held out his hand. 'Good-bye, my friend. I shall be discreet. You may depend upon it.'

'Discreet?' demanded Madame Mathis suspiciously. 'What is there to be discreet about?'

'Ah, you may ask!' He winked at Graham. 'Monsieur and I have made a plot to blow up the Bank of France, seize the Chamber of Deputies, shoot the two hundred families and set up a Communist government.'

She looked round apprehensively. 'You should not say such things, even for a joke.'

'A joke!' He scowled at her malevolently. 'You will see if it is a joke or not when we drag these capitalist reptiles from their great houses and cut them to pieces with the machine-guns.'

'Robert! If someone should hear you say such things . . .'

'Let them hear!'

'I only asked you to shut the window, Robert. If it had not been so stiff I would have done it myself. I . . .'

The door closed behind them.

Graham stood for a moment looking out of the window at the distant searchlights: grey smudges moving restlessly among the clouds low down on the horizon. It was not, he reflected, unlike the skyline that he could see from his bedroom window where there were German planes about over the North Sea.

He turned and made his way back to his beer and sandwiches.

ERIC AMBLER

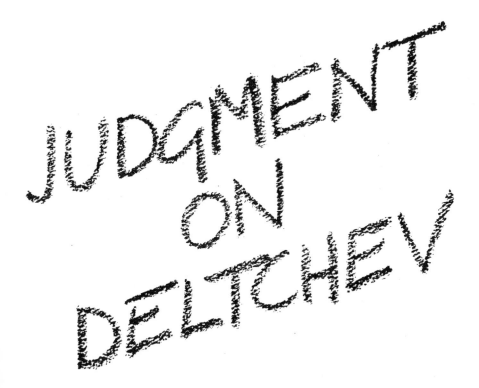

JUDGMENT ON DELTCHEV

Judgment on Deltchev

'Many things in your good people cause me disgust, and, verily, not their evil. I would that they had a madness by which they succumbed, like this pale criminal!'

NIETZSCHE: *Thus Spake Zarathustra*

Chapter One

Where treason to the state is defined simply as opposition to the government in power, the political leader convicted of it will not necessarily lose credit with the people. Indeed, if he is respected or loved by them, his death at the hands of a tyrannical government may serve to give his life a dignity it did not before possess. In that event his enemies may in the end be faced not by the memory of a fallible human being but by a myth, more formidable than the real man could ever have been, and much less vulnerable. His trial, therefore, is no formality, but a ceremony of preparation and precaution. He must be discredited and destroyed as a man so that he may safely be dealt with as a criminal. Sometimes he is induced to confess abjectly to the crimes of which he is accused; but unless he has himself been a member of the party that now seeks to destroy him, such confessions are not always believed by the people; and when, for example, he is the leader of an unliquidated opposition party, it is better to observe outwardly the old legal forms, to bring witnesses, produce evidence, and let him try to defend himself.

So it was with Nikolai Petkov in Bulgaria, with Julius Maniu and Ion Mihalache in Rumania, and with many other liberals in eastern Europe. Petkov they hanged. Maniu and Mihalache were condemned to solitary confinement for life. When Yordan Deltchev's trial took place, the pattern for such occasions had been already set.

The charges against him were of 'treason and the preparation of a terrorist plot to assassinate the head of the state.' The trial began before a People's Court on the 11th of June. He was described in the indictment as 'president of the Agrarian Socialist Party and formerly a member of the Provisional Government of National Unity.' In fact, he had been head of that Government and also its Foreign Minister. He was still the leader of the only effective opposition to the People's Party regime that remained.

I had been asked to attend the trial and write a series of articles about it by an American newspaper publisher whom I had met once or twice when he had been visiting London. The request had surprised me. I had never written anything of that kind before and had thought at first that my name had been mistaken for someone else's. There had been no mistake, however, and I had decided to accept.

At some time or other, I suppose, most writers who have never done newspaper work indulge in the belief that, should the occasion arise, they would make brilliant reporters. Some of them, of course, are right. My case is different. With a solemnity that in retrospect seems pathetic, I looked up an old *Times* article on Deltchev, bought some of the likely books, and lunched with an economist who had once read a paper before the Royal

Institute of International Affairs. I felt that I ought to learn something about the country I was going to visit, its people, and its problems.

The odd part is that I did learn one thing. It was over that luncheon that I first heard about the Officer Corps Brotherhood. It was referred to as a kind of joke.

Originally, it seemed, this Brotherhood had been a welfare association formed to protect and to help financially the families of a number of army officers who had been shot after the Macedonian *Putsch* of 1925. The founders were brother officers of the victims and sympathetic to their cause; but they were not wealthy men and it was not long before some of them became convinced that the most honourable way of helping and protecting the bereaved families would be to kill those who had condemned their men to death.

By the early thirties the Brotherhood had become a secret society of reactionary extremists and been responsible for at least twenty-eight political murders. Moreover, it was concerned no longer with simple acts of vengeance, but rather with eliminating potential sources of injustice that would later call for vengeance. As in the Brotherhood's dogma any politician or highly placed official with even remotely liberal ideas was a potential source of injustice, the problem of the Brotherhood became a matter of interest to all parties.

Attempts made by successive prewar governments to bring actual murderers to justice and to suppress the organization had been only partly successful because never quite wholehearted. It was easy enough to disapprove of the Brotherhood, but courage was required to become actively concerned with an attack upon it. The Brotherhood had survived and although its earlier 'officers only' membership qualification had been relaxed and psychotics from many other sections of the community had found it congenial, it had retained much of its traditional military background. The symbolic revolver and dagger of other Balkan terrorist organizations had become for the Officer Corps Brotherhood the symbolic rifle and bayonet; and during the occupation the Brotherhood had snobbishly preferred to collaborate with the German Army authorities rather than with the Gestapo.

This latter piece of discrimination, however, had not deterred the Provisional Government, set up after the liberation, from making the first serious effort to stamp out the Brotherhood once and for all. Emergency powers had been used to the full. Membership in the organization had been made a capital offence, and arrests, summary trials and executions had continued over months. So effective, indeed, had been the Government's campaign that there was little doubt in most minds that the Brotherhood had been betrayed from within. Interest in this aspect of the affair, however, had soon faded. When, during the elections, there had been none of the usual Brotherhood murders, it had been assumed with general relief that the organization was at last dead and buried. Now, astonishingly, the corpse had been exhumed and was being declared alive. For part of the case against Deltchev contained the incredible allegation that he, who as head of the Provisional Government had set out to destroy the Brotherhood, was in fact a member of it and the organizer of a plot to assassinate the head of the

People's Party Government.

I left London at the end of May and arrived in the capital the day before the trial began.

Chapter Two

Over much of south eastern Europe the heaviest summer rains have fallen by early June, and the hardening mud of the roads is being grated into dust. The tinted walls of the villages glow in the strong sun, and the shadows on them are black and sharply defined. Only the higher Balkan peaks still have snow upon them. The corn is becoming tall and rich, and in the river valleys east of the Yugoslav frontier the fields of roses and white poppies that you see from the train are alive with blossom. But in the cities the air is humid, and the insects that swirl in the sunshine over the refuse in the streets or crawl from the dark recesses of hotel beds are in their lush heyday. At that time the human animal has a strange feeling of lassitude; strange because, although the body is sluggish, the mind is uneasily alert, as if it fears that something is being prepared for its discomfort.

I was met at the Central Station by my employer's local representative. His name was Georghi Pashik.

I saw him standing on the platform as my train drew in: a short, dark, flabby man in rimless glasses and a tight seersucker suit with an array of fountain pens in the handkerchief pocket. Under his arm he carried a thin, black dispatch case with a silver medallion hanging from the zipper tag. He stood by a pillar gazing about him with the imperious anxiety of a wealthy traveller who sees no porter and knows that he cannot carry his own baggage. I think it was the fountain pens that identified him for me. He wore them like a badge.

I know a lot about Pashik. I know, for instance, that the black dispatch case that he carried so importantly rarely contained anything but a stale meat sandwich and a revolver, that the seersucker suit was given to him when he was working in a Displaced Persons camp, that one of the fountain pens came from Passaic, New Jersey, and that those facts can be related directly to his death. I know now some of the ways in which his mind worked and of the strange fantasies that possessed it. Then he was merely a name in conversation—'our man there, Pashik, will fix you up with all the permits you need'—a figure waiting on a station platform. I was not expecting a man of destiny to meet me.

He shook my hand and smiled in a friendly way.

'I'm delighted to know you, Mr Foster. Have you had breakfast?'

'Not yet. It's very kind of you to meet me.'

He gestured a denial. 'I have my car outside. We'll have to carry your luggage, Mr Foster. There are no porters at this hour.'

He spoke English well with an accent both foreign and American. He was not a prepossessing person. He had a plump, sallow face with several chins and a two days' growth of beard, and his eyes, as brown and limpid as a spaniel's, squinted slightly through the rimless glasses. He was businesslike and very courteous.

'Good journey, Mr Foster?' he asked as we walked out to his car.

'Not bad.'

'Any trouble at the frontier?'

'No more than usual, I imagine.'

'I'm very glad of that.'

In the station yard he put my suitcase in a battered Opel with no cushions on the back seats. He took my typewriter from me to put it with the suitcase and then paused, looking at it thoughtfully.

'You know, Mr Foster,' he said, 'sometimes the authorities make a great deal of trouble for visitors who they think may not be favourable to the regime.'

'Yes?'

'Oh yes.' He put the typewriter in the car and then, with his hand still on the carrying handle of it, turned his head. For a moment he seemed about to say something very important. It was on the tip of his tongue. Then he changed his mind. He shrugged. 'Things are difficult right now, Mr Foster,' he said. 'I'm glad they made no trouble for you.'

He had an office in a building just off the Boulevard Marshal Sokolovsky. He called himself the Pan-European Press Service and represented a number of American and a few British newspapers whose proprietors had not found it necessary after the war to re-establish their own offices in the capital. He was energetic and gave an impression of efficiency. I had to be registered as a foreigner with the police and as a newspaper correspondent with the Ministries of the Interior and Propaganda; I also had to have a special permit for the trial. It was early evening before we had finished.

Although there was a good deal of waiting about in the various offices we visited, as well as the ordinary opportunities for conversation, our relationship did not progress during the day. For the most part he remained courteous but reserved, avoiding all discussion of Deltchev or the trial on the grounds, plainly insufficient at times, that we might be overheard, and introducing me to officials with a measured politeness that took no responsibility at all for my subsequent behaviour. He had very much the air of the man on the spot who, while giving the specialist from the head office all reasonable assistance, feels entitled to suspect that the results may not justify the trouble taken. This I could well understand; indeed, I would have shared the suspicion. What puzzled me as the day wore on was the growing realization that, understandable and appropriate though his attitude might be, it was only partly a disguise for professional jealousy and that he had some quite different anxiety about me to conceal. It manifested itself in curious ways: sudden bursts of cordiality followed by strained silences, moments when I looked up to find his brown myopic eyes contemplating me furtively, as if to assess my bank balance, and other moments, like that at the station, when he changed his mind about what he was going to say as he opened his mouth to say it. Evidently some bad news had arrived for me while I had been travelling, or he had a request to make that I would be likely to receive badly. The thought bothered me. Unfortunately, I already had a bad conscience about Pashik. I disliked him because of his smell.

I had become aware of it when we entered his car at the station. It was sour and musty and at first I was not sure whether it came from the car or its owner. I don't think that I have an unduly fastidious nose or that the stinks of urban humanity specially distress me. I have known other people afflicted with what is daintily called body odour without disliking them. Yet Pashik I did dislike. Perhaps it was that the personality expressed by his appearance and manner—the suit, the American glasses, the dispatch case, the touch of complaisance—did not in some peculiar way allow for a bad smell. I remember that when I found that he was the source and not his car, I took note of those with whom we came in contact in case what I was finding offensive was the body smell of a city rather than that of one particular inhabitant. But no; it was Pashik. And then, unreasonably, I had begun to dislike him and so was at a disadvantage for what followed.

The sun had not yet set, but the shadows of a church spire and the dome of a mosque stretched like a finger and thumb across the St Mihail Square when we left the Propaganda Ministry for the last time that day and walked back to Pashik's car; but I had my permit for the trial.

He waved my thanks aside mock-modestly.

'We do what we can, Mr Foster.' He had one of his moments of cordiality. 'If you do not mind coming with me and waiting while I clear up at my office, I will then take you to dinner. There is a special restaurant I use.'

I should have liked to refuse; instead, I thanked him again.

There was a minute anteroom to his office, with a frosted glass door on which were painted the names of all the newspapers he represented. The list was long and imposing, and after it the office was an anticlimax. It contained a desk, a table, two chairs, and several filing cabinets. The window looked out on a tall fire-escape well. It admitted warm stagnant air and a grey twilight that left the corners of the room in darkness. Standing on one of the filing cabinets and framed as importantly as if it were a picture of his wife was a publicity photograph of Myrna Loy, with a reproduction of her signature on it.

He turned on the desk lamp and began to go through a pile of message flimsies. Most of them he crumpled and tossed aside; two or three he scribbled on and handed to a youth with a glazed peak cap who had been awaiting his return; others he clipped together in a folder. When he reached the last of the messages, he gave the youth some money and sent him off. Then he picked up the telephone and had a conversation, to me quite unintelligible, with a woman whose voice I could hear vibrating tinnily in the receiver. It ended with a brief crescendo of negatives. He stood up and began to tidy the desk. He was frowning and ill at ease.

I watched him from the darkness outside the ring of light shed by the desk lamp. His small hands no longer moved surely. He was making up his mind to a difficult task. He stopped tidying to look out at me. Then he sat down again, leaned back, and, taking out a packet of American cigarettes, began to open it.

'Mr Foster,' he said very carefully, 'there is a matter about which I have not yet spoken to you.'

Here it was.

'Yes?'

He kept his eyes on the cigarette packet. 'The matter of censorship. You know there is a strict censorship here, of course?'

'I was told so.'

'In the ordinary way the procedure is that I submit the matter to the censorship office and then file it as a cable or airmail it.'

'I see.'

'That is in the ordinary way.' He laid peculiar emphasis on the words.

'You mean that you would like me to give my stuff to you for submission to the censorship and onward transmission. Is that it?'

He did not reply for a moment or two and began to rock slowly on the back legs of his chair. 'Mr Foster, these are not ordinary times here in this country,' he said.

I waited. His glasses, reflecting the light of the desk lamp, winked steadily as he rocked. He went on: 'As I understand it, your articles may contain satirical matter hostile and derogatory to this regime.'

'They might do so, yes.'

He shook his head solemnly. 'I can tell you now, Mr Foster. That's out. Right out.'

'Well, we'll see.'

'Didn't they warn you at head office that things might be difficult here?'

I smiled amiably. 'They said that you might be, Mr Pashik.'

He stopped rocking. 'Oh now, Mr Foster, please. You don't at all understand. The censorship is very powerful here. For writing matter antagonistic to the People's Party regime you would be liable under the February decrees to imprisonment and a heavy fine.'

'Yes, but only liable.'

'I agree. In your case there would naturally be no question of enforcing the decree, but your permit for the trial would certainly be cancelled and you would have a very disagreeable interview with the police.'

'I could make an article out of that, too.'

His lips tightened. 'Obviously your papers would be confiscated, Mr Foster. If it amuses you to write articles so that they may be confiscated, that is your affair. I am concerned with practical newspaper work.'

He had me there; I was not. But I felt that at the moment he was not either. I thought he was trying to show me how helpless I would be without him. I said as calmly as I could: 'Very well, you're the paper's representative here and you tell me it's all very difficult. I understand. Now, how do we get over the difficulty?'

I had to wait while he lit a cigarette and blew smoke at the end of it like a bad actor pretending to think. 'You could try going down into Greece over Saturday night and Sunday and sending your work from there.' He blew some more smoke. 'Of course, the police would guess what you were attempting. An American on a Chicago paper tried it.'

'Yes?'

Now he looked directly at me. 'He just wasted a lot of time, Mr Foster. Of course he had no written matter when they searched him at the frontier; it was memorized; but they made difficulties about his visa, took his passport away to get it fixed, and kept him at the frontier station for a week. He had a very uncomfortable time.'

'I see. Well, now you've told me how it can't be done, what's the answer?' He was rocking again. 'There is no answer, Mr Foster. Other ways have been tried. The crews of foreign air liners were used as couriers for a while, but no longer. It is too dangerous for them. I have tried to make all this clear to the head office, but what is real here does not seem so in New York and London.'

'In fact, you think it's a great waste of time my being here at all.'

'No, I do not say that.'

'In effect you say it.'

'You misunderstand me. I am in favour of these articles. This trial is *dramatisch*–er—' He broke off, feeling for the word.

'Theatrical?'

'Yes, theatrical. Thank you. The trial of a political leader on ideological grounds is most theatrical to Western ways of thinking. So I say that to have a distinguished playwright, such as you, Mr Foster, write matter about the Deltchev trial is a very cute editorial idea. I am myself looking forward to reading the series. But–' he leaned forward impressively–'you cannot write it here and send it or take it out of the country; that is, not unless you paraphrase the Propaganda Ministry's official matter and get every page stamped by the censorship. You must resign yourself to that.'

'But—'

'See the trial, Mr Foster, memorize'–he stabbed his forehead with a finger to show me where–'and then go home and write your articles. That is what you must do.'

For a moment or two I did not answer.

I had been in a train for four days and had had very little sleep on the journey. I had arrived at seven o'clock that morning in a strange city under a hot sun and in a sticky, enervating atmosphere. I had left my luggage in a hotel that might, for all I could remember of the geography of the streets, be a hundred yards away or three miles from where I was now; and even if I found the hotel and remembered the room number, I would not know how to ask for the key. I had trailed round cafés and Government offices, listening to conversations that concerned me conducted in a language I did not begin to understand, at the heels of an aggrieved, self-important eastern European with fat hips and a bad smell. I had a blister on the sole of my right foot and a grimy face. I was also hungry and well on the way to wishing I had not come. Now I was being told that the fact that I had come at all was a pity, but that if I behaved myself and cared to waste my time, I might stay and see the fun. Or so it seemed to me then. I felt myself losing my temper and then managed to wait until the moment had passed before replying. I tried to keep my voice level.

'Mr Pashik, you know as well as I do that these articles are meant for publication during the trial as a commentary on it. They'd be useless afterwards.'

'Do you think so?' He looked knowing. 'Deltchev will be condemned to death. Your articles will be part of the campaign against the sentence.'

'That's not what I was told. I was asked to send the stuff in as I did it.'

'And why?' He threw up his hands, smiling with teeth like salted almonds. 'In case you, Mr Foster, the distinguished playwright, should find time to enjoy yourself on the expense account, or get an idea for a new play about life behind that sinister Iron Curtain and forget your commission. Editors treat us all like children.'

'Nevertheless, the articles are expected.'

'No, Mr Foster, they are not. I sent a cable to head office saying that they will not be available until you return.'

'I think you should have consulted me before you did that.'

'I am responsible, Mr Foster.'

There was a thin-lipped silence. Then I said: 'Mr Pashik, are you a member of the People's Party? I didn't think to ask you before.'

He smiled again, but the American accent became more pronounced. 'Ah, Mr Foster, you are mad at me. I don't blame you. I will be frank with you.'

'Good.'

'If there is any trouble with the censorship over anything that goes out of this office, it will be closed up. That means that *I* will be closed up, finished. I am responsible.'

'Then you'll still be responsible if the articles are published after the trial.'

'Ah no. If the Propaganda Ministry admits you to the country, it is their affair if you produce hostile matter when you leave. While you are here the responsibility rests with this office that you should not prejudge the trial by sending hostile matter.' He shrugged. 'It is no doubt for them an expedient. For myself, I am hostile to the regime; but I have been expelled for my opinions before, and Pan-European, representing twenty-seven foreign newspapers, has a responsibility to others besides your editor. So you see I must play ball with the regime, Mr Foster.'

I did not know quite what to say. My impulse was to take the trial permit from my pocket, put it on his desk, and say that I would leave in the morning. Certainly that is what he hoped I would do. It was only my awareness of disliking him for a poor reason that made me hesitate. He pushed the cigarettes towards me.

I shook my head. 'When did you send that cable?'

'Four days ago, Mr Foster.'

'Why not before?'

'It was not certain that you were coming.'

'It was settled three weeks ago that I was coming.'

'I did not know that.'

'Have you had a reply?'

'Yes, Mr Foster.'

'May I see it, please?'

'Certainly.' He opened a drawer in the desk and brought out a cable and put it in front of me. I read:

YOUR 109 OF 6 JUNE UNDERSTOOD ADVISE FOSTER AND ARRANGE AIR PASSAGE LONDON SOONEST CLOSE TRIAL.

'You could have shown me this before,' I said.

'I did not realize that you did not trust me, Mr Foster,' he replied gently. 'The cable only says to advise you of something and secure an air passage for you. It does not explain what I have been telling you. You still have to believe that I am telling you the truth.'

His smile said that this was the moment when I should feel silly and apologize. Perhaps it was the smile that prevented my doing so. Instead I said: 'I take it that the other foreign correspondents will be under the same restriction?'

'If they are hostile to the regime they will have to be equally discreet.'

'That story about the American who tried to go to Greece for the week-end—I suppose you made that up in case I thought of the idea myself and didn't tell you.'

'It was a way of warning you that the method was known.'

'You go at things in rather a roundabout way, don't you?'

He looked at me thoughtfully. 'One gets in the habit of it, Mr Foster,' he said, and then paused. 'Roundabout ways are sometimes safer. However'—his expression changed and he stood up expansively, his smell billowing around him—'it is good to meet a person who cares for frankness. We can understand one another.' He smiled cheerfully. 'We shall get on well, Mr Foster. We can help each other, and that is as it should be. I will show you.'

He went over to a filing cabinet in the outer darkness, opened one of the drawers, and began to search through it.

'You know, Mr Foster,' he murmured as he picked through the files, 'being expelled from a country is not dignified and not at all rewarding. For a few hours you are the brave man who dared to tell the truth. But for the next day, when the handclasp of friends is forgotten, you are just another reporter without a job.'

He came back to the desk with an untidy bundle of papers and a large envelope.

'When did it happen to you?' I asked.

'Italy, 1930. I was a married man then, too,' he said. He hesitated for an instant, then stuffed the papers into the envelope and handed it to me with the rueful smile of a rich uncle for the rascally nephew whom he likes.

'The office file on Yordan Deltchev, Mr Foster. It will help you.'

'Thank you.'

'Please.' He put up a protesting hand. 'I want to help you, Mr Foster. And I want you to know that I want to. And that is frank. *Avanti!* Now we go to dinner, eh?'

That night I was too tired to sleep. For a while I tried to do so; then I gave up, switched on the light, and began to read the file Pashik had given to me.

At that point I still had the illusion that I could report the Deltchev trial.

Chapter Three

This is what I learned from the file.

Until the spring of 1940, when his country had joined two of its Balkan neighbours in coming to terms with the Axis, Yordan Deltchev, although an important figure in the councils of the Agrarian Socialist Party, had had no popular following. Originally a lawyer by profession, he had been deputy for a provincial manufacturing area and then, having served the monarchy and later the Republic in various subordinate capacities, had become Minister of Posts and Telegraphs.

At that time he had been regarded by the knowledgeable as a very able man and as either honest or so far insufficiently tempted. That he was not then even considered as potentially a great popular leader is understandable. His special talent was for organization; and while as a speaker he was not without force, the cool logic, drily delivered, that made him effective in debate seemed unlikely ever to capture the hearts of audiences of peasants. That it did ultimately do so was a phenomenon produced by a peculiar combination of circumstances. Deltchev himself had very little to do with it.

He had been one of the few deputies, and the only Minister, who had opposed the alliance with the Axis at all vigorously; and during the summer of 1940, at the request of German authorities, he had been interned. Toward the end of the year he was released, but kept under police surveillance. Two years passed before the surveillance became sufficiently negligent for him to embark on the underground political activity with which his name was to become associated.

Before that time, opposition to the pro-German Government and its allies had been expressed chiefly by acts of sabotage against war-supply installations and by propaganda against the recruitment of divisions for the Russian front. This work had been done by groups led by militant People's Party men, but containing a good proportion of Agrarian Socialists. Yet, although it was sometimes spectacular and always dangerous, the amount of inconvenience it caused the enemy was small and its effect on popular morale disappointing. To Deltchev's way of thinking, the policy of the underground opposition should be to leave the winning of the war to those who could fight effectively and to concentrate on planning for the future of the country during the period immediately following the inevitable German collapse. He saw that her fate at the hands of the victorious powers would depend very much on the speed with which she could herself establish a provisional government sufficiently uncompromised to negotiate without cringing and strong enough to prevent civil war.

The resultant Committee of National Unity was not created by Deltchev alone, but it was he who made it effective. Clandestine organizations are mostly recruited from among the dedicated, the romantic, and the mentally ill-adjusted men and women of a community; and in them courage and devotion are more easily found than high-level planning ability and political skill. Because he was the clearest thinker the Committee had and the only member of it with any practical experience of government, Deltchev became in effect (though in fact he never held any specific appointment) its president, its secretary-general, and, eventually, its spokesman. Hundreds of thousands of people who had never heard of Deltchev the Minister of Posts and Telegraphs now came to know of and exult in Yordan Deltchev the patriot. And when the time came for him to speak to them, the dry steady voice and the cool logic seemed, after the hysterical oratory of the war years, to derive from a special kind of sanity and goodness. They felt he possessed the truth.

If the Provisional Government of National Unity set up by the Committee in the spring of 1944 had done no more than sue for peace so promptly, it would have justified its existence; for by this action it saved all but one of the northern frontier provinces from devastation and kept the minute army intact and available for police duties. Yet it did do more. It was able to secure recognition, qualified but sufficient, by the United Nations, and contrived, in those days of hasty negotiation and shifting authority, to confuse and postpone discussions of such matters as territorial claims and the dismantling of industrial installations. It ensured, at a minimum cost both to the national economy and to the national pride, that most of the vital decisions affecting the country's future were made not in the heat of the newly won battle, but in the milder atmosphere of delayed peace conferences. The credit for these benefits was given to Deltchev. He began to be nicknamed, affectionately, 'Papa' Deltchev.

Perhaps but for that nickname there would have been no People's Party regime, and no Deltchev trial.

When the Provisional Government came into power, it was said by neglected members of his own party that the motives behind Deltchev's actions had all along been those of a shrewd, ambitious politician and that, while he could not be blamed for having had greatness thrust upon him, he should not now behave toward his old friends as if he had achieved it. They were soon to wish that they had been entirely right.

One of the main articles of the Committee's original programme had been that of insisting on the need for free elections at the earliest possible moment. Its conclusion and the sanctimonious style of its wording were concessions to Anglo-American susceptibilities, which, it had been felt, could hurt nobody. Not that the men of the Committee were cynically indifferent to elections; it was simply that, faced with the task of planning for a great emergency of which nothing was then known and only the worst could be expected, they found such talk unrealistic. A cultivated sense of emergency is not easy to discard, and, later on, the early state of mind about elections tended to persist. When, therefore, the People's Party members of the Provisional Government began to press for redemption of the election promise, their action was interpreted, and correctly interpreted, as a demand for more power; that is, a larger share of the important posts. Only to Deltchev, apparently, did it mean anything different.

The People's Party had lately grown enormously in numbers and influence. The participation of the Agrarian Socialists in the formation and work of the Committee had achieved its object of enlisting wide popular support; but it had also had the secondary effect of making the Committee a powerful recruiting agency for the People's Party. This mishap had long been a subject of complaints and bitter exchanges within the Government, and on one occasion Petra Vukashin, the leader of the People's Party men, had been too frank. 'If,' he had said, 'you are fool enough to introduce your wife to a handsome young man with a bad reputation, you must not complain when you find them in bed together.'

When, to the manifest discomfort of Vukashin and the rest of the People's Party faction, Deltchev took the election proposal seriously and began to argue in favour of it, it was assumed at first by his pathetically gleeful colleagues that 'Papa' Deltchev was merely calling the enemy's bluff. They knew, had known for some time, that the Provisional Government had the approval and support of the Western powers, who would not press for the promised elections while the country was in Soviet occupation. They had evidence that the Russians, not unimpressed by Deltchev's efficiency, were content to let things stay as they were for the present. Some of its members had even wondered if the word 'provisional' might not be dropped from the title of a government with so rich an expectation of life. They could not know that their leader, Deltchev, had already numbered its days.

Many attempts were made later to offer more reasonable explanations of Deltchev's actions at that time than the one accepted by the simpler members of the public—namely, that he was a self-sacrificing patriot who had been directly inspired by God. Since, however, most of their other explanations relied on the assumption that he was monumentally corrupt, none of them was much more convincing.

The material facts were simple.

After the meeting at which the election promise was discussed Deltchev seemed preoccupied and unwilling to pursue the matter in private conversation. To one persistent man, however, he said: 'If we have clean hands they cannot accuse us.' The man took this to be a comment on the strength of the Government's position and the absurdity of the People's Party manoeuvre.

That was on a Thursday. For the next few days Deltchev was at home in bed with a severe chill. On the following Tuesday he was due to make a radio speech about a national campaign then in progress for conserving winter foodstuffs for livestock.

He came to the radio station straight from his bed, looking, according to the director of the station, 'like a man who has been fighting with devils.' In his speech he talked briefly about the conservation campaign and then, after a momentary hesitation, produced a handwritten script from his pocket and began to read a statement.

Five minutes later the people knew that, in the considered opinion of 'Papa' Deltchev, the time had now come for the Government to redeem the Committee's solemn pledge to hold free elections at the earliest possible moment.

At the beginning of the statement he had declared that he was speaking only for himself and not for the Provisional Government of National Unity. This declaration was both seized upon as evidence of his cynical contempt for his audience and pointed to as marking his absolute integrity. For the former view it was said that no one but a fool would suppose that, whether he wanted to do so or not, Deltchev could in fact dissociate his private opinions on such a question from those of the Government he led; for the latter it was argued that if you accepted the fact of his honesty (and who could deny it?) you would see that his disclaimer was a simple statement of the truth, which he had been bound to make if he were not to deceive the public. As equally divergent constructions could be placed on every other sentence in the statement, neither side could score points. Deltchev himself had returned from the radio station to his bed and, having issued through his secretary the statement that the broadcast speech was 'self-explanatory,' remained there, silent and inaccessible. But by the time two days had passed, it was clear that the storm over the speech, which raged with mounting fury among the politicians, was no longer of interest to the people. In their eyes the Provisional Government was now committed quite irrevocably to holding elections in the near future and anyone who attacked Deltchev was attempting to deny the fact. Yet it was the People's Party that profited most from the situation.

Those of the unfortunate Agrarian Socialists who had the wit to see that, whatever they might now say in private about Deltchev, they could not hope to win without him as a figurehead were in the majority; but they were terribly hampered by a considerable and vindictive minority whose only concern now seemed to be to oppose and revile him in public. The People's Party, while taking full advantage of this mistake, took care not to make it themselves. By referring to Deltchev patronizingly but respectfully as a kind of elder statesman (he was in fact only sixty then) they managed to convey the impression that he was in a state of derelict senility. How else could one explain his continued association with the Agrarian Socialists? Also, by securing the postponement of the elections until the early summer, they gave themselves time to prepare a *coup d'état* that anticipated publication of the election results by a few hours. In the event, it was almost unnecessary. Thanks to Deltchev, they very nearly came into power by constitutional means.

His response to these events was at first curiously passive. True, he protested against the *coup*, but rather formally, as if expressing an appropriate but not heartfelt sentiment; and in the Chamber his attacks upon the new Government had about them the studied moderation of a fencing master with a new pupil. For a long time he seemed unaware or unwilling to be aware of the Government's quick, wary moves to make themselves secure. Soon the anti-Deltchev faction within his own party began to find people ready at last to listen to their tale of a great fortune deposited abroad in Deltchev's name the day after his election statement. Even among the general public he seemed to be losing popularity. It was understandable that the Government's supporters should have come to think of Deltchev almost as one of themselves.

Then came the incident of 'Deltchev's football match.'

The occasion was the official opening of a sports stadium. It had been completed in 1940 and immediately requisitioned for use by the German Army as a transit camp. Later the Red Army had used it as a garrison headquarters. Its return was a gesture of Soviet goodwill, which the new Government had dutifully decided to celebrate with as much publicity as possible. It was probably the presence of Western diplomatic representatives at the ceremony that determined that Deltchev as leader of the 'opposition' should be asked to speak.

He began, deceptively, with a tribute to the Red Army and expressions of his party's recognition of the generous motives that had prompted the early return of the stadium. He hoped that in the near future it would be the scene of a memorable football match with the local Red Army team.

Then, during the mild applause that greeted this suggestion, he moved nearer to the microphones. But this time he took no script from his pocket. He knew exactly what he wanted to say.

'But meanwhile, my countrymen, there is another, more deadly battle for us to fight—the battle for freedom within the state.'

He paused. There was a silence, in which the long banners could be heard flapping in the wind. He went on.

'Two days ago I was invited by the leader of the People's Party, Petra Vukashin, to take the office of Minister of Justice in the Government that now has power. My answer was promised for tonight. I take this opportunity of giving him the answer now. I answer that if he thinks that by so betraying my brothers in the Agrarian Socialist Party I should change in any way their determination to fight until this new tyranny is utterly destroyed—if he thinks that, then he is stupid. If our opposition to his party's criminal plans is such that he must try to buy us off with a share of the loot, then he is also frightened. My countrymen, there is no time to lose. These stupid, frightened men are dangerous, not for what they are now, but for what they mean to become—your masters. They are not . . .'

At this point the booming public-address system in the stadium was cut off. In the deathly pause that followed, Deltchev's voice, high and thin in the wind, could only be heard by those near him as he completed the sentence.

Then the cheering began. It came across the packed stadium as a rolling, sighing wave of sound that surged up and broke with a roar that shook the air like an explosion. It lasted nearly a minute and subsided only when another sound came to replace it: the steady, massive chanting of Deltchev's name. Suddenly on the far side of the stadium there was a wide swirling movement in the crowd as a fight developed, and from closer at hand there was angry shouting. Deltchev, who during the cheering had stood motionless in front of the dead microphones, now waved his hand and turned away. There was another tremendous cheer and more shouting. At that moment the officer in command of a Russian military band, which had been waiting to lead into the arena the squads who were giving the gymnastics display, decided not to wait for an order to do so. It was a sensible decision. As the band began to play and march in, the cheering became ragged and in places gave way to laughter and clapping. In less than a minute the incident of 'Deltchev's football match' was over; over, that is, except for the breathless excitement of discussing it and of reporting it to those who had merely heard it on the radio. But nothing about it was forgotten and much that had not happened was remembered. 'Papa' Deltchev had come back to them. He had spoken his mind and they had shown that they were with him in his fight against the 'masters.'

Four nights later an attempt was made to assassinate him.

His house was of the old kind with a walled courtyard. As he got out of his car to enter the house, a grenade was thrown. It hit the wall by the entrance and bounced back into the road before exploding, so that Deltchev, who had gained the doorway, was partly shielded from the blast. There were few people about at the time and the man who had thrown the grenade escaped.

The driver of the car was badly cut about the head and neck, but Deltchev, although he had been flung against the half-open door and much shaken, was not seriously hurt. In the ensuing confusion, however, his protests that the pain in his shoulder was caused only by a bruise were ignored and he was taken to hospital with the driver. Within an hour rumours that he was dead or dying were circulating in the cafés, and a large crowd gathered outside the hospital. By this time Deltchev had returned to his home, where the police were collecting fragments of the grenade in the presence of an even larger crowd. There was a great deal of hostility toward the police.

It is said that when the Chief of Police reported to Vukashin later that night that the attempt on Deltchev was being described openly as the Government's reply to the stadium speech, the Minister exclaimed: 'Did they think we would reply in the Chamber?' The story may be untrue, but, in the light of what followed, it is not incredible. Certainly from that moment on there was an ominous change in the Propaganda Ministry's public attitude toward Deltchev, and it is likely that the decision to try him was made at this time. The Ministry's official statement on the affair had a sort of angry jocularity about it that did nothing to change the general belief that the Government had known of the attempt in advance. It asserted that the grenade was of American manufacture, and went on to suggest that the obvious place to seek the criminal was in the ranks of Deltchev's own party, where there were many criminals with Anglo-American imperialist connections.

The editor of a newspaper that described this statement as 'unsatisfactory, but significantly so,' was immediately imprisoned. A series of savage attacks on the Agrarian Socialist Party now began. Their violent tone and the barely concealed threats that accompanied every allusion to Deltchev conveyed unmistakable warnings. The opposition had become intolerable and was going to be liquidated; but first Deltchev must be disposed of. He had a choice. He could escape abroad and be condemned or stay at home and be condemned. In any event he would be condemned.

Deltchev chose to stay. A month later he was arrested.

That was all. For a while I looked out of my hotel window across the flat roofs and Byzantine spires of the city, as still in the moonlight as the landscape of a dead world; and at last I became sleepy.

As I collected up the mass of news cuttings, notes, and manuscript that composed Pashik's file and began to put it all back in the envelope, I noticed a paper that I had not seen before. It had been clipped to the back of a wad of sheets with cuttings pasted on them and therefore easily overlooked.

It was a page from a memo pad of the kind I had seen on Pashik's desk. On it was typed: '*Case of K. Fischer, Vienna '46 – Aleko's band?*'

For me, then, it was not the most interesting thing about the file. I went to sleep.

Chapter Four

Pashik had promised to drive me to the trial, and we met for breakfast. He nodded at the envelope I was carrying with the approving smile of a friendly schoolmaster.

'Ah, Mr Foster, you have been reading.'

'Yes. There's a lot of material there. Did you collect it?'

He fingered his chin self-consciously for a moment; he had shaved. 'Why do you ask, Mr Foster?'

'Because a lot of the unpublished stuff was obviously done by someone who knew Deltchev very well and liked him. You?'

'Ah, the memoir'; he looked embarrassed; 'that was commissioned by one of my papers from Petlarov.'

'Who's he?'

'He was Deltchev's secretary and friend—until the elections. Then they quarrelled. He was paid for the memoir, but it was not used. It was not the moment.'

'Where is Petlarov now? Is he here?'

'He may be.'

'I should like to talk to him.'

'He will know nothing about the trial, Mr Foster.'

'I'd still like to talk to him.'

'He may not wish to see you.'

'Then he will say so. You said you wanted to be helpful, Pashik. Here's your opportunity.'

He wriggled unhappily. 'Please, Mr Foster. I see I must explain to you.' He lowered his voice. 'You do not understand. After the arrest of Deltchev, Petlarov was naturally arrested too. He is released now, but he is still suspect. It would be most indiscreet to have relations with him. I cannot take the risk.'

'You don't have to. Just get a message to him from me. I suppose he can speak German?'

'I do not know. Perhaps not.'

'Send a message as if from me asking him to telephone me at my hotel this evening.'

He sighed. 'Very well, Mr Foster. But I think it will be useless.'

I held up the envelope with the file in it. 'We don't want to take this with us do we? We could leave it at your office on the way and write a note to Petlarov at the same time. Your office boy can deliver it.'

He pursed his lips together at this. 'I see you still do not trust me, Mr Foster,' he said.

'What do you mean?'

He saw the danger of explaining just in time. 'It is not important,' he said with dignity.

He took the envelope from me. Then I remembered. 'Oh, by the way,' I said, 'what does this refer to?' I showed him the paper with the *Aleko* note on it.

He looked at it blankly for a moment. 'Oh, that, Mr Foster,' he said, and taking it from me put it in his pocket; 'that is nothing. Something from another file.'

When once you know how a person lies, it is difficult for him to deceive you again. With Pashik it was a special tone of voice he used for direct lies that gave him away—a cold, too matter-of-fact tone. He had used it before in telling me the untrue story of the American journalist who had tried to go to Greece for the week-end. I supposed the fact that he had lied about this piece of paper to be equally unimportant.

The large courtroom at the Ministry of Justice had been thought too small for a political trial of such moment. It was being staged, therefore, in the main lecture hall of the Army School of Aeronautics, a modern building on the outskirts of the city.

The walls, ordinarily decorated with engineering charts and war trophies, had been hung with flags—those of the Republic and of the Soviet Union, and, at greater intervals, those of the other sympathetic nations of eastern Europe. Just above and on either side of the judges' dais two draped Soviet flags bulged over (but, tactlessly, did not quite conceal) one of the trophies, the tail plane of a Russian aircraft presented by a German flak unit during the war. Pinned to some of the flags were notices printed in four languages saying that smoking was prohibited. In the balcony a row of soundproof booths had been erected for the interpreters relaying translations of the proceedings to the earphones of the foreign diplomatic and press representatives below. In the balcony, too, on heavy stands or clamped to the balcony rail, were big floodlights pointing down into the court to illuminate it for the Propaganda Ministry's film cameras. Besides the judges' dais, on both sides of the prisoner's rostrum, at the corners of the hall, in the balcony, by the doors, and below every flag on the walls guards were posted. They were all officers or N.C.O.'s and armed with machine pistols, which they did not sling, but held ready in their hands. It had been explained by the Propaganda Ministry that when the evidence against the criminal Deltchev was publicly known, attempts might be made by the people he had deceived to kill him before justice could be done.

The courtroom was crowded. My place and Pashik's were in the foreign-press section, below the edge of the balcony and to one side. In the centre was the diplomatic section. On the ledge in front of each seat in these two sections was a pair of earphones and four plug sockets marked with letters distinguishing the Russian, French, English, and German interpretation channels. Also on the ledge was a duplicated copy of the indictment in

French. There seemed to be no seats for members of the public without tickets, but several rows behind us were prominently labelled with notice cards bearing initials, which Pashik said were those of prominent trade-union organizations. The occupants of these seats were obviously in their best clothes and on their best behaviour. They all wore badges, and in one row there was a group of peasants in national costume. They looked as if they were attending a prize-giving. The front rows, however, had a different look about them. These seats were reserved for the important party members and functionaries. Their occupants wore dark neat clothes and either sat with self-conscious, preoccupied frowns or conversed in *affairé* undertones with their neighbours. Aware of being on the public eye, they were concerned to show that they had business there and were not merely favoured spectators. It was warm, and most of the women and many of the men had highly coloured paper fans.

At about ten o'clock the floodlights in the balcony were turned on and the fluttering sound of film cameras began. A buzz of anticipation went round the courtroom; then, as the three black-robed judges came slowly in, all stood up. The judges went to their places on the dais but did not sit down until the national anthem had been played through a loudspeaker. It was all curiously reminiscent of a royal visit to the opera. Even the low murmur of conversation that began as we sat down again was familiar. All that was different was that instead of the lowering of lights and the rise of a curtain somebody stood up and called out the name of Yordan Deltchev, and all eyes turned toward a pair of glazed doors beside the dais. Then there was silence except for the sound of the cameras and the distant throbbing of the generator set that supplied the power for the floodlights.

After a moment or two the glazed doors were flung open and three men entered the court. Inside the door they paused for a moment, blinking in the lights that poured down on them. Two of them were uniformed guards, tall, smart young fellows. Between them was an elderly man with a thin grey face, deep-set eyes, and white hair. He was short and had been stocky, but now his shoulders were rounded and he was inclined to stoop. He stood with his hands thrust deep into his jacket pockets, looking about him uncertainly. One of the guards touched his arm and he walked over to the rostrum and stepped on to it. A chair had been placed for him, but for a moment he stood there looking round at the flags upon the walls. He smiled faintly. He still had his hands in his pockets. Then, with a curt nod to each of the judges, he sat down and closed his eyes. This was Yordan Deltchev.

There were twenty-three counts listed in the published indictment against him. They charged (principally in count number eight, though the same charge was paraphrased in two other counts) that he had 'prepared terrorist plots against the state and conspired with reactionary organizations, including the criminal Officer Corps Brotherhood, to secure, for financial and other personal advantages, the occupation of the motherland by troops of a foreign power.' There were other charges concerned with terrorist activity, the smuggling of arms, and plots to assassinate members of the People's Party Government, 'in particular P. I. Vukashin.' Sprinkled throughout were dark references to 'various confederates,' 'notorious foreign agents,' 'hired saboteurs and murderers,' 'reactionary gangsters,' and so on, while the name of the Officer Corps Brotherhood recurred with the persistence of a typewriter bell. It was soon evident that the indictment was a propaganda document intended for foreign consumption. It said, in effect, or hoped to say: 'He is the kind of man against whom such charges may seriously be brought'; and: 'He is accused of so much that of some he must be guilty.'

The public prosecutor conducted his case in person. His name was Dr Prochaska and he was one of the few members of the legal profession who had joined the People's Party before it had come into power. He was an authority on questions of land tenure, and most of his practice had been concerned with cases involving them. He had had little experience of court advocacy of any kind and none at all in criminal proceedings. A stout, pugnacious-looking man with quick, jerky movements and a habit of licking his lips every few seconds, he seemed more concerned to defend himself against accusations of weakness than to present his case effectively. He made scarcely any reference to the official indictment and dealt with only two of the charges in it. If he could prove, or seem to prove, those, then Deltchev would stand convicted on the whole indictment. That, at least, was the impression I had of it. From the commencement of his long opening address he adopted a tone of ranting denunciation that carried little conviction and confused even the more reasoned passages. In spite of the earphones on my head, and the voice of the interpreter quietly translating the speech, I was constantly distracted by the sight and half-heard sounds of its originator.

His case, however, was dangerously simple.

It was generally known that at the time of the German retreat in 1944 Deltchev, who had been secretly in touch with both the Russians and the Western powers, had gone to great lengths to secure Anglo-American rather than Soviet occupation of the country. Against the wishes of a majority of the Committee of National Unity, he had at one point gone as far as to propose to the Western powers that the national army should continue to resist the Russians in the north so as to give the Americans and British time to prepare an airborne invasion from Middle East bases.

It was now suggested by the prosecution that this proposal had come in fact from the Western powers themselves and that Deltchev's support of it had been bought with the promise that he would have control of the reallocation of the German oil concessions. In other words, he had tried to sell his countrymen's lives for money and power.

The other favoured charge was the one that had so amused my economist friend. It was that Deltchev had planned to assassinate Vukashin, the head of the People's Party Government, and that he was, in fact, a member of the Officer Corps Brotherhood. If this could seem to be proved, he could quite legally and with full popular approval be sentenced to death. The case against Deltchev was designed to destroy him, and the Agrarian Socialist Party which had produced him, forever.

I left the court that day in a peculiar frame of mind. I felt as if I had been to the first night of what had seemed to me a very bad play only to find that everyone else had enjoyed it immensely. A Propaganda Ministry bureau had been set up in a room adjoining the court. On the way out Pashik stopped to get the official bulletin on the day's proceedings. The room was crowded and I waited in the doorway. There were a number of tables, each signposted with the name of one of the official languages. As I stood there, I saw a bald young man whom I thought I knew coming away from the English table. I had noticed him earlier in the day and been unable to place him. Now as he pushed his way out we came face to face. He nodded.

'You're Foster, aren't you?'

'Yes. We've met before.'

'Sibley, Consolidated Press.'

'Oh yes.' I remembered, too, that I had not liked him.

'What are you doing here?' he asked. 'Getting local colour for a new play?'

I explained. He raised his eyebrows. 'Very nice too. Still, I expect you'll make a play out of it sometime, won't you?'

'I don't know.'

'I should have thought that there were masses of material for you. It'd make quite a nice little paragraph, your being here. Do you mind if I use it?'

'Yes, I do.' I smiled as I said it, but not very cordially.

He laughed. 'All right, I'll spare you. But it'd be nice to send something even a *little* more interesting than these hand-outs.' He waved the sheets in his hand. 'I'm at our Paris office really. I've been lent for the trial. Why I can't think. An office boy could file this junk for all of us.' He turned his head as Pashik came up. 'Hullo, Georghi, we were just talking about you.'

'Good evening, Mr Sibley. We must be going, Mr Foster. I have to get to the office.'

'That's our Georghi. Always on the job.' Sibley grinned. 'Where are you staying, Foster?'

I told him.

'We must have a drink together,' he said.

In the car Pashik gave me the bulletin. I glanced through it. Most of it was composed of extracts from Dr Prochaska's address. They were even more idiotic to read than to listen to. I put the bulletin down. The streets leading back to the centre of the city were narrow and crowded and Pashik was a driver who twitched at the wheel instead of steering with it. He squeezed his way none too skilfully between two carts.

'Mr Foster,' he said then, 'there is a suggestion which I think I must make to you.' He looked round at me soulfully. 'You will not, I hope, be offended.'

'Not at all. Look out.'

He twitched away from a cyclist just in time. The cyclist shouted. Pashik sounded the horn unnecessarily and put on speed.

'It is a small thing,' he said—the car swayed unpleasantly across some protruding tram lines—'but I would not, if I were in your place, be too friendly here with Mr Sibley.'

'Oh? What's the matter with him?'

'It is nothing personal, you understand.'

'But what?'

'He drinks too much and becomes indiscreet.'

'I don't see that that has anything to do with me.'

'His associates will be suspect.'

I thought for a moment. 'Mr Pashik,' I said then, 'as a newspaperman don't you think you're a bit too anxious about the censorship and the Propaganda Ministry and the police and all the rest of it?'

A woman missed death by an inch. He sounded the horn absently and shook his head. 'I do not think so. It is difficult to explain.'

'What's so difficult about it?'

'You are a stranger here, Mr Foster. You look on our life from the outside. You are interested in the trial of a man whose name you scarcely know because his situation seems to you to contain the elements of a spiritual conflict. Naturally so. You are a writer of fiction and you make the world in your own image. But be careful. Do not walk upon the stage yourself. You may find that the actors are not what they have seemed.'

'Is Sibley one of the actors?'

'I was speaking generally, Mr Foster.'

'Then I'm sorry, but I don't understand what we're talking about.'

He sighed. 'I was afraid not. But perhaps it does not matter.'

I let that one go. A few moments later he pulled up outside my hotel. I got out of the car.

'Shall we meet for dinner, Mr Foster?'

I hesitated. The air outside the car smelt good. I shook my head. 'I think I'll get to bed early tonight,' I said.

Chapter Five

The Hotel Boris had been built by a German company in 1914 and was one of those hotels in which footsteps echo and only the sound of a toilet flushing in the distance reminds you that you are not alone there. The foyer was a cavernous place with a tessellated floor and a hydraulic lift in a wrought-iron cage. The reception clerk was a slow-moving, mentally deficient youth with a charming smile. He spoke a little English.

'There is a message for you, sir,' he said. He glanced at a scrap of paper that he had taken out of the key rack. 'Mr Stanoiev called to see you and will call again.'

'Stanoiev? I don't know anyone of that name. Are you sure it was for me?'

He looked stupid. 'I don't know, sir. He went away.'

'I see.'

The lift was deserted. I walked up the wide shallow stairs to the sixth floor.

My room was at the end of a long corridor with upholstered benches set against the wall at intervals along it. As I started down the corridor, I noticed that at the far end there was a man sitting on one of the benches. He was reading a newspaper.

It made an odd picture; one never expects corridor furniture to be used except as shelves for trays and chambermaids' dusters. As I approached he looked up casually, then went back to his newspaper. I glanced at him as I passed by.

He was a thin, dried-up man with pale, haggard eyes and grey hair cropped so that the bone of his skull was visible. He had a peculiarly blotchy complexion like that of someone just cured of a skin disease. The hands holding up the newspaper were long and yellow. There was a black soft hat beside him on the bench.

I went on past him to my room. I put the key in the lock and turned it. Then someone spoke from just behind me.

'Herr Foster?'

It made me jump. I turned round. The man who had been on the bench was standing there with his hat under his arm.

I nodded.

'Petlarov,' he said, and then added in German: 'I can speak French or German, whichever you prefer.'

'German will be all right. I'm glad to see you.' I finished opening the door. 'Will you come in?'

He bowed slightly. 'Thank you.' He walked in and then turned and faced me. 'I must apologize,' he said in a clipped, businesslike way, 'for answering your note in this fashion. A native of this country would not find it strange, but as you are a foreigner I must make an explanation.'

'Please sit down.'

'Thank you.' In the light of the room his clothes were shabby and he looked ill. His precise, formal manner, however, seemed to ignore both facts. He chose a hard chair as if he did not intend to stay long.

'First,' he said, 'I think you should know that I am under surveillance; that is to say, I have to report to the police every day. Second, I am officially listed as an "untrustworthy person." That means that if you were to be seen entering my house or talking to me in a public place, you would attract the attention of the police, and yourself become suspect. That is why I have used this unconventional means of seeing you. I discovered your room number by leaving a note for you in the name of Stanoiev and noticing which box it was put into. Then I came discreetly up here and waited for you to return. You need therefore have no fear that my name is in any way connected with yours or my presence here known about.' He bowed curtly.

'I am most grateful to you for coming.'

'Thank you. May I ask how you obtained my address?'

'From a man named Pashik.'

'Ah, yes. I thought it must be him.' He looked thoughtfully into space.

'Do you know him well, Herr Petlarov?'

'You mean what is my opinion of him?'

'Yes.'

He considered for a moment. 'Let us say that I do not subscribe to the common belief that he is merely a disagreeable person whose political views change with the person he talks to. But now that I am here, what do you want of me?'

I had held out my cigarettes. His hand had gone out to them as he was speaking, but now he hesitated. He looked up from the cigarettes, and his eyes met mine.

'I have some more,' I said.

He smiled in a deprecatory way. 'If you had perhaps a bar of chocolate or a biscuit, Herr Foster, it would, I think, be better for my stomach than tobacco.'

'Of course.' I went to my suitcase. 'I have no chocolate, but here are some biscuits.'

I had a box, bought in Paris for the train journey and then forgotten. I opened it. The biscuits were the kind with pink icing sugar on them.

'Not very good for a bad stomach,' I remarked.

He took one with a polite smile. 'Oh yes. Excellent.' He nibbled at it with very white false teeth.

'Pashik gave me your piece on Deltchev to read,' I said.

'Oh, yes? It was considered unsuitable for publication.'

'By Pashik?'

'Yes, but I was not surprised or upset. I knew that it had been commissioned in the belief that because I had had a difference of opinion with Yordan I would therefore write about him in an unfavourable way. If Pashik had asked me, I would have told him what to expect. Fortunately he did not ask.'

'Fortunately?'

'If he had known he would not have commissioned the article, and I needed the money.'

'Oh, I see. I have a bottle of whisky here. Would it be safe to ask the floor waiter for some glasses?'

'I think not. Perhaps I may have another biscuit.'

'Of course, please help yourself. You know, Herr Petlarov, I came here to write a series of articles about the trial of Deltchev. But Pashik seems afraid that I shall offend the censor if I do them here.'

'He is probably right,' he said calmly. 'He is usually right about these things. Yes, I can see. If you offend he will be blamed.'

I must have looked disbelieving. He took another biscuit. 'I will tell you a little story about the regime. A member of the People's Party wrote a novel about the fight of a group of workmen with the capitalists who wish to close a factory. It was a naïve story in which the capitalists were all monsters of evil and the workmen's leader a People's Party man. The Propaganda Minister, whose name is Brankovitch, would not, however, allow its publication. He said that the hero was not positive.'

'I don't understand.'

'The author had not demonstrated that the hero member of the party was a *good* man.'

'But surely that was inferred.'

'Brankovitch would say that you were in intellectual error, Herr Foster. Inference is not positive. The public must be *instructed* that the man is good, as they must be instructed in all things.'

'You must be exaggerating.'

'In London or New York I would be exaggerating. Here, no. The sequel to this is that the writer was angry and made a little propaganda of his own. He has now been sent to forced labour. Pashik does not see that fate for himself. You see, Herr Foster, those who must be persuaded to obey are no longer important, for shortly we shall cease to exist. Our liquidation has begun.' He smiled significantly.

'What do you mean?'

He took another biscuit and held it up. 'This is the third biscuit I have taken,' he said. 'There are twenty-one left in the box. I can eat nine more.'

'You can have the box.'

He inclined his head. 'Thank you. I had hoped that you would give it to me. I had based my calculations on your doing so. If I eat nine more I shall have eaten twelve. That will leave twelve for my wife. Luckily we have no children to share with us.'

I was silent.

'I will explain. It is quite simple. Persons who are listed as untrustworthy are not allowed to work at anything but manual labour. I tried that, but I am not strong enough. So, as I cannot work, my wife and I may not have ration cards. We are, of course, very often hungry, and that can make a good argument for obedience.'

I got up and went to the wardrobe for the whisky. Out of the corner of my eye I saw him reaching for another biscuit. He glanced over his shoulder at me.

'Please do not distress yourself, Herr Foster. A bad conscience can, I know, be as unpleasant in some ways as an empty stomach, and the person with the biscuits so often has a bad conscience. The trouble is that most of us with empty stomachs also have bad consciences. That combination will prove deadly.'

'I have a metal cup,' I said, 'and also a tooth glass. If you like whisky—'

'I tasted it once,' he said courteously. 'I thought it better than schnapps and more interesting than our plum brandy. You need not fear, however, that I shall insist on taking it away with the biscuits.'

I gave him the tooth glass. He took a small sip and looked at me. 'I know that you will forgive me telling you that before I came to see you this evening I looked up your name in an English reference book I have.'

'You'd like to know what a playwright is doing writing articles about a political trial?'

'Oh no, I see the connection. I was putting myself in your place for a moment. You have been in this city for two or three days perhaps. You do not know the country or the people. You are present at a trial that is like a game played for counters of which you do not know the value. Yet you have to interpret it for Western eyes.'

'Something of the kind has already been said to me once today.'

He nodded calmly. 'As a guide you have Pashik, a man so preoccupied with a problem of his own—self-preservation possibly, but we cannot be sure—that he can lead you only to the counter of the Propaganda Ministry.' He took another biscuit. 'Have you seen the official bulletin of the trial today?'

'This?' I took it out of my pocket. 'They gave out copies as we left the courtroom.'

'They will do so every day. Tell me, Herr Foster, what will there be in your articles that a clever, malicious journalist sitting in London could not contrive for himself from a set of these reports?'

'I'm sure you have your own answer ready.'

'Ah, I have offended you.' He smiled. 'But not seriously, I think, if you reflect. What I am suggesting to you, Herr Foster, is that you might find it useful to employ my services.'

'Yes, that's what I thought you meant. How?'

'As a guide. I make this suggestion without embarrassment. You were kind enough to invite me to tell you some things about Yordan and of course I will do so.' He touched the biscuit box. 'I should have been well paid for that. But I think that I could be of further use to you.' His haggard eyes looked up at me with a cold little smile in them. He licked a crumb off his lower lip.

'I'm sure you could,' I said, and waited.

'For instance,' he went on, 'I wonder if you have considered that some of the evidence against Yordan Deltchev might not be as stupid as the prosecution makes it.' He looked into the tooth glass.

An unpleasant suspicion crossed my mind. 'Your difference of opinion with him,' I said, 'was over his radio speech approving the election, wasn't it?'

He was very quick. He said calmly: 'If I were an enemy of his I would not need to beg a gift of biscuits, Herr Foster. I should be a witness at his trial. And if, as your caution may suggest, I am here as an emissary of the Propaganda Ministry to try to corrupt your judgment, then you cannot yet have identified the man whose task it will be to do so.'

'I'm sorry. I don't know what you're talking about. What man?'

'Our friend Brankovitch has been forced to admit a number of hostile foreign journalists for the purpose of reporting this trial. Do you suppose that while they are here he will make no attempt to neutralize their hostility? Of course he must try. I can even tell you the procedure he will adopt. Tomorrow perhaps, or the next day, after Vukashin's evidence has been heard, Brankovitch will call a foreign-press conference and answer questions. Then, perhaps the next day, someone will approach you privately with a great secret. This person will tell you that he has discovered a way of getting uncensored messages out of the country. He will let you persuade him to share the discovery. Of course, your messages will not be sent, but they will serve as a guide to your intentions, which can then be anticipated in the official propaganda. Brankovitch likes, for some reason, to use *agents provocateurs*.' He looked at me sardonically. 'I know his sense of humour. It was I who recommended him to Yordan for a place on the Committee.'

I offered him a cigarette again. He hesitated. 'If I might take two?' he said.

'One for your wife?'

'Yes.'

'Please take the packet.'

'Thank you.'

'It was not quite full. He counted the cigarettes in it carefully.

'How did you meet Deltchev?' I asked.

He looked up. 'He was my partner,' he said. He seemed surprised that I did not know.

I gave him a box of matches and he lit a cigarette.

'Thank you.' He blew smoke. 'When Yordan first practised as a lawyer, I was his clerk. Later I became his partner. When he was appointed Minister of Posts and Telegraphs, I became his assistant and secretary. I was also his friend.'

'What sort of man is he? Superficially, I mean.'

'Quiet, deliberate, very patient. A sound lawyer. If you were a journalist interviewing him in his office, you would probably be irritated by a habit he has of looking past you when he is talking. He keeps his desk very tidy and empties the ashtray as soon as you have put your cigarette out. Yet polite. He would tend to put words into your mouth–criticisms of himself–and then answer them. A bad habit for a lawyer, that. A man with a family–wife, son, daughter–of whom he is very fond, but not a family man. A good man, but not at ease with himself.'

'The sort of man who would betray a principle for a bribe?'

'Yordan has never valued money enough to be corrupt in that way. Power might have tempted him once. You speak, of course, of his actions over the election promise.'

'Yes.'

'If he was paid to make that radio speech, he gave up what he might value–power–to gain what he did not value–money.' He shrugged. 'I have had plenty of time for thinking, and much bitterness has gone. At one time I thought of killing Yordan for what he did then, but even in hate I never supposed that he had been bribed.'

'What is your explanation?'

'I have none. Yordan was often accused of being merely a shrewd politician. In retrospect that seems as ridiculous as the accusation now that he is a murderer. By unnecessarily bringing about the November elections he committed political suicide and betrayed all the people who were loyal to him. You ask for an explanation.' He threw up his hands. 'It is as easy to say that he was insane as to deny that he was bribed. When I faced him in his room that night he did not look insane. He looked strangely at peace with himself. That made me more angry, and, you know, in anger many things seem clear. "Why?" I shouted at him; "why?" "It is better so," was all he replied. Then, when I had finished abusing him, I said: "Papa Deltchev has gone and the Minister of Posts and Telegraphs has returned. Papa Deltchev was not strong enough to bear a people's love!"' Petlarov looked across at me and smiled slightly. 'But now I cannot remember what I meant,' he added.

After a moment I asked: 'Will the election matter be raised at the trial?'

He shook his head. 'Not by the prosecutor. For the regime, the less said about the election the better. But they might tolerate the defence's making play with it to suggest Yordan's fundamental sympathy with the regime.'

'Who is defending?'

'His name is Stanoiev. It amused me to use it here. He is the party member appointed to defend. His arguments in mitigation will be given prominence. They will serve as the final condemnation.' He frowned. 'What I do not understand is this affair of the Officer Corps Brotherhood. Yordan's attitude toward Soviet occupation–yes, that is something to argue and misinterpret, to deal with speciously. But the Officer Corps

Brotherhood is another matter. They make so much of it that they must have something. Yet the idea is absurd.'

'Surely it's easy enough to manufacture evidence?'

'Yes, but that is not their way. Consider the case of Cardinal Mindszenty. He was accused of an offence against the currency regulation. We know that it was only technically an offence and not committed for his own gain, but he was guilty of it and that was the reason it was used. If he had been charged as a corrupter of youth it would have made better propaganda, and no doubt the evidence could have been manufactured. But no–the currency offence could be proved. The lie stands most securely on a pinpoint of truth.' He took the last of his twelve biscuits and shut the box. 'What do you want of me, Herr Foster?'

'You have already given me a great deal.'

'I have a suggestion. Why do you not talk to Madame Deltchev?'

'Is it possible?'

'Yes, for you. She and her household are under protection–that is, they are not permitted to leave the house, which is guarded–but your permits will allow you to pass. I will give you a letter to her. She will see no other journalist, I assure you. You will make a coup.'

'Yes, I see that. What kind of woman is she?'

'She was a schoolteacher in the town where we practised years ago. She came of a Greek family. If she had married me instead of Yordan, perhaps I should have become a minister. But better that you should form your own opinion. If you wish, I will come here every evening at this time to give you what information and comment I can.' He leaned forward and touched my knee with his forefinger. 'Is it agreed?'

'Agreed. But what is my part of the agreement?'

He hesitated. 'Money–a little, what you consider fair–and your ration card. Not the restaurant tickets–those you will need and I could not use–but the ration card for bread, meat, butter, milk, eggs, and green vegetables. As a foreigner, you have one on the highest scale, I think.'

'Yes.'

'You still have it? You have not already disposed of it?'

'No. It's yours. I'll get it now.'

He sighed. 'It is as well that my wife is not here,' he said. 'She would weep.'

Later, when he had gone, I sat by the window and had a whisky and water in the tooth glass. I was beginning to feel perceptive and understanding.

That was the point at which I should have packed my bag and gone home.

Chapter Six

In the afternoon of the second day of the trial the prosecutor completed his opening address to the court and began to call witnesses.

The first was Vukashin, the head of the Government. There was a stir as he went into the witness box.

He was one of those politicians who in their dealings with the public are like small-part actors who specialize in playing such things as shrewd lawyers, family doctors, and wise fathers; their mannerisms of speech and gesture have been cultivated to fit the stock characters their physical peculiarities suggest. He was square and solid, with a short neck, and he stood awkwardly in the witness box, his big hands clasping the ledge in front of him, the shoulders of his ill-fitting jacket hunched about his ears. He had blunt features, with a muscular jaw and full, determined lips. His forehead was low and permanently knitted in a frown of concentration. In the popular edition of his biography published by the Propaganda Ministry he was referred to as a 'veteran front fighter in the class struggle,' and from the illustrations you received the impression that he had spent most of his life marching up steep hills at the head of fist-brandishing processions of angry revolutionaries. The role he affected was that of 'simple workman.'

In fact he was not simple nor, strictly speaking, had he ever been a workman. His father had been a small but fairly prosperous tradesman, and Vukashin himself had been a bookkeeper in a timber warehouse during the early part of his political career. It had been a natural talent for accountancy and office organization rather than revolutionary ardour that had raised him first to the secretaryship of a trade union and later to a leadership of the party. He had a reputation for the kind of wit that makes a political statement in terms of some excretory or sexual function. He was a powerful man physically and was said to have once made a brutal assault on a colleague who had opposed him. But it was also said that the victim had been a boring speaker and unpopular and that the assault had been calculated quite coolly for its disturbing effect on the morale of other intransigent colleagues. He was himself a brusque, direct speaker and very effective with big audiences. 'What are the *real* facts behind this problem?' he would shout; and although he never answered such questions, the sturdy conviction with which he pretended to do so, and his way of enumerating his sentences so emphatically that they sounded like hammer strokes of logic, usually concealed the deception.

The prosecutor's self-effacing deference to him was so abject that it was not even amusing. From a ranting bully who at least existed, Dr Prochaska became suddenly no more than a disembodied, impersonal voice, a prompter who fed the witness with a short question and then waited until the speech in reply was over and another question was wanted from him.

'Minister Vukashin, in March of 1944 when the armistice negotiations began, what was the attitude of the prisoner, Deltchev?'

'Our policy was peace, immediate peace to save the country from devastation by reactionary-led forces seeking to continue their losing battle with our Soviet ally. Every hour of it meant another cottage, another farm destroyed, every day a fresh horror for our peasant workers in the frontier areas. Who could have said "Go on"? Not a man with heart and bowels! Only a blood-maddened beast. But there was such a creature. His name was Deltchev!'

'Minister Vukashin, in what ways did the prisoner Deltchev work against the peace?'

'It would be easier, Public Prosecutor, to tell the court in what ways he did *not* work against the peace, for then I could answer shortly: "in *no* way." From the beginning of the negotiations he used his position on the Committee to hinder their conclusion. You may ask why this was tolerated, why he was not immediately removed from his post. The answer to that is simple. We believed at that time that he was in misguided but honest doubt about the terms of the negotiations that were under discussion. We were a responsible group acting not for a defeated country—we were never defeated—but for a resurgent nation. The terms offered us by Russia, however, contained, as was natural in the circumstances, military clauses that involved our surrendering certain rights of government. The interpretation put upon them depended upon one thing and one thing only—whether or not Russia could be trusted. We of the People's Party did trust Russia, and in the event we have been justified. All the rights surrendered by us then have now been restored. The prisoner took a contrary view—or said that he did, for we know better now—and it was this view that he urged upon us as a justification for delay and for continuing his negotiations with the Anglo-Americans.'

'Did he contend that better terms would be obtained from them than from our Soviet ally?'

'No. The terms were no different in essence. They had been agreed to by the Foreign Ministers at the Moscow Conference of '43. According to the prisoner, what would be different was the way in which they would be enforced. Or so he said.'

'Minister Vukashin, did the prisoner take part in the discussions with Soviet representatives?'

'Very little. He was too busy licking the backsides of the Anglo-Americans.'

Laughter.

'Minister Vukashin, in presenting his arguments for negotiations with them, what advantages did the prisoner claim would follow?'

'He claimed so many advantages that you would have supposed us conquerors about to impose our will upon the defeated. But what were the facts at that time? First . . .'

The earphones softly droned out the translation, but above this sound his own voice persisted. It was loud and, in the harsh, penetrating quality of its lower notes, disquietingly aggressive. He claimed hostility as urgently as another might claim love, and to hate him was to submit to a seduction. In a way he was impressive.

The voice went on and the grotesque rubbish it talked was passively received in evidence. I watched the judges' faces as they listened.

The floodlights for the cameras were on all the time now. The day was warm, and soon, as the afternoon sun poured in through the high steel-framed windows, those in the lights began to sweat. Most of them wiped their heads frequently and fanned themselves; but the judges, sweltering in their black gowns and biretta-like caps, seemed unwilling to acknowledge their discomfort before the eyes of the cameras. They had been judges before the People's Party had come into power and it was known that all such appointments were under review by the Government. Later, perhaps, in a cool cinema at the Propaganda Ministry, the film would be examined by subtle, hostile men able to construe the wiping of hands or forehead as gestures of disrespect to the Minister and his evidence. No momentary relief from discomfort was worth that risk to the judges. Two of their older colleagues had already been dismissed for showing reluctance to preside at this trial. Now, behind the sweating impassivity of those who had not shown reluctance, there was the terrible anxiety of men who, having sacrificed their principles, fear that the sacrifice may after all go unrewarded.

Only the prisoner did not sweat. He sat with his hands in his jacket pockets and his eyes closed, the back of his white head resting against the wooden rail that separated the lawyers' tables from the body of the courtroom. His face was livid in the glare of the lights and he looked as if he might faint; but, strangely, he did not sweat. But for the pricking of your own skin you might have fancied that the heat of the place was an illusion and that all the perspiration you could see was simply a visible manifestation of collective guilt.

The afternoon crept on and the shadows moved slowly across the courtroom until there were only narrow strips of sunlight on the walls. There were no more than ten minutes to go before the day's adjournment when the 'incident' occurred.

Vukashin had almost completed his evidence and the prosecutor was asking him a series of questions about the meeting of the Committee at which it had been finally decided to accept the armistice terms.

'Minister Vukashin, what was the attitude of the prisoner when it was clear that the majority of the Committee favoured acceptance?'

'As always, he attempted to obstruct the wish of the majority. He repeated all his former arguments and, when these were rejected again by the rest of the Committee, he said that he had had further discussions with the Anglo-American representatives and that something might yet be done with them.'

'He gave the impression that *he* was making proposals to *them*?'

'He had always given that impression. But now in the heat of the moment he made a slip that revealed his true colours. He said that the Anglo-Americans were only waiting for the word and at the snap of his fingers they would come.'

At that moment a strange voice in the court said something loudly and sharply, and, in the dead silence that followed, the interpreter automatically translated:

'That is a lie.'

Deltchev had risen to his feet and was facing the witness box. His hands were still in his jacket pockets, but he was standing very straight.

Vukashin looked startled for a moment, then turned his head to the judges.

'The prisoner objects to the truth.'

The centre judge leaned forward. 'The prisoner will be silent.'

Deltchev took no notice. 'I do not object to the truth,' he said. 'Nor do I object to the fantastic perversions of the truth that the court has been listening to today, for no person in his senses will accept them. I do,

however, object to lies that attribute to me statements which I have never
made.'

The judge shouted angrily: 'Be silent. You will have an opportunity of
speaking later.'

'Will the Minister Vukashin be available to me for cross-examination?'

'Your counsel may examine the witness if he wishes to do so.'

'He does not propose to do so. He values his own skin too much.'

There was a commotion at this, and the thin, dark man whom I took to be
Stanoiev began to make some sort of appeal to the judges. As several others,
including Dr Prochaska, were speaking at the same time, the interpreter
became tongue-tied. One of the judges began to shout.

'The presiding judges call for silence,' said the interpreter.

Vukashin had been standing in the witness box looking on with a grim
smile. Now he raised a hand and, as the noise subsided, spoke: 'I have given
my evidence. Let him say what he wants.'

Deltchev faced him again. There was complete silence now. The
prisoner's voice was light but very clear and precise.

'Minister Vukashin,' he said, 'was it with the Committee's knowledge
that I made the proposal to the Anglo-American representatives in 1944
that we should fight a delaying action in the north?'

Vukashin hesitated a fraction of a second. 'Be careful how you answer,'
Deltchev put in quickly. 'The facts can be checked. The minutes of the
Committee still exist.'

Vukashin made an impatient gesture. 'I am aware of that.'

'Then you see the need for caution. Will you answer the question,
please?'

'The reply is not as simple as you try to suggest. The Committee was
aware that a proposal was made, but it was not aware that you had
instructions from your Anglo-American friends to make it appear that the
proposal came from the Committee.'

'Your answer is that I *was* authorized by the Committee to make the
proposal.'

'Yes, but . . .'

'Let me continue, Minister. If the Committee authorized the proposal
and if, as you say, the Anglo-American representatives wished it to be
made, will you explain then why they did not immediately accept it?'

'Do you please ask me to explain the actions of the Anglo-Americans.'

Laughter.

'It is not the actions of the Anglo-Americans I am asking you to explain,
but your own account of them.'

Vukashin turned angrily to the judges. 'I am here to give evidence, not to
answer political riddles. That is enough.'

'You have been very patient. The court thanks you, Minister. The
prisoner will be silent.'

Vukashin left the witness box and sat down. As he did so, Deltchev
turned with a pale smile to face the courtroom. 'The Minister is afraid to
answer,' he said.

It was at that point that Dr Prochaska made a foolish mistake. He had
been standing there impotent and forgotten during this exchange. He was

irritated. He was the prosecutor and yet matters had been taken out of his, the responsible, hands, and an important battle of words had taken place without him. More serious still, the Minister, whom he should have protected, had had the worst of the battle. Now he saw his chance of retrieving not only his own dignity but that of the Minister as well. Never once since the trial opened had Deltchev taken his hands from his pockets, and Dr Prochaska had found the fact irritating. He suddenly thought he saw just how he might humiliate the prisoner.

'Afraid?' he exclaimed derisively. 'The Minister is *afraid* to answer?' He gave a short laugh. 'It is not the Minister who is afraid. It is you, Deltchev! No wonder you seek to accuse and discredit the witnesses against you. You are in fear of your life. No wonder you tremble. No wonder you keep your hands in your pockets. Do you think we do not notice? Ah, but the people have eyes, Deltchev. You cannot deceive them forever. You may disguise your fear in other ways, but your trembling hands you dare not let us see. Come, show us your hand, Deltchev. Or else be silent while justice is done.'

In the breathless hush that descended, there was one single quickly suppressed giggle and then no sound but the fluttering of the cameras. The prosecutor had a hard, ugly little smile on his lips. At that moment he was not absurd. Vukashin looked down at his own hands, frowning. Deltchev stood quite still, his face expressionless. He was making up his mind.

Then he took his hands out of his pockets and held them out, palms downward, in front of him. They shook with a coarse tremor that must have been visible at the back of the court.

'The prisoner's hands are more truthful than his tongue,' said the prosecutor.

Without a glance in his direction Deltchev put his hands back in his pockets and raised his head.

'I speak,' he said loudly, 'to the members of the diplomatic corps present here and to the representatives of the foreign press.'

There was another commotion in the front of the court, and the prosecutor began to protest to the judges. The interpreter began to translate the protest and I took my earphones off. Others beside me were doing the same. Deltchev had spoken in German.

'You may have formed your own conclusions,' he went on, 'about the quality of the evidence that will be given by the prosecution in this court. In case you are in doubt, this demonstration will convince you. The evidence of my own hands has now been offered against me. I will explain what it is worth.'

With an elaborately satirical bow in the direction of the diplomatic and foreign-press sections, the prosecutor abandoned his protest and stood, his arms akimbo and an unsuccessful attempt at a smile on his face, looking up at the ceiling.

'I make no defence of myself in offering this explanation,' Deltchev was saying; 'my defence is in the safe hands of the prosecution.' He smiled faintly. 'But perhaps you will be interested in this fact. I give it to you merely as a point of interest.'

He paused and then went on very deliberately: 'Gentlemen, I am a diabetic and have been so for several years now. That has meant, of course, a careful diet balanced with injections of insulin. The amount of insulin I need is not great—twenty units in the morning and twenty at night. I can, of course, call medical witnesses to prove this. When I was first arrested, the prison doctor was authorized to supply me with insulin. He even increased the injections slightly to compensate for the change in diet. Five weeks ago I was moved to another part of the prison and was not allowed to see the prison doctor. For just over four weeks I have been without insulin. The symptoms of diabetes have therefore returned—thirst, fatigue and other disagreeable manifestations, which I shall not trouble you with. The trembling of my hands is part of my general weakness and debility. If the prosecutor had asked me to show you my knees, you would have seen that they also tremble.' He looked round at the prosecutor for a moment and then turned back to us. 'I think that if he had known of this illness he would not have drawn your attention to it in this way. It is no part of his task to create sympathy for me. I merely ask you to note that he makes wrong deductions even from facts. The fantasies that he will create from the falsehoods his case rests upon I leave to your imagination.'

Then he sat down.

The prosecutor said something quickly to the judges. The centre judge said something in reply. I put the earphones on again and caught the translation.

'The presiding judges rule that the remarks of the prisoner shall not be entered in the record, as they were made in a foreign language not intelligible to the court. The case is adjourned until tomorrow.'

The court rose.

When the judges had gone, Deltchev stepped down from the rostrum and with his two guards walked slowly toward the glazed doors. Nobody else in the court moved. They watched him. At the door he paused and looked back. Then with a small, friendly nod he turned away again and went on through the doors.

I looked at Pashik. He was standing stiffly and awkwardly as if caught in the act of rising. He did not seem to notice his discomfort. 'A good man, Mr Foster,' he said to me softly; 'in his way a great man.'

But I did not pay much attention to him. Even now I can remember everything that went through my mind during the next half-hour. I was very shocked by what I had seen and heard and full of hatred for the People's Party regime. I think that if I had met Dr Prochaska in the corridor outside the courtroom I might have hit him. But soon I began to think more reasonably.

Nobody, I thought, could share the experience I had just had without also sharing my passionate indignation at what was being done in that sunny courtroom. If I could convey the scene with even a tenth of the impact it had in reality, I would arouse a storm of anger that might damage the regime appreciably. And then an idea began to form in my mind of how I might write about the Deltchev trial.

This, I thought suddenly, was more than just the crooked trial of a politician by his more powerful opponents. Here, epitomized, was the eternal conflict between the dignity of mankind and the brutish stupidity of the swamp. Deltchev, sick and alone, knowing that nothing could save him from a verdict and a sentence already decided upon, was yet prepared to go on fighting for the truth he believed in. Dimitrov at the Reichstag fire trial had fought for his life and won. Deltchev's life was already forfeit, but he was fighting none the less and might win a greater victory. And the fight was of his own choosing. Months back he could have escaped abroad and made the Government's task easy. He had not done so. Long-forgotten sentences began to run through my mind. '*Will you then flee from well-ordered cities and virtuous men? and is existence worth having on these terms? Or will you go to them without shame, and talk to them, Socrates? And what will you say to them? What you say here about virtue and justice and institutions and laws being the best things among men? Would that be decent of you? Surely not? . . . Will there be no one to remind you that in your old age you were not ashamed to violate the most sacred laws from a miserable desire of a little more life?*' . . . *This, dear Crito, is the voice I seem to hear murmuring in my ears, like the sound of a flute in the ears of a mystic. . . .*

I was deeply moved. I was also beginning to enjoy myself.

And then I got back to my hotel, and Petlarov was waiting in the corridor.

We went into my room and I told him what had happened.

He nodded coolly when I had finished. 'Oh yes. Poor Yordan. He is certainly not strong. But how foolish of them not to tell Prochaska how the victim was being prepared! But we may expect foolishness. You see, they have always been able to rely before upon the folly of others. Now that they have to rely on themselves, their deficiencies are revealed. Of course an incident like that will make no difference to the outcome of the trial.'

'No, but it will make a great difference to the comments on the trial in the Atlantic countries.'

'The comments of the West did not save Petkov or Mindszenty. I think it is interesting, however, in quite a different way.' He smiled thinly. 'Why do you think Yordan made this demonstration? What did he hope to gain by it?'

'He saw an opportunity of hitting back and he took it. Surely, that's obvious. It was splendid.'

'He saw an opportunity and took it, certainly. What exactly did he say finally–the last two sentences?'

I had scribbled down Deltchev's words as he had said them. I read the last two sentences again. ' "I merely ask you to note that he makes wrong deductions even from facts. The fantasies that he will make from the falsehoods his case rests upon I leave to your imagination." '

Petlarov showed his white teeth. 'What a clever lawyer Yordan is!' he said. 'Do you not see what he has done, Herr Foster? Oh, certainly he has won the sympathy of the foreign diplomatists and press representatives, and that is very nice; but what else?'

'He made the prosecutor look a fool.'

'He did more. Consider. He makes the speech in German. Why?'

'Obviously so that he would be allowed to speak. The interpreters didn't relay what he said, of course. As far as the public was concerned, he was unintelligible. Obviously it was the American and British representatives who mattered to him, and Vukashin and the judges and Prochaska didn't want to antagonize them unnecessarily by shutting him up. If they don't care much anyway about Western opinion, they could afford to let him talk.'

'If it was the American and British who mattered, why did he not speak in English? Yordan speaks very good English.'

'Oh.'

'The educated persons of most small nations need a second language to their own. With us it is mostly German. Many of the party members in that courtroom speak German, and some of them are not unfriendly to Yordan. Those were the persons who interested him. What he wanted to do—and what he has done, perhaps—is to discredit the prosecution's evidence in advance.'

'That's not difficult. It discredits itself.'

'So far, yes. But perhaps Yordan was wiser than we yet know.'

'I don't understand you.'

'It is quite simple.' He leaned forward with a chilling smile. 'You see, Herr Foster,' he said, 'some of the evidence against him may not discredit itself. Some of it may be true.'

Chapter Seven

Deltchev's house was on the edge of the city in an old residential quarter behind the Presidential Park. Petlarov had drawn a sketch map for me of the way there, and after an early dinner I walked to it from the hotel. There was a slight breeze and the air seemed cooler. The main streets and cafés were full of people, the women in their shapeless dresses and cheap wedge shoes, the men in their cloth caps, with their jackets over their arms, and their shirts undone at the neck; but beyond the park, where there were few shops and scarcely any cafés, the streets were almost deserted and the only sounds came from the radios in apartment houses.

I found the quarter without difficulty. It was off the Boulevard Dragutin; six quiet streets, paved for a short distance from the boulevard and then ending casually in a hillside wasteland of scrub and tamarisks. The streets were lined with plane trees and with square, solid old houses, each isolated within its own courtyard by a high wall with a heavy wooden door in it. The spaces between the walls of adjacent houses formed narrow lanes, some of which connected parallel streets, but mostly were shut off by tall iron gates and choked with wild vines.

The numbers on the houses were on blue enamel plates over the wall doors, and when I came to the right street I saw that Deltchev's house must be the last in it. But the setting sun was in my eyes and I did not see the guards outside the house until I was nearly upon them.

They were standing in the shadow of the plane tree just by the door. The trunk of this tree was scarred and the lower branches were leafless; the grenade of American manufacture must have exploded just by it. The guards' faces turned toward me as I approached.

They were in the uniform of what I referred to in my own mind as the 'military police,' though perhaps '*gardes mobiles*' would have contained a more accurate comparison. They wore the same grey-green uniform as the courtroom guards; but these had rifles instead of machine pistols, and instead of tunics they had blouses bunched in at the waist by greasy leather belts with ammunition pouches. From a difference in their badges I guessed that they were a corporal and a private. They were young, bronzed, and rather stupid-looking. Our eyes met as I came up, and I nodded, but they did not reply in any way or make any movement to intercept me. I stopped by the door, looked up at the plate to confirm that I was at the right house, and then reached up to pull a bell handle bracketed to the wall.

The next moment I received a violent blow on the shoulder. The shock of it made me gasp. I lurched against the door and twisted round. The private had his rifle raised to prod me again. The corporal had his rifle pointed at my stomach, and his finger was on the trigger. I raised my hands.

The corporal shouted something and took a pace backwards. I moved away from the door. I started to say in German that I did not understand what he was saying, but he shouted again, and this time I caught the word for 'papers.' With the heel of my hand I indicated my breast pocket and said: '*Papieren.*' The private jabbed the muzzle of his rifle into my ribs. Then the corporal, stepping forward, tore open my jacket, snatched out my wallet, and stepped smartly away from me.

It all happened in a few seconds. I was absurdly shaken. I must have looked it, for the private grinned at me then in quite a friendly way as if my discomfort were a tribute to his efficiency. The corporal was frowning over my press permit. He looked at the photograph on it and he looked at me. Then he folded the permit, put it back in the wallet, and, coming up to me, began to speak very slowly and distinctly, waving the wallet under my nose to emphasize what he was saying. It was clearly an admonishment. I nodded. Then he gave me back the wallet, saluted negligently, and moved away. Behind me the private stretched up and pulled the bell handle. A bell clanged inside the courtyard. Then he, too, went back to his post under the tree.

They watched me as I waited, the private still grinning, the corporal frowning. My shoulder hurt abominably and I badly wanted to rub it; but a curious shame and perhaps, too, a fear of pleasing them prevented my doing so. I was disconcerted by these unfamiliar and, I could not help thinking, rather childish emotions. I had behaved stupidly and had been roughly treated and humiliated in consequence; but it was no use; my hatred of them welled up like a sickness.

Then I heard footsteps crossing the courtyard inside: the clacking, slithering footsteps of wooden-soled sandals without heel straps. There was a pause and a rattling of bolts. Then the door opened a few inches and an old woman looked out. She had a face like a walnut shell, with woolly grey hair and bright little eyes very deep in their sockets.

She looked past me to the guards.

'I would like to see Madame Deltchev,' I said in German.

She snapped out a reply I did not understand.

From behind me the corporal shouted something. I looked round in time to see him raise his rifle threateningly. She snapped again, then very slowly she opened the door. I heard the private laugh as I went inside.

The wall of the courtyard was about fourteen feet high and decorated all the way round with big frescoes of pastoral scenes: peasants dancing, a young man wooing a dairymaid, a village wedding. They were crude and conventional like the decorations on Russian toys. The predominant colours were cobalt blue, terracotta, and ochre, but in some places the paint had flaked so badly that only a faint discolouration of the stones showed where it had been. The floor of the courtyard was paved with square flags, on which stood potted plants of various kinds, some of them in brilliant flower. Out of a square space in the flagstones grew a big cherry tree. Beyond it, in a corner, there was a neat woodpile, with vine poles leaning against the wall by it.

The old woman had stopped to bolt the door again, but now she straightened up and faced me grimly, her arms folded, her eyes bright and full of malice. She said something that must have been: 'Well, now you're in, what do you want?' In German I replied that I did not understand. She did not understand that. I got out Petlarov's letter addressed to Madame Deltchev and gave it to her. She took it in her clawed, arthritic hands and looked without comprehension at the writing. I guessed that she could not read. She looked up at me suspiciously for a moment, then held up a hand for me to wait and clacked away round the side of the house.

I rubbed my shoulder and looked at the front of the house. It was about twenty feet from the wall, a blank symmetrical façade in grey stone with white painted metal shutters fastened over all the windows. Double steps curved up to the front door, which was flanked by potted azaleas and looked as if it were rarely opened. I heard the old woman's footsteps on a bare floor inside and a distant murmur of voices. Then for a bit there was silence. I was a small boy again, calling for a friend with rich parents.

The breeze stirred the leaves of the cherry tree and there were other footsteps inside the house. A moment or two later the front door opened and a girl came out. At the top of the steps she paused.

'Herr Foster?'

'Yes.'

She came down the steps with the preoccupied frown of a busy person whose time is being wasted. She was in the early twenties, dark and very pale, with high Slavic cheekbones. It was an intelligent face, too, but had an expression of bland self-assurance too determined to be real.

'I am Katerina Deltchev,' she said.

'I'm glad to meet you.' She had only a remote facial resemblance to her father.

'What is it you wish, Herr Foster?'

'To see your mother. Perhaps Petlarov's letter did not explain that.' I knew that it did.

'At the moment I am afraid that is quite impossible. She is very upset, you understand.'

'Naturally. Is she specially upset today?'

'Please?'

'I am sure that these are all terrible days for her. I merely wondered if the proceedings today had specially affected her.'

'I don't think so.'

'Then perhaps you would ask her when I may see her, Fräulein.'

'I can tell you anything you wish to know, Herr Foster.' She smiled, but not very warmly. 'Would you like a drink?'

'No, thank you. Are you quite sure that your mother wishes to be protected from someone who may be of help to her?'

'I don't understand.'

'If you will take Petlarov's letter to her, I'm sure she will explain to you.'

She stopped smiling. 'My mother does not see journalists.'

'So I believe. That is why Petlarov gave me the letter to her.'

She hesitated, then pressed her lips together. 'Very well. Please wait.'

She turned on her heel and went into the house again. She was wearing white shorts, a *maillot*, and sandals. I felt a little sorry for her. It is difficult, even for an attractive woman, to make a dignified exit in shorts.

I waited a few more minutes. The light was going. Then the front door opened again and this time the old woman came out. She beckoned to me and I followed her.

Inside, there was a large hallway, with curtained doorways on either side and a slippery hardwood floor. There was a radiator against the wall between two of the doors. It was all very clean and smelt of polish. Motioning me to follow her, the old woman climbed up the stairs. On the landing there was a shuttered window, and by the half-light filtering through the slits in the metal I could see a passage running along the width of the house. The old woman turned to the right along it and, going to a door at the end, scratched on the panel. There was a voice from within. She opened the door.

Red light from the setting sun streamed into the passage through tall unshuttered windows in the room beyond, and as I came to the doorway I could see the bare khaki hills outside the city.

The windows gave on to a wooden terrace with an awning and vines growing over trellises at the sides. There was an iron table there with books on it and some cane chairs.

The room was large and filled with massive red plush drawing-room furniture of the kind made for the wealthy tradesmen of pre-Sarajevo Vienna. On the walls there were heavy gilt mirrors and girandoles, and coloured prints in polished wood and ormolu frames. Overhead there was a large gilt electric chandelier. The upholstery was red cut velvet. In winter the room would be quite cheerless, but now with the windows opened on the terrace and with the gilt touched by the glow of the sunset it had a certain richness and warmth.

As I came into the room, a woman sitting just out of the sun by the far window put a book down and rose to her feet.

I had a slight shock.

She was someone who had once been a provincial schoolteacher. Petlarov had said: 'Perhaps if she had married me instead of Yordan, I should have become a minister.' There was the diabetic husband under sentence of death. There were my pilgrimage to this old house to see her and my interview with the attractive young woman whose mother did not see journalists. There was the quiet shuttered house, the smell of furniture polish. Out of all these things an image of the Madame Deltchev I would find had been composed in my mind's eye. She had been an old woman with white hair, in a wheel chair perhaps or even bedridden; a wiry matriarch with the evidence of her youthful beauty still discernible in her face, and the vitality, which had served the young lawyer and then driven the ambitious politician, still there in the brightness of her glance and the impatient directness of her speech. How this irascible crone had borne a daughter twenty years ago or what disease now immobilized her my untidy imagination had not troubled to inquire. What I had been prepared for in Madame Deltchev was a female counterpart of the grey, shaking man I had seen in court that day and with whose mystery and fate I was preoccupied; and I had visualized no other.

What I saw was a slim, erect woman of about fifty in a striped silk blouse and well-cut skirt, and with sleek, black hair only slightly touched with grey. Her forehead was broad and high and she had gentle, very intelligent eyes. The bold regular features, which her daughter had inherited, were in her more masculine, but her complexion was perfect.

She smiled politely as she greeted me. 'Herr Foster, I'm so sorry that you were kept waiting outside.'

'It's very kind of you to see me.'

'Please sit down.' She sat down again herself. She had a small lace fan that she fluttered unobtrusively by the side of her face farthest from me. 'My daughter had the best of intentions, but she did not understand Petlarov's motives.'

The girl stood behind the chair. She did not look at me.

'With Petlarov,' she said angrily, 'there is only one motive. He does only what he is paid for.'

Her mother said quietly: 'Please get us some tea, Katerina.'

Katerina laughed shortly. 'English journalists drink only whisky and soda, Mother. It is traditional.' She went over to the samovar. 'Isn't that right, Herr Foster?'

Madame Deltchev frowned and said something quickly in their own language. The girl made a sharp retort. Madame Deltchev smoothed her hair.

'I think that Herr Foster will excuse you, Katerina, if you wish to leave us to talk,' she said calmly.

The girl stood still looking at her for a moment, her face dark with anger. Then with a bang she put down the tea glass she had been holding and walked out of the room.

Her mother rose and, going over to the samovar, began to pour the tea herself.

'All nerves in this house,' she said, 'are greatly strained, Herr Foster.'

'Yes, I can imagine.'

'For my daughter it is perhaps most difficult,' she went on; 'unfortunately she is in political disagreement with my husband. She sympathizes with that section of the Agrarian Socialists which blames Yordan for the present situation. So her love for her father is in conflict with her feelings toward the man who betrayed his party. It is difficult for her and I cannot help much.' She handed me some tea. 'You see, Herr Foster, it is not without reason that I avoid speaking to journalists. I do not guard my tongue. The regime would be glad to use the fact that Yordan's own children oppose him politically. But Petlarov says that you are friendly and to be trusted.'

'I was wondering, madame, what there was about Petlarov's motives to be understood.'

She took her tea back to her chair. 'Petlarov is a good friend,' she said. 'Even after his disagreement with Yordan he remained a friend. When he was released from prison I was able to see him for a short while and I asked his advice about the press. We were already an object of interest, you see. He told me that I should see no one until he sent somebody who could be trusted.'

'That is very flattering, but, frankly, I do not see the reason for his choice.'

'Did you not read his letter?' She held it up.

'I'm afraid I couldn't.'

'Oh yes, the language.' She looked at the letter. 'He says that you are going to write a series of articles about the trial and sentence which will be published in America and England. He says that your articles will be well written and acceptable and that although they will be politically naïve—' She broke off and looked at me apologetically. 'He means, of course, that he does not regard you as primarily a political person.'

'He's right.'

She smiled. 'So many of our circle would be offended.' She returned to the letter. '. . . although they will be politically naïve, their simplification of obvious issues and the evident sincerity of their indignation will be admirably suited to the campaign against the outcome of the trial.' She folded the letter. 'Petlarov is interesting, is he not?'

'Very.'

'So very wise, and yet not a whole man.' She picked up her tea reflectively. 'His nerves were never strong enough for power.'

'Unlike your husband's.'

She looked up, a little sharply, as if I had interrupted a train of thought. 'Yes, let us talk about Yordan,' she said; 'and about the trial. That is why you are here.'

'I don't wish to distress you, but I should like you to know about something that happened today.'

She nodded. 'Yordan made one of his demonstrations. I already know about it.'

'It wasn't in the official bulletin.'

'No. Every evening since we have been under house arrest an old friend of our family has come to see us. Every evening he is searched by the sentries and every evening the sentries find some money in his handkerchief. They let him pass.'

'I see. The demonstration was very moving.'

'Yes, I was told that. It is a great relief. After this they will not dare to withhold his insulin injections.'

There was a curious lack of emotion in the way she said it. We might have been discussing a common acquaintance.

'Do you think that was all he hoped to gain from it?'

'What else is there, Herr Foster? Please do not think that you must spare my feelings. Yordan will be condemned.'

'Petlarov had another explanation. He said that your husband seized the chance of discrediting the evidence of the prosecution.'

'Yordan is a good lawyer.'

'From the way your husband used his opportunity Petlarov deduced that there might be some evidence against him that can only be dealt with by discrediting it.'

She looked slightly puzzled. 'Evidence that can only be dealt with by discrediting it?' she repeated.

'Yes.'

She shrugged. 'There will no doubt be many things too absurd even for denial.'

'There is no true evidence that can be brought to support any of the charges?'

She looked surprised. 'Of course not.'

'No facts at all that could be twisted into evidence of corrupt negotiations in 1944?'

'Most facts can be twisted, Herr Foster.'

'But in this case not credibly?'

'No.'

'That would be true also of the alleged association with the Officer Corps Brotherhood?'

'Doubly so. The idea is absurd. My husband was the man primarily responsible for the destruction of the Brotherhood.'

'You think that false evidence will be brought?'

'They have no alternative,' she said with a touch of impatience.

'Then it will be easy for your husband to disprove the evidence?'

'If he is allowed to do so, yes. But I do not follow the trend of your questions, Herr Foster. The charges are obviously absurd.'

'That is what troubles me, madame. If there is no vestige of a case to support them, they are too absurd. As Petlarov points out, if they had to fake evidence, there were less fantastic charges available.'

'Petlarov is sometimes too clever. It is perfectly simple. Association with the Brotherhood is a capital offence and today also a disgrace.'

'You do not expect to be surprised by any of the evidence?'

'Nothing that the People's Party can contrive would surprise me.'

For a moment or two I sipped my tea. There was something difficult I wanted to say. She was sitting attentively waiting for me to go on. The sun was dying and in the faint after-light her face was astonishingly youthful. I might have been looking at the young schoolteacher whom the lawyer Deltchev had married, the young woman of Greek family whose lips may have had even then the same gentle, inflexible determination that I saw now.

'Madame Deltchev,' I said, 'when you were speaking of your daughter you referred to your husband as the man who betrayed his party.'

'I was representing him as my daughter sees him.'

'But you do not see him that way?'

'I understand him better than that, Herr Foster.'

'That might not be a reply to the question, madame.'

'Is the question important for your understanding of the trial?'

'I do not know your husband. It seems to me important that I should.'

She sat back in her chair. She had just put her tea down on the table beside her, and her hands rested lightly on the chair arms. There they could reveal nothing.

'You saw my husband in court today. You could see the evidence of most of the qualities you wish to know about–his courage, his cleverness, his sense of timing, his determination. One thing the circumstances would not let you see–his absolute integrity, and I, who know his heart, will vouch for that.'

The light was very dim now, and in the shadow of the chair her face was difficult to see. Then she leaned forward and I saw her smile.

'And in case you wish to ask me about his weaknesses, Herr Foster, I will tell you. He cannot accept people as they are, but only as his reason dictates they should be. Feeling he suspects, reason never, and the idea that in him the two may be connected he rejects completely. Therefore he is often mistaken about people and just as often about himself.'

I was silent for a moment. Then I got up to go.

'May I come and see you again, Madame?'

'Of course, Herr Foster, please do.' Then she paused. 'I shall in any case be here,' she added.

'Afterwards, if you are allowed to do so, will you leave the country?'

'When Yordan is dead, do you mean?'

'When there is no more to be done here.'

'Then I shall go on living behind our wall,' she said. 'Did you not notice our wall?'

'It's very fine.'

'You will see such walls round most of our old houses. In Bulgaria and in Greece, in Yugoslavia, in all the countries of Europe that have lived under Turkish rule it is the same. To put a wall round your house then was not only to put up a barrier against the casual violence of foreign soldiers, it was in a way to deny their existence. Then our people lived behind their walls in small worlds of illusion that did not include an Ottoman Empire. Sometimes, as if to make the illusion more complete, they painted the walls with scenes of national life; but only on the inside, for that was where life was lived. Now that we are again inside our walls, the habits of our parents and our childhood return quietly like long-lost pets. I surprise them in myself. This room, for instance. Since Yordan's arrest it has been the only room on this floor of the house that has had the shutters open in the daytime. My feelings tell me it is better so. But why? No reason except that from all the other windows on this floor one can see the street.'

'Isn't it dangerous to deny the street?'

'For my children, yes. For me, no, for I shall not try to impose my private world upon the real. My son Philip is a student in Geneva. He will be a lawyer like his father. Already he promises to be brilliant, and Switzerland is a better place for study than here. I hope to make it possible for Katerina to join him there.' She paused. 'Yes, by all means come again, Herr Foster. When you wish.' She pressed a bell-push. 'Rana will unbolt the doors and show you out. I will tell her also to admit you if you come again.'

'Thank you.'

We shook hands and said good night. As I went to the door I heard the old woman's sandals flapping along the passage outside.

'Herr Foster.'

'Yes, madame?'

'It might be misleading to pay too much attention to Petlarov's views.'

'I will remember what you say. Good night.'

'Good night.'

The door opened and a shaft of electric light from the passage struck across the darkened room. I glanced back; I wanted to see her face again in the light; but she had turned away.

I went past the old woman into the passage and waited while she was given her instructions. Then she shut the door of the room and led the way downstairs.

The girl was standing in the hall. She was waiting for me. She had changed into a blouse and skirt.

'Herr Foster, may I speak to you a moment?'

'Of course.' I stopped.

She said something to the old woman, who shrugged and went away.

'I will show you out myself,' the girl said; 'but I wanted to speak to you first. I wanted to apologize to you for my behaviour.'

'That's all right.'

'It was unforgivable.'

She looked so solemn that I smiled.

Her pale cheeks coloured slightly. 'I have something to ask of you, Herr Foster.'

'Yes, Fräulein?'

She dropped her voice. 'Tell me, please. Were you searched by the guards when you came in?'

'No. One of them pushed me in the back with his rifle and they looked at my press permit, but that's all.'

'A foreign press permit. Ah, yes.' Her eyes became intent. 'Herr Foster, I have a favour to ask of you.' She paused, watching to see how I took it.

'What is it you want me to do?'

'To deliver a letter for me.'

'What letter?'

She took a letter from her blouse pocket.

'Can't you post it?'

'I am not permitted. Besides—' She hesitated.

'You just want me to post it for you?'

'To deliver it, Herr Foster.'

'Why can't I post it?'

'There is internal censorship.'

'Where is it to be delivered?'

'Inside the city, Herr Foster,' she said eagerly. 'Near the station.'

'Who is it to?'

She hesitated again. 'A young man,' she said.

'Supposing I'm caught with it?'

'You will not be, Herr Foster. Rana said that when she opened the door the guards were friendly to you. Please, Herr Foster.'

I thought for a moment of the guards and of their friendliness. The muscles in my shoulder had stiffened slightly.

'All right, Fräulein. A pleasure.'

'Thank you, Herr Foster.'

I took the letter and glanced at the envelope. The address was in block letters and quite clear. I put it in my pocket.

Her smile was replaced suddenly by a look of anxiety. 'When will you deliver it?'

'Tomorrow sometime. When I can.'

She would have liked to ask me to deliver it that night, but I was not going to do that. I made as if to go.

'Thank you,' she said again. 'I will show you out now if you wish.'

She had a small hand-lamp. We went out and across the dark courtyard to the door in the wall. She undid the bolts.

'Good night, Herr Foster,' she whispered, and then, standing behind the door so that she could not be seen from outside, she opened it.

The beam of a powerful flashlight shone in my face, blinding me. I stepped through the wall, and the door closed behind my back. I stood still.

'*Papieren*,' said a remembered voice.

I got out my wallet and opened it with the press permit showing. The private was holding the flashlight. The corporal came into the beam of it. He glanced at the permit without touching it and then, smiling at me grimly, he nodded and with his thumb motioned me on my way. He said something and the private laughed. They were pleased that I had so quickly learned my lesson.

It was only as I walked away up the street and the beating of my heart began to return to normal that I realized that, for a moment or two, while the light had been shining on my face and while I had wondered if they might be going to search me after all, I had been very frightened. I fingered the pocket with the letter. It crackled faintly. I smiled to myself. I was childishly pleased. I did not know that I had just performed one of the most foolish actions of my life.

Chapter Eight

As usual now, I had breakfast with Pashik.

'Last night, Mr Foster,' he said, 'I telephoned your hotel.'

'I was out.'

'Yes. It does not matter.' In his brown eyes was the faint hostility of the lover determined not to be possessive. 'It was to tell you that Monsieur Brankovitch, the Minister of Propaganda, has called a foreign-press conference for this evening. We, of course, have been invited.'

'Oh?' What Petlarov had said about the tactics of the Propaganda Ministry came into my mind.

'Monsieur Brankovitch will speak and also answer questions,' said Pashik solemnly. 'It will be very interesting. The food and drink will be excellent.'

'And there will be a collection taken for the poor of the parish.'

'I beg pardon.'

'Nothing. A bad joke.'

'The conference will be in the state rooms of the Ministry at six o'clock.'

'Good.'

He dabbed his bread in his coffee. 'Have you seen Petlarov again, Mr Foster?'

'Yes. I thought you'd rather not know about it.' For a moment I wondered if I should also tell him that I had been to see Madame Deltchev, and then decided not to.

'As long as there is no indiscretion, Mr Foster.'

'He comes privately to my hotel room. The reception clerk does not know him.'

He sighed unhappily. 'No doubt he will be discreet for his own sake. Is he still of interest to you?'

'Yes. He is an intelligent man, don't you think?'

'If he had used his intelligence, Mr Foster, I should be more sympathetic towards him.'

'You mean if he had played ball with the regime?'

'Of course. That is the realistic attitude.'

We went off to the trial.

That day, the third, six witnesses were heard. All of them had been members of the Committee of National Unity, and all, except one, were members of the People's Party. The exception was a man named Lipka, and he was a member of the anti-Deltchev section of the Agrarian Socialists.

For the most part, the evidence consisted of repetitions of the assertions made by Vukashin the day before. A mass of documents, including the minutes of the Committee meetings for the critical period, was produced, and there was a great deal of pseudo-legal fuss about which documents could and which could not be admitted as exhibits. The minutes were naturally well to the fore. As minutes they were quite often worse than useless, but as ammunition for the prosecutor they were just the thing. I remember one typical item: 'After some discussion the Committee agreed that Y. Deltchev should meet again with the Anglo-American repre-sentatives and urge them to delay the final decision on the proposals previously made.' The prosecutor's witnesses declared that the 'discussion' in question had been an effort by Deltchev and his henchmen to stampede the Committee into accepting a set of Anglo-American proposals it had not even seen and that the Committee's decision had made Deltchev 'grind his teeth with rage.' The judges had a word or two to say and even the defendant's counsel, Stanoiev, felt it safe to join in this sort of argument. At one point, indeed, there was a fair simulation of a legal battle between the two advocates—a battle between two clowns with rubber swords—and, in the approved fashion, high words were exchanged.

The only effective witness was Lipka. He was one of those angry, embittered men who bear the news of their defeat in their faces; prepared always for hostility, they succeed in provoking no more than weary impatience. A talentless but ambitious man, he had been an Agrarian Socialist deputy for many years without achieving office, and his membership on the Committee had seemed to him the long-awaited recognition of his worth and the beginning of his period of fulfilment. In fact, his value to the unconstitutional Committee had resided simply in his status as an elected deputy, and when posts in the Provisional Government were being allotted he had been passed over without a thought. From that moment he had nursed an almost pathological hatred of Deltchev. At one time that hatred had been something over which people smiled and shrugged. Now, at last, the People's Party had turned it to account. His mode of attack was stupid but damaging.

Most of those whose work is directly related to the moods and behaviour of the public are inclined to refer to it on occasion in disparaging, even insulting terms. But, while a gibe at popular stupidity from a harassed bus conductor may be amusing, the same gibe from the mouth of a leading politician has, for many, an uglier sound. What Lipka did was to quote Deltchev's private comments on various matters and contrast them with public utterances made by him at the same time.

'Papa' Deltchev had made a speech officially regretting an incident in which some peasants, misunderstanding or ignoring a Red Army order to keep out of a certain area, had been shot down by Russian sentries. In private he had said: 'It might not be a bad thing if a few more of the damn fools were shot.' After a speech congratulating the farmers on their public-spirited efforts to send more food to the towns 'Papa' Deltchev had said privately: 'Thank God, they've had sense enough at last to find the black market.' On his own proposals for dealing with the fuel shortage 'Papa' Deltchev had remarked: 'And if they're still cold we can always print a few more copies of the regulations for them to burn.'

There were altogether about a dozen examples given of the prisoner's 'contemptuous disregard of the welfare of the people whose interests he pretended to have at heart.' No doubt there were, as Lipka claimed, many others that could have been quoted. The muttered asides of an overworked minister of state grappling with administrative chaos are unlikely to be distinguished for their sweetness or reason, and if he is an impatient man with crude notions of humour, they may be better forgotten. Certainly they cannot fairly be used as evidence of his true mind and intentions.

In his only interruption of the day Deltchev made this point himself. He said: 'The doctor called out in the middle of a cold night may privately curse all mankind, but that curse does not prevent his doing his best for the patient.'

This remark was immediately excluded from the record as irrelevant. It had its effect in court, but I was beginning to see that it was not in the court that Deltchev was being tried.

Petlarov's comments were not reassuring.

'After sitting for three days in that courtroom,' he said, 'you may realize that not one single piece of evidence that could be called evidence in a civilized court of law has been offered in support of the charges and that the only piece of sense uttered has been supplied by the prisoner in his own defence. And yet already much damage has been done. The grocer I now visit again–thanks to you, my friend–is an intelligent man and a supporter of Deltchev. He detests the People's Party and suspects what he reads in the controlled press. Yet the trial is important to him, and as he cannot attend in person, he must read the official reports in the newspapers. He reads with great suspicion, of course, and he discounts much of what he reads. But where is his standard of measurement? How can he discriminate? He reads that Minister Vukashin's evidence proves conclusively certain accusations against Deltchev. Can he ask by what rules of evidence Vukashin's statements are held to constitute a proof of anything except their own dishonesty? Of course not. He is a cautious man and hard to convince, but when I ask him today what he thinks, he is uneasy and does not like to meet my eye. "Evidently," he says to me, "there was much evil that we did not know about. Even if these pigs must find out, it is best that we know. We are in a mess all right." And you know, Herr Foster, for the Vukashins and the Brankovitches, that is success. The disillusioned do not fight.'

'I thought that it was the possible truth of some of the allegations that was worrying you.'

'The foreign press is not so easily disturbed by official bulletins as my grocer. What did Madame have to say about the Brotherhood?'

'She said quite confidently that the charges were absurd.'

'Did you believe her?'

'I believe she sincerely thinks they are absurd.'

'You were impressed, eh?'

'Yes. She said she thought you were being over-clever.'

'It is possible. I hope so. But remember that the only parts of the indictment which make statements that can be proved or disproved are those referring to the Brotherhood. You may create a haze of misrepresentation to prove that a man had evil intentions and cast doubts on his denials; but if you claim that on a certain date he went to a certain place and saw a certain person and he can prove that he did not, you are lost. Because the court invites your contempt, do not suppose that Prochaska and Brankovitch are fools.'

'What does Katerina Deltchev do?'

'She was an art student.'

'Was?'

'Is, for all I know. But of course she cannot attend classes at present.' He looked at my wrist watch. 'It is time for you to go. You must not miss Brankovitch.'

I went to the press conference in a gloomy frame of mind.

The Ministry of Propaganda occupied one of the wings of what had once been the royal palace. It had been built, during a period of national prosperity toward the end of the eighteenth century, to the design of an Italian architect who had seen Versailles. Only a quarter of the building planned had been completed, but the resultant structure was imposing and quite large enough to contain three ministries and the national bank. The Propaganda Minister's press conference took place in a large state room with a painted ceiling and two vast chandeliers. Chairs had been ranged in a semicircle round the marquetry desk at which the Minister was to stand. To one side there was a long table arranged as a buffet, with napkins covering the food on it.

Among the American and British correspondents Brankovitch was known as Creeping Jesus; he had a peculiar way of walking with his head and shoulders slightly in front of the rest of his body while his arms remained at a position of attention at his sides. By the French correspondents it was said that the posture was imposed upon him, as, in his imagination, Brankovitch carried two portfolios under his arms: that of his own Ministry on one side and that of the head of the Government on the other. He was a pale, dark man with a massive head and supercilious eyes. A graduate of Warsaw University, he had once been a mining engineer and his connection with politics had begun with pamphleteering. He had made a name for himself before the war as the arch-opponent of the foreign oil companies. He was a clever, ambitious man who never missed a chance of referring most emphatically to his loyalty to and admiration of Vukashin. There were many jokes made about these fulsome references to his leader; but it was said that, while he did not laugh at the jokes when they were reported to him, neither did he frown. It was believed that Vukashin disliked him personally but respected his judgment.

There were about sixty persons in the room; about half of us were foreigners. Brankovitch came in briskly, followed by two male secretaries bearing files and notebooks, and those who had been standing about talking took their seats. Brankovitch waited, looking round, until the movements had ceased. Then he began.

'Gentlemen of the press,' he said, 'I have invited you to meet me here with three objects in mind. First, I wish to help you as far as possible in your work by giving you certain information necessary to your understanding of the evidence soon to be given in the criminal trial you are reporting. Next, I wish to give you an opportunity of asking me questions on matters of fact, and also'–he smiled slightly–'on matters of opinion to which you may feel you already know the answers. Thirdly, I wished for the pleasure of renewing acquaintance with those of you I already know and of meeting those I don't know. But business before pleasure, as the English say. I will speak briefly and then there will be time for questions.'

He glanced at his watch. He had a sort of brusque amiability that was not displeasing; he did not much care what we thought of him or mind if his amiability were not reciprocated. He was the busy man prepared to waste a little time on fools and so, logically, indifferent to foolishness.

'Let me tell you,' he said, 'about the Officer Corps Brotherhood; not about its origins–I feel sure you know about those–but about its later activities and its methods. Terrorist societies are not recent institutions. Most countries have suffered from them. Many countries, including the United States of America, still do suffer from them occasionally. It is the duty of all civilized governments, when these occasions arise, to seek out and destroy the criminals. It is the duty, I say; yet, of course, the duty is not always performed. Sometimes the government is itself terrorized. In other cases the government may sympathize with the terrorists' aims and secretly wish them well. I need hardly tell you that the Government of the People's Party is neither intimidated by nor in any degree sympathetic to the Officer

Corps Brotherhood. We will not tolerate crime of any sort. The workman who kills his mate in a moment of rage and the fanatic who kills his ideological enemy in cold blood shall have the same justice.'

'From a People's Court?' somebody in the row behind me murmured; but if Brankovitch heard, he took no notice. He went on:

'Under the reactionary governments of the prewar years the Brotherhood became a great and terrible burden to our people. It is not known for certain how many murders it was responsible for. Without doubt the number must be reckoned in hundreds. I can tell you with more precision that the number of violent attacks on the person committed by the Brotherhood in the ten years between 1930 and 1940 was about one thousand four hundred. This figure includes only those cases serious enough to need hospital treatment. The reason for the greater precision is, of course, that those persons lived to explain what had happened. The injuries included bullet wounds–approximately six hundred cases; stabbings–approximately two hundred cases; acid-throwing–approximately thirty cases; flogging–approximately two hundred cases; and severe bruising and beating with truncheons, rods, and other weapons made up the remainder.'

He had been referring to notes in front of him. Now he pushed them aside.

'But statistics can give little idea of the emotional consequences of this state of affairs, of the hatreds and fears aroused and of the effect on the social life of the community. I will tell you, therefore, of one typical case among the known cases and leave the rest to your imaginations. It is the case of Kyril Shatev, who was prefect of this city in 1940. A man named Brodno, a criminal pervert and a member of the Brotherhood, had been arrested on suspicion of murder. There was plenty of evidence on this occasion and Shatev determined to bring this man to trial. Immediately he began to receive the usual threats from the Brotherhood. He ignored them. I will be quite honest with you; past experience told him that when the case came for trial the attentions of the Brotherhood would turn from him to the judge trying the case. The judge might yield, but that was not Shatev's business. However, he miscalculated. The probability is that the evidence against Brodno incriminated senior members of the Brotherhood and was for them too dangerous to be heard. The Sunday before the date of the trial was to be set, Shatev, with his wife, his two young children, and two female servants, was at his house about ten kilometres out of the city. They were about to sit down to the midday meal when a car drove up and three men got out. They said they wanted water for the car. A servant unthinkingly opened the outer door and the men pushed past her, knocking her senseless with a pistol butt. Then they went into the house. Shatev tried to defend his family and was immediately shot. Unfortunately for him, he did not die at once. The men had a bayonet, and the two children were killed with it. Shatev's wife was then forced to witness her husband's sexual mutilation, also with the bayonet. She was then killed herself. The other servant was not harmed. She was to serve as a witness, they said, that the sentence of the Brotherhood had been carried out. She was threatened, however, that if she attempted to identify the murderers she too would be killed. The murderers were never identified and Brodno was never tried.'

He paused for a moment and looked round. 'One typical case,' he said, and sighed. 'No doubt,' he went on, 'much could be said about a government that allowed itself to be intimidated by such means, but it is easy to miss the point. There were, in fact, many members of the Brotherhood in Government circles. This we found out later, for, of course, membership was always secret. Who were these men? We know of two who were ministers and twenty-seven in posts of high authority in the civil service, the police, and the army. There were certainly others in these high places. The plain truth is that membership in the Brotherhood ran through every class of our society except that of the ordinary workman. This Brotherhood is a bourgeois disease. It is difficult to conceive, I grant you, that a man, presumably of more than average intelligence and ability, who has made his way to a position of authority and responsibility, could have any direct relationship with, for example, the murderous perverts who entered the Shatevs' house that Sunday or with others equally vile. But we found it so. When, during the life of the Provisional Government, we began the attack upon this evil, we had many terrible surprises. Yes, I say, *terrible*. To despise a man politically is one thing. To discover that he is a criminal lunatic is another. It is difficult to believe the most incontrovertible evidence in such cases. Yet we must.'

He paused again and there was dead silence. We knew that now he was talking about Deltchev. He clasped his hands in front of him.

'Let me give you an example from history, gentlemen,' he said; 'not the history of our own country, but that of Italy and France. In 1830 there was in Italy a young exile named Louis Bonaparte, a nephew of the first Napoleon and once his adopted grandson. In Italy also at that time there was a secret terrorist society called the Carbonari–the Charcoal-Burners. Among the members were nobles, officers, landlords, Government officials, peasants, and priests. The members called each other "cousin" and the only form of resignation ever accepted from a member was his death. This young Bonaparte became a member of the Carbonari and a year after was imprisoned by the Austrian police for his part in a murderous affair. He was not then a very important or responsible person. But twenty-eight years later, when that same man was Napoleon III, Emperor of France, the Carbonari had need of him and sent a reminder by an assassin named Orsini. The reminder was a gift of three bombs, and they exploded one evening in the January of 1858 as the Emperor was arriving at the Opera in Paris. Eight innocent bystanders were killed and a hundred and fifty wounded, but Cousin Bonaparte was quite safe. What the Carbonari wanted from him was help to make a bourgeois revolution in Italy. He did not hesitate. The responsibilities of Napoleon III, Emperor of France, toward the people he ruled were as nothing beside those of Cousin Bonaparte toward the Carbonari terrorists. And so the Italian Risorgimento was paid for with the blood of the French soldiers that soaked the fields of Montebello and Turbigo and Solferino. It is not a pretty story–no prettier than that of Shatev and his family.'

There was silence for a moment.

He added quietly: 'Gentlemen, our people will fertilize no more fields for the "cousins" or "brethren" of this century. We intend to seek out all the murderers whether they sit on café chairs or on the thrones they have made for themselves above the heads of the people. The People's Party and its great leader Vukashin are pledged to that.' He looked round at us again and then sat down. 'I will answer questions,' he said.

It was quite well done and for a space nobody moved; then an American in front of me got up.

'In December of last year, Minister,' he said, 'the People's Party Government announced that the Officer Corps Brotherhood had been completely–*eliminated*. I think that was the word used. Are we to understand now that that announcement was incorrect?'

Brankovitch nodded. 'Unfortunately, yes. At the time, of course, we believed it to be true. Later developments have shown that we were mistaken.'

'What later developments, Minister?'

'I would prefer not to anticipate the court proceedings.'

A small dark man got up.

'Minister, was not Deltchev himself responsible for the very vigorous proceedings taken to eliminate the Brotherhood?'

'He was certainly responsible for the action against the Brotherhood that we now know to have been ineffective, but the decision that there *should* be action was taken by the Provisional Government as a whole. In other words, the People's Party participated in the decision but not in the carrying-out of it.'

Others began to rise and now the questions came quickly.

'Minister, can your allusion to Napoleon III be taken to mean that the Government links the allegations about Deltchev's peace negotiations with the allegations about his membership in the Brotherhood?'

'You may draw that conclusion if you wish.'

'The charge is that Deltchev was to be paid for his efforts. Aren't the two suggestions inconsistent?'

'Possibly. But remember that Napoleon III also had his reward–Nice, the Riviera, Savoy.'

'Minister, do you consider that the evidence heard so far in court has gone any way toward proving any of the charges against Monsieur Deltchev?'

'The evidence must be considered as a whole.'

'By whom was defending counsel appointed, Minister?'

'By the Government. In all cases when a prisoner fails to appoint counsel to defend him that is done.'

'Did this prisoner fail to appoint counsel? Did he not, as an advocate, wish to defend himself?'

'On a criminal charge a prisoner is not by law permitted to conduct his own defence. The law was made for the benefit of poor persons certain of conviction who feared to burden their families with legal costs.'

'Minister, could not the law, clearly not intended for persons in Monsieur Deltchev's position, be waived in this case?'

'Are laws waived in England for the benefit of persons in high position?'

'Then you agree, Minister, that it would be to Monsieur Deltchev's benefit if he could defend himself?'

'It would be to the benefit of you gentlemen, I have no doubt. I apologize for our reluctance to have the court turned into a circus entertainment.'

'Will the Minister say if, as a result of the prosecutor's unhappy efforts yesterday to provide the court with entertainment, the prisoner will now be allowed proper medical attention in the prison?'

Brankovitch rose to his feet with a smile. 'The prisoner is receiving ample medical attention,' he said, 'and as much insulin as he wishes. It was nothing more sinister than a stupid administrative blunder that prevented his having attention for a few days. Disciplinary action has been taken against those responsible. Naturally the prisoner took the utmost advantage of his plight to gain sympathy—'

'When driven to do so by the prosecutor?'

'Or when a favourable opportunity presented itself.' Brankovitch smiled again. 'We interpret motives from the standpoint of our own prejudices. But please note that the prisoner was not prevented from addressing you.'

'What he said was not reported in the official press, Minister.'

'Quite properly. The fact that a man is diabetic surely does not affect his responsibility to the community for criminal acts. Gentlemen, perhaps you would care to continue our discussion over the refreshments. I hope you will not think I am attempting to corrupt you if I say that there is champagne and caviar for you to sample. I am merely performing another of my functions as a Minister in introducing to you two products of our agricultural and fishing industries which we are anxious to export. The champagne is not French, of course, but it is a dry, sparkling wine of pleasing character and I think you will like it.'

There were one or two murmurs of amused assent and a scraping of chairs. Waiters entered, obviously in response to a signal, and whisked away the napkins from the buffet.

'He is clever, the Minister,' said Pashik seriously.

'Yes, he is. Shall we go?'

He looked shocked. 'Do you not wish to ask questions, Mr Foster?'

'What about? Napoleon III?'

'I think it would be impolite to go,' said Pashik earnestly. 'The Minister will surely wish to meet you. There is protocol to be observed.'

'There are others going.' Though most of those present had moved over to the buffet and stood in groups talking, I noticed several making unobtrusive exits.

'Those are local agency men, Mr Foster. They have met the Minister before.'

'All right. Shall we go over?' Brankovitch was talking to a group that included Sibley, the man who drank too much and was indiscreet.

'No, Mr Foster. Let us quietly have some refreshments. Presently matters will arrange themselves.'

We were joined after a moment or two by an American I had chatted with once or twice at the courthouse. A waiter brought us wine and caviar sandwiches. One of the secretaries delivered copies of a long blood-curdling piece on the Officer Corps Brotherhood.

'Did you know that Byron was a member of the Carbonari?' the American was saying. 'I think we ought to rechristen our friend Brankovitch. When Ferdinand of Italy tried to liquidate the Carbonari he had his Minister of

Police set up another secret society called "the Braziers of the counter-poise," *Calderai del Contrappeso.* The Minister recruited all the worst characters in the country for it and what they did to the Italian liberals makes Little Bopeep of that Shatev story. The Minister was a man called Prince Canosa. What about Creeping Canosa for our friend?'

Pashik had left us. I talked to the American and ate sandwiches. After a few minutes Pashik came back rather breathlessly with one of the secretaries, a stony-eyed young man with over-neat clothes.

'This is Monsieur Kovitch,' he said; 'he is of the Minister's bureau.' The secretary bowed and we shook hands. 'The Minister is most anxious to meet you, Herr Foster,' he said stiffly.

'I shall be honoured.' I caught the American's eye and he put his tongue very obviously in his cheek.

The secretary stared hard at me. 'Have you yet had time, Herr Foster,' he said, 'to visit any of the well-known beauty spots that abound in the vicinity of our city?'

'I'm afraid I haven't.'

'At this time of year,' the secretary continued steadily, 'there are many varieties of the most remarkable rose blooms in the world to be seen and savoured. Our country is very beautiful. However, it is to be hoped that you will wish to be present on Saturday at the official parade and celebration in honour of the twenty-seventh anniversary of the founding of the People's Party.'

'I don't—'

'Herr Foster's special pass has already been applied for,' Pashik put in smartly.

'Ah, then he will see some of the beauties of the country brought to the city,' pursued the secretary steadily. 'This year the parade will be a symbolic integration of peaceful husbandry and armed might—the plough and the sword in harmony together.'

'Very interesting.'

'Yes. It is of the utmost importance that all our visitors leave us with a correct impression. I will myself see that you have an advantageous place, Herr Foster. Here, now, is the Minister.'

He stepped aside nimbly, like a *compère* effacing himself for the entry of the star. Brankovitch, with the other secretary in attendance, had stopped to say a word to a Scandinavian group. Now he turned in my direction. The secretary beside me said something in his own language with my name in it. Brankovitch held out his hand and turned on a watery smile.

'How do you do?' he said in English. His warm hand released mine almost as soon as it touched it. He nodded to Pashik as I answered him. 'You have not been to our country before, Mr Foster?'

'No, Minister. But I'm finding my first visit most interesting.'

He nodded. 'Much fiction has already been written about it, but mostly by strangers. Now that cultural activities are being widely encouraged, however, perhaps a native school of writers will emerge. There is the language difficulty, of course. A knowledge of our language is rare. Yet Ibsen, also writing in a narrowly spoken language, achieved world fame.'

'Ibsen's heroes and heroines were not obliged to be positive, Minister.'

'Ah, I see you have heard of our special problems. Yes, we are compelled to consider the standard of education of the public here. We must pay still for past injustices. The percentage of illiteracy is high and those who are literate are for the most part still uneducated in the Western sense of the word. But in other cultural fields–the visual arts and music, for example–greater freedom is already possible.'

'Ideas do not have to be expressed in words to be dangerous, Minister.'

'We do not hinder truth, Mr Foster–only the facile repetition of lies. But we must have a long undisturbed conversation about such things, for I would be glad to hear your opinions. Tell me, how did you find Madame Deltchev last night? In good health?'

I sensed rather than heard Pashik's sharply indrawn breath. Brankovitch's gaze rested on me with unwavering affability.

'She seemed very well.'

He smiled again. 'She is not being persecuted?'

'Not that I'm aware of.'

'We have tried to spare her as much as possible. Naturally her position is difficult and we have to protect her against possible demonstrations. But I am glad to hear that she is well. You are the only journalist who has interviewed her, I think.'

'I think so.'

He nodded vaguely. 'I am so glad to have had this opportunity of meeting you, Mr Foster,' he said. 'We must have another talk. Most interesting.'

He nodded again and turned away. The secretary slid past me after him. The interview was at an end.

I looked at Pashik. His face was quite expressionless. He stepped up to me.

'Do you wish to go now, Mr Foster?'

'Yes, I think so.'

'You did not tell me that you had seen Madame Deltchev,' he said as we walked away.

'No. I thought you'd prefer not to know.'

'We must hope no harm is done.'

'What harm can be done?'

He shrugged. 'Such things attract attention.'

'Does that matter?'

'We must hope not. But I would have preferred that you had told me. I could at least have prevented the embarrassment.'

'What embarrassment? The sentries on the house looked at my permit. They reported. What of it?'

'You do not understand.'

'I'm afraid I don't. I think you're over-anxious, as I've said before.'

'I think my opinion about that may be better informed, Mr Foster.'

'I'm sorry, Pashik. I certainly have no wish to compromise you, but I have a job to do.'

'I have the responsibility, Mr Foster.'

'You must try to shoulder it.'

Before he could answer, there were quick footsteps behind us. Pashik turned round as if he expected to be attacked. It was Sibley.

'Hullo there,' he said breezily; 'how are you, Foster? And you, Georghi my friend? What a dreadful party! When are we going to have that drink? Now? I feel the need.'

'Please excuse me,' said Pashik hastily, 'I must go to my office. Mr Foster, you have messages to send.'

'I'll see you tomorrow.'

He hesitated. We had reached the door. He gave up. 'Very well. Good night, Mr Foster. Good night, Mr Sibley.'

'Good night.'

He went, leaving a slip-stream of malodorous disapproval.

Sibley chuckled. 'Poor little man,' he said.

Chapter Nine

We went to a near-by café and ordered drinks. Then Sibley disappeared to make a telephone call. When he came back the drinks had arrived. He picked his up, peered into it as if it were a crystal ball, then downed it at a gulp.

'Well, what do you think?' he said grimly.

'About this evening's performance?'

'Performance! Exactly.' He snapped his fingers at the waiter for another drink. 'Incredible, isn't it?'

'In what way do you mean?'

'Oh, all of it. That old, old routine! Prejudice, friends? Not a bit of it! Anyway, judge for yourselves, friends. Here are the simple facts given as simply as we know how–the facts about the Brotherhood. What has that to do with Deltchev? Who said it had anything to do with him? You're drawing the conclusions, friends, not us. We're only giving you the nasty facts. And to show you that the facts are really nasty we'll pull an old atrocity story out of the bag. Castration and rape, friends! Yes, we thought that'd get you where it hurts. What has that to do with Deltchev? Well, we don't say definitely that it *has* anything to do with him but–well, you're drawing the conclusions and we can't stop you, can we? In fact, although we're not exactly saying so, the same ugly thought is beginning to cross our minds now. How clever of you to think of it first, friends! But it does seem fantastic, doesn't it? Though, wait! Isn't there a historical precedent that fits the situation like a glove? Of course there is. And doesn't history repeat itself? Of course it does. In fact, there is one point of coincidence we didn't mention. When Murat decided to destroy the Carbonari he gave the job to his police chief. The police chief destroyed a lot of people, and Murat thought the job was done until he found out that the police chief had always been a Carbonaro himself and that the cousins were stronger than ever. Strange, isn't it, friends? How clever of you to remember without our telling you! Any more questions? Yes? Well, let's not get into tiresome arguments. Let's have some caviar and a nice glass of aerated cat water.

They make me tired.' He swallowed another large plum brandy and sat back.

'Another drink?'

'For God's sake, yes.' He leaned forward, his face slightly flushed, his lips still wet with brandy. 'How does one deal with it, Foster?'

'Brankovitch's press conference?' I signalled to the waiter.

'All of it. The whole phony business. Perhaps it's all right for you. You've got plenty of time. A series of articles, weeks hence. But I'm supposed to be sending news. All I've got through so far are those damned official bulletins. I suppose Pashik sends those to your people?'

'Yes.'

'Do you know what I'd like to do?' His dull, hot eyes brooded on mine.'

'No, what?'

'I'd like to put it across them. I'd like to split the whole damn business wide open.' He frowned suddenly as if with irritation at himself. 'Take no notice. I had drinks before the party.' He smiled slyly and lowered his voice. 'Can you keep a secret, Foster?'

'Yes.'

'The funny thing is I can do it.'

'Do what?'

'What I said—break it open.' He looked round cautiously and leaned farther forward. 'I've found a way round this bloody censorship.'

'Oh, yes?' My heart began to beat rather unpleasantly.

'I can't tell you the details because I swore not to, but there's a little man in the Propaganda Ministry who doesn't like the regime any more than we do and he'll play. Of course, if he was found out he'd be lucky if they hanged him quickly, but he's prepared to take the risk. There's only one snag.' He paused. I waited. 'He can't do it more than once and the deadline's tomorrow.'

'That should give you time.'

'It's a risk.' He frowned at the table as the waiter put fresh drinks down. 'A big risk. If I'm caught, I'm out. Of course, that wouldn't matter to you. It's not your living. But, by God, it's a risk I'd like to take.'

'The little man in the Propaganda Ministry must think it worth while.'

He laughed shortly. 'You're right. It's funny, isn't it? One minute I'm breathing fire and murder, and the next I'm worrying about a little risk.' He laughed again. His performance was deteriorating rapidly. I was not helping him and he would have to come to the point himself. I waited, fascinated.

'Would *you* take the risk?' he asked suddenly.

'I don't know. The question would have to arise.'

'All right, supposing'—I thought I detected a note of genuine exasperation in his voice—'just supposing you had a chance to file a short message with mine. Would you take it?'

'Is that an offer?'

'Don't be silly. Why should I give you a beat?'

'I don't know. Why should you?'

'You'd have to make it worth my while.'

'What's that mean?'

He did not answer. He was pretending to debate with himself. 'Look, Foster,' he said then, 'let's be serious for a moment. If I'd thought you were going to fasten on to the thing like this, I tell you frankly I wouldn't have mentioned it.' He paused. 'But since I have, I tell you what I'll do. If you'll undertake to confine your message to pure comment on the trial as a whole, I'll get it through with mine.'

'If you do send one, of course.'

'Oh, I'm going to send it all right. Don't you worry. And now you can buy me another drink.' He sat back with a tremendous air of having sold his birthright. 'I make only one stipulation. I'll have to read your stuff before I pass it on. Honestly, I wouldn't trust my own brother in a thing like this. Right?'

'I understand.' To give myself time to think I looked round for the waiter. I had had it all now: the confidence-promoting diatribe against the regime, the brandy-laden indiscretion, the indignant denial, the burst of generosity, the second thoughts, the grudging commitment. Petlarov would be amused. Pashik would purse his lips. I looked at my watch. I did not want to have to talk to Sibley any more. The waiter had disappeared. I put some money on the table.

'I have to go,' I said.

It took me five minutes and another hastily swallowed drink to do so, but at last I stood up and put on my hat.

'About you-know-what,' he said; 'you'd better give me the stuff tomorrow morning. Two hundred words maximum.'

'Oh, that.' I smiled and shook my head. 'I don't think I'll bother.'

'Are you mad?'

'No. It's different for you. For me it's not worth the risk.'

He looked at me coldly for a moment. Then very elaborately he shrugged. 'As you will, *mon brave*,' he said.

'Good night.'

Still seated at the table, he gave me a heavily ironic bow. 'Don't change your mind tomorrow, Foster *mio*,' he answered, 'it'll be too late.'

'I won't change my mind.' I nodded to him and walked out of the café. Outside I hesitated. Now that the disagreeable part of the encounter was over, I was curious. Sibley the *agent provocateur* and employee of Brankovitch interested me as Sibley the breezy newspaperman never could. I had an impulse to go back into the café, sit down, and try to lure him into explaining himself. I did look back. He was sitting looking down at his drink, his elbows on the table, the thin, fair down on his sunburnt scalp glistening faintly in the evening sun. As I looked, he put his hands up to his head and there was something so hopeless about the gesture that it was quite moving. Then one hand dropped to the stem of his glass and twirled it between a finger and thumb. The other came down too. The money I had put on the table was still there, and now a finger of this other hand crept out rather stealthily toward it and gently sorted it over to see how much was there. Then he looked round for the waiter. I turned away. For the moment there was nothing more I wanted to know about Sibley.

I went back to my hotel. I did not eat much dinner. I remembered that in one dim corner of the hotel foyer I had seen a framed map of the city on the wall. After dinner I went to it and got out Katerina Deltchev's letter. The address on the envelope was short: '*Valmo, Patriarch Dimo 9.*'

With some difficulty I located the street on the map and set out. The girl had said that the street was near the station. It was, but it was also on the other side of the main line, and to get there I had to make a wide detour through a crowded street market to a bridge and walk back along the far side of a freight yard. By the time I had found the church that I had noted as a reference point on the map, it was almost too dark to read the lettering of the street names.

It was not an inviting locality. On one side of the main road there were tall warehouses and a power station interspersed with ugly apartment blocks; on the other side were small shops and steep lanes of wooden houses, the roofs of which were patched here and there with sheets of rusty corrugated iron; the old slum. There was a tram terminus a short distance down the road and I considered riding straight back into the city without troubling further about the letter. Then I decided to give the search for the street five minutes. If, as I hoped, I had not found it by then, I would go back. I found it almost immediately.

The street of the Patriarch Dimo was one of the steeper and shabbier lanes. There was a dimly lit wine shop at the corner, and behind it a decrepit wooden building that seemed to be used as a stable for oxen. I walked up the hill slowly. The girl had said hesitantly that her letter was to 'a young man.' I had, I think, imagined Valmo to be a fellow art student of hers, a handsome lad with other girl friends who would have no scruples about taking advantage of Katerina's enforced absence. Now my ideas had to change.

Number 9 was a house much like the rest, but with the ground-floor shutters crossed with planks and nailed up. There were no lights in any of the upper rooms and the greasy-walled entrance passage at the side was littered with pebbles and marked with chalk lines as if children had been playing a game in it. The house looked empty. I walked along the passage to the door and struck a match.

At some time recently the building had been a lodging house, for there was a board with names painted on it. The match went out and I struck another. None of the painted names was Valmo. Then, as the second match was going out, I saw it. The top name had been scratched over with the point of a knife and under it the word 'Valmo' was crudely written in pencil. I dropped the burnt-out match and stood in the darkness for a moment. I was becoming curious about this Valmo. By the light of another match I looked for a bell and, seeing none, tried the door. It was open.

I went in.

There was a small lobby with a flight of stairs in it. The place was quite still and seemed deserted. I looked round for a light. On the ceiling there was a hook and a smoke shield, but no lantern beneath it. I went up the stairs striking matches. There were two doors on the first landing, both open. I looked in. The rooms were empty. In one of them some floorboards were missing. I went on up. I did not stop on the next landing; obviously the house was abandoned. Only one thing delayed my turning back. The rooms I had seen had been deserted for many months. But Katerina had not been confined to her house that long. It was possible, therefore, that Valmo had only recently moved away and had left a notice of his new address.

As I went up the last flight of stairs I noticed a peculiar smell. It was ammoniac and very sickly. It became stronger as I reached the landing under the roof. I struck another match. There was only one door here, and it was shut. There was no notice on it. I knocked and waited. The match burned out. I struck another and turned the handle of the door and pushed. The door opened. Then I had a shock; the room inside was furnished.

I raised the match above my head and moved forward into the doorway. As I did so, I became aware of a sound; there were flies buzzing in the room.

In the small light of the match I saw an unmade bed, a deal table, and a chair with some newspapers piled on it. There was also a packing-case.

The match burned down and I dropped it. Then, by the pale arc of light it made as it fell, I saw on the floor a dark mass like a crumpled curtain.

As I struck the next match I took a pace forward into the room. The light from the match flared up.

The next instant my heart jolted violently. It was not a curtain on the floor. It was a man; and his face was black.

I stepped back quickly and with some sort of shout, I think. The movement blew the match out or I should have run. I fumbled desperately with the box and managed to get another match alight. I forced myself to look again.

His hair was close-cropped and white except where the blackness spread. The blackness was congealed blood, and it lay on and about him like spilled wax. His mouth was open and there was a gaping wound by his ear. There was no telling what he had looked like. He was lying on his right side, his knees drawn up to his chest and his elbows nearly touching them. He had on a dark serge suit and leather sandals, but no socks. He had been small and thin. The flies buzzed round him. He had been dead for more than a few hours.

I began to retch and went out to the landing.

A minute passed and I was beginning to get my breath again when I thought I heard a sound from below.

The blood was thudding in my head so loudly and my breathing was so quick and shallow that it was difficult to be certain. Then I managed to hold my breath for just over a second and heard the sound again. Very slowly and quietly somebody was coming up the stairs.

I don't know who I thought it was; the murderer, I suppose; at that moment I would have panicked if a fly had settled on my hand. In the darkness I stumbled back into the room, shut the door, lighted a match, and looked feverishly for the bolt. There was a bolt, but the socket of it was missing. I looked round desperately for something to jam the door with. I tried to use the chair, but the door handle was too low. The match I was holding went out. I fumbled with the box again, opened it upside down, and the matches spilled on the floor. I was shaking with fear now. I went down on my knees and started to pick the matches up. At that moment I heard the footsteps on the landing just outside the door. I remained motionless. Under the door I saw a light flicker. The person outside had a flashlight.

Then the light went out and the door opened.

There was silence for a moment. Suddenly the flashlight went on and swept quickly round the room. It stopped on the body. Then it moved again quickly and stopped on me.

The end of a revolver barrel gleamed just in front of the flashlight. I did not move.

A voice said: 'What are you doing here, Mr Foster?'

It was Pashik.

Chapter Ten

I got to my feet.

'Why are you here, Mr Foster?' he repeated.

'I don't know,' I said. 'Do you mind taking that light off my face?'

He turned the light down to my feet. I could see him now and the revolver in his hand was still pointing at me. He had his dispatch case under his arm and the medallion on it winked faintly.

'Well, Mr Foster?'

'I might ask you the same question.'

'I followed you, Mr Foster.'

'With a gun?'

'It was possible that we might not be alone.'

'We're not.' I looked at the dead man on the floor, but he did not move the light from my feet.

'I want to know why you are here, Mr Foster, and who told you of this place. And I want to know right now.' There was a very sharp edge to his voice.

'Katerina Deltchev asked me to deliver a letter for her. This was the address on it.'

'Show me the letter.'

'Pashik, do we have to stay in this room? Can't we go outside? Anyway, shouldn't we be calling the police? This man's been murdered.'

'No, Mr Foster, we should not be calling the police. Show me that letter.'

I got it out. He came forward, took it from me, and turned the light on it.

'She told me that it was to a young man,' I said.

Without replying he put the letter in his pocket and swept the light round the room.

'Have you touched anything here, Mr Foster?'

'This chair. Why?'

'What did you touch it for?'

'When I heard you coming up the stairs I tried to jam it under the door handle.'

'Wipe the chair where you touched it and also both sides of the door with your handkerchief. Then pick up all the matches you dropped, including the burnt-out ones, please.'

I obeyed him. Just then the wish to get out of the room was stronger than my disposition to argue. He held the light down while I picked up the matches.

'Did anyone know you were coming here?'

'Only Katerina Deltchev.'

'You told nobody?'

'No.'

'Not Petlarov?'

'No.'

'Mr Sibley?'

'Nobody.'

'Did anyone see you come in here?'

'I shouldn't think so. There weren't many people about.'

'Your clothes are noticeably foreign. Did anyone turn to look at you?'

'You should know if you were following me.'

'I was not close enough to see. Was there anybody in the passage below when you arrived?'

'No.' I had collected all the matches. I straightened up. 'I can't stay in this room any longer,' I said, and went out on the landing.

'Wipe the door, Mr Foster.'

I did so. He ran the light round the room again and came out. 'Shut the door with your handkerchief in your hand, please. Yes, that will do. Now, Mr Foster, my car is at the end of the street by the wine shop. You have your matches. Go down as you came up, walk to my car, get in it, and wait for me.'

'What are you going to do?'

'We must not be seen leaving together.'

'Why not?'

'Get going, Mr Foster.'

He still had the revolver in his hand and he handled the thing as if he were used to it. Oddly, there was nothing incongruous about the look of Pashik with a gun.

He held the light for me as I went down the top flight of stairs. After that I struck matches again. It was a relief to get into the street. By the time I reached his car I had done a good deal of thinking.

I smoked the greater part of a cigarette before he joined me. Without a word he climbed into the driver's seat, took his gun and flashlight from the dispatch case and, putting them in the door pocket, stuffed a greasy rag over them. He started the car. 'And now,' he said, 'we'll go see a friend of mine.'

'What friend?'

'He will advise us what we must do. He is of a special kind of police.'

'What special kind?'

'You will see, Mr Foster. Perhaps the ordinary police should be told. I do not know.'

He twitched the wheel suddenly, swerved across the road, and swung round uncertainly into a turning on the left.

I threw away the cigarette I had been smoking and lit another.

'Why did you follow me, Pashik?'

'I had a hunch that you might be about to do something foolish, Mr Foster.'

'But you did follow me?'

'You will agree that I was justified.'

I looked at him. 'I came through a street market that was difficult to get through on foot. How did you follow me in a car?'

'I cannot answer questions while I am driving, Mr Foster.'

'Then let's stop for a few minutes. I have lots of questions and they won't keep.'

He drove on in silence.

'You've been to that house before, haven't you?' I said after a moment or two.

'Why should you think that, Mr Foster?'

'You knew that that man's body was there before you came in. That is, unless you're quite used to finding corpses with shotgun wounds lying about. You paid no attention to this one.'

He had been driving toward the centre of the city. Now we lurched into a quiet boulevard with trees along it.

'Another thing,' I said: 'if you followed me and expected to find me there, you wouldn't have shown your gun. As you came up the stairs you heard me move about. If you'd known it was me you'd have called my name. You didn't follow me. You went there on your own account and for your own reasons. What were they?'

'You are making things very difficult, Mr Foster,' he said gloomily.

'Yes. Who was the dead man? Valmo? Who killed him? You?'

He did not answer. Behind the trees that lined the road there were houses with portes-cochères. He slowed down, then turned suddenly into a space between the trees and drove through into one of the courtyards. He stopped and immediately turned off the lights. We were in pitch-darkness.

'Mr Foster,' he said, 'you are arrogant and very dumb. If I were truly a murderer you would be already dead. I have been very patient with you. Now we will see my friend.'

He switched on the flashlight and I saw that he had his revolver again. He put it in his dispatch case and we both got out. I looked up. The bulk of quite a large house was visible against the sky.

'Where is this?' I asked.

'My friend has an apartment here. This way.'

I could see very little. We went through a side door down some tiled steps to a small hydraulic lift with a rope control. The cage bounced as we got into it. Pashik hauled on the rope and we shot upwards with a faint hissing sound.

At the top floor the lift stopped automatically and we got out on a bare stone landing with a small doorway in it and a steel ladder up to a skylight. Pashik knocked on the door.

After a moment or two a woman in an apron opened the door. She had grey hair scragged back into a bun, and a bitter mouth. She obviously knew Pashik. He made some explanation to her. She nodded and looked at me curiously as we went in; then she led the way along a narrow passage and showed us into a drawing-room. She switched on the lights and left us, shutting the door behind us. If there had been a faint smell of disinfectant in the air, it would have seemed like an appointment with a dentist. The room we were in, indeed, had very much the look of a waiting-room. The chairs stood round the walls and there was a large table in the middle with one small ashtray on it. All that was wanting was a selection of magazines.

'What's your friend's name?' I asked.

Pashik sat on the edge of one of the chairs. 'I will introduce you to him, Mr Foster.'

'What did you go to that house for?'

'You do not believe me when I answer your questions, Mr Foster.' His brown eyes looked at me mournfully. He took off his glasses and began polishing them.

'You never do answer them. Why didn't you tell me that Sibley was working for the Propaganda Ministry? You must have known.'

'How do you know that, Mr Foster?'

'Petlarov warned me to expect an approach from someone pretending to have a way round the censorship. It came from Sibley. If you knew, why didn't you warn me?'

'Would you have believed me if I had, Mr Foster? No. You would have thought that I was trying to stop you sending news out.'

'Yes, I'm afraid you're right. I'm sorry.'

'It is unimportant, Mr Foster. It is simply that you do not like me.' He put his glasses on and stared at me. 'I am used to being disliked,' he added; 'I no longer mind.'

But I was spared the deathly embarrassment of replying to this. The grey woman appeared at the door, nodded to Pashik, and said something. He got up and turned to me.

'My friend wishes to see me privately for a moment, Mr Foster,' he said. 'Perhaps you will wait.'

He picked up his dispatch case and went out of the room.

I sat down.

Until that moment I had been feeling all right. Now, suddenly, the smell of the dead man was in my nostrils again. I felt sick and giddy. I put my head between my knees and tried to think of other things. I suppose that if Pashik had not arrived on the scene I would have hurried back to my hotel, had several large brandies and a sleeping-pill, and gone to bed. Instead, I was sitting in a strange room in a strange house with a desperate feeling of having lost all contact with reality. At that moment I would have given anything to be back in London, quietly doing in my own way the work I understood. I had realized that the delayed reaction to the horror of finding a decomposing corpse in a dark room was only the surface of my discomfort. Beneath, there were fears of another kind. I had thought to write about the trial and condemnation of an innocent man. Now, in spite of the obvious injustice of the trial itself, I was having to accept the disagreeable possibility that really the man might not be innocent, that the rubbish Prochaska was talking might have a basis in fact, that the trembling hands of the diabetic Deltchev might have clasped in friendship those of the murderers of the Shatev family; and the foolish trouble was that if those things were true, I feared to know about them. Petlarov's grocer, I reflected bitterly, was not alone in his ill-informed uneasiness; Mr Valiant-for-Truth, the great journalist, had also caught a whiff of the odour of corruption and was wishing his delicate nose elsewhere. It was curious how preoccupied I had become with smells; they seemed easier to deal with at that time than other ideas; the smell of the dead man, the smell of Pashik, the smell of furniture polish in Deltchev's house; those three things were related. And if I looked for reassurance to the other senses, I could recall the taste of the plum brandy I had had with Sibley, the feeling of the sentry's rifle butt on my shoulder, the image of Petlarov's white false teeth, and the sound of his voice saying: 'Some of the evidence may not discredit itself. Some of it may be true.'

I got up and began to wander round the room. I knew now that the train of thought I had been avoiding could be avoided no longer.

If you accepted the seemingly incredible proposition that Deltchev was, and for years had been, a member of the Officer Corps Brotherhood, it was possible to explain some things about him that had hitherto defied explanation. To begin with, you could explain the inexplicable election affair; Deltchev had done what he did, not because he had thought it right or necessary, or because he was a saint, or because he had been bought; he had done it in obedience to the orders of the Brotherhood. And having said that, you could also explain why he himself had been able to give no explanation for his action. You could explain, though with difficulty, how a prosaic, undistinguished Minister of Posts and Telegraphs had been able to become the leader of a secret nationalistic revolutionary movement and ultimately seize power. You could even explain the 'football match' incident in that context; the fanatically nationalistic Brotherhood, having through fear of the growing People's Party misjudged the election timing, had commanded their puppet Deltchev to retrieve the position. Napoleon III had done more for the Carbonari. Besides, had not Petlarov himself admitted that power was a bribe that might be used with Deltchev? In a fantastic way it all fitted. It might be objected that, as a lawyer, Deltchev would not have qualified for membership in the early days of the Brotherhood; but the class distinction between professional men and army officers was not great. His membership was not impossible. It was certainly not improbable. Idealistic young men very often joined societies supposedly dedicated to the human struggles for freedom and justice; and very often, too, they later regretted having done so. When, I wondered, had Deltchev begun to regret the association? Then another objection occurred to me. Why, if the Brotherhood had supported Deltchev, had it also collaborated with the German occupation forces? But this I disposed of easily. What better cover could there have been for the subversive activities of the Brotherhood than half-hearted collaboration with the German Army? Not with the sharp and sceptical Gestapo, mark you, but with the army. It would be interesting to know about the men who had made the Brotherhood's policy. Perhaps the trial would reveal them.

But meanwhile Deltchev's daughter had sent a letter to a cheap lodging where there was a murdered man. I thought about that. Who was Valmo? Katerina's middle-aged lover? I doubted it. This rather too knowing young woman had offered me whisky because she had thought that that would be the beguiling way with an irritable reporter; she had said that the letter was to 'a young man' because she had thought, perhaps less incorrectly, that that would be the beguiling way with a reluctant letter-smuggler. If I had had the presence of mind to do so, I might have looked more closely at the room for signs of a relationship with Katerina; her photographs perhaps, or a letter in her handwriting. A letter. And that brought me back to Pashik.

I had made a mistake about Pashik. I had thought of him as one of those hapless, over-anxious persons who cannot help entangling themselves in systems of small, unnecessary lies. It had not occurred to me that he might have anything of more than private importance to conceal. Now I had to reckon with the news not only that could he be concerned quite calmly with the body of a murdered man but also that his tiresome preoccupation with 'discretion' had its origins in something very unlike the old-maidish timidity to which I had attributed it.

At that moment, with a jolt, I came out of the haze of cowlike rumination in which I had been lost and began to think clearly. If Pashik had known that the body was there before he came to the house, why was it now necessary to consult his 'friend in the special police' so urgently? Answer: because I had been there, because I had seen the body, because I had seen Pashik, because I had drawn certain conclusions, because I might be indiscreet.

I had been pacing up and down the room. I stopped then went to the door. From another part of the apartment there came very faintly a murmur of voices. I glanced at my watch. Pashik had been gone five minutes. I was suddenly convinced that it would be wise to leave without waiting to be introduced to Pashik's friend—to leave now, quietly. I hesitated momentarily, then I made up my mind. I put my hand on the doorknob and turned it gently. Then I began to pull. But the door did not move. I had been locked in.

Chapter Eleven

For a moment or two I stood there looking stupidly at the door as if I expected it to open itself. To find oneself locked in a room and know that the locking cannot be accidental or a practical joke is, when one has forgotten the worst parts of childhood, an odd sensation. My feelings were confused and are not easily described; I was angry and frightened and depressed all at once. Then I broke out into a sweat. I tried the door again, then turned away from it. The room suddenly looked different, very large and empty, and I could see every detail in it. There was something familiar and yet not quite right about it.

When I had been walking about I had noticed an inch or two of string looped round one corner of the carpet. Now I saw it again; I was standing on the hardwood surround just by it. At that moment I was wondering if I should hammer on the door and demand to be let out, or sit there quietly and pretend not to have noticed that I had been locked in. Absently I reached down to pick up the string. I wanted something to fidget with. I got the string, but the corner of the carpet came up with it. The string was threaded through the edge of the carpet and tied to a label. The label had some figures written on it and a printed name, obviously that of the dealer who had sold it. It was an expensive carpet, a Sparta, yet the owner had not troubled to remove the price tag. It had simply been tucked away out of sight. I was puzzled. I let the carpet fall back into place and walked round the room again. At one end by the windows there was a buhl cabinet. I opened one of the drawers. There was a small brass screw in it and some dust. I tried the other drawers. All were empty except one, which contained a price tag from the same dealer who had supplied the carpet. I went round quickly looking at the wood of the chairs. They had been used a lot and yet there was a certain *un*used look about them. And then I knew what was familiar about the room: it was like a stage set when all the furniture has just been brought in and placed in position.

At that moment I heard voices and footsteps in the passage outside. I sat down. They came to the door and there was a slight pause. I knew why. The person who was about to open the door was preparing to turn the knob and the key simultaneously so that the sound of the latch would conceal that of the unlocking. If I did not know that I had been locked in, they did not want to tell me of the fact. My heart beat faster.

The door opened and after a momentary pause Pashik came in. He was followed slowly by a small man in a loose tussore suit and a black tie. I stood up.

Pashik put his hand on my shoulder and enveloped me in a broad smile. 'Herr Foster,' he said in German, 'let me introduce you to Herr Valmo.'

I had no time to digest this surprise. The other man came forward with a polite smile and held his hand out tentatively.

'So pleased, Herr Foster,' he said.

He was about fifty, short and very slight, with wispy and receding grey hair brushed back from a sunburnt forehead. It was a thin, pointed face with large, pale-blue eyes and an expression that might have been cruel or amused or both. He looked like a retired ballet dancer who has taken successfully to management. In his hand was Katerina Deltchev's letter. It had been opened.

'Herr *Valmo*?' I said.

He smiled. 'I am afraid a little explanation is due to you.' He had a quiet, monotonous voice.

'It was not possible for *me* to explain, Herr Foster,' said Pashik. 'I could not break a confidence.'

'Please sit down, Herr Foster, and you, my dear Pashik. A cigarette? Ah, you are already smoking. As our friend Pashik explained to you, I am, you might say, some sort of a policeman, a very'–he made a belittling gesture with his hand–'a very confidential sort of policeman.' The woman appeared at the door with a tray and he glanced round. 'Yes, come in Mentcha. Put it down.' He turned again, pulled round a chair, and sat facing me. 'Coffee and a little brandy, Herr Foster. You have had a very upsetting experience, our friend tells me. Thank you, Mentcha. Shut the door. And now,' he went on as she went out, 'we must set your mind at rest. In the coffee, the brandy?'

'Thank you.'

Pashik was sitting deferentially by as if at a conference between his superiors. The hand holding his cigarette was trembling slightly.

Valmo handed me a cup and went on talking as he filled the other two. 'There is one thing,' he said, 'that I must ask of you, Herr Foster. That is that you respect the confidence of what I am about to tell you.' He held a cup out to Pashik but he looked at me. 'Pashik tells me that you are not friendly to the regime here. I understand. But I am not a politician. I am a civil servant. Our country is a centre for many conspiracies against the law and it is my task to destroy them. Can I be certain that you will respect my confidence, Herr Foster?'

'Yes.' I tasted the coffee.

'Very well.' He put his cup behind him on the table and then leaned forward toward me with his elbows on his knees and his hands together. 'In my role of policeman, Herr Foster, it was my duty to seek out the perpetrators of the bomb outrage against Herr Deltchev that took place shortly before his arrest. I made certain secret inquiries and investigations. It was believed that the criminals had had the Deltchev family under surveillance, and members of the family co-operated with me in identifying them. I have said that my function is not political. Herr Deltchev's trial does not relieve me of the responsibility of tracing these criminals. You understand?'

I nodded.

'For reasons with which I will not trouble you,' he continued, 'it became necessary for me to install an agent in the Patriarch Dimo. For convenience and identification, the agent employed my name. Very well. Three days ago my agent reported to me that he had news of the men we were after. That night he was killed.' He paused impressively.

'Who found him dead?' I asked.

He stared at me for a moment. Then he turned round and picked up his coffee cup again. 'I did, Herr Foster,' he said blandly. 'However, let me continue. The agent had collected certain documentary evidence against the conspirators, which he kept hidden in the room. I discovered that this had not been stolen. Therefore, I argued, they did not know of its existence. Therefore, if they were made aware of its existence they would return for it. Therefore I replaced the true documents with some false ones and sat down to wait for results.'

'You mean you put a secret watch on the house to catch the murderer when he returned?'

He smiled gently and shook his head. 'I am afraid you do not know the street of the Patriarch Dimo, Herr Foster,' he said. 'That sort of secret could not be kept there. No. I set a different kind of trap. All I wanted was to get the false documents into the conspirators' hands. I had reason to believe that in fact that had happened. Tonight I asked Herr Pashik, who is a friend of mine and also sometimes a helper, to go to the house and make sure.' He spread his hands out like a conjuror. 'He finds you there.'

'With a letter addressed to you.'

'Exactly. Katerina Deltchev had recalled an important piece of evidence. She wrote to tell me of it.'

'Through your agent.'

'Naturally. This address is most confidential, Herr Foster. So you see how it has happened and the need for your discretion.' He sat back with a smile, clicked his lighter, and held the letter in the flame of it. As it caught fire, he smiled at me again. 'I'm sure you do,' he added.

I thought quickly. It was just not quite good enough. The man who called himself Valmo and said that he was of the secret police had had a certain initial advantage; he did not look like the conventional secret policeman of fiction. If he had been vaguer and more mysterious about his story, it might even have been convincing. There would have been nothing unlikely about a secret policeman who was secretive. But this man had seen the holes in his story as he was telling it and instead of leaving them had tried to cover them up. For instance, having indicated an official connection between the Deltchev household and Patriarch Dimo Street he had decided that it did not satisfactorily cover Katerina's letter, so he had added another detail; that weak one about her recalling an important piece of evidence. It would have been better to let me see the hole and question it. He could then have replied with a knowing shake of the head that he was afraid he could not permit himself to give me that information. And that, in turn, would have prevented my asking the awkward question I did in fact ask.

'Herr Valmo,' I said, 'what I don't understand is why Fräulein Deltchev, who is under house arrest, has to get me to smuggle out a letter to the head of the secret police. Why didn't she just give it to one of the sentries?'

He crushed the ashes of the letter on to the tray. 'She is a girl. No doubt she was afraid I would not get it.'

'She seemed more concerned about the censorship than anything else. She made me promise to deliver it by hand.'

'Confinement affects some people strangely.'

'Shall you go to see her?'

'It may be necessary. I do not know.' He was getting confused now. He pulled himself together a trifle impatiently. 'Those, however, are not matters of immediate concern, Herr Foster. It is your position that we must make clear.'

'Yes.'

'I have given you a great deal of confidential information. It must, please, remain confidential.' His pale eyes stared at me coldly. 'I may add, Herr Foster, that if you were not a distinguished journalist, it would have been considered advisable to put you in prison for a short while to make sure of your behaviour. That, however, we need not discuss. You have already assured me that you will be discreet. I require now three further undertakings from you. First'—he held up a finger—'that you will not return to the house in the Patriarch Dimo or tell anyone of it. Secondly, that you will not again visit the Deltchev house. Thirdly, that you will make no attempt to identify this house and that you forget its existence, and mine.'

I did not reply immediately. I knew now the kind of conversation that must have taken place between Valmo and Pashik while I was safely locked up and waiting. My one desire was to get out of the place as quickly as possible. But I had the sense to realize that if I showed my anxiety and agreed to the terms too hastily, they would not feel quite safe. They were both watching me narrowly. I frowned, then looked up and nodded.

'All right,' I said curtly. 'I agree. And now, if you don't mind, I'd like another brandy.'

Valmo stood up. 'Yes, of course,' he said perfunctorily. He poured a small one. He could not wait to get rid of me now. 'Herr Pashik?'

'Thank you, no.'

They stood looking at me impatiently while I sipped the brandy. It was the only moment of enjoyment I had had in the whole evening and it lasted about ten seconds. As I swallowed the first sip, I heard the front door of the apartment open and close and footsteps in the passage outside.

'It is my brother,' said Valmo quickly.

Then the door opened and a young man came into the room. He saw me and stopped.

'Good evening, Jika,' Valmo said. 'We are talking a little business. I shall be with you in a minute.'

He was about twenty-five, dark and very tired-looking. He had a raincoat on and his hair was blown about as if he had been in an open car. He looked at us suspiciously. For a moment he did not move; then he turned away slowly and went to the door.

'Don't be too long, Aleko,' he said. 'I have something for you.'

I raised the brandy to my mouth again. I was not looking directly at Pashik, but I could see his face and it had gone the colour of mud. He knew that I had seen the 'Aleko' note in the Deltchev file and for some reason was terrified lest I had remembered it. Aleko himself was waiting for me to finish my drink. The use of his Christian name had not visibly upset him. But the situation was delicate. I had seen something I should not have seen, but Pashik did not know if I realized it. The main thing then was to get out of the apartment before he could make up his mind what to do. I drank the brandy at a gulp and held out my hand to Aleko.

'Thank you, Herr Valmo, and goodbye.'

He smiled agreeably. 'I hope your stay is pleasant here, Herr Foster,' he said.

I turned to Pashik. 'Are you going to drive me back to my hotel, Pashik?'

'Yes, Mr Foster, yes.'

We went along the passage to the front door. Aleko came out to the lift with us. Aleko shook my hand again.

'I have liked you, Herr Foster,' he said; 'and with a journalist that is a new experience for me. I have faith in you. Goodbye.'

He might have been sending a promising young dancer on a first international tour.

Pashik was already in the lift. I got in after him. We went down in silence.

It was not until we were in his car and out on the road again that I broke the silence.

'Aleko Valmo,' I said. 'A curious name.'

'In these parts it is quite common, Mr Foster.'

He spoke calmly. He had made up his mind that I had forgotten the other name.

I was not feeling very friendly toward him, and for a moment or two I toyed with the idea of asking him suddenly: 'What was the case of K. Fischer, Vienna '46, about, Pashik, and what had Aleko to do with it?'

Then I decided not to. We did not speak again until he drew up outside my hotel. As I went to get out, he put his hand on my arm and his brown eyes sought mine.

'Mr Foster,' he said, 'it has been a lousy experience for you this evening and no doubt you will wish to forget all about it. That is, if you are wise.'

I did not answer. His voice took on its cautious round-about tone.

'I wish only to tell you,' he said, 'that I understand your feelings and share them. But you have your own profession and need not trouble about what happens to deadbeats and bums far away from your home. Men are dying all over the world for the causes they believe in. You cannot fight their battles.'

'Are you telling me that I should mind my own business?' I asked.

'Ah, please, Mr Foster!' He spread his hands out. 'You are mad at me.'

I was exasperated. 'I'm not mad at you, Pashik. I'm merely trying to get you to say straight out what you mean without all this double-talk. I don't mind being advised to mind my own business. That's all right. I don't have to take the advice if I don't want to. I'm still capable of deciding what is my own business and what isn't. I'm not fighting any battles. I'm trying to find out what goes on here.'

'That is what I mean, Mr Foster. It does no good to try.'

'You mean I won't be able to find out?'

He looked away from me and picked at the steering-wheel. 'You force me to be frank, Mr Foster.'

'What's the matter with frankness? Why has it to be forced?'

'You say you fight no battles, Mr Foster,' he said quietly; 'but I tell you, you are wandering like a fool between the opposing forces of those who are. That is a crazy thing to do. Once, years ago in Vienna, I saw street fighting between troops and revolutionaries. The fighting went on for many days. But there was one street that was swept equally by the fire of both sides, and neither could advance. Then one afternoon something very silly happened, as so often it happens in war. Into this empty, silent street there came a man. We heard his footsteps first. Then we saw him. He staggered from a side turning right into the middle of the street and stood there swaying. He belonged to neither side. He was drunk and did not know where he was or what he was doing. He began to sing and wave and call out for a woman. At first the soldiers laughed and shouted jokes at him. But after a while their officer noticed that the enemy was taking advantage of the distraction to run across the far end of the street in ones and twos so as to outflank the troops. He shouted a warning and they opened fire. The enemy replied with covering fire and the street was swept from end to end with machine-gun bullets. The drunk was killed immediately. You see, Mr Foster?'

'Which side were you on?'

'I was a soldier then. I have been many things, Mr Foster.'

'Yes. Tell me. The reason that your friend Valmo doesn't want me to go to the Deltchev house again is that he doesn't want me to ask Katerina Deltchev to confirm his story, isn't it?'

'I don't know, Mr Foster. As long as you keep faith with Mr Valmo it does not matter. One thing I have to ask of you myself, however. I thought it discreet not to mention your connection with Petlarov; it would have complicated the affair. None of these things must on any account be mentioned to Petlarov. Or Mr Sibley. That is most important.'

'All right.' I was tired of the whole business now. I wanted to get to bed. I opened the car door. Pashik put out his hand again.

'You will think over what I said, Mr Foster,' he said anxiously. 'It is for your own good I ask.'

I got out of the car. 'I'll be very sober,' I said. 'That I promise you. Good night.'

I was about to slam the door. He leaned across and held it open. His glasses flickered in the light from the hotel entrance as he looked up at me.

'I hope so,' he said slowly. 'But if you do not intend to take my advice, Mr Foster, it might be less painful to be drunk. Good night.'

Then he shut the door and drove off.

I did not sleep well that night.

Chapter Twelve

It was on the fourth day of the trial that the evidence connecting Deltchev with the Brotherhood was given.

When the court opened, a man named Kroum was called into the witness box. He was about fifty, with a bald head and glasses and an erect military appearance. He looked shrewd and brutal. He described himself as a brigadier of police in the detective department of the Ministry of the Interior.

Prochaska began his examination in what was for him an unexpected way.

'Brigadier Kroum, how long have you been a member of the police?'

'Thirty years, sir.'

'How long have you held your present appointment?'

'Twelve years, sir.'

'Are you a member of any political party?'

'No, sir.'

'Have you any political affiliations?'

'No, sir.'

'None at all?'

'I do not interest myself in politics, sir. I have my work to do.'

'An excellent citizen! Have you ever arrested a man or ordered his arrest for political reasons?'

'The only reason for any arrest, sir, is that a man breaks or is suspected of breaking the law. I do not make the law. It is my duty simply to enforce the law under the constitution. That is the duty of every police officer,' he added.

Someone near me sniggered at this; but my impression was that Brigadier Kroum meant what he said.

Prochaska glanced at a paper. 'In March,' he said, 'were you concerned with the arrest of eight persons on the charge of trading illicitly in prepared opium?'

'I was responsible for the arrests, sir.'

'Did you also examine the prisoners?'

Kroum hesitated. 'Unofficially, sir, and solely for the purpose of obtaining information about other members of the gang. The examining magistrate was responsible, of course, for the official interrogation.'

'You were not usurping the magistrate's function, but merely doing your duty as a police officer. Is that correct?'

'Yes, sir. That is correct.'

'But you gave the prisoners the impression that they were making official depositions?'

'It is sometimes necessary, sir.'

He had a blubbery mouth with bad-tempered creases round it. Interrogation by Brigadier Kroum would not be an agreeable experience.

'Was one of those arrested a man named Rila?'

'Yes, sir.'

'Did you interrogate him?'

'I did, sir.'

'Tell the court about this interrogation.'

'Yes, sir. This Rila is a criminal well known to the police. He is an old man who has served many prison sentences. I knew that his eldest granddaughter was pregnant for the first time. I told him that this time he would surely die in prison and never see his great-grandchild, but that if he assisted the police by telling all he knew, a permit might be obtained for the child to be brought for him to see.' He looked doubtfully at the prosecutor. 'It is customary to offer such inducements to prisoners. No regulations would be broken, sir.'

'No, no. Continue please.'

'At first he refused to talk. Said he knew nothing. The usual.' Kroum was gaining courage. 'But the following day, when I saw him again, he was in a better mood. He had thought over my offer and he was worried. After a while he asked if I would protect him from any consequences there might be of his talking. That, too, is usual with criminals informing,' he added confidentially.

'Yes. Continue please.'

'I asked him for the names of the other members of the gang. He said there were no other members and that we had them all and that there was no information he could give about that case. But he wanted to see his great-grandchild and there was other important information he could give in return for the concession. I said that if the information was valuable it might be possible.'

'Continue.'

'He then told me that there was in existence a conspiracy to assassinate Minister Vukashin and that the conspirators were members of the Officer Corps Brotherhood.' He paused.

'And did you believe him—this criminal who wished to purchase a concession with information?'

'No, sir. At first I thought it was merely an impudent lie and sent him back to his cell. But on thinking it over I decided to question him again. Even though I thought that what he had said must be fantastic, the suggestion was so serious that I felt it necessary to make quite sure. I felt it my duty,' he added virtuously.

'Yes, yes. So you questioned him again.'

'Yes, sir, and again he began by asking for protection. Again I reassured him. Then he told me a strange story. He lodged in a house in the Maria Louisa quarter. One of his fellow lodgers was a man named Pazar.' He paused. He was at his ease now, talking more as an experienced policeman and less as an applause-hungry functionary. 'We know that house,' he went on; 'it is a place for crooks; and because we do know it we let it be; but anyone living there is automatically suspect. Pazar, however, was new there. Rila was curious about him. For Rila there was always the possibility that a stranger might be a police spy. So he took note of this man's movements and was watchful. All he discovered to begin with was that on certain evenings Pazar would be visited by three or four men unknown in the Maria Louisa quarter. They did not look poor, and Rila wondered what they were up to. It is probable, I think, that all along he had an idea of joining in what he thought might be a profitable racket, but this, of course, he denied when I suggested it. He gave another explanation. However—'

'Just a moment, brigadier. What was the explanation he gave?'

Kroum looked embarrassed. 'He said, sir, that he was only interested in human nature.'

There was some laughter. Prochaska frowned. 'Go on,' he said shortly.

'Yes, sir. Rila said that Pazar had been living there for about a month when one day he stopped Rila on the stairs and asked to speak to him privately. Rila agreed and they went to his room. After a lot of talk Pazar came out with what he wanted. Someone had told him that Rila dealt in illicit drugs and Pazar wanted some heroin for a friend. Rila's first thought was that Pazar was a police spy after all and he pretended to be shocked. But after a little more talk Rila became convinced that Pazar himself was a heroin addict and needed the stuff badly. Now Rila is quite frank about what followed. Pazar had little money and asked for credit. Rila refused. With heroin addicts one might as well give the stuff away as give credit. Instead he referred to Pazar's well-dressed visitors and said that if he, Rila, could afford smart clothes like that he would be very grateful to the person who had helped him. In other words, he asked for a share in the profitable business he thought was being done by Pazar's friends. Pazar refused angrily and went away. Rila shrugged and waited. Pazar would have to have his stuff, and if he had been driven to asking Rila for it, that meant that his old source of supply had for some reason been stopped. Two days later Pazar came again to Rila, who repeated his price. Pazar again refused, but this time he did not get angry; he pleaded with Rila. His friends, he said, had nothing to do with any trade. They were political. He went on pleading and Rila went on refusing until Pazar became desperate. He begged on his knees, and when Rila told him to go away he broke down and wept. Then it came out. Pazar and the friends who visited him were members of the Brotherhood.'

Kroum paused. He had his audience now. There was dead silence. He went on:

'At first Rila did not believe him. When he did believe, he was worried.

Our criminals have never liked the Brotherhood. They have been resentful of the extra vigilance it has caused, but also they have been afraid. It is curious,' Kroum went on thoughtfully; 'a man who kills for money they understand, but the Brotherhood killer troubles them. This old criminal Rila talked about the Brotherhood as a boy might talk about ghosts and demons.'

'Yes, yes. Continue.'

'Pazar worried him very much, for he knew the ways of heroin addicts, as I have said, and he knew that they were treacherous and spiteful. If he refused Pazar and Pazar told his mysterious friends of the Brotherhood that their secret was known to Rila, then Rila would be in danger. So to keep Pazar quiet he gave him some heroin. After a few days Pazar came back for more, and soon Rila was supplying him regularly. Pazar would come into his room and stay and talk and gradually he became more indiscreet.'

That word! I glanced at Pashik next to me. His face was quite impassive, but his hands were tense.

Kroum had paused again. Now he went on very slowly:

'One day—Rila cannot remember which day—Pazar began to tell him of something he called the secret of power. He was very mysterious about this secret, but Rila let him talk and after a while Pazar took a round of machine-pistol ammunition from his pocket. "This is the secret of power, my friend," he said, "for this beautiful little thing can make a revolution." Rila was afraid to ask him what he meant, but Pazar told him eventually. The Brotherhood were planning to assassinate Minister Vukashin.'

The prosecutor nodded and looked up at the judges. 'The man Rila made a deposition to the effect of what the witness has told the court,' he said. 'The deposition is signed by him and properly witnessed.' He picked up a bundle of papers. 'I submit it to the court in evidence, together with three certified copies.'

The copies were passed to the clerk of the court, who handed them up to the dais. The centre judge glanced at the top paper, nodded gravely, and said something.

'The presiding judges accept the documents in evidence,' said the interpreter's voice, 'and call upon the prosecutor to continue.'

Prochaska turned to the witness box again. 'Brigadier Kroum, what action did you take as a result of what you had heard?'

Kroum had prepared this answer: 'I considered it my duty, sir, to inform the Minister of the Interior at once so that those responsible for the protection of Minister Vukashin might be warned.'

'And then?'

'Then, sir, I set about investigating the truth of the story.'

'You doubted it?'

Kroum very nearly permitted himself a tolerant grin. 'The police, sir, are obliged to think suspiciously of persons who wish to help them,' he said, 'especially if they may gain an advantage by doing so.'

'Very well. You investigated. What did you discover?'

'That there was a man named Pazar at the house in Maria Louisa, that he did occasionally receive the kind of visitors described, and that he had a reputation for drug-taking. He was not known as a criminal. He was believed to have been at one time a schoolmaster. He had also made a living as a language tutor.'

'And then what did you do?'

'There were three possible explanations, sir: that Rila had made up the rest of the story or that Pazar had invented it to impress Rila and get drugs from him; second, that Pazar was mentally unstable as a result of drug-taking and not only invented the story but also believed it to be true; thirdly, that it was in fact true. Although we believed this last possibility unlikely, we decided that no harm would be done by acting upon it. We therefore set a watch on the house with the idea of identifying Pazar's visitors and possibly confronting them in Pazar's room. On the evening of the third day Pazar did not return to the house at the customary time. That same evening a man arrived at the house and was identified by the woman who kept it as one of the regular visitors. He went straight to Pazar's room, which was on the second floor. He received, of course, no reply to his knock and waited for a time. Then he decided to go. When he was stopped by one of my men, he immediately drew a revolver and began to shoot, wounding two policemen. He then attempted to escape, but was shot down. He was identified as a man named Eftib, a university student with a reputation for fanatical views of the kind associated with the Officer Corps Brotherhood.'

'He was killed?'

'Unfortunately he died before we could question him, sir.'

'Continue.'

'The fact that Pazar had not returned and that only Eftib had arrived for a meeting suggested to us that Pazar had been warned of our activity and had passed the warning to the other conspirators. This view was confirmed by the fact that Eftib had been visiting his parents in the country and had only that evening returned. He, therefore, had not received the warning. In any case, our interest in the house was now exposed. We therefore entered Pazar's room and made a search of his belongings.'

'And you found?'

'The complete dossier of a conspiracy to assassinate Minister Vukashin on the occasion of the university celebration, including a plan of the operation and detailed orders for the five men participating in it.'

A stir ran round the court. Prochaska looked up at the judges. 'I ask the court for discretion in this matter,' he said. 'I have the dossier here and will with permission proceed to offer it in evidence. I ask leave, however, to withhold that part of it concerned with the actual plan of the attempt. It is of great ingenuity and, for reasons that will appear in a moment, unsafe for publication at present. It is in any case not essential to the prosecution's case.'

'The permission asked for is granted by the presiding judges.'

A bulky file was handed to the clerk of the court. Prochaska continued: 'The witness is, of course, not quite accurate in describing what he found as a dossier. He found the operation plan concealed under the floorboards of the room and in other hiding-places a number of documents. These things were later collected into dossier form.'

The centre judge nodded.

Prochaska turned to Kroum again. 'I will ask you now to identify the various items. Item one.' He nodded to the clerk, who handed Kroum a clipped wad of papers.

Kroum looked at it.

'Do you recognize those papers?' asked Prochaska.

'I do, sir. I identify them as those I found concealed beneath the tiles of the stove in Pazar's room.'

'Have you ever seen papers like that before?'

'Yes, sir. These are pledge forms used as part of the initiation ceremony of the Officer Corps Brotherhood. I recognized them at once. They were secretly printed by a member of the Brotherhood now dead. His name was Markoff. He was arrested, tried, and hanged in January '45. But these were his work.'

'Read the pledge to the court.'

Kroum cleared his throat. He said: 'The form is headed: *Brotherhood of the Officer Corps for the Holy Protection of all Kindred Families and of the Sacred Motherland which gave them Birth and Honour.* Then follows the pledge: *I, Brother X, having, from the dictates of my own heart and conscience and for no other reason, submitted myself to the judgment of my Brethren in honour, and having, through the mingling of my blood with theirs, received absolution before the Mother of God for all acts committed in their name, do hereby dedicate my soul and body to the service of the Brotherhood until and unto death. Recognizing that between Brothers thus specially united by ties of blood there may be no contention or preference or inequality, I swear unconditional and immediate obedience to all orders given to me by Brothers to whom authority has been delegated by the Brethren assembled, and should authority be so delegated to me I swear to accept it and use it faithfully in the knowledge that the responsibility is shared by all equally and that my loyalty to the Brotherhood is superior to all other loyalties and avowals, private or public. My reward for faithful service shall be the honour and love of my Brothers and their protection of me and of my family. But should I betray or in any other way fail the Brotherhood, my own death will be only part of the price to be paid for the offence, for by this oath now taken I bind my whole being, and in betrayal of it all that I hold dear is forfeit. All this I understand and accept. All this I believe just. All this I freely swear to on my blood, my honour, and my life and by this act became of you my Brothers.'* Kroum looked up. 'That is all, sir.'

'A licence to commit treason and murder,' commented Prochaska, 'as the acknowledged crimes of this fraternity have long since proved.' He nodded to the clerk, who handed up another document to Kroum.

Kroum looked at it.

'Do you recognize that document?'

'I do, sir. It was hidden in Pazar's room with the papers I have just read from.'

'What is it?'

'A list of names under the word "Active."'

'Is the name of Pazar there?'

'It is.'

'And Eftib?'

'Yes, sir.'

'Is there any other name there familiar to the police?'

'Yes.' He hesitated. 'The name of Deltchev.'

There was dead silence in the court now. Deltchev was sitting in his usual position with his eyes closed. He did not move.

'Is there any other peculiarity about the list?'

'Yes, sir. Certain names on it are underlined.'

'Which names?'

'Those of Pazar, Eftib, Vlahov, Pechanatz, Radiuje, and Deltchev.'

There was a faint murmur in the court. Deltchev opened his eyes and looked at Kroum thoughtfully.

'Did you say that the plan to assassinate Minister Vukashin required five persons to operate it?'

'Yes, sir.'

'Then the sixth person might be the leader?'

'It seemed likely, sir.'

'What action did you take?'

'I informed the Minister of the Interior, and warrants for the arrest of Pazar, Vlahov, Pechanatz, and Radiuje were issued.'

'Did you execute the warrants?'

'Pechanatz and Radiuje were found to have already left the country. Vlahov was arrested while attempting to do so. It was at the airport and he was placed in the waiting-room to await an escort. The arresting officer had neglected to search him and while in the waiting-room he shot himself. Pazar has not yet been traced.'

'What action has been taken about the other names on the list?'

'I ask permission not to answer that question, sir.'

'I understand, brigadier.' He turned to the judges. 'I would point out to the court that at least one man connected with the conspiracy is still in the country and free and that he may attempt to find other confederates even now. It is for that reason that all information cannot yet be made public.'

'The presiding judges acknowledge the point.'

Prochaska bowed and nodded to the clerk. More papers were handed to Kroum.

'Do you recognize those documents?'

'Yes, sir. I identify them as from Pazar's room.'

'Describe them.'

'They are messages, mostly typewritten or inked in block letters on plain paper.'

'Read from them.'

'The first reads: "*Meeting for Thursday to take place Friday. Notified V. and P.*"'

'No signature?'

'None is signed, sir.'

'Continue.'

'The second reads: "*Await advice as arranged.*" The third: "*P. remains incomplete. Progress others.*" The next: "*V. unsuccessful. Will expedite.*" Next—'

Prochaska interrupted him. 'One moment, brigadier. I do not think we need trouble you to read all the messages. I wished only to show their character. They continue like that?'

'Yes, sir. There are over thirty of them.'

'Do you understand their meaning?'

'I think so.'

'They have a direct dealing on the assassination plan?'

'Yes, sir.'

'Then we will be discreet. I come to another point. Do these messages constitute a correspondence or are they only messages received?'

'Messages received, sir.'

'What initials appear in the messages?'

'V., P., E., R., and D.'

'Referring to?'

'Vlahov, Pechanatz, Eftib, Radiuje, and Deltchev, I believe.'

'It seems likely. What is the general character of these messages? Are they, for example, instructions?'

'I would say they are reports.'

'To the leader of the conspirators?'

'I think not, sir. It is difficult to say, but in my opinion Pazar, who received the reports, was responsible for co-ordinating the information. We learned that he received no messages at the house. My belief is that the others used a café or a shop as a post office and that he collected the messages from there, copied them, and redistributed them for information to those concerned. The nature of the plan would call for constant communications of that sort during the period of preparation. No doubt each conspirator had an accommodation address.'

'Very well. The messages have been numbered for convenience. Please find message number twenty-seven.'

'I have it here.'

'Read it please.'

'It reads: "*V. in difficulty. Advise D. urgent.*"'

'Is that written or typewritten?'

'Typewritten.'

'Is there anything else on the paper?'

'Yes, sir, some pencil writing.'

'Read it please.'

'It reads: "*Strumitza, twelve.*"'

The courtroom stirred.

'Is that an address?'

'Yes, sir. It is the prisoner's address.'

'What explanation have you for its being there?'

'It is in Pazar's handwriting. I suggest that as the message was urgent he did not deliver it to the usual accommodation address for the prisoner, but took it direct to his home. The pencil note was a memorandum of an address that Pazar would not normally use.'

I looked at Deltchev. His eyes were closed again. He had not moved. It was impossible to believe. And yet—

Stanoiev did not cross-examine. Kroum left the witness box reluctantly, like an aging prima donna on a farewell tour, and one of his colleagues took his place. The questioning was resumed. What Kroum had said was now elaborately confirmed. I no longer paid much attention. I was trying to digest what I had already heard.

Chapter Thirteen

It was true; of that I had little doubt. Prochaska had an air of confidence that was not of the kind he could assume. Perhaps clever cross-examination could have made much of Kroum's evidence look weak; Deltchev was not an uncommon name, and when you pointed out that the prisoner's identification with the D. of the messages rested solely on a pencilled note of an address alleged to be in the handwriting of a man who could not be produced, you might have shaken a jury's belief in the whole story. But here there was no jury to be shaken and, after the massive certainties of Vukashin and the rest, the very flimsiness of the thing gave it probability. Someone named Deltchev who lived in Deltchev's house had been in close touch with persons desperate enough, as Eftib and Vlahov had been, to shoot when confronted by the police or to commit suicide when arrested. Madame Deltchev? Absurd. Katerina Deltchev? By the time the luncheon break came, I thought I was ready for Pashik.

'Well,' I said, 'what do you think?'

'It is very interesting.'

'Yes. Where do you think Pazar is now?'

He shrugged elaborately. 'It is a mystery.'

'So they say. When do you think they'll find that man in Patriarch Dimo?'

The brown eyes looked at me steadily. He did not reply.

I stared back at him. 'I would guess that it's Pazar's body in that room, wouldn't you?' I said.

'What makes you think that, Mr Foster?'

'Just an association of ideas. Someone in Deltchev's house sent messages to a man named Pazar. That man is now missing. Someone in Deltchev's house sends a message by me to a man who lived in Patriarch Dimo. That man is now dead.'

'That is bad logic, Mr Foster.'

'It might be good guessing. Do you believe that Deltchev was in a conspiracy to assassinate Vukashin?'

'It could be so.'

'Yes, it could be, but do you think yourself that it was so?'

'Who else could there be, Mr Foster?'

'Katerina Deltchev could be the D. of those messages.'

He showed his brown teeth in a smile. 'A nice young lady of twenty in a Brotherhood conspiracy? That is a very funny idea, but it is no more than funny. The Officer Corps Sisterhood! Ah, please, Mr Foster!'

'Yes, it's silly. I'm trying to find a reasonable explanation, that's all.'

'The reasonable explanation is the one already given. Mr Foster, we are newspapermen, not attorneys for the defence. We need only observe and report. We are lucky.'

He had a bland, noncommittal look on his face. At breakfast I had not mentioned the events of the night before. In the morning light they had assumed the proportions of a bad dream, and until I could talk to Petlarov I was content to leave them so. Besides, I was tired of Pashik's denials and warnings and had made up my mind to discover something about the case of 'K. Fischer, Vienna '46' before I tackled him again. It looked now as if he thought I had taken his advice. I put aside a temptation to correct the impression.

'What was the Brotherhood plan they're being so secretive about?' I asked.

'I know no more than you, Mr Foster.'

'Doesn't Valmo know? Surely a man in his position would know such things?'

'I am not in his confidence to that extent.'

'Did you know Pazar or Eftib?'

To my surprise, he nodded. 'Eftib I knew. He was a young man with a great dislike of dogs. A dog he found tied up one day he beat to death with a piece of chain. The other students disliked and feared him. He was not sane, I think.'

'How did you know him?'

'The dog he killed belonged to one of the professors at the university. There was a scandal. I reported it for a newspaper, but his family paid to avoid the publicity. By now,' he added thoughtfully, 'they may wish he had been safely put in prison.'

The waiter came up with our food. This particular section of the restaurant was reserved for the pressmen attending the trial and across the room I could see Sibley talking earnestly and confidentially to one of the Americans. Then out of the corner of my eye I saw Pashik looking at me. He looked away almost as I saw him, but not quite fast enough. He had to cover up.

'Yes,' he said, 'Mr Sibley is busy still. He may succeed with someone who has no reason to suspect him. It is very strange.'

I smiled. 'There's something I find even stranger, Pashik.'

'Yes, Mr Foster?' He was on his guard again.

'I find it strange that although you are quite ready to serve someone you say is of the Government secret police, you put obstacles in the way of Sibley, who is trying to serve the Propaganda Ministry.'

He stared at me for a moment and I thought that he was about to reply. Then he changed his mind, cleared his throat, and picked up his knife and fork. 'Mr Foster,' he said heavily, 'I think we should get on with our eating.'

I could get nothing more out of him. After the luncheon break the conspiracy evidence was resumed. Now that he had something like real evidence to deal with, Prochaska spread himself. Every detail of Kroum's evidence was sworn to by three or four different persons, every document certified and proved. Had you not heard the earlier days of the trial, you might from Prochaska's attitude have supposed the judges to be pettifogging martinets hostile to his case. When you remembered the rubbish that had already been admitted as evidence by that pathetic trio, the present solemnity was funny. But not for long. Presently it became boring. Only one thing kept me there: the possibility of Deltchev's speaking in his own defence. But he seemed as bored as I was. As witness after witness was brought in to swear to the authenticity of the message with his address on it, I expected a protest from him. It would have been easy enough:

'These conscientious policemen swear to the presence of my address on this piece of paper. Nobody disputes that it is there. Why waste the time they might be devoting to more useful duties? Produce a really serious witness: the man who wrote it or who saw it written or, even better, the man who can tell us *why* and in what circumstances it was written down there. Those questions are important, gentleman, for I, too, have been plotted against by assassins. They threw a bomb and badly wounded my chauffeur. That was outside my house, and to find my house you need the address, and to remember it you have to write it down. I have no wish to deprive Minister Vukashin of his martyr's laurels, but if I am to be convicted of plotting against his life, at least make sure that the evidence you use is not part of an old plot against *my* life. For a new plot new evidence should be manufactured. Economy in such matters is discourteous.'

But Deltchev said nothing at all and the afternoon drowsed on. Curiously, it was only the diplomatic and press sections who seemed bored. For most of the spectators it was an exciting afternoon. As each witness appeared, there would be a buzz of interest, then dead silence while he gave his evidence, then breathless whispering as he stepped down. It was the factual nature of the evidence that did it. There must have been many in that courtroom who had been unwilling to believe in Deltchev's guilt and privately uneasy about the trial. Now they were enjoying the illusion that the legal forms were being properly observed and that they were free of the responsibility of condoning an injustice. I was glad when the afternoon was over.

Pashik had nothing to say as he drove me back to my hotel. He knew that I was going to see Petlarov and he was saving himself for a farewell admonishment on the subject of discretion; so I thought, at least; and I was tired of him; I was tired of his smell, of his admonishments, of his evasions and mystery-making, of his long-suffering brown eyes, of his dirty seersucker suit, and of his bad driving.

He stopped jerkily outside the hotel and turned to me. 'Mr Foster—' he began.

I interrupted irritably. 'Look, do you have to go on calling me "Mr Foster" all the time? Can't you make it "Foster" or "you"? It would be easier for you and I shouldn't feel so stiff-necked.'

He began again picking at the vulcanite covering of the steering-wheel. He already had most of it off and the metal beneath looked bare and squalid.

'I am sorry, Mr Foster,' he said, 'I wished only to be polite.'

'Yes, of course. It's not important.'

But he was upset. 'I am afraid you are not a good-tempered man, Mr Foster,' he said.

'No, I'm not. I apologize. You wanted to tell me to be discreet again, didn't you?'

He picked for a moment or two in silence. He was working on a big piece and it peeled away like a strip of sunburnt skin.

'I don't know what more I can say to you, Mr Foster,' he said. 'I have tried to warn you, not because I like you or even because I have a responsibility to the New York office, but in the spirit of any man who sees another by accident going into a danger he does not realize. I can do no more. There are things more important than the safety of a stranger. You will not take advice; then you must take your chance. I will not discuss the case with you further. The services I am paid for are yours, however. Tomorrow I will be getting your press ticket for the anniversary celebration. When the end date of the trial is known, your return passage by air will be available. If there is any other service you wish performed, you must tell me. Meanwhile, when we meet we can talk of other things.' He turned and looked at me. 'Good night, Mr Foster.'

'Good night.'

I got out and went into the hotel. I was both impressed and depressed. As I walked up the stairs I decided that I would take his advice. I told myself that it was only my personal dislike of the man that had prevented my taking it before. That was really stupid. My task was to write articles about the trial, not to play policeman. I had stumbled on a political murder in a country where political murder was a commonplace. The fact that for me it was a novelty did not give me a licence to inquire into it. I should remember that I was a foreigner, there on sufferance, that I had a very lucrative profession to return to, and that in my temporary role of newspaper reporter I had done very well to get an exclusive interview with Madame Deltchev. That was enough. I would now mind my own business. And it might be a good idea to apologize to Pashik. He had been very patient with me and I had behaved with the bumptiousness of an amateur. And, by the way, since when had Mr Foster been entitled to object to being called Mr Foster by someone who wished to be courteous? Mr Foster was making a very tiresome fool of himself. He'd better stop.

Petlarov was sitting stiff and straight on his usual seat in the corridor. Without speaking he followed me into my room and sat down. I went to the wardrobe and got out the whisky. He took the tooth glass with his usual polite bow and then glanced up at me.

'You look tired, Herr Foster.'

'I've had a tiring twenty-four hours.'

He nodded politely. He did not even look a question.

'What about today's evidence? What do you think?' I asked. 'It's more or less what you feared, isn't it?'

He considered for a moment, then he shook his head. 'No. I don't think it is. You see, I expected something possible. I thought that Yordan might have committed some indiscretion capable of being shown badly. But not this. It is really very funny. I know Yordan and I know that he is incapable of this kind of association. And with men of the type of Eftib and Pazar it is grotesque.'

'He associated with Vukashin and Brankovitch?'

'He did not like them, but he recognized their importance. Both are considerable men, leaders. But conspiracy with this delinquent riffraff? It is impossible! Yordan is too much of a snob.'

'What sort of indiscretion did you expect?'

He shrugged. 'Many things are possible. For example, it would not have greatly surprised me to learn that some of the exiles were planning a *coup d'état* and had nominated Yordan their leader. If they appealed to him he would be flattered. He might temporize, but he would treat with them. In transactions of that kind many foolish things are written. Now with this, all is different. We have circumstantial evidence of the kind that is used to convict ordinary criminals–the piece of paper with the note on it, the scribbled address, the conspirators who escape and those who do not, the mysterious Pazar, who is missing but really dead–it is all of a different pattern.' He shrugged again. 'But that is only what I feel.'

'What did you mean by saying that Pazar is really dead?'

'If he were alive they would certainly have found him before the trial. They could not risk his being found unexpectedly. He might be an inconvenient witness and it would look bad if he, too, were killed resisting arrest.'

So then of course I told him. Whatever else was not my business, the problem of the evidence against Deltchev certainly was, and I had come to rely upon Petlarov's opinions. I told him about the letter I had carried, of the dead man in Patriarch Dimo 9, of Pashik's arrival, of the visit of Aleko, and of the Aleko note. He listened in silence and was silent for a time when I had finished. I noticed that he had gone very pale. Then he put down his drink and stood up.

'Herr Foster,' he said slowly, 'I too have something to tell you. Every two days I have to report to the police to get my papers stamped. It is part of the control to which, as an untrustworthy person, I am subject. Today when I reported, I was warned. I was told that I had recently made an undesirable association and that if I did not wish to be removed with my wife to a labour camp, the association must cease. That was all. Your name was not mentioned.' He hesitated. 'When I came here this evening, Herr Foster, I had almost made up my mind to ignore the warning. I thought that if it had been a serious matter I would not have been warned but arrested. I see now that I was wrong.'

'What do you mean?'

But he did not reply. He was fumbling agitatedly in his pocket. He got out the ration card I had given him and held it out to me.

'I am sorry, Herr Foster,' he said; 'I cannot keep our bargain.'

'That's all right. I understand.' I didn't, but he was so obviously upset that I wanted to soothe him. 'Keep the ration card anyway. I don't want it.'

He shook his head. His face looked pinched and there was sweat on his forehead. I had a curious sense of shock. I had come to think of Petlarov as some kind of genie who inhabited the corridor outside my hotel room, ready to explain, to enlighten, to serve when I needed him. Because his own account of himself had been quite calm and impersonal, because he had not exuded the self-pity I should have been so quick to condemn, I had not found it necessary to think of him as a human being. Now suddenly he was very much a human being; he was frightened. The realization gave me a curious feeling of discomfort.

'Herr Foster,' he said, 'please take the card. I cannot use it any more, and if I am arrested I do not wish to have it found in my pocket.'

I took it. He picked up his hat and went to the door.

'Just a moment,' I said.

He stopped. The effort he made to control his agitation was almost painful to watch. He just wanted to be gone.

'Can't you give me any idea what this is all about?' I asked.

For a moment I thought he was going without answering. Then he swallowed and licked his lips. He looked at his hat as he spoke. 'I will tell you one thing, Herr Foster. K. Fischer, Karl Fischer, you mentioned him.' He hesitated before he went on with a rush. 'He was a Left-wing politician, very popular in the working-class quarters of Vienna. A good man and a fearless speaker. He was in principle for the Soviets, but still in '46 he protested against the Soviet kidnappings of Austrians from the American sector. An honest man. He did what he thought right. He was murdered.' He hesitated and swallowed again.

'Yes?'

'In September it was,' he said. 'He went out one evening to see his married daughter in Favoriten. Next day the railway police found his body behind a shed in the marshalling yard outside the Ostbahnhof.' He paused and looked up at me. 'You said that the man you saw at Patriarch Dimo had been killed by a bullet wound in the back of the head, by the ear.'

'Yes.'

He nodded. 'That was how Karl Fischer died,' he said. 'That was the hand of Aleko.'

Then he went.

Chapter Fourteen

That was on Friday, the 14th of June. The assassination took place on the Saturday.

I have since been described in the People's Party press as 'a well-known agent of the English secret service,' 'the leader of a foreign murder gang,' 'Anglo-American spy and pervert,' and in other less reproducible ways. In one article the fact that I am a writer was acknowledged by a reference to 'the notorious pornographer and English murder-propaganda lackey Foster.'

That part of it has been less amusing than I would have thought. Some of the stuff was reproduced in London papers, and among my friends the 'notices of Foster's Balkan tour' were quoted hilariously for a day or two. But when the news of the Deltchev verdict came and the mass executions of Agrarian Socialists began, the attacks on me became related to events that were anything but funny. I began to be asked questions that the Foreign Office had suggested I should not answer.

With the newspapers it was not difficult; I did as I had been asked and referred them to the Foreign Office. With friends and acquaintances it was less simple. It is, I find, extraordinarily embarrassing to be described in print as a member of the British secret service. The trouble is that you cannot afterwards convince people that you are not. They reason that if you are a member you will still presumably have to say that you are not. You are suspect. If you say nothing, of course, you admit all. Your denials become peevish. It is very tiresome. Probably the only really effective denial would be a solemn, knowing acknowledgment that there *might* be some truth in the rumour. But I can never bring myself to it. Foreign Office or no Foreign Office, I have to explain what really happened.

To begin with, I think I should make it clear that I am not one of those persons who enjoy danger. I take pains to avoid it. Moreover, my timidity is speculative and elaborate. For instance, in Paris at the time of the Stavisky riots I was living in a hotel room overlooking a street in which the police fought a revolver battle with rioters. My first impulse was to lean out of the window and watch. The firing was several hundred yards away and I knew perfectly well that at that distance a revolver is about as dangerous as a water pistol. What I remembered, however, was that the author of *Way of Revelation* had had a similar impulse of curiosity in Mexico City and died of it, absurdly with a stray bullet through his head. Instead of leaning out of the window, therefore, I had knelt on the floor by it and tried to use my shaving-mirror as a periscope; but by the time I had arranged all this, the battle was over and I saw nothing but an indignant woman with an upset shopping-bag.

The war did nothing to make my attitude to danger bolder or more philosophic. I do not have heroic impulses. The news that a bomb had killed my wife in our London flat had many other effects on me, but it did not send me out in a murderous rage to exact retribution of the enemy, nor did it make me volunteer for some suicidal duty. For a long time my life felt less worth living than before, but I did not for that reason become careless of it. Accounts of great bravery sometimes move me deeply, but they arouse in me no desire to emulate them. The spirit of romantic derring-do runs somewhat thinly in my veins.

The truth about my part in the Deltchev affair is untidy. I did not even blunder into the danger; I strayed into it as if it were an interesting-looking tangle of streets in an old town. Certainly I had been warned that they were dangerous; but only to those who warned, I thought, not to me. When I found out that I was mistaken and tried to get out, I found also that I was lost. That was how it felt. The last moment at which I could have turned back was when Petlarov went out of my room that evening. If at that point I had shrugged my shoulders, had another drink, gone out to dinner, and spent the evening at a cinema, I should have been fairly safe. And I very nearly did do that. I had the drink—it was the last of the whisky—and I looked at a cinema I could see from my window. It was called LUX and was playing a dubbed version of a German film called *La Paloma* that I did not want to see. I considered opening a bottle of plum brandy I had bought, decided against it, and then caught sight of the typewriter I had brought with me but not yet used. I thought of the solemnity of my departure with it from London ten days or so before and felt absurd. Images came into my mind of those groups of toys you see mounted on highly coloured boards in the shops at Christmas time; the Boys' Conductor Set (complete with ticket punch), the Boys' Detective Set (complete with three disguises), the Boys' Tank Commander Set (complete with binoculars). I spent a self-abasing minute or two thinking of a new one: the Boys' Foreign Correspondent Set, complete with typewriter, whisky bottle, invisible ink, and a copy of John Gunther's *Inside Europe*. Then I did a foolish thing: I decided to pull myself together and be sensible.

What, I asked myself over dinner, were the facts? Quite simple. I was supposed to be reporting the trial of a man named Deltchev who was accused of planning an assassination. Probably he was innocent. Yet some of the evidence against him had a ring of truth about it. Moreover, his daughter had been in touch with someone concerned in the assassination plan. I had found that person dead, killed in the same way as an Austrian politician and most likely by the same man, Aleko. Aleko had pretended to be of the secret police but was probably an agent of another kind. Who had employed him? Deltchev? Or the People's Party to implicate Deltchev? But why should either employ Aleko when they had dangerous psychotics like Eftib and Pazar ready to hand? It didn't make sense. And where did Deltchev come in? That was the important thing. I was preparing to defend him before a very large public. It might be just as well (might it not?) to make sure that I had the facts right. *Might* be! A fine fool I should look if the noble Deltchev I had postulated turned out to be in reality as murderous as his persecutors but rather cleverer at concealing the fact. 'Mr Foster, what steps did you take to check the validity of your impressions?' 'Well, none really. I thought it better not to be inquisitive. Too risky.' Oh dear, oh dear! By the time the wine arrived I no longer had any doubts. Nothing I already knew about the case seemed either logical or in any other way satisfactory. Far too much was hidden. Well, it must be revealed; and if the intimidated Petlarov did not want to help me, I would find it out for myself. The first thing for me to do anyway was to see Madame Deltchev at once–that evening–and hear what she had to say about the day's evidence. Then I would give myself the pleasure of an interview with little Miss Katerina, tell her the news about her friend Valmo, and ask her the questions that Aleko did not want me to ask. After that I would decide what to do next.

I finished my dinner and walked out to the Deltchev house. As I turned into the street where it was, the mood of hearty resolution in which I had started out suddenly weakened. The guards I had passed before might not be on duty. A different set might have taken over. Then, as I approached, I saw that the same guards were there. It made no difference; my anxiety deepened. I realized that the real source of it had nothing to do with the guards but with the undertaking I had given to Aleko and my too ready disposal of it. If, I had reasoned, Aleko had really had any police powers he would not have asked for an undertaking not to visit the Deltchev house again; he would simply have issued an order to the guards not to admit me. Therefore, I had concluded, he had no police powers and I might call his bluff. But it was one thing to have arrived at a theoretical conclusion and quite another to act upon it in this way. All sorts of unconsidered possibilities occurred to me as I walked toward the house. Supposing, for instance, he really did have police powers and had planned to test my good faith by including this prohibition in the undertaking. For a moment I hesitated and was about to turn back; then I realized that the corporal had seen and recognized me. Retreat was impossible now. I walked on up to him and took out my press permit. He nodded curtly, but examined the permit carefully again while the doltish private stood grinning at me. At last the corporal handed back the permit with a faint shrug (ominous?) and nodded to the private. The latter hitched his rifle sling more snugly on his shoulder and, crossing to the door in the wall, pulled the bell.

It was as before. I waited. They watched me. There was the clacking of old Rana's sandals on the paving of the courtyard. The door opened cautiously. But then she recognized me and held the door for me to go in. Inside she said something and signed to me to wait. She was not long. Soon I heard her sandals flapping down the stairs inside the house. She opened the front door and beckoned me in.

I went upstairs. The same slippery floor, the same smell of furniture polish, but this time no Katerina. She, I thought, would be standing with her man-of-the-world air behind her mother's chair. I hoped, uncharitably, that my arrival would alarm her.

But Madame Deltchev was alone. She was standing facing me by the window as I came in. The light was behind her, but there was tension in the way she stood. On the table by her were two empty tea glasses. The old friend had delivered his report for the day.

She turned quickly. 'Good evening, Herr Foster. It is good of you to call again.'

'You are very kind, madame. I am afraid I have more questions.'

'Naturally. Please sit down.'

'Thank you.'

There was a *grande dame* artificiality about her manner that accentuated the feeling of strain she meant it to conceal. 'Although,' she went on, 'I think it unlikely that I shall be able to give you the information you need. Tea?'

'No, thank you.'

'Of course. You have dined, and the English do not drink tea after dinner.' She smiled mechanically and, picking up one of the glasses, went over to the samovar. 'With us it is a habit,' she said; 'Russian, of course. Most of our habits are Russian or Turkish or German or Greek. We have few of our own.' Boiling water spluttered from the tap into the glass. 'You see now why our patriots mean so much to us here. Their unquestioning belief that we are indeed a nation with our own cultural and political identities, and not merely a marginal tribe with some curious ethnological affinities, is a great comfort. The truth about many of our great traditional patriots is ugly or ludicrous; but it makes no difference. They are defended angrily. National feeling in small states is always angry; it must be so, for its roots are in fear and self-doubt, and for those things reason is no protection.'

She spoke as glibly as a journalist quoting without acknowledgment from an article he has just written. I was not sure whether she was talking for concealment or whether I was being offered an elaborately wrapped hint. Was there perhaps an ugly truth to be known about patriot Deltchev?'

'Your husband has meant a great deal to his people,' I said carefully.

'Yes, yes, he has.' She had carried her tea over to her chair. Now she sat down facing me. 'They will not give him up easily, no matter what lies are told about him. A cigarette, Herr Foster?'

'Thank you; I'm sure you are right. Have you heard about today's court proceedings, madame?'

'Yes, I have heard about them.'

I lit the cigarette she had given me. 'Do you consider that the evidence was false in itself or that it was false only in relation to your husband?'

'Some of his witnesses may be truthful, but their testimonies compose a lie.'

'May I put a hypothetical question? Supposing that the evidence were all true, that your husband had in fact been involved in this plot, would you have known about it, madame? Would he have confided in you?'

She did not answer immediately. Then: 'He always confided in me. I would have known.'

'It would be a dangerous secret to confide to anyone.'

'If it had existed; yes, very dangerous.'

'For comparison's sake, madame, can you tell me if your husband confided in you his intention to make that radio speech about the elections before he made it?'

She sat quite still for several moments, staring out through the window at the bare hills. I almost wondered if she had heard what I had said. She had heard, I knew, and understood too, but her air of preoccupation was very nearly convincing. Then, with a slight puzzled shake of the head as if to banish other thoughts and face the immediate reality, she turned her gentle, intelligent eyes toward me.

'I am very sorry, Herr Foster,' she said with a faint, confused smile, 'I am afraid I was not paying attention. I had other thoughts.' She put her hand to her forehead as if she had a headache. 'It was inexcusable.'

It was not badly done; I have known actresses make a worse job of it; but if I wanted to parody a particular style of drawing-room comedy I would have that speech, and the performance that goes with it, well in mind. She must have seen it in dozens of bad plays. Probably she was expecting from me one of the two conventional reactions to it, the guilty ('Forgive me, you're tired') or the aggrieved ('I'm a busy man and my time is valuable'). However, I felt neither guilty nor aggrieved. I did feel intensely curious.

I repeated the question.

Her lips twitched with annoyance. 'Herr Foster, what is the point of this question? Please be honest with me.'

'Certainly. You deny that there is a word of real truth in the evidence put before the court today. I wish to know what value I may put upon that denial. Is it based on knowledge or an emotional conviction? You must see that that is important.'

'What I see, Herr Foster,' she said coldly, 'is that this trial is beginning to have the effect intended by the Propaganda Ministry.'

I felt myself flush with anger. By the light of the setting sun she did not see that, but I did not reply and after a moment she began to apologize. I must forgive her; she was tired and overwrought; she had not slept for many nights; she was distracted with worry. I listened carefully. What she was saying was all quite reasonable and genuine, but it was also a protective screen. Something had happened to her since our first meeting; some inner certainty had gone. Before, she had been facing with calm courage the prospect of her husband's conviction and death. Perhaps that courage had rested upon a belief in his innocence which no longer went unquestioned. Perhaps the unworthy doubts of which she now accused me were merely the projections of her own misgivings.

I tried a different way.

'In the theatre,' I said, 'a little fact will sustain a lot of illusion. As Petlarov says, "the lie rests most securely on a pinpoint of truth." Brankovitch is not a fool. He knows that although he can impose any nonsense he likes upon the people of his own country, abroad it will not be so easy. With that trumped-up case he cannot hope to deceive the outside world. But what he can do is to confuse it by mixing with his lies a little truth. This plot against Vukashin. Why is it there? To prove that your husband is a member of the Brotherhood? Nonsense! Better evidence could be invented. Besides, even a stable government will regard an assassination plot as bad propaganda and try to conceal it if they can. No, this evidence is there because it is specially valuable. It is valuable because it is true. And those in court today recognized that it is true. It was not much—a few statements confirming a small set of facts—but it was true, and already in their minds this truth has grown and obscured the great mass of falsehood that surrounds it. You say, madame, that there may be truthful witnesses but that they compose a lie. But how much of a lie? Where does the truth end and the lie begin? You cannot defeat the prosecution's case with blank denials. It is not as simple as that. You have to give the whole truth, and that is what I want.'

There was a long silence. She looked stonily out of the window, and when she spoke she did not turn her head.

'Herr Foster, there is not a court of law in the civilized world that would accept the case against my husband. I have been well advised of that.'

'No civilized court of law is going to be asked to accept it,' I retorted. 'If the truth is not told, the final judgment will be delivered here. A few persons may doubt and speculate, but they must all come to the same conclusion.'

'What conclusion?'

'That there must have been something in the accusations against Deltchev, that the conspiracy evidence was never seriously disputed, that if he wasn't the criminal they tried to make him out, he was something very nearly as bad—a fool. Forgive me, madame, but what you do not seem to realize is that any protest against your husband's trial is a political act. No foreign office and no responsible newspaper is going to make that protest unless it is absolutely certain that he is innocent. They must know the truth.'

'It isn't true. The case against him is a lie. What else can I say?'

'To what extent did your husband confide in you?'

'What does it matter? If I tell you that he always confided in me you will say that this particular matter might have been too dangerous to confide. If I say that he did not confide it, it is no different.'

'If he were in any way involved in this conspiracy would you have known?'

'Yes. He was not involved.'

'Did you know that he was going to make that election broadcast before he made it?'

'Yes, I did.'

'Did you know why he was going to make it?'

'Yes.'

'Why was it?'

She shook her head hopelessly. I knew she was lying.

'Was it because at one time, long ago, your husband had been a member of the Officer Corps Brotherhood?'

For a moment she was quite still. Then, slowly, she raised her head and stared at me. 'Is that a serious question, Herr Foster?' she asked coolly.

I knew suddenly that it was not a serious question, but part of a fantasy in a locked room. I began to mumble: 'It was a faint possibility, madame.' She still stared at me. 'It could have been a youthful indiscretion, a mistake. . . .' I petered out.

She smiled in a twisted sort of way. 'Yordan does not make that kind of indiscretion. He is always an intelligent man. Are there any other questions, Herr Foster?' she added.

If I had had any advantage it was suddenly quite gone. 'Have you ever heard the name of Pazar before?'

'It is a Turkish name. I know no one who has it.'

'Or Eftib?'

'No. Nor any of the other persons mentioned today.'

'Aleko?'

'Was that name mentioned?'

'No. Do you know it?'

'It is a short name for Alexander. That is all I know.'

'Valmo?'

'It is a fairly common surname, but it means nothing in particular to me. Should it do so?'

'I don't know.' I stood up. 'Thank you for receiving me, madame.'

'It is nothing.' She stood up too and switched on a reading-lamp.

'Before I go, I should like, if I may, to speak to your daughter,' I said.

She stiffened. 'Why?'

'I should like to ask her some questions.'

'Perhaps I can answer them for you.'

'Perhaps.' I hesitated. 'When I left here two nights ago, madame, your daughter asked me to take out a letter for her and deliver it to a man named Valmo.' I paused.

She tried unsuccessfully to smile. 'My daughter is an attractive young woman. She has her affairs of the heart.'

'Yes, that was the impression of the letter she succeeded in giving to me. I agreed to take it.'

'That was chivalrous of you.'

'The address on the letter was Patriarch Dimo, 9. I found the place. It is a disused house in a slum.'

'And did you find the young man?'

I shook my head. She relaxed perceptibly.

'If you will give me the letter, Herr Foster, I will see that it is returned to my daughter. It was good of you to take so much trouble.' She held out her hand.

I said: 'I did not find a young man, madame. I found a dead one. He had been shot.'

Very slowly she sat down. 'Had he shot himself?' she asked softly.

'No. The wound was in the back of the head.'

She did not move. 'A young man?'

'No. Grey-haired, about fifty I should think. Why do you ask?'

She straightened up a little. 'I thought perhaps some poor young student—' She broke off and drew a deep breath. 'There are so many tragedies. You must have gone to the wrong house, Herr Foster.'

'No. It was the right house. But if the dead man was the person who had called himself Valmo, then your daughter knew Pazar. For that was the dead man's real name.'

There was a silence. She did not look at me.

'Did the police tell you that?' she said at last.

'I did not go to the police. It would have been difficult to explain how I came to be visiting the Brotherhood assassin they are supposed to be searching for. Difficult and embarrassing for us all.'

'We are in your debt, Herr Foster.'

'Perhaps you would prefer your daughter to explain,' I said.

She looked at her handkerchief. 'My daughter is not here.'

I was silent.

She looked at me. 'I am speaking the truth, Herr Foster.'

'I understood that everyone here was under house arrest.'

'My daughter is not here. She has gone.'

'Do you mean that the police took her away?'

'No. She escaped.'

'How? What about the guards?'

'Katerina has lived in this house all her life, Herr Foster. There are other ways of leaving it than by the gates.'

I hesitated. 'A few minutes ago, madame, I asked you if you had heard of Pazar before. You said that you had not. Do you still say that?'

'Yes. It is the truth.'

'But others in this house do know him?'

'I do not.'

'Do you know where your daughter has gone?'

'No.'

'When did she go?'

'This evening.'

'Can you think of any reason why she should go?'

'Herr Foster, I am very tired.'

I waited a moment or two, but she did not look up again. 'I'm sorry,' I said; 'I think I might have been of help to you.'

'I have told you all I can.'

'You have told me all you think it advisable for me to know, madame.'

'Good night, Herr Foster.' She pressed the bell-push.

I said good night and picked up my hat, but as I got to the door she spoke again.

'Herr Foster.'

I stopped.

'My daughter's letter. Will you give it to me, please?'

'It is burned.'

'Are you sure?'

'Quite sure.'

She hesitated. 'Forgive me, but do you know what was in it?'

'I did not open it. In any case I cannot read your language.'

She came a little way across the room toward me. 'Herr Foster,' she said, 'I have not been helpful to you, but I would not like you to think that I am ungrateful for your kindness and patience. I do most sincerely thank you.'

I bowed. I could not think of anything coherent to say that would not have deepened my embarrassment. The sound of Rana's sandals flapping along the passage outside came like the answer to a prayer.

'Good night, madame,' I said, and got out of the room as quickly as I could. It did not occur to me until I was walking down the stairs that my twinges of guilt were unnecessary. Beside the monumental evasions to which I had been listening for the past half-hour my own reticences were slight indeed.

Chapter Fifteen

It was very dark outside the house. The old woman had no lamp to guide us and I blundered rather than walked after her across the courtyard. The fact contributed somehow to the feelings of inadequacy, futility, and blank exasperation which were beginning to grow in me.

I stubbed my foot against the edge of a flagstone and said: 'Damn!' violently. The old woman opened the door in the wall and the flashlight from outside shone in my face. I scowled at it and hauled out my wallet as the door closed behind me. The light left my face and I saw the corporal.

'*Passieren, vorwärts!*' he snapped, and waved me on peremptorily.

'Don't you want to see my permit, you fool?' I inquired in English.

'*Passieren, passieren!*' he repeated, and waved me on again.

'Grinning lout,' I said with a smile to the private.

He nodded, grinning, and saluted.

I walked away. The corporal was not troubling to examine my permit any more. The corporal had decided that I was harmless. The corporal was absolutely right. Tomorrow, I decided, I would send a cable to the man who was paying me, tell him that he was wasting his money and my time, then take the first plane I could get out of the place. It was high time I stopped this foolishness and got back to work again. Not, I thought savagely, that the trip had been a complete loss. I had increased my knowledge of

Napoleon III. I had also had two interesting experiences: that of finding a dead body in a strange house, and that of being locked in a room in another strange house. In the unlikely event of my ever wanting to write the kind of play in which incidents like that occurred, the knowledge would be useful. Meanwhile, to hell with it!

I turned into the Boulevard Dragutin.

It ran in a gentle curve round the high boundary wall of the Presidential Park. It was a wide road, lined with big plane trees and cobbled. Most of the buildings in it were apartment houses; there were no shops or cafés. The lights were on tall standards set among the trees on the building side of the road. I walked on the other side. Beneath the dense foliage of the trees it was very dark.

I walked slowly. The air was pleasant and after a while something happened to make me forget my immediate troubles. Before I had left London I had been trying to write the third act of a new play and had got into difficulties with it. Indeed, I had practically made up my mind to scrap the whole thing. The commission to report the Deltchev trial had come at an opportune moment; it had given me a reason for suspending work on the play that left the real reasons for doing so in abeyance. But now, quite suddenly, I found myself thinking about the play again and seeing quite clearly the point of the problem that I had missed before. The shape of a third act began to emerge. Of course! The wife's lover wasn't her own choice, but her husband's, and it was her realization of this fact that made it possible for her to leave him. Of course! It was the key to her whole attitude toward her lover. He was not *her* choice. Of course! How curious it was! I had practically sign-posted the thing all the way through without realizing the fact. Why? My mind nosed round the discovery suspiciously like a terrier at a strange lamp-post. There must be a mistake. But no, it was all right. I had been too close to it before and too anxious. Now all was well. I drew a deep breath. Forgotten were the Deltchevs and the enigma they represented. I had just finished a play. I felt light-hearted and alive. I quickened my pace.

Then I heard it. It was only a slight sound and it went almost immediately; a sort of ringing of my footsteps on the paving stones. But I was very much aware of everything at that moment; of the soft, warm breeze that was beginning to stir the air, of the smell of the trees, and of the slow movement of a distant point of light. At this moment of heightened sensibility the ringing of my footsteps was a matter for appreciation and curiosity. The pavement was solid enough. Where did the rest of the sound come from? I slowed down a little and heard it again, a kind of echo. From the wall? I stepped out again, but in a more emphatic way this time. Then I understood. It was not an echo I was hearing. Someone was walking behind me.

It is easy to separate sounds once you know they are there. As I walked on, I could hear the other set of footsteps quite plainly. I slowed down again. The sounds separated and then again they coincided. Even then it took me a moment or two to grasp what was happening. The person behind me was varying his pace with mine. He did not want to change the distance between us. I was being followed.

My heart suddenly beat faster. I looked round. I could just see him, a faint thickening of the shadows under the trees about thirty yards behind me. I walked on, fighting down a desire to run. Perhaps I was imagining it all, like a neurotic spinster with fantasies of being raped. But no; the footsteps kept pace with mine. Wild ideas of turning quickly and challenging the follower went through my mind, but I kept on walking for a bit. The calves of my legs began to ache. Then, suddenly, I turned and crossed the road to the lighted side. Out of the corner of my left eye I tried to see if he was crossing too. I could hear his footsteps. They had slowed down. He wasn't going to cross. He was going to stay among the shadows. For a moment or two a feeling of relief flooded over me. It was not until I was nearly to the pavement that I realized why he had not crossed. A hundred yards or so ahead there was a stretch of road with no buildings and no lights. I remembered walking along it earlier. He was going to cross there.

I reached the pavement and hesitated. Then I bent down and pretended to tie my shoelace. I wanted time to think. If I went back the way I had come, I could stay in the lights. I remembered also that I had seen two policemen yawning and spitting on a corner. But what was I to do then? Explain to them? But there was nothing to explain. The only thing was to wait about like a frightened child until someone else came along with whom I could walk in company through the darkness. Ridiculous! What was there to be afraid of? Someone was following me. Very well. Let him follow. What did it matter? There was nothing to be afraid of in that. Nothing at all.

I stood up again and walked on stiffly toward the darkness.

It lay at the end of the lighted strip of pavement like the black mouth of a tunnel. The building I had to pass before I reached it was a huge baroque mansion that, judging from the lighted windows, had been converted into flats. I looked across the road. I could see him moving along under the trees now, a little behind me but at the same speed. The darkness came nearer and I began to see a short way into it. The footpaths ran on between a stone wall and the trees, but the surface of it changed from stone pavement to dust. At the end of the pavement I paused. The leaves above stirred faintly; there was a radio playing somewhere and the breathing sounds of distant traffic, but that was in the background; the darkness before me was quiet and still. The gritty dust crunched beneath my feet, and the branches seemed to close in as I walked on again. I had gone about thirty paces when I heard the sound of an approaching car. It passed, going in the opposite direction. Then, as the sound died away, I heard footsteps on the road; the man from the shadows was crossing it behind me. I went on faster, stumbling slightly over the swellings in the path made by tree roots. My heart was beating sickeningly now and I could feel the cold sweat stealing down my body. I fought against the desire to run. It was absurd, I told myself. I had been in situations fifty times more dangerous. Here there were no mines to tread on, no machine guns or mortars waiting to open fire. All I had to do was to walk along a path beneath some trees in a badly lighted street, followed by someone who might or might not be ill-intentioned. He might be a detective, one of Brankovitch's men instructed to report on my movements. Petlarov had been warned off me by the police. They might now be checking to see if I had any other contacts. Indeed, the man could have been following me about for days without my having noticed the fact. Yes, that must be it. I almost chuckled with relief and slowed down, listening for the footsteps behind me. But there were none. Perhaps they were muffled by the dust. Perhaps—

I stopped dead. Something had moved in front of me.

I stood quite still for a moment, trying to control the thudding of the blood in my head so that I could hear. Something had moved—a shadow, something. I took a step forward and my foot grated on a pebble. The next instant there was a blinding flash of light.

It came from a powerful hand-lamp a few yards in front of me and lasted for less than a second. And that, too, was the time I took to react. As the light went out I fell sideways, sprawling at the foot of a tree.

I only heard the first shot, a thudding crack that made my ears sing; but the next two I saw—yellow blots of flame that seemed to be exploding in my face as I rolled over and clawed for cover behind the tree. Then there was a silence.

I was gasping for breath as if I had been held under water, but my brain was working all right. He had missed me three times and then lost track of me. He would have to risk another flash from the lamp to locate me again, and it would be a risk; he could not be sure that I was unarmed. In any case, I was prepared now, and unless he was a first-rate shot or very lucky he had not much of a chance. For the moment I had forgotten the man behind me.

Five seconds went by. I was slowly straightening up and easing round away from the tree when the light flashed on again. It was not directly on me, and in the fraction of a second it took him to realize that, I had begun to move. I was halfway toward the next tree when he fired. The bullet whipped past my head. I reached the tree and swung round it as if to take cover again, but immediately scrambled on to the next one. The shot he fired at that moment was yards wide. But he had learned one thing; I was not going to fire back. The lamp shone out again, and this time it stayed on. He did not fire. He moved forward. He was going to make sure of it this time. Bent double, I scuttled on again. I saw my shadow twist among the long casts of the trees as the light swung round. Then, as I pulled up against the next tree, a different pistol fired.

The bullet tore through the bark an inch or two from my right eye, and a splinter of wood stung my cheek. I dived for the ground again. The other gun, I thought, had been a ·38, but this had a heavier sound. I could see how it was. If I had not crossed the road, the man behind me would have shot me in the back. The second man had been there to make sure I did not get away. Probably he had crossed ahead of me while I was still in the lighted section.

I was out of the light for a moment now, but both pistols fired again and the bullet from one of them ricocheted off the road. They were getting worried. Nearly half a minute had gone by since the first shot, and I could hear shouting in the distance. The lighted stretch was only a hundred yards away now, but if I broke cover and made a dash for it, I would have to pass the heavy pistol with the other man's light behind me. It would not do.

At that moment the man with the light began to run forward, yelling hoarsely. The heavy pistol fired again as I rolled sideways and found myself

on the edge of the road. I hesitated for only a split second. Then I scrambled
to my feet and ran, swerving like a rabbit, for the trees on the other side of
the road. They both fired, but by then I was a hopeless target for a pistol. I
dived through the trees, came up against the boundary wall, and ran along it
toward the lighted section.

I was safe now. I stopped to get my breath. There were people from the
houses standing on the pavement opposite, talking and pointing toward the
trees where the sound of the firing had come from. The two policemen I had
passed farther back were approaching at a run. I was out of sight. My breath
was beginning to come back, and with it my wits. I had not seen either of the
attackers. I had no information about them to give. But even that would take
a lot of explaining to the police, and they would certainly detain me while an
interpreter was found and my story checked. If I could avoid the police
altogether, I should do so. If, while they searched among the trees for the
dead and wounded that were not there, I could make myself scarce, I would
be saving them trouble. If, in fact, I now did what I should have done five
minutes earlier–kept my head, walked back to a café, and there telephoned
to the hotel for a car to fetch me–everyone would be much better off. I had
begun to tremble violently. My ears were singing and felt deaf. I leaned
against the Presidential wall fighting down a desire to vomit. Through the
singing in my ears I could hear shouts from farther up the road. Then my
head began to clear. Reaction or no reaction, if I was going to get away
unobtrusively I would have to be quick about it. Keeping close to the wall, I
started to walk.

It was an hour before the car arrived at the café, and by that time I had
had several plum brandies. I was not drunk but I felt sleepy. It was silly of
Aleko, I thought, to want to kill me. Very silly. I was perfectly harmless.
However, I had now acquired another useless piece of information: I knew
what it felt like to be shot at in civilian clothes; it was exactly the same as it
felt when you wore a uniform. That was interesting. In the car I went to
sleep and had to be wakened by the driver when we got to the hotel.

The reception clerk was asleep. I took my room key from the rack myself.
The lift was not working. I walked upstairs slowly, yawning. I was really
very tired. I was also beginning to feel stiff and bruised. If the water was hot
(and late at night when nobody wanted it, it usually was hot) I would have a
bath and attend to the knee I had cut on a stone. My suit was a mess too, but
that could wait until the morning. A bath, then sleep; that was it. I felt
curiously relaxed and happy. The odd thing was that this feeling had almost
nothing to do with the plum brandy. It was because I had survived an
ordeal.

I opened the door of my room. There was a small foyer with a cupboard
and a hat rack between the door and the bedroom itself. I switched on the
foyer light, remembered with a twinge of irritation that I had lost my hat
and would have to buy one of the local Homburgs next day, and went into
the bedroom.

My hand was on the bedroom light-switch when I saw what was there. I
stood quite still.

A woman was lying face-downwards across the bed. By the foyer light I
could see that she had a loose raincoat of some kind spread about her as if it

had been thrown there to cover her up.

I pressed the light-switch, and the room was flooded with the bright hard light from the naked lamps in the gilt chandelier.

Her hair was dark and one of her tightly clenched hands concealed her face. I walked over to the bed, and a loose board cracked loudly. I looked down.

She stirred. Her hands moved and she rolled on to her side. The light poured down on her face and she raised a hand to shield her eyes.

It was Katerina Deltchev.

Chapter Sixteen

I shook the bed, not gently, and she sighed. Then, with a start and a gasp, she was awake. She sat up quickly and the thin raincoat she had thrown over her slipped to the floor.

'Good evening,' I said.

For a moment she stared at me, then she scrambled off the bed and looked round defiantly.

'There's no one else here,' I added.

She drew herself up as if she were about to deliver an oath of allegiance. 'Herr Foster,' she said formally, 'I must apologize for this intrusion, but it was unavoidable. I will explain. I—' She broke off and looked down as she realized that she was in her stockinged feet.

'They're down there,' I said. Her shoes had slipped off while she had been asleep and were lying beside the bed.

She opened her mouth to say something, then shut it again, went over to the bed, and put her shoes on thoughtfully. She was a young woman who was used to being in charge of a situation; now she was casting about for a way of taking charge of this one.

'I am sorry—' she began.

'Quite all right,' I said. 'You wanted to see me, so you came here. I was out. You waited. You fell asleep. I am afraid I can't offer you anything but a cigarette. Will you smoke?'

For a fraction of a second she weighed the possible moral advantage of a refusal; then she shrugged her shoulders. 'Yes. Thank you.'

She took a cigarette and I lit it for her. She sat down again on the bed and looked at me calmly.

'Herr Foster,' she said, 'it is not really quite as simple as that for you, is it?'

'No, not quite.'

I went into the bathroom, dipped a towel in water, and wrung it out. Then I went back into the bedroom, sat down in the armchair, rolled the trouser leg up, and went to work with the towel on my cut knee. She watched uncertainly.

'Who told you I was staying here?' I asked.

'There were three hotels where you might have been staying. This was the second one I telephoned.'

'How did you know the room number?'

'By asking for another room number when I telephoned. Of course I got the wrong number. The operator corrected me.'

'Who let you in here?'

'The floor waiter. I said I was your lover and gave him some money. Does it matter?'

'Not a bit. It's just that at the moment I am in a suspicious mood. Now, then. How do you get out of the house without being seen? What do you do?'

'Our neighbours are friendly. Between our wall and theirs there is a tree. With two vine poles one can crawl from the top of our wall to the tree. From the tree one uses the branches to reach their wall. For a child it is easy. For a heavier person there is some danger, but it can be done.'

'Then why did you ask me to deliver that letter for you, Fräulein? If it was so important you could have delivered it yourself.'

'I did not wish to risk my life if there was another way.'

'Are you risking your life now?'

'Yes, Herr Foster. I am also risking yours.'

'That I guessed.'

'But only if I am found here.'

'Splendid.'

'If I get back tonight without being seen, I shall be safe too. The guards inspect us only in the morning.'

'Good.'

'I would not have come, Herr Foster,' she said severely, 'if it had not been absolutely necessary to see you.'

'You didn't have to leave the house to do that. I was there myself an hour ago.'

She shrugged. 'I did not know. I wished to see you because—'

I interrupted her. 'Do you know a man called Aleko?'

'Aleko? It is common.'

'Who was the Valmo you sent that letter to?'

'I don't know.'

'I see.'

'It is true. Valmo was only a name I was given to send letters to. The letter was for someone else.'

'Who?'

'My brother, Philip.'

I sighed. 'The one who's studying law in Geneva?'

'He is not in Geneva.'

'Your mother said he was.'

'My mother was lying.'

'I didn't think so.'

'She did not intend you to think so. Will you please listen to me without interruption for a moment?'

'All right, I'm listening.'

'My brother has been in hiding here since before Papa was arrested. My brother, Herr Foster, had five friends. Their names were Pazar, Eftib, Vlahov, Pechanatz, and Radiuje.'

I dropped the towel. 'Do you know what you're saying?'

'Perfectly. That is what I came to tell you. This evidence that they have brought against my father is quite true. Only it is not he who is guilty. It is my brother, Philip.'

I sat back and stared at her. She was telling the truth. A lot of things were suddenly and appallingly clear.

'When did your mother find out?'

'She did not tell me.'

'Does your father know.'

'He must have known from the beginning of the trial, or guessed. But what can he do? He cannot accuse his own son, and Brankovitch would certainly not let Philip give evidence.'

'Nobody would believe it anyway. They'd laugh. Dutiful son takes blame for father's crimes? I'd laugh myself.' I thought about it for a moment. It explained quite a lot of things, but not everything by any means. I looked up at her again. 'What's the idea of telling this to me, Fräulein?'

'I want you to publish my brother's evidence.'

'Does he want to give it?'

She set her lips firmly. 'He must.'

'Does your mother know of this idea?'

'I would not tell her. She would say that it would not help Papa, only condemn Philip.'

'She'd be right.'

'But abroad they must know the truth.'

'Would your mother agree with that?'

'I do not know. She is too clever to be simple. She would discuss the idea and think of possibilities nobody else had dreamed of. Then she would say she was tired. You would not know her real thoughts.'

'What was your brother up to? Is he crazy?'

She shook her head slowly. 'When Papa betrayed the party,' she said, 'he and Philip quarrelled. They were always in conflict, but this time my mother could do nothing.' Tears came to her eyes. 'We were all against him, even I was; and when the People's Party came to power, Philip joined a student political club that had for secretary this man Pazar. Pazar always needed money, but the students liked him. He talked very amusingly and they used to pay him for coaching. When they formed a club they would sometimes make him secretary and give him a commission on the subscriptions. Philip soon felt that the club was not serious, but he became very friendly with Pazar. Then, one day, Pazar told him that he was a member of the Brotherhood.'

'There must have been pleasure in telling that to the son of the man who had done so much to destroy it,' I remarked. It was all too easy to catch the flavour of those dangerous exchanges of confidences between the middle-aged drug addict and the fanatical youth.

She shrugged. 'Perhaps. I know that when Philip joined the Brotherhood it was only to revenge himself on Papa. He did not mean then to do more than join.'

'But once he had joined, he found that they expected more than a gesture. Was that it?'

She nodded. 'There were six of them elected, and Philip was named the leader. Their task was to kill Vukashin at the anniversary-celebration parade. But—'

'Just a moment. Who was the man who gave them the job?'

'It was not one man, but a group of men. They called themselves the Survivors.'

'When did Philip tell you all this?'

'Before he went to Switzerland. Mamma had become worried about him. He looked so ill and tired. She persuaded Papa to send him there to study. Naturally, he refused to go at first, but after a day or two he said no more. That was at Christmas. He had arranged to return in secret when Pazar sent for him.' She paused before she added: 'I knew then that he was not the real leader, but had been given the role of leader because of his name.'

'Did you say that to him?'

'He already knew it, I think. But if I had said it he would have made some other foolishness to prove to me that I was wrong. Besides, I thought that in Geneva he might change his mind and forget about it.'

'But he didn't.'

'No. We had arranged a code for our letters, and when the attempt on Papa was made, I heard from him that he was returning. I only saw him once. We met secretly at a place near the station.'

'Patriarch Dimo 9?'

'No, another. But he gave me two addresses which I might send letters to. Valmo, Patriarch Dimo 9, was one of them. The other he told me I must use only in case of an extreme emergency if I had to find him.'

'What was in the letter you gave me?'

'I begged him to escape to Greece and publish the truth about the conspiracy against Vukashin from there.'

'What made you decide to come to me?'

She frowned impatiently. 'Today's evidence, Herr Foster. Surely you see. The police know everything. Philip and Pazar are the only two left. They must be in hiding somewhere, helpless. Philip can do nothing now even if he wished. It must be done for him.'

I thought hard for a moment or two, then I shook my head. 'I don't think that it's as simple as you believe, Fräulein.'

'What do you mean?'

'Well, to begin with, Valmo was the name Pazar was hiding under. When I tried to deliver your letter, I found him dead. He'd been shot through the back of the head and had been there some days.'

'What happened to my letter?'

'That was burnt by a man named Aleko who said that he was of the secret police and that *his* name was Valmo. He also said that your letter was addressed to him and was something to do with the attempt on your father.' I described Aleko. 'Does that mean anything to you?' I added.

She looked utterly bewildered. 'No, Herr Foster.'

'What does your brother look like?'

She gave me a description.

I nodded. 'A young man who looks like that came into Aleko's apartment while I was there. I only saw him for a moment. Aleko called him Jika.'

She stood up quickly. 'That is Philip. He likes his friends to call him that. Herr Foster, where is this place?'

'I don't know for certain, but I should think that it may be another address your brother gave you. Have you got it?'

'Philip made me remember it. He said it was too dangerous to write down.'

'What is it?'

'Pashik, Pan-Eurasian Press Service, Serdika Prospek 15,' she said.

I went to the wardrobe, got out the bottle of plum brandy, and poured myself a big drink.

'Do you like this stuff?' I asked.

She shook her head.

'All right, Fräulein. You'd better go back now. I think I know how to reach your brother.'

Chapter Seventeen

Pashik lived in a modern apartment house near his office. He had pointed out the place to me on the day I had arrived. I thought now that I could find it without much difficulty. There were no taxis. I walked.

The way there lay through the business quarter, and by that time the streets were mostly empty and still. Earlier that day they had been decorated in preparation for the anniversary parade, and the bright moonlight striking obliquely through the flags overhead cast a multiplicity of shadows that stirred and twisted in the warm breeze. It was like walking through the dark forest of a dream. But I had gone some distance before I became frightened.

It was a very unpleasant sensation. The brandy-engendered resolution with which I had set out seemed to drain suddenly away. I began to shiver uncontrollably and an icy, numbing kind of logic invaded the small corner of my conscious mind not whimpering with the effort required to keep on walking. What I was doing was incredibly foolish. Not three hours ago two men had tried to kill me in the street. I had been very lucky to escape. Now here I was in the streets again, giving them another chance. For obviously they must be waiting for me. Ruthless determination of the kind they possessed would be intensified by failure. They would not fail a second time.

Soon every shadow had become a man with a gun, every doorway the place of an ambush. I kept on simply because I was afraid to go back. I walked now simply because I was afraid to break into a run that might precipitate action. My legs ached with the strain. My shirt clung to my back. I had so completely lost my head that I went on fifty yards past my destination without seeing it. There was a frantic ten seconds on the corner of the Boulevard Sokolovsky while I got my bearings. Then I saw the apartment house from a familiar angle. I ran the fifty yards back.

It was a tall, narrow building with massive ferroconcrete balconies, from the sides of which rusty weather stains drooled down the walls. In the daylight these stains gave the place a tired, unhappy air—you wanted someone to wipe its face for it—but in the moonlight they were hard shadows that made the balconies seem to project like freakish upper lips. The main entrance doors, ornate affairs of wrought iron and rolled glass, were still open, and the lobby beyond was dimly illuminated by a light from the concierge's room.

As I stood for a moment or two recovering my breath, I looked back along the street. There were two or three empty cars parked in it, but they had been there already. Nobody had followed me. I went in and pressed the concierge's bell. Nothing happened. After a minute or so I went over to the lift. Beside it was a list of the tenants. Pashik was on the fourth floor. The lift did not work, of course. I found the stairs and walked up.

At the moment of deciding to see Pashik that night I had had a clear image of the sort of interview it would be. I had seen him already in bed and asleep when I arrived. In response to my insistent ringing he had at last appeared, a bleary, nightshirted figure (I had been sure he wore nightshirts), fetid and protesting. I had cut through his protests decisively. I had given him no time to build up his defences. I had pelted him with the facts I had discovered and watched his features grow pinched as he realized how much I knew. Then, at last, wearily he had shrugged. 'Very well. Since you already know so much, Mr Foster, you had better hear the rest.' And I had sat down to listen.

The reality was somewhat different.

The door to his apartment was at the end of a short passage near the main staircase landing. As I turned into the passage, I saw that the door was ajar and that there were lights in the apartment. I went along the passage and up to the door. Then, with my hand on the bell, I paused. Inside, someone was speaking on the telephone. Or listening rather; there was a series of grunts, then two or three words I did not understand. The voice, however, was not Pashik's. I hesitated, then rang the bell.

The voice ceased abruptly. There was a movement from within. Then silence. Suddenly the door swung open and clattered gently against a picture on the wall behind it. For a moment the small lobby beyond looked empty. Then I saw. Between the doors of the two rooms facing me was a narrow strip of wall. On that wall was a mirror and, reflected in it, the face of the man who had pushed the door open with his foot. It was Sibley.

He moved slowly out from the wall just inside the entrance and looked at me. There was a heavy bottle-glass ashtray in his hand. He put it down on the hall table and grinned.

'Well, Foster dear,' he said archly, 'this *is* a nice surprise! A small world, I always say. Do *you* always say that? Of course you don't! Come to see our smelly friend?'

'Naturally. What are you doing here?'

He looked at me oddly. 'I've come to see him too, and also naturally. Doesn't seem to be about, though, does he? I've looked high and low.'

'Who were you expecting to have to beat over the head with that ashtray?'

'Somebody else who shouldn't be here. Like me. You're quite a logical visitor, of course. Been here before, I shouldn't wonder.'

'No.'

He grinned again. 'I thought not. Come on in and make yourself at home. I was telephoning.'

'Yes, I heard.'

'Don't speak the language though, do you?'

'No.'

'I thought not. This way.'

He went through the left-hand door. I hesitated and then followed.

It was a sitting-room that had obviously been furnished by the owners of the building. There were built-in cupboards and bookcases and a built-in sofa. There were cube-like chairs, glass-topped circular tables, and an oatmeal-coloured rug. You could have seen the same sort of things in any other furnished apartment building in any other European city. The extraordinary thing about this room was the decoration on the walls.

They were covered, every square foot of them, with pages cut from American magazines and stuck on with Scotch tape. There were pictures of film stars (all women), there were near-nude 'studies' of women who were not film stars and there were artlessly erotic colour drawings of reclining seductresses in lace step-ins. All would have looked quite at home in the room of an adolescent youth. Yet that was the comprehensible part of the display; it was not remarkable that Pashik should have the emotional development of a sixteen-year-old boy. The startling thing was that for every Ann Sheridan, for every sandal-tying beach beauty, for every long-legged houri, there was a precisely arranged frame of advertisement pages. The nearest Betty Grable was surrounded by Buick, Frigidaire, Lux and American Airlines, all in colour. A sun-tanned blonde glistening with sea water had Coca-Cola, U.S. Steel, Dictaphone and Lord Calvert whisky. A gauze-veiled brunette with a man's bedroom slipper in her hand and a speculative eye was framed by Bell Telephones, Metropolitan Life Insurance, General Electric and Jello. The baffling thing was that the selection and grouping of advertisements seemed quite unrelated to the pictures. There was no wit, no hint of social criticism, in the arrangements. Many of the advertisements were not particularly distinguished as such. It was fantastic.

Sibley had gone back to the telephone. He had said something into it, listened again, and then, with a last word, hung up. He flicked his fingers at the wall as if he were launching a paper pellet.

'Lots of fun, isn't it?'

'Lots. How did you get in?'

'The concierge has a pass key and is corrupt. Would you like a drink? There must be some about.' He opened one of the cupboards and peered inside.

'Do you know Pashik well?' I said.

'Would you believe me if I said yes?'

'No.'

'Then let's say that I think I know a bit more about him than you do.

Cigars but no drinks,' he added, producing a box. 'Cigar?'

'No, thanks.'

'No, it's a drink you need. You're not looking your usual cheerful self, *amigo*. A bit pinched round the gills and upset. Let's try this one.' He went to another cupboard.

'I take it you're not afraid of Pashik's suddenly turning up and finding you here searching his room. That wouldn't embarrass you?'

'Not a bit.'

'Was that why you came? Because you knew he wouldn't be here?'

He looked up from the cupboard he was searching and shook his head. 'No, Foster *mio*,' he said softly, 'that wasn't why. I just wanted a little chat with him. When there was no answer, I had another thought and fetched the concierge. Silly of me, wasn't it?–but I actually thought our Georghi might be dead.'

'Why should you think that?'

'It was just a thought I had.' He straightened up suddenly with a bottle in his hand. 'There now! Our old friend plum brandy!' And then he looked directly at me. 'You know about Pazar, of course?'

'What about him?'

'Tonight's police statement that they've found him shot in a derelict house.'

'Oh yes, that.' I tried to make it casual.

He reached down and brought out two glasses. 'A house in some street with a funny name,' he said slowly. 'What was it?'

'Patriarch Dimo.' My voice sounded unnatural to me.

'That's it. Who told you? Georghi?'

'Yes. He had the statement.'

He brought the bottle and glasses over and put them on the table. 'When did you see him?'

'Oh, earlier on.'

He shook his head. 'It won't do, Foster dear,' he said. 'No, don't get cross. I set a little trap and you fell into it, that's all. That statement was only issued half an hour ago. I was on the phone to the office when you came in. That's how I know.' He thrust his head forward. 'How did *you* know?'

I was feeling sick again. I sat down.

'*Did* Georghi tell you?'

I shook my head. 'I found him by accident.'

He whistled softly. 'My, my! You *do* get around! What sort of an accident was it that took you to Patriarch Dimo? The same sort that got you into the Deltchev house?'

'Not quite.'

'Doing a little private investigating perhaps?'

'That's the idea.'

He shook his head regretfully. 'Someone must be very cross with you.'

Another wave of sickness came. I drew a deep breath. 'Then that's probably why someone's just tried to kill me,' I said.

He stared at me expressionlessly for a moment. 'A joke, Foster dear?' he said gently. 'A joke in bad taste?'

'No joke.'

'Where was it?'

'In that road which runs round the park.'

'When.'

'An hour or two ago.'

'One man or two?'

'Two.'

'One of them couldn't have been Georghi by any chance?'

'No.'

He seemed to relax again. 'Well, well! Poor Foster! No wonder you look peaky. And here I am chattering away instead of pouring the much-needed drink. There.'

I swallowed the drink and sat back for a moment with my eyes closed. I hoped that he would believe that I was feeling faint. I had to think and it was difficult. Sibley was Brankovitch's paid man and already I had given myself away appallingly. Pashik was involved with Aleko and Philip Deltchev in a Brotherhood plot to assassinate Vukashin. The wreckage of that plot was being used to convict the elder Deltchev. Now, the dead Pazar, probably murdered by Aleko, had been officially discovered on the eve of the anniversary parade at which Vukashin was to be assassinated. There was a contrived, bad-third-act feeling about the whole thing; as if . . .

'Feeling better?' said Sibley.

'Yes, thanks.' I opened my eyes. He was looking down at me coldly. I had not deceived him. He smiled.

'What a busy week you've had! Have you any idea, I wonder, what you know that makes you worth killing?'

'None at all.'

He sat down opposite me. 'Maybe if you were to tell me what you do know, I could make a suggestion about that.'

'Or perhaps find a way through the censorship with it? By the way, how is your little man at Propaganda Ministry?'

He drank his drink down and looked at the empty glass as if waiting for someone to fill it. 'Do I detect a note of bitchiness and distrust, Foster dear?'

'Yes, you probably do.'

He looked at the bottle and poured himself another. 'Drink will be the death of me,' he said. 'I was tiddly, of course, but it seemed such a good joke at the time. Although, *amigo*, I won't deny that I would also have been interested to see what your angle on the affair was going to be.'

'My angle was and is that your little man in the Propaganda Ministry was Brankovitch.'

He giggled. 'Who told you they played that trick? Georghi?'

'Not Georghi.'

He giggled again. 'Oh dear! Not Georghi, you mean, but someone else whose name you don't want to mention in case I'm a Ministry spy who might get him into trouble. Oh dear, oh dear! I do see. I played right into your hands, didn't I? No wonder you were so maddening. The thing was that they'd tried it on me days before. I could send anything I wanted if I knew how. That was the line. It would cost a bit, of course, but that was to make it sound right.' He sighed. 'I don't like being taken for a fool, do you? I was a bit vexed, so I decided to amuse myself. I thought at first of pretending I'd fallen for it and sending a really dreadful story I'd heard about Vukashin's sex life. Then I sobered up and thought again. In the end all I did was to lift their dialogue and try it on someone else. Georghi was my first customer and I frightened him out of his wits—or he pretended I did. And that was the crazy part of it; because it wasn't until I saw him looking at me with those big brown eyes of his and got a breath of that subtle perfume that I remembered where I'd seen him before. Do I convince you?'

'By no means.'

He gazed upwards soulfully. 'It's so sad. I can never make the truth sound convincing. Of course, I *look* so shifty. I should stick to lying, shouldn't I?'

'Where was it you saw Pashik before?'

'Ah, I have your interest. If only I can keep it until the knock-out drops that I slipped into your drink begin to work, all will be well.'

Involuntarily I looked down at my glass.

He grinned. 'You're really very tiresome, aren't you, Foster dear? If I didn't want badly to know what makes you worth killing, I wouldn't say another word.'

'It's late. I'm very tired. And—'

'And it's always so upsetting to be shot at,' he said quickly. 'How inconsiderate of me not to remember that!'

'I wasn't apologizing.'

'Of course you weren't. You were just hoping that I'd cut the cackle. I do understand. These affectations of mine are such a bore. All right. Let's talk about Georghi Pashik—why he exists and in whose image he is made. What has he told you about himself?'

'He was expelled from Italy for writing something Mussolini didn't agree with. He did his military service in Austria. He admires Myrna Loy. The last item I deduced for myself from a picture in his office.'

'She must be his spiritual Mum, don't you think? All right, here it is. Technically, a stateless person. Born in the Trentino, of Macedonian Greek parents who were themselves of doubtful national status. He takes Hungarian nationality. Treaty of Trianon muddle. He does his military service in Austria. He goes eventually to Paris and works for Havas as a messenger. Intelligent, ambitious, a worker. He writes odd pieces. He gets on. Eventually they give him a job in the Rome office. He gets important. Then he's expelled, which is all very difficult because he's married an Italian girl and the *squadristi* make it hot for her family. He has a lot of trouble squaring things. After a bit his wife dies and he returns here to the home of his forefathers with very peculiar ideas about the way the world ought to be run.'

'What sort of ideas?'

'I'm coming to that. Well, the war breaks out and in 1940 Georghi skips to Cairo. For a time he's on a newspaper there, then he decides that it's time to do a little war work and gets taken on as an interpreter by the British. Later on, when the United States Middle East contingent arrives, he is transferred to them. In 1945 he turns up in an American Civil Affairs unit in Germany.'

'Still as an interpreter?'

'Still as an interpreter. Only by now he has a bastard sort of uniform and is working in a D.P. camp near Munich. He worked under an American major named Macready. I had business there, and that's where I first saw Georghi and got to know about him.'

'What was your business?'

'Intelligence—the British lot.' He caught a glance I gave him. 'Oh dear me, no! Not any more. I was just the wartime variety, uniform and everything. I was liaising with an American who was on the same job as me—checking up on the bad boys who'd gone to earth in the D.P. camps and then digging them out—and it was this man who told me about Georghi. Another drink?'

'I think I will.'

'That's good. There's another bottle in there if we run short or if Georghi comes home. All right, then. We go back to the time Georghi went over to the Americans in Cairo. Almost the first thing that happened was that he was sent up to a small hill town in the Lebanon with a lieutenant, a tech sergeant, and an enlisted man. The job was to operate a radio station monitoring an intelligence network operating in the Balkans. I believe there was some short-wave oddity that determined their position, but that's not important. The thing was that our Georghi was stuck out in the wilderness for nearly a year with three Americans who didn't like it either and talked about home. I don't know anything about the sergeant and the enlisted man, but the lieutenant was a radio engineer named Kromak and he came from Passaic, New Jersey. Do you know the Lebanon?'

I shook my head.

'In the evenings the sky is like wine and the shadows falling across the terraces have purple edges to them. Overhead, vines—grape and other things with big flowers and a wonderful smell. Everything is very still and warm and soft. It's the kind of atmosphere in which myths are born and the pictures in your mind's eye seem more real than the chair you're sitting on. I wax lyrical, you see. However, the point is that Lieutenant Kromak talked about Passaic, New Jersey, and read aloud his wife's letters while Georghi listened. He heard about Molly's graduation and Michael's camp counsellor, about Sue's new baby and the seeding of the front lawn. He heard about the new refrigerator and the shortage of gasoline, about his friend Pete Staal, the dentist, and the Rotary Anns. He heard about the mouse in the cedar closet and the new screens that had been bought for the porch. And when the weekly letter was exhausted, the reminiscences would begin. "Pete Staal, Pete Staal," Kromak would say dreamily, "a good dentist and a lovable son-of-a-bitch, but what a crazy guy! I remember the night Kitty and me, the Deckers, and the Staals went to Rossi's—that's an Italian restaurant at the far end of Franklin Street—and had ravioli. Ever had ravioli? At Rossi's they make the best ravioli in the world. Well, we didn't want to take two cars, so we rode down in mine. A Dodge I had then. Well, right after we'd eaten, Helen said she wanted to go over to the Nutley Field Club. That made Pete mad and he said that if she was going to Nutley he was going to fly down to Wilmington to see his mother. Of course, he knew what Helen really wanted—to see Marie and Dane Schaeffer—I told you about them, remember? Well . . ." And on he went while Georghi listened and drank it in. Do you know Passaic, New Jersey?'

'No.'

'Chemical plants and some light industry and the homes of the people who have to work there. But to Georghi Pashik, looking through the eyes of Lieutenant Kromak, who wanted so much to be back with the wife and kids, it must have represented a paradise of domestic security and gracious living. You know how it is? Lots of quite intelligent Europeans have fantastic notions about the way most Americans live. Sitting on that terrace in a Lebanon hill town, poor, unhappy, exiled Georghi must have been a push-over for the American way of life. Just to put it in terms of food—reason might tell him that the ravioli he'd get in Rossi's on Franklin Street, Passaic, would not be as good as he'd eaten already in Rome and Florence, but Rossi's ravioli had become the desirable ones. They had the approval of those legendary figures the Staals, the Deckers, and the Schaeffers, and that was what mattered. He began to understand why the Americans didn't like the Lebanese they came in contact with. Lebanese standards of sanitation and behaviour are not those of Passaic, New Jersey. Georghi heard local ways that he had accepted or failed even to notice condemned quite angrily. He was troubled and began to question himself. You see what was happening, of course? Along with his dream of Passaic, New Jersey, he was beginning to acquire an American conscience.'

He paused for a moment to swallow another drink and fill my glass.

'How much are you embroidering this story?' I asked.

He shrugged. 'Not much. But the man who told me was an American and he could reproduce that Kromak stuff so you'd think you were really listening to him. I just give you the bits I remember and fill in the rest. The effect's the same, though. Anyway, after nearly a year of the American Way and Purpose according to Lieutenant Kromak, Georghi was shifted back to Cairo. Americans again, only this time the high priest was a dairy chemist from Minnesota and the dream was in a slightly higher income bracket. Georghi read the Declaration of Independence, the Constitution of the United States and the Gettysburg address. After that there was a filling-station proprietor from Oakland, California. He was followed by an insurance man from Hagerstown, Maryland. Then came 1944 and the surrender negotiations between Deltchev and the Anglo-American repre-sentatives. There was a British military mission operating with the partisans in Macedonia at that time. They controlled quite a large area and had a landing strip, so it wasn't too difficult to arrange the meetings. The Anglo-Americans flew in from Foggia. Deltchev travelled overland somehow. They met in a village schoolroom. Georghi was one of the interpreters. It was after the second meeting that Georghi's little cap went over the windmill.'

'Wait a minute. Had he known Deltchev before?'

'Known of him, that's all. Well now, we get to the second meeting. They had their meeting all right, but storms delayed their return and they had to wait for twenty-four hours in the village. The atmosphere of the nego-tiations had been quite friendly and the wait produced a lot of general conversation about conditions inside the country, the problems, what was to be done about them, and so on. The man who told me this was on that trip. Anyway, one of the subjects discussed was the Officer Corps Brotherhood. Deltchev was very frank about the problem and the difficulties of dealing with it. Some of his revelations, in fact, were deeply shocking to the Anglo-American brass and they didn't hesitate to tell him so. Deltchev must have wished he hadn't mentioned the thing. But that night Georghi went to see him privately. It must have been a curious meeting. After extracting from Deltchev a lot of secrecy and immunity pledges, Georghi revealed that he was a member of the Officer Corps Brotherhood, had been one since he had returned to the land of his fathers from Italy in '37. I told you he'd had peculiar ideas then about the way things ought to be. He'd expressed them by joining the Brotherhood. But now, he told Deltchev, all that was changed. He'd seen the light of Western democracy—all the way from Passaic, New Jersey, to Hagerstown, Mayland, he might have added—and wanted to make reparation. The long and short of it was that the Provisional Government's big clean-up of the Brotherhood was made possible because Georghi turned stool pigeon.'

'How do you know?'

'Because the man who told me was the officer Deltchev went to for a check-up on Georghi. The old man's first idea, of course, had been that Georghi was either an *agent provocateur* or crazy. So he was very careful. But after the next meeting he had another talk with Georghi and a plan was made.' Sibley grinned. 'You know, Georghi did a very brave thing really, when you come to think of it. He could have stayed safely with the Americans. Instead he asked them to lend him to Deltchev and came back here. The risk was really appalling, when you think. For all he knew the Brotherhood might have already condemned him as a traitor. He'd not stayed to collaborate. He'd been in the service of a foreign army. And now he'd turn up again, safe and sound at a time when for a civilian the journey from Athens was all but impossible. However, he took the risk and got away with it. I suppose that outside this place the Brotherhood's intelligence system didn't operate, and in all the confusion nobody bothered to ask many questions. Georghi rejoined his cell and the game began. There were ten Brothers to a cell. Georghi would turn in the names of seven of them to Deltchev. Then the three survivors, Georghi among them, would attach themselves to another cell and in the next cell-purge the survivors of the first one would go with the rest. All except Georghi. He was the permanent survivor. But because of the secret way the Brotherhood was organized, nobody could know how many purges our man had survived. He always arrived with the credentials and code words of the cell just betrayed and he'd always see that those who came with him were at the top of his next list. So there was never anyone to say that where he went disaster followed. It was always the first time with him. But still risky. After a time the word got round that there was treachery, and the remainder of the Brotherhood disintegrated. As a safety measure, Georghi had himself arrested on suspicion and then released. He'd done all he could. Deltchev had him quietly shipped back to the Americans. That's when I met him.'

'But why didn't you recognize him at once?'

'He had a moustache then and, as I told you, a uniform. As a matter of fact, he was so American it was difficult to believe that he'd never been out of Europe. His boss in Germany, Colonel Macready, was the last of the prophets as far as Georghi was concerned. He came from Texas. You know that seersucker suit Georghi wears? Macready gave it to Georghi as a going-away present. It came from a department store in Houston. It was also a kind of consolation prize. Georghi had tried every way he could to get a quota number for America, but it was no good. So he came back here and claimed his reward.' He paused.

'What do you mean?'

'Well, just think. Four or five years ago he came back here without a penny to his name. Now he's got this place, which I can tell you is quite expensive by local standards, and an established press agency with a dollar income. How did he do it?'

'He's quite efficient.'

'But no genius. Besides, the Pan-Eurasian was a going concern long before the war.'

'You know the answer?'

'Yes. I did a bit of checking up. The Pan-Eurasian was originally a French company incorporated in Monaco. It took a bit of doing, but I managed to find out all about it through our Paris office. I got word today from them. Like a little surprise?'

'Yes.'

'All right, then. All the shares in the Pan-Eurasian Press Service were purchased in 1946 from the French syndicate that owned them. Forty-nine per cent of them are in the name of Georghi Pashik. All of them were bought with a draft signed by the person who owns the other fifty-one per cent.' He stopped and grinned again.

'Well, who is it?'

'Madame Deltchev.'

My mind turned a somersault. 'Are you sure?'

'Sure? Of course I'm sure.'

'She'd be a nominee, of course.'

He laughed. 'Nominee? That woman? Don't be silly. She ran Papa Deltchev as if he were a family business. And if you've fallen for that holier-than-thou line of hers, you'd better think again. I'm a newspaper reporter, Foster dear, and I've met some very tough ladies and gentlemen, but that one is up near the top of the list. When I was here two years ago, she was running the country. If there were any nominees around they were her husband and that secretary of his, Petlarov. She did the thinking. She wrote the speeches. She made the policy. Do you think that dried-up little lawyer could have got to power on his own? Not on your life! The only thing he ever did without consulting her was to make a damn-fool radio speech that virtually handed over the whole country to the People's Party. Papa Deltchev? Don't make me laugh! They're not trying a man in that courtroom. It's a legend they're after and I bet she's still fighting like a steer to preserve it. Why shouldn't she? It's her work. She's the only Deltchev they're sitting in judgment on.'

I shook my head. 'Oh no, she isn't.'

He stared. 'No?'

'No. You may be right about her husband, but she didn't control all the Deltchevs.'

'What are you talking about?'

'Her son, Philip. He's a member of the Brotherhood. He was recruited by Pazar. And he's the Deltchev who was the leader of the conspiracy against Vukashin. You see, they're using the evidence against the son to convict the father and they know it.'

Sibley stared at me, his face sagging.

'What's more,' I went on dully, 'the conspiracy is still in existence. And Philip Deltchev is still alive. I carried a letter from his sister, Katerina, to him. The address was Patriarch Dimo 9 and instead of Philip I found Pazar shot through the back of the head. Then Pashik turned up. Where he is in this I don't know. But he turned up and took me to see a man named Aleko, who says he is of the secret police, but isn't. In fact he's a professional assassin who makes a habit of shooting people through the back of the head. He seemed to be in charge of the whole affair. Philip Deltchev was there under the name of Jika. The Patriarch Dimo thing was explained to me as part of a cunning police trap to catch the man who tried to kill Deltchev before he was arrested. I pretended to accept that and agreed not to make any further visits to the Deltchev house. Of course, they didn't want me to ask Katerina any questions. Pashik warned me privately too.'

'But, all the same, you went?' Sibley's face was the colour of dirty chalk.

'Yes.'

'And you wonder why they tried to kill you?'

'Not any more. Of course, if the fact that Philip Deltchev was the Deltchev of the evidence were known it would make the trial look rather silly.'

He jumped up.

'Rather silly!' His voice rose. 'You poor bloody fool! Don't you know anything about this country? Don't you see what's happened? The People's Party has taken over the whole conspiracy. Aleko's *their* man, not the Brotherhood's, and he's going to do the shooting. Young Deltchev's only the scapegoat.'

'Scapegoat for what?'

'For tomorrow's assassination, you nitwit! Don't you see? It's Judgment Day! The People's Party are going to liquidate their boss, Vukashin!'

Chapter Eighteen

Sibley had his office car and he drove me back to my hotel or nearly to it. He was so frightened that I thought at first he was going to refuse to do even that. But in my own panic I had made up my mind to kill him if he tried to leave me to walk, and he must have known it. From the moment we left Pashik's apartment until we arrived we did not exchange a word. He stopped at the corner of the street by the hotel. I looked at him.

'I'm not driving up to the entrance,' he said curtly; 'you can get out here,' 'All right.'

The moment I was out of the car he slammed the door and drove off. I could see his point. If Aleko's men were waiting at the hotel for me, it would not be a good place to stop at. I turned the corner and paused. There was a police van outside the hotel entrance. I walked slowly toward it. The revolving doors were set back slightly, and as I approached I saw the sleeve of a uniform in the recess. I walked on more boldly. If the police were there, there would at least be no gunmen in ambush.

I reached the entrance and went in, stared at by the policeman. Inside the foyer there was a group of military police and the night clerk in his shirt sleeves. They seemed to be questioning him. Then, as I came through the revolving doors, they all looked at me. The night clerk pointed.

'Herr Foster,' he said.

An officer stepped forward and two of his men moved round behind me.

'Your papers please?' He spoke in German.

I fumbled them out somehow. My hands were trembling. He glanced at them, pulled my jacket open to see if I had a gun, then nodded to the men behind me. 'You are under arrest,' he said to me as the escort closed in. 'You will come with us.'

I turned round and walked toward the revolving door again. I just managed to get through it before, very violently and painfully, I vomited.

I sat with the escort on benches in the van. The officer locked us in and got up beside the driver. I did not see where we went. It was not far. I managed to recover sufficiently to ask what I was charged with, and found that the escort spoke no German. The van turned on to cobbles and stopped. I heard the officer get out. Then there was silence. We stayed there for about ten minutes. When the van was stationary, the roof ventilators did not revolve and soon the air inside became warm and stagnant. I could smell the uniforms and greased-leather equipment of the escort and their sour, wine-laden breaths. At last there were footsteps on the cobbles, and the door of the van opened. The officer shone a flashlight.

'Get out.'

The escort clambered down and I followed. We were in a quadrangle with a high entrance arch. On the three other sides the space was enclosed by a building with barred windows. A prison, I thought. The only light came from a narrow doorway near the van.

'Forward!'

Going toward the doorway I stumbled on the cobbles and one of the escort held me by the arm. I shook his hand away and went inside. There was a long stone passage with the smell of a barracks about it. Led by the officer, we marched the passage and up some stone stairs. Then there was another passage and more stairs. The place was certainly not a prison. At the end of the second passage there was a wooden door with a guard on it. As we approached he unbolted the door. The officer went through ahead of us, and the ring of his footsteps was suddenly muted. The corridor we now entered was carpeted. We walked on between heavily ornamented walls reaching up to a vaulted ceiling. At intervals there were marble pedestals with busts standing on them and gilt wall brackets with electric candle lamps. There were no doors. Before we reached the end of the corridor, however, we turned off into a narrow passage like the alleyway of a liner. Then there were several doors. The officer peered at each in turn, then opened one of them and motioned me in.

It was evidently a committee room. There was a long table with a dozen or so chairs placed round it, a table with a telephone, and a bookcase. Over the rich marble fireplace there was a portrait of Vukashin in a gilt frame draped with the national flag. There were green linen blinds over the windows and beside the fireplace a curtained door. The room smelt of stale cigarette smoke.

The door by which I had entered shut behind me and I heard the key turn in the lock. I turned round and found that I was alone. I looked at the time. It was two o'clock. I sat down at the table. My head was aching and there was a horrible taste in my mouth. There was a water carafe and glass on the table in front of me. I drank some of the water. It was strongly chlorinated and made me want to be sick again. I lit a cigarette. Minutes went by. Every now and then I would hear a movement or a cough from the passage outside. The escort was still there. When I had finished one cigarette, I lit another. If I were going to be put into a jail, my cigarettes would certainly be taken away. I might as well smoke while I could. However, this feeble effort at a philosophical approach to the situation was not successful. Whether or not I had cigarettes to smoke would probably not seem of much importance in the near future. If Sibley was right—and I knew that he was—my arrest could mean only one thing: that Aleko, having failed to kill me himself, had left me to be dealt with by his employers. It was not a pleasant thought. On the other hand, the party might have decided that to murder a foreign journalist would not be a wise move at a time when they would be busy denying their guilt of a more serious crime. But supposing their wisdom was of a different kind. Supposing they decided that the inconvenience of killing somebody who knew too much was as nothing compared with the inconvenience of being revealed as the accomplices of their leader's murder. Death seemed very near at that moment. I hoped it would come mercifully. Perhaps if the hand were that of Aleko—

I turned sharply, my heart pounding, my skin crawling. The curtain over the door on the far side of the room had moved.

I stood up. The fantastic thought went through my mind that if I were going to be shot from behind the curtain, I must stand up so as to present an easy target.

The curtain moved again. A draught from somewhere had caught it. There was the sound of a door closing in the adjoining room, footsteps; then the door behind the curtain opened and a hand brushed the folds aside.

Brankovitch came into the room.

He glanced at me casually before turning to shut the door behind him; then came round the table toward me.

'Sit down, Mr Foster.' He nodded to a chair and sat down himself facing me. His face was haggard and he needed a shave, but he did not look as if he had been roused from his bed. Probably he had been attending a meeting. The hours before a *coup d'état* that was to begin with an assassination would be busy ones for a propaganda minister. I must be one of the inevitable hitches.

He sighed. 'A cigarette?' He brought out a case.

'I have one, thank you.' This was idiotic. 'I'm glad to find that you allow prisoners under arrest to smoke,' I added.

He pursed his lips. 'I think it will be better, Mr Foster, if you avoid facetious comment. You are being treated with great consideration, as I think my presence here indicates. It would be polite of you to recognize the fact. You realize, I hope, that you are in a very serious position.'

'It's difficult for me to realize anything, Minister. All I know is that I have been arrested and brought here. I should like to know what the charge against me is and I should like the British Consul-General informed.'

His dark, supercilious eyes stared at me coldly. 'It would be convenient if you would abandon your pretence of innocence, Mr Foster. It wastes time. If you prefer to be treated as a common criminal, that can be arranged. If you will recognize the fact of my sitting here talking to you as evidence of consideration toward a distinguished foreign writer, we may make progress.'

I was silent.

He lit a cigarette. 'Very well, then. Early tonight on the avenue that runs round the Presidential Park, shots were fired by two men at a third. Police pursued the men who had fired the shots. They escaped. So did the other man. But something was found by the police. A hat. It had your name in it, Mr Foster. Was it your hat?'

I hesitated. 'Yes, it was my hat.'

'Why do you hesitate? Were you thinking of lying, Mr Foster?'

His eyes were on mine and at that moment I understood the nature of the interview. Brankovitch knew what Aleko knew. He knew about the letter to Philip Deltchev and my finding of Pazar. He knew that Aleko had forbidden me the Deltchev house and that I had that night ignored the prohibition. He knew that Aleko had tried to kill me and failed. He might know that Katerina had talked to me. What he was trying to find out now was how much I knew, how dangerous I was. If I did not know the truth about the conspiracy against Vukashin, I was unimportant. If I did know or if I had an inkling of the truth, I must be eliminated.

I leaned forward and put my cigarette out in the ashtray by him. Then I smiled ruefully. 'Surely you understand my position, Minister. The last thing I want to do is get involved in police proceedings. Two armed men attempted to hold me up. Luckily, I managed to get away from them. It happened on a very dark stretch of road. I didn't see either of their faces. What use would I have been to the police?'

'It was your duty to report the occurrence to them. By running away in that fashion you have raised a grave question in the minds of the police.'

'What question?'

'It might be that you were one of the men who fired shots.'

'Do you believe that, Minister?'

'What I believe is not important. This is a police affair. It is referred to me initially as a matter of policy because of your status here as a newspaper representative. But I cannot prevent their dealing with you as a criminal. I can merely advise them of my opinion.'

'If I were a criminal, Minister, would I have been so careless as to leave behind a hat with my name in it?'

'The police argue from the stupidity of the criminal, not from his cleverness. But assuming, Mr Foster, that your version of the affair is true, what do you think was the motive for this attack on you?'

Here it was. I looked puzzled. 'Motive? Robbery, I imagine. What else could it be?'

He pretended to think this over. Then: 'You have not, for instance, made any enemies here?'

I felt relieved. If this was the best he could do, I had nothing to worry about.

'Enemies? I don't think so.'

'You have been involved, for instance, in no unusual circumstances that might give a clue to the police?'

I hesitated again.

'I should advise you to be frank, Mr Foster. You see, armed robbery of that kind is a most unusual crime here. I do not imply that we have no violent criminals, but that it is unusual for them to be armed with revolvers. The reason is that to carry a revolver here is in itself an offence punishable by death. The law was made to deal with the Brotherhood criminals, but of course it applies to all. Robbers would try to kill you with knives. These men did not. If they were not robbers, then who were they? That is what the police ask.'

I still hesitated. I was in a terrifying quandary. Obviously, the 'unusual circumstances' he was inviting me to tell him about were my finding of Pazar and my meeting with Aleko. But to which would it be better to pretend—frankness or cunning? Which would conceal from him more effectively my actual knowledge? Frankness had its dangers. He would be able to cross-examine and perhaps catch me out. Or he might decide from my manner that I was less artless than I seemed and unlikely to have been genuinely taken in by Aleko's explanation of the affair. Perhaps an obstinate silence would be better. The silence itself would have a useful meaning. It would say to him: 'This man does not know that I know what he is concealing. His pretence of ignorance shows, therefore, that he is truly ignorant of the important facts.' But it might also add: 'And that is just what he hoped I would think. Clearly he is bluffing.'

'Yes, Mr Foster?' He was watching every movement of my face.

Suddenly, hopelessly, I decided. I drew a deep breath. 'Very well, Minister. I will be frank. I have a confession to make.'

'A confession, Mr Foster?'

'Yes.' And then I had a desperate inspiration. I looked at him angrily. 'That was what you were expecting, wasn't it?'

'Expecting?'

'Minister, with all due respect, I've had enough of this cat-and-mouse game. I've been silly. I stuck my nose into something that was none of my business and found out some things that I wasn't supposed to know. All right, I admit it. I didn't think Herr Valmo would bother you with it. I was hoping he wouldn't. But since he has, I'm sorry. One thing I can promise you is that no reference to it will be made in any of my articles. I can't say more than that.'

He stared at me. The skin of his face was stretched tightly. It was for a moment a most extraordinary and horrible mask. The lips moved.

'Can't you, Mr Foster?'

'What is there to say? I found a dead body that your secret-police people had baited a trap with. Naturally Herr Valmo was annoyed. But he didn't blame me. I acted in all innocence. I don't see what all the fuss is about.'

'Did you make certain very solemn promises to Herr Valmo?'

I looked embarrassed. 'Yes, I did.'

'And yet you again went to the Deltchev house.'

'Unfortunately, I did.'

'Why did you go?'

'I felt I had to have Madame Deltchev's comments on the trial evidence. To be quite frank, I thought it more important to have those comments than to obey an instruction I couldn't really see the point of.'

'Did you speak to Katerina Deltchev?'

I looked puzzled. 'No, it was the old servant who let me in.'

'Who do you think were the two men who tried to kill you tonight?'

'I've no idea. I told you. I didn't see their faces.'

'I think you are pretending to be more stupid than you really are, Mr Foster. How on reflection do you explain those men? If they weren't robbers, what were they?'

For an instant I thought that I had failed after all. It was the phrase 'on reflection' that did it. If he was thinking ahead to a moment when, with Vukashin assassinated, I was beginning to put two and two together, I was really done for. If he thought that there was the remotest chance of my getting at the truth, he would decide against me. I made a last attempt.

I stared at him with sudden horrified comprehension. 'You mean that they were Brotherhood men?'

For about ten long seconds he did not answer. Then, slowly, he nodded. 'You see, Mr Foster, this prohibition of Valmo's that you so irresponsibly ignored was not without reason. Naturally, Valmo did not tell you all the facts, but there was reason to believe that the Brotherhood was interested in reaching Madame Deltchev. You were mistaken tonight for one of Valmo's men. You are lucky to be still alive.'

He had swallowed the suggestion whole. And he had given himself away. I sat back with a sigh which could have meant anything but which came actually from a feeling of relief that was almost painful. Fortunately, I still had my wits about me. There was one thing he had not mentioned. If he did not bring it up I would have to and I did not know how. I took another risk.

I frowned suddenly. 'There's only one thing I don't understand,' I said. 'Your office issued a statement this evening saying that Pazar had been found shot. The details sounded as if he was the man *I* found. Why didn't Valmo tell me who he was? Why the secrecy?'

'Would you have respected the confidence, Mr Foster?'

'Of course.'

'As you did your undertaking to Herr Valmo?' He was quite sure of me now.

I tried to look embarrassed.

He smiled unpleasantly. 'I will speak plainly, Mr Foster. I think your behaviour here has been, to say the least of it, unethical. If you were a professional newspaperman I should make a very strong complaint both to your employers and to the British Chargé d'Affaires here. As it is, I shall recommend to the police that you are released in the morning. However, I shall withdraw from you all facilities for attending the Deltchev trial. I also advise you unofficially to leave the country immediately—let us say by tonight's train at the latest. In case you decide to ignore that advice, I propose to have your visa and *permis de séjour* cancelled forthwith. Do I make myself clear?'

I protested as convincingly as I could, demanded that an official expulsion order be issued, became angry, and finally pleaded. He was obviously and satisfactorily bored with me. It has occurred to me since that he must have been nearly as relieved as I was that the problem I represented had been disposed of. He may even have disliked the idea of having to have me killed. It is possible. The last thing he said to me could be taken that way. To stop me talking he rapped on the door to summon the escort. When they came in he gave them an instruction and turned to go. Then he paused and looked back.

'Mr Foster,' he said, 'I once saw a performance of a play of yours and I enjoyed it. Why not stay in the theatre I think, for you, it would be much safer.'

I was taken out of the building by the way I had come in. It must have been a wing of the Propaganda Ministry. There was another ride in the van, another oppressive wait, then a cell in a police station. The cell had a bug-infested plank bed, but I was too exhausted and shaken to care much about bugs. As the patch of sky I could see got lighter, I fell into a headache-ridden doze. I even slept a little. At nine o'clock the cell door opened and I was taken to a sort of waiting-room near the entrance.

There, dirty and unshaven, in his seersucker suit with the three fountain pens in the pocket and his briefcase resting on his knees, sat Pashik.

He rose to his feet as he saw me, and nodded.

'Good morning, Mr Foster.'

'How did you get here?' I said.

His eyes flickered warningly in the direction of my escort. He spoke in German. 'I have just been informed that you were arrested by mistake and were here. I understand that an apology has already been given and accepted.'

'Yes. Am I free to go?'

'I am told so.'

I shook hands with the escort and followed Pashik down the steps into his car. He drove off and turned a corner before he spoke. His tone was bleak and noncommittal.

'What happened, Mr Foster?'

'I was interrogated by Brankovitch.'

'Yes?'

'He wanted to find out how much I knew and how much I suspected.'

He turned to look at me. The car wandered in the direction of an obelisk.

'If we're going to talk hadn't you better stop?' I added quickly.

He straightened up but did not stop. 'And what did you know and suspect, Mr Foster?'

'That the Brotherhood plot to assassinate Vukashin has been taken over by the anti-Vukashin movement in the People's Party. That Aleko has been brought in to organize the job efficiently. That Philip Deltchev was involved in the original plot and is still involved. That when Vukashin is assassinated at the anniversary parade today, Philip Deltchev will be executed for the crime. That the story will be that when his father was arrested Philip took over the conspiracy and with the knowledge and approval of the Agrarian Socialist executive carried it through. That the Agrarian Socialist Party will be made illegal and liquidated. That Branko-vitch will take over the Government.'

He kept his eyes on the road. 'And what did you tell him you knew?'

'Only what he must have been already told by Aleko—that I found the body of Pazar and believed Herr Valmo's explanations.'

'And you convinced him!'

'Do you think I'd still be alive if I hadn't?'

'No, Mr Foster, I don't. May I say that I have always had the greatest respect for your intelligence?'

'Thank you.'

'You must have talked with Mr Sibley, of course.'

'Yes.'

'I was sure he had recognized me and that someone had been indiscreet. How much does he know, do you think?'

'He's got the general idea. And he's very frightened.'

'I see. We have much to tell each other, Mr Foster.'

'Yes. By the way, my permit for the trial has been withdrawn and I've got to be out of the country tonight.'

He nodded. 'That was to be expected. There is a train for Athens at five, which I strongly recommend.'

'Athens? Why Athens?'

'Because that is where Philip Deltchev is.'

I stared at him. He had a curious smirk on his face. He even began a wheezy kind of chuckle.

'What on earth are you talking about?' I demanded.

He swung exuberantly into the street that had the Hotel Boris in it. Already crowds were beginning to line the avenues in preparation for the parade. He looked at his watch and nearly mowed down a family group in national costume.

'It is now twenty of nine,' he said. 'In an hour Philip Deltchev will be at the Hotel Splendid Palace in Athens. Apart from Madame Deltchev and myself, you are the only person who knows this. You can be the first newspaperman to interview him, the first to expose the People's Party's political murder conspiracy.'

'But how did you know?'

'I think you could have guessed, Mr Foster. I saw him across the frontier myself last night.'

Chapter Nineteen

When Pashik was secretly rewarded for his services to the Provisional Government with shares in and management of the Pan-Eurasian Press Service he was not unduly grateful. He had risked his life to serve a political ideal; but it was an ideal that in his mind belonged exclusively to the United States of America; elsewhere it was not valid. He had performed his service somewhat in the spirit of the prosperous immigrant to that country who endows a public or a childbirth clinic in his native land. The act is charitable, but it is also a reparation, a propitiatory rite that makes the separation final and complete. For Pashik there was little satisfaction in the knowledge that his contribution had been so frankly and practically recognized. His pleasure in the gift resided in the fact that the agency's clients were nearly all American and that he could feel, not preposterously, that as their representative he was in a sense an outpost of the American way of life. One day, perhaps, he would go on a visitor's visa to America; and, perhaps one day, before he was old, he would get an immigration quota number. Meanwhile he was in touch. For Pashik, who had learned not to expect too much of life, that was a singular blessing and he enjoyed it. After a while he could almost forget that the Brotherhood had existed.

The reminder that it had indeed existed and the news that in an attenuated way it still did exist came as a blow. The messenger was Pazar. He told of cautious overtures being made, of small, tentative meetings, of wary soundings, and of half-formed plans. It was as if the Brotherhood had been decimated by a plague and as if the survivors had now begun to raise their heads and look about them, uncertain whether or not the infection still persisted. Gradually, in an atmosphere of intense suspicion and extravagant fears, contacts were being re-established. The security precautions were formidable. All surviving members were invited to reapply for membership and submit to the most searching investigation. Refusal to reapply when asked was to be deemed evidence of guilt. There had been no refusals so far, Pazar told Pashik grimly. The Brothers awaited him.

Pashik nodded and went to see his principal shareholder, Madame Deltchev. This was just about election time and Madame Deltchev advised Pashik to reapply. Apart from the fact that it would be dangerous for him not to do so—Pashik did not think that this alone would have weighed heavily with Madame Deltchev—she felt that it would be advisable to be informed of the new Brotherhood's activities. She had always had in mind the possibility of the People's Party's manipulating the Brotherhood for its own ends. This resurgence might not be only what it appeared to be.

So began again a double life for Pashik. He was reinitiated into the

Brotherhood and sat in judgment on the applications of others. The purges had proved fatal for nearly all the senior members and soon he found himself being admitted into the higher councils of the organization. Some two months before the arrest of Yordan Deltchev he heard of the membership of Philip and of the plot against Vukashin.

For once Madame Deltchev was at a loss. She had already planned the football-match incident and was manoeuvring as best she could to bring about an Agrarian-Socialist *coup* before the People's Party was quite secure. Her son's activities imperilled everything. Whether he succeeded or failed, it made no difference. As far as the people were concerned, Philip Deltchev was an extension of Papa Deltchev. The murder of Vukashin by Brother Philip would serve to unite the People's Party as never before and shatter the Agrarian Socialists irretrievably. She could not betray the boy, for to do so would bring the same evil consequences. It was useless, she knew, to attempt to persuade him, for he was too deeply committed. She could not even discuss it with him lest he should identify Pashik as her informant. Not that she would have minded sacrificing Pashik; it was simply that she saw no point in sacrificing him to no purpose. All she could do was to instruct Pashik to work within the Brotherhood to keep in touch with Philip and perhaps undermine his belief in the project. It was a feeble plan, but for the moment she could think of nothing better. Then events began in the most curious way to play into her hands.

In the days before the purges Pazar had been a comparatively unimportant member of the Brotherhood whose weaknesses had been clearly perceived and carefully reckoned with. He would certainly not have been allowed so much as to know about a plan as important as that he now administered. That he should tell someone of it was inevitable. That it should be the petty crook Rila whom he told was very nearly lucky. If Rila had not happened at that time to get into the hands of the police, things might have turned out very differently.

The casualties in the assassination group put the Brotherhood in a panic. The survivors had raised their heads only to find that the plague was still with them. It was another betrayal, another purge. Within a few hours the great majority of the readmitted Brothers were dispersed and in hiding. The rest—those who had no means of hiding—sat in their rooms rehearsing denials. Only Pashik was in a position to know that the plague had not returned and that there must be a different explanation of this disaster. He made his report to Madame Deltchev and waited.

A week later, things began to move. One night Philip Deltchev came to see him. He brought news. He and Pazar had escaped and were for the moment safe. Meanwhile the Brotherhood had reorganized. Pazar had been superseded as administrator—his nerves were bad—and a new man had taken over. His name was Aleko and he was a dynamo of a man with great determination and drive. But others were needed. Several Brothers had refused, cravenly. Would he, Pashik, come in with them? The plan would now go on to success, in which all would share.

Pashik accepted and reported to Madame Deltchev. She agreed with him that the whole affair felt peculiar. Their suspicions were aroused in the first place because of the failure of the police to arrest Pazar and Philip. Pashik knew that there was documentary evidence against them and that in such a dangerous case—a Brotherhood plot against Vukashin—the price of concealment was beyond the fugitives' capacity to pay. And there was Philip's name. Why was the People's Party not publicizing the affair? By way of reply to this question Madame Deltchev produced her theory that the People's Party would ultimately take over the Brotherhood. Pashik listened respectfully. But he had an unworthy thought: that Madame Deltchev's preoccupation with the idea was dictated by her annoyance at having failed to take over the Brotherhood herself. She was, to Pashik's way of thinking, a remarkable woman, but inclined to underrate the cleverness of others.

A day or two later he was summoned to meet Aleko. The meeting took place in the apartment I had been in, and it was soon evident to Pashik that Aleko was not what he pretended to be. For one thing, he noticed—as I had noticed—that the furnishings had been assembled from second-hand stores and arranged hurriedly in an unlikely way. But there might have been reasonable explanations for that. What decided him was Aleko's way of talking. Pashik had met many members of the Brotherhood and he had learned to recognize the habits of thought and speech that were the private currency of their relationships. For instance, the Brethren scarely ever talked of killing anybody without at some point using the phrase 'removing an obstacle.' Aleko used the word 'eliminate.' It was a small difference, but it was one of many. And there was a mannerism he had that was peculiar. When he spoke of firing a gun he would point with his forefinger at the back of his head and make a clicking noise with his tongue. For the Brethren a gun was a serious matter; you did not click facetiously with your tongue to convey its moment of power. The whole gesture reminded Pashik of something he knew he would remember later. By the end of that meeting he was sure that Aleko was not a bona-fide member of the Brotherhood. Yet he was dispensing money and making sound plans to assassinate Vukashin. In the early hours of the morning Pashik came to the conclusion that Madame Deltchev had been very nearly right. Someone had employed Aleko; someone who could hamstring police action and also pay well; someone in the People's Party. But not necessarily the People's Party as a whole. A faction within the party, then? It was probable. Somebody was going to get killed and somebody else was paying for the event. Pashik decided to learn more before deciding upon the identity of the principal.

The attempt to assassinate Deltchev had been organized, Pashik thought, by Vukashin himself and without Brankovitch's knowledge or approval. The press releases that came from the Propaganda Ministry bore marks of haste, improvisation and uncertainty of line which suggested that Brankovitch had been caught unprepared. Moreover, Aleko was disconcerted and talked vaguely about 'bungling.' The term could have referred to the failure of the attempt, but Pashik's impression was that it was more in the nature of a comment on a situation that permitted the attempt to take place at all. That was interesting because if the impression was correct, it meant that Brankovitch and Aleko had one thing at least in common—ignorance of Vukashin's intentions. And that in turn might mean that they had other things in common too.

The arrest of Deltchev created a new problem for Pashik. Hitherto he had

had no difficulty in arranging for private meetings with Madame Deltchev. Now that she was under house arrest, it was impossible to see her personally. He knew that all visitors would be reported and he could not afford to have his name on the list. His whole position was, indeed, highly equivocal. He was certainly known to Aleko's employers as a member of the Brotherhood. The faintest breath of suspicion as to his motives would result in his being informed upon and promptly hanged. He had Philip Deltchev on his hands and an obligation to extricate the young man if he could. He did not know exactly what was afoot. He was without allies. All he could do for the present was to remain as inconspicuous as possible, cultivate Philip Deltchev, and check up on Aleko. But for a while he did not make much progress with either intention. Philip Deltchev did not like him. The best he had been able to do about Aleko was to remember what the gun-pointing gesture had reminded him of. The 'K. Fischer' note that I had found was the result. It was Pazar who finally supplied the essential information.

When Aleko had taken over the conspiracy, Pazar had been in a pitiable state of exhaustion and terror. The arrest of Rila had cut off his drug supplies. He was without money or lodging and was hunted by the police. Philip, who then had (in the name Valmo) the room in the Patriarch Dimo, had taken him in, and for nearly a week the two had remained there, hungry, because they feared to go out to buy food, and in constant fear of discovery. The night Aleko arrived on the scene, Pazar had collapsed and was in a state almost of coma. It took him several days of ready access to the supplies of heroin that Aleko had miraculously procured to bring him back to anything like normality; and when he did come back, it was to find that he had been superseded.

Pazar was not unintelligent. Quite soon he perceived what Pashik already knew—that Aleko was not of the Brotherhood—but, unlike Pashik, he drew a wrong conclusion. His drug-twisted mind linked his discovery with his own fall from power and also with the memory of the traitor who had never been unmasked. All the paranoid projections of his mind focused suddenly upon a single object—Aleko. From that moment he began to plot against Aleko and to spy on him. Philip had moved into Aleko's apartment, and Pazar had the Patriarch Dimo room to himself. It was easy, therefore, for him to keep track of Aleko's movements outside the apartment. One night he followed Aleko to a house in the suburbs. It was a big house and there was a car outside of the kind that usually has a chauffeur. Aleko was there an hour. When he came out Pazar did not follow him, but stayed to watch the house and the car. Ten minutes after Aleko had gone, a man came out, got into the car, and drove off. As he passed by, Pazar recognized him. It was Brankovitch. Two days later, seething with malice and excitement, he told Pashik of his discovery.

It took Pashik ten seconds to make up his mind what he had to do. The first thing was to control Pazar and urge discretion. The second thing was to make him tell the story to Philip Deltchev in Pashik's presence so that while the boy would at last realize what was really happening, his desire for revenge could be usefully canalized. Obviously, Brankovitch's idea was to destroy his rival within the party and to put the guilt for the crime on the Deltchev family. In other words, he would manipulate the original conspiracy so as to convict the father and use the second conspiracy, his own, to dispose of Vukashin and have in his hands the perfect scapegoat, Philip. Pashik's idea was to remove the scapegoat when it was too late to change the assassination plan and let the whole affair recoil on Brankovitch. What was more, Pashik knew just how the idea could be put into practice. But everything depended on Philip.

It was a ticklish business. When Philip's first neurotic outbursts were spent he lapsed into a hopeless depression, which persisted for some days and which was noticed by Aleko. Fortunately, Pashik had managed to make his proposals understood, and Philip Deltchev had presence of mind enough to play the part he had been given. It was not too difficult. All he had to do was to continue to appear fanatically devoted to the task of killing Vukashin; and fanatics do not have to make much sense. The problem was Pazar. His hatred of Aleko soon wore so thin a disguise that an outburst of some sort was inevitable. All Pashik could do was to remind him constantly of the need for absolute secrecy, and hope that when the explosion came, Pazar the drug addict would be more in evidence than Pazar the conspirator. And so it turned out. The occasion was one of the biweekly meetings at which Aleko insisted on going over the entire plan of campaign afresh and rejustifying each part of it. The plan itself was simple enough, and clearly the object of the meetings was to keep the conspirators in hand; but that night Pazar chose to put a different interpretation on the meeting. Quite suddenly and fantastically he accused Aleko of having police hidden in an adjoining room to listen to the conversation. Without a word Aleko rose and showed the next room to be empty. Pazar replied that there were microphones hidden and began to tear up the carpet to prove it. Philip Deltchev sat as if he had not heard. Pashik sat sweating for what was to come. Aleko watched with a smile, but listened attentively to Pazar's babbling. There was just enough sense in it for him to guess what Pazar had discovered. When, in the end, Pazar collapsed, sobbing, Aleko gave him a big injection of heroin. When Pazar was quiet, Aleko looked at the others and shook his head. 'We cannot rely upon him,' he said. 'He will compromise us all.'

The other two nodded quickly. They were in heartfelt agreement.

Aleko smiled. 'Leave everything to me,' he said.

At the next meeting Pazar did not appear and Aleko announced briefly that he had committed suicide in his room, that the body would be left for the police to find, and that, as his services had never really been necessary, no Brother would be sought to replace him.

It was on the day after that meeting that I arrived.

I presented a serious problem to the harassed Pashik. To have someone in and about his office, poking and prying, hampering his movements, possibly endangering his neutral relations with the Propaganda Ministry—that was bad enough. To have someone directly concerned with him in contact with Petlarov was alarming, for who knew what that might not suggest to Brankovitch? He had already recognized and been recognized by Sibley, whom he remembered as one of the intelligence officers who could know his story.

Sibley knew me. Another potential danger. Especially as I was inquisitive. My interview with Madame Deltchev threw him into a panic. The night he learned of it, he faced Aleko with his gun in his pocket instead of in his briefcase. But nothing unusual happened at that meeting. It was after it that Aleko took him aside, gave him a wad of papers, and asked him to put them in Pazar's room to 'mislead' the police who found them. Pashik guessed that Brankovitch wished to take the opportunity afforded by Pazar's death of planting further incriminating evidence against Deltchev. When he got to Pazar's room, he found me there.

His dilemma was awful. I could be explained in several ways. I was telling him the truth or I was lying. But even if I was telling the truth I might still be an unwitting agent of Brankovitch's and this might be a trap to catch him out. On the other hand, I was doing work for one of the American clients and was therefore under the protection of the Pan-Eurasian Press Sevice. If this was a trap, then the only safe thing to do was to take me to Aleko for questioning. If it was not a trap, however, he might be taking the representative of an American client to his death.

'What made you decide to take me?' I asked.

Pashik blinked at me sheepishly. 'I did not quite decide, Mr Foster,' he said; 'I compromised. I left part of the decision to you.'

'What do you mean?'

'While I hid the papers Aleko had given me in the room, you were walking to my car at the end of the street. I thought you might take the opportunity to escape. If you did not—' He shrugged.

'Do you know why I didn't run?'

'Because you were not alarmed?'

'No. Because I wanted to ask you questions.'

He sighed. 'You have been very lucky, Mr Foster,' he said. 'It was difficult to persuade Aleko that you were harmless, and very embarrassing when he found that you were not. I certainly did not expect to find you alive this morning. And when you tell me of Katerina's foolishness I marvel.'

'I suppose she got back all right.'

'If she had not done so you would not be here. The check on the Deltchev house is carried out at eight every morning.'

'Does Madame Deltchev know what's happened?'

'I have been able to send her brief messages.'

'By that old friend of the family who drops in for tea?'

'You are too well informed, Mr Foster.'

I finished my fourth cup of coffee. 'When you begin to make flattering remarks, I am suspicious,' I said. 'You really mean that I still don't know at all what's going on.'

His brown eyes contemplated me through his rimless glasses. He was smelling strongly that morning. The seersucker suit was horribly dirty. He shrugged. 'As for instance, Mr Foster?'

'As for instance—why are you here at all at this moment? Why aren't you in Athens with Philip?'

We were in my hotel room. He opened his briefcase, took out a battered meat sandwich, and began eating it. He had his mouth full before he answered. 'You forget, Mr Foster, that there is to be an assassination here today.'

'I hadn't forgotten it. What I was wondering was why you've been so cagey about it. What exactly is going to happen? What's the plan? When did Philip come into it? What happens now he isn't here?'

'They do not know he is not here. He did not leave until after the final meeting last night.'

'But what's going to happen?'

'I will tell you. Pazar's original plan was simple and stupid. The celebration march takes place in the St Mihail Square. The parade marches in along the boulevard and out along the prospect. The saluting base is the stone platform halfway down the great steps that lead up to the portico in front of the Ministry of the Interior. It was the main state entrance to the old palace. From the bronze statues at the bottom up to the platform there are forty steps. On these occasions the steps are flanked with troops, forty each side. They are a bodyguard and they are armed with machine pistols. It was Pazar's idea to kidnap four of these men and replace them with his men. They would shoot Vukashin as he stood on the platform and hope to escape in the confusion, because it would seem to be the real troops who had fired. This, I may tell you, was the plan that the prosecutor at the trial did not wish to explain.'

'Why not?'

'Because the absurdity of it would make people laugh. Does it not make you laugh, Mr Foster?'

'It might have worked.'

He shook his head mournfully. 'I can see, Mr Foster, that you would not be a good conspirator. One has only to think for a moment of the kidnapping—'

'What were all those messages about?'

'The uniforms, naturally. They could not buy them. Instead they stole them from the soldiers' brothels. It was all very childish. When Aleko took over he made a new plan. Uniforms were wanted, but those of ordinary line troops, not those of the bodyguard. Three men only would be needed. It was a good plan. You know, when there is a parade great care is taken to guard against assassins. The occupants of rooms overlooking the square are carefully checked by the police, and the flat roofs of the buildings round it are guarded by troops from outside the city. The first part of the plan was to conceal a machine gun and ammunition on one of the flat roofs. Then just before the parade men in uniform would go up to the roof and tell the troops already there that the guards were being doubled as trouble was expected. As the real troops were from outside, these would not expect to recognize men who said they were from a city battalion. The false men would have bottles of brandy and things to eat in their haversacks. After a while they would offer to share it. The brandy would be heavily dosed with morphine. The soldiers would go to sleep; the gun would be produced and set up and trained on the platform. All would be in readiness for the appearance of Vukashin. And when the thing was done, escape would be possible. It would be difficult in the surprise and confusion to say exactly where the shots had come from. The troops on near-by roofs might think they were from a window below. But there would be doubt. And while there was doubt, there would be time for us to descend to the street and mingle with the crowd. Who is going to suspect three soldiers? Until the real ones wake up, hours later, nobody will know how it was done, and by then it will be too late.'

'Philip Deltchev will have escaped?'

'Exactly, Mr Foster. That was why the plan seemed so good at first to Philip and Pazar and so strange to me. Until I knew that Brankovitch was deeply involved and saw that it would be quite easy for him to arrange for the police to be warned that, say, thieves disguised as soldiers would be raiding such-and-such a building during the parade and that a patrol waiting at the exits could catch them redhanded.'

'So as there will be no Philip, there will be no assassination. Is that it?'

'No, Mr Foster, that is not it. There were to be three on the gun—Philip, myself, and one of Aleko's men.'

'One of those who tried to kill me?'

'That is so. But there is another man and Aleko himself. What, I asked myself, would they be doing while Vukashin was being assassinated?'

'Leaving the country, I should think.'

'Yes, I thought that. But three days ago there was a serious complication. Aleko told us that there would be a second gun on another roof and that he and the other man would man it. Philip would have the honour of firing first, but Aleko would be there in case of an emergency. What would that suggest to you, Mr Foster?'

'That he was suspicious? That he didn't trust Philip?'

'Yes, I considered those possibilities. But then another thought occurred to me, a very interesting idea. Luckily I was able to check it. The following night the guns were hidden on the roofs we had selected—'

'Which are they?'

He smiled. 'That I think I will not tell you, Mr Foster. You will discover.'

There was something very disturbing about that smile. I suddenly became uneasy.

'Go on,' I said.

'The guns were wrapped in sacking and hung by wires inside the brick chimneys. Very early in the morning I returned by myself and examined them.' He paused, smiling again.

'And—'

'The gun on Philip's roof had no firing pin. It had been taken out.'

I looked blank. 'I'm sorry. I don't see—'

'Don't you, Mr Foster?' His eyes gleaming through the spectacles were no longer sad. 'Power is a great thing, you know. To be able to move and control great affairs—not the characters and situations on a stage, Mr Foster, but the real—that is the greatest of all pleasures. You feel it in the stomach.' He patted his own. 'Here. I feel it now.'

'Yes?' I wondered suddenly if he were mad.

'Consider.' He stood up and strode over to the window. 'A man in Aleko's profession is always in a difficult position. He must always be sure that his master has the power to protect him. He must always be sure that the master wishes to protect him. And he must consider the future. It is dangerous for him to serve one powerful person at the expense of another who may later do him harm. Aleko is clever. He would not have survived if he had not been. He is used to weighing advantages. And so I ask myself questions. Why are there two guns? Why is there no firing pin in a gun that Aleko expects to pour bullets into Vukashin. I answer, because it is Vukashin who is Aleko's best master and has been so perhaps from the first. What ultimate chance has Brankovitch in a struggle for power over Vukashin's dead body? None! He would go down in the end. His own intelligence would trip him. The sort of brutal cunning that lets him dig his own grave will always win. That is Vukashin's strength and Aleko knows it. Philip would have pressed the trigger of a gun aimed at Vukashin and nothing would have happened. Aleko would have pressed the trigger of the second gun, aimed at Brankovitch, and the gun would have fired. Philip and I and Aleko's man would have been arrested and hanged. The gun that would be used in evidence would be the one Aleko left on the other roof. The two murderous Deltchevs would hang together. The murderous Agrarian Socialists would be punished. Vukashin would be secure both from the opposition and from the plots and ambitions of Brankovitch. Aleko, who loves skiing, would be waiting, rich and happy, for the snow at St Moritz. A pretty picture, Mr Foster!'

'Yes.' There seemed nothing else to say.

'But a picture that will not be seen.'

'Because Philip is in Athens.'

He held up a finger. 'And because I am here.'

'I don't understand.'

'You will see now why I wish you to understand. The one obstacle is Aleko's man—one of those who tried to kill you—the one who was to have been with Philip and me. In one hour's time he will go to a rendezvous to meet us. If we do not arrive he will go to Aleko to warn him, and when Aleko knows that Philip is not there he will not fire. Brankovitch's life will be saved.'

'I see.'

'But if I stop this man, Aleko will fire. Brankovitch will die, and because there is no Philip to arrest, Vukashin will have to take Aleko. And when Philip has told his story to you and it is ringing round the world, Vukashin's day will begin to end. That is, if I stop this man.'

I said nothing.

For a moment he continued to stare out of the window; then he turned to face me, his self-assurance gone, his face working grotesquely. 'Do I stop him, Mr Foster?' he demanded. '*You* tell me!'

I stared at him, and he read my thoughts.

He shook his head. 'No, Mr Foster, it is not in your hands. There is nobody here for you to tell this story to. That is if you yourself wish to live. Warn Brankovitch, and you will be rewarded by him with a bullet. Warn Vukashin and it will be the same. You know too much for either's safety.'

'There's our Consulate. They could warn Brankovitch.'

'Then you would be killing me instead. I do not think you will choose that alternative. You have no moral dilemma, Mr Foster. It is my own I put to you.'

I was silent.

He sat down and gazed sullenly into space for a moment. 'Do you know America well?' he asked suddenly.

'Not very well.'

'No,' he said slowly, 'neither do I.'

He was silent again. I did not speak. I knew, as if he were thinking aloud, that he was submitting his problem to the judgment of Passaic, New Jersey, Oakland, California, and Hagerstown, Maryland. It was perhaps as good a way of resolving it as any other.

When at last he stood up he was calm and businesslike as the day we had met. He took an envelope out of his pocket and handed it to me.

'Your ticket for the press box at the anniversary parade, Mr Foster. I should have given it to you before. Even after what has happened, I do not see that there can be any objection to your using it. Your train, I would remind you, is at five. Have you money?'

'Yes, thanks.'

He held out his hand. 'I will try to get to the station to look after you, but there will be the cables and so on to attend to. You will forgive me if I cannot make it.'

I shook hands with him. 'Yes, of course. Thank you very much for all your help.'

He put up a protesting hand. 'A pleasure, Mr Foster.'

He turned away briskly, picked up his briefcase, and walked to the door. Then he paused.

'You're welcome,' he added, and went.

Chapter Twenty

The parade began at two o'clock.

It was only a quarter of a mile or so from the hotel to the square, but the crowds along the route of the parade and in the streets approaching the square were dense. It took me a long time to get through. The day was very warm and I felt tired and ill and frightened. I had not eaten any lunch. My legs were like paper and I kept thinking that I had lost something valuable. The sensation was curiously familiar. I had felt like that once before. And then I remembered: it had been when I was walking back to a hotel in Seville after seeing my first and only bullfight.

The press box was in a wooden stand built over the cathedral steps and at right angles to the front of the palace. The parade would pass below it, then bear left to march past the saluting base halfway up the palace steps. There a waist-high balustrade had been erected. It was draped with flags, and on the step below, flowers were banked to give an appearance of depth to the structure. Behind and above it were the crowded boxes of the lesser dignitaries. The whole square was a mass of flags and brilliantly coloured flowers. The façades of the buildings that formed the square were mostly of a honey-coloured stone, but the paving had been spread with white sand, and in the bright hot sunshine the effect was dazzling.

It was five minutes to the hour when I got there, and all but a few seats in the box were already filled. I could see the back of Sibley's head near the front. Nearly everyone had sunglassess, but I had forgotten mine, and the glare from the sand was painful. Somewhere a military band was playing, and every now and then a section of the crowd would raise a cheer. Heads would turn at the sound, but the cheer would die away. I looked at the rooftops. There was a canopy over the stand I was in and I could see only a small section of them. From there to the saluting base was a little over two hundred yards. At that range even a recruit could hit a man with one burst from an automatic gun. Perhaps even now an eye was peering through sights at the palace steps.

I wiped my face and neck with my handkerchief and looked at the official programme. A duplicated translation had been slipped into it for the benefit of us foreigners. The parade would symbolize the plough and the sword in harmony together. First would come the floats carrying the tableaux of the various industries and crafts. Then the massed representatives of sport and culture. Finally the parade of military and air power. The whole parade would be led by a special tableau depicting the victory of the People's Party. This tableau would halt before the Ministry of the Interior to summon the party leaders to witness the parade, the visible demonstration of the triumph of their work for the motherland.

I had seen this float lurking in a side street just off the square. It was a huge affair mounted on a platform carried by an aircraft transportation truck. Art, Science, Industry, Agriculture and Armed Might, each with its subsidiary tableau, were grouped round a white flag-decked plinth supporting a huge Winged Victory in wood and plaster. The subsidiary tableaux had the usual props: for Industry there was an anvil, for Science a retort on a bench, for Agriculture a plough, and so on. There were brackets and ledges jutting out from the sides of the plinth obviously for the use of the girls in voluminous white robes who would presently drape themselves round the feet of the Victory.

At eight minutes past two another band entered into the square and formed up round the statue in the centre. Then the bodyguards marched in with machine pistols at the ready and to the accompaniment of excited cheers took up their positions on the steps below the saluting base. The stage was being set. At two-eleven a squadron of cavalry clattered round from the far side and halted in line beneath the stand I was in. An order was shouted. The cavalry drew their sabres, and a single note on a bugle sounded. With a crash the bands began to play the national anthem. All those who had seats rose to their feet. Then, with a roar of cheering, a waving of flags and hats and another crash of music, the Winged Victory float began to move into the square.

My heart was beating so quickly and the blood was thudding so violently in my head that the din of brass bands and cheering was like a continuous rushing sound. I sat down, but it was no better. I stood up again. A man's voice came through the loudspeakers. He was talking very quickly—giving a description of the tableaux, I suppose. The Victory, preceded by a small detachment of troops on foot, turned jerkily and passed our stand. The statue was wobbling as it moved along and the girls posing on the plinth wobbled with it; but I had no desire to laugh. I found myself staring at the tableaux of Industry on one corner of the platform. A man in a leather apron had a sledge hammer raised above the anvil as if to strike. His arms were already feeling the strain and I watched the head of the hammer gradually getting lower. Then the float began to turn again and he was out of sight. On the far side of the square, troops presented arms as the Victory came into view. It crawled on until it was nearly level with the centre statue, then swung across to the foot of the steps exactly facing the saluting base and stopped. The girls on the plinth took up a new pose so that they all faced the palace.

Suddenly there was a tremendous roll of drums, and over the entire square the crowd fell silent. The drums ceased abruptly. Then the band began to play the People's Party marching song. All heads were turned toward the palace portico and the aisle of steps that ran down between the upper boxes to the saluting base. Through the loudspeakers came the sound of a choir singing the song. The crowd joined in. The air seemed to quiver with the sound. Then, as the song reached its climax—the great shout of affirmation that came on the final note—Vukashin appeared at the top of the steps and the cheering began.

He was wearing a black suit and had a cloth cap in his hand. For a moment he stood there motionless. Then he raised a hand in salute and began to walk down the steps toward the saluting base, while the cheering swelled up. When he was about two steps down, a man in the uniform of a marshal stepped from the group behind him and began to follow. The Minister of the Interior came next. And then Brankovitch started down.

He, too, was dressed in black, but very neatly, and he wore a grey Homburg. He walked down slowly and deliberately as if he were unaware of what was going on in the square below. As he passed the upper boxes, the occupants of which were clapping, he nodded casually to someone he knew there.

Vukashin had reached the base. Now he walked forward to the balustrade and looked down. A fresh storm of cheering greeted him. The marshal and the Minister of the Interior moved to left and right of him. Brankovitch moved to the balustrade beside the Minister of the Interior and said something to him. The latter smiled and pointed to the Victory. By this time the whole length of the balustrade was occupied. There were two or three uniforms, but most wore dark suits with grey Homburgs. There was only one cloth cap—Vukashin's. On the other side of Brankovitch was a stout man who held himself as if he had a boil on his neck. They were about a foot apart. Brankovitch turned sideways to say something to him.

Vukashin raised his hand to salute the Victory tableau, and with a jerk it set off again. At the same moment the bands struck up and the main procession began to move in.

It was headed by a detachment of men in white dungarees marching eight abreast. But I barely noticed them. My eyes were on Brankovitch. He was still talking to the man at his side.

As clapping and cheering broke out again, I began desperately to try to reassure myself. It just could not be! I had been listening to the babblings of a lunatic. Or—better, far better!—the verdict of Passaic and Oakland and Hagerstown had been that those things which were God's should be rendered unto God, that—Article something-or-other-of-the-Constitution-of-the-United-States-of-America—nobody can do anything that affects the life, liberty, or person of anybody, without the aforesaid democratic procedure having been properly and faithfully observed, and that the best thing Georghi Pashik could do would be to move his fat arse the hell out of it and send that suit to the cleaner's.

I was suddenly sure that it was going to be all right. At any moment now Pashik would appear beside me, businesslike, courteous, and all for playing ball with the regime. I almost laughed with relief. The time was two-nineteen.

And then it happened.

The head of the parade had curved into the straight in front of the saluting base, and Brankovitch turned to look at them. For a second or two he stopped talking and was absolutely still. The next moment the toneless, tearing rattle of a burst of Spandau fire echoed round the square. And almost, it seemed, before the echo of the first had done one leg of its journey, a second burst came.

I had my eyes on Brankovitch. There must have been some sort of stool or bench behind each of them to rest against during the parade, for he lurched back as if he were falling and then stopped for a moment. I saw the second burst hit him in the neck. Then he turned slightly sideways as if he were going to talk to the Minister of the Interior again and crumpled out of sight behind the balustrade.

The man with the boil was the quickest-witted. He took cover behind the balustrade a second after Brankovitch fell. There might, after all, have been other bullets on the way. The Minister of the Interior just stood staring. Vukashin gave one quick look round, then went as if to help Brankovitch. I think that for about ten seconds only a very few of the spectators realized that there was anything amiss at the saluting base. Most of them had just shifted their attention to the parade. But someone screamed. At the same moment men began shouting above the noise of the bands, and the bodyguard closed in defensively round the saluting base with their guns pointed at the crowd. Then a wave of panic came.

All at once everyone seemed to be shouting or screaming. The bands stopped and the parade slowed uncertainly. The Winged Victory, now on the far side of the square, jerked to a standstill. I saw one of the girls fall off the plinth as a great mass of people trying to get out of the square surged forward round the thing. A man near me in the press box was shouting like a maniac. I was very near the exit. I stumbled to it and got down the steps. An official coming up shouted something and tried to stop me, but I pushed past him and made for the narrow street that ran between the cathedral and the adjoining building in the square. This street had been closed by the police and made to serve as a main entrance for box-ticket-holders and I thought that if I could get behind the cathedral before the crowds in the square were completely out of control and the surrounding streets impassable, I might reach the hotel in time to finish what I had to do.

Others in the boxes had had the same idea. The street was filling rapidly and most of the people were running. I began to run too. By the time I reached it, the police barrier at the end had been swept away and people

were clambering over the remains of it to join the frantic stream pouring out
of the square. It would have been difficult to walk then even if I had wished
to, for to the shouting and screaming in the square behind us was now added
the sound of shooting as the bodyguard fired over the heads of the panic-
stricken crowds. Everybody ran. I must have run about a quarter of a mile
before it seemed safe to walk. People had begun to sink down exhausted on
the pavements. Many of them were crying. I walked on and found myself in
a street of small shops. The shopkeepers had put their shutters up for the
day and I did not want to try asking directions of anyone who knew what
had happened. It was not a good moment to reveal oneself as a foreigner.

I walked on aimlessly, looking for a familiar landmark. What I felt I had
to do was to see Madame Deltchev and tell her about Pashik before I went.
In the confusion I had had the absurd idea that I might get my bag and
typewriter from the hotel, be driven to the Deltchev house in a hotel car,
and go straight on to the station from there. I knew now that that was out of
the question. Even if I managed to find my way to the hotel and hire a car,
the chance of finding anyone that day who was willing to drive to Yordan
Deltchev's house was small. And that made me realize something else.
Unless I could get to the house before news of the assassination reached the
sentries on the door, the chances were that I would not be allowed in. It was
twenty to three now. Almost certainly the radio had shut down the moment
the thing had happened. It would be at least an hour before any official
statement was issued; but meanwhile the news and wild distortions of it
would be spreading all over the city by word of mouth. I would have to be
quick.

I hurried on. The sun was in my eyes. If I kept on walking west I must
eventually come to the wall of the Presidential Park. Then, if I followed the
wall round, I must come eventually to the quarter in which the house was.

I got there, but it took me well over half an hour and toward the end I
began to think that I must be too late. The atmosphere of the city was
extraordinary. Just by looking along a street you could see that something
serious had happened. People stood about in small groups on the pavements
outside their houses, talking very quietly. I had guessed right about the
radio being off. Not a sound came from the open windows of the apartment
houses. There were armoured cars about, too, parked at road junctions or
slowly cruising. Vukashin must have been ready to put a standard
emergency control plan into operation the instant he got back into the
Ministry. As I walked along in the hot sun, I began to see that I might have
difficulty in leaving the city that night.

To my dismay, there were several groups of people standing about
outside the Deltchev house, and as I drew nearer, I saw that there were
extra guards on the door. I wondered if Vukashin yet knew that there was no
Philip Deltchev to be arrested. The chances were that, with Vukashin
unable to admit to any precise understanding of the situation, things at the
palace were still confused. The people waiting here in the street must have
heard fantastic rumours and gravitated to the Deltchev house simply because
it was the nearest place with important political associations. I could even
reflect brutally that, with Brankovitch dead, the worst thing that could
happen to me here now was that I would be refused admittance. The same

corporal was there. He was looking more sullen than usual and anxious. That probably meant that he knew nothing. I went up to him and he recognized me with a nod. I produced my papers. He glanced at them doubtfully and handed them back, but made no signal to let me through.

'I don't know, *mein Herr*,' he said in German. 'I must await orders.'

'What orders?'

'Something has happened.'

'What?'

He shook his head uneasily. 'There are many rumours.'

'You mean the riot?'

He looked at me keenly. 'You know what it is?'

'There was a riot in the square during the parade. The troops had to fire.'

'A riot? You are sure it is nothing more?'

'It was very serious, I heard. Many were killed.'

'But a riot?' he insisted.

'But of course. I was told by an officer ten minutes ago.'

'An officer told you?'

'Yes. I have said—'

He sighed impatiently. 'These sheep!' he exclaimed, nodding toward the waiting people. 'These silly sheep, with their gossip! They tell me the Agrarian Socialists have attempted a *coup* and that a revolution has broken out. Sheep!' He spat and then grinned. 'A riot, you say. I know a way with rioters.'

I grinned back. He nodded to one of the sentries. The bell pealed and after a bit came the familiar sound of Rana's sandals in the courtyard. I felt the eyes of the street upon me as I went in.

There was the same smell of furniture polish and the same slippery floors. There was the same room, and she rose from the same chair to greet me. There were the same gentle, intelligent eyes below the same broad forehead and there was the same polite smile. And yet for me nothing was the same; I saw her now in a different context.

The smile went out. 'Herr Foster,' she said quickly, 'I am so glad you have come. What has happened? Something has. Rana says that there are people waiting outside in front of the house and additional guards. I don't understand it.'

I did not answer for a moment. Then I said: 'If you are asking me whether Aleko has succeeded, the answer is yes.'

'Aleko?'

'I have a train to catch, madame. Perhaps it will save time if I tell you that Pashik and I have talked very frankly and that at this moment, and because it has been difficult for Pashik to keep you fully informed, I know a great deal more about the affair than you do. I came to tell you what you don't already know.'

She stared at me and then very calmly sat down. 'I see. You are a messenger from Pashik.'

'No. Pashik doesn't know I'm here.'

'Where is he? With my son?'

'Your son is in Athens. Pashik is in the city somewhere.'

'You tell me Vukashin is dead. You saw it happen?'

'I did not say Vukashin was dead, madame. I said that Aleko had succeeded. Brankovitch was assassinated just about an hour ago.'

'Brankovitch?' Her hands came down on the wooden arms of the chair with a violence that would have been painful if she had been able to feel pain at that moment.

'Yes, Brankovitch.'

'You saw it yourself?'

'Yes.'

'Well? Go on.'

I went on. It was difficult, for she kept interrupting with questions to not all of which I knew the answers. I said nothing of Katerina's visit. There was no reason to do so. She probably knew of it anyway. When I had finished, she sat back slowly and shut her eyes. Her face was very smooth and beautiful.

'I am leaving for Athens on the five-o'clock train. That's if they'll let me out, of course. I'll see Philip tomorrow. His signed statement and mine will be in New York, Paris, and London by Tuesday at the latest. That will give Vukashin two days to make a fool of himself. After that he hasn't got a chance.'

Slowly she opened her eyes. 'My dear Herr Foster,' she said wearily, 'do you suppose that you can defeat men like Vukashin with external propaganda? The conception is naïve.'

'I rather thought it was yours.'

'Mine?' She stood up angrily. 'Pashik's, perhaps. Not mine. Don't you understand? They have defeated us.'

'Then you were defeated anyway.'

She shook her head. 'No. You see, Herr Foster, we could have come to terms with Brankovitch. He would have needed the Agrarian Socialists. He would have thought he was using them.'

'And your husband?'

She looked vague. 'Agreement could have been reached about that. An acquittal and then temporary retirement.'

In a very short space of time a lot of things went through my mind. Above them all, however, was the memory of my own voice asking if it were not dangerous to deny the street, and of the reply, the beautiful, saintly reply: '*For my children, yes. For me, no, for I shall not try to impose my private world upon the real.*'

I was aware then of a profound dislike of her and did not trouble to keep it out of my voice.

'Do you really believe that?' I answered.

She turned away to the window. 'Herr Foster,' she said thoughtfully, 'do you think you are safe here?'

It was very unexpected. My wretched stomach jerked unpleasantly. 'Safe?' I said.

'Aleko must realize by now what has been done by Pashik, and by you, to trick him. You say he has already tried to kill you once. He might guess you were here.'

I saw then. I was being punished. I laughed. 'If Aleko realizes what has been done, he will be far too busy getting out of the country to trouble me. I can't hurt him. If he doesn't know what's happened, then he is most probably under arrest by now. In that case I don't think he would talk until he knew whether Vukashin was going to save him or not.'

'You are very confident,' she said coldly. 'I think you are unwise to stay here.'

'Then I shall go. I should like to say goodbye to your daughter if I may.'

'I will give her your message.'

'Is there any message you would like me to give your son?'

'Yes, Herr Foster. You may tell him if you will that he did well and that it is not our fault, his and mine, that we are defeated. If it is possible Katerina and I will join him soon in Athens.'

'I'll tell him. There's one thing I should like to know.'

'Yes?'

'What induced your husband to make that election speech? What had gone wrong?'

'Nothing that would make a newspaper story, Herr Foster.'

'It is for my own information that I ask.'

She shrugged. 'As you please. It is no longer important, I suppose, what sort of man my husband was.'

When she had told me, I left.

I did not go back to the hotel. I reached the station with half an hour to spare. My passport got me on the train. The delay was at the frontier. It took me thirty-six hours to get to Athens, and by that time the Vukashin account of the Brankovitch assassination was out. The assassin was a man named Alexander or Aleko Gatin and he, together with an accomplice named Pashik, had been shot and killed while resisting arrest.

Philip Deltchev–Jika–was a pompous but amiable young man and very grateful for his mother's message. He said that it made him feel much better about everything. He was quite sure that she would contrive to join him. He did not mention his father.

Chapter Twenty-one

I saw the end of the Deltchev trial in the projection room of a newsreel company in London.

In the hard blacks and whites of the Propaganda Ministry's cameramen the scene looked more real than the one I remembered. Perhaps the film gave it an authority the original had lacked. Or it may have been the soundtrack that produced the effect; there was no interpreter to divide one's attention. With the six reels of film that Brankovitch's successor had selected for foreign consumption a translation of the proceedings had been sent; but for the moment I wanted just to look at it, and to look at Deltchev.

There was not a great deal of footage that included him. Only one of the three cameras had covered the dock, and the film had been received in an edited form that favoured the judges and Dr Prochaska; but during one evident denunciation of the prisoner there was a shot that showed him frowning anxiously and shifting his position in a way that made him look guilty. Most likely the shot had some other true explanation–boredom or some physical discomfort–but for me, as for the Propaganda Ministry, it had another significance. The Propaganda Ministry saw a scheming villain brought to book. I saw a prewar Minister of Posts and Telegraphs struggling to be a statesman. But then, I had listened to his wife.

It was the word 'Papa' that had defeated him.

The first time Deltchev saw the word printed in front of his name it pleased him; for, knowing his countrymen, he recognized the note of wry affection in it. It meant that they trusted him and that, although they might grumble, they would accept hardship at his hands and would not hate him too intensely. With amused pride he showed the newspaper to his wife and son. The small pang of anxiety he experienced he found unaccountable and ignored.

The nickname soon gained currency, and its use was no longer an occasion for comment; but he did not, for some reason, get used to it. On the contrary; as time went by, he began to experience discomfort whenever he saw it or heard it used. It had begun to feel to him like an accusation.

'Yordan always invites criticism,' his wife had said, 'and always fears it.'

Deltchev was aware of the jokes about his motives and had hitherto thought himself a better and not more prejudiced judge of them. Shrewd he might be; yet in 1940 he had opposed the Nazis, not for any personal advantage–unless internment and oblivion were advantages–but because he had thought it right to do so. Ambitious he might be; yet he had organized the Committee of National Unity, not for the risk of dying a martyr's death at the hands of the Gestapo, but because he thought it right to do so. But now, with his power increasing daily and that word 'Papa' fastened to his name, he was no longer sure of himself. The whole climate of his thought and feeling seemed to be changing. If he were held in affection, trusted, he might be worthy. His conscience told him that he was not.

'Yordan is a self-torturer,' his wife had said.

A terrible conflict now began within him; and the battleground chosen was the question of the election promise.

Reason and experience told him that the Provisional Government was the best that could be devised for the country in the present situation and that elections might well mean the accession of the People's Party to power. He believed that would be a disaster for the country. Reasoning, a lawyer's reasoning, told him, too, that the promise had been one of *free* elections and that the essential condition of freedom was not at present obtainable.

Yet the other voice, the cruel, accusing, contemptuous, punishing voice that haunted him, offered arguments of a different kind. 'Why are you so anxious?' it inquired. 'Why do you hesitate? Is it because you know in your heart that you have become corrupt and that these reasons you invent for keeping the power in your hands are mere devices to conceal the fact? Is it? You dictators are all the same! You whine that what you do is for the people's good and that they love and trust you. But when there is a chance that you may have to put that love and trust to the test, you find reasons–oh, excellent reasons!–why you should not do so. And the reasons are always to the same tune. It is for the people's good, you cry. That, my friend, is the spiral of corruption you are ascending. Government by consent of the governed! You know the phrase? Who are you to determine what government they shall consent to? Your power and their trust in you give you a responsibility above your party interests. You see now the distinction between a statesman and a politician. The statesman has courage. Did you speak? Ah no! Not the courage of his convictions. (How you twist and turn, my friend, to avoid the truth!) The statesman has the courage to be impartial—even at the risk of his own destruction.'

He told no one until after it was over, and then he told his wife.

'My hands are clean,' he said. It was as though by violating all his own beliefs and interests, as well as those of other honest men, he had performed an act of absolution for some unnamable sin.

'Last reel,' said the cutter who was supervising the running. 'Judges' summing up and sentence.'

I looked at the screen again. I looked at the tired shell of a man who had been Yordan Deltchev, and at the presiding judge delivering the sentence of death by hanging which had since been carried out.

There was silence in the courtroom after the sentence. Probably the spectators were expecting him to say something. But there was nothing. He nodded his head slightly and turned to go. The guards stepped forward. Then he climbed down from the dock and walked slowly away between them.

I recalled another departure he had made from the courtroom and the parallel I had attempted to draw from the trial of Socrates. My memory of it was better now. There were words more apt than the others I had chosen.

'*But, sirs, it may be that the difficulty is not to flee from death, but from guilt. Guilt is swifter than death.*'

'That's the lot,' said the cutter. 'Would you like to see the assassination of Brankovitch? I've got it here.'

'No, thanks,' I said. 'I've seen it.'

ERIC AMBLER

THE
SCHIRMER
INHERITANCE

The Schirmer Inheritance

To Sylvia Payne

Prologue

In 1806, Napoleon set out to chastise the King of Prussia. Both at Auerstadt and at Jena the Prussian armies suffered crushing defeats. Then, what remained of them marched east to join a Russian army under Bennigsen. In the following February, Napoleon met this combined force at the town of Preussisch-Eylau near Königsberg.

Eylau was one of the bloodiest and most terrible of Napoleon's battles. It began in a blizzard and in a temperature well below freezing-point. Both armies were half-starved and fought with desperate ferocity for the bleak shelter of the buildings of Eylau itself. Casualties on both sides were heavy, nearly a quarter of those engaged being killed. When, at nightfall on the second day, the fighting ended, it was from exhaustion rather than because a decision had been reached. Then, during the night, the Russian army began to retreat northwards. The survivors of the Prussian corps, whose flank-guard action against Ney's troops had nearly served to win the day, now had no reason to remain. They made their withdrawal through the village of Kuttschitten to the east. The cavalry screen of their rearguard was provided by the Dragoons of Ansbach.

The relationship between this unit and the rest of the Prussian army was absurd, but, in the Middle-Europe of the period, not unusually so. Not many years before, and well within the memories of the old soldiers in it, the regiment had been the only mounted force in the independent principality of Ansbach, and had taken its oaths of allegiance to the ruling Margrave. Then, Ansbach had fallen upon evil times, and the last Margrave had sold his land and his people to the King of Prussia. Fresh oaths of allegiance had had to be sworn. Yet their new lord had eventually proved as fickle as the old. In the year before Eylau, the Dragoons had experienced a further change of status. The province of Ansbach had been ceded by the Prussians to Bavaria. As Bavaria was an ally of Napoleon, this meant that, strictly speaking, the Ansbachers should now have been fighting against the Prussians, not beside them. However, the Dragoons themselves were as indifferent to the anomaly they constituted as they were to the cause for which they fought. The conception of nationality meant little to them. They were professional soldiers in the eighteenth-century meaning of the term. If they had marched and fought and suffered and died for two days and a night it was neither for love of the Prussians nor from hatred of Napoleon; it was because they had been trained to do so, because they hoped for the spoils of victory and because they feared the consequences of disobedience.

Thus, as his horse picked its way through the woods on the outskirts of Kuttschitten that night, Sergeant Franz Schirmer was able to consider his situation, and make plans for extricating himself from it, without much inconvenience to his conscience. Not many of the Dragoons of Ansbach were left, and, of those who were, few would survive the hardships to come. The wounded and the badly frost-bitten would die first, and then, when the horses had been lost or eaten, starvation and sickness would kill off all but the youngest and strongest of the remainder. Twenty-four hours earlier, the Sergeant could reasonably have expected to be one of the enduring few. Now, he could not. Late that afternoon, he had himself been wounded.

The wound had affected him strangely. A French cuirassier had slashed with a sabre and the Sergeant had taken the blow on his right arm. The blade had sliced obliquely through the heavy deltoid muscles and down to the bone just above the elbow. It was an ugly wound, but the bone had not broken, and it had therefore been unnecessary for him to seek torture at the hands of the army surgeons. A comrade had bound up the wound for him and strapped the arm against his chest with a crossbelt. It throbbed painfully now, but the bleeding seemed to have stopped. He was very weak, but that, he thought, might be due to hunger and the cold rather than to any serious loss of blood. The thing he found so strange was that with all his physical distress there went an extraordinary feeling of well-being.

It had come upon him as the wound was being bandaged. The feelings of surprise and terror with which he had first regarded the blood pouring down his useless arm had suddenly gone, and in their place had been an absurd, splendid sense of freedom and light-heartedness.

He was a bovine young man of a practical turn of mind, not given to fancies. He knew something about wounds. His had been bound up in its own blood and could, therefore, be reckoned healthy; but there was still no more than an even chance of his escaping death from gangrene. He knew something about war, too, and could see not only that the battle was probably lost, but also that retreat would take them into a countryside already picked clean by armies on the move. Yet this knowledge brought no despair with it. It was as if he had received with his wound some special forgiveness for his sins; an absolution more potent and complete than that which any mortal priest could give. He felt that he had been touched by God Himself, and that any drastic steps he might be obliged to take in order to stay alive would have Divine approval.

His horse stumbled as it fought its way clear of a snowdrift, and the Sergeant reined in. Half the officers had been killed and he had been put in command of one of the outlying detachments. He had orders to keep well out on the flank away from the road, and for a while it had been easy to do so; but now they had emerged from the forest, and in the deep snow the going was bad. One or two of the Dragoons behind him had already dismounted and were leading their horses. He could hear them floundering about in the snow at the rear of the column. If it proved necessary for him to lead his own horse, he might not have the strength to get back into the saddle.

He thought about this for a moment. After a two-day battle fought so desperately, the chances of there being any French cavalry still capable of harrying the retreat from a flank were remote. The flank guard was, therefore, no more than a drill-book precaution. Certainly, it was not worth taking risks for. He gave a brief word of command and the column began to turn into the forest again towards the road. He had no great fear of his disobedience being discovered. If it were, he would simply say that he had lost his way; he would not be severely punished for failing to do an officer's duty. In any case, he had more important matters to consider.

Food was the first thing.

Luckily, the haversack beneath his long cloak still contained most of the frozen potatoes he had looted from the farm building the previous day. They must be eaten sparingly; and secretly. At times like these, a man known to have private stores of food went in some danger, whatever his rank. However, the potatoes would not last long, and there would be no soup pots bubbling at the end of this march. Even the horses would be better off. None of the supply wagons had been lost and there was a day's fodder still in them. The men would starve first.

He fought off a surprise wave of panic. He would have to do something soon and panic would not help.

Already he could feel the cold eating into him. Not many hours could elapse before fever and exhaustion took irrevocable charge of the situation. His knees tightened involuntarily on the saddle-flaps, and, at that moment, the idea came to him.

The horse had started and passaged a little at the pressure. Sergeant Schirmer relaxed his thigh muscles and, leaning forward, patted the animal's neck affectionately with his left hand. He was smiling to himself as the horse walked on again. By the time the detachment reached the road his plan was made.

For the rest of that night and most of the next day, the Prussian corps moved slowly eastward towards the Masurian lakes; then, it turned north to Insterburg. Soon after nightfall, and on the pretext of rounding up a straggler, Sergeant Schirmer left the detachment and rode south across the frozen lakes in the general direction of Lotzen. By morning, he was south of that town.

He was also nearly at the limit of his strength. The march from Eylau to the point at which he had deserted had been bad enough; the cross-country journey from there would have taxed even an unwounded man. Now, the pain of his arm was at moments intolerable, and he was shaking so much from fever and the bitter cold that he could scarcely stay in the saddle. He was beginning to wonder, indeed, if he might not have been mistaken in his estimate of God's intentions, and if what he had supposed to be a sign of Divine favour might not prove to have been an intimation of approaching death. He knew, at all events, that if he did not very soon find shelter of the kind his plan called for, he would die.

He reined in and with an effort raised his head again to look about him. Far away to the left across the white desolation of a frozen lake he could see the low black shape of a farmhouse. His eyes moved on. It was just possible that there was a nearer building to investigate. But there was nothing. Hopelessly, he turned his horse's head in the direction of the farmhouse and resumed his march.

The area into which the Sergeant had ridden was, although at that date part of the Kingdom of Prussia, inhabited mainly by Poles. It had never been very prosperous; and after the Russian Army had passed through it, commandeering the winter stores of grain and fodder and herding away the livestock, it was little more than a wasteland. In some villages the Cossack horses had eaten the very thatch from the roofs, and in others the houses had been gutted by fire. The campaigns of the armies of Holy Russia could be more devastating for her allies than for her enemies.

The Sergeant, himself an experienced campaigner, had not been unprepared for devastation. Indeed, his plan had depended upon it. Country that had just supplied a Russian army would not attract another army for some time to come. A deserter might consider himself reasonably safe there. What he had not been prepared for, however, was the absence of a starving population. Since dawn, he had passed several farmhouses, and every one had been abandoned. He had realized by now that the Russians had been more exacting even than usual (perhaps because they had been dealing with Poles) and that the inhabitants, unable to conceal enough food to keep them alive until the spring, had trekked to places farther south that might have been spared. For him, therefore, the situation was desperate. He could, perhaps, stay in the saddle for another hour. If all the peasants in the immediate vicinity had gone with the rest, he was finished. He raised his head again, blinking to free his eyelashes from the ice that clung to them, and peered ahead.

At that moment he saw the smoke.

It came in a thin wisp from the roof of the building he was heading for, and he saw it for only a moment before it disappeared. He was still some way off, but he was in no doubt as to what he had seen. This was a peat–burning area, and that was smoke from a peat fire. His spirits rose as he urged his horse forward.

It took him another half-hour to reach the farmhouse. As he approached he saw that it was a wretched and dilapidated place. There was a low wooden building which was both barn and living quarters, an empty sheep-pen, and a broken-down wagon almost hidden under a drift of snow. That was all.

The horse's hoofs made only a faint crunching sound in the frozen snow. As he drew nearer, he let go the reins and carefully eased his carbine from its long saddle holster. When he had primed it he wedged the weapon across the saddle-bags and against the rolled blankets at the pommel. Then he took up the reins again and went on.

At one end of the building, there was a small shuttered window and, beside it, a door. The snow outside had been trodden since the last fall, but, except for the slight trickle of peat smoke from the roof, there was no other sign of life. He stopped and looked about him. The gate of the sheep pen was open. Near the cart was a slight mound of snow that probably covered the remains of a hay-rick. There were no cattle droppings on the fresh snow, no sounds of poultry. But for the faint sighing of the wind, the silence was absolute. The Russians had taken everything.

He let the reins slip through his fingers and the horse shook its head. The jangling of the bit seemed very loud. He looked quickly at the door of the building. If the sound had been heard, the first response to it would be that of fear; and, providing that it led to the immediate opening of the door and prompt compliance with his wishes, fear would be useful. If it led to the door's being barricaded against him, however, he was in a difficulty. He would have to break the door down, and he could not risk dismounting until he were sure that this was to be the end of his journey.

He waited. There was no sound from within. The door remained shut. His Dragoon's instinct was to slam the butt of his carbine against it and yell at those inside to come out or be killed; but he put the temptation aside. The carbine butt might have to come into play later, but for the present he would try the friendly approach he had planned.

He tried to call 'Ho!' but the sound that came from his throat was no more than a sob. Disconcerted, he tried again.

'Ho!'

He managed to croak the word this time but a deadly feeling of helplessness swept over him. He, who a moment ago had been thinking of battering on a door with his carbine and even of breaking it down, had not enough strength left to shout. There was a roaring in his ears, and he thought he was going to fall. He shut his eyes, fighting down the horrible sensation. As he opened his eyes again, he saw the door slowly open.

The face of a woman who stood in the doorway looking up at him was so ravaged by hunger that it was hard to tell what her age might be. But for the braids of hair wound round her neck, even her sex would have been in doubt. The voluminous peasant rags she wore were quite shapeless, and her feet and legs were bound with sacking like a man's. She stared at him dully, then said something in Polish and turned to go inside. He leaned forward and spoke in German.

'I am a Prussian soldier. There has been a great battle. The Russians are defeated.'

He said it as if he were announcing a victory. She stopped and looked up again. Her sunken eyes were quite expressionless. He had the curious idea that they would remain so even if he were to draw his sabre and cut her down.

'Who else is here?' he said.

Her lips moved again and this time she spoke in German. 'My father. He was too weak to go with our neighbours. What do you want here?'

'What's the matter with him?'

'He has the wasting fever.'

'Ah!' If it had been the plague he would have chosen to die in the snow rather than stay.

'What do you want?' she repeated.

To answer her, he undid the fastenings of his cloak and threw it back to reveal his wounded arm.

'I need shelter and rest,' he said; 'and someone to cook my food until my wound is healed.'

Her eyes flickered from his bloodstained tunic to the carbine and the bulging saddle-bags beneath it. He guessed that she was thinking that if she had the strength she might seize the gun and kill him. He put his hand on it firmly, and her eyes met his again.

'There is no food to cook,' she said.

'I have plenty of food,' he answered; 'enough to share it with those who help me.'

She still stared at him. He nodded reassuringly, then, holding his carbine firmly in his left hand, he brought his right leg across the saddle and slid to the ground. As his feet touched it, his legs gave way under him and he sprawled in the snow. A burning shaft of agony shot from his arm through every nerve in his body. He screamed, and then, for a moment or two after, lay there sobbing. At last, still clutching the carbine, he clambered dizzily to his feet.

The woman had made no attempt to help him. She had not even moved. He pushed past her through the doorway into the hovel beyond.

Inside, he looked round warily. By the light from the doorway that filtered through the peat smoke he could dimly see a rough wooden bed with what looked like a pile of sacking on it. A whimpering sound came from it now. The peat fire glowed dully in a crude clay stove in the centre. The dirt floor was soft with ash and peat dust. The reeking air made him choke. He blundered round the stove and between the roof supports into the space where the animals had been kept. The straw under his feet here was filthy, but he kicked a pile of it together against the back of the stove. He knew that the woman had followed him in and gone over to the sick man. Now he heard a whispered conversation. He arranged the pile of straw into the semblance of a bed and when he had finished spread his cloak on it. The whispers had ceased. He heard a movement behind him and turned.

The woman stood there facing him. She had a small axe in her hands.

'The food,' she said.

He nodded and went out into the yard again. She followed and stood watching as, with his carbine held between his knees, he awkwardly unstrapped the blankets. He succeeded at last and flung the roll in the snow.

'The food,' she said again.

He raised the carbine and, pressing the butt against his left hip, slid his hand down to the lock. With an effort he managed to cock it and move his forefinger on to the trigger. Then he put the muzzle to the horse's head just below the ear.

'Here is our food,' he said and pulled the trigger.

His ears sang with the noise of the shot as the horse sank kicking to the ground. The carbine had leapt from his hand and lay in the snow smoking. He picked up the blankets and tucked them under his arm before retrieving it. The woman still stood watching him. He nodded to her and, motioning to the horse, went towards the house.

Almost before he reached the door, she was on her knees by the dying animal at work on it with the axe. He looked back. There was the saddle and its contents; his sabre too. She might easily kill him with it while he lay helpless. There was a fortune, by her standards, in the flat leather pouch beneath his tunic. For a moment, he watched the quick, desperate movements of her arms and the dark mess of blood spreading in the snow beneath her. His sabre? She would not need a sabre if she had a mind to kill him.

Then he felt the periodic agony of his arm returning and heard himself beginning to moan. He knew suddenly that there was nothing more he could do now to order the world outside his own body. He stumbled through the doorway and to his bed. The carbine he put on the ground under the cloak. Then, he took off his helmet, unrolled his blankets, and lay down in the warm darkness to fight for his life.

The woman's name was Maria Dutka, and she was eighteen when Sergeant Schirmer first set eyes on her. Her mother had died when she was young, and as there were no other children and her father had failed to find a second wife, Maria had been brought up to do the work of a son and heir on the holding. Moreover, the chronic disease from which Dutka suffered was now of long standing, and the periods of relief from it had become rarer. She was already accustomed to thinking and acting for herself.

She was not headstrong, however. Although the idea of killing the Sergeant, in order to avoid having to share the dead horse with him, did occur to her, she discussed the matter with her father first. She was by nature deeply superstitious, and when he suggested that some supernatural agency might have had a hand in the Sergeant's providential appearance, she saw the danger of her plan. She saw, too, that even if the Sergeant were to die of his wound—and he was very near to death in those first days—the supernatural powers might consider that her murderous thoughts about him had turned the scale.

She nursed him, accordingly, with a kind of anxious devotion which it was easy for the grateful Sergeant to misunderstand. Later, however, she did something that appealed to him still more. When, during his convalescence, he made an attempt to thank her for so faithfully keeping her part of their bargain, she explained her motives to him with great simplicity and candour. At the time, he was both amused and impressed. Afterwards, when he thought about what she had said and the fact that she had said it, he experienced rather more surprising sensations. As the food they shared restored her youthful appearance and vitality, he began to watch the movements of her body and to modify pleasurably his earlier plans for the future.

He stayed in the Dutka house for eight months. Preserved under the snow, the carcass of the horse supplied them all with fresh meat until the thaw came, and then with the smoked and dried remains. By that time, too, the Sergeant was able to take his carbine into the woods and bring back deer. Vegetables began to grow. Then, for a few remarkable weeks, old Dutka rallied and, with the Sergeant and Maria doing a horse's work in the traces, was even able in the end to plough his land.

The Sergeant's continued presence was taken as a matter of course now. Neither Maria nor her father ever referred to his military past. He was a victim of war, as they were. The returning neighbours found nothing strange in his presence. They themselves had spent the winter working for strangers. If old Dutka had found a strong, hard-working Prussian to help him set things right, so much the better. And should the curious wonder how old Dutka paid him, or why a Prussian should trouble to work so poor a patch of land, there was always someone to remind them of Maria's broad hips and strong legs, and of the harvest to be reaped between them by such a lusty young fellow.

The summer came. The battle of Friedland was fought. The Emperors of France and Russia met on a raft moored in the river Niemen. The Treaty of Tilsit was signed. Prussia was stripped of all her territories west of the Elbe and all her Polish provinces. Bialla, only a few miles south of the Dutkas' holding, was suddenly on the Russian frontier, and Lyck had become a garrison town. Prussian infantry patrols came seeking recruits, and the Sergeant took to the woods with the other young men. He was away on one of these excursions when Maria's father died.

After the burial ceremonies, he got out his leather money pouch and sat down with Maria to count his savings. The proceeds of many looting forays and the peculations of four years as an N.C.O., they were more than sufficient to match the small amount that Maria would get from the sale of her father's holding to a neighbour. For there was no question now of their remaining to work the land. They had seen what could happen when the Russian armies came, and with this new frontier, the Russians were no more than a day's march away. To them this seemed a weightier argument for leaving the holding than the Sergeant's precarious position as a deserter. The place for them to go was clearly somewhere where there were neither Russians nor Prussians, and where Maria, already pregnant, could bring up their children in the certainty of being able to feed them.

Early in the November of 1808, they set out, with a handcart contrived from Dutka's old wagon, to walk towards the West. It was a hard, dangerous journey, for their road lay through Prussia and they dared travel only at night. But they did not go hungry. They had brought their food with them in the cart and it lasted until they reached Wittenberg. That was the first town they entered in broad daylight, too. They were free of Prussian soil at last.

They did not remain in Wittenburg, however. To the Sergeant, it seemed uncomfortably near the Prussian border. Toward the middle of December they arrived in Mühlhausen, newly incorporated into the Kingdom of Westphalia. There, Maria's first son, Karl, was born; and there, Maria and the Sergeant were married. For a time, the Sergeant worked as an ostler; but later, when he had added to their savings, he set up in business as a horse coper.

He prospered. The tides of the Napoleonic wars washed gently in the harbour that he and Maria had found. For several years it seemed as though the evil days were over. Then, the disease from which her father had suffered, attacked Maria herself. Two years after the birth of her second son, Hans, she died.

Eventually, Sergeant Schirmer married again and had ten more children by his second wife. He died in 1850, a respected and successful man.

Only once during all those happy years in Mühlhausen was Franz Schirmer disturbed by memories of the military crime he had committed. In 1815, by the Treaty of Paris, Mühlhausen became a Prussian city.

It was the year of the Sergeant's second marriage, and, while he did not think it likely that church records would be combed for the names of the deserters, there was always a chance that they might be used in checking mobilization lists. He could not bring himself to be fatalistic about the risk. After so many years of immunity from arrest he had lost the habit of living for the moment. The prospect of death before a firing squad, however remote it might be, could never be endured with the old fortitude.

Then what was to be done? He gave the matter careful thought. In the past, he reminded himself, he had trusted in God; and, in times of great danger, God had been good to him. But could he still simply trust in God again? And was this, he asked himself critically, a time of *great* danger? After all, there were plenty of other Schirmers in the Prussian Army records; and some of them, no doubt, were men named Franz. Was it really necessary to call upon God to insure against the possibility of the list of those citizens who had purchased army exemptions in Mühlhausen being compared with the list of army deserters in Potsdam? Or really wise to do so? Might not God, who had done so much for His servant, be displeased at having this minor responsibility thrust upon him and so neglect it? Was there not, therefore, something that His servant could do for himself in the matter, without invoking the aid of the Almighty?

Yes, indeed, there was!

He decided to change his name to Schneider.

He encountered only one slight difficulty. It was simple to change his own surname and that of the baby, Hans. He had good friends in the mayor's office, and his excuse that there was another horse dealer of the same name in a nearby town was readily accepted. But the first son, Karl, presented a problem. The boy, now seven years old, had just been classified for future conscription by the Prussian military authorities, and the Sergeant neither had nor wanted friends in Prussian military circles. Moreover, any official move to change the boy's name might easily invite the very inquiries into origins that he most dreaded. In the end, he did nothing about Karl's name. So it was that, although the sons of Franz and Maria were baptized in the name of Schirmer, they grew up with different surnames. Karl remained Karl Schirmer; Hans became Hans Schneider.

The Sergeant's change of name never caused him a moment's anxiety or inconvenience in his lifetime. The anxiety and inconvenience resulting from it descended, over a hundred years later, on the head of Mr George L. Carey.

Chapter One

George Carey came from a Delaware family that looked like an illustration to an advertisement for tooth paste. His father was a prosperous doctor with snow-white hair. His mother came from an old Philadelphia family, and was an important member of the garden club. His brothers were tall, solid and handsome. His sisters were slim, strong and vivacious. All had fine regular teeth which showed when they smiled. The whole family, indeed, looked so happy, so secure and so successful that it was difficult not to suspect that the truth about them might be different. But no, they actually were happy, secure and successful. They were also inclined to be smug.

George was the youngest son and, although his shoulders were not as broad as those of his brothers nor his smile as self-satisfied, he was the most talented and intelligent member of the family. When the glories of their football-playing days had departed, his brothers had made their ways aimlessly into business. George's plans for the future had been clear-cut from the moment he left High School. Despite his father's hopes for a successor in his practice, George had declined to pretend to an interest in medicine that he did not feel. What he wanted to go in for was law; and not the criminal, court-room kind, but the kind that led in early middle age to the presidencies of blue-chip corporations to high political office. But while the war, which came just after he had graduated from Princeton, had removed much of his solemnity and smugness and had had beneficial effects upon his sense of humour, it had done nothing to change his mind about his chosen profession. After four and a half years as a bomber pilot, he went to Harvard Law School. He graduated, *cum laude*, early in 1949. Then, having spent a useful year as secretary to a learned and famous judge, he joined Lavater's.

The firm of Lavater, Powell and Sistrom of Philadelphia is one of the really important law offices of the Eastern United States, and the long list of partners reads like a selection of promising candidates for a vacancy in the Supreme Court. No doubt its massive reputation still derives to some extent from memories of the vast utilities manipulations with which it was concerned in the 'twenties; but there have been few corporation cases of any magnitude during the last thirty years in which the firm has not held an important brief. It remains a virile, forward-looking concern and to be invited to join it is a mark of approbation most flattering to a young lawyer.

Thus, as he arranged his belongings in one of Lavater's comfortably furnished offices, George had reason to feel satisfied with the progress of his career. Admittedly, he was a little old for the somewhat junior position he was shrewd enough to realize that his four years in the Air Corps had not been wholly wasted from a professional point of view, and that the distinction of his war record had had quite as much to do with his presence at Lavater's as his work at Law School or the warm recommendation of the learned judge. Now, if all went well (and why shouldn't it?), he could look forward to a rapid advancement, valuable contacts and an expanding personal reputation. He felt that he had arrived.

The news that he was to do some work on the Schneider Johnson case came, then, as a disagreeable blow. It was also a surprise of another kind. The sort of business that Lavater's normally handled was the sort that made reputations as surely as it made money. From what George had remembered of the Schneider Johnson case, it was just the sort of slapstick affair that a corporation lawyer with a thought for his reputation would pay to stay clear of.

It had been one of the notorious missing-heir-to-a-fortune absurdities of the pre-war years.

In 1938, Amelia Schneider Johnson, a senile woman of eighty-one, had died in Lamport, Pennsylvania. She had lived alone in the decrepit frame house which had been the late Mr Johnson's wedding present to her, and her declining years had been passed in an atmosphere of genteel poverty. When she had died, however, it had been found that her estate included three million dollars in bonds which she had inherited in the nineteen-twenties from her brother, Martin Schneider, a soft-drinks tycoon. She had had an eccentric distrust of banks and safe-deposit boxes, and had kept the bonds in a tin trunk under her bed. She had also distrusted lawyers and had made no will. In Pennsylvania, at the time, the law governing intestacy had been determined by an act of 1917 which said, in effect, that anyone with even a remote blood relationship to the deceased might be entitled to a share in the estate. Amelia Schneider Johnson's only known relative had been an elderly spinster, Miss Clothilde Johnson; but she had been a sister-in-law and therefore had not qualified under the act. With the enthusiastic and disastrous co-operation of the newspapers, a search for Amelia's blood-relations had begun.

It was, George thought, all too easy to understand the newspapers' eagerness. They had scented another Garrett case. Old Mrs Garrett had died in 1930, leaving seventeen million dollars and no will, and here was the case eight years later, still going strong, with three thousand lawyers still chiselling away, twenty-six thousand claimants to the money and a fine smell of corruption over all. The Schneider Johnson thing could last as long. True, it was smaller, but size wasn't everything. It had plenty of human angles—a fortune at stake, the romantic isolation of the old lady's declining years (she had lost her only son in the Argonne), the lonely death without a relative at the bedside, the fruitless search for a will—there was no reason why it should not have staying power, too. The name Schneider and its American modifications were widely distributed. The old girl must have had blood-relatives somewhere even if she had not known them. Or him! Or her! Yes, there might even turn out to be a one-hundred-per-cent non-sharing heir! All right then, where was he? Or she? On a farm in Wisconsin? In a real estate office in California? Behind the counter of a drugstore in Texas? Which of the thousands of Schneiders, Snyders and Sniders in

America was going to be the lucky one? Who was the unsuspecting millionaire? Corn? Well maybe, but always good for a follow-up, and of nation-wide interest.

And of nation-wide interest it had proved. By the beginning of 1939, the administrator of the estate had been notified of over eight thousand claims to be the missing heir, an army of disreputable lawyers had moved in to exploit the claimants, and the whole case had begun to soar rapidly into the cloud-cuckoo-land of high fantasy, skulduggery and court-room farce in which it was to remain until, on the outbreak of war, it had fallen suddenly into oblivion.

What business Lavater's could have with the resurrection of so unsavoury a business, George could not imagine.

It was Mr Budd, one of the senior partners, who enlightened him.

The main burden of the Schneider Johnson estate had been borne by Messrs Moreton, Greener and Cleek, an old-fashioned Philadelphia law firm of great respectability. They had been Miss Clothilde Johnson's attorneys and had conducted the formal search for a will on her instructions. The intestacy duly established, the matter had come before the Orphans' Court in Philadelphia, and the Register of Wills had appointed Robert L. Moreton as administrator of the estate. He had remained the administrator until the end of 1944.

'And very nice too,' said Mr Budd. 'If only he'd had the sense to leave it at that, I wouldn't have blamed him. But no, the cockle-brained old coot retained his *own* firm as attorneys for the administrator. Jeepers! In a case like that it was suicidal!'

Mr Budd was a pigeon-chested man with a long head, a neat clipped moustache and bifocal glasses. He had a ready smile, a habit of using out-of-date colloquialisms and an air of careless good humour of which George was deeply suspicious.

'The combined fees,' George said carefully, 'must have been pretty big on an estate of that size.'

'No fees,' declared Mr Budd, 'are big enough to make it worth while for a decent law office to get mixed up with a lot of ambulance chasers and crooks. There are dozens of these inheritance cases hanging fire all over the world. Look at the Abdul Hamid estate! The British got tied up in that one and it's been going on for thirty years or more. That'll probably never be settled. Look at the Garrett case! Think how many reputations that's damaged. Shucks! It's always the same. Is A an imposter? Is B out of his mind? Who died before whom? Is the old photograph Aunt Sarah or Aunt Flossie? Has a forger been at work with faded ink?' He waved his arms disparagingly. 'I tell you, George, the Schneider Johnson case pretty well finished Moreton, Greener and Cleek as a regular law firm. And when Bob Moreton got sick in 'forty-four and had to retire, that was the end. They dissolved.'

'Couldn't Greener or Cleek have taken over as administrator?'

Mr Budd pretended to look shocked. 'My dear George, you don't take over an appointment like that. It's a reward for good and faithful service. In this case, our learned, highly respected and revered John J. Sistrom was the lucky man.'

'Oh. I see.'

'The investments do the work, George, our John J. takes the fees as administrator. However,' Mr Budd continued with a trace of satisfaction in his voice, 'it doesn't look as if he's going to do so much longer. You'll see why in a moment. From what old Bob Moreton told me at the time, the position was originally this. Amelia's father was named Hans Schneider. He was a German who'd immigrated in 1849. Bob Moreton and his partners were pretty well convinced in the end that if there were anybody at all entitled to take the estate it was one of the old man's relatives back in Germany. But the whole thing was complicated by the representation question. Do you know anything about that, George?'

'Bregy, discussing the 1947 act, gives a very clear summary of the former rules.'

'That's dandy.' Mr Budd grinned. 'Because, frankly, I don't know a thing about it. Now, leaving out all the newspaper nonsense, the history of the case, was, briefly, this. In 'thirty-nine, old Bob Moreton went off to Germany to check up on the other side of the Schneider family. Self-preservation, of course. They needed facts to go on if they were going to deal with all those phony claims. Then, when he got back, the damnedest thing happened. The damnedest things were always happening on that screwy case. It seemed that the Nazis had gotten wind of old Bob's inquiries. What they did was to take a quick look into the things themselves and produced an old man named Rudolph Schneider. Then they claimed the whole estate on his behalf.'

'I remember that,' George said. 'They hired McClure to act for them.'

'That's right. This Rudolph was from Dresden or some such place and they said that he was a first cousin of Amelia Johnson. Moreton, Greener and Cleek fought the claim. Said the documents the Krauts produced were forged. Anyway, the case was still before the courts when we got into the war in 'forty-one, and that finished it as far as they were concerned. The Alien Property Custodian in Washington moved in and filed the claim. Because of the German claim, of course. The case froze. When he retired, Bob Moreton handed over all the documents to John J. There were over two tons of them and they're down in our vaults right now, just where they were left when Moreton, Greener and Cleek delivered them in 'forty-four. Nobody's ever troubled to look them over. No reason to. Well, now there *is* a reason.'

George's heart sank. 'Oh, yes?'

By choosing this moment to fill his pipe Mr Budd avoided George's eyes as he went on. 'This is the situation, George. It seems that with the appreciation of values and interest the estate is worth over four million now, and the Commonwealth of Pennsylvania has decided to exercise its rights under the act and claim the lot. However, they've asked John J., as administrator, if he proposes to fight them on it, and, just for form's sake, he feels we ought to check through the documents to make sure that there's no reasonable claim outstanding. So that's what I want you to do, George. Just check through for him. Make sure he's not overlooking anything. O.K.?'

'Yes, sir. O.K.'

But he did not quite succeed in keeping a note of resignation out of his voice. Mr Budd looked up with a sympathetic chuckle. 'And if it'll make you feel any better about the job, George,' he said, 'I can tell you that we've been getting short of vault space for some time now. If you can get that load of junk out of the way you'll be earning the heartfelt thanks of the entire office.'

George managed to smile.

Chapter Two

He had no difficulty in finding the Schneider Johnson records. They were parcelled up in damp-proof wrappings, and had a storage vault to themselves which they filled from floor to ceiling. It was clear that Mr Budd's estimate of their total weight had not been exaggerated. Fortunately, all the parcels had been carefully labelled and arranged systematically. Having made sure that he understood the system which had been employed, George made a selection of the parcels and had them carried up to his office.

It was late in the afternoon when he started work and, with some idea of getting a general picture of the case before settling down to work seriously on the claims, he had brought up a bulky parcel labelled "Schneider Johnson Press Cuttings". The label proved to be slightly misleading. What in fact the parcel contained was the record of Messrs Moreton, Greener and Cleek's hopeless battle with the press and their effort to stem the flood of nonsensical claims that was overwhelming them. It made pathetic reading.

The record began two days after Mr Moreton had been appointed administrator of the estate. A New York tabloid had discovered that Amelia's father, Hans Schneider ('The Old Forty-Niner', as the paper called him), had married a New York girl named Mary Smith. This meant, the paper had contended excitedly, that the name of the missing heir could be Smith as well as Schneider.

Messrs Moreton, Greener and Cleek had properly hastened to deny the contention; but instead of pointing out, more or less simply, that, as Amelia's first cousins on her mother's side had all been dead for years, the Smith family of New York did not qualify in law as heirs, they had stuffily contented themselves with quoting the act as saying that 'there could be no representation admitted among collaterals after the grandchildren of brothers and sisters and children of aunts and uncles.' This unfortunate sentence, quoted derisively under the sub-heading 'Double-Talk', was the only part of the statement that had been printed.

Most of the partners' subsequent statements had suffered the same kind of fate. From time to time some of the more responsible papers had made serious efforts to interpret the intestacy laws to their readers, but never, as far as George could see, had the partners attempted to assist them. The fact that, as Amelia had no close relatives living, the only possible heirs were any nephews and nieces of the late Hans Schneider who had still been alive when Amelia had died, was never explicitly stated by the partners. The nearest they had come to clarity had been in a statement suggesting that it was unlikely that there were any 'first cousins of the intestate decedent who had survived the decedent' in America, and that if any did exist they would most probably be found in Germany.

They might have saved themselves the trouble. The suggestion that the legal heir to the estate might be in Europe instead of somewhere like Wisconsin had not been interesting to the newspapers of 1939; the possibility of his not existing at all they had preferred to ignore altogether. Besides, the enterprise of a Milwaukee paper had just then given the story yet another twist. With the help of the Immigration Authorities, this paper's Special Investigator had been able to discover the number of families named Schneider who had immigrated from Germany in the latter half of the nineteenth century. The number was large. Was it too much to suppose, the paper had asked, that at least one of the Old Forty-Niner's younger brothers had followed his example in immigrating? No, indeed! The hunt had been on again, and squads of Special Investigators had gone forth to pad hopefully through city records, land registers and state archives in the footsteps of the immigrant Schneiders.

George re-packed the parcel with a sigh. He knew already that he was not going to enjoy the next few weeks.

The total number of claims made was just over eight thousand, and he found that there was a separate file for each. Most had only two or three letters in them, but many were quite thick, while some had parcels to themselves and bulged with affidavits, photostats of documents, tattered photographs and genealogical tables. A few had old Bibles and other family souvenirs in them, and one, for some inexplicable reason even contained a greasy fur cap.

George set to work. By the end of his first week he had been through seven hundred of the claims, and was feeling sorry for Messrs Moreton, Greener and Cleek. Many, of course, had come from lunatics and cranks. There was the angry man in North Dakota who said that *his* name was Martin Schneider, that he was *not* dead, and that Amelia Johnson had stolen money from him while he lay sleeping. There was a woman who claimed the estate on behalf of a Californian society for the propagation of the Cataphrygian heresy, on the grounds that the spirit of the late Amelia had entered into Mrs Schultz, the society's honorary treasurer. And there was a man, writing in multi-coloured inks from a state hospital, who said that he was the legitimate son of Amelia by a secret first marriage to a coloured man. But the majority of the claimants seemed to be persons who, while not actually insane, had rudimentary notions of what constituted evidence. For instance, a chicago man named Higgins who had evolved an elaborate claim from the memory of having heard his father say that Cousin Amelia was a wicked old miser; and another man who had pressed for a share of the estate on the strength of an old letter from a Danish relative named Schneider. Then there were those who warily declined to send evidence to support their claims lest it should be stolen and used to prove the case of another claimant, and others who demanded travelling and hotel expenses so that they might present their cases in person to the administrator. Above all there were the lawyers.

Only thirty-four out of the first seven hundred claims which George examined had been handled by attorneys, but it took him over two days to get through those particular files. The claims in question were mostly of doubtful validity, and one or two were patently dishonest. In George's view, no reputable lawyer would have touched any of them. But these had been disreputable lawyers. They had both touched and held on. They had quoted non-existent precedents and photographed useless documents. They had hired dishonest inquiry agents to conduct pointless investigations and quack genealogists to draw up faked family trees. They had written portentous letters and uttered obscure threats. The only thing, apparently, that none of them had ever done had been to advise his client to withdraw a claim. In one of these files there was a letter to the administrator from an old woman named Snyder regretting that she had no more money left to pay her attorney to act for her, and asking that her claim should not on this account be overlooked.

In his second week on the records, George managed, in spite of a severe cold in the head, to push his score of examined claims up to nineteen hundred. In the third week he topped three thousand. By the end of the fourth week he was at the halfway mark. He was also feeling very depressed. The boring nature of the work and the cumulative effects of so much evidence of human stupidity were lowering themselves. The amused commiseration of his new colleagues and knowledge that he was beginning his career in Lavater's at the wrong end of an office joke had done nothing to improve matters. Mr Budd, when last encountered in the elevator on his way back from lunch, had talked cheerfully about baseball and had not even troubled to ask for a progress report. On the Monday morning of the fifth week, George surveyed with loathing the stacks of records that still remained to be examined.

'Finish the O's, Mr Carey?' The speaker was the janitor who looked after the vaults, cleaned up the parcels and carried them to and from George's office.

'No, I'd better start on the P's now.'

'I can ease the rest of the O's out if you like, Mr Carey.'

'All right, Charlie. If you can do it without bringing the lot down.' The inroads he had already made on the towering stacks of parcels had gradually reduced the stability of the remainder.

'Sure, Mr Carey,' said Charlie. He took hold of a section near the floor and pulled. There was a slithering noise and a crash as an avalanche of parcels engulfed him. In the cloud of dust that followed the subsidence, he stumbled to his feet coughing and swearing, his hand held to his head. Blood began to pour from a long cut over his eye.

'For God's sake, Charlie, how did that happen?'

The janitor kicked something solid under the heap of parcels about him. 'This damned thing caught me on the head, Mr Carey,' he explained. 'Must have been stacked up in the middle somewhere.'

'Do you feel all right?'

'Oh, sure. It's only a scratch. Sorry, Mr Carey.'

'You'd better get it fixed, anyway.'

When he had handed the janitor over to the care of one of the elevator men and the dust in the vault had settled again, George went in and examined the confusion. Both the O's and the P's had vanished under a rubble of S's and W's. He pushed several of the parcels aside and saw the reason for the janitor's cut eye. It was a large black japanned deed box of the kind that used to line the walls of old family lawyers. Stencilled on it in white paint were the words, 'SCHNEIDER–CONFIDENTIAL'.

George dragged the box clear of the parcels and tried to open it. It was locked, and there was no key attached to either of the handles. He hesitated. His business in this case was with the claims files and it was foolish to waste time satisfying his curiosity about the contents of an old deed box. On the other hand, it would take an hour to straighten out the mess at his feet. There was little point in his covering himself with dust and cobwebs in order to hasten the process, and Charlie would be back in a few minutes. He went into the janitors room, took a cold chisel and a hammer from the tool rack and returned to the box. A few blows cut through the thin metal round the tongue of the lock and he was able to wrench the lid open.

At first sight, the contents seemed to be simply some personal belongings from Mr Moreton's office. There was a calf-bound appointment book with his initials stamped on it in gold, an onyx desk set, a carved teak cigar-box, a tooled leather blotting-pad and a pair of leather-covered letter trays to match it. In one of the trays there was a hand towel, some aspirin tablets and a bottle of vitamin capsules. George lifted the tray. Beneath it was a thick loose-leaf binder labelled: 'GERMAN INQUIRY RE SCHNEIDER BY ROBERT L. MORETON, 1939'. He glanced through a page or two, saw that it was in diary form and put it aside for later reading. Underneath was a manilla folder containing a mass of photographs, mostly, it appeared, of German legal documents. The only other things in the box were a sealed package and a sealed envelope. On the package was written: 'Correspondence between Hans Schneider and his wife, with other documents found by Hilton G. Greener and Robert L. Moreton among effects of late Amelia Schneider Johnson Sept. 1938'. On the envelope was written: 'Photograph handed to R.L.M. by father Weichs at Bad Schwennheim'.

George put Mr Moreton's personal things back in the deed box and took the rest of the contents up to his office. There, the first thing he did was to open the sealed parcel.

The letters in it had been carefully numbered and initialled by Mr Greener and Mr Moreton. There were seventy-eight of them, all tied up in small packets with silk ribbon and with a pressed flower in each. George undid one of the packets. The letters in it belonged to the courtship period of Amelia's parents, Hans Schneider and Mary Smith. They showed that Hans had been working in a warehouse at the time and learning English, and that Mary had been learning German. George thought them formal, graceless and dull. However, their value to Mr Moreton must have been considerable, for they had probably made possible the speedy tracing of the Smith family concerned and led to its happy elimination from the list of claimants.

George tied the packet up again and turned to an album of old photographs. In it there were photographs of Amelia and Martin as children, of their brother Frederick, who had died at the age of twelve, and, of course, of Hans and Mary. More interesting, because it was even older, was a daguerreotype portrait of an old man with a vast beard.

He sat, erect and very stern, his big hands grasping the arms of the photographer's chair, his head pressed hard against the back of it. The lips were full and determined. There was a heavy, strong face beneath the beard. The silvered copper plate on which the portrait had been made was glued to a red velvet mount. Beneath it Hans had written. '*Mein geliebt Vater, Franz Schneider. 1782-1850.*'

The only other document was a thin, leather-bound notebook filled with Hans spidery writing. It was written in English. On the first page, elaborately decorated with ornamental pen strokes, was a description of the book's contents: 'An Account of My Beloved Father's Heroic Part in the Battle of Preussisch-Eylau, fought in the year 1807, of his Wounding, and of His Meeting with My Beloved Mother who Saved His Life. Set down by Hans Schneider for his Children in June 1867, that They may be Proud of The Name They Bear'.

The account began with the events leading up to Eylau, and went on with descriptions of the various actions in which the Ansbach Dragoons had engaged the enemy, and of spectacular incidents in the battle: a Russian cavalry charge, the capture of a battery of guns, the decapitation of a French officer. Obviously, what Hans had written down was a legend learned at his father's knee. Parts of it still had the artless quality of a fairy tale; but as the account progressed the middle-aged Hans could be seen perplexedly trying to reconcile his boyhood memories with his adult sense of reality. The writing of the Account, George thought, must have been a strange experience for him.

After his description of the battle, however, Hans's touch had become surer. The emotions of the wounded hero, his certainty that God was with him, his determination to do his duty until the end; these things were described with practised unction. And when the terrible moment of treachery came; when the cowardly Prussians had abandoned the wounded hero while he was helping a stricken comrade, Hans had let loose a torrent of Biblical denunciation. If God had not guided the hoofs of the hero's horse to the farmhouse of the gentle Maria Dukta, all would certainly have been over. As it was, Maria had been understandably suspicious of the Prussian uniform and (as she later confessed to the hero) her humane instincts had been all but overcome by her fears for her virtue and for her ailing father. In the end, of course, all had been well. When his wound was healed, the hero had brought his rescuer home in triumph. In the following year, Han's elder brother, Karl had been born.

The Account concluded with a sanctimonious homily on the subjects of prayer-saying and the obtaining of forgiveness for sins. George skipped it and turned to Mr Moreton's diary.

Mr Moreton and an interpreter whom he had engaged in Paris had arrived in Germany toward the end of March in 1939.

His plan had been simple; simple in intention at all events. First he would retrace Hans Schneider's steps. Then, when he had found out where the Schneider family had lived, he would set about discovering what had happened to all Han's brothers and sisters.

The first part of the plan had proved simple of execution. Hans had come from somewhere in Westphalia; and, in 1849, a man of military age had had to have a permit to leave it. In Münster, the old state capital, Mr Moreton had been able to find the record of Han's departure. Hans had come from Mühlhausen and gone to Bremen.

In Bremen, a search in the port authority files of old ships' manifests had revealed that Hans Schneider of Mühlhausen had sailed in the *Abigail*, an English ship of six hundred tons, on May 10th, 1849. This had checked with a reference, in one of Han's letters to Mary Smith, to his voyage from Germany. Mr Moreton had now concluded that he was tracing the right Hans Schneider. He had gone next to Mühlhausen.

Here, however, a baffling situation had awaited him. He had found that, although the church registers recorded marriages, baptisms and burials as far back as the Thirty Years War, none of them covering the years 1807 and 1808 contained any reference to the name of Schneider.

Mr Moreton had brooded on this disappointment for twenty-four hours; then, he had had an idea. He had gone back to the registers.

This time, he had turned to those for 1850, the year of Franz Schneider's death. The facts of his death and burial had been recorded, and the location of the grave. Mr Moreton had gone to inspect it. Now he had had a most disturbing surprise. A decaying memorial stone had supplied the confusing information that this was the resting place of Franz Schneider and his much beloved wife, Ruth. According to Han's Account, his mother's name was Maria.

Mr Moreton had returned to the registers again. It had taken him a long time to work back from 1850 to 1815, but by the time he had done so he had had the names of no less than ten of Franz Schneider's children and the date of his marriage to Ruth Vogel. He had also learned to his dismay that none of the children's names had been either Hans or Karl.

The idea that there must have been a previous marriage in some other city had soon occurred to him. But where could this earlier marriage have taken place? With what other towns had Franz Schneider been associated? From what town, for instance, had he been recruited into the Prussian Army?

There had been only one place where that sort of question might be answered. Mr Moreton and his interpreter had gone to Berlin.

It had taken Mr Moreton until the end of March to cut through the swathes of Nazi red tape and dig far enough into the archives at Potsdam to get at the Napoleonic war diaries of the Ansbach Dragoons. It had taken him less than two hours to find out that, between 1800 and 1815, the name of Schneider had figured only once in the nominal rolls of the regiment. A Wilhelm Schneider had been killed by a fall from his horse in 1803.

It had been a bitter blow. Mr Moreton's entry in his diary for that day ended with the despondent words: 'So I guess it's a wild-goose chase after all. Nevertheless I will make a check search tomorrow. If no result will abandon inquiry as I consider inability to link Hans Schneider positively with Mühlhausen family in records makes further efforts pointless.'

George turned the page and then stared blankly. The next entry in the diary consisted entirely of figures. They filled the page, line after line of them. The next page was the same, and the page after that. He flicked the pages over rapidly. With the exception of the date headings, every entry in the diary from then on–and it continued for over three months–was in figures. Moreover the figure were in groups of five. Not only had Mr Moreton decided after all *against* abandoning his inquiries in Germany, but he had thought it necessary to record the results of them in cypher.

George abandoned the diary and glanced throught the file of photographed documents. He did not read German with great confidence even when it was printed in roman type. German hand-writing of the traditional kind defeated him completely. These were all hand-written. Careful scrutiny of two or three of them revealed the fact that they referred to the births and deaths of people named Schneider, but this was scarcely surprising. He put them aside and opened the sealed envelope.

The photograph 'handed to R.L.M. by Father Weichs at Bad Schwennheim' proved to be a dog-eared, postcard-size portrait of a young man and a young woman sitting side by side on a professional photographer's rustic bench. The woman had a certain fluffy prettiness, and was possibly pregnant. The man was nondescript. Their clothes were of the early 'twenties. They looked like a prosperous working-class couple on their day off. There was a painted background of snow-covered pines behind them. Across the corner of it was written in German script, '*Johann und Ilse*'. The photographer's imprint on the mount showed that it had been taken in Zürich. There was nothing else in the envelope.

Charlie, the janitor, came in with a piece of sticking-plaster on his forehead and another load of parcels and George got back to work on the claims. But that night he took the contents of the deed box back to his apartment and went through it carefully again.

He was in a difficulty. He had been asked to check on the claims to the estate received by the former administrator; nothing else. If the deed box had not fallen and cut the janitor's head, he would probably not have noticed it. It would have been moved out of the way of the parcels of claims files and then left in the vault. He would have worked his way through the claims and then, no doubt, simply reported to Mr Budd what Mr Budd wanted to hear; that there were no outstanding claims worth discussing, and that the Commonwealth of Pennsylvania could go ahead. Then, he, George, would have been free of the whole mess and ready to be rewarded with an assignment more suited to his abilities. Now, it looked as if he had a choice of two days of making a fool of himself. One was by forgetting about the contents of the deed box and so running the risk of allowing Mr Sistrom to make a serious blunder; the other was by plaguing Mr Budd with idle fancies.

High political office and the presidencies of corporations seemed very far away that night. It was not until the early hours of the morning that he thought of a tactful way of putting the things to Mr Budd.

Mr Budd received George's report with impatience.

'I don't even know if Bob Moreton's still alive,' he said, irritably. 'In any case, all that this cypher stuff suggests to me is that the man was in an advanced stage of paranoia.'

'Did he seem O.K. when you saw him in 'forty-four, sir?'

'He may have *seemed* O.K., but from what you show me it looks very much as if he wasn't.'

'But he *did* go on with the inquiry, sir.'

'What if he did?' Mr Budd sighed. 'Look George, we don't want any complications in this business. We just want to unload. I appreciate that you want to be thorough but I should have thought it was very simple really. You just get a German translator on these photographed documents, find out what they're all about,' then check through the claims from people named Schneider and see if the documents refer in any way. That's straight-forward enough, isn't it?'

George decided that the time for tactful handling had arrived. 'Yes, sir. But what I had in mind was a way of speeding up the whole thing. You see, I haven't gotten through to the Schneider claims yet, but, judging by the volume of paper in the vault, there must be at least three thousand of them. Now it's taken me nearly four weeks to check through that number of ordinary claims. The Schneider files are certain to take longer. But I've been looking into things and I have a hunch that if I can check with Mr Moreton it may save a lot of time.'

'Why? How do you mean?'

'Well, sir, I checked through some of the reports on that case they fought against the Rudolph Schneider claim and the German Government. It seemed to me quite clear that Moreton, Greener and Cleek had a whole lot of facts at their disposal that the other side didn't have. I think they had very definite information that there was no Schneider heir alive.'

Mr Budd looked at him shrewdly. 'Are you suggesting, George, that Moreton went on and established beyond doubt that there was no heir, and that he and his partners then kept quiet about the fact so that they could go on drawing fees from the estate?'

'It could be, sir, couldn't it?'

'Terrible minds some of you young men have!' Mr Budd suddenly became jovial again. 'All right, what's the pitch?'

'If we could have the results of Moreton's confidential inquiries, we might have enough information to make any further examination of all these claims unnecessary.'

Mr Budd stroked his chin. 'I see. Yes, not bad, George.' He nodded briskly. 'O.K. If the old chap's alive and in his right mind, see what you can do. The quicker we can get out from under the whole thing the better.'

'Yes, sir, said George.

That afternoon he had a call from Mr Budd's secretary to say that a check with Mr Moreton's former club had disclosed that he was now living in retirement at Montclair, New Jersey. Mr Budd had written to the old man asking him if he would see George.

Two days later a reply came from Mrs Moreton. She said that her husband had been bedridden for some months, but that in view of former associations, and providing that Mr Carey's visit was brief, Mr Moreton would be glad to put his memory at Mr Carey's disposal. Mr Moreton slept in the afternoons. Perhaps Friday morning at eleven o'clock would be convenient to Mr Carey.

'That must be his second wife,' said Mr Budd. Early on the Friday morning, George put the deed box and all its original contents into the back of his car and drove up to Montclair.

Chapter Three

The house was a comfortable-looking place, surrounded by several acres of well-kept garden, and it occurred to George that the financial fate of Messrs Moreton, Greener and Cleek had not been quite as disastrous as Mr Budd had implied. The second Mrs Moreton proved to be a lean, neat woman in the late forties. She had a straight back, a brisk manner, and a patronizing smile. It seemed probable that she had been Mr Moreton's nurse.

'Mr Carey, is it? You won't tire him, will you? He's allowed to sit up in the morning at present, but we have to be careful.' She led the way through to a glass-enclosed porch at the rear of the house.

Mr Moreton was big and pink and flabby, like an athlete gone to seed. He had short white hair and very blue eyes, and there was still a trace of boyish good looks visible in the slack, puffy face. He was lying, propped up by cushions and swathed in a blanket, on a day bed fitted with a book rest. He greeted George eagerly, thrusting the book rest aside and struggling into a sitting posture in order to shake hands. He had a soft, pleasant voice and smelt faintly of lavender water.

For a minute or two he asked after the people at Lavater's whom he had known, and then about a number of men in Philadelphia of whom George had never heard. At last he sat back with a smile.

'Don't ever let anyone persuade you to retire, Mr Carey,' he said. 'You live in the past and become a bore. A dishonest bore, too. I ask you how Harry Budd is. You tell me he's fine. What I really want to know is whether he's bald.'

'He is,' George said.

'And whether, in spite of all that studied *bonhomie*, he's got ulcers yet, or high blood pressure.'

George laughed.

'Because if he has,' continued Mr Moreton amiably, 'that's fine. He's one son-of-a-bitch I don't have to envy.'

'Now, Bob!' his wife said reproachfully.

He spoke without looking at her. 'Mr Carey and I are going to talk a little business now, Kathy,' he said.

'Very well. Don't overtire yourself.'

Mr Moreton did not reply. When she had gone, he smiled. 'Drink, my boy?'

'No, thank you, sir. I think Mr Budd explained why I wanted to see you.'

'Sure. The Schneider Johnson matter. I could have guessed, anyway.' He looked sideways at George. 'So you found it, did you?'

'Found what, sir?'

'The diary and the photographs and all Hans Schneider's stuff. You found it, eh?'

'It's outside in the car, sir, with some of your personal belongings that were put in the box with it.'

Mr Moreton nodded. 'I know. I put them there myself–on top. I figured that, with any luck, a person opening the box would think that it was just my personal junk.'

'I'm afraid I don't quite follow you, sir.'

'Of course you don't. I'll explain. As administrator, I was ethically bound to hand over everything, lock, stock and barrel. Well, that confidential stuff was something I didn't want to hand over. I wanted to destroy it, but Greener and Cleek wouldn't let me. They said that if anything came up afterwards and John J. found out, I'd be in trouble.'

George said: 'Oh.' He had not really believed in his suggestion that Moreton, Greener and Cleek had concealed important information. It had merely occurred to him that the notion might be congenial to Mr Budd. Now, he was a trifle shocked.

Mr Moreton shrugged. 'So all I could do was to try and camouflage it. Well, I didn't succeed.' He stared out gloomily at the garden for a moment, then turned to George briskly as if to dismiss an ugly memory. 'I suppose the Commonwealth of Pennsylvania's after the loot again, eh?'

'Yes. They want to know if Mr Sistrom's going to fight them on it.'

'And Harry Budd, who doesn't like soiling his dainty fingers with such things, can't wait to get the thing out of the office, eh? No, you don't have to answer that, my boy. Let's get down to business.'

'Would you like me to get the papers out of the car, sir?'

'We won't need them,' said Mr Moreton. 'I know what's in that box as well as I know my own name. Did you read that little book Hans Schneider wrote for his children?'

'Yes.'

'What did you think of it?'

George smiled. 'After reading it I made a resolution. If I have children, I'm never going to tell them a thing about my war experiences.'

The old man chuckled. 'They'll get it out of you. The thing you want to watch out for is having a fool son like Hans who writes down what you say. That's dangerous.'

'How do you mean?'

'I'll tell you. I was administrator all right, but I went to Germany because my partners sent me. The case had been in our hair too long and they wanted to have done with it. My instructions were to confirm what we already believed–that there was no legitimate heir to the estate. Well, when I found that Hans was probably a son of Franz Schneider's first marriage, I had to know about that marriage in order to complete the picture. As you know, I went to Potsdam to see if I could trace him through the regimental archives. To begin with I failed.'

'But next day you went back for another check through?'

'Yes, but I'd had a night to think. And I'd thought again about what Hans had written. If there was any truth in the thing at all, Sergeant Schneider had become a casualty at the battle of Eylau and been lost in the retreat.

Surely the war diary would record that fact in a casualty list. So that next day, instead of going all over the nominal rolls again, I had the interpreter translate the regimental account of the battle for me.' He sighed reminiscently. 'There are some moments in life, my boy, that always feel good no matter how many times you go over them again in your mind. That was one of them. It was late morning and getting very warm. The interpreter was having trouble with that old writing and was stumbling over the translation of it. Then, he began on the account of the long march from Eylau to Insterburg. I was only half-listening. As a matter of fact, I was thinking about a bad march I'd done in Cuba during the Spanish-American War. And then something the interpreter had said made me jump right out of my skin.'

He paused.

'What was that?' George asked.

Mr Moreton smiled. 'I remember the words exactly. "During this night"–I quote from the war diary–"Franz Schirmer, a sergeant, left the detachment under his command, saying that he was going to succour a dragoon who had lagged behind because of a lame horse. When morning came, Sergeant Schirmer had not rejoined his detachment. There was found to be no other man missing from it, nor any who had lagged behind. Accordingly, the name of Franz Schirmer was posted in the list of deserters."'

For a moment or two there was silence. 'Well?' added Mr Moreton. 'What do you think of that?'

'Schirmer, did you say?'

'That's right. Sergeant Franz Schirmer, S-C-H-I-R-M-E-R.'

George laughed. 'The old bastard,' he said.

'Exactly.'

'So all that stuff he told his son Hans about the cowardly Prussians leaving him for dead was . . .'

'Bull,' said Mr Moreton, dryly. 'But you see the implications.'

'Yes. What did you do?' George asked.

'The first thing I did was to take security precautions. We'd already had trouble enough with the newspapers finding out stuff about the case and printing it, and before I went to Germany I agreed a policy with my partners. I was to keep what I was doing as a secret as possible, and to make sure that I didn't get an interpreter with German newspaper contacts, I was to engage him in Paris. The other thing we'd agreed was a cypher for confidential matters. It may sound funny to you but if you've ever had experience of . . .'

'I know,' George said. 'I saw the newspaper clippings.'

'Ah. Well, I'd been sending my partners progress reports in diary form. When I found out about Schirmer, I began to use the cypher. It was a simple key-word affair, but good enough for our purpose. You see, I had visions of the newspaper getting hold of the Schirmer name and starting another flood of claims from Schirmers, Shermans and the rest. The final thing I did was to fire the interpreter. I said I was abandoning the inquiry and paid him off.'

'Why was that?'

'Because I was going on with it, and I didn't want anyone outside the firm to have a complete picture. It was just as well I did fire him, too, because later on, when the Nazis were after the estate and France was occupied, the Gestapo pulled in the second man I used. Pulled him in for questioning. If he'd known what the first one knew, we'd have been in a spot. I got the second one through our Paris Embassy. By the time he arrived, I'd had the war diary entry photographed–you'll find it in the file–and was ready to move on.'

'To Ansbach?'

'Yes. There I found the record of Franz Schirmer's baptism. Back in Mühlhausen again I found the register entries for the marriage of Franz and Maria. But the really important thing I found was when I went back to Münster. The boy Karl was down in the recruits muster roll for 1824 as Karl *Schirmer*. Franz had changed his own name but not his eldest boy's.'

George thought quickly. 'I suppose Franz changed his name when Mühlhausen was ceded to Prussia.'

'That's what I thought. As far as the Prussians were concerned, he'd be a deserter. But I guess he just didn't trouble about Karl.'

'He changed Han's name.'

'But Hans was a baby then. He'd naturally grow up a Schneider. Anyway, whatever reason, there it was. Hans had had six brothers and five sisters. All were surnamed Schneider except one, Karl. His surname was Schirmer. All I had to do was to find out which of those persons had had children–cousins of Amelia–and whether any one of those children was alive.'

'That must have been quite a job.'

Mr Moreton shrugged. 'Well, it wasn't quite as bad as it sounds. Death rates were higher in the last century. Out of the eleven brothers and sisters, two boys and two girls died before they were twelve in a typhoid epidemic and another of the girls was killed by a runaway horse when she was fifteen. That meant I had only six to worry about. Four of them I handed over to a private inquiry agent specializing in that kind of thing. The other two, I looked after.'

'Karl Schirmer was one of your two?'

'He was. And by the middle of July, I had finished with the Schneiders. There had been children all right, but none of them had survived Amelia. So there was still no heir. The only one left to check on was Karl Schirmer.'

'Did he have any children?'

'Six. He'd been apprenticed to a printer in Coblenz, and married the boss's daughter. I spent from mid-July on chasing around the towns and villages of the Rhineland. By mid-August I'd traced all but one of the six, and there was still no heir. The missing child was a son, Fredrich, born in 1863. All I knew about him was that he'd married in Dortmund in 1887, and that he was a book-keeper. And then I had trouble with the Nazis.'

'What sort of trouble.'

'Well, in the summer of 1939, any foreigner who travelled about the Rhineland asking questions, checking official records and sending cables in cypher was bound to become suspect, but, like a dope, I hadn't thought of that. In Essen, I was interviewed by the police and asked to give an account of myself. I explained as best as I could and they went away, but the next day they came again. This time they had a couple of Gestapo boys with them.' Mr Moreton smiled ruefully. 'I don't mind telling you, my boy, I was glad I had an American passport. Still, I made them believe me in the end. The fact that I was trying to prevent the papers knowing what I was doing helped, I guess. They didn't like newspapers either. The main thing was that I managed to keep the name Schirmer out of it. But they made trouble all the same. Within two weeks, I had a cable from my partners to say that the German Embassy in Washington had notified the State Department that in future the German Government would represent any German national claiming the Schneider Johnson estate, and had requested information about the present state of the administrator's inquiries in the matter.'

'You mean the Gestapo had reported what you were doing to their Foreign Office?'

'They certainly had. That's how that phony Rudolph Schneider claim of their's started. You have no idea how difficult it is, politically and in every other way, to challenge the validity of documents produced and attested by the government of a friendly power—I mean a power enjoying normal diplomatic relations with your own government. It's like accusing them of forging their own banknotes.'

'And what about the Schirmer side of the family, sir? Did the Nazis ever get on to that?'

'No, they didn't. You see, they didn't have Amelia's documents to help them as we did. They didn't even have the right Schneider family, but it was difficult to prove.'

'And Friedrich Schirmer, Karl's son? Did you trace him?'

'Yes, my boy, I traced him all right, but I had hell's own job doing it. I got on his trail at last through a clerical employment agency in Karlsruhe. They found out for me that there had been an elderly book-keeper named Friedrich Schirmer on their files five years previously. They'd found him a job in a button factory at Freiburg-im-Breisgau. So I went to the button factory. There they told me that he had retired three years earlier at the age of seventy and gone into a clinic at Bad Schwennheim. Bladder trouble they said. They thought he'd probably be dead.'

'And was he?'

'Yes, he was dead.' Mr Moreton looked out at the garden as if he hated it. 'I don't mind telling you, my boy,' he said, 'that I was feeling pretty old and tired myself by then. It was the last week in August and there wasn't much doubt, from what the radio was saying, that Europe was going to be at war within the week. I wanted to go home. I've never been the sort of man who likes being in the thick of things. Besides, I was having trouble with the interpreter. He was a Lorrainer, France was mobilizing, and he was afraid he wouldn't have time to see his wife before he was called to his regiment. It was getting difficult to buy gasoline for the car, too. I was tempted to forget about Friedrich Schirmer and get out. And yet I couldn't quite bring myself to go without just making a final check-up. Twenty-four hours more, that was all I needed.'

'And so you did check up.' Now that he had the facts he wanted. George was getting impatient with Mr Moreton's reminiscences.

'Yes. I checked up. But without the interpreter. He was so darned scared that I told him to take the car, and drive it to Strasbourg and wait for me there. That was a lucky thing, too. When the Gestapo got hold of him later, he knew no more than that I'd gone to Bad Schwennheim. Real luck. I went there by train. Do you know it? It's near Triburg in Baden.'

'I never got down that way.'

'It's one of those scattered little resort towns—pensions, family hotels and small villas on the edge of the fir forest. I'd found that the best person to make for on those inquiries was the priest, so I set out to find him. I could see the church—like a cuckoo-clock it was on the side of the hill—and I had just about enough German to find out from a passer-by that the priest's house was beyond it. Well, I sweated up there and saw the priest. Luckily, he spoke good English. I told him the usual lies, of course . . .'

'Lies?'

'About its being a trifling matter, a small legacy, all that stuff. You have to play it down. If you go telling the truth on a job like that you're a dead duck. Greed! You'd be surprised what happens to perfectly sane people when they start thinking in millions. So I told the usual lies and asked the usual questions.'

'And the priest said Friedrich Schirmer was dead?'

'Yes.' Mr Moreton smiled shyly. 'But he also said what a pity it was that I'd come too late.'

'Too late for what?'

'For the funeral.'

'George's heart sank. 'You mean he'd survived Amelia?'

'By over ten months.'

'Had he a wife?'

'She's been dead for years.'

'Children?'

'A son named Johann. That's his photograph in the box you have. Ilse was the son's wife. Johann would be in his fifties now, I should think.'

'You mean he's alive?'

'I haven't any idea, my boy,' said Mr Moreton cheerfully. 'But if he is, he's certainly the Schneider Johnson heir.'

George smiled. '*Was* the heir you mean, don't you, sir? As a German, he could never receive the estate. The Alien Property Custodian would vest himself with the claim.'

Mr Moreton chuckled and shook his head. 'Don't be so certain, my boy. According to the priest, Friedrich spent over twenty years of his life working for a German electrical manufacturer with a plant near Schauffhausen in Switzerland. Johann was born there. Technically, he'd be Swiss.'

George sat back in his chair. For a moment or two he was too confused to think clearly. Mr Moreton's pink, puffy jowls quivered with amusement. He was pleased with the effect of his statement. George felt himself getting angry.

'But where did he live?' he asked. 'Where *does* he live?'

'I don't know that either. Neither did the priest. As far as I could make out, the family returned to Germany in the early 'twenties. But Friedrich

Schirmer hadn't seen or heard from his son and daughter-in-law in years. What's more, there was nothing in the papers he left to show that they'd ever existed, barring the photograph and some things he'd said to the priest.'

'Did Friedrich make a will?'

'No. He had nothing to leave worth troubling about. He had lived on a small annuity. There was scarcely enough money to bury him properly.'

'But surely you made an effort to find this Johann?'

'There wasn't much I could do right then. I asked Father Weichs–that was the priest–to let me know immediately if anything was heard of or from Johann, but the war broke out three days later. I never heard any more about it.'

'But when the German Government claimed the estate, didn't you tell them the situation and ask them to produce Johann Schirmer?'

The old man shrugged impatiently. 'Of course, if it had got to the point where they had a real chance of substantiating their Schneider claim we'd have had to. But, as it was, it was better not to show our hand. They'd already produced a phony Schneider. What was to stop them producing a phony Johann Schirmer? Supposing they'd discovered that Johann and Ilse were dead and without heirs! Do you think they'd have admitted it? Besides, we didn't expect the war to last more than a month or two; we were thinking all the time that at any moment one of us would be able to go back to Germany and clear the whole matter up in a proper way and to our own satisfaction. Then, of course, Pearl Harbour came and that was the end of the case as far as we were concerned.'

Mr Moreton sank back on to his cushions and closed his eyes. He had had his fun. Now he was tired.

George was silent. Out of the corner of his eye, he could see the second Mrs Moreton hovering in the background. He got to his feet. 'There's only one thing I'm not clear about, sir,' he said hesitantly.

'Yes, my boy?'

'You said that when you handed over to Mr Sistrom in 'forty-four, you didn't want these facts to come to his attention. Why was that?'

Slowly Mr Moreton opened his eyes. 'Early in 'forty-four,' he said, 'my son was murdered by the S.S. after escaping from a prisoner-of-war camp in Germany. My wife wasn't too well at the time and the shock killed her. When the time came to hand it all over to Sistrom, I guess I just couldn't accept the idea of a German getting anything out of this country as a result of my efforts.'

'I see.'

'Not professional,' the old man added disapprovingly. 'Not ethical. But that's the way I felt. Now—' he shrugged and his eyes were suddenly amused again–'now, all I'm wondering is what Harry Budd's going to say when you tell him the news.'

'I've been wondering the same thing myself,' said George.

Mr Budd said, 'Oh, my God!' with great force, and asked his secretary to see if Mr Sistrom was available for consultation.

John J. Sistrom was the most senior partner in the firm (Lavater and

Powell had been dead for years) and had been well thought of by the elder J. P. Morgan. A remote, portentous figure who entered and left his office by a private door, he was rarely seen except by other senior partners. George had been presented to him on joining the firm and received a perfunctory handshake. He was very old, much older than Mr Moreton, but skinny and spry; an energetic bag of bones. He fidgeted with a gold pencil while he listened to Mr Budd's disgusted explanation of the position.

'I see,' he said at last. 'Well, Harry, what do you want me to do? Retain someone else, I suppose.'

'Yes, John J. I thought that someone like Lieberman might be interested.'

'Maybe he would. What's the exact value of the estate now?'

Mr Budd looked at George.

'Four million three hundred thousand, sir,' George said.

Mr Sistrom pursed his lips. 'Let's see. Federal tax will account for quite a bit. Then, the thing has been held up for over seven years, so the nineteen-forty-three legislation applies. That means eighty per cent of what's left to the commonwealth.'

'If a claimant were to get half a million out of it, he'd be lucky,' said Mr Budd.

'Half a million free of tax is a lot of money these days, Harry.'

Mr Budd laughed. Mr Sistrom turned to George. 'What's your opinion of this Johann Schirmer's claim, young man?' he asked.

'On the face of it, sir, the claim looks sound to me. A big point in its favour would seem to be the fact that although the intestacy itself comes under the nineteen-seventeen act, this Schirmer claim would satisfy the tougher provisions of the 'forty-seven act. There's no question of representation. Friedrich Schirmer was a *first* cousin *and* he survived the old lady.'

Mr Sistrom nodded. 'you agree with that, Harry?'

'Oh, sure. I think Lieberman will be glad to act.'

'Funny things some of these old inheritance cases,' observed Mr Sistrom absently. 'They make perspectives. A German dragoon of Napoleon's time deserts after a battle and has to change his name. Now, here we sit, over a hundred years later and four thousand miles away, wondering how to deal with a situation arising out of that old fact.' He smiled vaguely. 'It's an interesting case. You see, we could argue that Friedrich inherited the estate prior to the appointment of the Alien Property Custodian and that it should, therefore, have descended to Johann Schirmer under the German law. There have been one or two cases of German-Swiss claims against the Custodian which have succeeded. There are all sorts of possibilities.'

'And won't the papers have fun when they get hold of them!' said Mr Budd.

'Well, they don't have to get hold of them, do they? Not for the present, anyway.' Mr Sistrom seemed to have come to a decision. 'I don't think we ought to be too hasty about this business, Harry.' he said. 'Naturally, we're not going to get involved in any newspaper nonsense, but we're in the possession of certain information that nobody else has access to. We're in a strong position. I think that before we come to any decision about this matter we ought at least to send someone quietly to Germany to see if this

Johann Schirmer can be traced. I don't like the idea of just letting the Commonwealth take all this money because we can't be bothered to fight them. If he's dead and without issue or heir, or we can't find him, then we can think again. Maybe I'll just tell the Commonwealth the facts and leave it to them in that case. But if there is some chance that the man may be alive, no matter how slight, we should bend our efforts to find him. There is no need to hand over a substantial fee to another firm for doing so. Our charge for services is made irrespective of whether we are successful or not. I see no reason for turning down the opportunity.'

'But, my God, John J. . . .!'

'It's perfectly ethical for the administrator's attorneys to endeavour to find the heir and be paid for their efforts.'

'I know it's ethical, John J., but jeepers . . .!'

'In this kind of office one can get too narrow,' said Mr Sistrom firmly. 'I don't think that, just because we're afraid of being annoyed by a little newspaper publicity, we should let the business go out of the family.'

There was a silence. Mr Budd heaved a sigh. 'Well, if you put it that way, John J. But suppose this man's in the Russian zone of Germany or in jail as a war criminal?'

'Then we can think again. Now, who will you send?'

Mr Budd shrugged. 'I'd say a good reliable private inquiry agent was what we needed.'

'Inquiry agent!' Mr Sistrom dropped his gold pencil. 'Look, Harry, we're not going to make a million dollars out of it. Competent private inquiry agents are far too expensive for a gamble like this. I think I have a better idea.' He turned in his chair and looked at George.

George waited with a sinking heart.

The blow came.

Mr Sistrom smiled benevolently. 'How would you like a trip to Europe, Mr Carey?' he said.

Chapter Four

Two weeks later George went to Paris.

As the plane from New York banked slowly and began to lose height in preparation for the landing at Orly, he could see the city turning lazily into view beneath the port wing. He craned his head to see more of it. It was not the first time he had flown over Paris; but it was the first time he had done so as a civilian, and he was curious to see if he could still identify the once familiar landmarks. He was, besides, at the beginning of a new relationship with the place. For him it had been, successively, an area on a map, the location of an Army Air Corps headquarters establishment, a fun fair in which to spend leave periods, and a grey wilderness of streets to wander in while you sweated it out waiting for transportation home, Now, it had become a foreign capital in which he had business to attend to; the point of departure for what, in a facetious moment, he had thought of as an Odyssey. Not even the knowledge that he was acting merely as an inexpensive substitute for a competent private inquiry agent could quite dispel a pleasurable feeling of anticipation.

His attitude toward the Schneider Johnson case had changed somewhat during those two weeks. Though he still regarded his connection with it as a misfortune, he no longer saw it as a major disaster. Several things had conspired to fortify his own good sense in the matter. There had been Mr Budd's protest against sending so able a man on so pedestrian a mission. There had been his colleagues' blasphemously expressed conviction that, having become bored with examining claims, he had cunningly misrepresented the facts in order to get himself a free vacation. Above all, there had been Mr Sistrom's decision to take a personal interest in the case. Mr Budd had crossly attributed his to vulgar greed; but George suspected that Mr Sistrom's apparently simple desire to milk the estate while he had the chance contained elements of other and less business-like desires. It was fantastic, no doubt, to suggest that, in a financial matter of any kind, a partner in Lavater's could be influenced by romantic or sentimental considerations; but, as George had already perceived, fantasy and the Schneider Johnson case had never been very far apart. Besides, the belief that a schoolboy lurked in Mr Sistrom was somehow reassuring; and reassurance was a thing of which he now stood in need.

After a further visit to Montclair, he had set to work de-cyphering Mr Moreton's diary. By the time he had completed the task and identified all the photographed documents in the deed box he was aware of an unfamiliar feeling of inadequacy and self-doubt. Münster, Mühlhausen, Karlsruhe and Berlin—he had dropped bombs on many cities in which Mr Moreton had worked to piece together the history of the Schirmer family. And killed quite a few of their inhabitants, no doubt. Would he have had the patience and ingenuity to do what Mr Moreton had done? He was inclined to doubt it. It was humiliating to be comforted by the knowledge that his own task was likely to prove simpler.

The morning after his arrival in Paris, he went to the American Embassy, established relations with the Legal Department there, and asked them to recommend a German-English interpreter whom they had themselves used and whose sworn depositions would later be accepted by the Orphans' Court in Philadelphia and by the Alien Property Custodian.

When he returned to his hotel a letter awaited him. It was from Mr Moreton.

My Dear Mr Carey,
Thank you very much for your letter. I am, of course, very interested to hear that my old friend John Sistrom has decided to take the Schirmer inquiry further, and very pleased to know that you are to have the responsibility. I congratulate you. You must stand well with John J. to be entrusted with this job. You may be sure that no newspaper will get a word out of me on the subject. I note with pleasure your flattering intention of taking the same precautionary measures as I did to ensure secrecy. If you will premit me to give you a word of advice on the interpreter question—don't take anyone you feel you do not like personally. You will be so much together that if you do not quite like

him to begin with, you will end by hating the sight of him.

As to the points in my diary on which you were not clear, I have set out my answers to your questions on a separate sheet of paper. Please remember, however, that I am relying upon my memory which in some instances may have failed me. The answers are given 'to the best of my knowledge and belief'.

I have given some thought to your problems in Germany, and it seems to me likely that Father Weichs, the Bad Schwennheim priest, will be among those with whom you will be getting in touch at an early stage. But when I tried to recall what I had said to you about my interview with him, it seemed to me that I had left out several important things. My diary, I know gives only the barest facts. It was my last interview in Germany and I was in a hurry to get home. But, as you may imagine, I remember the occasion vividly. A more detailed account of it may prove of some service to you.

As I told you, he informed me of Friedrich Schirmer's death and I gave him a cautious account of my reasons for inquiring about the man. We then had some conversation which, as it concerned Johann Schirmer to some extent, I will give you as I remember it.

Father Weichs is, or was, a tall, fair man with a bony face and sharp blue eyes. And nothing passive about him. My halting German set the muscles of his jaws twitching impatiently. Fortunately, he speaks English well, and after the courtesies were over that was the language we used.

'I hoped you might be a relative,' he said. 'He spoke once of an uncle in America whom he had never seen.'

'Had he no relatives here? No wife?' I asked.

'His wife died about sixteen years ago, in Shaffhausen. She was a Swiss. They had lived there for over twenty years. Their son was born there. But, when she died he returned to Germany. During his last illness he used to speak of his son, Johann, but he had not seen him for many years. Johann was married and he had lived with the couple for a time, but there had been a quarrel and he had left their house.'

'Where did they live?'

'In Germany, but he did not tell me where. The whole subject was very painful to him. He spoke of it only once.'

What did they quarrel about?'

Father Weichs hesitated at this question. Evidently he knew the answer to it. What he said was: 'I cannot say.'

'You don't know?' I persisted.

He hesitated again, then answered very carefully: 'Friedrich Schirmer was not, perhaps, as simple a man as he appeared. That is all I can say.'

'I see.'

'De mortuis . . . the old man was very sick.'

'You have absolutely no idea then, Father, of the whereabouts of Johann?'

'I regret, none. I looked among the old man's things for the address of someone to tell of his death, but I did not find anything. He lived at the sanatorium for old people. The woman director there said that he received no letters, only his annuity every month. Will the son receive the legacy now?'

I had been prepared for the question. At one moment I had thought of trusting this priest, but the habit of caution was very strong. I answered evasively. 'The money is in trust,' I said, and changed the subject by asking what had happened to his belongings.

'There was little more than the clothes he was buried in,' he said.

'No will?'

'No. There were a few books and some old papers—records of his army service, such things. Nothing of value. I have charge of them until the authorities tell me they may be destroyed.'

Naturally, I was determined to go through these things myself but tact was necessary. 'I wonder if I might see them, Father,' I said. 'It would be fitting, perhaps, if I could tell his relatives in America that I had done so.'

'Certainly, if you wish.'

He had made a package of the papers and put the dead man's rosary in with them. I looked through them.

It was, I must tell you, a pathetic collection. There were old Swiss concert programmes and catalogues of Swiss trade exhibitions, an accountancy diploma from a commercial college in Dortmund and the autographed menu of a banquet held in 1910 for the German employees of the Schauffhausen plant he had worked in. There were letters from business houses all over Germany replying to applications for bookkeeping posts. The applicant had written from Dortmund, Mainz, Hanover, Karlsruhe and Freiburg, in that date order. There were the army papers and the documents connected with the annuity he had purchased with his savings. In expansive moments, I have been known to contend that the apparently unimportant things a man keeps, the private souvenirs, the clutter he accumulates during his lifetime, are an index to the secrets of his soul. If this is so, then Friedrich Schirmer must have led a singularly uneventful inner life.

There were two photographs—the one you have seen of Johann and Ilse and another of the late Frau (Friedrich) Schirmer. I knew that I must have the one of Johann at all costs. I put them down casually.

'Nothing of interest, you see.' said Father Weichs.

I nodded. 'But,' I said, 'I wonder if it would not be a kindly action for me to take some remembrance of him back to his relatives in America. If these things are to be destroyed, it seems a pity not to save something of him.'

He thought for a moment but could see no objection. He suggested the rosary. I immediately agreed and only brought up the matter of the photograph as an afterthought. 'If, by any chance, it should be wanted, I could always copy it and return the original to you,' I said.

So I took it with me. I also had his promise that in the event of his learning anything of the whereabouts of Johann Schirmer, I should be informed. As you know, I have never heard from him. In the early hours of the following day, the German army crossed the frontier and began to advance into Poland.

Well, there it is, my boy. My wife has been good enough to type it all out for me and I hope it will be of some use to you. If there is anything else I can do, let me know. And if you feel that you can, without betraying your firm's confidence, let me know how you get on, I shall be more than pleased to hear. You know, the only one of all the Schneiders and Schirmers I got to know about that I really liked was that old Sergeant Franz. I imagine that he was quite a tough proposition. What happens to blood like that? Oh yes, I know that only certain physical characteristics get transmitted, and that it's all a matter of genes and chromosomes; but if you do happen to run across a Schirmer with a beard like Franz's, let me know. Good luck anyway.

Sincerely,

Robert L. Moreton.

George refolded the letter and looked at the accompanying sheet of paper with the answer to his questions. As he did so, the telephone by his bed buzzed harshly and he turned to answer it.

'Mademoiselle Kolin to see you, sir.'

'All right. I'll come down.'

This was the interpreter who had been recommended to him by the Embassy.

'Miss Kolin?' George had said. 'A woman?'

'Sure, she's a woman.'

'I assumed you'd get a man. You know I've got to travel all over the place staying at hotels. It's going to be awkward if . . .'

'Why? You don't have to sleep with her.'

'Isn't there a man available?.

'Not as good as Miss Kolin. You said you wanted someone we could vouch for if it came to getting the interpreter's testimony accepted in an American court. We could vouch for Kolin all right. We always use her or Miss Harle for important rogatory commissions and so do the British. Harle's on another job in Geneva right now, so we got Kolin. You're lucky she's available.'

'All right. How old is she?'

'Early thirties, and quite attractive.'

'For God's sake.'

'You don't have to worry.' The Embassy man had chuckled in an odd way.

George had ignored the chuckle and asked about Miss Kolin's history.

She had been born in one of the Serbian towns of Yugoslavia, and was a graduate of the University of Belgrade. She had an almost phenomenal talent for languages. A British major working with a relief organization had found her in a displaced persons' camp in 1945 and employed her as a secretary. Later, she had worked as an interpreter for an American legal team doing preparatory work for the Nuremberg trials. When the team's work had ended, one of the lawyers, impressed as much by her secretarial ability as by the fact that she was multi-lingual, had given her introductions to the International Standards Organization and the American Embassy in Paris and advised her to try to work up a connection as an interpreter and verbatim reporter. She had soon established herself. She now had a solid reputation at international trade conferences for the speed and reliability of her work. Her services were much in demand.

There were several women waiting in the foyer of the hotel and George had to ask the concierge to point his visitor out to him.

Maria Kolin was indeed attractive. She had the sort of figure and posture that make inexpensive clothes look good. The face and features were broad, the complexion brown against sleek straw-coloured hair. Her eyes were prominent and heavily-lidded. The only make-up she wore was lipstick, but this was boldly applied. She looked as if she had just returned from a ski-ing holiday.

However, although she had obviously seen the concierge point her out to him, she remained staring blankly into the middle distance as George approached, and gave an unreal start of surprise when he spoke.

'Miss Kolin? I'm George Carey.'

'How do you do?' She touched the hand he held out to her as if it were a rolled-up newspaper.

'I'm very glad you could come along,' George said.

She shrugged stiffly. 'Naturally, you would wish to interview me before deciding to employ me.' Her English was very clear and precise with only the faintest trace of an accent.

'They told me at the Embassy that you were a busy person and that I was lucky you were available.' He put as much friendliness as he could into his smile.

She looked past him vaguely. 'Ah, yes?'

George felt himself beginning to be irritated by her. 'Shall we sit down somewhere and talk, Miss Kolin?'

'Of course.'

He led the way across the foyer to some comfortable chairs near the bar. She followed a little too slowly. His irritation increased. She might be an attractive woman, but there was no reason for her to behave as if she were fending off a clumsy attempt at seduction. She was here about a job. Did she want it or didn't she? If she didn't, why waste time by coming at all?

'Now, Miss Kolin,' he said as they sat down; 'how much did the Embassy people tell you about this job?'

'That you were going to Germany to interview various persons there in connection with a law suit. That you would want verbatim reports of the interviews transcribed. That it might be necessary to attend later at an American Embassy to have these transcriptions notarized. The length of time for which you would require me would be not less than one month and not more than three. I should receive my normal fees on a monthly basis and all travelling and hotel expenses would be paid in addition.' She looked past him again, her head held high–a lady of quality importuned by a lascivious workman.

'Yes, that's about right,' George said. 'Did they tell you which law suit it was?'

'They said that it was a highly confidential matter and that you would, no doubt, explain what it was necessary for me to know.' A faint, indifferent smile–men are such children with their little secrets.

'Right. What passports do you have, Miss Kolin?'

'French.'

'I understood you were a Yugoslav citizen.'

'I am naturalized French. My passport *is* valid for Germany.'

'Yes, that was what I wanted to know.'

She nodded but did not say anything. One could be patient with the slow-witted, but one was not obliged to pander to them.

Several sentences came to the tip of George's tongue at that moment, most of them designed to bring the interview to an abrupt conclusion. He swallowed them. Just because she wouldn't pretend to be stupider or more eager for the work than she really was, he didn't have to insult the woman. She had an unfortunate manner. All right! Did that make her a bad interpreter? And what did he expect her to do? Cringe?

He offered her a cigarette.

She shook her head. 'Thank you, I prefer these.' She brought out a packet of Gitanes.

He struck a match for her. 'Are there any questions about the job you would like to ask me?' he said.

'Yes.' She blew smoke out. 'Have you had any experience of using an interpreter, Mr Carey?'

'None at all.'

'I see. Do you speak any German?'

'A little, yes.'

'How little? It is not a pointless question.'

'I'm sure it isn't. Well, I speak the German I learned at High School. I was stationed in Germany for a few months after the war and heard a fair amount of German spoken there. I can understand the drift of most conversations between Germans, but I sometimes misunderstand so completely that I might think I was listening to an argument about politics when what I was really hearing was a discussion of the finer points of chicken farming. Does that answer your question?'

'Very clearly. I will explain the point. When you are using an interpreter it is not always easy to avoid listening also to the conversation being interpreted. That way confusion may arise.'

'In fact, it's better to trust to the interpreter and not try to do the work for her.'

'Exactly.'

The barman was hovering in the background. George ignored him. The interview was as good as over, and he did not want to prolong it. Her cigarette was half-smoked now. When it had burned down another quarter of an inch he would get up.

'I expect you know Germany pretty well, Miss Kolin.'

'Only certain parts.'

'The Rhineland?'

'A little.'

'You worked on the preparations for the Nuremburg trials, I hear.'

'Yes.'

'As a Yugoslav you must have found that very satisfactory.'

'You think so, Mr Carey?'

'You didn't approve of the trials?'

She looked down at her cigarette. 'The Germans took my father as a hostage and shot him,' she said crisply. 'They sent my mother and me to work in a factory in Leipzig. My mother died there of bloodpoisoning from an infected wound which they refused to treat. I do not know exactly what happened to my brothers, except that eventually they were tortured to death in an S.S. barracks at Zagreb. Oh yes, I approved of the trials. If they made the United Nations feel strong and righteous, certainly I approved. But do not ask me to applaud.'

'Yes, I can see you must have wished for a more personal revenge.'

She had leaned forward to stub her cigarette out. Now she turned her head slowly and her eyes met his.

'I'm afraid that I have not your belief in justice, Mr Carey,' she said.

There was a curious, persecuted little half-smile on her lips. He realized suddenly that he was on the verge of losing his temper.

She rose to her feet and stood in front of him smoothing down her dress. 'Is there anything else you would like to know?' she asked calmly.

'I don't think so, thank you.' He stood up. 'It was very kind of you to come along, Miss Kolin. I'm not sure yet when I shall be leaving Paris. I'll get in touch with you as soon as I know.'

'Of course.' She picked up her bag. 'Good-bye, Mr Carey.'

'Good-afternoon, Miss Kolin.'

With a nod she went.

For a moment he looked down at the cigarette she had stubbed out and the lipstick on it; then he went to the lift and was taken up to his room.

He telephoned the Embassy man immediately.

'I've just seen Miss Kolin,' he said.

'Good. All fixed up?'

'No, *not* all fixed up. Look, Don isn't there somebody else I can get?'

'What is the matter with Kolin?'

'I don't know, but whatever it is I don't like it.'

'You must have caught one of her bad days. I told you she'd had some pretty rugged experiences as a refugee.'

'Look, I've talked to lots of refugees who've had rugged experiences. I've never talked to one before who made me sympathize with the Gestapo.'

'Too bad. Her work's O.K., though.'

'She's not.'

'You wanted the best interpreter available.'

'I'll take the next best.'

'Nobody who's actually worked with Kolin has ever had anything but praise for her.'

'She may be fine for conferences and committees. This is different.'

'What's different about it? You're not on a vacation trip, are you?' There was a note of irritation in the voice now.

George hesitated. 'No, but . . .'

'Supposing there's a dispute later over the testimony. You're going to look pretty silly explaining that you passed up the chance of getting a reliable interpreter because you didn't like her personally, aren't you, George?'

'Well, I . . .' George broke off and then sighed. 'O.K.–if I come back a raving alcoholic I shall send the doctor's bills to you.'

'You'll probably end by marrying the girl.'

George laughed politely and hung up.

Two days later he and Maria Kolin left for Germany.

Chapter Five

A book-keeper named Friedrich Schirmer had died at Bad Schwennheim in 1939. He had had a son named Johann. Find this son. If he were dead, then find his heir.

Those were George's instructions.

There were probably thousands of Johann Schirmers in Germany, but certain things were known about this one. He had been born in about 1895, in Schaffhausen. He had married a woman whose given name was Ilse. There was a photograph of them taken in the early twenties. George had a copy. It would probably be of little help in making a positive identification at this stage, but it might serve to remind former neighbours or acquaintances of the pair. Appearances were usually better remembered than names. The photograph itself supplied another faint clue; the photographer's imprint on the mount showed that it had been taken in Zürich.

However, the first move in the plan of campaign which Mr Sistrom had mapped out for him was, as Mr Moreton had surmised, to go to Bad Schwennheim and start where the former inquiry had stopped.

When Friedrich Schirmer had died, he had been estranged from his son for several years; but there was always a chance that the war might have changed things. Families tended to draw together in emergencies. It would have been natural, Mr Sistrom had contended, for Johann to try to get in touch with his father at that time. If he had done so, he would have been officially notified of the death. There might be a record of that notification giving his address. True, Mr Moreton had heard nothing on the subject from Bad Schwennheim, but that proved nothing. The priest might have forgotten his promise or neglected it; his letter could have been lost in the uncertain war-time mails; he might have gone off into the German Army as a chaplain. There were endless possibilities.

In the train on the way to Basel, George explained it all to Miss Kolin.

She listened attentively. When he had finished she nodded. 'Yes, I see. You can, of course, reject no possibility.' She paused. 'Do you hope much from Bad Schwennheim, Mr Carey?'

'Not much, no. I don't know exactly what the German procedure is, but I would say that when an old man like this Friedrich dies, the authorities don't fall over backwards finding relations to notify. We wouldn't, anyway. What's the point? There's no estate. And supposing Johann did write. The letter would go to the sanatorium and most likely get returned through the mail marked "addressee deceased" or whatever it is they put. The priest could easily not have heard about it.'

She pursed her lips. 'It is curious about this old man.'

'Not very. That sort of thing happens every day you know.'

'You say that Mr Moreton found nothing of the son except this one photograph among the old man's papers. No letters, no other photographs, except of his dead wife, nothing. They quarrelled, we are told. It would be interesting to know why.'

'The wife got tired of having him around, probably.'

'What disease did he die of?'

'Bladder trouble of some sort.'

'He would know he was dying, and yet he did not write to his son before the end or even ask the priest to do so?'

'Perhaps he just didn't care any more.'

'Perhaps.' She thought for a moment. 'Do you know the name of the priest?'

'It was a Father Weichs.'

'Then I think you could make inquiries before going to Bad Schwennheim. You could find out if Father Weichs is still there from the church authorities at Freiburg. If he is not still there they will be able to tell you where he is. You might save much time that way.'

'That's a good idea, Miss Kolin.'

'At Freiburg you may also be able to find out if the old man's belongings were claimed by a relative.'

'I think we may have to go to Baden for that information, but we can try at Freiburg.'

'You do not object that I make these suggestions, Mr. Carey?'

'Not a bit. On the contrary, they're very helpful.'

'Thank you.'

George did not find it necessary to mention that the ideas she had put forward had, in fact, already occurred to him. He had given some thought to Miss Kolin since taking his reluctant decision to employ her.

He disliked her and, if Mr Moreton were to be believed, would end by detesting her. She was not somebody he had chosen freely to serve him. She had, to all intents and purposes, been imposed upon him. It would be senseless, therefore, to behave towards her as if she ought to represent—as a good secretary ought to represent, for instance—an extension of part of his own mind and will. She was rather more in the position of an unsympathetic associate with whom it was his duty to collaborate amicably until a specific piece of work was done. He had encountered and dealt philosophically with such situations in the army; there was no reason why he should not deal philosophically with this one.

Thus, having prepared himself for the worst, he had found the Miss Kolin who had presented herself with suitcase and portable typewriter at the Gare de l'Est that morning an agreeable modification of it. True, she had marched along the platform as if she were going out to face a firing squad, and, true, she looked as if she had been insulted several times already that day, but she had greeted him in quite a friendly fashion and had then disconcerted him by producing an excellent map of Western Germany on which she had drawn for his convenience the boundaries of the various occupation zones. She had accepted with businesslike comprehension his patently guarded outline of the case, and shown herself alert and practical when he had gone on to explain in detail the nature of the work they had to do in Germany. Now, she was making intelligent and helpful suggestions. Kolin on the job was evidently a very different person from Kolin being interviewed for one. Or perhaps the man at the Embassy had been right, and that, having experienced one of her bad days, he was now enjoying a good one. In that case, it would be as well to discover how, if at all, the bad might be avoided. In the meantime, he could hope.

After two good days in Freiburg, his attitude toward his collaborator had undergone a further change. He was no nearer liking her, but he had acquired a respect for her ability which, from a professional standpoint, at any rate, was far more comforting. Within two hours of their arrival, she had discovered that Father Weichs had left Bad Schwennheim in 1943, having been called to the Hospital of the Sacred Heart, an institution for disabled men and women, just outside Stuttgart. By the end of the following day she had unearthed the facts that Friedrich Schirmer's belongings had been disposed of under a law dealing with the intestacy of paupers and that the dead man's next-of-kin was recorded as 'Johann Schirmer, son, whereabouts unknown'.

To begin with he had attempted to direct each step of the inquiry himself, but as they were passed from one official to another, the laborious time-wasting routine of question and interpretation followed by answer and interpretation became absurd. At his suggestion she began to interpret the substance of conversations. Then, in the middle of one interview, she had broken off impatiently.

'This is not the person you want,' she had told him. 'You will waste time here. There is, I think, a simpler way.'

After that he had stood back and let her go ahead. She had done so with considerable energy and self-assurance. Her methods of dealing with people were artless but effective. With the co-operative she was brisk, with the obstructive she was imperious, for the suspicious she had a bright, metallic smile. In America, George decided, the smile would not have beguiled an over-sexed schoolboy; but in Germany it seemed to work. Its final triumph was the persuasion of a dour functionary in the police department to telephone to Baden-Baden for the court records of the disposal of Friedrich Schirmer's estate.

It was all very satisfactory and George said so as handsomely as he could.

She shrugged. 'It does not seem necessary for you to waste your time with these simple routine inquiries. If you feel you can trust me to take care of them I am glad to do so.'

It was that evening that he found out something rather more disconcerting about Miss Kolin.

They had fallen into the habit of discussing the next day's work briefly over dinner. Afterwards, she would go to her room and George would write letters or read. This particular evening, however, they had been drawn into conversation with a Swiss businessman in the bar before dinner, and were later invited by him to sit at his table. His motive was quite evidently the seduction of Miss Kolin, if that could be accomplished without too much trouble, and if George had no objection. George had none. The man was agreeable, and spoke good English; George was interested to see how he would make out.

Miss Kolin had had four brandies before dinner. The Swiss had had several Pernods. With dinner she drank wine. So did the Swiss. After dinner he invited her to have brandy again, and again ordered large ones. She had four. So did the Swiss. With the second of them he became coyly amorous and tried to stroke her knee. She repelled the advance absently but efficiently. By the time he had finished his third, he was haranguing George bitterly on the subject of American fiscal policies. Shortly after his fourth, he went very pale, excused himself hurriedly and did not reappear. With a nod to the waiter Miss Kolin ordered a fifth for herself.

George had noticed before that she liked brandy, and that she rarely ordered anything else to drink. He had even noticed when they had been going through the Customs in Basel that she carried a bottle of it in her suitcase. He had not, however, observed that it affected her in any way. Had he been questioned on the point he would have said that she was a model of sobriety.

Now, as she sipped the new arrival, he watched her, fascinated. He knew that had he been drinking level with her he would by now have been unconscious. She was not even talkative. She was holding herself very upright in the chair and looking like an attractive, but very prudish, young schoolmistress about to deal for the first time with a case of juvenile exhibitionism. There was a suspicion of drool at one corner of her mouth. She retrieved it neatly with her tongue. Her eyes were glassy. She focused them with care on George.

'We go then tomorrow to the sanatorium at Bad Schwennheim?' she said precisely.

'No, I don't think so. We'll go and see Father Weichs at Stuttgart first. If he knows something it may be unnecessary to go to Schwennheim.'

She nodded. 'I think you are right, Mr Carey.'

She looked at her drink for a moment, finished it at a gulp and rose steadily to her feet.

'Good-night, Mr Carey,' she said firmly.

'Good-night, Miss Kolin.'

She picked up her bag, turned round and positioned herself facing the door. Then she began to walk straight for it. She missed a table by a hairsbreadth. She did not sway. She did not teeter. It was a miraculous piece of self-control. George saw her go out of the restaurant, change direction towards the concierge's desk, pick up her room key and disappear up the stairs. To a casual observer she might have had nothing stronger to drink than a glass of Rhine wine.

The Hospital of the Sacred Heart proved to be a grim brick building some way out of Stuttgart, off the road to Heilbronn.

George had taken the precaution of sending a long telegram to Father Weichs. In it he had recalled Mr Moreton's visit to Bad Schwennheim in 1939, and expressed his own wish to make the priest's acquaintance. He and Miss Kolin were kept waiting for only a few minutes before a nun appeared to guide them through a wilderness of stone corridors to the priest's room.

George remembered that Father Weichs spoke good English, but it seemed tactful to begin in German. The Priest's sharp blue eyes flickered from one to the other of them as Miss Kolin translated George's polite explanation of their presence there, and his hope that the telegram (which he could plainly see on the priest's table) had arrived to remind him of an occasion in 1939 when . . .

The muscles of Father Weich's jaws had been twitching impatiently as he listened. Now, he broke in, speaking English.

'Yes, Mr Carey. I remember the gentleman and, as you see, I have had your telegram. Please sit down.' He waved them to chairs and walked back to his table.

'Yes,' he said, 'I remember the gentleman very well. I had reason to.'

A twisted smile creased the lean cheeks. It was a fine, dramatic head, George thought. You were sure at first that he must hold some high office in the Church; and then you noticed the cracked, clumsy shoes beneath the table and the illusion went.

'He asked me to give you his good wishes,' George said.

'Thank you. Are you here on his behalf?'

'Unfortunately, Mr Moreton is now an invalid and retired.' It was difficult not to be stilted with Father Weichs.

'I am sorry to hear that, of course.' The priest inclined his head courteously. 'However, it was not the gentleman himself who gave me special cause to remember him. Consider! A lonely old man dies. I am his confessor. Mr Moreton comes to me asking questions about him. That is all. It is not as unusual as you think. An old person who has been neglected by relatives for many years becomes interesting to them when he dies. It is not often, of course, that an American lawyer comes, but even that is not remarkable in itself. There are many German families who have ties with your country.' He paused. 'But the incident becomes memorable,' he added dryly, 'when it proves to be a matter of importance for the police.'

'The police?' George tried hard not to look as guilty as he suddenly felt.

'I surprise you, Mr Carey?'

'Very much. Mr Moreton was making inquiries on behalf of a perfectly respectable American client in the matter of a legacy . . .' George began.

'A legacy,' interposed the priest, 'which he said was for a small amount of money.' He paused and gave George a wintry smile before he went on. 'I understand, of course, that size is relative, and that in America it is not measured with European scales, but even in America it seems an exaggeration to call three million dollars a small amount.'

Out of the corner of his eye George saw Miss Kolin looking startled for once; but it was a poor satisfaction at that moment.

'Mr Moreton was in a spot, Father,' he said. 'He had to be discreet. The American papers had already caused trouble by giving the case too much publicity. There had been a whole lot of false claims. Besides, the case was very complicated. Mr Moreton didn't want to raise anybody's hopes and then have to disappoint them.'

The priest frowned. 'His discretion placed me in a very dangerous position with the police. And with certain other authorities,' he added bleakly.

'I see. I'm sorry about that, Father. I think if Mr Moreton had known . . .' He broke off. 'Do you mind telling me what happened?'

'If it is of interest to you. A little before Christmas in 1940, the police came to me to ask questions about Mr Moreton's visit of the year before. I told them what I knew. They wrote it down and went away. Two weeks later they came back with some other men, not of the police, but the Gestapo. They took me to Karlsruhe.' His face hardened. 'They accused me of lying about Mr Moreton's visit. They said that it was a matter of the highest importance to the Reich. They said that if I did not tell them what they wished to know, I would be treated as some of my brothers in the Church had been treated.' He had been looking at his hands. Now he raised his head and his eyes met George's. 'Perhaps you are able to guess what they wanted to know, Mr Carey.'

George cleared his throat. 'I should say they wanted to know about someone named Schneider.'

He nodded. 'Yes, someone named Schneider. They said that Mr Moreton had been searching for this person, and that I was concealing my knowledge. They believed that I knew where this person was who was entitled to the American money, and that Mr Moreton had bought my silence so that the money could go to an American.' He shrugged. 'The sadness of evil men is that they can believe no truth that does not paint the world in their colours.'

'They weren't interested in Friedrich Schirmer?'

'No. I think that they believed in the end that it was a trick of Mr Moreton's to mislead them. I do not know. Perhaps they only became tired of me. In any case, they let me go. But you see, I have reason to remember Mr Moreton.'

'Yes. But I don't see how he could have anticipated the trouble he would cause you.'

'Oh, I have no bitterness, Mr Carey.' He sat back in his chair. 'But I should like to know the truth.'

George hesitated. 'Friedrich Schirmer's family was a branch of the Schneider family in question. The actual connection would take a long time to explain but I can tell you that the German Government did not know of it.'

The priest smiled. 'I see that it is still necessary to be discreet.'

George flushed. 'I'm being as frank as I can, Father. This has always been a pretty funny sort of a case. There have been so many phony claimants to the estate already that, even if a legitimate one were found, it would be enormously difficult now to establish the claim in the American courts. The fact is that, in all probability, no claim ever will be established. The money will just go to the Commonwealth of Pennsylvania.'

'Then why are you here, Mr Carey?'

'Partly because the law firm I work for succeeded Mr Moreton in the matter. Partly because it is our duty to find the heir. Partly because the matter has to be cleared up so that our firm may be paid.'

'That, at least, is frank.'

'Maybe I should add, too, that if there *is* a rightful heir then he or she ought to have the money and not the Commonwealth of Pennsylvania. The Federal Government and the State will get most of it in taxes in the end, anyway, but there's no reason why someone else shouldn't enjoy it, too.'

'Mr Moreton mentioned a trust.'

'Well . . .'

'Ah, I see. That also was discretion.'

'I'm afraid so.'

'Was Friedrich Schirmer the rightful heir?'

'Mr Moreton thought so.'

'Then why did Mr Moreton not tell the courts so?'

'Because Friedrich Schirmer was dead, and because he was afraid that if Friedrich were found to have no living heir, the German Government would fake one to get the money. In fact they did produce an old man they claimed to be the heir. Mr Moreton fought the claim for over a year.'

Father Weichs was silent for a moment, then he sighed. 'Very well. How can I help you now, Mr Carey?'

'Mr Moreton said that you promised to let him know if Friedrich Schirmer's son, Johann, appeared. Did he?'

'No.'

'Do you know if any letters ever came for Friedrich Schirmer to the sanatorium where he died?'

'Up to the middle of 1940 no letter came.'

'You would have known?'

'Oh, yes. I visited the sanatorium often.'

'And after the middle of 1940?'

'The sanatorium was commandeered by the army. It became the headquarters of a training school for radio operators.'

'I see. Well, that seems to be fairly conclusive.' George stood up. 'Thanks a lot, Father.'

But Father Weichs had made a movement of protest. 'One moment, Mr Carey. You asked if Johann Schirmer came to Bad Schwennheim.'

'Yes?'

'He did not come, but his son did.'

'His son?' Slowly, George sat down again.

'He would be of interest to you, the son?'

'If he were a grandson of Friedrich Schirmer, he would interest me very much.'

Father Weichs nodded. 'He came to see me. I must explain that, when the army occupied the sanatorium, I visited the Commandant of the school to offer the services of my church to those who wished them. The Commandant was not himself of the religion, but he was sympathetic and made it as easy as possible for those who wished to come to Mass.'

He looked thoughtfully at George. 'I do not know if you served in the army, Mr Carey,' he went on after a moment or two. George nodded. 'So! Then you may have noticed that there were some men—among the young front-fighters, I mean—who were not religious, and yet found it necessary sometimes to seek some of the consolations of religion. It was when they had to find the courage to face death or mutilation, after they had seen what those things were, that the need seemed to come. Then, the elaborate materialism of the intelligent among them proved as useless and sterile as the hero myths they had brought with them from the Hitler *Jugend*. They found that they needed something else, and sometimes they went to a priest to look for it.' He smiled faintly. 'Of course, it never appeared as simple as that at the time. They came to me for many commonplace reasons, these young men—to talk about their families, to ask advice on some material problem, to borrow a book or a magazine, to show photographs they had taken, to enjoy the privacy of a garden. But the outward reason was unimportant. Though they might not always realize it, what they wanted was, in some way, to come to terms with me as a priest. They wanted something that in their hearts they thought I might be able to give them—an inner peace and strength.'

'And Schirmer's grandson was one of them?'

Father Weichs shrugged. 'I was not sure. Perhaps, yes. But I will tell you. He had been sent to the school for special training. He was a . . .'

He broke off, hesitating, and then, glancing at Miss Kolin, said the word '*Fallschirmjäger*'.

'He was a paratrooper,' she said.

The priest nodded. 'Thank you, yes. He came to see me one day in September or October—I do not quite remember. He was a tall, strong-looking young man, very much a soldier. He had been wounded in Belgium in the attack on the fortress of Eben-Emael, and was not yet well enough to return to combatant duty. He came to ask me if I knew of his grandfather, Friedrich Schirmer.'

'Did he say where his home was?' asked George, quickly.

'Yes. He came from Köln.'

'Did he say what his father's occupation was?'

'No. I cannot remember that he did.'

'Had he any brothers or sisters?'

'No, he was an only child.'

'Did he know when he came that his grandfather was dead?'

'No. It was a great disappointment to him. When he was a boy, the grandfather had lived in his parents' house and been kind to him. Then, one day, there had been a quarrel and the old man had gone.'

'Did he say how he knew that the old man had lived at Bad Schwennheim?'

'Yes. The quarrel had been serious and, after Friedrich left, his name was never mentioned by the boy's parents. But the boy loved his grandfather. Even before he went to school the old man had taught him how to write and to rule his exercise book properly. Later, the grandfather helped him with arithmetic problems and talked to him much of commercial affairs. You knew Friedrich Schirmer was a book-keeper?'

'Yes.'

'The boy did not forget him. When he was about fourteen, his parents received a letter from the old man saying that he was retiring to live at Bad Schwennheim. He had heard them discussing it. They destroyed the letter, but he remembered the name of the town, and when he was sent to the army school there he tried to find his grandfather. He did not know until I told him that, by a strange chance, he was living in the building where the old man had died.'

'I see.'

Father Weichs looked down at his hands. 'You would not have thought, to see him or speak with him, that he was a young man whom it was necessary to protect from disillusion. I think I failed him. I did not understand him until it was too late. He came to see me several times. He asked many questions about his grandfather. I saw afterwards that he wanted to make a hero of him. At the time I did not think. I answered the questions as kindly as I could. Then, one day, he asked me if I did not think that his grandfather Friedrich had been a fine and good man.' He paused and then went on slowly and carefully as if choosing words in his own defence. 'I made the best answer I could. I said that Friedrich Schirmer had been a hard-working man, and that he had suffered his long, painfull illness with patience and courage. I could say no more. The boy took my words for agreement and began to speak with great bitterness of his father who had, he said, sent the old man away in a moment of jealous hatred. I could not allow him to speak so. It was against the truth. I said that he was doing his father a great injustice, that he should go to his father and ask for the truth.' He raised his eyes and looked at George sombrely. 'He laughed. He said that he had never yet had anything from his father that was good, and would not get the truth. He went on to talk jokingly of his father as if he despised him.

Then, he went away. I did not see him again.'

Outside, on the iron balconies of the hospital, the shadows were getting longer. A clock tolled the hour.

'And what *was* the truth, Father?' asked George, quietly.

The priest shook his head. 'I was Friedrich Schirmer's confessor, Mr Carey.'

'Of course. I'm sorry.'

'It would not help you to know.'

'No, I see that. But tell me this, Father. Mr Moreton made a rough list of the documents and photographs that were found after Friedrich Schirmer's death. Was that all he had? Was nothing else ever found?'

To his surprise he saw a look of embarrassment come over the priest's face. His eyes avoided George's. For a moment or two there was something positively furtive about Father Weichs's expression.

'Old documents,' George added, quickly, 'can be very important evidence in cases like these.'

Father Weichs's jaw muscles tightened. 'There were no other documents,' he said.

'Or photographs?'

'None that could possibly have been of any value to you, Mr Carey,' the priest replied, stiffly.

'But there *were* other photographs?' George insisted.

Father Weichs's jaw muscles began to twitch. 'I repeat, Mr Carey, that they would have had no bearing on your inquiry,' he said.

' "*Would* have had"?' George echoed. 'Do you mean they no longer exist, Father?'

'I do. They no longer exist. I burnt them.'

'I see,' said George.

There was a heavy silence while they looked at one another. Then Father Weichs got to his feet with a sigh and looked out of the window.

'Friedrich Schirmer was not a pleasant man,' he said at last. 'I see no harm in telling you that. You may even have guessed from what I have already said. There were many of these photographs. They were never of importance to anyone but Friedrich Schirmer–and possibly to those from whom he bought them.'

George understood. 'Oh,' he said blankly. 'Oh, I see.' He smiled. He had a strong desire to laugh.

'He had made his peace with God,' said Father Weichs. 'It seemed kinder to destroy them. The secret lusts of the dead should end with the flesh that created them. Besides,' he added briskly, 'there is always the risk of such erotica getting into the hands of children.'

George got to his feet. 'Thanks, Father. There are just a couple more things I'd like to ask you. Did you ever know what unit of the paratroopers young Schirmer was serving in?'

'No. I regret that I did not.'

'Well, we can find that out later. What were his given names, Father, and his rank? Do you remember?'

'I only knew one name. Franz, it was, I think. Franz Schirmer. He was a Sergeant.'

Chapter Six

They stayed that night in Stuttgart. Over dinner, George summed up the results of their work.

'We can go straight to Cologne and try to find the Johann Schirmers by going through the city records,' he went on; 'or we can go after the German army records, turn up Franz Schirmer's papers and get hold of his parents' address that way.'

'Why should the army have his parents' address?'

'Well, if it were our army he'd been in, his personal file would probably show the address of his parents, or wife if he's married, as next-of-kin. Someone they can notify when you've been killed is a thing most armies like to have. What do you think?'

'Cologne is a big city, nearly a million persons before the war. But I have not been there.'

'I have. It was a mess when I saw it. What the R.A.F. didn't do to it our army did. I don't know whether the city archives were saved or not, but I'm inclined to go for the army records first just in case.'

'Very well.'

'In fact, I think the army is a better bet all round. Two birds with one stone. We'll find out what happened to Sergeant Schirmer at the same time as we trace his parents. Do you have any ideas about where his German army records would be?'

'Bonn is the West German capital. Logically they should be there now.'

'But you don't really think they will be, eh? Neither do I. Anyway, I think we'll go to Frankfurt tomorrow. I can check up with the American army people there. They'll know. Another brandy?'

'Thank you.'

A further thing he had discovered about Miss Kolin was that, although she probably consumed, in public or in the privacy of her room, over half a bottle of brandy every day, she did not seem to suffer from hangovers.

It took them nearly two weeks to find out what the German army knew about Sergeant Schirmer.

He had been born in 1917, the son of Johann Schirmer (mechanic) and Ilse his wife, both of pure German stock. From the Hitler *Jugend* he had joined the army at the age of eighteen and been promoted to Corporal in 1937. He had been transferred from the engineers to a special air training unit (*Fallschirmjäger*) in 1938, and promoted to Sergeant in the following year. At Eben-Emael, he had received a bullet wound in the shoulder from which he had satisfactorily recovered. He had taken part in the invasion of Crete and had been awarded the Iron Cross (Third Class) for distinguished conduct. In Benghazi later in that year he had suffered from dysentery and malaria. In Italy, in 1943, while acting as a parachutist instructor, he had fractured a hip. There had been a court of inquiry to determine who had been responsible for giving the order to jump over wooded country. The court had commended the Sergeant's conduct in refraining from transmitting an order he believed to be incorrect while obeying it himself. After four months in hospital and at a rehabilitation centre and a further period of sick leave, a medical board had declared him unfit for further duty as a paratrooper or any other combatant duty which called for excessive marching. He had been posted to the occupation forces in Greece. There he had served as weapons instructor to the Ninety-Fourth Garrison Regiment in a Lines of Communication Division stationed in the Salonika area, until the following year. After an action against Greek guerrillas during the withdrawal from Macedonia, he had been reported 'missing, believed killed'. The next-of-kin, Ilse Schirmer, Elsass Str. 39, Köln, had been duly notified.

They found Elsass Strasse, or what was left of it, in the remains of the old town off the Neumarkt.

Before the stick of bombs which had destroyed it had fallen, it had been a narrow street of small shops with offices above them, and a tobacco warehouse halfway along. The warehouse had obviously received a direct hit. Some of the other walls still stood, but, with the exception of three shops at one end of the street, every building in it had been gutted. Lush weeds grew now out of the old cellar floors; notices said that it was forbidden to trespass among the ruins and to deposit rubbish.

Number thirty-nine had been a garage set back from the street in a space behind two other buildings and approached by an arched drive-in between them. The arch was still standing. Fastened to its brickwork was a rusty metal sign. The words on it could be read: '*GARAGE UND REPARATURWERKSTATT. J. SCHIRMER—Bereifung, Zubehör, BENZIN.*'

They walked through the archway to the place where the garage had stood. The site had been cleared, but the plan of the building was still visible. It could not have been a very big garage. All that remained of it now was a repair pit. It was half full of rainwater, and there were pieces of an old packing-case floating in it.

As they stood there it began to rain again.

'We'd better see if we can find out anything from the shops at the end of the street,' George said.

The proprietor of the second of the shops they tried was an electrical contractor, and he had some information. He had only been there three years himself and knew nothing of the Schirmers; but he did know something about the garage site. He had considered renting it for his own use. He had wanted to put up a workshop and storeroom there, and use the rooms over his shop to live in. The ground had no street frontage, and was therefore of little value. He had thought to get it cheaply; but the owner had wanted too much, and so he had made other arrangements. The owner was a Frau Gresser, wife of a chemist in the laboratories of a big factory out at Leverkusen. When women started bargaining, you understand, it was best to . . . Yes, he had her address written down somewhere, though if the gentleman was considering the property, he personally would advise him to think twice before wasting his time arguing with . . .

Frau Gresser lived in an apartment on the top floor of a newly reconstructed building near the Barbarossa Platz. They had to call three times before they found her in.

She was a stout, frowzy, breathless woman in the late fifties. Her apartment was furnished in the cocktail-bar-functional style of pre-war Germany, and crammed with Tyrolean knick-knacks. She listened suspiciously to their explanations of their presence before inviting them to sit down. Then she went and telephoned her husband. After a while she came back and said that she was prepared to answer questions.

Ilse Schirmer, she said, had been her cousin and childhood friend.

'Are the Schirmers alive now?' George asked.

'Ilse Schirmer and her husband were killed in the big air attacks on the city in May, 1942,' Miss Kolin interpreted.

'Did Frau Gresser inherit the garage land from them?'

Frau Gresser showed signs of indignation when the question was put and spoke rapidly in reply.

'By no means. The land was hers, hers and her husband's, that is. Johann Schirmer's own business went bankrupt. She and her husband had set him up in business again for the sake of Ilse. Naturally, they had hoped also to make a profit, but it was goodness of heart that motivated them in the first place. The business, however, was theirs. Schirmer was only the manager. He had a percentage of the takings, and an apartment over the garage. No one could say that he had not been generously treated. Yet, after so much had been done for him by his wife's friends, he had tried to cheat them over the takings.'

'Who was his heir? Did he leave a will!'

'If he had anything to leave except debts, his heir would have been his son Franz.'

'Did the Schirmers have any other children?'

'Fortunately, no.'

'Fortunately?'

'It was hard enough for poor Ilse to feed and clothe one child. She was never strong, and with a husband like Schirmer, even a strong woman would have become ill.'

'What was the matter with Schirmer?'

'He was lazy, he was dishonest, he drank. When poor Ilse married him she did not know. He deceived everyone. When we met him, he had a prosperous business in Essen. We thought him clever. It was not until his father went away that the truth was known.'

'The truth?'

'It was his father, Friedrich, who had the business head. He was a good accountant, and he kept the son properly under control. Johann was only a mechanic, a workman with his hands. The father had the brains. He understood money.'

'Did Friedrich own the business?'

'It was a partnership. Friedrich had lived and worked for many years in

Switzerland. Johann was brought up there. He did not fight for Germany in the first war. Ilse met him in 1915 while she was staying with friends in Zürich. They married and remained in Switzerland to live. All their savings were in Swiss francs. In 1923, when the German mark failed, they all came back to Germany–Friedrich, Johann, Ilse and the child Franz–and bought the garage in Essen cheap with their Swiss money. Old Friedrich understood business.'

'Then Franz was born in Switzerland?'

'Winterthur is near Zürich, Mr Carey,' said Miss Kolin. 'It was mentioned in the army papers, you remember. But he would still have to apply for Swiss nationality.'

'Yes, I know all about that. Ask her why the partnership broke up.'

Frau Gresser hesitated when she heard the question.

'As she has said, Johann had no head for . . .'

Frau Gresser hesitated again and was silent. Her plump face had become red and shiny with embarrassment. At last she spoke.

'She would prefer not to discuss the matter,' said Miss Kolin.

'All right. Ask her about Franz Schirmer. Does she know what happened to him?'

He saw the relief in Frau Gresser's face when she understood that the subject of Friedrich Schirmer's departure was not going to be pursued. It made him curious.

'Franz was reported missing in Greece in 1944. The official letter addressed to his mother was forwarded to Frau Gresser.'

'The report said "missing believed killed". Did she ever receive official confirmation of his death?'

'Not officially.'

'What does she mean?'

'One of Franz's officers wrote to Frau Schirmer to tell her what had happened to her son. That letter also was forwarded to Frau Gresser. Having read it, she had no doubt that Franz was dead.'

'Did she keep the letter? Is it possible for us to see it?'

Frau Gresser considered the request for a moment; finally, she nodded and, going to a chest-of-drawers shaped as if to reduce its wind resistance, brought out a tin box full of papers. After a long search, the officer's letter was found, together with the original army casualty notification. She handed both documents to Miss Kolin, making some explanation as she did so.

'Frau Gresser wishes to explain that Franz neglected to report to the army authorities that his parents had been killed, and that it was the postal authorities who forwarded the letters.'

'I see. What's the letter say?'

'It is from Lieutenant Herman Leubner of the Engineer Company, Ninety-Fourth Garrison Regiment. It is dated the first of December, 1944.'

'What's the date that Franz was reported missing on that army notification?'

'October thirty-first.'

'All right.'

'The Lieutenant writes: "Dear Frau Schirmer. You will, no doubt, already have been notified by the army authorities of the fact that your son Sergeant Franz Schirmer has been listed as missing. I write as his officer to tell you of the circumstances in which this sad occurrence took place. It was on the twenty-fourth of October . . ."' she broke off to recheck the date.

'They were pulling out. They wouldn't trouble to send casualty returns every day,' George said.

Miss Kolin nodded. 'It continues: "The regiment was moving westwards from Salonika towards the Greek frontier in the general direction of Florina. Sergeant Schirmer, as an experienced soldier and a responsible man, was sent with three trucks and ten men to a petrol dump several kilometres off the main road near the town of Vodena. His orders were to load as much of the petrol as he could on to the trucks, destroy the remainder, and return, bringing the troops who had been guarding the dump with him. Unfortunately, his detachment was ambushed by one of the Greek terrorist bands that had been attempting to hinder our operations. Your son was in the first truck, which exploded a mine laid by the terrorists. The third truck was able to stop in time to avoid most of the machine-gun fire of the terrorists, and two men from it were able to escape and rejoin the regiment. I myself led a force immediately to the place of the ambush. Your son was not among the dead we found and buried, nor was there any other trace of him. The driver of his truck was also missing. your son was not a man to surrender unwounded. It is possible that he was rendered unconscious by the explosion of the mine and so captured. We do not know. But I would be failing in my duty if I encouraged you to hope that if he were captured by these Greeks he would be alive. They have not the military codes of honour of us Germans. It is, of course, also possible that your son evaded capture, but was unable to rejoin his comrades immediately. If so, you will be informed by the authorities when there is news of him. He was a brave man and a good soldier. If he is dead, then you will have the pride and consolation of knowing that he gave his life for his Führer and the Fatherland."'

George sighed. 'That all?'

'He adds "Heil Hitler" and signs it.'

'Ask Frau Gresser if she heard any more about it from the army authorities?'

'No, she did not.'

'Did she make any attempts to find out more? Did she try the Red Cross?'

'She was advised that the Red Cross could do nothing.'

'When did she ask them?'

'Early in 1945.'

'And not since?'

'No. She also asked the *Volksbund Deutsche Kriegsgräberfürsorge*—that is the war graves organization—for information. They had none.'

'Was any application ever made to have him presumed dead?'

'There was no reason for such action.'

'Does she know if he married?'

'No.'

'Did she ever correspond with him?'

'The Christmases of 'forty and 'forty-one she wrote a letter of sympathy to him when his parents were killed, but received no more than a bare acknowledgment from him. He did not even ask where they were buried. He showed a want of feeling, she thought. She sent him a parcel soon afterwards. He did not trouble to write to thank her for it. She sent no more.'

'Where did his reply come from in 1942?'

'From Benghazi.'

'Did she keep any of his letters?'

'No.'

Frau Gresser spoke again. George watched her plump face quivering and her small, resentful eyes flickering between her two visitors. He was getting used now to interpretation and had learned not to try to anticipate the translation while he waited. He was thinking at the moment that it would be unpleasant to be under any sort of obligation to Frau Gresser. The rate of emotional interest she would charge would be exorbitantly high.

'She says,' said Miss Kolin, 'that she did not like Franz, and had never liked him even as a child. He was a sullen, sulky boy, and always ungrateful for kindness. She wrote to him only as a duty to his dead mother.'

'How did he feel about foreigners? Had he any particular girl friends? What I'm getting at is this—does she think he'd be the kind of man to marry a Greek girl, say, or an Italian, if he had the chance?'

Frau Gresser's reply was prompt and sour.

'She says that, where women were concerned, he was the sort of man who would do anything that his selfish nature suggested. He would do anything if he had the chance—except marry.'

'I see. All right, I think that's about the lot. Would you ask her if we can borrow these papers for twenty-four hours to have photostats made?'

Frau Gresser considered the request carefully. Her small eyes became opaque. George could feel the documents suddenly becoming precious to her.

'I'll give her a receipt for them, of course, and they'll be returned tomorrow,' he said. 'Tell her the American Consul will have to notarize the copies or she could have them back today.'

Frau Gresser handed them over reluctantly. While he was writing the receipt George remembered something.

'Miss Kolin, have another try at finding out why Friedrich Schirmer left the business at Essen.'

'Very well.'

He lingered over the writing out of the receipt. He heard Miss Kolin put the question. There was a momentary pause, then Frau Gresser replied with a positive volley of words. Her voice rose steadily in pitch as she spoke. Then she stopped. He signed the receipt and looked up to find her staring at him in a flustered, accusing sort of way. He handed her the receipt and put the documents in his pocket.

'She says,' said Miss Kolin, 'that the matter is not one which can be discussed in the presence of a man, and that it can have no bearing on your inquiries. She adds, however, that if you do not believe that she is telling the truth, she will make the explanation confidentially to me. She will say no more on the subject while you are here.'

'O.K. I'll wait for you downstairs.' He rose and bowed to Frau Gresser. 'Thank you very much indeed, madam. What you have told me is of inestimable help. I will see that your papers are safely returned to you tomorrow. Good day.'

He smiled affably, bowed again and went. He was outside the apartment almost before Miss Kolin had finished interpreting his farewell speech.

She joined him in the street below ten minutes later.

'Well,' he said, 'what was it all about?'

'Friedrich made advances to Ilse Schirmer.'

'To his son's wife, you mean?'

'Yes.'

'Well, well. Did she go into details?'

'Yes. She enjoys herself that one.'

'But the old man must have been around sixty then.'

'You remember the photographs that Father Weichs destroyed?'

'Yes.'

'He showed them to the wife.'

'Just that?'

'His meaning apparently was unmistakable. He also proposed in a veiled way that he should take similar photographs of her.'

'I see.' George tried to picture the scene.

He saw a shabby room in Essen, and an elderly bookkeeper sitting there pushing dog-eared photographs, one by one, across the table to where his son's wife could see them as she sat bent over her needlework.

How the man's heart must have beat as he watched her face! His mind must have seethed with questions and doubts.

Would she smile or would she pretend to be shocked? She was sitting still, absolutely still, and she had stopped working. Soon she would smile, for certain. He could not see her eyes. After all, there was nothing wrong in a little private joke between a father and daughter-in-law, was there? She was a grown-up woman, and knew a thing or two, didn't she? She liked him, he knew. All he wanted to do was show her that he wasn't too old for a bit of fun and that, even if Johann were no good, there was one man about the house for her to turn to. And now the last photograph, the sauciest of the lot. An eye-opener, eh? Good fun? She still hadn't smiled, but she hadn't frowned either. Women were funny creatures. You had to choose your moment; woo gently and then be bold. She was slowly raising her head now and looking at him. Her eyes were very round. He smiled and said what he had planned to say; that subtle remark about new pictures being better than old. But she did not smile back. She was getting to her feet and he could see that she was trembling. With what? Excitement? And then, suddenly, she had let out a sob of fear and run from the room out to the workshop where Johann was decarbonizing that Opel taxi. After that everything had become a nightmare, with Johann shouting at and threatening him, and Ilse weeping, and the boy Franz standing there listening, white-faced, not understanding what it was all about; only knowing that in some way the world was coming to an end.

Yes, George thought, a pretty picture; though probably an inaccurate one. Still, it was the sort of scene about which nobody could ever be quite accurate; least of all those who had taken part in it. He would never know what had really happened. Not that it mattered very much. Friedrich, Johan and Ilse, the principal actors, were certainly dead. And Franz? He glanced at Miss Kolin marching along beside him.

'Do you think Franz is dead?' he asked.

'The evidence seemed conclusive. Did you not think so?'

'In a way, yes. If the man had been a friend of mine and had a wife and family he was fond of back home, I wouldn't try to kid his wife that he might still be alive. And if she were crazy enough to go on believing that he wasn't dead, I'd tell her as gently as I could to face the facts. But this is different. If we took the evidence we've got to court and asked for leave to presume Franz Schirmer dead, they'd laugh at us.'

'I do not see why.'

'Look. The man's in a truck ambushed by these guerrillas. That Lieutenant comes along some time afterwards and has a look at the scene. There are lots of dead bodies about, but not the dead body of our man. So maybe he's escaped and maybe he's a prisoner. If he's a prisoner, says the Lieutenant, then he hasn't a hope because the Greek guerrillas had the habit of killing their prisoners. "Just a minute," says the judge; "are you claiming that *all* Greek guerrillas operating in 1944 *invariably* killed *all* their prisoners? Are you prepared to prove that there were no cases at all of German soldiers surviving after capture?" What does the Lieutenant say to that? I don't know anything about the Greek campaign–I wasn't there–but I do know if all those guerrillas were so well-trained and so well-organized and so trigger-happy that no German who fell into their hands was ever smart enough or lucky enough to get away with it, they'd have had the Germans pulling out of Greece long before the Normandy landings. All right then, let's alter the wording of the evidence. Let's say that Greek guerrillas *often* kill their prisoners. Now then . . .'

'But do you think he is *not* dead?' she asked.

'Of course I think he's dead. I'm just trying to point out there's a whole lot of difference between an ordinary everyday probability and the calculated kind that the law prefers. And the law's right. You'd be surprised how often people turn up when they've been thought dead. A man gets fired from his job and quarrels with his wife. So he goes down to the shore, takes off his coat, leaves it with a suicide note on the beach and that's the last seen of him. Dead? Maybe. But sometimes he's found by accident, years later, living under a different name, and with a different wife, in a city on the other side of the world.'

She shrugged. 'This is different.'

'Not so very. Look at it this way. It's 1944. Let's suppose that Franz Schirmer is captured by the guerrillas, but by luck or skill manages to get away alive. What is he to do? Rejoin his unit? The German occupation forces are trying to escape through Yugoslavia, and having a tough time doing it. If he leaves his hide-out and tries to catch them up, he's certain to be recaptured by the guerrillas. They're all over the place now. It's better to stay where he is for a while. He is a resourceful man, trained to live off the country. He can stay alive. When it is safe for him to do so, he will go. Time passes. The country is under Greek control once again. Hundreds of miles now separate him from the nearest German unit. Civil war breaks out in Greece. In the resultant confusion, he is able to make his way to the Turkish frontier and cross it without being caught. He is an engineer and does not mind work. He takes a job.'

'By February, 1945, Turkey was at war with Germany.'

'Maybe it's before February.'

'Then why does he not report to the German Consul?'

'Why should he? Germany is collapsing. The war is virtually over. Maybe he likes it where he is. Anyway, what has he to return to post-war Germany for? To see Frau Gresser? To see what's left of his parents' home? Maybe he married an Italian girl when he was in Italy and wants to get back there. He may even have children. There are dozens of possible reasons why he shouldn't go to the German Consul. Maybe he went to the Swiss one.'

'If he had married, his army record would show it.'

'Not if he married someone he wasn't supposed to marry. Look at the rules the Americans and British had about their troops marrying German girls.'

'What do you propose?'

'I don't know yet. I'll have to think.'

When he got back to the hotel, he sat down and wrote a long cable to Mr Sistrom. First, he set out briefly the latest developments in the inquiry, then he asked for instructions. Should he return home now or should he go on and make an attempt to confirm Franz Schirmer's death?

The following afternoon he had the reply.

'HAVING LOOKED UNDER SO MANY STONES', it said, 'SEEMS PITY LEAVE ONE UNTURNED STOP GO AHEAD TRY CONFIRM OR OTHERWISE FRANZ DEATH STOP SUGGEST GIVING IT THREE WEEKS STOP IF IN YOUR JUDGMENT NO SERIOUS HEADWAY MADE OR LIKELY BY THEN LETS FORGET IT. SISTROM.'

That night, George and Miss Kolin left Cologne for Geneva.

Miss Kolin had interpreted at conferences for the International Red Cross Committee and knew the people at headquarters who could be of help. George was soon put in touch with an official who had been in Greece for the Red Cross in 1944; a lean, mournful Swiss who looked as if nothing again could ever surprise him. He spoke good English, and four other languages besides. His name was Hagen.

'There is no doubt at all, Mr Carey,' he said, 'that the *andartes* did often kill their prisoners. I am not saying that they did it simply because they hated the enemy or because they had a taste for killing, you understand. It is difficult to see what else they could have done much of the time. A guerrilla band of thirty men or less is in no position to guard and feed the people they take. Besides, Macedonia is in the Balkan tradition and, there, the killing of an enemy can seem of small importance.'

'But why take prisoners? Why not kill them at once?'

'Usually they were taken for questioning.'

'If you were in my position, how would you go about establishing the death of this man?'

'Well, as you know where the ambush took place, you might try getting in touch with some of the *andartes* who were operating in that area. They might remember the incident. But I think I should say that you may find it difficult to persuade them to refresh their memories. Was it an ELAS band, do you know, or an EDES?'

'EDES?'

'The Greek initials stand for the National Democratic Liberation Army—the anti-Communist *andartes*. ELAS were the Communist *andartes*—the National Popular Liberation Army. In the Vodena area it would most likely be ELAS.'

'Does it matter which it was?'

'It matters a great deal. There have been three years of civil war in Greece, you must remember. Now that the rebellion is over, those who fought on the Communist side are not easy to find. Some are dead, some in prison, some in hiding still. Many are refugees in Albania and Bulgaria. As things are, you would probably find it difficult to get in touch with ELAS men. It is complex.

'Yes, it sounds it. What real chance would there be, do you think, of my finding out what I want to know?'

Monsieur Hagen shrugged. 'Often in such matters I have seen chance operate so strangely that I no longer try to estimate it. How important is your business, Mr Carey?'

'There is a good deal of money at stake.'

The other sighed. 'So many things could have happened. You know, there were hundreds of men reported "missing, believed killed" who had simply deserted. Salonika had plenty of German deserters towards the end of 1944.'

'Plenty?'

'Oh, yes, of course. ELAS recruited most of them. There were many Germans fighting for the Greek Communists around Christmas of that year.'

'Do you mean to say that in late 1944 a German soldier could go about in Greece *without* getting killed?'

A pale smile drifted across Monsieur Hagen's mournful face. 'In Salonika, you could see German soldiers sitting in the cafés and walking about the streets.'

'In uniform?'

'Yes, or part uniform. It was a curious situation. During the war, the Communists in Yugoslavia, Greece and Bulgaria had agreed to create a new Macedonian state. It was all part of a larger Russian plan for a Balkan Communist Federation. Well, the moment the Germans had gone, a force called the Macedonian Group of Divisions of ELAS took over Salonika and prepared to put the plan into execution. They didn't care any more about Germans. They had a new enemy to fight—the lawful Greek Government. What they wanted to fight with were trained soldiers. It was Vafiades who had the idea of recruiting German deserters. He was the ELAS commander in Salonika then.'

'Can't I get in touch with this Vafiades?' George asked.

He saw Miss Kolin stare at him. Monsieur Hagen now wore an expression of anxious perplexity.

'I'm afraid that would be a little difficult, Mr Carey.'

'Why? Is he dead?'

'Well, there seems to be some doubt as to just what has happened to him.' Monsieur Hagen seemed to be choosing his words. 'The last we heard of him directly was in 1948. He then told a group of foreign journalists that, as head of the Provisional Democratic Government of Free Greece, he proposed to establish a capital on Greek soil. That was just about the time his army captured Karpenissi, I believe.'

George looked blankly at Miss Kolin.

'Markos Vafiades called himself General Markos,' she murmured. 'He commanded the Greek Communist rebel army in the civil war.'

'Oh, I see.' George felt himself reddening. 'I told you I didn't know anything about the Greek set-up,' he said. 'I'm afraid this kind of name-dropping misses with me.'

Monsieur Hagen smiled, 'Of course, Mr Carey. We are closer to these things here. Vafiades was a Turkish-born Greek, a tobacco worker before the war. He was a Communist of many years standing, and had been to prison on that account. No doubt he had a respect for revolutionary tradition. When the Communists gave him command of the rebel army he decided to be known simply as Markos. It has only two syllables, and is more dramatic. If the rebels had won he might have become as big a man as Tito. As it was, if you will forgive the comparison, he had something in common with your General Lee. He won his battles but lost the war. And for the same kind of reasons. For Lee, the loss of Vicksburg and Atlanta, especially Atlanta, meant the destruction of his lines of communication. For Markos, also faced by superior numbers, the closing of the Yugoslav frontier had the same sort of effect. As long as the Communists of Yugoslavia, Bulgaria and Albania helped him, he was in a strong position. By retiring across those frontiers, he was able to break off any action that looked like developing unfavourably. Then, behind the frontier, he could regroup and reorganize in safety, gather reinforcements and appear again with deadly effect on a weakly-held sector of the Government front. When Tito quarrelled with Stalin and withdrew his support of the Macedonian plan, he cut Markos's lateral lines of communication in two. Greece owes much to Tito.'

'But wouldn't Markos have been beaten in the end, anyway?'

Monsieur Hagen made a doubtful face. 'Maybe. British and American aid did much. I do not dispute that. The Greek Army and Air Force were completely transformed. But the denial of the Yugoslav frontier to Markos made it possible to use that power quickly and decisively. In January of 1949, after over two years' fighting, the Markos forces were in possession of Naoussa, a big industrial town only eighty miles from Salonika itself. Nine months' later, they were beaten. All that was left was a pocket of resistance on Mount Grammos, near the Albanian frontier.'

'I see.' George smiled. 'Well, there doesn't seem to be much likelihood of my being able to talk to General Vafiades, does there?'

'I'm afraid not, Mr Carey.'

'And even if I could, there wouldn't be much sense in my asking him about a German sergeant who got caught in an ambush in 1944.'

Monsieur Hagen bowed his head politely. 'None.'

'So let me get it straight, sir. In 1944, the guerrillas–*andartes,* you call them, do you?—the *andartes* killed some Germans and recruited others. Is that right?'

'Certainly.'

'So that if the German soldier I'm interested in managed to get away alive after that ambush, it would not be fantastic to give him a fifty-fifty chance of staying alive?'

'Not at all fantastic. Very reasonable.'

'I see. Thanks.'

Two days later George and Miss Kolin were in Greece.

Chapter Seven

'Forty-five thousand killed including three thousand five hundred civilians murdered by the rebels, and seven hundred blown up by their mines. Twice as many wounded. Eleven thousand houses destroyed. Seven hundred thousand persons driven from their homes in rebel areas. Twenty-eight thousand forcibly removed to Communist countries. Seven thousand villages looted. That is what Markos and his friends cost Greece.'

Colonel Chrysantos paused and, leaning back in his swivel chair, smiled bitterly at George and Miss Kolin. It was an effective pose. He was a very handsome man with keen, dark eyes. 'And I have heard it said by the British and the Americans,' he added, 'that we have been too firm with our Communists. Too firm!' He threw up his long, thin hands.

George murmured vaguely. He knew that the Colonel's ideas of what constituted firmness were very different from his own, and that a discussion of them would not be profitable. Monsieur Hagen, the Red Cross man, who had given him the letter of introduction to Colonel Chrysantos, had made the position clear. The Colonel was a desirable acquaintance only in so far as he was a senior officer in the Salonika branch of Greek Military Intelligence, who could lay his hands on the kind of information George needed. He was not a person toward whom it was possible to have very friendly feelings.

'Do these casualty figures include the rebels, Colonel?' he asked.

'Of the killed, yes. Twenty-eight of the forty-five thousand were rebels. About their wounded, we have naturally no accurate figures; but in addition to those we killed, we captured thirteen thousand, and twenty-seven thousand more surrendered.'

'Do you have lists of the names?'

'Certainly.'

'Would it be possible to see if the name of this German is on one of those lists?'

'Of course. But you know we did not take more than a handful of Germans.'

'Still it might be worth trying, though, as I say, I don't even know yet if the man survived the ambush.'

'Ah, yes. Now we come to that. The twenty-fourth of October, 1944, was the date of the ambush, you say, and it was near a petrol point at Vodena. The *andartes* might have come from the Florina area, I think. We shall see. So!'

He pressed a button on his desk and a young Lieutenant with horn-rimmed glasses came in. The Colonel spoke sharply in his own language for nearly half a minute. When he stopped, the Lieutenant uttered a monosyllable, and went out.

As the door shut the Colonel relaxed. 'A good boy, that,' he said. 'You westerners sometimes pride yourselves that we cannot be efficient, but you will see—like that!' He snapped his fingers, smiled seductively at Miss Kolin, and then glanced at George to see if he minded having his girl smiled at in that way.

Miss Kolin merely raised her eyebrows. The Colonel passed round cigarettes.

George found the situation entertaining. The Colonel's curiosity about the nature of the relationship between his visitors had been evident from the first. The woman was attractive; the man looked passably virile; it was absurd to suppose that they could travel about together on business without also taking advantage of the association for their pleasure. Yet, of course, the man was an Anglo-Saxon, and so one could not be sure. In the absence of any positive evidence as to whether the pair were lovers or not, the Colonel was beginning to probe for some. He would try again in a moment or two. Meanwhile, back to business.

The Colonel smoothed his tunic down. 'This German of yours, Mr Carey—was he an Alsatian?'

'No, he came from Cologne.'

'Many of the deserters were Alsatian. You know, some of them hated the Germans as much as we did.'

'Ah, yes? Were you in Greece during the war, Colonel?'

'Sometimes. At the beginning, yes. Later, I was with the British. In their raiding forces. It was a type of Commando, you understand. That was a happy time.'

'Happy?'

'Were you not a soldier, Mr Carey?'

'I was a bomber pilot. I don't remember ever feeling particularly happy about it.'

'Ah, no—but the air is different from soldiering. You do not see the enemy you kill. A machine war. Impersonal.'

'It was personal enough for me,' George said; but the remark went unheard. There was the light of reminiscence in the Colonel's eyes.

'You missed much in the air, Mr Carey,' he said, dreamily. 'I remember once, for example . . .'

He was off.

He had taken part, it seemed, in numerous British raids on German garrisons on Greek territory. He went on to describe in great detail what he obviously felt to be some of his more amusing experiences. Judging by the relish with which he recalled them, he had indeed had a happy time.

'. . . splashed his brains over the wall with a burst from a Bren gun . . . put my knife low in his belly and ripped it open to the ribs . . . the grenades killed all of them in the room except one so I dropped him out of the window . . . ran away without their trousers so we could see what to shoot at . . . tried to come out of the house to surrender, but he was slow on his feet, and the phosphorus grenade set him alight like a torch . . . I let him have a burst from the Sten and nearly cut him in two . . .'

He spoke rapidly, smiling all the time and gesturing gracefully. Occasionally he broke into French. George made little attempt to follow. It did not matter, for the Colonel's whole attention now was concentrated on Miss Kolin. She was wearing her faintly patronizing smile, but there was something more in her expression besides—a look of pleasure. If you had been watching the pair of them without knowing what was being said, George thought, you might have supposed that the handsome Colonel was entertaining her with a witty piece of cocktail-party gossip. It was rather disconcerting.

The Lieutenant came back into the room with a tattered folder of papers under his arm. The Colonel stopped instantly and sat up straight in his chair to receive the folder. He looked through it sternly as the Lieutenant made his report. Once he rapped out a question and received an answer which appeared to satisfy him. Finally, he nodded, and the Lieutenant went out. The Colonel relaxed again and smirked complacently.

'It will take time to check the lists of prisoners,' he said; 'but as I hoped, we have some other information. Whether it will be of help to you or not, I cannot say.' He glanced down at the bundle of torn and greasy papers before him. 'This ambush you mention was most likely one of several operations undertaken in that week by an ELAS band based in the hills above Florina. There were thirty-four men, most of them from Florina and the villages about there. The leader was a Communist, named Phengaros. He came from Larisa. A German army truck was destroyed in the action. Does that sound like the case you know of?'

George nodded. 'That's it. There were three trucks. The first hit a mine. Does it say anything about any prisoners?'

'Prisoners would not be reported, Mr Carey. Fortunately, however, you can ask.'

'Ask whom?'

'Phengaros.' The Colonel grinned. 'He was captured in 1948. We have him under lock and key.'

'Still?'

'Oh, he was released under an amnesty, but he is back now. He is a Party member, Mr Carey, and a dangerous one. A brave man, perhaps, and a good one for killing Germans, but such politicals do not change their ways. You are lucky he has not long ago been shot.'

'I was wondering why he wasn't.'

'One could not shoot all of these rebels,' the Colonel said with a shrug. 'We are not Germans or Russkis. Besides, your friends in Geneva would not have liked it.'

'Where can I see this man?'

'Here in Salonika. I shall have to speak to the commandant of the prison. Do you know your Consul here?'

'Not yet, but I have a letter to him from our Embassy in Athens.'

'Ah, good. I will tell the Commandant that you are a friend of the American Ambassador. That should be sufficient.'

'What exactly is this man Phengaros in prison for?'

The Colonel referred to the folder. 'Jewel robbery, Mr Carey.'

'I thought you said he was a political prisoner.'

'In America, Mr Carey, your criminals are all capitalists. Here, in these times, they are occasionally Communists. Men like Phengaros do not steal for themselves, but for the Party funds. Of course, if we catch them they go to the criminal prison. They cannot be sent to the islands as politicals. They have made some big coups lately. It is quite traditional. Even the great Stalin robbed a bank for the Party funds when he was a young man. Of course, there are some of these bandits from the hills who only pretend to rob for the Party, and keep what they get for themselves. They are clever and dangerous, and the police do not catch them. But Phengaros is not of that kind. He is a simple, deluded fanatic of the type that always gets caught.'

'When can I see him?'

'Tomorrow, perhaps. We shall see.' He pressed the button again for the Lieutenant. 'Tell me,' he said, 'are you and Madame by chance without an engagement this evening? I should so much like to show you our city.'

Twenty minutes later, George and Miss Kolin left the building and came again into the heat and glare of a Salonika afternoon. George's excuse that he had a long report to write that evening had been accepted with ready understanding. Miss Kolin had seemed to have rather more difficulty in evading the Colonel's hospitality. The conversation, however, had been conducted in Greek and George had understood nothing of it.

They crossed to the shade on the other side of the street.

'How did you manage to get out of it?' he asked as they turned towards the hotel.

'I explained that my stomach was upset by the food and the flies, and that I should probably be sick all night.'

George laughed.

'I spoke the truth.'

'Oh, I'm sorry. Do you think you ought to see a doctor?'

'It will pass off. You have no stomach trouble yet?'

'No.'

'It will come later. This is a bad place for the stomach when one is not used to it.'

'Miss Kolin,' George said after a while, 'what did you really think of Colonel Chrysantos?'

'What can one think of such a man?'

'You didn't like him? He was very helpful and obliging.'

'Yes, no doubt. It soothes his vanity to be helpful. There is only one thing that pleases me about that Colonel.'

'Oh?'

She walked on several paces in silence. Then she spoke quietly; so quietly, that he only just heard what she said.

'He knows how to deal with Germans, Mr Carey.'

It was at that moment that George received the first intimations of coming discomfort in his stomach and intestines. At that moment also, he forgot about Colonel Chrysantos and Germans.

'I begin to see what you mean about the food and the flies,' he remarked as they turned the corner by the hotel. 'I think, if you don't mind, that we'll call in at a drugstore.'

The following day, the Colonel's Lieutenant arrived at their hotel in an army car and drove them out to the prison.

It was a converted barracks, built near the remains of an old Turkish fort on the western outskirts of the city. With its high surrounding wall and the Kalamara Heights across the bay as a background, it looked from the outside rather like a monastery. Inside, it smelt like a large and inadequately tended latrine.

The Lieutenant had brought papers admitting them, and they were taken to the administration block. Here they were introduced to a civilian official in a tight tussore suit, who apologized for the absence of the Commandant on official business, and offered coffee and cigarettes. He was a thin, anxious man, with a habit of picking his nose, of which he seemed to be trying, none too successfully, to break himself. When they had had their coffee, he took a heavy bunch of keys and led them through a series of passages with steel doors at both ends which he unlocked and relocked as they went along. They were shown eventually into a room with whitewashed walls and a steel grille running down the middle from floor to ceiling. Through the grille they could see another door.

The official looked apologetic and mumbled something in bad French.

'Phengaros,' Miss Kolin translated, 'is not a good prisoner and sometimes behaves violently. The Commandant would not wish us to be exposed to any trouble. It is for that reason that the interview must take place in these uncomfortable surroundings. He apologizes for them.'

George nodded. He was not at ease. He had spent a disagreeable and exhausting night, and the smell of the place was making it difficult for him to forget the fact. Moreover, he had never been inside a prison before, and, while he had not supposed the experience would be anything but depressing, he had been unprepared for the lively sense of personal guilt that it aroused.

There was a sound from the door beyond the grille, and he looked round. A Judas window had opened in it, and a face was peering through. Then, a key turned in the lock and the door opened. A man slowly entered the room.

The prisoner was thin and sinewy, with dark, sunken eyes, and a long beak of a nose. His skin was brown and leathery, as if he worked a lot in the sun. His shaven head had a black stubble of growth on it. He wore a cotton singlet and canvas trousers tied in at the waist with a strip of rag. His feet were bare.

He hesitated when he saw the faces on the other side of the grille, and the warder behind him prodded him with a club. He came forward into the light. The warder locked the door and stood with his back to it. The official nodded to George.

'Ask him what his name is,' George said to Miss Kolin.

She relayed the question. The prisoner licked his lips, his dark eyes looking beyond her at the men, as if she were the bait in a trap of their devising. He looked from her to the official and muttered something.

'What is the game?' Miss Kolin translated. 'You know my name well enough. Who is this woman?'

The official shouted something at him violently, and the warder prodded him again with the club.

George spoke quickly. 'Miss Kolin, explain to him in as friendly a way as you can that I am an American lawyer, and that my business has nothing to do with him personally. It is a private, a legal matter. Say we only want to question him about that ambush at Vodena. There is no political angle to it. Our only object in questioning him is to confirm the death of a German soldier reported missing in 1944. Make it good.'

As she spoke, George watched the prisoner's face. The dark eyes flickered suspiciously towards him as she went on. When she had finished, the prisoner thought for a moment. Then, he answered.

'He will listen to the questions and decide whether he will answer when he has heard them.'

Behind George the Lieutenant was beginning to mutter angrily to the official. George took no notice.

'O.K.,' he said, 'ask him his name. He's got to identify himself.'

'Phengaros.'

'Ask him if he remembers the ambush of the trucks.'

'Yes, he remembers.'

'He was in command of those particular *andartes*?'

'Yes.'

'What happened, exactly?'

'He does not know. He was not there.'

'But he said . . .'

'He was leading an attack on the petrol dump at the time. It was his second-in-command who caught the trucks.'

'Where is his second-in-command?'

'Dead. He was shot a few months later by the Fascist murder gangs in Athens.'

'Oh. Well, ask him if he knows of any German prisoners taken from the trucks.'

Phengaros thought for a moment, then nodded. 'Yes. One.'

'Did he see this prisoner?'

'He interrogated him.'

'What rank was he?'

'A Private, he thinks. The man was the driver of the truck that hit the mine. He was wounded.'

'Is he sure that there was no other prisoner?'

'Yes.'

'Tell him we have information that there were two men in that first truck who did not return, and whose bodies were not found by the German party that came on the scene later. One was the driver of the truck, who he says he interrogated. The other was the Sergeant in charge of the detachment. We want to know what happened to the Sergeant.'

Phengaros began gesturing emphatically as he talked.

'He says he was not there, but that if there had been a German Sergeant alive his men would certainly have taken him prisoner for questioning. A Sergeant would have more information to give than a driver.'

'What happened to the driver?'

'He died.'

'How?'

There was a hesitation. 'Of his wounds.'

'O.K., we'll skip that. When he served in the army of General Markos, did he come across any Germans fighting with it?'

'A few.'

'Any whose names he can remember?'

'No.'

'Ask him if he knows of anyone who actually took part in the truck ambush who's still alive.'

'He knows of nobody.'

'Surely they can't *all* be dead. Ask him to try and remember.'

'He knows of nobody.'

Phengaros was no longer looking at Miss Kolin now but staring straight ahead.

There was a pause. George felt a touch on his arm. The Lieutenant drew him aside.

'Mr Carey, this man does not wish to give information that might compromise his friends,' he said in English.

'Oh, I see. Of course.'

'Excuse me for a moment, please.'

The Lieutenant went to the official and held a whispered conversation with him. Then he returned to George.

'The information might be obtained for you, Mr Carey,' he murmured, 'but it would take time to do so.'

'How do you mean?'

'This Phengaros is a difficult man to persuade, it seems, but, if you wish, some disciplinary pressure might be applied . . .'

'No, no.' George spoke hastily; his knees were beginning to tremble. 'Unless he gives the information quite voluntarily it can have no legal value as evidence.' It was a dishonest excuse. Phengaros's evidence had no legal value, anyway; it was the evidence of eye-witnesses (if any) that would be important. But George could think of nothing better.

'As you please. Is there anything else you wish to ask?' The Lieutenant's manner was bored now. He had seen through George. If the inquiry could be pursued with such lily-livered timidity, it could not be of very great importance.

'I don't think so, thanks.' George turned to Miss Kolin. 'Ask this prison man if it's against the rules to give the prisoner some cigarettes.'

The official stopped picking his nose when he heard the question. Then, he shrugged. If the American wished to waste cigarettes on such an unco-operative type he might do so; but they must be examined first.

George took out a packet of cigarettes and handed it to him. The official glanced inside, pinched the packet and handed it back. George held it through the grille.

Phengaros had been standing there with a faint smile on his face. His eyes met George's. With an ironic bow he took the cigarettes. As he did so he began to speak.

'I understand the feelings of embarrassment that prompt you to offer this gift, sir,' translated Miss Kolin. 'If I were a criminal I would gladly accept them. But the fate of my comrades at the hands of the fascist reactionaries already rests too lightly on the conscience of the world. If your own conscience is troubling you, sir, that is to your credit. I am not yet so corrupted here as to allow you to ease it for the price of a packet of cigarettes. No. Much as I should have enjoyed smoking them, sir, I think that their destination must be that of all other American aid.'

With a flick of his wrist he tossed the cigarettes to the warder behind him.

They fell to the floor. As the warder snatched them up, the official began shouting to him angrily through the grille, and he hastened to unlock the door.

Phengaros nodded curtly and went out.

The official stopped shouting and turned apologetically to George. '*Une espèce de fausse-couche*,' he said; '*je vous demande pardon, Monsieur.*'

'What for?' said George. 'If he thinks I'm a lousy crypto-fascist imperialist lackey, he's quite right in refusing to smoke my cigarettes.'

'*Pardon?*'

'He also had the good manners not to heave the cigarettes right back in my face. In his place, I might have done just that.'

'*Qu'est ce que Monsieur a dit?*'

The official was looking desperately at Miss Kolin.

George shook his head. 'Don't bother to translate, Miss Kolin. He won't get it. You understand me, though, don't you, Lieutenant? Yes, I thought so. Now if you don't mind, I'd like to get the hell out of here before something very inconvenient happens inside my stomach.'

When they got back to the hotel there was a note from Colonel Chrysantos awaiting them. It contained the information that a search of all the relevant lists had failed to discover anybody named Schirmer who had been either killed or captured in the Markos campaign; nor had an amnesty been granted to anyone of that name.

'Miss Kolin,' George said, 'what can you drink when you have this stomach thing?'

'Cognac is the best thing.'

'Then we'd better have some.'

Later, when the experiment had been tried, he said: 'When we were in Cologne my office gave me permission to go on with the investigation for three more weeks, if I thought we were making progress. One of them's gone, and all we've found out is that Franz Schirmer most likely didn't get taken prisoner by the people who shot up the trucks.'

'Surely, that is something.'

'It's mildly interesting at best. It doesn't get us anywhere. I'm giving it one more week. If we're no nearer the truth by then, we go home. O.K.?'

'Perfectly. What will you do with the week?'

'Do what I have an idea I should have done before. Go to Vodena and look for his grave.'

Chapter Eight

Vodena, which used to be called Edessa and was once the seat of the Kings of Macedon, is some fifty miles west of Salonika. It hangs, amid lush growths of vine and wild pomegranate, fig and mulberry trees, in the foothills of Mount Chakirka six hundred feet above the Yiannitsa Plain. Sparkling mountain streams cascade lyrically down the hillsides into Nisia Voda, the tributary of the Vadar which flows swiftly past the town on its way to the parent river. The old tiled houses glow in the sun. There are no tourist hotels.

George and Miss Kolin were driven there in a car hired in Salonika. It was not an enjoyable trip. The day was hot and the road bad. The condition of their stomachs denied them even the consolation of a good lunch and a bottle of wine at their destination. While the chauffeur went off heartily in search of food and wine, they went into a café, fought the flies for long enough to drink some brandy and then dragged themselves off dispiritedly in search of information.

Almost immediately luck was with them. A sweetmeat pedlar in the market not only remembered the ambush well, but had actually been working in a nearby vineyard at the time. He had been warned to keep clear by the *andartes* who had arrived an hour before the German trucks came.

When the chauffeur returned, they persuaded the pedlar to leave his tray of fly-blown titbits with a friend and guide them to the scene.

The fuel dump had been near a railway siding about three miles out of Vodena, on the side road to Apsalos. The trucks had been caught about two miles along this stretch of road.

It was an ideal place for an ambush. The road was climbing steadily, and at that point made a hairpin turn below a hillside with plenty of cover for the attackers among its trees and thickets. Below and beyond the road there was no cover at all. The mines had been placed well past the turn, so that when the first truck hit it would block the road for those following. At that point they could neither turn their vehicles nor find cover from which to reply to the fire from above. For the *andartes* concealed on the hillside the business must have been easy. The remarkable thing was that as many as two of the eleven Germans in the truck had managed to get back down the road alive. They must have been exceptionally nimble or the fire from the hillside very wild.

Those who had died had been buried lower down the hill in a patch of level ground just off the road. According to the pedlar, the ground had been damp with rain at the time. The neat row of graves was still discernible in the undergrowth. Lieutenant Leubner and his men had piled a small cairn of stones on each. George had seen wayside German graves in France and Italy and guessed that originally each grave had also borne its occupant's steel helmet, and perhaps a wooden stake with his number, name and rank. It depended on how much time there had been to spare for such refinements. He looked for the stakes, but if they had ever existed there was now no sign of them. Under a nearby bush he found a rusty German helmet; that was all.

'Seven graves,' remarked Miss Kolin as they walked up the hill again; 'that is what one would expect from the Lieutenant's letter to Frau Schirmer. Ten men and the Sergeant went. Two men return. The bodies of the Sergeant and the driver of the first truck are missing. Seven are buried.'

'Yes, but Phengaros said that there was only one prisoner–the driver. So where was the Sergeant? Look! The driver was wounded when the truck hit the mine, but not killed. Most likely the Sergeant was in the cab beside him. Probably he was wounded, too. Lieutenant Leubner said he wasn't a man to surrender without a fight. Supposing he managed somehow to get clear of the road and was hunted down and killed some distance from it.'

'But how, Mr Carey? How could he get clear?'

They had reached the place of the ambush again. George walked along the edge of the road away from the hillside and looked down.

The bare rocky ground fell away precipitously to the valley below. It was absurd to suppose that even an unwounded man would attempt to scramble down it under fire from the hillside and the road above. The two men who had escaped had been able to do so because they had been in the last truck. The Sergeant had been a full two hundred yards farther away from cover. He had had no chance at all of getting clear.

George climbed a short way up the hillside to look at the scene from the attackers' point of view. From there, the plight of the men in the trucks seemed even more hopeless. He could imagine the scene: the trucks grinding up the hill, the ear-splitting detonation of the mine, the rattle of machine-gun and rifle fire, the thudding explosions of grenades lobbed on to the road, the hoarse shouts, the screams of the dying.

He clambered down to the car again.

'All right, Miss Kolin,' he said; 'what do *you* think happened?'

'I think that he was taken prisoner with the driver and that both were wounded. I think that the Sergeant died of his wounds or was killed trying to escape on the way to the *andartes*' rendezvous with Phengaros. Naturally, Phengaros would think that only one prisoner had been taken.'

'What about the Sergeant's papers? They would have taken them to Phengaros.'

'They would also take the papers of those they had killed here.'

George considered. 'Yes, you may be right. At least it's a reasonable explanation. There's still only one way we can find out for certain though, and that's by getting hold of someone who was there.'

Miss Kolin nodded towards the pedlar. 'I have been talking to this man. He says that the *andartes* who did this were from Florina. That agrees with the Colonel's information.'

'Did he know any of them by name?'

'No. They just said they were from Florina.'

'Another dead end. All right, we'll go there tomorrow. We'd better start back now. How much money do you think I should give the old man?'

It was early evening when they arrived back in Salonika. Something unusual seemed to have happened while they had been away. There were extra police on duty in the streets and shopkeepers stood in the roadway conferring volubly with their neighbours. The cafés were crowded.

At the hotel they heard the news.

Just before three o'clock that afternoon, a closed army truck had driven up to the entrance of the Eurasian Credit Bank in the Rue Egnatie. It had waited there for a moment or so. Then, suddenly, the covers at the back had been flung open and six men had jumped out. They had been armed with machine-pistols and grenades. Three of them had immediately stationed themselves in the entrance portico. The other three had gone inside. Within little more than two minutes, they had been out again with several hundred thousand dollars' worth of foreign currency in American dollars, escudos and Swiss francs. Ten seconds later, and almost before the passers-by had noticed that anything was wrong, they had been back in the truck and away.

The affair had been perfectly organized. The raiders had known exactly which safe the money was kept in, and exactly how to get it. No one had been shot. A clerk, who had courageously tried to set off an alarm bell, had received no more than a blow in the face from a gun butt for his audacity. the alarm bell had not sounded for the simple reason, discovered later, that the wires had been disconnected. The raiders had saluted with the clenched fist. Quite clearly, they had had a Communist confederate inside the bank. Quite clearly, the robbery was yet another in a series organized to replenish the Communist Party funds. Quite naturally, suspicion as to the identity of the confederate had fallen upon the courageous clerk. Would he have dared to do what he did unless he had known in advance that he was running no risk? Of course not! The police were questioning him.

That was the receptionist's excited account of the affair.

The hotel barman confirmed the facts, but had a more sophisticated theory about the motives of the criminals.

How was it, he asked, that every big robbery that now took place was the work of Communists stealing for the Party funds? Did nobody else steal any more? Oh, yes, no doubt there *had* been political robberies, but not as many as people supposed. And why should the brigands give the clenched fist salute as they left? To show that they were Communists? Absurd! They were merely seeking to give that impression in order to deceive the police by directing attention away from themselves. They could count on the police preferring to blame Communists. Everything bad was blamed on the Communists. He himself was not a Communist, of course, but . . .

He went on at length.

George listened absently. At that moment, he was more interested in the discovery that his appetite had suddenly begun to return and that he could contemplate without revulsion the prospect of dinner.

Florina lies at the entrance to a deep valley nine miles south of the Yugoslav frontier. About forty miles away across the mountains to the west is

Albania. Florina is the administrative centre of the province which bears its name and is an important railhead. It has a garrison and a ruined Turkish citadel. It has more than one hotel. It is neither as picturesque as Vodena, nor as ancient. It came into existence as an insignificant staging point on a Roman road from Durazzo to Constantinople, and far too late to share in the short-lived glories of the Macedonian Empire. In a land which has contained so many of the springs of Western civilization, it is a parvenu.

But if Florina has no history of much interest to the compilers of guide books, it has, in the Edwardian sense of the word, a Past.

In the summer of 1896, sixteen men attended a meeting in Salonika. There, they founded a political organization which in later years was to become the most formidable secret terrorist society the Balkans, or for that matter Europe, has known. It was called the International Macedonian Revolutionary Organization; IMRO, for short. Its creed was 'Macedonia for the Macedonians', its flag, a red skull and crossbones on a black ground, its motto, 'Freedom or Death'. Its arguments were the knife, the rifle and the bomb. Its armed forces, who lived in the hills and mountains of Macedonia, enforcing IMRO laws and imposing IMRO taxes on the villagers and townspeople, were called *comitadjis*. Their oath of allegiance was sworn upon a Bible and a revolver, and the penalty for disloyalty was death. Among those who took this oath and served IMRO there were rich men as well as peasants, poets as well as soldiers, philosophers as well as professional murderers. In the cause of Macedonian autonomy it killed Turks and Bulgars, Serbs and Vlachs, Greeks and Albanians. It also killed Macedonians in the same cause. By the time of the First Balkan War, IMRO was a serious political force capable of bringing considerable influence to bear upon events. The Macedonian *comitadji* with his cartridge belts and his rifle was becoming a legendary figure, an heroic defender of women and children against the savagery of the Turks, a knight of the mountains who preferred death to dishonour and treated his captives with courtesy and forbearance. The facts, harped upon by cynical observers, that the savageries of the Turks were generally committed by way of reprisal for atrocities committed by the *comitadjis*, and that the chivalrous behaviour was only in evidence when there was a chance of its impressing foreign sympathizers, seemed to have little effect on the legend. It persisted remarkably and has to some extent continued to do so. In the main square of Gorna-Djoumaia, the capital of Bulgarian Macedonia, there is even a monument to 'The Unknown *Comitadji*'. True, it was put up in 1933 by the IMRO gangsters who ran the city; but the Bulgarian Central Government of the time did not object to it, and it is almost certainly still there. If IMRO is no longer served by poets and idealists, it remains a political force, and has from time to time sold itself with nice impartiality to both Fascists and Communists. IMRO is, and always has been, a very Balkan institution.

Florina was one of the 'founder' strongholds of IMRO. Soon after the momentous Salonika meeting in 1896, an ex-sergeant of the Bulgarian Army named Marko began recruiting an IMRO band in Florina which rapidly became the most powerful in the area. And the most distinguished. The Bulgarian poet, Yavorov, and the young writer, Christo Silianov, were

among those who chose to join it and (though Silianov the writer, disgraced
himself by showing an effeminate aversion to cutting his prisoners' throats)
both saw much active service with the Florina men. Marko himself was
killed by Turkish soldiers, but the band remained an effective unit, and
played a prominent part in the rebellion of 1903. The irredentist techniques
of sabotage, ambush, kidnapping, intimidation, armed robbery and murder
are part of Florina's cultural heritage; and although it now takes invasion
and a war to induce the law-abiding inhabitants of the province to turn to
these old skills, there are always, even in times of peace, a few daring spirits
ready to take to the mountains and remind their unfortunate neighbours
that the traditions of their forefathers are still very much alive.

George and Miss Kolin arrived by train from Salonika.

The Parthenon Hotel was a three-storey building, near the centre of the
town. There was a café beneath it, and a restaurant which could be entered
directly from the street. It was about the size of a third-class commercial
hotel in a town like Lyons. The rooms were small, and the plumbing
primitive. The bedstead in George's room was of iron, but there was a
wooden frame round the springs. At Miss Kolin's suggestion, George spent
his first half-hour there with an insufflator and a cannister of D.D.T.,
spraying the crevices in the woodwork. Then he went down to the café.
Presently, Miss Kolin joined him.

The proprietor of the Parthenon was a small grey-faced man with grey
hair cut *en brosse,* and a crumpled grey suit. When he saw Miss Kolin
appear, he left a table by the bar counter, at which he had been standing
talking to an army officer, and came over to them. He bowed and said
something in French.

'Ask him if he'll join us for a drink,' George said.

When the invitation had been interpreted, the little man bowed again, sat
down with a word of apology and snapped his fingers at the barman.

They all had *oyzo.* Politenesses were exchanged. The proprietor
apologized for not speaking English, and then began discreetly to pump
them about their business in the town.

'We had few tourists here,' he remarked: 'I have often said that it is a
pity.'

'The scenery is certainly very fine.'

'If you have time while you are here you should take a drive. I shall be
happy to arrange a car for you.'

'Very kind of him. Say that we heard in Salonika that there was excellent
hunting to be had near the lakes to the west.'

'The gentleman is intending to go hunting?'

'Not this time, unfortunately. We are on business. But we were told that
there was plenty of game up there.'

The little man smiled. 'There is game of all sorts in the neighbourhood.
There are also eagles in the hills,' he added slyly.

'Eagles who do a little hunting themselves, perhaps?'

'The gentleman learned that in Salonika, too, no doubt.'

'I have always understood that this is a most romantic part of the
country.'

'Yes, the eagle is a bird of romance to some,' the proprietor said, archly.

Obviously, he was the kind of person who could not let the smallest joke go once he had got his teeth into it.

'It's a bird of prey, too.'

'Ah, yes, indeed! When armies disintegrate there are always a few who prefer to stay together and fight a private war against society. But here in Florina the gentleman need have no fear. The eagles are safe in the hills.'

'That's a pity. We were hoping you might be able to help us to find one.'

'To find an eagle? The gentleman deals in fine feathers?'

But George was getting bored. 'All right,' he said, 'we'll cut the double talk. Tell him I'm a lawyer and that we want, if possible, to talk to someone who was in the ELAS band led by Phengaros in 1944. Explain that it's nothing political, that we just want to check up on the grave of a German sergeant who was killed near Vodena. Say I'm acting for the man's relatives in America.'

He watched the little man's face as Miss Kolin translated. For a moment or two a quite extraordinary expression came over its loose grey folds; an expression compounded of equal parts of interest, amazement, indignation and fear. Then a curtain came down and the face went blank. Its owner picked up his drink and drained the glass.

'I regret,' he said precisely, 'that that is not a matter in which I can be of any assistance to you at all.'

He rose to his feet.

'Wait a minute,' said George. 'If he can't help me, ask him if he knows of anyone here who can.' The proprietor hesitated, then glanced across at the officer sitting at the table by the bar. 'One moment,' he said curtly. He went over to the officer and, bending over the table, began talking in a rapid undertone.

After a moment or two, George saw the officer look across quickly at him, then say something sharply to the proprietor. The little man shrugged. The officer stood up and came over to them.

He was a lean, dark young man with lustrous eyes, very wide riding breeches and a waist like a girl. He wore the badges of a captain. He bowed to Miss Kolin and smiled pleasantly at George.

'I beg your pardon, sir,' he said in English. 'The patron tells me that you are here making inquiries.'

'That's right.'

He clicked his heels. 'Streftaris, Captain,' he said. 'You are an American, Mister . . .?'

'Carey's my name. Yes, I'm an American.'

'And this lady?'

'Miss Kolin is French. She is my interpreter.'

'Thank you. Perhaps I can be of assistance to you, Mr Carey.'

'That's very kind of you, Captain. Sit down, won't you.'

'Thank you.' The Captain spun the chair round, swung the seat between his legs and sat down with his elbows resting on the back. There was something curiously insolent about the gesture. He smiled less pleasantly. 'You have made the patron feel very uneasy, Mr Carey.'

'I'm sorry about that. All I asked him was to put me in touch with someone who was in the Phengaros band in 1944. I told him there was nothing political about my business.'

The Captain sighed elaborately. 'Mr Carey,' he said, 'if I were to come to you in America and ask you to put me in touch with a gangster wanted by the police, would you be prepared to help me?'

'Is that a true comparison?'

'Certainly. I do not think you quite understand our problems here. You are a foreigner, of course, and that excuses you, but it is very indiscreet to inquire into matters of this kind.'

'Do you mind telling me why?'

'These men are Communists . . . outlaws. Do you know that Phengaros himself is in prison on a criminal charge?'

'Yes. I interviewed him two days ago.'

'Pardon?'

'Colonel Chrysantos in Salonika was kind enough to arrange for me to see Phengaros in prison.'

The Captain's smile faded. He took his elbows off the back of the chair.

'I beg your pardon, Mr Carey.'

'What for?'

'I did not understand that you were on official business.'

'Well, to be exact . . .'

'I do not think we have received orders from Salonika. Had we done so, of course, the commandant would have instructed me.'

'Now, just a moment, Captain, let's get this straight. My business is legal rather than official. I'll explain.'

The Captain listened carefully to the explanation. When George had finished he looked relieved.

'Then it is not on the advice of Colonel Chrysantos that you are here, sir?'

'No.'

'You must know, Mr Carey, that I am military intelligence officer for the district. It would be most unfortunate for me if Colonel Chrysantos thought . . .'

'Sure, I know. A very efficient man the Colonel.'

'Ah, yes.'

'And a busy one. So, you see, I thought it might be better if I didn't trouble the Colonel again, but just got the names of some of these people unofficially.'

The Captain looked puzzled. 'Unofficially? How unofficially?'

'I could buy the names, couldn't I?'

'But from whom?'

'Well, that was what I was hoping the patron might be able to tell me.'

'Ah!' the Captain at last permitted himself to smile again. 'Mr Carey, if the patron knew the names that you want could be bought, he would not be so foolish as to admit the fact to a stranger.'

'But haven't you a line on *any* of these people? What happened to them all?'

'Some were killed with the Markos forces, some are across the border with our neighbours. The rest—' he shrugged—'they have taken other names.'

'But they're somewhere around here, surely.'

'Yes, but I cannot recommend you to go looking for them. There are cafés in this town where, if you asked the questions you asked the patron here tonight, there would be much unpleasantness for you.'

'I see. What would you do in my place, Captain?'

The Captain thought carefully for a moment, then he leaned forward. 'Mr Carey, I would not wish you to believe that I am not anxious to give you all the assistance I can.'

'No, of course not.'

But the Captain had not finished. 'I wish to help you all I can. Please, however, explain to me one thing. You simply wish to know if this German Sergeant was killed or not killed in the ambush. Is that right?'

'That's right.'

'You do not specially wish to know the name of the person who saw him die?'

George considered. 'Well, let's put it this way,' he said finally; 'the probability is that the Sergeant *did* die. If he did and I can be reasonably certain of the fact, then that's all I want to know. My business is finished.'

The Captain nodded. 'Ah. Now let us suppose for a moment that such information could be obtained in some way. Would you be prepared to pay, perhaps three hundred dollars for that information without knowing where it came from?'

'Three hundred! That's rather a lot, isn't it?'

The Captain waved the subject away deprecatingly. 'Let us say two hundred. The sum is not important.'

'Then let's say one hundred.'

'As you will. But would you pay, Mr Carey?'

'Under certain conditions, yes.'

'What conditions, please?'

'Well, I can tell you right now that I'm not going to pay out a hundred dollars just for the pleasure of having someone tell me that he knows somebody else who knows a man who was in that ambush and says that the German Sergeant was killed. I'd want some kind of evidence that the story was genuine.'

'I understand that, but what evidence could there be?'

'Well, for one thing, what I'd want is a reasonable explanation of the fact that the Sergeant's body was not found by the German patrol that came along afterwards. There were dead men there, but the Sergeant wasn't among them. A genuine witness ought to know the answer to that one.'

'Yes, that is logical.'

'But is there any chance of getting the information?'

'That is what I have been thinking about. I see a chance, perhaps, yes. I can promise nothing. Do you know anything of police methods?'

'Only the usual things.'

'Then you will know that when one is dealing with criminals, it is sometimes wise to give the less dangerous ones temporary immunity, and even encouragement, if by doing so one can know a little of what is going on among the rest.'

'You mean paid informers?'

'Not quite. The paid informer is rarely satisfactory. One pays and pays for nothing and then, when he is about to be useful, he is found with his throat cut and the Government's money is wasted. No, the types I am discussing are the lesser criminals whose activities can be tolerated because they know and are trusted by those whom we may wish to put our hands on. Such types will not inform, you understand, but by seeming to be friendly and ready to overlook their little games one can learn much of what goes on that is interesting.'

'I understand. If there were money in it and nobody risked incriminating himself, such a person might find out what I wanted to know.'

'Exactly.'

'Have you someone in mind?'

'Yes, but I must make a discreet inquiry first to see if an approach can safely be made. I think that Colonel Chrysantos would be very annoyed with me, Mr Carey, if I put your life in danger—' he flashed a lustrous smile at Miss Kolin–'or that of Madame.'

Miss Kolin looked down her nose.

George grinned. 'No, we mustn't annoy the Colonel. But all the same, it's very kind of you to take all this trouble, Captain.'

The Captain raised a protesting hand. 'It is nothing. If you should happen to mention to the Colonel that I was of some small assistance to you, I should be well repaid.'

'Naturally, I shall mention it. But, who is this person you think might fix it up?'

'It is a woman. Outwardly, she is the proprietress of a wine shop. In fact, she deals secretly in arms. If a man wishes a rifle or a revolver, he goes to her. She gets it for him. Why do we not arrest her? Because then someone else would begin to deal, someone we might not know and could not so easily keep under surveillance. One day, perhaps, when we can be sure of stopping her sources of supply, we will take her. Until then, things are better as they are. She has a love of gossip, and for your purpose is most suitable.'

'But doesn't she know she's under surveillance?'

'Ah, yes, but she bribes my men. The fact that they take her money makes her feel safe. It is all quite friendly. But we do not wish to alarm her, so she must be consulted first.' He rose to his feet, suddenly businesslike. 'Perhaps tonight.'

'That's good of you, Captain. Won't you stay and have a drink?'

'Ah, no, thank you. Just now I have various appointments. Tomorrow I will send a note to you here to give you the address to go to if she has agreed, and any other necessary instructions.'

'O.K. Fine.'

There was a lot of heel-clicking and politeness, and he went. George signalled to the barman.

'Well, Miss Kolin,' he said when they were served again, 'what do you think?'

'I think that the Captain's various appointments are almost certainly with his mistress.'

'I meant do you think there's anything in this. You know this part of the world. Do you think he'll do what he said about contacting this woman?'

She shrugged. 'I think that for a hundred dollars the Captain would do almost anything.'

It took a moment or two for George to appreciate the implication of this statement. 'But the Captain's not getting the money,' he said.

'No?'

'No. That's for the wine-shop woman, if she comes through with the information.'

'I do not think he will give her a hundred dollars. Perhaps twenty. Perhaps nothing.'

'You're kidding.'

'You asked me for my impression.'

'He's the Keen Young Executive type. All he wants is a pat on the back from the boss. You see.'

Miss Kolin smiled sardonically.

George did not get much rest that night. The precautions he had taken against bed-bugs had somehow served to convince him that the mattress frame must be alive with the creatures. In the darkness he had soon begun to imagine that he was being attacked by them. Useless now to remind himself of the D.D.T. he had applied; Balkan bugs probably ate the stuff like ice-cream. After a fourth panic inspection had failed to reveal even one attacker, he had become desperate, stripped the bed, and made a further assault on the mattress with the insufflator. A rose-coloured dawn had been glowing among the mountain peaks before he had succeeded in going to sleep.

He awoke, resentfully, at nine o'clock. While he was at breakfast in the café downstairs, a letter arrived from the Captain.

> Dear Sir (*George read*),
> The woman is Madame Vassiotis at the wine shop in the rue Monténégrine. She will expect you, but not until this afternoon. Say that you come from Monsieur Kliris. Do not refer to me. She has been told what you want and might have an answer for you. The price will be U.S. dollars 150, but do not give it to the woman herself or speak of it. I wish to be assured personally that you are satisfied before you pay. If, when I have seen you this evening, you tell me that all is well, I will see that the money goes to her by Monsieur Kliris.

The letter was written on plain paper and unsigned.

George did not show it to Miss Kolin.

The rue Monténégrine proved to be a steep, refuse-strewn lane in the poorer quarter of the town. The houses were broken down and ugly. Lines of dingy washing were strung across the lane between some of the upper windows, others had bedding hung out over the sills. There were a great many children about.

The wine shop was near the top of the lane by a builder's yard. It had no display window. There was a bead-curtained doorway in a wall, and two or three steps leading down to the interior. George and Miss Kolin entered, and found themselves in a kind of cellar, with wine barrels stacked on their sides against the walls, and a massive wooden bench in the centre. Light came from an oil-lamp on a shelf. The air was cool, and there was a smell of stale wine and old barrels that was not unpleasant.

There were two persons in the shop. One of them, an old man in blue denim trousers, sat on the bench drinking a glass of wine. The other was Madame Vassiotis.

She was amazingly fat, with huge pendulous breasts and a vast lap. She was sitting on, and almost completely enveloping, a low stool by a doorway at the back of the shop. When they entered, she rose slowly to her feet and waddled forward into the light.

Her head was small for her body, with dark hair drawn tightly away from the brow. The face seemed as though it ought to belong to someone younger or less gross. it was still firm and delicately-shaped, and the eyes under their heavy lids were dark and clear.

She murmured a word of greeting.

Miss Kolin replied. George had briefed her in readiness for the interview, and she did not trouble to interpret the preliminaries. He saw Madame Vassiotis nod understandingly and glance at the old man. He promptly finished his wine and went out. Then she bowed slightly to George and, with a gesture of invitation, led the way through a doorway at the back into a sitting-room.

There, there were Turkish carpets on the walls, a divan with plush cushions, and a few pieces of rickety Victorian furniture. It reminded him of a fortune-teller's booth in a travelling fair. Only the crystal ball was missing.

Madame Vassiotis poured three glasses of wine, sank down heavily on to the divan and motioned them to chairs. When they were seated, she folded her hands in her lap and looked placidly from one to the other of them as if waiting for someone to propose a parlour game.

'Ask her,' George said, 'if she has been able to get any reply to the questions put to her by Monsieur Kliris.'

Madame Vassiotis listened gravely to the translation and then, with a nod, began to speak.

'She states,' said Miss Kolin, 'that she has been able to speak with one of the *andartes* who took part in the affair near Vodena. Her information is that the German Sergeant was killed.'

'Does she know how he was killed?'

'He was in the first truck of the German convoy. It exploded a mine.'

George thought for a moment. He had not mentioned either of those facts to the Captain. It was promising.

'Did the informant see the Sergeant dead?'

'Yes.'

'Was he on the road?'

'He was where he fell when the truck was hit.'

'What happened to the body afterwards?'

He saw Madame Vassiotis shrug.

'Does she know that the body was not there when the German patrol came along afterwards?'

'Yes, but her informant can offer no explanation of this.'

George thought again. This was awkward. An experienced man would probably know that the N.C.O. in charge of a German column would ride in the leading truck; and certainly anyone who had taken any part at all in the ambush would know that the leading truck had hit a mine. The informant might well have been farther down the road, firing on the other trucks. With the prospect of earning a few dollars for his trouble, however, he would be ready to oblige with a reasonable guess.

'Ask her if her friend knows what the Sergeant's injuries were.'

'She cannot say exactly. The Sergeant was lying in a pool of blood.'

'Is she absolutely sure in her own mind . . .?' Then he broke off. 'No, wait a minute. Put it another way. If the Sergeant were her own son, would she be satisfied in her own mind that he was dead from what her friend has told her?'

A smile appeared on the delicately-curved lips, and a chuckle shook the massive body as their owner understood his question. Then, with a grunting effort, she heaved herself up from the divan and waddled to a drawer in the table. From it she took a slip of paper which she handed to Miss Kolin with an explanation.

'Madame anticipated your doubts and asked for proof that her friend saw the body. He told her that they stripped the dead Germans of their equipment and that he got the Sergeant's water-bottle. He still has it. It has the Sergeant's number and name burnt into the strap. They are written on this paper.'

Madame Vassiotis sat down again and sipped her wine as George looked at the paper.

The army number he knew well; he had seen it before on several documents. Beneath it in block letters had been written: 'SCHIRMER F'.

George considered it carefully for a moment or two, then nodded. He had not mentioned the name Schirmer to the Captain. Trickery was quite out of the question. The evidence was conclusive. What had happened afterwards to the body of Sergeant Schirmer might never be known, but there was no shadow of doubt that Madame Vassiotis and her mysterious acquaintance were telling what they knew of the truth.

He nodded and, picking up his glass of wine, raised it politely to the woman before he drank.

'Thank her for me, please, Miss Kolin,' he said as he put the glass down, 'and tell her that I am well satisfied.'

He got out a fifty-dollar note and put it on the table as he stood up.

He saw an expression of hastily concealed amazement flicker across the fat woman's face. Then, she rose to her feet bowing and smiling. She was clearly delighted. If her dignity had permitted it she would have picked up the note to have a closer look. She pressed them to have more wine.

When, eventually, they were able to bow themselves out of the shop, George turned to Miss Kolin. 'You'd better tell her not to mention that fifty dollars to Monsieur Kliris,' he said; 'I shan't mention it to the Captain. With any luck she may get paid twice.'

Miss Kolin was on her sixth after-dinner brandy, and her eyes were glazing rapidly. She was sitting very straight in her chair. At any moment now she would decide that it was time for her to go to bed. The Captain had long since departed. He had had the air of a man of whose good nature unfair advantage had been taken. However, he had not refused the hundred dollars George had offered him. Presumably, he was now celebrating the occasion with his mistress. For George, there was nothing more to be done in Florina.

'We'll leave tomorrow morning, Miss Kolin,' he said. 'Train to Salonika. Plane to Athens. Plane to Paris. All right?'

'You have definitely decided?'

'Can you think of one reason for going on with the thing?'

'I never had any doubt that the man was dead.'

'No, that's right, you didn't. Going to bed now?'

'I think so, yes. Good-night, Mr Carey.'

'Good-night, Miss Kolin.'

Watching her meticulous progress to the door of the café, George wondered gloomily if she kept her rigid self-control until she got into bed or whether, in the privacy of her room, she allowed herself to pass out.

He finished his own drink slowly. He felt depressed, and wished to account for the fact. According to the lights of the ambitious young corporation lawyer who, only a few weeks back, had been pleased to watch his name being painted on an office door in Philadelphia, he should have been delighted by the turn of events. He had been given an irksome and unrewarding task, and performed it quickly and efficiently. He could now return with confidence to more serious and useful business. Everything was fine. And yet, he was deriving no pleasure from the fact. It was absurd. Could it be that, in his heart, he had hoped, ludicrously, to find the Schneider Johnson claimant and take him back in triumph to that juvenile dotard, Mr Sistrom? Could it be that what was now troubling him was merely an idiotic feeling of anti-climax? That must be it, of course. For a moment or two he almost succeeded in convincing himself that he had discovered the reason for his state of mind. Then, the even less palatable truth of the matter dawned on him. He had been enjoying himself.

Yes, there it was. The talented, ambitious, pretentious Mr Carey, with his smug, smiling family, his Brooks Brothers suits and his Princeton and Harvard degrees, *liked* playing detectives, *liked* looking for non-existent German soldiers, *liked* having dealings with dreary people like Frau Gresser, disagreeable people like Colonel Chrysantos and undesirables like Phengaros. And why? For the value of such experiences in a corporation law practice? Because he loved his fellow-men and was curious about them? Rubbish. More likely that the elaborate defences of his youth, the pompous fantasies of big office chairs and panelled boardrooms, of hidden wealth and power behind the scenes, were beginning to crumble, and that the pimply adolescent was belatedly emerging into the light. Was it not possible that, in finding out something about a dead man, he had at last begun to find out something about himself?

He sighed, paid the bar bill, got his key and went up to his room.

It was in the front of the hotel on the second floor, and at night the light streaming down from unshuttered windows across the street was almost strong enough to read by.

When he opened the door, therefore, he did not immediately look for the light switch. The first thing he saw as he took the key out of the lock was his brief-case lying open on the bed with its contents scattered about the covers.

He started forward quickly. He had taken about two steps when the door slammed behind him. He swung round.

A man was standing just beside the door. He was in the shadow but the pistol in his hand was clearly visible in the light from across the street. It moved forward as the man spoke.

He spoke very softly but, even to George with totally scattered senses, the strong Cockney accent in the voice was unmistakable.

'All right, chum,' it said. 'Gently does it. No, don't move. Just put your hands behind your head, keep absolutely quiet and hope you won't get hurt. Got it?

Chapter Nine

George's experience of extreme danger had been gained in the cockpits of heavy bombers, and in circumstances for which he had been carefully prepared by long periods of training. Of dangers such as those which lurk behind doors in Macedonian hotels, dangers unrelated to the wearing of a uniform and the organized prosecution of a war, he had had no experience, and neither Princeton nor Harvard Law School had done anything to prepare him for one.

As, therefore, he raised his hands obediently, and put them behind his head, he was suddenly aware of an overwhelmingly, unreasoning and quite impracticable desire to run away somewhere and hide. He struggled against it for a moment; then the man spoke again, and the desire went as suddenly as it had arrived. The blood began to pound unpleasantly in his head.

'That's right, chum,' the voice was saying soothingly. 'Now just go over to the window there and pull the shutters to. Then we'll have a little light on the scene. Slowly does it. Yes, you'll have to use your hands, but watch what you do with them or we'll have an accident. Don't try calling out or anything, either. All nice and quiet. That's the ticket.'

George pulled the shutters to, and at the same moment the light in the room went on. He turned.

The man who stood by the light switch, watching him, was in the middle thirties, short and thick-set, with dark, thinning hair. His suit was obviously a local product. Just as obviously he was not. The raw-boned, snub-nosed face, and the sly, insolent eyes originated, as did the Cockney accent, from somewhere within the Greater London area.

'That's better, eh?' the visitor said. 'Now we can see what's what without the neighbours across the street getting nosey.'

'What the hell's the idea of all this?' said George. 'And who the hell are you?'

'Easy, chum,' the visitor grinned. 'No names, no pack drill. You can call me Arthur if you like. It's not my name, but it'll do. Lots of people call me Arthur. You're Mr Carey, aren't you?'

'You should know.' George looked at the papers strewn over the bed.

'Ah, yes. Sorry about that, Mr. Carey. I meant to clear it up before you came back. But I didn't have time for more than a glance. I haven't taken anything, naturally.'

'Naturally. I don't leave money in hotel rooms.'

'Oh, what a *wicked* thing to say!' said the visitor, skittishly. 'Tongue like a whip-lash, haven't we?'

'Well, if you're not here for money, what are you here for?'

'A bit of a chat, Mr Carey. That's all.'

'Do you usually come calling with a gun?'

The visitor looked pained. 'Look, chum, how was I to know you'd be reasonable? Finding a stranger in your room! Supposing you'd started yelling blue murder and throwing the furniture about. I had to take precautions.'

'You could have asked for me downstairs.'

The visitor grinned slyly. 'Could I? Ah, but maybe you don't know much about these parts, Mr Carey. All right—' his tone suddenly became businesslike–'I'll tell you what I'll do with you. You promise not to start calling up the management or getting Charlie with me, and I'll put the gun away. O.K.?'

'All right. But I'd still like to know what you're doing here.'

'I told you. I want a little private chat. That's all.'

'What about?'

'I'll tell you.' Arthur put his gun away inside his jacket and produced a packet of Greek cigarettes. he offered them to George. 'Smoke, Mr Carey?'

George produced a packet of his own. 'No, thanks. I'll stick to these.'

'Chesterfields, eh? Long time no see. Mind if I try one?'

'Help yourself.'

'Thanks.' He fussed about the business of giving George a light, like an over-anxious host. Then he lit his own cigarette and drew on it apprec-iatively. 'Nice tobacco,' he said. 'Very nice.'

George sat down on the edge of the bed. 'Look,' he said impatiently, 'what exactly is this all about? You break into my room, go through my business papers, threaten me with a gun and then say you only want a private chat. All right, so we're chatting. Now what?'

'Mind if I sit down, Mr Carey?'

'Do anything you like, but for Pete's sake come to the point.'

'All right, all right, give us a chance.' Arthur sat down gingerly on a cane-backed chair. 'It's a private sort of a matter, Mr Carey,' he said. 'Confidential, if you know what I mean.'

'I know what you mean.'

'I wouldn't like it to go any further,' he persisted, maddeningly.

'I've got that.'

'Well, now—' he cleared his throat–'I have been given to understand by certain parties,' he said carefully, 'that you, Mr Carey, have been making certain inquiries of a confidential nature in the town.'

'Yes.'

'This afternoon you had a certain conversation with a certain women who shall be nameless.'

'Madame Vassiotis, you mean?'

'That's right.'

'Then why say she shall be nameless?'

'No names, no pack drill.'

'Oh, all right. Get on.'

'She gave you certain information.'

'What about it?'

'Easy does it, Mr Carey. Your inquiries were *re* a certain German N.C.O. named Schirmer. Correct?'

'Correct.'

'Do you mind telling me why you are making the said inquiries, Mr Carey?'

'If you were to tell me first just why you wanted to know, I might tell you.'

Arthur digested this reply for a moment or two in silence.

'And, just to make matters simpler, Arthur,' George added, 'I'll tell you that, although I'm a lawyer, I'm quite capable of understanding ordinary English. So what about letting your hair down and coming to the point?'

Mr Arthur's low forehead creased with the effort of thinking. 'You see, it's confidential, that's the trouble, Mr Carey,' he said, unhappily.

'So you explained. But if it's so confidential that you can't talk about it, you'd better go home and let me get some sleep, hadn't you?'

'Now don't talk like that, Mr Carey. I'm doing my best. Look! If you were to tell me what you want to know about this chap for, I could tell certain persons who might be able to help you.'

'What persons?'

'Persons with information to give.'

'You mean information to *sell*, don't you?'

'I said *give*.'

George examined his guest thoughtfully. 'You're British, aren't you, Arthur?' he said after a moment. 'Or is that confidential?'

Arthur grinned. 'Want to hear me speak Greek? I speak it like a native.'

'All right, then. You're a citizen of the world, then, eh?'

'Goldsmith!' said Arthur, unexpectedly.

'Pardon?'

'Oliver Goldsmith,' repeated Arthur; 'he wrote a book called *The Citizen of the World*. We had it at school. Lot of crap about a Chinaman who comes to London and sees the sights.'

'What part of London do you come from, Arthur?'

Arthur wagged a finger coyly. 'Ah, naughty, naughty! That would be telling!'

'Afraid I'll check up on the British War Office lists of troops reported missing in Greece, and find out which ones came from where you came from?'

'What do *you* think, chum?'

George admitted. 'O.K., Arthur. Here it is. This man, Schirmer, I've been inquiring about, was entitled to some money left by a distant relative of his in America. He was reported missing. I came here really to get confirmation of his death, but I'd also like to know if he ever had any children. That's all. I found out today that he's dead.'

'From old Ma Vassiotis?'

'That's right. And now I'm on my way home.'

'I get it.' Arthur was thinking hard now. 'Much money, is there?' he said at last.

'Just enough to make it worth my while coming here.'

'And that little bit of homework you've got with you?'

'Miss Kolin, you mean? She's an interpreter.'

'I get you.' Arthur came to a decision. 'Supposing–just supposing, mind–that there was a bit more information you could find out about this German. Would it be worth your while to stay another couple of days?'

'That would depend on the information.'

'Well, supposing he'd had a wife and kids. They'd be in line for the cash, wouldn't they?'

'*Did* he have a wife and kids?'

'I'm not saying he did, and I'm not saying he didn't. But just supposing . . .'

'If there was clear legal proof of that to be had, I'd certainly stay. But I'm not staying just in order to listen to a lot of unconfirmed hearsay, and I'm not paying out another cent to anyone.'

'Nobody's asked you to, have they?'

'Not so far.'

'Nasty suspicious nature you got, eh?'

'Yes.'

Arthur nodded gloomily. 'Can't blame you. Tricky lot of sods in this part of the world. Look, if I give you my sacred word of honour that it'll be worth your while to stay a couple of days, will you do it?'

'You're asking rather a lot, aren't you?'

'Listen, chum, *You're* the one that's going to get a favour done. Not me!'

'That's what you say.'

'Well, I can't do more. Here's the proposition. Take it or leave it. If you want the information my friends have got, stay here and do what I tell you.'

'And what might that be?'

'Well, first of all, you don't say one word to that little bastard of a Captain you were chin-wagging with last night. O.K.?'

'Go on.'

'All you do is go to that big café with the yellow blinds next door to the Acropolis Hotel between four and five tomorrow afternoon. Just sit there and have a cup of coffee. That's all. If you get no message from me while you're there, it's all off. If you do get a message, it'll be an appointment. Just say nothing and keep it.'

'What about the interpreter?'

'If she keeps her mouth shut she can come too.'

'Where would the appointment be?'

'You'd be taken to it by car.'

'I see. Just one question. I'm not exactly timid, but I would like to know a bit more about these friends of yours before I do anything about meeting them. Would they be ELAS people, for instance?'

Arthur grinned. 'Ask no questions and you'll be told no lies. You don't have to come if you don't want to.'

'Maybe not. But I'm not half-witted. You say these friends of yours don't want money for their information. O.K.–what do they want? For that matter, what do you want?'

'Sweet Fanny Adams,' said Arthur, cheerfully.

'Let's quit kidding.'

'All right. Maybe they want to see justice done.'

'Justice?'

'Yes. Ever heard of it?'

'Sure. I've heard of kidnapping, too.'

'Oh, blimey!' Arthur laughed. 'Look, if you're as nervous as that, chum, forget it.' He stood up. 'I'll have to be getting along now. If you want to come, be at the café tomorrow like I said. Otherwise . . .' He shrugged.

'O.K. I'll think about it.'

'Yes, you do that. Sorry to mess up all your papers like that, but I expect you'd sooner tidy them up yourself really. Bye-bye, for now.'

'Good-bye,' said George.

Almost before the word was out of his mouth, Arthur was out of the room and shutting the door noiselessly behind him.

It was not his uncertainty about bed bugs that kept George from sleeping soundly that night.

The café with the yellow blinds was in an exposed position on a busy corner, and everyone sitting in it could be clearly seen from anywhere in the main square. It was, George thought, the very last place he would have associated with the transaction of clandestine business. But then, he was not a practised conspirator. The café's air of having nothing to conceal was probably its greatest asset. In Arthur's world, no doubt, such matters were elaborately calculated.

Miss Kolin had listened blandly to George's account of his interview with Arthur and accepted without comment his decision to postpone their departure. When, however, he had gone on to say that, in view of the possible risks involved, he would leave her to decide for herself whether she would accompany him or not, she had been quite obviously amused.

'Risks, Mr Carey. But what sort of risks?'

'How should I know?' George was irritated. 'The point is that this isn't exactly the most law-abiding part of the world, and this guy Arthur's way of introducing himself for a cosy chat wasn't exactly according to Emily Post, was it?'

She had shrugged. 'It served its purpose.'

'What do you mean?'

'Frankly, Mr Carey, I think that it was a mistake to give the Vassiotis woman so much money.'

'From my point of view she'd earned it.'

'Your point of view, Mr Carey, is that of an American lawyer. The points of view of the Vassiotis and her friends are different.'

'I see. You think that this Arthur proposition is just another shake-down, then?'

'I do. You gave that Captain a hundred dollars and the Vassiotis fifty. Now, Mr Arthur and his friends would like some dollars, too.'

'He emphasized that there was no question of money involved. I told you.'

'You believed him?'

'All right, then, I'm the prize sucker. But, for some reason, I did believe him. For some reason, equally idiotic, no doubt, I still do.'

She had shrugged again. 'Then you are right to keep the appointment. It will be interesting to see what happens.'

That had been over breakfast. By lunch-time, his confidence in his first estimate of Arthur's intentions had completely evaporated. Sitting in the café with the yellow blinds, glumly sipping coffee, he had only one consoling thought in his head: no matter what happened, no matter what they did, neither Arthur nor any of Arthur's friends was going to get one red cent for his trouble.

It was after five o'clock now. The café was three parts empty. Nobody who looked as if he might conceivably have a message to deliver had been near them.

George had finished his coffee. 'All right, Miss Kolin,' he said, 'let's pay and go.'

She signalled to the waiter. When his change came, George noticed a fold of grey paper underneath it. He put it in his pocket with the change. When they had left the café he took out the paper and unfolded it.

The message was written in a careful schoolboy hand, and in pencil:

> A car with the registration number 19907 will be waiting for you outside the Cinema at 20.00 hrs (*it said*). If anyone wants to know where you are going you are going for a drive to get some air. The driver is O.K. Ask no questions. Do what he tells you. Wear comfortable shoes. Arthur.

The car was an old open Renault that George remembered having seen once before in the town. On that occasion it had been piled high with furniture. Now, it was empty, and the driver stood beside it, cap in hand, gravely holding open the door for them. He was a fierce, sinewy old man, with a long white moustache and skin like leather. He wore a patched shirt and a pair of old striped trousers belted in at the waist with lighting flex. The back of the car showed signs of having recently carried vegetables as well as furniture. the old man scooped up a handful of decaying stalks and threw them in the road before getting into his seat and driving off.

Soon they had left the town and were on a road with a sign-post pointing to Vevi, a station on the railway east of Florina.

It was getting dark now, and the old man turned on a single headlight. He drove to save petrol, coasting down the hills with the ignition switched off, and starting up again only just before the car rolled to a standstill. The battery was down, and when the engine was not running the headlight dimmed until it was useless. With the disappearance of the last of the daylight, every descent became a hair-raising plunge into blackness. Fortunately, they met no other traffic but, after one particularly sickening moment, George protested.

'Miss Kolin, tell him to go slower down the hills or keep the motor running for the light. He'll kill us if he's not careful.'

The driver turned right round in his seat to reply.

'He says the moon will be up presently.'

'Tell him to look where he's going, for God's sake!'

'He says that there is no danger. He knows the road well.'

'All right, all right. Don't say any more. Let him keep his eyes on the road.'

They had been driving for nearly an hour, and the promised moon had begun to rise, when the road joined another coming from the north. Ten minutes later, they turned to the left and began a long, steady climb through the hills. They passed one or two isolated stone barns, then the road began to get steadily worse. Soon the car was bounding and sliding along over a surface littered with loose stones and rocks. After a mile or two of this, the car suddenly slowed down, lurched across the road to avoid an axle-deep pothole and stopped dead.

The lurch and the sudden stop had flung George against Miss Kolin. For a moment he thought that the car had broken down, then, as they disentangled themselves, he saw that the driver was standing there with the door open, motioning them to get out.

'What's the idea?' George demanded.

The old man said something.

'He says that this is where we get out,' reported Miss Kolin.

George looked round. The road was a narrow ledge of track running across a bleak hillside of thorn scrub. In the bright moonlight it looked utterly desolate. From the scrub there came a steady chorus of cicadas.

'Tell him we're staying right here until he takes us where we're supposed to go.'

There was a torrent of speech when this was translated.

'He says that this is as far as he can take us. This is the end of the road. We must get out and walk on. Someone will meet us on the road beyond. He must wait here. Those are his orders.'

'I thought he said it was the end of the road.'

'If we will come with him he will show us that he speaks the truth.'

'Wouldn't you prefer to wait here, Miss Kolin?'

'Thank you, no.'

They got out and began to walk on.

For about twenty yards the old man walked ahead of them, explaining something and making large dramatic gestures, then he stopped and pointed.

They had indeed come to the end of the road; or, at least, to the end of that stretch of it. At some time, a big stone culvert had carried a mountain stream beneath the road bed. Now, the remains of it lay in a deep boulder-strewn gully that the stream had cut for itself in the hillside.

'He says that it was blown up by the Germans, and that the winter rains have made it bigger every year.'

'Are we supposed to cross it?'

'Yes. The road continues on the other side, and there we will be met. He will stay by the car.'

'How far on the other side will we be met?'

'He does not know.'

'That advice about comfortable shoes should have warned me. Well, I suppose that now we're here we may as well go through with it.'

'As you wish.'

The bed of the stream was dry, and they were able to pick their way over the stones and between the boulders without much trouble. Clambering up on the far side, however, was less easy as the gully was deeper there. The night was warm, and George's shirt was clinging stickily to his body by the time he had helped Miss Kolin up on to the road.

They stood for a moment getting their breath and looking back. The old man waved and went back to his car.

'How long do you think it would take us to walk back to Florina from here, Miss Kolin?' George asked.

'I think he will wait. He has not been paid yet.'

'*I* didn't hire him.'

'He will expect you to pay all the same.'

'We'll see about that. We'd better do what he says, anyway.'

They began to walk.

Except for the chirruping of cicadas and the grating of their footsteps, there was no sound on the road. Once, they heard the faint tinkle of a distant sheep bell, but that was all. They had been walking steadily and in silence for some minutes, when Miss Kolin spoke quietly.

'There is someone on the road ahead.'

'Where? I can't see anyone.'

'By those bushes we are coming to. He moved out of the shadow for a moment, and I saw the moonlight on his face.'

George felt his calves tightening as they walked on. He kept his eyes fixed on the bushes. Then, he saw a movement in the shadows and a man stepped out into the road.

It was Arthur; but a rather different Arthur from the one George had talked to in the hotel. He wore breeches, a bush shirt open at the neck and a peaked cap. The thin-pointed shoes had been replaced by heavy ankle boots. There was a pistol holster on the broad leather belt round his waist.

'Evening, chum,' he said as they came up to him.

'Hullo,' said George. 'Miss Kolin, this is Arthur.'

'Pleased to meet you, Miss.' The tone was humbly respectful, but George could see the shrewd, insolent eyes summing her up.

Miss Kolin nodded. 'Good-evening.' Her hostility was clearly audible.

Arthur pursed his lips at the sound. 'No trouble getting here, I hope, Mr Carey?' he asked anxiously. He was suddenly like a week-end host apologizing for the inadequacies of the local train service.

'None to speak of. Will that old man wait for us?'

'Oh, you don't want to worry about him. Shall we go?'

'Sure. Where to?'

'It's not far. I've got transport. Just up the road here.'

He led the way. They followed in silence. About a quarter of a mile further on, the road ended again. This time the obstruction was due to a landslide from the hill above which had obliterated a section of about fifty yards. However, a narrow track had been beaten out over the debris, and they stumbled along this cautiously until the road reappeared. That is, George and Miss Kolin stumbled; Arthur went forward as surefootedly as if he were in a city street. He was waiting for them when they got back to the road.

'Only a little way now,' he said.

They walked on for another quarter of a mile. There were tamarisks growing out of the hillside here, and the moonlight cast their distorted shadows across the road. Then the shadows became solid and Arthur slowed down. Parked on a section of road which was wide enough for a vehicle to turn, was a small covered truck.

'Here we are, chums. You hop in the back.'

He shone a flashlight below the tailboard as he spoke. 'You first, Miss. Now, careful. We don't want to spoil the nylons, do we? See that stirrup there? Well, just put your foot . . .'

He broke off as Miss Kolin climbed easily into the back of the truck. 'I have been in a British army truck before,' she said coldly.

'*Have* you, now, Miss? Well, Well! That's nice, isn't it? By the way,' he went on as George followed her, 'I'm going to have to do the canvas up. It'll be a bit warmish, I'm afraid, but we haven't got far to go.'

George groaned. 'Do you have to?'

'Afraid so, chum. My pals are a bit touchy about people knowing where they are. You know–security.'

'This had better be worth while. All right. Let's get on.'

George and Miss Kolin sat on two box-shaped fixtures in the body of the truck, while their escort lashed down the canvas flaps. When he had finished, they heard him get into the driving seat and start up. The truck lurched off over the stones.

Arthur was a forceful driver, and the truck bucked and swayed about fantastically. Inside, it was impossible to remain seated, and they stood crouched under the canvas top clinging to the metal supports. The air inside, which was soon mixed with exhaust fumes, became almost unbreathable. George was dimly aware of the truck turning several hair-pin bends, and he knew that they were climbing steeply, but he quickly lost all sense of direction. After ten minutes or more of excruciating discomfort, he was beginning to think that he would have to shout to Arthur to pull up, when, after yet another turn, the truck ran on to a comparatively smooth surface and stopped. A moment later the rear canvas was unlashed, moonlight and air streamed in, and Arthur's face appeared at the tailboard.

He grinned. 'Bit bumpy, was it?'

'Yes.'

They climbed out stiffly and found themselves standing on what had once been the flagged courtyard of a small house. All that remained of the house itself was a ruined wall and a pile of debris.

'ELAS boys did that,' Arthur explained, 'the other lot were using it as a strong point. We go this way.'

The ruined house was on the summit of a pine-clad hill. They followed Arthur along a track which led from the house down through the trees.

They walked silently over pine needles for about fifty yards, then Arthur halted.

'Wait a tick,' he said.

They waited while he went on ahead. It was very dark under the trees, and there was a strong smell of pine resin. After the atmosphere in the truck, the soft, cool air was delicious. A faint murmur of voices came from the darkness ahead.

'Did you hear that, Miss Kolin?'

'Yes. They were speaking Greek, but I could not distinguish the words. It sounded like a sentry challenging and receiving a reply.'

'What do you make of all this?'

'I think we should have left word with someone where we were going.'

'We didn't know where we were going, but I did what I could. If we're not back by the time the *femme de chambre* cleans my room in the morning, she'll find a letter addressed to the manager on my bureau. In it there's the number of the old man's car, and a note of explanation for the Captain.'

'That was wise, Mr Carey. I have noticed something . . .' She broke off. 'He's coming back.'

Her hearing was very acute. Several seconds went by before George was able to hear the soft rustle of approaching footsteps.

Arthur appeared out of the darkness. 'O.K., chums,' he said. 'Here we go. We'll have a bit of light on the scene in half a tick.'

They followed him down the path. It was getting less steep now. Then, as it levelled off, Arthur switched on a flashlight and George saw the sentry leaning against a tree with his rifle under his arm. He was a thin, middle aged man in khaki drill trousers and a ragged singlet. He watched them intently as they went by.

They were clear of the pine trees now, and there was a house in front of them.

'Used to be a village down the hill there,' said Arthur. 'Wiped out by some of the boys. All flat except our place, and we had to patch that up a good bit. Left to rot, it was. Belonged to some poor bastard of a deviationist who got his throat cut.' He had become the week-end host again; proud and fond of his house and wanting his guests to share his enthusiasm.

It was a two-storey building with stuccoed walls and broad overhanging eaves. The shutters over the windows were all closed.

There was another sentry by the door. Arthur said something to him, and the man shone a light on their faces before nodding to Arthur and motioning them on. Arthur opened the door and they followed him into the house.

There was a long narrow hall with a staircase and several doorways. An oil-lamp hung from a hook by the front door. There was no plaster on the ceiling and very little left on the walls. It looked like what it was; a house which had been gutted by bomb blast or shellfire and temporarily repaired.

'Here we are,' said Arthur; 'H.Q. mess and anteroom.'

He had opened the door of what appeared to be a dining-room. There was a bare trestle table with benches on either side. On the table there were bottles, glasses, a pile of knives and forks and another oil-lamp. In the corner of the room, on the floor, there were empty bottles.

'Nobody at home,' said Arthur. 'I dare say you could do with a snifter, eh? Help yourselves. The you-know-what is just across the hall on the right if anybody's interested. I'll be back in a jiffy.'

He went out of the room shutting the door after him. They heard him clattering up the stairs.

George looked at the bottles. There was Greek wine and plum brandy. He looked at Miss Kolin.

'Drink, Miss Kolin?'

'Yes, please.'

He poured out two brandies. She picked hers up, drank it down at a gulp and held the glass out to be filled again. He filled it.

'Pretty strong stuff this, isn't it?' he said, tentatively.

'I hope so.'

'Well, I didn't expect to be taken to a place like a military headquarters. What do you think it is?'

'I have an idea.' She lit a cigarette. 'You remember four days ago in Salonika there was a bank robbery?'

'I remember something about it. Why?'

'Next day, in the train to Florina I read the newspaper reports of it. It gave an exact description of the truck that was used.'

'What about it?'

'We came here in that truck tonight.'

'What? You're kidding.'

'No.' She drank some more brandy.

'You're mistaken, then. After all, there must be dozens, hundreds, maybe, of these British army trucks still about in Greece.'

'Not with slots for false number plates.'

'What do you mean?'

'I noticed the slots when he was shining the flashlight for me to get in. The false plates were on the floor in the back of the truck. When we stopped, I put them where the moonlight would shine as we got out. The part of the number I could see was the same as the one in the newspaper report.'

'Are you absolutely sure?'

'I do not like it any more than you, Mr Carey.'

But George was remembering something that Colonel Chrysantos had said: '*They are clever and dangerous, and the police do not catch them.*'

'If they get half a suspicion we know anything . . .' he began.

'Yes. It could be most disagreeable.' She raised her glass to drink again and then stopped.

There was the sound of footsteps coming down the stairs.

George drank his brandy down quickly and got out a cigarette. The learned judge, whose secretary he had been, had once said that it was impossible to practise law for many years without learning that no case, however matter-of-fact it might seem, could be considered entirely proof against the regrettable tendency of reality to assume the shape and proportions of melodrama. At the time George had smiled politely, and wondered if he would be given to making such half-baked generalisations when he became a judge. Now, he remembered.

The door opened.

The man who came into the room was fair and deep-chested, with heavy shoulders and big hands. He might have been any age between thirty and forty. The face was strong with muscular cheeks, a determined mouth and cool, watchful eyes. He held himself very erect, and the bush shirt he wore stretched tightly across his chest. With the revolver belt at his waist he looked almost as if he were wearing uniform.

He glanced swiftly from George to Miss Kolin as Arthur, who had followed him in, shut the door and bustled forward.

'Sorry to keep you waiting,' he said. 'Mr Carey, this is my chief. He speaks a bit of English. I taught him, but go easy on the long words. He knows who you are.'

The newcomer clicked his heels and gave the slightest of bows.

'Schirmer,' he said curtly, 'Franz Schirmer. I think you wish to speak with me.'

Chapter Ten

The German forces which withdrew from Greece in October, 1944 were very different both in numbers and quality from the field army which had invaded the country just over three years earlier. If the Twelfth Army of General von List, with its crack panzer divisions and its record of success in the Polish campaign, had epitomized the irresistible strength of the *Wehrmacht*, the occupation forces, setting out to make their way home while there was still a road home open to them, epitomized no less strikingly the *Wehrmacht's* ultimate exhaustion. The earlier practice of resting troops from the fighting fronts by giving them tours of occupation duty, had long been abandoned as a luxury. The Lines of Communication Division which garrisoned the Salonika area in 1944 was, for the most part, made up of men who, for one reason or another, were considered unfit for combatant duty; debilitated survivors from the Russian front, the older men, the weaklings, and those who, because of either wounds or sickness, were of low medical categories.

For Sergeant Schirmer, the war had ended on that day in Italy when he had obeyed the order of an inexperienced officer to make a parachute jump over a wood. The comradeship of fighting men in a *corps d'élite* has meant a great deal to a great many men. To Sergeant Schirmer, it had given something that his upbringing had always denied him—his belief in himself as a man. The months in hospital which had followed the accident, the Court of Inquiry, the rehabilitation centre, the medical examinations and the posting to Greece, had been a bitter epilogue to the only period of his life in which he felt he had known happiness. Many times, he had wished that the tree branch which had merely broken his hip had pierced his breast and killed him.

If the Ninety-Fourth Garrison Regiment at Salonika had been the kind of unit in which a soldier like Sergeant Schirmer could have come to take even a grudging pride, many things no doubt would have been very different. But it was not a unit in which any self-respecting man could have taken pride. The officers (with a few exceptions such as Lieutenant Leubner) were the army's unemployables, the kind of officers whom unit commanders hasten to get rid of when they have the chance, and who spend most of their service lives held on depot establishments awaiting postings. The N.C.O.s (again with a few exceptions) were incompetent and corrupt. The rank and file were a disgruntled and decrepit assembly of old soldiers, chronic invalids, dullards and petty delinquents. Almost the first order which the Sergeant had received from an officer on joining, had been an order to remove his paratrooper's badge. That had been his introduction to the regiment, and, as time went by, he had learned to fortify and console himself with his contempt for it.

The German withdrawal from Thrace was an ignominious affair. The depot soldiers responsible for the staff work had had little experience of moving troops in the field and still less of supplying them while they were on the move. Units like the Ninety-Fourth Garrison Regiment, and there was more than one, could do little to make good the deficiencies. The knowledge that British raiding forces were advancing rapidly from the south in order to harass the retreat, and that *andarte* bands were already hovering aggressively on the flanks, may have lent urgency to the withdrawal but, in doing so, it also added to the confusion. It was traffic congestion rather than any brilliant planning by Phengaros that led to the ambushing of Sergeant Schirmer's convoy.

He was one of the last of his regiment to leave the Salonika area. Contempt for his regiment he might have, but that did not prevent his doing his utmost to see that the fraction of it that he controlled carried out its orders properly. As headquarters weapons instructor, he had no platoon responsibilities and came under the command of an engineer officer in charge of a special rearguard party. This officer was Lieutenant Leubner, and he had been detailed to carry out a series of important demolitions in the wake of the retreat.

The Sergeant liked Lieutenant Leubner who had lost a hand in Italy; he felt that the Lieutenant understood him. Between them, they organized the party in two detachments, and the Sergeant was given command of one of them.

He drove himself and his men unmercifully, and succeeded in completing his part of the work in accordance with the time-table issued with the movement order. During the night of 23rd of October, his detachment loaded the trucks they were to take with them and moved out of Salonika. They were exactly on schedule.

His orders were to go through Vodena, deal with the petrol dump on the Apsalos road and then rendezvous with Lieutenant Leubner at the bridge by Vodena. It had been anticipated that the laying of the demolition charges for the bridge would call for the united efforts of the two detachments if it were to be done to schedule. The time of the rendezvous had been fixed for dawn.

At first light that day, Sergeant Schirmer was at Yiannitsa, only a little over half-way along the road to Vodena, and trying desperately to force a way for his detachment past a column of tank transporters. The transporters should have been fifty miles farther on, but had themselves been held up by a column of horse-drawn wagons which had debouched from the Naoussa road twelve hours behind schedule. The Sergeant was two hours late when he passed through Vodena. Had he been on time, Phengaros's men would have missed him by an hour.

It had rained during the night, and with the rising sun the air became stiflingly humid; moreover, the Sergeant had had no sleep for thirty hours. Yet, as he sat beside the driver of the leading truck, he had little difficulty in staying awake. The machine-pistol lying across his knees reminded him of the need for vigilance, and the dull pain of his over-worked hip prevented his settling into too comfortable a position. But his fatigue manifested itself in other ways. His eyes, scouring an area of hillside above the bend in the road towards which they were climbing, kept shifting focus suddenly, so that he had to shake his head before he could see properly; and his thoughts wandered with dream-like inconsequence from the problems of the task in hand, and the possible plight of Lieutenant Leubner's detachment, to the attack on Eben-Emael, to a girl he had had in Hanover, and then, uneasily, to the moment in Salonika forty-eight hours earlier when Kyra had wept as he had said goodbye to her.

The weeping of women always made the Sergeant feel uneasy. It was not that he was sentimental where women were concerned; it was simply that the sound of weeping always seemed to presage his own misfortunes. There had been the time in Belgium, for instance, when that old woman had stood bleating because they had killed her cow. Two days after that he had been wounded. There had been the time in Crete, when it had been necessary for discipline to put some of the married men up against a wall and shoot them. A month later, in Benghazi, he had gone down with dysentery. There had been the time in Italy when some of the lads had fooled about with a young girl. Two days before his jumping accident, *that* had been. He would never admit to such an unreasoning and childish superstition, of course; but if he ever married it would be to some girl who would not weep even if he beat the living daylights out of her. Let her scream as much as she liked, let her try to kill him if she wanted to, and dared, but let there be no weeping. It meant bad luck.

It was the offside front wheel of the truck that exploded the mine. The Sergeant felt the lift of it a split second before his head hit the canopy of the driver's cab.

Then, there was something wet on his face and a thin, high singing in his ears. He was lying face downwards, and everything was dark except for one winking disc of light. Something gave him a violent blow in the side, but he was too tired to cry out or even to feel pain. He could hear men's voices, and knew that they were speaking Greek. Then the sounds of their voices faded and he began to fall through the air towards the trees below, defending himself against the cruel branches by locking his ankles tightly and pointing his toes, as he had been taught in the parachute jumping school. The trees engulfed him with a sigh that seemed to come from his own lips.

When he began to regain consciousness for the second time, there was nothing wet on his face but something stretching the skin of it. The disc of light was still there, but it no longer winked. He became aware now of his arms stretched out above his head, as if he were going to dive into water. He could feel his heart beating, sending pain from all over his body into his head. His legs felt warm. He moved his fingers and they dug into grit and pebbles. Consciousness began to flood back. There was something the matter with his eyelids, and he could not see properly, but he kept looking at the disc of light and moved his head slightly. Suddenly, he realized that the disc was a small, white pebble lying in a patch of sunlight. Then, he remembered that he was in Greece and had been in a truck that had been hit. With an effort, he rolled on to his side.

The force of the explosion had overturned the truck and smashed the floor of it to matchwood, but the main blast had missed the driver's cab. The Sergeant had been lying in an oil-drenched litter of empty petrol cans and debris, with his face in the mess of blood which had poured from his head wound. The blood had congealed now on his cheeks and in his eyes. The wreckage of the truck hung over him shading all but his legs from the sun. There was no sound except the chirping of cicadas and faint dripping noises from the truck.

He began to move his limbs. Though he knew that he had hurt his head, he did not as yet know the extent of his injuries. His great fear was that his hip had been broken again. For several long seconds all he could think of was the X-ray picture the surgeon had shown him of the thick metal pin which had been inserted to strengthen the neck of the damaged bone. If that had been torn away, he was finished. He moved his leg carefully. The hip was very painful, but it had been painful before the mine had exploded. Fatigue always made it painful. He became bolder and, drawing the leg up under him, began to sit up. It was then that he noticed that all his equipment had gone. He remembered the Greek voices and the blow he had felt, and began to realize what had happened.

His head was throbbing horribly, but the hip seemed to be all right. He dragged himself to his knees. A moment later, he vomited. The effort exhausted him, and he lay down again to rest. He knew that the head wound might be serious. It was not the amount of the bleeding that concerned him—he had seen plenty of scalp wounds and knew that they bled profusely—but the possibility of there being internal bleeding from the concussion. However, he would know soon enough if there were, and there was, in any case, nothing he could do about it. His immediate task was to find out what had happened to the rest of the detachment, and, if possible, take steps to deal with the situation. He made another effort to get to his feet and, after a bit, succeeded.

He looked about him. His watch had gone, but the position of the sun told him that less than an hour had elapsed since the crash. The wreckage of the truck lay across the road completely blocking it. The body of the driver was nowhere to be seen. He moved out cautiously into the middle of the road and looked down the hill.

The second truck had stopped, slewed across the road a hundred yards away. Three German soldiers lay in the road by it. Beyond he could just see the canopy of the driver's cab belonging to the third truck. He set off slowly down the hill, pausing every now and then to get his strength back. The sun beat down, and the flies buzzed round his head. It seemed an enormous distance to the second truck. He began to feel that he was going to vomit again and lay down in the shade of a bush to recover. Then he went on.

The soldiers in the road were quite dead. One of them, who looked as if he had first been wounded by a grenade burst, had his throat cut. All the arms and equipment had been taken, but the contents of two haversacks were strewn on the ground. The truck had some bullet-holes in it and was scarred by grenade bursts, but it seemed all right otherwise. For several wild moments he considered turning it round and driving back to Vodena, but the road was not wide enough to turn in, and he knew that, even if it had been, he would not have had the strength to do the job.

He could see the third truck plainly now, and with it more dead men. One of them was hanging over the side of it, his arms dangling grotesquely. It seemed probable that the whole of his detachment had become casualties. In any case, there was little point in investigating further. Militarily speaking, it had certainly ceased to exist. It would be in order for him, then, to look to his own safety.

He leaned against the side of the truck to rest again, and caught sight of his face in the driving mirror. The blood had congealed all over his hair as well as in his eyes and on his face; his whole head looked as inhuman as if it had been smashed to a pulp; it was easy to see why the *andartes* had taken him for dead.

His heart leapt suddenly with fear and sent a shaft of pain to the top of his head. The *andartes* had gone for the moment, but there was more than a possibility that they would return with drivers for the two serviceable trucks. It was even possible that they had left a sentry, and that, somewhere on the hillside above, the sights of a rifle were being steadied on him at that very moment. But, at the same moment, reason told him that there was very probably no sentry and that, even if there were, the man had already had more than enough time to shoot if he had intended to do so.

Nevertheless, the place was dangerous. Whether the *andartes* returned or whether they did not, it would not be very long before the local inhabitants ventured on to the scene. There were still plenty of pickings for them; the boots of the dead, the petrol cans, the tyres on the trucks, the tool kits. The *andartes* had taken scarcely anything. He would have to get away quickly.

For a moment or two, he thought of trying to go ahead on foot in the hope of reaching the fuel dump, but he soon abandoned the idea. Even if he had had enough strength to walk that distance, the chance of his being able to do so in broad daylight unseen by the local inhabitants would be remote. In that area and at that time, a solitary German soldier, wounded and unarmed, would be lucky if he were not tortured before he was stoned to death by the women. The road back to Vodena would be even more dangerous. He must wait for darkness, therefore; and that might give him time to recover his strength, too. His immediate course of action, then, was plain enough; he must find water, food, and a place to hide. Later on, if he were still alive, he would decide what to do next.

The water-bottles had all been taken. He dragged an empty petrol can out of the truck and began to drain the radiator into it. When it was half full he realized that he would not have the strength to carry more. There was still plenty left in the radiator, and it was not too hot to drink now. When he had slaked his thirst, he soaked his handkerchief in the water and sponged the blood from his face and eyes. His head he did not touch for fear of starting the bleeding again.

Next, he looked for food. The *andartes* had taken the sack with the supplies in it, but he knew the ways of army truck drivers and went to the tool-box. There were two emergency rations there, some sticks of chocolate and the driver's greatcoat. He put the rations and the chocolate in the greatcoat pockets and slung it over his shoulder. Then, he took the can of water and limped back slowly up the road.

He had already decided on his hiding-place. He remembered how innocent the hillside above had looked when he had been coming up the road in the truck, and how well it had concealed the attackers. It would conceal him in the same way. He left the road and started to climb.

It took him half an hour to climb a hundred yards. Once he lay for nearly ten minutes, too exhausted to move, before he could bring himself to crawl painfully on. The hillside was very steep, and he had to drag the heavy petrol can behind him. Several times he thought of leaving it and returning later to pick it up, but some instinct warned him that water was more necessary to him now than food and that he could not risk losing it. He crawled on until at last he could go no farther, and lay for a time retching helplessly, unable even to crawl out of the sun. Flies began to settle on his face without his being able to brush them away. After a while, tortured by the flies, he opened his eyes to see where he was.

There was a clump of thorn bushes a yard or so away, with a tamarisk growing among them. With a tremendous effort he dragged the can of water into the shade of the tree and crawled in among the thorn bushes with the greatcoat. The last thing he saw was a column of dense black smoke rising from somewhere beyond the hill in the direction of the fuel dump. Then, realizing that one at least of his decisions had been made for him, he lay face downwards on the coat and slept.

It was dark when he awoke. The pain in his head was agonizing and, although the night was warm, he was shivering violently. He crawled to the can of water and dragged it nearer to his bed. He knew now that he had a bout of malaria to add to his troubles, and to reduce his resistance to a possible infection of the head wound. He might be going to die; but the knowledge did not trouble him. He would fight for life as long as he was able. If he were defeated it would not matter. He had done the best he could.

He lay among the thorn bushes for nearly four days. For most of the time he was in a sort of half-waking dream state, dimly aware of the changes from darkness to light but little else that was outside him. At some moments he would know with one bit of his mind that he was delirious and talking to people who were not there; at others, he would be lost in the recurrent nightmare of the fall through the trees that never seemed to end twice in the same way.

On the third day, he awoke from a deep sleep to find that the pain in his head had lessened, that he could think clearly and that he felt hungry. He ate part of one of the emergency rations and then inspected his water supply. The can was nearly empty, but there was enough to last for that day. For the first time since he had crawled up the hill, he got to his feet. He felt horribly weak, but he forced himself to walk out of his hiding-place and look down at the road.

The two serviceable trucks had disappeared and, to his astonishment, the damaged one had been set on fire and burned out. The charred wreckage of it looked like a black stain on the limestone grit of the road. He had neither seen or heard anything of this bonfire.

He went back to his hiding-place and slept again.once, during the night, he awoke to the sound of many planes flying overhead and knew that the final stage of the withdrawal had been reached. The *Luftwaffe* was evacuating the Yidha airfield. He lay awake for a time, listening and feeling very much alone, but eventually he went back to sleep. The following morning he felt stronger and was able to go in search of water. He kept away from the road and, about half a mile down the hill, found a stream in which he washed after replenishing his drinking-water supply.

He had crossed a terraced vineyard to get to the stream, and on his way back he almost ran into a man and a woman working there. However, he saw them just in time and, retracing his steps, made his way round the vineyard. In doing so, he came near the road, and found the seven freshly-dug graves, with a steel helmet and a cairn of stones on each. There was a stake driven into the ground with a note fastened to it, giving the number and names of those buried there, and asking that the site should not be disturbed. It was signed by Lieutenant Leubner.

Sergeant Schirmer was strangely moved. It had not once occurred to him that the Lieutenant might find time to interest himself in the fate of the lost detachment. No doubt it had been he who had burnt the damaged truck and removed the others. A good officer, the Lieutenant.

He looked at the note again. Seven dead. That meant that three, including the missing driver, had been made prisoner or escaped. The paper was already somewhat tattered, and it had probably been there for over two days. It was bitter to know that friendly hands had been so near while he had lain hidden and oblivious among the thorn bushes. For the first time since the mine had exploded he was conscious of a feeling of despair.

He thrust it away angrily. What had he to despair of? His inability to rejoin the Ninety-Fourth Garrison Regiment, fumbling its way back to the Fatherland with its tail between its legs? The lack of someone to ask for orders? How the instructors at the parachute training school would have laughed!

He looked down again at the graves. He had no cap or helmet and so could not salute. He drew himself up into the position of attention and clicked his heels respectfully. Then, he picked up his petrol can and made his way back to the hillside and the thorn bushes.

After he had finished the remains of the first emergency ration he lay down to think things out.

The expedition for water had tired him sufficiently for him to realize that he was still very weak. Another twenty-four hours must elapse before he was fit to move. The food he had left could probably be made to last that long. After that he must forage.

And then what?

The German forces had probably left Vodena two days or more ago. It was idle to suppose that he could catch them up now. He would have hundreds of miles of difficult country to travel before he could do that. His only chance of getting through unseen would be to avoid the roads; yet if he did that, the long hard marches would soon lame him. He could try the railway, of course, but that was amost certainly in the hands of the Greeks again by now. His despair returned, and this time it was not so easily dismissed. The plain fact was that there was nowhere he could reasonably go. He was completely cut off in hostile territory where capture or surrender meant death, and the ways of escape were all closed. The only thing he could do, it seemed, was to go on living under the thorn bush like an animal, stealing what food he could from the fields. An escaped prisoner of war would be in a better position; at least he would have had time to prepare for the venture. He, Schirmer, was relatively helpless. He had no civilian clothes, no money, no papers, no food worth speaking of; moreover, he was still suffering from the after-effects of being blown up by a mine and an attack of malaria. He needed time to recover completely and time to plan. Above all, he needed someone to help him to get identity papers. Clothes and money he might steal, but to steal papers printed in a language he could not read and risk using them as his own would be folly.

And then he thought of Kyra; Kyra who had wept so bitterly when he had had to say goodbye to her, who had implored him, foolishly, to desert; the one friend he possessed in this hostile, treacherous land.

She had a small photographic processing business in Salonika. He had seen the bold AGFA advertisement sign outside her shop one day and gone in to see if he could buy some film for his camera. She had had no film to sell—it had been hard to come by at the time—but he had been attracted by her and had returned to the shop whenever he had had time off. There was little processing work to be had, and to make more money she had set up a small curtained 'studio' for the taking of identity card and passport photographs. When a local military identity card had been issued to the occupation forces, he had been able to suggest to the officer responsible for the issue in his own unit that she should be commissioned to do all the photographic work. He had also brought her army food. She lived with her brother in two rooms over the shop. However, the brother was a night-duty clerk in a hotel which had been commandeered by the occupation headquarters, and was only at home in the daytime. Quite soon, the Sergeant had been able to apply for a sleeping-out pass. Kyra was a full-blooded young woman with simple and readily fulfillable demands to make. The Sergeant was both lusty and skilful. The relationship had proved most satisfactory.

Now, it could be made to serve another purpose.

Salonika was seventy-four kilometres away by road. That meant that he would have to cover at least a hundred kilometres in order to keep away from the towns and villages. If he marched in daylight it would probably take him about four days to get there. If he played for safety and moved only at night it would take much longer. He must not work his hip too hard. He must allow, too, for the time he would have to spend getting food. The sooner he started the better. His spirits rose. The following night, having eaten the last of the army rations and with only the chocolate in his pocket for emergencies, he set off.

It took him eight days to reach his destination. Travelling at night, without map and compass to guide him, had proved too difficult. He had lost himself repeatedly. After the third night, he had decided that he must accept the greater risk and travel by day. He had found it easier than he expected. Even in the plain, there was plenty of cover to move in, and it had been possible, except in the vicinity of Yiannitsa, to keep fairly close to the road. Food was the greatest difficulty. From an isolated farm he was able to steal some eggs, and on another day he milked a straying goat; but mostly he lived on the wild fruit he could pick. It was not until the end of the seventh day that he decided that the situation had become desperate enough for him to eat his chocolate.

It was about ten o'clock in the morning when he reached the outskirts of Salonika. He was near the railway, and in an area that offered reasonable opportunities for concealment. He decided to stop there and wait until nightfall before entering the city.

Now that his journey was nearly done, the thing that most concerned him was his appearance. The wound on his scalp was healing well and would not excite much curiosity. He disliked the stubble of beard he had grown, but only because it was unsoldierly; he did not think that it would make him too conspicuous. The trouble was his uniform. It seemed to him that to walk through the streets of Salonika in a German uniform now would be to invite arrest or assassination. Something would have to be done.

He moved nearer to the railway and began to reconnoitre along it. Eventually, he came upon what he was looking for—a platelayer's hut. It was padlocked, but there were some heavy iron rail chairs on the ground nearby, and he used one to smash the hasp through which the padlock was fastened.

He had hoped to find a pair of overalls or a workman's blouse of some sort in the hut, but there was no clothing there of any kind. There was, however, a workman's dinner wrapped in a sheet of newspaper; a piece of bread, some olives and half a bottle of wine.

He took it back to his hiding-place and swallowed it greedily. The wine made him drowsy, and he slept for a while afterwards. When he awoke, he felt much refreshed and began to reconsider the problem of his clothing.

He had on a grey cotton singlet under his tunic. If he discarded the tunic and belted his uniform trousers, the top part of him would look like a dock labourer. At night, when the colour and material of the trousers could not be seen clearly, the only things that would give him away would be his jack-boots. He tried to conceal them by wearing the trousers over the boots instead of tucked inside them. The result was not altogether satisfactory, but he decided eventually that it was sufficiently so. The risks he would have to run to steal clothing were probably greater than the risk of having his boots identified in the darkness. So far, good fortune had been with him. It would be foolish to try it too hard within sight of his objective.

By eight o'clock that night it was quite dark, and he set off for the city.

He had a disagreeable surprise when he reached it. The quarters which he had to pass were ablaze with lights. The citizens of Salonika were celebrating their liberation from the occupation forces and the arrival of the 'Macedonian Group of Divisions' of ELAS.

It was a fantastic scene. Along the waterfront, long chains of screaming, singing people swayed and capered to music blaring from cafés and bars. The restaurants were jammed. Shrieking mobs danced on the chairs and tables. Everywhere, there were groups of drunken *andartes*, many of them Bulgars, staggering about, shouting wildly, firing rifles into the air and fetching women out of brothels to dance with them in the street. To the Sergeant, hurrying along discreetly in what shadows he could find, the city seemed like some vast orgiastic fair ground.

Kyra's shop was in a narrow street near the Eski Juma. There were no bars or cafés in it, and it was relatively quiet. The shopkeepers with shutters had taken the precaution of putting them up; others had nailed boards across their windows. Kyra's windows were protected in this way and the shop was in darkness; but there was a light in the window above it.

He was relieved at this. He had feared that she might be out taking part in the carnival in the streets, and that he would have to wait for her return. The fact that she was in also meant that she did not share in the popular rejoicing. That was all to the good.

He looked round carefully to see that his arrival had not been witnessed by anyone who might know him by sight; then, satisfied on this point, he rang the bell.

After a moment or two, he heard her come down the stairs and cross the shop to the door. The boards prevented his seeing her. He heard her stop, but the door did not open.

'Who is it?' she said in Greek.

'Franz.'

'God in heaven!'

'Let me in.'

He heard her fumbling with the bolts and then the door opened. He stepped inside, shut the door quickly behind him and took her in his arms. He could feel her trembling as he kissed her, and then she pressed away from him with a gasp of fear.

'What are you doing here?'

He told her what had happened to him and what he planned.

'But you cannot stay.'

'I have to.'

'No, you cannot.'

'Why not, my beloved? There is no risk.'

'I am already suspect because I have loved a German.'

'What can they do?'

'I may be arrested.'

'Absurd. If they arrested every woman in this place who had loved a German they would need an army to guard them.'

'It is different with me. The *andartes* have arrested Niki.'

'What for?' Niki was her brother.

'He is accused of spying for the Germans and informing. When he has confessed and accused others, they will kill him.'

'The swine! Nevertheless, I must stay, beloved.'

'You must surrender. You would be a prisoner of war.'

'Don't you believe it. They would cut my throat.'

'No. There are many German soldiers here. Deserters. No harm comes to them if they say they are sympathizers.'

'If they say they are Communists, you mean?'

'What does it matter?'

'You class me with these deserter swine?'

'Of course not, beloved. I wish only to save you.'

'Good. First, I need food. Then, a bed. I will use Niki's room tonight. I am fit for nothing but sleep.'

'But you cannot stay here, Franz. You cannot.' She began to sob.

He gripped her arms. 'No tears, my beloved, and no arguments. You understand? I give the orders. When I have eaten and rested, then we can talk. Now, you can show me what there is to eat.'

He had driven his fingers deep into her arm muscles, and when she stopped weeping he knew that he had frightened her as well as hurt her. That was as it should be. There would be no more disobedience for the present.

They went up to the apartment. When she saw him in the light, she gave a cry of dismay, but he cut short her further lamentations impatiently.

'I am hungry,' he said.

She put together a meal for him and watched him while he ate it. She was silent now and thoughtful, but he scarcely noticed her. He was planning. First, he would sleep and then he would see about getting a civilian suit. It was a pity that her brother Niki was so undersized; his clothes would be far too small. She would have to buy a secondhand suit somewhere. Then, she could find out exactly what papers he would need in order to move about freely. There was the language difficulty, of course; but perhaps he could overcome that by pretending to be a Bulgar or an Albanian; there would be plenty of that sort of scum about now. After that, he would have to decide where to go. It would be an awkward problem. There were not many countries left in which a German would be welcomed and assisted to repatriate himself. There was Spain, of course–he might get there by sea–or Turkey . . .

But his head was drooping on his chest now and his eyes would no longer stay open. He roused himself sufficiently to go into the bedroom. At the bed, he turned and looked back. Kyra was standing in the door watching him. She smiled reassuringly. He sank down on to the bed and went to sleep.

It was still dark, and he could not have been asleep for much more than two hours, when he awoke in response to a violent shaking of his arm and a blow in the back.

He rolled over and opened his eyes.

Two men with pistols in their hands were standing looking down at him. They wore the elementary kind of uniform which he had seen on the *andartes* rioting about in the streets a few hours earlier. Those, however, had all been very drunk; these were very sober and businesslike. They were lean, sour-looking young men with smart belts and brassards on their arms. He guessed that they were *andarte* officers. One of them spoke sharply in German.

'Get up.'

He obeyed slowly, overcoming a longing for sleep more desperate than any sensation of fear. He hoped that they would kill him quickly so that he could rest.

'Your name?'

'Schirmer.'

'Rank?'

'Sergeant. Who are you?'

'You'll find out. She says you were a paratrooper and an instructor. Is that correct?'

'Yes.'

'Where did you win your Iron Cross?'

The Sergeant was sufficiently awake now to appreciate the necessity of lying. 'In Belgium,' he said.

'Do you want to live?'

'Who doesn't?'

'Fascists don't. They are death-lovers, so we kill them. True democrats want to live. They prove their desire by fighting with their class comrades against the Fascists and the capitalist-imperialist aggressors.'

'Who are these aggressors?'

'Reactionaries and their Anglo-American bosses.'

'I don't know anything about politics.'

'Naturally. You have had no chance of learning about them. They are simple enough, however. Fascists die, true democrats live. You can, of course, choose freely which you are to be, but as time is short and there is much work to be done, you can have only twenty seconds to make up your mind. The usual time allowed is ten seconds, but you are an N.C.O., a skilled soldier and a valuable instructor. Also you are not a deserter. You are entitled to think carefully before you accept the sacred responsibility which is offered to you.'

'If I claim the rights of a prisoner of war?'

'You are no prisoner, Schirmer. You have not surrendered. You are still in the thick of the fight. At present you are an enemy of Greece and—' the *andarte* raised his pistol—'we have much to avenge.'

'And if I accept?'

'You will be given an early opportunity of demonstrating your political reliability, your loyalty and your skill. The twenty seconds have long ago departed. What do you wish to say?'

The Sergeant shrugged. 'I accept.'

'Then salute,' the *andarte* said sharply.

For an instant, the Sergeant's right arm started to move, and in that instant he saw the *andarte's* finger tighten on the trigger. He clenched the fist of his left hand and raised it above his head.

The *andarte* smiled thinly. 'Very good. You may come with us in a moment.' He went to the bedroom door and opened it. 'But first there is another matter to attend to.'

He beckoned Kyra into the room. She walked stiffly, her face a tear-stained mask of fear. She did not look at the Sergeant.

'This woman,' the *andarte* said with a smile, 'was good enough to inform us that you were here. Her brother was a Fascist-collaborationist spy. Her object in betraying you was to convince us that she has a true democratic spirit. What do you think about that, Comrade Schirmer?'

'I think she is a Fascist bitch,' said the Sergeant, shortly.

'Excellent. That was my own thought. You will learn fast.'

The *andarte* glanced at his companion and nodded.

The companion's gun jerked up. Before Kyra could scream or the Sergeant could even think of protesting, three shots had crashed out. The shock waves brought down a small piece of plaster from the ceiling. The Sergeant felt it tap his shoulder as he saw the girl, her mouth still open, slammed against the wall by the force of the heavy bullets. Then, she sank to the floor without a sound.

The *andarte* officer looked at her intently for a moment, then nodded again and walked out of the room.

The Sergeant followed. He knew that some time when he was not so tired and confused he would feel horror at what had just happened. He had liked Kyra.

Sergeant Schirmer served in the Democratic Army of General Markos for just over four years.

After the December rebellion of 1944, and the promotion of Markos to the command of the army, he had been sent to Albania. There, he had been an instructor in a training camp set up to discipline the guerrilla bands then being organized in larger formations, in preparation for the campaign of 1946. It was in this camp that he met Arthur.

Arthur had been in a British Commando force which had raided a German headquarters in North Africa. He had been wounded and captured. The German officer in charge had chosen to ignore the standing order about shooting captured Commando men and had put Arthur in with a batch of other British prisoners who were being sent to Germany via Greece and Yugoslavia. In Yugoslavia, Arthur had escaped and spent the rest of the war fighting with the Tito Partisans. He had not troubled to return to England when the war ended, and had been one of the instructors provided by Tito to assist Markos.

In Arthur, the Sergeant found a kindred spirit. They were both professional soldiers, and had both served in *corps d'élite* as N.C.O.s. Neither had any emotional ties with his native land. Both loved soldiering for its own sake. Above all, they shared the same outlook on matters of politics.

During his service with the Partisans, Arthur had listened to so much Marxist patter that he knew a great deal of it by heart. At moments of stress or boredom he would recite it at length and at lighting speed. It had disconcerted the Sergeant when he had heard it for the first time, and he had approached Arthur privately on the subject.

'I was not aware, Corporal,' he had said in the clumsy mixture of Greek, English and German they used in order to converse; 'I did not think that you were a Red.'

Arthur had grinned. 'No? I'm one of the most politically reliable men in the outfit.'

'So?'

'So. Don't I prove it? Look how many slogans I know. I can talk like the book.'

'I see.'

'Of course, I don't know what this dialectical materialism stuff means, but then I could never understand what the Bible was all about either. At school we had to say bits of the Bible. I always used to get top marks for scripture. Here, I'm politically reliable.'

'You do not believe in the cause for which we fight?'

'No more than you do, Sergeant. I leave that to the amateurs. Soldiering's my job. What do I want with causes?'

The Sergeant had nodded thoughtfully, and glanced at the medal ribbons on Arthur's shirt. 'Do you think, Corporal, that there is any possibility of our general's plans succeeding?' he had asked. Although they both held commissions in the Markos forces they had chosen to ignore the fact in private. They had been N.C.O.s in proper armies.

'Could be,' Arthur said. 'Depends on how many mistakes the other lot make, same as always. Why? What are you thinking about, Sarge? Promotion?'

The Sergeant had nodded. 'Yes, promotion. If this revolution were to succeed there might be big opportunities for men able to take them. I think that I, too, must take steps to become politically reliable.'

The steps he had taken had proved effective, and his qualities as a natural leader had soon been recognized. By 1947 he was commanding a brigade, with Arthur as his second-in-command. When, in 1949, the Markos forces began to disintegrate, their brigade was one of the last to hold out in the Grammos area.

But they knew by then that the rebellion was over, and they were bitter. Neither of them had ever believed in the cause for which they had fought so long and hard and skilfully; but its betrayal by Tito and the Moscow Politburo had seemed an infamous thing.

' "Put not your trust in princes",' Arthur had quoted, gloomily.

'Who said this?' the Sergeant had asked.

'The Bible. Only these aren't princes, they're politicians.'

'It is the same.' A faraway look had come into the Sergeant's eyes. 'I think, Corporal, that in future we must trust only ourselves,' he had said.

Chapter Eleven

It was just after dawn and the mountains above Florina were outlined against a pink glow in the sky, when the old Renault deposited George and Miss Kolin outside the cinema where it had picked them up ten hours earlier. On George's instructions, Miss Kolin paid the driver and arranged with him to pick them up again that evening to make the same journey. They went to their hotel in silence.

When he got to his room, George destroyed the precautionary letter he had left there for the manager and sat down to draft a cable to Mr Sistrom.

'CLAIMANT LOCATED IN STRANGE CIRCUMSTANCES,' he wrote, 'IDENTITY BEYOND
REASONABLE DOUBT STOP COMPLEX SITUATION PREVENTS STRAIGHTFORWARD
ACTION TO DELIVER HIM YOUR OFFICE STOP MAILING FULL EXPLANATORY REPORT
TODAY STOP MEANWHILE CABLE IMMEDIATELY TERMS OF EXTRADITION TREATY IF
ANY BETWEEN U.S. AND GREECE WITH SPECIAL REFERENCE ARMED BANK ROBBERY.
CAREY.'

That, he thought grimly, should give Mr Sistrom something to gnaw on.
He read it through again, striking out the unnecessary prepositions and
conjunctions, and then translated it into the code they had agreed for highly
confidential messages. When he had finished he looked at the time. The post
office would not be open for another hour. He would write to Mr Sistrom
and mail the letter at the same time as he sent the cable. He sighed. It had
been an exhausting night—exhausting in some unexpected ways. When the
coffee and buttered rolls he had ordered from the restaurant arrived, he sat
down to compose his report.

'In my last report,' he began, 'I told you of the evidence I had been given
by Madame Vassiotis and of my consequent decision to return home as soon
as possible. Since then, as you will have gathered from my cable, the picture
has completely changed. I knew, of course, that the inquiries instituted by
Madame Vassiotis would reach the ears of all sorts of persons who, for one
reason or another, were regarded as criminals by the authorities. I scarcely
expected them to come to the attention of the man we have been looking for.
Nevertheless, that is what happened. Twenty-four hours ago, I was
approached by a man who stated that he had friends who had information to
give about Schirmer. Subsequently, Miss Kolin and I took a very
uncomfortable trip to a secret destination somewhere up in the mountains
near the Yugoslav frontier. At the end of the journey we were taken to a
house and confronted by a man who said he was Franz Schirmer. When I
had explained the purpose of our visit I asked him various pertinent
questions, all of which he answered correctly. I asked him then about the
ambush at Vodena and his subsequent movements. He told a fantastic
story.'

George hesitated; then he erased the word 'fantastic'—Mr Sistrom would
not like that sort of adjective—and typed the word 'curious' in its place.

And yet it *had* been fantastic, to sit there in the light of the oil-lamp
listening to the great-great-grandson of the hero of Preussisch-Eylau
telling, in his broken English, the story of his adventures in Greece. He had
spoken slowly, sometimes with a faint smile at the corners of his mouth,
always with his watchful grey eyes on his visitors, reading and assessing
them. The Dragoon of Ansbach, George thought, must have been very
much the same kind of man. Where other men would succumb to physical
disaster, men like these two Schirmers would always endure and survive.
One had been wounded, had put his trust in God, had deserted, and lived to
become a prosperous tradesman. The other had been left for dead, had put
his trust in himself, had kept his wits about him, and lived to fight another
day.

What the second Sergeant Schirmer had become, however, was a
question that the Sergeant himself had made no attempt to answer.

His own account of his adventures had ended inconclusively at the time of the closing of the Yugoslav frontier by Tito, and with a bitter complaint against the manoeuvrings of the Communist politicians that had defeated the Markos forces. But George had very little doubt now about the nature of the Sergeant's subsequent activities. They had conformed to an ancient pattern. When defeated revolutionary armies disintegrated, those soldiers who feared for political reasons to go back home, or who had no homes to go back to, turned to brigandage. And since, quite clearly, neither the Sergeant nor Arthur was, to use Colonel Chrysantos's words, a 'simple, deluded fanatic of the type that always gets caught,' their gleanings in Salonika had almost certainly gone into their own pockets, and those of their men-at-arms. It was a delicate situation. Moreover, if he were not to seem suspiciously incurious, he would have to invite them somehow to explain their set-up in their own way.

It had been Arthur who had provided the opening.

'Didn't I tell you it'd be worth your while to come, Mr Carey?' he said triumphantly when the Sergeant had finished.

'You did indeed, Arthur, and I'm very grateful. And of course, I understand now the reason for all the secrecy.' He looked at the Sergeant. 'I had no idea that fighting was still going on in this area?'

'No?' The Sergeant drained his glass and set it down with a bang. 'It is the censorship,' he said. 'The Government hide the truth from the world.'

Arthur nodded gravely. 'Proper Fascist-imperialist lackeys, they are,' he said.

'But we do not talk politics, eh?' The Sergeant smiled as he filled Miss Kolin's glass. 'It is not interesting for the beautiful lady.'

She said something coldly in German, and his smile faded. For a moment he seemed to be reconsidering Miss Kolin; then he turned to George cheerfully.

'Let us all fill our glasses and come to business,' he said.

'Yes, let's do that,' said George. He had given them the reassuring impression that he was content with his picture of them as simple revolutionaries still fighting for a lost cause. That was enough. 'I expect you'd like to know a bit more about the whole affair, wouldn't you, Sergeant?' he added.

'That is what I wish.'

George told him the history of the case from the beginning.

For a time the Sergeant listened politely, interrupting only to ask for the explanation of a legal word or phrase he did not understand. When Miss Kolin translated it into German he acknowledged the service each time with a nod. He seemed almost indifferent, as if he were listening to something that was really no concern of his. It was when George came to the part played in the case by the account of the first Sergeant Schirmer's exploits at Eylau that his attitude changed. Suddenly he leaned forward across the table and began interrupting with abrupt, sharp-voiced questions.

'You say Franz Schirmer? He had the same name and rank as me, this old man?'

'Yes. And he was roughly the same age as you were when you dropped into Crete.'

'So! Go on, please.'

George went on, but not for long.

'Where was he wounded?'

'In the arm.'

'As I was at Eben-Emael.'

'No, he had a sabre cut.'

'It does not matter. It is the same. Go on, please.'

George went on again. The Sergeant's eyes were fixed on him intently. He interrupted again.

'Food? What food had he?'

'Some frozen potatoes he'd taken from a barn.' George smiled. 'You know, Sergeant, I've got the complete account of all this written out by Franz Schirmer's second son, Hans. That's the one who emigrated to America. He wrote it out for his children, to show them what a fine man their grandfather had been.'

'You have this here?'

'I have a copy at the hotel in Florina.'

'I may see it?' He was eager now.

'Sure. You can have it. You'll probably have the original eventually. I guess all the family papers are rightfully yours.'

'Ah, yes. The family papers,' He nodded thoughtfully.

'But what Hans wrote isn't the whole story by any means. There were some things Franz Schirmer didn't tell his children.'

'So? What things?'

George went on to tell him then about the meeting with Maria, about Mr Moreton's investigation and about his discovery of the truth in the army records at Potsdam.

The Sergeant listened without interruption now; and when George finished he remained silent for a moment or two staring down at the table in front of him. At last he looked up and there was a quiet smile of satisfaction on his face.

'That was a man,' he said to Arthur.

'One of the boys, all right,' Arthur agreed, nodding; 'same name and rank, too. Let's see—dragoons were mounted infantry, weren't they?'

But the Sergeant had turned to George again. 'And this Maria. She was my great *Urgrossmutter*?'

'That's right. Her first son, Karl, was your *Urgrossvater*. But, you see, the strong case we have through knowing about the change of name. Amelia Schneider's first cousin was your grandfather Friedrich, and he survived her. You remember him?'

The Sergeant nodded vaguely. 'Yes. I remember.'

'Legally, he inherited the money. You will inherit from him through your father. Of course, there's a hell of a lot to be done before it can all be fixed up. Your claim may have to be advanced through the German or even the Swiss courts. You may have to apply for Swiss papers first. I don't know. It depends on the attitude of the Pennsylvania Court. Certainly, we can expect the Commonwealth of Pennsylvania to fight. What the attitude of the Alien Property Custodian will be we don't know yet. Anyway, it'll be tough. I guess you won't mind that though, eh?'

'No.' But he did not appear to be paying much attention to what George was saying. 'I have never been to Ansbach,' he said slowly.

'Well, you'll have plenty of time later on, I guess. Now, about the business side of it all. The law firm I represent are the attorneys for the administrator of the estate so we couldn't act for you ourselves. You'd have to retain someone else. I don't know whether or not you can afford to put up money for the costs of fighting the case. They'd be pretty heavy. If you didn't want to do that we could recommend a good firm who would act for you on a contingency basis. That is, they would take a percentage of what you got out of it. Explain it all, Miss Kolin, will you please?'

She explained. He listened absently, and then nodded.

'You agree?' George asked.

'Yes. I agree. You do all.'

'O.K. How soon can you leave for America?'

George saw Arthur look at him sharply. Now, the trouble was going to start.

The Sergeant frowned. 'America?'

'Yes. We could travel together if you like.'

'But I do not wish to go to America.'

'Well, Sergeant, if you're going to claim your estate, I'm afraid you'll have to go.' George smiled. 'The case can't be fought without you.'

'You said that you would do all.'

'I said that we would recommend a firm of attorneys to represent you. But they can't fight the case without producing the claimant. They'll have to prove your identity and so on. The State and the Alien Property Custodian's lawyer will want to ask you a lot of questions.'

'What questions?'

'Every sort of question. We'd better be quite clear about that. You're liable to have to account for every moment of your life, especially the bit since you were reported missing.'

'That's torn it,' said Arthur.

George misunderstood the remark with great care.

'Oh, I don't think the Sergeant has any cause to worry on that score,' he said. 'This is purely a domestic legal matter. The fact that he's been fighting in a civil war here is of no interest to Pennsylvania. We might run into some trouble getting a visa, but I think we could get over that in view of the special circumstances. Of course, the Greeks could make it tough for him if he wanted to return here afterwards, but beyond that there's nothing they can do. After all, it's not as if he'd committed some felony for which he could be extradited by the Greek Government, is it?' He paused. 'You'd better translate that, Miss Kolin,' he added.

Miss Kolin translated. When she had finished there was a tense silence. The Sergeant and Arthur stared at one another grimly. At last, the Sergeant turned to George again.

'How much you say, this money?'

'Well, I'm going to be frank with you, Sergeant. Until I was quite sure who you were I didn't want to make it sound too attractive. Now, you'd better know the facts. After various tax deductions, you stand to get close on a million dollars.'

'Crikey!' said Arthur, and the Sergeant swore violently in German.

'Of course, that is only if you win the case. The Commonwealth is after the money, too. Obviously, they'll try to prove that you're an impostor, and you'll have to be able to prove that you're not.'

The Sergeant had risen impatiently, and was pouring himself another glass of wine. George went on talking without a pause.

'It shouldn't be difficult, I think if it's gone about in the right way. There are all sorts of possibilities. For instance, supposing for some reason you'd had your finger-prints taken—while you were in the German Army, say—why then you wouldn't have any more to worry about. On the other hand . . .'

'Please!' The Sergeant held up his hand. 'Please, Mr Carey, I must think.'

'Sure,' said George. 'I was being stupid. It must be quite a shock to realize that you're a rich man. It'll take time for you to get adjusted.'

There was silence again. The Sergeant looked at Arthur and then they both looked at Miss Kolin sitting there impassively with her notebook. They could not say what was on their minds in front of her in Greek or German. Arthur shrugged. The Sergeant sighed and sat down by George again.

'Mr Carey,' he said, 'I cannot so immediately decide what I must do. I must have time. There are so many things.'

George nodded sagely as if he had suddenly understood the true nature of the Sergeant's dilemma. 'Ah, yes. I should have realized that, other difficulties apart, this situation presents you with quite a problem in revolutionary ethics.'

'Please?'

Miss Kolin translated rapidly and with a faint sneer that did not please George in the least. But the Sergeant seemed not to notice it.

He nodded absently. 'Yes, yes. That is so. I must have time to think about many things.'

George thought that it was time for slightly plainer speaking. 'There's one point I'd like to be clear about,' he said. 'That is if you don't mind taking me into your confidence?'

'Yes? A point?'

'Are you known to the Greek authorities under your own name?'

'Now, chum . . .' Arthur began warningly.

But George interrupted him. 'Save it, Arthur' The Sergeant's going to have to tell me eventually, anyway, if I'm to be any use to him. You see that, don't you, Sergeant?'

The Sergeant thought for a moment, then nodded. 'Yes. It is a good question, Corporal. I see his reason. Mr Carey, I am known by another name to the police.'

'Very well, then. I'm not interested in helping the Greek police. I'm concerned with the disposal of a big estate. Supposing we could keep that alias of yours out of the proceedings altogether—and I don't see why we shouldn't—would that make your decision easier?'

The Sergeant's shrewd eyes watched him steadily. 'Would there be no photographs in the newspapers of such a lucky man, Mr Carey?'

'Sure, there'd be pictures all over the front pages. Oh, I see. You mean that, names or no names, the fact that you'd been in Greece would be bound to attract attention here and the pictures would identify you, anyway.'

'So many persons know my face,' said the Sergeant, apologetically. 'So you see, I must think.'

'Yes, I see that,' said George. He knew now that the Sergeant understood the position as clearly as he did. If the robbery or robberies in which he had been concerned were extraditable offences, then any kind of publicity would be fatal to him. Among those who would know his face, for instance, would be the clerks in the Salonika branch of the Eurasian Credit Bank. The only thing the Sergeant did not understand was that George was aware of the true position. No doubt a day would come when it would be safe to enlighten him; in Mr Sistrom's office, perhaps. For the present, discretion was advisable. 'How long do you want to think, Sergeant?' he said.

'Until tomorrow. If you will tomorrow night come back we will speak again.'

'O.K.'

'And you will bring also my family papers?'

'I'll do that.'

'Then *auf Wiedersehen*.'

'*Auf Wiedersehen*.'

'You will not forget the papers?'

'No, I won't forget, Sergeant.'

Arthur took them back to the truck. He was silent on the way. It was evident that he, too, had plenty to think about. But when they were in the truck again and he was about to do up the canvas he paused, and leaned on the tailboard.

'Do you like the Sarge?' he said.

'He's quite a guy, you must be very fond of him.'

'Best pal in the world,' said Arthur, curtly. 'I was just asking. I wouldn't like anything to happen to him, if you take my meaning.'

George chuckled. 'How would you like to be the most unpopular man in Philadelphia, Arthur?'

'Eh?'

'That's what I shall be if anything happens to Franz Schirmer.'

'Oh-la-la! Sorry I spoke.'

'Forget it. Say, what about taking it easy this time on some of those bends going down?'

'O.K., pal. You're the doctor. Easy it is.'

The opening between the driver's seat and the rear of the truck had a flap over it and during the drive down to the culvert George struck a match so that Miss Kolin could examine the false number plates again. She looked at them carefully and nodded. George extinguished the match impatiently. Any real hopes he might have had that the Sergeant would, after all, turn out to be only another simple-minded zealot of the Phengaros type, had long since been abandoned. It was absurd to go on clutching at straws.

Promising to meet them again the following night at the same place, Arthur left them at the culvert. They stumbled back to the car, roused the old man from his sleep and set out on the road back to Florina.

Although it was the first opportunity they had had of talking privately since they had met the Sergeant, neither of them spoke for several minutes. Then, it was Miss Kolin who at last broke the silence.

'What do you intend to do?' she asked.

'Cable the office for instructions.'

'You will not inform the police?'

'Not unless the office tells me to. In any case, I'm by no means certain that we have anything more than vague suspicions to tell them.'

'Is that your honest opinion?'

'Miss Kolin, I wasn't sent to Europe to act as a Greek police informer. I was sent to find the rightful claimant to the Schneider Johnson estate, and produce him in Philadelphia. Well, that's what I'm doing. It's no concern of mine *what* he is here. He can be a brigand, a bandit, an outlaw, a travelling salesman or the Metropolitan Archbishop of Salonika for all I care. In Philadelphia, he's the rightful claimant to the Schneider Johnson estate, and what he is here doesn't affect his claim in the least.'

'I should think it would considerably affect his value in court.'

'That's his lawyer's headache, not mine, and he can deal with it how he pleases. Anyway, why should you worry?'

'I thought that you believed in justice.'

'I do. That's why Franz Schirmer is going to Philadelphia if I can get him there.'

'Justice!' She laughed unpleasantly.

George was already tired; now, he began to get annoyed.

'Look, Miss Kolin. You are engaged as an interpreter not as a legal adviser or my professional conscience. Let's both stick to our jobs. At the moment, the only thing that matters is that, incredible as it may seem, this man is Franz Schirmer.'

'He is also a German of the worst type,' she said, sullenly.

'I'm not interested in what type he is. All I'm concerned with is the fact that he exists.'

There was silence for a moment, and he thought that the argument was ended. Then she began to laugh again.

'Quite a guy, the Sarge!' she said, derisively.

'Now look, Miss Kolin,' he began, 'I've been very . . .'

But she was not listening any more. 'The swine!' she exclaimed bitterly. 'The filthy swine!'

George stared at her. She began pounding her knees with her fists and repeating the word 'filthy'.

'Miss Kolin. Don't you think . . .'

She rounded on him. 'That girl in Salonika! You heard what he did?'

'I also heard what she did.'

'Only for revenge after he had seduced her. And how many more has he treated that way?'

'Aren't you being a bit silly?'

She did not hear him. 'How many more victims?' Her voice rose. 'They are always the same, these beasts—killing and torturing and raping wherever they go. What do the Americans and British know of them? Your armies do not fight in your own lands. Ask the French about the Germans in their streets and in their houses. Ask the Poles and Russians, the Czechs, the

Yugoslavs. These men are filthy slime on the land that suffers them. Filth! Beating and torturing, beating and torturing, bearing down with their strength, until they . . . until they . . .'

She broke off, staring blankly ahead as if she had forgotten what she had been going to say. Then, suddenly, she crumpled into a passionate storm of weeping.

George sat there as stolidly as his embarrassment and the lurching of the car would allow, trying to remember how many drinks he had seen her have since they had left Florina. It seemed to him that her glass had never once been empty while they had been at the Sergeant's headquarters, but he could not quite remember. Probably, she had kept refilling it. If that were so, she must have had the best part of a bottle of plum brandy, as well as her after-dinner cognacs. He had been too preoccupied to pay much attention to her.

She was sobbing quietly now. The old man driving had merely glanced round once and then taken no further interest. Presumably he was accustomed to distracted women. George was not. He was feeling sorry for her; but he was also remembering her pleasure in the anecdotes of Colonel Chrysantos, the man who knew 'how to deal with Germans'.

After a while, she went to sleep, her head cushioned in her arms against the back of the seat. The sky was beginning to lighten when she awoke. For a time she stared at the road, taking no notice of the wind blowing her hair about; then she took out a cigarette and tried to work her lighter. The breeze of the car was too strong for it and George, who was already smoking, passed his cigarette to her to light hers from. She thanked him quite normally. She had made no reference to her outburst. No doubt she had forgotten about it. With Miss Kolin, he had decided now, anything was possible.

He finished his report to Mr Sistrom and sealed it in an envelope. The post office might be open now, he thought. He took the report and the cable and went downstairs.

He had left Miss Kolin over an hour before, when she had gone to her room. To his surprise, he saw her sitting in the café with the remains of a breakfast on the table in front of her. She had changed her clothes and was looking as if she had had a good night's sleep.

'I thought you were going to bed,' he said.

'You said you were going to send a cable to your office. I was waiting to take it to the post office. They make so much *chi-chi* about cables there. They have so few. I did not think you would like to deal with them yourself.'

'That's very good of you, Miss Kolin. Here it is. I've done my report, too. Air-mail that, will you?'

'Of course.'

She left some money on the table for the breakfast and was going through the lobby to the street, when the desk clerk came after her and said something in French. George caught the word "*téléphone*'.

She nodded to the clerk and smiled at George; in an almost embarrassed way, he thought.

'My call to Paris,' she said. 'I had cabled my friends that I was on my way home. I wished to tell them that I would be delayed. How long do you think we will be?'

'Two or three days, I'd say.' He turned to go. 'Pretty good work that, to get through to Paris from here in an hour,' he added.

'Yes.'

He saw her enter the telephone booth and begin speaking as he went upstairs, back to his room to sleep.

At eight o'clock that evening they met the old man with the Renault again, and began their second journey to the Sergeant's headquarters.

George had slept fitfully for most of the day and felt a great deal wearier for having done so. In the faint hope that there might be a reply cable in from Mr Sistrom, he had risen in the late afternoon and gone down to check. There had been nothing in. He had been disappointed, but not surprised. Mr Sistrom would have some thinking to do and some inquiries to make before he could send a useful reply. Miss Kolin had been out and, sitting beside her in the car, he noted that the leather satchel, which she carried slung by a strap from her shoulder, looked bulkier than usual. He decided that she had bought a bottle of brandy with which to fortify herself on the journey. He hoped, uneasily, that she would not hit it too hard.

Arthur was waiting for them at the same place, and took the same precautions about shutting them in the back of the truck. The night was even warmer than the previous one, and George protested.

'Is all that still necessary?'

'Sorry, chum. Got to be done.'

'It is a wise precaution,' said Miss Kolin unexpectedly.

'Yes, that's right, Miss.' Arthur sounded as surprised as George felt. 'Did you bring the Sarge's papers, Mr Carey?'

'I did.'

'Good. He's been worrying in case you'd forget. Can't wait to know about his namesake.'

'I brought along a copy of an old photograph of him as well.'

'You'll get a medal.'

'What's been decided?'

'I don't know. We had a chat last night after you'd gone but . . . anyway, you talk to him about it. There we are! All tucked up now. I'll take it quiet.'

They set off up the twisting rock-strewn road to the ruined house and went through the same routine as before when they reached it. This time, however, while they stood waiting among the pine trees for Arthur to warn the sentry of their approach, George and Miss Kolin had nothing to say to one another. Arthur returned and led them to the house.

The Sergeant greeted them in the hall, shaking hands with George and clicking heels to Miss Kolin. He smiled, but seemed secretly ill at ease as though doubtful of their goodwill. Miss Kolin, George was relieved to note, was her usual impassive self.

The Sergeant led them into the dining-room, poured out drinks and eyed George's briefcase.

'You have brought the papers?'

'Sure.' George opened the case.

'Ah!'

'And a photo of the Dragoon,' George added.

'This is true?'

'It's all here.' George took out a folder which he had brought from Philadelphia. Inside it there was a photostat or photograph of every important document in the case. 'The Corporal didn't have time to read the interesting part when he searched my room,' he added with a grin.

'*Touché*,' said Arthur, unmoved.

The Sergeant sat down at the table, glass in hand, his eyes gleaming as if he were about to be served with some ambrosial meal. George began to lay the documents one by one in front of him, explaining as he did so the origin and importance of each. The Sergeant nodded understandingly at each explanation or turned to Miss Kolin for guidance; but George soon saw that there were only certain documents in which he was genuinely interested–those which directly concerned the first Franz Schirmer. Even a photograph of Martin Schneider, the soft drinks potentate who had amassed the fortune which the Sergeant might inherit, produced no more than a polite exclamation. The photostats of Hans Schneider's Account, on the other hand, the church register entries relating to the marriage of Franz, and the record of the baptism of Karl, he studied minutely, reading the German aloud to himself. The copy photograph of old Franz he handled as if it were a Holy relic. For a long time he stared at it without speaking; then he turned to Arthur.

'You see, Corporal?' he said quietly. 'Am I not like him?'

'Take away the beard and he's your spitting image,' Arthur agreed.

And, indeed, for one who knew of the relationship, there was a strong resemblance between the two Schirmers. There was the same heavy strength in the two faces, the same determination in the two mouths, the same erectness; while the big hands grasping the arms of the chair in the daguerreotype and those grasping the photographic copy of it, might, George thought, have belonged to the selfsame man.

There was a rap on the door and the sentry put his head in. He beckoned to Arthur.

Arthur sighed impatiently. 'I'd better see what he wants,' he said, and went out shutting the door behind him.

The Sergeant took no notice. He was smiling now over Hans Schneider's Account of Eylau and the photostat of a page of the Dragoons' war diary, the one recording Franz Schirmer's desertion, which George had placed beside it. The old act of desertion seemed to give him special pleasure. From time to time he would glance at the old man's photograph again. George supposed that the Sergeant's own failure to return to Germany when an opportunity presented itself (he could have taken advantage of one of the amnesties) had been a kind of desertion. Perhaps, what the Sergeant was enjoying now was the reassuring intimation from the past that, contrary to the beliefs of his childhood, sinners were not obliged to dwell with devils always, and the outlaws and deserters, no less than fairy princes, might live happily ever after.

'Have you decided yet what you're going to do?' George asked.

The Sergeant looked up and nodded. 'Yes. I think so, Mr Carey. But first I would like to ask you some questions.'

'I'll do my best to . . .' he began.

But he never learned what the Sergeant's questions were. At that moment the door was flung open and Arthur came back into the room.

He slammed the door behind him, walked over to the table and looked grimly at George and Miss Kolin. His face was pinched and grey with anger. Suddenly, he threw two small, bright yellow tubes on the table in front of them.

'All right?' he said. 'Which of you is it? Or is it both of you?'

The tubes were about an inch and a half long and half an inch thick. They looked as if they had been cut from bamboo and then coloured. The three round the table stared at them, then up at Arthur again.

'What is this?' snapped the Sergeant.

Arthur burst into an angry torrent of Greek. George glanced at Miss Kolin. Her face was still impassive, but she had gone very pale. Then, Arthur stopped speaking and there was silence.

The Sergeant picked up one of the tubes, then looked from it to George and Miss Kolin. The muscles of his face set. He nodded to Arthur.

'Explain to Mr. Carey.'

'As if he didn't know!' Arthur's lips tightened. 'All right. Someone left a trail of these things from the culvert up here. One every fifty metres or so for someone else to follow. One of the lads coming up with a light spotted them.'

The Sergeant said something in German.

Arthur nodded. 'I put the rest on collecting them all before I came to report.' He looked at George. 'Any idea who might have dropped them, Mr Carey? I found one of these two wedged between the canvas and the body of the truck, so don't start trying to play dumb.'

'Dumb or not,' George said steadily, 'I don't know anything about them. What are they?'

The Sergeant got slowly to his feet. George could see a pulse going in his throat as he drew George's open briefcase towards him and looked inside. Then he shut it.

'Perhaps one should ask the lady,' he said.

Miss Kolin sat absolutely rigid, looking straight in front of her.

Suddenly he reached down and picked up her satchel from the floor by her chair.

'You permit?' he said and, thrusting his hand into it, drew out a tangle of thin cord.

He pulled on the cord slowly. A yellow tube came into view and then another, then a handful of the things, red and blue as well as yellow. They were strings of wooden beads of the kind used for making bead curtains. George knew now that it was not a bottle of brandy that had made the satchel so bulky. He began to feel sick.

'So!' The Sergeant dropped the beads on the table. 'Did you know of this, Mr Carey?'

'No.'

'That's right, too,' Arthur put in suddenly. 'It was Little Miss Muffet here who wanted the canvas over the truck. Didn't want him to see what she was up to.'

'For God's sake, Miss Kolin!' George said angrily. 'What do you think you're playing at?'

She stood up resolutely, as if she were about to propose a vote of no-confidence at a public meeting, and turned to George. She did not even glance at Arthur or the Sergeant. 'I should explain, Mr Carey,' she said coldly, 'that, in the interests of justice and in view of your refusal to take any steps yourself in the matter, I considered it my duty to telephone Colonel Chrysantos in Salonika and inform him, on your behalf, that the men who robbed the Eurasian Credit Bank were here. On his instructions, I marked the route from the culvert, so that his troops could . . .'

The Sergeant's fist hit her full in the mouth, and she crashed into the corner of the room where the empty bottles stood.

George leapt to his feet. As he did so the barrel of Arthur's gun jabbed painfully into his side.

'Stand still, chum, or you'll get hurt,' Arthur said. 'She's been asking for this and now she's going to get it.'

Miss Kolin was on her knees, the blood trickling from her cut lip. They all stood watching her as she climbed slowly to her feet. Suddenly, she picked up a bottle and flung it at the Sergeant. He did not move. It missed him by a few inches and smashed against the opposite wall. He stepped forward and hit her hard across the face with the back of his hand. She went down again. She had made no sound. She still made no sound. After a moment she began to get to her feet again.

'I'm stopping this,' said George angrily and started to move.

The gun dug into his side. 'You try, chum, and you'll get a bullet in the kidneys. It's nothing to do with you, so shut up!'

Miss Kolin picked up another bottle. There was blood running from her nose now. She faced the Sergeant again.

'*Du Schuft!*' she said venomously, and hurled herself at him.

He brushed the bottle aside and hit her again in the face with his fist. When she fell this time she did not try to get up, but lay there gasping.

The Sergeant went to the door and opened it. The sentry who had summoned Arthur was waiting there. The Sergeant beckoned him in, pointed to Miss Kolin and gave an order in Greek. The sentry grinned and slung his rifle across his back. Then he went over to Miss Kolin and hauled her to her feet. She stood there swaying and wiping the blood from her face with her hand. He gripped her arm and said something to her. Without a word, and without looking at any of them, she began to walk towards the door.

'Miss Kolin . . .' George started forward.

She took no notice. The sentry pushed him aside and followed her out of the room. The door closed.

Sickened and trembling, George turned to face the Sergeant.

'Easy, chum,' said Arthur. 'None of the hero-to-the-rescue stuff. It won't wash here.'

'Where's she being taken?' George demanded.

The Sergeant was licking the blood off one of his knuckles. He glanced at George and then, sitting down at the table, took the passport from Miss Kolin's satchel.

'Maria Kolin,' he remarked. 'French.'

'I asked where she's being taken?'

Arthur was standing behind him still. 'I wouldn't try getting tough, Mr Carey,' he advised. 'Don't forget, you brought her here.'

The Sergeant was examining the passport. 'Born in Belgrade,' he said. 'Slav.' He shut the passport with a snap. 'And now we will talk a little.'

George waited. The Sergeant's eyes rested on his.

'How did you find out, Mr Carey?'

George hesitated.

'Talk fast, chum.'

'The truck the Corporal brought us up in—it had slots for false number plates, and the plates were lying inside on the floor of the truck. They were the same numbers as those mentioned in the Salonika papers.'

Arthur swore.

The Sergeant nodded curtly. 'So! You knew this last night?'

'Yes.'

'But *you* did not go to the police today?'

'What I did was to cable in code to my office to find out what the extradition treaty between America and Greece says about armed robbery.'

'Please?'

Arthur explained in Greek.

The Sergeant nodded. 'That was good. Did she know you do this?'

'Yes.'

'Then why does she tell Chrysantos?'

'She doesn't like Germans.'

'Ah, so?'

George looked down pointedly at the Sergeant's hands. 'I understand her feelings.'

'Easy, chum.'

The Sergeant smiled enigmatically. 'You understand her feelings? I do not think so.'

The sentry came in, gave the Sergeant a key with a word of explanation and went out again.

The Sergeant put the key in his pocket and poured himself a glass of plum brandy. 'And now,' he said, 'we must think what is to be done. Your little friend is safely in a room upstairs. I think we must ask you also to stay, Mr Carey. It is not that I do not trust you but that, at the moment, because you do not understand, you are feeling that you would like to destroy the corporal and me. In two days, perhaps, when the corporal and I have finished arranging our business, you may go.'

'Do you intend to keep me here by force?'

'Only if you are not wise and do not wish to stay.'

'Aren't you forgetting why I came here?'

'No. I will give you my decision in two days, Mr Carey. Until then, you stay.'

'Supposing I told you that unless Miss Kolin and I are released immediately you'll have as much chance of inheriting that estate as that sentry outside.'

'Your office in America will be very sad. Arthur explained to me.'

George felt himself reddening. 'Does it occur to you that, trail or no trail, Colonel Chrysantos won't take very long to find this place now? In two or three hours he may have you surrounded by Greek troops.'

Arthur laughed. The Sergeant smiled grimly.

'If that is so, Mr Carey, Chrysantos will be in trouble with his Government. But you need not worry. If this bad Colonel comes, we will protect you. A glass of wine? No? Brandy? No? Then, since you are tired, the Corporal will show you where you can sleep. Good-night.' He nodded dismissal and began to go through the photostats again, putting those that interested him specially into a separate pile.

'This way, chum.'

'Just a moment. What about Miss Kolin, Sergeant?'

The Sergeant did not look up. 'You do not have to worry about her, Mr Carey. Good-night.'

Arthur led the way; George followed him; the sentry brought up the rear. They went upstairs to a derelict room with a straw mattress on the floorboards. There was also a bucket. The sentry brought in an oil-lamp.

'It's only for a couple of nights, Mr Carey,' said Arthur–the hotel receptionist apologizing to a valued client who has arrived unexpectedly. 'You'll find the palliasse fairly clean. The Sarge is very keen on hygiene.

'Where's Miss Kolin?'

'Next room.' He jerked his thumb. 'But don't you worry about her. It's a better room than this.' 'What did the Sergeant mean about Chrysantos getting into trouble with the Government?'

'If he tried to surround us? Well, the Greek frontier's nearly a kilometre away. We're on Yugoslav territory. I'd have thought you'd have guessed.'

George digested this disconcerting news while Arthur adjusted the lamp wick.

'What about the frontier patrols?'

Arthur hung the lamp on a hook jutting out from the wall. 'You want to know too much, chum.' He went to the door. 'No lock on this door, but, just in case you're thinking of sleep-walking, there's a wide-awake sentry here on the landing, and he's trigger-happy. Get the idea?'

'I get it.'

'I'll give you a call when it's time for breakfast. Pleasant dreams.'

About an hour had gone by when George heard the Sergeant come upstairs and say something to the sentry.

The sentry replied briefly. A moment or two later George heard the sound of a key being inserted in the door of the next room–the room Arthur had said was Miss Kolin's.

With some idea of protecting her, George got up quickly from the mattress on which he had been lying, and went to the door. He did not open it immediately. He heard Miss Kolin's voice and the Sergeant's. There was a pause, then the sound of the door being shut. The key turned in the lock once more.

For a while, he thought the Sergeant had gone, and went back to the corner where his mattress was. Then, he heard the Sergeant's voice again, and hers. They were talking in German. He went to the wall and listened. The tone of their voices was curiously conversational. He was aware of a strange uneasiness, and his heart began to beat too fast.

The voices had ceased now, but soon they began once more, and softly, as if the speakers did not wish to be overheard. Then there was silence for a long time. He lay down again on the mattress. Minutes went by; then, in the silence, he heard her utter a fierce, shuddering cry of passion.

He did not move. After a while there were low voices again. Then nothing. He became aware for the first time of the sound of the cicadas in the night outside. He was at last beginning to understand Miss Kolin.

Chapter Twelve

George was kept for two days and three nights at the Sergeant's headquarters.

On the first day, the Sergeant left the house soon after dawn, and returned when it was dark. George spent the day in the room downstairs, and had his meals there with Arthur. He did not see either the Sergeant or Miss Kolin. After that first night, she was moved to another room in an annexe to the house, and food was taken to her by one of the sentries. When George asked if he could see her, Arthur shook his head.

'Sorry, chum. No can do.'

'What's happened to her?'

'I'll give you three guesses.'

'I want to see her.'

Arthur shrugged. 'I don't mind whether you see her or not. It's just that *she* doesn't want to see *you*.'

'Why not?'

'The Sarge is the only one she wants to see.'

'Is she all right?'

'Fit as a fiddle.' He grinned. 'Cut lip, of course, and a bruise or two, but radiant as a bride. You wouldn't know her.'

'How much longer is this going on?'

'Search me. I'd say it had only just started.'

'After what happened, it doesn't make sense.'

Arthur looked at him with some amusement. 'I expect you've been nicely brought up. I told you she'd been asking for it, didn't I? Well, she got it, and very nice too. I've never seen the Sarge take such a fancy to a girl before.'

'A fancy!' George was getting angry.

'I wouldn't mind betting she was a virgin,' Arthur mused; 'or as good as.'

'Oh, for God's sake!'

'What's the matter, chum? Sour grapes?'

'I don't think there's much point in discussing it. Did Colonel Chrysantos turn up?'

'The sheriff's posse, you mean? Sure. They're sitting on their backsides, like twerps, just on the other side of the frontier. Waiting for something to happen.'

'Or, maybe, waiting for Miss Kolin and me to turn up. Supposing the American Embassy's brought into this and they start complaining to Belgrade. Going to be a bit awkward for you, isn't it?'

'You'll be back before they finish even *talking* about doing anything. And when you do get back you'll begin to think again about all the fuss your office is going to make over the Sarge, and say it was all a mistake.'

'Got it all worked out, haven't you. I don't see what you had to get so mad about.'

'No? For one thing they've arrested that poor old sod who drove you. That's not funny, is it?'

'How do you know?'

'We had word from Florina this morning.'

'How?'

'Ask no questions you'll be told no lies. I'll tell you this, though. The *comitadjis* have been using these hills for fifty years or more. There's not much you can't get away with in these parts if you know the ropes. Don't forget that they're Macedonians on both sides of the frontier. When it comes to small-scale work like this, the Chrysantos boys haven't got an earthly.'

'What'll happen to the driver?'

'That depends. He's an old *comitadji*, so he won't say where he got his orders from, no matter what they do to him. But it's awkward. He isn't the only one in Florina. There's old Ma Vassiotis, for instance. They might have a go at her. You know, if the Sarge hadn't changed things round a bit, I'd be inclined to go up and give your Miss What's-her-name another bashing myself.'

'Supposing I were to tell Chrysantos that I hired the car and told the old man where to go?'

'He might believe you. But how did *you* know where to go?'

'I'd say you told me.'

Arthur laughed. 'Proper lawyer, aren't you?'

'Would it matter to you?'

'Not a tuppenny damn.'

'O.K., then.'

Arthur was cleaning a pistol. George watched him for a while in silence. At last he said: 'Supposing there had been no question of the Sergeant's going to America. Would you have gone on with this racket of yours?'

Arthur looked up, then shook his head. 'No. I reckon we've just about had it now.'

'Having pulled off the big job?'

'Maybe. Time to move on, anyway.' He bent over the pistol again.

'Got plenty of dough put away?' George said, after a moment or two.

Arthur looked up, startled. 'I've never met anyone with such terrible manners,' he said.

'Come off it, Arthur.'

But Arthur was genuinely shocked. 'How would you like it if I was to ask you how much money you had in the bank?' he said indignantly.

'All right. Tell me something else then. How did it start? The Sergeant kept very quiet about that. What happened in the end to that Markos brigade you both commanded?'

Arthur shook his head sadly. 'Always asking questions. I suppose it's being a lawyer.'

'I have an inquiring mind.'

'Just plain nosey-parkering my mother would have called it.'

'You forget that, at present, I'm the Sergeant's legal adviser. Between a man and his legal adviser there should be no secrets.'

Arthur uttered a four-letter word and went back to his cleaning.

But the following evening he came back to the subject of his own accord. George had still seen nothing of either the Sergeant or Miss Kolin and a suspicion had been forming in his mind. He began to ask questions again.

'What time's the Sergeant coming back today?'

'Don't know, chum. When we see him, I expect.' Arthur was reading a Belgrade newspaper which had arrived mysteriously during the day. Now he threw it down in disgust. 'Lot of nonsense in that paper,' he said. 'Ever read the *News of the World*? London paper that is.'

'No, I've never seen it. Is the Sergeant in Greece or Albania today?'

'Albania?' Arthur laughed, but, as George opened his mouth to ask another question, he went on: 'You were asking what happened to us when we packed up fighting. We were up near the Albanian frontier then.'

'Oh, yes?'

Arthur nodded reminiscently. 'You ought to have a look at Mount Grammos if you ever get the chance,' he said. 'Wonderful scenery up that way.'

The Grammos massif had been one of the first strongholds of the Markos forces; it came to be one of his last.

For weeks, the brigade's position in the area had been deteriorating steadily. The trickle of deserters had become a stream. There came a day in October when important decisions had to be taken.

The Sergeant had been on his feet for fourteen hours or more, and his hip was paining him when at last he gave orders to bivouac for the night. Later, the officer in charge of an outlying picket caught two deserters from another battalion and sent them to brigade headquarters to be dealt with.

The Sergeant looked at the men thoughtfully, and then gave orders for them to be executed. When they had been led away, he poured himself a glass of wine and nodded to Arthur to do the same. They drank their wine in silence. Then, the Sergeant refilled the glasses.

'Does it occur to you, Corporal,' he said, 'that those two men may have been setting their brigade commander and his second-in-command a good example?'

Arthur nodded. 'It's been occurring to me for days, Sarge. We haven't a hope in hell.'

'No. The best we can hope for is that they will starve us to death.'

'They're beginning to do that already.'

'I have no wish to be a martyr of the revolution.'

'Neither have I. We've done our jobs, Sarge, as well as we knew how and a bit over. *And* we've kept faith. That's more than those bastards at the top can say.'

' "Put not your trust in princes." I have remembered that, you see. I think the time has come to seek our independence.'

'When do we go?'

'Tomorrow night would not be too soon.'

'When they find out us two have gone, you won't see the rest of them for dust. I wonder how many'll get through.'

'The ones who always get through, the *comitadji* types. They will hide away in their hills as they have done before. They will be there when we want them.'

Arthur was startled. 'When we want them? I thought you said something about independence.'

The Sergeant filled his glass again before he replied. 'I have been thinking, Corporal,' he said at last, 'and I have a plan. The politicians have used us. Now we will use them.'

He stood up and limped over to his kit-bag for the tin box in which he kept his cigars.

Arthur watched him with something that he knew was very like love. He had a profound respect for his friend's planning ability. Surprising things sometimes emerged from that hard, heavy head.

'How use them?' he said.

'The idea came to me several weeks ago,' said the Sergeant. 'I was thinking of that history of the Party which we were once compelled to read. You remember?'

'Sure. I read mine without cutting the pages open.'

The Sergeant smiled. 'You missed some important things, Corporal. I will give you my copy to read.' He lighted a cigar luxuriously. 'I think that it is quite possible that from being mere soldiers we may soon become soldiers of fortune.'

'It was dead easy,' Arthur said. 'The Sarge had got hold of a list of all the secret Party members and sympathizers in the Salonika area, and we sorted out those that worked in banks and in the offices of businesses with big pay-rolls. Then, we approached them and gave them their big chance to serve the Party in its hour of need, just as the book said the old Bolshies had done. We could always say we'd denounce them if they got suspicious, but we haven't had any trouble of that kind. I tell you, every single job we've done, we've had a man or woman on the inside, helping us for the honour and glory of the Party.' He laughed contemptuously. 'Flies in the Ointment Unite! Expropriations! They couldn't wait to ditch the people they were working for. Some of them would torture their own mothers if the Party wanted them to, and be glad to do it. "Yes, Comrade. Certainly, Comrade. Glad to be of service, Comrade!" It's made me sick sometimes to hear them,' he added self-righteously.

'Still, you did pretty well out of it, didn't you?'

'Maybe we did, but I still don't like people who bite the hand that feeds them.'

'Surely, it must have taken quite a bit of courage for some of these people to act on their convictions to the extent of helping you.'

'I'm not so sure,' said Arthur sourly. 'If you ask me, these political convictions that make it O.K. to play someone else a dirty trick behind their backs, have something pretty phony about them.'

'Hypocrisy, Arthur. What about the trick *you* were playing?'

'I'm not pretending to be better than I am. It's these phonies I can't stand. You should talk to some of them. Clever. Know all the answers. Prove anything you like. The sort you *don't* want with you if you're going out on a patrol, because, if things get sticky, *they're* the ones who'll start looking for a reason for everybody to cop out and go home.'

'Does the Sergeant feel the same way about these things?'

'Him?' Arthur laughed. 'No. He doesn't bother. You see. *I* think there are all kinds of people. He doesn't. He thinks there are only two kinds—those you'd want with you when things are bad, and those you wouldn't have at any price.' He smiled slyly, and added: 'And he makes up his mind real quick.'

George lit his last cigarette and stared thoughtfully at Arthur for a moment. The suspicion suddenly became a certainty. He screwed up the empty packet and tossed it on the table.

'Where are they, Arthur? he said.

'Where are who?' Arthur's face was all innocence.

'Come on, Arthur! Let's stop playing games. They were here last night, I know, because I heard the Sergeant come in around midnight and start talking to you. But this morning, neither he nor Miss Kolin was here. At least, I didn't see him, and no food's been taken up to her. So where are they?'

'I don't know.'

'Think again.'

'I don't know, Mr Carey, and that's a fact.'

'Has he gone for good?'

Arthur hesitated and then shrugged. 'Yes, he has.'

George nodded. He had suspected, but, now that he knew for certain, the news came as a blow. 'What am I being kept here for?' he asked.

'He's got to have time to get clear.'

'Clear of me?'

'No, clear of this country.' Arthur leaned forward earnestly. 'You see, supposing you went back and Chrysantos started on you, and you blew the gaff about his being on the way out? I don't say you'd mean to, but he's a cunning bastard that one. You can see it might be awkward.'

'Yes, I see. He'd already decided what he was going to do. I think he might have told me.'

'He asked me to, Mr Carey. I was going to wait until after supper, just to be on the safe side, but you may as well know now. You see, there wasn't much time. We've been all fixed up to go for days. He made the final arrangements yesterday and just came back to ask her if she wanted to go too.'

'And she did?'

'Like a shot. Can't keep her hands off him. Proper case it is.'

'Isn't he afraid she'll try and turn him in again?'

Arthur laughed. 'Don't be silly, chum. She's been waiting for a man like that all her life.'

'I still don't get it.'

'I expect you're like me,' Arthur said, consolingly. 'I like it a little more on the quiet side myself. But about the money . . .'

'Yes, about the money.'

'We talked it over, him and me, Mr Carey, and we came to a conclusion. He couldn't have claimed it. You see that, don't you? You talked about extradition and all that, but that's not the point. Extradition or not, everything would have had to come out. That'd be no good. He's going to start a new life under a new name, with all this behind him. He hasn't got a million dollars or anything like, but he's got enough to go on with. If he claimed that money he'd be a marked man. You know that as well as I do.'

'He could have told me this the first time.'

'He only wanted his family papers, Mr Carey. You can't blame him for that.'

'And then, he just had me stringing along so that I wouldn't make trouble. I get it.' George sighed. 'All right. What's his new name going to be? Schneider?'

'Now you don't want to be bitter, chum. He liked you and he's very grateful.'

After a moment or two George looked up, 'What about you?'

'Me? Oh, I'll be getting along too, by and by. It's easier for me, being British. There are all sorts of places I can go. I might even join the Sarge if I feel like it.'

'Then you *do* know where he's going?'

'Yes, but I don't know *how* he's going. He might be on a ship in Salonika at this very moment for all I know. But I couldn't say for certain. What I don't know, nobody can make me tell.'

'So you're just here to look after me. Is that it?'

'Well, I've got to pay off the boys, too, and clear up generally. I'm the adjutant you might say.'

There was a silence. He looked round the room moodily. His eyes met George's. Unsuccessfully, for once, he tried to grin.

'I tell you what, chum,' he said. 'Now that the Sarge's gone and everything, I reckon we're both a bit down in the mouth today. We got hold of some German wine once. Kept it for special occasions, like last night. What about you and me having a bottle between us now?'

The sun was shining when George awoke the following morning. He looked at his watch and saw that it was eight o'clock. On the two previous mornings Arthur had roused him, with a good deal of military noise, at seven.

He listened. The house was quite silent, and the cicadas outside seemed very loud. He went and opened the door of his room.

There was no sentry on duty there. The 'boys' had evidently been paid off. He went downstairs.

In the room where they had eaten their meals, Arthur had left a note and a letter for him.

George looked at the note first.

Well chum (*it said*), I hope you have not got too much of a hangover. There's a letter here that Sergeant Schirmer left for you before he went. Sorry I can't lend you my razor today as it's the only one I've got. When you want to go back to dear old Civilization just walk up through the trees past the place we parked the truck and then take the right fork. You can't miss it. It's less than a mile away. Nobody on this side will interfere with you. You will soon meet a patrol on the other side. Don't forget to do your best for that old driver. It's been nice knowing you. All the best. Arthur.

The letter from the Sergeant was in Miss Kolin's angular handwriting.

Dear Mr Carey (*he read*),

I have asked Maria to write this for me so that the meaning of what I feel and have to say will be clear and properly expressed in your language.

First, allow me to apologize for having left you so suddenly and discourteously, without taking my leave of you. No doubt, by the time you read this, the Corporal will have explained to you the situation and also the reasons for my decision not to attempt to go with you to America. I trust that you will understand. I was naturally disappointed, as I always wished to see something of your country. Perhaps some day it will be possible.

And now, permit me to express my gratitude to you and to those of your office who sent you. Maria has told me of your persistence and determination to find a man you had so much reason to believe dead. It is a good thing to be able to go on a little further when those with less spirit are ready to turn back. I am sorry that you will have no more valuable a reward than my gratitude. Yet that I offer you sincerely, my friend. I would have been glad to receive so much money if it had been possible, but not more glad than I am now to possess the documents you brought me.

The money I cannot think of with great emotion. It is a large sum, but I do not think it has to do with me. It was earned in America by an American. I think it is just that, if there is no other heir but me, the American State of Pennsylvania should have it. My true inheritance is the knowledge you have brought me of my blood and of myself. So much has changed and Eylau is long ago, but hand clasps hand across the years and we are one. A man's immortality is in his children. I hope I shall have many. Perhaps Maria will bear them. She says that she will wish to.

The Corporal tells me that you will be so kind as to speak discreetly for the driver who was arrested. Maria asks that, if possible, you will give him her typewriter and the other things she left in Florina so that he may sell them and have the money. His name is Douchko. She sends you also her apologies and her thanks. So now, my friend, there is only left for me to thank you again and to wish you happiness in your life. I hope we may meet again.

Yours very sincerely,
Franz Schirmer.

The signature was in his own writing, very neat and clear.

George put the letters in his pocket, got his briefcase from his room and walked up through the pine trees. It was a fine, fresh morning and the air was good. He began to think out what he would have to say to Colonel Chrysantos. The Colonel was not going to be pleased; neither was Mr Sistrom. The whole situation, in fact, was most unfortunate.

George wondered why it was, then, that he kept laughing to himself as he walked on towards the frontier.

ERIC AMBLER

Passage of Arms

Passage . . .

9. A mutual act of transaction; something that goes on between two persons mutually; a negotiation; an interchange or exchange of vows, endearments, or the like; an interchange or exchange of blows; encounter; altercation; a fencing, as in argument; as, a *passage* at or of arms.

Webster's New International Dictionary

Chapter One

I

All that Mr Wright, the rubber estate manager, ever knew of the business was that an army patrol had ambushed a band of terrorists within a mile of his bungalow, that five months later his Indian clerk, Girija Krishnan, had reported the theft of three tarpaulins from the curing sheds, and that three years after that someone had removed the wheels from an old scooter belonging to one of his children. As it never occurred to him to look for a possible connection between the three incidents, he remained unaware even of that knowledge. In Malaya, at that time, there were more important facts to ponder and attempt to correlate. Stolen tarpaulins and missing scooter wheels were trivial mysteries; and, although the ambush itself was not forgotten, it was remembered more for its proximity than its novelty.

Mr and Mrs Wright had been at breakfast when they heard the sound of firing. It began with a flurry of sub-machine-gun bursts and continued intermittently for about two minutes.

The truck which took the tappers off to the work areas had not yet left the compound; and, although there was a lot of shouting and excitement, there was no panic and little confusion. Almost before the firing had ceased, the barbed-wire barricades were in position and the inner defence posts manned. During the long silence that followed, Mrs Wright, a woman of character, calmed the servants and ordered fresh toast and tea so that she and her husband could finish breakfast.

At eight-thirty the patrol appeared: fifteen Malay infantrymen under a British subaltern, and two R.A.F. radio operators. They had been in the jungle for several weeks and their success that morning would probably earn them a rest period. They were smiling and talking as they toiled up the steep track to the compound.

Shortly after they arrived, Girija was summoned to the bungalow. As he went up the veranda steps he could see the officer, a downy, blue-eyed Englishman with paratroop wings on his jungle-green bush shirt. Mrs Wright was pouring him a cup of tea.

'All Chinese, and on their way to mine the main road by the look of things,' he was saying. 'We got the lot.'

'Nice work,' said Mr Wright.

'Could have been better, sir.' The young officer grinned. 'They were all killed outright. You can't ask them questions about their chums when they're dead.'

Mr Wright chuckled and then, seeing his clerk waiting outside, beckoned him in.

'Girija, this is Lieutenant Haynes. He's just wiped out a gang of terrorists. I said we'd let him have some men to help bury them. Will you see to it?'

'Certainly, sir.' Girija turned with a slight bow to the officer.

Lieutenant Haynes nodded genially. 'I left two men there on guard,' he said. 'They'll give your chaps a hand if you send extra spades. The ground's quite soft, I think. Shouldn't take long. If you'll speak to my sergeant he'll detail a guide for you.'

'Thank you, sir. I will make all necessary arrangements.'

The officer's grin faded slightly. 'Seen many dead terrorists around these parts?' he asked.

'No, sir. Have not had that pleasure.'

'Well, mind you spread the good news.'

'I understand, sir. Two men from each kampong?'

'That's the idea. And tell them they'll be seeing plenty more before we're done.'

Girija smiled politely and withdrew to organize the burial party.

He was well aware of the reason for it. The Malay villages in the area had long been suspected by the authorities of aiding the Communist guerrillas with food and shelter. It was not that the villagers approved of the invaders, but simply that the savage reprisals that could follow any refusal of aid were more intimidating than the possibility of having fines or other collective punishments imposed by the British. They were not warlike people; their villages were often isolated; the British forces were scattered. In the past, glib official assurances that the police and army were at last gaining the upper hand and able to protect the outlying areas from the terrorists had been given too often, and too often proved baseless. Now, the villagers believed only what they saw themselves, or what had been seen by their own people. Dead terrorists had to be shown to be dead. The burial party was in the nature of a morale-building or public relations device.

Girija found the head tapper and explained what was wanted: two men from each of the four neighbouring villages, and picks and shovels. Then he went to the Malay sergeant and secured a guide. Within twenty minutes the party was ready to move. The head tapper was obviously hoping to go with it, but Girija sent him off with the truck and the remaining men to the work areas. He had decided to take charge of the burial party himself.

The action had taken place in a deep gully carved out of the red laterite hillside by the monsoon rains, and flanked on both sides by bamboo thickets, fern trees and dense tangles of croton undergrowth. It was a natural route for men to use on that otherwise trackless hillside, and a perfect site for an ambush.

There were ten bodies there; four within a few feet of one another, and the rest scattered along the gully for a distance of some twenty-five yards. It was easy to see what had happened. Concealed in the undergrowth along both lips of the gully, the patrol had been able to open fire at point-blank range without fear of hitting each other or the smallest chance of missing the enemy below them. One or two of the dead men were lying in attitudes which suggested desperate split second attempts to claw their way to cover behind the roots of a fallen tree. One had been hit in the back as he turned to run. One, the farthest away, had tried to return the patrol's fire; there were empty shells scattered on the ground by him; but he was as dead as the rest. Nobody in the patrol had been hit.

The two Malay soldiers left on guard were squatting on their heels by a Sterno fuel stove, heating cans of tea and smoking. They took no notice of the burial party. Beside them, on a groundsheet, were stacked the arms and equipment collected from the dead: machine pistols, boxes of ammunition and road mines, and canvas belts with pouches containing hand-grenades.

The soldier who had guided the party from the compound joined his friends at the stove. Girija knew that they would not help with the digging unless he told them what Lieutenant Haynes had said; but he made no attempt to do so. During his brief inspection of the gully he had made two small discoveries. They had aroused his curiosity and made him wish to know more about the dead terrorists. He put the burial party to work and sat down on the ground near-by.

The first thing he had noted was the fact that, although the bodies had been searched and stripped of all arms and equipment, there had been no cooking utensils of any kind found on them. This meant almost certainly that they were within a day's marching distance of their camp; which meant, in turn, that they were probably living off one or more of the four villages near the estate. They would be known, if only by sight, to at least two members of the burial party.

His second discovery had to do with the arms and equipment. He was sure that the machine pistols were new; not new in type necessarily, but newly acquired. His father had been a subahdar in the British Army and Girija had spent his childhood in barracks and cantonments. He knew the look of a new gun and how soon it acquired the patina of use from normal cleaning and handling. At least three of the machine pistols on the groundsheet had been so recently unpacked, and so little used and cleaned, that traces of brown preservative grease were still visible on them. The ammunition boxes, the mines and the grenades were also new. The grenades were of an old type with cast-iron fragmentation cases; but the grey paint on them was fresh and the pins were clean and bright.

The gully was only partly shaded by the overhanging trees, and by eleven o'clock the sun was shining directly into it. The tappers were craftsmen, used to the careful work of milking rubber trees without damaging them. Digging graves on a hillside, and in ground which, despite Lieutenant Haynes's assurances, had proved to be rock hard, was not a job which they could be expected to tackle with enthusiasm. The excitement of the occasion and the sight of ten bloody corpses were novelties that had soon palled. By the time the third grave had been dug, most of the men had lost their customary good humour. Criticism began to be voiced of the soldiers squatting in the shade and drinking tea while others cleaned up the mess they had made. There was even an exchange of remarks, meant to be overhead, to the effect that the tuan's clerk might, without serious loss of face, enhance his already considerable popularity by taking a shovel and doing a bit of digging himself.

Girija was able to ignore this unworthy suggestion with equanimity. The tappers' complaints interested him for reasons other than their substance. He was almost certain now that he knew the area in which the band had made their headquarters. Only two of the burial party had remained cheerful. Malays were not good at concealing their emotions, and although these two were trying hard to conform to the mood of the others, their satisfaction with the turn of events and the task in which they were engaged kept showing through their scowls. Girija watched them dump one of the bodies into its grave with unmistakable gusto, and then glance round guiltily when they caught themselves grinning at one another.

The two men came from a village named Awang on a river three miles away to the west. Once there had been tin mining in the district, but falling yields and rising operating costs had made the mines uneconomic. The small labour force of Awang had been gradually absorbed by the rubber estates.

Girija had been to the village once or twice to pay sick benefits to the families of men in hospital; but he did not know it well. It was at the end of a secondary road which had degenerated in recent years to no more than a cycle track. Beyond the old tin workings the jungle-covered hills stretched all the way to the borders of Thailand. In that lush wilderness, small groups of disciplined men with minds and bodies adapted to the environment could remain healthy and mobile almost indefinitely. At that period, it was impossible either to police the area effectively or to halt the stream of Chinese militants filtering down the peninsula from the north. Villages like Awang became staging points for the terrorist bands cautiously working their way southward towards the politically more sensitive areas of Selangor, Negri Sembilan, Malacca and Johore. The men now being buried had probably made their camp within a mile or so of it; going in at night to receive food, gather information, brow-beat the headman and talk earnestly to potential recruits.

Girija walked over to the two tappers and stood watching them as they filled in the grave. They had fallen silent as he approached. After a moment or two he moved in closer.

'A good day's work,' he remarked.

They looked at him warily.

He smiled. 'The past buries itself.'

That raised a sheepish grin.

'And honest men are free again,' he added.

They went on working. The body was covered now.

'The tuan was pleased,' Girija said thoughtfully; 'pleased that these pigs were all foreigners. To him that proved the loyalty and courage of our men here.'

They looked at him again. One of them mumbled: 'The tuan is a father to us.'

'It is unfortunate,' Girija went on, 'that the Lieutenant tuan does not agree with him.'

They stared at him in dismay.

Girija shrugged. 'He said that this gang was new to the district. He said that a week was no test of loyalty.'

He had them now. Dismay gave way to indignation.

The man who had spoken before spoke again. 'The tuan was right,' he said firmly. 'The Lieutenant tuan does not speak the truth.'

Girija shrugged again. 'It is not important.'

'The Lieutenant tuan is wrong,' the man insisted. 'It was many weeks.'

Girija made sympathetic sounds.

'Many weeks,' repeated the other man emphatically.

Girija spread out his hands. 'It is not my business. Perhaps you should tell this to the Lieutenant tuan.' He saw the sudden panic in their eyes and went on smoothly. 'Myself I do not think it necessary, or wise. The pigs are dead. They are best forgotten.'

'Yes, yes. It is best. We will forget.'

Girija smiled benignly and moved away. He knew that they were watching him and wondering fearfully if he would betray them to the Lieutenant. He had no intention of doing so; but there was no point in telling them that. They would not quite believe him; and in any case they had served their purpose. He had found out what he wanted to know.

<h1 style="text-align:center">2</h1>

Girija was born of Bengali parents at Cawnpore in the United Provinces of India. He had five sisters but no brothers. When he was six his father, the subahdar, went to London with a detachment of his regiment to march in the coronation procession of King George the Sixth. During his stay, the subahdar was taken on a conducted tour of the city which included visits to the Tower of London, Westminster Abbey, the Houses of Parliament, the British Museum, the Law Courts, Battersea power station, and, for some obscure reason, a factory in Acton where bus bodies were made. He returned to India laden with souvenirs and fired with ambition for his only son. The Law Courts had particularly impressed him. Girija would become a lawyer, or, failing that, a policeman.

Girija became neither. The subahdar was killed at the battle of Alamein, and Girija spent the next three years in a military orphanage at Benares. When the war ended, however, his mother wrote to a brother, who had a cotton goods business in Singapore, explaining that she had only her widow's pension and asking if she might join him with the children. The prospect of securing this windfall of cheap labour appealed to the brother, and he replied sending passage money. In December 1946 the family sailed as deck passengers from Calcutta. With them went the subahdar's medals and the precious souvenirs of his visit to London; the coronation mug, the picture postcards, the newspaper cuttings, the photographs, the ash-tray from the Warrant Officers' mess at Chelsea Barracks, and the bus body manufacturer's catalogue.

In his last year at the orphanage Girija had been taught book-keeping, office organization and the jargon of commercial letter writing. The uncle in Singapore found him useful; so useful, indeed, that after three months he got rid of the book-keeper to whom he had been paying forty dollars (Straits) a week and replaced him with Girija to whom he paid twenty. Girija was sixteen then. He stayed two years in Singapore. During them, he learned Malay and a smattering of Cantonese, and made friends with a Parsee who worked in the offices of a Chinese financial syndicate.

At that time, shortage of capital, ill health brought about by internment, or sheer hopelessness engendered by the early successes of the terrorists were persuading many British rubber planters in Malaya to sell out. The Chinese syndicate was buying. It was through his Parsee friend that Girija heard that the new manager of a recently acquired estate in the north was asking the Singapore office for a clerk.

His uncle was angered by Girija's decision to leave him, and talked darkly of getting a court order requiring Girija to repay the cost of his passage from Calcutta. To his astonishment the bluff failed. Girija, whom he had come to regard as a pliant and somewhat timid young man, not only laughed loudly and made a disrespectful noise with his lips, but also threatened to take his mother and sisters north with him unless their wages were immediately doubled. There was a shrill Bengali family quarrel during which Girija uttered a further and more compelling threat. He had made a secret analysis of his uncle's accounts which he was prepared to send to the Inspector of Taxes. The uncle wept and spoke of ingratitude, but capitulated. Girija's mother embraced her son proudly and said that he was his father's true heir.

When the time came for Girija to leave, however, he asked her for only one thing that had belonged to his father; the bus body manufacturer's catalogue. His sisters were relieved. They had been afraid that, as a man, he would feel himself entitled to the subahdar's medals.

The catalogue was a quarto size book with a brown cover on which the name of the manufacturer was embossed in green. Inside there were forty-eight pages of thick, shiny paper displaying the specifications of twenty different types of buses together with colour illustrations of the exteriors and interiors of each. There were double-deckers and single-deckers, buses designed to enable the driver to collect the fares, and buses designed to carry conductors. There were twelve seaters, twenty-four seaters and sixty seaters. There were buses for long distances and buses for local services in cities, for cold climates and for hot. The cover was dog-eared from much handling and some of the pages were loose. There was an ink stain on the title page. It was Girija's most treasured possession.

As a small boy he had sat for hours turning the pages, studying the illustrations and re-reading the text. He had, in the end, come to know it by heart. At the orphanage, when he had been separated both from his mother and the catalogue, he had found comfort in reciting it to himself, beginning with the Foreword by the Chairman ('*In presenting to our customers all over the world this, the Eighteenth Edition, of our Catalogue and Price List, we are proudly conscious that . . .*') and finishing with the specifications of a forty seat medium range staging coach (available on A.E.C. or Commer chassis) '*as supplied to the Argentine Government*. Price £8,586, f.o.b. London.'

One day, in the streets of Benares, he had seen a new bus that he thought he recognized as a modification of one of those listed in the catalogue. It had been just starting away and he had run for almost half a mile before he had caught up with it at a stopping place. Breathlessly he had searched for the body manufacturer's name-plate. The bus had been moving off again before he had found it; but it had been the right plate and a wave of excitement had swept over him. From that moment, he had known exactly what he wanted to do in the world. He would operate a bus service.

His first letter to the body manufacturer had been written from Singapore on his uncle's business stationery. He had been aware for some time that the original catalogue from London, precious though it was and always would be, was now very much out of date. Nevertheless, the decision to send for the latest edition had not been easily taken. For some reason that he had been unable to account for, it had seemed almost like an act of treachery.

However, the arrival of the new catalogue had given him other things to worry about. The catalogue itself had been magnificent. Unfortunately, it had been accompanied by a courteous letter from the sales manager, informing him that the company's Far Eastern Representative, Mr W.W.Belden, would shortly be visiting Singapore and would take the opportunity of meeting Mr Krishnan and discussing his fleet requirements with him personally. For weeks Girija had gone in fear of W.W.Belden's arrival at his uncle's office and the humiliating scenes that would ensue when the truth was known. But Mr Belden had never come, and eventually Girija had drawn the correct conclusion. Mr Belden had investigated the financial status of this new prospective customer and decided not to waste his time.

His prudence had been understandable. The cheapest twenty-four seater now cost over three thousand pounds; almost double the price of the cheapest bus in the 1936 catalogue. But one thing in the new edition had caught Girija's eye; a quotation from a trade journal devoted to the interests and activities of road transport operators. Girija had found that this journal could be obtained in Singapore, and had bought a subscription. From the articles it published he began to learn about the economics of public transportation. By the time he went to work for Mr Wright, he had acquired a reasonably realistic view of his chances of achieving his life's ambition. Unless he could find a working capital of at least twenty thousand dollars (Straits) his chances of starting even the most modest country bus service were non-existent.

3

Girija had a one-room atap house in the estate compound, and an arrangement with one of the servants at the Wrights' bungalow to keep it clean. There were Indian families of his own caste living in a village six miles away, and on Sundays he would cycle over there for tiffin. One of the families had an attractive daughter named Sumitra, whom he thought he would one day marry. However, during the week, the curfew kept him at home, and there he always cooked his own food. Sometimes, he would go back to the office after he had eaten his evening meal and do some more work before going to bed; at others, he would listen to Radio Malaya and read and dream.

On the evening of the day of the ambush, he stayed late in the office trying to make up for the time he had lost by going with the burial party. The following morning he would have to drive in with Mr Wright to the bank at Bukit Amphu to cash the weekly wages cheque, and he had not yet completed the time sheets.

The work required care and concentration and he was glad of it; for it postponed the moment when he would have to entertain once more the dangerous thoughts which had come to him in the morning.

The things he had observed at the scene of the ambush, and learned from the two tappers, had made it possible for him to reconstruct the recent history of the dead men with reasonable certainty.

They had only recently arrived from the north and were relatively inexperienced. Of that he was sure. Their use of the easy route offered by the gully showed that. True, they had had a lot to carry, but that did not excuse carelessness. In an area where British patrols were being supplied by the R.A.F., a fact which they could scarcely help knowing, they had not even troubled to send scouts on ahead to feel the way, but had blundered straight into the ambush in a body.

The Lieutenant's opinion was that they had been on their way to mine the main road. Girija did not agree with that. The quantity of ammunition they had been carrying was out of all proportion to the needs of such an operation. And how was the lack of cooking utensils and food supplies to be explained if they were going so far from their base? To Girija there seemed only one possible explanation. What the Lieutenant's patrol had ambushed was a supply column on its way to deliver mines and ammunition to another gang operating farther south.

It had been at this point in his argument with himself that Girija's heart had begun to beat faster, and that an unpleasant sensation had come to his stomach. If his reasoning were correct it could mean only one thing. The base camp near Awang was a guerrilla arms dump.

He finished his work, locked up the office and walked slowly back across the courtyard to his house. It was a warm, humid night. He took off his shirt and khaki drill shorts, washed himself carefully all over and then put on a dhoti. There was some lentil soup in an iron saucepan. He lit the oil burner under it and sat down to wait.

What had disconcerted him had been not so much the nature of his thoughts, as the way in which they had presented themselves. He did not regard himself as being fundamentally honest or dishonest, idealistic or corrupt, law-abiding or delinquent. He did not think of himself as definable in such terms. His dilemmas had always been capable of resolution into simple questions of choice. Choice A would be wise (advantageous). Choice B would be stupid (disadvantageous). The discovery that his mind could explore enthusiastically the possibility of his committing a major crime, with only a belated and distasteful glance at the path of rectitude, had been disturbing.

And a major crime it undoubtedly would be.

He had heard about these dumps and caches. It was known that the arms were brought in by professional smugglers operating from beyond the Thai border and employing different routes from those used by the guerrillas. A number of consignments had been intercepted; but it was generally believed that a far greater number always got through. Terrorists captured far to the south in the Kuala Lumpur area had been found to be in possession of substantial quantities of weapons, ammunition and explosives of the same pattern as those intercepted in the north. It was said that there were not enough troops in the whole of Malaya to patrol the border with Thailand effectively.

Just before the burial party had finished its work that morning the Malay sergeant and four more soldiers had arrived with packing crates strung on bamboo poles. When the ammunition and grenades had been loaded into the crates, they were taken off to the compound. While the machine pistols were being gathered up, Girija had asked the sergeant a question.

The sergeant had looked down at the machine pistol in his hands and shrugged. 'How should I know what they cost?'

'But don't you know how much your own cost, Sergeant? Supposing a man lost one.'

'He would be court-martialled.'

'But surely he would have stoppages of pay, too?'

'Oh yes. Two hundred dollars perhaps.'

'So much?'

'They do not grow on trees.'

The sergeant had gone. Girija had turned and looked at the row of graves. Each man had had a machine pistol; and ammunition was costly stuff. It was more than likely that what the ten men had been carrying between them was worth anything up to three thousand dollars. It would be interesting to know how much more there was where that had come from.

The soup began to bubble. He poured it into a bowl and, when it had cooled a little, began to eat.

The penalty for being found in the illegal possession of arms was death. Whether or not knowledge of the whereabouts of smuggled arms would constitute possession, and whether concealment of such knowledge carried the same penalty he did not know. One thing was clear. The illegal *selling* of smuggled arms would certainly be a hanging matter; at least while the emergency regulations remained in force. The best thing he could do was to go to Mr Wright immediately and make a clean breast of the matter.

But a clean breast of *what* matter? He did not really *know* anything about an arms dump. He only believed one to be there. And where was 'there'? Assuming that his deductions were correct, the dump was concealed in an area of jungle covering at least three square miles. It might prove quite impossible to find. Mr Wright would not thank him for starting a wild goose chase, and neither would the police. When the time came for him to apply for a local bus service franchise they might remember the trouble he had caused and hold it against him. No. The best thing he could do was nothing.

He finished his soup and felt better. He was an innocent man again quietly digesting his evening meal. What did he want with smuggled arms? Could he ever have sold them? Of course not. Who would buy? And supposing others knew of the dump, if dump there were. Ten men had been killed; but supposing that other members of the guerrilla band had stayed behind. It might be highly dangerous to start searching in the area for their camp. Besides, there was always a chance that one or two of the men living at Awang already knew where it was. Not a very big chance perhaps; the guerrillas would not have trusted their unwilling hosts to that extent; but someone might have found out by chance. Naturally, no man or woman from the village would dare to go to the police with the information; or not immediately anyway. A decent interval would have to elapse before the dump could be discovered 'accidentally'. More likely it would just be forgotten. And that perhaps was what he should do; forget about it. After all, he could always remember again later, if he wanted to.

There was a metal trunk in one corner of the room. In it he kept his catalogues and trade papers, and the schedule of a projected daily bus service linking ten of the principal rubber estates in the district with Bukit Amphu sixteen miles away. He took the schedule out, read it through very carefully, and then began to make one or two long-contemplated modifications.

4

A month went by before Girija made any move to locate the arms dump.

There had been no reports of any special patrol activity in the district, and guerrilla attacks in the province had been concentrated on areas nearer the coast. He had watched the men from Awang carefully without detecting anything unusual in their demeanour. But such reassurances came mingled with doubt. If no dump had been discovered, it could well be for the simple reason that none existed.

It was, in fact, the growing conviction that he must have been mistaken that gave him the courage he needed to go on. If there were nothing to find, he argued, there could be nothing incriminating in the search.

The first part of his plan called for a satisfactory cover for repeated visits to the Awang area. He might avoid going through the village itself, but he would have to use a mile or more of the road leading to it. Encounters with men who knew him, and who might gossip or ask questions, would be inevitable. The difficulty had seemed insurmountable at first; but finally he had had an idea.

The latex produced by the estate went thirty miles by road down to the port of Kuala Pangkalan and from there was shipped to Singapore. Since the emergency, the trucks from the coast had had to be provided with armoured car escorts, and, consequently, did not make the journey so often. Mr Wright had been talking for some time, and writing to Singapore, about the need for additional storage sheds. The Singapore office had been reluctant to authorize the expenditure. Girija's idea was to make the new sheds an excuse for his trips to Awang.

Near the abandoned mine workings there were a number of derelict corrugated-iron buildings which had been used as offices, stores and repair shops. Girija wrote to the head office of the mining company in Kota Bharu, and asked permission to inspect the property with a possible view to making an offer for the material of the buildings.

He did not tell Mr Wright. If Mr Wright found out no great harm would be done. Indeed, Mr Wright would probably give him a pat on the back for his zeal and initiative in attempting to solve the problem of the new storage sheds. But Mr Wright would also tell him something he already knew; that the mining company's rust-eaten buildings were not worth the cost of dismantling them, and that it would be a waste of time for him to go and inspect them.

The mining company replied with understandable enthusiasm that Mr Krishnan had their full permission to inspect the buildings any time he liked. That was all he needed. No one person he might encounter there would know exactly how many visits of inspection he had made, nor how many might be necessary. It would be assumed that he was acting on Mr Wright's instruction. If he were ever challenged he could produce the letter.

The following Sunday he cycled out to Awang. Just short of the village, he turned off the road on to the overgrown track which led to the mining company's property. He met nobody on the way.

Ground sluicing had cleared some twenty acres of land in the bend of the river. No topsoil had been left for the jungle to reclaim and the brown scars of the workings were still visible beneath a thin film of scrub and weed. Girija walked along the river bank until he came to the shell of a building that had housed a big rotary pump, and went through the motions of inspecting it and taking notes. This was for the benefit of anyone who might have seen him and be watching from across the river. After a few minutes he moved away, circling out of sight of the river bank until he reached the cover of some trees.

He had thought long and carefully about the problems of searching the area. The only large-scale map which covered it, and to which he might ordinarily have had access, was an ordnance survey sheet marked with the estate boundary lines. Unfortunately, a strict security regulation governed the distribution and custody of such maps at that time, and it had to be kept by Mr Wright in his personal safe. Girija was forced to rely on his none too vivid recollection of it.

The picture in his mind was one of the three parallel ridges, rather like steps, with contour lines very close together. That meant, he knew, that the sides of the ridges were steep and that there were deep ravines between them. It was not much to go on; but it was something. He did not believe that even inexperienced men would choose the floor of a ravine for a base camp, any more than they would choose to perch on the summit of a ridge. To that extent the likely areas of search were limited. And there was another factor to be considered. Even if they had had only small quantities of arms and ammunition to store, they would have tried to find a place for them which gave some protection from the weather. He thought it unlikely that there were caves there; but on the steeper hillsides there would be sizeable hollows made during the monsoons, when the heavier trees fell and tore their roots out of the ground. Such hollows could easily be made into shelters. All in all, it seemed sensible to start the search by working along the upper slopes.

He attempted to do so; and that first Sunday expedition was very nearly the last. It took him an hour to climb three hundred yards up the side of the first ridge, and almost as long to get down again. He tore his clothes, scratched his arms and legs, and ended by becoming completely exhausted. He also became frightened. If some patrolling policeman were to ask him to account for the tears and scratches, he would be hard put to it to invent a convincing explanation.

He succeeded in getting back to his house unobserved; but the experience had thoroughly unnerved him and he decided to abandon the whole project. For several days he did succeed in putting it out of his mind. Then, as the scratches on his arms and legs began to heal, he began to think again. None of the ambushed men had had scratches on the arms and legs. That meant that they must have found an easy route to and from their hiding place. The beauty of this deduction restored his confidence.

The next time he made no attempt to penetrate the jungle. Instead he worked his way round the fringes of it looking for easy ways in. He found several and noted them for future reference.

The following Sunday he began a systematic probe. He had learned well from his initial mistake. When the going became too hard, he made no attempt to force a path through, but went back and tried a different or more circuitous way. He knew by now that he could never hope to cover anything like the whole area; but he had become philosophical about the search; it was a kind of game now, and although he did not expect to win, he had not yet reached the point of conceding his defeat.

Eight weeks after he began, he received his first piece of encouragement. He had been following a dry stream bed up a fold in a hillside. On both sides there were cane thickets of a kind he had learned to avoid. It was useless to try and push your way through. You had to go round them; and they often covered wide areas. Then, as the stream bed bore away sharply to the left, he paused. There were a few pieces of dead cane lying on the ground. At first he thought that they had been broken away by some animal grubbing for food among the roots. Then he saw that they had been cut.

He stood still for a moment, staring. There was no mistaking the marks on the cane. They had been made by a metal cutting-edge. He examined the border of the thicket carefully. For a distance of about two feet the cane was thinner and greener, and near the ground he could see short stumps of older cane in amongst the new growth. At some time in the not too distant past, someone had cleared a path there.

It was getting late, and he was a mile and a half or more from the tin workings and the shed where he had left his bicycle. He decided to leave further investigation until the following Sunday. During the week, on the pretext of checking an inventory, he went to the tool store, borrowed one of the long chopping knives, called a parang, that the estate workers used for clearing underbrush, and hid it in his room. On Sunday morning he wrapped the parang in newspaper, tied it to the cross-bar of his bicycle and set off early for Awang.

He found his way back to the cane thicket without difficulty and started hacking a path through it with the parang. The new growth had not yet had time to harden, and the going was fairly easy. He had no fear of running into surviving members of the band. If this were indeed the way to their camp, it had not been used for several months.

The path was uphill. After he had gone fifteen yards, the cane thinned out and he found himself on a shallow ledge from which he could see down into the stream bed. On the ground there were some dead tree branches arranged to form a sort of chair. It looked as if the ledge had been used as a vantage point from which a sentry could cover the approach along the stream bed. A well-worn track led off to the right. He followed it, his heart pounding.

The camp was in a clearing shielded both from the sun and from air observation by the branches of a large flame-of-the-forest. The jungle apes had been there before him. Pieces of clothing had been torn apart and scattered over the clearing amid cooking pots, an earthenware chatty and empty rice bags. The only thing that seemed to have escaped the apes' attentions was a metal box. It was full of leaflets, printed in Malay and Chinese, calling upon the people of Malaya to rise against the imperialist exploiters and establish a people's democracy.

There was another path leading down from the clearing and Girija followed it. About twelve yards down, a hole had been dug and used as a latrine. He walked back slowly to the clearing. In the long search for the camp site his doubts had been forgotten. Now, he remembered them and faced the bitterness of defeat. Lieutenant Haynes had been right. He, Girija, had been wrong. For Sunday after Sunday he had exchanged the pleasures of tiffin with his future mother-in-law, and the soft glances of Sumitra, for senseless walks in the jungle and the pursuit of an illusion. There was no arms dump; there never had been.

He had started to retrace his footsteps when his foot struck something that tinkled. He looked down. Lying on the ground was a brass cartridge-case. As he bent down to pick it up he saw another one. A minute later he had found three more. He stared at them, puzzled. They were of .303 calibre. He went over the ground again and found what he was looking for; the clip which had held the five rounds.

There was no doubt about it. A .303 rifle had been fired there. But no rifle of any kind had been found at the scene of the ambush. And none of the weapons had been of .303 calibre. Where, then, was the rifle?

He searched the camp site thoroughly first. He found a small fixed frequency radio in a teak box; but no rifle. He began to search the hillside above the camp, taking any route that looked as if it might conceivably have been used before. After about an hour he came upon a clump of bamboo from which a number of thick stalks had been cut. Then, about twelve yards away, he saw it.

Braced between the steep hillside and the trunk of a tree was a triangular roof of bamboo. Cane screens had been plaited to enclose the sides of the structure and form a shelter.

Girija scrambled towards it, slipping and sliding on the spongy carpet of dead leaves and slashing wildly with the parang at the undergrowth in his path. When he reached the shelter, he stood for an instant, breathless and trying to prepare himself for the crushing disappointment of finding it empty. Then, he pulled one of the screens aside.

There was a sudden, swift rustle and his heart leapt as some small brown animal rushed out past him. He pulled the screen back farther and looked inside.

The hillside beneath the roof had been dug out to make the space roughly rectangular. It was about six feet high and ten feet long, and filled from floor to roof with wood and metal packing cases.

He sat down on the ground to get his breath back, and stared at the cases. A number of them, he could see, were long and narrow and had rope handles. One of these was near the screen, and looked as if it had been opened. He crawled over to it and prised the lid off with the parang.

Inside, carefully packed on slotted wood bearers were six .303 rifles. Five of them were heavily greased and wrapped in thick, oiled paper with the name of a Belgian manufacturer printed on it. One had been unwrapped. Girija took it out and opened the breach. It had been fired, presumably down at the camp site, and put back without being cleaned. The barrel was corroded.

Girija clucked disapprovingly. That was no way to treat valuable property. He returned the rifle to its case and began to examine the rest of his find. He soon discovered that there was more there than he had at first supposed. There were ten cases of rifles and at least thirty other boxes and cases of various sizes, in addition to ammunition containers.

He began to move some of these so as to get a look at the stencilled markings on the bigger cases, and then stopped. He would have to start back soon and there was no hope of taking an inventory that day. Besides, he had no need of an inventory.

He knew that all he had really found was hope. Of course, it would have been agreeable to dream of what was there in terms of wealth; but wealth that could only be realized, if at all, in some unmeasurable fullness of time was meaningless. It would be the hope that mattered in the days to come; and if he could draw from it the strength to go on quietly reading his transport trade journals, and turning the pages of his catalogues, and revising notional time-tables, and faithfully continuing to serve Mr Wright; if, in short, he could be patient and discreet, he might perhaps one day fulfil himself.

5

He waited, patiently and discreetly, for three years.

In the beginning it had been comparatively easy. There had been practical matters to attend to.

First, he thoroughly cleaned and greased the rifle that had been fired; then he gave some thought to the long-term problems of storage and preservation. The monsoon rains would arrive shortly, and the bamboo roof was not waterproof.

He decided to reconstruct the shelter. One Sunday he moved all the boxes out of it and laid a framework of bamboo on the ground to ensure a proper circulation of air. Over this he put a heavy tarpaulin taken from the estate compound, and then rearranged the boxes on top of it. Another tarpaulin went over the boxes and was lashed down firmly with wire rope. A third tarpaulin he incorporated in the roof. He also repaired the screens.

Thereafter, he only went to the place once a month to make sure that all was in order. He would have gone more often if he could have trusted himself; but, rather to his surprise, he had found patience easier to cultivate than discretion.

In spite of his initial resolution, it had proved hard not to make an inventory of what was in the shelter and keep it in his tin trunk. He knew that such a document was premature and pointless. He knew that, if through some mischance, Mr Wright happened to see it and ask questions, his lies would be unconvincing. Yet, the temptation had persisted. There had also been an insane desire to confide in Sumitra, to bask in her admiration and flattery, and bind her future more securely to his. He knew that she would certainly tell her mother, who would tell the father, who worked in the bank at Bukit Amphu and was a notorious chatterbox; but that temptation, too, had continued to haunt him.

During the second year he had other troubles. His mother died; and two of the cases resting on the lower tarpaulin were attacked by termites. Fortunately, he noticed the fact in good time and was able to minimize the damage. The ammunition boxes were metal and, having given them a thick coat of bitumen paint, he moved them to the bottom of the stack. The damaged boxes he repaired with strips of teak; and sprayed all the wood containers with a powerful solution benzine hexachloride.

The second year went by; and the third. General Templer's policy of winning the co-operation and goodwill of the people of Malaya, and enlisting them in the fight against the terrorists began to succeed; and, as success snowballed into victory, curfews were lifted and road blocks removed. Areas free of terrorists were declared 'white', and restrictions on unescorted civil transport movements cancelled.

The day that the province in which he worked was declared 'white', Girija wrote to England for a new bus body catalogue. The following Sunday, he went to the shelter and spent two of the happiest hours of his life, making an inventory.

Chapter Two

I

When the rubber estates in the Pangkalan district had latex for shipment, they generally notified the Anglo-Malay Transport Company at the port of Kuala Pangkalan. The company would then send their trucks to collect the latex, store it temporarily in their godowns, and finally, when instructions came through from Singapore, ship it out in one of their big motor junks.

The founder, manager and sole proprietor of this useful enterprise was a Chinese, Mr Tan Siow Mong.

Mr Tan had been educated at a mission school in Macao, and spoke Hokkien and Portuguese as well as Cantonese, Malay and English. His father had owned a fishing junk, and had divided his working years between snapper fishing and carrying cargoes of rattan up the coast to Hong Kong. When he died, in the early thirties, Mr Tan and his two brothers had taken over the junk and turned to the more lucrative business of opium smuggling. They had been caught, in the end, by a British gunboat, and their junk had been impounded. By that time, they had had a substantial sum of money saved and could accept the forfeiture of the junk with equanimity. However, a family council had considered it advisable for the Tans to leave the China Coast for a while, and seek their fortunes elsewhere. One brother had gone to Singapore, another to Manila. Tan Siow Mong, the eldest, had taken his mother to Kuala Pangkalan. There, with his share of the family capital, he had started to deal in copra and lend money to Malays at forty per cent. During the Japanese occupation he had accepted a disused godown in discharge of a debt. After the war he had tried to sell it. Unable to find a buyer, he had eventually decided to make it pay for itself. The Anglo-Malay Transport Company had grown from that decision.

Mr Tan was in the late forties now, with greying hair and rimless glasses. He wore well-cut tussore suits, and was never seen without a dark tie even in the hottest weather. He had an air of well-bred dignity that was much admired in the Chinese business community of Kuala Pangkalan.

His office was so placed that he could, without moving from his desk, see the trucks in the unloading bay of number one godown and the wooden quay at which the junks discharged and took on cargo. By turning his head he could also see, through a glass panel let into the wall beside the door, his four Chinese assistants. Mr Tan did not believe in elaborate organization. Working sixty-five hours a week, the four assistants were well able to take care of most of the routine paper work of the business. The accounts he preferred to look after himself.

Two of the trucks were unloading bales of latex which had come down that afternoon from one of the Cheang Thye Phu Syndicate estates, and he could see the Indian clerk from the estate office checking off the weights with the godown foreman.

Mr Tan did not like that. Mr Wright, the estate manager, had always, and rightly, trusted the company before. Why had he suddenly felt it necessary to send his clerk to check the weighing?

The clerk and the godown foreman had evidently agreed the figures now, for, as Mr Tan watched, the clerk smiled and turned away. Mr Tan had made a note to ask the foreman what reason, if any, had been given for this uncomplimentary change of procedure, when he saw that the clerk was walking across the yard towards his office.

Mr Tan looked down at the papers on his desk. It would be undignified to be seen peering out. A moment or two later one of his assistants came in to say that Mr Krishnan desired the pleasure of a few moments conversation with him.

Mr Tan disapproved of Indians. He had often found them to be disagreeably acute in business matters. He also disapproved of estate clerks, who, if they were not given occasional presents, could delay the payment of accounts and cause other inconveniences.

This one he remembered only from having seen him with Mr Wright, the estate manager. He was lean and very dark, with bright, intelligent eyes and a predatory mouth that smiled too much. It would be interesting to discover what price the fellow would put upon his nuisance value.

He greeted Girija with grave courtesy and asked him to sit down.

'It is not often,' he went on in English, 'that we have the pleasure of seeing you, Mr Krishnan.'

Girija smiled. 'Thank you. Mr Wright sends all compliments and best favours.'

Mr Tan congratulated himself on choosing English for the conversation. His own, he knew, was excellent. The clerk's was little better than the illiterate commercial patois that the British called 'Babu'. It placed him at a disadvantage, small but possibly useful.

'And are Mr and Mrs Wright well?'

'Both very well. We hope ditto for Mrs Tan, self and family.'

'Thank you, yes.'

Tea was brought in from the outer office and served in minute cups. Tentative moves might now be made towards a discussion of the real object of the visit.

'This must be a busy time for you at the estate,' observed Mr Tan.

What this banality was in effect asking was why Mr Wright had thought it necessary to waste his clerk's time by sending him in to Kuala Pangkalan to supervise a normal warehousing operation.

Girija smiled and answered in Malay. 'With the rubber market so firm, we are always busy now.'

Mr Tan nodded. He was wondering if by some faint flicker of expression he had revealed his amusement at the clerk's English. The Malay was fluent. Courteously, he answered in the same language.

'Let us hope the bad times are ended for good.'

'Good business for one is good business for all,' said Girija.

'Very true.' Now, Mr Tan decided, they were coming to the point. Reference to mutual advantage was the accepted preliminary to a squeeze.

'This tea is excellent, sir,' said Girija.

Mr Tan instantly sent for more. This again postponed pointed discussion and further inanities were exchanged. Grudgingly, Mr Tan had to admit to himself that the young man was handling the interview well. He found himself becoming interested.

When they were alone again, he said: 'Mr Wright is a very good manager. It must be a pleasure to work for such a man.'

Girija nodded. 'Indeed it is. He is, as you say, a fine manager. But he is also a man of good heart.'

'I can well believe that.'

'In fact,' Girija went on, 'when I asked him if he would allow me to come down to Kuala Pangkalan on personal business, he did not even question me before giving his permission.'

'One has always known that he values your services highly.' Mr Tan was making the pace again now. The use of the phrase 'values your services' would, he was sure, bring the matter to a head.

'And yet,' said Girija, 'I was glad he did not ask me questions.' He paused.

Mr Tan was silent. He was certain that the moment had arrived.

Girija flashed a smile. 'For if he had, I would have been forced to hurt his feelings or to lie. I would not wish to do either of those things.'

'Both are offences against good taste,' agreed Mr Tan sententiously.

'Mr Wright has been my father,' said Girija. 'How could I tell him that, being in need of the wisest advice on a matter of great importance, I was turning not to him but to Mr Tan Siow Mong?'

Mr Tan said nothing. He had nothing relevant to say. He was hurriedly revising his estimate of the situation. If the clerk were choosing this way of leading up to a request for money, he must have some absurdly large sum in mind.

Girija leant forward earnestly. 'Nowhere in Kuala Pangkalan is there a wiser head in important matters of business,' he said. 'It is well known.'

Mr Tan noted the qualifying phrase, 'in important matters of business'. He said: 'You pay me an undeserved compliment.'

'My friend,' continued Girija, 'could think of no one else whose advice on this matter would be so valuable.'

'Your friend?' Mr Tan was becoming confused again and in consequence also a little annoyed; but his tone remained polite.

'You do not know him, sir,' said Girija; 'and he knows you only from your high reputation. When I said that I would ask your advice on this important matter that is troubling him, he begged me not to mention him by name.

The matter is highly confidential.'

'Most business matters are.' Mr Tan spoke dryly. He guessed that 'confidential' in this context probably meant 'criminal'.

Girija's smile became tentative. For the first time, Mr Tan saw him ill at ease, and decided to offer a word of reassurance. It would be irritating if the man took fright and left without revealing the object of his visit.

'If your friend respects my wisdom,' he remarked, 'he must also acknowledge my discretion.'

Girija's smile went back into place and his eyes met Mr Tan's. 'Of course. But he is a nervous man. You will see why when I explain.' He paused to choose his words before going on. 'It appears that some years ago during the emergency, when the terrorists were bringing in arms from the north, my friend found some of these arms—rifles, machine-guns, ammunition.' He looked up to see how Mr Tan was taking this.

Mr Tan smiled; but very faintly. 'And so he turned them over to the police?'

'That, of course, is what he should have done.' Girija shrugged. 'But, as I said, my friend is a nervous man. He did not wish to call attention to himself. At the time, it seemed best to do nothing. Now, he is in a difficulty.'

'Yes?'

'My friend is in need of money. He thought of these arms. If he told the police about them now, there would be questions and trouble. But if a buyer for the arms could be found, perhaps his debts could be paid, and no one would be the worse. The emergency is over. No harm could come of it, only good for my friend.'

Mr Tan sat very still. 'You wish me to advise you friend?'

Girija nodded. 'That is what he hopes you may do, sir. Yes.'

'He should still take the matter to the police. It would be very wrong to try to sell them. He need not say that he found them long ago, but he should certainly go to the police.'

Girija spread out his hands. 'But, sir, my friend has debts.'

'It is better to go to a money-lender than to risk going to prison.'

Girija smiled triumphantly. 'That was exactly my own advice to him, sir. To risk going to prison for a few hundred dollars is the act of a fool. I told him so.'

Mr Tan hesitated. The agreement baffled him. He knew instinctively that somewhere, somehow, he had mismanaged the conversation. He knew that he was left with only one question to ask, and that when he had asked it he would have lost a battle of wits. But he also knew that his curiosity would have to be satisfied. Mentally he shrugged off the humiliation.

'And what was his reply?' he asked.

Girija's hand went to the row of ball-point pens in his shirt pocket, and drew from behind it a folded sheet of paper. He opened it out and handed it across the desk.

'This paper, sir,' he said; 'my friend gave me this paper.'

Mr Tan took the paper, spread it out on the desk in front of him and looked down. It was a typed list with the word 'INVENTORY' at the head of it. He read on:

DESCRIPTION	TYPE	QUANTITY	TODAY'S FREE MARKET VALUE ($ STRAITS)
Rifles	.303 Military S.A. Belge	54	16,000
.303 Ammo	For above	5,000 rds.	6,000
Machine pistols	Schmeisser	25	18,000
.300 Ammo	With magazines for above	8,000 rds.	7,000
Bazookas	U.S. Govt. pattern	4	6,000
Ammo for same	,, ,, ,,	35 rds.	1,000
Grenades	Mills unfused ⎫		
Fuses	For same ⎭	100	2,000
Land mines	Teller	40	4,000
			60,000

Equals £(Sterling)	7,500
Equals $(U.S.)	21,000

Note All items in brand new mint condition in original mnfrs.
   packings, containers etc.
Prices All prices f.o.b. vicinity Kuala Pangkalan.
Terms and Conditions Items sold separate subject 20% increase.

Mr Tan looked up.

'You see, sir,' said Girija softly; 'I was wrong. It is not just a matter of a few hundred dollars, but of many thousands.'

Mr Tan pretended to read the list through a second time in order to give himself time to think. He had little doubt that the 'friend' for whom the clerk claimed to be acting was non-existent. The Indian must have been desperate for money to take the risk of approaching a comparative stranger in this way; or very sure of himself as a judge of character. Mr Tan had an uneasy feeling that the latter explanation might be the more likely. The fellow looked confident enough, and not at all desperate. Of course, he could be lying, and the whole story could be a mere trick to get money; but Mr Tan did not really think so. In any case it would be simple to find out. He looked up again and met the clerk's eyes.

'My friend,' said Girija, 'would be willing to pay a commission of fifty per cent to anyone who found a buyer, and who would take delivery of the goods.'

Mr Tan shook his head. 'But this would be a serious criminal matter. Does your friend not understand that?'

'That was my first thought, too,' said Girija approvingly; 'but he did not agree. This is not stolen property, he says. It has no owner. If it should leave the country the police would have no interest in it. The emergency is over.'

'But the laws remain.'

'That is true.' Girija nodded thoughtfully. 'You think, then, sir, that I should tell my friend that you advise him to go to the police?'

'I think you should tell him to put the whole matter out of his mind.' Mr Tan paused and then added: 'Perhaps later the law will not be so strict.'

'Yes, that is so.'

'Such merchandise as this is always saleable.' Mr Tan looked down again at the list. 'Have you seen any of these items?'

'My friend is naturally careful.'

'But do you believe him? You say he wishes to find a buyer. A list is not proof that there is something to sell. Could he produce samples?'

'He would be more than ready to do that, sir.'

Mr Tan refolded the inventory. 'I know little about these matters,' he said; 'but I have heard that buyers in this market are not easy to reach. Contacts must be found. Time must be spent. There can be no urgency.'

'My friend is very patient.'

'Then, do as I suggest. Tell him to forget for a while.' He looked up at Girija. 'You agree?'

'Of course, sir.'

Mr Tan held up the list. 'And I may keep this paper?'

It was a test question.

Girija smiled. 'My friend will be happy for it to remain in such wise hands, sir.'

He rose. The interview was over. When the usual courtesies had been exchanged, he left.

Mr Tan watched him walk away across the yard, then sent for the Chiang Thye Phu Syndicate estate's files.

The first thing was to find out whether the clerk's discretion and sense of self-preservation were as lively as they had appeared to be. If he had been foolhardy enough to type out his list on Mr Wright's estate office typewriter and then leave it with someone who could, if it seemed advantageous, go to the authorities and gain credit by reporting the incident, Mr Tan wanted no more to do with him and would burn the paper at once. If, as he suspected, the young man had been careful to leave himself in a position to deny effectively all knowledge of the conversation they had just had, and of the list, then something might be made of the situation.

He looked through Mr Wright's office consignment notes and compared the typing on them with that of the list. It was obvious that the list had not been typed on the same machine. So far so good. He read through the list once more and then locked it in his private office safe.

Later that day, when he had had further time to think, he wrote to his brother in Singapore.

2

Tan Yam Heng was the disreputable member of the family. Such, at least, was the view of his brothers in Kuala Pangkalan and Manila.

He was one of the founders of the Singapore Democratic Action Party and organizer of a waterfront trade union which, though small in membership, had sufficient nuisance value to levy tribute on two of the bigger stevedoring companies. As the fruits of these negotiations were always handed over to him personally, privately, and in cash, he did not consider it necessary to report their receipt either to the union auditors or the income tax authorities. He had no time to waste on the pettifogging rituals of accountancy and other hindrances to social progress. He saw himself as a man of power, a manipulator of puppets, choosing to work behind the scenes until the strategic moment came for him to step forward and lead his party on to victory.

If that had been all there were to say of him his brothers would have been content. His political pretensions they could ignore and, devious men themselves, they did not seriously object to his methods of augmenting his income. What they did object to, strongly, was what he did with it.

Most Chinese like to gamble, and with some this liking becomes an addiction as compulsive as those of drugs or alcohol. Yam Heng was a gambler of this kind. Moreover, he was a stupid gambler. Games of chance are at least subject to the law of averages, race horses do sometimes run true to form, and skill can often qualify bad luck at poker; but Yam Heng's conceit and fantasies of omnipotence had in the end demanded more esoteric gratifications. He had taken to gambling on the 'pickle' market.

This unofficial market in raw rubber is conducted by freebooters operating outside the respectable Singapore brokerage houses, and they are speculating on small price fluctuations over short periods. On the pickle market a consignment of rubber in transit may theoretically change hands several times in the course of a day. Large sums of money are made and lost on feverish, bull-and-bear transactions. The successful speculators are Chinese with great experience, cool heads and reliable intelligence organizations. Much use is made of the time differences between the London and Singapore markets, and a few minutes lead on a piece of cabled information can make thousands of dollars for its possessor. It is the efficient who generally win, the gamblers who generally lose.

The pickle market was no place for Yam Heng. The acquaintance who had introduced him to it was one of a syndicate of small men, and they had been perfectly willing to let an outsider buy in; the stronger the syndicate the better; but his arrogant impatience with their wariness and caution had soon antagonized them. Eventually, he had taken his money out of the syndicate and started to plunge on his own.

If he had immediately and heavily lost, the blow to his self-esteem might have caused him to think twice about continuing. Unfortunately, he had won. After that, it had been too late.

His early appeals for loans had been received by his brothers with fraternal tolerance, and responded to in the belief that the money lent would be repaid. They had known, of course, that he was over-fond of gambling, but had believed his profligacy in that respect to be confined to horse-racing or fan-tan. The discovery of the true nature of the 'investments' they were so innocently subsidizing had been a disagreeable shock; so had the realization that Yam Heng had been deceitfully making his applications for loans simultaneously, and in identical terms, to both of them.

There had been worse to come. In the face of their joint refusals to lend him another cent, Yam Heng had blandly informed them that the various union funds in his charge were some thousands of dollars short, and that unless the shortages were made good before the annual audit, the consequences for the Tan name might be serious. There had been hasty consultation between Kuala Pangkalan and Manila. The brothers had paid up in the end; but only after both of them had been to Singapore and personally checked the union books. The days when Yam Heng could be trusted had gone. Thereafter, he had the status somewhat of a poor relation; a responsibility to be discharged as inexpensively as possible.

It was with this responsibility in mind that Mr Tan had written his letter. Some weeks earlier he had received one of Yam Heng's periodic requests for money and noted a veiled belligerence in the wording. It had reminded him that the annual audit of the union books was due shortly, and that Yam Heng would soon be making his annual attempt to extort money by hinting at another raid on the union funds. Mr Tan's nerves were strong, and for the previous three years he had successfully refused to be intimidated; but he knew gamblers, and there was always the chance that one day Yam Heng might become desperate.

At that moment, in fact, Yam Heng was merely depressed. He had had two small wins in the past two weeks, and a bigger loss which had cancelled out the winnings. His brother's letter annoyed him.

It contained a polite inquiry after his health, a detailed account of their mother's most recent illness, and a proposal that he visit Kuala Pangkalan at a convenient moment in the near future. It mentioned that the junk *Happy Dawn* would be unloading in Singapore the following week, and that the Master would be instructed to offer him a free passage. It gave no hint of a possible reason for the visit.

Yam Heng knew his brother too well to suppose that the visit had been proposed for any social or family reason. Their mother was senile. Her current state of health could only have been mentioned to make the invitation seem logical to some stranger reading the letter. Yam Heng disliked having his curiosity aroused unless he had the means on hand to satisfy it. The offer of the junk passage irritated him also. It was his brother's way of saying that, if he wanted to travel in comfort by train or plane, he could pay his own fare. He considered sending a dignified reply regretting that pressure of work compelled him to decline the invitation; but, finally, curiosity and the faint hope of another loan decided him to accept. He had just enough money for the train fare.

His brother met him at the station, greeted him warmly and drove him to the ornate brick and stucco house in Willoughby Road. The first evening was spent in celebrating the family reunion. Old Mrs Tan emerged from her room, an elaborate dinner was consumed, the young children made their Uncle Yam tell them about Singapore, and the eldest son showed his Voigtlander camera and some of the colour slide photographs of birds which he had made with it. Yam Heng found it all very agreeable. His brother remained friendly and courteous. There were no references, oblique or otherwise, to their long estrangement, nor to the reasons for it. He permitted himself a few restrained smiles, some delicate compliments to his sister-in-law, and a joke or two with the younger children.

It was not until the following day that his brother revealed the reason for the invitation. In the morning they toured the godowns, visited the truck maintenance shed, and watched one of the junks unloading fifty-gallon drums of fuel oil. Then, they went to the office and tea was served.

'And how,' Siow Mong inquired at last, 'is the pickle market?'

Yam Heng gave him an impassive stare.

'I ask,' Siow Mong continued after a pause, 'not in a spirit of criticism, but because I want information.'

For one wild moment Yam Heng wondered if his brother were contemplating a foray of his own. Then, he shrugged. 'Some make money, some lose.'

His brother nodded sagely as if he had had a suspicion confirmed. 'I did hear,' he went on, 'that there is another thriving market now in Singapore.'

'There are markets there in most things.'

'Yes. But I heard–I cannot remember from what source–that the market in arms is particularly active at present.'

'Oh yes.' Yam Heng spoke indifferently. 'The Indonesian rebels are trying to buy. They had several purchasing agents there.'

'Several?'

'There is one from Sumatra, one from Java, another from Celebes. They are united only in their opposition to the Central Government.'

'They compete?'

Yam Heng shrugged. 'They must. There is not so much to buy. It is not easy.'

'How do they pay? Rupiahs?'

'Nobody would take rupiahs. Pounds or dollars, I suppose.'

'Dollars U.S.?'

'Straits or Hong Kong dollars, I would think. Why?'

'Cash?'

'I suppose so.'

His brother nodded approvingly. 'I would think this a very satisfactory business.'

'No doubt it is.'

'These agents you speak of–you know them?'

'I know who they are, yes.'

'Have you not thought of taking an interest in the business yourself?'

Yam Heng smiled sourly. 'The pedlar cannot do business with an empty tray.'

'And if the tray were to be filled?'

Yam Heng hesitated. His brother was not in the habit of making idle remarks. 'That would require capital,' he said cautiously.

'Not necessarily.'

Siow Mong went over to his private safe, got out the piece of paper Girija had left with him and handed it to Yam Heng.

'That was brought to me by a man who wants a buyer for those goods,' he said.

Yam Heng read the list through carefully. His expression did not change. When he had finished he glanced up at his brother. 'It says that delivery must be taken in the *vicinity* of Kuala Pangkalan. What does that mean?'

Siow Mong told him about Girija's visit and summarized the conversation they had had.

Yam Heng listened without interrupting, and then read through the list again. He spoke as he read.

'This is dangerous, Siow Mong,' he said.

'Yes.'

'Is this Indian to be trusted?'

'I think so. If he gets what he wants.'

'I know very little about this market. Are these prices realistic?'

'I was able to make only one inquiry. There is a dealer in machinery here who used to import sporting rifles. Naturally, I had to be careful how I asked, but from what I was able to learn I would think these prices are three times what they should be. But in a sellers' market, who knows?'

'I could find out in Singapore.' Yam Heng paused. 'What is your proposal?'

Siow Mong sat down behind his desk and leant forward across it. 'You are a gambler, brother,' he said pleasantly; 'and you know what I think of that. Especially as, in the game you play, you cannot win. I am inviting you to try a different one.'

'Selling arms is no game.'

'It can be very profitable.' Siow Mong's smile faded. 'Let us have no misunderstandings. I have a good business here. I do not like risks. I do not have to take them. If you can find a way to handle this transaction without personal risk to me, I will help you, for a small handling charge of ten per cent. But I must know exactly what you intend to do first. If I agree with your plan I will put you in contact with the Indian. Is that understood?'

Yam Heng had been listening absently and did not reply to his brother's question. 'There are two problems here,' he said slowly. 'The first is to get the goods out of the country. That is a matter of careful organization. The second problem is more difficult. They must be made respectable.'

Siow Mong waited. Yam Heng might be a fool in many respects, but he could sometimes be shrewd.

'You see,' Yam Heng continued after a moment or two; 'if *I* were to sell these goods in Singapore, I might never receive payment. They would deal, yes; but these are not normal business dealings. There is no trust. "Payment on delivery," they would say. But when I had delivered they could give me a five thousand dollar tip and tell me to go to the police for the rest. What could I answer in such a case? You say that these are not stolen goods, and no doubt you are right. But I would be as helpless as if they were, if I had to deal illegally.'

'What is the alternative. How do you make such property respectable?'

'There must be an intermediary, someone who will sign papers, admit ownership if necessary, and take perhaps five per cent for his trouble.'

'What sort of person? An Englishman?'

'It would be better if he were not a subject of the Federation or of Singapore. I am thinking of the emergency regulations.'

'A Frenchman or an American, perhaps?'

'There are Americans doing such business.'

'Could you approach one of them?'

Yam Heng pursed his lips. 'This would be too small for those men, I think. Besides they would want too much for themselves. We do not need an experienced man.'

Siow Mong thought for a moment. Then he asked: 'Have you met Khoo Ah Au?'

'Who is he?'

'I was forgetting that you have been out of touch with family affairs. He married our niece in Manila last year. They live in Hong Kong now. Perhaps he would know of a suitable American. I shall be going there next month. I might discuss the requirements with him. Possibly . . .' He broke off. 'But this is all talk. You say that to ship the goods is only a matter of organization. How would you do it?'

Yam Heng told him.

His brother listened and was impressed. 'It might be done,' he admitted grudgingly at last.

They discussed some details and, later that day, Siow Mong telephoned Girija. He referred to their recent conversation and then said that although he, Mr Tan, could do nothing in the matter, he had heard of a Mr Lee who might be able to give useful advice. A meeting was arranged.

3

Girija never guessed that 'Mr Lee' was Mr Tan's brother. Mr Tan was refined. Mr Lee had coarse, heavy features, a sullen expression and a hectoring, impatient way of speaking that bordered on rudeness. Girija did not like him.

They met at a rest house not far from the estate. Mr Lee had taken a room there for the night and they identified one another without difficulty.

The first meeting was brief. Mr Lee produced Girija's list and asked him if he were prepared to prove the existence of the items listed by producing a sample of any one of them that Mr Lee himself selected.

Girija nodded. 'I have already said that my friend could give a sample if required. I ask only that the item chosen should be small and light.'

'How small? How light?'

'Small and light enough to be carried in the pocket. You would not ask me to cycle along the road with a rifle on my back.'

'Is a machine pistol loading clip small enough?'

'Yes. And I will bring a few rounds of ammunition with it.'

'When?'

'Monday.'

'Today is Thursday. Why not tomorrow?'

'It cannot be arranged before Monday.'

'Very well. But I have no time to waste.'

On Sunday, Girija went out to Awang and made his way up to the dump. It was several months since he had last repaired the shelter and the screens were in a bad state. The termites were back again, too. He hoped that Mr Lee was in as much of a hurry as he professed to be.

On Monday, he met Mr Lee again and showed him some ammunition and a clip.

Mr Lee wiped the grease off the clip and examined the German markings carefully. Finally, he put the clip in his pocket.

'That would seem to be in order,' he said. 'Naturally, I will have to check these marks. In the meantime I must have some information. Where would delivery take place?'

'In this area.'

'What do you consider would be needed to transport the goods?'

'One thirty hundredweight truck.'

'Are the goods near a road?'

'Not at present. They can be brought to a loading point fifty yards from a road, but that operation will require three days advance notice.'

'That may be difficult.'

'It must be allowed for.' Girija spoke with assurance. He had had three years to solve this problem in logistics, and knew that there was only one answer to it.

'You say fifty yards from a road. Would you and your friend be there to help with the loading? It would have to be done at night.'

'I or my friend would be there. Two men could do the loading in less than an hour. The heaviest boxes are those with the rifles. There are nine of them and they weigh about forty pounds each. But they have rope handles.'

Mr Lee looked at him with interest. 'You speak as if you have had experience before.'

'I am a business man, Mr Lee.' Girija paused. 'Perhaps, now that you have examined the samples, we should discuss financial arrangements and terms.'

Mr Lee took the list from his pocket. 'These prices you mention are foolish. You knew that, of course.'

Girija smiled. 'I knew that you would say they were foolish, Mr Lee. And, of course, I understand. These are always difficult goods to sell. The right buyer may not be found immediately. The demand fluctuates. Handling and storage charges are high. You must work on a very small margin of profit. That is why I am prepared to pay fifty per cent of these estimated prices to the selling agent.'

'*You* are prepared, Mr Krishnan? What about your friend?'

Girija was not disconcerted. 'I am authorized to speak for him at present,' he said. 'I say "at present" because my friend is considering the possibility of going to Singapore and investigating the market personally.'

'Could your friend move the goods?'

'He is a patient man. He could wait.'

Mr Lee did not reply immediately. He was tired of Girija's toothy smile and the knowing lilt in his voice. 'Your prices are foolish,' he repeated coldly.

Girija smiled again. 'Then I will reduce them, Mr Lee. I will accept thirty thousand dollars Malay net.'

'That is an insignificant reduction.'

'It is the only one I can make.'

'I will pay twenty thousand.'

They compromised in the end on twenty-five thousand, to be paid one month after the goods were handed over. A protocol for the transaction was also agreed. Under this, each of the high contracting parties was protected against murder or trickery on the part of the order. The meeting ended in an atmosphere of goodwill and mutual respect.

The following day Tan Yam Heng took the train back to Singapore.

The following week Tan Siow Mong flew up to Hong Kong. He was there for only two days; but he was able to spend an entertaining and constructive evening with his niece and her husband, Khoo Ah Au.

Chapter Three

I

Twelve hours out of Kobe, the *Silver Isle* ran into bad weather and more than half of her ninety passengers took to their cabins.

She was owned by the Isle Line which operated a freight run between San Francisco and Calcutta, calling at Yokohama, Kobe, Hong Kong, Manila, Saigon, Singapore and, occasionally, Rangoon. With the growing popularity of round-the-world trips, the company's passenger traffic had increased rapidly, and they had refitted two of their newer ships so as to enlarge and improve the cabin accommodation. The *Silver Isle* was one of these. Unfortunately, the improvements, which included an extra deck, had also added considerably to her top hamper, and in any but the calmest sea she rolled heavily.

For Greg Nilsen, however, the bad weather came as a blessing. Both he and Dorothy, his wife, were good sailors and could go down to the dining-room with their appetites unimpaired. True, Dorothy did complain that the incessant rolling made her tired; but he could only view that as a minor inconvenience. As far as he was concerned, any weather conditions that kept Arlene Drecker confined to her cabin were fine.

Greg was an engineer and the owner of a precision die-casting business in Wilmington, Delaware. He and Dorothy had been planning their round-the-world trip for over two years; ever since their younger boy had gone to college.

They could have done it earlier if they had been prepared to fly most of the way; but Dorothy had said no. She had wanted to do it properly; by sea, and in small, slow boats.

'After all,' she had said; 'we're only going to be able to do it once in our lives. All the tourists go to Tokyo and Hong Kong and Paris and Rome, places like that. I think we ought to see some of the little out-of-the-way places as well; the ones most people just read about, or see pictures of in photographic books; wonderful places like Tahiti, where the cruise ships don't go.'

Greg had agreed with her. However, a few evenings spent with maps, sailing lists and an eighteen-inch globe had modified their views. They had found, for example, that if they wanted to go to Japan and Hong Kong, a one-day visit to Tahiti would add two weeks to their travel schedule. In the end it was plain that, even if they compromised on the size and speed of the boats, confined themselves to the regular ports of call and cut out South America completely, the trip would still take at least two months. If they did not want to spend all the time travelling, it would take three.

Greg had some very capable men working for him; but, at the management level, Nilsen Die-Casting and Tools was very much a one man business. A three month vacation could not be embarked upon just when he felt like it; and, although he had for some time been planning a re-organization that would enable him to delegate more responsibility, it involved changes that could only be made gradually. He had allowed two years; one in which to make the changes, and one in which to see that they worked; but, even so, it had still not been easy to get away. There had been some moments in the month before they had sailed when difficulties over a new Government contract had made it look as if the trip would have to be called off. However, the difficulties had been ironed out in time and they had left Wilmington early in October. Because of the amount of baggage they were taking, they had gone by train to San Francisco. They had sailed on the seventh.

Neither of them had travelled much by ship before. During the war, Greg had gone to Europe in a troop-ship. Together they had been to England and France and back on the *United States* and the *America*. That was all. They had received much advice from more experienced friends. One of them, Greg remembered later, had had a solemn warning to deliver.

'It's the first two or three days you want to be careful of,' this man had said; 'and especially the first day just after you sail. You're going to be with those people for weeks. But you'll be feeling strange and want to be friendly. You'll go into the bar and have a drink to celebrate the start of the trip. Watch it. Don't start getting friendly with anyone. Wait. You start talking to someone, and before you know it, bingo, you're stuck with the ship's bore. It can ruin a trip.'

Arlene Drecker was not the ship's bore; but, as far as Greg was concerned, she became an even more maddening affliction.

After the ship had sailed, he and Dorothy had stayed on deck until they had cleared the Golden Gate. They had promised the boys to make a complete photographic record of the trip, and Greg had been up on the boat deck with the 8 mm. Bell and Howell for the best part of an hour. It had been a sunny day, with a cool breeze. They had been glad, when there was no more to see aloft, to get down into the warmth of the bar for a pre-lunch drink.

Arlene had been sitting by herself at a small table about six feet away from them. She had been writing radio telegrams and sipping a Martini. Then, the pen she had borrowed from the writing-room had run out of ink, and she had looked round in exasperation. Greg had politely offered her his. She had accepted. Later, when she returned his pen, she had asked them to have a drink.

'No, no. You join us,' Dorothy had said.

Arlene had smiled. 'You know, a gal travelling alone has one big problem–how to persuade people to sometimes let her buy a drink.'

Nevertheless, she had joined them and had another Martini. They had gone down to lunch together. Later that day, the chief steward had approached Greg with the permanent seating plan for the dining-room, and asked if he and Mrs Nilsen minded having Miss Drecker sit at their table. There were no single tables, he had explained, and Miss Drecker did not want to be with a crowd. Greg had had little choice but to agree.

That night, when they went down to dinner, there had been a bottle of champagne on the table; to thank them, Arlene had explained, for letting her sit with them, and to drink a toast to the voyage.

Later, in their cabin, Greg had grumbled about this. He did not care for champagne which always gave him indigestion; but Dorothy had not been sympathetic. It showed, she had said, that Arlene did not intend to impose on them. The champagne had been a very nice way of telling them that. The fact that it gave him indigestion was beside the point. Dorothy had taken a liking to Arlene.

She was a tall, angular blonde with large white teeth, a beige complexion and very thin legs. Dorothy deduced from things said that she was probably in her late forties; but she certainly looked younger. She dressed smartly and in a vaguely masculine style that suited her; although she was inclined sometimes to overload herself with chunky gold bracelets and wear earrings which accentuated the narrowness of her head. She talked freely, and not unamusingly, about herself in a carefully mellifluous voice which creaked slightly on each change of register. Her father had been a Los Angeles real estate man. During the war she had been in the American Red Cross and had stayed on with that organization in France and Germany until 1947. Then her father had died and she had gone back to California. She had a house in Palm Springs now, which she rented when she went away on her trips. She had never had any great desire to get married, although she liked married people and was crazy about kids. But things had to work out right, or it was no good. She had a sister who had been married four times, and what a mess and misery all that had been. Her attitude towards men was one of sardonic camaraderie tinged with disdain.

By the fourth day out, Greg's dislike of her had become intense. The bottle of champagne had been a minor irritant; but when at dinner on the second night a bottle of claret had appeared, he had objected.

'It was very thoughtful of you, Arlene,' he had said; 'but Dorothy and I don't drink wine as a regular thing. So if you don't mind . . .'

'But the steward's already opened it. Oh come on, Nilsen. Live dangerously.'

Dorothy had giggled. The steward had smiled and poured the wine.

'Now look, Dorothy,' Greg had said when they were alone; 'Arlene Drecker can drink all the wine she wants and so can you for that matter. But I'm not having her tell me what I'm going to drink.'

'She didn't mean it that way.'

'I don't care what way she meant it. The way it worked out was that I had to drink something I didn't want or seem boorish. Dammit, she's not our hostess on this ship. I wish she'd stop behaving as if she were.'

'She's only trying to be friendly.'

'Listen. If you want wine or we want wine, *I'll* order it.'

The following night Arlene had ordered burgundy; but Greg had taken the precaution of ordering in advance a bottle of *rosé* and the two wines arrived together.

'Too bad,' Greg had said blandly; 'what about joining us and having rosé, Arlene?'

'Rosé with roast beef?' Arlene had raised her eyebrows. 'Thanks, I prefer burgundy.'

But the next night, when the steward had produced the partly consumed bottle of burgundy, Arlene had not pressed them to share it with her. Greg had succeeded in making his point. It had not been until later in the evening that he had discovered that she had paid his bar bill for the day. Dorothy had not been able to help laughing.

Two days before they had reached Yokohama a notice had gone up announcing that during the ship's stay in port, conducted sight-seeing tours ashore had been arranged. Those passengers wishing to take advantage of the special rates offered should inform the purser's office within the next twenty-four hours.

Greg had put his and Dorothy's names down. At lunch Dorothy had mentioned the fact.

Arlene had stared at her incredulously. 'Sight-seeing tours! Honey, you must be out of your mind.'

'What's wrong with sight-seeing tours?' Greg had asked. 'After all, that's what we're making the trip for—to see sights.'

'Oh, Greg!' Arlene had laughed tolerantly. 'Have you ever been on a Japanese sight-seeing tour?'

'Have you?'

'Yes, and I can tell you it's the end. They just cram you into a bus, give you a box lunch and then drive you from one clip joint to another. They don't want to show you what you want to see. They just want you to buy things—cameras, fans, bits of fake jewellery.'

'That's not what it says on the notice-board.'

'Naturally. Look, if you want to go rubber-necking, let me take you. I've been before. All you do is hire a car and have the man drive you around. You're on your own. You can stop when you want and go on when you want.'

Dorothy had turned to him uncertainly. 'What do you think, Greg?'

'Well, we've put our names down now.'

Arlene had sighed. 'Well, take them off again. Why not? If you want to be tourists you may as well do it properly. This is not the best time of the year to come to Japan, but, since you are here, at least make yourselves comfortable.'

Unhappily, she had been right. Those who had gone on the sight-seeing tour had returned exhausted, ill-tempered and late for dinner. Dorothy had had a fascinating day and bought a pair of carved soapstone hair-pins which the barman said were worth at least three times what she had paid for them.

The following day, and then later at Kobe, the performance had been repeated. It could have been his fancy, but Greg suspected that both Dorothy and Arlene had a tacit agreement to ignore his leadership and run things their own way. When the table steward had reported that Miss Drecker was staying in her cabin, seasick, it had required an effort of will to utter the appropriate words of regret.

The bad weather lasted for two days and Greg thoroughly enjoyed them both. When, on the third day, Arlene made a wan appearance at lunch, he was almost as solicitous as Dorothy.

Then came the misunderstanding over the ship's shuffle-board tournament. The Doctor had wanted Greg and Dorothy on his team, and Greg, without consulting Dorothy, had accepted. When the first round was announced over the ship's loudspeakers, Dorothy was missing. Greg found her eventually in Arlene's cabin playing Scrabble. By the time he had explained what had happened and they had reached the deck, the teams had been rearranged and they were out of the tournament.

Greg was annoyed. He did not mind about the shuffle-board, which he thought an old man's game; but he did mind having to apologize to the Doctor.

Dorothy was very reasonable about it. 'I'm sorry, dear, but you didn't tell me, did you?'

'I thought you were around on deck.'

'Well, you were reading and Arlene suggested Scrabble. I know how you hate that, so I didn't bother you.'

'Did you have to play down in the cabin?'

'She's got a very comfortable cabin. You haven't seen it. It's twice the size of ours. Look, dear, I'm sure the Doctor didn't mind a bit. He understood.'

'Yes, I know. But all the same . . .'

All the same, he was annoyed. That evening, when Arlene and Dorothy began to talk about the shopping they were going to do in Hong Kong, his annoyance returned.

'The big stores are in Victoria,' Arlene was saying; 'that's on Hong Kong island itself. But for us gals the best places are over in Kowloon. That's on the mainland. There's one called Star of Siam in the Peninsular Hotel that's a must.'

'Shops in a hotel?' asked Dorothy.

'That's right. There are two whole floors of them.'

'Sounds like a tourist trap to me,' said Greg.

Arlene smiled at him. 'What would you say to a suit in the best English tropical worsted, made to order, for twenty-five dollars?'

'Oh sure, I know all about that. They just copy a suit you have and it falls to pieces the first time you wear it.'

Arlene smiled again, very gently. 'Is that what happens? I've never heard that, not from anyone who's really been there and bought one.'

'Why don't you try, dear?' said Dorothy. 'I mean twenty-five dollars for a suit is cheap. And you do need some more summer outfits.'

'Brooks Brothers is good enough for me.' He knew it was a dull, foolish remark even as he said it.

'Well, it's not important.' Dorothy spoke a trifle grimly.

Arlene's silence was monumentally tactful.

It was a Sunday night and there was no dancing after dinner. When Arlene had gone to her cabin, Dorothy suggested a walk round the deck before they went to bed.

After a while, she said: 'Darling, I'm worried. I'm having a good time, a wonderful time. You don't seem to be.'

'Because I don't happen to want to buy a suit in Hong Kong?'

'Now you're being tiresome.'

'All right. That woman gets on my nerves.'

'Arlene? But she's really a very nice person.'

'Well, I don't like her and I wish she'd get out of our hair.'

'She's not in *my* hair. I think she's being very sweet and helpful. Can you imagine what it would have been like in Tokyo if we hadn't been lucky enough to have her to show us around? It couldn't have been very exciting for her. She'd seen it all before. She went to a lot of trouble for us.'

'Well, I wish she'd go to a lot of trouble for somebody else. Anyway, if she's seen it all before, why does she come on the trip?'

'Greg dear, you're usually more understanding and tolerant. She's a very lonely woman.'

'And for some very good reasons.'

'That's an unkind thing to say. It doesn't sound like you.'

'Well, it is me. I told you, I don't like the woman. The chief steward told me she didn't want to sit with a crowd. Why not if she's so lonely? Why did she have to pick on us?'

Dorothy did not reply immediately and they walked once round the deck in silence.

'Look, darling,' she said finally; 'we didn't come on this trip just for a vacation, but because we wanted to travel and because we wanted to see something of the world outside America. If we were multi-millionaires maybe we could have done it in our own private yacht. As it is, we have to go with other people. We're not in a position to choose our travelling companions, any more than they're in a position to choose us. So, we've all got to make the best of one another. Isn't that common sense?'

Greg chuckled. 'It's a poem, and beautifully delivered.'

'Greg, I'm serious.'

'I know you are, dear.' He drew her arm through his. 'That's why you're so cute.'

He had recovered his good humour. Dorothy's homilies usually had that effect on him. Before they were married she had taught at a kindergarten school, and, in moments of stress, traces of the old Montessori manner were still discernible.

'You're maddening,' she said.

'I know it.' He stopped and kissed her cheek. 'All right, darling, we'll be nice, well-behaved American tourists spreading sweetness and light and hard currency wherever we go.'

'If you'll just spread a little of that sweetness in Arlene's direction, that's all I ask.'

'You said make the best of one another. Okay, I'll make the best of her, whatever that is.'

'Thank you, dear.'

He sighed. 'Anyway, I'll try.'

And, for some days, try he did.

2

The *Silver Isle* was to be in Hong Kong for forty-eight hours, discharging and taking on cargo, and she docked on the Kowloon side of the harbour by the wharfs on the Canton Road.

This was convenient for the passengers. They could go ashore any time they wanted, and were within easy walking distance of both the ferry to Victoria and the Peninsular Hotel.

Left to themselves, Greg and Dorothy would probably have taken the ferry straight away and gone across to see Hong Kong itself; but Arlene led them first to the hotel.

'There'll be plenty of time for sight-seeing later,' she told them. 'Let's get organized first. I suppose you've heard that these Chinese can make anything from a pair of ear-rings to a man's tuxedo overnight. Well, it just is not true. If you want anything properly made you have to give them at least thirty-six hours. So let's do our shopping first, and then we don't have to worry.'

They window-shopped for a while in the hotel; and then the girls left Greg with a tailor named Mr Yu, and went back to the Star of Siam to order Thai silk skirts. They had arranged to meet in the hotel lobby. When Greg had chosen his suit materials and had his measurements taken, he made his way down there.

He knew that he had at least half an hour to wait. It was too early for a drink. There was a row of travel agents' booths in the lobby, most of them offering sight-seeing tours. It might be a good idea, he thought, to see about renting a car and driver.

The moment that thought came into his head another one followed it: 'Maybe I'd better check with Arlene first.' It was enough. He said 'God dammit' between his teeth, and went over to the nearest booth.

A Chinese in a black business suit came forward.

'Good morning, sir. What can I do for you?'

'I want to rent a limousine with a driver to take us around. Do you have cars?'

'We do not have our own cars, but we can arrange that for you, sir. An American car if you wish. When and for how long would you want it?'

'Well, we only have two days. We'd like to see as much as we can. We could start right after lunch from here.'

'Then I would suggest, sir, that this afternoon you go across on the car ferry to Hong Kong and drive up to the Peak. There is a magnificent view from there. After that I would suggest a drive to Deep Water Bay and Repulse Bay with tea at the hotel there. Tomorrow you could tour Kowloon and the New Territories.'

'Would that take us as far as the Red Chinese border?'

'Certainly, sir. And you could lunch at Shatin. But I will get you a good driver who will know all these things and make helpful suggestions.'

'How much would it cost?'

By the time Arlene and Dorothy arrived it was all settled.

Arlene clearly resented having the arrangements taken out of her hands in this fashion, but had difficulty in finding anything in them to criticize. She did the best she could, however.

'We didn't have to have a car this afternoon,' she said. 'We could have gone across to the island by the Star ferry and taken a cab the other side.'

'In all this humidity?' said Dorothy. 'It's worse than August in New York.'

'Humidity?' Arlene smiled knowingly. 'You wait until we get to Singapore.'

Greg congratulated himself on this small rift in the female alliance; but his satisfaction was short-lived. They went to a Chinese restaurant for lunch and Arlene insisted on their all using chop-sticks. It was considered discourteous, she said, to use a fork. Dorothy thought it great fun; but Greg, who liked Chinese food and was hungry, became impatient and dropped some of the food on his tie.

After lunch they went back to the Peninsular Hotel to pick up the car and driver.

The car proved to be a three-year-old Chevrolet Bel-Air and Arlene looked at it disdainfully. The driver was a young Chinese wearing grey flannel trousers, a dark blue blazer and a chauffeur's cap. He took off the cap and stood respectfully at attention as he held the rear door open for the ladies.

'Want me to go in front with you?' Greg asked him.

'If you do not object, sir, I think you will be more comfortable.'

'Okay.'

When they were in the car the driver turned to him.

'I see you have a camera, sir. There are certain places on the road up to the Peak where particularly good shots can be obtained. Would you like me to stop at those places?'

'That'd be fine. By the way, what's your name?'

'My Chinese name is Khoo Ah Au, sir.' The driver smiled. 'American clients find it easier to call me Jimmy.'

3

Khoo Ah Au liked American tourists. He found them, on the whole, generous, easy-going and completely predictable. They were rarely ill-tempered, as the British often were, or eccentric in their demands, as were the French. They did not harass him with questions he had not been asked before, and listened politely, if sometimes inattentively, to the information he had to impart. They used their light meters conscientiously before taking photographs and bought their souvenirs dutifully at the shops which paid him commission. Above all, he found their personal relationships very easy to read. It was probably a matter of race, he thought. His own people were always very careful not to give themselves away, to expose crude feelings about one another. Americans seemed not to care how much was understood by strangers. It was almost as if they enjoyed being transparent.

This American and these two women, for example. You had only to listen for a few minutes to what they said and how they said it, and everything was clear. The woman called Arlene was attracted to the wife and the husband was jealous. Possibly, he had no cause; possibly, the two women had done no more than exchange confidences or touch each other's hands; but he was jealous. And the hungry woman was jealous of him. Only the wife, personable but middle-aged, seemed unconcerned. She did not appear flattered by the situation, or even aware of it. Perhaps she was more subtle than she sounded. When he had listened a little more, he would be able to decide.

They were on the car ferry when he heard something that interested him keenly. 'If we'd gone across by the passenger ferry,' the Arlene woman was saying, 'you'd have been able to get a beautiful shot of the boat in dock.'

'Well, maybe I'll do that tomorrow,' the American said. 'Anyway there'll be plenty of chances of seeing her in dock.'

It was the word 'boat' that had interested him. He had assumed that the trio were staying at the Peninsular Hotel because he had been engaged from there. The possibility of their being transit passengers off a boat had not occurred to him.

'You've come by boat, sir?' he inquired diffidently.

'Yes, the *Silver Isle*. Know her?'

'Oh yes, sir. And are you staying here?'

'No, we're going on in her. Manila, Saigon, Singapore, Rangoon, Calcutta. My wife and I are on a world trip.'

'Ah, that is very nice.'

They were coming in to the landing ramp now and his passengers had plenty to engage their attention. It gave him time to think.

Almost two months had elapsed since his wife's uncle had visited them, and, so far, all his attempts to find an American who would meet Mr Tan's specifications had failed. Moreover, his last attempt had been a frightening failure. The American, a department store executive from Cleveland, had accused him of trying to work a confidence trick, and threatened to go to the police. After that, he had made up his mind to do nothing further in the matter. Unfortunately, Mr Tan was a highly respected member of his wife's family, and she had begun nagging him about it; not in an angry way, but reproachfully, intimating that his failure to do what her uncle wanted would cause her to lose face. There was also the money to be considered. With the five hundred dollars (Hong Kong) that Mr Tan had offered for the service, he could go to Cheong Ming and Co. and buy a hi-fi set. But was it worth the risk?

He began to study the American beside him.

He was tall and thin with loose-fitting clothes and short, greying hair. He spoke quietly and with a slight smile in one corner of his mouth. His eyes were watchful and shrewd; but there might be innocence there, too. Not an easy man to deceive; but one who might sometimes deceive himself.

Ah Au drove up towards the Peak. Near the lower cable-car station he stopped so that they could admire the view of the port from the road. The American took his camera and got out of the car.

The Arlene woman said: 'There's a much better view from the top.'

She and the wife stayed in the car.

Ah Au went over to the American and began pointing out various landmarks in the panorama below them.

'Yes, it's a great place,' the American said. 'By the way, Jimmy, *is* the view better from up top?'

'There is a fine view there, too, sir, which I will show you in a minute, but this is better for photography. From the Peak there is more haze.'

'I see.' He was winding the camera.

'Are you using Kodachrome, sir?'

'Yes. Why?'

'From here, sir, at f8 with a haze filter you will get a very good picture.'

'Thanks. You take many pictures?'

'No, sir, but I have such information for my clients.'

The camera whirred. As they were walking back to the car, the American said: 'Is this your car or do you just drive for someone else?'

'It is my car, sir. I like to give personal service to clients.'

'I expect you make more money working for yourself, too.'

Ah Au smiled. 'There is also that, sir.'

The American smiled back.

Ah Au drove on up to the Peak. Some progress had been made, he thought. They had established a personal relationship.

The tour continued. His passengers had tea at the Repulse Bay Hotel. Then, he drove them on to the fishing village of Aberdeen and showed them the floating Chinese restaurants. At the Arlene woman's suggestion, it was decided he should drive them out there to dine the following night. It was on the way back to the ferry that Jimmy had the glimpse of his client's mind that he had been hoping for.

He was driving along Connaught Road, by the long quay where the junks tied up for unloading, when the American turned to him.

'Jimmy, what are all those barges lined up along there? I mean the green painted ones with the yellow stars on them.'

'They are junks from Canton, sir.'

'But that's in Red China.'

'Yes, sir. Canton is only ninety miles away.'

'Stop the car. I've got to have some shots of this.'

Ah Au parked the car, and, leaving the women sitting in it, walked back along the quay with the American. The man seemed curiously excited and was almost tripping over himself in his eagerness to get a closer look at the junks.

'What are they doing here?' he asked.

'They come and go all the time, sir.'

'Doing what?'

'Carrying cargo.' Ah Au was puzzled. He could not understand why the man was so interested.

'What sort of cargo?'

'Any sort of cargo, sir. That is rattan cane they are unloading. It is made into chairs and baskets here.'

'But I don't see any police about. Do you mean they're allowed just to come and go as they please?'

'They are ordinary people. They make no trouble, sir.'

'Well, I'll be . . .'

He began to take pictures. When they got back to the car, Ah Au listened thoughtfully as the American told his wife and her friend what he had found out.

The women were interested, and the Arlene one said that it showed what the British had come to when they didn't worry about Communists going in and out of one of their colonies; but they were not interested the way the man was. As they drove on towards the ferry, Ah Au saw him looking about him intently, as if he were discovering a new meaning in everything he saw.

By the time they reached the mainland Ah Au had decided to take matters a stage further. As he drove them back along the Canton Road to the ship, he asked a question.

'Tomorrow morning, sir, for your tour of the New Territories, do you wish me to go to the Peninsular Hotel, or shall I take the car to the ship?'

'Can you do that?'

'Oh yes, sir. If I have your name to give at the dock gate.'

'My name's Nilsen. Would ten o'clock be okay?'

'Perfectly, sir.' He frowned as if making an effort of memory. 'Mr Nilsen, there was another Mr Nilsen here last year. He was in the textile business. He had a big plant at a place called Dayton, I think. Perhaps you know him.'

Mr Nilsen smiled tolerantly. 'No, Jimmy, I don't. I'm an engineer and I have a small die-casting plant at a place called Wilmington. Nilsen's a pretty common name in the United States.'

'I beg your pardon. I did not know that. Some day, perhaps, I will be able to go to America.'

He congratulated himself. The chances of his being caught out in the lie about a textile man named Nilsen from Dayton had been small. The information gained had been reassuring. Mr Nilsen was neither a government official, who might consider it his duty to notify the authorities, nor a newspaper man who might become indiscreet in other ways. He was a respectable business man of just the type that Mr Tan had described; and travelling by just the specified route. The problem now was to find a way of putting Mr Tan's proposition in an attractive light without being either compromised or misunderstood.

When he returned home, Ah Au said nothing to his wife about Mr Nilsen. He had already decided to make this further attempt to oblige Mr Tan; but only if the opportunity presented itself. He would take no more risks than he had to. The pressure of her expectations might distort his judgment.

During the night he lay awake for an hour going over every moment of the afternoon and re-examining his image of Mr Nilsen. When he was sure that nothing had escaped his attention, he went back to sleep.

The Arlene woman was late, and they did not leave the dock until nearly ten-thirty. Mr Nilsen controlled his impatience too obviously. It was an inauspicious beginning. Ah Au wanted Mr Nilsen in as relaxed a mood as possible, and took an early opportunity of suggesting that, as they had plenty of time in hand, they might like to stop at the Castle Peak Hotel for coffee. It was about four miles out on the Tai Po Road, and they would be passing it anyway.

Mrs Nilsen thought this a good idea, and the tension seemed to slacken. By the time they left Castle Peak and were heading for the frontier, the atmosphere had improved still further. Soon, as they began to pass farms and paddy fields, Ah Au was hearing the familiar exclamations–'Look at that wooden plough!' 'This is really old China!' 'What about those hats with curtains!' 'My God, the smell!'–which told him that his passengers were enjoying themselves.

He drove absently, answering the questions put to him promptly and fully, but not elaborating on his answers. He was waiting for a British Army truck to come along. Presently they overtook one, and he slowed to stay behind it. It was, happily, full of troops.

He glanced at Mr Nilsen and smiled. 'We are getting near Red China,' he said. 'This is the beginning of the military zone.'

Mr Nilsen was leaning forward staring at the truck. 'Are those British troops?'

'Yes, sir, a Scottish regiment. There is a camp farther along this road.'

'How many do they have to guard this frontier?'

'One or two battalions, I think.'

'One or two battalions!' He turned round. 'Did you hear that, Dorothy? Only one or two battalions to guard this frontier. My God, the Reds could walk in here any time they wanted. Isn't that right, Jimmy?'

Ah Au smiled. 'Oh yes, sir. But I think they could do that even if there were two divisions to guard the frontier.'

Mr Nilsen nodded grimly. 'You could be right at that. How near to the frontier can we get?'

'About a mile, sir. It is dangerous you see.'

'How dangerous?'

'Sometimes they shoot from the other side at persons moving too close to the frontier line.'

'Nice people.'

The army truck turned off the road into the camp entrance, and Ah Au put on speed again. He could feel the mounting excitement of the man beside him and wanted to satisfy it.

About a mile and a half from the frontier, the road turned sharply to the right and ran parallel to it. However, there was a narrow cart track heading straight on, and Ah Au drove down it until they reached a small farmhouse. The track continued; but a few yards past the house there was a large signboard prohibiting movement beyond that point. Ah Au stopped the car, took a pair of binoculars from the glove compartment, and they all got out.

For about a mile ahead the landscape was flat. Then, there was a line of low hills, the sides of which were dotted with groups of burial urns, and a ridge. Along the ridge and near the top of it ran a thin black line.

'That is the frontier, sir.' Ah Au handed Mr Nilsen the binoculars.

'That black line?'

'Yes, it is a barbed-wire fence. There are machine-gun towers, too, but you cannot see them well from here.'

Mr Nilsen scanned the line of the fence from side to side, then handed the binoculars to his wife and got out his camera.

'F11 with the haze filter,' Ah Au murmured.

Mr Nilsen nodded and went to work. He did a panning shot first, beginning close on his wife as she looked through the binoculars, then going on to the signboard, then moving into an extreme long shot of the frontier. Then, he switched the turret on to the telephoto lens. He used two magazines of film before he was finished.

The Arlene woman became bored and went back to the car. Small children from the farmhouse soon began to peer at her through the car windows, and hold out their hands for money. Ah Au had to chase them away.

Mr Nilsen returned to the car reluctantly, and insisted on taking some shots of the farmhouse and the giggling children before he could be persuaded to leave. Even as they bumped along the track back to the road, he kept looking over his shoulder towards the frontier. Ah Au was pleased with the impression it had made.

When they passed the Kowloon–Canton Railway where it curved towards the frontier station, there were more questions.

'Is there a lot of railroad traffic between Kowloon and Canton?'

'Oh yes, sir. People go to see friends and family in Canton.'

'I don't get it. You mean they just go?'

'They must get a permit from the Chinese government office in Hong Kong, but it is quite easy.'

'Hear that, Dorothy? So that's the bamboo curtain!'

'You wish to go to Canton, sir?'

'Me? No thanks!' He laughed. 'I have United States government contracts to think about.'

They stopped at Tai Po market so that the two women could look at the small shops there and buy coolie hats. Ah Au bargained for the hats, and, when they had been paid for, took them back to the car.

He was about to return and render further assistance, when Mr Nilsen joined him.

'They've gone into a silk shop,' he said. 'They're not going to buy, but they'll be there an age. You smoke?'

'Not when driving, sir. But now, thank you.'

They sat in the car and smoked. A ring of children collected to stare at them, but Mr Nilsen took no notice.

'Have you ever been to Canton?' he asked.

'No, sir. I have been to Macao where my wife has some relatives, but my family is in Manila.'

'Is that so? Don't you like the Philippines?'

'My family went there from here, sir. But I was born here and I am

British. There are more opportunities here, I think.'

'I don't get it. I should have thought this was the last place where you could look forward to any sort of security for your family. This section for instance. You call it the New Territories. But it's leased, isn't it, from the Government of China.'

'Yes, sir, in 1898. It was leased for ninety-nine years.'

'So in 1997 you'll have to give it back to the Reds, if they're still in business.'

'That is so.'

'Or if they don't walk in and take it back before.'

'There is always the possibility, sir, but I do not think the risk is great. Hong Kong is no danger to them, and it is a useful outlet to the west. That is why, too, the Portuguese are allowed to stay in Macao.'

Ah Au spoke almost without thinking. He had planned to wait until after lunch at Shatin before attempting to broach the subject of Mr Tan's proposition. Now, he was being offered an opening of a kind he could not possibly have contrived. His heart began to beat faster. Then, he made up his mind.

'All that could change overnight,' Mr Nilsen was saying; 'some shift in the Cold War or another Korea over the Formosa situation, and I wouldn't give you a nickel for the Peninsular Hotel.'

Ah Au smiled. 'You are probably right, sir. But, meanwhile, there are advantages to both sides, and not only for the big bankers and trading companies here.'

'That so?'

'In fact I can tell you a story that may amuse you, sir.'

'What's that?'

'Well, sir, it is a little confidential, but you are not a policeman or a newspaper man, so I can tell you.' He paused.

'Sure, go ahead.'

'You see, sir, we Chinese are all pirates at heart.' He shrugged. 'Chinese piracy is as old as history. When the Reds began sending arms and ammunition down by sea in junks to the terrorists in Malaya, there were naturally some men, both here and in Macao, who thought it a pity that such valuable cargoes should arrive at their destinations. It was a great temptation. So as often as they could, they . . .' He spread his hands deprecatingly.

'They hijacked them?' Mr Nilsen smiled.

'Yes, though that was not the best part of the joke, sir. You know that arms and ammunition are very valuable in this part of the world.'

'They are in most places.'

'Particularly in the Far East, sir. But the trouble is that there are government regulations and embargoes that make it difficult to sell military equipment. It was not easy to seize these cargoes, and although the Reds could not make international complaints without admitting openly that they were supplying the terrorists, these pirates, these hijackers you would call them, they ran great risks. There had to be profit.' He paused again. He could see that he had Mr Nilsen's whole attention.

'Well, how did they get rid of the stuff?'

'It was very simple, sir. They took the Communist arms down to Indonesia, and sold them to the *anti*-Communist rebels.'

Mr Nilsen stared and then began to laugh.

Ah Au sighed inwardly with relief. He saw the holes in his own story so clearly that he had been afraid Mr Nilsen would see them, too.

He did see one an instant later. When he had stopped laughing, he said: 'What I don't see is why the Reds sent the stuff down by sea at all. What about the British Navy? Couldn't they intercept the shipments to Malaya?'

'They intercepted many, sir, but, you know, there are a lot of junks in the China Seas. Last year there were over twenty-five thousand of them using Hong Kong alone. You cannot intercept and search every junk at sea between here and Singapore.'

'I suppose not.'

'Though you are right, sir. The illegal arms traffic was stopped in the end. A friend of mine in Manila was very sad about that.'

'Yes?'

'Some time ago he took a shipment of arms and ammunition out of a Red junk off Hainan. It was modern equipment, rifles, machine-guns, bazookas, worth sixty thousand dollars. And it is still in Manila.'

'Why? Aren't there any more anti-Communists in Indonesia?'

'Plenty, sir, but it is not as simple as it was before. This is no longer a small business. The buying agents for the rebels are in Singapore and they must be careful. They will not buy illegal arms any more. My friend has tried to sell. Now he says he must try to make the arms legal.'

'How does he propose to do that?'

But Ah Au had seen the two women approaching and was already getting out of the car to open the door for them. Mr Nilsen's forecast that they would buy nothing had proved incorrect. His wife had a shantung dress-length and the Arlene woman had some jade ear-rings. They got into the car showing their purchases and chattering about the other things that the shop had for sale.

Ah Au drove on towards Shatin.

The interruption of his conversation with Mr Nilsen had not dismayed him. On the contrary; he was glad of it. He was quite sure that Mr Nilsen was sufficiently intrigued to want an answer to his last question; and it was much better that he should be the one to return to the subject.

Ah Au did not have to wait long. When the three Americans had had lunch at the Shatin Hotel, the women went for a walk in the gardens overlooking the valley. Mr Nilsen had gone to the toilet; but, when he came out, he did not join the women in the garden. Instead, he came out to Ah Au who was sitting in the car.

Ah Au got out to open the door, but Mr Nilsen waved him back.

'I've seen enough sights for the moment,' he said with a smile; 'I want to hear more about your friend in Manila.'

'Yes, sir?'

'What did you mean about making that shipment of arms legal?'

'You understand, sir, this is very confidential.'

'Sure, I understand.'

'For arms to be legal, sir, they have to have a legal owner and a legal place of origin. What my friend needs is a nominee.'

'How do you mean?'

'What my friend would like to do is ship the arms to be held in bond at Singapore, and then sell them.'

'Why can't he do that?'

'Sir, the authorities at Singapore would not accept the consignment in bond without a proper certified bill of lading from a reputable shipper at the port of origin. Unfortunately, residents of Manila cannot trade in arms without a government permit. That is difficult and expensive to obtain. So, he must have a foreign nominee.'

'Why? I don't get it.'

'After the war in Manila, sir, a lot of surplus American war material was sold to dealers who exported it. The regulations about permits do not apply to non-resident foreigners exporting arms.'

'I see.'

'Also, sir, the nominee would have to go to Singapore to sign clearance papers. My friend has tried to find the right person, but although he is willing to pay as much as five per cent for the service, he has been unsuccessful. He will not deal with crooks.'

'Hijackers aren't usually so particular.'

'A crook would cheat him, sir. Once the papers are signed what is to prevent the nominee from claiming the goods are his and keeping all the money. Sixty thousand Straits dollars is a lot. Twenty-one thousand dollars American.'

'And five per cent of that is a thousand and fifty.' Mr Nilsen grinned amiably. 'Jimmy, you couldn't be telling me all this for a reason, could you?'

Ah Au's heart missed a beat. Was Mr Nilsen going to be like the man from Cleveland after all?

'A reason, sir? But you asked me.'

'I know it. But you sort of raised the question in the first place. Come on now, Jimmy. Didn't you have some idea that I might be suckered into acting as your friend's nominee?'

Ah Au looked amazed. 'You, sir? I had not thought of it.'

'All right. Never mind.' He started to turn away.

Ah Au spoke quickly. 'But would you consider such a proposition, sir?'

Mr Nilsen looked at him coldly. 'What's the angle, Jimmy?'

'Angle, sir?'

'What's your friend in Manila trying to smuggle? Opium?'

'Sir, that is not a good thing to say. You asked me questions. I answered the truth.'

'All right. Let me ask you some more questions. What's your friend's name?'

'Sir, if you believe that he is smuggling opium you will go to the police. How can I tell you?'

'All right, I promise not to go to the police. What's his name?'

Ah Au hesitated, then bowed slightly. 'As you promise, I must accept your promise. Please note that, sir. His name is Mr Tan Tack Chee.'

'Right, then why does Mr Tan Tack Chee have you touting for him? Why doesn't he find a nominee himself?'

'Because he has no contacts, sir, with passengers off boats. He cannot go up to strangers and make his request. And it has to be someone who is going to Singapore. How would he know?'

'Why doesn't he get hold of an officer on one of the ships and ask him to do it?'

'A ship's officer dealing in arms would be an object of suspicion to the authorities in Singapore, sir.'

'So would I.'

'No, sir. Many of the dealers in war material are American business men. You are an engineer with a business in America. You would be perfectly acceptable.'

'Don't you mean innocent-looking? Don't you mean I'd be a good cover? You say no opium. Okay, but there are other kinds of contraband. How do I know what'd be in that shipment.'

Ah Au smiled. 'Mr Nilsen, sir, no person who wished to make an illegal shipment of any kind would describe it on a bill of lading and a ship's manifest as arms and ammunition. That is asking for it to be examined by port authorities.'

'Is that how it would be described?'

'Of course, sir.' Ah Au spread out his hands. 'That is my friend's need, to be able to have the shipment legally bonded in Singapore. I explained this.'

Mr Nilsen thought for a moment, then nodded. 'Yes, you did. This Mr Tan, now. You say he's a friend of yours. How did you get to know him?'

Ah Au drew himself up a trifle stiffly. 'He is my wife's father, sir,' he said.

Mr Nilsen began to laugh, then checked himself. 'Sorry, Jimmy. I was just amused at the idea of a man calling his father-in-law his friend.'

'You are not friendly with Mrs Nilsen's father, sir?'

'Oh sure, but . . . no, skip it. I'd better go and see where those women have got to.'

He had started to go. Ah Au followed him.

'Then you will consider the proposition, sir?'

Mr Nilsen grinned affably. 'Oh sure, I'll consider it.'

'When will you decide, sir?'

'I'll let you know tonight. Now back the car up, Jimmy, will you. I have to stop off at the Peninsular Hotel for a fitting at the tailor's.'

4

Greg was feeling good that evening. The idea of his having been asked, in all seriousness, to act as front man for a Chinese pirate had appealed to his sense of humour.

At least, that is how he chose to explain the sudden lightness of heart that had come to him as he was changing for dinner. He regarded himself, not without reason, as a mature and level-headed man. If anyone had suggested that, somewhere in the back streets of his mind, another Greg Nilsen–a roistering, romantic, ten-year-old swashbuckler—had escaped from custody and was out enjoying a game of cops and robbers, he would have been angrily incredulous. It had not yet occurred to him to ask himself why, if the whole thing were simply a good joke, he had not told Dorothy about it.

Jimmy Khoo brought the car to the boat at seven o'clock and drove them across to Aberdeen.

The trouble with Arlene started in the sampan which took them out from the quayside to the floating restaurant. Half-way out across the harbour, she suddenly jumped up out of her seat.

'I've been bitten,' she said to Dorothy.

'Oh no!'

'I've been bitten.'

'Where?'

The light sampan rocked dangerously.

'Better sit down,' Greg cautioned them. 'You're rocking the boat.'

Dorothy sat down, but Arlene ignored him. 'I've been bitten,' she repeated maddeningly and, pulling up one side of her skirt, began examining the back of her leg.

The sampan lurched over in the other direction. The Chinese girl, standing on the stern counter with the oar, was thrown off balance. The old woman who owned the sampan screamed. Greg felt the wicker chair he was sitting on start to slide. He grabbed at the side of the boat.

'For God's sake sit down!' he shouted.

Arlene sat down, the Chinese girl giggled, and a minute later they were at the restaurant steps. Greg paid off the sampan and joined Dorothy and Arlene on the veranda. They appeared to be having some sort of argument.

He heard Dorothy saying: 'I'm sure Greg didn't mean to . . .' And then Arlene turned to face him. Her nose and mouth were pinched and white with anger.

'I'm not used to being yelled at like that,' she said.

'Arlene, I only asked you to sit down. That sort of boat upsets pretty easily.'

'There was no need to yell at me like that.'

'I yelled because I didn't want to have to swim the rest of the way.'

'Oh really, Greg!' This was Dorothy. 'I do think you ought to apologize to Arlene. I know you meant well, but it wasn't very polite.'

'All right, I'm sorry. Now, for goodness' sake, let's go eat.'

It was not a gracious apology and nobody attempted to pretend it was. The situation was not improved when they found that the desirable tables on the upper deck were all reserved, and that they would have to sit down below surrounded by very noisy mah jongg players. Arlene had said that it was unnecessary to make table reservations. Greg pointedly refrained from reminding her of the fact. The critical moment came, however, when they went with the waiter to the big traps moored alongside the vessel to choose the fish they would eat.

There was a man with a long-handled landing net standing by the traps. As the customers pointed to the fish they wanted, he would scoop them dextrously out of the water and fling them on to a long tiled slab which led to the kitchen.

One of the fish he pulled out was some kind of grouper. It was a heavy fish and it landed on the slab with a force that stunned it. For a moment or two it lay there almost still, its eyes staring vacuously, its big slack mouth gaping in an expression of the deepest gloom.

Arlene glanced at Dorothy. 'Isn't that someone we know?' she asked dryly.

She did not look at Greg; but Dorothy did, and then burst out laughing.

'Oh really, Arlene,' she said; 'he's not looking as miserable as all that.'

Then, she squeezed Greg's arm in affectionate apology; and, of course, he had to laugh, too.

But there was murder in his heart, and, at that moment, a resolution was born. Somewhere, somehow, their plans, his and Dorothy's, would have to be changed. He was not going to go all the way to Calcutta in the *Silver Isle* with Arlene Drecker.

When they arrived back at the ship, the two women went on board while Greg stayed to settle the account with Jimmy. He added a generous tip.

'Thank you very much indeed, sir.' Jimmy took off his cap and bowed, but made no move to leave. He was looking at Greg expectantly.

Greg smiled. 'Oh yes. You want to know about that proposition.'

'I hope you can accept, sir.'

'Well, I don't know, Jimmy.'

'Sir, all that is necessary is that you sign some papers in Manila and Singapore.'

'People have been hanged before now just for signing papers, Jimmy.'

'In this case, sir . . .'

'No. I tell you what I will do. When we get to Manila I'll see your Mr Tan if you'll have him contact me on the ship. And *then* I'll decide. Okay?'

Jimmy beamed. 'Certainly, sir. That will be entirely satisfactory. Thank you very much indeed, sir.'

'There's nothing to thank me for. And mind you explain the exact position to him. I don't want any misunderstandings.'

'There will be none. And may I say what a pleasure it has been to serve you, sir?'

'The pleasure's mutual. Be seeing you again some day, maybe.'

'I sincerely hope so, sir.'

When Greg got back on board, he found that some mail had been sent up to the cabin from the purser's office. Among it was a progress report from his vice-president in charge of production. Everything at the plant was running smoothly. He didn't have to worry about a thing; just enjoy the trip.

5

The following morning, Khoo Ah Au dispatched two cables; one to his wife's father in Manila, the other to his wife's uncle in Kuala Pangkalan.

The cable to Mr Tan Tack Chee read:

CONTACT POSSIBLE PROSPECT MR G. NILSEN PASSENGER S.S. SILVER ISLE ARRIVING MANILA 14TH RESPECTFUL AFFECTION WIFE AND SELF. KHOO.

The cable to Mr Tan Siow Mong read:

HAVE ADVISED MANILA SUITABLE PROSPECT ARRIVING S.S. SILVER ISLE 14TH RESPECTFUL AFFECTION WIFE AND SELF. KHOO.

That night Mrs Khoo had the unusual and elevating experience of receiving an overseas telephone call from her father in Manila. The only disappointing thing about it was that more time was devoted to the business talk with her husband than to the discussion of her possible pregnancy.

Chapter Four

I

Two days later the *Silver Isle* docked in Manila, and hordes of scarlet-shirted Filipino stevedores swarmed on board. They seemed to penetrate into every corner of the ship. Some even found their way into the writing-room, where they lounged with their feet up on the tables until indignant stewards shooed them away.

The passengers had been warned that Manila was one of the worst ports in the Far East for pilfering. Greg was depositing a package containing Dorothy's jewellery in the purser's safe, when a steward came up with the message that a Mr Tan Tack Chee would like to see him. The gentleman was in the bar.

Dorothy was waiting for him by the notice-board. They, or rather they and Arlene, had decided not to go ashore immediately, but wait until after lunch. When the purser's clerk had made out the receipt, Greg went over to her.

'Darling, I meant to tell you before. There's a man here who wants to see me on business. It'll only take a few minutes. I'll see you up on the sports deck.'

Dorothy pulled a face. 'Business? I thought we'd left that behind.'

'It's nothing important.'

'I didn't know you did any business here.'

'It's just a man I promised to see.' There was nothing untrue about the statement; nevertheless he did not feel quite easy about it. 'I'll tell you the story later,' he added. 'Look, darling, do you mind holding on to the camera for me?'

He went up to the bar. It was crowded with dock police, customs officials, and the usual collection of 'business' visitors thirsty for free drinks. The steward who had brought him the message pointed to a table in the corner of the bar. Greg made his way over.

Seated at the table with an open brief-case in front of him was a middle-aged Chinese. He wore a well-pressed light-grey suit and thick tortoiseshell glasses. He was writing busily in a loose-leaf notebook. As Greg approached, he glanced up.

'Mr Tan?'

'Mr Nilsen?' As he spoke he rose and they shook hands.

Mr Tan's voice and manner were subdued, and his hand was like a soft bag of chicken bones. It would have been difficult to conceive of anyone less piratical. Greg, whose imagination had had three days to prepare for the encounter, was disconcerted.

'My son-in-law in Hong Kong cabled me that you would be passing through Manila,' Mr Tan said easily. 'He hoped that I might perhaps be of some service to you and Mrs Nilsen.'

'Well, that's very kind of you, Mr Tan. But I rather understood that there was a matter of business you wanted . . .'

'Do you or Mrs Nilsen know Manila?' Mr Tan's interruption was so gentle in tone that Greg scarcely noticed the firmness of it.

'No, we don't.'

'Then, may I make a suggestion? I have my car on the wharf. It would be a favour if you would allow me to place it at your disposal.'

'Mr Tan, I don't think . . .'

Mr Tan held up a slender hand. 'And an additional favour if you would allow me to be your host at lunch. You understand, I do not have the professional skills of my son-in-law, but my driver knows Manila well and can show you what there is to see.'

'As a matter of fact, Mr Tan, we've sort of committed ourselves to taking another passenger along with us. A lady.'

'She is included in the invitation,' Mr Tan said promptly.

'I think . . .'

'I understand perfectly, Mr Nilsen. Please feel free to consult with your wife before you accept.'

Greg hesitated. 'Mr Tan, I think I had better explain that I have not mentioned to my wife the business we might have to discuss.'

'Naturally, Mr Nilsen, one does not trouble ladies with business.' He smiled. 'I am in the so-called import-export market. That is a very loose term covering everything from powdered milk to earth-moving equipment.'

Greg nodded uncertainly. 'I guess so. If you'll excuse me I'll go and find my wife.'

Half an hour later the four of them left the ship and walked along the quay to the car park. As they approached, a pink Cadillac swung out of the parking line and pulled up alongside them. A Filipino driver sprang out to open the doors and they all got in.

Mr Tan took them to his house for lunch. It was in the Spanish style and built on a hillside overlooking the bay. Mrs Tan, obviously a second wife, proved to be young, very attractive, and a graduate of the University of Southern California. She wore toreador pants, and barbecued steaks for them on the patio. Arlene was enchanted. Mr Tan talked about Philippine politics, skin diving and the amusing misfortunes of an American film company who were trying to shoot on location up in the hills. He did not once mention business.

After lunch, the car dropped him back at his office, which was in a modern, American-style building, and then the Filipino driver took them on a tour of the city. When they returned to the office Mr Tan's secretary informed them that he had had to go out, but that he hoped Mr and Mrs Nilsen and Miss Drecker would dine with him that evening. The car would call for them at seven. Mr Tan would wear a white tuxedo.

Dorothy glanced at Arlene with a smile of triumph. 'We're certainly getting the full treatment,' she said. 'He must want those die-castings pretty badly, eh, darling?'

Even Arlene was looking at him with approval.

Greg mumbled something non-committal. He was feeling thoroughly confused. His neglecting to tell Dorothy about the conversation with Jimmy Khoo in Hong Kong had been natural enough, he assured himself. The commercial technicalities about nominees, manifests and shipping in bond would only have bored her; and, besides, they had agreed from the start that business talk was to be taboo on the trip. The last thing he had been prepared for was having to account for Mr Tan in the rôle of a generous host. When he had first reported the invitation to lunch, Arlene had been there, and it had been impossible to go into long explanations. 'He's in the import-export business,' had been all he had said; but Dorothy had jumped to the conclusion that the man wanted to buy die-castings.

He had not realized it until later, or he could have said something to her in time. As it was, the first he had heard about it had been during the afternoon's sight-seeing. He had been listening to the driver talking about the village he came from, when a fragment of conversation from the back seat had caught his attention.

'You see,' Dorothy had been saying, 'Greg's plant only does this special precision work. Most of his contracts are with the Government, or people like airplane manufacturers, or those other people who develop the missiles. He's never had much time for export business before.'

'Well, you ought to encourage it.'

'Why?'

'Won't it make part of your trip tax deductible?'

Dorothy had laughed. 'I'd never thought of that.'

'I'll bet Greg has.'

Greg had pretended not to hear. An explanation at that moment would merely have made his wife look foolish and indulged Arlene's appetite for discord.

Now, he was almost sorry that he had not taken the risk. He had manoeuvred himself into one false position where Dorothy was concerned; and it looked very much as if Mr Tan had manoeuvred him into another. It was going to be embarrassing now to say 'no' to Mr Tan, or even to question him closely, when the question could only imply doubt of his good faith. The fact that Mr Tan's hospitality had a clear purpose was beside the point. Wisely or unwisely, the hospitality had been accepted; and so, an obligation, of courtesy at least, had been incurred.

Dinner was at a country club just outside the city, and had been specially ordered by Mr Tan. The rum drinks were innocent-tasting but very potent. Towards the end of the evening, Arlene became emotional and, in trying to express her gratitude for the wonderful day she had had, was moved to tears of joy. Her mascara ran and she was forced to retire to the powder room. Mrs Tan and Dorothy decided to join her there. Greg and Mr Tan were alone.

There was a pause.

'This has been a very enjoyable day,' Greg said.

Mr Tan smiled. 'For me, too, Mr Nilsen. Although–' he smiled again–'it would have been more enjoyable if you had not been so troubled by your suspicions.'

'Suspicions?'

'My son-in-law in Hong Kong is a very praiseworthy young man. He is not a man of great substance as yet, but he is honest and hard-working. Otherwise, I would not have allowed my daughter to marry him. But he has a weakness.'

'Oh yes?'

'A taste for melodrama. Did he mention piracy, Mr Nilsen?'

'He did, yes.'

'I was afraid so. He lives in the richly flavoured past of lions and dragons. It is an engaging weakness, but embarrassing in business.'

'I guess it would be.'

'You know, Mr Nilsen, this small parcel of arms was acquired by accident, but, as far as I am concerned, perfectly legally. I will confess to you that its existence is inconvenient, and I would like to disembarrass myself. A technicality makes this difficult. You, as you know, are in a position to overcome the technicality. That is the length and breadth of the problem.'

Greg pushed his drink away. 'Mr Tan, are you on the level?'

'Sir?'

'I want to get this straight. These are arms from Red China originally intended for Red terrorists in Malaya. Is that correct?'

'Perfectly correct. As I said, they fell into my hands by accident.'

'What sort of accident?'

'The man who seized them off Hainan left them with me as a pledge for a loan. Later, I am afraid, he went bankrupt.'

'And now you want to sell them to the *anti*-Red people in Indonesia. Is that correct?'

'Entirely correct, Mr Nilsen.'

Greg considered for a moment and then nodded. 'Okay, it's a deal.'

Mr Tan stroked his chin thoughtfully before he said: 'Very well. I will bring the papers to you to sign in the morning.' He hesitated and then went on. 'I will be frank with you, Mr Nilsen. I am not entirely happy with this arrangement.'

Greg stared at him. 'You mean you've changed your mind?'

'Indeed no. On the contrary, I am quite satisfied with the arrangement as far as it goes. My regret is that it does not go further.'

'How do you mean?'

'My brother in Singapore is capable of handling the shipping and delivery arrangements, but when it comes to dealing with the buyers, I am not sure that he is the best man. An American can always drive a harder bargain in that business. How long will you be in Singapore, Mr Nilsen?'

'Two days.'

'Not very long. I had hoped you might consider conducting the negotiations personally. For an additional consideration, of course.'

Greg shook his head. 'I don't think I'm qualified to do that, Mr Tan. And, as you say, I won't be there long enough.'

'I quite understand. Ah, here are the ladies.'

The ship was sailing at midday. At ten-thirty, Mr Tan arrived with the papers for signature.

The first was a consigner's note requesting the Anglo-Malay Transport Company of Kuala Pangkalan to ship the goods listed from the Tak Wah Godown and Storage Corporation, Manila, to the Chen Wharehouse Company, Singapore, to be held in bond there pending further instructions. The second was an export licence giving Greg's name and address in the United States and a list of the goods to be exported. This required his counter-signature and passport number to become effective.

When Greg had signed, Mr Tan gave him copies of the documents. 'As soon as you arrive in Singapore, Mr Nilsen,' he said, 'my brother, Tan Yam Heng, will contact you. I have written his name down here. He will have copies of the bill of lading and go with you to make the proper customs declaration. He will then ask you to sign a paper transferring the ownership of the goods in bond to a company or person to be designated later. When you have signed that paper, he will hand you a cheque for one thousand and fifty dollars U.S.'

'Not going to have any trouble with the customs people, am I?'

'No. The goods are being held in bond. It is merely a formality.' Mr Tan stood up. 'It has been a pleasure to meet and do business with you, Mr Nilsen.'

Dorothy was ashore with Arlene, doing some last-minute shopping and arranging the flowers to be sent with their note of thanks to Mrs Tan. She did not get back until half an hour before the ship sailed. By that time, Mr Tan had left.

'What a pity,' she said when Greg told her. 'I think he's nice. I hope you decided to let him have his castings after all.'

Greg hesitated and then side-stepped the question. 'As a matter of fact he wanted to see me about something else, something he wants me to do for him in Singapore.'

'Are you going to do it?'

'I think so.'

Dorothy nodded approvingly. 'After all, they did put themselves out for us, didn't they?'

2

That afternoon, a cable went from Manila to Kuala Pangkalan.

DOCUMENTS SIGNED AIRMAILED YOU TODAY. TACK CHEE.

That evening, Girija was in the estate office when the telephone rang. As he lifted it off the cradle he heard the operator telling Kuala Pangkalan to go ahead.

'Mr Krishnan?' said a voice a moment later.

'Yes.'

'I am speaking for Mr Lee.'

'Yes?' He did not recognize the voice, which was that of Mr Tan Siow Mong's eldest son.

'Mr Lee wished for delivery three days from now of the goods previously discussed.'

'Very well.'

'Mr Lee will be at the rest house on Thursday evening at eight o'clock, if you will meet him there.'

'Very well.'

The caller hung up.

Girija sat down again at his desk. His heart was pounding; but whether from excitement at the prospect of having a long-cherished dream realized, or from fear of the things he would now have to do, he did not know. He sat there for a while until he felt himself calmer. Then, he looked at his watch.

It was half-past six. He had three nights in which to move the arms and ammunition to the pick-up point near the road. If everything went according to plan, that was only just sufficient time. His instinct was to lock the office and set out at once for Awang; but he restrained himself. The first thing to remember was that his behaviour must not appear in any way unusual.

At seven o'clock he left the office and went to his house. There were the remains of some food which he had prepared at midday, and he forced himself to eat it. At eight o'clock, he took his bicycle and left the compound.

His first care was to see that he was not followed. The possibility of Mr Lee's attempting to discover where the arms were hidden, so that he could remove them without payment, had to be considered. All appeared to be well, however, and he reached the tin workings without encountering anyone he knew on the way.

He had been up to the camp site at night only once before. That had been months ago, when he had been planning the operation; but he still remembered the panic that had seized him when he left the open ground by the tin workings and entered the terrifying blackness of the jungle. The track to the lower end of the dried stream bed was the worst part. It was too near the village for him to risk using a flashlight, except intermittently, and, well as he knew it in daylight, at night there was always the danger of getting lost. Above all, there was his fear of leopards. It was at night that they raided villages on the edge of the jungle, carried off chickens and goats, and killed men. He knew the fear to be largely irrational; there had been no reports of leopards in the area for some time; but still it haunted every step he took. He plunged on desperately along the track, living for the moment when he would reach the stream bed and be able to keep the flashlight on all the time.

His plan for moving the boxes of arms and ammunition fell into three parts.

On the first night, he would move them from the shelter to the cane thicket at the edge of the stream bed. On the second night, he would move them to the foot of the stream bed where it met the track. On the third night, he would move them to a pick-up dump that he had contrived in one of the derelict mining company buildings.

It had taken a long time to prepare the dump. The building he had selected for it was a windowless Nissen hut that had formerly been used as a store for drums of diesel oil. The corrugated-iron sections were so badly rusted that it was possible to put a fist through them in most places; and there were several big holes near the ground where the rusting process was more advanced and the metal had simply disintegrated. From Girija's point of view it had three things to recommend it. There was still enough metal there to prevent a casual passer-by seeing inside; it contained some empty oil drums which had been punctured for some reason, and so had not been stolen for use as water-butts by the villagers; and it had a door with a hasp on it to take a padlock.

Once the arms and ammunition were out of the shelter, the risk of their being discovered increased as they were moved nearer the road. While they were in the cane thicket, the risk was small. The second stage at the foot of the stream bed was a greater risk; but, for twenty-four hours, an acceptable one. For the third stage, however, there had to be an effective hiding place. Girija had never read *The Purloined Letter*, but the technique he employed was similar in principle to that used in Poe's story; concealment by familiarity.

The first thing he had done was to buy a padlock, grease the interior mechanism carefully and leave it in the underbrush for the exterior to rust. Then, one day he had gone to the oil store and padlocked the door. A gleaming new padlock would have excited too much interest in a passer-by. The rusty one, if noticed at all, would only arouse mild curiosity. When he had returned a week later, the padlock had still been there; but there had been signs that someone had crawled through one of the holes near the ground to find out what was behind the locked door. As there had still been nothing inside but the useless oil drums, nothing had been touched. Girija's next move had been to move the oil drums inside, so as to cover the bigger holes in the corrugated iron, and draw a series of squares and circles on the dirt floor with a stick, to make it seem as if children had been playing there. The following week he had found that one of the drums had been pushed aside. He had replaced it. He had considered defecating on the floor as an additional discouragement to the curious, but had finally decided that it would require too many visits to make that form of deterrent completely effective. In the event, additional measures had not been needed. That had been the last time the drums had been touched. The former oil store with the padlocked door had become accepted as a place where children sometimes played, containing nothing worth stealing and nothing of interest. It would look no different during the twenty-four hours it held the arms and ammunition.

By the time he reached the camp site, it was after nine-thirty; but he rested a few minutes before starting work. He had calculated that it would take him less than two hours to move all the boxes to the cane thicket, and was determined to reserve his strength as much as possible. The hardest part of the job would come on the third night, and he must be prepared for that.

The problem of handling the boxes, he had solved almost by accident. At intervals, Mr Wright received catalogues from a mail order house in Singapore, and in one of them Girija had seen a device that had interested him. It was a gadget for those with heavy suitcases who did not wish to hire porters, and consisted of a strap attached to a bracket with two small trolley wheels mounted on it. The strap was fastened lengthwise round the suitcase, with the wheels at one corner. There was a handle on the strap. The owner of the suitcases simply grasped this handle and walked along, trailing the case behind him, with half the weight of it carried on the trolley wheels. The price was six dollars.

Girija had sent for one and experimented. The thing worked on firm ground; but up at the camp site, and with a heavy box of rifles, the small wheels sank into the spongy surface of the hillside and were useless. Larger wheels with broader tyres were needed. He had found them eventually on the estate. Before the Wright children had been sent away to school in England, one of them had had a scooter. It had been left in Mr Wright's garage, and Girija had had no difficulty in removing the wheels. Mounted on an axle made out of a spare jack handle, they worked quite well.

The transfer to the cane thicket was completed by midnight, and Girija began the journey back. In spite of his resolve to conserve his energies, he was very tired, and realized that he could no longer rely upon his wits to see him through. Now, it would be a question of stamina.

There was a compensation. As his weariness increased, his fears seemed to diminish. By the time he had completed the next night's work, he had forgotten about leopards, and feared the dark track from the stream bed to the tin workings only because it threatened his powers of endurance.

The nine boxes containing the rifles were the most awkward to handle, and only one could be moved at a time. It required twenty stumbling journeys each way to shift all the boxes and ammunition containers, and the final move from the stream bed to the oil store took five and a half hours. When he had secured the padlock he sank down on to the ground in a state of collapse. It was another hour before he could summon the strength to get on his bicycle and ride back to the estate; and only the fear of being seen returning to the estate compound at daybreak before he had had time to wash and put on clean clothes, drove him to make that final effort.

He was in the office that morning on time as usual; but he knew that unless he could get some rest during the day, he would be unable or unfit to keep his appointment with Mr Lee in the evening. If he pleaded sickness, Mrs Wright, a keen amateur physician, would dose him with pills and order him to bed; and she would see that he stayed there, too. In the end, on the pretext of looking into some minor pay dispute among the tappers, he left the compound, walked to a part of the estate which he knew was not being worked, and went to sleep under the trees. He awoke at sun-down and hurried back to the office. His body ached almost intolerably; but he was no longer stupid with fatigue. When Mr Wright looked in at the office on his way to the bungalow, he was able to report, with his usual air of efficiency, that the pay dispute had been satisfactorily settled.

Girija's business arrangements with Mr Lee were somewhat complex.

When they met at the rest house, Mr Lee would give him a draft on the Hong Kong and Shanghai Bank for twenty-five thousand Straits dollars, post-dated thirty days and guaranteed by Mr Tan. He would also give him a receipt for the arms and ammunition. Girija would, in return, give Mr Lee a promissory note for twenty-five thousand dollars, acknowledging the sum as a loan repayable within thirty days. Then, Girija would return alone to the estate compound, put the cheque in an envelope, marked 'To be opened in the event of my death', and leave it in a safe place of his own choosing.

An hour later, he would meet Mr Lee at a rendezvous on the Awang road. Mr Lee would have a truck. Guided by Girija, they would then drive to the dump, where Mr Lee would be allowed to inspect what he was buying.

This would be a critical moment for both of them; but both would feel reasonably secure. If there were no arms, and Girija had brought Mr Lee there merely in order to kill him and keep the cheque, Mr Tan would know and be in a position to inform on Girija. If, on the other hand, Mr Lee contemplated killing Girija and making off with the arms, there would be the tell-tale cheque to accuse Mr Lee. The promissory note and the receipt were safeguards of a more genteel nature. The promissory note was Mr Lee's insurance against Girija's making off with the cheque and failing to deliver the goods. The receipt for the arms was Girija's insurance against Mr Lee's declining to return the promissory note when the arms had been delivered. These two documents would be formally exchanged at the conclusion of the transaction.

Girija reviewed the procedure once more as he cycled out to the rest house. He knew that Mr Lee could trust him; he was quite certain that he could not trust Mr Lee. His tired mind began to imagine new ways in which he could be betrayed. Supposing Mr Lee had henchmen hiding in the truck? What was there to prevent them pouncing on him, retrieving the receipt for the arms, and then seizing the whole consignment? Mr Lee could still use the promissory note, and Girija would be in no position to complain of what had happened to the police. Or supposing Mr Lee had a confederate in the estate compound who would watch where he put the cheque, and then steal it while he was away delivering the arms. There were countless opportunities for treachery remaining in the situation. Only one possibility did he refuse to consider; that the cheque guaranteed by Mr Tan might not in the end be honoured.

Mr Lee was already at the rest house when he arrived. His attitude was wary but businesslike. He merely grunted a greeting, and then handed Girija the promissory note to sign. He then produced the cheque and the receipt. When the documents had changed hands, he nodded.

'That is satisfactory. Now, where do we meet?'

'At the twenty-one mile post near Awang.'

'Where is that?'

Girija told him how to get there, and then stood up to go. His whole body was aching, and a spasm of pain shot up his spine as he moved.

Mr Lee was eyeing him thoughtfully. 'Are you sick?' he asked.

'No, I am tired.'

'Will your friend be there?'

'No, but I will help you load the boxes.'

'Then I will meet you in one hour's time.'

The whole transaction had taken no more than five minutes. Girija cycled back to the estate compound and went to his house. When he had written the inscription on the envelope, he put the cheque inside and locked them in his tin trunk. If he did not return, Mr Wright would probably take charge of the trunk and ultimately hand it over to the authorities. It was not an ideal arrangement, but it was the best Girija could think of. As long as Mr Lee did not know how he had disposed of the cheque, that was all that mattered.

He had ten minutes to wait before setting out for the rendezvous. He considered opening up the tin trunk again and passing the time with his bus catalogues, but made no move to do so. Through his weariness, he knew that the time for dreams was over. The next time he looked at the catalogues, if there were to be a next time, he would be seeing them through different eyes. There was half a tin of butterscotch on the table by his charpoy. He sat and ate that until it was time to go.

The truck was already at the rendezvous when he arrived. About a hundred yards short of it, he dismounted, switched off his bicycle lamp, and walked along the edge of the road. As he approached, he saw that the canvases above the tailboard of the truck were drawn and tied. He did not like this, and made up his mind to see that the truck was empty before they moved off.

Mr Lee looked out of the driver's cab window as Girija came up.

'You are late,' he said.

'I am two minutes early,' Girija replied evenly. 'Would you open the back of the truck please?'

'Why?'

'I wish to put my bicycle inside.'

'Why can't you leave it among the trees there. No one will steal it. We have to come back this way.'

'I prefer to have it with me.'

Mr Lee got down impatiently and went to the rear of the truck. Girija joined him. In silence they unfastened the tailboard. Girija knew the truck. It belonged to a copra dealer in Kuala Pangkalan. The Anglo-Malay

Transport Company hired it sometimes when their own trucks were busy. Mr Lee must have learned of it from Mr Tan.

The back of the truck was empty. Girija put his bicycle inside and they set off. Mr Lee was a fast and bad driver. Luckily, they met little traffic on the way. After ten minutes they reached the road leading to the tin workings.

'You turn off here,' said Girija; 'and I must ask you to put your lights out.'

'On this cart track? We shall run into a tree.'

'If you drive slowly, you will be all right. If you keep your lights on, we may be seen from the kampong and someone will come to see what is happening.'

Mr Lee grumbled but submitted. The truck ground along the road as far as the derelict pump shed.

'We stop here,' said Girija.

They got down from the cab and Mr Lee looked round.

'What is this place?'

Girija told him. 'We go this way,' he added.

'One moment. Are the cases open?'

'Of course not.'

Mr Lee took a case-opener and a hammer from the cab of the truck. In his hands they looked like weapons. Girija's scalp crawled as he led the way to the oil store. However, Mr Lee's main concern at that moment seemed to be to avoid tripping on the uneven ground beneath the scrub. He muttered a complaint about the darkness.

Girija took no notice. Not until they were inside the oil store with the door firmly shut did he switch on his flashlight.

Mr Lee looked at the stacked boxes. 'Is this all of it?'

'Everything on the list is there.'

Mr Lee produced the list from his pocket. 'Which are the rifles?'

'Those long boxes there.'

Mr Lee began opening them. He opened every one. When Girija suggested that this was a waste of time, Mr Lee straightened up.

'Cases full of stones have been sold before now,' he said. 'I am buying only what I see. If you want to save time, you can refasten the cases after I have examined them.'

When he had finished with the rifles, he went on in the same methodical way with the rest—the machine pistols, the bazookas, the grenades, the landmines. Only when he approached the ammunition did Girija protest again.

'If you open those, Mr Lee, you will not be able to reseal them. You will reduce their market value.'

Mr Lee looked at the ammunition boxes. They were air-tight metal containers with soft inner lids which had to be cut or torn open with a tool. He nodded reluctantly.

'Okay. I will accept them unseen. Now, we can start loading.'

He grabbed the rope handle of one of the rifle boxes and looked up at Girija.

Girija smiled, but made no move to take the other handle. Once the boxes were in the truck, there was nothing to prevent Mr Lee's hitting him on the head with the case-opener, and taking the receipt from him while he was unconscious. He had a feeling that Mr Lee was aware of the fact.

'Do you not think, Mr Lee,' he said, 'that we should complete our business first?'

'There is plenty of time for that.'

Girija held up the flashlight. 'By the time we have finished the loading, this battery will be very weak. Let us complete our business now, Mr Lee, while there is light.'

Mr Lee stared at him resentfully, then shrugged. 'As long as you help with the loading, I do not care.'

'I will certainly help you.' Girija produced Mr Lee's receipt from his pocket and held it up.

Mr Lee shrugged again and got out the promissory note. The two pieces of paper changed hands. The moment he had his note, Girija lit a match and burned it. Mr Lee did the same with his receipt. The transaction was complete.

It took an hour to load the truck, and Mr Lee became abusive over Girija's refusal to use the flashlight to guide them across the scrub. When the job was finished, Girija went back alone to the oil store to replace the padlock on the door. As he did so, he heard the truck start up and drive off. Mr Lee had not had the elementary courtesy to wait and say good-bye.

Girija went back to the track, picked up his bicycle, and started for home. When he had gone about a mile, he remembered that he had left the trolley with the scooter wheels in the oil store. For a moment or two, he wondered if he should go back and get rid of it; then, the absurdity of the notion struck him. What could a pair of wheels and a strap tell anybody? He had nothing to hide any more; nothing, that is, except a cheque for twenty-five thousand dollars.

When he reached his house he examined the tin trunk to see that the lock had not been tampered with. He did not open it. He did not even wait to undress before he lay down on the charpoy and went to sleep.

3

It was one in the morning when Tan Yam Heng drove the truck up to the gate of the Anglo-Malay Transport Company's compound. The Sikh night watchman came out of his hut and opened the gate. Yam Heng told him to remain at the gate and then drove through to the unloading bay of number two godown.

The unloading platform was level with the tailboard of the truck. It did not take him long to drag the boxes out and stack them inside the two large machinery crates he had brought in some hours earlier. He had only been able to guess at the various dimensions of the boxes, and they had to be wedged and braced inside the crates; but he had anticipated this, and had provided himself with the wood and tools he would need to do the job. By two-thirty both crates were ready to ship. He left them on the platform and drove himself back to his brother's house in the truck. Tan Siow Mong had waited up for him.

'Was everything in order?' he asked.

'Yes.'

'Were the goods according to specification?'

'I opened and counted everything except the ammunition. Those boxes are sealed.'

'And he has the cheque.'

'Of course.'

'You do not seem pleased. Has anything gone wrong?'

'That Indian clerk is insufferable. He treated me as if I were a crook.'

His brother nodded calmly. 'I warned you he was no fool,' he said.

The following morning Tan Siow Mong had a brief interview with Kwong Kee, master of the Anglo-Malay Transport Company's motor junk, *Glowing Dawn*, just back from her weekly run to Manila.

Kwong Kee was a square, pot-bellied man with a cheerful disposition and a venereal appetite that bordered on satyriasis. He was not greatly interested in the commercial reasons Mr Tan gave him for switching the *Glowing Dawn* temporarily to the Singapore run. Nor was he interested in the cargo she carried. And if Mr Tan's young brother were fool enough to want to go home by sea instead of comfortably by train, that was no business of his either. He was quite content to do as he was told. It was some time since he had sampled the Singapore brothels.

The *Glowing Dawn* sailed that afternoon with a cargo of latex and two machinery crates. When she was well out to sea, Yam Heng went down into the hold and stencilled the consignee's name and address on the crates: 'G.NILSEN, C/O CHEN WHAREHOUSE CO. SINGAPORE. IN BOND.'

4

The night before the *Silver Isle* was due in at Saigon, there was a ship's gala dance. The notice had said: 'Fancy Dress Optional.'

On the advice of his cabin steward, who had lived through many of these occasions, Greg went as a Spanish hidalgo. It was easy. All he had to do was wear the black pants belonging to his tuxedo, an evening dress shirt with a black string tie, and two cummerbunds instead of one to raise the waist line. The steward provided the extra cummerbund and also a flat-topped black hat with a wide brim. He always carried them in his baggage. They had earned him many an extra tip. As he explained to Greg, the advantage of the costume was that a gentleman did not have to wear a jacket with it; and in the steamy heat of the South China Sea, that was a real blessing. Dorothy painted on the long sideburns he needed with her eyebrow pencil.

She herself had been undecided what to wear. She had discussed the problem with Arlene; but Arlene had been curiously unhelpful, and had even refused to say what she was going to wear herself; she wanted it to be a surprise. Finally, with the aid of the stewardess, Dorothy had settled for a German doll costume. The stewardess happened to have the dirndl skirt and the blouse with embroidered smocking. Dorothy made herself a coif with two white napkins from the dining-room, and put big dabs of rouge on her cheeks.

Both she and Greg were ready early, but lurked in their cabin with the door on the hook until, by watching their fellow passengers passing along the alleyway outside and listening to their conversation, they had assured themselves that they were not going to be the only ones who had opted for fancy dress. Then, they went up to the bar.

Most of the passengers had decided on some form of fancy costume for the evening; and, although many had contented themselves with funny hats, false noses and other easily discarded fripperies, a few had allowed their enthusiasm to run away with them. In the bar, the pirates, Al Jolsons, hoboes and Indian maharajahs were already drenched with sweat and in difficulty with their burnt cork make-ups. Over their Martinis, Greg and Dorothy congratulated themselves on having hit it off just right; they had taken trouble, but not too much trouble; and they were comfortable.

Arlene did not appear until just before the ship's speakers announced dinner. Then, she made a slow, regal entrance through the double doors leading to the lounge. She was wearing a *cheong sam*, the silk formal dress with the high collar and split skirt that Chinese women wear, and long jade ear-rings. Just inside the door, she stopped and smiled as if expecting a round of applause.

The *cheong sam* can be an attractive and becoming garment; but it makes certain demands on the wearer. She must be small-boned and very slender, with invisible hips and near-to-invisible buttocks, a flat stomach and minute breasts. Her arms and neck must appear fragile, and her face must be round with high cheek-bones. She must, in other words, be Chinese. On Arlene's shapely, but large and well-padded body, and surmounted by her equine head, it looked grotesque.

Greg said: 'My God!'

'She bought it in Hong Kong,' muttered Dorothy. 'It's the most lovely material.'

'It still looks ridiculous.'

'I didn't see it on her at the fitting.'

'She must be out of her mind!'

Arlene's entrance created a minor sensation, and there were one or two uncertain whoops of gallantry as she swayed over to the Nilsen's table. If she were kidding, everyone was prepared to laugh. If she were serious, they were ready to be polite. Meanwhile, they were embarrassed.

Arlene sat down beside Dorothy and the splits in her skirt gaped to reveal, on Greg's side, a large area of thigh and one pink suspender. She smiled archly.

'Well, what do you think of Chinese laundly girl?'

'It's a lovely dress,' said Dorothy eagerly.

'It certainly is,' said Greg. 'Martini?'

'No.' Her smile was challenging now. 'Tonight, I am drinking champagne.'

They went down to dinner twenty minutes late, and had to run a gauntlet of eyes as they crossed to their table. Arlene's half-bottle of champagne seemed to have gone to her head, and she began calling Greg 'Don Gregorio' and Dorothy 'Gretchen'. She was thoroughly pleased with herself, looking about her with the calm assurance of a woman who knows that she is the most attractive in the room.

When the dancing began, she became skittish, breaking away from her partners to execute little hip-waggling solos in the middle of the deck. Greg and Dorothy, dancing sedately on the outskirts, glanced at one another.

Dorothy was worried. 'I don't understand it,' she muttered; 'she usually has such good taste in clothes.'

'Yes.'

'Well, you must admit she *has*.'

'If you ask me,' said Greg; 'she had a few belts of gin in her cabin before she came up.'

'Now, darling, that's a nasty thing to say.'

'Well, look at her.'

Arlene, with her arms stretched out wide, her head turned over her right shoulder and her chin tilted imperiously, was now dancing a flamenco. Her partner, one of the ship's officers, was rotating around her somewhat helplessly. He had an uneasy grin on his face.

'She's just a little excited,' said Dorothy defensively. 'Anyway she's having a good time.'

'In my opinion, she's making a horse's ass of herself.'

'Really, Greg!'

Arlene did not return to their table. When a 'Leap Year' dance was announced, she made a bee-line for the Captain and after that dance returned with him to his table; whether by invitation or not it was impossible to determine.

The following morning, when they were going up the river to Saigon, she did not appear at her usual time; but Greg and Dorothy were too busy shooting with their movie camera and watching the sampans and the river banks go by to give her much thought. They found her, immaculate but a trifle pensive, sitting in the bar after the ship had docked.

'What happened to you last night?' she asked Dorothy as they joined her.

'We went down around eleven-thirty.'

'Four o'clock, me,' Arlene said grimly; 'the barman opened up a can of weinies. He's got an electric grill back there. That was after I'd switched to scotch.'

'Who else was there?' Dorothy asked.

'Nobody. Just the barman and me. He comes from L.A. and he's a Dodger fan,' she added sourly.

But after lunch she felt fine again and they all went ashore. At Arlene's suggestion they crushed into a small Renault taxi for a tour of the city.

It was insufferably humid, and the driver, a handsome young Vietnamese, smelt peculiarly of rotting fish. Arlene explained that the smell came from a sauce used in all Vietnamese cooking and was no reflection on the driver's personal cleanliness. The driver grinned.

'Is made from fish,' he said suddenly in English. 'You like me show where make it?'

Up to that moment he had spoken nothing but French, and Arlene had been the interpreter. Nobody had troubled to ask him if he understood English, Greg remembered. Arlene, proud of her French she had acquired in her Red Cross days, had just gone ahead and spoken for them. As a result, they had unwittingly hurt the man's feelings. That was precisely the sort of stupid incident, Greg thought, that made Americans unpopular abroad.

However, the driver did not seem offended. 'I show you on way back ship,' he went on. 'Make bad smell, but many vitamins.'

'That so?'

They were travelling along a broad, tree-lined street that reminded Arlene and Dorothy of Paris, when the driver turned to Greg.

'Now I show you where Quiet American made bomb explosion,' he said.

'How's that?'

'That café there.' The driver pointed. 'That was where Quiet American made bomb explosion. Many killed.'

They were crossing a square now. Greg looked from the café to the driver.

'But *The Quiet American* was a novel,' he said.

'Yes, sir. That is café back there. I was near at time of explosion. Was very bad.'

'But it was fiction,' Dorothy said. 'It didn't actually happen.'

'Apparently there was a bomb explosion there,' Arlene explained. 'I had this when I was here before. Somebody told me Graham Greene was in the city at the time.'

'Graham Greene, yes.' The driver nodded emphatically. 'Presently I will show you bridge where Fowler found dead body of correspondent, and place where there was restaurant where they talk. Real restaurant now gone, pulled down.'

'You mean people here believe that story?'

'Is true, sir. I show you the place.'

'But it was just a novel.'

'Look,' said Arlene impatiently; 'if you go to Marseille, they take you out to the Château d'If and show you the hole in the wall that the Count of Monte Cristo made when he scratched his way through to the Abbé Faria. They show you the dungeon occupied by the Man in the Iron Mask. It doesn't mean anything. It's just to make the tourists feel they're getting their money's worth.'

'But that was an anti-American novel. If they believe all that stuff, my God! We're giving these people millions in aid.'

'That's right,' said Dorothy.

Arlene smiled. 'I can see you two have got a few surprises coming to you on this trip.'

They returned to the ship, hot, tired and out of temper. On their way down to shower and change, Greg and Dorothy had to squeeze their way past a pile of baggage in the alleyway. Their steward told them that three new passengers had come on board. When they went up on deck, they saw Arlene sitting talking animatedly to a florid, thick-set man in a khaki bush shirt. They were drinking Pernod.

At cocktail time, Greg and Dorothy were sitting in their usual corner when Arlene appeared with the same man. He had changed into a white shark-skin suit. Evidently, he was one of the new passengers. They came over.

'Ce sont mes amis, Greg et Dorothy Nilsen,' said Arlene. 'Je veux vous présenter Monsieur Seguin.'

'How do you do?' said Monsieur Seguin.

They shook hands. Greg said: 'Will you join us?'

'Thank you.' With a courteous bow to Dorothy, Monsieur Seguin sat down.

He had small blue eyes, a merry smile, and large pudgy hands with little mats of gleaming blond hair on the backs of them.

'Monsieur Seguin est ingénieur civil,' Arlene explained. 'Il va nous accompagner jusqu'à Calcutta. Monsieur Nilsen est ingénieur aussi.'

'Indeed?' Monsieur Seguin looked interested. 'In what branch of our profession, sir?' His English was excellent.

'How do you say die-casting in French?' Arlene asked.

Greg shrugged helplessly.

'Oh, but I understand,' said Monsieur Seguin affably. 'Mr Nilsen makes the small pieces of all those things that the world thinks of when it hears an American use the phrase "standard of living".'

Arlene laughed heartily. Greg and Dorothy smiled. More Pernods were arriving.

'Isn't it lucky?' Arlene said. 'I had a word with the Chief Steward and he's fixed it for Monsieur Seguin to sit at our table.'

The *Silver Isle* was an American ship and most of her passengers were Americans. Not unnaturally the cooking was American, and served in the American style.

Monsieur Seguin did not like it. He did not like the shrimp cocktail and tried to remove all the sauce from it. He asked for his steak *bleu* and, when it came rare, regretted that it had been overcooked. He did not want his salad on the side, but as a separate course, and requested that the slices of avocado pear be removed. He ignored the baked Idaho potato, and refused the ice-cream. He took one mouthful of the Wisconsin Brie, made a face and ate no more. However, he remained, apparently, good-humoured. His only comment seemed mild enough for a Frenchman who had not enjoyed his dinner.

'I needed to lose some weight,' he said with a smile. 'This ship will be very good for me. Here, it will be easy to maintain a régime.'

'I don't know what they think they're doing,' Arlene burst out angrily. 'You could get better food at a drug store.'

Dorothy chuckled. 'The other day you were saying you thought the food was great.'

'Great is a relative term, dear. Even an American chef must be able to cook eatable food *one* day in thirty.' She was sharing a bottle of wine with Monsieur Seguin and now she drained her glass.

Monsieur Seguin refilled it. 'Mademoiselle, I think you are being very unfair to America,' he said. 'She has made some very important contributions to world civilization. Let us see–' he pretended to search his memory–'she has given us chewing gum, and Coca-Cola, and gangster films, and she has given us atomic bombs.' He smiled slyly at Greg. 'As well as a lot of advice.'

Greg raised his eyebrows. 'Aren't you forgetting popcorn?'

'Ah yes. Pardon. And I was forgetting democracy also. McCarthy style, of course.'

Arlene laughed. 'That's telling 'em!'

Dorothy's face froze.

Greg smiled placidly at Monsieur Seguin. 'I expect you have a lot of jokes about American tourists, too. And foreign aid.'

Monsieur Seguin shrugged. 'It is sad,' he said. 'You Americans give away billions of dollars to defend yourselves against Communism, but you ask everyone to believe that you give it because you are good and kind. Why?'

'Because big daddy-o wants to be loved,' said Arlene promptly.

'America,' said Monsieur Seguin, 'is rich, and behaves like the rich always behave. When they begin to fear death, they become philanthropists.'

'Well, most Americans aren't rich,' said Greg; 'and they certainly don't feel particularly philanthropic when they're paying their taxes.'

'That's just childish,' snapped Arlene. 'Monsieur Seguin was talking about us as a nation.'

Dorothy's face went pink. 'I don't think Greg's the one who's being childish,' she said.

'What I meant to say,' Monsieur Seguin went on evenly, 'was simply that American foreign policy has always, from the first, been made by men who saw the world through the eyes of money, of riches.'

'If you don't mind my saying so, Monsieur Seguin,' said Greg; 'that is one of the stupidest remarks I've ever heard.'

Monsieur Seguin smiled. 'You know, Mr Nilsen, there was an American who owned fifteen thousand acres of some of the best land in America. He owned land in New York and Pennsylvania and Virginia and Maryland and the City of Washington. When he died he was one of the richest men in your country.'

'Who was that, Rockefeller?'

'His name was George Washington,' said Monsieur Seguin quietly; 'but, of course, you knew that.'

Arlene laughed so much that she had the whole dining-room looking at their table.

Dorothy sat with a face like stone.

After dinner, she and Greg went straight to their cabin.

'I think Arlene behaved disgustingly,' Dorothy said; 'and as for that ghastly little Frenchman . . . Was it right what he said, about Washington, I mean?'

Greg shrugged. 'Probably. He's the sort of man who collects facts of that kind. Of course, they weren't relevant to the point he was trying to make, but that wouldn't interest him. He's a debater.'

'It's Arlene I don't understand. Encouraging him to go on talking all that anti-American nonsense. And on an American ship, too. I mean it's such bad taste. And how dared she ask the steward to put him at our table, without even consulting us?'

'I tell you one thing, dear,' said Greg; 'and you'd better be ready for it. The next time that guy starts any anti-American stuff, I'm going to take a poke at him.'

'You mean we have to go on eating with him?' Dorothy demanded.

Greg stared at her, a wild hope surging through him. 'Darling, the ship's full. You know that. They can't rearrange the seating now.'

'You mean we're stuck with them, all the way to Calcutta?'

'Unless we complain to the purser and make a personal issue of it, I'm afraid we are.'

'Oh, Greg!' She sat down miserably on her bed. 'Our lovely trip!'

He sat down beside her and put his arm round her waist. 'You said it yourself, darling. We're not in a position to choose our travelling companions.'

Dorothy stuck out her chin. 'Maybe not. But we *are* in a position to choose the way we travel.'

'Darling, we're booked through on this ship to Calcutta.'

'Maybe we are, but we can change our minds. We could stop over at Singapore, take a side trip or two and then go on by air to Calcutta. You said you were going to do something for Mr Tan in Singapore. All right! It's business. If you explained that, I know we could get a refund on the passage.'

Greg had never loved her more. 'That's right. Pan-Am and B.O.A.C. go via Bangkok. Maybe we could stop over there instead of Rangoon before we go on to Calcutta.'

'Bangkok! That would be wonderful!'

'As a matter of fact it wouldn't cost us any extra, even allowing for side trips. I didn't tell you, but this business that Mr Tan asked me to do'll net me a thousand dollars.'

'Hong Kong?'

'No, real American dollars. And I could make a thousand more if we spent a day or two extra in Singapore.'

'How?'

'Signing papers. Anyway I'll tell you about that later. The main thing is that we enjoy ourselves. We don't have to worry about the extra expense. If we decide we want to get off at Singapore, then that's all there is to it.'

Dorothy was silent for a moment. Then she said: 'I know you don't like Arlene. I suppose she's not really a very likeable person. I think that's why I felt sorry for her.'

Later that evening, Greg had a talk with the purser, and then sent a radiogram to Mr Tan Tack Chee in Manila.

Chapter Five

I

At the upper social levels of the British community in Singapore, Colonel Soames was known as 'The Policeman'.

There was nothing derogatory about the name. It had been applied originally to distinguish him from another Colonel Soames, who had been a retired Gurkha officer and a prominent member of the Turf Club. The fact that its use had continued after 'Gurkha' Soames's death, however, had been only partly the result of habit. Although Colonel Soames's status as a senior police official was well known, the nature of his duties was not. He never discussed them, and any attempt to draw him out on the subject was met by him with a frosty silence. It was generally assumed that he was not, strictly speaking, a policeman at all, but something to do with Intelligence. To go on calling him 'The Policeman' was a mildly sardonic way of underlining that assumption.

It was, in a sense, correct. Singapore was a naval, military and air base of crucial importance to the British Commonwealth; but it was also a free port and a trading post, largely dependent for its economic existence on international commerce. In the latter capacity it was obliged to receive many strange guests. Colonel Soames's job was to detect the undesirables among them, and to see that their interests and those of Singapore as a whole did not seriously conflict. He worked in collaboration with the immigration department, the service intelligence organizations, the port and airport authorities, and the customs. He never ordered arrests. If any major criminal activity came to his attention, he either turned the facts over to an appropriate colleague for action, or, if, in his judgment, inaction would be more productive, he merely watched and waited. Occasionally, he might suggest a deportation, or the refusal of an entry permit; but most of his results were obtained simply by contriving to let the objects of his attentions know that they were observed and understood. Officially, he was in charge of a branch of the internal security forces. His own definition of his function was 'discouraging the bad boys'.

His second-in-command was a plain-clothes inspector named Chow Soo Kee. Every morning at ten they met to discuss the reports of the previous day. It was at one of these meetings that the name 'Nilsen' first came to Colonel Soames's attention.

They had reviewed the current activities of a Belgian who was attempting to set up a central distribution agency for 'blue' films from Bangkok, an Austrian who was buying girls for a new brothel in Brunei, and an Australian couple who seemed to be doing too well at the badger game. They had discussed the steps to be taken in the case of the consul of a

Central American republic, who, comfortably shielded by his diplomatic immunity, was making money in the opium market. It had been decided to advise a man posing as a theatrical booking agent that his record had been forwarded by Scotland Yard. Inspector Chow was getting up to leave, when he remembered something.

'By the way, Colonel,' he said, 'we have another arms dealer.'

'Not that Italian again?'

'No, sir, a new one. Customs told me about him. There was a parcel of arms consigned in bond to a G. Nilsen from Manila.'

'How big?'

Inspector Chow told him. 'Probably Korean war surplus,' he added. 'They could be samples.'

'Rather a lot of samples, don't you think? Sounds more like a small man trying to get his toe in.'

'Well, that's the funny thing, sir. He isn't the usual type. Full name is Gregory Hull Nilsen. American citizen. Engineer. Comes from Wilmington, Delaware, where he has his own light engineering business. Travelling with his wife. They arrived on the *Silver Isle* two days ago. Staying at the Raffles Hotel. They have an air-conditioned suite. Highly respectable sort of people, apparently.'

'Well, that's a comfort.'

'Yes, sir.' Inspector Chow paused. 'Except for two things. He made a false statement to the immigration people. Said he and his wife were here just as tourists. Made no mention of the arms business.'

'How long did he ask for?'

'Two weeks. Immigration visa'd them for thirty days. The other thing was that he was brought to the hotel by Tan Yam Heng.'

'You mean that union thug who's always losing his shirt on the pickle market?'

'Yes, sir. Apparently on friendly terms with him. That's what I didn't like. Tan's a member of the Democratic Action Party.'

'Who else has this man seen?'

'Nobody, as far as I can gather. Yesterday he and his wife hired a car and drove round the island; to see the sights, they said. The driver says that's all they did do.'

'Could be establishing their cover. I wonder why he lied, though. Stupid thing to do, if he's just a dealer. Who'd be in the market now for what he's got to sell?'

Inspector Chow thought for a moment. He knew that what he had to say would not please Colonel Soames, and he wanted to phrase it as delicately as possible.

Indonesia, the young republic which claimed sovereignty over the three thousand islands of the former Dutch East Indies, was an uneasy neighbour. The Central Government in Java was weak, unstable and hagridden by Communism. In the big outer islands, especially Sumatra and Celebes, there were powerful revolutionary movements demanding secession and independence. The political thinking of these movements was religious in tone and strongly anti-Communist; and they had made fighting alliances. For three years or more, parts of Sumatra and Celebes had been virtually in a state of civil war, with insurgent forces in control of large areas and Central Government troops having in some places to defend even the big towns. With the long coastline of Sumatra only thirty miles away across the Straits of Malacca, Singapore was, whether it liked it or not, the natural supply base for the Sumatran insurgents. Their 'liaison officers' and purchasing agents were the bane of Colonel Soames's existence.

'As you pointed out, sir,' Inspector Chow said finally, 'it is a small consignment. I don't think the Darul Islam people would be interested at present. You know they had a shipment of eighty machine-guns and fifty three-inch mortars three weeks ago.'

'Not through here, I hope.'

'No, sir. Direct from Macao.'

'That Dutchman handle it?'

'Yes. But he shipped the ammunition separately, over three tons apparently, and an Indonesian Government destroyer intercepted it. They'll be wanting to replace that ammunition first. I don't think they'll bother about a few more rifles. I would say that, at the moment, the most interested buyer would be Captain Lukey.'

He was careful to say the last two words very casually. Captain Lukey was the liaison officer and representative in Singapore of a small insurgent force that had recently begun to operate in Northern Sumatra. Colonel Soames's dislike of him was personal and intense.

Herbert Henry Lukey had been a regular soldier in a British county regiment, and commissioned as a lieutenant-quartermaster during World War II. He had served, without distinction, until 1950, when the final period for which he had signed-on had expired. His regiment had been stationed in Egypt at the time, and much of his last six months of service had been spent answering questions at Courts of Inquiry appointed to investigate the virtual disappearance of a number of emergency petrol storage dumps of which he had been in charge. His answers had revealed qualities of imagination and ingenuity not hitherto apparent in his military career; and a secret, though unauthorized, investigation of his bank balance had shown him to be in the possession of funds far exceeding his total army pay for the previous five years. However, the smokescreen of confusion which he had succeeded in creating had, in the end, led to the inquiries being abandoned for lack of evidence. The petrol losses had been written off, in the way he had originally advocated as 'due to evaporation'. He could, and frequently did, claim that his army record was as clean as a whistle.

His subsequent record, as a civilian in North Borneo, Malaya and Singapore, was not. He had worked in minor executive posts for several big trading concerns, most of which had, like the army, suffered some evaporation of assets before dispensing with his services. Eventually, one of them had thought forthrightedly and unconfusedly enough about its losses to go to the police. There had been talk, too, of forged references. He had left Singapore hurriedly, and, after a while, the charges against him had been dropped. Occasional inquiries over the next three years from police authorities in Colombo, Cape Town, Mombasa and Bombay, had made it possible to chart his subsequent progress. The report of his return to Singapore had been referred immediately to Colonel Soames.

'The Policeman' was not an intolerant man. He disapproved of the crooked and the *louche*, but he did not generally dislike them. Admittedly, his attitude was not as objective as he thought it was, and had a paternalistic, schoolmasterish quality about it; but that was largely a result of his training. He had come late to police work, and was inclined to treat most of the adult transgressors who came his way as if they were delinquent members of a regiment of which he was in command, and to which both he and they owed a common loyalty.

However, with Captain Lukey it was different; and the difference resided in the word 'Captain'.

The day after Lukey had returned, Colonel Soames had summoned him to his office for an interview.

'According to your statement to the immigration authorities,' Colonel Soames had begun, 'you are here as a liaison officer and purchasing agent for the armed forces of the Independent Party of the Faithful of North Sumatra. Is that correct?'

'Perfectly correct.'

'You say you are a liaison officer. What is the liaison between, may I ask?'

'The army of the Party of the Faithful and other forces in Sumatra hostile to those Commies in Djakarta, sir.'

'I see. And in your rôle as purchasing agent, what are you intending to purchase?'

'Supplies, Colonel.'

'Arms?'

'Supplies of various kinds, Colonel.'

'Do you have funds for these purchases?'

'Naturally, Colonel.'

'And where do these funds come from?'

'They are subscribed by loyal Sumatrans and certain friendly parties.'

'Have you a banking account?'

'Yes, Colonel. Hong Kong and Shanghai, Orchard Road. All perfectly respectable.'

'Are you empowered to sign cheques?'

'With a counter-signature, yes.'

'Whose counter-signature?'

'A member of the Executive Committee of the Party of the Faithful.'

'Is the Committee aware of your previous record?'

'My British Army record, Colonel? Certainly.'

'I was thinking more of your record here, and in Borneo.'

'I wasn't aware that I had one, sir.'

'Weren't you?'

'I don't think I understand you, Colonel. Are you suggesting I have a criminal record in Singapore?'

That had been just what Colonel Soames had been suggesting; but he knew better than to say so. There had been no convictions recorded against the man in that area.

'All I am suggesting is that while you are in Singapore you are careful to respect the law. Do you understand, Mr Lukey?'

'*Captain* Lukey if you don't mind, Colonel.'

Colonel Soames had smiled unpleasantly. 'And that brings me to another point. I don't think that there is much sense in my pointing out that the use of a military title to which one is not entitled is bad form and caddish. Perhaps I should simply remind you that it is an offence in law.'

Captain Lukey had smiled back, equally unpleasantly. 'And perhaps I should simply tell you, Colonel, that the British Army isn't the only army in the world. Here, take a look at this.'

He had handed over a paper. It had been a commission from the Commander in Chief of the army of the Independent Party of the Faithful of North Sumatra, appointing his loyal servant 'Herbert Henry Lukey a staff captain.

It had touched Colonel Soames in a very sensitive place. He had lost his temper.

'This is meaningless. You cannot accept such a commission.'

'Why not, Colonel?'

'In the first place you are a British subject. In the second place you are, unhappily, an officer in the armed forces of Her Majesty the Queen.'

'Not any more, Colonel.'

'You may not be a serving officer, but you are on the reserve. You could be recalled to active duty if necessary.'

Captain Lukey had grinned. 'Do you take me for a fool, Colonel? I came off the reserve two years ago. I'm over age.'

'Well, that's something to be thankful for, but don't expect me to recognize this rubbish.' Colonel Soames had tossed the paper contemptuously back across the desk.

Captain Lukey had picked it up, folded it carefully and put it back in his pocket before speaking. Then he had said: 'Is that your considered opinion, Colonel?'

'It is.'

'Then you won't have any objection, I take it, if I report it back to my commanding officer in Sumatra, as the official British view.'

Colonel Soames had hesitated. The Independent Party of the Faithful was probably little more than a gang of dissident Sumatran officers greedy for the spoils of local political power. But in Sumatra anything might happen. Within a few months, those same officers could be members of a lawfully constituted government. A senior Singapore police official who had gratuitously insulted its leaders would find himself most unpopular with the British Foreign Office, to say nothing of Government House. The fact that H. H. Lukey was, in his opinion, a cad, would not excuse the indiscretion.

He had swallowed his annoyance. 'No, it's not an official British view. It merely represents my personal opinion of you.'

Captain Lukey had not been deceived by the evasion. He had grinned infuriatingly. 'Good show, Colonel. I'll tell my masters I'm getting full co-operation and all proper respect.'

'You can also tell them that if there's any hanky-panky here you'll be out on your ear, and pretty damn quick.'

It had been a feeble threat and Captain Lukey had known it. He had still been grinning when he left.

Colonel Soames had not forgotten the humiliation. He looked up sharply at Inspector Chow. 'Why Lukey?'

'He doesn't seem to have much money to spend, sir. I should think he could just about manage this deal though. Another thing. He's been trying to buy three-o-three ammunition. They must have rifles of that calibre already. It would make sense to buy more. Most of the stuff going about at present is three-o-o.'

'I see.' The Colonel was thoughtful for a moment, then he nodded. 'Put a man on to Tan Yam Heng. See if he tries to contact Lukey. Keep me posted.'

'Very good, sir.'

'What did you say that American's name was? Nilsen?'

'Yes, sir. Do you want me to . . . ?'

'No. I think I may look into that myself.'

2

Greg and Dorothy were enjoying Singapore. They had made two tours of the island and also crossed the causeway into Johore; and, although they had had to admit to themselves that there was not really all that much to see, they were so glad to be on their own again that it did not seem to matter. In any case, they were having fun arranging side trips. There was a Garuda Indonesian Airways flight that could take them down to Bali, and they had made provisional reservations for early the following week. The only snag was that they would have to have Indonesian tourist visas, and those took several days to get. Until those came through they would not know for certain what their plans were. So they had applied for the visas and decided that, if they did not come through in time, they would console themselves with a trip up to Penang. The man in Thos. Cook's had shown them some pictures of the island that made it look almost as enchanting as Bali.

The only area of dissension between them was that surrounding the Tan arms deal.

When Greg had, finally, explained it to her in detail, Dorothy had stared at him almost incredulously.

'But, darling, it sounds to me completely crooked.'

'What's crooked about it? It's just a question of helping Mr Tan to avoid a technicality in the Philippine law. Nothing more.'

'Well, that's something, isn't it? It's their law.'

'It wasn't made to cover this sort of eventuality.'

'What sort is that?'

'Well, I think the idea of selling Communist arms to the anti-Communists is a pretty good idea.'

'Maybe. But how do you know they *are* Communist arms? Who told you they were? How do you know he's telling the truth?'

It had been a long, inconclusive and uncomfortable discussion. One passage of it had stayed in his mind to trouble him later.

'Supposing someone back home had come to you with a proposition like this,' she had said.

'How could they?'

'But supposing they did. You know what? I think you'd call the police or the FBI.'

'Well, this isn't America, and the circumstances and the people are all entirely different.'

She had nodded calmly. 'That's just my point.'

'I don't get it.'

'Maybe we don't know *how* different they are.'

Their first encounter with Mr Tan Yam Heng in Singapore had not improved the situation. They had found his appearance unprepossessing and his manner furtive. Indeed, when he had contacted them on the boat, Greg had at first mistaken him for some sort of tout. Then, he had tried to hustle them through the immigration and customs before they had had a chance to say good-bye to anyone on the ship. Greg had had to be very firm.

Later, at the hotel, Tan had produced an airmail letter from Manila confirming that Greg would act as sole selling agent for Mr Tan Tack Chee, and revising their financial arrangements accordingly. That had been all right; but, although the letter had been addressed to Greg personally, Tan Yam Heng had already opened it and read the contents. When he had gone, Dorothy had raised her eyebrows.

'Not much like his brother, is he?'

'No.'

'Do you think opening other people's letters is an old Chinese custom?'

'Well, I don't suppose it matters. By the way, Mr Tan sends you and Arlene his best wishes.'

The meeting at the Customs House the following morning had been no more propitious. After Greg had signed the appropriate papers, they had gone outside.

'The next thing, Mr Nilsen,' Tan Yam Heng had said briskly, 'is for me to arrange meetings with buyers.'

Greg had smiled and shaken his head. 'No, Mr Tan. The next thing is for you to give me a cheque for one thousand and fifty dollars.'

'But that is not until you sign the papers transferring ownership of the goods. That is the arrangement.'

'That *was* the arrangement. You read your brother's letter. The arrangement is changed. The first five per cent is to be paid over on signature of the customs documents. The *second* five per cent will be paid when ownership is transferred to the actual buyer.'

It had been at that moment that Greg had understood why Mr Tan in Manila had been so anxious for him to act as his agent. Under the earlier arrangement, there would have been nothing to stop Mr Tan in Singapore from completing the blank transfer of ownership in his own favour. Under the new arrangement, ownership would only be transferred to the buyer. The explanation was simple. Mr Tan in Manila did not trust Mr Tan in Singapore; and probably for very good reasons.

Tan Yam Heng had scowled almost threateningly. 'Between associates in business enterprise,' he had said, 'there must be trust and personal dignity in all negotiations.'

'I couldn't agree more. And I think the best way of keeping that trust and personal dignity, Mr Tan, is for everyone to do just what they're agreed to do right along the line. No more, no less.'

Mr Tan Yam Heng had had the cheque, drawn on the Manila office of an American bank, ready in his pocket, and had handed it over in the end; but with a bad grace. He had left saying that he would telephone when he had arranged the meetings.

Since then, two days had elapsed and Greg had heard nothing. He had not told Dorothy about the argument over the cheque; nor had he thought it necessary to discuss with her his other misgivings. He was on the point of cabling to Mr Tan in Manila to remind him of the time limit they had agreed, when Tan Yam Heng called.

'Mr Nilsen,' he said, 'I have an interested buyer.'

'Oh.'

'He would like to meet with you and discuss the proposition.'

'Who is he?'

'A British Army captain, now acting for a group in Indonesia.'

'What sort of group?'

'I think it is religious.'

'What do you mean, religious?'

'Does it matter? We wish to sell, he wishes to buy.'

'It matters a great deal. Anyway, what's the man's name? How do I meet him?'

'His name is Captain Lukey, and, if convenient, I will bring him to your hotel this afternoon at five.'

'Okay.'

'And the price is agreed?'

'We ask seventy-five thousand, accept anything over sixty.'

'Yes. This is very confidential.'

'I'll see you at five.'

He told Dorothy.

'What's a religious group want with rifles and machine-guns?' she asked.

'How should I know? I don't think Tan knew what he was talking about. Anyway, there's a British officer acting for them, so they must be fairly respectable.'

'I suppose you'll have to see him alone.'

'You can stay in the bedroom and listen through the door, if you want.'

Tan Yam Heng arrived ten minutes early, and looking more furtive than ever.

'I wished,' he explained, 'to find the best route from the courtyard entrance to your suite. As soon as he arrives I will bring him straight here without telephoning from the reception desk first, if you agree.'

'It's all right with me.'

'The fewer people who see us together the better.'

'Why all the cloak and dagger stuff?'

'In such negotiations it is important to be secret. If some spy of the Indonesian Government got to know of this it would be dangerous.'

Greg avoided looking at Dorothy. 'I see.'

'Captain Lukey may wish to search the suite before discussions begin.'

'Well, he can't. My wife's going to be in the bedroom.'

'These are serious matters. I am sure Mrs Nilsen understands.'

'Look, there's not going to be any searching, and if the gallant Captain doesn't like it, he can do the other thing. How well do you know him?'

'I have talked to him.'

'Did he say he wanted to search the place?'

'No, but . . .'

'Then supposing we let him speak for himself. He'll be here in a minute. Now why don't you just go down and wait for him, Mr Tan.'

Tan Yam Heng went, sullenly. Twenty minutes later he returned with Captain Lukey.

The Captain was a tall man in the late forties with a slight paunch, a florid complexion, greying brown hair, and a large handlebar moustache stained on one side by nicotine. He wore the Singapore business uniform—white duck slacks, white long-sleeved shirt with breast pockets, and a regimental tie. He had a reverberating voice and a hearty manner. He came into the room with hand out-stretched.

'How do you do, Mr Nilsen? Sorry I'm late. Got held up in a spot of traffic.'

'Glad to know you, Captain,' said Greg. 'Won't you sit down?'

Captain Lukey seemed not to have heard the invitation. He smiled broadly, put his hands on his hips and looked round the room. 'Well now,' he said; 'the last time I was in this suite, General Blacklock had it. That was before he became C. in C. of course. I was his A.D.C. for a time. Rum bird, old Blackie.'

'Can I get you a drink?' Greg asked.

'Very handsome of you. I'll have a stengah if you don't mind.'

'That's scotch and soda, isn't it?'

'Little scotch, lot of soda. Got to keep the old water-works going in this climate.'

'Oh yes, I see.' Greg was having trouble placing Captain Lukey's accent. Behind the stage British there was another intonation that he could not identify. Colonel Soames could have told him that it came from Liverpool.

'You know,' said Captain Lukey, 'lots of people say business before pleasure.' He sat down heavily. 'Never been able to understand it myself. But then people say all sorts of things they've never thought about. They've got rule of thumb minds. The shortest distance between two points is a straight line. Agreed?'

'Agreed.'

'Is the hypotenuse of a right-angled triangle a straight line?'

'It is.'

'And the sum of the lengths of the other two sides is greater?'

'Yes.'

Captain Lukey gave him a cunning leer. 'Yet the *square* of the hypotenuse is *equal* to the sum of the squares of the other two sides. How do you account for that?'

'Euclid accounted for it quite satisfactorily.' Greg put some more soda in the Captain's drink. He was wondering if the man were as sober as he had at first appeared to be.

'Euclid!' The Captain laughed shortly, as if Greg had mentioned some long-discredited mutual acquaintance, and glanced over his shoulder at Tan Yam Heng. 'You never bothered your head about that sort of thing, eh, Tan?'

'I do not understand.' Tan Yam Heng had stationed himself in front of the door like a character in a trench coat melodrama.

The Captain eyed him sourly. 'I'll bet you don't. Shortest distances, maybe. Straight lines? Don't make me laugh.'

'Are you meaning to insult me, Captain?'

'Me? Perish the thought.'

Greg finished mixing the drinks and crossed over to them.

'Shall we talk business?' he said. There was a touch of impatience in his voice that he could not quite conceal.

Captain Lukey chuckled. 'That's what I like,' he said; 'American hustle. Okay, brother, where do we go from here? You name it.'

He was speaking now with what he evidently imagined to be an American accent.

Greg smiled. 'All right. I understand you're in the market for small arms and ammunition. Did Mr Tan show you a list of the stuff I have in bond here?'

'Yup,' said Captain Lukey sportively.

'He's told you the price?'

'Yup.'

'And I gather you're interested.'

'Nope.'

Greg stared at him coldly. 'Then, why are you here?'

'Because I just *might* become interested.' He had abandoned his American accent.

'In what circumstances?'

'Well, if the stuff were really new and not reconditioned, for instance.'

'You can inspect it.'

'And if you cut your asking price by fifty per cent, so that I could make a reasonable offer at something like the current market price.'

'There is no current market price.'

'Mr Nilsen, I'm just a simple soldier, but even I know better than that. I can buy rifles at twenty dollars apiece.'

'Then you should.'

'I'm not all that interested in rifles. Now, if you were to put a fair price on the machine pistols, we might talk. As it is . . .' He broke off, swallowed the rest of his drink and got to his feet. 'Tell you what. You think it over and we'll be in touch tomorrow. What do you say?'

'I might come down a little, but the price'll still be in the same range.'

Captain Lukey nodded, almost appreciatively. 'Well,' he said, 'there's no taste in nothing.'

Greg found the statement obscure, but he, too, nodded. The Captain wrung his hand and went, exuding goodwill.

The moment the door had shut Tan Yam Heng went to it, listened and then flung it open suddenly.

The corridor outside was empty. Tan shut the door again and turned to Greg.

'Of course, he is bluffing,' he said.

'How far? You did check the going prices thoroughly, I suppose?'

'Oh yes. If he does not come back to us it will only be because he does not have the money to pay.'

'What happens in that case?'

Tan looked shifty. 'There is another buyer, but he is away in Macao at present.'

'When's he coming back?'

'Next week, perhaps.'

'Well, he won't find me here. All right, Mr Tan, we'll check in the morning.'

When he had gone Dorothy came out of the bedroom.

'What a curious man,' she said. 'Do you think he really is a British officer?'

'Why not? I've met some pretty curious American officers in my time. Why shouldn't the British Army have some dogs, too.'

The telephone rang. Greg answered it.

'Mr Nilsen?' It was Captain Lukey.

'Yes.'

'I'm speaking from downstairs. I wonder if I could slip up and see you again for a tick.'

'Very well.'

'Be up in a brace of shakes.'

Greg looked at Dorothy. 'Lukey again.'

'I'll go back into the bedroom.'

'No, you stay here.'

Captain Lukey returned looking bland and businesslike. When he saw Dorothy, however, he became stickily gallant.

'Well, this is a delightful surprise. I'd no idea.'

Dorothy said: 'How do you do, Captain?'

The Captain did not miss the lack of warmth in her tone. 'Terribly sorry to butt in like this, Mrs Nilsen. Frightfully bad form, but I did want another word with your good husband. Ghastly shop talk I'm afraid.'

Dorothy sat down. 'That's quite all right, Captain.'

'I'm afraid Tan's not here,' said Greg.

'I know. Saw him go.' The Captain smiled boyishly. 'As a matter of fact I waited downstairs until he did.'

'Oh?'

'Mind if I sit down?'

'Do.'

'You see, it was a bit awkward.'

'What was?'

The Captain smoothed his moustache. 'Well, it's a funny sort of game, this. I didn't know quite what to expect here. No offence meant, of course. As soon as I met you I knew that you were a good type.' He hesitated.

'But . . . ?' said Greg encouragingly.

'Well, as I say, it's awkward.' Captain Lukey gave the impression of a simple man wrestling with an unfamiliar problem in ethics. 'I'm no saint myself, and if you tell me to run along and mind my own confounded business, I'll understand, but I do think white men ought to stick together a bit. Nothing against Asians, mind you, but well sometimes . . .' He broke off, his pale, anxious eyes searching Greg's face for understanding.

'Captain, if you'll just tell me what you're talking about.'

The Captain turned apologetically to Dorothy. 'So sorry about all this, Mrs Nilsen.'

Dorothy smiled sweetly. 'Oh, I'm just as interested as my husband.'

The Captain did not seem reassured. He went on with knitted brow. 'Well, it's awkward, you see,' he said again; and then appeared to make up his mind. 'Look, Nilsen, man to man, how long have you known this fellow Tan?'

'Three days. Why?'

'I see. Thought it might be like that.'

'Like what?'

'Nilsen, I'm not asking you how you came to meet him or who put him in touch with you or who recommended him as a contact man.' He paused and then added somewhat unexpectedly: 'Ask no questions and you'll be told no lies, I always say.'

Greg shrugged. 'I may not answer your questions, Captain, but I'm certainly not going to lie to you.'

'Very decent of you to put it that way.' Captain Lukey seemed genuinely pleased.

'Is it?'

'Frankness begets frankness, Nilsen. So I'll be frank with you. How much do you know about Tan?'

'Very little.'

'Do you know what he does for a living?'

'Import-export—at least that's what I gathered.'

'Did he tell you that?'

'Not in so many words, no.'

'What would you say if I told you that he ran a labour protection racket down at the docks?'

'How do you know?'

'Made inquiries about him. You see I know most of the people in this business. Part of my job. I didn't know you and I didn't know him. Could have been a trap.'

'A what?'

The Captain looked surprised. 'Well, of course. Naturally the Indonesian Government knows what's going on. You know as well as I do that they've only got a few old destroyers and gun boats to patrol a huge area. They can't stop more than a fraction of the stuff getting through. So, naturally, they go for our weak spot.'

'What's that?'

'Money. If they can get me tied up in a phony deal they will.'

'I'm afraid I don't get it. Are you suggesting I'm operating a phony deal?'

'Good God no! Please don't misunderstand. This is nothing personal.'

'Then what's the problem? You inspect the stuff first. You don't pay until you take delivery, do you?'

'No. But I take delivery in bond. As soon as I start to move it, things happen. First some cheap lawyer comes along and claims that the goods have been obtained by trickery and gets a court order holding them. By the time that's straightened out, there's some other stooge claiming that all the ammunition is phony, and that instead of having cordite inside them the cartridges are loaded with morphine. So then the narcotics people have a go. And so on.'

'But the stuff gets there in the end.'

'If you're lucky.'

'But you said yourself that the Indonesian Government can't maintain an effective patrol.'

'If they know exactly when the stuff is going, the size of the consignment, and the approximate delivery area, they've got at least a fifty-fifty chance of intercepting it. It stands to reason.'

'You said money was the weak spot.'

'You don't know these people, Nilsen.'

'What people?'

'The people I work for. Oh, they're good types in lots of ways, but when they pay out money that's something special.'

'Who are they? Tan said something about their being a religious group.'

'They're devout Muslims if that's what you mean. Most of the anti-Communists are. That doesn't mean they're not tough though. Life and death don't mean much to them. They'd kill a man or be killed themselves without turning a hair. But they're funny when it comes to money. If things go badly they give up.'

'And you think Tan's working for the Indonesian Government?'

'I don't know. In my opinion he's the type who'd work for anyone who paid enough. Anyway, I don't want to risk it.'

'Then you don't want to deal?'

'I didn't say that. I said I don't want to deal with Tan.'

'But Tan already knows about all this. If what you say is true, he can cause just as much trouble whoever deals.'

'Not if you're the principal. Are these goods bonded in your name?'

'They are.'

'Then we don't need Tan at all.'

Greg was silent. He was inclined to believe what the Captain had said, or some of it anyway; and his own instincts were against having business dealings of any kind with Mr Tan. Unfortunately, they were almost equally against having dealings with Captain Lukey. And there was the overriding complication of the fact that he was not in reality a principal at all, but an agent. To some extent he was deceiving Captain Lukey. He temporized.

'I'll have to think about that, Captain.'

'Sure. Don't get me wrong–' the Captain was Americanizing again–'I'm not trying to pressure you, old boy.'

The sudden lapse into British made Greg smile. 'Oh, I didn't think you were, Captain,' he said hastily.

His smile and his tone of voice combined to create an effect he had not intended.

'No need to apologize,' said Captain Lukey cheerfully. He suddenly snapped his fingers. 'I tell you what. Have you and Madame made any plans for the evening?'

Greg looked quickly at Dorothy. 'Well, we . . .'

But it was too late. The Captain swept on enthusiastically. 'I tell you what. Why don't we stop talking shop now and all go out to dinner, the four of us?'

'Four?' For one wild moment Greg thought that the Captain was proposing to include Tan in the invitation.

'I know my good lady will be dying to meet you. She's mad about America. Do you like Indian food? I mean the real stuff, not those ghastly Madras curries the planters ruin their livers on. There's a little restaurant we found where it's absolutely the real thing. You know India, of course?'

'Well, no. But I'm sure you don't want to . . .'

'Then that's settled, then.' The Captain smiled broadly at them both. 'Sorry to butt in again like this. Supposing I pick you up at seven. No jackets. Just a tie. We might have a spot of the cup that cheers first.'

He gave them a mock salute and left.

Greg looked at Dorothy. 'Sorry, darling,' he said, 'I didn't think fast enough.'

But Dorothy did not seem unduly put out. 'Well, at least we'll go somewhere we wouldn't have been to on our own,' she said. 'I wonder what Mrs Lukey's like.'

Promptly at seven, Captain Lukey called up from the lobby and they went downstairs. He was alone.

'Left my good lady outside in the taxi,' he explained.

It was dark and Mrs Lukey was sitting in the shadows at the back of the taxi; but even in the brief glimpse Greg had of her as they were introduced, he saw that she was strikingly beautiful. Her husband got in beside the driver and told him to go to the Cathay Hotel. On the way there he talked almost continuously, identifying buildings which they could not see, and having rapid conversations in Malay with the driver which they did not understand. Dorothy, sitting next to Mrs Lukey, exchanged one or two brief courtesies with her. From her English, which was fluent but over-precise, Greg deduced that Mrs Lukey was not British. It was not until they were in the elevator which took them up to the Cathay Hotel bar, that he saw her clearly.

She had dark hair, cut short, and a long face with a delicate, high-cheeked bone structure that reminded him of a bust of Queen Nefertiti which he had seen illustrated in *Life*. Her skin was pale without being pallid. She wore no powder and very little lipstick. Her figure was slender, with a small waist that the flared silk skirt she was wearing made seem even smaller. Only her legs were disappointing. Greg thought them too straight and shapeless. Nevertheless she was an exquisite creature and it was difficult to understand how she had been captivated by Captain Lukey. Beside her, he looked oafish and gross. She smiled readily, revealing excellent teeth. However, the smile did not reach her eyes, and at those moments she became less beautiful. It was possible, Greg thought, that she had a dull mind.

Her husband was an overpowering host. He drank deeply and talked incessantly, mostly about people whom he had known in South Africa and Egypt. Many of the stories he told seemed pointless to Greg, until he realized that, in deference to Dorothy, and possibly also to his own wife, the Captain was censoring his tongue. He was the kind of man who has a stock of anecdotes packed away in his mind like the contents of a kit-bag; he cannot rummage about and select what he wants, everything must be pulled out as it comes to hand, dirty clothes as well as clean. It was noticeable, too, as the evening progressed, that the social pretensions of those who peopled his memories became more and more modest. Brother army officers, generals, senior civil servants, important business men and embassy attachés gradually gave way to sergeant-majors, canteen managers, stewards, bartenders and seedy men encountered in pubs. Captain Lukey's accent also deteriorated, or at least changed; earthier tones and racier speech rhythms replacing the plummy affectations of the afternoon. Greg and Dorothy found him easier to understand, and, as some of his stories were quite funny, even began to warm to him. Captain Lukey the officer and gentleman might verge on the odious, but Lukey the soldier of fortune was not unengaging.

The Indian restaurant was in a street off Orchard Road. It was small and squalid. The waiters were Indians wearing dhotis and striped shirts with the tails hanging out. They spread sheets of white wrapping paper on the table instead of a cloth. A single fan stirred the warm, curry-laden air. There were a great many flies. Greg made up his mind that the first thing he and Dorothy would do when they got back to the hotel would be to take full doses of the Entero-Vioforme which they had bought in Saigon.

Mrs Lukey ordered dinner in a language which she told Dorothy was Urdu. It took a long time to prepare, and Captain Lukey had drunk four more stengahs and paid two visits to the toilet before it arrived. There were four dishes, two of them curries, and a bowl of boiled Patna rice. To Greg's surprise, it was all delicious. He often ate curried dishes; the University Club in Wilmington always had curried shrimps or curried turkey on the lunch menu; but he had never tasted curries like these. They were hot, but not harsh, and there were undertones of flavour that he could not begin to identify.

'In the west you use curry powder already made,' Mrs Lukey explained. 'Here, the spices are ground fresh and mixed according to the needs of the dish. In this case, for instance, there is less turmeric and more cumin. That is what you taste.'

A plate of Indian condiments was put on the table. Among the seeds and sauces and shredded coconut, there were sliced bananas.

'If a curry is too hot,' said Mrs Lukey, 'you add sliced banana and it becomes milder.'

'You mean it seems milder?'

'No. It *is* milder. I do not understand why. Some say it is the juice of the banana. Try.'

Dorothy tried and was impressed.

Mrs Lukey smiled. 'Some curries are so hot,' she said, 'that even I could not eat them without banana, even though I have lived many years in India.'

The Captain, returning from yet another visit to the toilet, overheard her.

'If you think this is a good curry,' he said, 'you wait until you taste Betty's. She's a wonderful cook.'

This was the first time they had heard Mrs Lukey's first name. The Captain's endearments, which had ranged from 'darling', through 'the mem-sahib', to 'old girl', had not hitherto included it.

Suddenly the Captain slapped the table. 'I tell you what. One night you must come over to our place and have a binge. The old girl will cook and if we can still move afterwards we'll have a rubber of bridge. You play bridge?'

Greg admitted that they did.

'Then, it's a date. As a matter of fact, why don't we go back now and have a drink. It's only a furnished place we've taken while we look around, but it's not all that bad, and at least we'll be able to drink some decent whisky.'

Greg had opened his mouth to hedge, but Dorothy spoke first. 'I think that would be a lovely idea,' she said.

The Lukeys' apartment was a few minutes' walk from the restaurant. It was over an electrical appliance showroom and was approached by a long steep stairway at the side. The living-room had pale green walls and contained a polished teak table and some bamboo-framed lounge chairs. In one corner there was a card table with some papers and a desk pad on it. Light came from a frosted glass ceiling fitting. The effect was bleak.

'Make yourselves at home,' said the Captain. Going to a wardrobe in the small hallway, he got out bottles and glasses.

Dorothy and Mrs Lukey retired to the bedroom. Greg sat down in one of the lounge chairs.

'You know,' Captain Lukey continued as he made the drinks, 'the trouble with my job is that you never know where you're going to be next. Can't put down any roots.'

'I suppose not.' Greg had not thought of the Captain's occupation as one about which it was possible to generalize in such terms. Acting as purchasing agent for Sumatran insurgent forces scarcely seemed the basis of a career. Whether the insurgents won or lost, their need for a foreign representative with Captain Lukey's special qualifications seemed bound eventually to disappear; and, while there might be other insurgent forces in other parts of the world who could use his services when available, the business of contacting them would be hazardous as well as difficult. The Captain did not strike him as being a particularly robust type of adventurer. 'How did you come to get into the job?' he asked.

'Oh, I don't know. Friends, influence.' The Captain grinned. 'Never could stand the ordinary desk job. "Sing ho for the open road", that's me.' He reached for the soda siphon. 'Say when.'

'That's enough, thanks.' Greg went over and took the drink.

'Yes, always on the go.' The Captain shook his head ruefully. 'Take next week now. I'll probably have to go off to Macao for a few days.'

'On business?'

'You can bet your sweet life I wouldn't go for pleasure.'

Greg was beginning to understand the Captain. When dissembling he had the too artless look of a boy telling a lie.

'I shouldn't have thought there'd be much for you there at the moment,' he said casually. 'My information is that the buyers are all moving in here.'

The Captain looked at him quickly. 'The Dutchman's still there.'

'I'm only telling you what I heard.'

The Captain stared at him gloomily for a moment and then, with a visible effort, relaxed. 'No shop in the mess,' he said. 'Cost you drinks all round in the old days. All the same, I'd like to know where we stand pretty soon. About Tan, for instance, you said you'd think it over. How long do you want?'

'Twenty-four hours.'

'Cards on the table, Nilsen. Got another buyer on ice?'

'Could be.' Greg was enjoying this.

'Is he dealing with Tan?'

'Look, I said I want twenty-four hours to think it over. Until tomorrow evening. I'd like to deal with you, Captain, and as long as there's no misunderstanding about price range, I'm sure we can work something out. If you want to save time, you can arrange with Tan to inspect the stuff at the warehouse in the morning.'

'I told you. I don't want to deal with Tan.'

'He's merely holding the customs documents at present. You wouldn't be committing yourself to anything.'

'All right. As long as we understand one another.'

The women came out of the bedroom and the Captain returned to his reminiscences. Soon, Greg and Dorothy left.

As they were walking to the taxi rank by the Cathay Greg told her about his brief business discussion.

'You know,' he added, 'I'm a bit sorry for that man.'

Dorothy laughed.

'Oh, I know he's a phony,' Greg said; 'all that gobbledy-gook he talks, all those stories, all that false bonhomie.'

'And all those trips to the men's room.'

'It's not his fault if he has a weak bladder.'

'He shouldn't drink so much.'

'I think he's a pretty depressed character. I think he has to have a few drinks to stay in one piece. You know he wants those arms badly and tried to pretend that he didn't. It was pathetic, bush league stuff. It made me feel like a con man.'

'Famous last words.'

'All right. We'll see.'

They walked on in silence for a moment or two. 'I liked her,' said Dorothy.

'Yes, what about that! How in the world did he do it? She looks like something out of *Vogue*. Do you think she really likes him?'

'Oh yes.'

'Attraction of opposites, I suppose. What nationality is she? Betty sounds British enough, but she's got a funny sort of accent.'

Dorothy glanced at him wonderingly. 'You mean you didn't get it?'

'Get what?'

'She's Eurasian.'

'She's what?'

'Well, Anglo-Indian she called it. Her mother came from Bombay. She didn't say much, but I think it must have been very important to her to marry an Englishman.'

Even that one?'

'I told you. She's very fond of him.'

He drew her arm through his. 'I'm glad we came on this trip together,' he said.

Dorothy smiled.

When they got back to the hotel, there was a message for Greg. Mr Lane Harvey of the American Syndicated Wire Service had telephoned, and would call again in the morning.

Before he went to sleep that night, Greg booked a person-to-person call to Mr Tan Tack Chee in Manila.

3

While they were at breakfast the following morning, the Singapore overseas operator called to say that Mr Tan was not then in Manila but was expected back that afternoon. Greg placed a call for 4.00 p.m. Manila time.

Just as he put the telephone down, it rang again.

'Mr Nilsen? This is Lane Harvey, American Syndicated Wire Service.'

'Yes?'

'You're from Wilmington, Delaware, I believe.'

'That's right.'

'And you have a die-casting business there?'

'Yes. What's all this about? The plant hasn't burned down, has it?'

Mr Harvey chuckled. 'No, nothing like that. It's just that I'd like to send back a story on you, if you could spare me half an hour sometime today.'

'Well, yes, of course. But, Mr Harvey, it's not a very big plant you know, and I'm not an important man. Mrs Nilsen and I are just tourists stopping over for a few days. I don't want to waste your time.'

'Mr Nilsen, you wouldn't be wasting my time. That's the very reason I want to talk to you. More Americans are travelling now than ever before. New York's doing a survey on the problems they run into, what they don't like, what they do like, and so on. We don't get many stopping over here in Singapore, so if you could spare the time I'd be grateful.'

'Okay, if you think it's worth it. When do you suggest?'

'Well, let's see. Are you doing anything for lunch?'

'I don't think so.'

'Then why don't you and Mrs Nilsen come along to the American Club?'

'Well, that's very kind of you, but . . .'

'Mr Nilsen, I've got to try and justify my expense account sometimes.'

Greg laughed. 'All right, Mr Harvey.'

'Twelve-thirty then? I'll send the office car for you.'

'We can take a cab.'

'No trouble. The car'll pick you up at twelve-thirty.'

Greg gave Dorothy the gist of the conversation.

'Isn't it a bit unusual?' she said. 'Why doesn't he just come over here?'

'I don't know. Perhaps that's the way they like to do things in Singapore.'

Lane Harvey was a balding man of about forty with an unhealthy complexion and sleepy eyes. He spoke slowly and carefully, as if he were under some pressure that he was striving to ignore, or as if he were listening all the time to the voice of a doctor telling him to relax or suffer the consequences.

'For a wire service man,' he said, 'this place is Siberia. Politically South-East Asia is one of the most important areas in the world. In Viet-Nam, Laos, Cambodia, Thailand, Sumatra, Java, the Islands, everywhere around, there's history being made. But all around. Not in Singapore. We're in the eye of the storm here.'

'So all you have to do is interview American tourists,' said Dorothy. 'It's a shame.'

Lane Harvey smiled. 'I'll tell you a secret, Mrs Nilsen. It's more comfortable here than those other places, and I like being comfortable. But an American correspondent who doesn't wail for the dangers and discomforts of the battle-front is guilty of unprofessional conduct.' He signalled to the waiter for another round of drinks. 'Now tell me about your trip.'

Greg began to do so. Lane Harvey listened attentively, nodding understandingly now and then, but asked no questions. After a few minutes, Greg, beginning to hear the sound of his own voice droning on, broke off.

'Look, Mr Harvey, this must be very boring for you.'

'No, no.'

'Isn't there something else we can talk about?'

'You've given me just what I wanted.' He looked across the ranch-style patio. 'By the way, I hope you don't mind. I asked someone else to join us for lunch. He's very British, pukka sahib and all that, but he knows a lot about Singapore. You might find him interesting.'

A lean, grey-haired man with a long, narrow head and a receding chin, was advancing across the patio towards them. He was one of the few men there wearing a jacket. He came up to the table.

'Hullo, Harvey. Hope I'm not late.'

'Not a bit. Sit down and have a drink. Mr and Mrs Nilsen, this is Colonel Soames.

Over lunch, Lane Harvey insisted on telling the Colonel all about their trip, the details of which he recalled with remarkable accuracy. Greg became embarrassed.

'Now wait a minute,' he said. 'Thousands of Americans must do this trip every year. There's nothing special about it.'

'Yes, but we ought to do more about them in Singapore,' said the Colonel.

'All we get as a rule are the transient passengers off the boats. They buy a few batik sarongs and that's the end of it. Now you, for instance. What made you decide to stay in Singapore? It would be interesting to know.'

Greg glanced at Dorothy and grinned. 'We were escaping,' he said.

The Colonel looked startled. 'Indeed?'

'From the ship's bore.'

'Oh now, that isn't fair,' Dorothy protested. 'Arlene may have been difficult, but she wasn't a bore.' She turned to the Colonel. 'You see we were going on to Calcutta, but, well, we thought it might be better to get off here and take a side trip. Anyway, there was some business Greg wanted to attend to here, so it fitted in quite well.'

The waiter came over and said something to Lane Harvey. He got up apologetically. 'Call from New York,' he said. 'I'll only be a few minutes but don't you wait for me, please.'

He left them. The Colonel nodded genially.

'Nothing like combining business with pleasure,' he remarked.

'Harvey was saying that you knew a lot about Singapore,' Greg said. 'Are you in the tourist business here?'

The Colonel began eating his steak. 'I suppose you might call it that,' he replied.

'Then I expect you know quite a lot of the local people.'

The Colonel shrugged. 'Big place, Singapore,' he said. 'Over a million now. Mostly Chinese of course.'

'I suppose you don't happen to know of a Chinese named Tan Yam Heng?'

Dorothy said: 'Oh, darling, I don't think you ought to bother the Colonel with all that.'

'No bother, Mrs Nilsen,' the Colonel said cheerfully. 'As a matter of fact I do happen to know the chap. Trade union organizer. That the one you mean?'

'Well, I heard it put a little more crudely,' Greg said.

'Labour thug?'

'Something like that.'

'Who told you?'

'A Captain Lukey. Perhaps you know him, too?'

'Met him, yes. Having trouble with Tan?'

'It's a long story. I won't bother you with it. Captain Lukey doesn't want to deal with Tan. I wondered why. You confirm what Lukey said. That answers the question. I'm much obliged to you.'

The Colonel gave him a toothy grin. 'Could be another answer though, couldn't there?'

'How do you mean?'

'You're selling something?'

'Yes.'

'Lukey wants to buy?'

'Yes.'

'And Tan Yam Heng's the contact man?'

'Yes.'

'Could be that Tan's trying to get a commission out of Lukey as well as you, couldn't it?' The Colonel smeared English mustard on a large piece of steak and popped it into his mouth.

Greg stared. 'But . . .' he began, then stopped. The possibility had simply not occurred to him.

The Colonel chewed for a moment or two and then swallowed. 'Squeeze,' he said. 'Old Chinese custom.'

'But why didn't Lukey tell me that?'

'Might think you already knew. Might think you didn't want to know. Might think a lot of things. What's your impression of Lukey?'

'I only met him yesterday. We had dinner. Do you happen to know anything about these people he represents?'

The Colonel shrugged. 'They're called the Army of the Independent Party of the Faithful,' he said. 'All I know about them is that their Committee seems to have some sense of self-preservation.'

'Oh?'

'They don't allow Lukey to sign cheques on his own. One of them has to counter-sign. Met that chichi wife of his?'

'Chichi, Colonel?' Dorothy said. 'What does that mean?'

'Indian slang for Eurasian, Mrs Nilsen.' He grinned. ' "Anglo-Indians" as they like to call themselves nowadays.'

The diversion had given Greg time to think. 'Colonel,' he said, 'you told us that your business was with tourists. You didn't mean that quite literally, did you?'

'I said you could call it that.'

'What are you really? Police of some kind?'

'I work for the Government, yes.'

'And this little party was prearranged, I take it.' Greg's smile was wide but hostile.

The Colonel nodded. 'We try to do these things in a friendly fashion.'

'What things? Is there something wrong, Colonel?'

'Wrong?' He appeared to consider the adjective. 'That rather depends upon your point of view, doesn't it? Of course there are some cranks who think that gun-running and the arms traffic are evil things in themselves, ethically indefensible. I think that's a lot of nonsense myself. In your country and mine the people can change their governments, if they want to, by voting. But there are a lot of places where it takes a revolution to do that. Look at Cuba. If somebody hadn't supplied that fellow Castro with arms, Batista would still be a dictator. Some people might say that those gun-runners deserved a vote of thanks. Take Sumatra. The people there are afraid that Java's going to go Communist. They want to secede from Indonesia before that happens. Maybe they're right. Sumatra could be a self-supporting country. There are quite a few people here who think that she might one day join the Federation of Malaya. But, whatever they do, they'll have to win their independence first. They won't do that with words. Mind you, these are only my personal views.'

'Do they conflict with your official views, Colonel?'

The Colonel shook his head. 'No, Mr Nilsen, they don't. And for a very simple reason. I have no official views. I am not entitled to any. My job is to obey orders. The British Government recognizes the Indonesian Government, and is in normal, friendly, diplomatic relations with it. That means that we don't like to add to its difficulties by helping its enemies. At the moment, that means you.'

'Well, that's certainly laying it on the line, Colonel.'

'I'll go further.' The Colonel took a cigar case from his pocket and offered it to Greg.

Greg shook his head. 'No thanks.'

The Colonel took a cigar for himself and glanced inquiringly at Dorothy. 'Do you mind, Mrs Nilsen?'

'Not in the least.' Dorothy's tone was icy.

'You were going further, Colonel,' said Greg.

'Yes. I should tell you that I was considering having you deported.'

'I beg your pardon.'

'Making false statements to the immigration authorities is a serious offence.'

'False statements? What the hell are you talking about?'

'Steady, darling,' Dorothy said quietly.

Greg took no notice. He was glaring across the table at the Colonel.

The Colonel stared back coldly. 'Nature of visit—tourism. Isn't that what you told the the immigration inspector?'

'Of course. It happened to be the truth.'

'No. Only part of the truth. You are also here dealing in arms.'

'Oh, for God's sake! Look, I also had a letter from the man I left in charge of my plant back in America. I even replied to it. So I'm in the die-casting business here, too.'

'There's no point in losing your temper, Mr Nilsen, and it's bad for the digestion. I said I had considered deporting you. Of course, now that I have met you and Mrs Nilsen I have no doubt of your good faith.'

'Is that intended as a compliment, Colonel?'

'No, reassurance.'

'The American Consul will be glad to hear that.'

The Colonel smiled. 'You can't threaten me with your Consul. I know him very well, and he doesn't have much patience with empty indignation.'

'How does he feel about petty officiousness?'

'If I'd wanted to be officious, Mr Nilsen, we would not be sitting at this table, but in my office. I don't expect you to like what I'm saying, but I think you might try to understand the political reasons for it. Singapore is a free port and a centre of international trade. I admit that legally there is nothing to stop you or anyone else using its warehouse facilities as you are using them. But we don't like it, and you can't expect us to welcome your presence here.' He smiled at Dorothy. 'I'm speaking officially, of course, Mrs Nilsen.'

'But you don't disapprove of selling arms to anti-Communists,' demanded Greg.

'Personally, not in the least.'

Greg laughed shortly. 'You change hats rather easily, don't you, Colonel?' he said, and had the satisfaction of seeing the Colonel redden.

'I'm sorry you think that,' he said stiffly. He looked at his watch. 'I think it's time I was getting back to my office.'

The look at the watch was evidently some sort of signal, for, almost immediately, Lane Harvey returned to the table.

'Sorry to have to leave you like that,' he said when the Colonel had gone. 'You know how it is.'

'Yes,' said Greg acidly. 'The Colonel explained.'

Lane Harvey was unembarrassed. He even grinned. 'Funny old guy, isn't he,' he said. 'I thought you'd like him.'

4

Late that afternoon, Inspector Chow interviewed the driver of the American Syndicated Wire Service car. Then, he reported to Colonel Soames.

'They went straight back from the American Club to the Raffles Hotel. The man was expecting a telephone call from Manila. The driver had no difficulty in hearing their conversation.'

'Well?'

'The man was very angry, sir.'

'I imagine he was.'

'With Mr Harvey, mainly. He used strong language and talked of reporting the incident to Mr Harvey's superiors in New York, with a view to having him dismissed.'

'He'll think better of that.'

'Yes, sir. He spoke of humiliation and feeling ridiculous. He also apologized to the woman and talked of forgetting the whole deal. That was a reference to the arms, I take it.'

'Pulling out, eh? Good show. I was pretty sure he was an amateur.'

'Later, sir, he changed his mind.'

'Oh?'

'The woman said that he had a business obligation to Captain Lukey.'

Colonel Soames stared. 'Mrs Nilsen said that? Are you sure?'

'That is what the driver reports, sir.'

'But she was on my side right from the start. I could see it.'

'According to the driver, sir, Mrs Nilsen made some highly unfavourable remarks about you. She appeared to think that you had insulted Mrs Lukey.'

'I?' Colonel Soames was genuinely bewildered. 'I only asked her if she'd met the woman.'

'Yes, sir.' Inspector Chow's face was quite expressionless. 'It appeared that you used the word "chichi".'

'What about it? She asked what it meant. I told her.'

'She appeared to think that it was equivalent to using the word "jigaboo" in America.'

'What the hell does that mean?'

'I don't know, sir, but I assume that it must be something to do with the race question.' Inspector Chow hesitated. 'The woman used one very unladylike phrase.'

'Well?'

Colonel Soames could not be quite certain, but he thought he detected a hint of relish in Inspector Chow's tone as he answered.

'She said you were a bigoted old bastard, sir.'

Chapter Six

I

The call to Manila came through on time.

Greg was still out of temper, and cut through Mr Tan's preliminary courtesies almost brusquely.

'Mr Tan, I'll come to the point. The prospective buyer doesn't want to deal through your brother.'

'Oh. Does he give a reason?'

'He says he doesn't trust him, but I have an idea that that's not the real reason.'

'I see. And what do you think the real reason is, Mr Nilsen?'

'Are you paying your brother a commission?'

'Of course.'

'Well, I think he's trying to make the buyer pay him a commission for the introduction as well.'

There was a pause. 'What do you propose, Mr Nilsen?'

'That I negotiate on my own with the buyer, and that you tell your brother to behave himself.'

'Leaving everything in your hands, Mr Nilsen?'

'You're covered. Your brother has the customs documents. He can hold on to those as security.'

There was another pause before Mr Tan said: 'Very well. I will cable to my brother.'

'Today?'

'At once. It is a pleasure to do business with you, Mr Nilsen.'

At five o'clock there was a call from Captain Lukey.

'Did you inspect the stuff?' Greg asked him.

'Yes. It seemed pretty fair. What about Tan?'

'He's taken care of.'

'Good show.'

'Do you want to talk business?'

'Be over in a jiffy.'

Despite his admitted eagerness to buy, the Captain proved to be a stubborn bargainer. It took an hour and three stengahs to force his price up to fifty thousand dollars. His method of haggling was to isolate two items, the machine pistols and the bazookas, admit their worth, and then insist on putting a nominal valuation on the remaining items. He wore a tortured expression throughout, gnawed steadily at his moustache as if it were hurting him, and covered sheets of hotel stationery with pointless calculations. In the end Greg became impatient.

'Captain, we're not getting anywhere. Sixty-five thousand is rock bottom. If you don't want the stuff just say so.'

'But if we disregard the rifles . . .'

'Well, let's not disregard them. They're there and that's the price.'

Eventually, at sixty-two thousand five hundred, there was a meeting of the minds. When they had shaken hands on the deal the Captain grinned.

'I'd have paid sixty-five if you'd stuck out.'

'Well, I'd have gone down to sixty if you'd stuck out,' Greg replied, 'so we're both happy. Now, about terms. Cash on delivery of course. Okay?'

'Okay.'

'Good. If you'll get a certified cheque made out and meet me at the Customs House tomorrow morning, we'll square it all away.'

The Captain stared at him indignantly. 'I'm afraid I can't do that, old boy.'

'Why not?'

'Well, I'm only the liaison officer, the agent. I have to follow the drill.'

'What drill?'

'Well, I told you. Those people are funny about money. They like to do the paying out themselves.'

'As long as it's clearly understood that the stuff stays where it is until I have sixty-two thousand five hundred dollars in my hand, I don't care who does the paying.'

'You needn't worry about that, old boy. They want that stuff and the sooner the better. This is how we handle it. I give you a draft on the Hong Kong and Shanghai Bank, made out but unsigned. It requires two signatures, mine and a member of the Central Committee's. When you present that cheque to him, he knows that I've inspected the stuff and agreed the price. He signs. Then, you and I go down to the Customs House, you sign the transfer, I countersign the cheque and Bob's your uncle.'

'Will the cheque be certified?'

'We can go to the bank and cash it first if you like.'

'Well, it sounds unnecessarily complicated to me, but if that's the way they want it, okay. Where do I see this Committee man?'

'In Labuanga.'

'Where's that?'

'Oh, it's only half an hour or so by air. Anyway, my good lady will arrange all that side of it.' He spoke rather too airily. Greg was suddenly suspicious.

'Where is it?'

'Just across the other side of the straits opposite Penang.'

'In Sumatra?'

'Well, naturally.'

Greg took a deep breath. 'Now wait a minute. Why didn't you say something about this before? I'm not going gallivanting off into the wilds of Sumatra in order to get a cheque signed.'

'Labuanga isn't in the wilds, old boy,' the Captain said patiently. 'It's a coast town with its own airport and a hotel. Pretty little place as a matter of fact.'

'I don't care how pretty it is.'

'But that's the drill. There's nothing to it really. It's always worked out fine. Don't misunderstand, old boy. I'm not asking you to pay your own expenses.'

'I tell you it's out of the question. Quite apart from anything else, I don't have an Indonesian visa.'

'Well, that's easily fixed.'

'Is it? I understood it took a week.'

The Captain threw up his hands in exasperation. 'Old boy, this isn't my idea. You want cash on delivery, Singapore. All right. Cash it is. I'm not arguing about that. But you've got to look at things from their point of view. They've been let down before now, and they like to know who they're dealing with. You only have to go the first time. After that it's plain sailing.'

'Don't they trust you?'

'Of course they trust me. I tell them what to buy and what they ought to pay. They just finalize the first deal.'

'Well, I don't like it. If you can't produce the money here without this drill, as you call it, the deal's off.'

The Captain drew himself up. 'I'm sorry, old boy, but I can't accept that. I thought we shook hands on it.'

'We didn't shake hands on a trip to Sumatra.'

'Old boy,' the Captain said wearily, 'there's a plane every day. You can be there and back in twenty-four hours. It's perfectly simple. Betty goes along with you, calls up when you get there, arranges the meeting, and takes you to it. You don't have to bother about a thing. Take Dorothy along with you for the ride, if you like.'

'I don't get this. Why does your wife have to go? Why don't you go yourself?'

'I would, but the Indonesians won't give me a visa anymore.'

'Why not?'

'Naturally, they know what I'm up to.'

'But they let your wife in?'

'She's got her passport in her maiden name. As a matter of fact she looks forward to these little trips. Makes a change for her. Look, old boy,' he went on persuasively, 'you admit the deal's a good one for you. All I'm asking you to do is finalize it.'

'You could have said something about this before.'

'It never occurred to me that you'd object, old boy. Most of you chaps are popping in and out all the time.'

'Well, I'm not.'

'A half-hour plane trip, that's all. Surely, old boy . . .'

'All right, all right,' Greg snapped irritably, 'I'll think about it.'

'I'll have to know tomorrow. They're waiting to hear about this stuff.' He was looking tortured again.

'I understand.'

The Captain smiled bitterly, shook his head, sighed, finished his stengah, and went.

Dorothy came out of the bedroom.

'You heard?' Greg said.

'Yes. Do you think he meant that if I went with you he'd pay my expenses too?'

Greg chuckled. 'I wonder. The Colonel was certainly right about his needing a counter-signature on cheques. What a way to do business?'

'What will you do?'

'I'm darned if I know. The trouble is that, as Mr Tan's appointed agent, I'm virtually the legal owner as far as Singapore Customs are concerned. If I don't sell it to Lukey what happens? After all, I do have an obligation to Tan. I can't just do nothing at this stage. As for that crooked brother of his, I'd be crazy if I expected him to find another buyer while I'm around to stop him picking up two commissions. It's got to be Lukey.'

Dorothy shrugged. 'Well, we'll never get another chance to see Sumatra.'

'Are you serious?'

'Why not? Why shouldn't we both go. You know, while you two were arguing about money, the Cook's man called up. He said our Indonesian visas have come through. All we have to do is take our passport round in the morning.'

2

Mrs Lukey, or, as her British passport somewhat incongruously proclaimed her, Miss Elizabeth O'Toole, met them at Singapore Airport with the tickets. The plane, a Garuda Indonesian Airways Convair with an Australian pilot, was reassuring. The discovery that the flying time to Labuanga was not thirty minutes, as the Captain had claimed, but a full two hours, seemed a matter for amusement rather than annoyance. They were getting off the beaten track; and not merely as tourists, but in order to sell arms to a band of freedom-loving anti-Communists. Moreover, they were travelling at someone else's expense. The spirit of high adventure tingled in their veins.

Mrs Lukey had explained the whole thing to them while they had been waiting in the departure lounge. The Captain's contact man in Labuanga was a Sumatran oil company employee who had legitimate reasons for cabling regularly to Singapore. This man also had access to a clandestine radio, through which he kept in touch with insurgent headquarters in the hills. On these cheque-signing occasions, he notified headquarters and arranged the rendezvous three days in advance. This gave the Committee member time to make the journey to the coast without running the risk of travelling by day.

'What sort of people are they?' Greg had asked her; 'the Committee members, I mean.'

'I've only seen two of them. One is a lawyer from Medan, the other is an army officer. I think those two are sent because they both speak English. A European comes with them, but only as a guard, I think. All the Committee members are Muslims.'

'What sort of European?'

'He is Polish. Hamid, who is our contact, said that he had been in the Foreign Legion in Indo-China, and was training them to use the arms.'

The plane reached its cruising altitude and headed north along the coast of Sumatra. The Malacca Strait moved slowly beneath them, green among the shoals of the off-shore islands, brown where the river mouths discharged the silt carried down from the hills, slate blue where the colder currents flowed down from the Bay of Bengal. Then, as the Strait widened, they altered course and began to fly over land. Soon, from their seats on the port side, all they could see below was something that looked like a vast sand dune covered with green moss.

'Jungle,' said Mrs Lukey.

The Indonesian stewardess began to serve bottled lemonade and stale cheese sandwiches. Twenty minutes before they were due at Labuanga, they ran into a local storm and had to fasten their seat belts. The plane bucketed about wildly for a time, and they came in to land under a huge black cloud and in a deluge of rain. A sheet of spray went up as the plane touched down; but by the time it had taxied in to the arrival apron, the rain had stopped and the sun was out again. Their first impression of Labuanga airport was the smell of steaming mud.

It was the most favourable impression they received.

Mrs Lukey had warned them about the immigration and customs officials. 'They are appointed from Djakarta,' she had said; 'and they are not friendly to anyone here. Europeans especially they do not like. The last time I was here, they made two Europeans undress to be searched; but the papers in Singapore were very angry about it, and I do not think we shall be troubled in that way if we are careful. It is better not to smile or look impatient.'

Greg and Dorothy did their best to remain impassive, but it was difficult, One immigration official took their passports away for examination, and did not return. A second official then demanded the production of the passports. When Mrs Lukey had explained to him what had happened, they were told to wait. It took an hour to recover the passports. Next, the currency control official ordered Greg to turn out his pockets, and, for some unexplained reason, decided to confiscate his Diner's Club credit card. Finally, the customs inspector insisted on taking the lens numbers of his camera and impounding the exposed film in it.

Mrs Lukey seemed to be as shaken as Greg and Dorothy by the experience. 'I am sorry,' she said. 'They have never been so bad before.'

'What the hell were they trying to prove?' demanded Greg. 'Why take a credit card? I don't particularly mind. I can replace that. But what's the idea?'

'Darling, at least they didn't make us undress.'

Greg, whose cotton and Dacron shirt was clinging wetly to his body, muttered that he wished they had. The loss of the film had particularly annoyed him.

The airport was three miles from the town and the airline bus had already gone. There were no taxis. They found that they had to wait for another bus. There was a painful silence.

Mrs Lukey made an unfortunate attempt to dispel the gloom. 'Well, anyway,' she said, 'I don't suppose the same men will be on duty tomorrow when we leave.'

'You mean we have to go through all that again?' asked Dorothy.

'If we are careful about our exit visas it will be all right.'

Greg swung round. 'What exit visas?'

'We have to get those tomorrow morning at the police office. As long as we give the man who makes them out a good tip, there will be no trouble.' She gave them an anxious smile.

There was another silence.

As the mud dried, other, more human smells were beginning to emerge from the vicinity of the airport. The heat was stupefying. Dorothy could feel the sweat trickling down her legs. She made a determined effort to be objective.

'Well,' she said lightly, 'it's their country.'

Mrs Lukey turned to her eagerly. 'Yes, they are really gay, laughing, happy people, but they are not always understood. It is the same in India. Because a European coming to Bombay cannot buy alcoholic drinks without a permit, he thinks that the Indians are not friendly people. That is not true. One must live in a country to know it. One should not judge a country from the airport. Nor from its customs officials.'

She had spoken quickly and vehemently, and, in doing so, had suddenly become more Asian than European. It was a disconcerting transformation.

Dorothy started to make some sort of reply. Fortunately, a bus drew into the yard at that moment and she did not have to complete it.

Almost as soon as the bus left the airport they passed through a village. The houses were of the small teak-framed atap kind with which they were becoming familiar; but on most of them the atap was faded and torn or patched. Only one house looked new and cared for. There was a signboard across the veranda. On it, painted in Malay and English, were the words: 'LABUANGA DISTRICT COMMUNIST PARTY.'

Dorothy and Mrs Lukey were on the other side of the bus. Greg did not draw their attention to it.

3

Labuanga was a port, and the terminal point of a system of pipe lines connecting the oil fields in the area. The town sprawled over a broad alluvial tongue of land jutting out into the sea beside a river delta. It had been built by the Dutch, and the tree-lined streets and public gardens of the civic centre had been laid out like those of a provincial town in Holland. The effect was bizarre. The trees were not lindens or sycamores, but casuarinas.

Flower-beds which should have contained orderly rows of tulips, narcissi and hyacinths, were lush with crotons, wild orchids and scarlet lilies. Hibiscus rioted over the iron railings surrounding a plinth which had supported a statue of Queen Wilhelmina. The portico of the Stadhuis looked raffish under the burden of a monstrous bougainvillaea. The centre of Labuanga was like a respectable Dutch matron seduced by the jungle and gone native.

Radiating out from it were the wide roads and bungalow compounds of the former European quarter. There were still a number of Europeans living there, mostly oil company employees; but many of the buildings had been taken over by the security forces and other agencies of the Central Government. It was now called the 'Inner Zone'.

The change had a military as well as a social significance. The District of Labuanga covered an area of several hundred square miles and included oil fields, pipe lines, copra plantations, over fifty villages, and substantial tracts of virgin jungle in addition to the city and port. An effective system of defences against the insurgents operating from the hills would have absorbed at least three divisions of reliable and well-equipped troops. Major-General Iskaq, the Military Governor of Labuanga, had at his disposal a garrison consisting of two demoralized infantry battalions, with three small field guns, ten decrepit armoured cars and sixty policemen. So far, the insurgents had confined themselves to night raids on outlying oil storage installations, the dynamiting of bridges, and harassing reconnaissances in force. But the General knew that the day must come when the Party of the Faithful would feel itself strong enough to mount an all-out assault on the city, capture it, defend it against counter-attack and proclaim an autonomous regional government. When that day (or night) did come the Inner Zone would become a fortress within which the garrison could hold out until help came from Medan. The problem had been to guard against surprise. At every road junction on the perimeter of the Zone, concrete defence positions had been built. Now, at the first sign of any insurgent activity at all in the vicinity of the city, an alarm button was pressed, the defence positions were manned, and the rest of the garrison withdrew behind them. Only a small mobile column was left outside the Zone to deal with the raiding party which had been the cause of the trouble.

The Inner Zone plan was one of those dreamlike pieces of military thinking which even their authors know to be unsound, but which are solemnly acted upon nevertheless, because any plan is preferable to none. The General was well aware of the illusory nature of this one. The Zone contained the police headquarters, the Stadhuis and a number of office buildings and houses. From a tactical point of view it was a mere geographical location, no easier to defend than any other part of the city. The power station, the water-pumping station, the port installations and the telephone exchange were all outside it, together with the bulk of the population. But there were similar disadvantages to every other area that had been considered. The truth was that, with only two infantry battalions, ten armoured cars and three field guns, there was no right way of defending a place the size of Labuanga against superior forces.

General Iskaq was a cunning and ambitious man with deep contempt for

Djakarta politicians and a sensitive regard for his own interests. He knew that many of his officers were in sympathy with the insurgents and that he had only to hint at such a sympathy himself to initiate secret negotiations with the Committee. He had a reputation as a patriot, and the price they would pay for his defection would be high. He had never heard the axiom 'If you can't lick 'em, join 'em' expressed in just those terms, but it exactly described his own ideas about power. Only one thing secured his allegiance to the Central Government.

His father had been a Javanese coolie. All through his childhood, the General had seen his father kicked, shouted at and bullied by white men, or *mandurs* working for white men. There had been nothing strange about this. His friends' fathers had been treated in the same way. That white men should drive Javanese coolies to work, coolies who would otherwise have idled in the shade, had been in the natural order of things; just as it had been natural to stop work when a white man drove by in his car or carriage, and turn towards him, and bow. Then, one day, a white man who had drunk too much gin had accused the General's father of smiling at him. When the General's father had denied it, the white man had started to beat him about the head and shoulders with a thick cane. The General's father had been strong, but the cane had been stronger and, as his face had become covered with blood, he had fallen to his knees crying like a child.

From that moment, and for many years after, the General had found nothing natural in a relationship with white men but hatred. It was not until the Japanese Army had surrendered and the white men had tried to reclaim Java as a colony, that he had been able to assuage much of his hatred by killing. What was left of it had, in time, been transformed into the irrational but unshakeable belief that white men and Asians could have no interests in common, and that what was good for one must be bad for the other. The Party of the Faithful was financed by white men, its forces were trained by white men, and, if it came to power, it would be friendly with white men. For the General, the idea of coming to terms with such an organization was totally unacceptable.

His repeated requests to the Area Commander for reinforcements had been refused; and for a good reason. The Area Commander had no reinforcements to send. The General had been in a mood of bitter desperation when his new Intelligence officer, Captain Gani, had come to him with an interesting proposal.

According to the Captain's estimates, the insurgents had roughly three thousand men in the hills and many unarmed sympathizers in the city, ready to help them when the time came. The General had only two thousand men at present. Yet, did he but know it, he could have a powerful ally with over fifteen hundred men to throw in on his side. That ally was the local Communist Party. If the General were prepared to arm the Party men, he would have a disciplined auxiliary force at his side and superior fire power.

The General had stared at him angrily. 'Are you mad?'

'Far from it, sir. What I am proposing is the creation of a loyal militia to meet an emergency.'

The General had laughed harshly. 'You know the Area Commander. He is one of Doctor Hatta's men. Are you fool enough to imagine that he would give me permission to arm the Labuanga Communists? He would have me arrested for suggesting it.'

'You are responsible for the defences here, sir, not the Area Commander. You are entitled to take emergency measures without consulting him. Besides, until it is equipped, the militia should remain a secret force.'

'Only the Area Commander can authorize the issue of arms and ammunition. What is your militia to be equipped with? Stones?'

Captain Gani had had an answer for that, too.

Two months later, the General had promoted him to Major and made him his personal aide.

4

The Harmonie Hotel was in the Inner Zone and consisted of a number of porticoed colonial bungalows built inside a rectangular, wire-fenced compound. The reception clerk, a handsome young Indonesian in European dress, was courteous but firm. The only accommodation he could offer them was a bungalow with three beds in it. All other bungalows in the hotel were occupied by permanent residents. This was by Government order.

Greg and Dorothy stared at one another in dismay, but Mrs Lukey nodded as if she had anticipated the difficulty. 'There is a sitting-room,' she said. 'I can sleep in there.'

The clerk took them along to the bungalow. The sitting-room was an unscreened veranda with a tiled floor. The bedroom beyond contained three cubicles completely enclosed by perforated zinc screens and looking rather like old-fashioned meat safes. As the clerk turned on the ceiling fan, a thing like a soft-shelled crab with black fur on it flopped on to the floor at their feet and begun scuttling towards the wardrobe.

Dorothy let out a yelp of fear. Giggling, the boy who had brought their bags in picked the creature up by one of its hairy legs and tossed it out through the sitting-room.

'My God!' said Greg. 'What was that?'

'They are quite harmless,' Mrs Lukey said. 'It is better to leave them. They eat the insects.'

But the thing had unnerved Dorothy. While Mrs Lukey was away telephoning the contact man, she insisted on Greg searching every inch of the bungalow. He found some lizards and a mildewed slipper, but no more of the black creatures. He did make the discovery that the bungalow contained no bathroom.

When Mrs Lukey returned, she showed them the row of bath-houses, separated for hygienic reasons from the living quarters. One of those gloomy cement caverns had the number of their bungalow on it. Inside, there was a toilet, a large urn full of water, and a metal scoop.

'It is a Siamese bath,' Mrs Lukey explained; 'you throw the cold water over you. It is very refreshing.'

The rendezvous was for seven o'clock at a house outside the Inner Zone.

It was then a little after four. They had had no lunch. They bathed awkwardly and, when they had changed, walked over to the hotel restaurant. There was a noisy group of Dutchman drinking in the veranda bar, and they did not stay there long. With some difficulty they found a waiter and persuaded him to produce some food. It was a warmed-up rice dish and not very appetising, but they were hungry enough to persevere with it. While they were eating, darkness fell, and the square on the far side of the gardens, which had been deserted before, suddenly came to life. Market stalls were set up among the trees, people congregated and food sellers appeared. A boy, squatting on his haunches by the roadside, began to play a bamboo xylophone.

It was a gentle, plaintive sound and curiously moving. Dorothy looked at Greg and he smiled at her understandingly. They were in a strange, far-off land, with no tourists within hundreds of miles of them. For a moment, the discomforts of the day were forgotten. It was a brief moment.

Mrs Lukey had said that it would take half an hour to walk to the rendezvous, and that they would probably be back at the hotel by eight o'clock. When they had had their coffee, they returned to the bungalow.

As soon as they switched the lights on, a large insect flew in and blundered about the sitting-room, hitting the walls and light-fittings with the force of a ricocheting pebble. Greg killed it eventually by knocking it down with a towel and treading on it. It was like a huge grasshopper made of brown plastic. Its hard shell crunched sickeningly beneath his foot. Two more came in immediately after.

Mrs Lukey said that they were harmless and that it was best to ignore them; but Dorothy had seen the one Greg had killed and was afraid of the things getting into her hair. The prospect of remaining there by herself, while Greg and Mrs Lukey went off to their business appointment, was becoming more unattractive every minute. She announced her intention of shutting herself inside one of the screened bed cubicles while they were gone.

Greg looked at Mrs Lukey. 'Is there any reason why all of us can't go? If we took a cab, Dorothy could sit and wait outside while we did our business.'

'Of course, if she will not be bored.'

'I'd sooner be bored than fighting these things,' Dorothy said.

They had some difficulty in getting a taxi, but the reception clerk sent boys out and eventually one was captured. Shortly after seven they set off.

The taxi was a diminutive Fiat, and Greg and Dorothy, crouching in the back, found it difficult to see where they were going. After they left the Inner Zone there were fewer lights in the streets, and soon they lost all sense of direction. They had glimpses of the port, of the flashing beacon, at the end of a mole, mirrored in the water, and of a cluster of oil storage tanks. Then, they turned on to a road with a bad surface and broken fences on either side, bumped along it for two or three hundred yards, and stopped.

The house was about twenty yards from the road, and surrounded by an untidy litter of banana trees. It was built on teak piles and there were steps leading up to the veranda. Light showed through the plaited window blinds.

Greg pressed Dorothy's hand. 'You'll be all right here?'

'Of course.'

As Greg clambered out to join Mrs Lukey, she said something to the taxi-driver. He switched off his lights. As they walked towards the house, Greg asked her if she had used this rendezvous before.

'Once,' she said.

The car's arrival had been heard, and, as they approached, a door opened on the veranda and a man came out. He had a flashlight in his hand. He shone it in their faces for a moment before motioning them up the steps.

He was very small and thin with slightly bowed shoulders. He wore a black *petji*, a sarong and bi-focal glasses. He inclined his head courteously to Mrs Lukey, and then looked at Greg.

'Mr Nilsen?'

'Yes.'

He held out his hand and said in good English: 'I am Mr Hamid. That is not my real name and this is not my house, of course, but you will understand that I have to be careful.'

'Sure.'

'Please come in.'

The walls were of corrugated iron. Nightfall had not brought any noticeable drop in temperature, and the single room interior was like an oven. In one corner there was a bed with a mosquito net looped back over it; but most of the space appeared to be used as an office. There was a desk, a steel filing-cabinet, and a table piled high with small cartons apparently in the process of being labelled. Against one wall were stacked some larger cartons with the words 'Fragile—Made in Japan' stencilled on their sides.

There were two men in the room; one Indonesian, one European. The Indonesian was a slender, graceful man and tall for his race. The skin of his face was stretched tightly over a prominent bone structure, and the veins on his forehead stood out too plainly. There was a look of hunger and tension about his face that seemed to contradict the ease and grace of his body. His hair was long and unkempt. The European was thick-set and muscular with cropped grey hair, lined grey cheeks and a thin half-smile which exposed a set of stainless steel false teeth. Both men were dressed in sweat-stained khaki shirts and slacks, and wore pistol belts. The Indonesian was sitting by the desk. The European lounged on the bed.

As Greg and Mrs Lukey came in, the Indonesian got to his feet.

'This is Major Sutan,' said Hamid.

The Major did not offer to shake hands. 'The woman can wait outside,' he said.

Mrs Lukey looked at Hamid, who nodded and ushered her out again. The Major moved across and shut the door after them before turning to face Greg again.

'Your passport, please,' he said.

Greg took the passport from his hip pocket and handed it over.

The Major examined the photograph in it and handed it back. 'This is

Captain Voychinski,' he said.

Greg nodded. 'How do you do, Captain?'

The man on the bed stared at him without speaking.

'Captain Voychinski is Polish,' said the Major. 'He is one of our technical advisers. Sit down please, Mr Nilsen.'

He himself sat down behind the desk. Greg got the Singapore cheque out and laid it on the desk. Major Sutan glanced at it.

'We have not done business together before,' he said; 'you will not object if I ask you some questions?'

Greg smiled amiably. 'As long as you don't object if I ask you a few, no.'

Major Sutan considered him for a moment before he said: 'Perhaps you had better ask your questions first.'

'All right. To begin with, why do I have to come all this way to get a cheque signed? Captain Lukey says you like to know whom you're dealing with. I don't get it. Don't you trust him?'

Major Sutan shrugged. 'We trust ourselves.'

Captain Voychinski got up off the bed and came over. 'That's right, mister,' he said. His English was only just intelligible. 'That fool in Singapore know nothing.'

'He knows how to drive a bargain.'

'Does he know *agent provocateur* when he see?' Captain Voychinski demanded. He spat the French words out as if they were fish-bones.

'Are you suggesting that's what I am?'

'How we know? You sell arms. How do we know you not take our money and tell the Central Government.'

'I went through all this with Captain Lukey,' Greg said patiently. 'It's not my business to deliver the arms here. I sell them in Singapore. When and how they reach you is your business.'

Major Sutan leaned forward. 'We have lost too many shipments lately, Mr Nilsen.'

'Sorry about that, but I don't know what it's got to do with me.'

'I am explaining our caution, Mr Nilsen.'

'Well, I'm not proposing to tell the Indonesian Government about the deal, and I don't know anyone who is. That's if there is to be any deal to tell about.'

'If, Mr Nilsen?'

'That's right—if. You like to know whom you're dealing with. So do I.'

Captain Voychinski laughed unpleasantly.

Greg turned and stared at him. 'You're a long way from home, Captain,' he said.

'Home?'

'Isn't Poland your home?'

'What is meant by that?' Captain Voychinski's hand had gone to his pistol.

Major Sutan intervened. 'Captain Voychinski is an ardent fighter against Communism,' he said. 'He fought in Russia and Italy and Viet-Nam.'

'Italy?' Greg raised his eyebrows.

'Captain Voychinski was an officer in a Polish division of the Wehrmacht.'

'I see.'

'Any more questions, Mr Nilsen?'

Greg shook his head. Captain Voychinski smiled grimly and took his hand from his pistol.

'Very well.' Major Sutan picked up the cheque and looked down at it. 'Where did these arms come from please?'

'Manila. Why?'

'You are not a regular dealer, Mr Nilsen, and the composition of the shipment is unusual. Naturally, we are curious.'

'I got the stuff from a man who'd taken it as collateral for a loan. He was left with it on his hands and wanted to get rid of it. I understand that it came originally from Red China.' ·

'How?'

'I was told that it was intercepted at sea on its way to Malaya.'

'At sea?'

'That's right. Does it matter? Captain Lukey has inspected the stuff.'

'Arms from China to Malaya do not go by sea.'

'Well, these did.'

'What is the name of the person who told you?'

'Tan Tack Chee.'

Major Sutan looked down at the cheque again, and then took a pen from his shirt pocket. 'I do not know this Tan, Mr Nilsen, but I would suggest you do not deal with him again.'

'Why not?'

'If you are not lying to me, then he lied to you. I do not think you can be lying.'

'Thanks.'

'On that point you would have no reason to lie.' He signed the cheque and pushed it across the desk. 'That is all, Mr Nilsen. Will you be returning to Singapore tomorrow?'

'Yes.' Greg picked up the cheque and slipped it inside his passport.

'Then the transaction could be completed the following day?'

'It could.'

Major Sutan got to his feet and held out his hand. 'Next time,' he said, 'I think that our dealings will be more friendly. It will not be necessary for you to come here again, I think.'

'Thanks.' Greg shook hands with Major Sutan, nodded to Captain Voychinski and went to the door.

Mrs Lukey and Hamid were waiting on the veranda.

'Is everything in order?' Hamid asked.

'Yes, the cheque's signed.' Greg glanced at Mrs Lukey. 'Shall we go? Good night, Mr Hamid.'

They had reached the bottom of the veranda steps when he heard Dorothy cry out.

He started to run towards the road.

There were lights there now and he saw the soldiers almost immediately. Two of them were dragging the driver out of the taxi. Three more were coming towards him across the clearing. From behind, near the house, there was a sudden confused shouting, and the ear-shattering din of a sub-machine-gun burst.

At that moment one of the soldiers saw him, yelled to the others, and started to bring his carbine up to his shoulder.

Mrs Lukey was screaming at him to stop.

Greg stopped; and then, as the other two soldiers ran towards him, he took a step backwards and put up his hands.

Chapter Seven

I

General Iskaq ate a second honey cake and poured himself a third cup of coffee. It was cool enough to drink, but he left it to get still cooler. He was in no hurry. He knew that he was going to enjoy the day which lay before him. A little delay in approaching it could only serve to increase the ultimate satisfaction. Meanwhile, there were more modest pleasures at hand. He picked up his binoculars.

From the window of his apartment on the top floor of the Stadhuis he could see the port, the river delta and the sea beyond. The sky was cloudless and, at that early hour, there was little heat haze. The previous day's rains were pouring down from the hills, and the silt-laden water was swirling out in fantastic patterns across the choppy waters of the bay. When the river was in flood like that, the currents interacted with the tides to produce a mill race effect at the harbour mouth. Plans had been made to eliminate this navigational hazard by extending the mole; but the Government had refused to pay for the work. Now, a tanker in ballast trying to get alongside the oil company's wharf was having to be warped in cautiously a foot at a time. The morning sun was glittering on her wheelhouse windows, and the General could see the white-topped caps of her European officers out on the wings of the bridge. Other white blobs on the wharf marked the presence of the oil company's Dutch under-manager and the English representative of the tanker's owners. They, too, would be impatient at the delay.

The General watched through his binoculars and was content. Admittedly, the situation had richer possibilities. For some minutes, he had toyed with the vision of one, or, better still, both of the warps parting under the strain, and of the tanker drifting helplessly across the basin to crunch into the side of a dredger moored there; but that, he knew, had been idle day-dreaming. One should not expect too much of life. It was enough that the Europeans were inconvenienced and irritated. Enough for the present anyway. One of them, the Englishman, was British Vice-Consul in Labuanga, and there were further tribulations in store for him.

The tanker was nearing the wharf now, and the brown water eddying round her sides was losing its power over her. The General continued to watch; but his thoughts began to stray. There was an important question to be decided. Whom should he tell first—the American Vice-Consul or his British colleague.

It was not easy. The Englishman, Mr Wilson, was the local agent of the North Borneo and Federation Shipping Company, and his post as British Vice-Consul was merely honorary. In fact, it was said that the only reason for appointing a British Vice-Consul in Labuanga had been to enable Mr Wilson to import his supplies of whisky and tobacco duty free. When told that a female British citizen had been arrested the night before and was in jail on charges of conspiracy against the government, illegal trading in arms, illegal entry, consorting with criminals, and espionage, the inexperienced Mr Wilson might well become confused and behave incorrectly. That would be most enjoyable. On the other hand, he might consult with the British Consul in Medan, or, worse, ask Mr Hallet, the American Vice-Consul, for advice. They were very friendly. In that case, Mr Hallett would have less of a shock when he discovered that there were two American citizens also in jail on the same charges.

The General wanted Mr Hallett to have a big shock. Mr Hallett's post was not honorary. He was a career member of the Foreign Service of the United States, and acted not only as his country's Vice-Consul, but as a local information officer as well, organizing subversive things like American book centres and documentary film shows, and corrupting promising young Indonesians by arranging for them to take courses in American technical institutions. He was also closely associated with the World Health Organization office in Labuanga, and had been known to accompany malaria control and B.C.G. field units into the interior. On occasions, he had even penetrated into insurgent held areas with such units, returning not only unscathed but impertinently unwilling to talk about what he had seen. There were a number of American technicians working in the oil fields; and, when they came into Labuanga, they could be as riotous as Dutchmen. Mr Hallett had a disagreeable way of making the arrest of one of those drunken gangsters appear as either a calculated affront to the President of the United States, or the result of some ridiculous mistake on the part of the security forces under the General's command. The prospect of confronting Mr Hallett with two American arms smugglers, disguised as tourists and caught red-handed in the company of notorious traitors, was infinitely alluring.

From the other end of the apartment he could hear his wife upbraiding one of the servants for not answering the door-bell promptly. A moment or two later he heard the voice of Major Gani. He decided to hear his aide's report before making up his mind how he would handle the situation.

The General did not really like Major Gani, who had spent a year as a student at a Japanese university and did not always trouble to conceal his belief that he was cleverer and more cultivated than his commanding officer. He had, too, an annoying habit of quietly snapping his fingers while the General was speaking. The General, a religious man himself, had also realized by now that Gani was a Communist. However, it was impossible to get rid of him at this juncture. The man had made himself indispensable;

and so had the Communist Party.

The idea of seizing the insurgent arms shipments in the Labuanga area had been a good one; he was at once arming his secret militia and denying arms to the enemy; but without the Communist intelligence network to discover the times and places of the shipments it would have been impossible. The insurgents had lost four substantial shipments before they had changed their delivery arrangements; and now, thanks to Gani and the Party, the new arrangements would soon be as unprofitable to the Committee as the old.

It had been Gani who had noted, in the immigration service's reports, the frequency and brevity of the visits to Labuanga of the British woman, Elizabeth O'Toole. A more detailed study had then shown that O'Toole had always arrived from Singapore, and in the company of a male European of one sort or another. She had always left with him the following day. Out of five visits, one had been made with a Belgian, one with an Italian, one with a German, and one each with two different Australians. Since nobody in his senses, Asian or European, would regularly choose Labuanga as a place of assignation for any amorous purpose, Gani had made a further investigation and noted a relationship between the dates of three of O'Toole's visits and the dates of three interceptions of arms shipments. The Party had alerted the comrades in Singapore and inquiries had been made about her there. Two days ago, a report of her true identity had been received, together with the information that she was about to make another visit to Labuanga. Arrangements had been made with the immigration service to delay the woman and her companion at the airport when they arrived, so that the necessary steps could be taken to place them under surveillance.

Major Gani came in briskly. As usual, his salute was more like an acknowledgment of applause than a mark of respect; but the General did not care today. He was hungry for information.

'Well, Major?'

Major Gani took off his cap and sat down before he answered. 'The traitor Hamid Osman,' he said, 'died of his wounds an hour ago, sir. It is a pity because I had hoped for much information from the man. The house they were meeting in belongs to a small importer. He is believed to be in Medan at the moment. We shall find out. Hamid Osman's house was most interesting.'

'Ah.'

'He was unmarried and lived with his brother who is a radio technician. We found a radio transmitter there. It was still warm from use.'

'You arrested the brother?'

'He had escaped. The two houses are only three hundred yards apart. He must have heard the firing.'

The General frowned. 'The radio was still warm, you say. Would he have had time to report to the traitors in the hills?'

'Perhaps.'

'It would have been better if we could have had complete secrecy.'

Major Gani shrugged. 'There cannot be complete secrecy, sir. The American and British Consuls here will have to be informed. And I believe there is a Polish Consul in Medan.'

There was a hint of malice in the way he said the last sentence. The General would have to be careful. If it became generally known that there were four non-Dutch whites under lock and key in Labuanga jail on charges other than disorderly conduct, the Area Commander in Medan would remove them from the General's jurisdiction within hours. The Area Commander had a weakness for personal publicity and would certainly not permit a subordinate to take charge of a situation of such lively interest to the Press.

'I will deal with the American and British Consuls myself,' the General replied casually. 'They will want to be discreet. The Polish Consul does not matter.' He brushed the subject aside with a wave of his coffee spoon. 'Now, about the prisoners. What information do we have from them?'

'It is a little soon, sir, to expect real information. I interrogated the taxi-driver who took them from the hotel. He heard only that the house had been used as a meeting place once before. Nothing of value. I released him.' He saw the General stiffen and added curtly: 'He is a good Party member.'

'But the O'Toole woman—what does she say?'

'Nothing, sir.' Major Gani began snapping his fingers.

'And the Americans?'

'Also nothing. The man Voychinski advised them to say nothing until instructed by their Consuls. It is not important. They are not important.'

The General threw his coffee spoon down with a clatter. 'Not important?' he demanded. 'Four European gangsters engaged in smuggling arms to the traitors, not important?'

Major Gani sighed patiently. 'Very important, sir, for propaganda purposes. But, for our purposes, we have someone much more useful—Major Sutan.'

The General controlled himself. In his day-dreaming about the white prisoners he had almost forgotten that a member of the insurgent Committee had been taken, too.

'What does Sutan say?' he asked.

'He refuses to speak.'

'Where are the prisoners?'

'In the police jail, sir.'

'Sutan as well?'

'Yes, sir.' And then Major Gani made a mistake. 'He is a strong man,' he went on blandly, 'and will not talk easily. I have put two good men on to the preliminary interrogating work, but we do not want to injure him too much in view of the public court martial that must follow, and it may be twenty-four hours or more before he can be persuaded. I thought it safer not to interrogate him at your own headquarters. He has many friends in the Army.'

'Yes.' The General pushed his cold coffee away and got to his feet. 'I was one of them.'

'Ah, then you understand, sir.'

Major Gani was an able and astute officer with a glib command of the Marxist dialectic and a keen eye for the weaknesses of other men; but he was also a deeply conceited man and in some respects grossly insensitive. To him, General Iskaq was merely a brutish and reactionary strong-arm guerrilla leader, whom circumstances had thrust into a temporary position of authority; a thick-skulled clod to be deferred to and pandered to now so that he could be exploited later. The possibility of the General's disliking the idea of torturing a former comrade had not occurred to him.

The General looked him in the eyes. 'Yes, I do understand. I shall take charge of these interrogations personally.'

'In the case of the foreigners, sir?'

'In the cases of all these prisoners. Then, we will see who will talk, and who will not.'

2

At the time of the arrest, Greg had been too bewildered to be really frightened; it had been as if they were in some nightmare traffic accident involving a truckload of uniformed maniacs instead of another car. Later, when Dorothy and Mrs Lukey were being yelled at, prodded with guns and searched in front of a roomful of policemen, he had been too angry. The butt of a carbine slammed into the pit of his stomach had ended that phase. Out of the consequent pain and nausea had come at last a cold realization of their predicament; and, with it, fear. On the way to the jail, Mrs Lukey had wept hysterically. It had been Dorothy, calm and collected, who had found the words of reassurance. Handcuffed to Voychinski and Major Sutan, he had sat there in numbed silence.

At the jail, a single storey brick building in a walled compound on the outskirts of the town, Dorothy and Mrs Lukey had been hustled off to the women's quarters. Major Sutan had been held in the administration block. Greg and Captain Voychinski had been put into a cell containing one iron-framed bed, an urn of water and a bucket. The whole place had a strong ammoniac smell thinly mingled with that of disinfectant.

Voychinski had taken their arrest philosophically, and, now that Greg's good faith had been so strikingly proved, his attitude became almost friendly. Unfortunately, he was one of those men who, in the face of danger, affect a sardonic facetiousness as nerve-racking after a while as any display of fear.

'How did they get on to us?' Greg asked him as soon as they were alone.

'When I know I send you letter.'

'What do you think they'll do?'

'To me? Pop-pop-pop.' He grinned, showing his steel teeth. 'Or perhaps . . .' He made the motion of castrating himself. 'With you? Big trial after six months. After two years, perhaps, they let you go. With the women? If they let you go they keep the women. If they let the women go they keep you. Don't worry.'

'Well, they'll have to inform our Consuls anyway.'

'Oh yes. Next week, perhaps.'

'What about Major Sutan?'

'He no have Consul here. Like me.'

As there was nothing to sit on except the bed, neither of them had any sleep. Voychinski seemed unconcerned. He began to talk about his experiences with the German Army in Russia and Italy. His facetiousness never flagged, but there was an unpleasant undercurrent of reality to all he said. Greg, who had served with the Fifth Army in Italy and understood what he was hearing about, listened with a mounting disgust that he found difficult to conceal. He had seen an Italian village after a unit of the sort Voychinski seemed to have enjoyed serving with had left it. He tried not to listen, and to pin his thoughts on to the moment when Dorothy and he would be regaling their friends with the hilarious account of how they were arrested in Labuanga and had to spend a night in the local hoosegow; but it was not a very convincing fantasy and was too easily overlaid by another in which Dorothy and he did not figure personally. In this, their friends were discussing with gloomy perplexity what the newspapers were referring to as 'the Nilsen arms racket inquiry' and wondering how come Greg Nilsen had made such a horse's ass of himself.

Soon after dawn, a guard brought them a pot of rice and fish which they had to eat with their fingers. Greg ate very little. His bowels were beginning to cause him uneasiness and he had been obliged more than once to make use of the bucket. Voychinski had some jokes to make about that, too. Greg's dislike of him was now complete.

The barred window of the cell gave on to an inner court, and, as the sun rose, they were able to see through the zinc mosquito screen that it was an exercise yard. About twenty male prisoners, bare-footed and wearing sarongs tucked between their legs like loin cloths, wandered about aimlessly or squatted in groups under the supervision of guards with carbines. Inside the cell, the heat and smell were becoming unbearable. When, shortly before noon, a guard unlocked the door and beckoned to him, Greg's fondest hope was that he was to be allowed out into the yard with the other prisoners.

Instead, he was taken by two guards to a room off a corridor leading to the main entrance. Except for a long table and six chairs, it was bare. The windows were barred. One guard entered with him, motioned him to a chair and stood by the door with his carbine at the ready. After a brief interval the door opened and an army officer entered. Greg recognized him as the officer who had attempted to interrogate him the previous night; a handsome man with angry eyes and an air of carefully controlled impatience. Behind him was a man of Greg's own race, in a very clean white shirt and gaberdine slacks. He was about thirty-five, stocky, and balding, with a round chubby face and square shoulders. He stood in the doorway with a lopsided smile on his face, and looked curiously at the guard.

As Greg got to his feet, the officer inclined his head. 'I am Major Gani,' he said.

Greg nodded. 'Major.'

'And this, as you requested, is the American Vice-Consul in Labuanga.'

Greg gave an audible sigh of relief and smiled. 'Am I glad to see you, Consul.'

The man in the doorway nodded but without looking at him. 'I wish I could say the same, Mr Nilsen. My name's Ross Hallett.'

Greg started to move towards him, but the guard raised his carbine threateningly. Hallett took no notice. He looked from the guard to Major Gani.

'Good-bye, Major,' he said.

Major Gani's lips tightened and he began to snap his fingers. 'The formalities have now been complied with,' he said. 'You have seen the prisoner. He is unharmed. It is now your duty to inform him that it is in order for him to be interrogated and to answer all questions.'

Hallett shook his head. 'Oh no, Major. That isn't my duty.'

'This is Labuanga, not Washington, Mr Hallett. The prisoner is under our law, and so are you.'

'Sure we are,' Hallett replied easily; 'and you have every right to ask Mr Nilsen any questions you like. But that doesn't mean he has to answer them. You see, I've had no opportunity yet of talking privately to him. I don't think that I can advise him to co-operate with you at this stage.'

He turned away as if to go, then paused as the Major said something sharply in his own language. Hallett answered him in the same language.

'What did he say?' Greg asked.

Hallett ignored him. Greg stood there, uncomprehending and irritated, while they argued. Finally, the Major gave a reluctant nod and motioned the guard out of the room.

'You may have ten minutes,' he said in English. 'There will be a guard on the door.'

He followed the guard outside.

Hallett's smile faded as the door closed.

'Sit down, please,' he said.

'Now look, Mr Hallett,' Greg began, 'all I'm worried about at the moment is my wife. You see . . .'

'I know, Mr Nilsen. But we don't have that much time, so supposing you let me run things. I've seen your wife and she seems to be okay. The British Vice-Consul is seeing Mrs Lukey, and she's okay, too.'

'You mean Miss O'Toole, don't you?'

Hallett sighed. 'Mr Nilsen, I don't have time for games. Whatever her passport says, these people know she's Mrs Lukey.'

'How did they find out?'

'I don't know. Anyway that's unimportant. If you'll just answer my questions we may get somewhere.' He took a notebook from his pocket. 'Now then. Mrs Nilsen gave me some basic facts and, according to her, you have a joint American passport. Where is it now?'

'They took it away.'

'The police or the military?'

'That officer who was just in here was in charge.'

'What else did they take from you?'

'Everything–money, wallet, watch, the lot.'

'They claim they have documentary evidence linking you with Major Sutan. What would that be?'

'I had a cheque for sixty-two thousand five hundred Malay dollars in my passport. It was drawn on the Hong Kong and Shanghai Bank and signed by Sutan.'

Hallett's lopsided smile returned for a moment; but it was anything but friendly. 'Do you know what sort of a spot you're in, Mr Nilsen?'

'I have a pretty good idea.'

'I wonder if you have. All right, give me the background. I want the whole history of this transaction.'

Greg gave it to him.

When he had finished, Hallett was staring at him in sour wonderment. Greg shrugged.

Hallett drew a deep breath. 'Mr Nilsen,' he said, 'I wish you could tell me something. Why is it that when an apparently normal, intelligent, law-abiding citizen like you gets hold of a passport and a steamship ticket, he suddenly turns into a juvenile . . .'

'Okay, Mr Hallett,' Greg broke in irritably. 'You can't say anything I haven't already said myself.'

'I wouldn't be too sure of that. Our country spends millions of dollars trying to help these people become a nation of free men, trying to give them confidence in democratic processes, trying to persuade them that some version of our way of doing things offers them a better chance of happiness than the Communist Party, and then people like you . . .' He broke off. 'I'll give you the rest of the lecture another time. Right now we've got to try to get you and Mrs Nilsen out of this mess.'

'Well, Mrs Nilsen anyway.'

'As they see it, she's guilty by association.' Hallett leaned forward. 'Now, tell me again. Your arrangement with Lukey was just as you've stated it? You had nothing to do with the delivery of this war material and know nothing about the arrangements that were to be made for that delivery? Is that right? Don't fool with me, Mr Nilsen. I have to know. Is that the true picture?'

'It is.'

Hallett sighed. 'That's too bad.'

'What do you mean?'

'The Military Governor's terms for your release are that you inform them when and how the stuff is being delivered, so that they can intercept and confiscate it.'

'But that's crazy. How can I tell them? Lukey doesn't even own the stuff until that cheque is cashed in Singapore.'

'They won't believe that.'

'But they'll have to.'

'There's no have to about it.'

'Major Sutan'll tell them I don't know anything. Voychinski, too.'

'A traitor and a hoodlum? Why should they believe what they say?'

Greg was silent for a moment. Then, he nodded. 'I see. It looks as if my wife and I are going to be here quite a while.'

Hallett made no comment. 'How much money did you have with you?' he asked.

Greg told him.

'All right, I'll try to get that released. While you're held without trial you can pay for a more comfortable cell and have food sent in from outside if you want.'

'Will I be able to see my wife?'

'I'll ask, but I doubt it.'

'I don't know how Mrs Lukey's fixed for money. If we can get these privileges for her, too, I'd be glad to pay.'

'I'll speak to the British Consul about that. Now, then. You're going to be interrogated by the Governor personally. His name is General Iskaq and what he'd really like to do is beat the daylights out of you. He won't, because he knows I'd raise hell in Medan and Djakarta if he did, but bear it in mind and don't push him. Do you know what xenophobia is?'

'Yes.'

'Well, the General has it badly. So watch yourself. Tell him the truth. He won't believe you, but go on telling it anyway. That cheque is your best talking point.'

'How do you mean?'

'It substantiates your story that the transaction was incomplete, and that there were, therefore, no delivery arrangements. Tell him about the second signature needed. Say that, if he doesn't believe you, he should send the cheque to the Indonesian Consulate in Singapore and ask them to try and cash it as it is. Ask him if he thinks you fool enough to trust Lukey with the goods before you had been paid.'

'He knows Lukey?'

'Of course. Lukey's a crook. The oil company filed embezzlement charges against him two years ago, but couldn't make them stick. The Government deported him.'

'I see.'

'Another thing. Don't get into any sort of political discussion. You had the stuff to sell. You were approached in Singapore. You thought you were dealing with an agent of the Central Government.'

'You said I was to tell the truth.'

'The Communist Party here will make all the propaganda use they can out of this. They'll try to say you're an American agent and that we're secretly backing the insurgents while pretending friendship with the Central Government. The less help they have from you the better.'

'How do I account for the meeting with Major Sutan?'

They could hear footsteps approaching along the corridor outside. Hallett began to speak quickly.

'You thought he was a Government official trying to get a secret commission on the deal. Play the innocent. You shouldn't find that too difficult.' He waved Greg into silence with a gesture. 'Do you smoke, Mr Nilsen?' he went on loudly.

'A cigar occasionally. Why?'

'I'll send you in some cigarettes anyway. They are currency here. There's a pack to go on with. Liquor is not allowed, I'm afraid.'

'Do you have something for an upset stomach?'

'I'll get you some pills from my doctor.'

The door opened as he was speaking and Hallett got to his feet. Greg rose with him.

The man who came into the room had a stunted, barrel-chested body the ugliness of which was only partially concealed by an immaculately laundered uniform. He had a heavy, pock-marked face with thick, rubbery lips and ears. His eyes were watchful and his movements deliberate, like those of some powerful yet cumbersome animal He wore a scrubbed webbing pistol belt, and carried a short leather-covered cane of the type Greg had seen carried by British officers during the war.

Just inside the door he stopped and looked distastefully from Hallett to Greg.

'This is Mr Nilsen,' Hallett said, and added to Greg: 'The Military Governor of Labuanga, General Iskaq.'

The General went over to the table and sat at the head of it. He was followed by Major Gani who motioned to Greg to stand facing the General.

Hallett said: 'Governor, I have advised Mr Nilsen to make a frank and full statement.'

The General seemed to take no notice.

'You will find that he acted in good faith and that no possible charge against him can be substantiated,' Hallett continued.

Major Gani smiled ironically and began to translate what had been said into Malay. Only then did Greg realize that the General could not understand English.

When the translation was finished, the General looked at Hallett and said something in a harsh, guttural voice.

Hallett inclined his head politely and turned to Greg. 'I am requested to leave now, Mr Nilsen,' he said. 'You will, of course, answer the Governor's questions as best you can. I have no doubt that you and Mrs Nilsen will be released very soon. In any case, I shall be watching your interests and will see you as often as I can. If it becomes necessary, I will get counsel for you.'

'Thanks.'

With a slight bow to the General, Hallett went. As the guard shut the door behind him, Major Gani sat down by the General.

Greg turned to face him.

Major Gani nodded. 'We will begin,' he said briskly. 'First, let us hear what you and Mr Hallett have arranged that you shall say. After that we will hear the truth.'

3

The General listened absently to the white man's voice speaking the language that always sounded to him like the chattering of apes, and watched the sweat pouring off him as he talked. In his mind's eye, however, all he could see was the room he had left ten minutes earlier, and his old friend Mohamad Sutan lying on the stone floor in a pool of bloody water, moaning and choking, with blood running from his mouth and nostrils and his stomach heaving. He had told the proudly smiling men who had done it to stop for the present and let the prisoner rest; but he could not leave matters there. Soon, he would have to tell them to go on again. Unless, of course, one of the whites should talk first.

As Major Gani started to tell him what the white man was saying, the General picked up the cane he had placed beside him on the table and began to tap the palm of his other hand.

4

'It's really my fault,' Dorothy was telling Mrs Lukey. 'We'd been planning this trip and looking forward to it for so long that the reality was bound to be an anti-climax. I was prepared for that, but Greg wasn't and I let him get angry and bored. I should have had more sense. When a man's worked so hard and successfully for so many years, and been such a wonderful husband and father, you tend to forget some things about him. Or maybe tell yourself that they're no longer there.'

'What sort of things?'

Dorothy sighed inwardly with relief. After the American and British Consuls had been there, Mrs Lukey had been calmer for a while; but gradually the effect of their visits had worn off and she had begun to weep again. She was going to be tortured, she was going to be raped, she was going to be shot. She had done nothing. She did not want to die.

As almost everything she said expressed Dorothy's own presentiments and fears, it had not been easy to reassure her with any sort of conviction. Despair can be infectious, and Dorothy had begun to cast about feverishly for some means of diverting her companion's thoughts from their immediate situation. She had found it, unexpectedly, in the subject of her relationship with Greg. Mrs Lukey was almost avidly curious about it. Dorothy guessed that she was trying indirectly to find the key to a more secure relationship with her own husband. It was the difficulties of marriage that interested her most. Her eyes were dry now, and, although she still held the damp white ball which had been Dorothy's last piece of Kleenex, her nose had at last stopped running.

'What sort of things?' she repeated.

'Oh, I don't know,' Dorothy said. 'Nothing very bad, really. You know those dolls with round weights at their feet? The ones that always stand up straight again however much you push them over? As long as he has work that's important to him, a man like Greg hardly ever does anything really silly. It's only when the weight is suddenly taken away that things go wrong. It was like that when he came home from the army. He'd been away four years working with mine detection equipment and explosives. It was dangerous work, but it had fascinated him. All that time he'd hardly thought of anything else. When he came home safely to me and the boys, I was so happy. I thought that all our troubles were over.' She paused. 'The first thing that happened was that he fell in love with another woman—or rather, a nineteen-year-old girl.'

Mrs Lukey looked at her quickly; but Dorothy's expression remained placid.

'I suppose that if it hadn't been for the children,' she said, 'we'd have broken up. But we didn't. Greg got his business going and gradually everything was all right again.'

'What about the other woman?'

Dorothy shrugged. 'The last time we talked about it was five years ago. Greg became very upset.'

'Because he was still in love with her?'

'No. Because he couldn't remember her second name.'

Mrs Lukey stared at her uncertainly for a moment. Dorothy was looking preternaturally solemn. Then, Mrs Lukey began to laugh. After a moment, Dorothy began to laugh with her. They did not hear the footsteps of the guard approaching, and were still laughing when the cell door opened. Mrs Lukey's laughter became a strangled cry as they turned.

Standing in the doorway was the old woman who acted as wardress, and one of the armed guards from the control section.

The wardress said something in Malay, and Mrs Lukey began to back away.

As Dorothy started to go to her, the guard came into the cell and, reaching out, grabbed Mrs Lukey by the arm. She screamed and tried to pull away. With a shout he flung her across the cell to the wardress, and then, using his carbine with both hands, thrust them out into the corridor. The cell door slammed behind him.

As the sound of Mrs Lukey's screams receded, Dorothy sat down on the bed and searched her bag frantically to see if by any chance there was one more piece of Kleenex that she had overlooked. There was none. She sobbed once and tried holding her breath. Then, she ceased trying. Kleenex or no Kleenex, it was better to cry.

5

When Greg was taken back to his cell, Voychinski was stretched out asleep on the bed.

He awoke at the sound of the cell door closing, but made no attempt to move. Greg took no notice of him. Heat, lack of sleep, stomach cramps and the insistent questioning had exhausted him to the point of indifference to discomfort. When he had used the bucket, he sat down on the floor and rested his back against the wall.

Voychinski sat up lazily and yawned. Greg took Hallett's cigarettes and matches from the shirt pocket and tossed them on to the bed.

'Compliments of the American Consul,' he said.

Voychinski picked up the cigarettes and smirked. 'You leave soon, hah?'

'Just as soon as I tell them when and how that stuff you were going to buy is being delivered.'

'They think you know?'

'That's right. They think I know.'

Voychinski swung his feet off the bed and looked down at him. 'Who question you?'

'General Iskaq and that Major.'

'So!' The pale eyes searched for hidden clues. 'What you say?'

'What could I say? I told them all I know. I told them fifty times.'

'About the delivery?'

'I don't know anything about the delivery. You know that as well as I do.'

'But you tell them something, a good story perhaps?'

'I told them what I know and that's all.'

'Nothing about delivery?'

'That's right.'

'You lie.'

Greg shut his eyes wearily. 'Anything you say.'

Voychinski got up off the bed and stared down beligerently. 'Gani would not permit you to say nothing.'

'Gani wasn't conducting the interrogation.'

'You are lucky.'

'It's not Gani I'm worried about.'

'That peasant Iskaq?' Voychinski spat derisively. 'Listen, my friend. Iskaq is a soldier, a good soldier, but stupid politically. Oh yes, he would wish to break your face, but he is not serious. Gani is the dangerous one. He want those guns to arm more of his party men.'

'What party men?'

'You do not know he is a Red?'

'How would I?'

'Mrs Lukey know it.'

'What difference does it make?'

'My friend, if Iskaq had political sense he would have come over to the Committee. Now, he secretly helps to arm the Reds and think he is fighting us when he only make firing squad for himself. It is stupid.' He sat down again and stared at Greg suspiciously. 'You did not tell Gani anything?'

'About the delivery? Don't be silly. I don't know anything. Is there anyone who does? Does Major Sutan? Do you?'

Voychinski's eyes narrowed unpleasantly. 'Did Gani tell you to ask that?'

'Oh, for God's sake!'

Voychinski shrugged. 'When a man is afraid and has nothing to lose he will do many things. And Gani means to find out from one of us.'

Greg glowered at him. 'What do you mean, "nothing to lose"?'

'Your arms are still in Singapore.'

'Exactly! So there's nothing for Major Gani to find out. That's what I keep trying to tell you.'

Voychinski sighed impatiently. 'My friend, do you think that you are the only man in the world who sell us arms?'

It took Greg several seconds to get the point. Then, he remembered something Captain Lukey had said. 'You only have to go the first time.

After that it's plain sailing.' With only one deal to consummate himself, he had not taken much notice of it then. He looked up at Voychinski.

'You mean there's another shipment from someone else already on the way?'

Voychinski showed his teeth but did not reply. From along the corridor there was the sound of a door opening and a rattle of keys. A moment later the cell door was opened and a guard outside motioned to Voychinski.

He got up slowly, stretched himself and walked out. He did not even glance at Greg. The door shut behind him.

6

Ross and Fran Hallett were playing bridge with Dr Subramaniam, the Indian director of the tuberculosis clinic, and his wife that evening when the lights went out. It was a little before eight o'clock.

They were not unduly concerned. Power failures were common enough. Dr Subramaniam lit some oil lamps and they went on with the rubber. Twenty minutes later the lights were still out, and Dr Subramaniam, wondering if the failure could after all be due to a fuse in his own house, went out to the road to see if there were lights elsewhere. He saw immediately that the failure was general; but as he walked back he heard the sound of distant machine-gun fire. It seemed to come from the other side of the town, by the port.

He called Ross Hallett. The sounds of firing were becoming more insistent and, intermingled with them now, there were faint thudding noises.

'What is it do you think?' asked the Doctor; 'another raid on the storage tanks?'

'Possibly. Difficult to tell from here.'

'What else could it be?'

'I wouldn't like to say. Anyway, I think I have to get back.'

'Why? There's nothing you can do. We've got a spare bed you and Fran can have for the night.'

Hallett shook his head. 'I'll be grateful if you'd let Fran stay, but I have to get back.'

'They'll have shut the Inner Zone.'

'I'll get through on my pass.'

Fran Hallett recognized what she called the 'State Department' look on her husband's face when he returned to the house, and made no attempt either to dissuade him from going or to insist on going along herself. She did not even tell him to take care. She merely reminded him that there were fresh eggs in the water cooler and kissed him good night.

He drove very slowly. Once, when a column of army troop carriers began to pass him, he pulled off the road and stopped. During these emergencies the Labuanga garrison became trigger-happy, and moving vehicles, including their own, were frequently shot at. As he approached the Inner Zone check point, he became even more cautious. A hundred yards short of it, he stopped the car, and, leaving the headlights on, got out and walked towards the guard-house. With the lights behind him the sentries could see clearly that he was unarmed and alone.

The N.C.O. in charge of the check point had never seen a diplomatic pass before, and could not read. An officer had to be summoned to approve the pass before he was allowed through. The sounds of firing were louder there and it was possible to determine the direction from which they were coming. The officer was excited and on edge, but Hallett decided to take a small risk.

'What do they want?' he asked. 'To burn one more oil tank?'

There was a local joke implicit in the form of the question. From time to time Government spokesmen had accused the oil company of secretly subsidizing the Party of the Faithful. Insurgent propaganda leaflets had indignantly denied the charge and listed the attacks made on oil company property. The list had been unconvincing and a Government newspaper had run a sarcastic article about it. Why was it, the writer had asked, that the insurgents were never able to blow up more than one oil storage tank at a time? Why didn't they use a little more explosive while they were about it, and blow up two or three? And why did they bother with oil storage tanks at all, when they could, at much less risk to themselves, cut the pipe lines? The writer had gone on to offer helpful suggestions of how this might be done, and to suggest that the insurgents apply to America for technical assistance. Even the strongly pro-Faithful had smiled a little at this.

The officer looked at Hallett uncertainly.

Hallett said: 'Maybe they brought two sticks of dynamite this time.'

The officer grinned. 'Tuan, it will take more than two sticks to blow up the power station.'

Hallett chuckled, but said nothing more. He had confirmed an earlier suspicion.

He went back to his car and drove through into the Inner Zone.

Chapter Eight

I

Keith Wilson, Her Britannic Majesty's Honorary Vice-Consul in Labuanga, had been born in Shanghai. When he was eight, his parents had sent him 'home' to school in England. When he was eighteen, he had returned to the Far East. Most of his working life had been spent in Borneo and Malaya. He looked, and, in a sense, was a typical middle-class, pipe-smoking Englishman. His wife had died in a Singapore internment camp during the war, and he had never remarried. The ruling passion of his life was cricket, and his only complaint against Labuanga was that there were not enough cricketers there to form two teams. He had a powerful radio receiver and spent much of his spare time listening to broadcast cricket commentaries on the Australian and B.B.C. short wave services. He held that the political stability of India and Pakistan owed as much to the legacy of cricket as to the existence of the British-trained Indian Civil Service. When not on the subject of cricket, he had an agreeable sense of humour. He also had the insights necessary to translate obscure Malay and Chinese jokes into colloquial English. The Halletts, who had read their Somerset Maugham, referred to him, not unaffectionately, as 'The Taipan'.

He answered Hallett's telephone call promptly. 'I tried to get you at the Subramaniams',' he said. 'They told me you were on your way back. Are you at home now?'

'Yes.' Hallett could hear the breathing of the switchboard operator listening to their conversation, and knew that Wilson could hear it, too. 'What about a drink?' he asked.

'Fine. Why don't you come over here and enjoy the view?'

'Be with you in a couple of minutes.'

Wilson's apartment was on the top floor of the oil company's building and overlooked the western half of the city. That was the area in which the power station was situated. Earlier, when the firing had started, he had been able to see through his binoculars a sparkle of tracer bullets in that direction. By the time Hallett telephoned, however, the firing had almost ceased. He had switched the radio over to battery operation, and was listening to the voices on the garrison communication frequency when Hallett arrived.

'What do you make of it, Keith?' Hallett asked.

'As far as I can gather, the Faithful sent a strong force in to take over the power station, and the army got in first. The Faithful took up encircling positions. Now they're all just sitting there. I don't understand it. If they wanted to dynamite the place, why didn't they use a small party and their usual hit and run tactics?'

'Why indeed?'

Wilson was lighting another candle. Something in Hallett's voice made him look up. 'Any ideas?'

'A hunch. You know the night defence plan. The moment there's an attack alarm, the main body concentrates in the Inner Zone. No dispersal of forces. All that's left outside is the mobile column. Where's that now?'

'Holding the power station.'

'Which is on the opposite side of town from the jail.'

'What about it?'

'That power station attack could be a diversion. The Faithful could be going for the jail to spring Major Sutan.'

Wilson thought for a moment. 'It's a possibility,' he said finally. 'Do you think Sutan's worth it to them?'

'He's an important member of the Committee. Besides, if they do nothing, don't they lose face?'

Wilson thought again. 'If they did get inside that jail,' he said, 'what they'd do there wouldn't be very nice.'

'That's what I was thinking. Once they started killing . . .'

'Yes. You know I tried to call our Consul in Medan earlier. I wanted him to go to the Area Commander and get Mrs Lukey moved out of here. They wouldn't put me through. Said the line was down.'

'I know. They gave me the same treatment. I'd made up my mind to fly over there in the morning if necessary. As it is . . .'

'What do we do? Call General Iskaq and request him to move troops out to the jail in case?'

Hallett frowned. 'I don't know. Let's think. Supposing he did take the idea seriously enough to send part of the garrison out there. Is that necessarily better for our people? Supposing the troops were given orders to shoot all prisoners in the case of an attack. It's happened before. Supposing someone like Major Gani decided to use them as hostages. Look at it another way. The more fighting there was, the more killing there would be after the fighting was over. After all, the jail doesn't matter to us, only those three persons inside it.'

'I gather you're against requesting reinforcements,' said Wilson dryly.

'I'm against hypothetical reinforcements in that hypothetical situation.'

Wilson switched the radio off. 'Well, it may be hypothetical, but I must confess you have me worried. Mrs Lukey's a highly-strung woman. Anglo-Indian, you know. Even with your Mrs Nilsen to help, she's in a pretty bad state. I didn't like leaving her there today.'

'Do you think she knows anything they want to know?'

Wilson hesitated before he said: 'I'm afraid she might do.'

Ross Hallett nodded. Mrs Lukey was a British subject and, common humanity aside, no concern of his. He thought about the Nilsens, who *were* his concern. To Fran he had referred to them as 'rogue tourists'. They had been irresponsible and stupid; more irresponsible and more stupid than the booziest oil-driller spoiling for a fight. So far, he had been able to view their predicament with a certain amount of detachment. Now it was beginning to frighten him. Men like General Iskaq and Major Gani were not easily deterred from violence by the fear of diplomatic consequences. The Nilsens could be murdered that very night, and he would be powerless except to protest and listen to polite expressions of regret.

'I'm going out to the jail,' he said. 'Do you want to come with me?'

'What are we going to do?'

'Ask to see the prisoners.'

'At this time of night? They won't let us.'

'No, but we'll be there. It can't do any harm and, if there is going to be trouble, it just might do some good.'

'Then we ought to put on a show. Flags on our cars, neckties, lots of protocol.'

'Whatever you say, Excellency.'

They had to make a wide detour to avoid going through the Inner Zone, and approached the section in which the jail was situated from the Chinese quarter to the south of it. It was probably that which saved them. If they had been coming from the Inner Zone, they would almost certainly have been fired upon before they had had time to identify themselves.

As Hallett's car was the more imposing, it had been agreed that he should lead the way. Skirting the Chinese quarter there was a deep drainage canal that was bridged in only two places. He was driving very slowly over the ruts and potholes of the approach road to one of the bridges, when something he saw in the headlights made him pull up quickly. He heard Wilson stopping behind him.

They were about fifty yards from the narrow earth ramp which led up to the bridge. At the foot of the ramp was an overturned cart completely blocking the way. Hallett got out of his car, Wilson joined him.

'What do you think, Keith?'

'We could probably move it out of the way between us.'

'Think we ought to try?'

'I don't know. Does it look like an accident to you?'

'Pretty funny sort of accident.'

On one side of the road there were a few small houses, but they were in complete darkness. The only sounds were those of crickets and of the car engines idling.

'What about leaving the cars here with the lights on and going a bit closer to have a look?'

'Okay.'

They walked forward into the beam of the headlights, heard the quick rustle of sandalled feet, and saw the long shadows of the men behind them flickering across the road ahead. As they swung round and stopped with their hands in the air, the men closed in.

2

It had been mid-afternoon when Voychinski had been taken away, and Greg had immediately used the opportunity to get some sleep.

It had been dark when he had wakened. Voychinski had not returned. After a while, a guard had come in with food and water. With it had been a package from Hallett containing a carton of cigarettes, two paperback novels, a tube of Entero-Vioforme, and a note saying that he hoped to secure further amenities the following day. The package had been opened and most of the cigarettes stolen. Greg had given one of the remaining packs to the guard, and received in return a cup of weak tea. His watch had been taken from him with the rest of his personal belongings, and he had had no means of telling the time. It had been about two hours later, it seemed, when the lights had gone out. He had thought that this must be part of the jail routine. Then, through the grille in the cell door, he had seen oil lamps being brought to light the corridor.

The cells had been left in darkness. As he could no longer read, he had gone to sleep again.

To Dorothy the power failure had brought a curious kind of relief.

Some time after nightfall, Mrs Lukey had been brought back to the cell sobbing incoherently. It appeared that after being questioned for over two hours by Major Gani, she had been taken to another room and confronted by Captain Voychinski. Already, he had been so badly beaten by his guards that he was scarcely able to stand; then, in front of her, they had knocked him down and kicked him until he became unconscious. After that, she had been taken out and warned, meaningly, that her own interrogation would shortly be resumed. Meanwhile, she should try to remember useful facts.

Dorothy had done her best to calm her; but without success. It had been all she could do to remain calm herself. If they could beat Captain Voychinski, they could beat Greg. The American Consul had said that Greg would not be physically harmed; but how could he be sure? These horrible little madmen might do anything.

'But what do they want to know?' she had asked. 'Mr Hallett said he was going to tell Greg to make a full statement.'

'There is another shipment already on the way.' Mrs Lukey had hesitated. 'They want to know about that.'

'Did you know about it?'

'Yes, I knew.'

'Did you tell them what they wanted?'

'I told them what was in the shipment. That is all I know. But they want the route so that they can intercept it. They said that if I did not know the route myself, I must tell them who did know.'

'What did you say?'

Mrs Lukey raised her panic-stricken eyes to Dorothy's. 'I told them Captain Voychinski knew.'

'And *does* he?' Dorothy was beginning to feel sick.

'He might.' The eyes pleaded for understanding and forgiveness. 'I could not help it. I had to say something or they would have beaten me.'

And then the lights had gone out, and Dorothy had no longer had to watch Mrs Lukey's eyes and wonder if, the next time she were questioned, she would become desperate enough to implicate Greg as well as Captain Voychinski.

There were two beds in that cell. After a while, Dorothy said: 'It looks as if we're not going to have any more light. I think we ought to try to get some sleep.'

'They will be coming for me again.'

'If you don't listen for them, maybe they won't.'

'I could not sleep.'

'Try.'

A few minutes later Mrs Lukey began, in a quiet, ladylike way, to snore.

Dorothy dozed fitfully. Hours seemed to go by. She was half awake, half asleep, when she heard a sound like a huge air-filled paper bag bursting somewhere near at hand. A moment later the sound came again. This time the bed shook a little. Mrs Lukey woke up and started to whimper.

3

Only convicted prisoners serving sentences of less than ninety days, and suspects on remand or awaiting trial, were held in Labuanga jail. It was built round two small quadrangles which were used as exercise yards; one for the male prisoners, one for the female. Separating the two quadrangles was the so-called 'control section'. This contained the guards' quarters, some interrogation rooms, a kitchen and the head jailer's office. A high outer wall enclosed the whole compound. The main gates, two imposing slabs of iron-braced teak, were opposite the control section entrance.

What Dorothy had heard were the explosions of two P.I.A.T. mortar bombs, stolen some months earlier from a British Army ordnance depot in Kuala Lumpur, and purchased from the thieves by Captain Lukey. They were fired, with some accuracy, from a projector which looked like a truncated Lewis gun, and the first one hit the junction of the gates just by the drop bar. Two of the brackets which supported it snapped, and a piece of the flying metal wounded one of the duty guards. The second bomb completed the work. The drop bar fell to the ground and one of the gates swung open. The unwounded guard was too dazed by the blast of the explosions to do more than stare as the attackers poured in. Then, as he turned and started to run, he tripped and fell to his knees. An instant later, a parang sliced down into the muscles of his neck, and he slid forward to die.

The grilles at the entrance to the control section were less imposing than the outer gates, but more efficient. A Very pistol was fired to give the P.I.A.T. crew light to aim by, but the bomb only bent and jammed the long sliding bolts. A second bomb aimed at the hinges was equally unsuccessful. By this time, too, the defenders had come to their senses. A flare was lobbed from the roof of the building on to the road, and a burst of rifle fire from behind the grille forced the P.I.A.T. crew to take cover behind the outer wall where they could do no more damage. The flare from the roof was now followed by grenades. Caught in the narrow space between the outer wall and the jail itself, the attackers began to suffer casualties.

However, they were well-trained and ably led. The surprise attack having failed, they set about blasting their way in. With the aid of smoke grenades and covering fire from across the road outside, more men were rushed through the broken outer gates. They had orders to work round the sides of the building, deal with the defenders on the roof, and then dynamite their way through from the rear.

Inside the control section, Major Gani, whose interrogation of Voychinski had been interrupted at an interesting point, was on the telephone to General Iskaq at his headquarters in the Inner Zone.

'No, sir,' he was saying, 'I cannot tell you how strong the attacking force is. It is impossible to estimate. But they are well armed, with machine-guns and an anti-tank weapon of some kind. Our guards are armed with only rifles and grenades. It is imperative that you send armoured cars and troops.'

'Anti-tank weapons?'

'They burst open the main gate with two shots.'

The General hesitated. Only four of his ten obsolete armoured cars were at that moment capable of taking the road. The rest had mechanical trouble of one sort or another. Three, which were awaiting spare parts from Italy, had been out of commission for months. The thought of exposing even one of the effective cars to the fire of anti-tank weapons made his heart sink.

He put a touch of impatience into his voice. 'Unless they destroy the outer wall first, they cannot use such long-range weapons against the building. The jail is of brick. Every window is barred. You have the main gate covered. Why do you need more troops?'

'These guards are not troops,' Major Gani replied. He knew that he had made a mistake in mentioning the anti-tank weapons, and tried to regain the initiative. 'I must remind you, sir,' he went on quickly, 'that we are holding prisoners here. This is an attempt to free them.'

'Of course. But they will not be freed.'

'Then send troops, sir.'

'They will not be freed,' the General repeated sharply. 'Better if they should all be killed.'

'You authorize me to kill those five prisoners, sir, including the American and British subjects?'

'It would be the insurgents who would be held responsible. But that will not be necessary. We will keep them. Has the white man talked yet?'

'No, sir. He . . .'

Somewhere overhead a grenade burst, and slabs of plaster fell down from the ceiling of the head jailer's office from which Major Gani was speaking. As the plaster dust billowed up, he heard the General asking if they had been cut off.

He managed to croak into the mouthpiece, 'Send troops,' before the dust forced him to start coughing; then, he hung up. If the General were left wondering what had happened, so much the better. The troops would be dispatched with more urgency.

He had misread the General's thought processes. The General was a hard man to stampede. So far, only about half of the available Party men had been armed with weapons from the intercepted shipments, and they had very little ammunition. Subsequent interceptions would no doubt improve that position, but, until they did, the 'militia' was not effective. As far as the General was concerned, the Inner Zone plan was still in force. That meant that the garrison did not dissipate its small strength by chasing off in all directions to fight wherever the rebels chose to attack. The thrust at the power station was obviously a diversion for the attempt on the jail; but that knowledge changed nothing. The power station was difficult to defend. The jail was virtually a stronghold. Gani was an Intelligence officer, unused to battle and therefore over-anxious. His reckless demand for armoured cars showed that. He must learn that there was more to soldiering than he had realized. The experience might make him more respectful.

The General's only misgiving at that moment concerned his authorization to kill the white prisoners. It would be annoying if Gani lost his head and killed them prematurely. For a moment or two he considered telephoning the jail and countermanding the authorization; but he concluded finally that any hint of indecision on his part could be misinterpreted just then. If there were a serious change in the situation at the jail, Gani would obviously report it. Meanwhile, it was best to leave things as they were.

At that moment, in fact, the situation at the jail was changing more rapidly than even Major Gani, knew. There had been fighting on the roof, and the jail guards up there had been cornered by the water tank. It was only a matter of time before the enemy winkled them out and gained access to the stairs leading below. With a steadiness and decision which would have surprised the General, Major Gani prepared to evacuate the control section and fall back behind the grilles and steel doors of the men's cell block. What he did not know was that, under cover of the roof fighting, a party had made its way to the rear of the building and was at that moment setting demolition charges in one of the drains.

Orders had been given to remove Sutan and Voychinski from the interrogation rooms and transfer them immediately to cells in the men's block, when the man who had taped the charges lighted the fuse.

4

Greg's cell was less than a hundred feet from the explosion. The blast wave slammed him against the wall, smashed the light fitting, and snatched the zinc screen out of the window embrasure as if it had been paper.

Since the attack had begun, he had been sitting there as wretched and perplexed as a child listening to a quarrel between adults. Outside in the corridor, there had been some confused shouting at first, and then the guards, apparently in response to an order, had all left. The other prisoners in that section had begun to carry on excited conversations in Malay through the door grilles. The exercise yard had been quiet. The sounds had been coming from the other side of the jail. He had started then to worry about Dorothy. If, as it seemed, there were some sort of jail riot going on, she could be in danger.

Now, as he got to his feet and went to the unscreened window, he could see a cloud of dust and smoke drifting across the moonlit yard. At the same moment, there was the crash of a grille opening along the corridor behind him and the sound of running, struggling, shouting men. Then, the air was shattered by a long burst of sub-machine-gun fire and the shouts changed to screams.

5

The Committee member in charge of the raiding force was a former army officer, Colonel Oda, whom Hallett had met on one of his trips into insurgent territory.

The Colonel had a protruding lower lip which curled inauspiciously at the smallest hint of opposition to his wishes; but he was not wholly unreasonable, and had been persuaded in the end that the proposal of his second-in-command to kill the American and British Vice-Consuls and commandeer their cars was both politically unsound and tactically unnecessary. On the subject of those in the jail, however, he had been adamant. He and he alone would decide what was to be done with them; prisoners and guards, white or brown. After further discussion he had agreed, reluctantly, to allow the foreign diplomatic representatives to accompany the attacking force. They would go as neutral observers of the justice meted out by the Committeee of the Faithful.

The reason for even that concession had soon become apparent. Neutral or no, the observers had been ordered, before the assault began, to park their beflagged cars bumper to bumper fifty yards from the jail entrance, in order to provide cover for the Colonel's battle headquarters among the trees beside the road. During the early stages of the fighting, Hallett and Wilson had been obliged to crouch behind the cars while carbine bullets from the roof of the jail had ripped through the door panels into the upholstery.

Half an hour after the first P.I.A.T. mortar bomb had been fired, the demolition charge blew out the rear wall of the control section. Two minutes after that, the sound of firing ceased. There was some shouting. Then, the second-in-command appeared at the main gate and called out that the place was taken. The Colonel walked across the road. He took no notice of Hallett and Wilson. They exchanged questioning glances, then left the cars and followed him.

As they went through the main gate the damaged grilles beyond were being levered open by the men inside. Lanterns had been brought. By their yellow light it was possible to see a group of guards huddled by an office door with their hands clasped behind their heads. The bodies of the guards who had been killed in the forecourt were lying face downwards at the foot of the steps. Their blood had drained into a broad puddle. The Colonel did not trouble to walk round it.

The blast of the demolition charge had brought down a great deal of plaster. The dust of it hanging in the air made Hallett and Wilson cough. It did not seem to affect the Colonel. He was talking to his second-in-command. When he saw the captured guards, however, he stopped and glanced over his shoulder at Hallett.

'Do you know where your American and British prisoners are in this place?' he asked.

'I know where they were, Colonel.' Hallett began coughing again.

The Colonel looked at one of the soldiers covering the guards. 'Keys,' he said.

The soldier looked at the six terrified guards. Three of them had long key chains at their belts. The soldier grinned and took out a knife. Then, he stepped forward and swung the knife upwards. The guard screamed as the double blade of the knife slashed through the belt and across his stomach simultaneously. As he doubled up in agony, the soldier snatched the belt away and handed the keys to the Colonel. The other two guards with keys hastily unfastened their belts and let them drop to the floor. The soldier with the knife laughed.

The Colonel pulled his lip in and nodded to Hallett. 'You may release your prisoners,' he said; 'but do not try to take them away from here.'

'Very well, Colonel.'

But the Colonel was already walking on. 'Voychinski can wait,' he was saying to the second-in-command. 'The one who matters is our Sutan.'

The guard with the stomach wound had sunk to the floor and was looking down stupidly at the blood pouring over his hands. Wilson picked up one of the belts and took the key chain off it. His face was white as he looked at Hallett.

'If you want to see that Nilsen's all right,' he said quietly, 'I'll look after the two women.'

Hallett nodded. 'Okay.'

He took the other belt and went on down the corridor. The demolition charge had wrecked the building here, and he had to pick his way over piles of rubble to get to the passage leading to the men's cell block. The soldiers there had seen him with their Colonel and made no move to stop him. In any case, they were too busy stripping the bodies of the dead guards to care much about a white man. He stumbled on, using the flashlight from his car to light the way and shutting his ears to the cries of two men who were not yet dead. From beyond the open grille ahead of him came the sound of prisoners calling to one another and pounding on the doors of their cells. One man was screaming hysterically that the place was on fire and that they would all be burnt alive. As Hallett went along trying to make out the cell numbers, he shouted in Malay that everything was all right and that all prisoners would soon be released. Under cover of the excited cries that followed this announcement he called out quietly: 'Mr Nilsen.'

'Here.'

He had already passed the cell. He went back, fumbling with the flashlight and the keys, and called again.

'Where are you? Keep talking.'

'Right here. Is that Hallett? What's going on? Is my wife all right? What's happened?' He was trying, not quite successfully, to keep a tremor out of his voice.

Hallett began trying the keys. 'Take it easy, Mr Nilsen. I've got to find the right key. The jail's been taken over temporarily by the insurgents. The

British Consul's gone along to get your wife and Mrs Lukey.'

'Is she all right?'

'There was no fighting on that side. They may be scared, but I'm pretty sure they're not hurt. Wait a minute. This looks as if it might be the right one.'

A moment later he had the cell door open, and saw the prisoner's face livid and desperate in the beam of the flashlight.

Hallett made himself smile. 'Dr Livingstone, I presume,' he said, and then: 'Steady, Mr Nilsen. Sit down a moment.'

'I just want to get out of here.' But he did as he was told. 'It sounded as if they'd blown the whole place up,' he added weakly.

'Only a bit of it. Now listen. We're in a curious sort of spot. Sutan's friends came to get him. Okay, they've got him. They won't hold this place for long, though. As soon as it starts to get light they'll be high-tailing it back to the hills. Where that leaves you and Mrs Nilsen, I don't know, unless you ask them to take you along. Even if they'd agree, I wouldn't advise that.'

'You mean we've got to stay here in jail?'

'I hope not. I don't know. I'm just warning you. At the moment it's all up to the commander of the raiding party, and he's a tough proposition. I'm taking you to him now. He doesn't speak much English, so he won't question you direct, but don't say anything unless I tell you to. Above all don't get mad or try to protest. Just keep quiet. Is that clear?'

'I don't have a protest left in me.'

'Good. How's your stomach?'

'Queasy.'

'Well, keep close to me and don't look around too much, or it may give you trouble.'

He led the way out of the cell and back towards the control section. He went quickly, holding the flashlight ahead of him and ignoring Nilsen's complaints that he could not see where he was going. Hallett judged that the man had reached a point of mental exhaustion at which he could very easily become unnerved. Anger was sometimes a useful restorative.

'Come on,' he said impatiently; we don't have much time.'

'Time for what?'

Hallett did not have to reply. They had reached the main corridor of the administration block and Colonel Oda's second-in-command was approaching. He was a square, muscular man with a wispy moustache and bright, stupid eyes. He had not forgotten that the Colonel had earlier accepted Hallett's arguments in preference to his own. He looked at Nilsen contemptuously.

'Is this your American?'

'This is Mr Nilsen, yes.'

'You will both come to the Colonel immediately.'

'Very well.'

The second-in-command turned on his heel and they followed him along the corridor. Hallett felt Nilsen's hand on his arm.

'What did he say?'

Hallett frowned warningly and told him loudly in Malay to hold his tongue. The second-in-command spoke no English and Hallett did not want to irritate him unnecessarily.

The room into which they were taken was the one in which Hallett had last seen Major Gani; and Major Gani was the first person he saw there now. He was standing against one of the barred windows, with a soldier on either side of him and blood running from his head and left shoulder. Sitting at the table beside Colonel Oda was a man whom Hallett guessed to be Major Sutan. His head was drooping and his face a deathly yellow in the lamplight. It was obviously all he could do to remain upright. The Colonel was talking to him quietly.

Across the table from them was Wilson with the two women. Mrs Lukey was crying. As soon as he saw his wife, Nilsen went over and put his arms round her. She began to cry, too. The Colonel looked up in exasperation and saw Hallett.

'Ah!' He rapped on the table as if for silence. 'I have told Mr Wilson. Now, I tell you, Mr Hallett. Major Sutan has confirmed the friendly status of these European prisoners. You may take them with you and go. That is all.'

Hallett's eyes met Wilson's. The latter shrugged resignedly.

The Colonel frowned. 'That is all,' he repeated sharply.

'Thank you.' Hallett bowed slightly. 'May I ask where you suggest they should go to?'

'That is their affair. They are free to go.'

'Just a moment, Colonel.' Hallett went forward to the table. 'You asked Mr Wilson and me to come here as neutral observers to witness the administration of justice by the Committee of the Faithful. You say now that Major Sutan has confirmed the friendly status of these persons. Yet you are prepared to send them away from here, without protection, to be re-arrested by the Central Government, put back into prison like common criminals, perhaps shot as your collaborators. Is that the justice of the Committee of the Faithful?'

'They are free to go. I do not understand what you want.'

'He understands all right,' Wilson said in English. 'I've just finished explaining it to him.'

Hallett kept his eyes on the Colonel. 'It has been instructive to see how the Committee of the Faithful keeps faith with its friends,' he said. He put a sarcastic inflection on the word 'Faithful'.

The second-in-command stepped forward. 'You do not have to hear these insults, Colonel. Give the order and I will see that they cause no further trouble.'

The Colonel ignored him. 'What can we do?' he demanded angrily. 'What do you expect?'

'A safe conduct for these persons to the airport, and permission to embark on the first Malayan Airways plane to Penang or Singapore.'

'You are a fool or mad.'

'I don't believe so.'

'This is a raiding force, not an army of occupation. Only General Iskaq could give such a safe conduct.'

'I know that.'

The Colonel laughed shortly. 'Then you must know also that you are wasting my time. We have released these persons. They are in your care. We can do no more.'

'You can obtain a safe conduct for them from General Iskaq.'

'Impossible.'

'Is it? Why not ask Major Gani?' Without waiting for a reply Hallett looked across the room at the man by the window. 'Major, do you think that General Iskaq values your services highly enough to grant a safe conduct for Mr and Mrs Nilsen and Mrs Lukey in exchange for your release unharmed?'

He saw Gani's eyes flicker. Then, there was a crash as Colonel Oda stood up quickly and his chair shot back against the wall.

Wilson started to move towards Hallett. The second-in-command snapped back the cocking handle of his machine pistol.

Hallett looked from the machine pistol to the Colonel's lower lip and shrugged. 'Violence is the fool's answer for every difficulty,' he remarked. 'I did not think it was yours, Colonel.'

'Get out, before we think too much.'

Hallett inclined his head. 'Very well. It is a pity. I had hoped that Mr Wilson and I could have been of help to you.'

The Colonel's lip curled proudly. 'We did not need your help to take this prison. We will not need your help to take all Labuanga when we wish.'

'Maybe not. But you will find that taking Labuanga is easier than keeping it. One day, soon perhaps, you will proclaim an autonomous government here and declare your independence of Djakarta and Medan. It is then you will need the help of friends.'

'These are our friends,' the Colonel tapped his pistol holster.

'They will not win your government recognition. Think, Colonel. The Central Government will denounce you as brigands and bandits and destroy you as they destroyed your comrades in Celebes. To whom will you appeal for justice? To the United Nations? The Central Government is there before you. To the Soviet Union? You are anti-Communists. The only ears that will hear you are in the United States and Britain. Our countries, Mr Wilson's and mine, admire good fighting men, but they also value moderation. No doubt Major Sutan has been vilely ill-treated by this man Gani. But how will you explain that, merely in order to have your revenge by torturing and killing Gani, you endangered the lives of two Americans and a British subject? Supposing General Iskaq puts them back here tomorrow, has them killed, and then tells the world that they were savagely murdered by you when the jail was attacked. How could you deny it?'

'You would know that was not true,' the Colonel said indignantly.

'Would I? It seems to me that there is a very small difference between that and what you are planning. And how foolish that plan is. Simply by using Gani as a hostage you could not only cause General Iskaq to lose face, but also show yourselves as humane and honourable men, infinitely more worthy of governing Labuanga than these lackeys from Djakarta. These things are not forgotten. When the day comes on which you need the friendship of the United States and the nations of the British Commonwealth, which memory will you prefer–that of killing Major Gani or that of having saved Americans and British lives?'

The Colonel stared at him for a moment and then sat down again. He looked at Sutan inquiringly.

Sutan's haggard eyes looked up at Hallett. 'Captain Voychinski has died from the beatings this man gave him,' he said slowly in English. 'Perhaps the gentleman does not know that. Voychinski was a white man. Perhaps, if the gentleman saw Voychinski's body, he would not feel so merciful.'

'It's not mercy he's asking for,' Wilson put in; 'but some protection for these people who came here to do business with you.'

'They came at their own risk.'

'Oh no. They came because you wanted them to. They were told there was no risk. Personally, I feel they were unwise, but I also feel that you people have a responsibility. Besides, have you thought about what would happen to your future arms deliveries if you turn these three persons over to the authorities? You wouldn't be able to buy a bow and arrow after that.'

The Colonel hammered on the table with his fist. 'We are *not* turning them over to the authorities,' he shouted.

'In effect you are.' Hallett had taken over again. 'That is unless they have a safe conduct out of the country.'

The Colonel turned to Sutan.

Sutan shrugged wearily. 'Gani learned nothing that matters. Do what is best.'

The Colonel looked with disgust from the white men to Major Gani. His eyes hardened.

'We had good plans for you, Gani,' he said. 'Perhaps, if your General does not love you enough, we shall still carry them out. Or perhaps, if you stay in Labuanga, there will be another day.'

'Perhaps,' said Major Gani.

The Colonel motioned to the telephone. 'Then see if your fine General will speak to you.'

6

General Iskaq had not been unduly worried by the absence of news from the jail. An explosion had been heard in that direction; but the sounds of firing had later ceased. He had assumed that the situation at the jail was now similar to that at the power station. When he heard Gani's voice on the telephone, he was prepared to be calm and matter-of-fact. By making no reference at all to Gani's hysterical behaviour earlier, he would emphasize its absurdity far more effectively than by drawing attention to it.

When he heard what Gani had to say, a spasm like an electric shock seemed to jolt him from his heels to the top of his head. His ears began to sing.

Through the singing he became aware of Gani's repeating urgently:

'General! General! Can you hear me?'

He controlled himself carefully before he answered: 'You say you are a hostage?'

'Yes, General. You see, the position is this . . .'

'Answer my questions!' He had heard the brisk self-assurance flowing back into Major Gani's voice, and, in a sudden rage, shouted the order.

'Certainly, General. But you see . . .'

'What steps were taken about the white prisoners?'

'Unfortunately, Captain Voychinski died. The others are alive. It is about those persons . . .'

'And Sutan?'

'Major Sutan is beside me, sir, and Colonel Oda.'

'Why have they not killed you?'

'If you will permit me to explain, sir.'

He explained.

The General listened with mounting bitterness. Fantasies began to crowd into his mind. He would countermand his standing orders about night operations and the Inner Zone, take his armoured cars and field guns out, and blast the jail into a heap of rubble. He would kill everyone in it, including Major Gani. The anti-tank weapons of the raiding force would be crushed beneath the wheels of the armoured cars. There would be a holocaust. Or, simpler, he would refuse the safe conduct, tell them to kill Gani, and then hang the three whites publicly in front of the Stadhuis. Or, wiser, more cunning, he would put a cordon round the jail area, cover it with the field guns, and starve them all into submission. He knew that none of those things was really going to happen, that he could never be sure that the power station and jail attacks were not tricks to lure him out of the Inner Zone so that the garrison could be chopped to pieces by the main body of the insurgents. He also knew that, however much he might want to discard Major Gani, the time had not yet come when he could safely do so. Without Gani, the arming of the militia could not be completed, and he, the Military Governor, would be left again to plead impotently for reinforcements which would never arrive. He knew, too, that he could never justify, even to himself, the proposition that the life of one Indonesian officer was worth sacrificing for the pleasure of punishing three whites.

He heard himself saying: 'Very well. I understand. But what guarantees do we have that they will keep the agreement?'

'One moment, sir.'

'I had better speak to Oda myself.'

'One moment, please, sir.'

There was a pause and silence. Gani had had the impertinence to put his hand over the microphone. Then another detested voice addressed him.

'Governor, this is Ross Hallett. I am at the jail in order to protect the lives of two American citizens. Colonel Oda, who commands the troops now in control of the jail compound, has requested my assistance and that of the British Vice-Consul in the matter of this proposed exchange of prisoners.'

'What kind of assistance?'

'As referees, Governor. It will be five hours before a Malayan Airways freight plane leaves that could take Mr and Mrs Nilsen and Mrs Lukey out of Indonesian territory. During that period, Colonel Oda's troops will leave the jail compound. They will take Major Gani with them. So that there will be no misunderstandings, or unfortunate incidents, Mr Wilson will accompany Major Gani and remain with him. I shall remain at the airport with Mr and Mrs Nilsen, Mrs Lukey and three of Colonel Oda's officers, until the plane leaves. I shall then telephone Mr Wilson and the exchange will be completed. Major Gani will report to you. Colonel Oda's officers will report back to him.'

'You expect me to trust you?'

'Colonel Oda is prepared to trust us, Governor. However, should either side attempt to take advantage of the situation, Mr Wilson and I will personally offer ourselves as hostages until the agreement is carried out.'

The General thought for a moment. The possibilities of trickery inherent in such a situation were many. Hallett had obviously envisaged some of them. For instance, he had stipulated a Malayan Airways plane. That precluded the use of an Indonesian plane to take the prisoners into the air and set them down at Labuanga again after Gani's release. But, what was to prevent Oda, on learning that his white accomplices were free, from killing Gani and laughing at Mr Wilson's protests? The lives of three expendable junior officers? The General sighed. He knew the answer to that. No insurgent leader who hoped to survive would dare to abandon so treacherously even the most useless of his men.

'How can I believe that you will not favour the traitors in arranging this exchange?' the General said at last.

'Do you really believe, Governor, that Mr Wilson and I are dishonest?'

The General examined his inner thoughts and found, somewhat to his surprise, that his truthful answer to that question would be 'no'. He decided to ignore it.

'Very well,' he said coldly.

'Then perhaps I may discuss the detailed arrangements for the exchange with a member of your staff.'

'I will discuss the arrangements personally.'

When the conversation was finished, the General made a few notes and sent for his senior colonel.

Only one thing puzzled him. Gani had tortured Sutan. Sutan and Oda were friends. How was it that such men, whom he himself knew and had once respected, could forego the satisfaction of tearing Gani to pieces with their own hands in order to permit three whites to escape without a scratch on their ugly skins? It seemed incredible. And yet, from another point of view, it showed how easily Asians became weak and corrupt through association with white men. It showed how right he had been himself to resist the temptation to come to terms with the Party of the Faithful. The thought was comforting.

7

It was four o'clock in the morning when Hallett set out in his bullet-scarred car to drive Greg, Dorothy and Mrs Lukey from the jail to the airport. Following him, in Major Gani's personal jeep, were the three insurgent officers who would replace them as hostages when the plane took off three and a half hours later.

Hallett had managed to retrieve the two passports and an envelope with Greg's valuables in it from the wreckage of the head jailer's officer; but, at his lukewarm suggestion that some other way might be found of picking up their other belongings from Harmonie Hotel, Greg had shaken his head.

'We've caused enough trouble,' he had said. 'As far as Dorothy and I are concerned they can keep everything, camera included. We just want out.'

Mrs Lukey had not been so accommodating. Hallett had explained briefly to Greg and Dorothy the substance of the negotiations for their release; but Mrs Lukey had understood them at the time and, as a result, had acquired an exaggerated idea of the strength of their position.

'I do not see why someone should not be sent from the hotel to the airport,' she had said. 'I have a very nice overnight case. It was very expensive. I do not want to lose it. These people are all thieves.'

Hallett had started to remind her that the Inner Zone was still closed, when Dorothy had firmly taken Mrs Lukey aside. Neither man had heard what she said, but, thereafter, Mrs Lukey had been subdued, and there had been no more talk of her overnight case.

The General had evidently decided that the opportunity of impressing three insurgent officers with the strength of the Labuanga garrison had been too good to miss, and the airport building was bristling with troops when they arrived. As Hallett presented himself to the officer in charge, an armoured car moved in menacingly, if pointlessly, to cover the approaches to the bus yard.

They were taken to a large store in the customs section to await the arrival of the plane. Hallett asked for food and tea, and rather to his surprise, some was presently brought. Access, under escort, to a near-by wash-room was also granted, providing that not more than two persons went at a time. Dorothy and Mrs Lukey were away taking advantage of this concession, when Greg raised a question that was beginning to trouble him.

'Does everybody know about all this?' he asked. 'I mean, will it get in the newspapers back home?'

Hallett's smile was not entirely free from malice. 'If it gets in the newspapers here,' he said, 'you can bet your life it'll be picked up back home. So far, it's all been kept secret. I don't imagine the General'll want to give it any publicity now. The Press do what they're told here anyway. Where you'll have to be careful is in Singapore.'

'How do you mean?'

'Well, you'll be put on this plane under armed guard. You can't stop the crew talking when they get back. You might be questioned when you arrive. If I were you, I'd have a nice dull story ready in advance for the pilot.'

'Like what?'

'Technically your visa's not in order. You were only cleared for Bali. You've been held here under guard. You could be pretty mad about it. Why didn't Garuda Indonesian Airlines check your visa carefully before flying you out from Singapore? Goddamn Asian inefficiency. That sort of stuff. I'm not telling you to say that, mind. That's just advice.'

'Thanks. I wish there were something I could do for you.'

'Don't worry about that, Mr Nilsen. There's no real harm been done.'

'Major Gani's going back to work, isn't he? That's harm. You can't have enjoyed making that deal.'

'No?' Hallett laughed. 'I was never so relieved in my life. When the General agreed to swap you three for that sadistic bastard, I thought he must be kidding.'

Greg stared. 'Why?'

'You don't know General Iskaq. I'd have said he'd have ditched his own wife for the chance of keeping his hands on you three. He hates the whites. Always has.'

'So you said. But you knew he couldn't ditch Gani.'

'Couldn't? I was almost sure he would. You don't know how lucky you are.'

'But in view of what he and Gani are doing, surely he *had* to have him back.'

Hallett frowned. 'What are you talking about?'

'Well, aren't they hijacking all these insurgent arms shipments to arm the Communists? Isn't Gani the Party go-between?'

Hallett said nothing for a moment, then looked across at the three officers. They were curled up on top of some packing cases, asleep. He looked again at Greg.

'Who told you that?'

'Voychinski. Didn't you know? He spoke as if it were common knowledge.'

'Well, it isn't. Can you remember exactly what he said?'

Greg could. He would remember every moment he had spent in that jail for the rest of his life.

'Is it important?' he ended.

'If it's true, and that could easily be checked, it's important enough to relieve Iskaq of his job and start a clean-up. Assuming the Area Commander in Medan were to find out, of course.'

'Will he?'

'That's not for me to say. All I'll have to do is send an information report through. You'll be quoted as the source, naturally.'

'Do I have to be?'

'I'll have to send through a report about your arrest and the reasons for it.' His smile was no longer unfriendly. 'This could just about square the account,' he added.

'That's something, I suppose.'

'It is. By the way, was that cheque of Sutan's with your other things? I didn't look to see.'

'I don't know.' Greg got his passport out and opened it. The cheque was still there. He looked up at Hallett. 'Did Major Sutan mention it to you at all?'

'No.'

'That's funny. He must have known they'd found it, but he said nothing to me before we left. I know he was in pretty bad shape, but you'd think he'd have been anxious about that.'

'Perhaps he took it for granted that an experienced arms peddler like you would have asked for another cheque if he needed it.' There was a gleam of amusement in his eyes.

Greg was silent for a moment, then he folded the cheque carefully and put it in another pocket. 'Did you see Voychinski's body?' he asked.

Hallett seemed to find nothing inconsequential in the question. He nodded. 'Major Sutan evidently felt that a mutilated corpse ought to prove something about the Central Government. All it proves really, of course, is that in civil wars there are always men around like Major Gani.'

'I think that Voychinski was that kind of man himself.' Greg remembered something. 'By the way, did you or Wilson tell Dorothy *how* he died?'

'I didn't, and I don't imagine Wilson would. Maybe Mrs Lukey told her. Why?'

'Well, she didn't appear to worry too much about those guards who were killed. But Voychinski dying, that really seemed to upset her.'

8

The freight plane from Koetaradja and Medan landed at seven-thirty and took off again for Singapore at eight. The captain was a New Zealander. Greg had no difficulty in boring him with complaints about Indonesian red tape and a garbled tale of mislaid overnight bags. He listened absently, lent Greg an electric shaver, and returned to his seat in the nose. They did not see him again.

Most of the interior space was taken up by pieces of machinery going to Singapore and beyond for repair, and mail-bags. The plane was unpressurized, cold and noisy. They sat on the mail-bags, dozing fitfully, until the Malay radio operator came aft to warn them that in five minutes they would be landing in Singapore. The plane taxied in to the freight sheds and the operator led them across to the passenger arrival section so that they could go through immigration and customs. He left them there, politely declining the tip Greg offered him.

It was the first time the three of them had been alone together and able to talk freely since the evening of their arrest. Mrs Lukey, hollow-eyed and plaintive when she had been awakened on the plane, now became flustered and embarrassed. As soon as they were through the customs, she hurried off to telephone her husband.

Greg sighed. 'Oh, my God! Do we have to wait for her? All I want in the world at the moment is the Raffles Hotel, a bath, and a drink.'

'Me, too, darling,' said Dorothy; 'but I think we have to wait a moment.'

'I suppose so. Don't you think one of us ought to tell her that we're not holding her responsible for anything.'

'I don't think so.' Dorothy's tone was surprisingly firm.

'Just as you say. Only she looked perfectly miserable to me.'

'I don't think we're feeling exactly gay, are we, darling?'

He kissed her, but she drew away.

'Don't. We both smell of that place still.'

'I know.'

They stood there unhappily until Mrs Lukey returned.

'I had to telephone,' she explained breathlessly. 'I knew he would be terribly worried when we did not get back yesterday. He sent a cable off but there was no reply. He is coming over immediately with the car.'

Dorothy nodded. 'That's good, but I don't think we'll wait, Betty.'

'Oh, but you must.'

'No. We'll get a cab to the Raffles.'

'That's right,' said Greg. 'Maybe we'll talk later, or tomorrow morning when we're rested up a bit.'

'But he said he wanted to see you.'

'Sure, but not right now, eh? We'll be in touch.'

She seemed both relieved and distressed to see them go.

In the taxi they were silent until, as they were nearing the hotel, Dorothy said: 'Did you get that cheque back?'

'Yes, it was still in the passport.' He paused. 'We don't even have a toothbrush,' he went on. 'I suppose we'd better stop at a drug store and buy a few things.'

By the time they had bathed it was twelve-thirty. Greg rang down to the bar for double dry Martinis, but neither he nor Dorothy wanted any lunch. While they were drinking the Martinis, he telephoned Cook's.

'This is Mr Nilsen . . . Yes, we're back from Indonesia . . . Yes . . . Well, we decided to cut it short. Now look. I'd like you to check up for me on boats sailing during the next couple of days for Calcutta . . . No, that doesn't matter. British, Norwegian, German, anything you like, as long as it's comfortable. We'd want a large stateroom with bath, air-conditioned if possible . . . I see. Okay, but not too slow and it's got to be comfortable with good food. At the same time I'd like to know about flights to Calcutta . . . Via Bangkok. We might want to stop there for a couple of days . . . Yes, that's right . . . No, not today. We'll come around and see you in the morning . . . Thanks.'

He hung up and his eyes met Dorothy's.

'Could we afford the Bangkok trip?' she asked.

'I don't know. Let's see what it would cost anyway.'

He smiled at her, but she was looking down at her drink now.

'Greg, what are you going to do about Captain Lukey?'

He got up with a sigh. 'I don't know. While we were in the plane I tried to think about it. We went to get a cheque signed and–' he hesitated–'get off the beaten track. Well, we did both. Logically, all I have to do now is go to the customs office with Tan and Lukey, sign some papers and collect sixty-two thousand five hundred dollars. But . . .' He broke off.

'But you don't know if you want to be logical.'

'That's right. What do you think?'

She went over and kissed his cheek. 'Maybe we should get some sleep,' she said.

Chapter Nine

I

Greg woke at six-thirty in the evening. His body ached all over and he had a metallic taste in his mouth. Dorothy was still asleep. He went into the sitting-room, shut the bedroom door softly behind him and rang for some ice. When it came, he got out the remains of the bottle of whisky purchased for his first meeting with Captain Lukey, and made himself a drink. As he drank it, he realized that he would be feeling very hungry, but for one thing: he could still smell the jail.

He thought carefully about that. Before they had gone to bed, both he and Dorothy had thoroughly washed every inch of themselves, their hair included; and they had given every stitch of clothing they had been wearing to the room boy with orders to burn or otherwise dispose of it. There could be only one reason for the phenomenon. 'Thank *you*, Doctor Freud,' he muttered sourly.

He reached for the telephone and asked the operator to see if Mr Lane Harvey of the American Syndicated Wire Service could be found at his office or at the American Club.

Harvey was at the Club, and sounded as if he had been there for some time.

'And how was fabulous Bali?' he asked.

'Great.'

'And those nubile young ladies with the fecund breasts and the sidelong looks? How were they? Or maybe I'd better ask Mrs N. about them.'

'Maybe you had. Look, I want to have a word with Colonel Soames. Do you mind telling me how I can get in touch with him?'

There was a momentary pause before Harvey answered. 'The Policeman? Sure. Just call up police admin. They'll put you through to his office.'

'I meant this evening.'

'Oh. Well, I don't have my book with me right now, but I'll be going back to my office some time. Supposing I call you later.'

'Thanks. I'm at the Raffles.'

'I'll call you.'

His tone was careless and he hung up almost before the last word was out. Greg suspected that the promise had already been forgotten. He put some more ice in his drink and then looked up the word 'Police' in the telephone directory. There was a long list of entries none of which was 'Police admin.'. He was edging his way through the listings under 'Government', when the telephone rang.

'This is Soames,' said a well-remembered voice.

'Colonel Soames, I was just trying to contact you.'

'So I gathered. That's why I'm phoning. What can I do for you?'

'I need advice. I'd like to see you as soon as I can.'

'Won't the morning do?'

'I was hoping . . .' Greg broke off. 'Look, I've been in Labuanga. I got back today. It's sort of urgent.'

There was a pause. 'Very well, Mr Nilsen. I'll meet you in the Raffles lounge in fifteen minutes. Will that be all right?'

'Fine. Thanks.'

He went back into the bedroom. Dorothy was fast asleep. Very quietly, he collected the clothes he needed and returned to the sitting-room. When he was dressed, he left a note for Dorothy telling her where he was, and went down to the lounge.

2

Colonel Soames arrived with the sandwiches Greg had ordered. He was wearing a white dinner jacket.

'Hope this won't take long,' he said briskly. 'I'm due at a dinner party at eight-thirty.'

'It's a longish story,' said Greg; 'but I'll cut it as short as I can. What are you drinking?'

'Is that coffee you've got there?'

'Yes.'

'I'll have some of that. Now, what's the trouble?'

The Colonel was a good listener. He did not stir as Greg told him the history of his dealings with the Tan brothers, Captain Lukey and the Party of the Faithful. Twice only, he interjected brief questions to obtain a clarification of detail. Once, he signalled to the waiter to bring some more coffee. When Greg had finished he sat back.

'That's all?'

'Yes.'

'What did you say that fellow's name was? Gani?'

'Yes. Major Gani.'

'Very interesting. Might come in handy to our people some time. Much obliged to you.' He paused. 'You said you wanted advice, though.'

'Help would be a better word.'

'For a rank amateur you don't seem to have done so badly without help. You've been lucky, of course, but didn't someone say luck was a form of genius?'

Greg leaned forward. 'Colonel, you said at lunch the other day that you'd considered having me deported.'

The Colonel chuckled amiably. 'If I'd known what I know now, I probably would have. Can't have amateurs fooling about in the arms racket. Disgraceful state of affairs!'

'Supposing you had deported me,' Greg went on; 'and supposing I'd just been on the point of concluding a piece of business that netted me sixty-two thousand five hundred Straits dollars. Would I have been allowed to complete it?'

The Colonel's smile faded and he eyed Greg curiously. 'That would have depended. I was only gingering you up a bit. You wouldn't have been deported unless the Indonesians had made a formal and specific complaint against you. In that case, naturally, we'd have tried to stop you completing.'

'Once I was out could I have come back?'

'Of course not.'

Greg nodded. 'That's what I wanted to know. Right, Colonel. As a favour to me, I'd like you to have a deportation order made out against me.'

'I beg your pardon?'

'Naturally, I'd like it done without any fuss or publicity. I figure there wouldn't be any, unless I tried to contest the order, and obviously I wouldn't do that. I'm sure that if I were to have a word with the American Consul first there'd be no trouble there.'

The Colonel was staring at him angrily. 'If this is your idea of humour, Nilsen, I think it's in very poor taste.'

'I'm quite serious.'

'Then you must be up to some game I don't know about. I think you'd better tell me what that is.'

'Certainly. I want to call this whole deal off.'

The Colonel scowled. 'I see. Had a better offer for the stuff. My dear chap, if you think you're going to use me to get you off the hook, you're very much mistaken.'

'I haven't another offer. I don't want another offer. I just want out from the whole filthy business.'

'But not neglecting to take your commission, I imagine.'

'No deal, no commission, nothing.'

The Colonel shook his head wearily. 'All right, what are you up to? Come on, let's hear it.'

'I've told you. I want out.' He paused, then shrugged. 'You may as well know the whole idiotic truth. When I went into this thing it was a sort of a joke. I was told these arms had been hijacked from the Communists. I thought it would be highly amusing to help put them into the hands of anti-Communists. Don't ask me how I managed to sucker myself into thinking that I was doing something pretty smart. That's another cute little story. The thing is, I fell for all that double talk of Tan's in Manila like a kid. No, that's unfair. My own sons would have had more sense.' He paused again.

'Well, then I got what I deserved. I had a chance of seeing a bit of both sides of this fascinating little war. Oh yes, I found a Communist bastard all right, and he was right where you might have expected him to be. But I found a Fascist bastard there as well.'

The Colonel laughed shortly. 'And wasn't *he* where you might have expected *him* to be?'

'I guess he was.' Greg's lips thinned. 'But you have to remember this, Colonel. I'd been dealing in make-believe. Now for a real hundred per cent Rover-boy like me, just a lick of reality can be terribly uncomfortable and disturbing. To say nothing of the fact that Rover-boy managed to put his wife as well as himself into a very dangerous situation, where they not only became a source of acute embarrassment to their country's representative, but had to be rescued by him as well. So you see, Colonel, the joke's now over. My wife's a very tolerant woman. She hasn't said "I told you so," and she won't. But I have a bad conscience and she knows it. I think she'd like me to do something about that. So, that's what I'm trying to do.'

The Colonel sneered. 'I see. You'd like to wash your hands of the whole thing, and make believe none of it ever happened.'

'Yes, that's about the size of it, I guess. More make-believe, as you say. Well, maybe that won't work, but there are some things I can do.'

'Like having yourself deported? What would that accomplish?'

'One thing. It would put Tan back right where he started. Originally, he couldn't move those arms from Manila because of some legal snag, or so he said. I'm his sole authorized agent. If I'm expelled from here, I can't sign them out of bond or transfer ownership. That means he can't move the arms from Singapore because of a legal snag. So he's back where he was before I came along, and those arms are back behind the eight ball. He can't take legal action against me because the circumstances are beyond my control. He can have his cheque for a thousand dollars back. Finish.'

The Colonel looked perplexed. 'I see your point, but, my dear fellow, you're not seriously asking me to have you deported, are you?'

'I am.'

'I'm not Himmler, you know. I'd have to justify such a request, and I don't see how I could.'

'Why not? You said yourself that a complaint from the Indonesian Government could do the trick. I bet there's one on the way right now.'

'If what you say about General Iskaq is true, I should think that extremely unlikely. He'd have to send his complaint through Medan and that'd mean he'd have to answer a lot of awkward questions first.' He shook his head. 'No, I'm afraid it won't do. If that's your idea of washing your hands, you can forget about it.'

'Well, thanks for listening.'

The Colonel glanced at his watch. 'I'll have to be off.' He hesitated. 'Of course, it's none of my business really, but I can't help thinking that you're being a bit hard on yourself, Nilsen.'

'Yes?'

'And on one or two other people as well.'

'Including Tan?' Greg asked sarcastically.

'I wasn't thinking of him. You see,' the Colonel went on thoughtfully,

'I'm something of a prig myself, too, on occasions, so I can understand how you feel. But one thing I have noticed. When all the hand-washing, clean slate stuff begins, it usually has the effect of landing someone else in the soup. Funny thing, moral indignation.'

Greg said nothing.

'This idea of yours, for instance.' The Colonel broke off to murmur something in Malay to a passing waiter. 'It wasn't such a bad idea really, selling Communist supplies to anti-Communist forces, hoisting them with their own petards or whatever the phrase is. Not bad at all.'

'Maybe. If they really had been Communist supplies.'

'They were that, all right.'

'You don't mean to say you believe that story of Tan's about collateral for a debt?'

'No, but I had one of my chaps take a closer look at the stuff. The types of weapons, the manufacturers, the ammunition batch numbers, the quantities—it all corresponds to a very familiar pattern.'

'What pattern?'

'Terrorist arms cache. That's exactly the kind of parcel the Chinese were shoving across the Thai border into Malaya four or five years ago. Couldn't mistake it.'

'Where did Tan get it then?'

'How should I know? Probably stole it. Does it matter?'

'No, except that, if he did, that makes me a receiver of stolen goods as well.'

The Colonel sighed. 'As well as what, my dear fellow? Of what other crimes against God or man are you accusing yourself?'

'Arrogance, ignorance, stupidity, and trying to make a fast buck out of men trying to kill one another. Will that do for the moment?'

The waiter put down two stengahs in front of them.

'As I doubt if I shall reach my hostess in time to be offered a drink before dinner, this is just a precaution,' the Colonel explained. 'After all the breast-beating you've been doing, you could probably use one, too.'

Greg was silent.

The Colonel drank half the contents of his glass, and then dabbed his lips with a black silk handkerchief. 'Nowadays,' he said, 'we don't hear the phrase "merchants of death" very much. It's all very sad. The idea that the act of selling arms somehow tricked people into making wars they didn't want never really stood up to very close inspection, did it? But it was good to have a fine, top-hatted bogey-man to put all the blame on. The trouble is we've learned a thing or two since 1939. Now, we can't even blame the politicians—not with much conviction anyway. The real bogey-man crawled out of the mud with our ancestors millions of years ago. Well, we all have a piece of him, and when we start to put the pieces together it's like one of those nuclear fission things—when the mass reaches a critical point a chain reaction starts and, poof!'

Greg raised his eyebrows. 'I always thought there was a standard justification for any sort of illicit peddling, whether it was in drugs, smut or arms. 'If I don't, somebody else will.' Isn't yours a bit new?'

'I wasn't talking about illicit peddling,' the Colonel replied huffily; 'and I wasn't attempting to justify anything. I was merely trying to correct your rather muddled view of your obligations at this moment. Selling arms or selling the wherewithal to make them—what's the difference? What does your Government do with the die-castings you make for them—feed the hungry or put them into ballistic missiles?'

'The United States Government isn't selling arms for profit.'

'I must remember that when the nuclear war starts. It'll be a great comfort.'

Greg's temper was beginning to fray at the edges. 'As I said before, Colonel, you change hats rather easily. Which one are you wearing at the moment?'

'Major Sutan's, probably.'

Greg looked at him, startled.

The Colonel picked up his drink and examined it dubiously. 'Of course,' he said slowly, 'you've had a trying time, a surprise or two, and not very much sleep. Apt to warp a man's judgment, those things. Same as a hangover. Alcoholic remorse and all that.' He looked up with a small smile.

'What are you getting at, Colonel?'

'Well now. Let's suppose I'm Sutan. Rightly or wrongly, I'm buying arms with which to fight for something—freedom, power, social justice or one of the other delusions. You offer to sell me arms and I accept your offer. We're both men of good faith, eh? I give you a cheque and then something unforeseen happens. As a result, I and my friends have a choice. We can wash our hands of you and your wife and leave you both to rot, or we can, at some cost to ourselves, see that you go free. It's not an easy choice, but we decide in your favour, and you go free. To show your appreciation, you promptly call the deal we've made off, and try and arrange things so that nobody else can call it on again. How does that sound to you?'

Greg sighed. 'As it was intended to sound, of course. However, the facts are a bit different.'

'I'm sure they are. But you began by asking for advice. Then you asked me to help you. I couldn't do that, so perhaps you'll accept some advice after all. It's not your conscience that's troubling you, Mr Nilsen, but a slight injury to your self-esteem. Officially, I'm not particularly interested now either in you or in what happens to those arms. Unofficially though, I would suggest that you do something about recovering your sense of humour.'

'So that I can laughingly go ahead with the deal as planned?'

'Oh, I've no doubt you'll find a way of penalizing yourself in the process, like sending that thousand dollar cheque back to Tan.' He got to his feet. 'I really must be going now. I think I'll let you pay for my drink.'

'Good-bye, Colonel.'

The Colonel hesitated, then sat down again. 'I don't like to leave you in this despondent mood,' he said. 'If it's laughter you need, it's just possible that I may be able to help you.'

'I'll stop you if I've heard it.'

The Colonel ignored the remark. 'What was your arrangement with Tan in Manila about payment?' he asked. 'What were you to do with the money from Lukey?'

'Pay it into the Merchants' Security Bank here for the credit of his account.'

'Was anything particular said about what you were to do if you received the money in cash?'

'No. Why? I seem to be missing the point of this story, Colonel. You know, I doubt very much if we laugh at the same things.'

'How about poetic justice? That can sometimes be quite entertaining, can't it?'

'Oh, sure.'

'Well, your Mr Tan in Manila wasn't what you might call frank with you, was he? Don't you think you're entitled to a little joke at his expense?'

'What sort of joke?'

'You could give Tan Yam Heng here the money to bank for his brother.'

'And give him a chance to take his double commission after all? Is that the idea?'

The Colonel pursed his lips. 'Something like that. Of course, you'd make the fellow give you a receipt in duplicate for the full amount. Keep one copy for yourself, send the other to Manila.'

Greg smiled doubtfully. 'Well, it's not exactly the biggest belly laugh of the year.' He shrugged. 'In fact it's sort of petty, isn't it?'

'I can assure you that Mr Tan won't think so.'

'You mean he'll lose face, or whatever they call it?'

'Undoubtedly.'

'Well, I'll think about it. There's no chance of Tan Yam Heng being restrained by any feelings of family loyalty, I suppose?'

The Colonel grinned. 'Don't worry. I know a little about that chap. No chance at all.'

When he had gone, Greg remained there for a few minutes, finishing his drink and thinking about what the Colonel had said.

He had, he reflected, been called, directly or by implication, a prig, a simpleton, a hypocrite, a pompous ass, a self-satisfied ingrate, and a man who could mistake his self-esteem for his conscience. Together with the adjectives he himself had applied it all made quite a picture. Dorothy would have been highly indignant. The odd thing was that he did not feel at all indignant himself. For the first time in several days, in fact, he felt like laughing; not at anything in particular, certainly not at the Colonel's feeble vision of poetic justice, but because he had suddenly seen his own face.

He signed a chit for the sandwiches and drinks, and went back up to the suite. Dorothy had not stirred. He undressed, brushed his teeth and got back into bed beside her.

3

The following morning he met Captain Lukey and Tan Yam Heng at the Orchard Road branch of the Hong Kong and Shanghai Bank.

The Captain was boisterously cheerful and countersigned the cheque with a flourish. The 'spot of bother in Labuanga', as he had called it over the telephone, had now, it seemed, been forgotten.

Greg watched Tan as the money was being paid out. His face did not move, but his eyes followed every bundle of notes as it was pushed across the counter, and the fingers of his right hand twitched in sympathy with the Captain's as he checked the bundles. It was more than likely, Greg decided, that the Colonel had been right. Once Tan Yam Heng had his hands on the money, brotherly love would not deter him from taking a triple or even quadruple commission if he had a mind to.

From the bank they went to the Customs House. There, Greg signed the necessary papers transferring the ownership of the arms and ammunition to Captain Lukey, and received the bulky canvas bag containing the money.

Captain Lukey beamed. 'Signed, sealed and delivered,' he said fatuously. 'What about a drink to celebrate?'

They went to the lounge bar of a near-by hotel. When the drinks had been ordered, Captain Lukey left them to go to the toilet. Greg looked at Tan.

'I think this is where you give me another cheque for a thousand and fifty dollars,' he said.

'Ah no.' Tan pointed to the bag on the table in front of Greg. 'That must be paid into the Merchants' Security Bank first.'

'Where is the bank?'

'In Coleman Road. We will take a taxi there.'

Greg frowned. 'I've got a lot to do today. Look, you're acting for your brother. Why don't I give you the money, and you pay it in? Then we can square everything away right now.'

He had been prepared for some visible indication that the suggestion met with Tan's approval, but had not expected the reaction to be so manifest. It was remarkable. Not a muscle of the man's face moved; but suddenly it was glistening with sweat.

His lips moved slowly. 'If that is what you wish, Mr Nilsen, I will go to the bank.'

'Fine. Just a moment.' Greg got up and, going over to one of the writing tables, wrote out on hotel stationery two copies of a receipt for sixty-two thousand five hundred Straits dollars cash received from Gregory H. Nilsen as payment in full for the goods listed on bill of lading number so-and-so, and the date. Then, he addressed an envelope to Tan Tack Chee in Manila, marked it 'airmail', and went back to the table.

Captain Lukey had stopped to talk to someone on his way back from the toilet, and they were able to complete the transaction before he returned. Tan filled in the bill of lading number on the receipts, signed both copies and handed Greg a cheque for a thousand and fifty dollars. Greg put the cheque and one copy of the receipt into his pocket. Across the other copy he wrote 'Compliments of Gregory H. Nilsen', then put it in the envelope and sealed it.

Tan was sitting tensely, watching. Greg pushed the canvas bag over to him and smiled. 'I guess you don't want to count that again.'

'No.' Tan took the bag and rested it on his knees.

Greg held up the envelope. 'You don't happen to have an airmail stamp for Manila do you?'

'I will get one from the barman.'

'Don't trouble. I'll get one later.'

'No trouble, Mr Nilsen.'

Tan put the bag under his arm and went to the bar. Captain Lukey came back to the table and began talking about the 'dear old chum' he had just run into. 'White man through and through, which is more than you can say for some of the murky types who work for Afro-Asian nowadays.'

Tan came back with a stamp and put it on the table at Greg's elbow. He did not sit down.

'If you will be good enough to excuse me now,' he said with strained civility, 'I think I will go to the bank.'

'Won't you have a drink first?'

'No, I will go to the bank.' He was still sweating, and obviously yearning to be gone.

'Okay. I'll be seeing you.'

'Good-bye, Mr Nilsen, Captain.'

He hurried away. Captain Lukey chuckled. 'You must have a trusting nature, old boy. If it was mine, I wouldn't let him hold that money even while I tied a shoe lace.'

Greg smiled. He was putting the stamp on the envelope. 'I don't think I need worry,' he said.

As they were leaving, Greg went over to the hotel mail box. He was about to drop the envelope in it, when Captain Lukey stopped him.

'By the way, old boy. Couldn't help noticing, but if you want that to go airmail to Manila you'll have to put some more stamps on. That's the surface rate. It may take a week or more to get there.'

Greg shrugged and put the envelope into the box. 'It's not particularly urgent,' he said.

4

On his way back to the hotel, Greg called in at the Chase National, who were his own bankers' agents, paid in Mr Tan's two American dollar cheques, and asked for a special clearance on them.

At the hotel, he wrote out a cheque for two thousand one hundred dollars payable to the Wilmington Chapter of the American Red Cross. Dorothy, who knew a woman on the Volunteer Service Co-ordination Committee, wrote a covering letter. They mailed it on their way to see the man at Thomas Cook's.

Chapter Ten

I

Tan Tack Chee and Tan Siow Mong were bland men with level heads and strong nerves; but the arrival of Yam Heng's receipt in Manila threw them into a state of flustered consternation that Greg would have found gratifying, if puzzling.

Tack Chee took one long, appalled look at the receipt and then put through an overseas call to the Raffles Hotel in Singapore. He was told that Mr and Mrs Nilsen had sailed two days previously on the S.S. *Camboge* for Colombo and Bombay. Next, he tried to call Yam Heng at the union office where he worked. A clerk there told him that Yam Heng had not been to his office for several days. He was presumed to be indisposed. Yam Heng had no telephone at his home, and Tack Chee knew that it would be useless to cable. Despairingly, he put through a call to the Merchants' Security Bank. The manager was helpful and efficient. No payment of any kind had been made into his account for the past month. Tack Chee hung up, turned his air-conditioner on to 'Full', and told his secretary to place a person-to-person call to his brother in Kuala Pangkalan.

Siow Mong had not been unduly concerned at the delay in collecting the twenty-five thousand dollars due to him in respect of Girija's cheque. He had received a satisfactory progress report from Singapore, saying that the sale was about to be completed. As there was still a clear week to go before the Indian could present the cheque for payment, he did not expect to have to draw upon his own resources in order to honour it. Only one thing was troubling him a little. So far, the clerk had shown himself to be shrewd, careful and discreet. The question was—would he go on being shrewd, careful and discreet with twenty-five thousand dollars in the bank? Money could affect people strangely; and for a young man in his position this would be a fortune. What did he propose to do with it? Something foolish, like buying an expensive sports car and driving about ostentatiously advertising his sudden wealth? And, if so, how was he proposing to explain where he had got it? Tan Siow Mong had decided to have a talk with him before the thirty days were up, to caution him if that seemed necessary, and to make sure that any explanations the young man contemplated using did not compromise either the Anglo-Malay Transport Company or its proprietor.

The telephone call from Manila came through late on Thursday afternoon.

As soon as he heard his brother's voice, Siow Mong knew that something was wrong; but Tack Chee was an ingenious breaker of bad news, and it was two minutes before Siow Mong fully realized what had happened. Then, he lost his temper, and for a further minute there was a loud and demeaning exchange of generalities in which words relating to the excretory organs and functions of the body were freely used. Finally, however, Siow Mong began to recover his self-possession and to think again.

'It is the American who is responsible,' he declared. 'If the money is gone, he must pay.'

'Impossible,' Tack Chee replied. 'Yam Heng signed the receipt as my authorized agent. We can only hope that he has not yet lost it all. You must go to Singapore immediately.'

'Both of us must go.'

'My expenses in this business have already been heavy enough. Twenty-one hundred dollars American plus entertainment, and now overseas telephone calls.'

'Those are trifles, brother.' Siow Mong was becoming angry again. 'When I stand to lose twenty-five thousand dollars Malay, plus five hundred dollars Hong Kong, plus shipping and other handling charges, I am surprised that you commit the indelicacy of speaking about them.'

'There is nothing indelicate about two thousand dollars American. The whole transaction was your idea.'

'You had no criticisms of it. If you had properly instructed this Nilsen . . .' He broke off. 'There is no sense in our bickering. It is a waste of time. Obviously, we shall get nothing unless Yam Heng can be persuaded to co-operate. You know what that means. This time it may be necessary to bring in the police, and threaten charges of embezzlement. You are the legal principal in this, and the receipt will be required as evidence. You must be there.'

'The police? He would know we were bluffing.'

'I am not bluffing,' Siow Mong said. 'This time he has gone too far. Charges of misappropriation of funds brought against him by that union would have been damaging to our names. We should have lost face. Charges brought against him by us would give rise to no such indignity, except for Yam Heng.'

'They might cause pain to our mother.'

'She has endured worse,' Siow Mong said unfeelingly. 'If I leave immediately for Kota Bharu, I can get a plane to Singapore tonight. I will meet you at the Cathay Hotel tomorrow morning.'

Yam Heng had had a bitterly frustrating week on the pickle market, and was querulous when the brothers eventually confronted him. He had, he explained indignantly, merely borrowed the money for a few days. Was not part of it due to him anyway, for all his work on their behalf? Why was he hounded in this way? Yes, he had incurred certain losses; but these would at any moment be more than offset by substantial gains. In three days' time, he would be able to give them a hundred thousand dollars if they needed money so badly.

Mention of the police, however, changed the character of the debate. There was abuse, and much harsh, contemptuous laughter and snapping of fingers. It was only when he realized that his brothers were not simply ready to press charges against him, but beginning to feel vindictive enough to relish the prospect of doing so, that Yam Heng agreed sulkily to an accounting.

Of the sixty-two thousand five hundred dollars there remained seventeen thousand three hundred; and threats of violence as well as police prosecution were necessary to persuade Yam Heng to part with that. His brothers left him, glutinous with self-pity, and returned to the Cathay Hotel.

Minor expenses disregarded, they were fourteen thousand Straits dollars out of pocket on the deal. They were also tired. They had little difficulty in agreeing how they should divide the salvaged remains. Tack Chee took the equivalent of eight hundred American dollars to set off against his outlay of twenty-one hundred. Siow Mong, as the heavier loser, took the balance of fifteen thousand Straits dollars.

He arrived back in Kuala Pangkalan late on Friday night. When he went to his office the following morning he found a message. Mr Krishnan had telephoned and would like to see Mr Tan. In the hope that Mr Tan would find it convenient to do so, he would call in on Saturday afternoon at four p.m.

2

Mr Tan, sitting gloomily at his desk, watched the Indian cross the yard from number one godown, and thought that he detected a certain impudent jauntiness in the fellow's walk.

In spite of its obvious absurdity, he could not quite rid himself of the fear that the Indian had somehow learned of the Singapore disaster, and had come there merely to gloat over and humiliate him. If that should indeed be the case, he told himself darkly, the fellow would regret his temerity.

As matters now stood, he, Siow Mong, was prepared to be generous. The

Indian would be solemnly warned of the dangers of so much sudden wealth, and of the impossibility of his being able to account satisfactorily to the police for its acquisition. It would then be relatively simple to persuade him to return the cheque. In exchange, he would be given a deed of annuity guaranteeing him a yearly income of two thousand five hundred dollars for ten years. Mr Tan was reasonably sure that he could buy such an annuity for around fifteen thousand dollars.

Should the fellow be in any way disagreeable, however, Mr Tan had an alternative scheme ready. He would stop payment of the cheque and invite the young blackguard to sue him in open court. There, if his challenge were accepted, he would tell the judge that the Indian had undertaken to buy for him, through a relative, a certain valuable tract of tin-bearing land, and that the post-dated cheque had been written, at the Indian's request, to impress the relative and to use as a deposit if the purchase went through. When he had discovered that the Indian's land-owning relative was non-existent, he had stopped the cheque. Perfectly simple. If the Indian chose to tell the truth, he would either be disbelieved and lose his case, or believed and prosecuted for selling arms. Mr Tan did not think that he would be fool enough to risk either of those alternatives.

When he was announced, Mr Tan assumed the mask of courtesy and ordered tea.

Girija flashed a smile as they shook hands. 'I am sure that if Mr Wright had been aware that I was to have the pleasure of seeing you, Mr Tan, he would have wished me to convey his personal regards.' He had a box file under his arm. He placed it on the floor beside him as he sat down.

'Mr and Mrs Wright are well and happy, I hope.'

'Oh yes, thank you. I trust that your own fine family are equally blessed.'

The tea came and was consumed to further light conversation. Then, Girija picked up the box file and rested it on his knees. Mr Tan accepted this as an intimation that business might begin.

'I was hoping to have the pleasure of seeing you again in the near future, Mr Krishnan,' he said. 'In fact, when I returned from Singapore yesterday, it was already in my mind to telephone you.'

'Perhaps there was the same thought in both our minds, Mr Tan.'

Mr Tan stiffened involuntarily.

'I refer,' Girija continued, 'to the thought, sad for me, that, under present arrangements, our very satisfactory association will shortly end.'

Mr Tan relaxed. He had noted the words 'under present arrangements' and decided to wait for the Indian to explain them.

'I am assuming,' Girija added politely, 'that the association also proved satisfactory from your point of view.'

'Oh yes. Very satisfactory,' Mr Tan replied manfully.

'And Mr Lee's?'

'Sufficiently so, I believe.'

'I am glad of that,' said Girija, 'because it gives me the courage to submit a further problem to you, in the hope of receiving further good advice.'

Mr Tan was silent.

Girija flashed another smile. 'I am so sorry to have to tell you that the friend I spoke of to you before has since died.'

Mr Tan permitted himself a faint twitch of the lips. 'You have my sympathy.'

'Thank you. However, as you know, my friend had money. That now passes to me. Unfortunately, he left no will. My difficulty at the moment is to find a substitute for that will.'

Mr Tan hid his satisfaction perfectly.

'I can appreciate the difficulty,' he said. 'In fact, if you will allow me to say so, I had anticipated it. I even had a possible solution to suggest to you if you were interested.'

'I am indeed most interested.'

Mr Tan proceeded, somewhat elliptically, to explain his annuity proposal. As he began to enlarge upon its virtues, however, he was disconcerted to see, for the first time, a smile of pure amusement spread over the Indian's face. He felt himself getting angry, and stopped in the middle of a sentence.

The smile vanished instantly and Girija leaned forward.

'Mr Tan, I beg your pardon. Perhaps I should have explained first. For the project that I have in mind, twenty-five thousand dollars will be the minimum capital required if we are to operate at a profit.'

Mr Tan never discovered whether the Indian had used the words 'we' and 'profit' at that moment intentionally; just as he was never quite clear how it had come about that, twenty minutes later, the contents of the box file had been scattered over his desk, and he had been listening bemused to a dissertation on the economics of public transport operational in rural areas. It had been quite difficult to break in and regain the initiative; and even then he did not keep it long.

'Why don't you begin with one bus? Why must you have two?'

'People must learn quickly that the buses are reliable or they will keep to their bicycles. The service must become indispensable, Mr Tan. With only one bus it cannot be guaranteed.'

'But if you were to buy one new one, you would have the reliability you want.'

'We cannot afford an experienced mechanic full time to begin with. Therefore we cannot carry out maintenance at night, as the big operators do. What I propose is that we buy two of these reconditioned buses. I know this firm at Acton in London. They have long experience of the work. The chassis are old, but very good. The engines are new. The bodies have been adapted for Far East work. Look, here is a picture.'

Mr Tan waved the picture aside. 'Yes, yes. It is all very interesting. But why have you brought this project to me?'

Girija returned to his seat on the other side of the desk before he replied, slowly and methodically: 'Firstly, Mr Tan, because a bus service such as I have described would be a logical extension of the Anglo-Malay Transport Company's business. Secondly, because of the trade journals I subscribe to, Mr Wright knows of my interest in such matters. He knows of my respect for you. He would not think it too strange that a new bus company which you owned should employ me as manager. Thirdly, because if a new company called Kuala Pangkalan Transport Limited were formed, with a nominal capital of fifty thousand dollars, and if, in consideration of my signing a service agreement as managing director of that company, I were allotted fifty per cent of the ordinary shares free, I could return your cheque to you without presenting it for payment. Fourthly, because a company with your reputation behind it would have no difficulty in securing a franchise to operate the service. Fifthly, because I think you know that I can be trusted and would serve our interests well.'

Mr Tan thought carefully. What the Indian had said about the need for a bus service was undoubtedly true. As a business venture it was probably sound. The capital of a new company would not have to be fully paid up. Fifteen thousand would buy the two reconditioned buses. On the other hand, if the project were a success, a fifty per cent interest in it was eventually to be worth a lot more than twenty-five thousand dollars. He would certainly be wise to keep the ordinary shares in his own hands. A counter-offer of non-voting preference shares might be the answer. Ingeniously worked out, it could, he was sure, be made to seem advantageous. Meanwhile, he would employ delaying tactics, wear the Indian down by keeping him waiting, and then, if necessary, dictate the terms. He fingered the papers from the box file as if they were of small importance, and then pushed them aside.

'Very well,' he said; 'I will look through these estimates and proposals, and perhaps make some other inquiries. Later, possibly, we could meet again and continue the discussion.'

Girija nodded. 'Of course, Mr Tan. On the terms I have mentioned, the whole matter can be very easily settled–' he paused and flashed his most annoying smile–'any day before your cheque falls due for payment next week.'

3

The day after Greg and Dorothy arrived back in Wilmington, Kuala Pangkalan Transport Limited took delivery of its first vehicle at Singapore.

W.W.Belden, the maker's Far Eastern representative, was on hand to promote an atmosphere of goodwill. The new owners' Managing Director, G.Krishnan, was there to sign the necessary documents on behalf of his company.

A ten-ton crane picked the bus off the deck of the ship and placed it on the dockside.

Privately, Mr Belden thought that the thing looked like a cattle truck; but, as most of its passengers would presumably be coolies, that probably did not matter. The important thing was that the Indian seemed to be pleased. With all this German competition in the low price field, you had to be on your toes. When the second reconditioned unit had been delivered, he would start plugging their own new economy job. Meanwhile, he had a luncheon date at the Yacht Club. As soon as he could gracefully do so, he left.

The two drivers Girija had brought with him had both spent some years on army vehicles, and knew the type of chassis well. When everything had been checked, the new battery installed, the temporary registration plates fitted, and the tank filled, the engine was started. It had a leisurely, powerful sound that was very satisfying.

One driver got up into the cab, the other sat behind him on one of the passenger benches.

The driver at the wheel grinned down at Girija.

'Can we drive the tuan to his hotel?'

Girija smiled and shook his head. 'I'll be waiting for you in Kuala Pangkalan,' he said.

He did not ride in buses; he operated them.

But he stood there, listening and watching, as the big gears grated, the big tyres began to turn and the bus rumbled away towards the dock gates and the journey north. He wished that his father, the subahdar, could have been there.

ERIC AMBLER

THE LIGHT OF DAY

The Light of Day

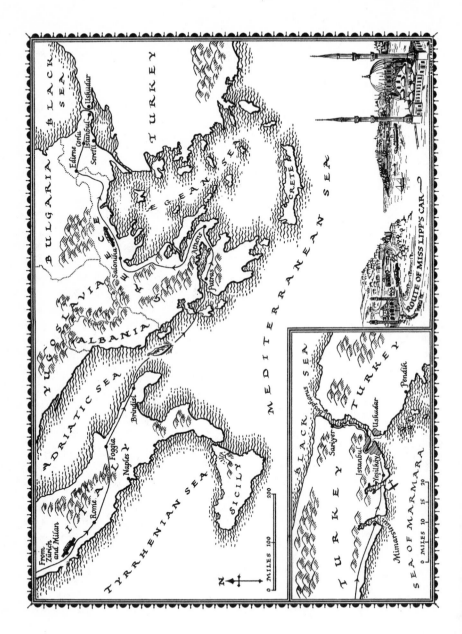

ROUTE OF MISS LIPP'S CAR

BLACK SEA

BULGARIA

YUGOSLAVIA

TURKEY

ALBANIA

GREECE

AEGEAN SEA

CRETE

MEDITERRANEAN SEA

ADRIATIC SEA

ITALY

TYRRHENIAN SEA

SICILY

Edirne
Corlu
Istanbul
Üsküdar
Şerefli

Salonika

Athens

Patras

Brindisi

Foggia
Naples
Rome

From
Zürich
and Milan

N

0 MILES 100 200

BLACK SEA

TURKEY

TURKEY

SEA OF MARMARA

Sarıyer
Bosphorus
Istanbul
Yeşilköy
Üsküdar
Pendik

Mimars

0 MILES 10 15 20

Chapter One

It came down to this: if I had not been arrested by the Turkish police, I would have been arrested by the Greek police. I had no choice but to do as this man Harper told me. He was entirely responsible for what happened to me.

I thought he was an American. He looked like an American–tall, with the loose, light suit, the narrow tie and button-down collar, the smooth, old-young, young-old face and the crew cut. He spoke like an American, too; or at least like a German who has lived in America for a long time. Of course, I now know that he is not an American, but he certainly gave that impression. His luggage, for instance, was definitely American: plastic leather and imitation gold locks. I know American luggage when I see it. I didn't see his passport.

He arrived at the Athens airport on a plane from Vienna. He could have come from New York or London or Frankfurt or Moscow and arrived by that plane–or just from Vienna. It was impossible to tell. There were no hotel labels on the luggage. I just assumed that he came from New York. It was a mistake anyone might have made.

This will not do. I can already hear myself protesting too much, as if I had something to be ashamed of; but I am simply trying to explain what happened, to be completely frank and open.

I really did not suspect that he was not what he seemed. Naturally, I approached him at the airport. The car-hire business is only a temporary sideline with me, of course–I am a journalist by profession–but Nicki had been complaining about needing more new clothes, and the rent was due on the flat that week. I needed money, and this man looked as if he had some. Is it a crime to earn money? The way some people go on you would think it was. The law is the law and I am certainly not complaining, but what I can't stand is all the humbug and hypocrisy. If a man goes to the red light district on his own, nobody says anything. But if he wants to do another chap, a friend or an acquaintance, a good turn by showing him the way to the best house, everyone starts screaming blue murder. I have no patience with it. If there is one thing I pride myself on it is my common sense–that and my sense of humour.

My correct name is Arthur Simpson.

No! I said I would be completely frank and open and I am going to be. My correct *full* name is Arthur Abdel Simpson. The Abdel is because my mother was Egyptian. In fact, I was born in Cairo. But my father was a British officer, a regular, and I myself am British to the core. Even my background is typically British.

My father rose from the ranks. He was a Regimental Sergeant-Major in the Buffs when I was born; but in 1916 he was commissioned as a Lieutenant-Quartermaster in the Army Service Corps. We were living in officers' married quarters in Ismaillyah when he was killed a year later. I was too young at the time to be told the details. I thought, naturally, that he must have been killed by the Turks; but Mum told me later that he had been run over by an army lorry as he was walking home one night from the officers' mess.

Mum had his pension, of course, but someone told her to write to the Army Benevolent Association for the Sons of Fallen Officers, and they got me into the British school in Cairo. She still kept on writing to them about me, though. When I was nine, they said that if there were some relative in England I could live with they would pay for my schooling there. There was a married sister of Father's living at Hither Green in south-east London. When the Benevolent Association said that they would pay twelve-and-six a week for my keep, she agreed to have me. This was a great relief to Mum because it meant that she could marry Mr Hafiz, who had never liked me after the day I caught them in bed together and told the Imam about it. Mr Hafiz was in the restaurant business and as fat as a pig. It was disgusting for a man of his age to be in bed with Mum.

I went to England on an army troop-ship in care of the sick-bay matron. I was glad to go. I have never liked being where I am not wanted. Most of the men in the sick bay were V.D. cases and I used to listen to them talking. I picked up quite a lot of useful information, before the matron, who was (there is no other word) an old bitch, found out about it and handed me over to the P.T. Instructor for the rest of the voyage. My aunt in Hither Green was a bitch, too, but I was wanted there all right. She was married to a book-keeper who spent half his time out of work. My twelve-and-six a week came in very handy. She didn't dare get too bitchy. Every so often, a man from the Benevolent Association would come down to see how I was getting on. If I had told him the tale they would have taken me away. Like most boys of that age, I suppose I was what is known nowadays as a 'bit of a handful'.

The school was on the Lewisham side of Blackheath and had a big board outside with gold lettering on it:

CORAM'S GRAMMAR SCHOOL
For the Sons of Gentlemen
Founded 1781

On top of the board there was the school coat of arms and motto, *Mens aequa in arduis*. The Latin master said it was from Horace; but the English master liked to translate it in Kipling's words: 'If you can keep your head when all about you are losing theirs . . . you'll be a Man, my son.'

It was not exactly a public school like Eton or Winchester—there were no boarders, we were all day boys—but it was run on the same lines. Your parents, or (as in my case) guardian, had to pay to send you there. There were a few scholarship boys from the local council schools—I think we had to have them because of the Board of Education subsidy—but never more than twenty or so in the whole school. In 1920 a new Head was appointed. His name was Brush and we nicknamed him 'The Bristle'. He'd been a master at a big public school and so he knew how things should be done. He made a lot of changes. After he came, we played rugger instead of soccer, sat in forms instead of in classes and were taught how to speak like gentlemen. One or two of the older masters got the sack, which was a good thing; and The Bristle made all the masters wear their university gowns at prayers in the morning. As he said, Coram's was a school with a good tradition, and, although we might not be as old as Eton or Winchester, we were a good deal older than Brighton or Clifton. All the swotting in the world was no good if you didn't have character and tradition. He made us stop reading trash like the *Gem* and *Magnet* and turn to worthwhile books by authors like Stevenson and Talbot Baines Reed.

I was too young when my father was killed to have known him well; but one or two of his pet sayings have always remained in my memory; perhaps because I heard him repeat them so often to Mum or to his army friends. One, I remember, was 'Never volunteer for anything', and another was 'Bullshit baffles brains'.

Hardly the guiding principles of an officer and a gentleman, you say? Well, I am not so sure about that; but I won't argue. I can only say that they were the guiding principles of a practical, professional soldier, and that at Coram's they worked. For example, I found out very early on that nothing annoyed the masters more than untidy handwriting. With some of them, in fact, the wrong answer to a question neatly written would get almost as many marks as the right answer badly written or covered with smears and blots. I have always written very neatly. Again, when a master asked something and then said 'Hands up who knows', you could always put your hand up even if you didn't know, as long as you let the eager beavers put their hands up first, and as long as you smiled. Smiling–pleasantly, I mean, not grinning or smirking–was very important at all times. The masters did not bother about you so much if you looked as if you had a clear conscience.

I got on fairly well with the other chaps. Because I had been born in Egypt, of course, they called me 'Wog', but, as I was fair-haired like my father, I didn't mind that. My voice broke quite early, when I was twelve. After a while, I started going up to Hilly Fields at night with a fifth-former named Jones iv, who was fifteen, and we used to pick up girls–'square-pushing' as they say in the army. I soon found that some of the girls didn't mind a bit if you put your hand up their skirts, and even did a bit more. Sometimes we would stay out late. That meant that I used to have to get up early and do my homework, or make my aunt write an excuse note for me to take to school saying that I had been sent to bed after tea with a feverish headache. If the worse came to the worst, I could always crib from a boy named Reese and do the written work in the lavatory. He had very bad acne and never minded if you cribbed from him; in fact I think he liked it. But you had to be careful. He was one of the bookworms and usually got everything right. If you cribbed from him word for word you risked getting full marks. With me, that would make the master suspicious. I got ten out of ten for a chemistry paper once, and the master caned me for cheating. I had never really liked the man and I got my revenge later by pouring a test-tube of sulphuric acid (conc.) over the saddle of his bicycle; but I have always remembered the lesson that incident taught me. Never try to pretend that you're better than you are. I think I can fairly say that I never have.

Of course, an English public-school education is mainly designed to build character, to give a boy a sense of fair play and sound values, teach him to take the rough with the smooth and make him look and sound like a gentleman.

Coram's at least did those things for me; and, looking back, I suppose that I should be grateful. I can't say that I enjoyed the process though. Fighting, for instance: that was supposed to be very manly, and if you did not enjoy it they called you 'cowardy custard'. I don't think it is cowardly not to want someone to hit you with his fist and make your nose bleed. The trouble was that when I used to hit back I always sprained by thumb or grazed my knuckles. In the end, I found that the best way to hit back was with a satchel, especially if you had a pen or the sharp edge of a ruler sticking out through the flap; but I have always disliked violence of any kind.

Almost as much as I dislike injustice. My last term at Coram's, which I should have been able to enjoy because it *was* the last, was completely spoiled.

Jones iv was responsible for that. He had left school by then, and was working for his father, who owned a garage, but I still went up to Hilly Fields with him sometimes. One evening he showed me a long poem typed out on four foolscap pages. A customer at the garage had given it to him. It was called 'The Enchantment' and was supposed to have been written by Lord Byron. It began:

> *Upon one dark and sultry day,*
> *As on my garret bed I lay,*
> *My thoughts, for I was dreaming half,*
> *Were broken by a silvery laugh,*
> *Which fell upon my startled ear,*
> *Full loud and clear and very near.*

Well, it turned out that the laugh was coming through a hole in the wall behind his bed, so he looked through the hole.

> *A youth and maid were in the room,*
> *And each in youth's most beauteous bloom.*

It then went on to describe what the youth and maid did together for the next half-hour—very poetically, of course, but in detail. It was really hot stuff.

I made copies and let some of the chaps at school read it. Then I charged them fourpence a time to be allowed to copy it out for themselves. I was making quite a lot of money, when some fourth-form boy left a copy in the pocket of his cricket blazer and his mother found it. Her husband sent it with a letter of complaint to The Bristle. He began questioning the boys one by one to find out who had started it, and, of course, he eventually got back to me. I said I had been given it by a boy who had left the term before—The Bristle couldn't touch *him*—but I don't think he believed me. He sat tapping his desk with his pencil and saying 'filthy smut' over and over again. He looked very red in the face, almost as if he were embarrassed. I remember wondering if he could be a bit 'queer'. Finally, he said that as it was my last term he would not expel me, but that I was not to associate with any of the younger boys for the rest of my time there. He did not cane me or write to the Benevolent Association, which was a relief. But it was a bad experience all the same and I was quite upset. In fact, I think that was the reason I failed my matric.

At Coram's they made a fetish out of passing your matric. Apparently, you couldn't get a respectable job in a bank or an insurance company without it. I didn't want a job in a bank or an insurance company–Mr Hafiz had died and Mum wanted me to go back and learn the restaurant business–but it was a disappointment all the same. I think that if The Bristle had been more broad-minded and understanding, not made me feel as if I had committed some sort of crime, things would have been different. I was a sensitive boy and I felt that Coram's had somehow let me down. That was the reason I never applied to join the Old Coramians' Club.

Now, of course, I can look back on the whole thing and smile about it. The point I am making is that persons in authority–headmasters, police officials–can do a great deal of damage simply by failing to understand the other fellow's point of view.

How could I have possibly known what kind of man this Harper was?

As I explained, I had simply driven out to the Athens airport looking for business. I spotted this man going through customs and saw that he was carrying his ticket in an American Express folder. I gave one of the porters two drachmas to get me the man's name from his customs declaration. Then I had one of the uniformed airline girls give him my card and the message: 'Car waiting outside for Mr Harper.'

It is a trick I have used lots of times and it has almost always worked. Not many Americans or British speak demotic Greek; and by the time they have been through the airport customs, especially in the hot weather, and been jostled by the porters and elbowed right and left, they are only too ready to go with someone who can understand what they're talking about and take care of the tipping. That day it was really very hot and humid.

As he came through the exit from the customs I went up to him.

'This way, Mr Harper.'

He stopped and looked me over. I gave him a helpful smile which he did not return.

'Wait a minute,' he said curtly. 'I didn't order any car.'

I looked puzzled. 'The American Express sent me, sir. They said you wanted an English-speaking driver.'

He stared at me again, then shrugged. 'Well, okay. I'm going to the Hôtel Grande Bretagne.'

'Certainly, sir. Is this all your luggage?'

Soon after we turned off the coast road by Glyfada he began to ask questions. Was I British? I side-stepped that one as usual. Was the car my own? They always want to know that. It is my own car, as it happens, and I have two speeches about it. The car itself is a 1954 Plymouth. With an American I brag about how many thousands of miles it has done without any trouble. For the Britishers I have a stiff-upper-lip line about part-exchanging it, as soon as I can save enough extra cash, for an Austin Princess, or an old Rolls-Royce, or some other real quality car. Why shouldn't people be told what they want to hear?

This Harper man seemed much like the rest. He listened and grunted occasionally as I told him the tale. When you know that you are beginning to bore them, you usually know that everything is going to be all right. Then, you stop. He did not ask how I happened to live and work in Greece, as they usually do. I thought that would probably come later; that is, if there were going to be a later with him. I had to find out.

'Are you in Athens on business, sir?'

'Could be.'

His tone as good as told me to mind my own business, but I pretended not to notice. 'I ask, sir,' I went on, 'because if you should need a car and driver while you are here I could arrange to place myself at your disposal.'

'Yes?'

It wasn't exactly encouraging, but I told him the daily rate and the various trips we could take if he wanted to do some sight-seeing—Delphi and the rest.

'I'll think about it,' he said. 'What's your name?'

I handed him one of my cards over my shoulder and watched him in the driving mirror while he read it. Then he slipped it into his pocket.

'Are you married, Arthur?'

The question took me by surprise. They don't usually want to know about your private life. I told him about my first wife and how she had been killed by a bomb in the Suez troubles in 1956. I did not mention Nicki. I don't know why; perhaps because I did not want to think about her just then.

'You did say you were British, didn't you?' he asked.

'My father was British, sir, and I was educated in England.' I said it a little distantly. I dislike being cross-examined in that sort of way. But he persisted just the same.

'Well, what nationality *are* you?'

'I have an Egyptian passport.' That was perfectly true, although it was none of his business.

'Was your wife Egyptian?'

'No, French.'

'Did you have any children?'

'Unfortunately no, sir.' I was definitely cold now.

'I see.'

He sat back, staring out of the window, and I had the feeling that he had suddenly put me out of his mind altogether. I thought about Annette and how used I had become to saying that she had been killed by a bomb. I was almost beginning to believe it myself. As I stopped for the traffic lights in Omonias Square I wondered what had happened to her, and if the gallant gentlemen she had preferred to me had ever managed to give her the children she had said she wanted. I am not one to bear a grudge, but I could not help hoping that she believed now that the sterility had been hers not mine.

I pulled up at the Grande Bretagne. While the porters were getting the bags out of the car Harper turned to me.

'Okay, Arthur, it's a deal. I expect to be here three or four days.'

I was surprised and relieved. 'Thank you, sir. Would you like to go to Delphi tomorrow? On the week-ends it gets very crowded with tourists.'

'We'll talk about that later.' He stared at me for a moment and smiled slightly. 'Tonight I think I feel like going out on the town. You know some good places?'

As he said it there was just the suggestion of a wink. I am sure of that.

I smiled discreetly. 'I certainly do, sir.'

'I thought you might. Pick me up at nine o'clock. All right?'

'Nine o'clock, sir. I will have the concierge telephone to your room that I am here.'

It was four-thirty then. I drove to my flat, parked the car in the courtyard and went up.

Nicki was out, of course. She usually spent the afternoon with friends—or said she did. I did not know who the friends were and I never asked too many questions. I did not want her to lie to me, and if she had picked up a lover at the Club I did not want to know about it. When a middle-aged man marries an attractive girl half his age, he has to accept certain possibilities philosophically. The clothes she had changed out of were lying all over the bed and she had spilt some scent, so that the place smelt more strongly of her than usual.

There was a letter for me from a British travel magazine I had written to. They wanted me to submit samples of my work for their consideration. I tore the letter up. Practically thirty years in the magazine game and they treat you like an amateur! Send samples of your work, and the next thing you know is that they've stolen all your ideas without paying you a penny-piece. It has happened to me again and again, and I am not being caught that way any more. If they want me to write for them, let them say so with a firm offer of cash on delivery, plus expenses in advance.

I made a few telephone calls to make sure that Harper's evening out would go smoothly, and then went down to the café for a drink or two. When I got back Nicki was there, changing again to go to work at the Club.

It was no wish of mine that she should go on working after our marriage. She chose to do so herself. I suppose some men would be jealous at the idea of their wives belly-dancing with practically no clothes on in front of other men; but I am not narrow-minded in that way. If she chooses to earn a little extra pocket money for herself, that is her affair.

While she dressed, I told her about Harper and made a joke about all his questions. She did not smile.

'He does not sound easy, Papa,' she said. When she calls me 'Papa' like that it means that she is in a friendly mood with me.

'He has money to spend.'

'How do you know?'

'I telephoned the hotel and asked for him in room two-three-two. The operator corrected me and so I got his real room number. I know it. It is a big air-conditioned suite.'

She looked at me with a slight smile and sighed. 'You do so much enjoy it, don't you?'

'Enjoy what?'

'Finding out about people.'

'That is my newspaper training, *chérie*, my nose for news.'

She looked at me doubtfully, and I wished I had given a different answer. It has always been difficult for me to explain to her why certain doors are now closed to me. Reopening old wounds is senseless as well as painful.

She shrugged and went on with her dressing. 'Will you bring him to the Club?'

'I think so.'

I poured her a glass of wine and one for myself. She drank hers while she finished dressing and then went out. She patted my cheek as she went, but did not kiss me. The 'Papa' mood was over. 'One day,' I thought, 'she will go out and not come back.'

But I am never one to mope. If that happened, I decided, then good riddance to bad rubbish. I poured myself another glass of wine, smoked a cigarette and worked out a tactful way of finding out what sort of business Harper was in. I think I must have sensed that there was something not quite right about him.

At five to nine I found a parking place on Venizelos Avenue just round the corner from the Grande Bretagne, and went to let Harper know that I was waiting.

He came down after ten minutes and I took him round the corner to the car. I explained that it was difficult for private cars to park in front of the hotel.

He said, rather disagreeably I thought: 'Who cares?'

I wondered if he had been drinking. Quite a lot of tourists who, in their own countries, are used to dining early in the evening start drinking *ouzo* to pass the time. By ten o'clock, when most Athenians begin to think about dinner, the tourists are sometimes too tight to care what they say or do. Harper, however, was all too sober. I soon found that out.

When we reached the car I opened the rear door for him to get in. Ignoring me, he opened the other door and got into the front passenger seat. Very democratic. Only I happen to prefer my passengers in the back seat where I can keep my eye on them through the mirror.

I went round and got into the driving seat.

'Well, Arthur,' he asked, 'where are you taking me?'

'Dinner first, sir?'

'How about some sea-food?'

'I'll take you to the best, sir.'

I drove him out to the yacht harbour at Tourcolimano. One of the restaurants there gives me a good commission. The waterfront is really very picturesque, and he nodded approvingly as he looked around. Then I took him into the restaurant and introduced him to the cook. When he had chosen his food and a bottle of dry Patras wine he looked at me.

'You eaten yet, Arthur?'

'Oh, I will have something in the kitchen, sir.' That way my dinner would go on his bill without his knowing it, as well as my commission.

'You come and eat with me.'

'It is not necessary, sir.'

'Who said it was? I asked you to eat with me.'

'Thank you, sir. I would like to.'

More democracy. We sat at a table on the terrace by the water's edge and he began to ask me about the yachts anchored in the harbour. Which were privately owned, which were for charter? What were charter rates like?

I happened to know about one of the charter yachts, an eighteen-metre ketch with twin diesels, and told him the rate—one hundred and forty dollars U.S. per day, including a crew of two, fuel for eight hours' steaming a day and everything except charterers' and passengers' food. The real rate was a hundred and thirty, but I thought that, if by any chance he was serious, I could get the difference as commission from the broker. I also wanted to see how he felt about that kind of money; whether he would laugh as an ordinary salaried man would, or begin asking about the number of persons it would sleep. He just nodded, and then asked about fast, sea-going motor-boats without crew.

In the light of what happened I think that point is specially significant.

I said that I would find out. He asked me about the yacht brokers. I gave him the name of the one I knew personally, and told him the rest were no good. I also said that I did not think that the owners of the bigger boats liked chartering them without their own crewmen on board. He did not comment on that. Later, he asked me if I knew whether yacht charter parties out of Tourcolimano or the Piraeus covered Greek waters only, or whether you could 'go foreign', say across the Adriatic to Italy. Significant again. I told him I did not know, which was true.

When the bill came, he asked if he could change an American Express traveller's cheque for fifty dollars. That was more to the point. I told him that he could, and he tore the fifty-dollar cheque out of a book of ten. It was the best thing I had seen that day.

Just before eleven o'clock we left and I drove him to the Club.

The Club is practically a copy of the Lido night-club in Paris, only smaller. I introduced him to John, who owns the place, and tried to leave him there for a while. He was still absolutely sober and I thought that if he were by himself he would drink more; but it was no good. I had to go in and sit and drink with him. He was as possessive as a woman. I was puzzled. If I had been a fresh-looking young man instead of, well, frankly, a pot-bellied journalist, I would have understood it—not approved, of course, but understood. But he was at least ten to fifteen years younger than me.

They have candles on the tables at the Club and you can see faces. When the floor-show came on, I watched him watch it. He looked at the girls, Nicki among them, as if they were flies on the other side of a window. I asked him how he liked the third from the left—that was Nicki.

'Legs too short,' he said. 'I like them with longer legs. Is that the one you had in mind?'

'In mind? I don't understand, sir.' I was beginning to dislike him intensely.

He eyed me. 'Shove it,' he said unpleasantly.

We were drinking Greek brandy. He reached for the bottle and poured himself another. I could see the muscles in his jaw twitching as if with anger. Evidently something I had said, or which he thought I had said, had annoyed him. It was on the tip of my tongue to mention that Nicki was my wife, but I didn't. I remembered, just in time, that I had only told him about Annette, and about her being killed by a bomb.

He drank the brandy down quickly and told me to get the bill.

'You don't like it here, sir?'

'What more is there to see? Do they start stripping later?'

I smiled. It is the only possible response to that sort of boorishness. In any case, I had no objection to speeding up my programme for the evening.

'There is another place,' I said.

'Like this?'

'The entertainment, sir, is a little more individual and private.' I picked the words carefully.

'You mean a cat-house?'

'I wouldn't put it quite like that, sir.'

He smirked. 'I'll bet you wouldn't. How about "*maison de rendezvous*"? Does that cover it?'

'Madame Irma's is very discreet and everything is in the best of taste, sir.'

He shook with amusement. 'Know something, Arthur?' he said. 'If you shaved a bit closer and had yourself a good haircut, you could hire out as a butler any time.'

From his expression I could not tell whether he was being deliberately insulting or making a clumsy joke. It seemed advisable to assume the latter.

'Is that what Americans call "ribbing", sir?' I asked politely.

This seemed to amuse him even more. He chuckled fatuously. 'Okay, Arthur,' he said at last, 'okay. We'll play it your way. Let's go to see your Madame Irma.'

I didn't like the '*your* Madame Irma' way of putting it, but I pretended not to notice.

Irma has a very nice house standing in its own grounds just off the road out to Kifissia. She never has more than six girls at any one time and changes them every few months. Her prices are high, of course, but everything is very well arranged. Clients enter and leave by different doors to avoid embarrassing encounters. The only persons the client sees are Irma herself, Kira, the manageress who takes care of the financial side, and, naturally, the lady of his choice.

Harper seemed to be impressed. I say 'seemed' because he was very polite to Irma when I introduced them, and complimented her on the decorations. Irma is not unattractive herself and likes presentable-looking clients. As I had expected, there was no nonsense about my joining him at *that* table. As soon as Irma offered him a drink, he glanced at me and made a gesture of dismissal.

'See you later,' he said.

I was sure then that everything was all right. I went into Kira's room to collect my commission and tell her how much money he had on him. It was after midnight then. I said that I had had no dinner and would go and get some. She told me that they were not particularly busy that night and that there need be no hurry.

I drove immediately to the Grande Bretagne, parked the car at the side, walked round to the bar, and went in and ordered a drink. If anyone happened to notice me and remember later, I had a simple explanation for being there.

I finished the drink, gave the waiter a good tip and walked through across the foyer to the lifts. They are fully automatic; you work them yourself with push-buttons. I went up to the third floor.

Harper's suite was on the inner court, away from the noise of Syntagmaios Square, and the doors to it were out of sight of the landing. The floor servants had gone off duty for the night. It was all quite easy. As usual, I had my pass-key hidden inside an old change purse; but, as usual, I did not need it. Quite a number of the sitting-room doors to suites in the older part of the hotel can be opened from outside without a key, unless they have been specially locked, that is; it makes it easier for room-service waiters carrying trays. Quite often the maid who turns down the beds last thing can't be bothered to lock up after her. Why should she? The Greeks are a particularly honest people and they trust one another.

His luggage was all in the bedroom. I had already handled it once that day, stowing it in the car at the airport, so I did not have to worry about leaving fingerprints.

I went to his briefcase first. There were a lot of business papers in it—something to do with a Swiss company named Tekelek, who made accounting machines—I did not pay much attention to them. There was also a wallet with money in it—Swiss francs, American dollars and West German marks—together with the yellow number slips of over two thousand dollars' worth of traveller's cheques. The number slips are for record purposes in case the cheques are lost and you want to stop payment on them. I left the money where it was and took the slips. The cheques themselves I found in the side pocket of a suitcase. There were thirty-five of them, each for fifty dollars. His first name was Walter, middle initial K.

In my experience, most people are extraordinarily careless about the way they look after traveller's cheques. Just because their counter-signature is required before a cheque can be cashed they assume that only they can negotiate it. Yet anyone with eyes in his head can copy the original signature. No particular skill is required; haste, heat, a different pen, a counter of an awkward height, writing standing up instead of sitting—a dozen things can account for small variations in the second signature. It is not going to be examined by a handwriting expert, not at the time that it is cashed anyway; and usually it is only at banks that the cashier asks to see a passport.

Another thing: if you have ordinary money in your pocket, you usually know, at least approximately, how much you have. Every time you pay for something, you receive a reminder; you can see and feel what you have. Not so with traveller's cheques. What you see, if and when you look, is a blue folder with cheques inside. How often do you count the cheques to make sure that they are all there? Supposing someone were to remove the *bottom* cheque in a folder. When would you find out that it had gone? A hundred to one it would not be until you had used up all the cheques which had been on top of it. Therefore; you would not know exactly *when* it had been taken;

and, if you had been doing any travelling, you probably would not even know *where*. If you did not know when or where, how could you possibly guess *who*? In any case you would be too late to stop its being cashed.

People who leave traveller's cheques about *deserve* to lose them.

I took just six cheques, the bottom ones from the folder. That made three hundred dollars, and left him fifteen hundred or so. It is a mistake, I always think, to be greedy; but unfortunately I hesitated. For a moment I wondered if he would miss them all that much sooner if I took two more.

So I was standing there like a fool, with the cheques right in my hands, when Harper walked into the room.

Chapter Two

I was in the bedroom and he came through from the sitting-room. All the same he must have opened the outer door very quietly indeed or I would certainly have heard the latch. I think he expected to find me there. In that case, the whole thing was just a cunningly planned trap.

I was standing at the foot of one of the beds, so I couldn't move away from him. For a moment he just stood there grinning at me, as if he were enjoying himself.

'Well now, Arthur,' he said, 'you ought to have waited for me, oughtn't you?'

'I was going back.' It was a stupid thing to say, I suppose; but almost anything I had said would have sounded stupid at that point.

And then, suddenly, he hit me across the face with the back of his hand.

It was like being kicked. My glasses fell off and I lurched back against the bed. As I raised my arms to protect myself he hit me again with the other hand. When I started to fall to my knees, he dragged me up and kept on hitting me. He was like a savage.

I fell down again and this time he let me be. My ears were singing, my head felt like bursting and I could not see properly. My nose began to bleed. I got my handkerchief out to stop the blood getting all over my clothes, and felt about among the cheques lying on the carpet for my glasses. I found them eventually. They were bent a bit but not broken. When I put them on, I saw the soles of his shoes about a yard from my face.

He was sitting in the armchair, leaning back, watching me.

'Get up,' he said, 'and watch that blood. Keep it off the rug.'

As I got to my feet, he stood up quickly himself. I thought he was going to start hitting me again. Instead, he caught hold of one lapel of my jacket.

'Do you have a gun?'

I shook my head.

He slapped my pockets, to make sure, I suppose, then shoved me away.

'There are some tissues in the bathroom,' he said. 'Go clean your face. But leave the door open.'

I did as I was told. There was a window in the bathroom; but even if it had been possible to escape that way without breaking my neck, I don't suppose I would have tried it. He would have heard me. Besides, where could I have escaped to? All he would have had to do was call down to the night concierge, and the police would have been there in five minutes. The fact that he had not called down already was at least something. Perhaps, as a foreigner, he did not want to get involved as a witness in a court case. After all, he had not actually lost anything; and if I were to eat enough humble pie, perhaps even cry a bit, he might decide to forget the whole thing; especially after the brutal way in which he had attacked me. That was my reasoning. I should have known better. You cannot expect common decency from a man like Harper.

When I came out of the bathroom, I saw that he had picked up the cheque folder and was putting it back in the suitcase. The cheques I had torn out, however, were lying on the bed. He gathered them up and motioned me towards the sitting-room.

'In there.'

As I went in, he moved past me to the door and bolted it.

There was a marble-topped commode against the side wall. On the commode was a tray with an ice-bucket, a bottle of brandy and some glasses. He picked up a glass then looked at me.

'Sit down right there,' he said.

The chair he motioned to was by a writing table under the window. I obeyed orders; there did not seem to be anything else to do. My nose was still bleeding, and I had a headache.

He slopped some brandy into a glass and put it on the table beside me. For a moment or two I felt encouraged. If you are going to have a man arrested you don't sit him down first and give him a drink. Perhaps it was just going to be a man-to-man chat in which I told him a hard-luck story and said how sorry I was, while he got dewy-eyed over his own magnanimity and decided to give me another chance.

That one did not last long.

He poured himself a drink and then glanced across at me as he put ice in the glass.

'First time you've been caught at it, Arthur?'

I blew my nose a little to keep the blood running before I answered. 'It's the first time I've ever been tempted, sir. I don't know what came over me. Perhaps it was the brandy I had with you. I'm not really used to it.'

He turned and stared at me. All at once his face was neither old-young nor young-old. It was white and pinched and his mouth worked in an odd way. I have seen faces go like that before and I braced myself. There was a metal lamp on the writing table beside me. I wondered if I could possibly hit him with it before he got to me.

But he did not move. His eyes flickered towards the bedroom and then back at me.

'You'd better get something straight, Arthur,' he said slowly. 'That was just a little roughing-up you had in there. If I really start giving you a going-over, you'll leave here on a stretcher. Nobody's going to mind about that except you. I came back and caught you stealing. You tried to strong-arm your way out of it and I had to defend myself. That's how it'll be. So cut out the bull, and the lies. Right?'

'I'm sorry, sir.'

'Empty your pockets. On this table here.'

I did as I was told.

He looked at everything, my driving licence, my *permis de séjour*, and he touched everything. Finally, of course, he found the pass-key in the change purse. I had sawn off the shank of it and cut a slot in the end so that I could use a small coin to turn it, but it was still over two inches long, and heavy. The weight gave it away. He looked at it curiously.

'You make this?'

'Not the key part. I just cut it down.' There seemed no point in trying to lie about that.

He nodded. 'That's better. Okay, we'll start over. We know you're a two-bit ponce and we know you heist traveller's cheques from hotel rooms when you get the chance. Do you write the counter-signature yourself?'

'Yes.'

'So that's forgery. Now, I'm asking again. Have you ever been caught before?'

'No, sir.'

'Sure?'

'Yes.'

'Do you have any sort of police record?'

'Here in Athens?'

'We'll start with Athens.'

I hesitated. 'Well, not exactly a police record. Do you mean traffic offences?'

'You know what I mean. Quit stalling.'

I sneezed, quite unintentionally, and my nose began bleeding again. He sighed impatiently and threw me a bunch of paper napkins from the drink-tray.

'I had you pretty well figured out at the airport,' he went on; 'but I didn't think you'd be quite so stupid. Why did you have to tell that Kira dame that you'd had no dinner?'

I shrugged helplessly. 'So that I could come here.'

'Why didn't you tell her you'd gone to gas up the car? I just might have bought that one.'

'It didn't seem important. Why should you suspect me?'

He laughed. 'Oh brother! I know what that car you have sells for here, and I know that gasoline costs sixty cents a gallon. At the rates you charge you couldn't break even. Okay, you get your pay-offs–the restaurant, the clip joint, the cat-house–but they can't amount to much, so there must be something else. Kira doesn't know what it is, but she knows there's something because you've cashed quite a few traveller's cheques through her.'

'She told you that?' This really upset me; the least one can expect from a brothel-keeper is discretion.

'Why shouldn't she tell me? You didn't tell her they were stolen, did you?' He drank his brandy down. 'I don't happen to like paying for sex, but I wanted to find out a bit more about you. I did. When they realized that I wasn't going to leave without paying, they were both real friendly. Called me a cab and everything. Now, supposing *you* start talking.'

I took a sip of brandy. 'Very well. I have had three convictions.'

'What for?'

'The charge in each case was representing myself as an official guide. In fact, all I did was to try to save one or two clients from those boring archaeological set speeches. The official guides have to learn them by heart before they can pass the examination. Tourists like to know what they are looking at, but they do not want to be bored.'

'What happened? Did you go to jail?'

'Of course not. I was fined.'

He nodded approvingly. 'That was what Irma thought. Now you just keep on playing straight like that and maybe we can keep the police out of this. Have you ever been jailed anywhere, to serve time I mean?'

'I do not see why I should . . .'

'Okay, skip it,' he broke in. 'What about Turkey?'

'Turkey? Why do you ask?'

'Have you been there?'

'Yes.'

'Any police record there?'

'I was fined in Istanbul for showing some people round a museum.'

'Which museum?'

'The Topkapi.'

'Were you posing as an official guide that time?'

'Guides must be licensed there. I did not have a licence.'

'Have you ever driven from here to Istanbul?'

'Is that a criminal offence?'

'Just answer. Have you?'

'Occasionally. Some tourists like to travel by road. Why?'

He did not answer. Instead he took an envelope from the writing desk and began to scribble something in pencil. I desperately needed a cigarette, but was afraid to light one in case it might look as if I were no longer worried. I *was* worried, and confused, too; but I wanted to be sure I looked that way. I drank the brandy instead.

He finished his scribbling at last and looked up. 'All right, Arthur. There's a pad of plain paper there and a pen. I'm going to dictate. You start writing. No, don't give me any arguments. Just do as I tell you.'

I was hopelessly bewildered now. I picked up the pen.

'Ready?'

'Yes.'

'Head it, "*To the Chief of Police, Athens*". Got that? Now go on. "*I, Arthur A. Simpson of—*" put in your address—"*do hereby confess that on June fifteenth, using an illegal pass-key, I entered the suite of Mr Walter K. Harper in the Hôtel Grande Bretagne and stole American Express traveller's cheques to the value of three hundred dollars. The numbers of the cheques were . . .*"'

As he felt in his pocket for the loose cheques, I started to protest.

'Mr Harper, I can't possibly write this. It would convict me. I couldn't defend myself.'

'Would you sooner defend yourself right now? If so, I can call the police and you can explain about that pass-key.' He paused and then went on more patiently: 'Look, Dad, maybe you and I will be the only ones who will ever read it. Maybe in a week's time it won't even exist. I'm just giving you a chance to get off the hook. Why don't you take it and be thankful?'

'What do I have to do for it?'

'We'll get to that later. Just you keep writing. *"The numbers of the cheques were P89.664.572 through P89.664.577, all in fifty-dollar units. I intended to forge Mr Harper's signature on them so that I could cash them illegally. I have stolen, forged and cashed other cheques in that way."* Shut up and keep writing! *"But now I find I cannot go through with it. Because of Mr Harper's great kindness to me during his visit to Athens and his Christian charity, I feel that I cannot rob him. I am, therefore, sending the cheques I stole from him back with this letter. By taking this decision, I feel that I have come out of the darkness into the light of day. I know now that, as a sinner of the worst type, my only chance is to make restitution, to confess everything, and to pay the penalties the law demands. Only in this way can I hope for salvation in the world to come."* Now sign it.'

I signed it.

'Now date it a week from today. No, better make it the twenty-third.'

I dated it.

'Give it to me.'

I gave it to him and he read it through twice. Then he looked at me and grinned.

'Not talking any more, Arthur?'

'I wrote down what you dictated.'

'Sure. And now you're trying to figure out what would happen if I sent it to the police.'

I shrugged.

'All right, I'll tell you what would happen. First they'd think you were a nut. They'd probably think that I was some kind of a nut, too, but they wouldn't be interested in me. I wouldn't be around anyway. On the other hand, they couldn't ignore the whole thing, because of the cheques. Three hundred dollars! They'd have to take that seriously. So they'd start by getting on to the American Express and finding out about all the cheque forgeries that have been traced back to accounts in Athens banks. Then they'd pull you in and grill you. What would you do, Arthur? Tell them about me and what really happened? You'd be silly to do that, wouldn't you? They'd throw the book at you. No, you're too smart for that. You'd go along with the reformation jazz. That way, you'd have a real defence—voluntary confession, restitution, sincere repentance. I'll bet you'd get away with just a nominal sentence, maybe no more than a year.'

'Thank you.'

He grinned again. 'Don't you worry, Arthur. You're not going to do any time at all.' He waved the paper I had written and the cheques. 'This is just a little insurance.' He picked up the brandy bottle and refilled my glass. 'You see, a friend of mine is going to trust you with something valuable.'

'What?'

'A car. You're going to drive it to Istanbul. You'll be paid a hundred bucks and expenses. That's all there is to it.'

I managed to smile. 'If that's all there is to it, I don't see why you have to blackmail me. I would gladly do the job every week for that money.'

He looked pained. 'Who said anything about blackmail? I said insurance. This is a seven-thousand-dollar Lincoln, Arthur. Do you know what it's worth now in Turkey?'

'Fourteen thousand.'

'Well, then, isn't it obvious? Supposing you drove it into the first garage you came to and sold it.'

'It wouldn't be so easy.'

'Arthur, you took a hell of a risk tonight for just three hundred bucks. For fourteen thousand you'd do pretty well, anything, now, wouldn't you? Be your age! As it is, I don't have to worry, and my friend doesn't have to worry. As soon as I know the car's delivered, that little confession 'll be torn up and the cheques 'll go back in my pocket.'

I was silent. I didn't believe a word he was saying and he knew it. He didn't care. He was watching me, enjoying himself. 'All right,' I said finally; 'but there are just one or two questions I'd like to ask.'

He nodded. 'Sure there are. Only that's the one condition there is on the job, Arthur—no questions.'

I would have been surprised if he said anything else. 'Very well. When do I start?'

'Tomorrow. How long does it take you to drive to Salonika?'

'About six or seven hours.'

'Let's see. Tomorrow's Tuesday. If you start about noon you can spend the night there. Then Wednesday night in Edirne. You should make Istanbul Thursday afternoon. That'll be okay.' He thought for a moment. 'I'll tell you what you do. In the morning, you pack an overnight bag and come here by cab or streetcar. Be downstairs at ten.'

'Where do I pick up the car?'

'I'll show you in the morning.'

'Whatever you say.'

He unbolted the door. 'Good deal. Now take your junk and beat it. I have to get some sleep.'

I put my belongings back in my pockets and went to the door.'

'Hey!'

As I turned, something hit me in the chest and then fell at my feet.

'You've forgotten your pass-key,' he said.

I picked it up and left. I didn't say good-night or anything. He didn't notice. He was finishing his drink.

The worst thing at school was being caned. There was a ritual about it. The master who had lost his temper with you would stop ranting, or, if it was one of the quiet ones, stop clenching his teeth, and say: 'Take a note to the Headmaster.' That meant you were for it. The note was always the same, *Request permission to punish*, followed by his initials; but he would always fold it twice before he gave it to you. You were not supposed to read it. I don't know why; perhaps because they didn't like having to ask for permission.

Well, then you had to go and find The Bristle. Sometimes, of course, he would be in his study; but more often he would be taking the sixth form in trigonometry or Latin. That meant you had to go in and stand there until he decided to notice you. You would have to wait five or ten minutes sometimes; it depended on the mood he was in. He was a tall, thick man with a lot of black hair on the backs of his hands, and a purple face. He spoke very fast while he was teaching, and after a while little flecks of white stuff would gather at the corners of his mouth. When he was in a good mood, he would break off almost as soon as you came in and start making jokes. 'Ah, the good Simpson, or perhaps we should say the insufficiently good Simpson, what can we do for you?' Whatever he said, the sixth form always rocked with laughter, because the more they laughed the longer he would go on wasting time. 'And how have you transgressed, Simpson, how have you transgressed? Please tell us.' You always had to say what you'd done or not done–bad homework, lying, flicking ink pellets–and you had to be truthful, in case he asked the master later. When he had made some more jokes, he initialled the note and you went. Before that 'Enchantment' business I think he rather liked me, because I pretended not to be able to help laughing at his jokes even though I was going to be caned. When he was in a bad mood he used to call you 'sir', which I always thought a bit stupid. 'Well, sir, what is this for? Cribbing under the desk? A pauper spirit, sir, a pauper spirit! Work for the night cometh! Now get out and stop wasting my time.'

When you returned to the form-room you gave the master the initialled note. Then he took his gown off, so that his arms were free, and got the cane out of his desk. The canes were all the same, about thirty inches long and quite thick. Some masters would take you outside into the coat lobby to do it, but others would do it in front of the form. You had to bend down and touch your toes and then he would hit you as hard as he could, as if he were trying to break the cane. It felt like a hot iron across your backside, and if he happened to hit you twice in exactly the same place, like a heavy club with spikes on it. The great thing was not to cry or make a fuss. I remember a boy once who wet himself after it and had to be sent home; and there was another one who came back into the room and threw up, so that the master had to send for the school porter to clean up the mess. (They always sent for the porter when a boy threw up, and he always said the same thing when he came in with his bucket and mop–'Is *this* all?–as if he were disappointed it wasn't blood.) Most boys, though, when they were caned, just got very red in the face and tried to walk back to their places as if nothing had happened. It wasn't pride; it was the only way to get any sympathy. When a boy cried you didn't feel sorry for him, merely embarrassed because he was so sorry for himself, and resentful because the master would feel that he had done something effective. One of the most valuable things I learned at Coram's was how to hate; and it was the cane that taught me. I never forgot and never began to forgive a caning until I had somehow evened the score with the master who had given it to me. If he were married, I would write an anonymous letter to his wife saying that he was a sodomite and that he had been trying to interfere with young boys. If he were a bachelor, I would send it as a warning to one of the other boys' parents. Mostly I never heard what happened, of course; but on at least two occasions I heard that the parents had questioned their boys and then forwarded my letters to The

Bristle. I never told anyone, because I did not want the others copying my idea; and as I was very good at disguising my writing the masters never knew for certain who had done it. Just as long as they had a suspicion they could not prove, I was satisfied. It meant that they knew I could hit back, that I was a good friend but a bad enemy.

My attitude to Harper was the same. He had given me a 'caning'; but instead of wallowing in self-pity, as any other man in my position might have done, I began to think of ways in which I could hit back.

Obviously, there was nothing much I could do while he had that 'confession'; but I knew one thing—he was a crook. I didn't yet know what kind of a crook—although I had some ideas—but I would find out for certain sooner or later. Then, when it was safe to do so, I would expose him to the police.

Nicki was in bed when I got back to the flat. I had hoped that she would be asleep because one side of my face was very red where he had hit me, and I didn't want to have to do any explaining; but she had the light on and was reading some French fashion magazine.

'Hullo, Papa,' she said.

I said hullo back and went to the bathroom to get rid of the handkerchief with all the blood on it. Then I went in and began to get undressed.

'You didn't stay long at the Club,' she said.

'He wanted to go on to Irma's.'

She did not like that, of course. 'Did you find out any more about him?'

'He is a business man—accounting machines, I think. He has a friend who owns a Lincoln. He wants me to drive it to Istanbul for him. I start tomorrow. He's paying quite well—a hundred dollars American.'

She sat up at that. 'That's very good, isn't it?' And then, inevitably, she saw my face. 'What have you done to yourself?'

'I had a bit of an accident. Some fool in a Simca. I had to stop suddenly.'

'Did the police come?'

She had a tiresome habit of assuming, just because I was once accused (falsely) of causing an accident through driving while drunk, that every little traffic accident in which I was involved was going to result in my being prosecuted by the police.

'It wasn't important,' I said. I turned away to hang up my suit.

'Will you be long away?' She sounded as if she had accepted the accident.

'Two or three days. I shall come back suddenly by air and surprise you with a lover.'

I thought that would amuse her, but she did not even smile. I got into bed beside her and she put the light out. After a few moments she said: 'Why does a man like Mr Harper want to go to a house?'

'Probably because he is impotent anywhere else.'

She was silent for a time. Then she put up a hand and touched my face. 'What really happened, Papa?'

I considered telling her; but that would have meant admitting openly that I had lied about the accident, so I did not answer. After a while, she turned away from me and went to sleep.

She was still asleep, or pretending to be, when I left in the morning.

Harper kept me waiting ten minutes; just long enough for me to remember that I had forgotten to disconnect the battery on my car. It did not hold its charge very well anyway, and the electric clock would have run it down by the time I returned. I was wondering if I would have time to telephone Nicki and tell her to ask the concierge to disconnect the battery, when Harper came down.

'All set?' he asked.

'Yes.'

'We'll get a cab.'

He told the driver to go to Stele Street out in the Piraeus.

As soon as we were on the way, he opened the briefcase and took out a large envelope. It had not been there the night before; of that I am certain. He gave it to me.

'There's everything you'll need there,' he said: '*carnet de tourisme* for the car, insurance Green Card, a thousand Greek drachmas, a hundred Turkish lira, and fifty American dollars for emergencies. The *carnet* has been countersigned authorizing you to take it through customs, but you'd better check everything out yourself.'

I did so. The *carnet* showed that the car was registered in Zürich, and that the owner, or at any rate the person in legal charge of it, was a Fräulein Elizabeth Lipp. Her address was Hotel Excelsior, Laufen, Zürich.

'Is Miss Lipp your friend?' I asked.

'That's right.'

'Are we going to meet her now?'

'No, but maybe you'll meet her in Istanbul. If the customs should ask, tell them she doesn't like eight-hundred-and-fifty-mile drives, and preferred to go to Istanbul by boat.'

'Is she a tourist?'

'What else? She's the daughter of a business associate of mine. I'm just doing him a favour. And by the way, if she wants you to drive her around in Turkey you'll be able to pick up some extra dough. Maybe she'll want you to drive the car back here later. I don't know yet what her future plans are.'

'I see.' For someone who had told me that I wasn't to ask questions, he was being curiously outgoing. 'Where do I deliver the car in Istanbul?'

'You don't. You go to the Park Hotel. There'll be a room reservation for you there. Just check in on Thursday and wait for instructions.'

'Very well. When do I get that letter I signed?'

'When you're paid off at the end of the job.'

Stele Street was down at the docks. By an odd coincidence there happened to be a ship of the Denizyollari Line berthed right opposite; and it was taking on a car through one of the side entry ports. I could not help glancing at Harper to see if he had noticed; but if he had he gave no sign of the fact. I made no comment. If he were simply ignorant, I was not going to enlighten him. If he still really thought that I was foolish enough to believe his version of Fräulein Lipp's travel needs and arrangements, so much the better. I could look after myself. Or so I thought.

There was a garage half-way along the street, with an old Michelin tyre sign above it. He told the cab-driver to stop there and wait. We got out and went towards the office. There was a man inside, and when he saw Harper through the window he came out. He was thin and dark and wore a greasy blue suit. I did not hear Harper address him by any name, but they appeared to know one another quite well. Unfortunately, they spoke together in German, which is a language I have never learned.

After a moment or two, the man led the way through a small repair shop and across a scrap yard to a row of lock-up garages. He opened one of them and there was the Lincoln. It was a grey four-door Continental, and looked to me about a year old. The man handed Harper the keys. He got in, started up and drove it out of the garage into the yard. The car seemed a mile long. Harper got out.

'Okay,' he said. 'She's all gassed up and everything. You can start rolling.'

'Very well.' I put my bag on the back seat. 'I would just like to make a phone call first.'

He was instantly wary. 'Who to?'

'The concierge at my apartment. I want to let him know that I may be away longer than I said, and ask him to disconnect the battery on my car.'

He hesitated, then nodded. 'Okay. You can do it from the office.' He said something to the man in the blue suit and we all went back inside.

Nicki answered the telephone and I told her about the battery. When she started to complain that I had not wakened her to say good-bye, I hung up. I had spoken in Greek, but Harper had been listening.

'That was a woman's voice,' he said.

'The concierge's wife. Is there anything wrong?'

He said something to the man in the blue suit of which I understood one word, '*adressat*'. I guessed that he had wanted to know if I had given the address of the garage. The man shook his head.

Harper looked at me. 'No, nothing wrong. But just remember you're working for me now.'

'Will I see you in Istanbul or back here?'

'You'll find out. Now get going.'

I spent a minute or two making sure that I knew where all the controls were, while Harper and the other man stood watching. Then, I drove off and headed back towards Athens and the Thebes-Larissa-Salonika road.

After about half a mile I noticed that the taxi we had used on the drive out there was behind me. I was driving slowly, getting used to the feel of the car, and the taxi would normally have passed me; but it stayed behind. Harper was seeing me on my way.

About five miles beyond Athens I saw the taxi pull off the road and start to turn around. I was on my own. I drove on for another forty minutes or so, until I reached the first of the cotton fields, then turned off down a side road and stopped in the shade of some acacias.

I spent a good half-hour searching that car. First, I looked in the obvious places: in the back of the spare-wheel compartment, under the seat cushions, up behind the dashboard. Then I took off all the hub-caps. It's surprising how big the cavities are behind some of them, especially on American cars. I knew of a man who had regularly smuggled nearly two kilos of heroin a time that way. These had nothing in them, however. So I tried the tank, poking about with a long twig to see if any sort of a compartment had been built into or on to it; that has to be done, too. Again I drew a blank. I would have liked to have crawled underneath to see if any new welding had been done, but there was not enough clearance. I decided to put the car into a garage greasing-bay in Salonika and examine the underside from below. Meanwhile, there was an air-conditioner in the car, so I unscrewed the cover and had a look inside that. Another blank.

The trouble was I did not have the slightest idea what I was looking for—jewellery, drugs, gold or currency. I just felt that there must be something. After a bit, I gave up searching and sat and smoked a cigarette while I tried to work out what would be worth smuggling into Turkey from Greece. I could not think of anything. I got the *carnet* out and checked the car's route. It had come from Switzerland, via Italy and the Brindisi ferry to Patras. The counterfoils showed that Fräulein Lipp had been with the car herself then. She, at least, *did* know about ferrying cars by sea. However, that only made the whole thing more mysterious.

And then I remembered something. Harper had spoken of the possibility of a *return* journey, of my being wanted to drive the car back from Istanbul to Athens. Supposing *that* was the real point of the whole thing. I drive from Greece into Turkey. Everything is perfectly open and above board. Both Greek and Turkish customs would see and remember car and chauffeur. Some days later, the same car and chauffeur return. 'How was Istanbul, friend? Is your stomach still with you? Anything to declare? No fat-tailed sheep hidden in the back? Pass, friend, pass.' And then the car goes back to the garage in the Piraeus, for the man in the blue suit to recover the packages of heroin concealed along the inner recesses of the chassis members, under the wheel arches of the body, and inside the cowling beside the automatic transmission. Unless, that is, there is a Macedonian son-of-a-bitch on the Greek side who's out to win himself a medal. In that event, what you get is the strange case of the respectable Swiss lady's disreputable chauffeur who gets caught smuggling heroin, and Yours Truly is up the creek.

All I could do was play it by ear.

I got the Lincoln back on the road again and drove on. I reached Salonika soon after six that evening. Just to be on the safe side, I pulled into a big garage and gave the boy a couple of drachmas to put the car up on the hydraulic lift. I said I was looking for a rattle. There were no signs of new welding. I was not surprised. By then I had pretty well made up my mind that it would be the return journey that mattered.

I found a small comfortable hotel, treated myself to a good dinner and a bottle of wine at Harper's expense, and went to bed early. I made an early start the following morning, too. It is an eight-hour run from Salonika across Thrace to the Turkish frontier near Edirne (Adrianople as it used to be called), and if you arrive late you sometimes find that the road-traffic customs post has closed for the night.

I arrived at about four-thirty and went through the Greek control without difficulty. At Karaagac, on the Turkish side, I had to wait while they cleared some farm trucks ahead of me. After about twenty minutes, however, I was able to drive up to the barrier. When I went into the customs post with the *carnet* and my other papers, the place was practically empty.

Naturally, I was more concerned about the car than with myself, so I simply left my passport and currency declaration with the security man, and went straight over to the customs desk to hand in the *carnet*.

Everything seemed to be going all right. A customs inspector went out to the car with me, looked in my bag and merely glanced in the car. He was bored and looking forward to his supper.

'*Tourisme?*' he asked.

'Yes.'

We went back inside and he proceeded to stamp and validate the *carnet* for the car's entry, and tear out his part of the counterfoil. He was just folding the *carnet* and handing it back when I felt a sharp tap on my shoulder.

It was the security man. He had my passport in his hand. I went to take it, but he shook his head and began waving it under my nose and saying something in Turkish.

I speak Egyptian Arabic and there are many Arabic words in Turkish; but the Turks pronounce them in a funny way and use a lot of Persian and old Turkish words mixed up with them. I shrugged helplessly. Then he said it in French and I understood.

My passport was three months out of date.

I knew at once how it had happened. Earlier in the year I had had some differences with the Egyptian consular people (or 'United Arab Republic' as they preferred to call themselves) and had allowed the whole question of my passport to slide. In fact, I had made up my mind to tell the Egyptians what they could do with their passport, and approach the British with a view to reclaiming my United Kingdom citizenship; to which, I want to make it clear, I am perfectly entitled. The thing was that, being so busy, I had just not bothered to fill in all the necessary forms. My Greek *permis de séjour* was in order, and that was all I normally needed in the way of papers. Frankly, I find all this paper regimentation we have to go through nowadays extremely boring. Naturally, with all the anxiety I had had over Harper, I had not thought to look at the date on my passport. If I had known that it was out of date, obviously I would have taken more trouble with the security man, kept him in conversation while he was doing the stamping or something like that. I have never had any bother like that before.

As it was, the whole thing became utterly disastrous; certainly through no fault of mine. The security man refused to stamp the passport. He said that I had to drive back to Salonika and have the passport renewed by the Egyptian vice-consul there before I could be admitted.

That would have been impossible as it happened; but I did not even have to try to explain why. The customs inspector chimed in at that point, waving the *carnet* and shouting that the car *had* been admitted and was now legally in Turkey. As *I* had *not* been admitted and was *not*, therefore, legally in Turkey, how was I, *legally*, to take the car out again? What did it matter if the passport was out of date? It was only a matter of three months. Why did he not just stamp the passport, admit me and forget about it?

At least that was what I think he said. They had lapsed into Turkish now and were bawling at one another as if I did not exist. If I could have got the security man alone, I would have tried to bribe him; but with the other one there it was too dangerous. Finally, they both went off to see some superior officer and left me standing there, without *carnet* or passport, but with, I

admit it frankly, a bad case of the jitters. Really, my only hope at that point
was that they would do what the customs inspector wanted and overlook the
date on the passport.

With any luck, that might have happened. I say 'with any luck', although
things would still have been awkward even if they had let me through. I
would have somehow to buy an Egyptian consular stamp in Istanbul and
forge the renewal in the passport—not easy. Or I would have had to have
gone to the British Consulate-General, reported a lost British passport and
tried to winkle a temporary travel document out of them before they had
had time to check up—not easy either. But at least those would have been the
sort of difficulties a man in my anomalous position would understand and
could cope with. The difficulties that, in fact, I did have to face were quite
outside anything I had ever before experienced.

I stood there in the customs shed for about ten minutes, watched by an
armed guard on the door who looked as if he would have liked nothing
better than an excuse for shooting me. I pretended not to notice him; but his
presence did not improve matters. In fact, I was beginning to get an attack
of my indigestion.

After a while, the security man came back and beckoned to me. I went
with him, along a passage with a small barrack-room off it, to a door at the
end.

'What now?' I asked in French.

'You must see the Commandant of the post.'

He knocked at the door and ushered me in.

Inside was a small bare office with some hard chairs and a green baize
trestle table in the centre. The customs inspector stood beside the table.
Seated at it was a man of about my own age with a lined, sallow face. He
wore some sort of officer's uniform. I think he belonged to the military
security police. He had the *carnet* and my passport on the table in front of
him.

He looked up at me disagreeably. 'This is your passport?' He spoke good
French.

'Yes, sir. And I can only say that I regret extremely that I did not notice
that it was not renewed.'

'You have caused a lot of trouble.'

'I realize that, sir. I must explain, however, that it was only on Monday
evening that I was asked to make this journey. I left early yesterday
morning. I was in a hurry. I did not think to check my papers.'

He looked down at the passport. 'It says here that your occupation is that
of journalist. You told the customs inspector that you were a chauffeur.'

So he had an inquiring mind; my heart sank.

'I am acting as a chauffeur, sir. I was, I *am* a journalist, but one must live
and things are not always easy in that profession.'

'So now you are a chauffeur, and the passport is incorrect in yet another
particular, eh?' It was a very unfair way of putting it, but I thought it as well
to let him have his moment.

'One's fortunes change, sir. In Athens I have my own car, which I drive
for hire.'

He peered, frowning, at the *carnet*. 'This car here is the property of

Elizabeth Lipp. Is she your employer?'

'Temporarily, sir.'

'Where is she?'

'In Istanbul, I believe, sir.'

'You do not know?'

'Her agent engaged me, sir–to drive her car to Istanbul where she is going as a tourist. She prefers to make the journey to Istanbul by sea.'

There was an unpleasant pause. He looked through the *carnet* again and then up at me abruptly.

'What nationality is this woman?'

'I don't know, sir.'

'What age? What sort of woman?'

'I have never seen her, sir. Her agent arranged everything.'

'And she is going from Athens to Istanbul by sea, which takes twenty-four hours, but she sends her car fourteen hundred kilometres and three days by road. If she wants the car in Istanbul why didn't she take the car on the boat with her? It is simple enough and costs practically nothing.'

I was only too well aware of it. I shrugged. 'I was paid to drive, sir, and well paid. It was not for me to question the lady's plans.'

He considered me for a moment, then drew a sheet of paper towards him and scribbled a few words. He handed the result to the customs inspector, who read, nodded and went out quickly.

The Commandant seemed to relax. 'You say you know nothing about the woman who owns the car,' he said. 'Tell me about her agent. Is it a travel bureau?'

'No, sir, a man, an American, a friend of Fräulein Lipp's father he said.'

'What's his name? Where is he?'

I told him everything I knew about Harper, and the nature of my relationship to him. I did not mention the disagreement over the traveller's cheques. That could have been of no interest to him.

He listened in silence, nodding occasionally. By the time I had finished, his manner had changed considerably. His expression had become almost amiable.

'Have you driven this way before?' he asked.

'Several times, sir.'

'With tourists?'

'Yes, sir.'

'Ever without tourists?'

'No, sir. They like to visit Olympus, Salonika and Alexandropolis on their way to Istanbul.'

'Then did you not think this proposal of Mr Harper's strange?'

I permitted myself to smile. '*Monsieur le Commandant*,' I said, 'I thought it so strange that there could be only two possible reasons for it. The first was that Mr Harper was so much concerned to impress the daughter of a valuable business associate with his *savoir faire* that he neglected to ask anyone's advice before he made his arrangements.'

'And the second?'

'That he knew that uncrated cars carried in Denizyollari ships to Istanbul must be accompanied by the owner as a passenger, and that he did not wish to be present when the car was inspected by customs for fear that something might be discovered in the car that should not be there.'

'I see.' He smiled slightly. 'But *you* had no such fear.'

We were getting cosier by the minute. '*Monsieur le Commandant*,' I said, 'I may be a trifle careless about having my passport renewed, but I am not a fool. The moment I left Athens yesterday, I stopped and searched the car thoroughly, underneath as well as on top, the wheels, everywhere.'

There was a knock on the door and the customs inspector came back. He put a sheet of paper down in front of the Commandant. The Commandant read it and his face suddenly tightened. He looked up again at me.

'You say you searched everywhere in the car?'

'Yes, sir. Everywhere.'

'Did you search inside the doors?'

'Well, no, sir. They are sealed. I would have damaged . . .'

He said something quickly in Turkish. Suddenly, the security man locked an arm round my neck and ran his free hand over my pockets. Then he shoved me down violently on to a chair.

I stared at the Commandant dumbly.

'Inside the doors there are–' he referred to the paper in his hand–'twelve tear-gas grenades, twelve concussion grenades, twelve smoke grenades, six gas respirators, six Parabellum pistols, and one hundred and twenty rounds of nine-millimetre pistol ammunition.' He put the paper down and stood up. 'You are under arrest.'

Chapter Three

The post had no facilities for housing prisoners, and I was put in the lavatory under guard while the Commandant reported my arrest to headquarters and awaited orders. The lavatory was only a few yards from his office, and during the next twenty minutes the telephone there rang four times. I could hear the rumble of his voice when he answered. The tone of it became more respectful with each call.

I was uncertain whether I should allow myself to be encouraged by this or not. Police behaviour is always difficult to anticipate, even when you know a country well. Sometimes Higher Authority is more responsive to a reasonable explanation of the misunderstanding, and more disposed to accept a dignified expression of regret for inconvenience caused, than some self-important or sadistic minor official who is out to make the most of the occasion. On the other hand, the Higher Authority has more power to abuse, and, if it comes to the simple matter of a bribe, bigger ideas about his nuisance value. I must admit, though, that what I was mainly concerned about at that point was the kind of physical treatment I would receive. Of course, every police authority, high or low, considers its behaviour 'correct' on all occasions; but in my experience (although I have only really been arrested ten or twelve times in my whole life) the word 'correct' can mean almost anything from hot meals brought in from a near-by restaurant and plenty of cigarettes, to tight-handcuffing in the cell and a knee in the groin if you dare to complain. My previous encounters with the Turkish police had been uncomfortable only in the sense that they had been inconvenient and humiliating; but then the matters in dispute had been of a more or less technical nature. I had to face the fact that 'being in possession of arms, explosives and other offensive weapons, attempting to smuggle them into the Turkish Republic, carrying concealed fire-arms and illegal entry without valid identification papers' were rather more serious charges. My complete and absolute innocence of them would take time to establish, and a lot of quite unpleasant things could happen in the interim.

The possibility that my innocence might *not* be established was something that, realist though I am, I was not just then prepared to contemplate.

After the fourth telephone call, the Commandant came out of his office, gave some order to the security man, who had been waiting in the passage, and then came into the lavatory.

'You are being sent at once to the garrison jail in Edirne,' he said.

'And the car I was driving, sir?'

He hesitated. 'I have no orders about that yet. No doubt it will be wanted as evidence.'

Direct communication with High Authority seemed to have sapped a little of his earlier self-confidence. I decided to have one more shot at bluffing my way out. 'I must remind you, sir,' I said loudly, 'that I have already protested formally to you against my detention here. I repeat that protest. The car and its contents are within your legal jurisdiction. I am not. I was refused entry because my papers were not in order. Therefore, legally, I was not in Turkey and should have been at once returned to the Greek side of the border. In Greece, I have a *permis de séjour* which *is* in order. I think that when your superiors learn these facts, you will find that you have a lot to answer for.'

It was quite well said. Unfortunately, it seemed to amuse him.

'So you are a lawyer, as well as a journalist, a chauffeur and an arms-smuggler.'

'I am simply warning you.'

His smile faded. 'Then let me give you a word of warning, too. In Edirne you will not be dealing with the ordinary police authorities. It is considered that there may be political aspects to your case and it has been placed under the jurisdiction of the Second Section, the Ikinci Büro.'

'Political aspects? What political aspects?' I tried, not very successfully, to sound angry instead of alarmed.

'That is not for me to say. I merely warn you. The Director Second Section is General Haki. It will be his men who will interrogate you. You will certainly end by co-operating with them. You would be well advised to begin by doing so. Their patience, I hear, is quite limited. That is all.'

He went. A moment or two later the security man came in.

I was driven to the garrison jail in a covered jeep with my right wrist handcuffed to a grab-rail, and an escort of two soldiers. The jail was an old stone building on the outskirts of the town. It had a walled courtyard, and there were expanded metal screens as well as bars over the windows.

One of the soldiers, an N.C.O., reported to the guard on the inner gate, and after a few moments two men in a different sort of uniform came out through a smaller side door. One of them had a paper which he handed to the N.C.O. I gathered that it was a receipt for me. The N.C.O. immediately unlocked the handcuffs and waved me out of the jeep. The new escort-in-charge prodded me towards the side door.

'*Girmek, girmek!*' he said sharply.

All jails seem to smell of disinfectants, urine, sweat and leather. This was no exception. I went up some wooden stairs to a steel gate which was opened from the inside by a man with a long chain of keys. Beyond it and to the right was a sort of reception-room with a man at a desk and two cubicles at the back. The guard shoved me up to the desk and rapped out an order. I said in French that I didn't understand. The man at the desk said: '*Vide les poches.*'

I did as I was told. They had taken all my papers and keys from me at the frontier post. All I had left in my pockets was my money, my watch, a packet of cigarettes and matches. The desk man gave me back the watch and the cigarettes, and put the money and the matches into an envelope. A man in a grubby white coat now arrived and went into one of the cubicles. He was carrying a thin yellow file folder. After a moment or two he called out an order and I was sent in to him.

The cubicle contained a small table and a chair and a covered bucket. In one corner there was a wash basin, and on the wall a white metal cabinet. The white-coated man was at the table preparing an inking plate of the kind used for fingerprinting. He glanced up at me and said in French: 'Take your clothes off.'

People who run jails are all the same. When I was naked, he searched the inside of the clothes and the shoes. Next, he looked in my mouth and ears with a flashlight. Then he took a rubber glove and a jar of petroleum jelly from the wall cabinet and searched my rectum. I have always deeply resented that indignity. Finally, he took my fingerprints. He was very businesslike about it all; he even gave me a piece of toilet paper to wipe the ink off my hands before he told me to dress and go into the next cubicle. In there, was a camera, set up with photofloods and a fixed focus bar. When I had been photographed, I was taken along some corridors to a green wooden door with the word ISTIFHAM lettered on it in white paint. *Istifham* is a Turkish word I know; it means 'interrogation'.

There was only one small screened and barred window in the room; the sun was beginning to set and it was already quite dark in there. As I went in, one of the guards followed me and switched on the light. His friend shut and locked the door from the outside. The guard who was to stay with me sat down on a bench against the wall and yawned noisily.

The room was about eighteen feet square. Off one corner there was a washroom with no door on it. Apart from the bench, the furniture consisted of a solid-looking table bolted to the floor and half a dozen chairs. On the wall was a telephone and a framed lithograph of Kemal Ataturk. The floor was covered with worn brown linoleum.

I got out my cigarettes and offered one to the guard. He shook his head and looked contemptuous as if I had offered him an inadequate bribe. I shrugged and, putting the cigarette in my own mouth, made signs that I wanted a light. He shook his head again. I put the cigarette away and sat down at the table. I had to assume that at any moment now a representative of the Second Section would arrive and start questioning me. What I needed, very badly, was something to tell him.

It is always the same with interrogation. I remember my father trying to explain it to Mum one night just before he was killed. It's no good for a soldier who is up on a charge before his C.O. just to tell the truth; he has to have something more, something fancy to go with it. If he got back to barracks half an hour after lights-out just because he'd had too much beer and missed the last bus, who cares about him? He's simply a careless bloody fool—seven days confined to barracks, next case. But if, when he's asked if he has anything to say, he can tell the tale so that the C.O. gets a bit of fun out of hearing it, things are different. He may be only admonished. My father said that there was a corporal in his old regiment who was so good at making up yarns for the orderly room that he used to sell them for half-a-crown apiece. They were known as 'well-sirs'. My father bought a well-sir once when he was 'crimed' for overstaying an evening pass. It went like this:

'Well sir, I was proceeding back along Cantonment Road towards the barracks in good time for lights-out and in a soldierly manner. Then, sir, just as I was passing the shopping arcade by Ordnance Avenue, I heard a woman scream.' Pause. *'Well sir, I stopped to listen and heard her scream again. There were also some confused cries. The sound was coming from one of the shops in the arcade, so I went to investigate.'* Pause again, then go on slowly. *'Well sir, what I found was one of these Wogs—beg pardon, sir, a native—molesting a white woman in a doorway. I could see she was a lady, sir.'* Let that sink in a bit. *'Well sir, the moment this lady saw me she appealed to me for help. She said she'd been on her way home to her mother's house, which was over on the other side of Artillery Park, when this native had attempted to—well, interfere with her. I told him to clear out. In reply, sir, he became abusive, calling me some very dirty names in his own lingo and using insulting language about the Regiment.'* Take a deep breath. *'Well sir, for the lady's sake I managed to hold on to my temper. As a matter of fact, sir, I think the man must have been drunk or under the influence of drugs. He had sense enough to keep his distance, but the moment I escorted the lady out of the arcade I realized that he was following us. Just waiting for a chance to molest her again, sir. She knew it, too. I've never seen a lady more frightened, sir. When she appealed to me to escort her to her mother's house, sir, I realized that it would make me late. But if I'd just gone on my way and something terrible had happened to her, I'd have never forgiven myself, sir.'* Stiffen up and look without blinking at the wall space over the C.O.'s head. *'No excuse to offer, sir, I'll take my medicine.'* C.O. can't think of anything else to say except, 'Don't let it happen again.' Charge dismissed.

The only trouble is that in the Army, unless you are always making a damned nuisance of yourself, they would sooner give you the benefit of the doubt than not, because it's easier for them that way. Besides, they know that even if you *have* made the whole thing up, at least they've had you sweating over it. The police are much more difficult. They don't *want* you to have the benefit of any doubt. They want to start checking up and double-checking your story, and getting witnesses and evidence, so that there *is* no doubt. 'What was the lady's name? Describe her. Exactly where was the house to which you escorted her? Was her mother in fact there? Did you see her? It takes twenty-two minutes to walk from the shopping arcade to the other side of Artillery Park, and a further thirty minutes to walk from there to the barracks. That makes fifty-two minutes. But you were two hours late getting in. Where did you spend the other hour and eight minutes? We have a witness who says that he saw you . . .' And so on. You can't buy well-sirs good enough for the police for half-a-crown. Intelligence people are even worse. Nine times out of ten they don't even have to worry about building up a case against you to go into court. *They* are the court—judge, jury and prosecutor, all in one.

I did not know anything about this Second Section which the Commandant had mentioned; but it was not hard to guess what it was. The Turks have always been great borrowers of French words and phrases. The Ikinci Büro sounded to me like the Turkish counterpart of the Deuxième Bureau. I wasn't far wrong.

I think that if I were asked to single out one specific group of men, one type, one category, as being the most suspicious, unbelieving, unreasonable, petty, inhuman, sadistic, double-crossing set of bastards in any language, I would say without any hesitation 'the people who run counter-espionage departments'. With them, it is no use having just one story; and especially not a true story; they automatically disbelieve that. What you must have is a series of stories, so that when they knock the first one down you can bring out the second, and then, when they scrub that out, come up with a third. That way they think they are making progress and keep their hands off you, while you gradually find out the story they really want you to tell.

My position at Edirne was hopeless from the start. If I had known what was hidden in the car *before* the post Commandant had started questioning me, I wouldn't have told him about Harper. I would have pretended to be stupid, or just refused to say anything. Then, later, when I had finally broken down and 'told all', they would have believed at least some of what I had said. As it was, I had told a story that happened to be true, but sounded as if I thought they were half-witted. You can imagine how I felt as I waited. With no room at all for manoeuvre, I knew that I must be in for a bad time.

The sun went down and the window turned black. It was very quiet. I could hear no sounds at all from other parts of the jail. Presumably, things were arranged so that there they could hear no sounds made in the interrogation room—screams etc. When I had been there two hours, there were footsteps in the corridor outside, the door was unlocked and a new guard came in with a tin bowl of mutton soup and a hunk of bread. He put these on the table in front of me, then nodded to his friend, who went out and relocked the door. The new man took his place on the bench.

There was no spoon. I dipped a piece of bread in the soup and tasted it. It was lukewarm and full of congealed fat. Even without my indigestion I could not have eaten it. Now, the smell alone made me want to throw up.

I looked at the guard. '*Su?*' I asked.

He motioned to the washroom. Evidently, if I wanted water I would have to drink from the tap. I did not relish the idea. Indigestion was bad enough; I did not want dysentery, too. I made myself eat some of the bread and then took out my cigarettes again in the hope that the new man might he ready to give me a match. He shook his head. I pointed to a plastic ash-tray on the table to remind him that smoking was not necessarily prohibited. He still shook his head.

A little before nine, a twin-engined plane flew over the jail and then circled as if on a landing pattern. The sound seemed to mean something to the guard. He looked at his watch and then absently ran his hands down the front of his tunic as if to make sure that the buttons were all done up.

More to break the interminable silence in the room than because I wanted to know, I asked: 'Is there a big airport at Edirne?'

I spoke in French, but it meant nothing to him. I made signs which he misunderstood.

'*Askeri ucak,*' he said briefly.

An Army plane. That concluded that conversation; but I noticed that he kept glancing at his watch now. Probably, I thought, it was time for his relief and he was becoming impatient.

Twenty minutes later there was the distant sound of a car door slamming. The guard heard it, too, and promptly stood up. I stared at him and he glowered back.

'*Hazirol!*' he snapped, and then exasperatedly, '*Debout! Debout!*'

I stood up. I could hear approaching footsteps and voices now. Then the door was unlocked and flung open.

For a moment nothing more happened, except that someone in the corridor, whom I could not see, went on speaking. He had a harsh peremptory voice which seemed to be giving orders that another voice kept acknowledging deferentially—'*Evet, evet efendim, derhal.*' Then the orders ceased and the man who had been giving them came into the room.

He was about thirty-five I would think, perhaps younger, tall and quite slim. There were high cheekbones, grey eyes and short brown hair. He was handsome, I suppose, in a thin-lipped sort of way. He was wearing a dark civilian suit that looked as if it had been cut by a good Roman tailor, and a dark-grey silk tie. He looked as if he had just come from a diplomatic corps cocktail party; and for all I know he may have done so. The hand below it was holding a large manila envelope.

He examined me bleakly for a moment, then nodded. 'I am Major Tufan, Deputy-Director Second Section.'

'Good evening, Major.'

He glanced at the guard, who was staring at him round-eyed, and suddenly snapped out an order: '*Defol!*'

The guard nearly fell over himself getting out of the room.

As soon as the door closed the Major pulled a chair up to the table and sat down. Then he waved me back to my seat by the bread.

'Sit down, Simpson. I believe that you speak French easily, but not Turkish.'

'Yes, Major.'

'Then we will speak in French instead of English. That will be easier for me.'

I answered in French. 'As you wish, sir.'

He took cigarettes and matches from his pocket and tossed them on the table in front of me. 'You may smoke.'

'Thank you.'

I was glad of the concession, though not in the least reassured by it. When a policeman gives you a cigarette it is usually the first move in one of those 'let's-see-if-we-can't-talk-sensibly-as-man-to-man' game in which he provides the rope and you hang yourself. I lit a cigarette and waited for the next move.

He seemed in no hurry to make it. He had opened the envelope and taken from it a file of papers which he was searching through and rearranging, as if he had just dropped the whole lot and was trying to get it back into the right order.

There was a knock at the door. He took no notice. After a moment or two the door opened and a guard came in with a bottle of *raki* and two glasses. Tufan motioned to him to put them on the table, and then noticed the soup.

'Do you want any more of that?' he asked.

'No thank you, sir.'

He said something to the guard, who took the soup and bread away and locked the door again.

Tufan rested the file on his knees and poured himself a glass of *raki*. 'The flight from Istanbul was anything but smooth,' he said; 'we are still using piston-engined planes on these short runs.' He swallowed the drink as if he were washing down a pill, and pushed the bottle an inch or two in my direction. 'You'd better have a drink, Simpson. It may make you feel better.'

'And also make me more talkative, sir?' I thought the light touch might show that I was not afraid.

He looked up and his grey eyes met mine. 'I hope not,' he said coldly; 'I have no time to waste'. He shut the file with a snap and put it on the table in front of him.

'Now then,' he went on, 'let us examine your position. First, the offences with which you are charged render you liable upon conviction to terms of imprisonment of at least twenty years. Depending on the degree of your involvement in the political aspects of this affair, we might even consider pressing for a death sentence.'

'But I am not involved at all, Major, I assure you. I am a victim of circumstances—an innocent victim.' Of course he could have been bluffing about the death sentence, but I could not be sure. There was that phrase 'political aspects' again. I had read that they had been hanging members of the former government for political crimes. I wished now that I had taken the drink when he had offered it. Now my hands were shaking, and I knew that, if I reached for the bottle and glass, he would see that they were.

Apparently, however, he did not have to see them; he knew what he was doing to me, and wanted me to know that he knew. Quite casually, he picked up the bottle, poured me half a glass of *raki* and pushed it across to me.

'We will talk about the extent of your involvement in a minute,' he said.

'First, let us consider the matter of your passport.'

'It is out of date. I admit that. But it was a mere oversight. If the post Commandant had behaved correctly I would have been sent back to the Greek post.'

He shrugged impatiently. 'Let us be clear about this. You had already committed serious criminal offences on Turkish soil. Would you expect to escape the consequences because your papers were not in order? You know better. You also know that your passport was not invalid through any oversight. The Egyptian Government had refused to renew it. In fact they revoked your citizenship two years ago on the grounds that you made false statements on your naturalization papers.' He glanced in the file. 'You stated that you had never been convicted of a criminal offence and that you had never served a prison sentence. Both statements were lies.'

This was such an unfair distortion of the facts that I could only assume that he had got it from the Egyptians. I said: 'I have been fighting that decision.'

'And also using a passport to which you were not entitled and had failed to surrender.'

'My case was still *sub judice.* Anyway, I have already applied for restoration of my British citizenship, to which I am entitled as the son of a serving British officer. In fact, I *am* British.'

'The British don't take that view. After what happened you can scarcely blame them.'

'Under the provisions of the British Nationality Act of 1948 I remain British unless I have specifically renounced that nationality. I have never formally renounced it.'

'That is unimportant. We are talking about your case here and the extent of your involvement. The point I wish to make is that our action in your case is not going to be governed in any way by the fact that you are a foreigner. No consul is going to intercede on your behalf. You have none. You are stateless. The only person who can help you is my Director.' He paused. 'But he will have to be persuaded. You understand me?'

'I have no money.'

It seemed a perfectly sensible reply to me, but for some reason it appeared to irritate him. His eyes narrowed and for a moment I thought he was going to throw the glass he was holding in my face. Then he sighed. 'You are over fifty,' he said, 'yet you have learned nothing. You still see other men in your own absurd image. Do you really believe that I could be bought, or that, if I could be, a man like you could ever do the buying?'

It was on the tip of my tongue to retort that that would depend on the price he was asking, but if he wanted to take this high-and-mighty attitude, there was no sense in arguing. Obviously, I had touched him in a sensitive area.

He lit a cigarette as if he were consciously putting aside his irritation. I took the opportunity to drink some of the *raki*.

'Very well.' He was all business again. 'You understand your position, which is that you have no position. We come now to the story you told to the post Commandant before your arrest.'

'Every word I told the Commandant was the truth.'

He opened the file. 'On the face of it that seems highly unlikely. Let us see. You stated that you were asked by this American, Harper, to drive a car belonging to a Fräulein Lipp from Athens to Istanbul. You were to be paid one hundred dollars. You agreed. Am I right?'

'Quite right.'

'You agreed, even though the passport in your possession was not in order?'

'I did not realize it was out-of-date. It has been months since I used it. The whole thing was arranged within a few hours. I scarcely had time to pack a bag. People are using out-of-date passports all the time. Ask anyone at any international airline. They will tell you. That is why they always check passengers' passports when they weigh their baggage. They do not want difficulties at the other end. I had nobody to check. The Greek control scarcely looked at the passport. I was leaving the country. They were not interested.'

I knew I was on safe ground here, and I spoke with feeling.

He thought for a moment then nodded. 'It is possible, and, of course, you had good reason not to think too much about the date on your passport. The Egyptians were not going to renew it anyway. That explanation is acceptable, I think. We will go on.' He referred again to the file. 'You told the Commandant that you suspected this man Harper of being a narcotics smuggler.'

'I did.'

'To the extent of searching the car after you left Athens.'

'Yes.'

'Yet you still agreed to make the journey.'

'I was being paid one hundred dollars.'

'That was the only reason?'

'Yes.'

He shook his head. 'It really will not do.'

'I am telling you the truth.'

He took a clip of papers from the file. 'Your history does not inspire confidence.'

'Give a dog a bad name.'

'You seem to have earned one. Our dossier on you begins in '57. You were arrested on various charges and fined on a minor count. The rest were abandoned by the police for lack of evidence.'

'They should never have been brought in the first place.'

He ignored this. 'We did, however, ask Interpol if they knew anything about you. It seemed they knew a lot. Apparently you were once in the restaurant business.'

'My mother owned a restaurant in Cairo. Is that an offence?'

'Fraud is an offence. Your mother was *part* owner of a restaurant. When she died, you sold it to a buyer who believed that you now owned all of it. In fact, there were two other shareholders. The buyer charged you with fraud but withdrew his complaint when the police allowed you to regularize the transaction.'

'I didn't know of the existence of these other shareholders. My mother had never told me that she had sold the shares.' This was perfectly true.

Mum was entirely responsible for the trouble I got into over that.

'In 1931 you bought a partnership in a small publishing business in Cairo. Outwardly it concerned itself with distributing foreign magazines and periodicals. Its real business was the production of pornography for the Spanish and English-speaking markets. And that became your real business.'

'That is absolutely untrue.'

'The information was supplied through Interpol in '54 by Scotland Yard. It was given in response to an inquiry by the New York police. Scotland Yard must have known about you for a long time.'

I knew it would do no good for me to become angry. 'I have edited and sometimes written for a number of magazines of a literary nature over the years,' I said quietly. 'Sometimes they may have been a little daring in their approach and have been banned by various censoring authorities. But I would remind you that books like *Ulysses* and *Lady Chatterley's Lover*, which were once described by those same authorities as pornographic or obscene, are now accepted as literary works of art and published quite openly.'

He looked at his papers again. 'In January '55 you were arrested in London. In your possession were samples of the various obscene and pornographic periodicals which you had been attempting to sell in bulk. Among them was a book called *Gents Only* and a monthly magazine called *Enchantment*. All were produced by your Egyptian company. You were charged under the British law governing such publications, and also with smuggling them. At your trial you said nothing about their being literary works of art. You pleaded guilty and were sentenced to twelve months' imprisonment.'

'That was a travesty of justice.'

'Then why did you plead guilty?'

'Because my lawyer advised me to.' In fact, the C.I.D. inspector had tricked me into it. He had as good as promised me that if I pleaded guilty I would get off with a fine.

He stared at me thoughtfully for a moment then shut the file. 'You must be a very stupid man, Simpson. You say to me, "I am telling you the truth," and yet when I try to test that statement all I hear from you is whining and protestation. I am not interested in how you explain away the past, or in any illusions about yourself that you may wish to preserve. If you cannot even tell the truth when there is nothing to be gained by lying, then I can believe nothing you tell me. You were caught by the British, smuggling pornography and trying to peddle it. Why not admit it? Then, when you tell me that you did not know that you were smuggling arms and ammunition this afternoon, I might at least think, "This man is a petty criminal, but it is remotely possible that for once he is being truthful." As it is, I can only assume that you are lying and that I must get the truth from you in some other way.'

I admit that 'some other way' gave me a jolt. After all, five minutes earlier he had been pouring me a glass of *raki*. He meant to put the fear of God into me, of course, and make me panic. Unfortunately, and only because I was tired, upset and suffering from indigestion, he succeeded.

'I am telling you the truth, sir.' I could hear my own voice cracking and quavering but could do nothing to control it. 'I swear to God I am telling you the truth. My only wish is to tell you all I can, to bring everything out of the darkness into the light of day.'

He stared at me curiously; and then, as I realized what I had said, I felt myself reddening. It was awful. I had used those absurd words Harper had made me write in that confession about the cheques.

A sour smile touched his lips for an instant. 'Ah yes,' he said. 'I was forgetting that you have been a journalist. We will try once more then. Just remember that I do not want speeches in mitigation, only plain statements.'

'Of course.' I was too confused to think straight now.

'Why did you go to London in '55? You must have known that Scotland Yard knew all about you.'

'How could I know? I hadn't been in England for years.'

'Where were you during the war?'

'In Cairo doing war work.'

'What work?'

'I was an interpreter.'

'Why did you go to London.'

I cleared my throat and took a sip of *raki*.

'Answer me!'

'I was going to answer, sir.' There was nothing else for it. 'The British distributor of our publications suddenly ceased making payments and we could get no replies from him to our letters. I went to England to investigate and found his offices closed. I assumed that he had gone out of business and began to look for another distributor. The man I eventually discussed the possibility with turned out to be a Scotland Yard detective. We used to send our shipments to Liverpool in cotton bales. It seems that the customs had discovered this and informed the police. Our distributor had been arrested and sent to prison. The police had kept it out of the papers somehow. I just walked into a trap.'

'Better, much better,' he said. He looked almost amused. 'Naturally, though, you felt bitter towards the British authorities.'

I should have remembered something he had let drop earlier, but I was still confused. I tried to head him off.

'I was bitter at the time, of course, sir. I did not think I had had a fair trial. But afterwards I realized that the police had their job to do–' I thought that would appeal to him–'and that they weren't responsible for making the laws. So I tried to be a model prisoner. I think I was. Anyway I received the maximum remission for good behaviour. I certainly couldn't complain of the treatment I had in Maidstone. In fact, the Governor shook hands with me when I left and wished me well.'

'And then you returned to Egypt?'

'As soon as my probationary period was up, yes. I went back to Cairo, sir.'

'Where you proceeded to denounce a British business man named Colby Evans to the Egyptian authorities as a British secret agent.'

It was like a slap in the face, but I managed to keep my head this time. 'Not immediately, sir. That was later, during the Suez crisis.'

'Why did you do it?'

I didn't know what to say. How could I explain to a man like that that I had to pay back the caning they had given me? I said nothing.

'Was it because you needed to prove somehow to the Egyptian authorities that you were anti-British, or because you didn't like the man, or because you were sincerely anti-British?'

It was all three, I suppose; I am not really sure. I answered almost without thinking.

'My mother was Egyptian. My wife was killed by a British bomb in the attack they made on us. Why shouldn't I feel sincerely anti-British?'

It was probably the best answer I had given so far; it sounded true, even though it wasn't quite.

'Did you really believe this man was an agent?'

'Yes, sir.'

'And then you applied for Egyptian citizenship.'

'Yes, sir.'

'You stayed in Egypt until '58. Was that when they finally decided that Evans had *not* been a British agent after all and released him?'

'He was convicted at his trial. His release was an act of clemency.'

'But the Egyptians did start to investigate you at that time.' It was a statement.

'I suppose so.'

'I see.' He refilled my glass. 'I think we are beginning to understand one another, Simpson. You now realize that it is neither my business nor my inclination to make moral judgments. I, on the other hand, am beginning to see how your mind works in the areas we are discussing—what holds the pieces together. So now let us go back to your story about Mr Harper and Fräulein Lipp.' He glanced again at the file. 'You see, for a man of your experience it is quite incredible. You suspect that Harper may be using you for some illegal purpose which will be highly profitable to him, yet you do as he asks for a mere hundred dollars.'

'It was the return journey I was thinking of, sir. I thought that when he realized that I had guessed what he was up to, he would have to pay me to take the risk.'

He sat back, smiling. 'But you had accepted the hundred dollars before that possibility had occurred to you. You would not have searched the car outside Athens otherwise. You see the difficulty?'

I did. What I didn't see was the way out of it.

He lit another cigarette. 'Come now, Simpson, you were emerging very sensibly from the darkness a few minutes ago. Why not continue? Either your whole story is a lie, or you have left something of importance out. Which is it? I am going to find out anyway. It will be easier for both of us if you just tell me now.'

I know when I am beaten. I drank some more *raki*. 'All right. I had no more choice with him than I have with you. He was blackmailing me.'

'How?'

'Have you got an extradition treaty with Greece?'

'Never mind about that. I am not the police.'

So I had to tell him about the traveller's cheques after all.

When I had finished, he nodded. 'I see,' was all he said. After a moment, he got up and went to the door. It opened the instant he knocked on it. He began to give orders.

I was quite sure that he had finished with me and was telling the guards to take me away to a cell, so I swallowed the rest of the *raki* in my glass and put the matches in my pocket on the off-chance that I might get away with them.

I was wrong about the cell. When he had finished speaking, he shut the door and came back.

'I have sent for some eatable food,' he said.

He did not stop at the table, but went across to the telephone. I lighted a cigarette and returned the matches to the table. I don't think he noticed. He was asking for an Istanbul number and making a lot of important-sounding noises about it. Then he hung up and came back to the table.

'Now tell me everything you remember about this man Harper,' he said.

I started to tell him the whole story from the beginning, but he wanted details now.

'You say that he spoke like a German who has lived in America for some years. When did you reach that conclusion? After you heard him speak German to the man at the garage?'

'No. Hearing him speak German only confirmed the impression I had had.

'If you were to hear me speak German fluently could you tell whether it was my mother tongue or not?'

'No.'

'How did he pronounce the English word "later", for example?'

I tried to tell him.

'You know, the German "l" is more formal than that,' he said; 'but in Turkish, before certain vowels, the "l" is like the English consonant you were pronouncing. If you were told that this man had a Turkish background, would you disbelieve it?'

'Not if I were told it was true perhaps. But is Harper a Turkish name?'

'Is it a German one?'

'It could be an anglicization of Hipper.'

'It could also be an anglicization of Harbak.' He shrugged. 'It could also be an alias. It most probably is. All I am trying to discover is if the man could be Turkish.'

'Because of the political aspects you mentioned?'

'Obviously. Tear-gas grenades, concussion grenades, smoke grenades, six pistols, six times twenty rounds of ammunition. Six determined men, equipped with that material, making a surprise attack on some important person or group of persons could accomplish a great deal. There are still many supporters of the former régime. They do not like the Army's firm hands.'

I refrained from telling him that I wasn't so very fond of those firm hands myself.

'But, of course,' he went on; 'we keep our eyes on them. If they wished to attempt anything they would need help from outside. You say he had Swiss francs and West German marks as well as dollars?'

'Yes.'

'Naturally it is possible that what we have here is only one small corner of a much larger plan. If so, there is a lot of money behind it. This man Harper went to a great deal of trouble and expense to get that material through. Perhaps . . .'

The telephone rang and he broke off to answer it. His call to Istanbul had come through. I understood about one word in ten of his side of the conversation. He was reporting to his boss; that much was easily gathered. My name was mentioned several times. After that he mostly listened, just putting in an occasional *evet* to show that he was getting the point. I could hear the faint quacking of the voice at the other end of the line. Finally, it stopped. Tufan asked a question and received a brief reply. That was all. Tufan made a respectful sound, then hung up and looked across at me.

'Bad news for you, Simpson,' he said. 'The Director does not feel disposed to help you in any way. He regards the charges against you as too serious.'

'I'm sorry.' There seemed nothing more to say. I downed another *raki* to try to settle my stomach.

'He considers that you have not been sufficiently helpful to us. I was unable to persuade him.'

'I've told you everything I know.'

'It is not enough. What we need to know is more about this man Harper, who his associates and contacts are, who this Fräulein Lipp is, where the arms and ammunition are going, how they are to be used. If you could supply that information or help to supply it, of course, your case might be reconsidered.'

'The only way I could possibly get information like that would be to drive on to Istanbul tomorrow as if nothing had happened, go to the Park Hotel and wait for somebody to contact me as arranged. Is that what you're telling me I have to do?'

He sat down facing me. 'It is what we might tell you to do, if we thought that we could trust you. My Director is doubtful. Naturally, he is thinking of your past record.'

'What has that to do with it?'

'Isn't it obvious. Supposing you warn these people that the car was searched. Perhaps they would reward you.'

'Reward me?' I laughed loudly; I think I must have been getting a bit tight. 'Reward me for telling them that they are under surveillance? Are you serious? You were talking about a group of men determined enough to risk their lives. At the moment, the only contact I can identify is Harper. He may or may not be in Istanbul. Supposing he's not. Someone has to contact me to get at the car. What do I do? Whisper "Fly, all is discovered" into his ear, and expect him to tip me before he leaves? Or do I wait until I've made a few more contacts before I tell them the good news, so that they can pass the hat round? Don't be ridiculous! They'd know at once that they wouldn't get far, because you'd pick me up again and make me talk. Reward? I'd be lucky if they let me stay alive.'

He smiled. 'The Director wondered if you would have the sense to see that.'

But I was too annoyed by what I thought was his stupidity to grasp the implication of what he had said. I went on in English. I didn't care any more whether he understood me or not. I said: 'In any case, what have *you* got to lose? If I don't turn up in Istanbul tomorrow, they'll know that something's gone wrong, and all you'll have is a couple of names that don't mean anything to you, and a second-hand Lincoln. You'll have me, too, of course, but you already know all I know about this, and you're going to look damn silly standing up in court trying to prove that I was going to carry out a one-man *coup d'état*. Your bloody Director may be one of these fine, upstanding, crap-packed bastards who thinks that everybody who doesn't smell to high heaven of sweetness and roses isn't worth a second thought, but if his brain isn't where his arse ought to be he must know he's got to trust me. He has no bloody alternative.'

Tufan nodded calmly and moved the *raki* bottle just out of my reach. 'Those were more or less the Director's own words,' he said.

Chapter Four

I woke up the next morning with a hangover; and not just because of the *raki*. Nervous strain always has that effect on me. It was a wonder that I had been able to sleep at all.

The 'eatable food' that Tufan had ordered had turned out to be yoghourt (which I detest) and some sort of sheep's milk cheese. I had just eaten some more bread while Tufan made telephone calls.

The Lincoln had been left out at the Karaagac customs post, which was closed for the night. He had had to get the Commandant out of bed to open the place up, and arrange for an army driver to take the car to the garrison repair shop. The grenades and arms, and my bag, had been removed to the local Army H.Q. for examination. That meant that more people, including the customs inspector who had searched the car, had then had to be rounded up so that the stuff could be put back inside the doors again exactly as it had been found.

Even with all the authority he had, it had taken an hour just to organize the work. Then, the question of a hotel room for me had come up. I was so exhausted by then that I would not have minded sleeping in a cell. I had told him so; but, of course, it had not been my comfort he had been thinking about. I had had to listen to a lecture. Supposing Harper asked me where I had spent the night; supposing this, supposing that. An agent sometimes had to take risks, but he should never take unnecessary ones. To be caught out through carelessness over trifles was unforgivable; and so on. That had been the first time he had referred to me as an 'agent'. It had given me an uncomfortable feeling.

He had told me to meet him outside a new apartment building near the hotel at nine o'clock. He was already there when I arrived. His clothes were still quite neat, but he hadn't shaved and his eyes were puffy. He looked as if he had been up all night. Without even saying 'good morning' he motioned me to follow him and led the way down a ramp to a small garage in the basement of the building.

The Lincoln was there and looking very clean.

'I had it washed,' he said. 'It had too many fingerprints on it. It'll be dusty again by the time you get to Istanbul. You had better look at the doors.'

I had warned him to be careful about the interior door panels. They were leather and had been quite clean when I had taken the car over in Athens. If some clumsy lout of an army fitter had made scratches or marks when replacing them, Harper would be bound to notice.

I could see nothing wrong, however. If I had not been told, I would not have known that the panels had ever been taken off.

'It's all inside there, just as it was before?' I asked.

'The customs inspector says so. All the objects were taped out of the way of the window glasses against the metal. Photographs were taken before they were removed.'

He had a set of prints in his pocket and he showed them to me. They didn't convey much. They looked like pictures of hibernating bats.

'Have you any idea where the stuff was bought?' I asked.

'A good question. The pistols and ammunition are German, of course. The grenades, all kinds, are French. That doesn't help us much. We do know that the packing was done in Greece.'

'How?'

'It was padded with newspapers to stop any rattling. There are bits of Athens papers dated a week ago.' He took a sealed envelope from the front seat of the car and opened it up. 'These are the things that were taken from you at the frontier post,' he said. 'You had better put them back in your pockets now and I will keep the envelope. I have a special tourist visa stamped in the passport validating it as a travel document within Turkey for one month. That is in case the hotel clerk should notice the expiry date or if you are stopped by the traffic police for any reason. If Harper or anyone else should happen to see it, you simply say that the security control made no difficulties when you promised to get the passport renewed in Istanbul. The *carnet* is in order, of course, and there are your other personal papers.' He handed them to me, then tore the envelope in four and put the pieces in his pocket.

'Now,' he went on, 'as to your orders. You know the information we want. First, the names and addresses of all contacts, their descriptions, what they say and do. Secondly, you will attempt, by keeping your ears and eyes open, to discover where and how these arms are to be used. In that connection you will take particular note of any place names mentioned, no matter in what context. Buildings or particular areas, too. Do you understand that?'

'I understand. How do I report?'

'I am coming to that. First, from the moment you leave here you will be under surveillance. The persons allocated to this duty will be changed frequently, but if you should happen to recognize any of them you will pretend not to. Only in an emergency or in a case of extreme urgency will you approach them. In that event they will help you if you say my name. You will report normally by telephone, but not from a telephone that goes through a private switchboard. Certainly not from the telephone in a hotel room. Use café telephones. Unless, for physical or security reasons, it is impossible, you will report at ten every night, or at eight the following morning if you have missed the ten o'clock call.' He took a box of matches from his pocket. 'The number is written here underneath the matches. As soon as you are certain that you will not forget it, throw the box away. If you want to communicate other than at the daily report times, a duty officer will pass your call or give you another number at which I can be reached. Is that all clear?'

'Yes.' I took the matches and looked at the number.

'Just one more thing,' he said. 'The Director is not an amiable or kindly man. You will keep faith with us because it would not be in your interests to do otherwise. He knows that, of course. But, for him, stupidity or clumsiness in carrying out orders are just as unacceptable as bad faith and have the same consequences. I would strongly advise you to be successful. That is all, I think, unless you have any questions.'

'No. No questions.'

With a nod, he turned away and walked up the ramp to the street. I put my bag in the back of the car again. Ten minutes later I was clear of Edirne and on the Istanbul road.

After a few miles I identified the surveillance car as a sand-coloured Peugeot two or three hundred yards behind me. It kept that distance, more or less, even when trucks or other cars got between us, or going through towns. It never closed up enough for me to see the driver clearly. When I stopped at Corlu for lunch he did not overtake me. I did not see the Peugeot while I was there.

The restaurant was a café with a few shaky tables under a small vine-covered terrace outside. I had a glass or two of *raki* and some stuffed peppers. My stomach began to feel a bit better. I sat there for over an hour. I would have liked to have stayed longer. There were moments like that at school, too; when one bad time had ended and the next had not yet begun. There can be days of it also, the days when one is on remand awaiting trial–not innocent, not guilty, not responsible, out of the game. I often wish that I could have an operation–not a painful or serious one, of course–just so as to be convalescent for a while after it.

The Peugeot picked me up again three minutes after I left Corlu. I stopped again only once, for petrol. I reached Istanbul just after four.

I put the Lincoln in a garage just off Taxim Square and walked to the hotel, carrying my bag.

The Park Oteli is built against the side of a hill overlooking the Bosphorus. It is the only hotel that I know of which has the foyer at the top, so that the lift takes you down to your room instead of up. My room was quite a long way down and on a corner overlooking a street with a café in it. The café had a gramophone and an inexhaustible supply of Turkish *caz* records. Almost level with the window and about fifty yards away was the top of a minaret belonging to a mosque lower down the hill. It had loudspeakers in it to amplify the voice of the *muezzin* and his call to prayer was deafening. When Harper had made the reservation, he had obviously asked for the cheapest room in the hotel.

I changed into a clean shirt and sat down to wait.

At six o'clock the telephone rang.

'Monsieur Simpson?' It was a man's voice with a condescending lilt to it and an unidentifiable accent. He wasn't an Englishman or an American.

'This is Simpson,' I answered.

'Miss Lipp's car is all right? You have had no accidents or trouble on the journey from Athens?'

'No. The car is fine.'

'Good. Miss Lipp has a pressing engagement. This is what you are to do. You know the Hilton Hotel?'

'Yes.'

'Drive the car to the Hilton at once and put it in the car-park opposite the entrance to the hotel and behind the Kervansaray night-club. Leave the *carnet* and insurance papers in the glove compartment and the ignition key beside the driver's seat on the floor. Is it understood?'

'It is understood, yes. But who is that speaking?'

'A friend of Miss Lipp. The car should be there in ten minutes.' He rang off abruptly as if my question had been impertinent.

I sat there wondering what I ought to do. I was certainly not going to do as he had told me. The only hope I had of my making any sort of contact with the people Tufan was interested in was through the car. If I just let it go like that I would be helpless. Even without Tufan's orders to carry out I would have refused. Harper had said that I would be paid and get my letter back when the job was done. He, or someone on his behalf, would have to fulfil those conditions before I surrendered control of the car. He must have known that, too. After what had happened in Athens he could scarcely have expected me to trust to his good nature. And what had happened to all that talk of driving for Miss Lipp while she was in Turkey?

I hid the *carnet* under some shelf-lining paper on top of the wardrobe and went out. It took me about ten minutes to walk to the Hilton.

I approached the car-park briskly, swinging my keys in my hand as if I were going to pick up a car already there. I guessed that either the man who had telephoned, or someone acting on his instructions, would be waiting for the Lincoln to arrive, all ready to drive it away the instant I had gone. In Instanbul it is unwise to leave even the poorest car unlocked and unattended for very long.

I spotted him almost immediately. He was standing at the outer end of the Hilton driveway smoking a cigarette and staring into the middle distance, as if he were trying to decide whether to go straight home to his wife or visit his girl-friend first. Remembering that I would have to give Tufan his description, I took very careful note of him. He was about forty-five and thick-set with a barrel chest and a mop of crinkly grey hair above a brown puffy face. The eyes were brown, too. He was wearing a thin light-grey suit, yellow socks and plaited leather sandals. Height about five-ten, I thought.

I walked through the car-park to make sure that there were no other possibilities there, then came out the other side and walked back along the street for another glimpse of him.

He was looking at his watch. The car should have been there by then if I were following instructions.

I walked straight back to the Park Hotel. As I unlocked the door to my room I could hear the telephone inside ringing.

It was the same voice again, but peremptory now.

'Simpson? I understand that the car is not yet delivered. What are you doing?'

'Who is that speaking?'

'The friend of Miss Lipp. Answer my question, please. Where is the car?'

'The car is quite safe and will remain so.'

'What are you talking about?'

'The *carnet* is in the hotel strong-room and the car is garaged. It will remain that way until I hand it over to Mr Harper or someone holding credentials from Mr Harper.'

'The car is the property of Miss Lipp.'

'The *carnet* is in the name of Miss Lipp,' I answered; 'but the car was placed in my care by Mr Harper. I am responsible for it. I don't know Miss Lipp except by name. I don't know you *even* by name. You see the difficulty?'

'Wait.'

I heard him start to say something to someone with him: '*Il dit que . . .*' And then he clamped a hand over the telephone.

I waited. After a few moments he spoke again. 'I will come to your hotel. Remain there.' Without waiting for my agreement, he hung up.

I went upstairs to the foyer and told the desk clerk that I would be out on the terrace if I were wanted. The terrace was crowded, but I eventually managed to find a table and order a drink. I was quite prepared to make the contact; but I had not liked the sound of the man on the telephone, and preferred to encounter him in a public place rather than in the privacy of my room.

I had left my name with the head waiter, and after about twenty minutes I saw him pointing me out to a tall, cadaverous man with a narrow, bald head and large projecting ears. The man came over. He was wearing a cream and brown striped sports shirt and tan linen slacks. He had a long, petulant upper lip and a mouth that drooped at the corners.

'Simpson?'

'Yes.'

He sat down facing me. Brown eyes, one gold tooth left side lower jaw, gold-and-onyx signet ring on little finger of left hand; I made mental notes.

'Who are you?' I asked.

'My name is Fischer.'

'Will you have a drink, Mr Fischer?'

'No. I wish to clear this misunderstanding relative to Miss Lipp's car.'

'There is no misunderstanding in my mind, Mr Fischer,' I answered. 'My orders from Mr Harper were quite explicit.'

'Your orders were to wait orders at the hotel,' he snapped. 'You have not complied with them.'

I looked respectfully apologetic. 'I am not doubting that you have a perfect right to give those orders, Mr Fischer, but I assumed, naturally, that Mr Harper would be here, or, if not here in person, that he would have given a written authorization. That is a very valuable car and I . . .'

'Yes, yes,' he broke in impatiently. 'I understand. The point is that Mr Harper has been delayed until tomorrow afternoon and Miss Lipp wishes her car at once.'

'I'm sorry.'

He leaned across the table towards me and I caught a whiff of after-shave lotion. 'Mr Harper would not be pleased that you put Miss Lipp to the trouble of coming to Istanbul herself to claim her car,' he said menacingly.

'I thought Miss Lipp *was* in Istanbul.'

'She is at the villa,' he said shortly. 'Now we will have no more of this nonsense, please. You and I will go and get the car immediately.'

'If you have Mr Harper's written authority, of course.'

'I have Mr Harper's authority.'

'May I see it, sir?'

'That is not necessary.'

'I'm afraid that is for me to decide.'

He sat back, breathing deeply. 'I will give you one more chance,' he said after a pause. 'Either you hand over the car immediately or steps will be taken to *compel* you to do so.'

As he said the word 'compel', his right hand came out and deliberately flicked the drink in front of me into my lap.

At that moment something happened to me. I had been through an awful twenty-four hours, of course; but I don't think it was only that. I suddenly felt as if my whole life had been spent trying to defend myself against people compelling me to do this or that, and always succeeding because they had all the power on their side; and then, just as suddenly, I realized that for once the power was mine; for once I wasn't on my own.

I picked up the glass, set it back on the table and dabbed at my trousers with my handkerchief. He watched me intently, like a boxer waiting for the other man to get to his feet after a knock-down, ready to move in for the kill.

I called the waiter over. 'If this gentleman wished to make a report about a missing car to the police, where should he go?'

'There is a police post in Taxim Square, sir.'

'Thank you. I spilled my drink. Wipe the table and bring me another, please.'

As the waiter got busy with his cloth, I looked across at Fischer. 'We could go there together,' I said. 'Or, if you would prefer it, I could go alone and explain the situation. Of course, I expect the police would want to get in touch with you. Where should I tell them to find you?'

The waiter had finished wiping the table and was moving away. Fischer was staring at me uncertainly.

'What are you talking about?' he said. 'Who said anything about the police?'

'You were talking of compelling me to hand over the car to you. Only the police could make me do that.' I paused. 'Unless, that is, you had some other sort of compulsion in mind. In that case, perhaps I should go to the police anyway.'

He did not know what to say to that. He just stared. It was all I could do not to smile. It was quite obvious that he knew perfectly well what was hidden in the car, and that the very last thing he wanted was the police taking an interest in it. Now he had to make sure that I didn't go to them.

'There is no need for that,' he said finally.

'I'm not so sure.' The waiter brought me the drink and I motioned to Fischer. 'This gentleman will pay.'

Fischer hesitated, then threw some money on the table and stood up. He was doing his best to regain control of the situation by trying to look insulted.

'Very well,' he said stiffly; 'we shall have to wait for Mr Harper's arrival. It is very inconvenient and I shall report your insubordinate behaviour to him. He will not employ you again.'

And then, of course, I had to go too far. 'When he knows how careless you can be, maybe he won't have much use for you either.'

It was a silly thing to say, because it implied that I knew that the situation was not what it appeared on the surface, and I wasn't supposed to know.

His eyes narrowed. 'What did Harper tell you about me?'

'Until tonight I didn't even know you existed. What should he have told me?'

Without answering he turned and went.

I finished my drink slowly and planned my movements for the evening. It would be best, I thought, to dine in the hotel. Apart from the fact that the cost of the meal would go on the bill, which Harper could be paying, I wasn't too keen on going out just then. Fischer had seemed to accept the situation; but there was just a chance that he might change his mind and decide to get rough after all. Tufan's men would be covering me, presumably, but I didn't know what their orders were. If someone were to beat me up it wouldn't be much consolation to know that they were standing by, taking notes. It was certainly better to stay in. The only problem was the ten o'clock telephone report. I had already noticed that the public telephones in the foyer were handled by an operator who put the calls through the hotel switchboard, so I would have to risk going out later. Unless, that is, I missed the ten o'clock call and left it until the morning at eight. The only trouble was that I would then have to explain to Tufan why I had done so, and I did not want to have to explain that I was afraid of anything that Fischer might do. My trousers were still damp where he had upset the drink over me, and I was still remembering how good it had felt to make him climb down and do what *I* wanted. I could not expect Tufan to realize how successfully I had handled Fischer if I had to start by admitting that I had been too nervous to leave the hotel afterwards.

All I could do was to minimize the risk. The nearest café I knew of was the one on the side street below my room. With so many lighted hotel windows above, the street would not be too dark for safety. The telephone would probably be on the bar, but with any luck the noise of the music would compensate for the lack of privacy. Anyway, it would have to do.

By the time I had finished dinner I was feeling so tired that I could hardly keep my eyes open. I went back to the terrace and drank brandy until it was time for the call.

As I walked from the hotel entrance to the road I had to get out of the way of a taxi and was able to glance over my shoulder casually as if to make sure that it was safe to walk on. There was a man in a chauffeur's cap about twenty yards behind me.

Because of the contours of the hill and the way the street twisted and turned, it took me longer than I had expected to get to the café. The man in the chauffeur's cap stayed behind me. I listened carefully to his footsteps. If he had started to close in, I would have made a dash for the café; but he kept his distance, so I assumed that he was one of Tufan's men. All the same it was not a very pleasant walk.

The telephone was on the wall behind the bar. There was no coin-box and you had to ask the proprietor to get the number so that he knew what to charge you. He couldn't speak anything but Turkish, so I wrote the number down and made signs. The noise of the music wasn't as bad inside the place as it sounded from my room, but it was loud enough.

Tufan answered immediately and characteristically.

'You are late.'

'I'm sorry. You told me not to call through the hotel switchboard. I am in a café.'

'You went to the Hilton Hotel just after six. Why? Make your report.'

I told him what happened. I had to repeat the descriptions of the man at the Hilton car-park and of Fischer so that he could write them down. My report on the meeting with Fischer seemed to amuse him at first. I don't know why. I had not expected any thanks, but I felt I had earned at least a grunt of approval for my quick thinking. Instead, he made me repeat the conversation and then began harping on Fischer's reference to a villa outside Istanbul and asking a lot of questions for which I had no answers. It was very irritating; although, of course, I didn't say so. I just asked if he had any additional orders for me.

'No, but I have some information. Harper and the Lipp woman have reservations on an Olympic Airways plane for Athens tomorrow afternoon. It arrives at four. The earliest you will hear from him probably will be an hour after that.'

'Supposing he gives me the same orders as Fischer—to hand over the car with its papers—what do I do?'

'Ask for your wages and the letter you wrote.'

'Supposing he gives them to me?'

'Then you must give up the car, but forget to bring the *carnet* and the insurance papers. Or remind him of his promise that you could work for Miss Lipp. Be persistent. Use your intelligence. Imagine that he is an ordinary tourist whom you are trying to cheat. Now, if there is nothing more, you can go to bed. Report to me again tomorrow night.'

'One moment, sir. There is something.' I had had an idea.

'What is it?'

'There is something that you could do, sir. If, before I speak to Harper, I could have a licence as an official guide with tomorrow's date on it, it might help.'

'How?'

'It would show that in the expectation of driving Miss Lipp on her tour, I had gone to the trouble and expense of obtaining the licence. It would look as if I had taken him seriously. If he or she really wanted a driver for the car it might make a difference.'

He did not answer immediately. Then he said: 'Good, very good.'

'Thank you, sir.'

'You see, Simpson, when you apply your intelligence to carrying out orders instead of seeing only the difficulties, you become effective.' It was just like The Bristle in one of his good moods. 'You remember, of course,' he went on, 'that as a foreigner you could not hold a guide's licence. Do you think Harper might know that?'

'I'm almost sure he doesn't. If he does, I can say that I bribed someone to get it. He would believe me.'

'I would believe you myself, Simpson.' He chuckled fatuously, enchanted by his own joke. 'Very well, you shall have it by noon, delivered to the hotel.'

'You will need a photograph of me for it.'

'We have one. Don't tell me you have forgotten so soon. And a word of caution. You know only a few words of Turkish. Don't attract attention to yourself so that you are asked to show the licence. It might cause trouble with museum guards. You understand?'

'I understand.'

He hung up. I paid the proprietor for the call and left.

Outside, the man in the chauffeur's cap was waiting up the street. He walked ahead of me back to the hotel. I suppose he knew why I had been to the café.

There was a guide to Istanbul on sale at the concierge's desk. I bought one with the idea of brushing up on my knowledge of the Places of Interest and how to get to them. On my way down to my room I had to laugh to myself. 'Never volunteer for anything,' my father had said. Well, I hadn't exactly volunteered for what I was doing now, but it seemed to me that I was suddenly getting bloody conscientious about it.

I spent most of the following morning in bed. Just before noon I got dressed and went up to the foyer to see if Tufan had remembered about the guide's licence. He had; it was in a sealed Ministry of Tourism envelope in my mail-box.

For a few minutes I felt quite good about that. It showed, I thought, that Tufan kept his promises and that I could rely on him to back me. Then I realized that there was another way of looking at it. I had asked for a licence and I had promptly received one; Tufan expected results and wasn't giving me the smallest excuse for not getting them.

I had made up my mind not to have any drinks that day so as to keep a clear head for Harper; but now I changed my mind. You can't have a clear head when there's a sword hanging over it. I was careful though and only had three or four *rakis*. I felt much better for them, and after lunch I went down to my room to take a nap.

I must have needed it badly because I was still asleep when the phone rang at five. I almost fell off the bed in my haste to pick it up, and the start that it gave me made my head ache.

'Arthur?' It was Harper's voice.

'Yes.'

'You know who this is?'

'Yes.'

'Car okay?'

'Yes.'

'Then what have you been stalling for?'

'I haven't been stalling.'

'Fischer says you refused to deliver the car.'

'You told me to wait for *your* instructions, so I waited. You didn't tell me to hand the car to a perfect stranger without any proof of his authority . . .'

'All right, all right, skip it! Where is the car?'

'In a garage near here.'

'Do you know where Sariyer is?'

'Yes.'

'Get the car right away and hit the Sariyer road. When you get to Yeniköy look at your mileage reading, then drive on towards Sariyer for exactly four more miles. On your right you'll come to a small pier with some boats tied up alongside it. On the left of the road opposite the pier you'll see a driveway entrance belonging to a villa. The name of the villa is Sardunya. Have you got that?'

'Yes.'

'You should be here in about forty minutes. Right?'

'I will leave now.'

Sariyer is a small fishing port at the other end of the Bosphorus where it widens out to the Black Sea, and the road to it from Istanbul runs along the European shore. I wondered if I should try to contact Tufan before I left and report the address I had been given, then decided against it. Almost certainly, he had had Harper followed from the airport, and in any case I would be followed to the villa. There would be no point in reporting.

I went to the garage, paid the bill and got the car. The early evening traffic was heavy and it took me twenty minutes to get out of the city. It was a quarter to six when I reached Yeniköy. The same Peugeot which had followed me down from Edirne was following me again. I slowed for a moment to check the mileage and then pushed on.

The villas of the Bosphorus vary from small waterfront holiday places, with window-boxes and little boat-houses, to things like palaces. Quite a lot of these *were* palaces once; and before the capital was moved from Istanbul to Ankara the diplomatic corps used to have summer embassy buildings out along the Bosphorus, where there are cool Black Sea breezes even when the city is sweltering. The Kösk Sardunya looked as if it had started out in some such way.

The entrance to the drive was flanked by huge stone pillars with wrought-iron gates. The drive itself was several hundred yards long and wound up the hillside through an avenue of big trees which also served to screen the place from the road below. Finally, it left the trees and swept into the gravel courtyard in front of the villa.

It was one of those white stucco wedding-cake buildings of the kind you see in the older parts of Nice and Monte Carlo. Some French or Italian architect must have been imported around the turn of the century to do the job. It had everything—a terrace with pillars and balustrades, balconies, marble steps up to the front portico, a fountain in the courtyard, statuary, a wonderful view out over the Bosphorus—and it was huge. It was also run down. The stucco was peeling in places and some of the cornice mouldings had crumbled or broken away. The fountain basin had no water in it. The courtyard was fringed with weeds.

As I drove in, I saw Fischer get up from a chair on the terrace and go through a french window into the house. So I just pulled up at the foot of the marble steps and waited. After a moment or two, Harper appeared under the portico and I got out of the car. He came down the steps.

'What took you so long?'

'They had to make out a bill at the garage, and then there was the evening traffic.'

'Well . . .' He broke off as he noticed me looking past him and over his shoulder.

A woman was coming down the steps.

He smiled slightly. 'Ah yes. I was forgetting. You haven't met your employer. Honey, this is Arthur Simpson. Arthur, this is Miss Lipp.'

Chapter Five

Some men can make a good guess at a woman's age just by looking at her face and figure. I never can. I think that this may be because, in spite of Mum, I fundamentally respect women. Yes, it must be that. If she is very attractive, but obviously not a young girl, I always think of twenty-eight. If she has let herself go a bit, but is obviously not elderly, I think of forty-five. For some reason I never think of any ages in between those—or outside them, for that matter—except my own, that is.

Miss Lipp made me think of twenty-eight. In fact she was thirty-six; but I only found that out later. She looked twenty-eight to me. She was tall with short brownish-blonde hair, and the kind of figure that you have to notice, no matter what dress covers it. She also had the sort of eyes, insolent, sleepy and amused, and the full good-humoured mouth which tell you that she knows you can't help watching the way her body moves, and that she doesn't give a damn whether you do so or not; watching is not going to get you anywhere anyway. She wasn't wearing a dress that first time; just white slacks and sandals, and a loose white shirt. Her complexion was golden brown and the only make-up she was wearing was lipstick. Obviously, she had just bathed and changed.

She nodded to me. 'Hullo. No trouble with the car?' She had the same combination of accents as Harper.

'No, madam.'

'That's good.' She did not seem surprised.

Fischer was coming down the steps behind her. Harper glanced at him.

'Okay, Hans, you'd better run Arthur into Sariyer.' To me he said: 'You can take the ferry-boat back to town. Are the *carnet* and Green Card in the glove compartment?'

'Of course not. They are in the hotel safe.'

'I told you to put them in the glove compartment,' said Fischer angrily.

I kept my eyes on Harper. '*You* didn't tell me,' I said; 'and you didn't tell me to take orders from your servant.'

Fischer swore angrily in German, and Miss Lipp burst out laughing.

'But isn't he a servant?' I asked blandly; 'he behaved like one, though not a very good one, perhaps.'

Harper raised a repressive hand. 'Okay, Arthur, you can cut that out. Mr Fischer is a guest here and he only meant to be helpful. I'll arrange to have the documents picked up from you tomorrow before you leave. You'll be paid off when you hand them over.'

My stomach heaved. 'But I understood, sir, that I was to act as Miss Lipp's driver while she is in Turkey.'

'That's okay, Arthur. I'll hire someone locally.'

'I can drive the car,' said Fischer impatiently.

Harper and Miss Lipp both turned on him. Harper said something sharply in German and she added in English: 'Besides you don't know the roads.'

'And I do know the roads, madam.' I was trying hard to make my inner panic come out sounding like respectful indignation. 'Only today I went to the trouble and expense of obtaining an official guide's licence so that I could do the job without inconvenience to you. I was a guide in Istanbul before.' I turned to Harper and thrust the licence under his nose. 'Look, sir!'

He frowned at it and me incredulously. 'You mean you really *want* the job?' he demanded. 'I thought all you wanted was this.' He took my letter out of his pocket.

'Certainly, I want that, sir.' It was all I could do to stop myself reaching out for it. 'But you are also paying me a hundred dollars for three or four days' work.' I did my best to produce a grin. 'As I told you in Athens, sir, for that money I do not have to be persuaded to work.'

He glanced at her and she answered, with a shrug, in German. I understood the last three words: '. . . man English speaks.'

His eyes came to me again. 'You know, Arthur,' he said thoughtfully, 'you've changed. You could be off the hook if you wanted, but now you don't want to be off. Why?'

This was just answerable. I looked at the letter in his hand. 'You didn't send that. I was afraid all the time that you'd sent it anyway, out of spite.'

'Even though it would have cost me three hundred dollars?'

'It wouldn't have cost you anything. The cheques would have been returned to you eventually.'

'That's true.' He nodded. 'Not bad, Arthur. Now tell me what you meant when you told Mr Fischer that he'd been careless. What did you think he'd been careless about?'

They were all three waiting for my answer to that. The men's suspicion of me was in the air and Miss Lipp had smelt it as well. What was more, she didn't look in the least puzzled by what Harper was saying. Whatever the game was, they were all in it.

I did the best I could. 'Why? Because of the way he'd behaved, of course. Because he *had* been careless. Oh, he knew your name all right and he knew enough to get in touch with me, but I knew he couldn't be acting on your orders.'

'How did you know?'

I pointed to the letter. 'Because of that. You told me it was your insurance. You'd know I wouldn't turn the car over to a complete stranger without getting my letter back. He didn't even mention it.'

Harper looked at Fischer. 'You see?'

'I was only trying to save time,' said Fischer angrily. 'I have said so. This does not explain why he used that word.'

'No, it doesn't,' I said. The only way was to bull it through. 'But this does. When he started threatening me I offered to go with him to the police and settle the matter. I've never seen anyone back down so fast in my life.'

'That is a lie!' Fischer shouted; but he wasn't so sure of himself now.

I looked at Harper. 'Anyone who pulls that sort of bluff without knowing what to do when it's called is careless to my way of thinking. If Mr Fischer had been a dishonest servant instead of your helpful guest, you'd have said I'd been pretty careless to let him get away with a fourteen-thousand-dollar car. I'd be lucky if that was all you said.'

There was a brief silence, then Harper nodded. 'Well, Arthur, I guess Mr Fischer won't mind accepting your apology. Let's say it was a misunderstanding.'

Fischer shrugged.

Just what Harper thought that I was making of the situation I cannot imagine. Even if I hadn't known what was hidden in the car, I would have realized by now that there was something really fishy going on. Miss Lipp, in Turkey for a little ten-day tourist trip with a Lincoln and a villa the size of the Taj Mahal, was sufficiently improbable. The shenanigans over the delivery of the car had been positively grotesque.

However, it was soon apparent that nothing I might think or suspect was going to give Harper any sleepless nights.

'All right, Arthur,' he said, 'you've gotten yourself a deal. A hundred a week. You still have that fifty dollars I gave you?'

'Yes, sir.'

'Will that take care of the bill at the Park?'

'I think so.'

'Right. Here's the hundred you have coming for the trip down. Go back to town now. In the morning check out of the hotel. Then, take a ferry-boat back to Sariyer pier so that you get there around eleven. Someone will meet you. We'll find a room for you here.'

'Thank you, sir, but I can find a room in a hotel.'

'There isn't a hotel nearer than Sariyer, and that's too far away. You'd have to use the car to get to and fro, and it'd always be there when we wanted it here. Besides, we've got plenty of rooms.'

'Very well, sir. May I have my letter?'

He put it back in his pocket. 'Sure. When you're paid off at the end of the job. That was the deal, remember?'

'I remember,' I said grimly.

Of course, he thought that by still holding the letter over me he was making sure that I toed the line, and that, if I happened to see or hear anything that I shouldn't, I would be too scared to do anything but keep my mouth shut about it. The fact that he wasn't being as clever as he thought was no consolation to me. I wanted to get back to Athens and Nicki, but I wanted that letter first.

'You will drive now to the ferry-boat,' said Fischer.

I said 'Good-night, madam,' to Miss Lipp, but she didn't seem to hear. She was already walking back up the steps with Harper.

Fischer got into the back seat. I thought at first that he merely intended, in a petty way, to show me who was boss; but, as I drove back down to the road, I saw him looking over the door panels. He was obviously still suspicious. I thanked my stars that the repacking had been carefully done. It was almost comforting to see the sand-coloured Peugeot in the driving mirror.

He didn't say anything to me on the way. In Sariyer, I stopped at the pier approach and turned the car for him. Then I got out and opened the door as if he were royalty. I'd hoped it would make him feel a bit silly, but it didn't seem to. Without a word he got in behind the wheel, gave me a black look and tore off back along the coast road like a maniac.

The Peugeot had stopped and turned about a hundred yards back, and a man was scrambling out of its front passenger seat. He slammed the door and the Peugeot shot away after the Lincoln. There was a ferry-boat already at the pier, and I did not wait to see if the man who had got out followed me. I suppose he did.

I was back at the Kabatas ferry pier soon after eight and shared a *dolmus* cab going up to Taxim Square. Then I walked down to the hotel and had a drink or two.

I needed them. I had managed to do what Tufan wanted, up to a point. I was in touch with Harper and would for the moment remain so. On the other hand, by agreeing to stay at the villa I had put myself virtually *out* of touch with Tufan; at least as far as regular contact was concerned. There was no way of knowing what life at the villa was going to be like, nor what would be expected of me there. It might be easy for me to get out to a safe telephone, or it might be quite difficult. If I were seen telephoning, Harper would immediately get suspicious. Who did I know in Istanbul? What was the number? Call it again—and so on. Yet I didn't see how I could have refused to stay there. If I had argued the point any further, Harper might have changed his mind about keeping me on. Tufan couldn't have it both ways; and I made up my mind to tell him so if he started moaning at me.

I had some dinner and went down to the café beside the hotel. A man with a porter's harness on his back followed me this time.

Tufan did not moan at me as a matter of fact; but when I had finished my report he was silent for so long that I thought he'd hung up. I said: 'Hullo.'

'I was thinking,' he said; 'it will be necessary for us to meet tonight. Are you in the café in the street by the hotel?'

'Yes.'

'Wait five minutes, then go up to the hotel and walk along the street past it for about a hundred yards. You will see a small brown car parked there.'

'The Peugeot that's been following me?'

'Yes. Open the door and get in beside the driver. He will know where to take you. Is that clear?'

'Yes.'

I paid for the telephone call and bought a drink. When the five minutes were up I left.

As I approached the Peugeot, the driver leaned across and pushed open the door for me to get in. Then he drove off past the hotel and down the hill towards the Necati Bey Avenue.

He was a young, plump, dark man. The car smelt of cigarettes, hair-oil and stale food. In his job, I suppose, he had to eat most of his meals sitting in the car. There was a VHF two-way taxi radio fitted under the dash and every now and again Turkish voices would squawk through the loud-speaker. He appeared not to be listening to them. After a minute or so he began to talk to me in French.

'Did you like driving the Lincoln?' he asked.

'Yes, it's a good car.'

'But too big and long. I saw the trouble you had in the narrow streets this afternoon.'

'It's very fast, though. Were you able to keep up with him when he drove back to the villa?'

'Oh, he stopped about a kilometre up the road and began looking at the doors. Did they rattle?'

'Not that I noticed. Did he stop long?'

'A minute or two. After that he did not go so fast. But this little . . .'

He broke off and picked up a microphone, as a fresh lot of squawks came over the radio.

'*Evet, efendi, evet*,' he answered, then put the microphone back. 'But this little machine can show those big ones a thing or two. On a narrow hill with corners I can leave them standing.'

He had turned on to the Avenue and we were running parallel to the shore.

'Where are we going?' I asked.

'I am not permitted to answer questions.'

We were passing the state entrance to the Dolmabahçe Palace now.

It was built in the last century when the Sultans gave up wearing robes and turbans and took to black frock-coats and the fez. From the sea it looks like a lakeside grand hotel imported from Switzerland; but from the road, because of the very high stone wall enclosing the grounds, it looks like a prison. There is about half a mile of this wall running along the right-hand side of the road, and just to look up at it gave me an uncomfortable feeling. It reminded me of the yard at Maidstone.

Then I saw a light high up on the wall ahead, and the driver began to slow down.

'What are we stopping here for?' I asked.

He did not answer.

The light came from a reflector flood and the beam of it shone down vertically on to an armed sentry. Behind him was a pair of huge iron-bound wooden gates. One of them was half-open.

The car stopped just short of the gates and the driver opened his door.

'We get out,' he said.

I joined him on the roadway and he led the way up to the gates. He said something to the sentry, who motioned us on. We went through the gap between the gates and turned left. There was a light burning in what I assumed was the guardroom. He led the way up a low flight of steps to the door. Inside was a bare room with a table and chair. A young lieutenant—I suppose he was orderly officer of the day—sat on the table talking to the sergeant of the guard, who was standing. As we came in, the officer stood up, too, and said something to the driver.

He turned to me. 'You have a guide's licence,' he said. 'You are to show it to this officer.'

I did so. He handed it back to me, picked up a flashlight and said in French: 'Follow me, please.'

The driver stayed behind with the sergeant of the guard. I followed the lieutenant down the steps again and across some uneven cobblestones to a narrow roadway running along the side of a building which seemed to be a barracks. The windows showed lights and I could hear the sound of voices and a radio playing *caz*. There were light posts at intervals, and, although the surface of the road was broken in places, it was just possible to see where one was walking. Then we went through a high archway out of the barracks area into some sort of garden. Here it was very dark. There was some moonlight and I could see parts of the white bulk of the palace looming to the left of us, but trees shadowed the ground. The lieutenant switched on his flashlight and told me to be careful where I walked. It was necessary advice. Restoration work seemed to be in progress. There were loose flagstones and masonry rubble everywhere. Finally, however, we came to a solidly paved walk. Ahead was a doorway and, beside it, a lighted window.

The lieutenant opened the door and went in. The light came from a janitor's room just inside, and, as the lieutenant entered, a man in a drab blue uniform came out. He had some keys in his hand. The lieutenant said something to him. The janitor answered briefly, and then, with a curious glance at me, led the way across a hall and up a staircase, switching on lights as he went. At the landing he turned off down a long corridor with a lot of closed doors along one side and grilled, uncurtained windows on the other. There was carpet on the floor with a narrow drugget running down the centre to save wear.

From the proportions of the staircase and the height of the ceilings it was obvious that we were in a large building; but there was nothing noticeably palatial about that part of it. We might have been in a provincial town hall. The walls were covered with dingy oil paintings. There seemed to be hundreds of them, mostly landscapes with cattle or battle scenes, and all with the same yellow-brown varnish colour. I don't know anything about paintings. I suppose they must have been valuable or they would not have been in a palace; but I found them depressing, like the smell of moth-balls.

There was a pair of heavy metal doors at the end of that corridor, and beyond it more corridors and more paintings.

'We are in what used to be the palace harem now,' the lieutenant said impressively. 'The steel doors guarded it. Each woman had her own suite of rooms. Now certain important government departments have their offices here.'

I was about to say, 'Ah, taken over by the eunuchs, you mean,' but thought better of it. He did not look as if he cared for jokes. Besides, I had

had a long day and was feeling tired. We went on through another lot of steel doors. I was resigned to more corridors, when the janitor stopped and unlocked the door of one of the rooms. The lieutenant turned on the lights and motioned me in.

It was not much larger than my room at the Park, but probably the height of the ceiling and the heavy red and gold curtains over the window made it seem smaller. The walls were hung with patterned red silk and several large paintings. There was a parquet floor and a white marble fireplace. A dozen gilt armchairs stood around the walls, as if the room had just been cleared for dancing. The desk and chairs standing in the centre looked like a party of badly-dressed gatecrashers.

'You may sit down and you may smoke,' the lieutenant said; 'but please be careful if you smoke to put out your cigarettes in the fireplace.'

The janitor left, shutting the door behind him. The lieutenant sat down at the desk and began to use the telephone.

The paintings in the room were, with one exception, of the kind I had seen in the corridors, only bigger. On one wall was a Dutch fishing-boat in a storm; facing it, alongside a most un-Turkish group of nymphs bathing in a woodland stream, was a Russian calvary charge. The painting over the fireplace, however, was undoubtedly Turkish. It showed a bearded man in a frock-coat and fez facing three other bearded men who were looking at him as if he had B.O. or had said something disgusting. Two of the group wore glittering uniforms.

When the lieutenant had finished telephoning, I asked him what the painting was about.

'That is the leaders of the nation demanding the abdication of Sultan Abdul Hamid the Second.'

'Isn't that rather a strange picture to have in a Sultan's palace?'

'Not in this palace. A greater man than any of the Sultans died here, greater even than Suleiman.' He gave me a hard, challenging look, daring me to deny it.

I agreed hastily. He went into a long rambling account of the iniquities of the Bayar-Menderes government and of the reasons why it had been necessary for the Army to clean out that rats' nest and form the Committee of National Union. Over the need to shoot down without mercy all who were trying to wreck the Committee's work, especially those members of the Democratic Party who had escaped justice at the Army's hands, he became so vehement that he was still haranguing me when Major Tufan walked into the room.

I felt almost sorry for the lieutenant. He snapped to attention, mumbling apologies like a litany. Tufan had been impressive enough in civilian clothes; in uniform and with a pistol on his belt he looked as if he were on his way to take charge of a firing squad—and looking forward keenly to the job. He listened to the lieutenant for about five seconds, then dismissed him with a flick of a hand.

As the door closed on the lieutenant, Tufan appeared to notice me. 'Do you know that President Kemal Ataturk died in this palace?' he asked.

'I gathered so from the lieutenant.'

'It was in 1938. The Director was much with him before the end and the

President talked freely. One thing he said the Director has always remembered. "If I can live another fifteen years I can make Turkey a democracy. If I die sooner, it will take three generations." That young officer probably represents the type of difficulty he had in mind.' He put the briefcase on the desk and sat down. 'Now, as to *your* difficulties. We have both had time to think. What do you propose?'

'Until I know what it's going to be like at the villa, I don't see how I can propose anything.'

'As you are their chauffeur it will obviously be necessary for you to attend to the fuelling of the car. There is a garage outside Sariyer that you could go to. It has a telephone.'

'I had thought of that, but it may not be reliable. It depends on how much the car is used. For example, if I only drive into Istanbul and back, I can't pretend to need petrol immediately. That car takes over a hundred litres. If I were always going to the garage at a fixed time to fill up, no matter what mileage I had driven, they would become suspicious.'

'We can dispense with the fixed time. I have arranged for a twenty-four-hour watch. And even if you foresee future difficulties, you should be able to make one single call to report on them. After that, if necessary, we will use a different method. It will entail more risk for you, but that cannot be avoided. You will have to write your reports. Then you will put the report inside an empty cigarette packet. The person following you at the time–I have arranged to have the car changed every day–will then pick the reports up.'

'You mean you expect me to throw them out of the window and hope they won't notice?'

'Of course not. You will drop them whenever you find a suitable moment when you have stopped and are outside the car.'

I thought it over; that part of it might not be so bad. I would just have to make sure that I had plenty of cigarette packets. What I did not like was having to write out the reports. I said so.

'There is a slight risk, I agree,' he said; 'but you will have to take it. Remember, they will only search you if you have given them reason to suspect you. You must be careful not to.'

'I still have to write the reports.'

'You can do that in the toilet. I do not imagine you will be observed there. Now, as to our communicating information and orders to you.' He opened his briefcase and took out a small portable transistor radio of the type I had seen German tourists carrying. 'You will carry this in your bag. If it should be seen, or you should be heard using it, you will say that it was given to you by a German client. Normally it receives only standard broadcast frequencies, but this one has been modified. I will show you.' He slipped it out of the carrying case, took the back off and pointed to a small switch just by the battery compartment. 'If you operate that switch it will receive UHF transmissions on a fixed frequency from up to half a mile away. The transmissions will be made to you from a surveillance car. It is a system we have tried out, and, providing there are no large obstacles such as buildings between the two points, it works. Your listening times will be seven in the morning and eleven at night. Is that clear? For security it will be better if you use the earphone attachment.'

'I see. You say it has been modified. Does that mean that it won't receive ordinary broadcasts? Because, if so, I couldn't explain it . . .'

'It will work normally unless you move this switch.' He replaced the back. 'Now then, I have some information for you. Both Harper and Miss Lipp are travelling on Swiss passports. We had no time at the airport to discover, without arousing suspicion, if the passports were genuine or not. The relevant particulars are as follows: Robert Karl Harper, aged thirty-eight, described as an engineer, place of birth Berne, and Elizabeth Maria Lipp, aged thirty-six, described as a student, place of birth Schaffhausen.'

'A student?'

'Anyone can be described as a student. It is meaningless. Now, as to the Kösk Sardunya.' He referred to a paper in the briefcase. 'It is the property of the widow of a former minister in the government of President Inönü. She is nearly eighty now and has for some years lived quietly with her daughter in Izmir. She has from time to time tried to sell Sardunya, but nobody has wished to buy at the price she asks. For the past two years, she has leased it furnished to a N.A.T.O. naval mission which had business in the zone. The mission's work ended at the beginning of the year. Her agent here in Istanbul was unable to find another tenant until three months ago. Then he received an inquiry from an Austrian named Fischer—yes, exactly—who was staying at the Hilton Hotel. Fischer's other names are Hans Andreas, and he gave an address in Vienna. He wanted a furnished villa for two months, not a particular villa, but one in that neighbourhood and near to the shore. He was willing to pay well for a short lease, and gave a deposit in Swiss francs. On the lease, which is in his name, his occupation is given as manufacturer. He arrived three weeks ago when the lease began and has not registered with the police. We have not yet traced the record of his entry, so we do not have all passport particulars about him.'

'What is he a manufacturer of?'

'We do not know. We have sent an inquiry to Interpol, but I expect a negative reply. We received negative replies on both Harper and Lipp. That increases the probability that they are politicals.'

'Or that they are using aliases.'

'Perhaps. Now, the other personnel at the villa. There are a husband and wife who live over what was the stabling. Their name is Hamul and they are old servants who have been there for some years as caretakers and who do cleaning work. Then there is the cook. Through the owner's agent, Fischer requested a cook with experience of Italian cooking. The agent found a Turkish Cypriot named Geven who had worked in Italy. The police here have had trouble with him. He is a good cook, but he gets drunk and attacks people. He served a short prison sentence for wounding a waiter. It is believed that the agent did not know this when he recommended the man to Fischer.'

'Is there anything against the couple?'

'No. They are honest enough.' He put his papers away. 'That is all we know so far, but, as you see, the shape of a conspiracy begins to unfold. One person goes ahead to establish a base of operations, a second person arranges for the purchase of weapons, a third arrives with the means of transporting them and a prepared cover story. Probably the real leaders have not yet arrived. When they do, it will be your duty to report the fact. Meanwhile, your orders are, specifically, first to ascertain whether the weapons have been removed from the car or not, and secondly, if they have been removed, where they are cached. The first will be easy, the second may be difficult.'

'If not impossible.'

He shrugged. 'Well, you must run no risks at this stage. Thirdly, you will continue to listen for any mention of names—names of persons or places—and report movements. Finally, you will listen particularly for any political content in their conversation. The smallest hint may be of importance in that connection. That is all, I think. Have you any questions?'

'Dozens,' I said; 'only I don't know what they are at the moment.'

I could see he hadn't liked that at once. It was a bit cheeky, I suppose; but I was really tired of him.

He pursed his lips at me. 'The Director is very pleased with you so far, Simpson,' he said. 'He even spoke of the possibility of helping you in some way beyond the withdrawal of the charges against you, perhaps in connection with your papers, if your co-operation brought about a successful disposal of this matter. It is your chance. Why don't you take it?'

This boy could do better. He should be encouraged to adopt a more positive attitude towards his schoolwork. Athletics: *Fair.* Punctuality: *Fair.* Conduct: *Has left much to be desired this term.* Signed: *G.D.Brush M.A. (Oxon.)* Headmaster.

I did my best. 'What do you mean by "political context"?' I asked. 'Do you mean, are they in favour of democratic ideals? Or against a military dictatorship?—that's what some people call your government, isn't it? Do they talk about capitalist oppression or Soviet domination or the welfare of mankind? Things like that? Because, if so, I can tell you now that the only section of mankind that Harper is interested in is the bit represented by himself.'

'That could be said of a great many political conspirators. Obviously, what we are concerned with is their attitudes to the political situation here, where the Army acts at present as a trustee for the republic.' He said that stiffly; he hadn't liked the bit about military dictatorship either. 'As I have said, Harper may be merely a hired operative, but we cannot say yet. Remember, there are six pistols and ammunition for six.'

'That's another thing I don't understand, sir. I know that there are all those grenades, too—but *pistols*? Is that enough for a *coup d'état*? If they were machine-guns now . . .'

'My dear Simpson, the head of a secret political organization in Belgrade once handed out four pistols to four rather stupid students. In the event only one was used, but it was used to assassinate the Archduke Ferdinand of Austria and it started a European war. Pistols can be carried in the pocket. Machine-guns cannot.'

'You think these people are out to assassinate somebody?'

'That is for you to help us discover. Have you any more questions?'

'Is there any information yet about this business machine company, Tekelek? Harper seemed to be using it as a cover.'

'We are still awaiting word from Switzerland. If it is of interest I will let you know.'

He handed me the portable radio, then, as I got up to go, went to the door and gave an order to the lieutenant waiting outside about taking me back to the gate. I had started to move when he had an afterthought and stopped me.

'One more thing,' he said: 'I do not wish you to take foolish risks, but I do wish you to feel confidence in yourself if you are obliged to take necessary ones. Some men have more confidence in themselves if they are armed.'

I couldn't help glancing at the polished pistol-holster on his belt. He smiled thinly. 'This pistol is part of an officer's uniform. You may borrow it if you wish. You could put it in your bag with the radio.'

I shook my head. 'No, thank you. It wouldn't make me feel better. Worse, more likely. I'd be wondering how to explain it away if anyone happened to see it.'

'You are probably wise. Very well, that is all.'

Of course, I hadn't the slightest intention of taking any sort of risk if I could help it. All I intended to do was to go through the motions of co-operating so as to keep Tufan happy, and somehow get my letter back from Harper before Tufan's people pulled him in. Of course, I was quite certain that he was going to be pulled in. He *had* to be!

Tufan stayed behind, telephoning. As I went back along the corridors with the lieutenant, I saw him glancing at me, wondering if it were better to make polite conversation with someone who seemed on such good terms with the powerful Major Tufan, or to say nothing and keep his nose clean. In the end, all he said was a courteous good-night.

The Peugeot was still outside. The driver glanced at the radio I was carrying. I wondered if he knew about the modification, but he made no comment on it. We drove back to the hotel in silence. I thanked him and he nodded amiably, patting the wheel of his car. 'Better on the narrow roads,' he said.

The terrace was closed. I went to the bar for a drink. I had to get the taste of the Dolmabahçe out of my mouth.

'Conspiracy,' Tufan had said. Well, that much I was prepared to concede. The whole Harper-Lipp-Fischer set-up was obviously a cover for something; but all this cloak and dagger stuff about *coups d'état* and assassination plots I really couldn't swallow. Even sitting in the palace with a painting about a Sultan being deposed staring down from the wall, it had bothered me. Sitting in a hotel bar with a glass of brandy—well, frankly I didn't believe a bloody word of it. The point was that I knew the people concerned—or, anyway, I had met them—and Tufan didn't know and hadn't met any of them. 'Political context', for Heaven's sake! Suddenly, Major Tufan appeared in my mind's eye not as a man in charge of a firing squad, but as a military old maid always looking for secret agents and assassins under her bed—a typical counter-espionage man in fact.

For a moment or two I almost enjoyed myself. Then I remembered the doors of the car and the arms and the respirators and the grenades, and went back to zero.

If it hadn't been for those things, I thought, I could have made two good guesses about the Harper set-up, and one of them would certainly have been right. My first guess would have been narcotics. Turkey is an opium-producing country. If you had the necessary technical personnel–Fischer, the 'manufacturer', Lipp, the 'student'–all you would need would be a quiet, secluded place like the Kösk Sardunya in which to set up a small processing plant to make heroin, and an organizer–Harper, of course–to handle distribution and sales.

My second guess would have been some *de luxe* variation of the old badger game. It begins in the romantic villa on the Bosphorus graced by the beautiful, blue-blooded Princess Lipp, whose family once owned vast estates in Romania, her faithful servitor Andreas (Fischer), and a multi-millionaire sucker enslaved by the lady's beauty. Then, just as the millionaire is preparing to dip his wick, in comes the mad, bad, dangerous husband Prince (Harper) Lipp, who threatens to spread the whole story (with pictures, no doubt) over the front pages of every newspaper from Istanbul to Los Angeles, *unless* . . . The millionaire can't wait to pay up and get out. Curtain.

On the whole, though, I would have made narcotics the first choice. Not that I didn't see Harper as a con man, or in the role of blackmailer (I knew all too well that he could play that), but the cost and extent of the preparatory work suggested that big profits were expected. Unless the supply of gullible millionaires had suddenly increased in the Istanbul area, it seemed more likely that the expectation was based on the promise of a successful narcotics operation.

It seemed to me so obviously the right answer that I began to think again about the grenades and pistols. Supposing they did fit into the narcotics picture after all, but in a subsidiary sort of way. Supposing they had no direct relationship to Harper, but had been carried for someone *outside* the villa group–someone Turkish with political intentions of the kind in which Tufan was interested. The narcotics picture had to include a supplier of illicit raw opium. Almost certainly that supplier would be Turkish. Why shouldn't the price for his illicit opium have included a small shipment of illicit arms? No reason at all. Or the delivery of the arms might merely have been one of those little gestures of goodwill with which businessmen sometimes like to sweeten their contractual relationships. 'I'm bringing a car in anyway. Why not let me take care of that other little matter for you? Just give me a letter to your man in Athens?'

There was only one thing that I could see that was not quite right about it–the time factor. The villa had been taken on a short lease. The car had been imported on a tourist *carnet*. I didn't know how long it took to set up a laboratory and process enough heroin to make a killing in the dope market; but, on the face of it, two months seemed a bit short. I decided in the end that, for safety, they might well want to avoid remaining for too long in any one place and intended to keep the laboratory on the move.

I think I knew, secretly, that it wasn't a highly convincing explanation; but, at that moment, it was the best that I could think of, and until a better one occurred to me I was prepared to be uncritical. I liked my arms-for-opium theory. At least it held out a promise of release. When Tufan realized that, as far as the arms were concerned, Harper was only an intermediary, his interest must shift from the villa group to someone somewhere else. My usefulness would be at an end. Harper would accept my resignation with a shrug, return my letter and pay me off. Tufan's delighted Director would help me over my papers. A few hours later I would be back in Athens, safe and sound.

I remembered that I hadn't yet written to Nicki. Before I went to bed, I bought a postcard from the concierge and wrote a few lines. '*Still on Lincoln job. Money good. Should last a few more days. Home mid-week latest. Be good. Love, Papa.*'

I didn't put the villa address, because that would have made her curious. I didn't want to have to answer a lot of questions when I got back. Even when I've had a good time, I don't like having to talk about it. Good or bad, what's over's done with. Anyway, there was no point really in giving an address. I knew she wouldn't write back to me.

The following morning I went out early, bought a dozen packets of cigarettes and then looked for a shop which sold tools. If I were to make sure that the stuff had been removed from the car doors I would have to look inside at least one of them. The only trouble was that the screws which fastened the leather panels had Phillips heads. If I tried to use an ordinary screwdriver on them, there would be a risk of making marks or possibly scratching the leather.

I could not find a tool shop, so, in the end, I went to the garage off Taxim Square, where they knew me, and persuaded the mechanic there to sell me a Phillips. Then I went back to the hotel, paid my bill and took a taxi to the ferry pier. There was no sign of the Peugeot following.

A ferry-boat came in almost immediately and I knew that I was going to be early at Sariyer. In fact, I was twenty minutes early, so I was all the more surprised to see the Lincoln coming along the road as the boat edged into the pier.

Miss Lipp was driving.

Chapter Six

As I came off the pier, she got out of the car. She was wearing a light yellow cotton dress that did even less to obscure the shape of her body than the slacks and shirt I had seen her in the day before. She had the keys of the car in her hand, and, as I came up, she handed them to me with a friendly smile.

'Good morning, Arthur.'

'Good morning, madam. It's good of you to meet me.'

'I want to do some sight-seeing. Why don't you put your bag in the trunk for now, then we won't have to stop off at the villa?'

'Whatever you say, madam.' I put my bag down and went to hold the rear door open for her, but she was already walking round to the front passenger seat, so I had to scuttle round to get to that door ahead of her.

When she was installed, I hurriedly put my bag in the luggage compartment and got into the driving seat. I was sweating slightly, not only because it was a warm day, but also because I was flustered. I had expected

Fischer to meet me with the car; I had expected to go straight to the villa, to be told where I would sleep, to be given a moment to orient myself, a chance to think and time to plan. Instead, I was on my own with Miss Lipp, sitting where she had been sitting until a few moments ago, and smelling the scent she used. My hand shook a little as I put the ignition key in, and I felt I had to say something to cover my nerves.

'Isn't Mr Harper joining you, madam?'

'He had some business to attend to.' She was lighting a cigarette. 'And by the way, Arthur,' she went on, 'don't call me madam. If you have to call me something, the name's Lipp. Now, tell me what you have on the tour menu.'

'Is this your first time in Turkey, Miss Lipp?'

'First in a long time. All I remember from before is mosques. I don't think I want to see any more mosques.'

'But you would like to begin with Istanbul?'

'Oh yes.'

'Did you see the Seraglio?'

'Is that the old palace where the Sultans' harem used to be?'

'That's it.' I smiled inwardly. When I had been a guide in Istanbul before, it had been the same. Every woman tourist was always interested in the harem. Miss Lipp, I thought to myself, was no different.

'All right,' she said, 'let's go see the Seraglio.'

I was regaining my composure now. 'If I may make a suggestion.'

'Go ahead.'

'The Seraglio is organized as a museum now. If we go straight there we shall arrive before it opens. I suggest that I drive you first to the famous Pierre Loti café, which is high up on a hill just outside the city. There you could have a light lunch in pleasant surroundings and I could take you to the Seraglio afterwards.'

'What time would we get there?'

'We can be there soon after one o'clock.'

'Okay, but I don't want to be later.'

That struck me as rather odd, but I paid no attention. You do get the occasional tourist who wants to do everything by the clock. She just had not impressed me as being of that type.

I started up and drove back along the coast road. I looked for the Peugeot, but it wasn't there that day. Instead, there was a grey Opel with three men in it. When we got to the old castle at Rumelihisari, I stopped and told her about the blockade of Constantinople by Sultan Mehmet Fatih in 1453, and how he had stretched a great chain boom across the Bosphorus there to cut off the city. I didn't tell her that it was possible to go up to the main keep of the castle because I didn't want to exhaust myself climbing up all those paths and stairs; but she didn't seem very interested anyway, so, in the end, I cut the patter short and pushed on. After a while, it became pretty obvious that she wasn't really much interested in anything in the way of ordinary sight-seeing. At least, that was how it seemed at the time. I don't think she was bored, but when I pointed places out to her she only nodded. She asked no questions.

It was different at the café. She made me sit with her at a table outside under a tree and order *raki* for us both; then she began asking questions by the dozen, not about Pierre Loti, the Turkophile Frenchman, but about the Seraglio.

I did my best to explain. To most people, the word 'palace' means a single very big building planned to house a monarch. Of course, there are usually a few smaller buildings around it, but the big building is the Palace. Although the word 'seraglio' really means 'palace', it isn't at all like one. It is an oval-shaped walled area over two miles in circumference, standing on top of the hill above Seraglio Point at the entrance to the Bosphorus; and it is a city within a city. Originally, or at least from the time of Suleiman the Magnificent until the mid-nineteenth century, the whole central govern-ment, ministers and high civil servants, as well as the Sultan of the time, lived and worked in it. There were household troops and a cadet school as well as the Sultan's harem inside the walls. The population was generally over five thousand, and there was always new building going on. One reason for this was a custom of the Ottomans. When a new Sultan came to the throne, he naturally inherited all the wealth and property accumulated by his father; but he could not take the personalized property for his own personal use without losing face. Consequently, all the old regalia had to be stored away and new pieces made, a new summer palace had to be built and, of course, new private apartments inside the Seraglio, and a new mosque. As I say, this went on well into the nineteenth century. So the Seraglio today is a vast rabbit-warren of reception rooms, private apartments, pavilions, mosques, libraries, gateways, armouries, barracks and so on, interspersed by a few open courtyards and gardens. There are no big buildings in the 'palace' sense. The two biggest single structures happen to be the kitchens and the stables.

Although the guide-books try to explain all this, most tourists don't seem to understand it. They think 'seraglio' means 'harem' anyway and all they are interested in apart from that is the 'Golden Road', the passage that the chosen girls went along to get from the harem to the Sultan's bed. The harem area isn't open to the public as a matter of fact, but I always used to take the tourists I had through the Mustafa Pasha pavilion at the back and tell them that that was part of the harem. They never knew the difference, and it was something they could tell their friends.

Miss Lipp soon got the idea, though. I found that she knew something about Turkish history; for instance, who the Janissaries had been. For someone who, only an hour or so earlier, had been asking if the Seraglio was the old palace, that was a little surprising. At the time, I suppose, I was too busy trying to answer her other questions to pay much attention. I had shown her the guide-book plan and she was going through all the buildings marked on it.

'The White Eunuchs' quarters along here, are they open?'

'Only these rooms near the Gate of Felicity in the middle.'

'The Baths of Selim the Second—can we see them?'

'That is part of the museum now. There is a collection of glass and silverware there, I think.'

'What about the Hall of the Pantry?'

'I think that building has the administration offices in it now.'

Some of the questions I couldn't answer at all, even vaguely, but she still kept on. Finally, she broke off, swallowed her second *raki* at a gulp and looked across at me.

'Are you hungry, Arthur?'

'Hungry? No, Miss Lipp, not particularly.'

'Why don't we go to the palace right now, then?'

'Certainly, if you wish.'

'Okay. You take care of the check here. We'll settle later.'

I saw the eyes of one or two men sitting in the café follow her as she went back to the car, and I noticed them glancing at me as I paid for the drinks. Obviously they were wondering what the relationship was–father, uncle or what? It was oddly embarrassing. The trouble was, of course, that I didn't know what to make of Miss Lipp and couldn't decide what sort of attitude to adopt towards her. To add to the confusion, a remark Harper had made at the Club in Athens, about Nicki's legs being too short, kept coming into my mind. Miss Lipp's legs were particularly long, and, for some reason, that was irritating as well as exciting; exciting because I couldn't help wondering what difference long legs would make in bed; irritating because I knew damn well that I wasn't going to be given the chance to find out.

I drove her to the Seraglio and parked in what used to be the Courtyard of the Janissaries, just outside the Ortakapi Gate by the Executioner's block. As it was so early, there were only two or three other cars besides the Lincoln. I was glad of that, because I was able to get off my piece about the gate without being overheard by official guides with other parties. The last thing I wanted at that moment was to have my guide's licence asked for and challenged.

The Ortakapi Gate is a good introduction to the 'feel' of the Seraglio. 'It was here at this gate that the Sultans used to stand to watch the weekly executions. The Sultan stood just there. You see the block where the beheading was done. Now, see that little fountain built in the wall there? That was for the Executioner to wash the blood off himself when he had finished. He was also the Chief Gardener. By the way, this was known as the Gate of Salvation. Rather ironic, don't you think? Of course, only high palace dignitaries who had offended the Sultan were beheaded here. When princes of the royal house were executed–for instance, when a new Sultan had all his younger brothers killed off to prevent arguments about the succession–their blood could not be shed, so they were strangled with a silk cord. Women who had offended were treated in a different way. They were tied up in weighted sacks and dropped into the Bosphorus. Shall we go inside now?'

Until Miss Lipp, I had never known it to fail.

She gave me a blank stare. 'Is any of that true, Arthur?'

'Every word of it.' It *is* true, too.

'How do you know?'

'Those are historic facts, Miss Lipp.' I had another go. 'In fact, one of the Sultans got bored with his whole harem and had them all dumped into the Bosphorus. There was a shipwreck off Seraglio Point soon after, and a diver was sent down. What he saw there almost scared him to death. There were all those weighted sacks standing in a row on the bottom and swaying to and fro with the current.'

'Which Sultan?'

Naturally, I thought it was safe to guess. 'It was Murad the Second.'

'It was Sultan Ibrahim,' she said. 'No offence, Arthur, but I think we'd better hire a guide.'

'Whatever you say, Miss Lipp.'

I tried to look as if I thought it a good idea, but I was really quite angry. If she had asked me right out whether I was an historical expert on the Seraglio, I would have told her, quite frankly, that I was not. It was the underhand way in which she had set out to trap me that I didn't like.

We went through the gate, and I paid for our admissions and selected an English-speaking guide. He was solemn and pedantic, of course, and told her all the things I had already explained all over again; but she did not seem to mind. From the way she bombarded him with questions you would have thought she was going to write a book about the place. Of course, that flattered him. He had a grin like an ape.

Personally, I find the Seraglio rather depressing. In Greece, the old buildings, even when they are in ruins and nothing much has been done in the way of restoration, always seem to have a clean, washed look about them. The Seraglio is stained, greasy and dilapidated. Even the trees and shrubs in the main courtyards are neglected, and the so-called Tulip Garden is nothing but a scrubby patch of dirt.

As far as Miss Lipp was concerned, though, the place might have been Versailles. She went everywhere, through the kitchens, through the museum rooms, the exhibition of saddles, this kiosk, that pavilion, laughing at the guide's standard jokes and scuffing her shoes on the broken paving stones. If I had known what was going on in her mind, of course, I would have felt differently; but as it was, I became bored. After a bit, I gave up following them everywhere and just took the short cuts.

I was looking forward to a sit-down by the Gate of the Fountain while they 'did' the textiles exhibition, when she called me over.

'Arthur, how long will it take us to get to the airport from here?'

I was so surprised that I must have looked at her a bit blankly. 'The airport?'

She put on a slight heaven-give-me-patience look. 'Yes, Arthur, the airport. Where the planes arrive. How long from here?'

The guide, who hadn't been asked, said: 'Forty minutes, *madame*.'

'Better allow forty-five, Miss Lipp,' I said ignoring him.

She looked at her watch. 'The plane gets in at four,' she said. 'I tell you what, Arthur. You go get yourself a sandwich or something. I'll meet you where you parked the car in an hour. Right?'

'As you wish, Miss Lipp. Are we meeting someone at the airport?'

'If that's all right with you.' Her tone was curt.

'I only meant that if I knew the line and flight number I could check if the plane is going to be on time.'

'So you could, Arthur. I didn't think of that. It's Air France from Geneva.'

I was in the sunshine of her smile again, the bitch.

There was a restaurant of sorts near the Blue Mosque, and when I had ordered some food I telephoned Tufan.

He listened to my report without comment until I had finished. 'Very well,' he said then, 'I will see that the passports of the Geneva passengers are particularly noted. Is that all?'

'No.' I started to tell him my theory about the drug operation and its necessary link with a raw opium supplier, but almost at once he began interrupting.

'Have you new facts to support this?'

'It fits the information we have.'

'Any imbecile could think of ways of interpreting the information we have. It is the information we do not have that I am interested in. Your business is to get it, and that is all you should be thinking about.'

'Nevertheless . . .'

'You are wasting time. Report by telephone, or as otherwise arranged, and remember your listening times. Now, if that is all, I have arrangements to make.'

The military mind at work! Whether he was right or wrong (and, as it happens, he was both right *and* wrong) made no difference. It was the arrogance of the man I couldn't stand.

I ate a disgusting meal of lukewarm mutton stew and went back to the car. I was angry with myself, too.

I have to admit it; what had really exasperated me was not so much Tufan's anxiety-bred offensiveness as my own realization that the train of thought which had seemed so logical and reasonable the previous night was not looking as logical and reasonable in the morning. My conception of the 'student' Miss Lipp as a laboratory technician was troublesome enough; but speaking again with Tufan had reminded me that the villa, which I had so blithely endowed with a clandestine heroin-manufacturing plant, also housed an elderly married couple and a cook. So that, in addition to the time factor improbability, I now had to accept another; either the plant was to be so small that the servants would not notice it, or Harper counted on buying their discretion.

Then, in sheer desperation, I did something rather silly. I felt that I had to know if the grenades and pistols were still in the car. If they had been taken out, at least one bit of my theory was still just tenable. I could assume that they had been delivered or were in process of delivery to the persons who wanted them.

I had about twenty minutes to spare before Miss Lipp came out of the Seraglio; but in case she was early I drove the car to the other end of the courtyard under some trees opposite the church of St Irene. Then I got the Phillips screwdriver out of my bag and went to work on the door by the driver's seat.

I wasn't worried about anyone seeing me. After all, I was only carrying out Tufan's orders. The men in the Opel wouldn't interfere; and, if some cab-driver became inquisitive, I could always pretend that I was having trouble with a door lock. All that mattered was the time, because I had to do it carefully to avoid making marks.

I loosened all the screws carefully first, and then began to remove them. It seemed to take an age. And then a horrible thing happened. Just as I was taking out the last screw but one, I happened to glance up and saw Miss

Lipp with the guide walking across the courtyard from the alleyway leading to the Archaeological Museum.

I knew at once that she had seen the car because she was walking straight towards it. She was about two hundred yards away, and on the opposite side of the car to the door I had been working on, but I knew that I couldn't get even one of the screws back in time. Besides, I was not in the place she had told me to be. There was only one thing I could do: stuff the screws and screwdriver into my pocket, start the car, drive around the courtyard to meet her and hope to God the two loose screws would hold the panel in place when I opened the door to get out.

I had one piece of luck. The guide practically fell over himself opening her door for her, so I didn't have to open the one on my side. I was able to get my apology in at the same time.

'I'm sorry, Miss Lipp. I thought you might be visiting the Saint Irene Church and I wanted to save you the walk back.'

That got by all right because she couldn't thank the guide and answer me at the same time. The guide was an unexpected help, too, as he immediately asked her if she would like to see the church, 'pure Byzantine, built in the reign of Justinian, and of great historical interest'.

'I'll leave that for another time,' she said.

'But you will be here tomorrow, *madame*, when the Treasury Museum is on view?'

'Well, maybe.'

'Otherwise, it must be Thursday, *madame*. That part and the pictures are on view only two days in the week, when all the other rooms are closed.' He was obviously panting for her to come again. I wondered how much she had tipped him.

'I'll try and make it tomorrow. Thank you again.' She gave him the smile. To me, she said: 'Let's go.'

I drove off. As soon as we got on to the cobbles the panel started to vibrate. I immediately pressed my knee against it and the vibration stopped; but I was really scared now. I didn't think that she would notice that the screws were out; but Fischer or Harper certainly would, and there was this unknown we were going to meet. I knew that I had somehow to replace the screws while the car was at the airport.

'Is the plane on time?' she asked.

A donkey cart came rattling out of a side street at that moment, and I made a big thing of braking and swerving out of its way. I didn't have to pretend that the cart had shaken me up. I was shaken up all right. My call to Tufan and the argument with him had made me forget completely about calling the airline. I did the best I could.

'They didn't know of any delay,' I said; 'but the plane was making an intermediate stop. Would you like me to check again?'

'No, it's not worth it now.'

'Did you enjoy the Seraglio, Miss Lipp?' I thought if I kept talking it might quieten my stomach down a bit.

'It was interesting.'

'The Treasury is worth seeing, too. Everything the Sultans used was covered with jewels. Of course, a great many of the things were gifts from kings and emperors who wanted to impress the Sultans with their greatness. Even Queen Victoria sent things.'

'I know.' She chuckled. 'Clocks and cut glass.'

'But some of the things are really incredible, Miss Lipp. There are coffee cups sculptured out of solid amethyst, and, you know, the largest emerald in the world is there on the canopy of one of the thrones. They even did mosaic work with rubies and emeralds instead of marble.' I went on to tell her about the gem-encrusted baldrics. I gave her the full treatment. In my experience every normal woman likes talking about jewels. But she didn't seem much interested.

'Well,' she said, 'they can't be worth much.'

'All those hundreds and thousands of jewels, Miss Lipp!' My leg was getting stiff trying to stop the panel vibrating. I wriggled surreptitiously into a new position.

She shrugged. 'The guide told me that the reason they have to close some rooms on the days they open up the others is because they're understaffed. The reason they're understaffed is because the government hasn't the money to spend. That's why the place is so shabby, too. Pretty well all of the money they have for restoration goes into the older, the Byzantine buildings. Besides, if all those stones were real gems they'd be in a strong-room, not a museum. You know, Arthur, quite a lot of these old baubles turn out in the end to be just obsidian and garnet.'

'Oh these are real gems, Miss Lipp.'

'What's the biggest emerald in the world look like, Arthur?'

'Well it's pear-shaped, and about the size of a pear, too.'

'Smooth or cut?'

'Smooth.'

'Couldn't it be green tourmaline?'

'Well, I suppose I don't know really, Miss Lipp. I'm not an expert.'

'Do you care *which* it is?'

I was getting bored with this. 'Not much, Miss Lipp,' I answered. 'It just makes a more interesting story if it's an emerald.'

She smiled. 'It makes a more amusing story if it's not. Have you ever been to the mysterious East?'

'No, Miss Lipp.'

'But you've seen pictures. Do you know what makes those tall pagodas glitter so beautifully in the moonlight?'

'No, Miss Lipp.'

'They're covered with little pieces of broken bottle glass. And the famous emerald Buddha in Bangkok isn't emerald at all; it's carved from a block of ordinary green jasper.'

'Little known facts,' I thought. 'Why don't you send it in to the *Reader's Digest?*' I didn't say it, though.

She took a cigarette from the gold case in her bag and I fumbled in my pocket for matches; but she had a gold lighter, too, and didn't notice the matches I held out to her. 'Have you always done this sort of work?' she asked suddenly.

'Driving? No, Miss Lipp. Most of my life I have been a journalist. That was in Egypt. When the Nasser crowd took over, things became impossible.

It was a matter of starting again.' Simple, straightforward–a man who has suffered the slings and arrows of outrageous fortune but wasn't looking for anyone's shoulder to weep on.

'I was thinking about the traveller's cheques,' she said. 'Is that what you meant by "starting again"?'

'I'm sorry Mr Harper had to tell you about that.' It was no surprise, of course, that Harper had told her; but with so many other things on my mind–driving, keeping the door panel from rattling, cramp in my leg and wondering how the hell I was going to replace the screws–all I could think of was that obvious reply.

'Did you think he wouldn't tell me?' she went on.

'I didn't think about it either way, Miss Lipp.'

'But since he did tell me and since you're driving this car, that must mean that I don't mind too much about things like that, mustn't it?'

For one idiotic moment I wondered if she were making some sort of pass at me; but it was a brief moment.

'I suppose so,' I answered.

'And that Mr Harper doesn't mind either?'

'Yes.'

'And that, in fact, we're all very sensible, tolerant persons?'

I couldn't help glancing at her. She was watching me in her amused, considering way, but there was nothing sleepy about her eyes now. They were steadily intent.

And then I got the message. I was being sounded, either to discover what I had made of the set-up and if they had left any shirt-tails showing, or to find out if I could be trusted in some particular way. I knew that how I answered would be very important indeed to me; but I didn't know what to say. It was no use pretending to be stupid any more, or trying to avoid the issue. A test was being applied. If I failed it, I was out–out with Harper, out with Tufan and his Director, out with the Turkish customs and, in all probability, out with the Greek police as well.

I felt my face getting red and knew that she would notice. That decided me. People get red when they feel guilty or nervous; but they also get red when they are angry. In order not to seem nervous or guilty, all I could do was to seem angry.

'Including Mr Fischer?' I asked.

'What about Mr Fischer?'

'Is he sensible, too, Miss Lipp?'

'Does that matter?'

I glanced at her again. 'If my personal safety–safety from some sort of bad luck, let us say–depended on Fischer's being sensible, I'd be quite worried.'

'Because he upset a drink over you?'

'Ah, he told you that, did he? No, that was only stupid. I'd be worried because he was careless, because he gave himself away.'

'Only himself?' There was quite an edge to her voice now. I knew that I had gone far enough.

'What else is there to give away, Miss Lipp?' *I am wary but not treacherous, Miss Lipp. I watch my own interests, Miss Lipp, but I know how to be discreet, too, no matter how phony the set-up looks.*

'What indeed?' she said shortly.

She said no more. The test was over. I did not know whether I had passed or not; but there was nothing more that I could do, and I was glad of the relief. I hoped she would not notice that I was sweating.

We arrived at the airport ten minutes before the plane was due. She got out and went into the arrivals section, leaving me to find a place to park. I quickly did the two loose screws up before I went to join her.

She was at the Air France counter.

'Fifteen minutes to wait,' she said.

'And at least another fifteen before they get through customs,' I reminded her. 'Miss Lipp, you have had no lunch. The café here is quite clean. Why not wait there and have some cakes and tea? I will keep a check on the plane and arrange for a porter to be ready. When the passengers are in customs I will let you know.'

She hesitated, then, to my relief, nodded. 'All right, you do that.'

'May I ask who it is that we are meeting?'

'Mr Miller.'

'I will take care of everything.'

I showed her where the café was, hung around long enough to make sure that she was going to stay there, and then hurried back to the car.

I was sweating so much by this time that my fingers kept slipping on the screwdriver. In fact, I did what I had been trying hard to avoid doing and scratched the leather; but it couldn't be helped. I rubbed some spit on the place and hoped for the best. The Opel was parked about a dozen yards away and I could see the men in it watching me. They probably thought I'd gone mad.

When the last screw was in place, I put the screwdriver back in my bag and went inside again to the Air France counter. The plane was just landing. I found a porter, gave him five lira and told him about Mr Miller. Then I went to the men's room and tried to stop myself sweating by running cold water over my wrists. It helped a little. I cleaned myself up and went back to the café.

'The passengers are beginning to come through now, Miss Lipp.'

She picked up her bag. 'Take care of the check, will you, Arthur?'

It took me a minute or two to get the waiter's attention, so I missed the meeting between Miss Lipp and Mr Miller. They were already on their way out to the car when I saw them. The porter was carrying two pieces of luggage, one suitcase and one smaller bag. I went ahead and got the luggage compartment open.

Mr Miller was about sixty with a long neck and nose, lined grey cheeks and a bald head with brown blotches on the skin. The backs of his hands had blotches, too. He was very thin and his light tussore suit flapped as he walked as if it had been made for someone with more flesh to cover. He had rimless glasses, pale lips, a toothy smile and that fixed stare ahead which says: 'You'll have to get out of my way, I'm afraid, because I haven't the time to get out of yours.'

As they came up to the car Miss Lipp said: 'This is Arthur Simpson who's driving for us, Leo.'

Before I could even say 'good afternoon' he had handed me the raincoat he had been carrying over his arm. 'Good, good,' he said and climbed into the back seat. She smiled slightly as she got in after him, though not at me, to herself.

The coat smelt of lavender water. I put it with the luggage, tipped the porter again and got into the driving seat.

'To the villa, Miss Lipp?'

'Yes, Arthur.'

'Wait a minute,' It was Miller. 'Where is my coat?'

'With your luggage, sir.'

'It will get dirty in there. It should be on a seat in here.'

'Yes, sir.'

I got out and retrieved the coat.

'What a fuss you make, Leo,' I heard her say. 'The car's quite clean.'

'The baggage in there is not clean. It has been in the belly of a plane with other baggage. It has been on the floor and table of the customs place. It has been handled by the man who searched it, handled again by the porter. Nothing is clean.' His accent had no American inflections, and he couldn't pronounce his 'th's'. I thought he might be French.

I draped the coat over the back of the seat in front of him. 'Will that be all right, sir?'

'Yes, of course,' he said impatiently.

That type is always the same. *They* make the difficulties and then behave as if *you're* the one who's being the nuisance.

'Let's go, Arthur,' said Miss Lipp. Her tone was non-committal. I couldn't tell whether she found him tiresome or not. I watched them in the driving mirror.

As soon as we were clear of the airport, he settled back and looked her over in a fatherly way.

'Well, my dear, you're looking healthy. How are Karl and Giulio?'

'Karl's fine. Giulio we haven't seen yet. He's with the boat. Karl was thinking of going over there tomorrow.'

'Have you anything planned for then?'

'We thought you might like to do a little sight-seeing. That is unless you're tired.'

'You are more considerate than a daughter, my dear.' The teeth leered at her and the pale eyes behind the rimless glasses flickered towards my back.

I had realized that this was a conversation conducted solely for my benefit, but now I saw her face stiffen. She knew that I was listening hard and was afraid that he was overdoing it.

'You must persuade Arthur to show you around the Seraglio Palace,' she said. 'He is quite an authority on it. Isn't that right, Arthur?'

That was as good as telling me that the old fool would believe any cock-and-bull story I cared to tell him. On the other hand it must be telling him something, too; perhaps warning him that the driver wasn't such a fool as he looked. I had to be careful.

'I would be happy to show Mr Miller what there is to see,' I said.

'Well, we must certainly think about that,' he replied; 'certainly, we must think about it.'

He glanced at her to see if he had said the right thing. A sentence of my father's came into my mind: 'One moment they're full of shit and the next moment . . .' At that point he would make a raspberry sound with his tongue. Vulgar, of course, but there was never any doubt about the kind of man he meant.

Mr Miller kept quiet after that. Once or twice she pointed out places of interest, in the manner of a hostess with a newly arrived guest; but the only thing he asked about was the tap water at the villa. Was it safe to drink or was there bottled water available? There was bottled water, she told him. He nodded, as if that had confirmed his worst fears, and said that he had brought plenty of Entero Vioforme for intestinal prophylaxis.

We reached the villa a little after five. Miss Lipp told me to sound the horn as I went up the drive.

The reception committee consisted of Harper and Fischer. Hovering in the background, ready to carry luggage, was an old man wearing an apron whom I took to be Hamul, the resident caretaker.

Tufan had said that Fischer was the lessee of the villa, but there was no doubt who was the real host there. All Fischer received from the incoming guest was a nod of recognition. Harper got a smile and an 'Ah, my dear Karl'. They shook hands with business-like cordiality, and then Harper, Miller and Miss Lipp went straight into the house. To Fischer were left the menial tasks of telling Hamul where Miller's bags were to go, and of showing me where to put the car and where I was to sleep.

At the back of the villa there was a walled stable yard. Part of the stabling had been converted into a garage with room for two cars. It was empty except for a Lambretta motor-scooter.

'The Lambretta belongs to the cook,' Fischer said; 'see that he does not steal gasoline from the car.'

I followed him across the yard to the rear entrance of the house.

Inside, I had a brief glimpse of the polished wood flooring of a passage beyond the small tiled hallway, before he led the way up a narrow staircase to the top floor. All too obviously we were in the old servants' quarters. There were six small attic cubicles with bare wood floors, bare wood partition walls and a single skylight in the roof for all of them. The sanitary arrangements consisted of an earthenware sink with a water tap in the wall at the head of the stairs. It was stiflingly hot under the low roof and there were dust and cobwebs everywhere. Two of the cubicles showed signs of having been swept out recently. Each contained an iron bedstead with a mattress and grey blankets. In one there was a battered composition leather suitcase. Fischer showed me the other.

'You will sleep here,' he said. 'The chef has the next bed. You will eat your meals with him in the kitchen.'

'Where is the toilet?'

'There is a *pissoir* across the yard in the stables.'

'And the bathroom?'

He waved his hand towards the sink. He was watching my face and enjoying himself just a bit too obviously. I guessed that this had been his own wonderful idea of punishment for the crime of calling him a servant, and that Harper probably did not know of it. In any case, I had to protest.

Without some privacy, especially at night, I could neither use the radio nor write reports.

I had put my bag down on the floor to rest my arm. Now I picked it up and started to walk back the way we had come.

'Where are you going?'

'To tell Mr Harper that I'm not sleeping here.'

'Why not? If it is good enough for the chef it is good enough for you, a driver.'

'It will not be good enough for Miss Lipp if I smell because I am unable to take a bath.'

'What did you expect–the royal apartment?'

'I can still find a hotel room in Sariyer. Or you can get another driver.'

I felt fairly safe in saying that. If he were to call my bluff I could always back down; but I thought it more likely that I had already called his. The very fact that he was arguing with me suggested weakness.

He glared at me for a moment, then walked to the stairs.

'Put the car away,' he said. 'It will be decided later what is to be done with you.'

I followed him down the stairs. At the foot of them, he turned off left into the house. I went out to the yard, left my bag in the garage and walked back to the car. When I had put it away, I went into the house and set about finding the kitchen. It wasn't difficult. The passage which I had glimpsed from the back entrance ran along the whole length of the house, with a servants' stairway leading to the bedroom floor, and, on the right, a series of doors which presumably gave the servants access to the various reception rooms in front. There was a smell of garlic-laden cooking. I followed the smell.

The kitchen was a big stone-floored room on the left of the passage. It had an old charcoal range along the rear wall with three battered flues over it, and a heavy pinewood table with benches in the middle. The table was cluttered with cooking debris and bottles, and scarred from years of use as a chopping block. Empty butcher's hooks hung from the beams. There was a barrel on a trestle, and beside it a sinister-looking zinc ice-box. A doorway to one side gave on to what appeared to be the scullery. A short man in a dirty blue denim smock stood by the range, stirring an iron pot. This was Geven, the cook. As I came in he looked up and stared.

He was a dark, moon-faced, middle-aged man with an upturned nose and large nostrils. The mouth was wide and full with a lower lip that quivered much of the time as if he were on the verge of tears. The thick, narrow chest merged into a high paunch. He had a three-day growth of beard, which was hardly surprising in view of the fact that he had nowhere to shave.

I remembered that he was a Cypriot and spoke to him in English. 'Good evening. I am the chauffeur, Simpson. Mr Geven?'

'Geven, yes.' He stopped stirring and we shook hands. His hands were filthy and it occurred to me that Mr Miller was probably going to need his Entero Vioforme. 'A drink, eh?' he said.

'Thanks.'

He pulled a glass out of a bowl of dirty water by the sink, shook it once and poured some *konyak* from an already opened bottle on the table. He also refilled his own half-empty glass, which was conveniently to hand.

'Here's cheers!' he said and swallowed thirstily. A sentence of Tufan's came into my mind–'He gets drunk and attacks people.' I had not thought to ask what sort of people he usually attacked, the person with whom he was drinking or some casual bystander.

'Are you British?' he asked.

'Yes.'

'How you know I speak English?'

An awkward question. 'I didn't know, but I don't speak Turkish.'

He nodded, apparently satisfied. 'You worked for these people before?'

'A little. I drove the car from Athens. Normally, I work there with my own car.'

'Driving tourists?'

'Yes.'

'Are these people tourists?' His tone was heavily ironical.

'I don't know. They say so.'

'Ah!' He winked knowingly and went back to his stirring again. 'Are you by the week?'

'Paid, you mean? Yes.'

'You had some money from them?'

'For the trip from Athens.'

'Who paid? The Fischer man?'

'The Harper man. You don't think they really are tourists?'

He made a face and rocked his head from side to side as if the question were too silly to need an answer.

'What are they, then?'

He shrugged. 'Spies, Russia spies. Everyone know–Hamul and his wife, the fishermen down below, everyone. You want something to eat?'

'That smells good.'

'It *is* good. It is for us. Hamul's wife cooks for him in their room before they come to wait table in the dining-room. Then I cook for the spies. Maybe, if I feel like it, I give them what is left after we eat, but the best is for us. Get two dishes, from the shelf there.'

It was a chicken and vegetable soup and was the first thing I had eaten with any pleasure for two days. Of course, I knew that I would have trouble with the garlic later; but, with my stomach knotted up by nerves the way it was, I would have had trouble with anything. Geven did not eat much. He went on drinking brandy; but he smiled approvingly when I took a second helping of the soup.

'Always I like the British,' he said. 'Even when you are backing the Greeks in Cyprus against us, I like the British. It is good you are here. A man does not like drinking alone. We can take a bottle upstairs with us every night.' He smiled wetly at the prospect.

I returned the smile. It was not the moment, I felt, to tell him that I hoped not to be sharing the servants' quarters with him.

And then Fischer had to come in.

He looked at the brandy bottle disapprovingly, and then at me. 'I will show you your room,' he said.

Geven held up an unsteadily protesting hand. '*Efendi*, let him finish his dinner. I will show him where to sleep.'

It was Fischer's opportunity. 'Ah no, chef,' he said; 'he thinks himself too good to sleep with you.' He nodded to me. 'Come.'

Geven's lower lip quivered so violently that I was sure he was about to burst into tears; but his hand went to the bottle as if he were about to throw it at me. It was possible, I thought, that he might be going to do both things.

I whispered hurriedly: 'Harper's orders, nothing to do with me,' and got out of the room as quickly as I could.

Fischer was already at the staircase in the passage.

'You will use these stairs,' he said; 'not those in the front of the house.'

The room to which he now showed me was at the side of the house on the bedroom floor. He pointed to the door of it.

'There is the room,' he said, and then pointed to another door along the corridor; 'and there is a bathroom. The car will be wanted in the morning at eleven.' With that he left, turning off the lights in the corridor as he went.

When he had gone, I turned the lights on again. The corridor had cream lincrusta dadoes with flowered wallpaper above. I had a look at the bathroom. It was a most peculiar shape and had obviously been installed, as an afterthought, in a disused storage closet. There was no window. The plumbing fixtures were German, *circa* 1905. Only the cold water taps worked.

The bedroom wasn't too bad. It had a pair of french windows, a brass bedstead, a chest of drawers and a big wardrobe. There was also a deal table with an ancient hand-operated sewing-machine on it. At the time when women guests in big houses always brought their ladies' maids with them to stay, the room had probably been given to one of the visiting maids.

There was a mattress on the bed, but no sheets or blankets. I knew it would be unwise to complain again. Before I got my bag from the garage, I went back up to the servants' quarters and took the blankets from the cubicle which Fischer had allocated to me. Then I returned to the room. The car radio transmission wasn't due until eleven; I had time to kill. I began by searching the room.

I always like looking inside other people's drawers and cupboards. You can find strange things. I remember once, when I was at Coram's, my aunt had pleurisy and the district nurse said that I would have to be boarded out for a month. Some people with an old house off the Lewisham High Road took me in. The house had thick laurel bushes all round it and big chestnut trees that made it very dark. I hated going past the laurel bushes at night, because at that time I believed (in the way a boy does) that a madman with a German bayonet was always lying in wait ready to pounce on me from behind and murder me. But inside the house it was all right. There was a smell of Lifebuoy soap and furniture polish. The people had had a son who had been killed on the Somme, and they gave me his room. I found all sorts of things in the cupboard. There was a stamp collection, for instance. I had never collected stamps, but a lot of chaps at school did and I took one or two of the stamps and sold them. After all, he was dead, so he didn't need them. The thing I liked most though was his collection of minerals. It was in a flat wooden case divided up into squares with a different piece of mineral in each one and labels saying what they were–graphite, galena, mica, quartz, iron pyrites, chalcocite, fluorite, wolfram and so on. There were exactly sixty-four squares and exactly sixty-four pieces of mineral, so at first I couldn't see how to keep any of them for myself because the empty square would have shown that something was missing. I did take one or two of them to school to show the chemistry master and try to get in his good books; but he only got suspicious and asked me where I had found them. I had to tell him that an uncle had lent them to me before he would let me have them back. After that, I just kept them in the box and looked at them; until I went back to my aunt's, that is, when I took the iron pyrites because it looked as if it had gold in it. I left a small piece of coal in the square instead. I don't think they ever noticed. I kept that piece of iron pyrites for years. 'Fools' gold', some people call it.

All I found in the room at Sardunya was an old Russian calendar made of cardboard in the shape of an ikon. There was a dark brown picture of Christ on it. I don't read Russian, so I couldn't make out the date. It wasn't worth taking.

I had the windows wide open. It was so quiet up there that I could hear the diesels of a ship chugging upstream against the Black Sea current towards the boom across the narrows above Sariyer. Until about eight-thirty there was a faint murmur of voices from the terrace in front. Then they went in to dinner. Some time after nine, I became restless. After all, nobody had told me to stay in my room. I decided to go for a stroll.

Just to be on the safe side, in case anyone took it into his head to go through my things, I hid the radio on top of the wardrobe. Then I went down, out through the rear door and skirted the front courtyard to the drive.

It was so dark there under the trees that I couldn't really see where I was going, and after I had gone a hundred yards or so I turned back. Miss Lipp, Harper, Miller and Fischer were coming out on to the terrace again when I reached the courtyard, and Hamul was lighting candles on the tables.

Along the side of the courtyard it was quite dark, and the weeds made it easy to move quietly over the gravel. At the entrance to the stable yard I stopped by the wall to see if I could hear anything they said.

I must have waited there for twenty minutes or more before I heard anything but an indistinct mumble. Then one of the men laughed loudly—Miller it was—and I heard him saying seven words as if they were the climax of a joke.

'Let the dogs be fed and clothed!' he cackled, and then repeated it. 'Let the dogs be fed and clothed!'

The others laughed with him, and then the mumbling began again. I went on in and up to my room.

I made the bed as comfortable as I could with the blankets, and then shaved to save myself the trouble of doing so in the morning.

Just before eleven, I took the radio out of its case, opened the back and turned the small switch. All I got was a hissing sound. I waited. I did not trouble to use the earphone, because I did not see any reason to then. I had not even shut the windows.

On the stroke of eleven, the set made a harsh clacking noise. A moment later, a voice crackled through the tiny loudspeaker at such a high volume level that I could feel the whole set vibrating in my hands. I tried to turn the thing down, but, with the UHF on, the control seemed to have no effect. All I could do was stuff the set under the blankets. Even there it seemed like a public address system. I scrambled to the windows and shut them. The loudspeaker began repeating its message:

'*Attention period report. Attention period report. New arrival is Leopold Axel Miller. Belgian passport gives following data: age sixty-three, described as importer, place of birth Antwerp. Data now also received concerning Tekelek S.A., a Swiss corporation registered in Berne. Nominal capital fifty thousand Swiss francs. Directors are K.W.Hoffman, R.E.Kohner, G.D.Bernadi and L.A.Mathis, all of whom are believed to have personal numbered accounts at Crédit Suisse, Zürich. Business of Tekelek said to be sale of electronic accounting machines manufactured in West Germany. Urgent you report progress. Attention period report . . .*'

I fumbled under the blankets, turned the UHF switch off and replaced the back on the set. Then I tuned in a Turkish station in case anyone had heard the noise and came to investigate.

Nobody did.

'Urgent you report progress.'

I had a cigarette packet with two cigarettes left in it. I lit one, put the other in my pocket and went to the bathroom for a piece of toilet paper.

When I returned I locked the door and sat down to write my progress report. It was quite short.

Cook, caretaker and local fishermen all believe suspects to be Russian spies.

I folded the toilet paper, put it inside the cigarette packet, crumpled the packet and put the result in my pocket ready for disposal in the morning.

I felt I had done my duty for that day.

Chapter Seven

I woke up very early in the morning and with that nasty sick feeling that I used to have when it was a school day and I hadn't done my homework properly the night before.

I got the cigarette packet out of my pocket and had another look at my toilet paper report. It really was not good enough. Unless I could think of something else to say, Tufan would think that I was trying to be funny. I went and had an extremely uncomfortable cold bath, collected some more sheets of toilet paper and started again.

Period report heard. Attempts to check door contents frustrated. Will try again today, I wrote.

I thought about the 'today'. Fischer had ordered the car for eleven o'clock. With that instruction to rely upon, it would be perfectly natural for me to go and fill up the car with petrol without asking anyone's permission; and, as long as I didn't keep them waiting, I could take my time about it. If, when I got back, they objected to my having taken the car out by myself or wanted to know why I had been so long, I could say that I had been to buy razor-blades or something, and be the injured innocent.

It was six-forty-five by then and in a few minutes I would have to get ready for the seven o'clock radio contact. Two other things occurred to me that I might add to my report.

Will telephone you from garage after inspection if time and circumstances allow, or will add to this report. During conversation Lipp–Miller yesterday name 'Giulio' was mentioned in connection with a boat. No other details.

Then I added the bit about the Russian spies. It didn't look quite so bald and stupid now.

I hid the report under the lining paper of one of the drawers, shut the french windows tight and got the radio ready with the earphone attachment plugged in. Promptly at seven the car began transmitting.

'Attention period report. Attention period report. Advice received from Swiss source that no passports have been legally issued to Harper and Lipp. In view Miller contact and Tekelek papers with Harper, possibility must be considered that correct names of Harper and Lipp are Hoffman and Kohner or vice versa. Miller may be Mathis. Imperative you report progress.'

As the voice began repeating I switched off. When I had packed the set away, I got the report out and added five words.

Hoffman, Kohner and Mathis, names noted.

At least, I ought to get an 'E' for Effort. I put the new report in the cigarette packet, burnt my earlier effort and started to get dressed. As I did so, I heard the Lambretta start up and then go whining off down the drive. About twenty minutes later, I heard the sound of it returning. I looked out of the window and saw it disappearing into the stable yard with a bundle of partially-wrapped loaves strapped to the rear seat.

Geven was back in the kitchen when I went down. He gave me a sullen look and did not answer when I said 'good morning'. He was probably hung over as well as disgusted with me; but he looked such a mess anyway that it was hard to tell.

There was a pot of coffee on the range and I looked from it to him inquiringly. He shrugged, so I got a cup and helped myself. He was slicing the bread by hacking at it with a heavy chopping knife. From the neat way the slices fell I knew that the chopping knife was as sharp as a razor. As I had no desire to lose my fingers, I waited until he had put it aside before taking a piece of bread.

The coffee did not taste much like coffee, but the bread was good. I considered attempting to heal the breach by offering him the use of my bathroom; but I only had one towel and the thought of what it would look like by the time he had finished with it kept me silent. Instead, I offered him a cigarette.

He took it and motioned to a basket of apricots on the table. I don't like apricots, but it seemed as well to accept the offer. Soon he began to mutter about the breakfasts which had to be served, each on a separate tray to the four 'lords and ladies' above. I offered to lay the trays and, although he waved away the offer, friendly relations seemed to be re-established. After a while, Mr and Mrs Hamul arrived and were introduced. Mrs Hamul was a small, stout, sad-looking old woman with the black dress and head-scarf of the conservative Turkish matron. As neither she nor her husband spoke a word of anything but Turkish, the formalities were brief. I lingered there, though, and had another piece of bread. The best time to leave without attracting attention, I had decided, would be while Harper and the rest were having their breakfasts.

As soon as the trays started going up, I told Geven that I had to buy petrol and asked if there was anything I could get for him while I was in town. At once he wanted to come with me. I got out of that by saying that I had to go immediately in order to be back at the time for which the car had been ordered. I left him, sulking, picked up the Phillips screwdriver from my room and went to the garage.

The Lincoln was a quiet car, and I knew that all they would probably hear of my going would be the sound of the tyres on the gravel of the courtyard; but I was so afraid of Harper or Fischer suddenly appearing on one of the bedroom balconies and yelling at me to stop that in my haste to reach the drive I almost hit the basin of the fountain. As I went on down the drive I broke into a sweat and my legs felt weak and peculiar. I wanted to stop and be sick. That may sound very stupid, but when you are like I am, the bad things that *nearly* happen are just as hard, in a way, as the bad things that do actually happen. They are certainly no easier to forget. I always envied those characters in *Alice* who only felt pain before they were hurt. I seem to feel things before, during and after as well; nothing ever goes completely away. I have often thought of killing myself, so that I wouldn't have to think or feel or remember any more, so that I could rest; but then I have always started worrying in case this after-life they preach about really exists. It might turn out to be even bloodier than the old one.

The Peugeot was back on duty again. I drove towards Sariyer for about half a mile, and then turned left on to one of the roads leading up to the forest. It was Sunday morning and families from Istanbul would soon be arriving at the municipal picnic grounds to spend the day; but at that early hour the car-parking areas were still fairly empty, and I had no difficulty in finding a secluded place under the trees.

I decided to try the same door again. I had scratched the leather on it once already; but if I were very careful it need not be scratched again. In any case, as long as I drove the car, scratches would be less noticeable on that door than on the others. The earlier attempt had taught me something, too. If I removed all the screws on the hinge side of the door first and only loosened the others, I thought it might be possible to ease the panel back enough to see inside the door without taking the whole panel and electric window mechanism completely away.

It took me twenty minutes to find out that I was right about the panel, and a further five seconds to learn that I had been completely wrong about the stuff having been removed. There it still was, just as I had seen it in the photographs Tufan had shown me at Edirne. In this particular door there were twelve small, paper-wrapped cylinders–probably grenades.

I screwed the panel back into place, and then sat there for a while thinking. The Peugeot was parked about a hundred yards away–I could see it in the mirror–and I very nearly got out and walked back to tell the driver what I had found. I wanted badly to talk to someone. Then I pulled myself together. There was no point in talking to someone who wouldn't, or couldn't, usefully talk back. The sensible thing would be to obey orders.

I took my report out of the cigarette packet and added to it.

9.20 a.m. inspected interior front door driver's side. Material still in place as per photo. In view of time absent from villa and inability to add to this report, will not telephone from garage now.

I replaced the toilet paper in the packet, tossed it out of the window and drove back on to the road. I waited just long enough to see a man from the Peugeot pick up the report, then I drove into Sariyer and filled the tank. I arrived back at the villa just before ten.

I half-expected to find an angry Fischer pacing the courtyard and demanding to know where the hell I'd been. There was nobody. I drove the car into the stable yard, emptied the ash-trays, brushed the floor carpeting and ran a duster over the body. The Phillips screwdriver in my pocket worried me. Now that I knew that the stuff was still in the car, it seemed an incriminating thing to have. I certainly did not want to put it back in my room. It might be needed again, so I could not throw it away. In the end, I hid it inside the cover of an old tyre hanging on the wall of the garage. Then I went and tidied myself up. Shortly before eleven o'clock I drove the car round to the marble steps in the front courtyard.

After about ten minutes Harper came out. He was wearing a blue sports shirt with blue slacks, and he had a map in his hand. He nodded in response to my greeting.

'Are we all right for gas, Arthur?'

'I filled it this morning, sir.'

'Oh, you did?' He looked agreeably surprised. 'Well, do you know a place called Pendik?'

'I've heard the name. On the other side somewhere, isn't it? There's supposed to be a good restaurant there, I think.'

'That's the place. On the Sea of Marmara.' He spread the map out and pointed to the place. From Uskudar, on the Asian side of the Bosphorus, it was twenty-odd miles south along the coast. 'How long will it take us to get there?'

'If we have luck with the car ferry, about an hour and a half from here, sir.'

'And if we don't have luck?'

'Perhaps ten or twenty minutes more.'

'All right. Here's what we do. First, we go into town and drop Miss Lipp and Mr Miller off at the Hilton Hotel. Then you drive Mr Fischer and me to Pendik. We'll be there a couple of hours. On the way back we stop off at the Hilton to pick the others up. Clear?'

'Yes, sir.'

'Who paid for the gas?'

'I did, sir. I still have some of the Turkish money you gave me. I have the garage receipt here.'

He waved it aside. 'Do you have any money left?'

'Only a few lira now.'

He gave me two fifty-lira notes. 'That's for expenses. You picked up a couple of checks for Miss Lipp, too. Take the money out of that.'

'Very well, sir.'

'And, Arthur—stop needling Mr Fischer, will you?'

'I rather thought that he intended to needle me, sir.'

'You got the room and bathroom you asked for, didn't you?'

'Yes, sir.'

'Well, then, cut it out.'

I started to point out that since I had been shown to the room the previous night I had not even set eyes on Fischer, much less 'needled' him, but he was already walking back to the house.

They all came out five minutes later. Miss Lipp was in white linen; Miller, draped with camera and extra lens case, looked very much the tourist; Fischer, in *maillot*, white jeans and sandals, looked like an elderly beach-boy from Antibes.

Harper sat in front with me. The others got into the back. Nobody talked on the way into Istanbul. Even at the time, I didn't feel that it was my presence there that kept them silent. They all had the self-contained air of persons on the way to an important business conference who have already explored every conceivable aspect of the negotiations that lie ahead, and can only wait now to learn what the other side's attitude is going to be. Yet two of them seemed headed for a sight-seeing tour, and the others for a seaside lunch. It was all rather odd. However, the Peugeot was following and, presumably, those in it would be able to cope with the situation when the party split up. There was nothing more I could do.

Miss Lipp and Miller got out at the door of the Hilton. A tourist bus blocked the driveway long enough for me to see that they went inside the hotel, and that a man from the Peugeot went in after them. The narcotics operation suddenly made sense again. The raw opium supplier would be waiting in his room with samples which Miller, the skilled chemist, would proceed to test and evaluate. Later, if the samples proved satisfactory, and *only* if they did, Harper would consummate the deal. In the meantime, a good lunch seemed to be in order.

We had to wait a few minutes for the car ferry to Uskudar. From the ferry pier it is easy to see across the water the military barracks which became Florence Nightingale's hospital during the Crimean War. Just for the sake of something to say, I pointed it out to Harper.

'What about it?' he said rudely.

'Nothing, sir. It's just that that was Florence Nightingale's hospital. Scutari the place was called then.'

'Look, Arthur, we know you have a guide's licence, but don't take it too seriously, huh?'

Fischer laughed.

'I thought you might be interested, sir.'

'All we're interested in is getting to Pendik. Where's this goddam ferry you talked about?'

I didn't trouble to answer that. The ferry-boat was just coming in at the pier, and he was merely being offensive—for Fischer's benefit, I suspected. I wondered what they would have said if I had told them what the sand-coloured Peugeot just behind us in the line of cars was there for, and whose orders its driver was obeying. The thought kept me amused for quite a while.

From Uskudar I took the Ankara road, which is wide and fast, and drove for about eighteen miles before I came to the secondary road which led off on the right to Pendik. We arrived there just before one o'clock.

It proved to be a small fishing port in the shelter of a headland. There were several yachts anchored in the harbour. Two wooden piers jutted out from the road, which ran parallel to the foreshore; one had a restaurant built on it, the other served the smaller boats and dinghies as a landing stage. The place swarmed with children.

I was edging my way along the narrow road towards the restaurant when Harper told me to stop.

We were level with the landing stage and a man was approaching the road along it. He was wearing a yachting cap now, but I recognized him. It was the man who had been waiting at the Hilton car-park on the night I had arrived in Istanbul.

He had obviously recognized the car and raised his hand in greeting as Harper and Fischer got out.

'Park the car and get yourself something to eat,' Harper said to me. 'Meet us back here in an hour.'

'Very good sir.'

The man in the yachting cap had reached the road and I heard Harper's greeting as the three met.

'Hi, Giulio. *Sta bene?*'

And then they were walking back along the landing stage. In the driving mirror, I could see a man from the Peugeot sauntering down to the quayside to see what happened next.

At the end of the landing stage they climbed into an outboard dinghy. Giulio started it up and they shot away towards a group of yachts anchored about two hundred yards out. They went alongside a sixty-foot cabin cruiser with a squat funnel. The hull was black, the upper works white, and the funnel had a single band of yellow round it. A Turkish flag drooped from the staff at the stern. There was a small gangway down, and a deck hand with a boat-hook to hold the dinghy as the three went on board. It was too far away for me to see the name on the hull.

I parked the car and went into the restaurant. The place was fairly full, but I managed to get a table near a window from which I could keep an eye on the cruiser. I asked the head waiter about her and learned her name, *Bulut*, and the fact that she was on charter to a wealthy Italian gentleman, Signor Giulio, who could eat two whole lobsters at a sitting.

I did not pursue my inquiries; Tufan's men would doubtless get what information was to be had from the local police. At least I knew now what Giulio looked like, and where the boat which Miss Lipp had mentioned to Miller was based. I could also guess that Giulio was no more the true charterer of the *Bulut* than was Fischer the true lessee of the Kösk Sardunya. Wealthy Italian gentlemen with yachts do not lurk in the Istanbul Hilton car-park waiting to drive away cars stuffed with contraband arms; they employ underlings to do such things.

Just as my grilled swordfish cutlet arrived, I saw that the *Bulut* was moving. A minute or two later, her bow anchor came out of the water and there was a swirl of white at her stern. The dinghy had been left moored to a buoy. The only people on the deck of the cabin cruiser were the two hands at the winches. She headed out across the bay towards an off-shore island just visible in the distant haze. I wondered whether the Peugeot men would commandeer a motor-boat and follow; but no other boat of any kind left the harbour. After about an hour, the *Bulut* returned and anchored in the same place as before. I paid my bill and went to the car.

Giulio brought Harper and Fischer back to the landing stage in the dinghy, but did not land with them. There was an exchange of farewells that I could see but not hear, and then they walked ashore to the car. Harper was carrying a flat cardboard box about two feet long by six inches wide. It was roughly tied with string.

'Okay, Arthur,' he said as he got into the car. 'Back to the Hilton.'

'Very good, sir.'

As I drove off he glanced back at the piers.

'Where did you lunch?' he asked. 'That restaurant there?'

'Yes, sir.'

'Good food?'

'Excellent, sir.'

He grinned over his shoulder at Fischer. 'Trust Giulio!'

'Our man Geven can cook well,' said Fischer defensively. 'And I intend to prove it to you.'

'He's a lush,' Harper said shortly.

'He cooked a *castradina* before you arrived which would have made you think you were in the Quadri.' Fischer was getting worked up now and leaning forward over the back of the front seat. His breath smelt of garlic and wine.

I could not resist the opportunity. 'If you don't mind my saying so, sir,' I said to Harper, 'I think Mr Fischer is right. Geven is an excellent cook. The chicken soup he gave me last night was perfect.'

'What soup?' Fischer demanded. 'We did not get soup.'

'He was upset,' I said. 'You remember, Mr Fischer, that you told him that he was not good enough to have a bathroom. He was upset. I think he threw away the soup he had made.'

'I told him no such a thing!' Fischer was becoming shrill.

'Wait a minute,' said Harper. 'The cook doesn't have a *bathroom?*'

'He has the whole of the servants' rooms for himself,' Fischer said.

'But no bathroom?'

'There is no bathroom there.'

'What are you trying to do, Hans—poison us?'

Fischer flung himself against the back seat with a force that made the car lurch. 'I am tired,' he declared loudly, 'of trying to arrange every matter as it should be arranged and then to receive nothing but criticism. I will not so to be accused, thus . . .' His English broke down completely and he went into German.

Harper answered him briefly in the same language. I don't know what he said, but it shut Fischer up. Harper lit a cigarette. After a moment or two he said: 'You're a stupid crook, aren't you, Arthur?'

'Sir?'

'If you were a smart one, all you'd be thinking about would be how much dough you could screw out of this deal without getting your fingers caught in the till. But not you. That miserable little ego of yours has to have its kicks, too, doesn't it?'

'I don't understand, sir.'

'Yes, you do. I don't like stupid people around me. They make me nervous. I warned you once before. I'm not warning you again. Next time you see a chance of getting cute, you forget it, quick; because if you don't that ego's liable to get damaged permanently.'

It seemed wiser to say nothing.

'You're not still saying that you don't understand, Arthur?' He flicked my knee viciously with the back of his hand. The pain startled me and I swerved. He flicked me again. 'Watch where you're going. What's the matter? Can't you talk while you're driving, or has the cat got your tongue?'

'I understand, sir.'

'That's better. Now you apologize like a little Egyptian gentleman to Mr Fischer.'

'I'm very sorry, sir.'

Fischer, appeased, signified his forgiveness with a short laugh.

The ferry from Uskudar was crowded with returning Sunday motorists and it took half an hour to get on a boat. Miss Lipp and Miller were waiting at the hotel entrance when I pulled up. Miller gave a wolfish grin and, as usual, leapt into the car ahead of Miss Lipp.

'You took your time,' he said to no one in particular.

'The ferry was crowded,' Harper replied. 'Did you have a good afternoon?'

It was Miss Lipp who answered him. 'Let the dogs be fed and clothed,' she said. It was the same sentence that I had heard Miller cackling over the previous night, and I wondered idly what it could mean.

Harper nodded to her. 'Let's get back to the villa, Arthur,' he said.

None of them uttered a word on the drive back. I sensed a feeling of tension between them, and wondered who was waiting to report to whom. As they got out of the car, Harper picked the cardboard box up off the floor and turned to me.

'That's it for today, Arthur.'

'What time tomorrow, sir?'

'I'll let you know.'

'The car is very dusty, sir, and there is no proper hose here. I would like to get it washed at a garage.'

'You do that.' He could not have cared less what I did.

I drove into Sariyer and found a garage where they would wash the car. I left it there and went to a café. I had a drink before I telephoned Tufan.

The written report of the morning had been supplemented by reports from the surveillance squad and he had more to tell me than I had to tell him. Giulio's other name was Corzo, and his Swiss passport gave his occupation as 'industrial designer'. His age was forty-five and his place of birth Lugano. The cabin cruiser had been chartered a week earlier, for one month, through a yacht-broker in Antalya. The crew of three were local men of good reputation. As for Miss Lipp and Miller, they had lunched in the Hilton grill-room, then hired a car. They had spent forty-five minutes sight-seeing and returned to the Hilton, where Miss Lipp had visited the hairdresser. She had had a shampoo and set. Miller had passed the time reading French newspapers on the terrace.

'Then it must have been the meeting with Giulio they wanted to hear about,' I said.

'What do you mean?'

I told him of the feeling I had had on the way back that they had been impatient for a chance to talk privately.

'Then why are you not at the villa? Go back there immediately.'

'If they wish to have private talk, there is nothing I can do to overhear it. Their part of the house on the ground floor is separate. I have not even seen those rooms.'

'Are there no windows?'

'Giving on to their private terrace, yes. I could have no excuse for being even near it, let alone on it.'

'Then do without an excuse.'

'You told me to take no risks.'

'No *unnecessary* risks. An important discussion justifies risk.'

'I don't *know* that it is important. I just had a feeling. I don't know that it's a discussion either. Harper may just have wanted to pass on a piece of private information he had received from Giulio to the others. The whole thing could have been over in a minute.'

'The meeting at Pendik was obviously important. We must know why. So far all you have learned is gossip from a fool of a cook. What do these people with arms and ammunition hidden in their car and false passports discuss when they are alone? What do they say? It is for you to find out.'

'I can tell you one thing they say—"Let the dogs be fed and clothed." I overheard it first last night. It seemed to be some sort of private joke.'

He was silent for a moment and I waited for another angry outburst. None came. Instead he said thoughtfully: 'That is quite an interesting joke.'

'What does it mean?'

'When one of the old Sultans was preparing to receive a certain class of persons, he would always keep them waiting a long time, perhaps a whole day. Then, when he thought that they had been sufficiently humbled, he would give that order—"Let the dogs be fed and clothed." After that, they would be admitted to the chamber of the Grand Vizier, given food and robed in caftans.'

'What class of persons?'

'The ambassadors of foreign powers.' He paused. Obviously, he was still thinking about it. Then he dismissed me curtly. 'You have your orders. Report as arranged.'

I went and got the car. The man at the garage who had the key to the petrol pump had gone home, and there was only the old man who had washed the car waiting for me. I wasn't too pleased about that, as it meant that I would have to fill the tank in the morning. Opportunities for making telephone reports to Tufan did not seem particularly desirable at that moment.

When I got back to the villa it was almost dark and the lights were on in the terrace rooms. I put the car away and went to the kitchen.

Geven was in a jovial mood. Fischer had moved him to a bedroom near mine and told him to share my bathroom. Whether this was due to spite on Fischer's part or a shortage of bathrooms, I couldn't tell. Geven, through some obscure reasoning process of his own, had decided that the whole thing had been my idea. In a way, I suppose, he was right; but there was nothing to be done about it. I took a tumbler of brandy from him and beamed like an idiot as if I had earned every drop. He had cooked a spaghetti *Bolognese* for the kitchen. The spies were having canned soup, and a shish kebab made with mutton which he proudly assured me was as tough as new leather. The spaghetti was really good. I had a double helping of it. As soon as the Hamuls arrived, I got away, giving as an excuse that I had work to do on the car. I went out to the yard.

The terrace ran along the front and right side of the house, I had noticed a door in the wall beside the garage. There was an orchard of fig trees beyond and I thought it possible that the side terrace might be accessible from there.

The door had no lock, only a latch, but the old hinges were rusty and I used the dip-stick from the car to run some oil into them before I attempted to open it. It swung inwards silently and I shut it behind me. I waited then, not only so that my eyes would get used to the dark, but because the spies had not yet gone into dinner. I could hear their voices faintly. I knew that Tufan would have wanted me to go closer and hear what they were saying; but I didn't. The ground was uneven and I would have to feel my way towards the terrace balustrade. I preferred to do that while they were well away from the terrace and trying to get their teeth into Geven's shish kebab.

After fifteen or twenty minutes, dinner was served and I edged forward slowly to the terrace. As soon as I reached it and was able to see through the balustrade, I realized that it would be impossible for me to get close enough to the windows of the room they had been using to hear anything. There was too much light coming from them. I suppose one of these daredevil agents you hear about would have concealed himself in the shadows; but that looked too risky for me. Getting to the shadows would have been easy enough; but if Harper and Co. decided to sit outside, as they had done the night before, there would have been no way of getting back without being seen.

I walked on through the orchard until I came to the outer edge of the front courtyard. This was the side which overlooked the Bosphorus and there were no trees to obstruct the view. A low stone balustrade ran along the edge with a statue on a plinth at each end. The first of these statues was over thirty feet from the corner of the terrace, but it was the nearest I could get and still remain in cover. The top of the plinth was chest-high. Using the balustrade as a stepping-stone, it wasn't difficult to climb up. The statue, a larger than life-size Vestal virgin with bird-droppings all over her, seemed quite steady, and I was able to hold on to her draperies. From the plinth I could see over the terrace balustrading and through the windows of the corner drawing-room. It was not much, but it was something. If they did decide to come out on to the terrace, I might even catch a word or two of what they said.

After about twenty minutes, they came back into the room. The bits of it
that I could see contained an old leather-topped library table, part of a faded
green settee, part of a wall mirror, a low round table and one or two gilt
chairs. The only person I could actually see at first was Miller, who took a
corner of the settee; but he was talking nineteen to the dozen and waving his
hands about, so he obviously wasn't alone. Then Mrs Hamul came in with a
coffee tray which she put on the round table, and I saw bits of the others as
they helped themselves. Somebody gave Miller a glass of brandy, which he
drank as if he needed it; he could have been trying to wash away the taste of
his dinner. After a bit, he stopped talking and appeared to be listening, his
head moving slightly as he shifted his attention from one speaker to another.
Then there was a flash of white in the mirror and his head turned. For a
moment, I saw Miss Lipp. She had changed into a green dress, though; the
white belonged to a large sheet of paper. Almost immediately it disappeared
from view. Miller's head lifted as he began to listen to someone who was
standing up. A minute or so went by and then the paper reappeared, as if
put aside, on the library table. I could see now that it was a map. At that
distance and at that angle it was impossible to tell what it was a map of, but it
looked to me like a roughly triangular island. I was still staring at it when
Harper moved in and folded it into four.

After that, nothing seemed to happen until, suddenly, Harper and Miss
Lipp came out on to the terrace from a window much farther away and
walked down the marble steps. There was nothing purposeful about their
movements—they were obviously just going for a stroll—but I thought it as
well to get out of the way. If they were going to admire the view from the
balustrade, I would be in an awkward spot.

I got down from the plinth and moved back into the shelter of the fig
trees. Sure enough, they made their way round to the balustrade. When
they turned to go back I was only twenty-five feet away from them. I heard a
snatch of conversation.

'. . . if I took over?' That was Miss Lipp.

'He was Leo's idea,' he answered. 'Let Leo take care of him. After
tomorrow, he doesn't matter too much anyway. Even Arthur could do the
rest of that job.'

She laughed. 'The indignant sheep? With his breath you wouldn't even
need the grenades, I guess. You'd get a mass surrender.'

He laughed.

She said: 'When does Giulio's man arrive?'

'Some time today. I didn't wait. Giulio knows . . .'

I heard no more.

As soon as they were well clear, I went back through the orchard to the
yard, and then up to my room. I locked the door. Geven would be free of the
kitchen at any moment, and I did not want to be bothered with him.

I had to think about what they had said and it was hard to do so, because
all I could think about was her laugh and the words she had used about me. I
felt sick. There was another time when it had been like that, too. Jones iv
and I had gone up to Hilly Fields to meet a couple of girls we knew. One of
them was named Muriel, the other was Madge. Madge didn't turn up
because, so Muriel said, she had a cold. So there were just the three of us.

Muriel was really Jones' girl, so I was more or less out of it. I tried to pick up another girl, but that was more difficult when you were alone and I didn't have any luck. After a while, I gave up and went back to where I had left the other two necking on a seat under the trees. I thought I'd come up quietly and give them a surprise. That is how I overheard it. She was saying that she had to get home early, for some reason or other, and he was asking her about Saturday night.

'With Arthur, too?' she said.

'I suppose so.'

'Well, Madge won't come.'

'She'll be over her cold by then.'

'She hasn't got a cold. She just didn't want to come. She says Arthur's a little twerp and gives her the creeps.'

I went away and they didn't know that I'd heard. Then I was sick behind the bushes. I hated that girl Madge so much that it was like a pain.

Geven came up and I heard him go into the bathroom. A little while afterwards he came out and knocked on my door. I had taken the precaution of switching out the light so that it wouldn't show under the door and he would think that I was asleep. He knocked again. After a few moments I heard him muttering to himself. Then he went away.

I nearly changed my mind and called him in. I could have done with a drink just then, and someone to talk to. But then I thought of how dirty he was and how the stink of his body would stay in the room—'the perfume of the great unwashed', as my father would have said. Besides, I couldn't be sure of getting rid of him when I wanted to, and I had the eleven o'clock radio call to take.

It came at last.

'*Attention period report. Attention period report. Passenger for yacht* Bulut *arrived Pendik seventeen hundred hours today. Name Enrico, other names unknown so far. Description: short, stocky, black hair, brown eyes, age about thirty-five. Casual observation of subject and hand luggage suggests workman rather than guest of charterer Corzo. Are you able to identify this man? Important that written notes of all conversations, with particular care as to political content, should be made. Essential you report progress. Repeat. Essential.*'

The outside of the body can be washed of sweat and grease; but inside there are processes which produce other substances. Some of these smell. How do you wash away the smells of the inside of the body?

Chapter Eight

The morning call was a repetition of that of the previous night, and made no more sense at seven a.m. than it had at eleven. I got up and went to the bathroom. Luckily, I had had the sense to remove my towel to my bedroom; but Geven had left a filthy mess. There was grey scum in the bath and shaving soap in the basin. Patience was necessary in order to flush the toilet successfully, and he had given up too soon.

Shaved, he looked more bleary-eyed than he had with the three-day growth, but his mood was one of jovial aggression. Fischer's complaints about the shish kebab, it seemed, had been loud and insolent. But the reprisal had already been planned–the spies' dinner that night would be boiled mutton in yoghourt *à la Turque*. Fischer would learn to his cost who was master in the kitchen; and if he didn't like the knowledge, well, then, the spies could go on eating pig-swill or find themselves another chef.

I had breakfast, got the car and drove out to the garage for petrol.

Tufan answered promptly. I made my report about the overheard conversation first, editing only slightly. 'If I took over. He was Leo's idea, let Leo take care of him. After tomorrow he doesn't matter too much anyway. Grenades . . . mass surrender.'

He made me repeat it slowly. When he started to complain that there wasn't more of it, I told him about the map. I had guessed that this would excite his interest, and it did.

'You say it looked like a map of an island?'

'I thought so. The shape was roughly triangular.'

'Was it a coloured map?'

'No, black and white.'

'Then it could have been a marine chart?'

'I suppose so.'

He said thoughtfully: 'A boat, the chart of an island, grenades, respirators, guns, surrender . . .'

'And something that Fischer is to do today,' I reminded him.

He ignored the interruption. 'You are sure the island had a triangular shape?'

'I thought so, but the map wasn't absolutely flat. It was hard to see. It could have been a design for a swimming pool.'

He ignored the frivolity. 'Could it have been kidney-shaped?'

'Perhaps. Would that mean something?'

'That is the shape of the island of Yassiada where certain political prisoners are held awaiting trial. It is only fifteen kilometres from Pendik. Have you heard the name Yassiada mentioned?'

'No.'

'Or Imrali?'

'No. Is that an island, too?'

'It is a town on an island sixty kilometres from Pendik. It is also the place where Menderes was hanged.'

'How is that island shaped?'

'Like the head of a dog. I must have another report from you this evening without fail, even if it is only negative.'

'I will do what I can.'

'Above all, you must search for this chart.'

'How can I?'

'You can search at night. In any case you must obtain a closer look at it.'

'I don't see how I can do that. Even if they bring it out again, I won't be able to get any closer.'

'With binoculars you could.'

'I have no binoculars.'

'On the way back to the villa, stop on the road. The Opel is on surveillance duty today. An agent from the car will give you binoculars.'

'Supposing Harper sees them. How do I explain them?'

'Don't let him see them. I expect a report tonight. If necessary, you will make direct contact with the surveillance personnel. Is that clear?' He hung up.

I drove back towards the villa. Just outside Sariyer on the coast road I pulled up. The Opel stopped a hundred yards behind me. After a minute or two, a man got out of it and walked towards the Lincoln. He was carrying a leather binocular case. He handed it to me without a word and went back to the Opel.

I put the binoculars on the seat and drove on. They were too big to put in my pocket. I would either have to smuggle them up to my room somehow or hide them in the garage. I was annoyed with myself. I should have known better. Any sort of map is cat-nip to intelligence people. I should have kept quiet about it.

Even without the binoculars, though, I would have been irritated, and I did have sense enough to realize that. The binoculars were only a nuisance. It was really the conclusion he had come to that bothered me.

What he'd wanted to see all along, and, quite evidently, what he now *did* see, was yet another conspiracy against the Committee of National Union, yet another *coup* in preparation. The last attempt to overthrow the Committee had been made by a group of dissident army officers *inside* the country. What more likely than that the next attempt would be made with the help of money and hired terrorists from *outside* the country? What more likely than that it would begin with a daring rescue of officer prisoners awaiting trial? As he had said: 'A boat, the chart of an island, grenades, respirators, guns, surrender.' It all added up so neatly.

The trouble was, as it had been all along, that he didn't know the people concerned. I did. I knew how vile they were, too. In fact, there was nothing I wanted more at that moment than to see them get hell. But they just didn't strike me as the sort of people who would be hired terrorists. I could not have said why. If he had countered by asking me what sort of people *were* hired terrorists and how many I had met, I would have had no sensible answer. All I could have said would have been: 'These people wouldn't take that kind of risk.'

When I got back to the villa, Fischer was standing on the terrace at the top of the steps. He motioned to me to pull up there. As he came down the steps, I remembered, just in time, to shove the binoculars on to the floor by my feet.

'You will not be wanted today, Simpson,' he said. 'We are going on a private excursion. I will drive the car.'

'Very good, sir. It is full of petrol, but I was going to dust it.' I was all smiles above, and all binoculars below.

'Very well.' He waved me off in his high-handed way. 'The car must be here in half an hour.'

'Yes, sir.'

I drove round the courtyard into the garage, and hid the binoculars behind an empty oil-drum before I gave the car a flick over with a wet duster.

Just before ten I drove it to the courtyard and left it there with the ignition key in. Then I went back to the yard, through the door into the orchard, and found a place from which I could see the car without being seen. When they went out, I wanted to make sure that they had all gone—Fischer, Harper, Miss Lipp and Miller.

After forty minutes or so, all four came out and got into the car. As soon as they had gone, I went to the kitchen. Geven was there, chopping meat and sipping brandy. I had a drink myself and let him talk for a while before asking whether they were expected back for lunch. They were not. He would make an omelette *pour le personnel*.

I went upstairs to the bedroom floor. At the head of the back stairs the corridor ran left and right, parallel to the rear wall of the villa. If you turned right, you came to my room and Geven's, among others; if you turned left, you were faced by a pair of double doors. Beyond them were the master bedrooms and guest suites.

The double doors were half-open when I went up. Through the opening, I caught a glimpse of a wickerwork trolley full of dirty linen, and of old Hamul working on the floor of the corridor with a carpet-sweeper. Mrs Hamul was presumably changing the sheets on the beds.

I went to my room, waited an hour, and then strolled back along the corridor.

The door was still open and the Hamuls were still messing about in the bedrooms. I went down to the kitchen and had another drink with Geven. He was busy with the stewpot and another hour went by before he decided to make the omelette. I heard the Hamuls come down at about the same time and go through to the laundry. As soon as I had finished eating. I told Geven that I was going to have a sleep and went upstairs again.

First, I locked my room from the outside in case he looked in to see if I were there; then I went through the double doors and shut them behind me.

What I was looking for was the map, and it was difficult to know where to start. There were about eighteen rooms there, and they were of all shapes and sizes. Some were bedrooms, some sitting-rooms; some were so sparsely furnished that it was hard to tell what they had been. Where there was furniture, it was all in the same bilious-looking French-hotel style. The only things not in short supply were mirrors and chandeliers; every room had those.

I identified Miller's room first, because his suitcase was open on the bed, then Fischer's because of the shirts in one of the drawers. I found no map in either room. Miss Lipp's suite was over the centre portico, with Harper's next to it on the corner. There was a connecting door. I looked through all the drawers and cupboards, I looked inside the suitcases, I looked above and below every piece of furniture. The only maps I found were in a copy of *Europa Touring* that was on Miss Lipp's writing desk, along with some Italian paper-back novels.

Beyond Harper's suite, and on the side of the building overlooking the orchard, there was a room that had been fitted up as a studio. Architect's drawers had been built along one wall. It seemed a good place to look for a large flat map, and I was carefully going through every drawer when I heard the sound of car doors slamming.

I scrambled through Harper's bedroom, which had windows on to the courtyard, and saw the roof of the Lincoln in front of the portico. Then I panicked. I missed the door which led to the passage and got into his bathroom instead. By the time I had found the right door, I could hear Fischer's voice from the stairs. It was hopeless to try to dodge round the rooms. I didn't know the way well enough. All I could do was retreat back through Harper's bedroom into the studio and shut the door. From there, there was no other way out, except through the window, but it was the only hiding place I could find.

I heard him come into the room, then a clink of money, then a sort of slap. He was emptying his pockets on to the table. The door didn't latch properly and I could hear every move he made. I knew that he would hear any move I made, too. I froze there.

'My God, that city's worse than New York in August,' he said.

I heard Miss Lipp answer him. The door connecting the suites, which I had shut, must have been opened by her.

'I wonder if Hamul fixed that water. Undo me will you, *Liebchen?*'

He moved away. I tiptoed over to the studio window and looked out. There was a small balcony outside and, a few feet below, the roof of the terrace. If I could get down there, I thought it might be possible to reach the orchard without breaking my neck. The trouble was that I would have to open the french window to the balcony. It had one of those long double bolts that you work by twisting a handle in the centre. They can make a clattering noise when they spring open, and this one looked as if it would. I went back to the door.

It sounded as if they were in his sitting-room. I heard her give a soft chuckle.

'Too many clothes on,' she said.

He came back into the bedroom and, then, after a moment or two went into the bathroom. Water began to run. I went to the window again and gingerly tried the handle. It moved easily enough. The bottom bolt slid out and the door sprang inward with a slight thud; but then I saw that one side of the connecting link was broken and that the top bolt hadn't moved. I tried to pull it down by hand, but it was too stiff. I would have to push it down through the slot at the top. I put a chair against the window and looked about for something metal I could use to push with.

The noise of running water from the bathroom stopped, and I stood still again. I tried to think what I had in my pockets that might move the bolt; a key perhaps.

'I will have to do something about my tan when we get back,' said Miss Lipp. She was in the next room now.

'It's holding up.'

'Your hair's wet.'

Silence, then a deep sigh from her and the bed creaked.

For about two minutes I clung to the hope that they were going to have a siesta. Then movements began. After a while I could hear their breathing and it wasn't the breathing of sleep. More minutes went by and there were other sounds. Then the beast with two backs was at work, and soon it was making its usual noises, panting and grunting and moaning, while I stood there like a half-wit, picturing her long legs and slim thighs and wondering how on earth I was going to get out of there without anybody seeing me. I was sweating so much that it was running into my eyes and misting my glasses. I couldn't have seen to get the bolt open just then, even if I had dared to try.

They seemed to go on interminably; but the noisy finales arrived at last. I waited, hopefully, for them to go to their bathrooms, but they didn't. There was just another long silence, until I heard him say, 'Here,' and a lighter clicked. Another silence, until he broke it.

'Where shall we eat tonight?'

'Les Baux. I will have the *feuilleté de ris de veau*. You?'

'Avallon, Moulin des Ruats, the *coq au vin*.'

'With the *Cuvée du Docteur*?'

'Of course. Though right now, frankly, I'd settle for a ham sandwich and a glass of beer.'

'It's not for long, *Liebchen*. I wonder who told Hans that this man could cook.'

'He can cook all right, but he's one of those lushes who has to be wooed. If he isn't, he gets into a white rage and says "The hell with you". Hans doesn't know how to handle him. I'll bet Arthur eats better than we do. In fact, I know damn well he does. Where's the ash-tray?'

'Here.' She giggled. 'Careful!'

'*Merde, alors!*'

'That is not the place for an ash-tray.'

Soon it began all over again. Eventually, when they were exhausted, they did have the decency to go to the bathrooms. While the water was running, I got up on to the chair and worked on the bolt with my room key. By the time he had finished in the bathroom, I had the window unlatched. I had to wait then until they were asleep; though it was not until I heard her voice again that I knew that she had returned to his bed.

'*Liebchen*,' she said drowsily.

'What is it?' He was half-asleep, too.

'Be careful, please, tomorrow.'

'*Entendu.*'

There was the sound of a kiss. I looked at my watch. It was twenty past three. I gave them ten minutes, then carefully edged over to the window and pulled one side open. I did it very slowly because there was a slight breeze outside and I did not want the draught to open the bedroom door while I was still there. Then I edged my way out on to the balcony.

It was a four-foot drop to the roof of the terrace and I made scarcely any noise getting down. I had more trouble at the end of the terrace. I am really not built for climbing, and I tried to use the trellis-work as a step-ladder. It gave way, and I slithered to the ground, clutching at the branches of an espaliered peach tree.

I managed to get to my room without anyone seeing the mess I was in.

When I had cleaned up and changed my shirt, I went down to the car and put it away in the garage.

If I had noticed then that the door panels had been taken off, things would have turned out very differently for Harper, Lipp and Miller; but I didn't notice. It didn't even occur to me to look at them. I was still too flustered to do anything except try to behave naturally. Garaging the car was just a way of showing that I was outside and on the job.

I went back into the kitchen. There was nobody there. I found a bottle of Geven's brandy and had a drink and a cigarette. When I was quite calm again, I went out and walked down the drive to the road.

The Opel was parked near the fishing-boat pier. I strolled across to it and saw the men inside watching me. As I passed, I said: 'Tufan.'

When I had gone on a few paces I heard a car door open. A moment or so later a man fell in step beside me.

'What is it?' He was a dark, hard-eyed police type in an oatmeal-coloured shirt with buttoned pockets. He spoke in French.

'Something dangerous is to be attempted tomorrow,' I said. 'I do not know what. I overheard part of a conversation. Major Tufan should be informed.'

'Very well. Why did you not drive today?'

'They told me I wasn't needed. Where did they go?'

'To Istanbul, Beyoglu. They drove to a garage by the Spanish Consulate. It is a garage that has spare parts for American cars. The driver, Fischer, remained there with the car for ten minutes. The other two men and the woman walked to the Divan Hotel. They had lunch there. Fischer joined them there and also had lunch. Then they walked back to the garage, picked up the car and returned here. Major Tufan says that you are to report on a chart later.'

'If I can. Tell him I made a search of the bedrooms while they were out, but could not find the chart. I will try to search the living-rooms tonight. It may be quite late before I can report. Will you be here?'

'Someone will be.'

'All right.'

As we turned and walked back towards the Opel, I crossed the road and re-entered the drive. I had something to think about now. From what I had overheard in the courtyard the night before, I knew that Fischer had some special task to perform that day. Had he already performed it, or was it yet to be performed? Driving the car into Istanbul so that he and the others could have some eatable food didn't seem very special. On the other hand, it was odd that I should have been told to stay behind, and odd about that visit to the garage. There was nothing wrong with the car and it needed no spare parts. And why had Fischer not walked to the Divan with the other three? Why had he stayed behind?

It is obvious that I should have thought of the car doors first. I didn't do so for a very simple reason: I knew from personal experience how long it took to remove and replace one panel, and Fischer had not been at the garage long enough to empty one door, let alone four. The possibility that his function might have been to give orders instead of doing the actual work didn't occur to me, *then*. And, I may say, it didn't occur to Tufan *at all*. If it had, I should have been spared a ghastly experience.

Anyway, when I went back through the yard to take a look at the car, my mind was on spare parts. I looked in the luggage compartment first to see if anything had been stowed away there; then I examined the engine. You can usually tell by the smudges and oil-smears when work has been done on an engine. I drew a blank, of course. It wasn't until I opened the door to see if anything had been left in the glove compartment that I saw the scratches.

Whoever had taken the panels off had made the very mistake I had been so careful to avoid; he had used an ordinary screwdriver on the Phillips heads. There were scratches where the tool had slipped. Of course, nobody would have noticed them on a casual inspection, but I was so conscious of the panels and what I had seen behind them that the slightest mark stood out. I went over all four and knew at once that they had all been taken off and replaced. I also knew, from the different feel of the doors when I swung them on their hinges, that the heavy things which had been concealed inside were no longer there. Presumably, they had been removed in the garage near the Spanish Consulate. Where they were at that moment was anybody's guess.

I wondered whether I should go down to the road again immediately and report to the surveillance car, or wait until I reported later about the map. I decided to wait. If the stuff was still in the garage, it would probably still be there in the morning. If, as seemed more likely, it had already been moved somewhere else, than the damage was done and two or three hours would make no difference. Anyway, I didn't *want* to go back down the road. I felt that I had run enough risks for one day already; and I still had to go looking for that damned map. I think I did the sensible thing. I can't stand people who are wise after the event, but it must be obvious now that it was Tufan who made the mistakes, not me.

The trouble with Geven began while we were in the kitchen eating our dinner; or, rather, while I was eating and he was putting away more brandy. It was about seven o'clock, and he had been drinking steadily since six. In that hour he must have had nearly a third of a bottle. He wasn't yet quite drunk, but he was certainly far from sober.

He had made a perfectly delicious risotto with finely chopped chicken livers and pimentos in it. I was on my second helping and trying to persuade him to eat what he had on his plate, when Fischer came in.

'Geven!'

Geven looked up and gave him his wet smile. '*Vive la compagnie,*' he looked convivially, and reached for a dirty glass. '*Un petit verre, monsieur?*'

Fischer ignored the invitation. 'I wish to know what you are preparing for dinner tonight,' he said.

'It is prepared.' Geven gave him a dismissive wave of his hand and turned to me again.

'Then can you tell me what it is.' At that moment Fischer caught sight of my plate. 'Ah, I see. A risotto, eh?'

Geven's lip quivered. 'That is for us servants. For the master and his guests there is a more important dish in the manner of the country.'

'What dish?'

'You would not understand.'

'I wish to know.'

Geven answered in Turkish. I understood one word of what he said: *kuzu*, baby lamb.

To my surprise, and to Geven's, too, I think, Fischer answered in the same language.

Geven stood up and shouted something.

Fischer shouted back, and then walked from the room before Geven had time to answer.

Geven sat down again, his lower lip quivering so violently that, when he tried to drain his glass, most of the brandy ran down his chin. He refilled the glass and glowered at me.

'*Pislik!*' he said. '*Domuz!*'

Those are rude words in Turkish. I gathered that they were meant for Fischer, so I said nothing and got on with my food.

He refilled my glass and shoved it towards me. 'A toast,' he said.

'All right.'

'There'll be no promotion this side of the ocean, so drink up, my lads, bless 'em all!'

Only he didn't say 'bless'. I had forgotten that he had been educated in Cyprus when it was under British rule.

'Drink!'

I drank. 'Bless 'em all.'

He began to sing. 'Bless all the sergeants and W.O. ones, bless all the corporals and their bleeding sons! Drink!'

I sipped. 'Bless 'em all.'

He drained the glass again and leaned across the chopping table, breathing heavily. 'I tell you,' he said menacingly; 'if that bastard says one more word, I kill him.'

'He's just a fool.'

'You defend him?' The lower lip quivered.

'No, no. But is he *worth* killing?'

He poured himself another drink. Both lips were working now, as if he had brought another thought agency into play in order to grapple with the unfamiliar dilemma my question had created.

The Hamuls arrived just then to prepare for the service of the evening meal. He began talking to Geven. He spoke a country dialect and I couldn't even get the drift of what he was saying; but it seemed to improve matters a little. Geven grinned occasionally and even laughed once. However, he still went on drinking, and, when I tried to slip away to my room, there was a sudden flare of temper.

'Where you go?'

'You have work to do here. I am in the way.'

'You sit down. You are my guest in the kitchen. You drink nothing. Why?'

I had a whole tumbler full of brandy in front of me by now. I took another sip.

'Drink!'

I drank and tried to look as if I were enjoying myself. When he wasn't looking, I managed to tip half the brandy in my glass down the sink. It didn't do much good. As soon as he noticed the half-empty glass, he filled it up again.

Dinner had been ordered for eight-thirty, and by then he was weaving. It was Mrs Hamul who did the dishing up. He leaned against the range, glass in hand, smiling benignly on her while she ladled the loathsome contents of the stewpot on to the service platters. Dinner was finally served.

'Bless 'em all!'

'Bless 'em all!'

'Drink!'

At that moment there was an indistinct shout from the direction of the dining-room. Then a door along the passage was flung open, and there were quick footsteps. I heard Miss Lipp call out 'Hans!' Then Fischer came into the kitchen. He was carrying a plateful of food.

As Geven turned unsteadily to confront him, Fischer yelled something in Turkish and then flung the plate straight at his head.

The plate hit Geven on the shoulder and then crashed to the floor; but quite a lot of food went on to his face. Gravy ran down his smock.

Fischer was still shouting. Geven stared at him stupidly. Then, as Fischer flung a final insult and turned to go, a most peculiar expression came over Geven's face. It was almost like a wide-eyed smile. '*Monsieur est servi,*' he said. At the same instant, I saw his hand dart out for the chopping knife.

I shouted a warning to Fischer, but he was already out in the passage. Geven was after him in a flash. By the time I got through the door, Fischer was already backing away and yelling for help. There was blood streaming from a gash on his face and he had his hands up trying to protect himself. Geven was hacking and slashing at him like a madman.

As I ran forward and clung on to the arm wielding the chopping knife, Harper came into the passage from the dining-room.

'*Senden illâllah!*' bawled Geven.

Then Harper hit him in the side of the neck and he went down like an empty sack.

Fischer's arms and hands were pouring blood now, and he stood there looking down at them as if they did not belong to him.

Harper glanced at me. 'Get the car around, quick.'

I stopped the car at the foot of the steps and went in through the front of the house. It did not seem to be a moment for standing on ceremony.

Fischer was sitting in a marble-floored washroom just off the main hall. Harper and Miss Lipp were wrapping his hands and arms in towels; Miller was trying to staunch the face wound; the Hamuls were running round in circles.

Harper saw me and motioned to Hamul. 'Ask the old guy where the nearest doctor is. Not a hospital, a private doctor.'

'I will ask him,' muttered Fischer. His face was a dirty grey.

I caught Hamul's arm and shoved him forward.

There were two doctors in Sariyer, he said, but the nearest was outside Bülyükdere in the other direction. He would come to the villa if called by telephone.

Harper shook his head when Fischer told him this. '*We'll* go to *him*,' he said. 'We'll give him five hundred lira and tell him you tripped over an electric fan. That should fix it.' He looked at Miss Lipp. 'You and Leo had better stay here, honey. The fewer, the better.'

She nodded.

'I don't know the way to this doctor's house,' I said. 'May we take Hamul as a guide?'

'Okay.'

Harper sat in the back with Fischer and a supply of fresh towels; Hamul came in front with me.

The doctor's house was two miles along the coast road. When we got there, Fischer told Hamul to wait outside in the car with me; so it was not possible for me to walk back and tell the men in the Opel what was going on. Presumably, they would find out from the doctor later on. Hamul fingered the leather of the seat for a while, then curled up on it and went to sleep. I tried to see if I could get out without waking him, but the sound of the door opening made him sit up instantly. After that, I just sat there and smoked. I suppose that I should have written a cigarette packet message about the car-doors and dropped it then – Hamul wouldn't have noticed that – but at that point, I still thought that I was going to be able to make a verbal report later.

They were inside well over an hour. When he came out, Fischer didn't look too bad at first sight. The cut on his face had a lint dressing taped over it, and his left arm was resting in a small sling of the kind that suggests comfort for a minor sprain rather than a serious injury. But when he got closer I could see that both his hands and forearms were quite extensively bandaged, and that the left hand was cupped round a thick pad taped so as to immobilize his fingers. I got out and opened the door for him. He smelt of disinfectant and surgical spirit.

He and Harper got in without a word, and remained silent on the way back to the villa.

Miller and Miss Lipp were waiting on the terrace. As I pulled up into the courtyard, they came down the steps. I opened the door for Fischer. He got out and walked past them into the house. Still, nothing was said. Hamul was already making for his own quarters at the back. Miller and Miss Lipp came up to Harper.

'How is he?' Miller asked. There was nothing solicitous about the question. It was a grim request for information.

'The left hand has seven stitches on one cut, four on another, more stitches on the arm. The right forearm has seven stitches. The other cuts weren't so deep. The doctor was able to tape those up. He gave him some shots and a sedative.' His eyes went to Miss Lipp. 'Where's the cook?'

'Gone,' she said. 'When he woke up, he asked if he could go to his room. We let him. He just packed his things and went off on that scooter of his. We didn't try to stop him.'

He nodded.

'But about Fischer . . .' Miller began, his teeth showing as if he wanted to eat someone.

Harper broke in firmly. 'Let's go inside, Leo.' He turned to me. 'You can put the car away for now, Arthur, but I may want it again later to drive to Pendik, so you stick around. Make yourself some coffee in the kitchen, then I'll know where to find you.'

'Very good, sir.'

When I got to the kitchen I found that someone, Mrs Hamul no doubt, had washed the dishes and cleaned the place up. The charcoal fires on the range were not quite dead, but I made no attempt to revive them. I found a bottle of red wine and opened that.

I was getting anxious. It was nearly ten-thirty and the radio call was due at eleven; but I didn't so much mind missing another '*Essential you report progress*'; it was the undelivered report on the car doors that bothered me. Obviously, Fischer's getting hurt had thrown some sort of spanner into the works and changes of plan were being made. If those changes meant that I was going to be up all night driving Harper to Pendik and back, I would have to deliver the message via a cigarette packet after all. I went into the scullery, in case Harper should suddenly come into the kitchen, and wrote the message—*Car doors now empty, check garage near Spanish Consulate*—on a piece of paper torn off a shelf-lining. I felt better when I had done that. My other assignment for the night, the search for the mysterious map, didn't worry me at all. In fact, though it may seem funny now, at that point in the proceedings I had completely forgotten about it.

It was after eleven-thirty and I had finished the last of the wine, when there was a sound of a door opening and Harper came through from the dining-room. I got to my feet.

'Sorry to keep you up this late, Arthur,' he said, 'but Mr Miller and I are having a friendly argument, and we want you to help us decide who's right. Come in.'

I followed him through the dining-room and along the passage to the room in which I had seen them the previous night.

It was L-shaped and even bigger than I had thought. When I had looked through the windows, all I had seen had been the short arm of the L. The long arm went all the way to the main entrance hall. There was a low platform with a concert-size grand piano on it. The room looked as if it had been used at some time for 'musical *soirées*'.

Miss Lipp and Miller were sitting at the library desk. Fischer was in the background, sitting in an armchair with his head thrown back so that he stared at the ceiling. I thought for a moment that he had passed out, but as I came in he slowly raised his head and stared at me. He looked terrible.

'Sit down, Arthur.' Harper motioned me to a chair facing Miller.

I sat down. Miss Lipp was watching Miller. Miller was watching me through his rimless glasses. The toothy smile was there as ever, but it was the most unamused smile I have ever seen; it was more like a grimace.

Harper leaned against the back of the settee.

'It's really two problems, Arthur,' he said. 'Tell me this. How long does it take to get to Pendik at this time of night? The same as during the day?'

'Less, perhaps; but it would depend on the ferry to Uskudar.'

'How often does that run at night?'

'Every hour, sir.'

'So if we missed one it could take us well over two hours?'

'Yes.'

He looked at Miller. 'Two hours to Pendik, two hours to persuade Giulio, two more hours to persuade Enrico . . .'

'If he would be persuaded,' Miss Lipp put in.

Harper nodded. 'Of course. And then two hours back. Not a very restful night, Leo.'

'Then postpone,' Miller snapped.

Harper shook his head. 'The overheads, Leo. If we postpone, it means abandon. What will our friends say to that?'

'It is not their necks.' Miller looked resentfully at Fischer. 'If you had not . . .' he began, but Harper cut him off sharply.

'We've been over all that, Leo. Now, why don't you at least give it a whirl?'

Miller shrugged.

Harper looked at me. 'We want to make an experiment, Arthur. Do you mind going over there and standing against the wall with your back against it?'

'Over here?'

'That's right. Your back touching the wall.' He went over to Fischer, picked up a length of thick cord which was lying across the bandaged hands and threw one end of it to me. I saw that the other end was attached to a leg of the settee. 'Now here's what it is, Arthur,' he went on. 'I've told Mr Miller that you can pull that settee six feet towards you just with the strength of your arms. Of course, your back's leaning against the wall, so you can't use your weight to help you. It has to be just your arms. Mr Miller says you can't do it, and he's got a hundred-dollar bill that says he's right. I've got one that says he's wrong. If he wins, I pay. If I win you and I split fifty-fifty. How about it?'

'I'll try,' I said.

'Very well, begin,' said Miller. 'Your shoulders against the wall, your heels not more than ten centimetres from it and together.' He moved over so that he could see that I didn't cheat.

I have always detested that kind of parlour trick; in fact, I dislike any sort of trial of physical strength. They always remind me of a lot of boys I once saw in the school lavatories. They were standing in a row seeing who could urinate the farthest. Suddenly, they started laughing and then began to aim at each other. I happened to get in the way and it was very unpleasant. In my opinion, rugger is the same kind of thing—just childish, smelly, homosexual horseplay. I always got out of it whenever I could. Today, any sort of exercise brings on my indigestion immediately.

Frankly, then, I didn't think that there was the slightest chance of my being able to pull that heavy settee one foot, much less six. I am not particularly strong in the arms anyway. Why should I be? I have enough strength to lift a suitcase and drive a car; what more do I want?

'Go on,' said Miller. 'Pull with all your strength!'

I should have done as he said and fallen flat on my face. Then Harper would have lost a hundred dollars, and I should have been spared the ordeal. But Miss Lipp had to interfere.

'Just a minute, Arthur,' she said. 'I tried this and I couldn't do it. But you're a man with a good pair of shoulders on you, and I think you *can* do it.'

Even if I had never heard her use the phrase 'indignant sheep' about me,

I would have known this heavy-handed guile for what it was. I do *not* have a good pair of shoulders on me. I have narrow, sloping ones. Women who think they can get away with that childish sort of flattery make me sick. I was really annoyed. Unfortunately, that made me go red. She smiled. I suppose she thought I was blushing because of her bloody compliment.

"I'm not much good at this sort of game,' I said.

'The thing is to pull on the cord steadily, Arthur. Don't jerk it. Pull steadily, and when it starts moving keep pulling steadily hand over hand. It's an easy fifty dollars. I *know* you can do it.'

I was getting really browned-off with her now. 'All right, you bitch,' I thought to myself; 'I'll show you!' So I did the exact opposite of what she'd said. I jerked on the cord as hard as I could.

The settee moved a few inches; but, of course, what I'd done by jerking it was to get the feet out of the dents they'd made for themselves in the thick carpet. After that, I just kept on pulling and it slid some more. As it got nearer it became easier because I was pulling up as well as along.

Harper looked at Miller. 'What about it, Leo?'

Miller felt my arms and shoulders as if he were buying a horse. 'He is flabby, out of condition,' he said sourly.

'But he did the trick,' Harper reminded him.

Miller spread out his hand as if to abandon the argument.

Harper took a note from his wallet. 'Here, Arthur,' he said, 'fifty dollars.' He paused and then went on quietly: 'How would you like to earn two thousand?'

I stared at him.

'Sit down,' he said.

I sat down and was glad to do so. My legs were trembling. With two thousand dollars I could buy a Central American passport that would be good for years; and it would be a real passport, too. I know, because I have looked into such matters. As long as you don't actually go to the country concerned, there's no trouble at all. You just buy the passport. That's the way their consuls abroad line their pockets. Of course, I knew it was all a pipe-dream. Even if I did whatever it was they wanted, Harper wasn't going to be in a position to pay me because the chances were that Tufan would have him in jail by then. Still, it was a good dream.

'I'd like that very much,' I said.

They were all watching me intently now.

'Don't you want to know what you have to do for it?' Harper asked.

I wasn't going to let him walk all over me. I sat back. 'What Mr Fischer was going to do, I suppose,' I answered; 'that is, if he hadn't had that little accident this evening.'

Miss Lipp laughed. 'I told you Arthur wasn't as simple as he looks,' she said.

'What else do you know, Arthur?' This was Harper again.

'Only what Miss Lipp told me, sir—that you are all very sensible, tolerant persons, who are very broad-minded about things that the law doesn't always approve of, but who don't like taking risks.'

'I told you all that, Arthur?' She pretended to be surprised.

'It was what I gathered, Miss Lipp.'

Harper smiled. 'All right,' he said; 'suppose we just leave it there. We have a deal.'

'I think I'm entitled to know a little more than that.'

'And you will, Arthur. We'll be leaving here tomorrow afternoon around three, bags packed and everything because we won't be coming back. Before we go you'll have a complete briefing. And don't worry. All you have to do is just pull on a rope at the right place and time. Everything else is taken care of.'

'Is this a police matter?'

'It would be if they knew about it, but they don't. I told you, you don't have to worry. Believe me you've taken bigger risks in Athens for a lot less than two thousand.'

'On that subject, sir, I think I am now entitled to have my letter back.'

Harper looked questioningly at Miller and Fischer. The latter began to talk in German. He spoke slowly and wearily now, and I guessed that the sedative had taken effect, but his attitude was clear enough. So was Miller's. Harper turned to me and shook his head regretfully.

'I'm sorry, Arthur, that'll have to wait. In fact, my friends seem to feel that you may be quite a security risk for the next twelve hours or so.'

'I don't understand.'

'Sure you do.' He grinned. 'I'll bet the idea's been churning around in that cute little brain of yours for the last five minutes. "If two hands on a rope are worth two thousand dollars to these people, what would a tip-off be worth to the police?"'

'I assure you . . .'

'Of course you do, Arthur. I was only kidding.' His tone was quite friendly. 'But you see the problems. We like to feel safe. Even that letter doesn't mean much here. Do you have the car keys?'

'Yes.'

'Let me have them.'

I handed them to him.

'You see, we wouldn't want you to have second thoughts and maybe walk out on us,' he explained.

'And we would not like him to use the telephone,' said Miller.

'That's right.' Harper thought for a moment. 'Hans is going to need help undressing,' he said, 'and the doctor's given him another antibiotic he has to take. I think it would be best if we made up an extra bed in his room and Arthur slept there.'

'So that he can kill me when I am helpless and get out by the window?' Fischer demanded thickly.

'Oh, I don't think Arthur would do that. Would you, Arthur?'

'Of course not.'

'That's right. But we don't want Hans to be worrying, do we? The doctor says he really needs to sleep. And you should have a good night's sleep, too, Arthur. You won't get any tomorrow night. You wouldn't mind taking a couple of good strong sleeping pills, would you? Or maybe even three?'

I hesitated.

'Oh, they won't hurt you, Arthur.' Miss Lipp gave me a fond smile. 'I'll tell you what. If you'll be a good boy and take your pills, I'll take one, too. We'll all need our sleep tomorrow.'

What could I say?

Chapter Nine

My head felt as if it had been stuffed with steel wool. There was even a metallic taste in my mouth. It took me some time to remember where I was. I could hear a loud buzzing noise. When, at last, I managed to open my eyes, I saw Fischer. The buzzing came from an electric shaver which he was holding, awkwardly, in his right hand.

My bed consisted of a mattress on the floor and the blankets from my old room. I rolled off the mattress and got to my feet unsteadily. Fischer gave me a disagreeable look.

'You snore like a pig,' he said.

He had a shirt and slacks on, I was glad to see; Harper or Miller must have helped him. Undressing him, the night before, had been an unpleasant task. It had meant touching him, and I hate touching anyone I dislike–another man especially.

'What's the time?' I asked.

They had taken everything from me after they had made me swallow the sleeping pills, even my watch. All I had been allowed had been my pyjama coat.

'About eleven,' he answered. 'Your clothes have been put in there.' He indicated a door.

I went through and found myself in one of the part-furnished rooms I had seen the day before. My things were piled on a brown, cut-velvet *chaise-longue*. I disposed of a minor anxiety first. The cigarette packet with the message inside it was still in my hip pocket and apparently undetected. I left it where it was. With any luck, I thought, I might be able to add to it. My papers were there. The radio was in its case.

From the bedroom Fischer said: 'I have finished with this bathroom. You may use it.'

'I think I will go and get some coffee first.'

'Then bring all your papers and money in here.'

There was no point in arguing. I did as he said, put some trousers on and found my way downstairs to the kitchen.

Mrs Hamul was there. The sight of the hired driver, unshaven and wearing a pyjama jacket at eleven in the morning must have seemed odd to her. She looked at me as if I were raving mad. I asked her for coffee. She gave me tea, and some of the previous day's bread toasted. The tea wasn't bad. My head began to clear. As I ate the toast, I wondered if I could muster enough Turkish to persuade her or her husband to take a message to the surveillance people on the road. Then Miss Lipp came in, well-groomed and very chic in white with yellow stripes.

'Good morning, Arthur. How do you feel?'

'Good morning, Miss Lipp. I feel terrible, thank you.'

'Yes, you look it, but I expect you'll feel better when you've cleaned up a bit. What's the Turkish for eggs?'

'"*Yumurta*", I think.'

Mrs Hamul heard the word and they began a sign-language conversation about eggs. I went back upstairs.

Miller was helping Fischer to pack. I slipped the empty cigarette packet and a pencil into my shaving kit and went into the bathroom. There was a lock on the door. While my bath was running, I added to the message I had written the previous night. *Am forced replace injured Fischer and closely watched. Event planned for tonight. Details unknown. Miller may be key person.*

The bedroom was empty when I returned to it. I dressed, packed my bag and went back down to the kitchen.

Miss Lipp was supervising the Hamuls' preparations for lunch. She looked up as I came in.

'The others are out on the terrace, Arthur,' she said. 'Why don't you go out there and get yourself a drink?'

'Very well.'

I went through the dining-room into the main hall. There, I hesitated. I was still trying to think of a way of getting down to the road and back without their knowing. As they were on the terrace it was, of course, hopeless to attempt to cross the courtyard. I would have to find some other way round the back and down through the trees. But that might take twenty minutes or more. And supposing Miss Lipp came out to the terrace and asked where I was, I gave up, and decided to rely upon dropping the cigarette packet.

The first thing I saw on the terrace was the cardboard box which Harper had brought back with him from Pendik. It was open and discarded on a chair. Harper, Fischer and Miller were contemplating something laid out across two tables.

It was a block-and-tackle, but of a kind I had not seen before. The blocks were triple-sheaved and made of some light metal alloy. They were so small that you could hold both of them in one hand. The 'rope' was a white cord about a quarter of an inch in diameter and there was a lot of it. On another table there was a thing that looked like a broad belt with hooks at each end, like those you see on dog-leashes.

Fischer looked up and stared at me haughtily.

'Miss Lipp told me to come here and have a drink,' I said.

Harper waved to a table with bottles and glasses on it. 'Help yourself. Then you'd better have a look at this.'

I gave myself some *raki* and looked at the cord of the tackle. It was like silk.

'Nylon,' Harper said; 'breaking strain over a ton. What you have to remember about it is that it's also slightly elastic. There's a lot of give in this tackle. You know how these things work?'

'Yes.'

'Show me,' said Miller. He picked up the belt and hooked it around one of the terrace pillars. 'Show me how you would pull this pillar down.'

I hooked one block to the belt, tied the other to the balustrade and pulled on the tackle.

'Okay,' said Harper, 'that'll do. Leo, I think you'd better carry the tackle. Arthur's too fat. It'll show on him. He can take the sling and the anchor rope. I don't think Hans should carry anything except his gun and the water-flask.'

'It is only because my skin is very sensitive that I object,' said Miller.

'Well, it won't be for long. As soon as you're inside you can take it off.'

Miller sighed irritably but said no more.

'May I know what it is I have to do?' I asked.

'Just pull on this tackle, Arthur. Oh, you mean about taking this gear along? Well, you'll have to carry that sling–' he indicated the belt–'and this extra rope here, wound around that beautiful body of yours under your shirt, so that nobody can see it. It'll be a bit warm for a while, but you'll have plenty of time to cool off. Any other questions?'

I had a dozen and he knew it, but there isn't any sense in asking when you know you're not going to be answered.

'Who is going to carry the bag?' asked Miller.

'You'd better take that, folded in your pocket.'

Miss Lipp came out. 'Lunch in thirty minutes,' she said.

'Lunch!' Miller looked sour.

'You can eat eggs, Leo. You've got to eat something.' She took the drink Harper handed her. 'Does Arthur know that he's going to have to wait for his dinner tonight?'

'I don't know anything, Miss Lipp,' I said calmly; 'but I will say this. I was told that I would be given a briefing today. So far, all I have been given is a bad attack of nervous indigestion. Whether I eat dinner or not, and, for that matter, whether I eat lunch or not, are matters of complete indifference to me.'

She went quite red in the face, and I wondered for a moment if I had said anything offensive; then I realized that the damned woman was trying not to laugh. She looked at Harper.

'Okay,' he said. 'Come in here.' He led the way through a french window into the drawing-room. Only Miss Lipp followed with me. I heard Fischer asking Miller to pour him another drink and Miller telling him that he ought to exercise the hand not pamper it. Then I no longer listened. Harper had walked to the library table, opened a drawer in it and pulled out the 'map'.

'Recognize this place?' he asked.

'Yes.'

It was a plan of part of the Seraglio area and of the roads adjacent to the walls. The triangular shape I had noted was formed by the coastline.

'This is what we are going to do,' he went on. 'When we leave here, we will drive to a garage in Istanbul. Our bags will be in the trunk of the Lincoln. At the garage, Mr Miller, Mr Fischer, you and I will get out of the Lincoln and into a different car which will be waiting there. I will then drive you to the Seraglio Palace. Then, Mr Miller, Mr Fischer and you will get out. The Palace is open to the public until five. The three of you will buy tickets and enter in the ordinary way as tourists. You will then cross the

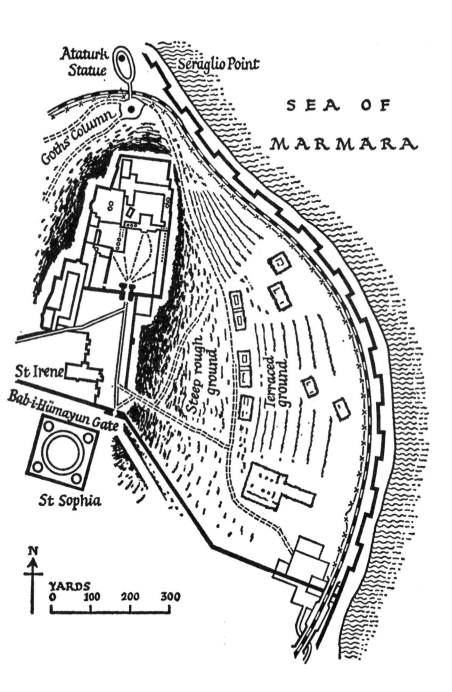

Ataturk
Statue

Seraglio Point

Goths' Column

SEA OF

MARMARA

Steep rough ground

Terraced ground

St Irene

Bab-i-Hümayun Gate

St Sophia

N

YARDS
0   100   200   300

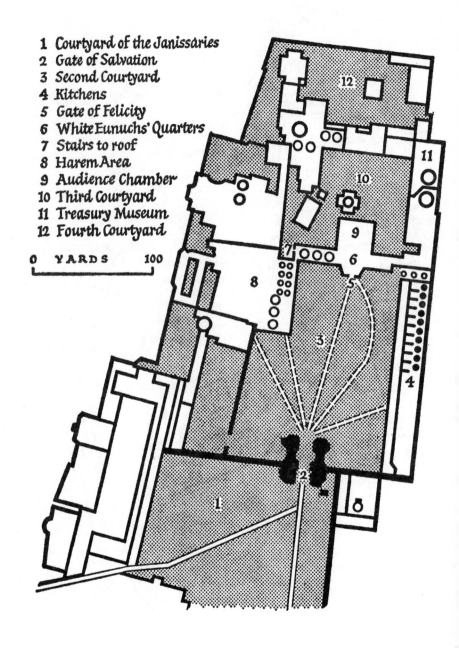

1 Courtyard of the Janissaries
2 Gate of Salvation
3 Second Courtyard
4 Kitchens
5 Gate of Felicity
6 White Eunuchs' Quarters
7 Stairs to roof
8 Harem Area
9 Audience Chamber
10 Third Courtyard
11 Treasury Museum
12 Fourth Courtyard

0 YARDS 100

second courtyard to the Gate of Felicity. When you are sure that the guides have lost interest in you, you will go through into the third courtyard and turn left. You then have a short walk—exactly sixty paces—before you come to a big bronze gate in a courtyard to the left with a small door beside it. Both gate and door are kept locked, but Mr Miller will have a key to the door. Beyond the door is a passage with a stairway leading up to the roof of the White Eunuchs' apartments'—he pointed to the plan—'here. Then you lock the door behind you and wait. Clear so far?'

'Quite clear, except about why we're doing all this.'

'Oh, I thought you'd have guessed that.' He grinned. 'We're just going to have ourselves a piece of the old Sultans' loot. Just a little piece, that's all—about ten million dollars' worth.'

I looked at Miss Lipp.

'I was being cagey, Arthur,' she said. 'There is some obsidian and garnet there, and green tourmaline, too. But a lot of that stuff's the real thing. There are six pigeon's blood rubies in that throne-room that must be over twenty carats apiece. Do you know what just one ruby like that is worth, Arthur? And the emeralds on those Koran caskets! My God!'

Harper laughed. 'All right, honey, I think Arthur has the picture. Now'—he turned again to the plan—'there are civilian watchmen on duty, but not very many of them, and the night-shift comes on at eight. You give them an hour to settle down. At nine you move. You go up the stairs to the roof and turn left. There are three little domes, cupolas they call them, on the roof there, and you walk along to the right of them. After that the roof is more or less flat until you get to the gate arch. You go around that over the roof of the audience chamber and on until you see the chimneys of the kitchens on your right. Then you turn left again, cross the roof of the place where they have the miniatures and tapestries. At the end of it there's a three-foot drop on to the roof of the Treasury museum. That's where you have to be careful. The Treasury roof is thirty-five feet wide, but it's vaulted. There is a flat area around the cupola, though, so you climb down there. All quite safe. The cupola is ten feet in diameter and that'll be your anchor for the tackle. Mr Miller'll tie the knots for you. When he's got the sling hooked up, he'll sit in it. Then all you have to do is lower him over the side until he's level with a steel shutter eighteen feet below. He'll do the rest.'

'Mr Miller will?'

He looked at me with amusement. 'You think he's too old for that sort of thing? Arthur, when Mr Miller gets busy he makes a fly look like a man in diving boots.'

'You said there was a steel shutter?'

'You could open it with a toothpick. The wall's four feet thick and solid stone. I guess it'd stand up to a six-inch shell. But the shutters over the window apertures are just quarter-inch plate with ordinary draw bolts on them. They don't even fit properly. And no alarm system.'

'But if this jewellery is so valuable . . .'

'Have you ever looked through one of those window apertures, Arthur? There's a sheer drop of three hundred feet below. It's quite impossible to get up or down there. That's why we're going in from above. The trick is getting out again. What their security set-up relies on is the fact that the whole area is walled like a fortress. There are gates, of course, and the gates have troops guarding them at night; but gates can be opened if you know how. That'll all be taken care of. You'll walk out of there just as easily as you walked in.' His eyes found mine and held them. 'You see, Arthur, we're professionals.'

I forced myself to look away. I looked at Miss Lipp; but her eyes had the same intent look as his. 'I'm sorry,' I said; 'I'm not a professional.'

'*You* don't have to be,' she said.

'I can't do it, Mr Harper.'

'Why not?'

'Because I'd be too afraid.'

He smiled. 'That's the best thing I've heard you say, Arthur. You had me worried for a moment.'

'I mean it.'

'Sure you do. Who wouldn't be scared? *I'm* scared. In a few hours' time I'll be even more scared. That's good. If you aren't a bit scared you don't stay on your toes.'

'I'm not talking about being a bit scared, Mr Harper. I'm talking about being *too* scared. I'd be no use to you.' And I meant it. I was thinking of myself on top of that roof with a three-hundred foot drop down to the road. 'I can't stand heights, you see.'

There was a silence, and then Miss Lipp laughed. 'I don't believe you. Arthur,' she said. 'You? You with two good arms and hands to hold on with, scared of going where Hans Fischer isn't afraid to go with only *half* a hand? It doesn't make sense.'

'I'm sorry,' I said again.

There was another silence and then Harper glanced at her and moved his head slightly. She walked out on to the terrace.

'Let's get a couple of things straight, Arthur,' he said. 'All I'm asking you to do is take a little ride and then a little walk, and then handle a rope for twenty minutes. You'll be in no danger. Nobody's going to take pot-shots at you. And when it's done you get two thousand bucks. Right?'

'Yes, but . . .'

'Let me finish. Now, supposing you chicken out, what do we do?'

'Get someone else, I suppose.'

'Yes, but what do we do about *you*?' He paused. 'You see, Arthur, it's not just a question of getting the job done. You know too much now not to be a part of it. If you're going to be on the outside, well, we'll have to protect ourselves another way. You follow me?'

He could see that I did. I had a choice: I could either frighten myself to death on the roof of the Seraglio, or take a shorter, quicker route to the police mortuary.

'Now go get yourself another drink and stop worrying,' he said; 'just think of the two thousand bucks.'

I shrugged. 'All right. I'm merely telling you how I feel, that's all.'

'You'll be okay, Arthur.' He led the way back on to the terrace.

It was on the tip of my tongue to ask him how okay Mr Miller would be if the height got me down and I passed out while I was handling the tackle;

but I thought better of it. If he realized that I really wasn't just being timid, that I really couldn't stand heights, he might decide that I was too dangerous a liability in every way. Besides, I was coming to my senses again now. Tufan's 'politicals' had turned out to be big-time crooks after all. I had been right all along, and he had been hopelessly wrong; but he was still a powerful ally, and I still had a good chance of being able to stop the whole thing. All I had to do was add just three words—*raiding Seraglio treasury*—to the note in the cigarette packet and drop it for the surveillance people. After that, my worries would be over, and Harper's would begin. I had a pleasing vision of the lot of them, rounded up and in handcuffs, watching Tufan hand me a brand-new British passport.

'What are you grinning at, Arthur?' Harper asked.

I was pouring myself the second drink he had prescribed. 'You told me to think of the two thousand dollars, Mr Harper,' I answered. 'I was just carrying out orders.'

'You're a screwball, Arthur,' he said amiably; but I saw a reflective look in his eyes and decided that I had better watch myself. All the same, I couldn't help wondering what he would have said and done if he had been warned, at that moment, that the customs people in Edirne had looked inside the doors of the car, and that every move he had made since had been made with the knowledge and by permission of the security police—if, in other words, he had been told how vulnerable he was. Not that I had the slightest desire to warn him; I hadn't forgotten the caning he had given me in Athens; but if it had been safe to do so, I would have liked to have told him that it was my lousy out-of-date Egyptian passport that had done the job. I would have liked to have seen the bastard's face. I still would.

Hamul shuffled out and made signs to Miss Lipp that lunch was served. She glanced at me. 'Bring your drink in with you, Arthur.'

Presumably I was being promoted to eating with the gentry so that they could keep an eye on me.

Miller was a gloomy feeder, and made the omelette less appetizing than it could have been by talking about infectious diseases all the time. How did they grow virus cultures in laboratories? Why, in eggs, of course! He discussed the possible consequences at length. The others took no notice; evidently they were used to him; but it got me down. I hadn't felt much like eating anyway.

When the fruit came Harper looked across at me. 'As soon as the Hamuls have cleared away,' he said, 'you had better start getting the bags down. They think we're going to Ankara for a couple of days, so it doesn't matter if they see us. The important thing is that we leave ourselves time to clean up the rooms.'

'Clean them up?'

'For fingerprints. With any luck we'll never be connected with this place. The rent was paid in advance and the owner couldn't care less if we don't show up again. The Hamuls will dust off most of it automatically. They're great polishers, I've noticed. But things they could miss, like window handles and closet mirrors, we should take care of ourselves—just in case.'

By two o'clock I had all the bags down and asked Harper if I could go to my old room to clean up there. He nodded. 'Okay, Arthur, but don't be too long. I want you to give Mr Fischer a hand.'

I hurried upstairs. In the bathroom, I completed the cigarette packet message. Then I went through the motions of 'cleaning up'–Tufan already had *my* fingerprints–and returned to Fischer's room.

At a quarter to three Harper drove the car from the garage to the courtyard and I loaded the bags. There wasn't room for all of them in the luggage compartment, so some had to go on the floor by the back seat.

At three, Harper, Miller and I went up to Miller's room. There, Miller and I took our shirts off and swathed ourselves in the tackle, Harper assisting and rearranging things until he was satisfied that nothing would show. I had the spring hooks of the sling hanging down inside my trouser-legs. It was dreadfully uncomfortable. Harper made me walk up and down so that he could see that all was in order.

'You look as if you've wet your pants,' he complained. 'Can't you walk more naturally?'

'The hooks keep hitting one another.'

'Well, wear one higher and one lower.'

After further adjustments, he was satisfied and we went downstairs to be inspected by Miss Lipp. She had to find fault with Miller–he had developed the same trouble with the blocks as I had with the hooks–and while they were putting it right I managed to transfer the cigarette packet from my hip to my shirt pocket, so that it would be easier to get at when the time came.

Fischer was getting edgy now. The bandages prevented his wearing a wrist-watch and he kept looking at Miller's. Miller suddenly got irritated.

'You cannot help, so do not get in the way,' he snapped.

'It is time we were leaving. After four-thirty, they count the people going in.'

'I'll tell you when it's time to leave,' Harper said. 'If you can't keep still, Hans, go sit in the car.'

Fischer sulked, while Miller returned to his bedroom for final adjustments. Harper turned to me.

'You're looking warm, Arthur. Better you don't drive with all that junk under your shirt. You'll only get warmer. Besides, Miss Lipp knows the way. You ride in the back.'

'Very well.' I had hoped that I might be able to drop the packet while I was making a hand signal; but I knew it was no use arguing with him.

At three-thirty we all went out and got into the car. Miller, of course, was first in the back. Harper motioned me to follow then Fischer got in after me and Harper shut the door. So I wasn't even next to a window.

Miss Lipp drove with Harper beside her.

From where I was sitting, the driving mirror did not reflect the road behind me. After a minute or two, and on the pretext of giving Fischer more room for the arm that was in the sling, I managed to make a half-turn and glance through the rear window. The Peugeot was following.

Miss Lipp drove steadily and very carefully, but there wasn't much traffic and we made good time. At ten to four we were past the Dolmabahçe Palace and following the tram-lines up towards Taxim Square. I had assumed that the garage Harper had spoken of would be the one near the Spanish

Consulate, which I had heard about from the surveillance man. It looked at that point as if the assumption were correct. Then, quite suddenly, everything seemed to go wrong.

Instead of turning right at Taxim Square, she went straight on across it and down the hill towards Galata. I was so surprised that I nearly lost my head and told her she was going the wrong way. Just in time, I remembered that I wasn't supposed to know the way. But Miller had noticed my involuntary movement.

'What is the matter?'

'That pedestrian back there—I thought he was going to walk straight across into us.' It is a remark that foreigners driving in Istanbul make every other minute.

He snorted 'They are peasants. They deny the existence of machinery.'

At that moment, Miss Lipp turned sharply left and we plunged down a ramp behind a service station.

It wasn't a large place underground. There was garage space for about twenty cars and a greasing bay with an inspection pit. Over the pit stood a Volkswagen Minibus van. In front of it stood a man in overalls with a filthy rag in his hand.

Miss Lipp pulled the Lincoln over to the left and stopped. Harper said: 'Here we are! Out!'

Miller and Harper had their doors open, and Harper opened Fischer's side as well. As I slid out after Miller, I got the cigarette packet from my shirt pocket into the palm of my hand.

Now Harper was climbing up into the driving seat of the van.

'Move yourselves,' he said, and pressed the starter.

The other door of the van was at the side. Miller wrenched it open and got in. As I followed, I pretended to stumble and then dropped the cigarette packet.

I saw it land on the greasy concrete and climbed on in. Then, the door swung to behind me and I heard Fischer swear as it caught him on the shoulder. I leaned back to hold it open for him, so I was looking down and saw it happen. As he put out his good hand to grasp the hand-rail and climb in, his left foot caught the cigarette packet and swept it under the van into the pit. It wasn't intentional. He wasn't even looking down.

Miller shut the door and latched it.

'Hold tight,' Harper said and let in the clutch.

As the van lurched forward, the back of my legs hit the edge of a packing case and I sat down on it. My face was right up against the small window at the back.

We went up to the top of the ramp again, waited a moment or two for a bus to go by, and then, made a left turn on down towards the Galata Bridge. Through the window, I could see the Peugeot parked opposite the garage.

It was still there when I lost sight of it. It hadn't moved. It was waiting, faithful unto death, for the Lincoln to come out.

Chapter Ten

For a minute or two I couldn't believe that it had happened, and kept looking back through the window expecting to see that the Peugeot was following after all. It wasn't. Fischer was swearing and massaging his left shoulder where the door had caught him. Miller was grinning to himself as if at some private joke. As we bounced over the tram-lines on to the Galata Bridge, I gave up looking back and stared at the floor. At my feet, amid some wood shavings, there were torn pieces of an Athens newspaper.

Of the six packing cases in the van, three were being used as seats. From the way the other three vibrated and slid about they appeared to be empty. From the way Miller and Fischer were having to hold on to steady themselves on the corners, it looked as if their cases were empty, too. Mine was more steady. It seemed likely that the case that I was sitting on now held the grenades, the pistols and the ammunition that had come from Athens inside the doors of the car. I wished the whole lot would blow up then and there. It didn't even occur to me, then, to wonder how they were going to be used. I had enough to think of with my own troubles.

As Harper drove past Aya Sophia and headed towards the gate in the old Seraglio wall, he began to talk over his shoulder to us.

'Leo goes first. Hans and Arthur together a hundred yards behind him. Arthur, you pay for Hans so that he doesn't have to fumble for money with those bandages on. Right?'

'Yes.'

He drove through into the Courtyard of the Janissaries and pulled up under the trees opposite St Irene.

'I'm not taking you any nearer to the entrance,' he said. 'There'll be guides hanging around and we don't want them identifying you with this van. On your way, Leo. See you tonight.'

Miller got out and walked towards the Ortakapi Gate. He had about a hundred and fifty yards to go.

When he had covered half the distance, Harper said: 'Okay, you two. Get ready. And, Arthur, you watch yourself. Leo and Hans both have guns and they'll use them if you start getting out of line in any way.'

'I will think of the two thousand dollars.'

'You do that. I'll be right behind you now, just to see that you make it inside.'

'We'll make it.'

I wanted to appear as co-operative as I could just then, because, although I was sick with panic, I had thought of a way of stopping them they couldn't blame on me—at least in a dangerous way. I still had my guide's licence.

Tufan had warned me against attracting attention to myself as a guide in case I was challenged and had to show it. He had said that, because I was a foreigner, that would cause trouble with museum guards. Well, trouble with museum guards was the one kind of trouble I needed at that moment; and the more the better.

Fischer and I began to walk towards the gate. Miller was within a few yards of it, and I saw a guide approach him. Miller walked straight on in without a glance at the man.

'That's the way,' Fischer said and began to walk a little faster.

The hooks began to thump against my legs. 'Not so fast,' I said; 'if these hooks swing too much they'll show.

He slowed down again immediately.

'You needn't worry about the guides,' I said, 'I've got my licence. I'll be your guide.'

As we got nearer the Gate, I began to give him the set speech, all about the weekly executions, the block, the fountain, the Executioner who was also the Chief Gardener.

The guide who had approached Miller was watching us, so I raised my voice slightly to make sure that he heard me and knew what I was up to. What I hoped was that he would follow us and complain about me to the guard at the gate. Instead, he lost interest and turned away.

It was disappointing, but I had another plan worked out by then.

Just inside the gate-house there is a counter where you pay to go in. When I got to it, I handed the man three separate lira and said: 'Two tickets, please.' At the same time I showed him my guide's licence.

From his point of view I had done three wrong things, I had shown a guide's licence, and yet, by asking for two tickets, revealed that I didn't know that guides were admitted free; I had given him three lira, which a real guide would have known was enough to buy six tickets; and I had spoken to him in English.

He was a haggard man with a small black moustache and a disagreeable expression. I waited for trouble. It never came. He did absolutely nothing but glance at the licence, push across one ticket, take one of the lira and give me sixty kurush change. It was maddening. I picked the change up very slowly, hoping he would start to think.

'Let's go,' Fischer said.

Out of the corner of my eye I could see Harper approaching the gate. There was nothing for it but to go on. Usually there are one or two guides touting for customers inside the Second Courtyard. In fact, it had been there that I had been challenged three years previously. *That* episode had ended up in my being jailed for the night. I could only count on the same thing happening again.

Of course, the same thing did *not* happen again. Because it was the last hour of the museum day, all the courtyard guides were either out with parties of suckers completing tours of the palace, or cooling their fat arses in the nearest café.

I did my best. As we walked on along the right side of the Second Courtyard, I gave Fischer the set speech on the Seraglio kitchens—all about the Sung, Yuan and Ming porcelains—but nobody as much as looked at us.

Miller had already reached the Gate of Felicity and was standing there gawking at it like a tourist. When he heard our footsteps behind him, he walked through into the Third Courtyard.

I hesitated. Once we were through the gate, the Audience Chamber and the Library of Ahmed the Third would screen us from the buildings across the courtyard that were open to the public. Unless a guard came out of the manuscript library, and there was no reason why one should, there would be nothing to stop us getting to the door to which Miller had the key.

'Why are you stopping?' Fischer asked.

'He said that we were to stop here.'

'Only if there were guides watching.'

There were footsteps on the paving stones behind us. I turned my head. It was Harper.

'Keep going, Arthur,' he said; 'just keep going.' His voice was quite low, but it had an edge to it.

He was only about six paces away now, and I knew suddenly from the look on his face that I dare not let him reach me.

So I went on with Fischer through the Gate of Felicity. I suppose that obedience to Harper had become almost as instinctive with me as breathing.

As he had said, the walk was exactly sixty paces. Nobody stopped us. Nobody noticed us. Miller already had the door open when Fischer and I got there. All I remember about the outside of the door was that it had wood mouldings on it arranged in an octagon pattern. Then, with Fischer behind me, I was standing in a narrow stone passage with a vaulted ceiling and Miller was re-locking the door.

The passage was about twenty feet long and ended in a blank wall with a coiled fire hose inside a glass-fronted box fastened to it. The spiral stairway to the roof was of iron and had the name of a German company on it. The same company had supplied the fire hose. Miller walked to the bottom of the staircase and looked up at it appreciatively. 'A very clever girl,' he said.

Fischer shrugged. 'For someone who interpreted air photos for the Luftwaffe it was not difficult,' he said. 'A blind man could have seen this on the enlarged photo she had. It was I who had to find the way to it, and I who had to get a key and make all the other arrangements.'

Miller chuckled. 'It was she who had the same idea, Hans, and Karl who worked out the arrangements. We are only the technicians. They are the artists.'

He seemed to be enjoying himself thoroughly, and looked more wolfish than ever. I felt like being sick.

Fischer sat on the stairs. Miller took off his coat and shirt and unwound the tackle from his skinny waist. There didn't seem any point in being uncomfortable as well as frightened, so I unbuttoned, too, and got rid of the sling and anchor rope. He attached them to the tackle. Then he took a black velvet bag from his pocket. It was about the size of a man's sock and had a draw string at the top and a spring clip. He attached the clip to one of the hooks on the sling.

'Now,' he said, 'we are ready.' He looked at his watch. 'In an hour or so Giulio and Enrico will be on their way.'

'Who are they?' I asked.

'Friends who will bring the boat for us,' said Miller.

'A boat? How can a boat reach us?'

'It doesn't,' said Fischer. 'We reach the boat. You know the yards along the shore by the old city wall, where the boats land the firewood?'

I did. Istanbul is a wood-burning city in winter. The firewood yards stretch for nearly a mile along the coast road south-east of Seraglio Point, where the water is deep enough for coasters to come close inshore. But we were two miles from there.

'Do we fly?'

'The Volkswagen will call for us.' He grinned at Miller.

'Hadn't you better tell me more than that?'

'That is not part of the operation,' Miller said. 'Our part is this. When we leave the Treasury we go quietly back over the kitchens until we come to the wall of the Courtyard of the Janissaries above the place where the cars park during the day. The wall is only twenty feet high and there are trees there to screen us when we lower ourselves to the ground with the tackle. Then . . .'

'Then,' Fischer broke in, 'we take a little walk to where the Volkswagen will be waiting.'

I answered Miller. 'Is Mr Fischer to lower himself to the ground with one hand?'

'He will seat himself in the sling. Only one hand is needed to hold on to the buckles.'

'Even in the outer courtyard we are still inside the walls.'

'There will be a way through them.' He dismissed the subject with an impatient wave of his hand and looked about him for a place to sit down. There was only the iron staircase. He examined the steps of it. 'Everything here is very dirty,' he complained. 'That these people do not all die of disease is incredible. Immunity, perhaps. There was a city here even before Constantine's. Two thousand years or more of plague are in this place—cholera, bubonic, *la vérole*, dysentery.'

'Not any more, Leo,' said Fischer; 'they have even cleaned the drains.

'It is all waiting in the dust,' Miller insisted gloomily.

He arranged the nylon rope so as to make a seat on the stairs before he sat down. His exuberance had gone. He had remembered about viruses and bacteria.

I sat on the bottom step wishing that I had an irrational anxiety like his to occupy my mind, instead of the real and immediate fear that occupied my lungs, my heart and my stomach.

At five o'clock, bells were sounded in the courtyards and there were one or two distant shouts. The guards were herding everyone out and closing up for the night.

I started to light a cigarette, but Miller stopped me. 'Not until it is dark,' he said. 'The sun might happen to illuminate the smoke before it dispersed above the roof. It is better also that we talk no more. It will become very quiet outside and we do not know how the acoustics of a place like this may work. No unnecessary risks.'

That was what Tufan had said. I wondered what he was doing. He must, I thought, already know that he had lost everyone and everything, except

Miss Lipp and the Lincoln. The Peugeot would have radioed in. The question was whether the surveillance people had remembered the Volkswagen van or not. If they had, there would be a faint possibility of Tufan's being able to trace it, using the police; but it seemed very faint. I wondered how many thousand Volkswagen vans there were in the Istanbul area. Of course, if they happened to notice the registration number–if this, if that. Fischer began to snore and Miller tapped his leg until he stopped.

The patch of sky at the top of the staircase turned red and then grey and then blue-black. I lit a cigarette and saw Miller's teeth gleaming yellowly in the light of the match.

'What about flashlights?' I whispered. 'We won't be able to see a thing.'

'There will be a third-quarter moon.'

At about eight there was a murmur of voices from one or other of the courtyards–in there it was impossible to tell which–a man laughed. Presumably, the night watchmen were taking over. Then there was silence again. A plane going over became an event, something to think about. Was it preparing to land at Yesilköy airport or had it just taken off?

Fischer produced a flask of water with a metal cup on the base, and we each had a drink. Another age went by. Then there was the faint sound of a train pulling out of the Sirkeci station and chugging round the sharp curve at Seraglio Point below. Its whistle sounded shrilly, like a French train, and then it began to gather speed. As the sound died away, a light glared almost blinding me. Miller had a pen-light in his hand and was looking at his watch. He sighed contentedly.

'We can go,' he whispered.

'The light a moment, Leo,' Fischer said.

Miller held the light up for him. With his good hand, Fischer eased a small snub-nosed automatic from his breast pocket, worked the safety-catch and then transferred the thing to a side pocket. He gave me a meaning look as he patted it.

Miller got up, so I stood up, too. He came down the steps with the tackle and looped it around one shoulder like a bandolier. 'I will go first,' he said. 'Arthur will follow me. Then you, Hans. Is there anything else? Ah yes, there is.'

He went and relieved himself in the corner by the fire hose. When he had finished Fischer did the same thing.

I was smoking. 'Put that out now,' Miller said. He looked at Fischer. 'Are you ready?'

Fischer nodded, then, an instant before the light went out, I saw him cross himself. That is something I don't understand. I mean, he was asking a blessing, or whatever it is, when he was going to commit a sin.

Miller went up the stairs slowly. At the top he paused, looking all round, getting his bearings. Then he bent his head down to mine.

'Karl said that you may have vertigo,' he said softly; 'but it is all quite simple. Follow me at three paces. Do not look sideways or back, only ahead. There is one step down from this ironwork. Then there is lead sheet. I will step down, go three paces and wait a little so that your eyes can adjust themselves.'

I had been so long in the darkness that the intermittent glare of the pen-light had been almost painful. Outside on the roof, the moonlight seemed to make everything as bright as day; too bright for my liking; I was certain that someone would see us from the ground and start shooting. Fischer must have had the same feeling. I heard him swear under his breath behind me.

Miller's teeth gleamed for an instant; then he started to move forwards past the three cupolas over the quarters of the White Eunuchs. There was a space of about five feet between the cupolas and the edge of the roof. Staying close to the cupolas and looking only ahead as Miller had instructed me. I had no sensation at all of being on a high place. For a while, my only problem was keeping up with him. Harper had compared him to a fly. To me he looked more like an earwig as he slithered round the last of the three cupolas and scuttled on, leaning inwards over the slight hump in the centre of the roof. He stopped only once. He had crossed the roof of the Audience Chamber, to avoid what looked like three large fanlights over the Gate of Felicity, and was returning to the Eunuchs' roof when another fanlight appeared and the flat surface narrowed slightly. The way across was only about two feet wide.

I saw the ground below and started to go down on my knees—I might just have been able to crawl across by myself, I suppose—when he reached back, gripped my forearm and drew me after him. It was done so quickly that I had no time to get sick and lose my balance. His fingers were like steel clamps.

Then we were level with the kitchens and I could see the conical bases of their ten squat chimneys stretching away to the right. Miller led the way to the left. The flat space here was over thirty feet wide and I had no trouble. There was a four-foot rise then, which brought us over the big room with the exhibition of miniatures and glass in it. Ahead, I could see the whole of one cupola and, beyond it, the top of another smaller one. The smaller one, I knew, was the one on the roof of the Treasury Museum.

Miller began to move more slowly and carefully as he skirted the big cupola. Every now and again he stopped. Then I saw him lower himself over a ledge. When his feet found whatever there was below, only his head and shoulders were showing.

I was following round the big cupola, and had started to move away from it towards the ledge, when Miller turned and beckoned to me. He had moved a yard or two towards the outer edge of the roof, so I changed direction towards him. That is how it was that when I came to the ledge I saw too much.

There was the vaulted roof of the Treasury, and the cupola with a flat space about four feet wide all around the base of it. That is where Miller was standing. But beyond him there was nothing, just a great black emptiness, and then, horribly far away below, the faint white hairline of a road in the moonlight.

I felt myself starting to lose my balance and fall, so I knelt down quickly and clung to the lead surface of the roof. Then I began retching. I couldn't help it; I've never been able to help it. From what I've heard from people who get sea-sick, that must be the same sort of feeling; only my feeling about heights is worse.

I had nothing in my stomach to throw up, but that didn't make any difference. My stomach went on trying to throw up.

Fischer began kicking me and hissing at me to be silent. Miller reached up and dragged me by the ankles down over the ledge, then made me sit with my back against the side of the cupola. He shoved my head hard between my knees. I heard a scuffling noise as he helped Fischer down off the ledge, then their whispering.

'Will he be all right?'

'He will have to be.'

'The fat fool.' Fischer kicked me as I started to retch again.

Miller stopped him. 'That will do no good. You will have to help. As long as he gets no nearer the edge it may be possible.'

I opened my eyes just enough to see Miller's feet. He was laying out the anchor rope round the cupola and presently he pulled one end of it down between my back and the part I was leaning against. A moment or two later, he crouched down in front of me and began knotting the rope. When that was done, he slipped on the upper block of the lifting tackle. Then he brought his head close to mine.

'Can you hear me, Arthur?'

'Yes.'

'If you didn't have to move, you'd feel safe here, wouldn't you?'

'I don't know.'

'You *are* safe now, aren't you?'

'Yes.'

'Then listen. You can handle the tackle from here. Open your eyes and look up at me.'

I managed to do so. He had taken his coat off and looked skinnier than ever. 'Hans will be at the edge,' he went on, 'and with his good hand will hold my coat in place there. In that way the ropes will run smoothly over it and not be cut. You understand?'

'Yes.'

'And you will not have to go near the edge—only let out rope and pull in when you are told.'

'I don't know. Supposing I let it slip?'

'Well, that would be bad, because then you would have only Hans to deal with, and he would certainly make sure that you slipped, too.'

The teeth, as he smiled, were like rows of gravestones. Suddenly, he picked up a coil of rope from the lead beside him and put it in my hands.

'Get ready to take the strain,' he said, 'and remember that it stretches. I don't mind how slowly I go down or how quickly I come up. Hans will give you the signals to lower, stop and raise.' He pointed to a ridge in the lead. 'Brace your feet against this. So.'

The day Mum died, the Imam came and intoned verses from the Koran: *'Now taste the torment of the fire you called a lie.'*

Miller slipped the end of the rope around my chest and knotted it firmly. Then he hauled in the slack. 'Are you ready, Arthur?'

I nodded.

'Then look at Hans.'

I let my eyes go to Fischer's legs and then his body. He was lying on his right side with his shoulder on Miller's coat and his right hand on the tackle ready to guide it. I dared not look any nearer the edge. I knew I would pass out if I did.

I saw Miller put a pair of gloves on, step into the sling, then crouch down and move out of sight.

'Now,' Fischer whispered.

The strain didn't come suddenly; the stretch in the nylon had to be taken up first. My hands were slippery with sweat and I had looped the rope round the sleeve of my left arm to give me more purchase. When the full strain came, the loop tightened like a tourniquet. Then the pressure fluctuated and I could feel Miller bouncing in the sling as the tackle settled down.

'Steady.' Fischer held his right hand palm downwards over the tackle.

The movement in the block by the anchor rope beside me ceased.

'Lower slowly.'

I let the rope slide round my arm and the bouncing began again.

'Keep going, smoothly.'

I went on paying out the rope. There was less bouncing now, just an occasional vibration. Miller was using his feet to steady himself against the wall as he descended. I watched the coil of rope beside me growing smaller and had another terror to fight. The end of the rope was tied round my chest. I couldn't untie it now without letting go. If there were not enough rope in the coil to reach the shutter below. Fischer would make me move nearer to the edge.

There were about six feet left to go when he raised his hand. 'Stop. Hold still.'

I was so relieved that I didn't notice the pain in my arm from the tightened loop; I just closed my eyes and kept my head down.

There were slight movements on the rope, and, after a moment or two, faint clicking sounds as he went to work on the metal shutters. Minutes went by. My left arm began to go numb. Then there was another sound from below, a sort of hollow tapping. It only lasted a moment, before Fischer hissed at me. I opened my eyes again.

'Lower a little, very slowly.'

As I obeyed I felt the tension in the rope suddenly slacken. Miller was inside.

'Rest.'

I loosened the rope on my arm and massaged it until the pins-and-needles began. I didn't try to massage them away. They kept my mind on my arm and away from other things, such as the day the games master had made me dive. When you got into the cadet corps you had to be able to swim, and, once a week, all the boys in each squad who couldn't do so were marched to the Lewisham Public Baths to take lessons. When you had learned to swim you had to dive. I didn't mind the swimming part, but when my head went under water I was always afraid of drowning. For a time I didn't have to, because I kept telling the games master that I had bad ears; but then he said that I would have to get a doctor's certificate. I tried to write one myself, but I didn't know the proper words to use and he caught me out. I expected him to send me with a note to The Bristle, but instead he made me dive. I say

'dive'. What he did was pick me up by one arm and a leg and throw me in the
deep end; and he kept on doing it. Every time I managed to get out, even
while I was still choking up water, he would throw me in again. One of the
attendants at the Baths had to stop him in the end. He was married, so I
wrote a letter to his wife telling her how he messed about with certain boys
in the changing cubicles and pestered them to feel him. I was careless,
though, because I used the same handwriting as I had used on the
certificate, and he knew for certain it was me. He couldn't prove it, of
course, because he had torn up the certificate. He took me into a lobby and
accused me and called me an 'unspeakable little cad'; but that was all he did.
He was really shaken. When I realized it, I could have kicked myself. If I
had known that he actually had been messing about with boys in the
cubicles, I could have put the police on to him. As it was, I had simply
warned him to be more careful. He had thin, curly brown hair with an
officer's moustache, and walked as if he had springs on the soles of his feet.
The term after that he left and went to another school.

Fischer hissed at me and I opened my eyes.

'Take the strain.'

I wrapped the rope round my waist this time so that I could use my
weight to push away from the edge if necessary.

'Ready?'

I nodded and held on tight. There was a jerk as Miller got his weight into
the sling again. Then Fischer nodded.

'Up.'

I started to pull. The friction of the rope against the coat on the edge of
the roof made it terribly hard. The sweat ran into my eyes. Twice I had to
stop and knot the rope round my waist so that I could wipe my hands and
ease the cramp in my fingers; but the coil got larger again and then Fischer
began to use his good hand on one of the ropes in the tackle.

'Slow . . . slower . . . stop.'

Suddenly, the tackle ran free and Miller, grinning, was crawling across
the roof towards me. He patted my leg.

'*Merci, mon cher collègue,*' he said.

I shut my eyes and nodded. Through the singing in my ears I could hear
him reporting to Fischer as he gathered in the tackle.

'All those we counted on and a few more to garnish the dish. I even
fastened the shutters again.'

I felt him untying the rope from my chest. When I opened my eyes he was
clipping the velvet bag to his belt. Fischer was fumbling with the knots in
the anchor rope. I crawled over and began to help him. All I wanted was to
get away, and I knew that they would have to help me.

Fischer with his injured hand needed help to get back on to the upper roof
level. Then Miller somehow managed to heave me up high enough for me to
claw my way over the ledge. I crawled then on my hands and knees to the
shelter of the big cupola. By the time Miller reached me, I was able to stand
up.

We started back, as we had started out, with Miller in the lead. This time,
however, there was no turn to make. We left the White Eunuchs' quarters
on our right and went on over the kitchen roofs to the wall by the Gate of

Salvation. There was one awkward place—for me, that is—by the old water tower, but I somehow got past it on my hands and knees. Then we were on the wall overlooking the Courtyard of the Janissaries.

There was a row of tall plane trees close to the wall, and Miller used an overhanging branch as an anchor for the tackle. He lowered Fischer first, in the sling, and then me; but he wouldn't use the sling himself, because that would have meant leaving the tackle in the tree. It was not the tackle itself he cared about, he said; he didn't want to leave any traces behind of how the job had been done. He got off the wall by looping the anchor rope over the branch and sliding down it. Doubled like that, it wasn't quite long enough to reach the ground, so he dropped the last six feet, pulling one end of the rope with him. He landed as lightly as a cat and began gathering in the rope. After all he had done, he wasn't even out of breath.

Fischer took over the lead now, and headed for the outer wall on a line parallel with the road the tourist cars used during the day. Miller walked behind me. After a minute or two, we could see the lights of the guard-room beside the huge Bab-i-Hümayun Gate and Fischer slowed down. We had been walking in the shadow of a row of trees, but now they came to an end. Fifty yards across the road to the right was the bulk of St Irene; ahead the road forked, the right prong going to the gate, the left prong narrowing and curving inwards down the hill towards the sea.

Fischer stopped, staring at the gate.

It was no more than fifty yards away and I could see the sentry. He had his carbine slung over his shoulder and was picking his nose.

Fischer put his mouth to my ear. 'What time is it?'

'Five to ten.'

'We have time to wait.'

'Wait for what?'

'We have to go left down the hill. The guard changes in five minutes. It will be safer then.'

'Where are we going to?'

'The railroad—where it bridges the wall.'

A section of the railway ran along the shore-line just inside the big wall for about three-quarters of a mile; but I knew that there were guard posts at both ends of it. I said so.

He grinned. 'Guard posts, yes. But no gates.'

Miller hissed a warning.

An oblong of light glowed as the door of the guard-room opened. For an instant two men were outlined in the doorway. Then, as the business of changing sentries began, Fischer touched my arm.

'Now.'

He moved forward out of the shadow of the trees and cut across a patch of rough grass to the road. It descended sharply and narrowed to little more than a track. Within thirty seconds the top of the slope hid us from the sentries. Fischer glanced back to see that we were with him, and then walked on at a more leisurely pace.

Ahead was a strip of sea and beyond it the lights of Selimiye and Haydarpasar on the Asian side. Other lights moved across the water—a ferry and small fishing-boats. In the daylight, tourists with ciné-cameras waste hundreds of feet of film on the view. I suppose it's very beautiful. Personally, I never want to see it again—in any sort of light.

After a couple of minutes' walking we came to another track, which led off to the right towards the outer wall. Fischer crossed it and went straight on down over a stretch of waste land. There were piles of rubble from archaeological diggings, and part was terraced as if it had at some time been cultivated as a vineyard. At the bottom was the railway embankment.

There was a wooden fence running alongside it, and Miller and I waited while Fischer found the damaged section which he had chosen on an earlier reconnaissance as the best way through. It was about thirty yards to the right. We clambered over some broken boards to the side of the embankment and walked along the drainage ditch. Five minutes later it was possible to see the big wall again. We walked on another hundred feet, and there the embankment ended. If we were to go any farther we had to climb up and walk along the track over the bridge.

Fischer stopped and turned. 'What is the time?'

'Ten-fifteen,' said Miller. 'Where is the guard post exactly?'

'On the other side of the bridge, a hundred metres from here.' He turned to me. 'Now listen. A train will be coming soon. When it starts to cross the bridge we go to the top of the embankment. As soon as the last wagon has passed us we start to follow along the tracks at walking speed. When we have gone about twenty metres we will hear a loud explosion ahead. Then we start to run, but not too fast. Have you ever smelt tear-gas?'

'Yes.'

'You will smell it again, but do not worry. It is our tear-gas, not theirs. And there will be smoke, too, also ours. The train will have just gone through. The guard post will not know what is happening. They may think the train has blown up. It does not matter. The tear-gas and the smoke will make it hard for them to think, or see. If any of them tries too hard he will get a bullet or a plastic grenade to discourage him. In the confusion we run through. And then, as I told you, the Volkswagen will be waiting for us.'

'What about our confusion?' I said. 'How do we see where to go with tear-gas and smoke?'

Miller nodded. 'I asked the same question, my friend. We should have had respirators. But Karl's argument was good. With so much to conceal, how could we carry respirators, too?'

'I made the experiment,' Fischer said defensively. 'I tried to take a respirator in. They stopped me because of the bulge in my pocket. They thought I was trying to smuggle a camera into the Seraglio. They are strict about that, as you know. It was embarrassing.'

'How did you explain it?' Miller asked.

'I said I was a doctor.'

'They believed you?'

'If you say you are a doctor, people will believe anything. We need not worry where to go. We simply follow the rail tracks and leave everything to Karl. We have done our work for this evening. Now we only wait for our train.'

We waited twenty-five minutes.

It was a mixed train, Fischer said, carrying newspapers, mail-bags, local freight, and a few passengers, to the small towns between Istanbul and Pehlivanköy. It chuffed towards the bridge as noisily and importantly as the Orient Express. There was a slight off-shore breeze blowing. The thick black smoke from the engine rolled along our side of the embankment and engulfed us.

'*Los! Vorwärts!*' Fischer shouted, and coughing and spluttering, Miller and I scrambled after him up the embankment.

For half a minute we stayed there with the train wheels clacking over a join in the rails about three feet from our noses. Then the last axle-box went by.

'*Los!*' said Fischer again, and we were stumbling along the side of the tracks between the jutting ends of the sleepers and the parapet of the bridge.

We must have been about seventy yards from the guard post when the concussion grenade went off, and even at that distance the detonation made my ears sing. In front of me Fischer began to trot. Almost immediately he tripped over something and fell. I heard him gasp with pain as his left arm hit a sleeper; but he was on his feet and moving again before I got to him.

There was shouting ahead now, and I could hear the plunking, sizzling noise of tear-gas and smoke grenades detonating. The train smoke was still billowing around, but a moment later I got the first whiff of chemical smoke. Three yards more and I saw the white bandage on Fischer's right hand go to his forehead. Then I was in the tear-gas, too, and the first excruciating reaction of the sinuses began to spread into my eyes. I blundered on, choking. As the tears began to blind me, another concussion grenade went off. Then a shape loomed up out of the smoke and a respirator goggled at me; a hand gripped my arm and steered me to the right. I had vague, tear-blurred impression of a lighted room and a man in uniform with his hands above his drooping head leaning against a wall. Then the arm belonging to the hand was supporting me as I stumbled down a long flight of steps.

I was out of the smoke now and I could just see the door of the Volkswagen van. The arm shoved me towards it. I almost fell inside. Fischer was already there, hawking and coughing. More grenades were exploding on the bridge above as Miller scrambled in after me. Then there was a sound of running feet and the men in the respirators piled in. Someone pressed the starter. A moment later the van was on the move. I was crouched on the floor against one of the empty packing cases and somebody was treading on my feet. The stink of tear-gas was everywhere. I heard Harper's voice from the front passsenger seat.

'Everything okay, Leo?'

Miller was coughing and chuckling at the same time. 'The dogs have fed and clothed themselves,' he wheezed.

Chapter Eleven

There were five men besides Harper in the respirators, but my eyes were still so painful that I didn't see any of their faces well enough to be able to identify them. One of them was named Franz and he spoke German as well as Turkish. I know, because I heard him use both languages–the German to Fischer. The other four only spoke Turkish, I think. I can't be certain because I was only with them a few minutes, and I was coughing most of the time.

The van must have gone about three miles when it slowed down, made a wide U-turn and stopped.

Harper opened the door from the outside.

Miller was nearest the door and he got out first. I followed, with Fischer behind me. The other men just moved enough to make way for us. Then Harper shut the door again and the van was driven off.

'This way,' Harper said.

We were opposite one of the big wood yards by an unloading pier and some beached caïques. He led the way along the pier. I was beginning to see well enough again now to recognize Giulio standing up in the *Bulut*'s outboard dinghy. We climbed down into it. I heard Giulio ask who I was and be told that he would find out later. Then the motor started, and we shot away from the pier.

The *Bulut* was anchored a quarter of a mile away, and a man on deck, Enrico presumably, was at the small gangway waiting to help us on board. I followed the others to the saloon.

By the time I reached the bottom of the narrow companionway that led down to it, Harper was already untying the drawstring of Miller's velvet bag, while the others crowded round to look. I saw the glitter of dozens of green and red stones and I heard Giulio draw in his breath. The stones didn't look all that large to me; but of course, I am no judge of such things.

Harper was grinning his head off. 'Nothing but the best, Leo,' he said. 'You're a great man.'

'How much?' said Fischer.

'Better than ten million that's for sure,' Harper replied. 'Let's be on our way as soon as we can, Giulio.'

'*Pronto.*'

Giulio brushed past me and went up the companionway. There were sandwiches and drinks set out at the other end of the table. While they drooled over the stones, I poured myself a large whisky.

Harper looked across at me. 'Aren't you interested in the loot, Arthur?'

I had a sudden desire to hit him. I shrugged indifferently. 'I'm not interested in counting chickens,' I said. 'I'll settle for two thousand dollars, cash on the barrel.'

They all stared at me in silence for a moment. The deck began to vibrate as the boat's diesels started up.

Harper glanced at Miller. 'I take it Arthur behaved himself this evening.'

'He was a damned nuisance,' Fischer said spitefully.

Harper ignored him. 'Well, Leo?'

'He was afraid,' Miller answered; 'but what he did was enough. Under the circumstances I think he did well.'

Harper looked at me again. 'Why the cracks, Arthur? What's the problem?'

'How do you imagine you're going to get away with it?'

'Oh, I see.' He relaxed again, all smiles. 'So our Arthur's worried that the bloodhounds are going to start snapping at his butt, is he? Well, forget it. They won't. All they know so far is that a bunch of armed men in a Volkswagen van roughed up one of their guard posts. So the first thing they'll do is set up blocks on all the roads leading out of the city and look for the van. They'll find it, abandoned, over in Galata. Then they'll start the usual routine–Who's the owner? Where is he? What did he look like?–and get no place. By then, though, they'll have done some thinking, too, and some big brain will be starting to wonder why it had to be that particular post and why nobody got killed–why a lot of things. He may even think of checking out the Treasury Museum and so come up with the right answer. When he does, they'll double up on the road-blocks and throw out the dragnet. Only we won't be inside it. We'll be going ashore at a little place sixty miles from here and two hours' easy driving from Edirne and the frontier.' He patted my arm. 'And where we go ashore, Arthur, Miss Lipp will be waiting to pick us up.'

'With the Lincoln?'

'What else? We wouldn't want to walk, would we, or leave without our bags?'

I had to laugh. I couldn't help it. And it didn't matter, because Harper thought that it was the beauty of his plan that I found so amusing, and not the bloody great hole in it. I thought of the customs inspector's face when the Lincoln drove up for clearance–if Tufan allowed it to get that far–and when he saw me again. I laughed so much that Fischer began to laugh, too. It was the best moment I had had in days. I ate some sandwiches and had another drink. There was garlic sausage in the sandwiches, but I didn't even have a twinge of indigestion. I thought my worries were over.

The place we were to go ashore was a port called Serefli, a few miles south of Corlu. Harper said that it would take five hours to get there. I cleaned off the filth I had collected from the Seraglio roof as best I could and went to sleep in the saloon. The others used the cabins. Giulio and Enrico ran the boat between them. I found out later that they had sent the boat's regular crew ashore at Pendik for an evening on the town, and then slipped out of the harbour after dark. The patrol boat that was supposed to be keeping an eye on the *Bulut* missed it completely.

It was getting light when voices in the saloon woke me. Harper and Miller were drinking coffee, and Fischer was trying to make his dirty bandages look more presentable by brushing them. He seemed to be having some sort of discussion with Harper. As it was in German I couldn't understand. Then Harper looked at me and saw that I was awake.

'Arthur can use a screwdriver,' he said, 'if you just show him what to do.'

'Which door?' Fischer asked.

'Does it matter? How about the right rear?'

'We were talking about a safe place for the loot,' Harper said to me. 'Inside one of the car doors seems a good place for the customs people to forget about.'

'Arthur would not know about such things,' Miller said waggishly.

They had a good laugh over that gem of wit, while I tried to look mystified. Luckily, Enrico came in just then and said that we would be entering port in ten minutes.

I had some of the coffee and a stale sandwich. Harper went up to the wheel-house. Half an hour later, the sun was up and we were moored alongside a stone jetty.

Fishermen are early risers and the harbour was already busy. Cuttlefish boats were unloading the night's catch at the quayside. Caïques with single-cylinder engines were chugging out to sea. A port official came aboard to collect dues. After a while, Harper came down and said that he was going ashore to make sure that Miss Lipp was there. He left the velvet bag with Fischer.

He returned fifteen minutes later and reported that the Lincoln was parked in a side street beside a café-restaurant on the main square. Miss Lipp was in the restaurant eating breakfast. The side street was a quiet one. Fischer and I could get busy on the door. We would be allowed half an hour to complete the job.

Fischer borrowed a screwdriver from Enrico and we went ashore. Nobody seemed to take any notice of us, probably because we looked so scruffy. I couldn't see the Opel or the Peugeot anywhere about, but that didn't worry me. I knew that one or other of them would be on tap. We found the car without difficulty and I started on the door. It was an ordinary screwdriver I had to work with, but the earlier removals of the panel had eased the screws and I didn't do any more damage to the leather. It took me ten minutes to take the panel off, five seconds for Fischer to wedge the velvet bag in clear of the window mechanism, and fifteen minutes for me to replace the panel. Then Fischer and I got into the back seat. Two minutes later, Miss Lipp came out of the restaurant and got behind the wheel. If she had slept the previous night it could only have been at the inn in Corlu; but she looked as fresh as she always did.

'Good morning, Hans. Good morning, Arthur. The others are just coming across the square now,' she said.

They arrived a moment after. Harper got in the front seat with her, Miller sat on my left. She said good morning to Miller, and drove off the moment she heard the door close.

From Serefli to Corlu, where we would join the main Istanbul-Edirne road, there are twelve miles of narrow secondary road. The first mile or so is winding, and I waited until we got to a straighter part before I risked a look back.

The Peugeot was there, and I caught a glimpse of another car behind it. The Opel was on the job as well.

Harper had started telling Miss Lipp about the night's work and the size of the haul. Miller was putting in his word, too. There was a lot of mutual congratulation. It was like being in the winning team's bus. I wasn't needed in the conversation, and didn't have to listen to it either. I could think.

There were several possible explanations for the two cars being there. Miss Lipp had probably driven straight to Corlu from the garage, after dropping us the previous afternoon. By the time she had left the Istanbul area, Tufan must have been told that the men were no longer in the car, and realized that his only hope of re-establishing contact lay in keeping track of the Lincoln. The Opel could have been sent to make sure that there were no further mistakes. Or it may have been to compensate for lack of radio communication outside the Istanbul area. The two cars could talk to one another; if an urgent report became necessary, one car could stop and reach Istanbul by telephone while the other continued the surveillance. Then a third possibility occurred to me. Tufan must have been told about the attack on the guard post. As soon as he heard the details—smoke, tear-gas, concussion grenades, six men in respirators—he would know that the attack and the Lincoln were related. If he also knew that the *Bulut* had left Pendik and that the Lincoln had stopped at Corlu, he might have decided that reinforcements were necessary in that area.

The only certainty, I decided sourly, was that Tufan would not be the 'big brain' who would think of checking the Treasury Museum. He would still be off on his political wild goose chase. Well, he would have some surprises coming.

At that moment Miss Lipp said sharply: 'Karl!'

Miller had been in the middle of saying something and he broke off abruptly.

'What is it?' Harper said.

'That brown car behind us. It was behind me yesterday when I drove out from Istanbul. I thought then that I'd noticed it before, earlier in the day. In fact, I was so sure that when I stopped at Corlu I waited to get a look at it. When it didn't show up I figured it had turned off somewhere and thought no more about it.'

'Don't look around, anyone,' Harper said. He swivelled the driving mirror so that he could look behind. After a moment, he said: 'Try slowing down.'

She did so. I knew what would happen. The Peugeot would keep its distance. After about a minute, Harper twisted the mirror back into position. 'Do you think you could lose it?' he said.

'Not on these roads.'

'Okay. Just keep going. Doesn't look like a police car. I wonder . . .'

'Franz!' Fischer said suddenly.

'All set for a little hi-jacking operation, you mean?'

'Why not?'

'He could have done that better last night when he had us in the van,' said Miller.

'I'm not so sure,' said Harper. 'He might have figured that it would be safer to wait until we were all outside the city.'

'But Franz didn't know this end of the plan,' Miss Lipp objected.

'If he put a tail on you,' Fischer said, 'he could have guessed.'

'Well, we'll soon find out,' Harper said grimly. 'There are only two of them in that car. If it's Franz we're dealing with, that probably means that he's set up an ambush somewhere ahead with his other two mugs. That makes five. We only have three guns, so we'd better take care of this lot first. We'll pick a spot with some trees and then pull off the road. Okay?'

'May I look round at this car?' I asked.

'Why?'

'To see if I recognize it.'

I knew that I had to do something. If they started shooting at Turkish agents, Turkish security agents were going to start shooting back—and they weren't going to stop to ask questions or worry about who got hit.

'Okay,' he said; 'but make it casual.'

I looked back.

'Well?' he asked.

'I don't recognize the brown one,' I said; 'but there's another one behind it, a grey Opel.'

'That's right,' Miss Lipp said; 'it's been there some time. But so what? The road's too narrow for passing.'

'I'm almost sure it was outside that garage yesterday afternoon.' I tried to sound like a really worried man. It wasn't very difficult.

'There are many grey Opels,' Miller said.

'But not with such a very long radio aerial. That is why I noticed it.'

Harper had swivelled the mirror again and was peering into it. 'You'd better look, too, Leo,' he said grimly. 'See the antenna?'

Miller looked and swore. 'It could be a coincidence,' he said.

'Could be. Do you want to take a chance on it?'

'No,' said Fischer.

'I agree,' said Miller; 'but what do we do about them?'

Harper thought for a moment. Then he asked: 'How much farther to Corlu?'

'About three kilometres,' Miss Lipp answered.

'Then he must have it set up somewhere between Corlu and Edirne.'

'So?'

'So, instead of turning left at Corlu and going to Edirne, we change our plans and turn right.'

'But that would take us back to Istanbul,' Miller objected.

'Not all the way,' Harper said; 'only as far as the airport and the first plane out.'

'Leaving the car behind?' asked Miss Lipp.

'Don't worry, sweetie. We'll all be able to buy fleets of Lincolns when we cash in this pile of chips.'

Suddenly, they were all smiles again.

I tried to think. It was barely seven-thirty and the run from Corlu to the Istanbul Airport at Yesilköy would take little more than an hour. It was Wednesday, which meant that the Treasury Museum would normally stay closed until the following day. Unless the big brain had already started working, or unless Tufan had decided to stop uncovering non-existent terrorist plots and let the police know what was going on, there was every chance that, within a couple of hours, Harper and the rest would be out of the country. In that case, if anyone were going to stop them it would have to be me. The question was–did I *want* to stop them? Why didn't I just go along with them and collect my two thousand dollars?

I was still tired and confused or I would have remembered that there could be only one answer to that–my passport was not valid and an airline would not carry me. But instead of the answer, another stupid question came into my mind; and, stupidly, I asked it.

'Am I included in this?'

Harper turned round in his seat to face me, and gave me the cold, unpleasant smile I liked least.

'Included, Arthur? Why? Did you have something else in mind–like making a quick deal with Franz, for instance, or even the police?'

'Of course not. I just wanted to be certain.'

'Well that makes five of us who want to be certain. Don't you worry, Arthur. Until we're on that plane with the loot all safe and sound, you're not even going to the can by yourself. That's how much you're included.'

Fischer and Miller thought that hilariously amusing. Miss Lipp, I noticed, was keeping her attention divided between the road ahead and the cars behind.

We came to Corlu and turned right on to the main Istanbul road. Harper began to organize the change of plan.

'The first thing is to get the stuff out of the doors. Hans, you'd better change places with Arthur. He can get busy now.'

'He can't Fischer said. 'There are seven screws on the rear doors. With the door shut he cannot get at them. The door has to be open.'

'All the way open?'

'Nearly.'

Harper looked at the heavy doors. They were hinged at the rear, and would swing open against the wind. We were doing over sixty. It was obviously out of the question to take the panel off while we were on the move. He nodded. 'All right. Here's what we'll do. As soon as we get to the airport, Elizabeth and Leo will take all the passports and get busy buying tickets and filling out passport cards and customs forms for all of us. Right?'

They nodded.

'Then I follow them inside just to check on the flight number and boarding time so that we all know what the score is. As soon as I have that, I return the car and Arthur drives us to the parking lot. There, we open the door and get the stuff. When it's out, Hans gets porters and we unload the baggage. We leave the car on the park. Any questions?'

'You could unload the baggage first,' said Miller, 'while the car is in front.'

'Maybe. If we have plenty of time. If we don't have too much, I'd sooner make sure of the loot first.'

'We must have some baggage for the customs,' Miss Lipp put in. 'People without baggage get a personal search.'

'All right. We'll unload just the stuff from inside the car and leave the rest until later.'

There was a murmur of agreement. Miller asked: 'If there are two flights available within a short time, which do we take?'

'If one of them flies over a lot of Turkish territory–say to Aleppo or Beirut–we take the other. Otherwise, we take the first.'

They went on discussing which city they would prefer as a destination. I was wondering what would happen if I told them about my passport. From Harper, I decided, there would be only one reaction; if they could not take me with them, yet dared not leave me because I knew too much, I would have to be eliminated from the picture altogether. There would be a corpse on the floor of the car they left behind them. On the other hand, if I waited until the passport was challenged at the airport, there wasn't much they could do. I could yell my head off, demand to see a security official and tell him to contact Tufan. True, the three men had guns; but even if they managed to shoot their way out of the place, I would stand a better chance of coming out of it alive.

'Any more problems?' Harper asked, 'No? Okay, then, let's have the passports.'

I nearly threw up, but managed to cough instead.

Fischer asked me to get his out of his inside pocket for him. Miller passed his over and Harper flipped through the pages. I gave him Fischer's.

Miss Lipp said: 'My bag is on the floor, if you want to put them in it now.'

'Okay. Where's yours, Arthur?' *Has any boy not handed in his homework?*

I handed the wretched thing to him and waited.

He lingered over my vital statistics. 'Know something Arthur? I'd have said you were a good three years older. Too much *ouzo* and not enough exercise, that's your trouble.' And then, of course, his tone changed. 'Wait a minute! This is over two months out-of-date!'

'Out-of-date? But it can't be!' *I know I handed in my homework with the rest, sir.*

'Look at it!' He leaned over and jammed it under my nose.

'But I had no trouble coming in. You see, there's the visa!'

'What difference does that make, you stupid slob? It's out-of-date!' He glowered at me and then, unexpectedly, turned to Miss Lipp. 'What do you think?'

She kept her eyes on the road as she answered. 'When you leave here the immigration people are mostly interested in seeing that the exit cards are properly filled in. He'll get by there. It's the airline counter check that matters. They are responsible at the port of disembarkation if papers are not in order. We'll have to write in a renewal.'

'Without a consular stamp?'

She thought for a moment. 'There's a Swiss postage stamp in my purse, we could use that. Ten to one they won't look at it closely if there is writing across it. Anyway, I'll keep them talking.'

'What about where we land?' asked Miller. 'Supposing they catch it there?'

'That's *his* worry,' Harper said.

'Not if they send him back here.'

'They wouldn't trouble to do that. It's not that serious. The airport police would hold him until the airline could get the Egyptian Consul to come out and fix the renewal.'

'He has been nothing but a nuisance from the beginning.' This was Fischer, of course.

'He was useful enough last night,' remarked Miss Lipp. 'By the way, that renewal had better be in his handwriting. Would it be in Arabic?'

'French and Arabic, both.' Harper stuck the stamp on the renewal space. 'Okay, Arthur. Here you are. Write across the centre of the stamp. *"Bon jusqu'au,"* let's see—make it April ten of next year. Then do it in Arabic. You can, I suppose?'

I did as I was told—as ever—and handed the passport back to him.

I didn't know *where* I stood now. If the plane went to Athens I might be able to get away with it; I still had my Greek *permis de séjour* to fall back on. But if I went to Vienna, or Frankfurt, or Rome, or (hideous thought) Cairo, then I'd be completely up the creek. I would have to wait until I knew whether they were going to Athens or not before I decided whether I would go along or try to stay. If I wanted to stay, though, it would be more difficult now. With Harper and Fischer keeping their eyes on me, and no official to single me out because of my invalid passport, yelling for help wouldn't do much good. A quick clip of the jaw from Harper and some fast talking—'So sorry. Our friend tripped and hit his head on a suitcase. He'll be all right in a moment. We'll take care of him.'—would be the end of *that*. I would have to rely upon the surveillance cars. The only trouble was that before they regained direct contact with Tufan we would be at the airport. I would have to give the men in the cars time to draw the right conclusions and issue the necessary orders.

I could only think of one way of causing a delay. When I had finished putting back the door panel, I had slipped the screwdriver into my pocket. There wasn't another one in the car, I knew.

While we were going through Mimarsinan, fifteen minutes or so away from the airport, I managed to ease the screwdriver from my pocket and let it slide back on the seat until I was sitting on it. A minute or two later, I pretended to stretch my legs and stuffed it deep down behind the seat cushion and below the back of the seat. If I wanted to go, I could 'find' it; if I wanted to delay I could look for it in vain on the floor. That way, I thought, I would at least have some sort of control over the situation.

And then Miss Lipp began to worry again about the Peugeot and the Opel.

'They're still tailing us,' she said. 'I don't get it. Franz must have guessed where we're heading for by now. What does he think he's going to do?'

'Supposing it isn't Franz?' Miller said suddenly.

'If it isn't Franz, who is it?' Fischer demanded irritably. 'They can't be police or they would have stopped us. Could it be Giulio?'

'That is an imbecile suggestion,' Miller retorted. 'Giulio is of our company. You are not. If you were, you would not say such a stupid thing.'

I have a unique capacity for self-destruction. I said, helpfully: 'Perhaps it is Franz. Perhaps he thinks that we are going back to the villa. If we were, we would still be on this road.'

Harper looked back. 'When will he know better, Arthur?'

'Not until we turn right for the airport.'

'How far is the turn-off?'

'About six miles.'

'How far then?'

'A mile and a half.'

He looked at Miss Lipp. 'Do you think you could lose them so that they wouldn't see us make the turn?'

'I could try.'

The Lincoln surged forward. Seconds later I saw the red speedometer needle swing past the ninety mark.

Harper looked back. After a minute, he said: 'Leaving them cold.'

'We're going too fast for this road,' was all she said. It didn't seem to be worrying her unduly, though. She passed two cars and a truck going in the same direction as if they were standing still.

I already knew that I had made a bad mistake, and did my best to retrieve it. 'There's a bridge a mile or so ahead,' I warned her. 'The road narrows. You'll have to slow down for that.'

She didn't answer. I was beginning to sweat. If the surveillance cars lost us, that was really the end as far as I was concerned.

She beat a convoy of army trucks to the bridge by fifty yards. On the other side, the road wound a little and she had to slow down to seventy; but when I looked back there wasn't a car in sight. As she braked hard and turned right on to the airport road, Harper chuckled.

'For that extra ounce of get-up-and-go,' he announced facetiously, 'there is nothing, but *nothing*, like a Lincoln Continental.'

There's nothing like feeling a complete bloody half-wit either. When we drove up outside the airport building, my legs were quivering like Geven's lower lip.

Miller was out of the car and into the building almost before the car had stopped. Miss Lipp and Harper followed while Fischer and I handed the bags inside the car, mine included, to a porter.

I couldn't help looking back along the airport approach road and Fischer noticed. He smiled at my lily-livered anxiety.

'Don't be afraid. They are on their way to Sariyer by now.'

'Yes.' I knew that at least one of them would be; but I also knew that the men in the cars were not incompetent. When they failed to pick up the Lincoln again, the second car would turn back and try the airport road. How long would it take them to get the idea, though? Five minutes? Ten?

Harper came out of the building and hurried to the car.

'There's an Air France jet to Rome,' he said. 'Seats available. Boarding in twenty minutes. Let's get moving.'

I drove to the car-park, a chain-fenced area just off the loop of road in front of the building and beyond the taxi rank. There were only a few cars already there and, on Harper's instructions, I backed into an empty space between two of them.

'Where is the screwdriver?' Fischer asked.

'On the floor.' I was still backing the car and could see that he was already searching for it.

'It must have rolled under one of the seats,' Harper said impatiently. 'Okay, Arthur, that'll do. Let's get the doors open so we can see.'

I pulled up, got out and immediately began trying to peer under the seats. With a Lincoln there is not much to see. The seats are snug against the floor.

'Oh, for God's sake!' Harper said angrily. Suddenly, he grabbed at my jacket. 'You must have put it in your pocket.' He started slapping them to find out.

'I put it on the floor.'

'Well, it isn't there now,' Fischer said.

Harper glanced at his watch. 'It must have been pulled out with the baggage.'

'Shall I go back and look?'

'No, get one out of the tool-kit.'

'There isn't one there,' Fischer said. 'I noticed that before.'

'Okay, see if it's on the ground back there.' As Fischer hurried off, Harper looked at the next car to us, a Renault, and tried the front doors. They were locked, of course. Then he tried the front luggage compartment. To my horror, it opened. The next moment he had a tool-roll in his hand and was taking a screwdriver from it.

He grinned. 'If the owner comes back, we'll buy it off him as a souvenir,' he said, and quickly went to work on the door panel of the Lincoln.

I was utterly desperate or I could never have done what I did; but as I stood there gaping at him I became aware of the sound of an engine running. I hadn't finished backing the car into line with the others when he made me stop. Then I had simply forgotten to switch off.

The door to the driving seat was open and so were both back doors. He was crouched over the panel of the right-hand one on the opposite side of the car from me.

I glanced at the car-park entrance to make sure that Fischer wasn't coming back, and then I moved. I went to the door by the driver's seat, leaned across it as if I were going to switch off the engine and looked across the back of the seat.

Harper was bending down to undo one of the screws by the hinge.

I slid in to the driving seat gently so as not to rock the car, and eased the transmission lever from 'Park' to 'Drive'. The car gave a slight jerk. At the same moment I stamped on the accelerator.

I heard a thump as the door sent him flying, then I spun the wheel and was heading for the car-park entrance.

About twenty feet from it, I jammed on the brakes and the two rear doors swung shut with a slam. Through the rear window I could see Harper scrambling to his feet. As I closed the door beside me I accelerated again and went through on to the road. A moment later I was half way round the loop. Another car ahead slowed me for a moment. In the driving mirror I saw Harper running towards the taxi rank. I leaned on the horn ring and the car in front swerved. Then I was out of the loop and on the approach road.

I had gone about a mile when the Opel passed me, going in the opposite direction. I waved frantically, but kept on going. I didn't care whether they thought I'd gone mad or not. All I wanted was to get away from Harper.

I went on driving fast towards Istanbul until I saw in the mirror that the Opel was behind me. Only then did I stop.

It wasn't my fault that they took all that time to catch up with me.

Chapter Twelve

'The Director is not pleased with you,' Tufan informed me.

It was on the tip of my tongue to tell him what the Director could go and do to himself; but I managed to keep my temper. 'You got the stuff back,' I reminded him sharply; 'you have the names and descriptions of the people who took it. You know what was done and how it was done. What more do you want?'

'The woman and the three men,' he snapped.

The nerve of it! 'It wasn't I who let them get on that plane to Rome,' I said.

'It was your stupidity that did. If you hadn't panicked, if you had stopped immediately you saw the Opel instead of driving off like a madman, they would be in prison now. As it was, they got a close enough look at my men to realize their mistake. We had had no information from you. By the time we were able to re-establish contact with you, naturally they had gone.'

'They can be arrested in Rome. You can extradite them.'

'Not without a case strong enough to justify extradition proceedings.'

'You have it. I've told you what happened.'

'And what do you think your evidence would be worth in an Italian court?' he demanded. 'You smuggled the explosives in. Who is there to confirm your story of the subsequent robbery? They would have your record from Interpol to discredit you. Is the court to extradite four persons on your unsupported word that you have told the truth? They would laugh at us!'

'What about Giulio and Enrico?'

'Very sensibly, for them, they are saying nothing useful. They chartered a yacht. They decided to go for a night cruise. They were hailed by some men in a caïque who said that their motor had broken down. They took them to Serefli and put them ashore. Is that a crime? Tomorrow the police will have to let them go. There is nothing we can do. Your mistake, Simpson, was in not carrying out orders.'

'What orders, for God's sake?'

'The orders I gave you in this very room. You were told to report. You failed to do so. It was unfortunate that the packet you dropped in the garage was overlooked, but you had other opportunities. You could have reported at Serefli. You could have dropped your guide's licence at the guard post as you were taken through. There was want of imagination. We have no choice but to abandon the inquiry.'

'Including the inquiry about the attack on the guard post?'

He looked more po-faced than ever. 'That has already been officially described to the newspapers as an unsuccessful attempt by dissident elements to blow up a train.'

There was no polite comment I could make on that one, so I just shrugged and looked over his head at the picture of Abdul Hamid being deposed.

He stood up, as if to end the discussion, and smoothed down the front of his tunic. 'Luckily for you,' he said, 'the Director is not entirely dissatisfied with the affair. The Bureau has recovered the proceeds of a serious robbery which the Criminal Police did not even know about. It shows that *we* are not at the mercy of events, but in charge of them, that we anticipate. You were not entirely useless to us. As a result the Director has authorized the payment to you of a bonus.'

'So I should think. How much?'

'Five thousand lira, together with permission to sell them for foreign exchange, dollars or pounds sterling, at the official rate.'

For a moment I thought he must have made a mistake.

'Lira, Major? You mean dollars, don't you?'

'I mean Turkish lira,' he said stiffly.

'But that's only five hundred dollars—two hundred pounds!'

'Approximately. The fact that your suitcase and other personal belongings were lost has also been taken into consideration. In addition, arrangements are being made to have the various smuggling charges against you withdrawn. A favourable report on you will be made to Interpol. I think you will agree that you have been generously treated.'

A kick in the stomach couldn't have been more generous.

I opened my mouth to tell him that I wished now that I had taken my chance in Rome; but then I gave up. These policemen are all piss and wind anyway. Why add to it?

'You were going to say something?' he asked.

'Yes. How do I get out of this country?'

'The Director has persuaded the British Consul-General to issue to you a travel document good for one journey from here to Athens. I may say that it was not easy. The Consul agreed in the end only as a personal favour to the Director. In addition, an air passage has been reserved for you on the five o'clock Olympic Airways flight to Athens. A representative from the Consul-General will meet you with the travel document at the Olympic Airways office by the Hilton Hotel at three-thirty. If you will tell me in what currency you would like the bonus paid, a representative from the Bureau will also be there to give you the money.'

'I'll take it in dollars.'

'Very well. That is all, I think. You do not seem as pleased as you should be.'

'What is there to be pleased about?'

He shrugged. 'Perhaps you think you would have been better off in Rome. You wouldn't, you know. If those jewels had left the country, we would have known enough to get them back, and you would have been the first to be arrested. Why not consider yourself lucky?'

'Aren't you forgetting that Harper still has a certain letter of mine?'

'Why should he send it now?'

'To get his own back on me, of course.'

He shook his head. '*You* are forgetting. He can never be sure now how much you found out about them and how much you told us. Even I cannot be quite sure of that. As far as he is concerned, the less you see of policemen the better.' He smiled slightly. 'You see, you both have an interest in common.'

'Very gratifying.'

'You might even consider becoming an honest man.'

Work, Simpson, for the night cometh.

I ought to have blown the smug bastard a raspberry; but I was afraid he might call off the bonus if I did. Even a crumb is better than no bread. So I just gave him an imitation of Harper's most unpleasant grin, and tried to let him see how much I despised him. I don't really think I succeeded. He had a hide as thick as an elephant's.

There was a sergeant on duty this time to escort me back to the guard-room gate. He watched me all the time as if he thought I might try to steal one of the pictures. Then, when I got outside there were no taxis. You never can get a taxi from outside the Dolmabahçe Palace. I had to walk a mile before I found one, and that made me angrier still.

The representative from the Bureau looked like a plain-clothes police-man. He watched me carefully as I signed for the money and kept his fingers on the paper all the time in case I snatched it away. There were no flies on *him*. He knew how careful you had to be when dealing with crooks.

The representative from Her Britannic Majesty's Consulate-General in Istanbul was a snotty-nosed clerk who made me sign a paper saying that I understood that the granting of the travel document did not constitute recognition of any claim I had made or might make to United Kingdom citizenship. When I had signed it, I told him what he could do with it.

But on the way back to Athens in the plane, it gave me an idea.

I had been thinking about Nicki and wondering whether I would stop on my way to the flat and buy her a stone marten stole. She'd been hankering after one for a long while, and I thought that with the American notes I had I might get a good fur really cheaply—for thirty or forty dollars perhaps. I would be a 'papa' for at least a month. That is, if she hadn't moved out while I had been away. I was deciding that I had better make sure of that first when the stewardess stopped by my seat.

'Your nationality, sir?'

'British,' I said.

She handed me a passport control card to fill in and moved on to the next seat.

I had said 'British' without thinking. Why? Because I consider myself British, because I *am* British.

I took out the travel document and looked at it carefully. It, too, said I was British. And yet they had made me sign a paper which said in effect that I wasn't. There, the travel document could be considered an admission of my claim. The paper was unimportant because I had signed that under duress. You cannot take away a man's nationality by refusing to recognize his right to it. The 1948 Act is quite clear. The only way you can lose British nationality is by renouncing it. I haven't renounced mine at any time. Specifically, I did not renounce it by taking that Egyptian passport. Since the Egyptians say that my Egyptian naturalization is null and void because I made false statements, then it *is* null and void—*all* of it.

The British Government can't have it both ways. Either I am Egyptian or I am British. The Egyptians say I am not Egyptian and never have been. *I* say that I am not Egyptian and never have been. My father was a British officer. I am British.

That is why I have been so completely frank and open. I am not asking to be loved. I am not asking to be liked. I do not mind being loathed, if that will make some pettifogging government official happier. It is a matter of principle. If necessary, I shall take my case to the United Nations. They caned the British after Suez; they can cane them again for me. Sheep I may be; and perhaps certain persons find my breath displeasing; but I am no longer merely indignant. I am angry now.

I give the British Government fair warning. I refuse to go on being an anomaly. Is that quite clear? I *refuse!*

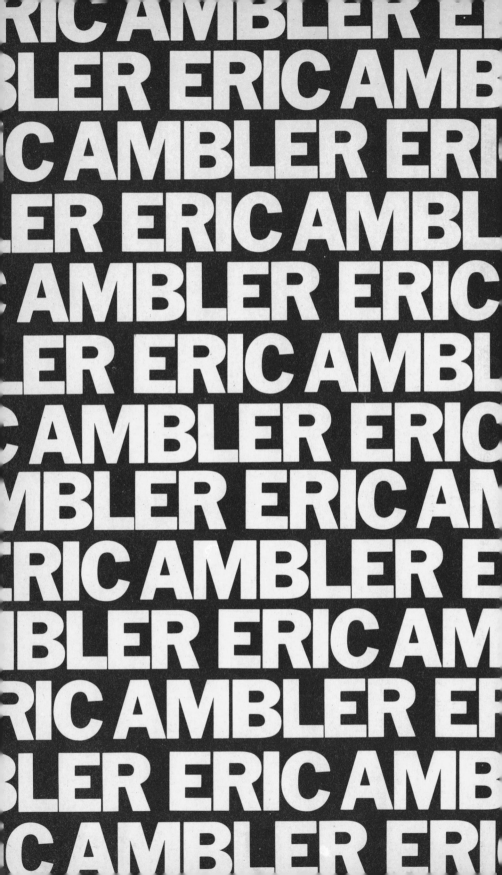